High Praise for
DIANA GABALDON
and her novels

"*VOYAGER* IS, FRANKLY, AN AMAZING READ. An unusual mix of romance, suspense and history. . . . If you can put this huge tome down before dawn, you're made of sterner stuff than I am."—*Arizona Tribune*

"ROUSING . . . AUDACIOUS . . . EXCITING . . . Gabaldon masterfully weaves . . . flashbacks . . . crossing time periods with abandon but never losing track of the story."—*Locus*

"INTRICATELY DETAILED . . . RICH IMAGINATION . . . THIS COULD BE THE START OF A SERIES TO RIVAL JAMES CLAVELL'S ORIENTAL SAGAS."—*The Oak Ridger* (Tennessee)

"SUPERIOR QUALITY . . . A TALENT THAT GOES BEYOND SUPERB, BEYOND INTELLIGENT STORYTELLING."
—*The Grand Prairie News* (Texas)

"UNCONVENTIONAL . . . MEMORABLE STORYTELLING"
—*The Seattle Times*

"ELABORATE AND COMPELLING . . . GABALDON [IS] A NATURAL STORYTELLER. *VOYAGER* IS . . . A LAVISH AND ENTERTAINING MIX OF HISTORY AND FANTASY."
—*Blade-Citizen* (San Diego, California)

"They are middle-aged lovers now, but their passion is just as strong (and Gabaldon had *Voyager* in her sights long before there was Robert James Waller). The language is right, the feeling is right, and if [Gabaldon] wants to write about Jamie and Claire when they're 50-something, I'd be happy to spend another 870 pages with them."
—*Detroit Free Press*

"GABALDON MAKES . . . HER STORY SING FOR ANYONE! [*VOYAGER*] is an involved tale that smoothly blends several popular genres. After reading the final chapter, you'll wish there were more."
—*The Cleveland Plain Dealer*

Books by Diana Gabaldon
(in order of publication)

THE OUTLANDER SERIES
OUTLANDER
DRAGONFLY IN AMBER
VOYAGER
DRUMS OF AUTUMN
THE OUTLANDISH COMPANION
(non-fiction)
THE FIERY CROSS
A BREATH OF SNOW AND ASHES

THE LORD JOHN GREY SERIES
LORD JOHN AND THE PRIVATE MATTER
LORD JOHN AND THE BROTHERHOOD OF THE BLADE
LORD JOHN AND THE HAND OF DEVILS

DIANA GABALDON

VOYAGER

DELTA TRADE PAPERBACKS

VOYAGER
A Delta Book

PUBLISHING HISTORY
Delacorte Press hardcover edition published 1994
Delta trade paperback edition / August 2001
Delta trade paperback reissue / September 2007

Published by Bantam Dell
A Division of Random House, Inc.
New York, New York

Book design by Virginia Norey

Delta is a registered trademark of Random House, Inc., and the
colophon is a trademark of Random House, Inc.

ISBN 978-0-385-33599-7

Printed in the United States of America
Published simultaneously in Canada

www.bantamdell.com

BVG 19 18 17 16 15 14 13 12 11

To my children,
    Laura Juliet,
        Samuel Gordon,
            and Jennifer Rose,

Who gave me the heart, the blood, and the bones of this book.

Acknowledgments

The author's deepest thanks to:

Jackie Cantor, as always, for being the rare and marvelous sort of editor who thinks it's all right if a book is long as long as it's good; my husband, Doug Watkins, for his literary eye, his marginal notes (e.g., "nipples *again*?"), and the jokes he insists I steal from him to give to Jamie Fraser; my elder daughter, Laura, who says, "If you come talk to my class about writing again, just talk about books and don't tell them about whale penises, okay?"; my son, Samuel, who walks up to total strangers in the park and says, "Have you read my mother's book?"; my younger daughter, Jenny, who says, "Why don't you wear makeup like on your book covers *all* the time, Mommy?"; Margaret J. Campbell, scholar; Barry Fodgen, english poet; and Pindens Cinola Oleroso Loventon Greenpeace Ludovic, dog; for generously allowing me to use their personae as the basis for the excesses of imagination (Mr. Fodgen wishes to note for the record that his dog Ludo has never actually tried to copulate with anyone's leg, wooden or not, but does understand the concept of artistic license); Perry Knowlton, who as well as being an excellent literary agent is also a fount of knowledge about bowlines, mainsails, and matters nautical, as well as the niceties of French grammar and the proper way to gut a deer; Robert Riffle, noted authority on what plants grow where, and what they look like while doing so; Kathryn (whose last name was either Boyle or Frye; all I remember is that it had to do with cooking), for the useful information on tropical diseases, particularly the picturesque habits of loa loa worms; Michael Lee West, for detailed descriptions of Jamaica, including regional dialect and folklore anecdotes; Dr. Mahlon West, for advice on typhoid fever; William Cross, Paul Block (and Paul's father), and Chrystine Wu (and Chrystine's parents), for invaluable assistance with Chinese vocabulary, history, and cultural attitudes; my father-in-law, Max Watkins, who, as always, provided useful comments on the appearance and habits of horses, including which way they face when the wind is blowing; Peggy Lynch, for wanting to know what Jamie would say if he saw a picture of his daughter in a bikini; Lizy Buchan, for telling me the story about her husband's ancestor who escaped Culloden; Dr. Gary Hoff, for medical detail; Fay Zachary, for lunch and critical comment; Sue Smiley, for critical reading and suggesting the blood vow; David Pijawka, for the materials on Jamaica and his most poetic description of what the air feels like after a Caribbean rainstorm; Iain

MacKinnon Taylor, and his brother Hamish Taylor, for their most helpful suggestions and corrections of Gaelic spelling and usages; and as always, the various members of the CompuServe Literary Forum, including Janet McConnaughey, Marte Brengle, Akua Lezli Hope, John L. Myers, John E. Simpson, Jr., Sheryl Smith, Alit, Norman Shimmel, Walter Hawn, Karen Pershing, Margaret Ball, Paul Solyn, Diane Engel, David Chaifetz, and many others, for being interested, providing useful discussion, and laughing in the right places.

Prologue

When I was small, I never wanted to step in puddles. Not because of any fear of drowned worms or wet stockings; I was by and large a grubby child, with a blissful disregard for filth of any kind.

It was because I couldn't bring myself to believe that that perfect smooth expanse was no more than a thin film of water over solid earth. I believed it was an opening into some fathomless space. Sometimes, seeing the tiny ripples caused by my approach, I thought the puddle impossibly deep, a bottomless sea in which the lazy coil of tentacle and gleam of scale lay hidden, with the threat of huge bodies and sharp teeth adrift and silent in the far-down depths.

And then, looking down into reflection, I would see my own round face and frizzled hair against a featureless blue sweep, and think instead that the puddle was the entrance to another sky. If I stepped in there, I would drop at once, and keep on falling, on and on, into blue space.

The only time I would dare to walk through a puddle was at twilight, when the evening stars came out. If I looked in the water and saw one lighted pinprick there, I could splash through unafraid—for if I should fall into the puddle and on into space, I could grab hold of the star as I passed, and be safe.

Even now, when I see a puddle in my path, my mind half-halts —though my feet do not—then hurries on, with only the echo of the thought left behind.

What if, this time, you fall?

PART ONE

Battle, and

the Loves of Men

1

The Corbies' Feast

Many a Highland chieftain fought,
Many a gallant man did fall.
Death itself were dearly bought,
All for Scotland's King and law.

—"Will Ye No Come Back Again"

APRIL 16, 1746

He was dead. However, his nose throbbed painfully, which he thought odd in the circumstances. While he placed considerable trust in the understanding and mercy of his Creator, he harbored that residue of elemental guilt that made all men fear the chance of hell. Still, all he had ever heard of hell made him think it unlikely that the torments reserved for its luckless inhabitants could be restricted to a sore nose.

On the other hand, this couldn't be heaven, on several counts. For one, he didn't deserve it. For another, it didn't look it. And for a third, he doubted that the rewards of the blessed included a broken nose, any more than those of the damned.

While he had always thought of Purgatory as a gray sort of place, the faint reddish light that hid everything around him seemed suitable. His mind was clearing a bit, and his power to reason was coming back, if slowly. Someone, he thought rather crossly, ought to see him and tell him just what the sentence was, until he should have suffered enough to be purified, and at last to enter the Kingdom of God. Whether he was expecting a demon or an angel was uncertain. He had no idea of the staffing requirements of Purgatory; it wasn't a matter the dominie had addressed in his schooldays.

While waiting, he began to take stock of whatever other torments he might be required to endure. There were numerous cuts, gashes, and bruises here and there, and he was fairly sure he'd broken the fourth finger of his right hand again—difficult to protect it, the way it stuck out so stiff, with the joint frozen. None of that was too bad, though. What else?

Claire. The name knifed across his heart with a pain that was more racking than anything his body had ever been called on to withstand.

If he had had an actual body anymore, he was sure it would have doubled up in agony. He had known it would be like this, when he sent her back to the stone circle. Spiritual anguish could be taken as a standard condition in Purgatory, and he had expected all along that the pain of separation would be his chief punishment—sufficient, he thought, to atone for anything he'd ever done: murder and betrayal included.

He did not know whether persons in Purgatory were allowed to pray or not, but tried anyway. *Lord,* he prayed, *that she may be safe. She and the child.* He was sure she would have made it to the circle itself; only two months gone with child, she was still light and fleet of foot—and the most stubbornly determined woman he had ever met. But whether she had managed the dangerous transition back to the place from which she had come—sliding precariously through whatever mysterious layers lay between then and now, powerless in the grip of the rock—that he could never know, and the thought of it was enough to make him forget even the throbbing in his nose.

He resumed his interrupted inventory of bodily ills, and became inordinately distressed at the discovery that his left leg appeared to be missing. Sensation stopped at the hip, with a sort of pins-and-needles tingling at the joint. Presumably he would get it back in due time, either when he finally arrived in Heaven, or at the least, at Judgment Day. And after all, his brother-in-law Ian managed very well on the wooden peg he wore to replace *his* missing leg.

Still, his vanity was troubled. Ah, that must be it; a punishment meant to cure him of the sin of vanity. He mentally set his teeth, determined to accept whatever came to him with fortitude, and such humility as he could manage. Still, he couldn't help reaching an exploratory hand (or whatever he was using for a hand) tentatively downward, to see just where the limb now ended.

The hand struck something hard, and the fingers tangled in wet, snarled hair. He sat up abruptly, and with some effort, cracked the layer of dried blood that had sealed his eyelids shut. Memory flooded back, and he groaned aloud. He had been mistaken. This *was* hell. But James Fraser was unfortunately not dead, after all.

The body of a man lay across his own. Its dead weight crushed his left leg, explaining the absence of feeling. The head, heavy as a spent cannonball, pressed facedown into his abdomen, the damp-matted hair a dark spill on the wet linen of his shirt. He jerked upward in sudden panic; the head rolled sideways into his lap and a half-open eye stared sightlessly up behind the sheltering strands of hair.

It was Jack Randall, his fine red captain's coat so dark with the wet it looked almost black. Jamie made a fumbling effort to push the body away, but found himself amazingly weak; his hand splayed feebly against Randall's shoulder, and the elbow of his other arm buckled suddenly as he tried to support himself. He found himself lying once more flat on his back, the sleeting sky pale gray and whirling dizzily overhead. Jack Randall's head moved obscenely up and down on his stomach with each gasping breath.

He pressed his hands flat against the boggy ground—the water rose up cold through his fingers and soaked the back of his shirt—and wriggled sideways. Some warmth was trapped between them; as the limp dead weight slid slowly free, the freezing rain struck his newly exposed flesh with a shock like a blow, and he shivered violently with sudden chill.

As he squirmed on the ground, struggling with the crumpled, mud-stained folds of his plaid, he could hear sounds above the keening of the April wind; far-off shouts and a moaning and wailing, like the calling of ghosts in the wind. And overall, the raucous calling of crows. Dozens of crows, from the sound.

That was strange, he thought dimly. Birds shouldn't fly in a storm like this. A final heave freed the plaid from under him, and he fumbled it over his body. As he reached to cover his legs, he saw that his kilt and left leg were soaked with blood. The sight didn't distress him; it seemed only vaguely interesting, the dark red smears a contrast to the grayish green of the moor plants around him. The echoes of battle faded from his ears, and he left Culloden Field to the calling of the crows.

He was wakened much later by the calling of his name.

"Fraser! Jamie Fraser! Are ye here?"

No, he thought groggily. I'm not. Wherever he had been while unconscious, it was a better place than this. He lay in a small declivity, half-filled with water. The sleeting rain had stopped, but the wind hadn't; it whined over the moor, piercing and chilling. The sky had darkened nearly to black; it must be near evening, then.

"I saw him go down here, I tell ye. Right near a big clump of gorse." The voice was at a distance, fading as it argued with someone.

There was a rustle near his ear, and he turned his head to see the crow. It stood on the grass a foot away, a blotch of wind-ruffled black feathers, regarding him with a bead-bright eye. Deciding that he posed no threat, it swiveled its neck with casual ease and jabbed its thick sharp bill into Jack Randall's eye.

Jamie jerked up with a cry of revulsion and a flurry of movement that sent the crow flapping off, squawking with alarm.

"Ay! Over there!"

There was a squelching through boggy ground, and a face before him, and the welcome feel of a hand on his shoulder.

"He's alive! Come on, MacDonald! D'ye lend a hand here; he'll no be walkin' on his own." There were four of them, and with a good deal of effort, they got him up, arms draped helpless about the shoulders of Ewan Cameron and Iain MacKinnon.

He wanted to tell them to leave him; his purpose had returned to him with the waking, and he remembered that he had meant to die. But the sweetness of their company was too much to resist. The rest had restored the feeling in his dead leg, and he knew the seriousness of the wound. He would die soon in any case; thank God that it need not be alone, in the dark.

"Water?" The edge of the cup pressed against his lip, and he roused himself long enough to drink, careful not to spill it. A hand pressed briefly against his forehead and dropped away without comment.

He was burning; he could feel the flames behind his eyes when he closed them. His lips were cracked and sore from the heat, but it was better than the chills that came at intervals. At least when he was fevered, he could lie still; the shaking of the chills woke the sleeping demons in his leg.

Murtagh. He had a terrible feeling about his godfather, but no memory to give it shape. Murtagh was dead; he knew that must be it, but didn't know why or how he knew. A good half of the Highland army was dead, slaughtered on the moor—so much he had gathered from the talk of the men in the farmhouse, but he had no memory of the battle himself.

He had fought with armies before, and knew such loss of memory was not uncommon in soldiers; he had seen it, though never before suffered it himself. He knew the memories would come back, and hoped he would be dead before they did. He shifted at the thought, and the movement sent a jolt of white-hot pain through his leg that made him groan.

"All right, Jamie?" Ewan rose on one elbow next to him, worried face wan in the dawning light. A bloodstained bandage circled his head, and there were rusty stains on his collar, from the scalp wound left by a bullet's graze.

"Aye, I'll do." He reached up a hand and touched Ewan's shoulder in gratitude. Ewan patted it, and lay back down.

The crows were back. Black as night themselves, they had gone to roost with the darkness, but with the dawn they were back—birds of war, the corbies had come to feast on the flesh of the fallen. It could as well be his own eyes the cruel beaks picked out, he thought. He could feel the shape of his eyeballs beneath his lids, round and hot, tasty bits of jelly rolling restless to and fro, looking vainly for oblivion, while the rising sun turned his lids a dark and bloody red.

Four of the men were gathered near the single window of the farmhouse, talking quietly together.

"Make a run for it?" one said, with a nod outside. "Christ, man, the best of us can barely stagger—and there's six at least canna walk at all."

"If ye can go, be going," said a man from the floor. He grimaced toward his own leg, wrapped in the remains of a tattered quilt. "Dinna linger on our account."

Duncan MacDonald turned from the window with a grim smile, shaking his head. The window's light shone off the rough planes of his face, deepening the lines of fatigue.

"Nay, we'll bide," he said. "For one thing, the English are thick as lice on the ground; ye can see them swarm from the window. There's no man would get away whole from Drumossie now."

"Even those that fled the field yesterday will no get far," MacKinnon put in softly. "Did ye no hear the English troops passing in the night at the quick-march? D'ye think it will be hard for them to hunt down our ragtag lot?"

There was no response to this; all of them knew the answer too well. Many of the Highlanders had been barely able to stand on the field before the battle, weakened as they were by cold, fatigue, and hunger.

Jamie turned his face to the wall, praying that his men had started early enough. Lallybroch was remote; if they could get far enough from Culloden, it was unlikely they would be caught. And yet Claire had told him that Cumberland's troops would ravage the Highlands, ranging far afield in their thirst for revenge.

The thought of her this time caused only a wave of terrible longing. God, to have her here, to lay her hands on him, to tend his wounds and cradle his head in her lap. But she was gone—gone away two hundred years from him —and thank the Lord that she was! Tears trickled slowly from under his closed lids, and he rolled painfully onto his side, to hide them from the others.

Lord, that she might be safe, he prayed. *She and the child.*

Toward midafternoon, the smell of burning came suddenly on the air, wafting through the glassless window. It was thicker than the smell of black-powder smoke, pungent, with an underlying odor that was faintly horrible in its reminiscent smell of roasting meat.

"They are burning the dead," said MacDonald. He had scarcely moved from his seat by the window in all the time they had been in the cottage. He looked like a death's-head himself, hair coal-black and matted with dirt, scraped back from a face in which every bone showed.

Here and there, a small, flat crack sounded on the moor. Gunshots. The coups de grace, administered by those English officers with a sense of compassion, before a tartan-clad wretch should be stacked on the pyre with his luckier fellows. When Jamie looked up, Duncan MacDonald still sat by the window, but his eyes were closed.

Next to him, Ewan Cameron crossed himself. "May we find as much mercy," he whispered.

They did. It was just past noon on the second day when booted feet at last approached the farmhouse, and the door swung open on silent leather hinges.

"Christ." It was a muttered exclamation at the sight within the farmhouse. The draft from the door stirred the fetid air over grimed, bedraggled, bloodstained bodies that lay or sat huddled on the packed-dirt floor.

There had been no discussion of the possibility of armed resistance; they had no heart and there was no point. The Jacobites simply sat, waiting the pleasure of their visitor.

He was a major, all fresh and new in an uncreased uniform, with polished boots. After a moment's hesitation to survey the inhabitants, he stepped inside, his lieutenant close behind.

"I am Lord Melton," he said, glancing around as though seeking the leader of these men, to whom his remarks might most properly be addressed.

Duncan MacDonald, after a glance of his own, stood slowly, and inclined his head. "Duncan MacDonald, of Glen Richie," he said. "And others"—he waved a hand—"late of the forces of His Majesty, King James."

"So I surmised," the Englishman said dryly. He was young, in his early thirties, but he carried himself with a seasoned soldier's confidence. He looked deliberately from man to man, then reached into his coat and produced a folded sheet of paper.

"I have here an order from His Grace, the Duke of Cumberland," he said. "Authorizing the immediate execution of any man found to have engaged in the treasonous rebellion just past." He glanced around the confines of the cottage once more. "Is there any man here who claims innocence of treason?"

There was the faintest breath of laughter from the Scots. Innocence, with the smoke of battle still black on their faces, here on the edge of the slaughter-field?

"No, my lord," said MacDonald, the faintest of smiles on his lips. "Traitors all. Shall we be hanged, then?"

Melton's face twitched in a small grimace of distaste, then settled back into impassivity. He was a slight man, with small, fine bones, but carried his authority well, nonetheless.

"You will be shot," he said. "You have an hour, in which to prepare yourselves." He hesitated, shooting a glance at his lieutenant, as though afraid to sound overgenerous before his subordinate, but continued. "If any of you wish writing materials—to compose a letter, perhaps—the clerk of my company will attend you." He nodded briefly to MacDonald, turned on his heel, and left.

It was a grim hour. A few men availed themselves of the offer of pen and ink, and scribbled doggedly, paper held against the slanted wooden chimney for lack of another firm writing surface. Others prayed quietly, or simply sat, waiting.

MacDonald had begged mercy for Giles McMartin and Frederick Murray, arguing that they were barely seventeen, and should not be held to the same account as their elders. This request was denied, and the boys sat together, white-faced against the wall, holding each other's hands.

For them, Jamie felt a piercing sorrow—and for the others here, loyal friends and gallant soldiers. For himself, he felt only relief. No more to worry, nothing more to do. He had done all he could for his men, his wife, his unborn child. Now let this bodily misery be ended, and he would go grateful for the peace of it.

More for form's sake than because he felt the need of it, he closed his eyes and began the Act of Contrition, in French, as he always said it. *Mon Dieu, je regrette* . . . And yet he didn't; it was much too late for any sort of regret.

Would he find Claire at once when he died, he wondered? Or perhaps, as he expected, be condemned to separation for a time? In any case, he would see her again; he clung to the conviction much more firmly than he embraced the tenets of the Church. God had given her to him; He would restore her.

Forgetting to pray, he instead began to conjure her face behind his eyelids, the curve of cheek and temple, a broad fair brow that always moved him to kiss it, just there, in that small smooth spot between her eyebrows, just at the top of her nose, between clear amber eyes. He fixed his attention on the shape of her mouth, carefully imagining the full, sweet curve of it, and the taste and the feel and the joy of it. The sounds of praying, the pen-scratching and the small, choked sobs of Giles McMartin faded from his ears.

It was midafternoon when Melton returned, this time with six soldiers in attendance, as well as the Lieutenant and the clerk. Again, he paused in the doorway, but MacDonald rose before he could speak.

"I'll go first," he said, and walked steadily across the cottage. As he bent his head to go through the door, though, Lord Melton laid a hand on his sleeve.

"Will you give your full name, sir? My clerk will make note of it."

MacDonald glanced at the clerk, a small bitter smile tugging at the corner of his mouth.

"A trophy list, is it? Aye, well." He shrugged and drew himself upright. "Duncan William MacLeod MacDonald, of Glen Richie." He bowed politely to Lord Melton. "At your service—sir." He passed through the door, and shortly there came the sound of a single pistol-shot from near at hand.

The boys were allowed to go together, hands still clutched tightly as they passed through the door. The rest were taken one by one, each asked for his name, that the clerk might make a record of it. The clerk sat on a stool by the door, head bent to the papers in his lap, not looking up as the men passed by.

When it came Ewan's turn, Jamie struggled to prop himself on his elbows, and grasped his friend's hand, as hard as he could.

"I shall see ye soon again," he whispered.

Ewan's hand shook in his, but the Cameron only smiled. Then he leaned across simply and kissed Jamie's mouth, and rose to go.

They left the six who could not walk to the last.

"James Alexander Malcolm MacKenzie Fraser," he said, speaking slowly to allow the clerk time to get it down right. "Laird of Broch Tuarach." Patiently, he spelled it, then glanced up at Melton.

"I must ask your courtesy, my lord, to give me help to stand."

Melton didn't answer him, but stared down at him, his expression of remote distaste altering to one of mingled astonishment and something like dawning horror.

"Fraser?" he said. "Of Broch Tuarach?"

"I am," Jamie said patiently. Would the man not hurry a bit? Being resigned to being shot was one thing, but listening to your friends being killed in your hearing was another, and not just calculated to settle the nerves. His arms were trembling with the strain of propping him, and his bowels, not sharing the resignation of his higher faculties, were twitching with a gurgling dread.

"Bloody hell," the Englishman muttered. He bent and peered at Jamie where he lay in the shadow of the wall, then turned and beckoned to his lieutenant.

"Help me get him into the light," he ordered. They weren't gentle about it, and Jamie grunted as the movement sent a bolt of pain from his leg right up through the top of his head. It made him dizzy for a moment, and he missed what Melton was saying to him.

"Are you the Jacobite they call 'Red Jamie'?" he asked again, impatiently.

A streak of fear went through Jamie at that; let them know he was the notorious Red Jamie, and they wouldn't shoot him. They'd take him in chains to London to be tried—a prize of war. And after that, it would be the hangman's rope, and lying half strangled on the gallows platform while they slit his belly and ripped out his bowels. His bowels gave another long, rumbling gurgle; they didn't think much of the notion either.

"No," he said, with as much firmness as he could manage. "Just get on wi' it, eh?"

Ignoring this, Melton dropped to his knees, and ripped open the throat of Jamie's shirt. He gripped Jamie's hair and jerked back his head.

"Damn!" Melton said. Melton's finger prodded him in the throat, just above the collarbone. There was a small triangular scar there, and this appeared to be what was causing his interrogator's concern.

"James Fraser of Broch Tuarach; red hair and a three-cornered scar on his throat." Melton let go of the hair and sat back on his heels, rubbing his chin in a distracted sort of way. Then he pulled himself together and turned to the lieutenant, gesturing at the five men remaining in the farm cottage.

"Take the rest," he ordered. His fair brows were knitted together in a deep frown. He stood over Jamie, scowling, while the other Scottish prisoners were removed.

"I have to think," he muttered. "Damme, I must think!"

"Do that," said Jamie, "if you're able. I must lie down, myself." They had propped him sitting against the far wall, his leg stretched out in front of him, but sitting upright after two days of lying flat was more than he could manage; the room was tilting drunkenly, and small flashing lights kept coming before his eyes. He leaned to one side, and eased himself down, hugging the dirt floor, eyes closed as he waited for the dizziness to pass.

Melton was muttering under his breath, but Jamie couldn't make out the words; didn't care greatly in any case. Sitting up in the sunlight, he had seen his leg clearly for the first time, and he was fairly sure that he wouldn't live long enough to be hanged.

The deep angry red of inflammation spread from midthigh upward, much brighter than the remaining smears of dried blood. The wound itself was purulent; with the stench of the other men lessening, he could smell the faint sweet-foul odor of the discharge. Still, a quick bullet through the head seemed much preferable to the pain and delirium of death by infection. Did you hear the bang? he wondered, and drifted off, the cool pounded dirt smooth and comforting as a mother's breast under his hot cheek.

He wasn't really asleep, only drifting in a feverish doze, but Melton's voice in his ear jerked him to alertness.

"Grey," the voice was saying, "John William Grey! Do you know that name?"

"No," he said, mazy with sleep and fever. "Look, man, either shoot me or go away, aye? I'm ill."

"Near Carryarrick." Melton's voice was prodding, impatient. "A boy, a fair-haired boy, about sixteen. You met him in the wood."

Jamie squinted up at his tormentor. The fever distorted his vision, but there seemed something vaguely familiar about the fine-boned face above him, with those large, almost girlish eyes.

"Oh," he said, catching a single face from the flood of images that swirled erratically through his brain. "The wee laddie that tried to kill me. Aye, I mind him." He closed his eyes again. In the odd way of fever, one sensation seemed to blend into another. He had broken John William Grey's arm; the memory of the boy's fine bone beneath his hand became the bone of Claire's forearm as he tore her from the grip of the stones. The cool misty breeze stroked his face with Claire's fingers.

"Wake up, damn you!" His head snapped on his neck as Melton shook him impatiently. "Listen to me!"

Jamie opened his eyes wearily. "Aye?"

"John William Grey is my brother," Melton said. "He told me of his meeting with you. You spared his life, and he made you a promise—is that true?"

With great effort, he cast his mind back. He had met the boy two days before the first battle of the rebellion; the Scottish victory at Prestonpans. The six months between then and now seemed a vast chasm; so much had happened in between.

"Aye, I recall. He promised to kill me. I dinna mind if you do it for him, though." His eyelids were drooping again. Did he have to be awake in order to be shot?

"He said he owed you a debt of honor, and he does." Melton stood up, dusting the knees of his breeches, and turned to his lieutenant, who had been watching the questioning with considerable bewilderment.

"It's the deuce of a situation, Wallace. This . . . this Jacobite scut is famous. You've heard of Red Jamie? The one on the broadsheets?" The Lieutenant nodded, looking curiously down at the bedraggled form in the dirt at his feet. Melton smiled bitterly.

"No, he doesn't look so dangerous now, does he? But he's still Red Jamie Fraser, and His Grace would be more than pleased to hear of such an illustrious prisoner. They haven't yet found Charles Stuart, but a few well-known Jacobites would please the crowds at Tower Hill nearly as much."

"Shall I send a message to His Grace?" The Lieutenant reached for his message box.

"No!" Melton wheeled to glare down at his prisoner. "That's the difficulty! Besides being prime gallows bait, this filthy wretch is also the man who captured my youngest brother near Preston, and rather than shooting the brat, which is what he deserved, spared his life and returned him to his companions. Thus," he said through his teeth, "incurring a bloody great debt of honor upon my family!"

"Dear me," said the Lieutenant. "So you can't give him to His Grace, after all."

"No, blast it! I can't even shoot the bastard, without dishonoring my brother's sworn word!"

The prisoner opened one eye. "I willna tell anyone if you don't," he suggested, and promptly closed it again.

"Shut up!" Losing his temper entirely, Melton kicked the prisoner, who grunted at the impact, but said nothing more.

"Perhaps we could shoot him under an assumed name," the Lieutenant suggested helpfully.

Lord Melton gave his aide a look of withering scorn, then looked out the window to judge the time.

"It will be dark in three hours. I'll oversee the burial of the other executed prisoners. Find a small wagon, and have it filled with hay. Find a driver—pick someone discreet, Wallace, that means bribable, Wallace—and have them here as soon as it's dark."

"Yes, sir. Er, sir? What about the prisoner?" The Lieutenant gestured diffidently toward the body on the floor.

"What about him?" Melton said brusquely. "He's too weak to crawl, let alone walk. He isn't going anywhere—at least not until the wagon gets here."

"Wagon?" The prisoner was showing signs of life. In fact, under the stimulus of agitation, he had managed to raise himself onto one arm. Blood-shot blue eyes gleamed wide with alarm, under the spikes of matted red hair. "Where are ye sending me?" Turning from the door, Melton cast him a glance of intense dislike.

"You're the laird of Broch Tuarach, aren't you? Well, that's where I'm sending you."

"I dinna want to go home! I want to be shot!"

The Englishmen exchanged a look.

"Raving," the Lieutenant said significantly, and Melton nodded.

"I doubt he'll live through the journey—but his death won't be on my head, at least."

The door shut firmly behind the Englishmen, leaving Jamie Fraser quite alone—and still alive.

2

The Hunt Begins

"Of course he's dead!" Claire's voice was sharp with agitation; it rang loudly in the half-empty study, echoing among the rifled bookshelves. She stood against the cork-lined wall like a prisoner awaiting a firing squad, staring from her daughter to Roger Wakefield and back again.

"I don't think so." Roger felt terribly tired. He rubbed a hand over his face, then picked up the folder from the desk; the one containing all the research he'd done since Claire and her daughter had first come to him, three weeks before, and asked his help.

He opened the folder and thumbed slowly through the contents. The Jacobites of Culloden. The Rising of the '45. The gallant Scots who had rallied to the banner of Bonnie Prince Charlie, and cut through Scotland like a blazing sword—only to come to ruin and defeat against the Duke of Cumberland on the gray moor at Culloden.

"Here," he said, plucking out several sheets clipped together. The archaic writing looked odd, rendered in the black crispness of a photocopy. "This is the muster roll of the Master of Lovat's regiment."

He thrust the thin sheaf of papers at Claire, but it was her daughter, Brianna, who took the sheets from him and began to turn the pages, a slight frown between her reddish brows.

"Read the top sheet," Roger said. "Where it says 'Officers.' "

"All right. 'Officers,' " she read aloud, " 'Simon, Master of Lovat' . . ."

"The Young Fox," Roger interrupted. "Lovat's son. And five more names, right?"

Brianna cocked one brow at him, but went on reading.

" 'William Chisholm Fraser, Lieutenant; George D'Amerd Fraser Shaw, Captain; Duncan Joseph Fraser, Lieutenant; Bayard Murray Fraser, Major," she paused, swallowing, before reading the last name, " '. . . James Alexander Malcolm MacKenzie Fraser. Captain.' " She lowered the papers, looking a little pale. "My father."

Claire moved quickly to her daughter's side, squeezing the girl's arm. She was pale, too.

"Yes," she said to Roger. "I know he went to Culloden. When he left me . . . there at the stone circle . . . he meant to go back to Culloden Field, to rescue his men who were with Charles Stuart. And we know he did"—she nodded at the folder on the desk, its manila surface blank and innocent in the lamplight—"you found their names. But . . . but . . . Jamie . . ." Speaking the name aloud seemed to rattle her, and she clamped her lips tight.

Now it was Brianna's turn to support her mother.

"He meant to go back, you said." Her eyes, dark blue and encouraging, were intent on her mother's face. "He meant to take his men away from the field, and then go back to the battle."

Claire nodded, recovering herself slightly.

"He knew he hadn't much chance of getting away; if the English caught him . . . he said he'd rather die in battle. That's what he meant to do." She turned to Roger, her gaze an unsettling amber. Her eyes always reminded him of hawk's eyes, as though she could see a good deal farther than most people. "I can't believe he didn't die there—so many men did, and *he* meant to!"

Almost half the Highland army had died at Culloden, cut down in a blast of cannonfire and searing musketry. But not Jamie Fraser.

"No," Roger said doggedly. "That bit I read you from Linklater's book—" He reached to pick it up, a white volume, entitled *The Prince in the Heather.*

"*Following the battle,*" he read, "*eighteen wounded Jacobite officers took refuge in the farmhouse near the moor. Here they lay in pain, their wounds untended, for two days. At the end of that time, they were taken out and shot. One man, a Fraser of the Master of Lovat's regiment, escaped the slaughter. The rest are buried at the edge of the domestic park.*

"See?" he said, laying the book down and looking earnestly at the two women over its pages. "An officer, of the Master of Lovat's regiment." He grabbed up the sheets of the muster roll.

"And here they are! Just six of them. Now, we know the man in the farmhouse can't have been Young Simon; he's a well-known historical figure, and we know very well what happened to him. He retreated from the field—unwounded, mind you—with a group of his men, and fought his way north, eventually making it back to Beaufort Castle, near here." He waved vaguely at the full-length window, through which the nighttime lights of Inverness twinkled faintly.

"Nor was the man who escaped Leanach farmhouse any of the other four officers—William, George, Duncan, or Bayard," Roger said. "Why?" He snatched another paper out of the folder and brandished it, almost triumphantly. "Because they all *did* die at Culloden! All four of them were killed on the field—I found their names listed on a plaque in the church at Beauly."

Claire let out a long breath, then eased herself down into the old leather swivel chair behind the desk.

"Jesus H. Christ," she said. She closed her eyes and leaned forward, elbows on the desk, and her head against her hands, the thick, curly brown hair spilling forward to hide her face. Brianna laid a hand on Claire's back, face troubled as she bent over her mother. She was a tall girl, with large, fine bones, and her long red hair glowed in the warm light of the desk lamp.

"If he didn't die . . ." she began tentatively.

Claire's head snapped up. "But he *is* dead!" she said. Her face was strained, and small lines were visible around her eyes. "For God's sake, it's two hundred years; whether he died at Culloden or not, he's dead now!"

Brianna stepped back from her mother's vehemence, and lowered her head, so the red hair—her father's red hair—swung down beside her cheek.

"I guess so," she whispered. Roger could see she was fighting back tears. And no wonder, he thought. To find out in short order that first, the man you had loved and called "Father" all your life really *wasn't* your father, secondly, that your real father was a Highland Scot who had lived two hundred years ago, and thirdly, to realize that he had likely perished in some horrid fashion, unthinkably far from the wife and child he had sacrificed himself to save . . . enough to rattle one, Roger thought.

He crossed to Brianna and touched her arm. She gave him a brief, distracted glance, and tried to smile. He put his arms around her, even in his pity for her distress thinking how marvelous she felt, all warm and soft and springy at once.

Claire still sat at the desk, motionless. The yellow hawk's eyes had gone a softer color now, remote with memory. They rested sightlessly on the east wall of the study, still covered from floor to ceiling with the notes and memorabilia left by the Reverend Wakefield, Roger's late adoptive father.

Looking at the wall himself, Roger saw the annual meeting notice sent by the Society of the White Rose—those enthusiastic, eccentric souls who still championed the cause of Scottish independence, meeting in nostalgic tribute to Charles Stuart, and the Highland heroes who had followed him.

Roger cleared his throat slightly.

"Er . . . if Jamie Fraser didn't die at Culloden . . ." he said.

"Then he likely died soon afterward." Claire's eyes met Roger's, straight on, the cool look back in the yellow-brown depths. "You have no idea how it was," she said. "There was a famine in the Highlands—none of the men had eaten for days before the battle. He was wounded—we know that. Even if he escaped, there would have been . . . no one to care for him." Her voice caught slightly at that; she was a doctor now, had been a healer even then, twenty years before, when she had stepped through a circle of standing stones, and met destiny with James Alexander Malcolm MacKenzie Fraser.

Roger was conscious of them both; the tall, shaking girl he held in his arms, and the woman at the desk, so still, so poised. She had traveled through the stones, through time; been suspected as a spy, arrested as a witch, snatched by an unimaginable quirk of circumstance from the arms of her first husband, Frank Randall. And three years later, her second husband, James Fraser, had sent her back through the stones, pregnant, in a desperate effort to save her and the unborn child from the onrushing disaster that would soon engulf him.

Surely, he thought to himself, she's been through enough? But Roger was a historian. He had a scholar's insatiable, amoral curiosity, too powerful to be constrained by simple compassion. More than that, he was oddly conscious of the third figure in the family tragedy in which he found himself involved—Jamie Fraser.

"If he didn't die at Culloden," he began again, more firmly, "then perhaps I can find out what did happen to him. Do you want me to try?" He waited, breathless, feeling Brianna's warm breath through his shirt.

Jamie Fraser had had a life, and a death. Roger felt obscurely that it was his duty to find out all the truth; that Jamie Fraser's women deserved to know all they could of him. For Brianna, such knowledge was all she would ever have of the father she had never known. And for Claire—behind the question he had asked was the thought that had plainly not yet struck her, stunned with shock as she was: she had crossed the barrier of time twice before. She could, just possibly, do it again. And if Jamie Fraser had not died at Culloden . . .

He saw awareness flicker in the clouded amber of her eyes, as the thought came to her. She was normally pale; now her face blanched white as the ivory handle of the letter opener before her on the desk. Her fingers closed around it, clenching so the knuckles stood out in knobs of bone.

She didn't speak for a long time. Her gaze fixed on Brianna and lingered there for a moment, then returned to Roger's face.

"Yes," she said, in a whisper so soft he could barely hear her. "Yes. Find out for me. Please. Find out."

3

Frank and Full Disclosure

The foot traffic was heavy on the bridge over the River Ness, with folk streaming home to their teas. Roger moved in front of me, his wide shoulders protecting me from the buffets of the crowd around us.

I could feel my heart beating heavily against the stiff cover of the book I was clutching to my chest. It did that whenever I paused to think what we were truly doing. I wasn't sure which of the two possible alternatives was worse; to find that Jamie had died at Culloden, or to find that he hadn't.

The boards of the bridge echoed hollowly underfoot, as we trudged back toward the manse. My arms ached from the weight of the books I carried, and I shifted the load from one side to the other.

"Watch your bloody wheel, man!" Roger shouted, nudging me adroitly to the side, as a workingman on a bicycle plowed head-downward through the bridge traffic, nearly running me against the railing.

"Sorry!" came back the apologetic shout, and the rider gave a wave of the hand over his shoulder, as the bike wove its way between two groups of schoolchildren, coming home for their teas. I glanced back across the bridge, in case Brianna should be visible behind us, but there was no sign of her.

Roger and I had spent the afternoon at the Society for the Preservation of Antiquities. Brianna had gone down to the Highland Clans office, there to collect photocopies of a list of documents Roger had compiled.

"It's very kind of you to take all this trouble, Roger," I said, raising my voice to be heard above the echoing bridge and the river's rush.

"It's all right," he said, a little awkwardly, pausing for me to catch him up. "I'm curious," he added, smiling a little. "You know historians—can't leave a puzzle alone." He shook his head, trying to brush the windblown dark hair out of his eyes without using his hands.

I did know historians. I'd lived with one for twenty years. Frank hadn't wanted to leave this particular puzzle alone, either. But neither had he been willing to solve it. Frank had been dead for two years, though, and now it was my turn—mine and Brianna's.

"Have you heard yet from Dr. Linklater?" I asked, as we came down the arch of the bridge. Late in the afternoon as it was, the sun was still high, so far north as we were. Caught among the leaves of the lime trees on the riverbank, it glowed pink on the granite cenotaph that stood below the bridge.

Roger shook his head, squinting against the wind. "No, but it's been only a week since I wrote. If I don't hear by the Monday, I'll try telephoning. Don't worry"—he smiled sideways at me—"I was very circumspect. I just told him that for purposes of a study I was making, I needed a list—if one existed—of the Jacobite officers who were in Leanach farmhouse after Culloden, and if any information exists as to the survivor of that execution, could he refer me to the original sources?"

"Do you know Linklater?" I asked, easing my left arm by tilting the books sideways against my hip.

"No, but I wrote my request on the Balliol College letterhead, and made tactful reference to Mr. Cheesewright, my old tutor, who *does* know Linklater." Roger winked reassuringly, and I laughed.

His eyes were a brilliant, lucent green, bright against his olive skin. Curiosity might be his stated reason for helping us to find out Jamie's history, but I was well aware that his interest went a good bit deeper—in the direction of Brianna. I also knew that the interest was returned. What I didn't know was whether Roger realized that as well.

Back in the late Reverend Wakefield's study, I dropped my armload of books on the table in relief, and collapsed into the wing chair by the hearth, while Roger went to fetch a glass of lemonade from the manse's kitchen.

My breathing slowed as I sipped the tart sweetness, but my pulse stayed erratic, as I looked over the imposing stack of books we had brought back. Was Jamie in there somewhere? And if he was . . . my hands grew wet on the cold glass, and I choked the thought off. Don't look too far ahead, I cautioned myself. Much better to wait, and see what we might find.

Roger was scanning the shelves in the study, in search of other possibilities. The Reverend Wakefield, Roger's late adoptive father, had been both a good amateur historian, and a terrible pack rat; letters, journals, pamphlets and broadsheets, antique and contemporary volumes—all were crammed cheek by jowl together on the shelves.

Roger hesitated, then his hand fell on a stack of books sitting on the nearby table. They were Frank's books—an impressive achievement, so far as I could tell by reading the encomiums printed on the dust jackets.

"Have you ever read this?" he asked, picking up the volume entitled *The Jacobites.*

"No," I said. I took a restorative gulp of lemonade, and coughed. "No,"

I said again. "I couldn't." After my return, I had resolutely refused to look at any material dealing with Scotland's past, even though the eighteenth century had been one of Frank's areas of specialty. Knowing Jamie dead, and faced with the necessity of living without him, I avoided anything that might bring him to mind. A useless avoidance—there was no way of keeping him out of my mind, with Brianna's existence a daily reminder of him—but still, I could not read books about the Bonnie Prince—that terrible, futile young man—or his followers.

"I see. I just thought you might know whether there might be something useful in here." Roger paused, the flush deepening over his cheekbones. "Did—er, did your husband—Frank, I mean," he added hastily. "Did you tell him . . . um . . . about . . ." His voice trailed off, choked with embarrassment.

"Well, of course I did!" I said, a little sharply. "What did you think—I'd just stroll back into his office after being gone for three years and say, 'Oh, hullo there, darling, and what would you like for supper tonight?' "

"No, of course not," Roger muttered. He turned away, eyes fixed on the bookshelves. The back of his neck was deep red with embarrassment.

"I'm sorry," I said, taking a deep breath. "It's a fair question to ask. It's only that it's—a bit raw, yet." A good deal more than a bit. I was both surprised and appalled to find just how raw the wound still was. I set the glass down on the table at my elbow. If we were going on with this, I was going to need something stronger than lemonade.

"Yes," I said. "I told him. All about the stones—about Jamie. Everything."

Roger didn't reply for a moment. Then he turned, halfway, so that only the strong, sharp lines of his profile were visible. He didn't look at me, but down at the stack of Frank's books, at the back-cover photo of Frank, leanly dark and handsome, smiling for posterity.

"Did he believe you?" Roger asked quietly.

My lips felt sticky from the lemonade, and I licked them before answering.

"No," I said. "Not at first. He thought I was mad; even had me vetted by a psychiatrist." I laughed, shortly, but the memory made me clench my fists with remembered fury.

"Later, then?" Roger turned to face me. The flush had faded from his skin, leaving only an echo of curiosity in his eyes. "What did he think?"

I took a deep breath and closed my eyes. "I don't know."

The tiny hospital in Inverness smelled unfamiliar, like carbolic disinfectant and starch.

I couldn't think, and tried not to feel. The return was much more terrifying than my venture into the past had been, for there, I had been shrouded by a protective layer of doubt and disbelief about where I was and what was happening, and had lived in constant hope of escape. Now I knew only too well where I was, and I knew that there was no escape. Jamie was dead.

The doctors and nurses tried to speak kindly to me, to feed me and bring me things to drink, but there was no room in me for anything but grief and terror. I had told them my name when they asked, but wouldn't speak further.

I lay in the clean white bed, fingers clamped tight together over my vulnerable belly, and kept my eyes shut. I visualized over and over the last things I had seen before I stepped through the stones—the rainy moor and Jamie's face—knowing that if I looked too long at my new surroundings, these sights would fade, replaced by mundane things like the nurses and the vase of flowers by my bed. I pressed one thumb secretly against the base of the other, taking an obscure comfort in the tiny wound there, a small cut in the shape of a J. Jamie had made it, at my demand—the last of his touch on my flesh.

I must have stayed that way for some time; I slept sometimes, dreaming of the last few days of the Jacobite Rising—I saw again the dead man in the wood, asleep beneath a coverlet of bright blue fungus, and Dougal MacKenzie dying on the floor of an attic in Culloden House; the ragged men of the Highland army, asleep in the muddy ditches; their last sleep before the slaughter.

I would wake screaming or moaning, to the scent of disinfectant and the sound of soothing words, incomprehensible against the echoes of Gaelic shouting in my dreams, and fall asleep again, my hurt clutched tight in the palm of my hand.

And then I opened my eyes and Frank was there. He stood in the door, smoothing back his dark hair with one hand, looking uncertain—and no wonder, poor man.

I lay back on the pillows, just watching him, not speaking. He had the look of his ancestors, Jack and Alex Randall; fine, clear, aristocratic features and a well-shaped head, under a spill of straight dark hair. His face had some indefinable difference from theirs, though, beyond the small differences of feature. There was no mark of fear or ruthlessness on him; neither the spirituality of Alex nor the icy arrogance of Jack. His lean face looked intelligent, kind, and slightly tired, unshaven and with smudges beneath his eyes. I knew without being told that he had driven all night to get here.

"Claire?" He came over to the bed, and spoke tentatively, as though not sure that I really was Claire.

I wasn't sure either, but I nodded and said, "Hullo, Frank." My voice was scratchy and rough, unaccustomed to speech.

He took one of my hands, and I let him have it.

"Are you . . . all right?" he said, after a minute. He was frowning slightly as he looked at me.

"I'm pregnant." That seemed the important point, to my disordered mind. I had not thought of what I would say to Frank, if I ever saw him again, but the moment I saw him standing in the door, it seemed to come clear in my mind. I would tell him I was pregnant, he would leave, and I would be alone with my last sight of Jamie's face, and the burning touch of him on my hand.

His face tightened a bit, but he didn't let go of my other hand. "I know. They told me." He took a deep breath and let it out. "Claire—can you tell me what happened to you?"

I felt quite blank for a moment, but then shrugged.

"I suppose so," I said. I mustered my thoughts wearily; I didn't want to be talking about it, but I had some feeling of obligation to this man. Not guilt, not yet; but obligation nonetheless. I had been married to him.

"Well," I said, "I fell in love with someone else, and I married him. I'm sorry," I added, in response to the look of shock that crossed his face, "I couldn't help it."

He hadn't been expecting that. His mouth opened and closed for a bit and he gripped my hand, hard enough to make me wince and jerk it out of his grasp.

"What do you mean?" he said, his voice sharp. "Where have you been, Claire?" He stood up suddenly, looming over the bed.

"Do you remember that when I last saw you, I was going up to the stone circle on Craigh na Dun?"

"Yes?" He was staring down at me with an expression somewhere between anger and suspicion.

"Well"—I licked my lips, which had gone quite dry—"the fact is, I walked through a cleft stone in that circle, and ended up in 1743."

"Don't be facetious, Claire!"

"You think I'm being funny*?" The thought was so absurd that I actually began to laugh, though I felt a good long way from real humor.*

"Stop that!"

I quit laughing. Two nurses appeared at the door as though by magic; they must have been lurking in the hall nearby. Frank leaned over and grabbed my arm.

"Listen to me," he said through his teeth. "You are going to tell me where you've been and what you've been doing!"

"I am telling *you! Let go!" I sat up in bed and yanked at my arm, pulling it out of his grasp. "I told you; I walked through a stone and ended up two hundred years ago. And I met your bloody ancestor, Jack Randall, there!"*

Frank blinked, entirely taken aback. "Who?"

"Black Jack Randall, and a bloody, filthy, nasty pervert he was, too!"

Frank's mouth hung open, and so did the nurses'. I could hear feet coming down the corridor behind them, and hurried voices.

"I had to marry Jamie Fraser to get away from Jack Randall, but then —Jamie—I couldn't help it, Frank, I loved him and I would have stayed with him if I could, but he sent me back because of Culloden, and the baby, and—" I broke off, as a man in a doctor's uniform pushed past the nurses by the door.

"Frank," I said tiredly, "I'm sorry. I didn't mean it to happen, and I tried all I could to come back—really, I did—but I couldn't. And now it's too late."

Despite myself, tears began to well up in my eyes and roll down my cheeks. Mostly for Jamie, and myself, and the child I carried, but a few for Frank as well. I sniffed hard and swallowed, trying to stop, and pushed myself upright in the bed.

"Look," I said, "I know you won't want to have anything more to do with me, and I don't blame you at all. Just—just go away, will you?"

His face had changed. He didn't look angry anymore, but distressed, and slightly puzzled. He sat down by the bed, ignoring the doctor who had come in and was groping for my pulse.

"I'm not going anywhere," he said, quite gently. He took my hand again, though I tried to pull it away. "This—Jamie. Who was he?"

I took a deep, ragged breath. The doctor had hold of my other hand, still trying to take my pulse, and I felt absurdly panicked, as though I were being held captive between them. I fought down the feeling, though, and tried to speak steadily.

"James Alexander Malcolm MacKenzie Fraser," I said, spacing the words, formally, the way Jamie had spoken them to me when he first told me his full name—on the day of our wedding. The thought made another tear overflow, and I blotted it against my shoulder, my hands being restrained.

"He was a Highlander. He was k-killed at Culloden." It was no use, I was weeping again, the tears no anodyne to the grief that ripped through me, but the only response I had to unendurable pain. I bent forward slightly, trying to encapsulate it, wrapping myself around the tiny, imperceptible life in my belly, the only remnant left to me of Jamie Fraser.

Frank and the doctor exchanged a glance of which I was only half-conscious. Of course, to them, Culloden was part of the distant past. To me, it had happened only two days before.

"Perhaps we should let Mrs. Randall rest for a bit," the doctor suggested. "She seems a wee bit upset just now."

Frank looked uncertainly from the doctor to me. "Well, she certainly

does seem upset. But I really want to find out . . . what's this, Claire?"
Stroking my hand, he had encountered the silver ring on my fourth finger,
and now bent to examine it. It was the ring Jamie had given me for our
marriage; a wide silver band in the Highland interlace pattern, the links
engraved with tiny, stylized thistle blooms.

"No!" I exclaimed, panicked, as Frank tried to twist it off my finger. I
jerked my hand away and cradled it, fisted, beneath my bosom, cupped in
my left hand, which still wore Frank's gold wedding band. "No, you can't
take it, I won't let you! That's my wedding ring!"

"Now, see here, Claire—" Frank's words were interrupted by the doc-
tor, who had crossed to Frank's side of the bed, and was now bending
down to murmur in his ear. I caught a few words—"not trouble your
wife just now. The shock"—and then Frank was on his feet once more,
being firmly urged away by the doctor, who gave a nod to one of the nurses
in passing.

I barely felt the sting of the hypodermic needle, too engulfed in the fresh
wave of grief to take notice of anything. I dimly heard Frank's parting
words, "All right—but Claire, I will know!" And then the blessed dark-
ness came down, and I slept without dreaming, for a long, long time.

Roger tilted the decanter, bringing the level of the spirit in the glass up to
the halfway point. He handed it to Claire with a half-smile.

"Fiona's grannie always said whisky is good for what ails ye."

"I've seen worse remedies." Claire took the glass and gave him back the
half-smile in change.

Roger poured out a drink for himself, then sat down beside her, sipping
quietly.

"I tried to send him away, you know," she said suddenly, lowering her
glass. "Frank. I told him I knew he couldn't feel the same for me, no matter
what he believed had happened. I said I would give him a divorce; he must
go away and forget about me—take up the life he'd begun building without
me."

"He wouldn't do it, though." Roger said. It was growing chilly in the
study as the sun went down, and he bent and switched on the ancient electric
fire. "Because you were pregnant?" he guessed.

She shot him a sudden sharp look, then smiled, a little wryly.

"Yes, that was it. He said no one but a cad would dream of abandoning a
pregnant woman with virtually no resources. Particularly one whose grip on
reality seemed a trifle tenuous," she added ironically. "I wasn't quite without
resources—I had a bit of money from my uncle Lamb—but Frank wasn't a
cad, either." Her glance shifted to the bookshelves. Her husband's historical
works stood there, side by side, spines gleaming in the light of the desklamp.

"He was a very decent man," she said softly. She took another sip of her drink, closing her eyes as the alcoholic fumes rose up.

"And then—he knew, or suspected, that he couldn't have children himself. Rather a blow, for a man so involved in history and genealogies. All those dynastic considerations, you see."

"Yes, I can see that," Roger said slowly. "But wouldn't he feel—I mean, another man's child?"

"He might have." The amber eyes were looking at him again, their clearness slightly softened by whisky and reminiscence. "But as it was, since he didn't—*couldn't*—believe anything I said about Jamie, the baby's father was essentially unknown. If he didn't know who the man was—and convinced himself that I didn't really know either, but had just made up these delusions out of traumatic shock—well, then, there was no one ever to say that the child *wasn't* his. Certainly not me," she added, with just a tinge of bitterness.

She took a large swallow of whisky that made her eyes water slightly, and took a moment to wipe them.

"But to make sure, he took me clean away. To Boston," she went on. "He'd been offered a good position at Harvard, and no one knew us there. That's where Brianna was born."

The fretful crying jarred me awake yet again. I had gone back to bed at 6:30, after getting up five times during the night with the baby. A bleary-eyed look at the clock showed the time now as 7:00. A cheerful singing came from the bathroom, Frank's voice raised in "Rule, Britannia," over the noise of rushing water.

I lay in bed, heavy-limbed with exhaustion, wondering whether I had the strength to endure the crying until Frank got out of the shower and could bring Brianna to me. As though the baby knew what I was thinking, the crying rose two or three tones and escalated to a sort of periodic shriek, punctuated by frightening gulps for air. I flung back the covers and was on my feet, propelled by the same sort of panic with which I had greeted air raids during the War.

I lumbered down the chilly hall and into the nursery, to find Brianna, aged three months, lying on her back, yelling her small red head off. I was so groggy from lack of sleep that it took a moment for me to realize that I had left her on her stomach.

"Darling! You turned over! All by yourself!" Terrorized by her audacious act, Brianna waved her little pink fists and squalled louder, eyes squeezed shut.

I snatched her up, patting her back and murmuring to the top of her red-fuzzed head.

"Oh, you precious darling! What a clever girl you are!"

"What's that? What's happened?" Frank emerged from the bathroom, toweling his head, a second towel wrapped about his loins. "Is something the matter with Brianna?"

He came toward us, looking worried. As the birth grew closer, we had both been edgy; Frank irritable and myself terrified, having no idea what might happen between us, with the appearance of Jamie Fraser's child. But when the nurse had taken Brianna from her bassinet and handed her to Frank, with the words "Here's Daddy's little girl," his face had grown blank, and then—looking down at the tiny face, perfect as a rosebud— gone soft with wonder. Within a week, he had been hers, body and soul.

I turned to him, smiling. "She turned over! All by herself!"

"Really?" His scrubbed face beamed with delight. "Isn't it early for her to do that?"

"Yes, it is. Dr. Spock says she oughtn't to be able to do it for another month, at least!"

"Well, what does Dr. Spock know? Come here, little beauty; give Daddy a kiss for being so precocious." He lifted the soft little body, encased in its snug pink sleep-suit, and kissed her button of a nose. Brianna sneezed, and we both laughed.

I stopped then, suddenly aware that it was the first time I had laughed in nearly a year. Still more, that it was the first time I had laughed with Frank.

He realized it too; his eyes met mine over the top of Brianna's head. They were a soft hazel, and at the moment, filled with tenderness. I smiled at him, a little tremulous, and suddenly very much aware that he was all but naked, with water droplets sliding down his lean shoulders and shining on the smooth brown skin of his chest.

The smell of burning reached us simultaneously, jarring us from this scene of domestic bliss.

"The coffee!" Thrusting Bree unceremoniously into my arms, Frank bolted for the kitchen, leaving both towels in a heap at my feet. Smiling at the sight of his bare buttocks, gleaming an incongruous white as he sprinted into the kitchen, I followed him more slowly, holding Bree against my shoulder.

He was standing at the sink, naked, amid a cloud of malodorous steam rising from the scorched coffeepot.

"Tea, maybe?" I asked, adroitly anchoring Brianna on my hip with one arm while I rummaged in the cupboard. "None of the orange pekoe leaf left, I'm afraid; just Lipton's teabags."

Frank made a face; an Englishman to the bone, he would rather lap water out of the toilet than drink tea made from teabags. The Lipton's had been left by Mrs. Grossman, the weekly cleaning woman, who thought tea made from loose leaves messy and disgusting.

"No, I'll get a cup of coffee on my way to the university. Oh, speaking of which, you recall that we're having the Dean and his wife to dinner tonight? Mrs. Hinchcliffe is bringing a present for Brianna."

"Oh, right," I said, without enthusiasm. I had met the Hinchcliffes before, and wasn't all that keen to repeat the experience. Still, the effort had to be made. With a mental sigh, I shifted the baby to the other side and groped in the drawer for a pencil to make a grocery list.

Brianna burrowed into the front of my red chenille dressing gown, making small voracious grunting noises.

"You can't be hungry again," I said to the top of her head. *"I fed you not two hours ago."* My breasts were beginning to leak in response to her rooting, though, and I was already sitting down and loosening the front of my gown.

"Mrs. Hinchcliffe said that a baby shouldn't be fed every time it cries," Frank observed. *"They get spoilt if they aren't kept to a schedule."*

It wasn't the first time I had heard Mrs. Hinchcliffe's opinions on child-rearing.

"Then she'll be spoilt, won't she?" I said coldly, not looking at him. The small pink mouth clamped down fiercely, and Brianna began to suck with mindless appetite. I was aware that Mrs. Hinchcliffe also thought breast-feeding both vulgar and insanitary. I, who had seen any number of eighteenth-century babies nursing contentedly at their mothers' breasts, didn't.

Frank sighed, but didn't say anything further. After a moment, he put down the pot holder and sidled toward the door.

"Well," he said awkwardly. *"I'll see you around six then, shall I? Ought I to bring home anything—save you going out?"*

I gave him a brief smile, and said, *"No, I'll manage."*

"Oh, good." He hesitated a moment, as I settled Bree more comfortably on my lap, head resting on the crook of my arm, the round of her head echoing the curve of my breast. I looked up from the baby, and found him watching me intently, eyes fixed on the swell of my half-exposed bosom.

My own eyes flicked downward over his body. I saw the beginnings of his arousal, and bent my head over the baby, to hide my flushing face.

"Goodbye," I muttered, to the top of her head.

He stood still a moment, then leaned forward and kissed me briefly on the cheek, the warmth of his bare body unsettlingly near.

"Goodbye, Claire," he said softly. *"I'll see you tonight."*

He didn't come into the kitchen again before leaving, so I had a chance to finish feeding Brianna and bring my own feelings into some semblance of normality.

I hadn't seen Frank naked since my return; he had always dressed in bathroom or closet. Neither had he tried to kiss me before this morning's *cautious peck. The pregnancy had been what the obstetrician called "high-risk," and there had been no question of Frank's sharing my bed, even had I been so disposed—which I wasn't.*

I should have seen this coming, but I hadn't. Absorbed first in sheer misery, and then in the physical torpor of oncoming motherhood, I had pushed away all considerations beyond my bulging belly. After Brianna's birth, I had lived from feeding to feeding, seeking small moments of mindless peace, when I could hold her oblivious body close and find relief from thought and memory in the pure sensual pleasure of touching and holding her.

Frank, too, cuddled the baby and played with her, falling asleep in his big chair with her stretched out atop his lanky form, rosy cheek pressed flat against his chest, as they snored together in peaceful companionship. He and I did not touch each other, though, nor did we truly talk about anything beyond our basic domestic arrangements—except Brianna.

The baby was our shared focus; a point through which we could at once reach each other, and keep each other at arm's length. It looked as though arm's length was no longer close enough for Frank.

I could do it—physically, at least. I had seen the doctor for a checkup the week before, and he had—with an avuncular wink and a pat on the bottom—assured me that I could resume "relations" with my husband at any time.

I knew Frank hadn't been celibate since my disappearance. In his late forties, he was still lean and muscular, dark and sleek, a very handsome man. Women clustered about him at cocktail parties like bees round a honeypot, emitting small hums of sexual excitement.

There had been one girl with brown hair whom I had noticed particularly at the departmental party; she stood in the corner and stared at Frank mournfully over her drink. Later she became tearfully and incoherently drunk, and was escorted home by two female friends, who took turns casting evil looks at Frank and at me, standing by his side, silently bulging in my flowered maternity dress.

He'd been discreet, though. He was always home at night, and took pains not to have lipstick on his collar. So, now he meant to come home all the way. I supposed he had some right to expect it; was that not a wifely duty, and I once more his wife?

There was only one small problem. It wasn't Frank I reached for, deep in the night, waking out of sleep. It wasn't his smooth, lithe body that walked my dreams and roused me, so that I came awake moist and gasping, my heart pounding from the half-remembered touch. But I would never touch that man again.

"Jamie," I whispered, "Oh, Jamie." My tears sparkled in the morning

light, adorning Brianna's soft red fuzz like scattered pearls and diamonds.

It wasn't a good day. Brianna had a bad diaper rash, which made her cross and irritable, needing to be picked up every few minutes. She nursed and fussed alternately, pausing to spit up at intervals, making clammy wet patches on whatever I wore. I changed my blouse three times before eleven o'clock.

The heavy nursing bra I wore chafed under the arms, and my nipples felt cold and chapped. Midway through my laborious tidying-up of the house, there was a whooshing clank from under the floorboards, and the hot-air registers died with a feeble sigh.

"No, next week won't do," I said over the telephone to the furnace-repair shop. I looked at the window, where the cold February fog was threatening to seep under the sill and engulf us. "It's forty-two degrees in here, and I have a three-month-old baby!" The baby in question was sitting in her baby seat, swaddled in all her blankets, squalling like a scalded cat. Ignoring the quacking of the person on the other end, I held the receiver next to Brianna's wide open mouth for several seconds.

"See?" I demanded, lifting the phone to my ear again.

"Awright, lady," said a resigned voice on the other end of the line. "I'll come out this afternoon, sometime between noon and six."

"Noon and six? Can't you narrow it down a little more than that? I have to get out to the market," I protested.

"You ain't the only dead furnace in town, lady," the voice said with finality, and hung up. I glanced at the clock; eleven-thirty. I'd never be able to get the marketing done and get back in half an hour. Marketing with a small baby was more like a ninety-minute expedition into Darkest Borneo, requiring massive amounts of equipment and tremendous expenditures of energy.

Gritting my teeth, I called the expensive market that delivered, ordered the necessities for dinner, and picked up the baby, who was by now the shade of an eggplant, and markedly smelly.

"That looks ouchy, darling. You'll feel much better if we get it off, won't you?" I said, trying to talk soothingly as I wiped the brownish slime off Brianna's bright-red bottom. She arched her back, trying to escape the clammy washcloth, and shrieked some more. A layer of Vaseline and the tenth clean diaper of the day; the diaper service truck wasn't due 'til tomorrow, and the house reeked of ammonia.

"All right, sweetheart, there, there." I hoisted her up on my shoulder, patting her, but the screeching went on and on. Not that I could blame her; her poor bottom was nearly raw. Ideally, she should be let to lie about on a towel with nothing on, but with no heat in the house, that wasn't *feasible. She and I were both wearing sweaters and heavy winter coats, which made the frequent feedings even more of a nuisance than usual; excavating a breast could take several minutes, while the baby screamed.*

Brianna couldn't sleep for more than ten minutes at a time. Consequently, neither could I. When we did drift off together at four o'clock, we were roused within a quarter of an hour by the crashing arrival of the furnace man, who pounded on the door, not bothering to set down the large wrench he was holding.

Jiggling the baby against my shoulder with one hand, I began cooking the dinner with the other, to the accompaniment of screeches in my ear and the sounds of violence from the cellar below.

"I ain't promising nothin', lady, but you got heat for now." The furnace man appeared abruptly, wiping a smear of grease from his creased forehead. He leaned forward to inspect Brianna, who was lying more or less peacefully across my shoulder, loudly sucking her thumb.

"How's that thumb taste, sweetie?" he inquired. "They say you shouldn't oughta let 'em suck their thumbs, you know," he informed me, straightening up. "Gives 'em crooked teeth and they'll need braces."

"Is that so?" I said through my own teeth. "How much do I owe you?"

Half an hour later, the chicken lay in its pan, stuffed and basted, surrounded by crushed garlic, sprigs of rosemary, and curls of lemon peel. A quick squeeze of lemon juice over the buttery skin, and I could stick it in the oven and go get myself and Brianna dressed. The kitchen looked like the result of an incompetent burglary, with cupboards hanging open and cooking paraphernalia strewn on every horizontal surface. I banged shut a couple of cupboard doors, and then the kitchen door itself, trusting that that would keep Mrs. Hinchcliffe out, even if good manners wouldn't.

Frank had brought a new pink dress for Brianna to wear. It was a beautiful thing, but I eyed the layers of lace around the neck dubiously. They looked not only scratchy, but delicate.

"Well, we'll give it a try," I told her. "Daddy will like you to look pretty. Let's try not to spit up in it, hm?"

Brianna responded by shutting her eyes, stiffening, and grunting as she extruded more slime.

"Oh, well done!" I said, sincerely. It meant changing the crib sheet, but at least it wouldn't make the diaper rash worse. The mess attended to and a fresh diaper in place, I shook out the pink dress, and paused to carefully wipe the snot and drool from her face before popping the garment over her head. She blinked at me and gurgled enticingly, windmilling her fists.

I obligingly lowered my head and went "Pfffft!" into her navel, which made her squirm and gurgle with joy. We did it a few more times, then began the painstaking job of getting into the pink dress.

Brianna didn't like it; she started to complain as I put it over her head, and as I crammed her chubby little arms into the puffed sleeves, put back her head and let out a piercing cry.

"What is it?" I demanded, startled. I knew all her cries by now and mostly, what she meant by them, but this was a new one, full of fright and pain. "What's the matter, darling?"

She was screaming furiously now, tears rolling down her face. I turned her frantically over and patted her back, thinking she might have had a sudden attack of colic, but she wasn't doubled up. She was struggling violently, though, and as I turned her back over to pick her up, I saw the long red line running up the tender inside of her waving arm. A pin had been left in the dress, and had scored her flesh as I forced the sleeve up her arm.

"Oh, baby! Oh, I'm so sorry! Mummy's so sorry!" Tears were running down my own face as I eased the stabbing pin free and removed it. I clutched her to my shoulder, patting and soothing, trying to calm my own feelings of panicked guilt. Of course I hadn't meant to hurt her, but she wouldn't know that.

"Oh, darling," I murmured. "It's all right now. Yes, Mummy loves you, it's all right." Why hadn't I thought to check for pins? For that matter, what sort of maniac would package a baby's clothes using straight pins? Torn between fury and distress, I eased Brianna into the dress, wiped her chin, and carried her into the bedroom, where I laid her on my twin bed while I hastily changed to a decent skirt and a fresh blouse.

The doorbell rang as I was pulling on my stockings. There was a hole in one heel, but no time to do anything about it now. I stuck my feet into the pinching alligator pumps, snatched up Brianna, and went to answer the door.

It was Frank, too laden with packages to use his key. One-handed, I took most of them from him and parked them on the hall table.

"Dinner all ready, dear? I've brought a new tablecloth and napkins—thought ours were a bit shabby. And the wine, of course." He lifted the bottle in his hand, smiling, then leaned forward to peer at me, and stopped smiling. He looked disapprovingly from my disheveled hair to my blouse, freshly stained with spit-up milk.

"Christ, Claire," he said. "Couldn't you fix yourself up a bit? I mean, it's not as though you have anything else to do, at home all day—couldn't you take a few minutes for a—"

"No," I said, quite loudly. I pushed Brianna, who was wailing again with fretful exhaustion, into his arms.

"No," I said again, and took the wine bottle from his unresisting hand.

"NO!" I shrieked, stamping my foot. I swung the bottle widely, and he dodged, but it was the doorjamb I struck, and purplish splatters of

Beaujolais flew across the stoop, leaving glass shards glittering in the light from the entryway.

I flung the shattered bottle into the azaleas and ran coatless down the walk and into the freezing fog. At the foot of the walk, I passed the startled Hinchcliffes, who were arriving half an hour early, presumably in hopes of catching me in some domestic deficiency. I hoped they'd enjoy their dinner.

I drove aimlessly through the fog, the car's heater blasting on my feet, until I began to get low on gas. I wasn't going home; not yet. An all-night cafe? Then I realized that it was Friday night, and getting on for twelve o'clock. I had a place to go, after all. I turned back toward the suburb where we lived, and the Church of St. Finbar.

At this hour, the chapel was locked to prevent vandalism and burglary. For the late adorers, there was a push-button lock set just below the door handle. Five buttons, numbered one to five. By pushing three of them, in the proper combination, the latch could be sprung to allow lawful entry.

I moved quietly along the back of the chapel, to the logbook that sat at the feet of St. Finbar, to record my arrival.

"St. Finbar?" Frank had said incredulously. "There isn't such a saint. There can't possibly be."

"There is," I said, with a trace of smugness. "An Irish bishop, from the twelfth century."

"Oh, Irish," said Frank dismissively. "That explains it. But what I can't understand," he said, careful to be tactful, "is, er, well . . . why?"

"Why what?"

"Why go in for this Perpetual Adoration business? You've never been the least devout, no more than I have. And you don't go to Mass or anything; Father Beggs asks me every week where you are."

I shook my head. "I can't really say, Frank. It's just something . . . I need to do." I looked at him, helpless to explain adequately. "It's . . . peaceful there," I said, finally.

He opened his mouth as though to speak further, then turned away, shaking his head.

It was peaceful. The car park at the church was deserted, save for the single car of the adorer on duty at this hour, gleaming an anonymous black under the arc lights. Inside, I signed my name to the log and walked forward, coughing tactfully to alert the eleven o'clock adorer to my presence without the rudeness of direct speech. I knelt behind him, a heavyset man in a yellow windcheater. After a moment, he rose, genuflected before the altar, turned and walked to the door, nodding briefly as he passed me.

The door hissed shut and I was alone, save for the Sacrament displayed *on the altar, in the great golden sunburst of the monstrance. There were two candles on the altar, big ones. Smooth and white, they burned steadily in the still air, without a flicker. I closed my eyes for a moment, just listening to the silence.*

Everything that had happened during the day whirled through my mind in a disjointed welter of thoughts and feelings. Coatless, I was shaking with cold from the short walk through the parking lot, but slowly I grew warm again, and my clenched hands relaxed in my lap.

At last, as usually happened here, I ceased to think. Whether it was the stoppage of time in the presence of eternity, or only the overtaking of a bone-deep fatigue, I didn't know. But the guilt over Frank eased, the wrenching grief for Jamie lessened, and even the constant tug of mother-hood upon my emotions receded to the level of background noise, no louder than the slow beating of my own heart, regular and comforting in the dark peace of the chapel.

"O Lord," I whispered, "I commend to your mercy the soul of your servant James." And mine, I added silently. And mine.

I sat there without moving, watching the flickering glow of the candle flames in the gold surface of the monstrance, until the soft footsteps of the next adorer came down the aisle behind me, ending in the heavy creak of genuflection. They came once each hour, day and night. The Blessed Sacrament was never left alone.

I stayed for a few minutes more, then slid out of the pew, with my own nod toward the altar. As I walked toward the back of the chapel, I saw a figure in the back row, under the shadow of the statue of St. Anthony. It stirred as I approached, then the man rose to his feet and made his way to the aisle to meet me.

"What are you doing here?" I hissed.

Frank nodded toward the form of the new adorer, already kneeling in contemplation, and took my elbow to guide me out.

I waited until the chapel door had closed behind us before pulling away and whirling to confront him.

"What is this?" I said angrily. "Why did you come after me?"

"I was worried about you." He gestured toward the empty car park, where his large Buick nestled protectively next to my small Ford. "It's dangerous, a lone woman walking about in the very late night in this part of town. I came to see you home. That's all."

He didn't mention the Hinchcliffes, or the dinner party. My annoy-ance ebbed a bit.

"Oh," I said. "What did you do with Brianna?"

"Asked old Mrs. Munsing from next door to keep an ear out in case she cried. But she seemed dead asleep; I didn't think there was much chance. Come along now, it's cold out."

It was; the freezing air off the bay was coiling in white tendrils around the posts of the arc lights, and I shivered in my thin blouse.

"I'll meet you at home, then," I said.

The warmth of the nursery reached out to embrace me as I went in to check Brianna. She was still asleep, but restless, turning her russet head from side to side, the groping little mouth opening and closing like the breathing of a fish.

"She's getting hungry," I whispered to Frank, who had come in behind me and was hovering over my shoulder, peering fondly at the baby. "I'd better feed her before I come to bed; then she'll sleep later in the morning."

"I'll get you a hot drink," and he vanished through the door to the kitchen as I picked up the sleepy, warm bundle.

She had only drained one side, but she was full. The slack mouth pulled slowly away from the nipple, rimmed with milk, and the fuzzy head fell heavily back on my arm. No amount of gentle shaking or calling would rouse her to nurse on the other side, so at last I gave up and tucked her back in her crib, patting her back softly until a faint, contented belch wafted up from the pillow, succeeded by the heavy breathing of absolute satiation.

"Down for the night, is she?" Frank drew the baby blanket, decorated with yellow bunnies, up over her.

"Yes." I sat back in my rocking chair, mentally and physically too exhausted to get up again. Frank came to stand behind me; his hand rested lightly on my shoulder.

"He's dead, then?" he asked gently.

I told you so, I started to say. Then I stopped, closed my mouth and only nodded, rocking slowly, staring at the dark crib and its tiny occupant.

My right breast was still painfully swollen with milk. No matter how tired I was, I couldn't sleep until I took care of it. With a sigh of resignation, I reached for the breast pump, an ungainly and ridiculous-looking rubber contraption. Using it was undignified and uncomfortable, but better than waking up in an hour in bursting pain, sopping wet from overflowing milk.

I waved a hand at Frank, dismissing him.

"Go ahead. It will only take a few minutes, but I have to . . ."

Instead of leaving or answering, he took the pump from my hand and laid it down on the table. As though it moved of its own will, without direction from him, his hand rose slowly through the warm, dark air of the nursery and cupped itself gently around the swollen curve of my breast.

His head bowed and his lips fastened softly on my nipple. I groaned, feeling the half-painful prickle of the milk rushing through the tiny ducts. I put a hand behind his head, and pressed him slightly closer.

"Harder," I whispered. His mouth was soft, gentle in its pressure, nothing like the relentless grasp of a baby's hard, toothless gums, that fasten on like grim death, demanding and draining, releasing the bounteous fountain at once in response to their greed.

Frank knelt before me, his mouth a supplicant. Was this how God felt, I wondered, seeing the adorers before Him—was He, too, filled with tenderness and pity? The haze of fatigue made me feel as though everything happened in slow motion, as though we were under water. Frank's hands moved slowly as sea fronds, swaying in the current, moving over my flesh with a touch as gentle as the brush of kelp leaves, lifting me with the strength of a wave, and laying me down on the shore of the nursery rug. I closed my eyes, and let the tide carry me away.

The front door of the old manse opened with a screech of rusty hinges, announcing the return of Brianna Randall. Roger was on his feet and into the hall at once, drawn by the sound of girls' voices.

"A pound of best butter—that's what you told me to ask for, and I did, but I kept wondering whether there was such a thing as second-best butter, or worst butter—" Brianna was handing over wrapped packages to Fiona, laughing and talking at once.

"Well, and if ye got it from that auld rascal Wicklow, worst is what it's likely to be, no matter what he says," Fiona interrupted. "Oh, and ye've got the cinnamon, that's grand! I'll make cinnamon scones, then; d'ye want to come and watch me do it?"

"Yes, but first I want supper. I'm starved!" Brianna stood on tiptoe, sniffing hopefully in the direction of the kitchen. "What are we having— haggis?"

"Haggis! Gracious, ye silly Sassenach—ye dinna have haggis in the spring! Ye have it in the autumn when the sheep are killed."

"Am I a Sassenach?" Brianna seemed delighted at the name.

"Of course ye are, gowk. But I like ye fine, anyway."

Fiona laughed up at Brianna, who towered over the small Scottish girl by nearly a foot. Fiona was nineteen, prettily charming and slightly plump; next to her, Brianna looked like a medieval carving, strong-boned and severe. With her long, straight nose and the long hair glowing red-gold beneath the glass bowl of the ceiling fixture, she might have walked out of an illuminated manuscript, vivid enough to endure a thousand years unchanged.

Roger was suddenly conscious of Claire Randall, standing near his elbow. She was looking at her daughter, with an expression in which love, pride, and something else were mingled—memory, perhaps? He realized, with a slight shock, that Jamie Fraser too must have had not only the striking height and Viking red hair he had bequeathed to his daughter, but likely the same sheer physical presence.

It was quite remarkable, he thought. She didn't do or say anything so out of the ordinary, and yet Brianna undeniably drew people. There was some attraction about her, almost magnetic, that drew everyone near into the glow of her orbit.

It drew him; Brianna turned and smiled at him, and without consciousness of having moved, he found himself near enough to see the faint freckles high on her cheekbones, and smell the whiff of pipe tobacco that lingered in her hair from her expeditions to the shops.

"Hullo," he said, smiling. "Any luck with the Clans office, or have you been too busy playing dogsbody for Fiona?"

"Dogsbody?" Brianna's eyes slanted into blue triangles of amusement. *"Dogsbody?* First I'm a Sassenach, and now I'm a dogsbody. What do you Scots call people when you're trying to be *nice?*"

"Darrrrlin'," he said, rolling his *r*'s exaggeratedly, and making both girls laugh.

"You sound like an Aberdeen terrier in a bad mood," Claire observed. "Did you find anything at the Highland Clans library, Bree?"

"Lots of stuff," Brianna replied, rummaging through the stack of photo-copies she had set down on the hall table. "I managed to read most of it while they were making the copies—this one was the most interesting." She pulled a sheet from the stack and handed it to Roger.

It was an extract from a book of Highland legends; an entry headed "Leap O' the Cask."

"Legends?" said Claire, peering over his shoulder. "Is that what we want?"

"Could be." Roger was perusing the sheet, and spoke absently, his atten-tion divided. "So far as the Scottish Highlands go, most of the history is oral, up to the mid-nineteenth century or so. That means there wasn't a great distinction made between stories about real people, stories of historical fig-ures, and the stories about mythical things like water horses and ghosts and the doings of the Auld Folk. Scholars who wrote the stories down often didn't know for sure which they were dealing with, either—sometimes it was a combination of fact and myth, and sometimes you could tell that it was a real historical occurrence being described.

"This one, for instance"—he passed the paper to Claire—"sounds like a real one. It's describing the story behind the name of a particular rock formation in the Highlands."

Claire brushed the hair behind her ear and bent her head to read, squint-ing in the dim light of the ceiling fixture. Fiona, too accustomed to musty papers and boring bits of history to be interested, disappeared back into her kitchen to see to the dinner.

" 'Leap O' the Cask,' " Claire read. " *'This unusual formation, located some distance above a burn, is named after the story of a Jacobite laird and his servant. The laird, one of the few fortunates to escape the disaster of Culloden, made his way with difficulty to his home, but was compelled to lie hidden in a cave on his lands for nearly seven years, while the English hunted the Highlands for the fugitive supporters of Charles Stuart. The laird's tenants loyally kept his presence a secret, and brought food and supplies to the laird in his hiding place. They were careful always to refer to the hidden man only as the "Dunbonnet," in order to avoid any chance of giving him away to the English patrols who frequently crossed the district.*

" *'One day, a boy bringing a cask of ale up the trail to the laird's cave met a group of English dragoons. Bravely refusing either to answer the soldiers' questions, or to give up his burden, the boy was attacked by one of the dragoons, and dropped the cask, which bounded down the steep hill, and into the burn below.' "*

She looked up from the paper, raising her eyebrows at her daughter.

"Why this one? We know—or we think we know," she corrected, with a wry nod toward Roger, "that Jamie escaped from Culloden, but so did a lot of other people. What makes you think this laird might have been Jamie?"

"Because of the Dunbonnet bit, of course," Brianna answered, as though surprised that she should ask.

"What?" Roger looked at her, puzzled. "What about the Dunbonnet?"

In answer, Brianna picked up a hank of her thick red hair and waggled it under his nose.

"Dunbonnet!" she said impatiently. "A dull brown bonnet, right? He wore a hat all the time, because he had hair that could be recognized! Didn't you say the English called him 'Red Jamie'? They knew he had red hair—he had to hide it!"

Roger stared at her, speechless. The hair floated loose on her shoulders, alive with fiery light.

"You could be right," Claire said. Excitement made her eyes bright as she looked at her daughter. "It was like yours—Jamie's hair was just like yours, Bree." She reached up and softly stroked Brianna's hair. The girl's face softened as she looked down at her mother.

"I know," she said. "I was thinking about that while I was reading—trying to see him, you know?" She stopped and cleared her throat, as though something might be caught in it. "I could see him, out in the heather, hiding, and the sun shining off his hair. You said he'd been an outlaw; I just —I just thought he must have known pretty well . . . how to hide. If people were trying to kill him," she finished softly.

"Right." Roger spoke briskly, to dispel the shadow in Brianna's eyes.

"That's a marvelous job of guesswork, but maybe we can tell for sure, with a little more work. If we can find Leap O' the Cask on a map—"

"What kind of dummy do you think I am?" Brianna said scornfully. "I thought of that." The shadow disappeared, replaced by an expression of smugness. "That's why I was so late; I made the clerk drag out every map of the Highlands they had." She withdrew another photocopied sheet from the stack and poked a finger triumphantly near the upper edge.

"See? It's so tiny, it doesn't show up on most maps, but this one had it. Right there; there's the village of Broch Mordha, which Mama says is near the Lallybroch estate, and there"—her finger moved a quarter-inch, pointing to a line of microscopic print. "See?" she repeated. "He went back to his estate—Lallybroch—and that's where he hid."

"Not having a magnifying glass to hand, I'll take your word for it that that says 'Leap O' the Cask,' " Roger said, straightening up. He grinned at Brianna. "Congratulations, then," he said. "I think you've found him—that far, at least."

Brianna smiled, her eyes suspiciously bright. "Yeah," she said softly. She touched the two sheets of paper with a gentle finger. "My father."

Claire squeezed her daughter's hand. "If you have your father's hair, it's nice to see you have your mother's brains," she said, smiling. "Let's go and celebrate your discovery with Fiona's dinner."

"Good job," Roger said to Brianna, as they followed Claire toward the dining room. His hand rested lightly on her waist. "You should be proud of yourself."

"Thanks," she said, with a brief smile, but the pensive expression returned almost at once to the curve of her mouth.

"What is it?" Roger asked softly, stopping in the hall. "Is something the matter?"

"No, not really." She turned to face him, a small line visible between the ruddy brows. "It's only—I was just thinking, trying to imagine—what do you think it was like for him? Living in a cave for seven years? And what happened to him then?"

Moved by an impulse, Roger leaned forward and kissed her lightly between the brows.

"I don't know, darlin'," he said. "But maybe we'll find out."

PART TWO

Lallybroch

4

The Dunbonnet

he came down to the house once a month to shave, when one of the boys brought him word it was safe. Always at night, moving soft-footed as a fox through the dark. It seemed necessary, somehow, a small gesture toward the concept of civilization.

He would slip like a shadow through the kitchen door, to be met with Ian's smile or his sister's kiss, and would feel the transformation begin. The basin of hot water, the freshly stropped razor would be laid ready for him on the table, with whatever there was for shaving soap. Now and then it was real soap, if Cousin Jared had sent some from France; more often just half-rendered tallow, eye-stinging with lye.

He could feel the change begin with the first scent of the kitchen—so strong and rich, after the wind-thin smells of loch and moor and wood—but it wasn't until he had finished the ritual of shaving that he felt himself altogether human once more.

They had learned not to expect him to talk until he had shaved; words came hard after a month's solitude. Not that he could think of nothing to say; it was more that the words inside formed a logjam in his throat, battling each other to get out in the short time he had. He needed those few minutes of careful grooming to pick and choose, what he would say first and to whom.

There was news to hear and to ask about—of English patrols in the district, of politics, of arrests and trials in London and Edinburgh. That he could wait for. Better to talk to Ian about the estate, to Jenny about the children. If it seemed safe, the children would be brought down to say hello to their uncle, to give him sleepy hugs and damp kisses before stumbling back to their beds.

"He'll be getting a man soon" had been his first choice of conversation when he came in September, with a nod toward Jenny's eldest child, his namesake. The ten-year-old sat at the table with a certain constraint, immensely conscious of the dignity of his temporary position as man of the house.

"Aye, all I need's another of the creatures to worry over," his sister replied tartly, but she touched her son's shoulder in passing, with a pride that belied her words.

"Have ye word from Ian, then?" His brother-in-law had been arrested—for the fourth time—three weeks before, and taken to Inverness under suspicion of being a Jacobite sympathizer.

Jenny shook her head, bringing a covered dish to set before him. The thick warm smell of partridge pie drifted up from the pricked crust, and made his mouth water so heavily, he had to swallow before he could speak.

"It's naught to fret for," Jenny said, spooning out the pie onto his plate. Her voice was calm, but the small vertical line between her brows deepened. "I've sent Fergus to show them the deed of sasine, and Ian's discharge from his regiment. They'll send him home again, so soon as they realize he isna the laird of Lallybroch, and there's naught to be gained by deviling him." With a glance at her son, she reached for the ale jug. "Precious chance they have of provin' a wee bairn to be a traitor."

Her voice was grim, but held a note of satisfaction at the thought of the English court's confusion. The rain-spattered deed of sasine that proved transfer of the title of Lallybroch from the elder James to the younger had made its appearance in court before, each time foiling the Crown's attempt to seize the estate as the property of a Jacobite traitor.

He would feel it begin to slip away when he left—that thin veneer of humanity—more of it gone with each step away from the farmhouse. Sometimes he would keep the illusion of warmth and family all the way to the cave where he hid; other times it would disappear almost at once, torn away by a chill wind, rank and acrid with the scent of burning.

The English had burned three crofts, beyond the high field. Pulled Hugh Kirby and Geoff Murray from their firesides and shot them by their own doorsteps, with no question or word of formal accusation. Young Joe Fraser had escaped, warned by his wife, who had seen the English coming, and had lived three weeks with Jamie in the cave, until the soldiers were well away from the district—and Ian with them.

In October, it had been the older lads he spoke to; Fergus, the French boy he had taken from a Paris brothel, and Rabbie MacNab, the kitchenmaid's son, Fergus's best friend.

He had drawn the razor slowly down one cheek and round the angle of his jaw, then wiped the lathered blade against the edge of the basin. From the corner of one eye, he caught a faint glimpse of fascinated envy on the face of Rabbie MacNab. Turning slightly, he saw that the three boys—Rabbie, Fergus, and Young Jamie—were all watching him intently, mouths slightly open.

"Have ye no seen a man shave before?" he asked, cocking one brow.

Rabbie and Fergus glanced at each other, but left it to Young Jamie, as titular owner of the estate, to answer.

"Oh, well . . . aye, Uncle," he said, blushing. "But . . . I m-mean"— he stammered slightly and blushed even harder—"with my Da gone, and even when he's home, we dinna see him shave himself always, and well, you've just such a lot of *hair* on your face, Uncle, after a whole month, and it's only we're so glad to see you again, and . . ."

It dawned on Jamie quite suddenly that to the boys he must seem a most romantic figure. Living alone in a cave, emerging at dark to hunt, coming down out of the mist in the night, filthy and wild-haired, beard all in a fierce red sprout—yes, at their age, it likely seemed a glamorous adventure to be an outlaw and live hidden in the heather, in a dank, cramped cave. At fifteen and sixteen and ten, they had no notion of guilt or bitter loneliness, of the weight of a responsibility that could not be relieved by action.

They might understand fear, of a sort. Fear of capture, fear of death. Not the fear of solitude, of his own nature, fear of madness. Not the constant, chronic fear of what his presence might do to them—if they thought about that risk at all, they dismissed it, with the casual assumption of immortality that was the right of boys.

"Aye, well," he had said, turning casually back to the looking glass as Young Jamie stuttered to a halt. "Man is born to sorrow and whiskers. One of the plagues of Adam."

"Of Adam?" Fergus looked openly puzzled, while the others tried to pretend they had the slightest idea what Jamie was talking about. Fergus, as a Frenchie, was not expected to know everything.

"Oh, aye." Jamie pulled his upper lip down over his teeth and scraped delicately beneath his nose. "In the beginning, when God made man, Adam's chin was as hairless as Eve's. And their bodies both smooth as a newborn child's," he added, seeing Young Jamie's eyes dart toward Rabbie's crotch. Beardless Rabbie still was, but the faint dark down on his upper lip bespoke new sproutings elsewhere.

"But when the angel wi' the flaming sword drove them out of Eden, no sooner had they passed the gate of the garden, when the hair began to sprout and itch on Adam's chin, and ever since, man has been cursed with shaving." He finished his own chin with a final flourish, and bowed theatrically to his audience.

"But what about the other hair?" Rabbie demanded. "Ye dinna shave *there*!" Young Jamie giggled at the thought, going red again.

"And a damn good thing, too," his elder namesake observed. "Ye'd need the devil of a steady hand. No need of a looking glass, though," he added, to a chorus of giggles.

"What about the ladies?" Fergus said. His voice broke on the word "ladies," in a bullfrog croak that made the other two laugh harder. "Certainly *les filles* have hair there, too, but they do not shave it—usually not, anyway," he added, clearly thinking of some of the sights of his early life in the brothel.

Jamie heard his sister's footsteps coming down the hall.

"Oh, well, that's no a curse," he told his rapt audience, picking up the basin and tossing the contents neatly through the open window. "God gave that as a consolation to man. If ye've ever the privilege of seeing a woman in her skin, gentlemen," he said, looking over his shoulder toward the door and lowering his voice confidentially, "ye'll observe that the hair there grows in the shape of an arrow—pointing the way, ye ken, so as a poor ignorant man can find his way safe home."

He turned grandly away from the guffawing and sniggers behind him, to be struck suddenly with shame as he saw his sister, coming down the hall with the slow, waddling stride of advanced pregnancy. She was holding the tray with his supper on top of her swelling stomach. How could he have demeaned her so, for a crude jest and the sake of a moment's camaraderie with the boys?

"Be still!" he had snapped at the boys, who stopped giggling abruptly and stared at him in puzzlement. He hastened forward to take the tray from Jenny and set it on the table.

It was a savoury made of goat's meat and bacon, and he saw Fergus's prominent Adam's apple bob in the slender throat at the smell of it. He knew they saved the best of the food for him; it didn't take much looking at the pinched faces across the table. When he came, he brought what meat he could, snared rabbits or grouse, sometimes a nest of plover's eggs—but it was never enough, for a house where hospitality must stretch to cover the needs of not only family and servants, but the families of the murdered Kirby and Murray. At least until spring, the widows and children of his tenants must bide here, and he must do his best to feed them.

"Sit down by me," he said to Jenny, taking her arm and gently guiding her to a seat on the bench beside him. She looked surprised—it was her habit to wait on him when he came—but sat down gladly enough. It was late, and she was tired; he could see the dark smudges beneath her eyes.

With great firmness, he cut a large slab of the savoury and set the plate before her.

"But that's all for you!" Jenny protested. "I've eaten."

"Not enough," he said. "Ye need more—for the babe," he added, with inspiration. If she would not eat for herself, she would for the child. She hesitated a moment longer, but then smiled at him, picked up her spoon, and began to eat.

Now it was November, and the chill struck through the thin shirt and breeches he wore. He hardly noticed, intent on his tracking. It was cloudy, but with a thin-layered mackerel sky, through which the full moon shed plenty of light.

Thank God it wasn't raining; impossible to hear through the pattering of raindrops, and the pungent scent of wet plants masked the smell of animals. His nose had grown almost painfully acute through the long months of living outdoors; the smells of the house sometimes nearly knocked him down when he stepped inside.

He wasn't quite close enough to smell the musky scent of the stag, but he heard the telltale rustle of its brief start when it scented *him*. Now it would be frozen, one of the shadows that rippled across the hillside around him, under the racing clouds.

He turned as slowly as he possibly could toward the spot where his ears had told him the stag stood. His bow was in his hand, an arrow ready to the string. He would have one shot—maybe—when the stag bolted.

Yes, there! His heart sprang into his throat as he saw the antlers, pricking sharp and black above the surrounding gorse. He steadied himself, took a deep breath, and then the one step forward.

The crash of a deer's flight was always startlingly loud, to frighten back a stalker. This stalker was prepared, though. He neither startled nor pursued, but stood his ground, sighting along the shaft of the arrow, following with his eye the track of the springing deer, judging the moment, holding fire, and then the bowstring slapped his wrist with stinging force.

It was a clean shot, just behind the shoulder, and a good thing, too; he doubted he had the strength to run down a full-grown stag. It had fallen in a clear spot behind a clump of gorse, legs stuck out, stiff as sticks, in the oddly helpless way of dying ungulates. The hunter's moon lit its glazing eye, so the soft dark stare was hidden, the mystery of its dying shielded by blank silver.

He pulled the dirk from his belt and knelt by the deer, hastily saying the words of the gralloch prayer. Old John Murray, Ian's father, had taught him. His own father's mouth had twisted slightly, hearing it, from which he gathered that this prayer was perhaps not addressed to the same God they spoke to in church on Sunday. But his father had said nothing, and he had mumbled the words himself, scarcely noticing what he said, in the nervous excitement of feeling old John's hand, steady on his own, for the first time pressing down the knife blade into hairy hide and steaming flesh.

Now, with the sureness of practice, he thrust up the sticky muzzle in one hand, and with the other, slit the deer's throat.

The blood spurted hot over knife and hand, pumping two or three times, the jet dying away to a steady stream as the carcass drained, the great vessels of the throat cut through. Had he paused to think, he might not have done it, but hunger and dizziness and the cold fresh intoxication of the night had taken him far past the point of thinking. He cupped his hands beneath the running stream and brought them steaming to his mouth.

The moon shone black on his cupped, spilling hands, and it was as though he absorbed the deer's substance, rather than drank it. The taste of the blood was salt and silver, and the heat of it was his own. There was no startlement of hot or cold as he swallowed, only the taste of it, rich in his mouth, and the head-swimming, hot-metal smell, and the sudden clench and rumble of his belly at the nearness of food.

He closed his eyes and breathed, and the cold damp air came back, between the hot reek of the carcass and his senses. He swallowed once, then wiped the back of his hand across his face, cleaned his hands on the grass, and set about the business at hand.

There was the sudden effort of moving the limp, heavy carcass, and then the gralloch, the long stroke of mingled strength and delicacy that slit the hide between the legs, but did not penetrate the sac that held the entrails. He forced his hands into the carcass, a hot wet intimacy, and again there was an effortful tug that brought out the sac, slick and moon-shining in his hands. A slash above and another below, and the mass slid free, the transformation of black magic that changed a deer to meat.

It was a small stag, although it had points to its antlers. With luck, he could carry it alone, rather than leave it to the mercy of foxes and badgers until he could bring help to move it. He ducked a shoulder under one leg, and slowly rose, grunting with effort as he shifted the burden to a solid resting place across his back.

The moon cast his shadow on a rock, humped and fantastic, as he made his slow, ungainly way down the hill. The deer's antlers bobbed above his shoulder, giving him in shadowed profile the semblance of a horned man. He shivered slightly at the thought, remembering tales of witches' sabbats, where the Horned One came, to drink the sacrifice of goat's or rooster's blood.

He felt a little queasy, and more than a little light-headed. More and more, he felt the disorientation, the fragmenting of himself between day and night. By day, he was a creature of the mind alone, as he escaped his damp immobility by a stubborn, disciplined retreat into the avenues of thought and meditation, seeking refuge in the pages of books. But with the rising of the moon, all sense fled, succumbing at once to sensation, as he emerged into the fresh air like a beast from its lair, to run the dark hills beneath the stars, and hunt, driven by hunger, drunk with blood and moonlight.

He stared at the ground as he walked, night-sight keen enough to keep his footing, despite the heavy burden. The deer was limp and cooling, its stiff, soft hair scratching against the back of his neck, and his own sweat cooling in the breeze, as though he shared his prey's fate.

It was only as the lights of Lallybroch manor came into view that he felt at last the mantle of humanity fall upon him, and mind and body joined as one again as he prepared himself to greet his family.

5

To Us a Child Is Given

Three weeks later, there was still no word of Ian's return. No word of any kind, in fact. Fergus had not come to the cave in several days, leaving Jamie in a fret of worry over how things might be at the house. If nothing else, the deer he had shot would have gone long since, with all the extra mouths to feed, and there would be precious little from the kailyard at this time of year.

He was sufficiently worried to risk an early visit, checking his snares and coming down from the hills just before sunset. Just in case, he was careful to pull on the woolen bonnet, knitted of rough dun yarn, that would hide his hair from any telltale fingering of late sunbeams. His size alone might provoke suspicion, but not certainty, and he had full confidence in the strength of his legs to carry him out of harm's way should he have the ill luck to meet with an English patrol. Hares in the heather were little match for Jamie Fraser, given warning.

The house was strangely quiet as he approached. There was none of the usual racket made by children: Jenny's five, and the six bairns belonging to the tenants, to say nothing of Fergus and Rabbie MacNab, who were a long way from being too old to chase each other round the stables, screeching like fiends.

The house felt strangely empty round him, as he paused just inside the kitchen door. He was standing in the back hall, the pantry to one side, the scullery to the other, and the main kitchen just beyond. He stood stock-still, reaching out with all his senses, listening as he inhaled the overpowering smells of the house. No, there was someone here; the faint sound of a scrape, followed by a soft, regular clinking came from behind the cloth-padded door that kept the heat of the kitchen from seeping out into the chilly back pantry.

It was a reassuringly domestic sound, so he pushed open the door cautiously, but without undue fear. His sister, Jenny, alone and vastly pregnant, was standing at the table, stirring something in a yellow bowl.

"What are you doing in here? Where's Mrs. Coker?"

His sister dropped the spoon with a startled shriek.

"Jamie!" Pale-faced, she pressed a hand to her breast and closed her eyes. "Christ! Ye scairt the bowels out of me." She opened her eyes, dark blue like his own, and fixed him with a penetrating stare. "And what in the name of the Holy Mother are ye doing here now? I wasna expecting ye for a week at least."

"Fergus hasna come up the hill lately; I got worried," he said simply.

"Ye're a sweet man, Jamie." The color was coming back into her face. She smiled at her brother and came close to hug him. It was an awkward business, with the impending baby in the way, but pleasant, nonetheless. He rested his cheek for a moment on the sleek darkness of her head, breathing in her complex aroma of candle wax and cinnamon, tallow-soap and wool. There was an unusual element to her scent this evening; he thought she was beginning to smell of milk.

"Where is everyone?" he asked, releasing her reluctantly.

"Well, Mrs. Coker's dead," she answered, the faint crease between her brows deepening.

"Aye?" he said softly, and crossed himself. "I'm sorry for it." Mrs. Coker had been first housemaid and then housekeeper for the family, since the marriage of his own parents, forty-odd years before. "When?"

"Yesterday forenoon. 'Twasn't unexpected, poor soul, and it was peaceful. She died in her own bed, like she wanted, and Father McMurtry prayin' over her."

Jamie glanced reflexively toward the door that led to the servants' rooms, off the kitchen. "Is she still here?"

His sister shook her head. "No. I told her son they should have the wake here at the house, but the Cokers thought, everything being like it is"—her small moue encompassed Ian's absence, lurking Redcoats, refugee tenants, the dearth of food, and his own inconvenient presence in the cave—"they thought better to have it at Broch Mordha, at her sister's place. So that's where everyone's gone. I told them I didna feel well enough to go," she added, then smiled, raising an impish brow. "But it was really that I wanted a few hours' peace and quiet, wi' the lot of them gone."

"And here I've come, breakin' in on your peace," Jamie said ruefully. "Shall I go?"

"No, clot-heid," his sister said affably. "Sit ye down, and I'll get on wi' the supper."

"What's to eat, then?" he asked, sniffing hopefully.

"Depends on what ye've brought," his sister replied. She moved heavily about the kitchen, taking things from cupboard and hutch, pausing to stir the large kettle hung over the fire, from which a thin steam was rising.

"If ye've brought meat, we'll have it. If not, it's brose and hough."

He made a face at this; the thought of boiled barley and shin-beef, the last remnants of the salted beef carcass they'd bought two months before, was unappealing.

"Just as well I had luck, then," he said. He upended his game bag and let the three rabbits fall onto the table in a limp tumble of gray fur and crumpled ears. "And blackthorn berries," he added, tipping out the contents of the dun bonnet, now stained inside with the rich red juice.

Jenny's eyes brightened at the sight. "Hare pie," she declared. "There's no currants, but the berries will do even better, and there's enough butter, thank God." Catching a tiny blink of movement among the gray fur, she slapped her hand down on the table, neatly obliterating the minuscule intruder.

"Take them out and skin 'em, Jamie, or the kitchen will be hopping wi' fleas."

Returning with the skinned carcasses, he found the piecrust well advanced, and Jenny with smears of flour on her dress.

"Cut them into collops and break the bones for me, will ye, Jamie?" she said, frowning at *Mrs. McClintock's Receipts for Cookery and Pastry-Work*, laid open on the table beside the pie pan.

"Surely ye can make hare pie without looking in the wee book?" he said, obligingly taking the big bone-crushing wooden mallet from the top of the hutch where it was kept. He grimaced as he took it into his hand, feeling the weight of it. It was very like the one that had broken his right hand several years before, in an English prison, and he had a sudden vivid memory of the shattered bones in a hare pie, splintered and cracked, leaking salty blood and marrow-sweetness into the meat.

"Aye, I can," his sister answered abstractedly, thumbing through the pages. "It's only that when ye havena got half the things ye need to make a dish, sometimes there's something else you'll come across in here, that ye can use instead." She frowned at the page before her. "Ordinarily, I'd use claret in the sauce, but we've none in the house, save one of Jared's casks in the priest hole, and I dinna want to broach that yet—we might need it."

He didn't need telling what she might use it for. A cask of claret might grease the skids for Ian's release—or at least pay for news of his welfare. He stole a sidewise glance at the great round of Jenny's belly. It wasn't for a man to say, but to his not inexperienced eyes, she looked damn near her time. Absently, he reached over the kettle and swished the blade of his dirk to and fro in the scalding liquid, then pulled it out and wiped it clean.

"Whyever did ye do that, Jamie?" He turned to find Jenny staring at him. The black curls were coming undone from their ribbon, and it gave him a pang to see the glimmer of a single white hair among the ebony.

"Oh," he said, too obviously offhand as he picked up one carcass, "Claire —she told me ye ought to wash off a blade in boiling water before ye touched food with it."

He felt rather than saw Jenny's eyebrows rise. She had asked him about Claire only once, when he had come home from Culloden, half-conscious and mostly dead with fever.

"She is gone," he had said, and turned his face away. "Dinna speak her name to me again." Loyal as always, Jenny had not, and neither had he. He could not have said what made him say it today; unless perhaps it was the dreams.

He had them often, in varying forms, and it always unsettled him the day after, as though for a moment Claire had really been near enough to touch, and then had drawn away again. He could swear that sometimes he woke with the smell of her on him, musky and rich, pricked with the sharp, fresh scents of leaves and green herbs. He had spilled his seed in his sleep more than once while dreaming, an occurrence that left him faintly shamed and uneasy in mind. To distract both of them, he nodded at Jenny's stomach.

"How close is it?" he asked, frowning at her swollen midsection. "Ye look like a puffball mushroom—one touch, and poof!" He flicked his fingers wide in illustration.

"Oh, aye? Well, and I could wish it was as easy as poof." She arched her back, rubbing at the small of it, and making her belly protrude in an alarming fashion. He pressed back against the wall, to give it room. "As for when, anytime, I expect. No telling for sure." She picked up the cup and measured out the flour; precious little left in the bag, he noted with some grimness.

"Send up to the cave when it starts," he said suddenly. "I'll come down, Redcoats or no."

Jenny stopped stirring and stared at him.

"You? Why?"

"Well, Ian's not here," he pointed out, picking up one skinned carcass. With the expertise of long practice, he neatly disjointed a thigh and cut it free from the backbone. Three quick smacks with the boning mallet and the pale flesh lay flattened and ready for the pie.

"And a great lot of help he'd be if he was," Jenny said. "He took care of his part o' the business nine months ago." She wrinkled her nose at her brother and reached for the plate of butter.

"Mmphm." He sat down to continue his work, which brought her belly close to his eye-level. The contents, awake and active, was shifting to and fro in a restless manner, making her apron twitch and bulge as she stirred. He couldn't resist reaching out to put a light hand against the monstrous curve, to feel the surprising strong thrusts and kicks of the inhabitant, impatient of its cramped confinement.

"Send Fergus for me when it's time," he said again.

She looked down at him in exasperation and batted his hand away with the spoon. "Have I no just been telling ye, I dinna need ye? For God's sake, man, have I not enough to worry me, wi' the house full of people, and scarce enough to feed them, Ian in gaol in Inverness, and Redcoats crawling in at the windows every time I look round? Should I have to worry that ye'll be taken up, as well?"

"Ye needna be worrit for me; I'll take care." He didn't look at her, but focused his attention on the forejoint he was slicing through.

"Well, then, have a care and stay put on the hill." She looked down her long, straight nose, peering at him over the rim of the bowl. "I've had six bairns already, aye? Ye dinna think I can manage by now?"

"No arguing wi' you, is there?" he demanded.

"No," she said promptly. "So you'll stay."

"I'll come."

Jenny narrowed her eyes and gave him a long, level look.

"Ye're maybe the most stubborn gomerel between here and Aberdeen, no?"

A smile spread across her brother's face as he looked up at her.

"Maybe so," he said. He reached across and patted her heaving belly. "And maybe no. But I'm coming. Send Fergus when it's time."

It was near dawn three days later that Fergus came panting up the slope to the cave, missing the trail in the dark, and making such a crashing through the gorse bushes that Jamie heard him coming long before he reached the opening.

"Milord . . ." he began breathlessly as he emerged by the head of the trail, but Jamie was already past the boy, pulling his cloak around his shoulders as he hurried down toward the house.

"But, milord . . ." Fergus's voice came behind him, panting and frightened. "Milord, the soldiers . . ."

"Soldiers?" He stopped suddenly and turned, waiting impatiently for the French lad to make his way down the slope. "What soldiers?" he demanded, as Fergus slithered the last few feet.

"English dragoons, milord. Milady sent me to tell you—on no account are you to leave the cave. One of the men saw the soldiers yesterday, camped near Dunmaglas."

"Damn."

"Yes, milord." Fergus sat down on a rock and fanned himself, narrow chest heaving as he caught his breath.

Jamie hesitated, irresolute. Every instinct fought against going back into the cave. His blood was heated by the surge of excitement caused by Fergus's appearance, and he rebelled at the thought of meekly crawling back into hiding, like a grub seeking refuge beneath its rock.

"Mmphm," he said. He glanced down at Fergus. The changing light was beginning to outline the boy's slender form against the blackness of the gorse, but his face was still a pale smudge, marked with a pair of darker smudges that were his eyes. A certain suspicion was stirring in Jamie. Why had his sister sent Fergus at this odd hour?

If it had been necessary urgently to warn him about the dragoons, it would have been safer to send the boy up during the night. If the need was not urgent, why not wait until the next night? The answer to that was obvious—because Jenny thought she might not be able to send him word the next night.

"How is it with my sister?" he asked Fergus.

"Oh, well, milord, quite well!" The hearty tone of this assurance confirmed all Jamie's suspicions.

"She's having the child, no?" he demanded.

"No, milord! Certainly not!"

Jamie reached down and clamped a hand on Fergus's shoulder. The bones felt small and fragile beneath his fingers, reminding him uncomfortably of the rabbits he had broken for Jenny. Nonetheless, he forced his grip to tighten. Fergus squirmed, trying to ease away.

"Tell me the truth, man," Jamie said.

"No, milord! Truly!"

The grip tightened inexorably. "Did she tell you not to tell me?"

Jenny's prohibition must have been a literal one, for Fergus answered this question with evident relief.

"Yes, milord!"

"Ah." He relaxed his grip and Fergus sprang to his feet, now talking volubly as he rubbed his scrawny shoulder.

"She said I must not tell you anything except about the soldiers, milord, for if I did, she would cut off my cods and boil them like turnips and sausage!"

Jamie could not repress a smile at this threat.

"Short of food we may be," he assured his protégé, "but not that short." He glanced at the horizon, where a thin line of pink showed pure and vivid behind the black pines' silhouette. "Come along, then; it'll be full light in half an hour."

There was no hint of silent emptiness about the house this dawn. Anyone with half an eye could see that things were not as usual at Lallybroch; the wash kettle sat on its plinth in the yard, with the fire gone out under it, full of cold water and sodden clothes. Moaning cries from the barn—like someone being strangled—indicated that the sole remaining cow urgently required milking. An irritable blatting from the goat shed let him know that the female inhabitants would like some similar attention as well.

As he came into the yard, three chickens ran past in a feathery squawk, with Jehu the rat terrier in close pursuit. With a quick dart, he leaped forward and booted the dog, catching it just under the ribs. It flew into the air with a look of intense surprise on its face, then, landing with a yip, picked itself up and made off.

He found the children, the older boys, Mary MacNab, and the other housemaid, Sukie, all crammed into the parlor, under the watchful eye of Mrs. Kirby, a stern and rock-ribbed widow, who was reading to them from the Bible.

" *'And Adam was not deceived, but the woman being deceived was in the transgression,'* " read Mrs. Kirby. There was a loud, rolling scream from upstairs, that seemed to go on and on. Mrs. Kirby paused for a moment, to allow everyone to appreciate it, before resuming the reading. Her eyes, pale gray and wet as raw oysters, flickered toward the ceiling, then rested with satisfaction on the row of strained faces before her.

" *'Notwithstanding, she shall be saved in childbearing, if she continue in faith and charity and holiness with sobriety,'* " she read. Kitty burst into hysterical sobbing and buried her head in her sister's shoulder. Maggie Ellen was growing bright red beneath her freckles, while her elder brother had gone dead-white at the scream.

"Mrs. Kirby," said Jamie. "Be still, if ye please."

The words were civil enough, but the look in his eyes must have been the one that Jehu saw just before his boot-assisted flight, for Mrs. Kirby gasped and dropped the Bible, which landed on the floor with a papery thump.

Jamie bent and picked it up, then showed Mrs. Kirby his teeth. The expression evidently was not successful as a smile, but had some effect nonetheless. Mrs. Kirby went quite pale, and put a hand to her ample bosom.

"Perhaps ye'd go to the kitchen and make yourself useful," he said, with a jerk of his head that sent Sukie the kitchenmaid scuttling out like a windblown leaf. With considerably more dignity, but no hesitation, Mrs. Kirby rose and followed her.

Heartened by this small victory, Jamie disposed of the parlor's other occupants in short order, sending the widow Murray and her daughters out to deal with the wash kettle, the smaller children out to catch chickens under the supervision of Mary MacNab. The older lads departed, with obvious relief, to tend the stock.

The room empty at last, he stood for a moment, hesitating as to what to do next. He felt obscurely that he should stay in the house, on guard, though he was acutely aware that he could—as Jenny had said—do nothing to help, whatever happened. There was an unfamiliar mule hobbled in the dooryard; presumably the midwife was upstairs with Jenny.

Unable to sit, he prowled restlessly around the parlor, the Bible in his hand, touching things. Jenny's bookshelf, battered and scarred from the last incursion of Redcoats, three months ago. The big silver epergne. That was slightly dented, but had been too heavy to fit in a soldier's knapsack, and so had escaped the pilfering of smaller objects. Not that the English had got so much; the few truly valuable items, along with the tiny store of gold they had left, were safely tucked away in the priest hole with Jared's wine.

Hearing a prolonged moan from above, he glanced down involuntarily at the Bible in his hand. Not really wanting to, still he let the book fall open, showing the page at the front where the marriages, births, and deaths of the family were recorded.

The entries began with his parents' marriage. Brian Fraser and Ellen Mac-Kenzie. The names and the date were written in his mother's fine round hand, with underneath, a brief notation in his father's firmer, blacker scrawl. *Marrit for love*, it said—a pointed observation, in view of the next entry, which showed Willie's birth, which had occurred scarcely two months past the date of the marriage.

Jamie smiled, as always, at sight of the words, and glanced up at the painting of himself, aged two, standing with Willie and Bran, the huge deer-hound. All that was left of Willie, who had died of the smallpox at eleven. The painting had a slash through the canvas—the work of a bayonet, he supposed, taking out its owner's frustration.

"And if ye hadna died," he said softly to the picture, "then what?"

Then what, indeed. Closing the book, his eye caught the last entry— *Caitlin Maisri Murray, born December 3, 1749, died December 3, 1749.* Aye, if. If the Redcoats had not come on December 2, would Jenny have borne the child too early? If they had had enough food, so that she, like the rest of them, was no more than skin and bones and the bulge of her belly, would that have helped?

"No telling, is there?" he said to the painting. Willie's painted hand rested on his shoulder; he had always felt safe, with Willie standing behind him.

Another scream came from upstairs, and a spasm of fear clenched his hands on the book.

"Pray for us, Brother," he whispered, and crossing himself, laid down the Bible and went out to the barn to help with the stock.

There was little to do here; Rabbie and Fergus between them were more than able to take care of the few animals that remained, and Young Jamie, at ten, was big enough to be a substantial help. Looking about for something to do, Jamie gathered up an armful of scattered hay and took it down the slope to the midwife's mule. When the hay was gone, the cow would have to be slaughtered; unlike the goats, it couldn't get enough forage on the winter hills to sustain it, even with the picked grass and weeds the small children brought in. With luck, the salted carcass would last them through 'til spring.

As he came back into the barn, Fergus looked up from his manure fork.

"This is a proper midwife, of good repute?" Fergus demanded. He thrust out a long chin aggressively. "Madame should not be entrusted to the care of a peasant, surely!"

"How should I know?" Jamie said testily. "D'ye think I had anything to do wi' engaging midwives?" Mrs. Martin, the old midwife who had delivered all previous Murray children, had died—like so many others—during the famine in the year following Culloden. Mrs. Innes, the new midwife, was much younger; he hoped she had sufficient experience to know what she was doing.

Rabbie seemed inclined to join the argument as well. He scowled blackly at Fergus. "Aye, and what d'ye mean 'peasant'? Ye're a peasant, too, or have ye not noticed?"

Fergus stared down his nose at Rabbie with some dignity, despite the fact that he was forced to tilt his head backward in order to do so, he being several inches shorter than his friend.

"Whether I am a peasant or not is of no consequence," he said loftily. "I am not a midwife, am I?"

"No, ye're a fiddle-ma-fyke!" Rabbie gave his friend a rough push, and with a sudden whoop of surprise, Fergus fell backward, to land heavily on the stable floor. In a flash, he was up. He lunged at Rabbie, who sat laughing on the edge of the manger, but Jamie's hand snatched him by the collar and pulled him back.

"None of that," said his employer. "I willna have ye spoilin' what little hay's left." He set Fergus back on his feet, and to distract him, asked, "And what d'ye ken of midwives anyway?"

"A great deal, milord." Fergus dusted himself off with elegant gestures. "Many of the ladies at Madame Elise's were brought to bed while I was there—"

"I daresay they were," Jamie interjected dryly. "Or is it childbed ye mean?"

"Childbed, certainly. Why, I was born there myself!" The French boy puffed his narrow chest importantly.

"Indeed." Jamie's mouth quirked slightly. "Well, and I trust ye made careful observations at the time, so as to say how such matters should be arranged?"

Fergus ignored this piece of sarcasm.

"Well, of course," he said, matter-of-factly, "the midwife will naturally have put a knife beneath the bed, to cut the pain."

"I'm none so sure she did that," Rabbie muttered. "At least it doesna sound much like it." Most of the screaming was inaudible from the barn, but not all of it.

"And an egg should be blessed with holy water and put at the foot of the bed, so that the woman shall bring forth the child easily," Fergus continued, oblivious. He frowned.

"I gave the woman an egg myself, but she did not appear to know what to do with it. And I had been keeping it especially for the last month, too," he added plaintively, "since the hens scarcely lay anymore. I wanted to be sure of having one when it was needed.

"Now, following the birth," he went on, losing his doubts in the enthusiasm of his lecture, "the midwife must brew a tea of the placenta, and give it to the woman to drink, so that her milk will flow strongly."

Rabbie made a faint retching sound. "Of the *afterbirth*, ye mean?" he said disbelievingly. "God!"

Jamie felt a bit queasy at this exhibition of modern medical knowledge himself.

"Aye, well," he said to Rabbie, striving for casualness, "they eat frogs, ye know. And snails. I suppose maybe afterbirth isna so strange, considering." Privately, he wondered whether it might not be long before they were all eating frogs and snails, but thought that a speculation better kept to himself.

Rabbie made mock puking noises. "Christ, who'd be a Frenchie!"

Fergus, standing close to Rabbie, whirled and shot out a lightning fist. Fergus was small and slender for his age, but strong for all that, and with a deadly aim for a man's weak points, knowledge acquired as a juvenile pickpocket on the streets of Paris. The blow caught Rabbie squarely in the wind, and he doubled over with a sound like a stepped-on pig's bladder.

"Speak with respect of your betters, if you please," Fergus said haughtily. Rabbie's face turned several shades of red and his mouth opened and closed like a fish's, as he struggled to get his breath back. His eyes bulged with a look of intense surprise, and he looked so ridiculous that it was a struggle for Jamie not to laugh, despite his worry over Jenny and his irritation at the boys' squabbling.

"Will ye wee doiters no keep your paws off—" he began, when he was interrupted by a cry from Young Jamie, who had until now been silent, fascinated by the conversation.

"What?" Jamie whirled, hand going automatically to the pistol he carried whenever he left the cave, but there was not, as he had half-expected, an English patrol in the stableyard.

"What the hell is it?" he demanded. Then, following Young Jamie's pointing finger, he saw them. Three small black specks, drifting across the brown crumple of dead vines in the potato field.

"Ravens," he said softly, and felt the hair rise on the back of his neck. For those birds of war and slaughter to come to a house during a birth was the worst sort of ill luck. One of the filthy beasts was actually settling on the rooftree, as he watched.

With no conscious thought, he took the pistol from his belt and braced the muzzle across his forearm, sighting carefully. It was a long shot, from the door of the stable to the rooftree, and sighted upward, too. Still . . .

The pistol jerked in his hand and the raven exploded in a cloud of black feathers. Its two companions shot into the air as though blown there by the explosion, and flapped madly away, their hoarse cries fading quickly on the winter air.

"Mon Dieu!" Fergus exclaimed. *"C'est bien, ça!"*

"Aye, bonny shooting, sir." Rabbie, still red-faced and a little breathless, had recovered himself in time to see the shot. Now he nodded toward the house, pointing with his chin. "Look, sir, is that the midwife?"

It was. Mrs. Innes poked her head out of the second-story window, fair hair flying loose as she leaned out to peer into the yard below. Perhaps she had been drawn by the sound of the shot, fearing some trouble. Jamie stepped into the stableyard and waved at the window to reassure her.

"It's all right," he shouted. "Only an accident." He didn't mean to mention the ravens, lest the midwife tell Jenny.

"Come up!" she shouted, ignoring this. "The bairn's born, and your sister wants ye!"

Jenny opened one eye, blue and slightly slanted like his own.

"So ye came, aye?"

"I thought someone should be here—if only to pray for ye," he said gruffly.

She closed the eye and a small smile curved her lips. She looked, he thought, very like a painting he had seen in France—an old one by some Italian fellow, but a good picture, nonetheless.

"Ye're a silly fool—and I'm glad of it," she said softly. She opened her eyes and glanced down at the swaddled bundle she held in the crook of her arm.

"D'ye want to see him?"

"Oh, a him, is it?" With hands experienced by years of unclehood, he lifted the tiny package and cuddled it against himself, pushing back the flap of blanket that shaded its face.

Its eyes were closed tight shut, the lashes not visible in the deep crease of the eyelids. The eyelids themselves lay at a sharp angle above the flushed smooth rounds of the cheeks, giving promise that it might—in this one recognizable feature, at least—resemble its mother.

The head was oddly lumpy, with a lopsided appearance that made Jamie think uncomfortably of a kicked-in melon, but the small fat mouth was relaxed and peaceful, the moist pink underlip quivering faintly with the snore attendant on the exhaustion of being born.

"Hard work, was it?" he said, speaking to the child, but it was the mother who answered him.

"Aye, it was," Jenny said. "There's whisky in the armoire—will ye fetch me a glass?" Her voice was hoarse and she had to clear her throat before finishing the request.

"Whisky? Should ye not be having ale wi' eggs beaten up in it?" he asked, repressing with some difficulty a mental vision of Fergus's suggestion of appropriate sustenance for newly delivered mothers.

"Whisky," his sister said definitely. "When ye were lyin' downstairs crippled and your leg killin' ye, did I give ye ale wi' eggs beaten up in it?"

"Ye fed me stuff a damn sight worse than that," her brother said, with a grin, "but ye're right, ye gave me whisky, too." He laid the sleeping child carefully on the coverlet, and turned to get the whisky.

"Has he a name, yet?" he asked, nodding toward the baby as he poured out a generous cup of the amber liquid.

"I'll call him Ian, for his Da." Jenny's hand rested gently for a moment on the rounded skull, lightly furred with a gold-brown fuzz. A pulse beat visibly in the soft spot on top; it seemed hideously fragile to Jamie, but the midwife had assured him the babe was a fine, lusty lad, and he supposed he must take her word for it. Moved by an obscure impulse to protect that nakedly exposed soft spot, he picked up the baby once more, pulling the blanket up over its head.

"Mary MacNab told me about you and Mrs. Kirby," Jenny remarked, sipping. "Pity I didna see it—she said the wretched auld besom nearly swallowed her tongue when ye spoke to her."

Jamie smiled in return, gently patting the baby's back as it lay against his shoulder. Dead asleep, the little body lay inert as a boneless ham, a soft comforting weight.

"Too bad she didn't. How can ye stand the woman, living in the same house wi' ye? I'd strangle her, were I here every day."

His sister snorted and closed her eyes, tilting her head back to let the whisky slide down her throat.

"Ah, folk fash ye as much as ye let them; I dinna let her, much. Still," she added, opening her eyes, "I canna say as I'll be sorry to be rid of her. I have it in my mind to palm her off on auld Kettrick, down at Broch Mordha. His wife and his daughter both died last year, and he'll be wanting someone to do for him."

"Aye, but if I were Samuel Kettrick, I'd take the widow Murray," Jamie observed, "not the widow Kirby."

"Peggy Murray's already provided for," his sister assured him. "She'll wed Duncan Gibbons in the spring."

"That's fast work for Duncan," he said, a little surprised. Then a thought occurred to him, and he grinned at her. "Do either o' them know it yet?"

"No," she said, grinning back. Then the smile faded into a speculative look.

"Unless you were thinking of Peggy yourself, that is?"

"Me?" Jamie was as startled as if she had suddenly suggested he might wish to jump out of the second-story window.

"She's only five and twenty," Jenny pursued. "Young enough for more bairns, and a good mother."

"How much of that whisky have ye had?" Her brother bent forward and pretended to examine the level of the decanter, cupping the baby's head in one palm to prevent it wobbling. He straightened up and gave his sister a look of mild exasperation.

"I'm living like an animal in a cave, and ye wish me to take a wife?" He felt suddenly hollow inside. To prevent her seeing that the suggestion had upset him, he rose and walked up and down the room, making unnecessary small humming noises to the bundle in his arms.

"How long is it since ye've lain wi' a woman, Jamie?" his sister asked conversationally behind him. Shocked, he turned on his heel to stare at her.

"What the hell sort of question is that to ask a man?"

"You've not gone wi' any of the unwed lasses between Lallybroch and Broch Mordha," she went on, paying no attention. "Or I'd have heard of it. None of the widows, either, I dinna think?" She paused delicately.

"Ye know damn well I haven't," he said shortly. He could feel his cheeks flushing with annoyance.

"Why not?" his sister asked bluntly.

"Why *not*?" He stared at her, his mouth slightly open. "Have ye lost your senses? What d'ye think, I'm the sort of man would slink about from house to house, bedding any woman who didna drive me out wi' a girdle in her hand?"

"As if they would. No, you're a good man, Jamie." Jenny smiled, half sadly. "Ye wouldna take advantage of any woman. Ye'd marry first, no?"

"No!" he said violently. The baby twitched and made a sleepy sound, and he transferred it automatically to his other shoulder, patting, as he glared at his sister. "I dinna mean to marry again, so ye just abandon all thought of matchmaking, Jenny Murray! I willna have it, d'ye hear?"

"Oh, I hear," she said, unperturbed. She pushed herself higher on the pillow, so as to look him in the eye.

"Ye mean to live a monk to the end of your days?" she asked. "Go to your grave wi' no son to bury you or bless your name?"

"Mind your own business, damn ye!" Heart pounding, he turned his back on her and strode to the window, where he stood staring sightlessly out over the stableyard.

"I ken ye mourn Claire." His sister's voice came softly from behind him. "D'ye think I could forget Ian, if he doesna come back? But it's time ye went on, Jamie. Ye dinna think Claire would mean ye to live alone all your life, with no one to comfort ye or bear your children?"

He didn't answer for a long time, just stood, feeling the soft heat of the small fuzzy head pressed against the side of his neck. He could see himself dimly in the misted glass, a tall dirty gangle of a man, the round white bundle incongruous beneath his own grim face.

"She was with child," he said softly at last, speaking to the reflection. "When she—when I lost her." How else could he put it? There was no way to tell his sister where Claire was—where he hoped she was. That he could not think of another woman, hoping that Claire still lived, even knowing her truly lost to him for good.

There was a long silence from the bed. Then Jenny said quietly, "Is that why ye came today?"

He sighed and turned sideways toward her, leaning his head against the cool glass. His sister was lying back, her dark hair loose on the pillow, eyes gone soft as she looked at him.

"Aye, maybe," he said. "I couldna help my wife; I suppose I thought I might help you. Not that I could," he added, with some bitterness. "I am as useless to you as I was to her."

Jenny stretched out a hand to him, face filled with distress. "Jamie, *mo chridhe*," she said, but then stopped, eyes widening in sudden alarm as a splintering crash and the sound of screams came from the house below.

"Holy Mary!" she said, growing even whiter. "It's the English!"

"Christ." It was as much a prayer as an exclamation of surprise. He glanced quickly from the bed to the window, judging the possibilities of hiding versus those of escape. The sounds of booted feet were already on the stair.

"The cupboard, Jamie!" Jenny whispered urgently, pointing. Without hesitation, he stepped into the armoire, and pulled the door to behind him.

The door of the chamber sprang open with a crash a moment later, to be filled with a red-coated figure in a cocked hat, holding a drawn sword before him. The Captain of dragoons paused, and darted his eyes all round the chamber, finally settling on the small figure in the bed.

"Mrs. Murray?" he said.

Jenny struggled to pull herself upright.

"I am. And what in flaming hell are ye doing in my house?" she demanded. Her face was pale and shiny with sweat, and her arms trembled, but she held her chin up and glared at the man. "Get out!"

Disregarding her, the man moved into the room and over to the window; Jamie could see his indistinct form disappear past the edge of the wardrobe, then reappear, back turned as he spoke to Jenny.

"One of my scouts reported hearing a shot from the vicinity of this house, not long since. Where are your men?"

"I have none." Her trembling arms would not support her longer, and Jamie saw his sister ease herself back, collapsing on the pillows. "You've taken my husband already—my eldest son is no more than ten." She did not mention Rabbie or Fergus; boys of their age were old enough to be treated

—or mistreated—as men, should the Captain take the notion. With luck, they would have taken to their heels at the first sight of the English.

The Captain was a hard-bitten man of middle age, and not overly given to credulity.

"The keeping of weapons in the Highlands is a serious offense," he said, and turned to the soldier who had come into the room behind him. "Search the house, Jenkins."

He had to raise his voice in the giving of the order, for there was a rising commotion in the stairwell. As Jenkins turned to leave the room, Mrs. Innes, the midwife, burst past the soldier who tried to bar her way.

"Leave the poor lady alone!" she cried, facing the Captain with fists clenched at her sides. The midwife's voice shook and her hair was coming down from its snood, but she stood her ground. "Get out, ye wretches! Leave her be!"

"I am not mistreating your mistress," the Captain said, with some irritation, evidently mistaking Mrs. Innes for one of the maids. "I am merely—"

"And her not delivered but an hour since! It isna decent even for ye to lay eyes on her, so much as—"

"Delivered?" The Captain's voice sharpened, and he glanced from the midwife to the bed in sudden interest. "You have borne a child, Mrs. Murray? Where is the infant?"

The infant in question stirred inside its wrappings, disturbed by the tightened grip of its horror-stricken uncle.

From the depths of the wardrobe, he could see his sister's face, white to the lips and set like stone.

"The child is dead," she said.

The midwife's mouth dropped open in shock, but luckily the Captain's attention was riveted on Jenny.

"Oh?" he said slowly. "Was it—"

"Mama!" The cry of anguish came from the doorway as Young Jamie broke free of a soldier's grip and hurled himself at his mother. "Mama, the baby's dead? No, no!" Sobbing, he flung himself on his knees and buried his head in the bedclothes.

As though to refute his brother's statement, baby Ian gave evidence of his living state by kicking his legs with considerable vigor against his uncle's ribs and emitting a series of small snuffling grunts, which fortunately went unheard in the commotion outside.

Jenny was trying to comfort Young Jamie, Mrs. Innes was futilely attempting to raise the boy, who kept a death grip on his mother's sleeve, the Captain was vainly trying to make himself heard above Young Jamie's grief-stricken wails, and over all, the muted sound of boots and shouting vibrated through the house.

Jamie rather thought the Captain was inquiring as to the location of the infant's body. He clutched the body in question closer, joggling it in an attempt to prevent any disposition on its part to cry. His other hand went to the hilt of his dirk, but it was a vain gesture; it was doubtful that even cutting his own throat would be of help, if the wardrobe were opened.

Baby Ian made an irascible noise, suggesting that he disliked being joggled. With visions of the house in flames and the inhabitants slaughtered, the noise sounded as loud to Jamie as his elder nephew's anguished howls.

"You did it!" Young Jamie had gotten to his feet, face wet and swollen with tears and rage, and was advancing on the Captain, curly black head lowered like a small ram's. "You killed my brother, ye English prick!"

The Captain was somewhat taken aback by this sudden attack, and actually took a step back, blinking at the boy. "No, boy, you're quite mistaken. Why, I only—"

"Prick! Cod! *A mhic an diabhoil!*" Entirely beside himself, Young Jamie was stalking the Captain, yelling every obscenity he had ever heard used, in Gaelic or English.

"Enh," said baby Ian in the elder Jamie's ear. "Enh, enh!" This sounded very much like the preliminary to a full-fledged screech, and in a panic, Jamie let go of his dirk and thrust his thumb into the soft, moist opening from which the sounds were issuing. The baby's toothless gums clamped onto his thumb with a ferocity that nearly made him exclaim aloud.

"Get out! Get out! Get out or I'll kill ye!" Young Jamie was screaming at the Captain, face contorted with rage. The Redcoat looked helplessly at the bed, as though to ask Jenny to call off this implacable small foe, but she lay as though dead with her eyes closed.

"I shall wait for my men downstairs," the Captain said, with what dignity he could, and withdrew, shutting the door hastily behind him. Deprived of his enemy, Young Jamie fell to the floor and collapsed into helpless weeping.

Through the crack in the door, Jamie saw Mrs. Innes look at Jenny, mouth opening to ask a question. Jenny shot up from the bedclothes like Lazarus, scowling ferociously, finger pressed to her lips to enjoin silence. Baby Ian champed viciously at the thumb, growling at its failure to yield any sustenance.

Jenny swung herself to the side of the bed and sat there, waiting. The sounds of the soldiers below throbbed and eddied through the house. Jenny was shaking with weakness, but she reached out a hand toward the armoire where her men lay hidden.

Jamie drew a deep breath and braced himself. It would have to be risked; his hand and wrist were wet with saliva, and the baby's growls of frustration were growing louder.

He stumbled from the wardrobe, drenched with sweat, and thrust the infant at Jenny. Baring her breast with a single wrench, she pressed the small head to her nipple, and bent over the tiny bundle, as though to protect it.

The beginnings of a squawk disappeared into the muffled sounds of vigorous sucking, and Jamie sat down on the floor quite suddenly, feeling as though someone had run a sword behind his knees.

Young Jamie had sat up at the sudden opening of the wardrobe, and now sat spraddled against the door, his face blank with bewildered shock as he looked from his mother to his uncle and back again. Mrs. Innes knelt beside him, whispering urgently in his ear, but no sign of comprehension showed on the small, tear-streaked face.

By the time shouts and the creaking of harness outside betokened the soldiers' departure, Young Ian lay replete and snoring in his mother's arms. Jamie stood by the window, just out of sight, watching them go.

The room was silent, save for the liquid noise of Mrs. Innes, drinking whisky. Young Jamie sat close against his mother, cheek pressed to her shoulder. She had not looked up once since taking the baby, and still sat, head lowered over the child in her lap, her black hair hiding her face.

Jamie stepped forward and touched her shoulder. The warmth of her seemed shocking, as though cold dread were his natural state and the touch of another person somehow foreign and unnatural.

"I'll go to the priest hole," he said softly, "and to the cave when it's dark."

Jenny nodded, but without looking up at him. There were several white hairs among the black, he saw, glinting silver by the parting down the center of her head.

"I think . . . I should not come down again," he said at last. "For a time."

Jenny said nothing, but nodded once more.

6

Being Now Justified by His Blood

As it was, he did come down to the house once more. For two months, he stayed close hidden in the cave, scarcely daring to come out at night to hunt, for the English soldiers were still in the district, quartered at Comar. The troops went out by day in small patrols of eight or ten, combing the countryside, looting what little there was to steal, destroying what they could not use. And all with the blessing of the English Crown.

A path led close by the base of the hill where his cavern was concealed. No more than a rude track, it had begun as a deer path, and still largely served that use, though it was a foolish stag that would venture within smelling distance of the cave. Still, sometimes when the wind was right, he would see a small group of the red deer on the path, or find fresh spoor in the exposed mud of the track next day.

It was helpful as well for such people as had business on the mountainside —few enough as those were. The wind had been blowing downwind from the cave, and he had no expectation of seeing deer. He had been lying on the ground just within the cave entrance, where enough light filtered through the overhanging screen of gorse and rowan for him to read on fine days. There were not a great many books, but Jared managed still to smuggle a few with his gifts from France.

This violent rain forced me to a new work, viz., to cut a hole through my new fortification, like a sink, to let the water go out, which would else have drowned my cave. After I had been in my cave some time, and found still no more shocks of the earthquake follow, I began to be more composed; and now, to support my spirits, which indeed wanted it very much, I went to my little store and took a small sup of rum, which however, I did then and always very sparingly, knowing I could have no more when that was gone.

It continued raining all that night, and great part of the next day, so that I could not stir abroad; but my mind being more composed, I began to think . . .

The shadows across the page moved as the bushes above him stirred. Instincts attuned, he caught the shift of the wind at once—and on it, the sound of voices.

He sprang to his feet, hand on the dirk that never left his side. Barely pausing to put the book carefully on its ledge, he grasped the knob of granite that he used as a handhold and pulled himself up into the steep narrow crevice that formed the cave's entrance.

The bright flash of red and metal on the path below hit him with a blow of shock and annoyance. Damn. He had little fear that any of the soldiers would leave the path—they were poorly equipped for making their way even through the normal stretches of open, spongy peat and heather, let alone an overgrown, brambly slope like this—but having them so close meant he could not risk leaving the cave before dark, even to get water or relieve himself. He cast a quick glance at his water jug, knowing as he did so that it was nearly empty.

A shout pulled his attention back to the track below, and he nearly lost his grip on the rock. The soldiers had bunched themselves around a small figure, humped under the weight of a small cask it bore on its shoulder. Fergus, on his way up with a cask of fresh-brewed ale. Damn, and damn again. He could have done with that ale; it had been months since he'd had any.

The wind had changed again, so he caught only small snatches of words, but the small figure seemed to be arguing with the soldier in front of him, gesticulating violently with its free hand.

"Idiot!" said Jamie, under his breath. "Give it to them and begone, ye wee clot!"

One soldier made a two-handed grab at the cask, and missed as the small dark-haired figure jumped nimbly back. Jamie smacked himself on the forehead with exasperation. Fergus could never resist insolence when confronted with authority—especially English authority.

The small figure now was skipping backward, shouting something at his pursuers.

"Fool!" Jamie said violently. "Drop it and run!"

Instead of either dropping the cask or running, Fergus, apparently sure of his own speed, turned his back on the soldiers and waggled his rump insultingly at them. Sufficiently incensed to risk their footing in the soggy vegetation, several of the Redcoats jumped the path to follow.

Jamie saw their leader raise an arm and shout in warning. It had evidently dawned on him that Fergus might be a decoy, trying to lead them into ambush. But Fergus too was shouting, and evidently the soldiers knew enough gutter French to interpret what he was saying, for while several of the men halted at their leader's shout, four of the soldiers hurled themselves at the dancing boy.

There was a scuffle and more shouting as Fergus dodged, twisting like an eel between the soldiers. In all the commotion and above the whining wind, Jamie could not have heard the rush of the saber being drawn from its scabbard, but ever after felt as though he had, as though the faint swish and ring of drawn metal had been the first inkling of disaster. It seemed to ring in his ears whenever he remembered the scene—and he remembered it for a very long time.

Perhaps it was something in the attitudes of the soldiers, an irritableness of mood that communicated itself to him in the cave. Perhaps only the sense of doom that had clung to him since Culloden, as though everything in his vicinity were tainted; at risk by virtue only of being near him. Whether he had heard the sound of the saber or not, his body had tensed itself to spring before he saw the silver arc of the blade swing through the air.

It moved almost lazily, slowly enough for his brain to have tracked its arc, deduced its target, and shouted, wordless, *no!* Surely it moved slowly enough that he could have darted down into the midst of the swarming men, seized the wrist that wielded the sword and twisted the deadly length of metal free, to tumble harmless to the ground.

The conscious part of his brain told him this was nonsense, even as it froze his hands around the granite knob, anchoring him against the overwhelming impulse to heave himself out of the earth and run forward.

You can't, it said to him, a thready whisper under the fury and the horror that filled him. *He has done this for you; you cannot make it senseless. You can't,* it said, cold as death beneath the searing rush of futility that drowned him. *You can do nothing.*

And he did nothing, nothing but watch, as the blade completed its lazy swing, crashed home with a small, almost inconsequential thunk! and the disputed cask tumbled end over end over end down the slope of the burn, its final splash lost in the merry gurgle of brown water far below.

The shouting ceased abruptly in shocked silence. He scarcely heard when it resumed; it sounded so much like the roaring in his ears. His knees gave way, and he realized dimly that he was about to faint. His vision darkened into reddish black, shot with stars and streaks of light—but not even the encroaching dark would blot out the final sight of Fergus's hand, that small and deft and clever pickpocket's hand, lying still in the mud of the track, palm turned upward in supplication.

He waited for forty-eight long, dragging hours before Rabbie MacNab came to whistle on the path below the cave.

"How is he?" he said without preliminary.

"Mrs. Jenny says he'll be all right," Rabbie answered. His young face was pale and drawn; plainly he had not yet recovered from the shock of his friend's accident. "She says he's not fevered, and there's no trace of rot yet in the"—he swallowed audibly—"in the . . . stump."

"The soldiers took him down to the house, then?" Not waiting for an answer, he was already making his way down the hillside.

"Aye, they were all amoil wi' it—I think"—Rabbie paused to distentangle his shirt from a clinging brier, and had to hurry to catch up with his employer—"I think they were sorry about it. The Captain said so, at least. And he gave Mrs. Jenny a gold sovereign—for Fergus."

"Oh, aye?" Jamie said. "Verra generous." And did not speak again, until they reached the house.

Fergus was lying in state in the nursery, ensconced in a bed by the window. His eyes were closed when Jamie entered the room, long lashes lying softly against thin cheeks. Seen without its customary animation, his usual array of grimaces and poses, his face looked quite different. The slightly beaked nose above the long, mobile mouth gave him a faintly aristocratic air, and the bones hardening beneath the skin gave some promise that his face might one day pass from boyish charm to outright handsomeness.

Jamie moved toward the bed, and the dark lashes lifted at once.

"Milord," Fergus said, and a weak smile restored his face at once to its familiar contours. "You are safe here?"

"God, laddie, I'm sorry." Jamie sank to his knees by the bed. He could scarcely bear to look at the slender forearm that lay across the quilt, its frail bandaged wrist ending in nothing, but forced himself to grip Fergus's shoulder in greeting, and rub a palm gently over the shock of dark hair.

"Does it hurt much?" he asked.

"No, milord," Fergus said. Then a sudden belying twinge of pain crossed his features, and he grinned shamefacedly. "Well, not so much. And Madame has been most generous with the whisky."

There was a tumbler full of it on the sidetable, but no more than a thimbleful had been drunk. Fergus, weaned on French wine, did not really like the taste of whisky.

"I'm sorry," Jamie said again. There was nothing else to say. Nothing he *could* say, for the tightening in his throat. He looked hastily down, knowing that it would upset Fergus to see him weep.

"Ah, milord, do not trouble yourself." There was a note of the old mischief in Fergus's voice. "Me, I have been fortunate."

Jamie swallowed hard before replying.

"Aye, you're alive—and thank God for it!"

"Oh, beyond that, milord!" He glanced up to see Fergus smiling, though still very pale. "Do you not recall our agreement, milord?"

"Agreement?"

"Yes, when you took me into your service in Paris. You told me then that should I be arrested and executed, you would have Masses said for my soul for the space of a year." The remaining hand fluttered toward the battered greenish medal that hung about his neck—St. Dismas, patron saint of thieves. "But if I should lose an ear or a hand while doing your service—"

"I would support you for the rest of your life." Jamie was unsure whether to laugh or cry, and contented himself with patting the hand that now lay quiet on the quilt. "Aye, I remember. You may trust me to keep the bargain."

"Oh, I have always trusted you, milord," Fergus assured him. Clearly he was growing tired; the pale cheeks were even whiter than they had been, and the shock of black hair fell back against the pillow. "So I am fortunate," he murmured, still smiling. "For in one stroke, I am become a gentleman of leisure, *non?*"

Jenny was waiting for him when he left Fergus's room.

"Come down to the priest hole wi' me," he said, taking her by the elbow. "I need to talk wi' ye a bit, and I shouldna stay in the open longer."

She followed him without comment, down to the stone-floored back hall that separated kitchen and pantry. Set into the flags of the floor was a large wooden panel, perforated with drilled holes, apparently mortared into the floorstones. Theoretically, this gave air to the root cellar below, and in fact— should any suspicious person choose to investigate, the root cellar, reached by a sunken door outside the house, did have just such a panel set into its ceiling.

What was not apparent was that the panel also gave light and air to a small priest hole that had been built just behind the root cellar, which could be reached by pulling up the panel, mortared frame and all, to reveal a short ladder leading down into the tiny room.

It was no more than five feet square, equipped with nothing in the way of furniture beyond a rude bench, a blanket, and a chamber pot. A large jug of water and a small box of hard biscuit completed the chamber's accoutrements. It had in fact been added to the house only within the last few years, and therefore was not really a priest hole, as no priest had occupied it or was likely to. A hole it definitely was, though.

Two people could occupy the hole only by sitting side by side on the bench, and Jamie sat down beside his sister as soon as he had replaced the panel overhead and descended the ladder. He sat still for a moment, then took a breath and started.

"I canna bear it anymore," he said. He spoke so softly that Jenny was forced to bend her head close to hear him, like a priest receiving some penitent's confession. "I can't. I must go."

They sat so close together that he could feel the rise and fall of her breast as she breathed. Then she reached out and took hold of his hand, her small firm fingers tight on his.

"Will ye try France again, then?" He had tried to escape to France twice before, thwarted each time by the tight watch the English placed on all ports. No disguise was sufficient for a man of his remarkable height and coloring.

He shook his head. "No. I shall let myself be captured."

"Jamie!" In her agitation, Jenny allowed her voice to rise momentarily, then lowered it again in response to the warning squeeze of his hand.

"Jamie, ye canna do that!" she said, lower. "Christ, man, ye'll be hangit!"

He kept his head bent as though in thought, but shook it, not hesitating.

"I think not." He glanced at his sister, then quickly away. "Claire—she had the Sight." As good an explanation as any, he thought, if not quite the real truth. "She saw what would happen at Culloden—she knew. And she told me what would come after."

"Ah," said Jenny softly. "I wondered. So that was why she bade me plant potatoes—and build this place."

"Aye." He gave his sister's hand a small squeeze, then let go and turned slightly on the narrow seat to face her. "She told me that the Crown would go on hunting Jacobite traitors for some time—and they have," he added wryly. "But that after the first few years, they would no longer execute the men that were captured—only imprison them."

"Only!" his sister echoed. "If ye mun go, Jamie, take to the heather then, but to give yourself up to an English prison, whether they'll hang ye or no—"

"Wait." His hand on her arm stopped her. "I havena told it all to ye yet. I dinna mean just to walk up to the English and surrender. There's a goodly price on my head, no? Be a shame to let that go to waste, d'ye not think?" He tried to force a smile in his voice; she heard it and glanced sharply up at him.

"Holy Mother," she whispered. "So ye mean to have someone betray ye?"

"Seemingly, aye." He had decided upon the plan, alone in the cave, but it had not seemed quite real until now. "I thought perhaps Joe Fraser would be best for it."

Jenny rubbed her fist hard against her lips. She was quick; he knew she had grasped the plan at once—and all its implications.

"But Jamie," she whispered. "Even if they dinna hang ye outright—and that's the hell of a risk to take—Jamie, ye could be killed when they take ye!"

His shoulders slumped suddenly, under the weight of misery and exhaustion.

"God, Jenny," he said, "d'ye think I care?"

There was a long silence before she answered.

"No, I don't," she said. "And I canna say as I blame ye, either." She paused a moment, to steady her voice. "But *I* still care." Her fingers gently touched the back of his head, stroking his hair. "So ye'll mind yourself, won't ye, clot-heid?"

The ventilation panel overhead darkened momentarily, and there was the tapping sound of light footsteps. One of the kitchenmaids, on her way to the pantry, perhaps. Then the dim light came back, and he could see Jenny's face once more.

"Aye," he whispered at last. "I'll mind."

It took more than two months to complete the arrangements. When at last word came, it was full spring.

He sat on his favorite rock, near the cave's entrance, watching the evening stars come out. Even in the worst of the year after Culloden, he had always been able to find a moment of peace at this time of the day. As the daylight faded, it was as though objects became faintly lit from within, so they stood outlined against sky or ground, perfect and sharp in every detail. He could see the shape of a moth, invisible in the light, now limned in the dusk with a triangle of deeper shadow that made it stand out from the trunk it hid upon. In a moment, it would take wing.

He looked out across the valley, trying to stretch his eyes as far as the black pines that edged the distant cliffside. Then up, among the stars. Orion there, striding stately over the horizon. And the Pleiades, barely visible in the darkening sky. It might be his last sight of the sky for some time, and he meant to enjoy it. He thought of prison, of bars and locks and solid walls, and remembered Fort William. Wentworth Prison. The Bastille. Walls of stone, four feet thick, that blocked all air and light. Filth, stench, hunger, entombment . . .

He shrugged such thoughts away. He had chosen his way, and was satisfied with it. Still, he searched the sky, looking for Taurus. Not the prettiest of constellations, but his own. Born under the sign of the bull, stubborn and strong. Strong enough, he hoped, to do what he intended.

Among the growing night sounds, there was a sharp, high whistle. It might have been the homing song of a curlew on the loch, but he recognized the signal. Someone was coming up the path—a friend.

It was Mary MacNab, who had become kitchenmaid at Lallybroch, after the death of her husband. Usually it was her son Rabbie, or Fergus, who brought him food and news, but she had come a few times before.

She had brought a basket, unusually well-supplied, with a cold roast partridge, fresh bread, several young green onions, a bunch of early cherries, and a flask of ale. Jamie examined the bounty, then looked up with a wry smile.

"My farewell feast, eh?"

She nodded, silent. She was a small woman, dark hair heavily streaked with gray, and her face lined by the difficulties of life. Still, her eyes were soft and brown, and her lips still full and gently curved.

He realized that he was staring at her mouth, and hastily turned again to the basket.

"Lord, I'll be so full I'll not be able to move. Even a cake, now! However did ye ladies manage that?"

She shrugged—she wasn't a great chatterer, Mary MacNab—and taking the basket from him, proceeded to lay the meal on the wooden tabletop, balanced on stones. She laid places for both of them. This was nothing out of the ordinary; she had supped with him before, to give him the gossip of the district while they ate. Still, if this was his last meal before leaving Lallybroch, he was surprised that neither his sister nor the boys had come to share it. Perhaps the farmhouse had visitors that would make it difficult for them to leave undetected.

He gestured politely for her to sit first, before taking his own place, cross-legged on the hard dirt floor.

"Ye've spoken wi' Joe Fraser? Where is it to be, then?" he asked, taking a bite of cold partridge.

She told him the details of the plan; a horse would be brought before dawn, and he would ride out of the narrow valley by way of the pass. Then turn, cross the rocky foothills and come down, back into the valley by Feesy-hant's Burn, as though he were coming home. The English would meet him somewhere between Struy and Eskadale, most likely at Midmains; it was a good place for an ambush, for the glen rose steeply there on both sides, but with a wooded patch by the stream where several men could conceal themselves.

After the meal, she packed the basket tidily, leaving out enough food for a small breakfast before his dawn leaving. He expected her to go then, but she did not. She rummaged in the crevice where he kept his bedding, spread it neatly upon the floor, turned back the blankets and knelt beside the pallet, hands folded on her lap.

He leaned back against the wall of the cave, arms folded. He looked down at the crown of her bowed head in exasperation.

"Oh, like that, is it?" he demanded. "And whose idea was this? Yours, or my sister's?"

"Does it matter?" She was composed, her hands perfectly still on her lap, her dark hair smooth in its snood.

He shook his head and bent down to pull her to her feet.

"No, it doesna matter, because it's no going to happen. I appreciate your meaning, but—"

His speech was interrupted by her kiss. Her lips *were* as soft as they looked. He grasped her firmly by both wrists and pushed her away from him.

"No!" he said. "It isna necessary, and I dinna want to do it." He was uncomfortably aware that his body did not agree at all with his assessments of necessity, and still more uncomfortable at the knowledge that his breeches, too small and worn thin, made the magnitude of the disagreement obvious to anyone who cared to look. The slight smile curving those full, sweet lips suggested that she was looking.

He turned her toward the entrance and gave her a light push, to which she responded by stepping aside and reaching behind her for the fastenings to her skirt.

"Don't do that!" he exclaimed.

"How d'ye mean to stop me?" she asked, stepping out of the garment and folding it tidily over the single stool. Her slender fingers went to the laces of her bodice.

"If ye won't leave, then I'll have to," he replied with decision. He whirled on his heel and headed for the cave entrance, when he heard her voice behind him.

"My lord!" she said.

He stopped, but did not turn around. "It isna suitable to call me that," he said.

"Lallybroch is yours," she said. "And will be so long as ye live. If ye're its laird, I'll call ye so."

"It isna mine. The estate belongs to Young Jamie."

"It isna Young Jamie that's doing what you are," she answered with decision. "And it isna your sister that's asked me to do what I'm doin'. Turn round."

He turned, reluctantly. She stood barefoot in her shift, her hair loose over her shoulders. She was thin, as they all were these days, but her breasts were larger than he had thought, and the nipples showed prominently through the thin fabric. The shift was as worn as her other garments, frayed at the hem and shoulders, almost transparent in spots. He closed his eyes.

He felt a light touch on his arm, and willed himself to stand still.

"I ken weel enough what ye're thinkin'," she said. "For I saw your lady, and I know how it was between the two of ye. I never had that," she added, in a softer voice, "not wi' either of the two men I wed. But I know the look of a true love, and it's not in my mind to make ye feel ye've betrayed it."

The touch, feather-light, moved to his cheek, and a work-worn thumb traced the groove that ran from nose to mouth.

"What I want," she said quietly, "is to give ye something different. Something less, mayhap, but something ye can use; something to keep ye whole. Your sister and the bairns canna give ye that—but I can." He heard her draw breath, and the touch on his face lifted away.

"Ye've given me my home, my life, and my son. Will ye no let me gi'e ye this small thing in return?"

He felt tears sting his eyelids. The weightless touch moved across his face, wiping the moisture from his eyes, smoothing the roughness of his hair. He lifted his arms, slowly, and reached out. She stepped inside his embrace, as neatly and simply as she had laid the table and the bed.

"I . . . havena done this in a long time," he said, suddenly shy.

"Neither have I," she said, with a tiny smile. "But we'll remember how 'tis."

PART THREE

When I Am Thy Captive

7

A Faith in Documents

MAY 25, 1968

The envelope from Linklater arrived in the morning post.

"Look how fat it is!" Brianna exclaimed. "He's sent something!" The tip of her nose was pink with excitement.

"Looks like it," said Roger. He was outwardly calm, but I could see the pulse beating in the hollow of his throat. He picked up the thick manila envelope and held it for a moment, weighing it. Then he ripped the flap recklessly with his thumb, and yanked out a sheaf of photocopied pages.

The cover letter, on heavy university stationery, fluttered out. I snatched it from the floor and read it aloud, my voice shaking a little.

"'Dear Dr. Wakefield,'" I read. "'This is in reply to your inquiry regarding the execution of Jacobite officers by the Duke of Cumberland's troops following the Battle of Culloden. The main source of the quote in my book to which you refer, was the private journal of one Lord Melton, in command of an infantry regiment under Cumberland at the time of Culloden. I have enclosed photocopies of the relevant pages of the journal; as you will see, the story of the survivor, one James Fraser, is an odd and touching one. Fraser is not an important historical character, and not in line with the thrust of my own work, but I have often thought of investigating further, in hopes of determining his eventual fate. Should you find that he did survive the journey to his own estate, I should be happy if you would inform me. I have always rather hoped that he did, though his situation as described by Melton makes the possibility seem unlikely. Sincerely yours, Eric Linklater.'"

The paper rattled in my hand, and I set it down, very carefully, on the desk.

"Unlikely, huh?" Brianna said, standing on tiptoe to see over Roger's shoulder. "Ha! He did make it back, we know he did!"

"We think he did," Roger corrected, but it was only scholarly caution; his grin was as broad as Brianna's.

"Will ye be havin' tea or cocoa to your elevenses?" Fiona's curly dark head poked through the study doorway, interrupting the excitement. "There's fresh ginger-nut biscuits, just baked." The scent of warm ginger came into the study with her, wafting enticingly from her apron.

"Tea, please," said Roger, just as Brianna said, "Oh, cocoa sounds great!" Fiona, wearing a smug expression, pushed in the tea cart, sporting both tea cozy and pot of cocoa, as well as a plate of fresh ginger-nut biscuits.

I accepted a cup of tea myself, and sat down in the wing chair with the pages of Melton's journal. The flowing eighteenth-century handwriting was surprisingly clear, in spite of the archaic spelling, and within minutes, I was in the confines of Leanach farmhouse, imagining the sound of buzzing flies, the stir of close-packed bodies, and the harsh smell of blood soaking into the packed-dirt floor.

"*. . . in satisfaction of my brother's debt of honor, I could not do otherwise than to spare Fraser's life. I therefore omitted his name from the list of traitors executed at the farmhouse, and have made arrangement for his transport to his own estate. I cannot feel myself either altogether merciful toward Fraser in the taking of this action, nor yet altogether culpable with respect to my service toward the Duke, as Fraser's situation, with a great wound in his leg festering and pustulent, makes it unlikely that he will survive the journey to his home. Still, honor prevents my acting otherwise, and I will confess that my spirit was lightened to see the man removed, still living, from the field, as I turned my own attentions to the melancholy task of disposing of the bodies of his comrades. So much killing as I have seen these last two days oppresses me,*" the entry ended simply.

I laid the pages down on my knee, swallowing heavily. "*A great wound . . . festering and pustulent . . .*" I knew, as Roger and Brianna could not, just how serious such a wound would have been, with no antibiotics, nothing in the way of proper medical treatment; not even the crude herbal poultices available to a Highland charmer at the time. How long would it have taken, jolting from Culloden to Broch Tuarach in a wagon? Two days? Three? How could he have lived, in such a state, and neglected for so long?

"He did, though." Brianna's voice broke in upon my thoughts, answering what seemed to be a similar thought expressed by Roger. She spoke with simple assurance, as though she had seen all the events described in Melton's journal, and were sure of their outcome. "He did get back. He was the Dunbonnet, I know it."

"The Dunbonnet?" Fiona, tut-tutting over my cold cup of undrunk tea, looked over her shoulder in surprise. "Heard of the Dunbonnet, have ye?"

"Have *you*?" Roger looked at the young housekeeper in astonishment.

She nodded, casually dumping my tea into the aspidistra that stood by the hearth and refilling my cup with fresh steaming brew.

"Oh, aye. My grannie tellt me that tale, often and often."

"Tell us!" Brianna leaned forward, intent, her cocoa cupped between her palms. "Please, Fiona! What's the story?"

Fiona seemed mildly surprised to find herself suddenly the center of so much attention, but shrugged good-naturedly.

"Och, it's just the story of one o' the followers o' the Bonnie Prince. When there was the great defeat at Culloden, and sae many were killed, a few escaped. Why, one man fled the field and swam the river to get away, but the Redcoats were after him, nonetheless. He came to a kirk along his way, and a service going on inside, and he dashing in, prayed mercy from the minister. The minister and the people took pity on him, and he put on the minister's robe, so when the Redcoats burst in moments later, there he was, standing at the pulpit, preachin' the sermon, and the water from his beard and clothes puddled up about his feet. The Redcoats thought they were mistaken, and went on down the road, and so he escaped—and everyone in the kirk said 'twas the best sermon they ever heard!" Fiona laughed heartily, while Brianna frowned, and Roger looked puzzled.

"That was the Dunbonnet?" he said. "But I thought—"

"Och, no!" she assured him. "That was no the Dunbonnet—only the Dunbonnet was another o' the men who got away from Culloden. He came back to his own estate, but because the Sassenachs were hunting men all across the Highlands, he lay hidden there in a cave for seven years."

Hearing this, Brianna slumped back in her chair with a sigh of relief. "And his tenants called him the Dunbonnet so as not to speak his name and betray him," she murmured.

"Ye ken the story?" Fiona asked, astonished. "Aye, that's right."

"And did your grannie say what happened to him after that?" Roger prompted.

"Oh, aye!" Fiona's eyes were round as butterscotch drops. "That's the best part o' the story. See, there was a great famine after Culloden; folk were starvin' in the glens, turned out of their houses in winter, the men shot and the cots set afire. The Dunbonnet's tenants managed better than most, but even so, there came a day when the food ran out, and their bellies garbeled from dawn 'til dark—no game in the forest, nay grain in the field, and the weans dyin' in their mothers' arms for lack o' milk to feed them."

A cold chill swept over me at her words. I saw the faces of the Lallybroch inhabitants—the people I had known and loved—pinched with cold and starvation. Not only horror filled me; there was guilt, too. I had been safe, warm, and well-fed, instead of sharing their fate—because I had done as Jamie wanted, and left them. I looked at Brianna, smooth red head bent in absorption, and the tight feeling in my chest eased a bit. She too had been safe for these past years, warm, well-fed, and loved—because I had done as Jamie wanted.

"So he made a bold plan, the Dunbonnet did," Fiona was continuing.

Her round face was alight with the drama of her tale. "He arranged that one of his tenants should go to the English, and offer to betray him. There was a good price on his head, for he'd been a great warrior for the Prince. The tenant would take the gold o' the reward—to use for the folk on the estate, o' course—and tell the English where the Dunbonnet might be taken."

My hand clenched so convulsively at this that the delicate handle of my teacup snapped clean off.

"Taken?" I croaked, my voice hoarse with shock. "Did they hang him?"

Fiona blinked at me in surprise. "Why, no," she said. "They wanted to, my grannie said, and took him to trial for treason, but in the end, they shut him up in a prison instead—but the gold went to his tenants, and so they lived through the famine," she ended cheerfully, obviously regarding this as the happy ending.

"Jesus Christ," Roger breathed. He set his cup down carefully, and sat staring into space, transfixed. "Prison."

"You sound like that's *good,*" Brianna protested. The corners of her mouth were tight with distress, and her eyes slightly shiny.

"It is," Roger said, not noticing her distress. "There weren't that many prisons where the English imprisoned Jacobite traitors, and they all kept official records. Don't you see?" he demanded, looking from Fiona's bewilderment to Brianna's scowl, then settling on me in hope of finding understanding. "If he went to prison, I can find him." He turned then, to look up at the towering shelves of books that lined three walls of the study, holding the late Reverend Wakefield's collection of Jacobite arcana.

"He's in there," Roger said softly. "On a prison roll. In a document—real evidence! Don't you see?" he demanded again, turning back to me. "Going to prison made him a part of written history again! And somewhere in there, we'll find him!"

"And what happened to him then," Brianna breathed. "When he was released."

Roger's lips pressed tight together, to cut off the alternative that sprang to his mind, as it had to mine—"or died."

"Yes, that's right," he said, taking Brianna's hand. His eyes met mine, deep green and unfathomable. "When he was released."

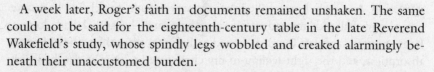

A week later, Roger's faith in documents remained unshaken. The same could not be said for the eighteenth-century table in the late Reverend Wakefield's study, whose spindly legs wobbled and creaked alarmingly beneath their unaccustomed burden.

This table normally was asked to accommodate no more than a small lamp, and a collection of the Reverend's smaller artifacts; it was pressed into service now only because every other horizontal surface in the study already overflowed with papers, journals, books, and bulging manila envelopes from antiquarian societies, universities, and research libraries across England, Scotland, and Ireland.

"If you set one more page on that thing, it's going to collapse," Claire observed, as Roger carelessly reached out, meaning to drop the folder he was carrying on the little inlaid table.

"Ah? Oh, right." He switched direction in midair, looked vainly for another place to put the folder, and finally settled for placing it on the floor at his feet.

"I've just about finished with Wentworth," Claire said. She indicated a precarious stack on the floor with her toe. "Have we got in the records for Berwick yet?"

"Yes, just this morning. Where did I put them, though?" Roger stared vaguely about the room, which strongly resembled the sacking of the library at Alexandria, just before the first torch was lit. He rubbed his forehead, trying to concentrate. After a week of spending ten-hour days thumbing the handwritten registers of British prisons, and the letters, journals, and diaries of their governors, searching for any official trace of Jamie Fraser, Roger was beginning to feel as though his eyes had been sandpapered.

"It was blue," he said at last. "I distinctly remember it was blue. I got those from McAllister, the History Lecturer at Trinity at Cambridge, and Trinity College uses those big envelopes in pale blue, with the college's coat of arms on the front. Maybe Fiona's seen it. Fiona!"

He stepped to the study door and called down the hall toward the kitchen. Despite the lateness of the hour, the light was still on, and the heartening scent of cocoa and freshly baked almond cake lingered in the air. Fiona would never abandon her post while there was the faintest possibility that someone in her vicinity might require nourishment.

"Och, aye?" Fiona's curly brown head poked out of the kitchen. "There'll be cocoa ready directly," she assured him. "I'm only waiting for the cake to be out of the oven."

Roger smiled at her with deep affection. Fiona had not the slightest use herself for history—never read anything beyond *My Weekly* magazine—but she never questioned his activities, tranquilly dusting the heaps of books and papers daily, without bothering about their contents.

"Thanks, Fiona," he said. "I was only wondering, though; have you seen a big blue envelope—a fat one, about so?" He measured with his hands. "It came in the morning post, but I've misplaced it."

"Ye left it in the upstairs bath," she said promptly. "There's that great thick book wi' the gold writing and the picture of the Bonnie Prince on the front up there, and three letters ye'd just opened, and there's the gas bill, too, which ye dinna want to be forgetting, it's due on the fourteenth o' the month. I've put it all on the top of the geyser, so as to be out of the way." A tiny, sharp ding! from the oven timer made her withdraw her head abruptly with a smothered exclamation.

Roger turned and went up the stairs two at a time, smiling. Given other inclinations, Fiona's memory might have made her a scholar. As it was, she was no mean research assistant. So long as a particular document or book could be described on the basis of its appearance, rather than its title or contents, Fiona was bound to know exactly where it was.

"Och, it's nothing," she had assured Roger airily, when he had tried to apologize earlier for the mess he was making of the house. "Ye'd think the Reverend was still alive, wi' such a moil of papers strewn everywhere. It's just like old times, no?"

Coming down more slowly, with the blue envelope in his hands, he wondered what his late adoptive father might have thought of this present quest.

"In it up to the eyebrows, I shouldn't wonder," he murmured to himself. He had a vivid memory of the Reverend, bald head gleaming under the old-fashioned bowl lamps that hung from the hall ceiling, as he pottered from his study to the kitchen, where old Mrs. Graham, Fiona's grandmother, would have been manning the stove, supplying the old man's bodily needs during bouts of late-night scholarship, just as Fiona was now doing for him.

It made one wonder, he thought, as he went into the study. In the old days, when a man's son usually followed his father's profession, was that only a matter of convenience—wanting to keep the business in the family—or was there some sort of family predisposition for some kinds of work? Were some people actually born to be smiths, or merchants, or cooks—born to an inclination and an aptitude, as well as to the opportunity?

Clearly it didn't apply to everyone; there were always the people who left their homes, went a-wandering, tried things hitherto unknown in their family circles. If that weren't so, probably there would be no inventors, no explorers; still, there seemed to be a certain affinity for some careers in some families, even in these restless modern times of widespread education and easy travel.

What he was really wondering about, he thought to himself, was Brianna. He watched Claire, her curly gold-shot head bent over the desk, and found himself wondering how much Brianna would be like her, and how much like the shadowy Scot—warrior, farmer, courtier, laird—who had been her father?

His thoughts were still running on such lines a quarter-hour later, when Claire closed the last folder on her stack and sat back, sighing.

"Penny for your thoughts?" she asked, reaching for her drink.

"Not worth that much," Roger replied with a smile, coming out of his reverie. "I was only wondering how people come to be what they are. How did you come to be a doctor, for instance?"

"How did I come to be a doctor?" Claire inhaled the steam from her cup of cocoa, decided it was too hot to drink, and set it back on the desk, among the litter of books and journals and pencil-scribbled sheets of paper. She gave Roger a half-smile and rubbed her hands together, dispersing the warmth of the cup.

"How did you come to be a historian?"

"More or less honestly," he answered, leaning back in the Reverend's chair and waving at the accumulation of papers and trivia all around them. He patted a small gilt traveling clock that sat on the desk, an elegant bit of eighteenth-century workmanship, with miniature chimes that struck the hour, the quarter, and the half.

"I grew up in the midst of it all; I was ferreting round the Highlands in search of artifacts with my father from the time I could read. I suppose it just seemed natural to keep doing it. But you?"

She nodded and stretched, easing her shoulders from the long hours of stooping over the desk. Brianna, unable to stay awake, had given up and gone to bed an hour before, but Claire and Roger had gone on with their search through the administrative records of British prisons.

"Well, it was something like that for me," she said. "It wasn't so much that I suddenly decided I must become a doctor—it was just that I suddenly realized one day that I'd *been* one for a long time—and then I wasn't, and I missed it."

She spread her hands out on the desk and flexed her fingers, long and supple, the nails buffed into neat, shiny ovals.

"There used to be an old song from the First World War," she said reflectively. "I used to hear it sometimes when some of Uncle Lamb's old army friends would come round and stay up late and get drunk. It went, 'How You Gonna Keep 'em Down on the Farm, After They've Seen Paree?' " She sang the first line, then broke off with a wry smile.

"I'd seen Paree," she said softly. She looked up from her hands, alert and present, but with the traces of memory in her eyes, fixed on Roger with the clarity of a second sight. "And a lot of other things besides. Caen and Amiens, Preston, and Falkirk, the Hôpital des Anges and the so-called surgery at Leoch. I'd *been* a doctor, in every way there is—I'd delivered babies, set bones, stitched wounds, treated fevers . . ." She trailed off, and shrugged. "There was a terrible lot I didn't know, of course. I knew how much I could learn—and that's why I went to medical school. But it didn't really make a difference, you know." She dipped a finger into the whipped cream floating on her cocoa, and licked it off. "I have a diploma with an M.D. on it—but I was a doctor long before I set foot in medical school."

"It can't possibly have been as easy as you make it sound." Roger blew on his own cocoa, studying Claire with open interest. "There weren't many women in medicine then—there aren't that many women doctors *now*, come to that—and you had a family, besides."

"No, I can't say it was easy at all." Claire looked at him quizzically. "I waited until Brianna was in school, of course, and we had enough money to afford someone to come in to cook and clean—but . . ." She shrugged and smiled ironically. "I stopped sleeping for several years, there. That helped a bit. And oddly enough, Frank helped, too."

Roger tested his own cup and found it almost cool enough to drink. He held it between his hands, enjoying the heat of the thick white porcelain seeping into his palms. Early June it might be, but the nights were cool enough to make the electric fire still a necessity.

"Really?" he said curiously. "Only from the things you've said about him, I shouldn't have thought he'd have liked your wanting to go to medical school or be a doctor."

"He didn't." Her lips pressed tight together; the motion told Roger more than words might, recalling arguments, conversations half-finished and abandoned, an opposition of stubbornness and devious obstruction rather than of open disapproval.

What a remarkably expressive face she had, he thought, watching her. He wondered quite suddenly whether his own were as easily readable. The thought was so unsettling that he dipped his face into his mug, gulping the cocoa, although it was still a bit too hot.

He emerged from the cup to find Claire watching him, slightly sardonic.

"Why?" he asked quickly, to distract her. "What made him change his mind?"

"Bree," she said, and her face softened as it always did at the mention of her daughter. "Bree was the only thing really important to Frank."

I had, as I'd said, waited until Brianna began school before beginning medical school myself. But even so, there was a large gap between her hours and my own, which we filled haphazardly with a series of more or less competent housekeepers and baby-sitters; some more, most of them less.

My mind went back to the frightful day when I had gotten a call at the hospital, telling me that Brianna was hurt. I had dashed out of the place, not pausing to change out of the green linen scrub-suit I was wearing, and raced for home, ignoring all speed limits, to find a police car and an ambulance lighting the night with blood-red pulses, and a knot of interested neighbors clustered on the street outside.

As we pieced the story together later, what had happened was that the latest temporary sitter, annoyed at my being late yet again, had simply put on her coat at quitting time and left, abandoning seven-year-old Brianna with instructions to "wait for Mommy." This she had obediently done, for an hour or so. But as it began to get dark, she had become frightened in the house alone, and determined to go out and find me. Making her way across one of the busy streets near our house, she had been struck by a car turning into the street.

She wasn't—thank God!—hurt badly; the car had been moving slowly, and she had only been shaken and bruised by the experience. Not nearly as shaken as I was, for that matter. Nor as bruised, when I came into the living room to find her lying on the sofa, and she looked at me, tears welling afresh on her stained cheeks and said, "Mommy! Where were you? I couldn't find you!"

It had taken just about all my reserves of professional composure to comfort her, to check her over, re-tend her cuts and scrapes, thank her rescuers—who, to my fevered mind, all glared accusingly at me—and put her to bed with her teddy bear clutched securely in her arms. Then I sat down at the kitchen table and cried myself.

Frank patted me awkwardly, murmuring, but then gave it up, and with more practicality, went to make tea.

"I've decided," I said, when he set the steaming cup in front of me. I spoke dully, my head feeling thick and clogged. "I'll resign. I'll do it tomorrow."

"Resign?" Frank's voice was sharp with astonishment. "From the school? What for?"

"I can't stand it anymore." I never took cream or sugar in my tea. Now I added both, stirring and watching the milky tendrils swirl through the cup. "I can't stand leaving Bree, and not knowing if she's well cared for—and knowing she isn't happy. You know she doesn't really like any of the sitters we've tried."

"I know that, yes." He sat opposite me, stirring his own tea. After a long moment, he said, "But I don't think you should resign."

It was the last thing I had expected; I had thought he would greet my decision with relieved applause. I stared at him in astonishment, then blew my nose yet again on the wadded tissue from my pocket.

"You don't?"

"Ah, Claire." He spoke impatiently, but with a tinge of affection nonetheless. "You've known forever who you are. Do you realize at all how unusual it is to know that?"

"No." I wiped my nose with the shredding tissue, dabbing carefully to keep it in one piece.

Frank leaned back in his chair, shaking his head as he looked at me.

"No, I suppose not," he said. He was quiet for a minute, looking down at his folded hands. They were long-fingered, narrow; smooth and hairless as a girl's. Elegant hands, made for casual gestures and the emphasis of speech.

He stretched them out on the table and looked at them as though he'd never seen them before.

"I haven't got that," he said quietly at last. "I'm good, all right. At what I do—the teaching, the writing. Bloody splendid sometimes, in fact. And I like it a good bit, enjoy what I do. But the thing is—" He hesitated, then looked at me straight on, hazel-eyed and earnest. "I could do something else, and be as good. Care as much, or as little. I haven't got that absolute conviction that there's something in life I'm meant to do—and you have."

"Is that good?" The edges of my nostrils were sore, and my eyes puffed from crying.

He laughed shortly. "It's damned inconvenient, Claire. To you and me and Bree, all three. But my God, I do envy you sometimes."

He reached out for my hand, and after a moment's hesitation, I let him have it.

"To have that passion for anything"—a small twitch tugged the corner of his mouth—"or anyone. That's quite splendid, Claire, and quite terribly rare." He squeezed my hand gently and let it go, turning to reach behind him for one of the books on the shelf beside the table.

It was one of his references, Woodhill's Patriots, *a series of profiles of the American Founding Fathers.*

He laid his hand on the cover of the book, gently, as though reluctant to disturb the rest of the sleeping lives interred there.

"These were people like that. The ones who cared so terribly much—enough to risk everything, enough to change and do things. Most people aren't like that, you know. It isn't that they don't care, but that they don't care so greatly." He took my hand again, this time turning it over. One finger traced the lines that webbed my palm, tickling as it went.

"Is it there, I wonder?" he said, smiling a little. "Are some people destined for a great fate, or to do great things? Or is it only that they're born somehow with that great passion—and if they find themselves in the right circumstances, then things happen? It's the sort of thing you wonder, studying history . . . but there's no way of telling, really. All we know is what they accomplished.

"But Claire—" His eyes held a definite note of warning, as he tapped the cover of his book. "They paid for it," he said.

"I know." I felt very remote now, as though I were watching us from a distance; I could see it quite clearly in my mind's eye; Frank, handsome, lean, and a little tired, going beautifully gray at the temples. Me, grubby in my surgical scrubs, my hair coming down, the front of my shirt crumpled and stained with Brianna's tears.

We sat in silence for some time, my hand still resting in Frank's. I could

*see the mysterious lines and valleys, clear as a road map—but a road to
what unknown destination?*

*I had had my palm read once years before, by an old Scottish lady
named Graham—Fiona's grandmother, in fact. "The lines in your hand
change as you change," she had said. "It's no so much what you're born
with, as what ye make of yourself."*

*And what had I made of myself, what was I making? A mess, that was
what. Neither a good mother, nor a good wife, nor a good doctor. A mess.
Once I had thought I was whole—had seemed to be able to love a man, to
bear a child, to heal the sick—and know that all these things were natural
parts of me, not the difficult, troubled fragments into which my life had
now disintegrated. But that had been in the past, the man I had loved
was Jamie, and for a time, I had been part of something greater than
myself.*

"I'll take Bree."

*I was so deep in miserable thought that for a moment, Frank's words
didn't register, and I stared at him stupidly.*

"What did you say?"

*"I said," he repeated patiently, "that I'll take Bree. She can come from
her school to the university, and play at my office until I'm ready to come
home."*

*I rubbed my nose. "I thought you didn't think it appropriate for staff to
bring their children to work." He had been quite critical of Mrs. Clancy,
one of the secretaries, who had brought her grandson to work for a month
when his mother was sick.*

He shrugged, looking uncomfortable.

*"Well, circumstances alter cases. And Brianna's not likely to be run-
ning up and down the halls shrieking and spilling ink like Bart Clancy."*

*"I wouldn't bet my life on it," I said wryly. "But you'd do that?" A
small feeling was growing in the pit of my clenched stomach; a cautious,
unbelieving feeling of relief. I might not trust Frank to be faithful to me
—I knew quite well he wasn't—but I did trust him unequivocally to care
for Bree.*

*Suddenly the worry was removed. I needn't hurry home from the hospi-
tal, filled with dread because I was late, hating the thought of finding
Brianna crouched in her room sulking because she didn't like the current
sitter. She loved Frank; I knew she would be ecstatic at the thought of
going to his office every day.*

*"Why?" I asked bluntly. "It isn't that you're dead keen on my being a
doctor; I know that."*

*"No," he said thoughtfully. "It isn't that. But I do think there isn't any
way to stop you—perhaps the best I can do is to help, so that there will be*

*less damage to Brianna." His features hardened slightly then, and he
turned away.*

"So far as he ever felt he had a destiny—something he was really meant to
do—he felt that Brianna was it," Claire said. She stirred her cocoa meditatively.

"Why do you care, Roger?" she asked him suddenly. "Why are you asking
me?"

He took a moment to answer, slowly sipping his cocoa. It was rich and
dark, made with new cream and a sprinkle of brown sugar. Fiona, always a
realist, had taken one look at Brianna and given up her attempts to lure
Roger into matrimony via his stomach, but Fiona was a cook the same way
Claire was a doctor; born to skill, and unable not to use it.

"Because I'm a historian, I suppose," he answered finally. He watched her
over the rim of his cup. "I need to know. What people really did, and why
they did it."

"And you think I can tell you that?" She glanced sharply at him. "Or that
I know?"

He nodded, sipping. "You know, better than most people. Most of a
historian's sources haven't your"—he paused and gave her a grin—"your
unique perspective, shall we say?"

There was a sudden lessening of tension. She laughed and picked up her
own cup. "We shall say that," she agreed.

"The other thing," he went on, watching her closely, "is that you're
honest. I don't think you *could* lie, even if you wanted to."

She glanced at him sharply, and gave a short, dry laugh.

"Everyone can lie, young Roger, given cause enough. Even me. It's only
that it's harder for those of us who live in glass faces; we have to think up our
lies ahead of time."

She bent her head and shuffled through the papers before her, turning the
pages over slowly, one by one. They were lists of names, these sheets, lists of
prisoners, copied from the ledger books of British prisons. The task was
complicated by the fact that not all prisons had been well-run.

Some governors kept no official lists of their inmates, or listed them haphazardly in their journals, in among the notations of daily expenditure and
maintenance, making no great distinction between the death of a prisoner
and the slaughter of two bullocks, salted for meat.

Roger thought Claire had abandoned the conversation, but a moment
later she looked up again.

"You're quite right, though," she said. "I'm honest—from default, more
than anything. It isn't easy for me *not* to say what I'm thinking. I imagine
you see it because you're the same way."

"Am I?" Roger felt absurdly pleased, as though someone had given him an unexpected present.

Claire nodded, a small smile on her lips as she watched him.

"Oh, yes. It's unmistakable, you know. There aren't many people like that —who will tell you the truth about themselves and anything else right out. I've only met three people like that, I think—four now," she said, her smile widening to warm him.

"There was Jamie, of course." Her long fingers rested lightly on the stack of papers, almost caressing in their touch. "Master Raymond, the apothecary I knew in Paris. And a friend I met in medical school—Joe Abernathy. Now you. I think."

She tilted her cup and swallowed the last of the rich brown liquid. She set it down and looked directly at Roger.

"Frank was right, in a way, though. It isn't necessarily easier if you know what it is you're meant to do—but at least you don't waste time in questioning or doubting. If you're honest—well, that isn't necessarily easier, either. Though I suppose if you're honest with yourself and know what you are, at least you're less likely to feel that you've wasted your life, doing the wrong thing."

She set aside the stack of papers and drew up another—a set of folders with the characteristic logo of the British Museum on the covers.

"Jamie had that," she said softly, as though to herself. "He wasn't a man to turn away from anything he thought his job. Dangerous or not. And I think he won't have felt himself wasted—no matter what happened to him."

She lapsed into silence, then, absorbed in the spidery tracings of some long-dead writer, looking for the entry that might tell her what Jamie Fraser had done and been, and whether his life had been wasted in a prison cell, or ended in a lonely dungeon.

The clock on the desk struck midnight, its chimes surprisingly deep and melodious for such a small instrument. The quarter-hour struck, and then the half, punctuating the monotonous rustle of pages. Roger put down the sheaf of flimsy papers he had been thumbing through, and yawned deeply, not troubling to cover his mouth.

"I'm so tired I'm seeing double," he said. "Shall we go on with it in the morning?"

Claire didn't answer for a moment; she was looking into the glowing bars of the electric fire, a look of unutterable distance on her face. Roger repeated his question, and slowly she came back from wherever she was.

"No," she said. She reached for another folder, and smiled at Roger, the look of distance lingering in her eyes. "You go on, Roger," she said. "I'll— just look a little longer."

When I finally found it, I nearly flipped right past it. I had not been reading the names carefully, but only skimming the pages for the letter "J." "John, Joseph, Jacques, James." There were James Edward, James Alan, James Walter, ad infinitum. Then it was there, the writing small and precise across the page: "Jms. MacKenzie Fraser, of Brock Turac."

I put the page down carefully on the table, shut my eyes for a moment to clear them, then looked again. It was still there.

"Jamie," I said aloud. My heart was beating heavily in my chest. "Jamie," I said again, more quietly.

It was nearly three o'clock in the morning. Everyone was asleep, but the house, in the manner of old houses, was still awake around me, creaking and sighing, keeping me company. Strangely enough, I had no desire to leap up and wake Brianna or Roger, to tell them the news. I wanted to keep it to myself for a bit, as though I were alone here in the lamp-lit room with Jamie himself.

My finger traced the line of ink. The person who had written that line had seen Jamie—perhaps had written this with Jamie standing in front of him. The date at the top of the page was May 16, 1753. It had been close to this time of year, then. I could imagine how the air had been, chilly and fresh, with the rare spring sun across his shoulders, lighting sparks in his hair.

How had he worn his hair then—short, or long? He had preferred to wear it long, plaited or tailed behind. I remembered the casual gesture with which he would lift the weight of it off his neck to cool himself in the heat of exercise.

He would not have worn his kilt—the wearing of all tartans had been outlawed after Culloden. Breeks, then, likely, and a linen shirt. I had made such sarks for him; I could feel the softness of the fabric in memory, the billowing length of the three full yards it took to make one, the long tails and full sleeves that let the Highland men drop their plaids and sleep or fight with a sark their only garment. I could imagine his shoulders broad beneath the rough-woven cloth, his skin warm through it, hands touched with the chill of the Scottish spring.

He had been imprisoned before. How would he have looked, facing an English prison clerk, knowing all too well what waited for him? Grim as hell, I thought, staring down that long, straight nose with his eyes a cold, dark blue—dark and forbidding as the waters of Loch Ness.

I opened my own eyes, realizing only then that I was sitting on the edge of my chair, the folder of photocopied pages clasped tight to my chest, so caught up in my conjuration that I had not even paid attention to which prison these registers had come from.

There were several large prisons that the English had used regularly in the eighteenth century, and a number of minor ones. I turned the folder over, slowly. Would it be Berwick, near the border? The notorious Tolbooth of

Edinburgh? Or one of the southern prisons, Leeds Castle or even the Tower of London?

"Ardsmuir," said the notecard neatly stapled to the front of the folder.

"Ardsmuir?" I said blankly. "Where the hell is *that*?"

8

Honor's Prisoner

"Ardsmuir is the carbuncle on God's bum," Colonel Harry Quarry said. He raised his glass sardonically to the young man by the window. "I've been here a twelvemonth, and that's eleven months and twenty-nine days too long. Give you joy of your new posting, my Lord."

Major John William Grey turned from the window over the courtyard, where he had been surveying his new domain.

"It does appear a trifle incommodious," he agreed dryly, picking up his own glass. "Does it rain *all* the time?"

"Of course. It's Scotland—and the backside of bloody Scotland, at that." Quarry took a deep pull at his whisky, coughed, and exhaled noisily as he set down the empty glass.

"The drink is the only compensation," he said, a trifle hoarsely. "Call on the local booze-merchants in your best uniform, and they'll make you a decent price. It's astounding cheap, without the tariff. I've left you a note of the best stills." He nodded toward the massive oaken desk at the side of the room, planted four-square on its island of carpet like a small fortress confronting the barren room. The illusion of fortifications was enhanced by the banners of regiment and nation that hung from the stone wall behind it.

"The guards' roster is here," Quarry said, rising and groping in the top desk drawer. He slapped a battered leather folder on the desktop, and added another on top of that. "And the prisoners' roll. You have one hundred and ninety-six at the moment; two hundred is the usual count, give or take a few deaths from sickness or the odd poacher taken up in the countryside."

"Two hundred," Grey said. "And how many in the guards' barracks?"

"Eighty-two, by number. In use, about half that." Quarry reached into the drawer again and withdrew a brown glass bottle with a cork. He shook it, heard it slosh, and smiled sardonically. "The commander isn't the only one to find consolation in drink. Half the sots are usually incapable at roll call. I'll leave this for you, shall I? You'll need it." He put the bottle back and pulled out the lower drawer.

"Requisitions and copies here; the paperwork's the worst of the post. Not a great deal to do, really, if you've a decent clerk. You haven't, at the moment; I had a corporal who wrote a fairish hand, but he died two weeks ago. Train up another, and you'll have nothing to do save to hunt for grouse and the Frenchman's Gold." He laughed at his own joke; rumors of the gold that Louis of France had supposedly sent to his cousin Charles Stuart were rife in this end of Scotland.

"The prisoners are not difficult?" Grey asked. "I had understood them to be mostly Jacobite Highlanders."

"They are. But they're docile enough." Quarry paused, looking out of the window. A small line of ragged men was issuing from a door in the forbidding stone wall opposite. "No heart in them after Culloden," he said matter-of-factly. "Butcher Billy saw to that. And we work them hard enough that they've no vigor left for troublemaking."

Grey nodded. Ardsmuir fortress was undergoing renovation, rather ironically using the labor of the Scots incarcerated therein. He rose and came to join Quarry at the window.

"There's a work crew going out now, for peat-cutting." Quarry nodded at the group below. A dozen bearded men, ragged as scarecrows, formed an awkward line before a red-coated soldier, who walked up and down, inspecting them. Evidently satisfied, he shouted an order and jerked a hand toward the outer gate.

The prisoners' crew was accompanied by six armed soldiers, who fell in before and behind, muskets held in marching order, their smart appearance a marked contrast to the ragged Highlanders. The prisoners walked slowly, oblivious to the rain that soaked their rags. A mule-drawn wagon creaked behind, a bundle of peat knives gleaming dully in its bed.

Quarry frowned, counting them. "Some must be ill; a work crew is eighteen men—three prisoners to a guard, because of the knives. Though surprisingly few of them try to run," he added, turning away from the window. "Nowhere to go, I suppose." He left the desk, kicking aside a large woven basket that sat on the hearth, filled with crude chunks of a rough dark-brown substance.

"Leave the window open, even when it's raining," he advised. "The peat smoke will choke you, otherwise." He took a deep breath in illustration and let it out explosively. "God, I'll be glad to get back to London!"

"Not much in the way of local society, I collect?" Grey asked dryly. Quarry laughed, his broad red face creasing in amusement at the notion.

"Society? My dear fellow! Bar one or two passable blowzabellas down in the village, 'society' will consist solely of conversation with your officers—

there are four of them, one of whom is capable of speaking without the use of profanity—your orderly, and one prisoner."

"A prisoner?" Grey looked up from the ledgers he had been perusing, one fair brow lifted in inquiry.

"Oh, yes." Quarry was prowling the office restlessly, eager to be off. His carriage was waiting; he had stayed only to brief his replacement and make the formal handover of command. Now he paused, glancing at Grey. One corner of his mouth curled up, enjoying a secret joke.

"You've heard of Red Jamie Fraser, I expect?"

Grey stiffened slightly, but kept his face as unmoved as possible.

"I should imagine most people have," he said coldly. "The man was notorious during the Rising." Quarry had heard the story, damn him! All of it, or only the first part?

Quarry's mouth twitched slightly, but he merely nodded.

"Quite. Well, we have him. He's the only senior Jacobite officer here; the Highlander prisoners treat him as their chief. Consequently, if any matters arise involving the prisoners—and they will, I assure you—he acts as their spokesman." Quarry was in his stockinged feet; now he sat and tugged on long cavalry boots, in preparation for the mud outside.

"*Seumas, mac an fhear dhuibh,* they call him, *or just Mac Dubh.* Speak Gaelic, do you? Neither do I—Grissom does, though; he says it means 'James, son of the Black One.' Half the guards are afraid of him—those that fought with Cope at Prestonpans. Say he's the Devil himself. Poor devil, now!" Quarry gave a brief snort, forcing his foot into the boot. He stamped once, to settle it, and stood up.

"The prisoners obey him without question; but give orders without his putting his seal to them, and you might as well be talking to the stones in the courtyard. Ever had much to do with Scots? Oh, of course; you fought at Culloden with your brother's regiment, didn't you?" Quarry struck his brow at his pretended forgetfulness. Damn the man! He *had* heard it all.

"You'll have an idea, then. Stubborn does not begin to describe it." He flapped a hand in the air as though to dismiss an entire contingent of recalcitrant Scots.

"Which means," Quarry paused, enjoying it, "you'll need Fraser's goodwill—or at least his cooperation. I had him take supper with me once a week, to talk things over, and found it answered very well. You might try the same arrangement."

"I suppose I might." Grey's tone was cool, but his hands were clenched tight at his sides. When icicles grew in hell, he might take supper with James Fraser!

"He's an educated man," Quarry continued, eyes bright with malice, fixed on Grey's face. "A great deal more interesting to talk to than the officers. Plays chess. You have a game now and then, do you not?"

"Now and then." The muscles of his abdomen were clenched so tightly that he had trouble drawing breath. Would this bullet-headed fool not stop talking and leave?

"Ah, well, I'll leave you to it." As though divining Grey's wish, Quarry settled his wig more firmly, then took his cloak from the hook by the door and swirled it rakishly about his shoulders. He turned toward the door, hat in hand, then turned back.

"Oh, one thing. If you do dine with Fraser alone—don't turn your back on him." The offensive jocularity had left Quarry's face; Grey scowled at him, but could see no evidence that the warning was meant as a joke.

"I mean it," Quarry said, suddenly serious. "He's in irons, but it's easy to choke a man with the chain. And he's a very large fellow, Fraser."

"I know." To his fury, Grey could feel the blood rising in his cheeks. To hide it, he swung about, letting the cold air from the half-open window play on his countenance. "Surely," he said, to the rain-slick gray stones below, "if he is the intelligent man you say, he would not be so foolish as to attack me in my own quarters, in the midst of the prison? What would be the purpose in it?"

Quarry didn't answer. After a moment, Grey turned around, to find the other staring at him thoughtfully, all trace of humor gone from the broad, ruddy face.

"There's intelligence," Quarry said slowly. "And then there are other things. But perhaps you're too young to have seen hate and despair at close range. There's been a deal of it in Scotland, these last ten years." He tilted his head, surveying the new commander of Ardsmuir from his vantage point of fifteen years' seniority.

Major Grey *was* young, no more than twenty-six, and with a fair-complexioned face and girlish lashes that made him look still younger than his years. To compound the problem, he was an inch or two shorter than the average, and fine-boned, as well. He drew himself up straight.

"I am aware of such things, Colonel," he said evenly. Quarry was a younger son of good family, like himself, but still his superior in rank; he must keep his temper.

Quarry's bright hazel gaze rested on him in speculation.

"I daresay."

With a sudden motion, he clapped his hat on his head. He touched his cheek, where the darker line of a scar sliced across the ruddy skin; a memento of the scandalous duel that had sent him into exile at Ardsmuir.

"God knows what you did to be sent here, Grey," he said, shaking his head. "But for your own sake, I hope you deserved it! Luck to you!" And with a swirl of blue cloak, he was gone.

"Better the Devil ye ken, than the Devil ye don't," Murdo Lindsay said, shaking his head lugubriously. "Handsome Harry was nain sae bad."

"No, he wasna, then," agreed Kenny Lesley. "But ye'll ha' been here when he came, no? He was a deal better than that shite-face Bogle, aye?"

"Aye," said Murdo, looking blank. "What's your meaning, man?"

"So if Handsome was better than Bogle," Lesley explained patiently, "then Handsome was the Devil we didna ken, and Bogle the one that we did —but Handsome was better, in spite of that, so you're wrong, man."

"I am?" Murdo, hopelessly confused by this bit of reasoning, glowered at Lesley. "No, I'm not!"

"Ye are, then," Lesley said, losing patience. "Ye're always wrong, Murdo! Why d'ye argue, when ye're never in the right of it?"

"I'm no arguin'!" Murdo protested indignantly. "Ye're takin' exception to *me,* not t'other way aboot."

"Only because you're wrong, man!" Lesley said. "If ye were right, I'd have said not a word."

"I'm not wrong! At least I dinna think so," Murdo muttered, unable to recall precisely what he had said. He turned, appealing to the large figure seated in the corner. "Mac Dubh, was I wrong?"

The tall man stretched himself, the chain of his irons chiming faintly as he moved, and laughed.

"No, Murdo, ye're no wrong. But we canna say if ye're right yet awhile. Not 'til we see what the new Devil's like, aye?" Seeing Lesley's brows draw down in preparation for further dispute, he raised his voice, speaking to the room at large. "Has anyone seen the new Governor yet? Johnson? MacTavish?"

"I have," Hayes said, pushing gladly forward to warm his hands at the fire. There was only one hearth in the large cell, and room for no more than six men before it at a time. The other forty were left in bitter chill, huddling together in small groups for warmth.

Consequently, the agreement was that whoever had a tale to tell or a song to sing might have a place by the hearth, for as long as he spoke. Mac Dubh had said this was a bard-right, that when the bards came to the auld castles, they would be given a warm place and plenty to eat and drink, to the honor of the laird's hospitality. There was never food or drink to spare here, but the warm place was certain.

Hayes relaxed, eyes closed and a beatific smile on his face as he spread his hands to the warmth. Warned by restive movement to either side, though, he hastily opened his eyes and began to speak.

"I saw him when he came in from his carriage, and then again, when I brought up a platter o' sweeties from the kitchens, whilst he and Handsome Harry were nattering to ain another." Hayes frowned in concentration.

"He's fair-haired, wi' long yellow locks tied up wi' blue ribbon. And big eyes and long lashes, too, like a lassie's." Hayes leered at his listeners, batting his own stubby lashes in mock flirtation.

Encouraged by the laughter, he went on to describe the new Governor's clothes—"fine as a laird's"—his equipage and servant—"one of they Sassenachs as talks like he's burnt his tongue"—and as much as had been overheard of the new man's speech.

"He talks sharp and quick, like he'll know what's what," Hayes said, shaking his head dubiously. "But he's verra young, forbye—he looks scarce more than a wean, though I'd reckon he's older than his looks."

"Aye, he's a bittie fellow, smaller than wee Angus," Baird chimed in, with a jerk of the head at Angus MacKenzie, who looked down at himself in startlement. Angus had been twelve when he fought beside his father at Culloden. He had spent nearly half his life in Ardsmuir, and in consequence of the poor fare of prison, had never grown much bigger.

"Aye," Hayes agreed, "but he carries himself well; shoulders square and a ramrod up his arse."

This gave rise to a burst of laughter and ribald comment, and Hayes gave way to Ogilvie, who knew a long and scurrilous story about the laird of Donibristle and the hogman's daughter. Hayes left the hearth without resentment, and went—as was the custom—to sit beside Mac Dubh.

Mac Dubh never took his place on the hearth, even when he told them the long stories from the books that he'd read—*The Adventures of Roderick Random, The History of Tom Jones, a Foundling,* or everyone's favorite, *Robinson Crusoe.* Claiming that he needed the room to accommodate his long legs, Mac Dubh sat always in his same spot in the corner, where everyone might hear him. But the men who left the fire would come, one by one, and sit down on the bench beside him, to give him the warmth that lingered in their clothes.

"Shall ye speak to the new Governor tomorrow, d'ye think, Mac Dubh?" Hayes asked as he sat. "I met Billy Malcolm, coming in from the peat-cutting, and he shouted to me as the rats were grown uncommon bold in their cell just now. Six men bitten this sennight as they slept, and two of them festering."

Mac Dubh shook his head, and scratched at his chin. He had been allowed a razor before his weekly audiences with Harry Quarry, but it had been five days since the last of these, and his chin was thick with red stubble.

"I canna say, Gavin," he said. "Quarry did say as he'd tell the new fellow of our arrangement, but the new man might have his own ways, aye? If I'm called to see him, though, I shall be sure to say about the rats. Did Malcolm ask for Morrison to come and see to the festering, though?" The prison had no doctor; Morrison, who had a touch for healing, was permitted by the guards to go from cell to cell to tend the sick or injured, at Mac Dubh's request.

Hayes shook his head. "He hadna time to say more—they were marching past, aye?"

"Best I send Morrison," Mac Dubh decided. "He can ask Billy is there aught else amiss there." There were four main cells where the prisoners were kept in large groups; word passed among them by means of Morrison's visits and the mingling of men on the work crews that went out daily to haul stone or cut peats on the nearby moor.

Morrison came at once when summoned, pocketing four of the carved rats' skulls with which the prisoners improvised games of draughts. Mac Dubh groped under the bench where he sat, drawing out the cloth bag he carried when he went to the moor.

"Och, not more o' the damn thistles," Morrison protested, seeing Mac Dubh's grimace as he groped in the bag. "I canna make them eat those things; they all say, do I think them kine, or maybe pigs?"

Mac Dubh gingerly set down a fistful of wilted stalks, and sucked his pricked fingers.

"They're stubborn as pigs, to be sure," he remarked. "It's only milk thistle. How often must I tell ye, Morrison? Take the thistle heads off, and mash the leaves and stems fine, and if they're too prickly to eat spread on a bannock, then make a tea of them and have them drink it. I've yet to see pigs drink tea, tell them."

Morrison's lined face cracked in a grin. An elderly man, he knew well enough how to handle recalcitrant patients; he only liked to complain for the fun of it.

"Aye, well, I'll say have they ever seen a toothless cow?" he said, resigned, as he tucked the limp greens carefully into his own sack. "But you'll be sure to bare your teeth at Joel McCulloch, next time ye see him. He's the worst o' them, for not believin' as the greens do help wi' the scurvy."

"Say as I'll bite him in the arse," Mac Dubh promised, with a flash of his excellent teeth, "if I hear he hasna eaten his thistles."

Morrison made the small amused noise that passed for a belly laugh with him, and went to gather up the bits of ointment and the few herbs he had for medicines.

Mac Dubh relaxed for the moment, glancing about the room to be sure no trouble brewed. There were feuds at the moment; he'd settled Bobby Sinclair and Edwin Murray's trouble a week back, and while they were not friends, they were keeping their distance from one another.

He closed his eyes. He was tired; he had been hauling stone all day. Supper would be along in a few minutes—a tub of parritch and some bread to be shared out, a bit of brose too if they were lucky—and likely most of the men would go to sleep soon after, leaving him a few minutes of peace and semiprivacy, when he need not listen to anyone or feel he must do anything.

He had had no time as yet even to wonder about the new Governor, important as the man would be to all their lives. Young, Hayes had said. That might be good, or might be bad.

Older men who had fought in the Rising were often prejudiced against Highlanders—Bogle, who had put him in irons, had fought with Cope. A scared young soldier, though, trying to keep abreast of an unfamiliar job, could be more rigid and tyrannical than the crustiest of old colonels. Aye well, and nothing to be done but wait to see.

He sighed and shifted his posture, incommoded—for the ten-thousandth time—by the manacles he wore. He shifted irritably, banging one wrist against the edge of the bench. He was large enough that the weight of the irons didn't trouble him overmuch, but they chafed badly with the work. Worse was the inability to spread his arms more than eighteen inches apart; this gave him cramp and a clawing feeling, deep in the muscle of chest and back, that left him only when he slept.

"Mac Dubh," said a soft voice beside him. "A word in your ear, if I might?" He opened his eyes to see Ronnie Sutherland perched alongside, pointed face intent and foxlike in the faint glow from the fire.

"Aye, Ronnie, of course." He pushed himself upright, and put both his irons and the thought of the new Governor firmly from his mind.

Dearest mother, John Grey wrote, later that night.

I am arrived safely at my new post, and find it comfortable. Colonel Quarry, my predecessor—he is the Duke of Clarence's nephew, you recall?—made me welcome and acquainted with my charge. I am provided with a most excellent servant, and while I am bound to find many things about Scotland strange at first, I am sure I will find the experience interesting. I was served an object for my supper which the steward told me was called a "haggis." Upon inquiry, this proved to be the interior organ of a sheep, filled with a mixture of ground oats and a quantity of unidentifiable cooked flesh. Though I am assured the inhabitants of Scotland esteem this dish a particular delicacy, I sent it to the kitchens and requested a plain boiled saddle of mutton in its place. Having thus made my first—humble!—meal here, and being somewhat fatigued by the long journey—of whose details I shall inform you in a subsequent missive—I believe I shall now retire, leaving further descriptions of my surroundings—with which I am imperfectly acquainted at present, as it is dark—for a future communication.

He paused, tapping the quill on the blotter. The point left small dots of ink, and he abstractedly drew lines connecting these, making the outlines of a jagged object.

Dared he ask about George? Not a direct inquiry, that wouldn't do, but a reference to the family, asking whether his mother had happened to encounter Lady Everett lately, and might he ask to be remembered to her son?

He sighed and drew another point on his object. No. His widowed mother was ignorant of the situation, but Lady Everett's husband moved in military circles. His brother's influence would keep the gossip to a minimum, but Lord Everett might catch a whiff of it, nonetheless, and be quick enough to put two and two together. Let him drop an injudicious word to his wife about George, and the word pass on from Lady Everett to his mother . . . the Dowager Countess Melton was not a fool.

She knew quite well that he was in disgrace; promising young officers in the good graces of their superiors were not sent to the arse-end of Scotland to oversee the renovation of small and unimportant prison-fortresses. But his brother Harold had told her that the trouble was an unfortunate affair of the heart, implying sufficient indelicacy to stop her questioning him about it. She likely thought he had been caught with his colonel's wife, or keeping a whore in his quarters.

An unfortunate affair of the heart! He smiled grimly, dipping his pen. Perhaps Hal had a greater sensitivity than he'd thought, in so describing it. But then, all his affairs had been unfortunate, since Hector's death at Culloden.

With the thought of Culloden, the thought of Fraser came back to him; something he had been avoiding all day. He looked from the blotter to the folder which held the prisoners' roll, biting his lip. He was tempted to open it, and look to see the name, but what point was there in that? There might be scores of men in the Highlands named James Fraser, but only one known also as Red Jamie.

He felt himself flush as waves of heat rolled over him, but it was not nearness to the fire. In spite of that, he rose and went to the window, drawing in great lungfuls of air as though the cold draft could cleanse him of memory.

"Pardon, sir, but will ye be wantin' your bed warmed now?" The Scottish speech behind him startled him, and he whirled round to find the tousled head of the prisoner assigned to tend his quarters poking through the door that led to his private rooms.

"Oh! Er, yes. Thank you . . . MacDonell?" he said doubtfully.

"MacKay, my lord," the man corrected, without apparent resentment, and the head vanished.

Grey sighed. There was nothing that could be done tonight. He came back to the desk and gathered up the folders, to put them away. The jagged object he had drawn on the blotter looked like one of those spiked maces, with which ancient knights had crushed the heads of their foes. He felt as though he had swallowed one, though perhaps this was no more than indigestion occasioned by half-cooked mutton.

He shook his head, pulled the letter to him and signed it hastily.

With all affection, your obt. son, John Wm. Grey. He shook sand over the signature, sealed the missive with his ring and set it aside to be posted in the morning.

He rose and stood hesitating, surveying the shadowy reaches of the office. It was a great, cold, barren room, with little in it bar the huge desk and a couple of chairs. He shivered; the sullen glow of the peat bricks on the hearth did little to warm its vast spaces, particularly with the freezing wet air coming in at the window.

He glanced once more at the prisoners' roll. Then he bent, opened the lower drawer of the desk, and drew out the brown glass bottle. He pinched out the candle, and made his way toward his bed by the dull glow of the hearth.

The mingled effects of exhaustion and whisky should have sent him to sleep at once, but sleep kept its distance, hovering over his bed like a bat, but never lighting. Every time he felt himself sinking into dreams, a vision of the wood at Carryarrick came before his eyes, and he found himself lying once more wide-awake and sweating, his heart thundering in his ears.

He had been sixteen then, excited beyond bearing by his first campaign. He had not got his commission then, but his brother Hal had taken him along with the regiment, so that he might get a taste of soldiering.

Camped at night near a dark Scottish wood, on their way to join General Cope at Prestonpans, John had found himself too nervous to sleep. What would the battle be like? Cope was a great general, all Hal's friends said so, but the men around the fires told frightful stories of the fierce Highlanders and their bloody broadswords. Would he have the courage to face the dreadful Highland charge?

He couldn't bring himself to mention his fears even to Hector. Hector loved him, but Hector was twenty, tall and muscular and fearless, with a lieutenant's commission and dashing stories of battles fought in France.

He didn't know, even now, whether it had been an urge to emulate Hector, or merely to impress him, that had led him to do it. In either case, when he saw the Highlander in the wood, and recognized him from the broadsheets as the notorious Red Jamie Fraser, he had determined to kill or capture him.

The notion of returning to camp for help *had* occurred to him, but the man was alone—at least John had thought he was alone—and evidently unawares, seated quietly upon a log, eating a bit of bread.

And so he had drawn his knife from his belt and crept quietly through the wood toward that shining red head, the haft slippery in his grasp, his mind filled with visions of glory and Hector's praise.

Instead, there had been a glancing blow as his knife flashed down, his arm locked tight round the Scot's neck to choke him, and then—

Lord John Grey flung himself over in his bed, hot with remembrance. They had fallen back, rolling together in the crackling oak-leaf dark, grappling for the knife, thrashing and fighting—for his life, he had thought.

First the Scot had been under him, then twisting, somehow over. He had touched a great snake once, a python that a friend of his uncle's had brought from the Indies, and that was what it had been like, Fraser's touch, lithe and smooth and horribly powerful, moving like the muscular coils, never where you expected it to be.

He had been flung ignominiously on his face in the leaves, his wrist twisted painfully behind his back. In a frenzy of terror, convinced he was about to be slain, he had wrenched with all his strength at his trapped arm, and the bone had snapped, with a red-black burst of pain that rendered him momentarily senseless.

He had come to himself moments later, slumped against a tree, facing a circle of ferocious-looking Highlanders, all in their plaids. In the midst of them stood Red Jamie Fraser—and the woman.

Grey clenched his teeth. Curse that woman! If it hadn't been for her—well, God knew what might have happened. What *had* happened was that she had spoken. She was English, a lady by her speech, and he—idiot that he was!—had leapt at once to the conclusion that she was a hostage of the vicious Highlanders, no doubt kidnapped for the purpose of ravishment. Everyone said that Highlanders indulged in rapine at every opportunity, and took delight in dishonoring Englishwomen; how should he have known otherwise!

And Lord John William Grey, aged sixteen and filled to the brim with regimental notions of gallantry and noble purpose, bruised, shaken, and fighting the pain of his broken arm, had tried to bargain, to save her from her fate. Fraser, tall and mocking, had played him like a salmon, stripping the woman half-naked before him to force from him information about the position and strength of his brother's regiment. And then, when he had told all he could, Fraser had laughingly revealed that the woman was his wife. They'd all laughed; he could hear the ribald Scottish voices now, hilarious in memory.

Grey rolled over, shifting his weight irritably on the unaccustomed mattress. And to make it all worse, Fraser had not even had the decency to kill him, but instead had tied him to a tree, where he would be found by his friends in the morning. By which time Fraser's men had visited the camp and —with the information *he* had given them!—had immobilized the cannon they were bringing to Cope.

Everyone had found out, of course, and while excuses were made because of his age and his noncommissioned status, he had been a pariah and an object of scorn. No one would speak to him, save his brother—and Hector. Loyal Hector.

He sighed, rubbing his cheek against the pillow. He could see Hector still, in his mind's eye. Dark-haired and blue-eyed, tender-mouthed, always smiling. It had been ten years since Hector had died at Culloden, hacked to pieces by a Highland broadsword, and still John woke in the dawn sometimes, body arched in clutching spasm, feeling Hector's touch.

And now this. He had dreaded this posting, being surrounded by Scots, by their grating voices, overwhelmed with the memory of what they had done to Hector. But never, in the most dismal moments of anticipation, had he thought he would ever meet James Fraser again.

The peat fire on the hearth died gradually to hot ash, then cold, and the window paled from deep black to the sullen gray of a rainy Scottish dawn. And still John Grey lay sleepless, burning eyes fixed on the smoke-blackened beams above him.

Grey rose in the morning unrested, but with his mind made up. He was here. Fraser was here. And neither could leave, for the foreseeable future. So. He must see the man now and again—he would be speaking to the assembled prisoners in an hour, and must inspect them regularly thereafter—but he would not see him privately. If he kept the man himself at a distance, perhaps he could also keep at bay the memories he stirred. And the feelings.

For while it was the memory of his past rage and humiliation that had kept him awake to begin with, it was the other side of the present situation that had left him still wakeful at dawn. The slowly dawning realization that Fraser was now *his* prisoner; no longer his tormentor, but a prisoner, like the others, entirely at his mercy.

He rang the bell for his servant and padded to the window to see how the weather kept, wincing at the chill of the stone under his bare feet.

It was, not surprisingly, raining. In the courtyard below, the prisoners were already being formed up in work crews, wet to the skin. Shivering in his shirt, Grey pulled in his head and shut the window halfway; a nice compromise between death from suffocation and death from the ague.

It had been visions of revenge that kept him tossing in his bed as the window lightened and the rain pattered on the sill; thoughts of Fraser confined to a tiny cell of freezing stone, kept naked through the winter nights, fed on slops, stripped and flogged in the courtyard of the prison. All that arrogant power humbled, reduced to groveling misery, dependent solely on his word for a moment's relief.

Yes, he thought all those things, imagined them in vivid detail, reveled in them. He heard Fraser beg for mercy, imagined himself disdaining, haughty.

He thought these things, and the spiked object turned over in his guts, piercing him with self-disgust.

Whatever he might once have been to Grey, Fraser now was a beaten foe; a prisoner of war, and the charge of the Crown. He was *Grey's* charge, in fact; a responsibility, and his welfare the duty of honor.

His servant had brought hot water for shaving. He splashed his cheeks, feeling the warmth soothe him, laying to rest the tormented fancies of the night. That was all they were, he realized—fancies, and the realization brought him a certain relief.

He might have met Fraser in battle and taken a real and savage pleasure in killing or maiming him. But the inescapable fact was that so long as Fraser was his prisoner, he could not in honor harm the man. By the time he had shaved and his servant had dressed him, he was recovered enough to find a certain grim humor in the situation.

His foolish behavior at Carryarrick had saved Fraser's life at Culloden. Now, that debt discharged, and Fraser in his power, Fraser's sheer helplessness as a prisoner made him completely safe. For whether foolish or wise, naive or experienced, all the Greys were men of honor.

Feeling somewhat better, he met his gaze in the looking glass, set his wig to rights, and went to eat breakfast before giving his first address to the prisoners.

"Will you have your supper served in the sitting room, sir, or in here?" MacKay's head, uncombed as ever, poked into the office.

"Um?" Grey murmured, absorbed in the papers spread out on the desk. "Oh," he said, looking up. "In here, if you please." He waved vaguely at the corner of the huge desk and returned to his work, scarcely looking up when the tray with his food arrived sometime later.

Quarry had not been joking about the paperwork. The sheer quantity of food alone required endless orders and requisitions—all orders to be submitted in duplicate to London, *if* he pleased!—let alone the hundreds of other necessities required by the prisoners, the guards, and the men and women from the village who came in by the day to clean the barracks and work in the kitchens. He had done nothing all day but write and sign requisitions. He *must* find a clerk soon, or die of sheer ennui.

Two hundred lb. wheat flowr, he wrote, *for prisoners' use. Six hogsheads ale, for use of barracks.* His normally elegant handwriting had quickly degenerated into a utilitarian scrawl, his stylish signature become a curt *J. Grey.*

He laid down his pen with a sigh and closed his eyes, massaging the ache between his brows. The sun had not bothered to show its face once since his arrival, and working all day in a smoky room by candlelight left his eyes burning like lumps of coal. His books had arrived the day before, but he had not even unpacked them, too exhausted by nightfall to do more than bathe his aching eyes in cold water and go to sleep.

He heard a small, stealthy sound, and sat up abruptly, his eyes popping open. A large brown rat sat on the corner of his desk, a morsel of plum cake held in its front paws. It didn't move, but merely looked at him speculatively, whiskers twitching.

"Well, God damn my eyes!" Grey exclaimed in amazement. "Here, you bugger! That's *my* supper!"

The rat nibbled pensively at the plum cake, bright beady eyes fixed on the Major.

"Get out of it!" Enraged, Grey snatched up the nearest object and let fly at the rat. The ink bottle exploded on the stone floor in a spray of black, and the startled rat leapt off the desk and fled precipitously, galloping between the legs of the even more startled MacKay, who appeared at the door to see what the noise was.

"Has the prison got a cat?" Grey demanded, dumping the contents of his supper tray into the waste can by his desk.

"Aye, sir, there's cats in the storerooms," MacKay offered, crawling backward on hands and knees to wipe up the small black footprints the rat had left in its precipitous flight through the ink puddle.

"Well, fetch one up here, if you please, MacKay," Grey ordered. "At once." He grunted at the memory of that obscenely naked tail draped nonchalantly over his plate. He had encountered rats often enough in the field, of course, but there was something about having his own personal supper molested before his eyes that seemed particularly infuriating.

He strode to the window and stood there, trying to clear his head with fresh air, as MacKay finished his mopping-up. Dusk was drawing down, filling the courtyard with purple shadows. The stones of the cell wing opposite looked even colder and more dreary than usual.

The turnkeys were coming through the rain from the kitchen wing; a procession of small carts laden with the prisoners' food; huge pots of steaming oatmeal and baskets of bread, covered with cloths against the rain. At least the poor devils had hot food after their wet day's work in the stone quarry.

A thought struck him as he turned from the window.

"Are there many rats in the cells?" he asked MacKay.

"Aye, sir, a great many," the prisoner replied, with a final swipe to the threshold. "I'll tell the cook to make ye up a fresh tray, shall I, sir?"

"If you please," Grey said. "And then if you will, Mr. MacKay, please see that each cell is provided with its own cat."

MacKay looked slightly dubious at this. Grey paused in the act of retrieving his scattered papers.

"Is there something wrong, MacKay?"

"No, sir," MacKay replied slowly. "Only the wee brown beasties do keep down the cockchafers. And with respect, sir, I dinna think the men would care to have a cat takin' all their rats."

Grey stared at the man, feeling mildly queasy.

"The prisoners eat the rats?" he asked, with a vivid memory of sharp yellow teeth nibbling at his plum cake.

"Only when they're lucky enough to catch one, sir," MacKay said. "Perhaps the cats would be a help wi' that, after all. Will that be all for tonight, sir?"

9

The Wanderer

Grey's resolve concerning James Fraser lasted for two weeks. Then the messenger arrived from the village of Ardsmuir, with news that changed everything.

"Does he still live?" he asked the man sharply. The messenger, one of the inhabitants of Ardsmuir village who worked for the prison, nodded.

"I saw him mysel', sir, when they brought him in. He's at the Lime Tree now, being cared for—but I didna think he looked as though care would be enough, sir, if ye take my meaning." He raised one brow significantly.

"I take it," Grey answered shortly. "Thank you, Mr.—"

"Allison, sir, Rufus Allison. Your servant, sir." The man accepted the shilling offered him, bowed with his hat under his arm, and took his leave.

Grey sat at his desk, staring out at the leaden sky. The sun had scarcely shone for a day since his arrival. He tapped the end of the quill with which he had been writing on the desk, oblivious to the damage he was inflicting on the sharpened tip.

The mention of gold was enough to prick up any man's ears, but especially his.

A man had been found this morning, wandering in the mist on the moor near the village. His clothes were soaked not only with the damp, but with seawater, and he was out of his mind with fever.

He had talked unceasingly since he was found, babbling for the most part, but his rescuers were unable to make much sense of his ravings. The man appeared to be Scottish, and yet he spoke in an incoherent mixture of French and Gaelic, with here and there the odd word of English thrown in. And one of those words had been "gold."

The combination of Scots, gold, and the French tongue, mentioned in this area of the country, could bring only one thought to the mind of anyone who had fought through the last days of the Jacobite rising. The Frenchman's Gold. The fortune in gold bullion that Louis of France had—according to rumor—sent secretly to the aid of his cousin, Charles Stuart. But sent far too late.

Some stories said that the French gold had been hidden by the Highland army during the last headlong retreat to the North, before the final disaster at Culloden. Others held that the gold had never reached Charles Stuart, but had been left for safekeeping in a cave near the place where it had come ashore on the northwestern coast.

Some said that the secret of the hiding place had been lost, its guardian killed at Culloden. Others said that the hiding place was still known, but a close-kept secret, held among the members of a single Highland family. Whatever the truth, the gold had never been found. Not yet.

French and Gaelic. Grey spoke passable French, the result of several years fighting abroad, but neither he nor any of his officers spoke the barbarous Gaelic, save a few words Sergeant Grissom had learned as a child from a Scottish nursemaid.

He could not trust a man from the village; not if there was anything to this tale. The Frenchman's Gold! Beyond its value as treasure—which would belong to the Crown in any case—the gold had a considerable and personal value to John William Grey. The finding of that half-mythical hoard would be his passport out of Ardsmuir—back to London and civilization. The blackest disgrace would be instantly obscured by the dazzle of gold.

He bit the end of the blunted quill, feeling the cylinder crack between his teeth.

Damn. No, it couldn't be a villager, nor one of his officers. A prisoner, then. Yes, he could use a prisoner without risk, for a prisoner would be unable to make use of the information for his own ends.

Damn again. All of the prisoners spoke Gaelic, many had some English as well—but only one spoke French besides. *He is an educated man,* Quarry's voice echoed in his memory.

"Damn, damn, *damn!*" Grey muttered. It couldn't be helped. Allison had said the wanderer was very ill; there was no time to look for alternatives. He spat out a shred of quill.

"Brame!" he shouted. The startled corporal poked his head in.

"Yes, sir?"

"Bring me a prisoner named James Fraser. At once."

⊱⊰

The Governor stood behind his desk, leaning on it as though the huge slab of oak were in fact the bulwark it looked. His hands were damp on the smooth wood, and the white stock of his uniform felt tight around his neck.

His heart leapt violently as the door opened. The Scot came in, his irons chinking slightly, and stood before the desk. The candles were all lit, and the office nearly as bright as day, though it was nearly full dark outside.

He had seen Fraser several times, of course, standing in the courtyard with the other prisoners, red head and shoulders above most of the other men, but never close enough to see his face clearly.

He looked different. That was both shock and relief; for so long, he had seen a clean-shaven face in memory, dark with threat or alight with mocking laughter. This man was short-bearded, his face calm and wary, and while the deep blue eyes were the same, they gave no sign of recognition. The man stood quietly before the desk, waiting.

Grey cleared his throat. His heart was still beating too fast, but at least he could speak calmly.

"Mr. Fraser," he said. "I thank you for coming."

The Scot bent his head courteously, but did not answer that he had had no choice in the matter; his eyes said that.

"Doubtless you wonder why I have sent for you," Grey said. He sounded insufferably pompous to his own ears, but was unable to remedy it. "I find that a situation has arisen in which I require your assistance."

"What is that, Major?" The voice was the same—deep and precise, marked with a soft Highland burr.

He took a deep breath, bracing himself on the desk. He would rather have done anything but ask help of this particular man, but there was no bloody choice. Fraser was the only possibility.

"A man has been found wandering the moor near the coast," he said carefully. "He appears to be seriously ill, and his speech is deranged. However, certain . . . matters to which he refers appear to be of . . . substantial interest to the Crown. I require to talk with him, and discover as much as I can of his identity, and the matters of which he speaks."

He paused, but Fraser merely stood there, waiting.

"Unfortunately," Grey said, taking another breath, "the man in question has been heard to speak in a mixture of Gaelic and French, with no more than a word or two of English."

One of the Scot's ruddy eyebrows stirred. His face didn't change in any appreciable way, but it was evident that he had grasped the implications of the situation.

"I see, Major." The Scot's soft voice was full of irony. "And you would like my assistance to interpret for ye what this man might have to say."

Grey couldn't trust himself to speak, but merely jerked his head in a short nod.

"I fear I must decline, Major." Fraser spoke respectfully, but with a glint in his eye that was anything but respectful. Grey's hand curled tight around the brass letter-opener on his blotter.

"You decline?" he said. He tightened his grasp on the letter-opener in order to keep his voice steady. "Might I inquire why, Mr. Fraser?"

"I am a prisoner, Major," the Scot said politely. "Not an interpreter."

"Your assistance would be—appreciated," Grey said, trying to infuse the word with significance without offering outright bribery. "Conversely," his tone hardened, "a failure to render legitimate assistance—"

"It is not legitimate for ye either to extort my services or to threaten me, Major." Fraser's voice was a good deal harder than Grey's.

"I did not threaten you!" The edge of the letter-opener was cutting into his hand; he was forced to loosen his grip.

"Did ye no? Well, and I'm pleased to hear it." Fraser turned toward the door. "In that case, Major, I shall bid ye good night."

Grey would have given a great deal simply to have let him go. Unfortunately, duty called.

"Mr. Fraser!" The Scot stopped, a few feet from the door, but didn't turn.

Grey took a deep breath, steeling himself to it.

"If you do what I ask, I will have your irons struck off," he said.

Fraser stood quite still. Young and inexperienced Grey might be, but he was not unobservant. Neither was he a poor judge of men. Grey watched the rise of his prisoner's head, the increased tension of his shoulders, and felt a small relaxation of the anxiety that had gripped him since the news of the wanderer had come.

"Mr. Fraser?" he said.

Very slowly, the Scot turned around. His face was quite expressionless.

"You have a bargain, Major," he said softly.

It was well past midnight when they arrived in the village of Ardsmuir. No lights showed in the cottages they passed, and Grey found himself wondering what the inhabitants thought, as the sound of hooves and the jingle of arms passed by their windows late at night, a faint echo of the English troops who had swept through the Highlands ten years before.

The wanderer had been taken to the Lime Tree, an inn so called because for many years, it had boasted a huge lime tree in the yard; the only tree of any size for thirty miles. There was nothing left now but a broad stump—the tree, like so many other things, had perished in the aftermath of Culloden, burned for firewood by Cumberland's troops—but the name remained.

At the door, Grey paused and turned to Fraser.

"You will recall the terms of our agreement?"

"I will," Fraser answered shortly, and brushed past him.

In return for having the irons removed, Grey had required three things: firstly, that Fraser would not attempt to escape during the journey to or from the village. Secondly, Fraser would undertake to give a full and true account of all that the vagrant should say. And thirdly, Fraser would give his word as a gentleman to speak to no one but Grey of what he learned.

There was a murmur of Gaelic voices inside; a sound of surprise as the innkeeper saw Fraser, and deference at the sight of the red coat behind him. The goodwife stood on the stair, an oil-dip in her hand making the shadows dance around her.

Grey laid a hand on the innkeeper's arm, startled.

"Who is that?" There was another figure on the stairs, an apparition, clothed all in black.

"That is the priest," Fraser said quietly, beside him. "The man will be dying, then."

Grey took a deep breath, trying to steady himself for what might come.

"Then there is little time to waste," he said firmly, setting a booted foot on the stair. "Let us proceed."

The man died just before dawn, Fraser holding one of his hands, the priest the other. As the priest leaned over the bed, mumbling in Gaelic and Latin, making Popish signs over the body, Fraser sat back on his stool, eyes closed, still holding the small, frail hand in his own.

The big Scot had sat by the man's side all night, listening, encouraging, comforting. Grey had stood by the door, not wishing to frighten the man by the sight of his uniform, both surprised and oddly touched at Fraser's gentleness.

Now Fraser laid the thin weathered hand gently across the still chest, and made the same sign as the priest had, touching forehead, heart, and both shoulders in turn, in the sign of a cross. He opened his eyes, and rose to his feet, his head nearly brushing the low rafters. He nodded briefly to Grey, and preceded him down the narrow stair.

"In here." Grey motioned to the door of the taproom, empty at this hour. A sleepy-eyed barmaid laid the fire for them and brought bread and ale, then went out, leaving them alone.

He waited for Fraser to refresh himself before asking.

"Well, Mr. Fraser?"

The Scot set down his pewter mug and wiped a hand across his mouth. Already bearded, with his long hair neatly plaited, he didn't look disheveled by the long night watch, but there were dark smudges of tiredness under his eyes.

"All right," he said. "It doesna make a great deal of sense, Major," he added warningly, "but this is all he said." And he spoke carefully, pausing now and then to recall a word, stopping again to explain some Gaelic reference. Grey sat listening in deepening disappointment; Fraser had been correct—it didn't make much sense.

"The white witch?" Grey interrupted. "He spoke of a white witch? And seals?" It scarcely seemed more farfetched than the rest of it, but still he spoke disbelievingly.

"Aye, he did."

"Say it to me again," Grey commanded. "As best you remember. If you please," he added.

He felt oddly comfortable with the man, he realized, with a feeling of surprise. Part of it was sheer fatigue, of course; all his usual reactions and feelings were numbed by the long night and the strain of watching a man die by inches.

The entire night had seemed unreal to Grey; not least was this odd conclusion, wherein he found himself sitting in the dim dawn light of a country tavern, sharing a pitcher of ale with Red Jamie Fraser.

Fraser obeyed, speaking slowly, stopping now and then to recall. With the difference of a word here or there, it was identical to the first account—and those parts of it that Grey himself had been able to understand were faithfully translated.

He shook his head, discouraged. Gibberish. The man's ravings had been precisely that—ravings. If the man had ever seen any gold—and it did sound as though he had, at one time—there was no telling where or when from this hodgepodge of delusion and feverish delirium.

"You are quite positive that is all he said?" Grey grasped at the slim hope that Fraser might have omitted some small phrase, some statement that would yield a clue to the lost gold.

Fraser's sleeve fell back as he lifted his cup; Grey could see the deep band of raw flesh about his wrist, dark in the gray early light of the taproom. Fraser saw him looking at it, and set down the cup, the frail illusion of companionship shattered.

"I keep my bargains, Major," Fraser said, with cold formality. He rose to his feet. "Shall we be going back now?"

They rode in silence for some time. Fraser was lost in his own thoughts, Grey sunk in fatigue and disappointment. They stopped at a small spring to refresh themselves, just as the sun topped the small hills to the north.

Grey drank cold water, then splashed it on his face, feeling the shock of it revive him momentarily. He had been awake for more than twenty-four hours, and was feeling slow and stupid.

Fraser had been awake for the same twenty-four hours, but gave no apparent sign of being troubled by the fact. He was crawling busily around the spring on his hands and knees, evidently plucking some sort of weed from the water.

"What are you doing, Mr. Fraser?" Grey asked, in some bewilderment.

Fraser looked up, mildly surprised, but not embarrassed in the slightest.

"I am picking watercress, Major."

"I see that," Grey said testily. "What for?"

"To eat, Major," Fraser replied evenly. He took the stained cloth bag from his belt and dropped the dripping green mass into it.

"Indeed? Are you not fed sufficiently?" Grey asked blankly. "I have never heard of people eating watercress."

"It's green, Major."

In his fatigued state, the Major had suspicions that he was being practiced upon.

"What in damnation other color ought a weed to be?" he demanded.

Fraser's mouth twitched slightly, and he seemed to be debating something with himself. At last he shrugged slightly, wiping his wet hands on the sides of his breeks.

"I only meant, Major, that eating green plants will stop ye getting scurvy and loose teeth. My men eat such greens as I take them, and cress is better-tasting than most things I can pick on the moor."

Grey felt his brows shoot up.

"Green plants stop scurvy?" he blurted. "Wherever did you get that notion?"

"From my wife!" Fraser snapped. He turned away abruptly, and stood, tying the neck of his sack with hard, quick movements.

Grey could not prevent himself asking.

"Your wife, sir—where is she?"

The answer was a sudden blaze of dark blue that seared him to the backbone, so shocking was its intensity.

Perhaps you are too young to know the power of hate and despair. Quarry's voice spoke in Grey's memory. He was not; he recognized them at once in the depths of Fraser's eyes.

Only for a moment, though; then the man's normal veil of cool politeness was back in place.

"My wife is gone," Fraser said, and turned away again, so abruptly that the movement verged on rudeness.

Grey felt himself shaken by an unexpected feeling. In part it was relief. The woman who had been both cause of and party to his humiliation was dead. In part, it was regret.

Neither of them spoke again on the journey back to Ardsmuir.

Three days later, Jamie Fraser escaped. It had never been a difficult matter for prisoners to escape from Ardsmuir; no one ever did, simply because there was no place for a man to go. Three miles from the prison, the coast of Scotland dropped into the ocean in a spill of crumbled granite. On the other three sides, nothing but empty moorland stretched for miles.

Once, a man might take to the heather, depending on clan and kinsmen for support and protection. But the clans were crushed, the kin dead, the Scottish prisoners removed far away from their own clan lands. Starving on the bleak moor was little improvement on a prison cell. Escape was not worth it—to anyone but Jamie Fraser, who evidently had a reason.

The dragoons' horses kept to the road; while the surrounding moor looked smooth as a velvet counterpane, the purpling heather was a thin layer, deceptively spread over a foot or more of wet, spongy peat moss. Even the red deer didn't walk at random in that boggy mass—Grey could see four of the animals now, stick figures a mile away, the line of their track through the heather seeming no wider than a thread.

Fraser, of course, was not mounted. That meant that the escaped prisoner might be anywhere on the moor, free to follow the red deer's paths.

It was John Grey's duty to pursue his prisoner and attempt his recapture. It was something more than duty that had made him strip the garrison for his search party, and urge them on with only the briefest of stops for rest and food. Duty, yes, and an urgent desire to find the French gold and win approval from his masters—and reprieve from this desolate Scottish exile. But there was anger, too, and an odd sense of personal betrayal.

Grey wasn't sure whether he was more angry at Fraser for breaking his word, or at himself, for having been fool enough to believe that a Highlander—gentleman or not—held a sense of honor equal to his own. But angry he was, and determined to search every deer path on this moor if necessary, in order to lay James Fraser by the heels.

They reached the coast the next night, well after dark, after a laborious day of combing the moor. The fog had thinned away over the rocks, swept out by the offshore wind, and the sea spread out before them, cradled by cliffs and strewn with tiny barren islets.

John Grey stood beside his horse on the clifftops, looking down at the wild black sea. It was a clear night on the coast, thank God, and the moon was at the half; its gleam painted the spray-wet rocks, making them stand out hard and shining as silver ingots against black velvet shadows.

It was the most desolate place he had ever seen, though it had a sort of terrible beauty about it that made the blood run cold in his veins. There was no sign of James Fraser. No sign of life at all.

One of the men with him gave a sudden exclamation of surprise, and drew his pistol.

"There!" he said. "On the rocks!"

"Hold your fire, fool," said another of the soldiers, grabbing his companion's arm. He made no effort to disguise his contempt. "Have you ne'er seen seals?"

"Ah . . . no," said the first man, rather sheepishly. He lowered his pistol, staring out at the small dark forms on the rocks below.

Grey had never seen seals, either, and he watched them with fascination. They looked like black slugs from this distance, the moonlight gleaming wetly on their coats as they raised restless heads, seeming to roll and weave unsteadily as they made their awkward way on land.

His mother had had a cloak made of sealskin, when he was a boy. He had been allowed to touch it once, marveling at the feel of it, dark and warm as a moonless summer night. Amazing that such thick, soft fur came from these slick, wet creatures.

"The Scots call them silkies," said the soldier who had recognized them. He nodded at the seals with the proprietary air of special knowledge.

"Silkies?" Grey's attention was caught; he stared at the man with interest. "What else do you know about them, Sykes?"

The soldier shrugged, enjoying his momentary importance. "Not a great deal, sir. The folk hereabout have stories about them, though; they say sometimes one of them will come ashore and leave off its skin, and inside is a beautiful woman. If a man should find the skin, and hide it, so she can't go back, why then—she'll be forced to stay and be his wife. They make good wives, sir, or so I'm told."

"At least they'd always be wet," murmured the first soldier, and the men erupted in guffaws that echoed among the cliffs, raucous as seabirds.

"That's enough!" Grey had to raise his voice, to be heard above the rash of laughter and crude suggestions.

"Spread out!" Grey ordered. "I want the cliffs searched in both directions —and keep an eye out for boats below; God knows there's room enough to hide a sloop behind some of those islands."

Abashed, the men went without comment. They returned an hour later, wet from spray and disheveled with climbing, but with no sign of Jamie Fraser—or the Frenchman's Gold.

At dawn, as the light stained the slippery rocks red and gold, small parties of dragoons were sent off to search the cliffs in both directions, making their way carefully down the rocky clefts and tumbled piles of stone.

Nothing was found. Grey stood by a fire on the clifftop, keeping an eye on the search. He was swathed in his greatcoat against the biting wind, and fortified periodically by hot coffee, supplied by his servant.

The man at the Lime Tree had come from the sea, his clothes soaked in saltwater. Whether Fraser had learned something from the man's words that he had not told, or had decided only to take the chance of looking for himself, surely he also would have gone to the sea. And yet there was no sign of James Fraser, anywhere along this stretch of coast. Worse yet, there was no sign of the gold.

"If he went in anywhere along this stretch, Major, you'll have seen the last of him, I'm thinking." It was Sergeant Grissom, standing beside him, gazing down at the crash and whirl of water through the jagged rocks below. He nodded at the furious water.

"They call this spot the Devil's Cauldron, because of the way it boils all the time. Fishermen drowned off this coast are seldom found; there are wicked currents to blame for it, of course, but folk say the Devil seizes them and pulls them below."

"Do they?" Grey said bleakly. He stared down into the smash and spume forty feet below. "I wouldn't doubt it, Sergeant."

He turned back toward the campfire.

"Give orders to search until nightfall, Sergeant. If nothing is found, we'll start back in the morning."

Grey lifted his gaze from his horse's neck, squinting through the dim early light. His eyes felt swollen from peat smoke and lack of sleep, and his bones ached from several nights spent lying on damp ground.

The ride back to Ardsmuir would take no more than a day. The thought of a soft bed and a hot supper was delightful—but then he would have to write the official dispatch to London, confessing Fraser's escape—the reason for it —and his own shameful failure to recapture the man.

The feeling of bleakness at this prospect was reinforced by a deep griping in the major's lower abdomen. He raised a hand, signaling a halt, and slid wearily to the ground.

"Wait here," he said to his men. There was a small hillock a few hundred feet away; it would afford him sufficient privacy for the relief he sorely needed; his bowels, unaccustomed to Scottish parritch and oatcake, had rebelled altogether at the exigencies of a field diet.

The birds were singing in the heather. Away from the noise of hooves and harness, he could hear all the tiny sounds of the waking moor. The wind had changed with the dawn, and the scent of the sea came inland now, whispering through the grass. Some small animal made a rustling noise on the other side of a gorse bush. It was all very peaceful.

Straightening up from what too late struck him as a most undignified posture, Grey raised his head and looked straight into the face of James Fraser.

He was no more than six feet away. He stood still as one of the red deer, the moor wind brushing over him, with the rising sun tangled in his hair.

They stood frozen, staring at each other. The smell of the sea came faintly on the wind. There was no sound but the sea wind and the singing of meadowlarks for a moment. Then Grey drew himself up, swallowing to bring his heart down from his throat.

"I fear you take me at a disadvantage, Mr. Fraser," he said coolly, fastening his breeches with as much self-possession as he could muster.

The Scot's eyes were the only part of him to move, down over Grey and slowly back up. Looked over his shoulder, to where six armed soldiers stood, pointing their muskets. Dark blue eyes met his, straight on. At last, the edge of Fraser's mouth twitched, and he said, "I think ye take me at the same, Major."

10

White Witch's Curse

Jamie Fraser sat shivering on the stone floor of the empty storeroom, clutching his knees and trying to get warm. He thought he likely would never be warm again. The chill of the sea had seeped into his bones, and he could still feel the churn of the crashing breakers, deep in his belly.

He wished for the presence of the other prisoners—Morrison, Hayes, Sinclair, Sutherland. Not only for company, but for the heat of their bodies. On bitter nights, the men would huddle close together for warmth, breathing each other's stale breath, tolerating the bump and knock of close quarters for the sake of warmth.

He was alone, though. Likely they would not return him to the large cell with the other men until after they had done whatever they meant to do to him as punishment for escaping. He leaned back against the wall with a sigh, morbidly aware of the bones of his spine pressing against the stone, and the fragility of the flesh covering them.

He was very much afraid of being flogged, and yet he hoped that would be his punishment. It would be horrible, but it would be soon over—and infinitely more bearable than being put back in irons. He could feel in his flesh the crash of the smith's hammer, echoing through the bones of his arm as the smith pounded the fetters firmly into place, holding his wrist steady on the anvil.

His fingers sought the rosary around his neck. His sister had given it to him when he left Lallybroch; the English had let him keep it, as the string of beechwood beads had no value.

"Hail Mary, full of grace," he muttered, "blessed art thou amongst women."

He hadn't much hope. That wee yellow-haired fiend of a major had seen, damn his soul—he knew just how terrible the fetters had been.

"Blessed is the fruit of thy womb, Jesus. Holy Mary, Mother of God, pray for us sinners . . ."

The wee Major had made him a bargain, and he had kept it. The major would not be thinking so, though.

He had kept his oath, had done as he promised. Had relayed the words spoken to him, one by one, just as he had heard them from the wandering man. It was no part of his bargain to tell the Englishman that he knew the man—or what conclusions he had drawn from the muttered words.

He had recognized Duncan Kerr at once, changed though he was by time and mortal illness. Before Culloden, he had been a tacksman of Colum MacKenzie, Jamie's uncle. After, he had escaped to France, to eke out what living might be made there.

"Be still, *a charaid; bi sàmhach,*" he had said softly in Gaelic, dropping to his knees by the bed where the sick man lay. Duncan was an elderly man, his worn face wasted by illness and fatigue, and his eyes were bright with fever. At first he had thought Duncan too far gone to know him, but the wasted hand had gripped his with surprising strength, and the man had repeated through his rasping breath, *"mo charaid."* My kinsman.

The innkeeper was watching, from his place near the door, peering over Major Grey's shoulder. Jamie had bent his head and whispered in Duncan's ear, "All you say will be told to the English. Speak wary." The landlord's eyes narrowed, but the distance between them was too far; Jamie was sure he hadn't heard. Then the Major had turned and ordered the innkeeper out, and he was safe.

He couldn't tell whether it was the effect of his warning, or only the derangement of fever, but Duncan's speech wandered with his mind, often incoherent, images of the past overlapping with those of the present. Sometimes he had called Jamie "Dougal," the name of Colum's brother, Jamie's other uncle. Sometimes he dropped into poetry, sometimes he simply raved. And within the ravings and the scattered words, sometimes there was a grain of sense—or more than sense.

"It is cursed," Duncan whispered. "The gold is cursed. Do ye be warned, lad. It was given by the white witch, given for the King's son. But the Cause is lost, and the King's son fled, and she will not let the gold be given to a coward."

"Who is she?" Jamie asked. His heart had sprung up and choked him at Duncan's words, and it beat madly as he asked. "The white witch—who is she?"

"She seeks a brave man. A MacKenzie, it is for Himself. MacKenzie. It is theirs, she says it, for the sake of him who is dead."

"Who is the witch?" Jamie asked again. The word Duncan used was *bandruidh*—a witch, a wisewoman, a white lady. They had called his wife that, once. Claire—his own white lady. He squeezed Duncan's hand tight in his own, willing him to keep his senses.

"Who?" he said again. "Who is the witch?"

"The witch," Duncan muttered, his eyes closing. "The witch. She is a soul-eater. She is death. He is dead, the MacKenzie, he is dead."

"Who is dead? Colum MacKenzie?"

"All of them, all of them. All dead. All dead!" cried the sick man, clutching tight to his hand. "Colum, and Dougal, and Ellen, too."

Suddenly his eyes opened, and fixed on Jamie's. The fever had dilated his pupils, so his gaze seemed a pool of drowning black.

"Folk do say," he said, with surprising clarity, "as how Ellen MacKenzie did leave her brothers and her home, and go to wed with a silkie from the sea. She heard them, aye?" Duncan smiled dreamily, the black stare swimming with distant vision. "She heard the silkies singing, there upon the rocks, one, and two, and three of them, and she saw from her tower, one and two, and three of them, and so she came down, and went to the sea, and so under it, to live wi' the silkies. Aye? Did she no?"

"So folk say," Jamie had answered, mouth gone dry. Ellen had been his mother's name. And that was what folk had said, when she had left her home, to elope with Brian Dubh Fraser, a man with the shining black hair of a silkie. The man for whose sake he was himself now called Mac Dubh— Black Brian's son.

Major Grey stood close, on the other side of the bed, brow furrowed as he watched Duncan's face. The Englishman had no Gaelic, but Jamie would have been willing to wager that he knew the word for gold. He caught the Major's eye, and nodded, bending again to speak to the sick man.

"The gold, man," he said, in French, loud enough for Grey to hear. "Where is the gold?" He squeezed Duncan's hand as hard as he could, hoping to convey some warning.

Duncan's eyes closed, and he rolled his head restlessly, to and fro upon the pillow. He muttered something, but the words were too faint to catch.

"What did he say?" the Major demanded sharply. "What?"

"I don't know." Jamie patted Duncan's hand to rouse him. "Speak to me, man, tell me again."

There was no response save more muttering. Duncan's eyes had rolled back in his head, so that only a thin line of gleaming white showed beneath the wrinkled lids. Impatient, the Major leaned forward and shook him by one shoulder.

"Wake up!" he said. "Speak to us!"

At once Duncan Kerr's eyes flew open. He stared up, up, past the two faces bending over him, seeing something far beyond them.

"She will tell you," he said, in Gaelic. "She will come for you." For a split second, his attention seemed to return to the inn room where he lay, and his eyes focused on the men with him. "For both of you," he said distinctly.

Then he closed his eyes, and spoke no more, but clung ever tighter to Jamie's hand. Then after a time, his grip relaxed, his hand slid free, and it was over. The guardianship of the gold had passed.

And so, Jamie Fraser had kept his word to the Englishman—and his obligation to his countrymen. He had told the Major all that Duncan had said, and the devil of a help to him that had been! And when the opportunity of escape offered, he had taken it—gone to the heather and sought the sea, and done what he could with Duncan Kerr's legacy. And now he must pay the price of his actions, whatever that turned out to be.

There were footsteps coming down the corridor outside. He clutched his knees harder, trying to quell the shivering. At least it would be decided now, either way.

". . . pray for us sinners now, and at the hour of our death, amen."

The door swung open, letting in a shaft of light that made him blink. It was dark in the corridor, but the guard standing over him held a torch.

"On your feet." The man reached down and pulled him up against the stiffness of his joints. He was pushed toward the door, stumbling. "You're wanted upstairs."

"Upstairs? Where?" He was startled at that—the smith's forge was downstairs from where he was, off the courtyard. And they wouldn't flog him so late in the evening.

The man's face twisted, fierce and ruddy in the torchlight. "To the Major's quarters," the guard said, grinning. "And may God have mercy on your soul, Mac Dubh."

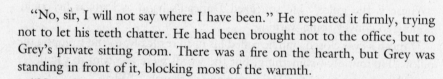

"No, sir, I will not say where I have been." He repeated it firmly, trying not to let his teeth chatter. He had been brought not to the office, but to Grey's private sitting room. There was a fire on the hearth, but Grey was standing in front of it, blocking most of the warmth.

"Nor why you chose to escape?" Grey's voice was cool and formal.

Jamie's face tightened. He had been placed near the bookshelf, where the light of a triple-branched candlestick fell on his face; Grey himself was no more than a silhouette, black against the fire's glow.

"That is my private affair," he said.

"Private affair?" Grey echoed incredulously. "Did you say your private affair?"

"I did."

The Governor inhaled strongly through his nose.

"That is possibly the most outrageous thing I have heard in my life!"

"Your life has been rather brief, then, Major," Fraser said. "If you will pardon my saying so." There was no point in dragging it out or trying to placate the man. Better to provoke a decision at once and get it over with.

He had certainly provoked something; Grey's fists clenched tight at his sides, and he took a step toward him, away from the fire.

"Have you any notion what I could do to you for this?" Grey inquired, his voice low and very much controlled.

"Aye, I have. Major." More than a notion. He knew from experience what they might do to him, and he wasn't looking forward to it. It wasn't as though he'd a choice about it, though.

Grey breathed heavily for a moment, then jerked his head.

"Come here, Mr. Fraser," he ordered. Jamie stared at him, puzzled.

"Here!" he said peremptorily, pointing to a spot directly before him on the hearthrug. "Stand here, sir!"

"I am not a dog, Major!" Jamie snapped. "Ye'll do as ye like wi' me, but I'll no come when ye call me to heel!"

Taken by surprise, Grey uttered a short, involuntary laugh.

"My apologies, Mr. Fraser," he said dryly. "I meant no offense by the address. I merely wish you to approach nearer. If you will?" He stepped aside and bowed elaborately, gesturing to the hearth.

Jamie hesitated, but then stepped warily onto the patterned rug. Grey stepped close to him, nostrils flared. So close, the fine bones and fair skin of his face made him look almost girlish. The Major put a hand on his sleeve, and the long-lashed eyes sprang wide in shock.

"You're wet!"

"Yes, I am wet," Jamie said, with elaborate patience. He was also freezing. A fine, continuous shiver ran through him, even this close to the fire.

"Why?"

"Why?" Jamie echoed, astonished. "Did you not order the guards to douse me wi' water before leaving me in a freezing cell?"

"I did not, no." It was clear enough that the Major was telling the truth; his face was pale under the ruddy flush of the firelight, and he looked angry. His lips thinned to a fine line.

"I apologize for this, Mr. Fraser."

"Accepted, Major." Small wisps of steam were beginning to rise from his clothes, but the warmth was seeping through the damp cloth. His muscles ached from the shivering, and he wished he could lie down on the hearthrug, dog or not.

"Did your escape have anything to do with the matter of which you learned at the Lime Tree Inn?"

Jamie stood silent. The ends of his hair were drying, and small wisps floated across his face.

"Will you swear to me that your escape had *nothing* to do with that matter?"

Jamie stood silent. There seemed no point in saying anything, now.

The little Major was pacing up and down the hearth before him, hands locked behind his back. Now and then, the Major glanced up at him, and then resumed his pacing.

Finally he stopped in front of Jamie.

"Mr. Fraser," he said formally. "I will ask you once more—why did you escape from the prison?"

Jamie sighed. He wouldn't get to stand by the fire much longer.

"I cannot tell you, Major."

"Cannot or will not?" Grey asked sharply.

"It doesna seem a useful distinction, Major, as ye willna hear anything, either way." He closed his eyes and waited, trying to soak up as much heat as possible before they took him away.

Grey found himself at a loss, both for words and action. *Stubborn does not begin to describe it,* Quarry had said. It didn't.

He took a deep breath, wondering what to do. He found himself embarrassed by the petty cruelty of the guards' revenge; the more so because it was just such an action he had first contemplated upon hearing that Fraser was his prisoner.

He would be perfectly within his rights now to order the man flogged, or put back in irons. Condemned to solitary confinement, put on short rations —he could in justice inflict any of a dozen different punishments. And if he did, the odds of his ever finding the Frenchman's Gold became vanishingly small.

The gold *did* exist. Or at least there was a good probability that it did. Only a belief in that gold would have stirred Fraser to act as he had.

He eyed the man. Fraser's eyes were closed, his lips set firmly. He had a wide, strong mouth, whose grim expression was somewhat belied by the sensitive lips, set soft and exposed in their curly nest of red beard.

Grey paused, trying to think of some way to break past the man's wall of bland defiance. To use force would be worse than useless—and after the guards' actions, he would be ashamed to order it, even had he the stomach for brutality.

The clock on the mantelpiece struck ten. It was late; there was no sound in the fortress, save the occasional footsteps of the soldier on sentry in the courtyard outside the window.

Clearly neither force nor threat would work in gaining the truth. Reluctantly, he realized that there was only one course open to him, if he still wished to pursue the gold. He must put aside his feelings about the man and take Quarry's suggestion. He must pursue an acquaintance, in the course of which he might worm out of the man some clue that would lead him to the hidden treasure.

If it existed, he reminded himself, turning to his prisoner. He took a deep breath.

"Mr. Fraser," he said formally, "will you do me the honor to take supper tomorrow in my quarters?"

He had the momentary satisfaction of having startled the Scottish bastard, at least. The blue eyes opened wide, and then Fraser regained the mastery of his face. He paused for a moment, and then bowed with a flourish, as though he wore a kilt and swinging plaid, and not damp prison rags.

"It will be my pleasure to attend ye, Major," he said.

MARCH 7, 1755

Fraser was delivered by the guard and left to wait in the sitting room, where a table was laid. When Grey came through the door from his bedroom a few moments later, he found his guest standing by the bookshelf, apparently absorbed in a copy of *Nouvelle Héloïse*.

"You are interested in French novels?" he blurted, not realizing until too late how incredulous the question sounded.

Fraser glanced up, startled, and snapped the book shut. Very deliberately, he returned it to its shelf.

"I *can* read, Major," he said. He had shaved; a slight flush burned high on his cheekbones.

"I—yes, of course I did not mean—I merely—" Grey's own cheeks were more flushed than Fraser's. The fact was that he *had* subconsciously assumed that the other did not read, his evident education notwithstanding, merely because of his Highland accent and shabby dress.

While his coat might be shabby, Fraser's manners were not. He ignored Grey's flustered apology, and turned to the bookshelf.

"I have been telling the men the story, but it has been some time since I read it; I thought I would refresh my memory as to the sequence of the ending."

"I see." Just in time, Grey stopped himself from saying "They understand it?"

Fraser evidently read the unspoken question in his face, for he said dryly, "All Scottish children are taught their letters, Major. Still, we have a great tradition of storytelling in the Highlands."

"Ah. Yes. I see."

The entry of his servant with dinner saved him from further awkwardness, and the supper passed uneventfully, though there was little conversation, and that little, limited to the affairs of the prison.

The next time, he had had the chess table set up before the fire, and invited Fraser to join him in a game before the supper was served. There had been a brief flash of surprise from the slanted blue eyes, and then a nod of acquiescence.

That had been a small stroke of genius, Grey thought in retrospect. Relieved of the need for conversation or social courtesies, they had slowly become accustomed to each other as they sat over the inlaid board of ivory and ebony-wood, gauging each other silently by the movements of the chessmen.

When they had at length sat down to dine, they were no longer quite strangers, and the conversation, while still wary and formal, was at least true conversation, and not the awkward affair of starts and stops it had been before. They discussed matters of the prison, had a little conversation of books, and parted formally, but on good terms. Grey did not mention gold.

And so the weekly custom was established. Grey sought to put his guest at ease, in the hopes that Fraser might let drop some clue to the fate of the Frenchman's Gold. It had not come so far, despite careful probing. Any hint of inquiry as to what had transpired during the three days of Fraser's absence from Ardsmuir met with silence.

Over the mutton and boiled potatoes, he did his best to draw his odd guest into a discussion of France and its politics, by way of discovering whether there might exist any links between Fraser and a possible source of gold from the French Court.

Much to his surprise, he was informed that Fraser had in fact spent two years living in France, employed in the wine business, prior to the Stuart rebellion.

A certain cool humor in Fraser's eyes indicated that the man was well aware of the motives behind this questioning. At the same time, he acquiesced gracefully enough in the conversation, though taking some care always to lead questions away from his personal life, and instead toward more general matters of art and society.

Grey had spent some time in Paris, and despite his attempts at probing Fraser's French connections, found himself becoming interested in the conversation for its own sake.

"Tell me, Mr. Fraser, during your time in Paris, did you chance to encounter the dramatic works of Monsieur Voltaire?"

Fraser smiled. "Oh, aye, Major. In fact, I was privileged to entertain Monsieur Arouet—Voltaire being his nom de plume, aye?—at my table, on more than one occasion."

"Really?" Grey cocked a brow in interest. "And is he as great a wit in person as with the pen?"

"I couldna really say," Fraser replied, tidily forking up a slice of mutton. "He seldom said anything at all, let alone much sparkling with wit. He only sat hunched over in his chair, watching everyone, wi' his eyes rolling about from one to another. I shouldna be at all surprised to hear that things said at my dinner table later appeared on the stage, though fortunately I never encountered a parody of myself in his work." He closed his eyes in momentary concentration, chewing his mutton.

"Is the meat to your taste, Mr. Fraser?" Grey inquired politely. It was gristled, tough, and seemed barely edible to him. But then, he might well think differently, had he been eating oatmeal, weeds, and the occasional rat.

"Aye, it is, Major, I thank ye." Fraser dabbed up a bit of wine sauce and brought the last bite to his lips, making no demur when Grey signaled MacKay to bring back the platter.

"Monsieur Arouet wouldna appreciate such an excellent meal, I'm afraid," Fraser said, shaking his head as he helped himself to more mutton.

"I should expect a man so feted in French society to have somewhat more exacting tastes," Grey answered dryly. Half his own meal remained on his plate, destined for the supper of the cat Augustus.

Fraser laughed. "Scarcely that, Major," he assured Grey. "I have never seen Monsieur Arouet consume anything beyond a glass of water and a dry biscuit, no matter how lavish the occasion. He's a weazened wee scrap of a man, ye ken, and a martyr to the indigestion."

"Indeed?" Grey was fascinated. "Perhaps that explains the cynicism of some of the sentiments I have seen expressed in his plays. Or do you not think that the character of an author shows in the construction of his work?"

"Given some of the characters that I have seen appear in plays and novels, Major, I should think the author a bit depraved who drew them entirely from himself, no?"

"I suppose that is so," Grey answered, smiling at the thought of some of the more extreme fictional characters with whom he was acquainted. "Though if an author constructs these colorful personages from life, rather than from the depths of imagination, surely he must boast a most varied acquaintance!"

Fraser nodded, brushing crumbs from his lap with the linen napkin.

"It was not Monsieur Arouet, but a colleague of his—a lady novelist— who remarked to me once that writing novels was a cannibal's art, in which one often mixed small portions of one's friends and one's enemies together, seasoned them with imagination, and allowed the whole to stew together into a savory concoction."

Grey laughed at the description, and beckoned to MacKay to take away the plates and bring in the decanters of port and sherry.

"A delightful description, indeed! Speaking of cannibals, though, have you chanced to be acquainted with Mr. Defoe's *Robinson Crusoe*? It has been a favorite of mine since boyhood."

The conversation turned then to romances, and the excitement of the tropics. It was very late indeed when Fraser returned to his cell, leaving Major Grey entertained, but no wiser concerning either the source or the disposition of the wanderer's gold.

APRIL 2, 1755

John Grey opened the packet of quills his mother had sent from London. Swan's quills, both finer and stronger than common goose-quills. He smiled faintly at the sight of them; an unsubtle reminder that his correspondence was in arrears.

His mother would have to wait until tomorrow, though. He took out the small, monogrammed penknife he always carried, and slowly trimmed a quill to his liking, composing in his mind what he meant to say. By the time he dipped his quill into the ink, the words were clear in his mind, and he wrote quickly, seldom pausing.

2 April, 1755
To Harold, Lord Melton, Earl of Moray

My dear Hal, he wrote, *I write to inform you of a recent occurrence which has much engaged my attention. It may amount in the end to nothing, but if there be any substance in the matter, it is of great import.* The details of the wandering man's appearance, and the report of his ravings followed swiftly, but Grey found himself slowing as he told of Fraser's escape and recapture.

The fact that Fraser vanished from the precincts of the prison so soon following these events suggests strongly to me that there was in truth some substance in the vagrant's words.

If this were the case, however, I find myself at a loss to account for Fraser's subsequent actions. He was recaptured within three days of his escape, at a point no more than a mile from the coast. The country-side beyond the prison is deserted for a great many miles beyond the village of Ardsmuir, and there is little likelihood of his meeting with a confederate to whom he might pass word of the treasure. Every house in the village has been searched, as was Fraser himself, with no trace discovered of any gold. It is a remote district, and I am reasonably sure that he communicated with no one outside the prison prior to his es-cape—I am positive that he has not done so since, for he is closely watched.

Grey stopped, seeing once more the windswept figure of James Fraser, wild as the red stags and as much at home on the moor as one of them.

He had not the slightest doubt that Fraser could have eluded the dragoons easily, had he so chosen, but he had not. He had deliberately allowed himself to be recaptured. Why? He resumed writing, more slowly.

It may be, of course, that Fraser failed to find the treasure, or that such a treasure does not exist. I find myself somewhat inclined to this belief, for if he were in possession of a great sum, surely he would have departed from the district at once? He is a strong man, well-accustomed to rough living, and entirely capable, I believe, of making his way overland to some point on the coast from which he might make an escape by sea.

Grey bit the end of the quill gently, tasting ink. He made a face at the bitterness, rose, and spat out the window. He stood there for a minute, looking out into the cold spring night, absently wiping his mouth.

It had finally occurred to him to ask; not the question he had been asking all along, but the more important one. He had done it at the conclusion of a game of chess, which Fraser had won. The guard was standing at the door, ready to escort Fraser back to his cell; as the prisoner had risen from his seat, Grey had stood up, too.

"I shall not ask you again why you left the prison," he had said, calmly conversational. "But I will ask you—why did you come back?"

Fraser had frozen briefly, startled. He turned back and met Grey's eyes directly. For a moment he said nothing. Then his mouth curled up in a smile.

"I suppose I must value the company, Major; I can tell ye, it's not the food."

Grey snorted slightly, remembering. Unable to think of a suitable response, he had allowed Fraser to leave. It was only later that night that he had laboriously arrived at an answer, at last having had the wit to ask questions of himself, rather than of Fraser. What would he, Grey, have done, had Fraser *not* returned?

The answer was that his next step would have been an inquiry into Fraser's family connections, in case the man had sought refuge or help from them.

And that, he was fairly sure, was the answer. Grey had not taken part in the subjugation of the Highlands—he had been posted to Italy and France—but he had heard more than enough of that particular campaign. He had seen the blackened stones of too many charred cottages, rising like cairns amid the ruined fields, as he traveled north to Ardsmuir.

The fierce loyalties of the Scottish Highlanders were legendary. A Highlander who had seen those cots in flames might well choose to suffer prison, irons, or even flogging, to save his family a visitation from English soldiers.

Grey sat and took up his quill, dipping it afresh.

You will know, I think, the mettle of the Scots, he wrote. That one in particular, he thought wryly.

It is unlikely that any force or threat I can exert will induce Fraser to reveal the whereabouts of the gold—should it exist, and if it does not, I can still less expect any threat to be effective! I have instead chosen to begin a formal acquaintance with Fraser, in his capacity as chief of the Scottish prisoners, in hopes of surprising some clue from his conversation. So far, I have gained nothing from this process. One further avenue of approach suggests itself, however.

For obvious reasons, he went on, writing slowly as he formed the thought, *I do not wish to make this matter known officially.* To call attention to a hoard that might well prove to be chimerical was dangerous; the chance of disappointment was too great. Time enough, if the gold were found, to inform his superiors and collect his deserved reward—escape from Ardsmuir; a posting back to civilization.

Therefore I approach you, dear brother, and ask your help in discovering what particulars may obtain regarding the family of James Fraser. I pray you, do not let anyone be alarmed by your inquiries; if such family connections exist, I would have them ignorant of my interest for the present. My deepest thanks for any efforts you may be able to exert on my behalf, and believe me always,

He dipped the pen once more and signed with a small flourish,

Your humble servant and most affectionate brother,
John William Grey.

MAY 15, 1755

"The men sick of *la grippe*," Grey inquired, "how do they fare?" Dinner was over, and with it their conversation of books. Now it was time for business.

Fraser frowned over the single glass of sherry that was all he would accept in the way of drink. He still had not tasted it, though dinner had been over for some time.

"None so well. I have more than sixty men ill, fifteen of them verra badly off." He hesitated. "Might I ask . . ."

"I can promise nothing, Mr. Fraser, but you may ask," Grey answered formally. He had barely sipped his own sherry, nor more than tasted his dinner; his stomach had been knotted with anticipation all day.

Jamie paused a moment longer, calculating his chances. He wouldn't get everything; he must try for what was most important, but leave Grey room to reject some requests.

"We have need of more blankets, Major, more fires, and more food. And medicines."

Grey swirled the sherry in his cup, watching the light from the fire play in the vortex. Ordinary business first, he reminded himself. Time enough for the other, later.

"We have no more than twenty spare blankets in store," he answered, "but you may have those for the use of the very sick. I fear I cannot augment the ration of food; the rat-spoilage has been considerable, and we lost a great quantity of meal in the collapse of the storeroom two months ago. We have limited resources, and—"

"It is not so much a question of more," Fraser put in quickly. "But rather of the type of food. Those who are most ill cannot readily digest the bread and parritch. Perhaps a substitution of some sort might be arranged?" Each man was given, by law, a quart of oatmeal parritch and a small wheaten loaf each day. Thin barley brose supplemented this twice each week, with a quart of meat stew added on Sunday, to sustain the needs of men working at manual labor for twelve to sixteen hours per day.

Grey raised one eyebrow. "What are you suggesting, Mr. Fraser?"

"I assume that the prison does have some allowance for the purchase of salt beef, turnips and onions, for the Sunday stew?"

"Yes, but that allowance must provide for the next quarter's supplies."

"Then what I suggest, Major, is that you might use that money now to provide broth and stew for those who are sick. Those of us who are hale will willingly forgo our share of meat for the quarter."

Grey frowned. "But will the prisoners not be weakened, with no meat at all? Will they not be unable to work?"

"Those who die of the grippe will assuredly not work," Fraser pointed out acerbically.

Grey snorted briefly. "True. But those of you who remain healthy will not be healthy long, if you give up your rations for so long a time." He shook his head. "No, Mr. Fraser, I think not. It is better to let the sick take their chances than to risk many more falling ill."

Fraser was a stubborn man. He lowered his head for a moment, then looked up to try again.

"Then I would ask your leave to hunt for ourselves, Major, if the Crown cannot supply us with adequate food."

"Hunt?" Grey's fair brows rose in astonishment. "Give you weapons and allow you to wander the moors? God's teeth, Mr. Fraser!"

"I think God doesna suffer much from the scurvy, Major," Jamie said dryly. "*His* teeth are in no danger." He saw the twitch of Grey's mouth and relaxed slightly. Grey always tried to suppress his sense of humor, no doubt feeling that put him at a disadvantage. In his dealings with Jamie Fraser, it did.

Emboldened by that telltale twitch, Jamie pressed on.

"Not weapons, Major. And not wandering. Will ye give us leave to set snares upon the moor when we cut peats, though? And to keep such meat as we take?" A prisoner would now and then contrive a snare as it was, but as often as not, the catch would be taken from him by the guards.

Grey drew a deep breath and blew it out slowly, considering.

"Snares? Would you not require materials for the construction of these snares, Mr. Fraser?"

"Only a bit of string, Major," Jamie assured him. "A dozen balls, no more, of any sort of twine or string, and ye may leave the rest to us."

Grey rubbed slowly at his cheek in contemplation, then nodded.

"Very well." The Major turned to the small secretary, plucked the quill out of its inkwell and made a note. "I shall give orders to that effect tomorrow. Now, as to the rest of your requests . . ."

A quarter-hour later, it was settled. Jamie sat back at last, sighing, and finally took a sip of his sherry. He considered that he had earned it.

He had permission not only for the snares, but for the peat-cutters to work an extra half-hour per day, the extra peats to provide for an additional small fire in each cell. No medicines were to be had, but he had leave for Sutherland to send a message to a cousin in Ullapool, whose husband was an apothecary. If the cousin's husband were willing to send medicines, the prisoners could have them.

A decent evening's work, Jamie thought. He took another sip of sherry and closed his eyes, enjoying the warmth of the fire against his cheek.

Grey watched his guest beneath lowered lids, seeing the broad shoulders slump a little, tension eased now that their business was finished. Or so Fraser thought. Very good, Grey thought to himself. Yes, drink your sherry and relax. I want you thoroughly off guard.

He leaned forward to pick up the decanter, and felt the crackle of Hal's letter in his breast pocket. His heart began to beat faster.

"Will you not take a drop more, Mr. Fraser? And tell me—how does your sister fare these days?"

He saw Fraser's eyes spring open, and his face whiten with shock.

"How are matters there at—Lallybroch, they call it, do they not?" Grey pushed aside the decanter, keeping his eyes fixed on his guest.

"I could not say, Major." Fraser's voice was even, but his eyes were narrowed to slits.

"No? But I daresay they do very well these days, what with the gold you have provided them."

The broad shoulders tightened suddenly, bunched under the shabby coat. Grey carelessly picked up one of the chessmen from the nearby board, tossing it casually from one hand to the other.

"I suppose Ian—your brother-in-law is named Ian, I think?—will know how to make good use of it."

Fraser had himself under control again. The dark blue eyes met Grey's directly.

"Since you are so well informed as to my connections, Major," he said evenly, "I must suppose that you also are aware that my home lies well over a hundred miles from Ardsmuir. Perhaps you will explain how I might have traveled that distance twice within the space of three days?"

Grey's eyes stayed on the chess piece, rolling idly from hand to hand. It was a pawn, a cone-headed little warrior with a fierce face, carved from a cylinder of walrus ivory.

"You might have met someone upon the moor who would have borne word of the gold—or borne the gold itself—to your family."

Fraser snorted briefly.

"On Ardsmuir? How likely is it, Major, that I should by happenstance encounter a person known to me on that moor? Much less that it should be a person whom I would trust to convey a message such as you suggest?" He set down his glass with finality. "I met no one on the moor, Major."

"And should I trust *your* word to that effect, Mr. Fraser?" Grey allowed considerable skepticism to show in his voice. He glanced up, brows raised.

Fraser's high cheekbones flushed slightly.

"No one has ever had cause to doubt my word, Major," he said stiffly.

"Have they not, indeed?" Grey was not altogether feigning his anger. "I believe you gave *me* your word, upon the occasion of my ordering your irons stricken off!"

"And I kept it!"

"Did you?" The two men sat upright, glaring at each other over the table.

"You asked three things of me, Major, and I have kept that bargain in every particular!"

Grey gave a contemptuous snort.

"Indeed, Mr. Fraser? And if that is so, pray what was it caused you suddenly to despise the company of your fellows and seek congress with the coneys on the moor? Since you assure me that you met no one else—you give me *your word* that it is so." This last was spoken with an audible sneer that brought the color surging into Fraser's face.

One of the big hands curled slowly into a fist.

"Aye, Major," he said softly. "I give ye *my word* that that is so." He seemed to realize at this point that his fist was clenched; very slowly, he unfolded it, laying his hand flat on the table.

"And as to your escape?"

"And as to my escape, Major, I have told you that I will say nothing." Fraser exhaled slowly and sat back in his chair, eyes fixed on Grey under thick, ruddy brows.

Grey paused for a moment, then sat back himself, setting the chess piece on the table.

"Let me speak plainly, Mr. Fraser. I do you the honor of assuming you to be a sensible man."

"I am deeply sensible of the honor, Major, I do assure you."

Grey heard the irony, but did not respond; he held the upper hand now.

"The fact is, Mr. Fraser, that it is of no consequence whether you did in fact communicate with your family regarding the matter of the gold. You might have done so. That possibility alone is sufficient to warrant my sending a party of dragoons to search the premises of Lallybroch—thoroughly—and to arrest and interrogate the members of your family."

He reached into his breast pocket and withdrew a piece of paper. Unfolding it, he read the list of names.

"Ian Murray—your brother-in-law, I collect? His wife, Janet. That would be your sister, of course. Their children, James—named for his uncle, perhaps?"—he glanced up briefly, long enough to catch a glimpse of Fraser's face, than returned to his list—"Margaret, Katherine, Janet, Michael, and Ian. Quite a brood," he said, in a tone of dismissal that equated the six younger Murrays with a litter of piglets. He laid the list on the table beside the chess piece.

"The three eldest children are old enough to be arrested and interrogated with their parents, you know. Such interrogations are frequently ungentle, Mr. Fraser."

In this, he spoke no less than the truth, and Fraser knew it. All color had faded from the prisoner's face, leaving the strong bones stark under the skin. He closed his eyes briefly, then opened them.

Grey had a brief memory of Quarry's voice, saying *"If you dine alone with the man, don't turn your back on him."* The hair rose briefly on the back of his neck, but he controlled himself, returning Fraser's blue stare.

"What do you want of me?" The voice was low, and hoarse with fury, but the Scot sat motionless, a figure carved in cinnabar, gilded by the flame.

Grey took a deep breath.

"I want the truth," he said softly.

There was no sound in the chamber save the pop and hiss of the peats in the grate. There was a flicker of movement from Fraser, no more than the twitch of his fingers against his leg, and then nothing. The Scot sat, head turned, staring into the fire as though he sought an answer there.

Grey sat quietly, waiting. He could afford to wait. At last, Fraser turned back to face him.

"The truth, then." He took a deep breath; Grey could see the breast of his linen shirt swell with it—he had no waistcoat.

"I kept my word, Major. I told ye faithfully all that the man said to me that night. What I didna tell ye was that some of what he said had meaning to me."

"Indeed." Grey held himself still, scarcely daring to move. "And what meaning was that?"

Fraser's wide mouth compressed to a thin line.

"I—spoke to you of my wife," he said, forcing the words out as though they hurt him.

"Yes, you said that she was dead."

"I said that she was *gone*, Major," Fraser corrected softly. His eyes were fixed on the pawn. "It is likely she is dead, but—" He stopped and swallowed, then went on more firmly.

"My wife was a healer. What they call in the Highlands a charmer, but more than that. She was a white lady—a wisewoman." He glanced up briefly. "The word in Gaelic is *ban-druidh;* it also means witch."

"The white witch." Grey also spoke softly, but excitement was thrumming through his blood. "So the man's words referred to your wife?"

"I thought they might. And if so—" The wide shoulders stirred in a slight shrug. "I had to go," he said simply. "To see."

"How did you know where to go? Was that also something you gleaned from the vagrant's words?" Grey leaned forward slightly, curious. Fraser nodded, eyes still fixed on the ivory chess piece.

"There is a spot I knew of, not too far distant from this place, where there is a shrine to St. Bride. St. Bride was also called 'the white lady,' " he explained, looking up. "Though the shrine has been there a verra long time —since long before St. Bride came to Scotland."

"I see. And so you assumed that the man's words referred to this spot, as well as to your wife?"

Again the shrug.

"I did not know," Fraser repeated. "I couldna say whether he meant anything to do with my wife, or whether 'the white witch' only meant St. Bride—was only meant to direct me to the place—or perhaps neither. But I felt I must go."

He described the place in question, and at Grey's prodding, gave directions for reaching it.

"The shrine itself is a small stone in the shape of an ancient cross, so weathered that the markings scarce show on it. It stands above a small pool, half-buried in the heather. Ye can find small white stones in the pool, tangled among the roots of the heather that grows on the bank. The stones are thought to have great powers, Major," he explained, seeing the other's blank look. "But only when used by a white lady."

"I see. And your wife . . . ?" Grey paused delicately.

Fraser shook his head briefly.

"There was nothing there to do with her," he said softly. "She is truly gone." His voice was low and controlled, but Grey could hear the undertone of desolation.

Fraser's face was normally calm and unreadable; he did not change expression now, but the marks of grief were clear, etched in the lines beside mouth and eyes, thrown into darkness by the flickering fire. It seemed an intrusion to break in upon such a depth of feeling, unstated though it was, but Grey had his duty.

"And the gold, Mr. Fraser?" he asked quietly. "What of that?"

Fraser heaved a deep sigh.

"It was there," he said flatly.

"What!" Grey sat bolt upright in his chair, staring at the Scot. "You found it?"

Fraser glanced up at him then, and his mouth twisted wryly.

"I found it."

"Was it indeed the French gold that Louis sent for Charles Stuart?" Excitement was racing through Grey's bloodstream, with visions of himself delivering great chests of gold louis d'or to his superiors in London.

"Louis never sent gold to the Stuarts," Fraser said, with certainty. "No, Major, what I found at the saint's pool was gold, but not French coin."

What he had found was a small box, containing a few gold and silver coins, and a small leather pouch, filled with jewels.

"Jewels?" Grey blurted. "Where the devil did they come from?"

Fraser cast him a glance of mild exasperation.

"I havena the slightest notion, Major," he said. "How should I know?"

"No, of course not," Grey said, coughing to cover his flusterment. "Certainly. But this treasure—where is it now?"

"I threw it into the sea."

Grey stared blankly at him.

"You—what?"

"I threw it into the sea," Fraser repeated patiently. The slanted blue eyes met Grey's steadily. "Ye'll maybe have heard of a place called the Devil's Cauldron, Major? It's no more than half a mile from the saint's pool."

"Why? Why would you have done such a thing?" Grey demanded. "It isn't sense, man!"

"I wasna much concerned with sense at the time, Major," Fraser said softly. "I had gone there hoping—and with that hope gone, the treasure seemed no more to me than a wee box of stones and bits of tarnished metal. I had no use for it." He looked up, one brow slightly raised in irony. "But I didna see the 'sense' in giving it to King Geordie, either. So I flung it into the sea."

Grey sat back in his chair and mechanically poured out another cup of sherry, hardly noticing what he was doing. His thoughts were in turmoil.

Fraser sat, head turned away and chin propped on his fist, gazing into the fire, his face gone back to its usual impassivity. The light glowed behind him, lighting the long, straight line of his nose and the soft curve of his lip, shadowing jaw and brow with sternness.

Grey took a good-sized swallow of his drink and steadied himself.

"It is a moving story, Mr. Fraser," he said levelly. "Most dramatic. And yet there is no evidence that it is the truth."

Fraser stirred, turning his head to look at Grey. Jamie's slanted eyes narrowed, in what might have been amusement.

"Aye, there is, Major," he said. He reached under the waistband of his ragged breeches, fumbled for a moment, and held out his hand above the tabletop, waiting.

Grey extended his own hand in reflex, and a small object dropped into his open palm.

It was a sapphire, dark blue as Fraser's own eyes, and a good size, too.

Grey opened his mouth, but said nothing, choked with astonishment.

"There is your evidence that the treasure existed, Major." Fraser nodded toward the stone in Grey's hand. His eyes met Grey's across the tabletop. "And as for the rest—I am sorry to say, Major, that ye must take my word for it."

"But—but—you said—"

"I did." Fraser was as calm as though they had been discussing the rain outside. "I kept that one wee stone, thinking that it might be some use, if I were ever to be freed, or that I might find some chance of sending it to my family. For ye'll appreciate, Major"—a light glinted derisively in Jamie's blue eyes—"that my family couldna make use of a treasure of that sort, without attracting a deal of unwelcome attention. One stone, perhaps, but not a great many of them."

Grey could scarcely think. What Fraser said was true; a Highland farmer like his brother-in-law would have no way of turning such a treasure into money without causing talk that would bring down the King's men on Lallybroch in short order. And Fraser himself might well be imprisoned for the rest of his life. But still, to toss away a fortune so lightly! And yet, looking at the Scot, he could well believe it. If ever there was a man whose judgment would not be distorted by greed, James Fraser was it. Still—

"How did you keep this by you?" Grey demanded abruptly. "You were searched to the skin when you were brought back."

The wide mouth curved slightly in the first genuine smile Grey had seen.

"I swallowed it," Fraser said.

Grey's hand closed convulsively on the sapphire. He opened his hand and rather gingerly set the gleaming blue thing on the table by the chess piece.

"I see," he said.

"I'm sure ye do, Major," said Fraser, with a gravity that merely made the glint of amusement in his eyes more pronounced. "A diet of rough parritch has its advantages, now and again."

Grey quelled the sudden urge to laugh, rubbing a finger hard over his lip.

"I'm sure it does, Mr. Fraser." He sat for a moment, contemplating the blue stone. Then he looked up abruptly.

"You are a Papist, Mr. Fraser?" He knew the answer already; there were few adherents of the Catholic Stuarts who were not. Without waiting for a reply, he rose and went to the bookshelf in the corner. It took a moment to find; a gift from his mother, it was not part of his usual reading.

He laid the calf-bound Bible on the table, next to the stone.

"I am myself inclined to accept your word as a gentleman, Mr. Fraser," he said. "But you will understand that I have my duty to consider."

Fraser gazed at the book for a long moment, then looked up at Grey, his expression unreadable.

"Aye, I ken that fine, Major," he said quietly. Without hesitation, he laid a broad hand on the Bible.

"I swear in the name of Almighty God and by His Holy Word," he said firmly. "The treasure is as I told you." His eyes glowed in the firelight, dark and unfathomable. "And I swear on my hope of heaven," he added softly, "that it rests now in the sea."

11

The Torremolinos Gambit

With the question of the French gold thus settled, they returned to what had become their routine; a brief period of formal negotiation over the affairs of the prisoners, followed by informal conversation and sometimes a game of chess. This evening, they had come from the dinner table, still discussing Samuel Richardson's immense novel *Pamela*.

"Do you think that the size of the book is justified by the complexity of the story?" Grey asked, leaning forward to light a cheroot from the candle on the sideboard. "It must after all be a great expense to the publisher, as well as requiring a substantial effort from the reader, a book of that length."

Fraser smiled. He did not smoke himself, but had chosen to drink port this evening, claiming that to be the only drink whose taste would be unaffected by the stink of tobacco.

"What is it—twelve hundred pages? Aye, I think so. After all, it is difficult to sum up the complications of a life in a short space with any hope of constructing an accurate account."

"True. I have heard the point made, though, that the novelist's skill lies in the artful selection of detail. Do you not suppose that a volume of such length may indicate a lack of discipline in such selection, and hence a lack of skill?"

Fraser considered, sipping the ruby liquid slowly.

"I have seen books where that is the case, to be sure," he said. "An author seeks by sheer inundation of detail to overwhelm the reader into belief. In this case, however, I think it isna so. Each character is most carefully considered, and all the incidents chosen seem necessary to the story. No, I think it is true that some stories simply require a greater space in which to be told." He took another sip and laughed.

"Of course, I admit to some prejudice in that regard, Major. Given the circumstances under which I read *Pamela*, I should have been delighted had the book been twice as long as it was."

"And what circumstances were those?" Grey pursed his lips and blew a careful smoke ring that floated toward the ceiling.

"I lived in a cave in the Highlands for several years, Major," Fraser said wryly. "I seldom had more than three books with me, and those must last me for months at a time. Aye, I'm partial to lengthy tomes, but I must admit that it is not a universal preference."

"That's certainly true," Grey agreed. He squinted, following the track of the first smoke ring, and blew another. Just off target, it drifted to the side.

"I remember," he continued, sucking fiercely on his cheroot, encouraging it to draw, "a friend of my mother's—saw the book—in Mother's drawing room—" He drew deeply, and blew once more, giving a small grunt of satisfaction as the new ring struck the old, dispersing it into a tiny cloud.

"Lady Hensley, it was. She picked up the book, looked at it in that help-less way so many females affect and said, 'Oh, Countess! You are so *coura-geous* to attack a novel of such stupendous size. I fear I should never dare to start so lengthy a book myself.' " Grey cleared his throat and lowered his voice from the falsetto he had affected for Lady Hensley.

"To which Mother replied," he went on in his normal voice, " 'Don't worry about it for a moment, my dear; you wouldn't understand it any-way.' "

Fraser laughed, then coughed, waving away the remnants of another smoke ring.

Grey quickly snuffed out the cheroot, and rose from his seat.

"Come along then; we've just time for a quick game."

They were not evenly matched; Fraser was much the better player, but Grey could now and then contrive to rescue a match through sheer bravado of play.

Tonight, he tried the Torremolinos Gambit. It was a risky opening, a queen's knight opening. Successfully launched, it paved the way for an un-usual combination of rook and bishop, depending for its success upon a piece of misdirection by the king's knight and king bishop's pawn. Grey used it seldom, for it was a trick that would not work on a mediocre player, one not sharp enough to detect the knight's threat, or its possibilities. It was a gambit for use against a shrewd and subtle mind, and after nearly three months of weekly games, Grey knew quite well what sort of mind he was facing across the tinted ivory squares.

He forced himself not to hold his breath as he made the next-to-final move of the combination. He felt Fraser's eyes rest on him briefly, but didn't meet them, for fear of betraying his excitement. Instead, he reached to the sideboard for the decanter, and refilled both glasses with the sweet dark port, keeping his eyes carefully on the rising liquid.

Would it be the pawn, or the knight? Fraser's head was bent over the board in contemplation, small reddish lights winking in his hair as he moved slightly. The knight, and all was well; it would be too late. The pawn, and all was likely lost.

Grey could feel his heart beating heavily behind his breastbone as he waited. Fraser's hand hovered over the board, then suddenly decided, swooped down and touched the piece. The knight.

He must have let his breath out too noisily, for Fraser glanced sharply up at him, but it was too late. Careful to keep any overt expression of triumph off his face, Grey castled.

Fraser frowned at the board for a long moment, eyes flicking among the pieces, assessing. Then he jerked slightly, seeing it, and looked up, eyes wide.

"Why ye cunning wee bastard!" he said, in a tone of surprised respect. "Where in the bloody hell did ye learn *that* trick?"

"My elder brother taught it to me," Grey answered, losing his customary wariness in a rush of delight at his success. He normally beat Fraser no more than three times in ten, and victory was sweet.

Fraser uttered a short laugh, and reaching out a long index finger, delicately tipped his king over.

"I should have expected something like that from a man like my Lord Melton," he observed casually.

Grey stiffened in his seat. Fraser saw the movement, and arched one brow quizzically.

"It is Lord Melton ye mean, is it not?" he said. "Or perhaps you have another brother?"

"No," Grey said. His lips felt slightly numb, though that might only be the cheroot. "No, I have only one brother." His heart had begun to pound again, but this time with a heavy, dull beat. Had the Scottish bastard remembered all the time who he was?

"Our meeting was necessarily rather brief," the Scot said dryly. "But memorable." He picked up his glass and took a drink, watching Grey across the crystal rim. "Perhaps ye didna know that I had met Lord Melton, on Culloden Field?"

"I knew. I fought at Culloden." All Grey's pleasure in his victory had evaporated. He felt slightly nauseated from the smoke. "I didn't know that you would recall Hal, though—or know of the relationship between us."

"As I have that meeting to thank for my life, I am not likely to forget it," Fraser said dryly.

Grey looked up. "I understand that you were not so thankful when Hal met you at Culloden."

The line of Fraser's mouth tightened, then relaxed.

"No," he said softly. He smiled without humor. "Your brother verra stubbornly refused to shoot me. I wasna inclined to be grateful for the favor at the time."

"You wished to be shot?" Grey's eyebrows rose.

The Scot's eyes were remote, fixed on the chessboard, but clearly seeing something else.

"I thought I had reason," he said softly. "At the time."

"What reason?" Grey asked. He caught a gimlet glance and added hastily, "I mean no impertinence in asking. It is only—at that time, I—I felt similarly. From what you have said of the Stuarts, I cannot think that the loss of their cause would have led you to such despair."

There was a faint flicker near Fraser's mouth, much too faint to be called a smile. He inclined his head briefly, in acknowledgment.

"There were those who fought for love of Charles Stuart—or from loyalty to his father's right of kingship. But you are right; I wasna one of those."

He didn't explain further. Grey took a deep breath, keeping his eyes fixed on the board.

"I said that I felt much as you did, at the time. I—lost a particular friend at Culloden," he said. With half his mind he wondered why he should speak of Hector to this man, of all men; a Scottish warrior who had slashed his way across that deadly field, whose sword might well have been the one . . . At the same time, he could not help but speak; there was no one to whom he *could* speak of Hector, save this man, this prisoner who could speak to no one else, whose words could do him no damage.

"He made me go and look at the body—Hal did, my brother," Grey blurted. He looked down at his hand, where the deep blue of Hector's sapphire burned against his skin, a smaller version of the one Fraser had reluctantly given him.

"He said that I must; that unless I saw him dead, I should never really believe it. That unless I knew Hector—my friend—was really gone, I would grieve forever. If I saw, and knew, I would grieve, but then I should heal— and forget." He looked up, with a painful attempt at a smile. "Hal is generally right, but not always."

Perhaps he had healed, but he would never forget. Certainly he would not forget his last sight of Hector, lying wax-faced and still in the early morning light, long dark lashes resting delicately on his cheeks as they did when he slept. And the gaping wound that had half-severed his head from his body, leaving the windpipe and large vessels of the neck exposed in butchery.

They sat silent for a moment. Fraser said nothing, but picked up his glass and drained it. Without asking, Grey refilled both glasses for the third time.

He leaned back in his chair, looking curiously at his guest.

"Do you find your life greatly burdensome, Mr. Fraser?"

The Scot looked up then, and met his eyes with a long, level gaze. Evidently, Fraser found nothing in his own face save curiosity, for the broad shoulders across the board relaxed their tension somewhat, and the wide mouth softened its grim line. The Scot leaned back, and flexed his right hand slowly, opening and closing it to stretch the muscles. Grey saw that the hand had been damaged at one time; small scars were visible in the firelight, and two of the fingers were set stiffly.

"Perhaps not greatly so," the Scot replied slowly. He met Grey's eyes with dispassion. "I think perhaps the greatest burden lies in caring for those we cannot help."

"Not in having no one for whom to care?"

Fraser paused before answering; he might have been weighing the position of the pieces on the table.

"That is emptiness," he said at last, softly. "But no great burden."

It was late; there was no sound from the fortress around them save the occasional step of the soldier on sentry in the courtyard below.

"Your wife—she was a healer, you said?"

"She was. She . . . her name was Claire." Fraser swallowed, then lifted his cup and drank, as though trying to dislodge something stuck in his throat.

"You cared very much for her, I think?" Grey said softly.

He recognized in the Scot the same compulsion he had had a few moments earlier—the need to speak a name kept hidden, to bring back for a moment the ghost of a love.

"I had meant to thank you sometime, Major," the Scot said softly.

Grey was startled.

"Thank me? For what?"

The Scot looked up, eyes dark over the finished game.

"For that night at Carryarrick where we first met." His eyes were steady on Grey's. "For what ye did for my wife."

"You remembered," Grey said hoarsely.

"I hadna forgotten," Fraser said simply. Grey steeled himself to look across the table, but when he did so, he found no hint of laughter in the slanted blue eyes.

Fraser nodded at him, gravely formal. "Ye were a worthy foe, Major; I wouldna forget you."

John Grey laughed bitterly. Oddly enough, he felt less upset than he had thought he would, at having the shameful memory so explicitly recalled.

"If you found a sixteen-year-old shitting himself with fear a worthy foe, Mr. Fraser, then it is little wonder that the Highland army was defeated!"

Fraser smiled faintly.

"A man that doesna shit himself with a pistol held to his head, Major, has either no bowels, or no brains."

Despite himself, Grey laughed. One edge of Fraser's mouth turned slightly up.

"Ye wouldna speak to save your own life, but ye would do it to save a lady's honor. The honor of my own lady," Fraser said softly. "That doesna seem like cowardice to me."

The ring of truth was too evident in the Scot's voice to mistake or ignore.

"I did nothing for your wife," Grey said, rather bitterly. "She was in no danger, after all!"

"Ye didna ken that, aye?" Fraser pointed out. "Ye thought to save her life and virtue, at the risk of your own. Ye did her honor by the notion—and I have thought of it now and again, since I—since I lost her." The hesitation in Fraser's voice was slight; only the tightening of the muscles in his throat betrayed his emotion.

"I see." Grey breathed deep, and let it out slowly. "I am sorry for your loss," he added formally.

They were both quiet for a moment, alone with their ghosts. Then Fraser looked up and drew in his breath.

"Your brother was right, Major," he said. "I thank ye, and I'll bid ye good e'en." He rose, set down his cup and left the room.

It reminded him in some ways of his years in the cave, with his visits to the house, those oases of life and warmth in the desert of solitude. Here, it was the reverse, going from the crowded, cold squalor of the cells up to the Major's glowing suite, able for a few hours to stretch both mind and body, to relax in warmth and conversation and the abundance of food.

It gave him the same odd sense of dislocation, though; that sense of losing some valuable part of himself that could not survive the passage back to daily life. Each time, the passage became more difficult.

He stood in the drafty passageway, waiting for the turnkey to unlock the cell door. The sounds of sleeping men buzzed in his ears and the smell of them wafted out as the door opened, pungent as a fart.

He filled his lungs with a quick deep breath, and ducked his head to enter.

There was a stir among the bodies on the floor as he stepped into the room, his shadow falling black across the prone and bundled shapes. The door swung closed behind him, leaving the cell in darkness, but there was a ripple of awareness through the room, as men stirred awake to his coming.

"You're back late, Mac Dubh," said Murdo Lindsay, voice rusty with sleep. "Ye'll be sair tuckered tomorrow."

"I'll manage, Murdo," he whispered, stepping over bodies. He pulled off his coat and laid it carefully over the bench, then took up the rough blanket and sought his space on the floor, his long shadow flickering across the moon-barred window.

Ronnie Sinclair turned over as Mac Dubh lay down beside him. He blinked sleepily, sandy lashes nearly invisible in the moonlight.

"Did Wee Goldie feed ye decent, Mac Dubh?"

"He did, Ronnie, thank ye." He shifted on the stones, seeking a comfortable position.

"Ye'll tell us about it tomorrow?" The prisoners took an odd pleasure in hearing what he had been served for dinner, taking it as an honor that their chief should be well fed.

"Aye, I will, Ronnie," Mac Dubh promised. "But I must sleep now, aye?"

"Sleep well, Mac Dubh," came a whisper from the corner where Hayes was rolled up, curled like a set of teaspoons with MacLeod, Innes, and Keith, who all liked to sleep warm.

"Sweet dreams, Gavin," Mac Dubh whispered back, and little by little, the cell settled back into silence.

He dreamed of Claire that night. She lay in his arms, heavy-limbed and fragrant. She was with child; her belly round and smooth as a muskmelon, her breasts rich and full, the nipples dark as wine, urging him to taste them.

Her hand cupped itself between his legs, and he reached to return the favor, the small, fat softness of her filling his hand, pressing against him as she moved. She rose over him, smiling, her hair falling down around her face, and threw her leg across him.

"Give me your mouth," he whispered, not knowing whether he meant to kiss her or to have her take him between her lips, only knowing he must have her somehow.

"Give me yours," she said. She laughed and leaned down to him, hands on his shoulders, her hair brushing his face with the scent of moss and sunlight, and he felt the prickle of dry leaves against his back and knew they lay in the glen near Lallybroch, and her the color of the copper beeches all around; beech leaves and beechwood, gold eyes and a smooth white skin, skimmed with shadows.

Then her breast pressed against his mouth, and he took it eagerly, drawing her body tight against him as he suckled her. Her milk was hot and sweet, with a faint taste of silver, like a deer's blood.

"Harder," she whispered to him, and put her hand behind his head, gripping the back of his neck, pressing him to her. "Harder."

She lay at her length upon him, his hands holding for dear life to the sweet flesh of her buttocks, feeling the small solid weight of the child upon his own belly, as though they shared it now, protecting the small round thing between their bodies.

He flung his arms about her, tight, and she held him tight as he jerked and shuddered, her hair in his face, her hands in his hair and the child between them, not knowing where any of the three of them began or ended.

He came awake suddenly, panting and sweating, half-curled on his side beneath one of the benches in the cell. It was not yet quite light, but he could see the shapes of the men who lay near him, and hoped he had not cried out. He closed his eyes at once, but the dream was gone. He lay quite still, his heart slowing, and waited for the dawn.

June 18, 1755

John Grey had dressed carefully this evening, with fresh linen and silk stockings. He wore his own hair, simply plaited, rinsed with a tonic of lemon-verbena. He had hesitated for a moment over Hector's ring, but at last had put it on, too. The dinner had been good; a pheasant he had shot himself, and a salad of greens, in deference to Fraser's odd tastes for such things. Now they sat over the chessboard, lighter topics of conversation set aside in the concentration of the midgame.

"Will you have sherry?" He set down his bishop, and leaned back, stretching.

Fraser nodded, absorbed in the new position.

"I thank ye."

Grey rose and crossed the room, leaving Fraser by the fire. He reached into the cupboard for the bottle, and felt a thin trickle of sweat run down his ribs as he did so. Not from the fire, simmering across the room; from sheer nervousness.

He brought the bottle back to the table, holding the goblets in his other hand; the Waterford crystal his mother had sent. The liquid purled into the glasses, shimmering amber and rose in the firelight. Fraser's eyes were fixed on the cup, watching the rising sherry, but with an abstraction that showed he was deep in his thoughts. The dark blue eyes were hooded. Grey wondered what he was thinking; not about the game—the outcome of that was certain.

Grey reached out and moved his queen's bishop. It was no more than a delaying move, he knew; still, it put Fraser's queen in danger, and might force the exchange of a rook.

Grey got up to put a brick of peat on the fire. Rising, he stretched himself, and strolled behind his opponent to view the situation from this angle.

The firelight shimmered as the big Scot leaned forward to study the board, picking up the deep red tones of James Fraser's hair, echoing the glow of the light in the crystalline sherry.

Fraser had bound his hair back with a thin black cord, tied in a bow. It would take no more than a slight tug to loosen it. John Grey could imagine running his hand up under that thick, glossy mass, to touch the smooth, warm nape beneath. To touch . . .

His palm closed abruptly, imagining sensation.

"It is your move, Major." The soft Scots voice brought him to himself again, and he took his seat, viewing the chessboard through sightless eyes.

Without really looking, he was intensely aware of the other's movements, his presence. There was a disturbance of the air around Fraser; it was impossible not to look at him. To cover his glance, he picked up his sherry glass and sipped, barely noticing the liquid gold taste of it.

Fraser sat still as a statue of cinnabar, only the deep blue eyes alive in his face as he studied the board. The fire had burned down, and the lines of his body were limned with shadow. His hand, all gold and black with the light of the fire on it, rested on the table, still and exquisite as the captured pawn beside it.

The blue stone in John Grey's ring glinted as he reached for his queen's bishop. *Is it wrong, Hector?* he thought. *That I should love a man who might have killed you?* Or was it a way at last to put things right; to heal the wounds of Culloden for them both?

The bishop made a soft thump as he set the felted base down with precision. Without stopping, his hand rose, as though it moved without his volition. The hand traveled the short distance through the air, looking as though it knew precisely what it wanted, and set itself on Fraser's, palm tingling, curved fingers gently imploring.

The hand under his was warm—so warm—but hard, and motionless as marble. Nothing moved on the table but the shimmer of the flame in the heart of the sherry. He lifted his eyes then, to meet Fraser's.

"Take your hand off me," Fraser said, very, very softly. "Or I will kill you."

The hand under Grey's did not move, nor did the face above, but he could feel the shiver of revulsion, a spasm of hatred and disgust that rose from the man's core, radiating through his flesh.

Quite suddenly, he heard once more the memory of Quarry's warning, as clearly as though the man spoke in his ear this moment.

If you dine with him alone—don't turn your back on him.

There was no chance of that; he could not turn away. Could not even look away or blink, to break the dark blue gaze that held him frozen. Moving as slowly as though he stood atop an unexploded mine, he drew back his hand.

There was a moment's silence, broken only by the rain's patter and the hissing of the peat fire, when neither of them seemed to breathe. Then Fraser rose without a sound, and left the room.

12

Sacrifice

The rain of late November pattered down on the stones of the courtyard, and on the sullen rows of men, standing huddled under the downpour. The Redcoats who stood on guard over them didn't look much happier than the sodden prisoners.

Major Grey stood under the overhang of the roof, waiting. It wasn't the best weather for conducting a search and cleaning of the prisoners' cells, but at this time of year, it was futile to wait for good weather. And with more than two hundred prisoners in Ardsmuir, it was necessary to swab the cells at least monthly in order to prevent major outbreaks of illness.

The doors to the main cell block swung back, and a small file of prisoners emerged; the trustys who did the actual cleaning, closely watched by the guards. At the end of the line, Corporal Dunstable came out, his hands full of the small bits of contraband a search of this sort usually turned up.

"The usual rubbish, sir," he reported, dumping the collection of pitiful relics and anonymous junk onto the top of a cask that stood near the Major's elbow. "Just this, you might take notice of."

"This" was a small strip of cloth, perhaps six inches by four, in a green tartan check. Dunstable glanced quickly at the lines of standing prisoners, as if intending to catch someone in a telltale action.

Grey sighed, then straightened his shoulders. "Yes, I suppose so." The possession of any Scottish tartan was strictly forbidden by the Diskilting Act that had likewise disarmed the Highlanders and prevented the wearing of their native dress. He stepped in front of the rows of men, as Corporal Dunstable gave a sharp shout to attract their attention.

"Whose is this?" The corporal raised the scrap high, and raised his voice as well. Grey glanced from the scrap of bright cloth to the row of prisoners, mentally ticking off the names, trying to match them to his imperfect knowledge of tartans. Even within a single clan, the patterns varied so wildly that a given pattern couldn't be assigned with any certainty, but there were general patterns of color and design.

MacAlester, Hayes, Innes, Graham, MacMurtry, MacKenzie, MacDonald . . . stop. MacKenzie. That one. It was more an officer's knowledge of men than any identification of the plaid with a particular clan that made him sure.

MacKenzie was a young prisoner, and his face was a shade too controlled, too expressionless.

"It's yours, MacKenzie. Isn't it?" Grey demanded. He snatched the scrap of cloth from the corporal and thrust it under the young man's nose. The prisoner was white-faced under the blotches of dirt. His jaw was clamped hard, and he was breathing hard through his nose with a faint whistling sound.

Grey fixed the young man with a hard, triumphant stare. The young Scot had that core of implacable hate that they all had, but he hadn't managed to build the wall of stoic indifference that held it in. Grey could feel the fear building in the lad; another second and he would break.

"It's mine." The voice was calm, almost bored, and spoke with such flat indifference that neither MacKenzie nor Grey registered it at once. They stood locked in each other's eyes, until a large hand reached over Angus MacKenzie's shoulder and gently plucked the scrap of cloth from the officer's hand.

John Grey stepped back, feeling the words like a blow in the pit of his stomach. MacKenzie forgotten, he lifted his eyes the several inches necessary to look Jamie Fraser in the face.

"It isn't a Fraser tartan," he said, feeling the words force their way past wooden lips. His whole face felt numb, a fact for which he was dimly grateful; at least his expression couldn't betray him before the ranks of the watching prisoners.

Fraser's mouth widened slightly. Grey kept his gaze fastened on it, afraid to meet the dark blue eyes above.

"No, it isn't," Fraser agreed. "It's MacKenzie. My mother's clan."

In some far-off corner of his mind, Grey stored away another tiny scrap of information with the small hoard of facts kept in the jeweled coffer labeled "Jamie"—his mother was a MacKenzie. He knew that was true, just as he knew that the tartan didn't belong to Fraser.

He heard his voice, cool and steady, saying "Possession of clan tartans is illegal. You know the penalty, of course?"

The wide mouth curled in a one-sided smile.

"I do."

There was a shifting and a muttering among the ranks of the prisoners; there was little actual movement, but Grey could feel the alignment changing, as though they were in fact drawing toward Fraser, circling him, embracing him. The circle had broken and re-formed, and he was alone outside it. Jamie Fraser had gone back to his own.

With an effort of will, Grey forced his gaze away from the soft, smooth lips, slightly chapped from exposure to sun and wind. The look in the eyes above them was what he had been afraid of; neither fear nor anger—but indifference.

He motioned to a guard.

"Take him."

Major John William Grey bent his head over the work on his desk, signing requisitions without reading them. He seldom worked so late at night, but there had not been time during the day, and the paperwork was piling up. The requisitions must be sent to London this week.

"Two hundred pound wheat flowr," he wrote, trying to concentrate on the neatness of the black squiggles under his quill. The trouble with such routine paperwork was that it occupied his attention but not his mind, allowing memories of the day to creep in unawares.

"Six hogsheds ale, for use of barracks." He set down the quill and rubbed his hands briskly together. He could still feel the chill that had settled in his bones in the courtyard that morning. There was a hot fire, but it didn't seem to be helping. He didn't go nearer; he had tried that once, and stood mesmerized, seeing the images of the afternoon in the flames, roused only when the cloth of his breeches began to scorch.

He picked up the quill and tried again to banish the sights of the courtyard from his mind.

It was better not to delay execution of sentences of this kind; the prisoners became restless and nervy in anticipation and there was considerable difficulty in controlling them. Executed at once, though, such discipline often had a salutary effect, showing the prisoners that retribution would be swift and dire, enhancing their respect for those who held their guardianship. Somehow John Grey suspected that this particular occasion had not much enhanced his prisoners' respect—for him, at least.

Feeling little more than the trickle of ice water through his veins, he had given his orders, swift and composed, and they had been obeyed with equal competence.

The prisoners had been drawn up in ranks around the four sides of the courtyard square, with shorter lines of guards arranged facing them, bayonets fixed to the ready, to prevent any unseemly outbreak.

But there had been no outbreak, seemly or otherwise. The prisoners had waited in a chill silence in the light rain that misted the stones of the courtyard, with little sound other than the normal coughs and throat-clearings of any assemblage of men. It was the beginning of winter, and catarrh was almost as common a scourge in the barracks as it was in the damp cells.

He had stood watching impassively, hands folded behind his back, as the prisoner was led to the platform. Watched, feeling the rain seep into the shoulders of his coat and run in tiny rivulets down the neck of his shirt, as Jamie Fraser stood on the platform a yard away and stripped to the waist, moving without haste or hesitation, as though this were something he had done before, an accustomed task, of no importance in itself.

He had nodded to the two privates, who seized the prisoner's unresisting hands and raised them, binding them to the arms of the whipping post. They gagged him, and Fraser stood upright, the rain running down his raised arms, and down the deep seam of his backbone, to soak the thin cloth of his breeches.

Another nod, to the sergeant who held the charge sheet, and a small surge of annoyance as the gesture caused a cascade of collected rain from one side of his hat. He straightened his hat and sodden wig, and resumed his stance of authority in time to hear the charge and sentence read.

". . . in contravention of the Diskilting Act, passed by His Majesty's Parliament, for which crime the sentence of sixty lashes shall be inflicted."

Grey glanced with professional detachment at the sergeant-farrier designated to give the punishment; this was not the first time for any of them. He didn't nod this time; the rain was still falling. A half-closing of the eyes instead, as he spoke the usual words:

"Mr. Fraser, you will take your punishment."

And he stood, eyes front and steady, watching, and hearing the thud of the landing flails and the grunt of the prisoner's breath, forced past the gag by the blow.

The man's muscles tightened in resistance to the pain. Again and again, until each separate muscle stood hard under the skin. His own muscles ached with tension, and he shifted inconspicuously from one leg to another, as the brutal tedium continued. Thin streams of red ran down the prisoner's spine, blood mixed with water, staining the cloth of his breeches.

Grey could feel the men behind him, soldiers and prisoners both, all eyes fixed on the platform and its central figure. Even the coughing was silenced.

And over it all like a sticky coat of varnish sealing off Grey's feelings was a thin layer of self-disgust, as he realized that his eyes were fixed on the scene not out of duty, but from sheer inability to look away from the sheen of mingled rain and blood that gleamed on muscle, tightened in anguish to a curve of wrenching beauty.

The sergeant-farrier paused only briefly between blows. He was hurrying it slightly; everyone wanted to get it over and get out of the rain. Grissom counted each stroke in a loud voice, noting it on his sheet as he did so. The farrier checked the lash, running the strands with their hard-waxed knots between his fingers to free them of blood and bits of flesh, then raised the cat once more, swung it slowly twice round his head, and struck again. "Thirty!" said the sergeant.

Major Grey pulled out the lowest drawer of his desk, and was neatly sick, all over a stack of requisitions.

*His fingers were dug hard into his palms, but the shaking
wouldn't stop. It was deep in his bones, like the winter cold.*

"Put a blanket over him; I'll tend him in a moment."

*The English surgeon's voice seemed to come from a long way off;
he felt no connection between the voice and the hands that gripped
him firmly by both arms. He cried out as they shifted him, the torsion
splitting the barely clotted wounds on his back. The trickle of warm
blood across his ribs made the shaking worse, despite the rough blanket they laid over his shoulders.*

*He gripped the edges of the bench on which he lay, cheek pressed
against the wood, eyes closed, struggling against the shaking. There
was a stir and a shuffle somewhere in the room, but he couldn't take
notice, couldn't take his attention from the clenching of his teeth
and the tightness of his joints.*

*The door closed, and the room grew quiet. Had they left him
alone?*

*No, there were footsteps near his head, and the blanket over him
lifted, folded back to his waist.*

"Mm. Made a mess of you, didn't he, boy?"

*He didn't answer; no answer seemed expected, in any case. The
surgeon turned away for a moment; then he felt a hand beneath his
cheek, lifting his head. A towel slid beneath his face, cushioning it
from the rough wood.*

*"I'm going to cleanse the wounds now," the voice said. It was
impersonal, but not unfriendly.*

*He drew in his breath through his teeth as a hand touched his
back. There was an odd whimpering noise. He realized he had made
it, and was ashamed.*

"How old are you, boy?"

*"Nineteen." He barely got the word out, before biting down hard
on a moan.*

*The doctor touched his back gently here and there, then stood up.
He heard the sound of the bolt being shot to, then the doctor's steps
returning.*

*"No one will come in now," the voice said kindly. "Go ahead and
cry."*

"Hey!" the voice was saying. "Wake up, man!"

He came slowly to consciousness; the roughness of wood beneath his
cheek brought dream and waking together for a moment, and he couldn't

remember where he was. A hand came out of the darkness, touching him tentatively on the cheek.

"Ye were greetin' in your sleep, man," the voice whispered. "Does it pain ye much?"

"A bit." He realized the other link between dreaming and waking as he tried to raise himself and the pain crackled over his back like sheet lightning. He let out his breath in an involuntary grunt and dropped back on the bench.

He had been lucky; he had drawn Dawes, a stout, middle-aged soldier who didn't really like flogging prisoners, and did it only because it was part of his job. Still, sixty lashes did damage, even if applied without enthusiasm.

"Nah, then, that's too hot by half. Want to scald him, do ye?" It was Morrison's voice, scolding. It would be Morrison, of course.

Odd, he thought dimly. How whenever you had a group of men, they seemed to find their proper jobs, no matter whether it was a thing they'd done before. Morrison had been a cottar, like most of them. Likely a good hand with his beasts, but not thinking much about it. Now he was the natural healer for the men, the one they turned to with a griping belly or a broken thumb. Morrison knew little more than the rest, but the men turned to him when they were hurt, as they turned to Seumus Mac Dubh for reassurance and direction. And for justice.

The steaming cloth was laid across his back and he grunted with the sting of it, pressing his lips tight to keep from crying out. He could feel the shape of Morrison's small hand, lightly laid in the center of his back.

"Bide ye, man, 'til the heat passes."

As the nightmare faded, he blinked for a moment, adjusting himself to the nearby voices and the perception of company. He was in the large cell, in the shadowy nook by the chimney breast. Steam rose from the fire; there must be a cauldron boiling. He saw Walter MacLeod lower a fresh armful of rags into its depths, the fire touching MacLeod's dark beard and brows with red. Then, as the heated rags on his back cooled to a soothing warmth, he closed his eyes and sank back into a half-doze, lulled by the soft conversation of the men nearby.

It was familiar, this state of dreamy detachment. He had felt much the same ever since the moment when he had reached over young Angus's shoulder and closed his fist on the scrap of tartan cloth. As though with that choice, some curtain had come down between him and the men around him; as though he were alone, in some quiet place of infinite remoteness.

He had followed the guard who took him, stripped himself when told, but all without feeling as though he had truly waked. Taken his place on the platform and heard the words of crime and sentence pronounced, without really listening. Not even the rough bite of the rope on his wrists or the cold rain on his naked back had roused him. These seemed all things that had happened before; nothing he said or did could change a thing; it was all fated.

As for the flogging, he had borne it. There was no room then for thought or regret, or for anything beyond the stubborn, desperate struggle such bodily insult required.

"Still, now, still." Morrison's hand rested on his neck, to prevent his moving as the sodden rags were taken off and a fresh, hot poultice applied, momentarily rousing all the dormant nerves to fresh startlement.

One consequence of his odd state of mind was that all sensations seemed of equal intensity. He could, if he tried, feel each separate stripe across his back, see each one in his mind's eye as a vivid streak of color across the dark of imagination. But the pain of the gash that ran from ribs to shoulder was of no more weight or consequence than the almost pleasant feeling of heaviness in his legs, the soreness in his arms, or the soft tickling brush of his hair across his cheek.

His pulse beat slow and regular in his ears; the sigh of his breath was a thing apart from the heave of his chest as he breathed. He existed only as a collection of fragments, each small piece with its own sensations, and none of them of any particular concern to the central intelligence.

"Here, Mac Dubh," said Morrison's voice, next to his ear. "Lift your head, and drink this."

The sharp scent of whisky struck him, and he tried to turn his head away.

"I don't need it," he said.

"That ye do," Morrison said, with that firm matter-of-factness that all healers seemed to have, as though they always knew better than you did what you felt like or what you required. Lacking strength or will to argue, he opened his mouth and sipped the whisky, feeling his neck muscles quiver under the strain of holding his head up.

The whisky added its own bit to the chorus of sensations that filled him. A burn in throat and belly, sharp tingle up the back of the nose, and a sort of whirling in his head that told him he had drunk too much, too fast.

"A bit more, now, aye, that's it," Morrison said, coaxing. "Good lad. Aye, that'll be better, won't it?" Morrison's thick body moved, so his vision of the darkened room was obscured. A draft blew from the high window, but there seemed more stir about him than was accounted for by the wind.

"Now, how's the back? Ye'll be stiff as a cornstook by the morrow, but I think it's maybe no so bad as it might be. Here, man, ye'll have a sup more." The rim of the horn cup pressed insistently against his mouth.

Morrison was still talking, rather loudly, of nothing in particular. There was something wrong about that. Morrison was not a talkative man. Something was happening, but he couldn't see. He lifted his head, searching for what was wrong, but Morrison pressed it down again.

"Dinna trouble yourself, Mac Dubh," he said softly. "Ye canna stop it, anyway."

Surreptitious sounds were coming from the far corner of the cell, the sounds Morrison had tried to keep him from hearing. Scraping noises, brief mutters, a thud. Then the muffled sound of blows, slow and regular, and a heavy gasping of fright and pain, punctuated with a small whimpering sound of indrawn breath.

They were beating young Angus MacKenzie. He braced his hands beneath his chest, but the effort made his back blaze and his head swim. Morrison's hand was back, forcing him down.

"Be still, Mac Dubh," he said. His tone was a mixture of authority and resignation.

A wave of dizziness washed through him, and his hands slipped off the bench. Morrison was right in any case, he realized. He couldn't stop them.

He lay still then under Morrison's hand, eyes closed, and waited for the sounds to stop. Despite himself, he wondered who it was, that administrator of blind justice in the dark. Sinclair. His mind supplied the answer without hesitation. And Hayes and Lindsay helping, no doubt.

They could no more help themselves than he could, or Morrison. Men did as they were born to. One man a healer, another a bully.

The sounds had stopped, except for a muffled, sobbing gasp. His shoulders relaxed, and he didn't move as Morrison took away the last wet poultice and gently blotted him dry, the draft from the window making him shiver in sudden chill. He pressed his lips tight, to make no noise. They had gagged him this afternoon, and he was glad of it; the first time he had been flogged, years ago, he had bitten his lower lip nearly in two.

The cup of whisky pressed against his mouth, but he turned his head aside, and it disappeared without comment to some place where it would find a more cordial reception. Milligan, likely, the Irishman.

One man with the weakness for drink, another with a hatred of it. One man a lover of women, and another . . .

He sighed and shifted slightly on the hard plank bed. Morrison had covered him with a blanket and gone away. He felt drained and empty, still in fragments, but with his mind quite clear, perched at some far remove from the rest of him.

Morrison had taken away the candle as well; it burned at the far end of the cell, where the men sat hunched companionably together, the light making black shapes of them, one indistinguishable from another, rimmed in gold light like the pictures of faceless saints in old missals.

He wondered where they came from, these gifts that shaped a man's nature. From God?

Was it like the descent of the Paraclete, and the tongues of fire that came to rest on the apostles? He remembered the picture in the Bible in his mother's parlor, the apostles all crowned with fire, and looking fair daft with the shock of it, standing about like a crowd of beeswax candles, lit for a party.

He smiled to himself at the memory, and closed his eyes. The candle shadows wavered red on his lids.

Claire, his own Claire—who knew what had sent her to him, had thrust her into a life she had surely not been born to? And yet she had known what to do, what she was meant to be, despite that. Not everyone was so fortunate as to know their gift.

There was a cautious shuffling in the darkness beside him. He opened his eyes and saw no more than a shape, but knew nonetheless who it was.

"How are ye, Angus?" he said softly in Gaelic.

The youngster knelt awkwardly by him, and took his hand.

"I am . . . all right. But you—sir, I mean . . . I—I'm sorry . . ."

Was it experience or instinct that made him tighten his own hand in reassurance?

"I am all right, too," he said. "Lay ye down, wee Angus, and take your rest."

The shape bent its head in an oddly formal gesture, and pressed a kiss on the back of his hand.

"I—may I stay by ye, sir?"

His hand weighed a ton, but he lifted it nonetheless and laid it on the young man's head. Then it slipped away, but he felt Angus's tension relax, as the comfort flowed from his touch.

He had been born a leader, then bent and shaped further to fit such a destiny. But what of a man who had not been born to the role he was required to fill? John Grey, for one. Charles Stuart for another.

For the first time in ten years, from this strange distance, he could find it in himself to forgive that feeble man who had once been his friend. Having so often paid the price exacted by his own gift, he could at last see the more terrible doom of having been born a king, without the gift of kingship.

Angus MacKenzie sat slumped against the wall next to him, head bowed upon his knees, his blanket over his shoulders. A small, gurgling snore came from the huddled form. He could feel sleep coming for him, fitting back the shattered, scattered parts of himself as it came, and knew he would wake whole—if very sore—in the morning.

He felt relieved at once of many things. Of the weight of immediate responsibility, of the necessity for decision. Temptation was gone, along with the possibility of it. More important, the burden of anger had lifted; perhaps it was gone for good.

So, he thought, through the gathering fog, John Grey had given him back his destiny.

Almost, he could be grateful.

13

Midgame

It was Roger who found her in the morning, curled up on the study sofa under the hearthrug, papers scattered carelessly over the floor where they had spilled from one of the folders.

The light from the floor-length windows streamed in, flooding the study, but the high back of the sofa had shaded Claire's face and prevented the dawn from waking her. The light was just now pouring over the curve of dusty velvet to flicker among the strands of her hair.

A glass face in more ways than one, Roger thought, looking at her. Her skin was so fair that the blue veins showed through at temple and throat, and the sharp, clear bones were so close beneath that she might have been carved of ivory.

The rug had slipped half off, exposing her shoulders. One arm lay relaxed across her chest, trapping a single, crumpled sheet of paper against her body. Roger lifted her arm carefully, to pull the paper loose without waking her. She was limp with sleep, her flesh surprisingly warm and smooth in his grasp.

His eyes found the name at once; he had known she must have found it.

"James MacKenzie Fraser," he murmured. He looked up from the paper to the sleeping woman on the sofa. The light had just touched the curve of her ear; she stirred briefly and turned her head, then her face lapsed back into somnolence.

"I don't know who you were, mate," he whispered to the unseen Scot, "but you must have been something, to deserve her."

Very gently, he replaced the rug over Claire's shoulders, and lowered the blind of the window behind her. Then he squatted and gathered up the scattered papers from the Ardsmuir folder. Ardsmuir. That was all he needed for now; even if Jamie Fraser's eventual fate was not recorded in the pages in his hands, it would be somewhere in the history of Ardsmuir prison. It might take another foray into the Highland archives, or even a trip to London, but the next step in the link had been forged; the path was clear.

Brianna was coming down the stairs as he pulled the door of the study closed, moving with exaggerated caution. She arched a brow in question and he lifted the folder, smiling.

"Got him," he whispered.

She didn't speak, but an answering smile spread across her face, bright as the rising sun outside.

PART FOUR

The Lake District

14

Geneva

"I think," Grey said carefully, "that you might consider changing your name."

He didn't expect an answer; in four days of travel, Fraser had not spoken a single word to him, managing even the awkward business of sharing an inn room without direct communication. Grey had shrugged and taken the bed, while Fraser, without gesture or glance, had wrapped himself in his threadbare cloak and lain down before the hearth. Scratching an assortment of bites from fleas and bedbugs, Grey thought that Fraser might well have had the better end of the sleeping arrangements.

"Your new host is not well disposed toward Charles Stuart and his adherents, having lost his only son at Prestonpans," he went on, addressing the iron-set profile visible next to him. Gordon Dunsany had been only a few years older than himself, a young captain in Bolton's regiment. They might easily have died together on that field—if not for that meeting in the wood near Carryarrick.

"You can scarcely hope to conceal the fact that you are a Scot, and a Highlander at that. If you will condescend to consider a piece of well-meant advice, it might be judicious not to use a name which would be as easily recognized as your own."

Fraser's stony expression didn't alter in the slightest particular. He nudged his horse with a heel and guided it ahead of Grey's bay, seeking the remains of the track, washed out by a recent flood.

It was late afternoon when they crossed the arch of Ashness Bridge and started down the slope toward Watendlath Tarn. The Lake District of England was nothing like Scotland, Grey reflected, but at least there were mountains here. Round-flanked, fat and dreamy mountains, not sternly forbidding like the Highland crags, but mountains nonetheless.

Watendlath Tarn was dark and ruffled in the early autumn wind, its edges thick with sedge and marsh grass. The summer rains had been more generous even than usual in this damp place, and the tips of drowned shrubs poked limp and tattered above water that had run over its banks.

At the crest of the next hill, the track split, going off in two directions. Fraser, some distance ahead, pulled his horse to a stop and waited for direction, the wind ruffling his hair. He had not plaited it that morning, and it blew free, the flaming strands lifting wild about his head.

Squelching his way up the slope, John William Grey looked up at the man above him, still as a bronze statue on his mount, save for that rippling mane. The breath dried in his throat, and he licked his lips.

"O Lucifer, thou son of the morning," he murmured to himself, but forbore to add the rest of the quotation.

For Jamie, the four-day ride to Helwater had been torture. The sudden illusion of freedom, combined with the certainty of its immediate loss, gave him a dreadful anticipation of his unknown destination.

This, with the anger and sorrow of his parting from his men fresh in memory—the wrenching loss of leaving the Highlands, with the knowledge that the parting might well be permanent—and his waking moments suffused with the physical pain of long-unused saddle muscles, were together enough to have kept him in torment for the whole of the journey. Only the fact that he had given his parole kept him from pulling Major John William Grey off his horse and throttling him in some peaceful lane.

Grey's words echoed in his ears, half-obliterated by the thrumming beat of his angry blood.

"As the renovation of the fortress has largely been completed—with the able assistance of yourself and your men"—Grey had allowed a tinge of irony to show in his voice—"the prisoners are to be removed to other accommodation, and the fortress of Ardsmuir garrisoned by troops of His Majesty's Twelfth Dragoons.

"The Scottish prisoners of war are to be transported to the American Colonies," he continued. "They will be sold under bond of indenture, for a term of seven years."

Jamie had kept himself carefully expressionless, but at that news, had felt his face and hands go numb with shock.

"Indenture? That is no better than slavery," he said, but did not pay much attention to his own words. America! A land of wilderness and savages—and one to be reached across three thousand miles of empty, roiling sea! Indenture in America was a sentence tantamount to permanent exile from Scotland.

"A term of indenture is not slavery," Grey had assured him, but the Major knew as well as he that the difference was merely a legality, and true only insofar as indentured servants would—if they survived—regain their freedom upon some predetermined date. An indentured servant *was* to most other intents and purposes the slave of his or her master—to be misused, whipped or branded at will, forbidden by law to leave the master's premises without permission.

As James Fraser was now to be forbidden.

"You are not to be sent with the others." Grey had not looked at him while speaking. "You are not merely a prisoner of war, you are a convicted traitor. As such, you are imprisoned at the pleasure of His Majesty; your sentence cannot be commuted to transportation without royal approval. And His Majesty has not seen fit to give that approval."

Jamie was conscious of a remarkable array of emotions; beneath his immediate rage was fear and sorrow for the fate of his men, mingled with a small flicker of ignominious relief that, whatever his own fate was to be, it would not involve entrusting himself to the sea. Shamed by the realization, he turned a cold eye on Grey.

"The gold," he said flatly. "That's it, aye?" So long as there remained the slightest chance of his revealing what he knew about that half-mythical hoard, the English Crown would take no chance of having him lost to the sea demons or the savages of the Colonies.

The Major still would not look at him, but gave a small shrug, as good as assent.

"Where am I to go, then?" His own voice had sounded rusty to his ears, slightly hoarse as he began to recover from the shock of the news.

Grey had busied himself putting away his records. It was early September, and a warm breeze blew through the half-open window, fluttering the papers.

"It's called Helwater. In the Lake District of England. You will be quartered with Lord Dunsany, to serve in whatever menial capacity he may require." Grey did look up then, the expression in his light blue eyes unreadable. "I shall visit you there once each quarter—to ensure your welfare."

He eyed the Major's red-coated back now, as they rode single-file through the narrow lanes, seeking refuge from his miseries in a satisfying vision of those wide blue eyes, bloodshot and popping in amazement as Jamie's hands tightened on that slender throat, thumbs digging into the sun-reddened flesh until the Major's small, muscular body should go limp as a killed rabbit in his grasp.

His Majesty's pleasure, was it? He was not deceived. This had been Grey's doing; the gold only an excuse. He was to be sold as a servant, and kept in a place where Grey could see it, and gloat. This was the Major's revenge.

He had lain before the inn hearth each night, aching in every limb, acutely aware of every twitch and rustle and breath of the man in the bed behind him, and deeply resentful of that awareness. By the pale gray of dawn, he was keyed to fury once more, longing for the man to rise from his bed and make some disgraceful gesture toward him, so that he might release his fury in the passion of murder. But Grey had only snored.

Over Helvellyn Bridge and past another of the strange grassy tarns, the red and yellow leaves of maple and larch whirling down in showers past the lightly sweated quarters of his horse, striking his face and sliding past him with a papery, whispering caress.

Grey had stopped just ahead, and turned in the saddle, waiting. They had arrived, then. The land sloped steeply down into a valley, where the manor house lay half-concealed in a welter of autumn-bright trees.

Helwater lay before him, and with it, the prospect of a life of shameful servitude. He stiffened his back and kicked his horse, harder than he intended.

Grey was received in the main drawing room, Lord Dunsany being cordially dismissive of his disheveled clothes and filthy boots, and Lady Dunsany, a small round woman with faded fair hair, fulsomely hospitable.

"A drink, Johnny, you must have a drink! And Louisa, my dear, perhaps you should fetch the girls down to greet our guest."

As Lady Dunsany turned to give orders to a footman, his Lordship leaned close over the glass to murmur to him. "The Scottish prisoner—you've brought him with you?"

"Yes," Grey said. Lady Dunsany, now in animated conversation with the butler about the altered dispositions for dinner, was unlikely to overhear, but he thought it best to keep his own voice low. "I left him in the front hall—I wasn't sure quite what you meant to do with him."

"You said the fellow's good with horses, eh? Best make him a groom then, as you suggested." Lord Dunsany glanced at his wife, and carefully turned so that his lean back was to her, further guarding their conversation. "I haven't told Louisa who he is," the baronet muttered. "All that scare about the Highlanders during the Rising—country was quite paralyzed with fear, you know? And she's never got over Gordon's death."

"I quite see." Grey patted the old man's arm reassuringly. He didn't think Dunsany himself had got over the death of his son, though he had rallied himself gamely for the sake of his wife and daughters.

"I'll just tell her the man's a servant you've recommended to me. Er . . . he's safe, of course? I mean . . . well, the girls . . ." Lord Dunsany cast an uneasy eye toward his wife.

"Quite safe," Grey assured his host. "He's an honorable man, and he's given his parole. He'll neither enter the house, nor leave the boundaries of your property, save with your express permission." Helwater covered more than six hundred acres, he knew. It was a long way from freedom, and from Scotland as well, but perhaps something better either than the narrow stones of Ardsmuir or the distant hardships of the Colonies.

A sound from the doorway swung Dunsany around, restored to beaming joviality by the appearance of his two daughters.

"You'll remember Geneva, Johnny?" he asked, urging his guest forward. "Isobel was still in the nursery last time you came—how time does fly, does it not?" And he shook his head in mild dismay.

Isobel was fourteen, small and round and bubbly and blond, like her mother. Grey didn't, in fact, remember Geneva—or rather he did, but the scrawny schoolgirl of years past bore little resemblance to the graceful seventeen-year-old who now offered him her hand. If Isobel resembled their mother, Geneva rather took after her father, at least in the matter of height and leanness. Lord Dunsany's grizzled hair might once have been that shining chestnut, and the girl had Dunsany's clear gray eyes.

The girls greeted the visitor with politeness, but were clearly more interested in something else.

"Daddy," said Isobel, tugging on her father's sleeve. "There's a *huge* man in the hall! He watched us all the time we were coming down the stairs! He's scary-looking!"

"Who is he, Daddy?" Geneva asked. She was more reserved than her sister, but clearly also interested.

"Er . . . why, that must be the new groom John's brought us," Lord Dunsany said, obviously flustered. "I'll have one of the footmen take him—" The baronet was interrupted by the sudden appearance of a footman in the doorway.

"Sir," he said, looking shocked at the news he bore, "there is a Scotchman in the hall!" Lest this outrageous statement not be believed, he turned and gestured widely at the tall, silent figure standing cloaked behind him.

At this cue, the stranger took a step forward, and spotting Lord Dunsany, politely inclined his head.

"My name is Alex MacKenzie," he said, in a soft Highland accent. He bowed toward Lord Dunsany, with no hint of mockery in his manner. "Your servant, my lord."

For one accustomed to the strenuous life of a Highland farm or a labor prison, the work of a groom on a Lake District stud farm was no great strain. For a man who had been mewed up in a cell for two months—since the others had left for the Colonies—it was the hell of a sweat. For the first week, while his muscles reaccustomed themselves to the sudden demands of constant movement, Jamie Fraser fell into his hayloft pallet each evening too tired even to dream.

He had arrived at Helwater in such a state of exhaustion and mental turmoil that he had at first seen it only as another prison—and one among strangers, far away from the Highlands. Now that he was ensconced here, imprisoned as securely by his word as by bars, he found both body and mind growing easier, as the days passed by. His body toughened, his feelings calmed in the quiet company of horses, and gradually he found it possible to think rationally again.

If he had no true freedom, he did at least have air, and light, space to stretch his limbs, and the sight of mountains and the lovely horses that Dunsany bred. The other grooms and servants were understandably suspicious of him, but inclined to leave him alone, out of respect for his size and forbidding countenance. It was a lonely life—but he had long since accepted the fact that for him, life was unlikely ever to be otherwise.

The soft snows came down upon Helwater, and even Major Grey's official visit at Christmas—a tense, awkward occasion—passed without disturbing his growing feelings of content.

Very quietly, he made such arrangements as could be managed, to communicate with Jenny and Ian in the Highlands. Aside from the infrequent letters that reached him by indirect means, which he read and then destroyed for safety's sake, his only reminder of home was the beechwood rosary he wore about his neck, concealed beneath his shirt.

A dozen times a day he touched the small cross that lay over his heart, conjuring each time the face of a loved one, with a brief word of prayer—for his sister, Jenny; for Ian and the children—his namesake, Young Jamie, Maggie, and Katherine Mary, for the twins Michael and Janet, and for Baby Ian. For the tenants of Lallybroch, the men of Ardsmuir. And always, the first prayer at morning, the last at night—and many between—for Claire. *Lord, that she may be safe. She and the child.*

As the snow passed and the year brightened into spring, Jamie Fraser was aware of only one fly in the ointment of his daily existence—the presence of the Lady Geneva Dunsany.

Pretty, spoilt, and autocratic, the Lady Geneva was accustomed to get what she wanted when she wanted it, and damn the convenience of anyone standing in her way. She was a good horsewoman—Jamie would give her that—but so sharp-tongued and whim-ridden that the grooms were given to drawing straws to determine who would have the misfortune of accompanying her on her daily ride.

Of late, though, the Lady Geneva had been making her own choice of companion—Alex MacKenzie.

"Nonsense," she said, when he pleaded first discretion, and then temporary indisposition, to avoid accompanying her into the secluded mist of the foothills above Helwater; a place she was forbidden to ride, because of the treacherous footing and dangerous fogs. "Don't be silly. Nobody's going to see us. Come on!" And kicking her mare brutally in the ribs, was off before he could stop her, laughing back over her shoulder at him.

Her infatuation with him was sufficiently obvious as to make the other grooms grin sidelong and make low-voiced remarks to each other when she entered the stable. He had a strong urge, when in her company, to boot her swiftly where it would do most good, but so far had settled for maintaining a strict silence when in her company, replying to all overtures with a mumpish grunt.

He trusted that she would get tired of this taciturn treatment sooner or later, and transfer her annoying attentions to another of the grooms. Or—pray God—she would soon be married, and well away from both Helwater and him.

It was a rare sunny day for the Lake Country, where the difference between the clouds and the ground is often imperceptible, in terms of damp. Still, on this May afternoon it was warm, warm enough for Jamie to have found it comfortable to remove his shirt. It was safe enough up here in the high field, with no likelihood of company beyond Bess and Blossom, the two stolid drayhorses pulling the roller.

It was a big field, and the horses old and well-trained to the task, which they liked; all he need do was twitch the reins occasionally, to keep their noses heading straight. The roller was made of wood, rather than the older kind of stone or metal, and constructed with a narrow slit between each board, so that the interior could be filled with well-rotted manure, which dribbled out in a steady stream as the roller turned, lightening the heavy contrivance as it drained.

Jamie thoroughly approved this innovation. He must tell Ian about it; draw a diagram. The gypsies would be coming soon; the kitchenmaids and grooms were all talking of it. He would maybe have time to add another installment to the ongoing letter he kept, sending the current crop of pages whenever a band of roving tinkers or gypsies came onto the farm. Delivery might be delayed for a month, or three, or six, but eventually the packet would make its way into the Highlands, passed from hand to hand, and on to his sister at Lallybroch, who would pay a generous fee for its reception.

Replies from Lallybroch came by the same anonymous route—for as a prisoner of the Crown, anything he sent or received by the mails must be inspected by Lord Dunsany. He felt a moment's excitement at the thought of a letter, but tried to damp it down; there might be nothing.

"Gee!" he shouted, more as a matter of form than anything. Bess and Blossom could see the approaching stone fence as well as he could, and were perfectly well aware that this was the spot to begin the ponderous turnabout. Bess waggled one ear and snorted, and he grinned.

"Aye, I know," he said to her, with a light twitch of the rein. "But they pay me to say it."

Then they were settled in the new track, and there was nothing more to do until they reached the wagon standing at the foot of the field, piled high with manure for refilling the roller. The sun was on his face now, and he closed his eyes, reveling in the feel of warmth on his bare chest and shoulders.

The sound of a horse's high whinny stirred him from somnolence a quarter-hour later. Opening his eyes, he could see the rider coming up the lane from the lower paddock, neatly framed between Blossom's ears. Hastily, he sat up and pulled the shirt back over his head.

"You needn't be modest on my account, MacKenzie." Geneva Dunsany's voice was high and slightly breathless as she pulled her mare to a walk beside the moving roller.

"Mmphm." She was dressed in her best habit, he saw, with a cairngorm brooch at her throat, and her color was higher than the temperature of the day warranted.

"What are you doing?" she asked, after they had rolled and paced in silence for some moments.

"I am spreading shit, my lady," he answered precisely, not looking at her.

"Oh." She rode on for the space of half a track, before venturing further into conversation.

"Did you know I am to be married?"

He did; all the servants had known it for a month, Richards the butler having been in the library, serving, when the solicitor came from Derwentwater to draw up the wedding contract. The Lady Geneva had been informed two days ago. According to her maid, Betty, the news had not been well received.

He contented himself with a noncommittal grunt.

"To Ellesmere," she said. The color rose higher in her cheeks, and her lips pressed together.

"I wish ye every happiness, my lady." Jamie pulled briefly on the reins as they came to the end of the field. He was out of the seat before Bess had set her hooves; he had no wish at all to linger in conversation with the Lady Geneva, whose mood seemed thoroughly dangerous.

"Happiness!" she cried. Her big gray eyes flashed and she slapped the thigh of her habit. "Happiness! Married to a man old enough to be my own grandsire?"

Jamie refrained from saying that he suspected the Earl of Ellesmere's prospects for happiness were somewhat more limited than her own. Instead, he murmured, "Your pardon, my lady," and went behind to unfasten the roller.

She dismounted and followed him. "It's a filthy bargain between my father and Ellesmere! He's selling me, that's what it is. My father cares not the slightest trifle for me, or he'd never have made such a match! Do you not think I am badly used?"

On the contrary, Jamie thought that Lord Dunsany, a most devoted father, had probably made the best match possible for his spoilt elder daughter. The Earl of Ellesmere *was* an old man. There was every prospect that within a few years, Geneva would be left as an extremely wealthy young widow, and a countess, to boot. On the other hand, such considerations might well not weigh heavily with a headstrong miss—a stubborn, spoilt bitch, he corrected, seeing the petulant set of her mouth and eyes—of seventeen.

"I am sure your father acts always in your best interests, my lady," he answered woodenly. Would the little fiend not go away?

She wouldn't. Assuming a more winsome expression, she came and stood close to his side, interfering with his opening the loading hatch of the roller.

"But a match with such a dried-up old man?" she said. "Surely it is heartless of Father to give me to such a creature." She stood on tiptoe, peering at Jamie. "How old are *you*, MacKenzie?"

His heart stopped beating for an instant.

"A verra great deal older than you, my lady," he said firmly. "Your pardon, my lady." He slid past her as well as he might without touching her, and leaped up onto the manure wagon, whence he was reasonably sure she wouldn't follow him.

"But not ready for the boneyard yet, are you, MacKenzie?" Now she was in front of him, shading her eyes with her hand as she peered upward. A breeze had come up, and wisps of her chestnut hair floated about her face. "Have you ever been married, MacKenzie?"

He gritted his teeth, overcome with the urge to drop a shovelful of manure over her chestnut head, but mastered it and dug the shovel into the pile, merely saying "I have," in a tone that brooked no further inquiries.

The Lady Geneva was not interested in other people's sensitivities. "Good," she said, satisfied. "You'll know what to do, then."

"To do?" He stopped short in the act of digging, one foot braced on the shovel.

"In bed," she said calmly. "I want you to come to bed with me."

In the shock of the moment, all he could think of was the ludicrous vision of the elegant Lady Geneva, skirts thrown up over her face, asprawl in the rich crumble of the manure wagon.

He dropped the shovel. "*Here?*" he croaked.

"No, silly," she said impatiently. "In bed, in a proper bed. In my bedroom."

"You have lost your mind," Jamie said coldly, the shock receding slightly. "Or I should think you had, if ye had one to lose."

Her face flamed and her eyes narrowed. "How dare you speak that way to me!"

"How dare ye speak so to *me*?" Jamie replied hotly. "A wee lassie of breeding to be makin' indecent proposals to a man twice her age? And a groom in her father's house?" he added, recollecting who he was. He choked back further remarks, recollecting also that this dreadful girl *was* the Lady Geneva, and he *was* her father's groom.

"I beg your pardon, my lady," he said, mastering his choler with some effort. "The sun is verra hot today, and no doubt it has addled your wits a bit. I expect ye should go back to the house at once and ask your maid to put cold cloths on your head."

The Lady Geneva stamped her morocco-booted foot. "My wits are not addled in the slightest!"

She glared up at him, chin set. Her chin was little and pointed, so were her teeth, and with that particular expression of determination on her face, he thought she looked a great deal like the bloody-minded vixen she was.

"Listen to me," she said. "I cannot prevent this abominable marriage. But I am"—she hesitated, then continued firmly—"I am *damned* if I will suffer my maidenhood to be given to a disgusting, depraved old monster like Ellesmere!"

Jamie rubbed a hand across his mouth. Despite himself, he felt some sympathy for her. But *he* would be damned if he allowed this skirted maniac to involve him in her troubles.

"I am fully sensible of the honor, my lady," he said at last, with a heavy irony, "but I really cannot—"

"Yes, you can." Her eyes rested frankly on the front of his filthy breeches. "Betty says so."

He struggled for speech, emerging at first with little more than incoherent sputterings. Finally he drew a deep breath and said, with all the firmness he could muster, "Betty has not the slightest basis for drawing conclusions as to my capacity. I havena laid a hand on the lass!"

Geneva laughed delightedly. "So you didn't take her to bed? She said you wouldn't, but I thought perhaps she was only trying to avoid a beating. That's good; I couldn't possibly share a man with my maid."

He breathed heavily. Smashing her on the head with the shovel or throttling her were unfortunately out of the question. His inflamed temper slowly calmed. Outrageous she might be, but essentially powerless. She could scarcely force him to go to her bed.

"Good day to ye, my lady," he said, as politely as possible. He turned his back on her and began to shovel manure into the hollow roller.

"If you don't," she said sweetly, "I'll tell my father you made improper advances to me. He'll have the skin flayed off your back."

His shoulders hunched involuntarily. She couldn't possibly know. He had been careful never to take his shirt off in front of anyone since he came here.

He turned carefully and stared down at her. The light of triumph was in her eye.

"Your father may not be so well acquent' with me," he said, "but he's kent *you* since ye were born. Tell him, and be damned to ye!"

She puffed up like a game cock, her face growing bright red with temper. "Is that so?" she cried. "Well, look at this, then, and be damned to *you*!" She reached into the bosom of her habit and pulled out a thick letter, which she waved under his nose. His sister's firm black hand was so familiar that a glimpse was enough.

"Give me that!" He was down off the wagon and after her in a flash, but she was too fast. She was up in the saddle before he could grab her, backing with the reins in one hand, waving the letter mockingly in the other.

"Want it, do you?"

"Yes, I want it! Give it to me!" He was so furious, he could easily have done her violence, could he get his hands on her. Unfortunately, her bay mare sensed his mood, and backed away, snorting and pawing uneasily.

"I don't think so." She eyed him coquettishly, the red of ill temper fading from her face. "After all, it's really my duty to give this to my father, isn't it? He ought really to know that his servants are carrying on clandestine correspondences, shouldn't he? Is Jenny your sweetheart?"

"You've read my letter? Ye filthy wee bitch!"

"Such language," she said, wagging the letter reprovingly. "It's my duty to help my parents, by letting them know what sorts of dreadful things the servants are up to, isn't it? And I am a dutiful daughter, am I not, submitting to this marriage without a squeak?" She leaned forward on her pommel, smiling mockingly, and with a fresh spurt of rage, he realized that she was enjoying this very much indeed.

"I expect Papa will find it very interesting reading," she said. "Especially the bit about the gold to be sent to Lochiel in France. Isn't it still considered treason to be giving comfort to the King's enemies? *Tsk*," she said, clicking her tongue roguishly. "How wicked."

He thought he might be sick on the spot, from sheer terror. Did she have the faintest idea how many lives lay in that manicured white hand? His sister, Ian, their six children, all the tenants and families of Lallybroch—perhaps even the lives of the agents who carried messages and money between Scotland and France, maintaining the precarious existence of the Jacobite exiles there.

He swallowed, once, and then again, before he spoke.

"All right," he said. A more natural smile broke out on her face, and he realized how very young she was. Aye, well, and a wee adder's bite was as venomous as an auld one's.

"I won't tell," she assured him, looking earnest. "I'll give you your letter back afterward, and I won't ever say what was in it. I promise."

"Thank you." He tried to gather his wits enough to make a sensible plan. Sensible? Going into his master's house to ravish his daughter's maidenhood —at her request? He had never heard of a less sensible prospect.

"All right," he said again. "We must be careful." With a feeling of dull horror, he felt himself being drawn into the role of conspirator with her.

"Yes. Don't worry, I can arrange for my maid to be sent away, and the footman drinks; he's always asleep before ten o'clock."

"Arrange it, then," he said, his stomach curdling. "Mind ye choose a safe day, though."

"A safe day?" She looked blank.

"Sometime in the week after ye've finished your courses," he said bluntly. "You're less likely to get wi' child then."

"Oh." She blushed rosily at that, but looked at him with a new interest.

They looked at each other in silence for a long moment, suddenly linked by the prospect of the future.

"I'll send you word," she said at last, and wheeling her horse about, galloped away across the field, the mare's hooves kicking up spurts of the freshly spread manure.

Cursing fluently and silently, he crept beneath the row of larches. There wasn't much moon, which was a blessing. Six yards of open lawn to cross in a dash, and he was knee-deep in the columbine and germander of the flowerbed.

He looked up the side of the house, its bulk looming dark and forbidding above him. Yes, there was the candle in the window, as she'd said. Still, he counted the windows carefully, to verify it. Heaven help him if he chose the wrong room. Heaven help him if it was the right one, too, he thought grimly, and took a firm hold on the trunk of the huge gray creeper that covered this side of the house.

The leaves rustled like a hurricane and the stems, stout as they were, creaked and bent alarmingly under his weight. There was nothing for it but to climb as swiftly as possible, and be ready to hurl himself off into the night if any of the windows should suddenly be raised.

He arrived at the small balcony panting, heart racing, and drenched in sweat, despite the chilliness of the night. He paused a moment, alone beneath the faint spring stars, to draw breath. He used it to damn Geneva Dunsany once more, and then pushed open her door.

She had been waiting, and had plainly heard his approach up the ivy. She rose from the chaise where she had been sitting and came toward him, chin up, chestnut hair loose over her shoulders.

She was wearing a white nightgown of some sheer material, tied at the throat with a silk bow. The garment didn't look like the nightwear of a modest young lady, and he realized with a shock that she was wearing her bridal-night apparel.

"So you came." He heard the note of triumph in her voice, but also the faint quaver. So she hadn't been sure of him?

"I hadn't much choice," he said shortly, and turned to close the French doors behind him.

"Will you have some wine?" Striving for graciousness, she moved to the table, where a decanter stood with two glasses. How had she managed that? he wondered. Still, a glass of something wouldn't come amiss in the present circumstances. He nodded, and took the full glass from her hand.

He looked at her covertly as he sipped it. The nightdress did little to conceal her body, and as his heart gradually slowed from the panic of his ascent, he found his first fear—that he wouldn't be able to keep his half of the bargain—allayed without conscious effort. She was built narrowly, slim-hipped and small-breasted, but most definitely a woman.

Finished, he set down the glass. No point in delay, he thought.

"The letter?" he said abruptly.

"Afterward," she said, tightening her mouth.

"Now, or I leave." And he turned toward the window, as though about to execute the threat.

"Wait!" He turned back, but eyed her with ill-disguised impatience.

"Don't you trust me?" she said, trying to sound winsome and charming.

"No," he said bluntly.

She looked angry at that, and thrust out a petulant lower lip, but he merely looked stonily over his shoulder at her, still facing the window.

"Oh, all right then," she said at last, with a shrug. Digging under the layers of embroidery in a sewing box, she unearthed the letter and tossed it onto the washing stand beside him.

He snatched it up and unfolded the sheets, to be sure of it. He felt a surge of mingled fury and relief at the sight of the violated seal, and Jenny's familiar hand within, neat and strong.

"Well?" Geneva's voice broke in upon his reading, impatient. "Put that down and come here, Jamie. I'm ready." She sat on the bed, arms curled around her knees.

He stiffened, and turned a very cold blue look on her, over the pages in his hands.

"You'll not use that name to me," he said. She lifted the pointed chin a trifle more and raised her plucked brows.

"Why not? It's yours. Your sister calls you so."

He hesitated for a moment, then deliberately laid the letter aside, and bent his head to the laces of his breeches.

"I'll serve ye properly," he said, looking down at his working fingers, "for the sake of my own honor as a man, and yours as a woman. But"—he raised his head and the narrowed blue eyes bored into hers—"having brought me to your bed by means of threats against my family, I'll not have ye call me by the name they give me." He stood motionless, eyes fixed on hers. At last she gave a very small nod, and her eyes dropped to the quilt.

She traced the pattern with a finger.

"What must I call you, then?" she asked at last, in a small voice. "I *can't* call you MacKenzie!"

The corners of his mouth lifted slightly as he looked at her. She looked quite small, huddled into herself with her arms locked around her knees and her head bowed. He sighed.

"Call me Alex, then. It's my own name, as well."

She nodded without speaking. Her hair fell forward in wings about her face, but he could see the brief shine of her eyes as she peeped out from behind its cover.

"It's all right," he said gruffly. "You can watch me." He pushed the loose breeches down, rolling the stockings off with them. He shook them out and folded them neatly over a chair before beginning to unfasten his shirt, conscious of her gaze, still shy, but now direct. Out of some idea of thoughtfulness, he turned to face her before removing the shirt, to spare her for a moment the sight of his back.

"Oh!" The exclamation was soft, but enough to stop him.

"Is something wrong?" he asked.

"Oh, no . . . I mean, it's only that I didn't expect . . ." The hair swung forward again, but not before he had seen the telltale reddening of her cheeks.

"You've not seen a man naked before?" he guessed. The shiny brown head swayed back and forth.

"Noo," she said doubtfully, "I have, only . . . it wasn't . . . ."

"Well, it usually isn't," he said matter-of-factly, sitting down on the bed beside her. "But if one is going to make love, it has to be, ye see."

"I see," she said, but still sounded doubtful. He tried to smile, to reassure her.

"Don't worry. It doesna get any bigger. And it wilna do anything strange, if ye want to touch it." At least he hoped it wouldn't. Being naked, in such close proximity to a half-clad girl, was doing terrible things to his powers of self-control. His traitorous, deprived anatomy didn't care a whit that she was a selfish, blackmailing little bitch. Perhaps fortunately, she declined his offer, shrinking back a little toward the wall, though her eyes stayed on him. He rubbed his chin dubiously.

"How much do you . . . I mean, have ye any idea how it's done?"

Her gaze was clear and guileless, though her cheeks flamed.

"Well, like the horses, I suppose?" He nodded, but felt a pang, recalling his wedding night, when he too had expected it to be like horses.

"Something like that," he said, clearing his throat. "Slower, though. More gentle," he added, seeing her apprehensive look.

"Oh. That's good. Nurse and the maids used to tell stories, about . . . men, and, er, getting married, and all . . . it sounded rather frightening." She swallowed hard. "W-will it hurt much?" She raised her head suddenly and looked him in the eye.

"I don't mind if it does," she said bravely, "it's only that I'd like to know what to expect." He felt an unexpected small liking for her. She might be spoiled, selfish, and reckless, but there was some character to her, at least. Courage, to him, was no small virtue.

"I think not," he said. "If I take my time to ready you" (if he *could* take his time, amended his brain), "I think it will be not much worse than a pinch." He reached out and nipped a fold of skin on her upper arm. She jumped and rubbed the spot, but smiled.

"I can stand that."

"It's only the first time it's like that," he assured her. "The next time it will be better."

She nodded, then after a moment's hesitation, edged toward him, reaching out a tentative finger.

"May I touch you?" This time he really did laugh, though he choked the sound off quickly.

"I think you'll have to, my lady, if I'm to do what you asked of me."

She ran her hand slowly down his arm, so softly that the touch tickled, and his skin shivered in response. Gaining confidence, she let her hand circle his forearm, feeling the girth of it.

"You're quite . . . big." He smiled, but stayed motionless, letting her explore his body, at as much length as she might wish. He felt the muscles of his belly tighten as she stroked the length of one thigh, and ventured tentatively around the curve of one buttock. Her fingers approached the twisting, knotted line of the scar that ran the length of his left thigh, but stopped short.

"It's all right," he assured her. "It doesna hurt me anymore." She didn't reply, but drew two fingers slowly along the length of the scar, exerting no pressure.

The questing hands, growing bolder, slid up over the rounded curves of his broad shoulders, slid down his back—and stopped dead. He closed his eyes and waited, following her movements by the shifting of weight on the mattress. She moved behind him, and was silent. Then there was a quivering sigh, and the hands touched him again, soft on his ruined back.

"And you weren't afraid, when I said I'd have you flogged?" Her voice was queerly hoarse, but he kept still, eyes closed.

"No," he said. "I am not much afraid of things, anymore." In fact, he was beginning to be afraid that he wouldn't be able to keep his hands off her, or to handle her with the necessary gentleness, when the time came. His balls ached with need, and he could feel his heartbeat, pounding in his temples.

She got off the bed, and stood in front of him. He rose suddenly, startling her so that she stepped back a pace, but he reached out and rested his hands on her shoulders.

"May I touch *you*, my lady?" The words were teasing, but the touch was not. She nodded, too breathless to speak, and his arms came around her.

He held her against his chest, not moving until her breathing slowed. He was conscious of an extraordinary mixture of feelings. He had never in his life taken a woman in his arms without some feeling of love, but there was nothing of love in this encounter, nor could there be, for her own sake. There was some tenderness for her youth, and pity at her situation. Rage at her manipulation of him, and fear at the magnitude of the crime he was about to commit. But overall there was a terrible lust, a need that clawed at his vitals and made him ashamed of his own manhood, even as he acknowledged its power. Hating himself, he lowered his head and cupped her face between his hands.

He kissed her softly, briefly, then a bit longer. She was trembling against him as his hands undid the tie of her gown and slid it back off her shoulders. He lifted her and laid her on the bed.

He lay beside her, cradling her in one arm as the other hand caressed her breasts, one and then the other, cupping each so she felt the weight and the warmth of them, even as he did.

"A man should pay tribute to your body," he said softly, raising each nipple with small, circling touches. "For you are beautiful, and that is your right."

She let out her breath in a small gasp, then relaxed under his touch. He took his time, moving as slowly as he could make himself do it, stroking and kissing, touching her lightly all over. He didn't like the girl, didn't want to be here, didn't want to be doing this, but—it had been more than three years since he'd touched a woman's body.

He tried to gauge when she might be readiest, but how in hell could he tell? She was flushed and panting, but she simply lay there, like a piece of porcelain on display. Curse the girl, could she not even give him a clue?

He rubbed a trembling hand through his hair, trying to quell the surge of confused emotion that pulsed through him with each heartbeat. He was angry, scared, and most mightily roused, most of which feelings were of no great use to him now. He closed his eyes and breathed deeply, striving for calm, seeking for gentleness.

No, of course she couldn't show him. She'd never touched a man before.

Having forced him here, she was, with a damnable, unwanted, unwarrantable trust, leaving the conduct of the whole affair up to him!

He touched the girl, gently, stroking her between the thighs. She didn't part them for him, but didn't resist. She was faintly moist there. Perhaps it would be all right now?

"All right," he murmured to her. "Be still, *mo chridhe*." Murmuring what he hoped sounded like reassurances, he eased himself on top of her, and used his knee to spread her legs. He felt her slight start at the heat of his body covering her, at the touch of his cock, and he wrapped his hands in her hair to steady her, still muttering things in soft Gaelic.

He thought dimly that it was a good thing he was speaking Gaelic, as he was no longer paying any attention at all to what he was saying. Her small, hard breasts poked against his chest.

"Mo nighean," he murmured.

"Wait a minute," said Geneva. "I think perhaps . . ."

The effort of control made him dizzy, but he did it slowly, only easing himself the barest inch within.

"Ooh!" said Geneva. Her eyes flew wide.

"Uh," he said, and pushed a bit farther.

"Stop it! It's too big! Take it out!" Panicked, Geneva thrashed beneath him. Pressed beneath his chest, her breasts wobbled and rubbed, so that his own nipples leapt erect in pinpoints of abrupt sensation.

Her struggles were accomplishing by force what he had tried to do with gentleness. Half-dazed, he fought to keep her under him, while groping madly for something to say to calm her.

"But—" he said.

"Stop it!"

"I—"

"Take it *out*!" she screamed.

He clapped one hand over her mouth and said the only coherent thing he could think of.

"No," he said definitely, and shoved.

What might have been a scream emerged through his fingers as a strangled "Eep!" Geneva's eyes were huge and round, but dry.

In for a penny, in for a pound. The saying drifted absurdly through his head, leaving nothing in its wake but a jumble of incoherent alarms and a marked feeling of terrible urgency down beween them. There was precisely one thing he was capable of doing at this point, and he did it, his body ruthlessly usurping control as it moved into the rhythm of its inexorable pagan joy.

It took no more than a few thrusts before the wave came down upon him, churning down the length of his spine and erupting like a breaker striking rocks, sweeping away the last shreds of conscious thought that clung, barnacle-like, to the remnants of his mind.

He came to himself a moment later, lying on his side with the sound of his own heartbeat loud and slow in his ears. He cracked one eyelid, and saw the shimmer of pink skin in lamplight. He must see if he'd hurt her much, but God, not just this minute. He shut his eye again and merely breathed.

"What . . . what are you thinking?" The voice sounded hesitant, and a little shaken, but not hysterical.

Too shaken himself to notice the absurdity of the question, he answered it with the truth.

"I was wondering why in God's name men want to bed virgins."

There was a long moment of silence, and then a tremulous intake of breath.

"I'm sorry," she said in a small voice. "I didn't know it would hurt you too."

His eyes popped open in astonishment, and he raised himself on one elbow to find her looking at him like a startled fawn. Her face was pale, and she licked dry lips.

"Hurt me?" he said, in blank astonishment. "It didna hurt *me*."

"But"—she frowned as her eyes traveled slowly down the length of his body—"I thought it must. You made the most terrible face, as though it hurt awfully, and you . . . you *groaned* like a—"

"Aye, well," he interrupted hastily, before she could reveal any more unflattering observations of his behavior. "I didna mean . . . I mean . . . that's just how men act, when they . . . do that," he ended lamely.

Her shock was fading into curiosity. "Do all men act like that when they're . . . doing that?"

"How should I—?" he began irritably, then stopped himself with a shudder, realizing that he did in fact know the answer to that.

"Aye, they do," he said shortly. He pushed himself up to a sitting position, and brushed the hair back from his forehead. "Men are disgusting horrible beasts, just as your nurse told you. Have I hurt ye badly?"

"I don't think so," she said doubtfully. She moved her legs experimentally. "It did hurt, just for a moment, like you said it would, but it isn't so bad now."

He breathed a sigh of relief as he saw that while she had bled, the stain on the towel was slight, and she seemed not to be in pain. She reached tentatively between her thighs and made a face of disgust.

"Ooh!" she said. "It's all nasty and sticky!"

The blood rose to his face in mingled outrage and embarrassment.

"Here," he muttered, and reached for a washcloth from the stand. She didn't take it, but opened her legs and arched her back slightly, obviously expecting him to attend to the mess. He had a strong urge to stuff the rag down her throat instead, but a glance at the stand where his letter lay stopped him. It was a bargain, after all, and she'd kept her part.

Grimly, he wet the cloth and began to sponge her, but he found the trust with which she presented herself to him oddly moving. He carried out his ministrations quite gently, and found himself, at the end, planting a light kiss on the smooth slope of her belly.

"There."

"Thank you," she said. She moved her hips tentatively, and reached out a hand to touch him. He didn't move, letting her fingers trail down his chest and toy with the deep indentation of his navel. The light touch hesitantly descended.

"You said . . . it would be better next time," she whispered.

He closed his eyes and took a deep breath. It was a long time until the dawn.

"I expect it will," he said, and stretched himself once more beside her.

"Ja—er, Alex?"

He felt as though he had been drugged, and it was an effort to answer her. "My lady?"

Her arms came around his neck and she nestled her head in the curve of his shoulder, breath warm against his chest.

"I love you, Alex."

With difficulty, he roused himself enough to put her away from him, holding her by the shoulders and looking down into the gray eyes, soft as a doe's.

"No," he said, but gently, shaking his head. "That's the third rule. You may have no more than the one night. You may not call me by my first name. And you may not love me."

The gray eyes moistened a bit. "But if I can't help it?"

"It isna love you feel now." He hoped he was right, for his sake as well as her own. "It's only the feeling I've roused in your body. It's strong, and it's good, but it isna the same thing as love."

"What's the difference?"

He rubbed his hands hard over his face. She *would* be a philosopher, he thought wryly. He took a deep breath and blew it out before answering her.

"Well, love's for only one person. This, what you feel from me—ye can have that with any man, it's not particular."

Only one person. He pushed the thought of Claire firmly away, and wearily bent again to his work.

He landed heavily in the earth of the flowerbed, not caring that he crushed several small and tender plants. He shivered. This hour before dawn was not only the darkest, but the coldest, as well, and his body strongly protested being required to rise from a warm, soft nest and venture into the chilly blackness, shielded from the icy air by no more than a thin shirt and breeks.

He remembered the heated, rosy curve of the cheek he had bent to kiss before leaving. The shapes of her lingered, warm in his hands, curving his fingers in memory, even as he groped in the dark for the darker line of the stableyard's stone wall. Drained as he was, it was a dreadful effort to haul himself up and climb over, but he couldn't risk the creak of the gate awakening Hughes, the head groom.

He felt his way across the inner yard, crowded with wagons and packed bales, ready for the journey of the Lady Geneva to the home of her new lord, following the wedding on Thursday next. At last he pushed open the stable door and found his way up the ladder to his loft. He lay down in the icy straw and pulled the single blanket over him, feeling empty of everything.

15

By Misadventure

Appropriately enough, the weather was dark and stormy when the news reached Helwater. The afternoon exercise had been canceled, owing to the heavy downpour, and the horses were snug in their stalls below. The homely, peaceful sounds of munching and blowing rose up to the loft above, where Jamie Fraser reclined in a comfortable, hay-lined nest, an open book propped on his chest.

It was one of several he had borrowed from the estate's factor, Mr. Grieves, and he was finding it absorbing, despite the difficulty of reading by the poor light from the owl-slits beneath the eaves.

> *My lips, which I threw in his way, so as that he could not escape kissing them, fix'd, fir'd and embolden'd him: and now, glancing my eyes towards that part of his dress which cover'd the essential object of enjoyment, I plainly discover'd the swell and commotion there; and as I was now too far advanc'd to stop in so fair a way, and was indeed no longer able to contain myself, or wait the slower progress of his maiden bashfulness, I stole my hand upon his thighs, down one of which I could both see and feel a stiff hard body, confin'd by his breeches, that my fingers could discover no end to.*

"Oh, aye?" Jamie muttered skeptically. He raised his eyebrows and shifted himself on the hay. He had been aware that books like this existed, of course, but—with Jenny ordering the reading matter at Lallybroch—had not encountered one personally before. The type of mental engagement demanded was somewhat different from that required for the works of Messieurs Defoe and Fielding, but he was not averse to variety.

> *Its prodigious size made me shrink again; yet I could not, without pleasure, behold, and even ventur'd to feel, such a length, such a breadth of animated ivory! perfectly well turn'd and fashion'd, the proud stiffness of which distended its skin, whose smooth polish and*

velvet softness might vie with that of the most delicate of our sex, and whose exquisite whiteness was not a little set off by a sprout of black curling hair round the root; then the broad and blueish casted incarnate of the head, and blue serpentines of its veins, altogether compos'd the most striking assemblage of figures and colors in nature. In short, it stood an object of terror and delight!

Jamie glanced at his own crotch and snorted briefly at this, but flipped the page, the crash of thunder outside meriting no more than a twinge of his attention. He was so absorbed that at first he failed to hear the noises down below, the sound of voices drowned in the heavy rush and beat of the rain on the planks a few feet above his head.

"MacKenzie!" The repeated stentorian bellow finally penetrated his awareness, and he rolled hastily to his feet, quickly straightening his clothes as he went toward the ladder.

"Aye?" He thrust his head over the edge of the loft to see Hughes, just opening his mouth for another bellow.

"Oh, there 'ee are." Hughes shut his mouth, and beckoned with one gnarled hand, wincing as he did so. Hughes suffered mightily from rheumatics in damp weather; he had been riding out the storm snug in the small chamber beside the tack room, where he kept a bed and a jug of crudely distilled spirits. The aroma was perceptible from the loft, and grew substantially stronger as Jamie descended the ladder.

"You're to help ready the coach to drive Lord Dunsany and Lady Isobel to Ellesmere," Hughes told him, the moment his foot touched the flags of the stable floor. The old man swayed alarmingly, hiccuping softly to himself.

"Now? Are ye daft, man? Or just drunk?" He glanced at the open half-door behind Hughes, which seemed a solid sheet of streaming water. Even as he looked, the sky beyond lit up with a sudden flare of lightning that threw the mountain beyond into sudden sharp relief. Just as suddenly, it disappeared, leaving its afterimage printed on his retina. He shook his head to clear the image, and saw Jeffries, the coachman, making his way across the yard, head bowed against the force of wind and water, cloak clutched tight about him. So it wasn't only a drunken fancy of Hughes's.

"Jeffries needs help wi' the horses!" Hughes was forced to lean close and shout to be heard over the noise of the storm. The smell of rough alcohol was staggering at close distance.

"Aye, but why? Why must Lord Dunsany—ah, feckit!" The head groom's eyes were red-rimmed and bleary; clearly there was no sense to be got out of him. Disgusted, Jamie pushed past the man and mounted the ladder two rungs at a time.

A moment to wrap his own worn cloak about him, a moment more to thrust the book he had been reading under the hay—stable lads were no respecters of property—and he was slithering down the ladder again, and out into the roar of the storm.

It was a hellish journey. The wind screamed through the pass, striking the bulky coach and threatening to overturn it at any moment. Perched aloft beside Jeffries, a cloak was little protection against the driving rain; still less was it a help when he was forced to dismount—as he did every few minutes, it seemed—and put his shoulder to the wheel to free the miserable contrivance from the clinging grip of a mudhole.

Still, he scarcely noticed the physical inconvenience of the journey, preoccupied as he was with the possible reasons for it. There couldn't be many matters of such urgency as to force an old man like Lord Dunsany outside on a day like this, let alone over the rutted road to Ellesmere. Some word had come from Ellesmere, and it could only concern the Lady Geneva or her child.

Hearing through the servants' gossip that Lady Geneva was due to be deliverd in January, he had counted quickly backward, cursed Geneva Dunsany once more, and then said a hasty prayer for her safe delivery. Since then, he had done his best not to think about it. He had been with her only three days before her wedding; he couldn't be sure.

A week before, Lady Dunsany had gone to Ellesmere to be with her daughter. Since then, she had sent daily messengers home, to fetch the dozen things she had forgotten to take and must have at once, and each of them, upon arrival at Helwater, had reported "No news yet." Now there was news, and it was plainly bad.

Passing back toward the front of the coach, after the latest battle with the mud, he saw the Lady Isobel's face peering out from beneath the isinglass sheet that covered the window.

"Oh, MacKenzie!" she said, her face contorted in fear and distress. "Please, is it much farther?"

He leaned close to shout in her ear, over the gurgle and rush of the gullies running down both sides of the road.

"Jeffries says it's four mile yet, milady! Two hours, maybe." If the damned and hell-bent coach didn't tip itself and its hapless passengers off the Ashness Bridge into Watendlath Tarn, he added silently to himself.

Isobel nodded her thanks, and lowered the window, but not before he had seen that the wetness upon her cheeks was due as much to tears as to the rain. The snake of anxiety wrapped round his heart slithered lower, to twist in his guts.

It was closer to three hours by the time the coach rolled at last into the courtyard at Ellesmere. Without hesitation, Lord Dunsany leapt down and, scarcely pausing to give his younger daughter an arm, hurried into the house.

It took nearly another hour to unharness the team, rub down the horses, wash the caked-on mud from the coach's wheels, and put everything away in Ellesmere's stables. Numb with cold, fatigue, and hunger, he and Jeffries sought refuge and sustenance in Ellesmere's kitchens.

"Poor fellows, you're gone right blue wi' the cold," the cook observed. "Sit ye down 'ere, and I'll soon 'ave yer a hot bite." A sharp-faced, spare-framed woman, her figure belied her skill, for within minutes, a huge, savoury omelet was laid before them, garnished with liberal amounts of bread and butter, and a small pot of jam.

"Fair, quite fair," Jeffries pronounced, casting an appreciative eye on the spread. He winked at the cook. "Not as it wouldn' go down easier wi' a drop o' something to pave the way, eh? You look the sort would have mercy on a pair o' poor half-frozen chaps, wouldn't ye, darlin'?"

Whether it was this piece of Irish persuasion or the sight of their dripping, steaming clothes, the argument had its effect, and a bottle of cooking brandy made its appearance next to the peppermill. Jeffries poured a large tot and drank it off without hesitation, smacking his lips.

"Ah, that's more like! Here, boyo." He passed the bottle to Jamie, then settled himself comfortably to a hot meal and gossip with the female servants. "Well, then, what's to do here? Is the babe born yet?"

"Oh, yes, last night!" the kitchen maid said eagerly. "We were up all night, with the doctor comin', and fresh sheets and towels called for, and the house all topsle-turvy. But the babe's the least of it!"

"Now, then," the cook broke in, frowning censoriously. "There's too much work to be standin' about gossiping. Get yer on, Mary Ann—up to the study, and see if his Lordship'll be wantin' anything else served now."

Jamie, wiping his plate with a slice of bread, observed that the maid, far from being abashed at this rebuke, departed with alacrity, causing him to deduce that something of considerable interest was likely transpiring in the study.

The undivided attention of her audience thus obtained, the cook allowed herself to be persuaded into imparting the gossip with no more than a token demur.

"Well, it started some months ago, when the Lady Geneva started to show, poor thing. His Lordship'd been nicer than pie to 'er, ever since they was married couldn't do enough for 'er, anything she wanted ordered from Lunnon, always askin' was she warm enough, 'ad she what she wanted to eat —fair dotin', 'is Lordship was. But then, when 'e found she was with child!" The cook paused, to screw up her face portentously.

Jamie wanted desperately to know about the child; what was it, and how did it fare? There seemed no way to hurry the woman, though, so he composed his face to look as interested as possible, leaning forward encouragingly.

"Why, the shouting, and the carrryings-on!" the cook said, throwing up her hands in dismayed illustration, " 'im shoutin', and 'er cryin', and the both of 'em stampin' up and down and slammin' doors, and 'im callin' 'er names as isn't fit to be used in a stableyard—and so I told Mary Ann, when she told me. . . ."

"Was his lordship not pleased about the child, then?" Jamie interrupted. The omelet was settling into a hard lump somewhere under his breastbone. He took another gulp of brandy, in hopes of dislodging it.

The cook turned a bright, birdlike eye on him, eyebrow cocked in appreciation at his intelligence. "Well, you'd think as 'e would be, wouldn't yer? But no indeed! Far from it," she added with emphasis.

"Why not?" said Jeffries, only mildly interested.

" 'E said," the cook said, dropping her voice in awe at the scandalousness of the information, "as the child wasn't 'is!"

Jeffries, well along with his second glass, snorted in contemptuous amusement. "Old goat with a young gel? I should think it like enough, but how on earth would his Lordship know for sure whose the spawn was? Could be his as much as anyone's, couldn't it, with only her ladyship's word to go by, eh?"

The cook's thin mouth stretched in a bright, malicious smile. "Oh, I don't say as 'e'd know whose it *was*, now—but there's one sure way 'e'd know it wasn't *'is*, now isn't there?"

Jeffries stared at the cook, tilting back on his chair. "What?" he said. "You mean to tell me his Lordship's incapable?" A broad grin at this juicy thought split his weatherbeaten face. Jamie felt the omelet rising, and hastily gulped more brandy.

"Well, *I* couldn't say, I'm sure." The cook's mouth assumed a prim line, then split asunder to add, "though the chambermaid did say as the sheets she took off the weddin' bed was as white as when they'd gone on, to be sure."

It was too much. Interrupting Jeffries's delighted cackle, Jamie set down his glass with a thump, and bluntly said, "Did the child live?"

The cook and Jeffries both stared in astonishment, but the cook, after a moment's startlement, nodded in answer.

"Oh, yes, to be sure. Fine 'ealthy little lad, 'e is, too, or so I 'ear. I thought you knew a'ready. It's 'is mother that's dead."

That blunt statement struck the kitchen with silence. Even Jeffries was still for a moment, sobered by death. Then he crossed himself quickly, muttered, "God rest her soul," and swallowed the rest of his brandy.

Jamie could feel his own throat burning, whether with brandy or tears, he could not say. Shock and grief choked him like a ball of yarn wedged in his gullet; he could barely manage to croak, "When?"

"This morning," the cook said, wagging her head mournfully. "Just afore noon, poor girl. They thought for a time as she'd be all right, after the babe was born; Mary Ann said she was sittin' up, holdin' the wee thing and laughin'." She sighed heavily at the thought. "But then near dawn, she started to bleed again bad. They called back the doctor, and he came fast as could be, but—"

The door slamming open interrupted her. It was Mary Ann, eyes wide under her cap, gasping with excitement and exertion.

"Your master wants you!" she blurted out, eyes flicking between Jamie and the coachman. "The both of ye, at once, and oh, sir"—she gulped, nodding at Jeffries—"he says for God's sake, to bring your pistols!"

The coachman exchanged a glance of consternation with Jamie, then leapt to his feet and dashed out, in the direction of the stables. Like most coachmen, he carried a pair of loaded pistols beneath his seat, against the possibility of highwaymen.

It would take Jeffries a few minutes to find the arms, and longer if he waited to check that the priming had not been harmed by the wet weather. Jamie rose to his feet and gripped the dithering maidservant by the arm.

"Show me to the study," he said. "Now!"

The sound of raised voices would have led him there, once he had reached the head of the stair. Pushing past Mary Ann without ceremony, he paused for a moment outside the door, uncertain whether he should enter at once, or wait for Jeffries.

"That you can have the sheer heartless effrontery to make such accusations!" Dunsany was saying, his old man's voice shaking with rage and distress. "And my poor lamb not cold in her bed! You blackguard, you poltroon! I will not suffer the child to stay a single night under your roof!"

"The little bastard stays here!" Ellesmere's voice rasped hoarsely. It would have been apparent to a far less experienced observer that his Lordship was well the worse for drink. "Bastard that he is, he's my heir, and he stays with me! He's bought and paid for, and if his dam was a whore, at least she gave me a boy."

"Damn you!" Dunsany's voice had reached such a pitch of shrillness that it was scarcely more than a squeak, but the outrage in it was clear nonetheless. "Bought? You—you—you dare to suggest . . ."

"I don't suggest." Ellesmere's voice was still hoarse, but under better control. "You sold me your daughter—and under false pretenses, I might add," the hoarse voice said sarcastically. "I paid thirty thousand pound for a virgin of good name. The first condition wasn't met, and I take leave to doubt the second." The sound of liquid being poured came through the door, followed by the scrape of a glass across a wooden tabletop.

"I would suggest that your burden of spirits is already excessive, sir," Dunsany said. His voice shook with an obvious attempt at mastery of his emotions. "I can only attribute the disgusting slurs you have cast upon my daughter's purity to your apparent intoxication. That being so, I shall take my grandson, and go."

"Oh, your *grand*son, is it?" Ellesmere's voice was slurred and sneering. "You seem damned sure of your daughter's 'purity.' Sure the brat isn't yours? She said—"

He broke off with a cry of astonishment, accompanied by a crash. Not daring to wait longer, Jamie plunged through the door, to find Ellesmere and Lord Dunsany entangled on the hearthrug, rolling to and fro in a welter of coats and limbs, both heedless of the fire behind them.

He took a moment to appraise the situation, then, seizing a fortuitous opening, reached into the fray and snatched his employer upright.

"Be still, my lord," he muttered in Dunsany's ear, dragging him back from Ellesmere's gasping form. Then, "Give over, ye auld fool!" he hissed, as Dunsany went on mindlessly struggling to reach his opponent. Ellesmere was almost as old as Dunsany, but more strongly built and clearly in better health, despite his drunkenness.

The Earl staggered to his feet, balding hair disheveled and bloodshot eyes glaring fixedly at Dunsany. He wiped his spittle-flecked mouth with the back of his hand, fat shoulders heaving.

"Filth," he said, almost conversationally. "Lay hands . . . on me, would you?" Still gasping for breath, he lurched toward the bell rope.

It was by no means certain that Lord Dunsany would stay on his feet, but there was no time to worry about that. Jamie let go of his employer, and lunged for Ellesmere's groping hand.

"No, my lord," he said, as respectfully as possible. Holding Ellesmere in a crude bear-leading embrace, he forced the heavyset Earl back across the room. "I think it would be . . . unwise . . . to involve your . . . servants." Grunting, he pushed Ellesmere into a chair.

"Best stay there, my lord." Jeffries, a drawn pistol in each hand, advanced warily into the room, his darting glance divided between Ellesmere, struggling to rise from the depths of the armchair, and Lord Dunsany, who clung precariously to a table edge, his aged face white as paper.

Jeffries glanced at Dunsany for instructions, and seeing none forthcoming, instinctively looked to Jamie. Jamie was conscious of a monstrous irritation; why should he be expected to deal with this imbroglio? Still, it was important that the Helwater party remove themselves from the premises with all haste. He stepped forward and took Dunsany by the arm.

"Let us go now, my lord," he said. Detaching the wilting Dunsany from the table, he tried to edge the tall old nobleman toward the door. Just at this moment of escape, though, the door was blocked.

"William?" Lady Dunsany's round face, splotched with the marks of recent grief, showed a sort of dull bewilderment at the scene in the study. In her arms was what looked like a large, untidy bundle of washing. She lifted this in a movement of vague inquiry. "The maid said you wanted me to bring the baby. What—" A roar from Ellesmere interrupted her. Heedless of the pointing pistols, the Earl sprang from his chair and shoved the gawking Jeffries out of the way.

"He's mine!" Knocking Lady Dunsany roughly against the paneling, Ellesmere snatched the bundle from her arms. Clutching it to his bosom, the Earl retreated toward the window. He glared at Dunsany, panting like a cornered beast.

"Mine, d'ye hear?"

The bundle emitted a loud shriek, as if in protest at this asseveration, and Dunsany, roused from his shock by the sight of his grandson in Ellesmere's arms, started forward, his features contorted in fury.

"Give him to me!"

"Go to hell, you codless scut!" With an unforeseen agility, Ellesmere dodged away from Dunsany. He flung back the draperies and cranked the window open with one hand, clutching the wailing child with the other.

"Get—out—of—my—house!" he panted, gasping with each revolution that edged the casement wider. "Go! Now, or I'll drop the little bastard, I swear I will!" To mark his threat, he thrust the yelling bundle toward the sill, and the empty dark where the wet stones of the courtyard waited, thirty feet below.

Past all conscious thought or any fear of consequence, Jamie Fraser acted on the instinct that had seen him through a dozen battles. He snatched one pistol from the transfixed Jeffries, turned on his heel, and fired in the same motion.

The roar of the shot struck everyone silent. Even the child ceased to scream. Ellesmere's face went quite blank, thick eyebrows raised in question. Then he staggered, and Jamie leapt forward, noting with a sort of detached clarity the small round hole in the baby's trailing drapery, where the pistol ball had passed through it.

He stood then rooted on the hearthrug, heedless of the fire scorching the backs of his legs, of the still-heaving body of Ellesmere at his feet, of the regular, hysterical shrieks of Lady Dunsany, piercing as a peacock's. He stood, eyes tight closed, shaking like a leaf, unable either to move or to think, arms wrapped tight about the shapeless, squirming, squawking bundle that contained his son.

◆

"I wish to speak to MacKenzie. Alone."

Lady Dunsany looked distinctly out of place in the stable. Small, plump, and impeccable in black linen, she looked like a china ornament, removed from its spot of cherished safety on the mantelpiece, and in imminent and constant peril of breakage, here in this world of rough animals and unshaven men.

Hughes, with a glance of complete astonishment at his mistress, bowed and tugged at his forelock before retreating to his den behind the tack room, leaving MacKenzie face-to-face with her.

Close to, the impression of fragility was heightened by the paleness of her face, touched faintly with pink at the corners of nose and eyes. She looked like a very small and dignified rabbit, dressed in mourning. Jamie felt that he should ask her to sit down, but there was no place for her to sit, save on a pile of hay or an upturned barrow.

"The coroner's court met this morning, MacKenzie," she said.

"Aye, milady." He had known that—they all had, and the other grooms had kept their distance from him all morning. Not out of respect; out of the dread for one who suffers from a deadly disease. Jeffries knew what had happened in the drawing room at Ellesmere, and that meant all the servants knew. But no one spoke of it.

"The verdict of the court was that the Earl of Ellesmere met his death by misadventure. The coroner's theory is that his lordship was—distraught"— she made a faint moue of distaste—"over my daughter's death." Her voice quivered faintly, but did not break. The fragile Lady Dunsany had borne up much better beneath the tragedy than had her husband; the servants' rumor had it that his lordship had not risen from his bed since his return from Ellesmere.

"Aye, milady?" Jeffries had been called to give evidence. MacKenzie had not. So far as the coroner's court was concerned, the groom MacKenzie had never set foot on Ellesmere.

Lady Dunsany's eyes met his, straight on. They were a pale bluish-green, like her daughter Isobel's, but the blond hair that glowed on Isobel was faded on her mother, touched with white strands that shone silver in the sun from the open door of the stable.

"We are grateful to you, MacKenzie," she said quietly.

"Thank ye, milady."

"Very grateful," she repeated, still gazing at him intently. "MacKenzie isn't your real name, is it?" she said suddenly.

"No, milady." A sliver of ice ran down his spine, despite the warmth of the afternoon sun on his shoulders. How much had the Lady Geneva told her mother before her death?

She seemed to feel his stiffening, for the edge of her mouth lifted in what he thought was meant as a smile of reassurance.

"I think I need not ask what it is, just yet," she said. "But I do have a question for you. MacKenzie—do you want to go home?"

"Home?" He repeated the word blankly.

"To Scotland." She was watching him intently. "I know who you are," she said. "Not your name, but that you're one of John's Jacobite prisoners. My husband told me."

Jamie watched her warily, but she didn't seem upset; no more so than would be natural in a woman who has just lost a daughter and gained a grandson, at least.

"I hope you will forgive the deception, milady," he said. "His Lordship—"

"Wished to save me distress," Lady Dunsany finished for him. "Yes, I know. William worries too much." Still, the deep line between her brows relaxed a bit at the thought of her husband's concern. The sight, with its underlying echo of marital devotion, gave him a faint and unexpected pang.

"We are not rich—you will have gathered that from Ellesmere's remarks," Lady Dunsany went on. "Helwater is rather heavily in debt. My grandson, however, is now the possessor of one of the largest fortunes in the county."

There seemed nothing to say to this but "Aye, milady?" though it made him feel rather like the parrot who lived in the main salon. He had seen it as he crept stealthily through the flowerbeds at sunset the day before, taking the chance of approaching the house while the family were dressing for dinner, in an attempt to catch a glimpse through a window of the new Earl of Ellesmere.

"We are very retired here," she went on. "We seldom visit London, and my husband has little influence in high circles. But—"

"Aye, milady?" He had some inkling by now of where her ladyship was heading with this roundabout conversation, and a feeling of sudden excitement hollowed the space beneath his ribs.

"John—Lord John Grey, that is—comes from a family with considerable influence. His stepfather is—well, that's of no consequence." She shrugged, the small black-linen shoulders dismissing the details.

"The point is that it might be possible to exert sufficient influence on your behalf to have you released from the conditions of your parole, so that you might return to Scotland. So I have come to ask you—do you want to go home, MacKenzie?"

He felt quite breathless, as though someone had punched him very hard in the stomach.

Scotland. To go away from this damp, spongy atmosphere, set foot on that forbidden road and walk it with a free, long stride, up into the crags and along the deer trails, to feel the air clearing and sharpening with the scent of gorse and heather. To go home!

To be a stranger no longer. To go away from hostility and loneliness, come down into Lallybroch, and see his sister's face light with joy at the sight of him, feel her arms around his waist, Ian's hug about his shoulders and the pummeling, grasping clutch of the children's hands, tugging at his clothes.

To go away, and never to see or hear of his own child again. He stared at Lady Dunsany, his face quite blank, so that she should not guess at the turmoil her offer had caused within him.

He had, at last, found the baby yesterday, lying asleep in a basket near the nursery window on the second floor. Perched precariously on the branch of a huge Norway spruce, he had strained his eyes to see through the screen of needles that hid him.

The child's face had been visible only in profile, one fat cheek resting on its ruffled shoulder. Its cap had slipped awry, so he could see the smooth, arching curve of the tiny skull, lightly dusted with a pale gold fuzz.

"Thank God it isn't red," had been his first thought, and he had crossed himself in reflexive thanksgiving.

"God, he's so small!" had been his second, coupled with an overwhelming urge to step through the window and pick the boy up. The smooth, beautifully shaped head would just fit, resting in the palm of his hand, and he could feel in memory the small squirming body that he had held so briefly to his heart.

"You're a strong laddie," he had whispered. "Strong and braw and bonny. But my God, you are so small!"

Lady Dunsany was waiting patiently. He bowed his head respectfully to her, not knowing whether he was making a terrible mistake, but unable to do otherwise.

"I thank ye, milady, but—I think I shall not go . . . just yet."

One pale eyebrow quivered slightly, but she inclined her head to him with equal grace.

"As you wish, MacKenzie. You have only to ask."

She turned like a tiny clockwork figure and left, going back to the world of Helwater, a thousand times more his prison now than it had ever been.

16

Willie

To his extreme surprise, the next few years were in many ways among the happiest of Jamie Fraser's life, aside from the years of his marriage.

Relieved of responsibility for tenants, followers, or anyone at all beyond himself and the horses in his charge, life was relatively simple. While the coroner's court had taken no notice of him, Jeffries had let slip enough about the death of Ellesmere that the other servants treated him with distant respect, but did not presume on his company.

He had enough to eat, sufficient clothes to keep warm and decent, and the occasional discreet letter from the Highlands reassured him that similar conditions obtained there.

One unexpected benefit of the quiet life at Helwater was that he had somehow resumed his odd half-friendship with Lord John Grey. The Major had, as promised, appeared once each quarter, staying each time for a few days to visit with the Dunsanys. He had made no attempt to gloat, though, or even to speak with Jamie, beyond the barest formal inquiry.

Very slowly, Jamie had realized all that Lady Dunsany had implied, in her offer to have him released. "John—Lord John Grey, that is—comes from a family with considerable influence. His stepfather is—well, that's of no consequence," she had said. It was of consequence, though. It had not been His Majesty's pleasure that had brought him here, rather than condemning him to the perilous ocean crossing and near-slavery in America; it had been John Grey's influence.

And he had not done it for revenge or from indecent motives, for he never gloated, made no advances; never said anything beyond the most common-place civilities. No, he had brought Jamie here because it was the best he could do; unable simply to release him at the time, Grey had done his best to ease the conditions of captivity—by giving him air, and light, and horses.

It took some effort, but he did it. When Grey next appeared in the stable-yard on his quarterly visit, Jamie had waited until the Major was alone, admiring the conformation of a big sorrel gelding. He had come to stand beside Grey, leaning on the fence. They watched the horse in silence for several minutes.

"King's pawn to king four," Jamie said quietly at last, not looking at the man beside him.

He felt the other's start of surprise, and felt Grey's eyes on him, but didn't turn his head. Then he felt the creak of the wood beneath his forearm as Grey turned back, leaning on the fence again.

"Queen's knight to queen bishop three," Grey replied, his voice a little huskier than usual.

Since then, Grey had come to the stables during each visit, to spend an evening perched on Jamie's crude stool, talking. They had no chessboard and seldom played verbally, but the late-night conversations continued— Jamie's only connection with the world beyond Helwater, and a small pleasure to which both of them looked forward once each quarter.

Above everything else, he had Willie. Helwater was dedicated to horses; even before the boy could stand solidly on his feet, his grandfather had him propped on a pony to be led round the paddock. By the time Willie was three, he was riding by himself—under the watchful eye of MacKenzie, the groom.

Willie was a strong, courageous, bonny little lad. He had a blinding smile, and could charm birds from the trees if he liked. He was also remarkably spoilt. As the ninth Earl of Ellesmere and the only heir to both Ellesmere and Helwater, with neither mother nor father to keep him under control, he ran roughshod over his doting grandparents, his young aunt, and every servant in the place—except MacKenzie.

And that was a near thing. So far, threats of not allowing the boy to help him with the horses had sufficed to quash Willie's worst excesses in the stables, but sooner or later, threats alone were not going to be sufficient, and MacKenzie the groom found himself wondering just what was going to happen when he finally lost his own control and clouted the wee fiend.

As a lad, he would himself have been beaten senseless by the nearest male relative within earshot, had he ever dared to address a woman the way he had heard Willie speak to his aunt and the maidservants, and the impulse to haul Willie into a deserted box stall and attempt to correct his manners was increasingly frequent.

Still, for the most part, he had nothing but joy in Willie. The boy adored MacKenzie, and as he grew older would spend hours in his company, riding on the huge draft horses as they pulled the heavy roller through the high fields, and perched precariously on the hay wagons as they came down from the upper pastures in summer.

There was a threat to this peaceful existence, though, which grew greater with each passing month. Ironically, the threat came from Willie himself, and was one he could not help.

"What a handsome little lad he is, to be sure! And such a lovely little rider!" It was Lady Grozier who spoke, standing on the veranda with Lady

Dunsany to admire Willie's peregrinations on his pony around the edge of the lawn.

Willie's grandmother laughed, eyeing the boy fondly. "Oh, yes. He loves his pony. We have a terrible time getting him even to come indoors for meals. And he's even more fond of his groom. We joke sometimes that he spends so much time with MacKenzie that he's even starting to *look* like MacKenzie!"

Lady Grozier, who had of course paid no attention to a groom, now glanced in MacKenzie's direction.

"Why, you're right!" she exclaimed, much amused. "Just look; Willie's got just that same cock to his head, and the same set to his shoulders! How funny!"

Jamie bowed respectfully to the ladies, but felt cold sweat pop out on his face.

He had seen this coming, but hadn't wanted to believe the resemblance was sufficiently pronounced as to be visible to anyone but himself. Willie as a baby had been fat and pudding-faced, and resembled no one at all. As he had grown, though, the pudginess had vanished from cheeks and chin, and while his nose was still the soft snub of childhood, the hint of high, broad cheek-bones was apparent, and the slaty-blue eyes of babyhood had grown dark blue and clear, thickly fringed with sooty lashes, and slightly slanted in appearance.

Once the ladies had gone into the house, and he could be sure no one was watching, Jamie passed a hand furtively over his own features. Was the resemblance truly that great? Willie's hair was a soft middle brown, with just a tinge of his mother's chestnut gleam. And those large, translucent ears—surely his own didn't stick out like that?

The trouble was that Jamie Fraser had not actually seen himself clearly for several years. Grooms did not have looking glasses, and he had sedulously avoided the company of the maids, who might have provided him with one.

Moving to the watering trough, he bent over it, casually, as though inspecting one of the water striders that skated over its surface. Beneath the wavering surface, flecked with floating bits of hay and crisscrossed by the dimpling striders, his own face stared up at him.

He swallowed, and saw the reflection's throat move. It was by no means a complete resemblance, but it was definitely there. More in the set and shape of the head and shoulders, as Lady Grozier had observed—but most definitely the eyes as well. Fraser eyes; his father, Brian, had had them, and his sister, Jenny, as well. Let the boy's bones go on pressing through his skin; let the child-snub nose grow long and straight, and the cheekbones still broader —and anyone would be able to see it.

The reflection in the trough vanished as he straightened up, and stood, staring blindly at the stable that had been home for the last several years. It was July and the sun was hot, but it made no impression on the chill that numbed his fingers and sent a shiver up his back.

It was time to speak to Lady Dunsany.

By the middle of September, everything had been arranged. The pardon had been procured; John Grey had brought it the day before. Jamie had a small amount of money saved, enough for traveling expenses, and Lady Dunsany had given him a decent horse. The only thing that remained was to bid farewell to his acquaintances at Helwater—and Willie.

"I shall be leaving tomorrow." Jamie spoke matter-of-factly, not taking his eyes off the bay mare's fetlock. The horny growth he was filing flaked away, leaving a dust of coarse black shavings on the stable floor.

"Where are you going? To Derwentwater? Can I come with you?" William, Viscount Dunsany, ninth Earl of Ellesmere, hopped down from the edge of the box stall, landing with a thump that made the bay mare start and snort.

"Don't do that," Jamie said automatically. "Have I not told ye to move quiet near Milly? She's skittish."

"Why?"

"You'd be skittish, too, if I squeezed your knee." One big hand darted out and pinched the muscle just above the boy's knee. Willie squeaked and jerked back, giggling.

"Can I ride Millyflower when you're done, Mac?"

"No," Jamie answered patiently, for the dozenth time that day. "I've told ye a thousand times, she's too big for ye yet."

"But I *want* to ride her!"

Jamie sighed but didn't answer, instead moving around to the other side of Milles Fleurs and picking up the left hoof.

"I *said* I want to ride Milly!"

"I heard ye."

"Then saddle her for me! Right now!"

The ninth Earl of Ellesmere had his chin thrust out as far as it would go, but the defiant look in his eye was tempered with a certain doubt as he intercepted Jamie's cold blue gaze. Jamie set the horse's hoof down slowly, just as slowly stood up, and drawing himself to his full height of six feet four, put his hands on his hips, looked down at the Earl, three feet six, and said, very softly, "No."

"Yes!" Willie stamped his foot on the hay-strewn floor. "You *have* to do what I tell you!"

"No, I don't."

"Yes, you do!"

"No, I . . . ." Shaking his head hard enough to make the red hair fly about his ears, Jamie pressed his lips tight together, then squatted down in front of the boy.

"See here," he said, "I havena got to do what ye say, for I'm no longer going to be groom here. I told ye, I shall be leaving tomorrow."

Willie's face went quite blank with shock, and the freckles on his nose stood out dark against the fair skin.

"You can't!" he said. "You can't leave."

"I have to."

"No!" The small Earl clenched his jaw, which gave him a truly startling resemblance to his paternal great-grandfather. Jamie thanked his stars that no one at Helwater had likely ever seen Simon Fraser, Lord Lovat. "I won't *let* you go!"

"For once, my lord, ye have nothing to say about it," Jamie replied firmly, his distress at leaving tempered somewhat by finally being allowed to speak his mind to the boy.

"If you leave . . ." Willie looked around helplessly for a threat, and spotted one easily to hand. "If you leave," he repeated more confidently, "I'll scream and shout and scare all the horses, so there!"

"Make a peep, ye little fiend, and I'll smack ye a good one!" Freed from his usual reserve, and alarmed at the thought of this spoiled brat upsetting the highly-strung and valuable horses, Jamie glared at the boy.

The Earl's eyes bulged with rage, and his face went red. He took a deep breath, then whirled and ran down the length of the stable, shrieking and waving his arms.

Milles Fleurs, already on edge from having her hoofs fiddled with, reared and plunged, neighing loudly. Her distress was echoed by kicks and high-pitched whinnying from the box stalls nearby, where Willie was roaring out all the bad words he knew—no small store—and kicking frenziedly at the doors of the stalls.

Jamie succeeded in catching Milles Fleurs's lead-rope and with considerable effort, managed to get the mare outside without damage to himself or the horse. He tied her to the paddock fence, and then strode back into the stable to deal with Willie.

"Damn, damn, *damn*!" the Earl was shrieking. "Sluire! Quim! Shit! Swive!"

Without a word, Jamie grabbed the boy by the collar, lifted him off his feet and carried him, kicking and squirming, to the farrier's stool he had been using. Here he sat down, flipped the Earl over his knee, and smacked his buttocks five or six times, hard. Then he jerked the boy up and set him on his feet.

"I *hate* you!" The Viscount's tear-smudged face was bright red and his fists trembled with rage.

"Well, I'm no verra fond of you either, ye little bastard!" Jamie snapped.

Willie drew himself up, fists clenched, purple in the face.

"I'm not a bastard!" he shrieked. "I'm not, I'm not! Take it back! Nobody can say that to me! Take it *back,* I said!"

Jamie stared at the boy in shock. There *had* been talk, then, and Willie had heard it. He had delayed his going too long.

He drew a deep breath, and then another, and hoped that his voice would not tremble.

"I take it back," he said softly. "I shouldna have used the word, my lord."

He wanted to kneel and embrace the boy, or pick him up and comfort him against his shoulder—but that was not a gesture a groom might make to an earl, even a young one. The palm of his left hand stung, and he curled his fingers tight over the only fatherly caress he was ever likely to give his son.

Willie knew how an earl should behave; he was making a masterful effort to subdue his tears, sniffing ferociously and swiping at his face with a sleeve.

"Allow me, my lord." Jamie did kneel then, and wiped the little boy's face gently with his own coarse handkerchief. Willie's eyes looked at him over the cotton folds, red-rimmed and woeful.

"Have you really got to go, Mac?" he asked, in a very small voice.

"Aye, I have." He looked into the dark blue eyes, so heartbreakingly like his own, and suddenly didn't give a damn what was right or who saw. He pulled the boy roughly to him, hugging him tight against his heart, holding the boy's face close to his shoulder, that Willie might not see the quick tears that fell into his thick, soft hair.

Willie's arms went around his neck and clung tight. He could feel the small, sturdy body shake against him with the force of suppressed sobbing. He patted the flat little back, and smoothed Willie's hair, and murmured things in Gaelic that he hoped the boy would not understand.

At length, he took the boy's arms from his neck and put him gently away.

"Come wi' me to my room, Willie; I shall give ye something to keep."

He had long since moved from the hayloft, taking over Hughes's snuggery beside the tack room when the elderly head groom retired. It was a small room, and very plainly furnished, but it had the twin virtues of warmth and privacy.

Besides the bed, the stool, and a chamber pot, there was a small table, on which stood the few books that he owned, a large candle in a pottery candlestick, and a smaller candle, thick and squat, that stood to one side before a small statue of the Virgin. It was a cheap wooden carving that Jenny had sent him, but it had been made in France, and was not without artistry.

"What's that little candle for?" Willie asked. "Grannie says only stinking Papists burn candles in front of heathen images."

"Well, I am a stinking Papist," Jamie said, with a wry twist of his mouth. "It's no a heathen image, though; it's a statue of the Blessed Mother."

"You are?" Clearly this revelation only added to the boy's fascination. "Why do Papists burn candles before statues, then?"

Jamie rubbed a hand through his hair. "Aye, well. It's . . . maybe a way of praying—and remembering. Ye light the candle, and say a prayer and think of people ye care for. And while it burns, the flame remembers them for ye."

"Who do you remember?" Willie glanced up at him. His hair was standing on end, rumpled by his earlier distress, but his blue eyes were clear with interest.

"Oh, a good many people. My family in the Highlands—my sister and her family. Friends. My wife." And sometimes the candle burned in memory of a young and reckless girl named Geneva, but he did not say that.

Willie frowned. "You haven't got a wife."

"No. Not anymore. But I remember her always."

Willie put out a stubby forefinger and cautiously touched the little statue. The woman's hands were spread in welcome, a tender maternity engraved on the lovely face.

"I want to be a stinking Papist, too," Willie said firmly.

"Ye canna do that!" Jamie exclaimed, half-amused, half-touched at the notion. "Your grandmama and your auntie would go mad."

"Would they froth at the mouth, like that mad fox you killed?" Willie brightened.

"I shouldna wonder," Jamie said dryly.

"I want to do it!" The small, clear features were set in determination. "I won't tell Grannie or Auntie Isobel; I won't tell anybody. Please, Mac! Please let me! I want to be like you!"

Jamie hesitated, both touched by the boy's earnestness, and suddenly wanting to leave his son with something more than the carved wooden horse he had made to leave as a farewell present. He tried to remember what Father McMurtry had taught them in the schoolroom about baptism. It was all right for a lay person to do it, he thought, provided that the situation was an emergency, and no priest was to hand.

It might be stretching a point to call the present situation an emergency, but . . . a sudden impulse made him reach down the jug of water that he kept on the sill.

The eyes that were like his watched, wide and solemn, as he carefully brushed the soft brown hair back from the high brow. He dipped three fingers into the water and carefully traced a cross on the lad's forehead.

"I baptize thee William James," he said softly, "in the name o' the Father, the Son, and the Holy Ghost. Amen."

Willie blinked, crossing his eyes as a drop of water rolled down his nose. He stuck out his tongue to catch it, and Jamie laughed, despite himself.

"Why did you call me William James?" Willie asked curiously. "My other names are Clarence Henry George." He made a face; Clarence wasn't his idea of a good name.

Jamie hid a smile. "Ye get a new name when you're baptized; James is your special Papist name. It's mine, too."

"It is?" Willie was delighted. "I'm a stinking Papist now, like you?"

"Aye, as much as I can manage, at least." He smiled down at Willie, then, struck by another impulse, reached into the neck of his shirt.

"Here. Keep this, too, to remember me by." He laid the beechwood rosary gently over Willie's head. "Ye canna let anyone see that, though," he warned. "And for God's sake, dinna tell anyone you're a Papist."

"I won't," Willie promised. "Not a soul." He tucked the rosary into his shirt, patting carefully to be sure that it was hidden.

"Good." Jamie reached out and ruffled Willie's hair in dismissal. "It's almost time for your tea; ye'd best go on up to the house now."

· Willie started for the door, but stopped halfway, suddenly distressed again, with a hand pressed flat to his chest.

"You said to keep this to remember you. But I haven't got anything for you to remember me by!"

Jamie smiled slightly. His heart was squeezed so tight, he thought he could not draw breath to speak, but he forced the words out.

"Dinna fret yourself," he said. "I'll remember ye."

17

Monsters Rising

Brianna blinked, brushing back a bright web of hair caught by the wind. "I'd almost forgotten what the sun looks like," she said, squinting at the object in question, shining with unaccustomed ferocity on the dark waters of Loch Ness.

Her mother stretched luxuriously, enjoying the light wind. "To say nothing of what fresh air is like. I feel like a toadstool that's been growing in the dark for weeks—all pale and squashy."

"Fine scholars the two of you would make," Roger said, but grinned. All three of them were in high spirits. After the arduous slog through the prison records to narrow the search to Ardsmuir, they had had a run of luck. The records for Ardsmuir were complete, in one spot, and—in comparison to most others—remarkably clear. Ardsmuir had been a prison for only fifteen years; following its renovation by Jacobite prison-labor, it had been converted into a small permanent garrison, and the prison population dispersed—mostly transported to the American Colonies.

"I still can't imagine why Fraser wasn't sent along to America with the rest," Roger said. He had had a moment's panic there, going over and over the list of transported convicts from Ardsmuir, searching the names one by one, nearly letter by letter, and still finding no Frasers. He had been certain that Jamie Fraser had died in prison, and had been in a cold sweat of fear over the thought of telling the Randall women—until the flip of a page had showed him Fraser's parole to a place named Helwater.

"I don't know," Claire said, "but it's a bloody good thing he wasn't. He's —he *was*—" she caught herself quickly, but not quickly enough to stop Roger noticing the slip—"terribly, terribly seasick." She gestured at the surface of the loch before them, dancing with tiny waves. "Even going out on something like that would turn him green in minutes."

Roger glanced at Brianna with interest. "Are you seasick?"

She shook her head, bright hair lifting in the wind. "Nah." She patted her bare midriff smugly. "Cast-iron."

Roger laughed. "Want to go out, then? It's your holiday, after all."

"Really? Could we? Can you fish in there?" Brianna shaded her eyes, looking eagerly out over the dark water.

"Certainly. I've caught salmon and eels many a time in Loch Ness," Roger assured her. "Come along; we'll rent a wee boat at the dock in Drumnadrochit."

The drive to Drumnadrochit was a delight. The day was one of those clear, bright summer days that cause tourists from the South to stampede into Scotland in droves during August and September. With one of Fiona's larger breakfasts inside him, one of her lunches stowed in a basket in the boot, and Brianna Randall, long hair blowing in the wind, seated beside him, Roger was strongly disposed to consider that all was right with the world.

He allowed himself to dwell with satisfaction on the results of their researches. It had meant taking additional leave from his college for the summer term, but it had been worth it.

After finding the record of James Fraser's parole, it had taken another two weeks of slog and inquiry—even a quick weekend trip by Roger and Bree to the Lake District, another by all three of them to London—and then the sight that had made Brianna whoop out loud in the middle of the British Museum's sacrosanct Reading Room, causing their hasty departure amid waves of icy disapproval. The sight of the Royal Warrant of Pardon, stamped with the seal of George III, *Rex Angleterre,* dated 1764, bearing the name of "James Alex*drl* M'Kensie Frazier."

"We're getting close," Roger had said, gloating over the photocopy of the Warrant of Pardon. "Bloody close!"

"Close?" Brianna had said, but then had been distracted by the sight of their bus approaching, and had not pursued the matter. Roger had caught Claire's eye on him, though; she knew very well what he meant.

She would, of course, have been thinking of it; he wondered whether Brianna had. Claire had disappeared into the past in 1945, vanishing through the circle of standing stones on Craigh na Dun and reappearing in 1743. She had lived with Jamie Fraser for nearly three years, then returned through the stones. And she had come back nearly three years past the time of her original disappearance, in April of 1948.

All of which meant—just possibly—that if she were disposed to try the trip back through the stones once more, she would likely arrive twenty years past the time she had left—in 1766. And 1766 was only two years past the latest known date at which Jamie Fraser had been located, alive and well. If he had survived another two years, and if Roger could find him . . .

"There it is!" Brianna said suddenly. " 'Boats for Rent.' " She pointed at the sign in the window of the dockside pub, and Roger nosed the car into a parking slot outside, with no further thought of Jamie Fraser.

———————

"I wonder why short men are so often enamored of very tall women?" Claire's voice behind him echoed Roger's thoughts with an uncanny accuracy—and not for the first time.

"Moth and flame syndrome, perhaps?" Roger suggested, frowning at the diminutive barman's evident fascination with Brianna. He and Claire were standing before the counter for rentals, waiting for the clerk to write up the receipt while Brianna bought bottles of Coca-Cola and brown ale to augment their lunch.

The young barman, who came up approximately to Brianna's armpit, was hopping to and fro, offering pickled eggs and slices of smoked tongue, eyes worshipfully upturned to the yellow-haltered goddess before him. From her laughter, Brianna appeared to think the man "cute."

"I always told Bree not to get involved with short men," Claire observed, watching this.

"Did you?" Roger said dryly. "Somehow I didn't envision you being all that much in the motherly advice line."

She laughed, disregarding his momentary sourness. "Well, I'm not, all that much. When you notice an important principle like that, though, it seems one's motherly duty to pass it along."

"Something wrong with short men, is there?" Roger inquired.

"They tend to turn mean if they don't get their way," Claire answered. "Like small yapping dogs. Cute and fluffy, but cross them and you're likely to get a nasty nip in the ankle."

Roger laughed. "This observation is the result of years of experience, I take it?"

"Oh, yes." She nodded, glancing up at him. "I've never met an orchestra conductor over five feet tall. Vicious specimens, practically all of them. But tall men"—her lips curved slightly as she surveyed his six-feet-three-inch frame—"tall men are almost always very sweet and gentle."

"Sweet, eh?" said Roger, with a cynical glance at the barman, who was cutting up a jellied eel for Brianna. Her face expressed a wary distaste, but she leaned forward, wrinkling her nose as she took the bite offered on a fork.

"With women," Claire amplified. "I've always thought it's because they realize that they don't have anything to prove; when it's perfectly obvious that they can do anything they like whether you want them to or not, they don't need to try to prove it."

"While a short man—" Roger prompted.

"While a short one knows he can't do anything unless you let him, and the knowledge drives him mad, so he's always trying something on, just to prove he can."

"Mmphm." Roger made a Scottish noise in the back of his throat, meant to convey both appreciation of Claire's acuity, and general suspicion of what the barman might be wanting to prove to Brianna.

"Thanks," he said to the clerk, who shoved the receipt across the counter to him. "Ready, Bree?" he asked.

The loch was calm and the fishing slow, but it was pleasant on the water, with the August sun warm on their backs and the scent of raspberry canes and sun-warmed pine trees wafting from the nearby shore. Full of lunch, they all grew drowsy, and before long, Brianna was curled up in the bow, asleep with her head pillowed on Roger's jacket. Claire sat in the stern, blinking, but still awake.

"What about short and tall women?" Roger asked, resuming their earlier conversation as he sculled slowly across the loch. He glanced over his shoulder at the amazing length of Brianna's legs, awkwardly curled under her. "Same thing? The little ones nasty?"

Claire shook her head meditatively, the curls beginning to work their way loose from her hairclip. "No, I don't think so. It doesn't seem to have anything to do with size. I think it's more a matter of whether they see men as The Enemy, or just see them as men, and on the whole, rather like them for it."

"Oh, to do with women's liberation, is it?"

"No, not at all," Claire said. "I saw just the same kinds of behavior between men and women in 1743 that you see now. Some differences, of course, in how they each behave, but not so much in how they behave to each other."

She looked out over the dark waters of the loch, shading her eyes with her hand. She might have been keeping an eye out for otters and floating logs, but Roger thought that far-seeing gaze was looking a bit farther than the cliffs of the opposite shore.

"You like men, don't you?" he said quietly. "Tall men."

She smiled briefly, not looking at him.

"One," she said softly.

"Will you go, then—if I can find him?" he rested his oars momentarily, watching her.

She drew a deep breath before answering. The wind flushed her cheeks with pink and molded the fabric of the white shirt to her figure, showing off a high bosom and a slender waist. Too young to be a widow, he thought, too lovely to be wasted.

"I don't know," she said, a little shakily. "The thought of it—or rather, the *thoughts* of it! On the one hand, to find Jamie—and then, on the other, to . . . go through again." A shudder went through her, closing her eyes.

"It's indescribable, you know," she said, eyes still closed as though she saw inside them the ring of stones on Craigh na Dun. "Horrible, but horrible in a way that isn't like other horrible things, so you can't say." She opened her eyes and smiled wryly at him.

"A bit like trying to tell a man what having a baby is like; he can more or less grasp the idea that it's painful, but he isn't equipped actually to understand what it feels like."

Roger grunted with amusement. "Oh, aye? Well, there's some difference, you know. I've actually heard those bloody stones." He shivered himself, involuntarily. The memory of the night, three months ago, when Gillian Edgars had gone through the stones, was not one he willingly called to mind; it had come back to him in nightmares several times, though. He heaved strongly on the oars, trying to erase it.

"Like being torn apart, isn't it?" he said, his eyes intent on hers. "There's something pulling at you, ripping, dragging, and not just outside—inside you as well, so you feel your skull will fly to pieces any moment. And the filthy noise." He shuddered again. Claire's face had gone slightly pale.

"I didn't know you could hear them," she said. "You didn't tell me."

"It didn't seem important." He studied her a moment, as he pulled, then added quietly, "Bree heard them as well."

"I see." She turned to look back over the loch, where the wake of the tiny boat spread its V-shaped wings. Far behind, the waves from the passage of a larger boat reflected back from the cliffs and joined again in the center of the loch, making a long, humped form of glistening water—a standing wave, a phenomenon of the loch that had often been mistaken for a sighting of the monster.

"It's there, you know," she said suddenly, nodding down into the black, peat-laden water.

He opened his mouth to ask what she meant, but then realized that he *did* know. He had lived near Loch Ness for most of his life, fished for eels and salmon in its waters, and heard—and laughed at—every story of the "fearsome beastie" that had ever been told in the pubs of Drumnadrochit and Fort Augustus.

Perhaps it was the unlikeliness of the situation—sitting here, calmly discussing whether the woman with him should or should not take the unimaginable risk of catapulting herself into an unknown past. Whatever the cause of his certainty, it seemed suddenly not only possible, but sure, that the dark water of the loch hid unknown but fleshly mystery.

"What do you think it is?" he asked, as much to give his disturbed feelings time to settle, as out of curiosity.

Claire leaned over the side, watching intently as a log drifted into view.

"The one I saw was probably a plesiosaur," she said at last. She didn't look at Roger, but kept her gaze astern. "Though I didn't take notes at the time." Her mouth twisted in something not quite a smile.

"How many stone circles are there?" she asked abruptly. "In Britain, in Europe. Do you know?"

"Not exactly. Several hundred, though," he answered cautiously. "Do you think they're all—"

"How should I know?" she interrupted impatiently. "The point is, they may be. They were set up to mark something, which means there may be the hell of a lot of places where that something has happened." She tilted her head to one side, wiping the windblown hair out of her face, and gave him a lopsided smile.

"That would explain it, you know."

"Explain what?" Roger felt fogged by the rapid shifts of her conversation.

"The monster." She gestured out over the water. "What if there's another of those—places—under the loch?"

"A time corridor—passage—whatever?" Roger looked out over the purling wake, staggered by the idea.

"It would explain a lot." There was a smile hiding at the corner of her mouth, behind the veil of blowing hair. He couldn't tell whether she was serious or not. "The best candidates for monster are all things that have been extinct for hundreds of thousands of years. If there's a time passage under the loch, that would take care of that little problem."

"It would also explain why the reports are sometimes different," Roger said, becoming intrigued by the idea. "If it's different creatures who come through."

"And it would explain why the creature—or creatures—haven't been caught, and aren't seen all that often. Maybe they go back the other way, too, so they aren't in the loch all the time."

"What a marvelous idea!" Roger said. He and Claire grinned at each other.

"You know what?" she said. "I'll bet that isn't going to make it on the list of popular theories."

Roger laughed, catching a crab, and droplets of water sprayed over Brianna. She snorted, sat up abruptly, blinking, then sank back down, face flushed with sleep, and was breathing heavily within seconds.

"She was up late last night, helping me box up the last set of records to go back to the University of Leeds," Roger said, defensive on her behalf.

Claire nodded abstractedly, watching her daughter.

"Jamie could do that," she said softly. "Lie down and sleep anywhere."

She fell silent. Roger rowed steadily on, toward the point of the loch where the grim bulk of the ruins of Castle Urquhart stood amid its pines.

"The thing is," Claire said at last, "it gets harder. Going through the first time was the most terrible thing I'd ever had happen to me. Coming back was a thousand times worse." Her eyes were fixed on the looming castle.

"I don't know whether it was because I didn't come back on the right day—it was Beltane when I went, and two weeks before, when I came back."

"Geilie—Gillian, I mean—she went on Beltane, too." In spite of the heat of the day, Roger felt slightly cold, seeing again the figure of the woman who had been both his ancestor and his contemporary, standing in the light of a blazing bonfire, fixed for a moment in the light, before disappearing forever into the cleft of the standing stones.

"That's what her notebook said—that the door is open on the Sun Feasts and the Fire Feasts. Perhaps it's only partly open as you near those times. Or perhaps she was wrong altogether; after all, she thought you had to have a human sacrifice to make it work."

Claire swallowed heavily. The petrol-soaked remains of Greg Edgars, Gillian's husband, had been recovered from the stone circle by the police, on May Day. The record concluded of his wife only, "Fled, whereabouts unknown."

Claire leaned over the side, trailing a hand in the water. A small cloud drifted over the sun, turning the loch a sudden gray, with dozens of small waves rising on the surface as the light wind increased. Directly below, in the wake of the boat, the water was darkly impenetrable. Seven hundred feet deep is Loch Ness, and bitter cold. What can live in a place like that?

"Would you go down there, Roger?" she asked softly. "Jump overboard, dive in, go on down through that dark until your lungs were bursting, not knowing whether there are things with teeth and great heavy bodies waiting?"

Roger felt the hair on his arms rise, and not only because the sudden wind was chilly.

"But that's not all the question," she continued, still staring into the blank, mysterious water. "Would you go, if Brianna were down there?" She straightened up and turned to face him.

"Would you go?" The amber eyes were intent on his, unblinking as a hawk's.

He licked his lips, chapped and dried by the wind, and cast a quick look over his shoulder at Brianna, sleeping. He turned back to face Claire.

"Yes. I think I would."

She looked at him for a long moment, and then nodded, unsmiling.

"So would I."

PART FIVE

You Can't Go Home Again

18

Roots

The woman next to me probably weighed three hundred pounds. She wheezed in her sleep, lungs laboring to lift the burden of her massive bosom for the two-hundred-thousandth time. Her hip and thigh and pudgy arm pressed against mine, unpleasantly warm and damp.

There was no escape; I was pinned on the other side by the steel curve of the plane's fuselage. I eased one arm upward and flicked on the overhead light in order to see my watch. Ten-thirty, by London time; at least another six hours before the landing in New York promised escape.

The plane was filled with the collective sighs and snorts of passengers dozing as best they might. Sleep for me was out of the question. With a sigh of resignation, I dug into the pocket in front of me for the half-finished romance novel I had stashed there. The tale was by one of my favorite authors, but I found my attention slipping from the book—either back to Roger and Brianna, whom I had left in Edinburgh, there to continue the hunt, or forward, to what awaited me in Boston.

I wasn't sure just what *did* await me, which was part of the problem. I had been obliged to come back, if only temporarily; I had long since exhausted my vacation, plus several extensions. There were matters to be dealt with at the hospital, bills to be collected and paid at home, the maintenance of the house and yard to be attended to—I shuddered to think what heights the lawn in the backyard must have attained by now—friends to be called on . . .

One friend in particular. Joseph Abernathy had been my closest friend, from medical school on. Before I made any final—and likely irrevocable—decisions, I wanted to talk to him. I closed the book in my lap and sat tracing the extravagant loops of the title with one finger, smiling a little. Among other things, I owed a taste for romance novels to Joe.

I had known Joe since the beginning of my medical training. He stood out among the other interns at Boston General, just as I did. I was the only woman among the budding doctors; Joe was the only black intern.

Our shared singularity gave us each a special awareness for the other; both of us sensed it clearly, though neither mentioned it. We worked together very well, but both of us were wary—for good reason—of exposing ourselves, and the tenuous bond between us, much too nebulous to be called friendship, remained unacknowledged until near the end of our internship.

I had done my first unassisted surgery that day—an uncomplicated appendectomy, done on a teenaged boy in good health. It had gone well, and there was no reason to think there would be postoperative complications. Still, I felt an odd kind of possessiveness about the boy, and didn't want to go home until he was awake and out of Recovery, even though my shift had ended. I changed clothes and went to the doctors' lounge on the third floor to wait.

The lounge wasn't empty. Joseph Abernathy sat in one of the rump-sprung stuffed chairs, apparently absorbed in a copy of *U.S. News & World Report*. He looked up as I entered, and nodded briefly to me before returning to his reading.

The lounge was equipped with stacks of magazines—salvaged from the waiting rooms—and a number of tattered paperbacks, abandoned by departing patients. Seeking distraction, I thumbed past a six-month-old copy of *Studies in Gastroenterology,* a ragged copy of *Time* magazine, and a neat stack of *Watchtower* tracts. Finally picking up one of the books, I sat down with it.

It had no cover, but the title page read *The Impetuous Pirate.* "A sensuous, compelling love story, boundless as the Spanish Main!" said the line beneath the title. The Spanish Main, eh? If escape was what I wanted, I couldn't do much better, I thought, and opened the book at random. It fell open automatically to page 42.

> *Tipping up her nose scornfully, Tessa tossed her lush blond tresses back, oblivious to the fact that this caused her voluptuous breasts to become even more prominent in the low-necked dress. Valdez's eyes widened at the sight, but he gave no outward sign of the effect such wanton beauty had on him.*
>
> *"I thought that we might become better acquainted, Señorita,"*
> *he suggested, in a low, sultry voice that made little shivers of antici-*
> *pation run up and down Tessa's back.*
>
> *"I have no interest in becoming acquainted with a . . . a . . .*
> *filthy, despicable, underhanded pirate!" she said.*
>
> *Valdez's teeth gleamed as he smiled at her, his hand stroking the*

handle of the dagger at his belt. He was impressed at her fearlessness; so bold, so impetuous . . . and so beautiful.

I raised an eyebrow, but went on reading, fascinated.

> *With an air of imperious possession, Valdez swooped an arm about Tessa's waist.*
>
> *"You forget, Señorita," he murmured, the words tickling her sensitive earlobe, "you are a prize of war; and the Captain of a pirate ship has first choice of the booty!"*
>
> *Tessa struggled in his powerful arms as he bore her to the berth and tossed her lightly onto the jeweled coverlet. She struggled to catch her breath, watching in terror as he undressed, laying aside his azure-blue velvet coat and then the fine ruffled white linen shirt. His chest was magnificent, a smooth expanse of gleaming bronze. Her fingertips ached to touch it, even though her heart pounded deafeningly in her ears as he reached for the waistband of his breeches.*
>
> *"But no," he said, pausing. "It is unfair of me to neglect you, Señorita. Allow me." With an irresistible smile, he bent and gently cupped Tessa's breasts in the heated palms of his calloused hands, enjoying the voluptuous weight of them through the thin silken fabric. With a small scream, Tessa shrank away from his probing touch, pressing back against the lace-embroidered feather pillow.*
>
> *"You resist? What a pity to spoil such fine clothing, Señorita . . ." He took a firm grasp on her jade-silk bodice and yanked, causing Tessa's fine white breasts to leap out of their concealment like a pair of plump partridges taking wing.*

I made a sound, causing Dr. Abernathy to look sharply over the top of his *U.S. News & World Report*. Hastily rearranging my face into a semblance of dignified absorption, I turned the page.

> *Valdez's thick black curls swept her chest as he fastened his hot lips on Tessa's rose-pink nipples, making waves of anguished desire wash through her being. Weakened by the unaccustomed feelings that his ardor aroused in her, she was unable to move as his hand stealthily sought the hem of her gown and his blazing touch traced tendrils of sensation up the length of her slender thigh.*
>
> *"Ah,* mi amor,*" he groaned. "So lovely, so pure. You drive me mad with desire,* mi amor. *I have wanted you since I first saw you, so proud and cold on the deck of your father's ship. But not so cold now, my dear, eh?"*
>
> *In fact, Valdez's kisses were wreaking havoc on Tessa's feelings. How, how could she be feeling such things for this man, who had*

cold-bloodedly sunk her father's ship, and murdered a hundred men with his own hands? She should be recoiling in horror, but instead she found herself gasping for breath, opening her mouth to receive his burning kisses, arching her body in involuntary abandon beneath the demanding pressure of his burgeoning manhood.

"Ah, mi amor," he gasped. "I cannot wait. But . . . I do not wish to hurt you. Gently, mi amor, gently."

Tessa gasped as she felt the increasing pressure of his desire making its presence known between her legs.

"Oh!" she said. "Oh, please! You can't! I don't want you to!"
[Fine time to start making protests, I thought.]

"Don't worry, mi amor. Trust me."

Gradually, little by little, she relaxed under the touch of his hypnotic caresses, feeling the warmth in her stomach grow and spread. His lips brushed her breast, and his hot breath, murmuring reassurances, took away all her resistance. As she relaxed, her thighs opened without her willing it. Moving with infinite slowness, his engorged shaft teased aside the membrane of her innocence . . .

I let out a whoop and lost my grasp on the book, which slid off my lap and fell on the floor with a plop near Dr. Abernathy's feet.

"Excuse me," I murmured, and bent to retrieve it, my face flaming. As I came up with *The Impetuous Pirate* in my sweaty grasp, though, I saw that far from preserving his usual austere mien, Dr. Abernathy was grinning widely.

"Let me guess," he said. "Valdez just teased aside the membrane of her innocence?"

"Yes," I said, breaking out into helpless giggling again. "How did you know?"

"Well, you weren't too far into it," he said, taking the book from my hand. His short, blunt fingers flicked the pages expertly. "It had to be that one, or maybe the one on page 73, where he laves her pink mounds with his hungry tongue."

"He *what?*"

"See for yourself." He thrust the book back into my hands, pointing to a spot halfway down the page.

Sure enough, "*. . . lifting aside the coverlet, he bent his coal-black head and laved her pink mounds with his hungry tongue. Tessa moaned and . . .*" I gave an unhinged shriek.

"You've actually *read* this?" I demanded, tearing my eyes away from Tessa and Valdez.

"Oh, yeah," he said, the grin widening. He had a gold tooth, far back on the right side. "Two or three times. It's not the best one, but it isn't bad."

"The best one? There are *more* like this?"

"Sure. Let's see . . ." He rose and began digging through the pile of tattered paperbacks on the table. "You want to look for the ones with no covers," he explained. "Those are the best."

"And here I thought you never read anything but *Lancet* and the *Journal of the AMA,*" I said.

"What, I spend thirty-six hours up to my elbows in people's guts, and I want to come up here and read 'Advances in Gallbladder Resection?' Hell, no—I'd rather sail the Spanish Main with Valdez." He eyed me with some interest, the grin still not quite gone. "I didn't think you read anything but *The New England Journal of Medicine,* either, Lady Jane," he said. "Appearances are deceiving, huh?"

"Must be," I said dryly. "What's this 'Lady Jane'?"

"Oh, Hoechstein started that one," he said, leaning back with his fingers linked around one knee. "It's the voice, that accent that sounds like you just drank tea with the Queen. That's what you've got, keeps the guys from bein' worse than they are. See, you sound like Winston Churchill—if Winston Churchill was a lady, that is—and that scares them a little. You've got somethin' else, though"—he viewed me thoughtfully, rocking back in his chair. "You have a way of talking like you expect to get your way, and if you don't, you'll know the reason why. Where'd you learn that?"

"In the war," I said, smiling at his description.

His eyebrows went up. "Korea?"

"No, I was a combat nurse during the Second World War; in France. I saw a lot of Head Matrons who could turn interns and orderlies to jelly with a glance." And later, I had had a good deal of practice, where that air of inviolate authority—assumed though it might be—had stood me in good stead against people with a great deal more power than the nursing staff and interns of Boston General Hospital.

He nodded, absorbed in my explanation. "Yeah, that makes sense. I used Walter Cronkite, myself."

"Walter *Cron*kite?" I goggled at him.

He grinned again, showing his gold tooth. "You can think of somebody better? Besides, I got to hear him for free on the radio or the TV every night. I used to entertain my mama—she wanted me to be a preacher." He smiled, half ruefully. "If I talked like Walter Cronkite where we lived in those days, I wouldn't have *lived* to go to med school."

I was liking Joe Abernathy more by the second. "I hope your mother wasn't disappointed that you became a doctor intstead of a preacher."

"Tell you the truth, I'm not sure," he said, still grinning. "When I told her, she stared at me for a minute, then heaved a big sigh and said, 'Well, at least you can get my rheumatism medicine for me cheap.'"

I laughed wryly. "I didn't get *that* much enthusiasm when I told my husband I was going to be a doctor. He stared at me, and finally said if I was bored, why didn't I volunteer to write letters for the inmates of the nursing home."

Joe's eyes were a soft golden brown, like toffee drops. There was a glint of humor in them as they fixed on me.

"Yeah, folks still think it's fine to say to your face that you can't be doing what you're doing. 'Why are you here, little lady, and not home minding your man and child?' " he mimicked.

He grinned wryly, and patted my hand. "Don't worry, they'll give it up sooner or later. They mostly don't ask me to my face anymore why I ain't cleanin' the toilets, like God made me to."

Then the nurse had come with word that my appendix was awake, and I had left, but the friendship begun on page 42 had flourished, and Joe Abernathy had become one of my best friends; possibly the only person close to me who truly understood what I did, and why.

I smiled a little, feeling the slickness of the embossing on the cover. Then I leaned forward and put the book back into the seat pocket. Perhaps I didn't want to escape just now.

Outside, a floor of moonlit cloud cut us off from the earth below. Up here, everything was silent, beautiful and serene, in marked contrast to the turmoil of life below.

I had the odd feeling of being suspended, motionless, cocooned in solitude, even the heavy breathing of the woman next to me only a part of the white noise that makes up silence, one with the tepid rush of the air-conditioning and the shuffle of the stewardesses' shoes along the carpet. At the same time, I knew we were rushing on inexorably through the air, propelled at hundreds of miles per hour to some end—as for it being a safe one, we could only hope.

I closed my eyes, in suspended animation. Back in Scotland, Roger and Bree were hunting Jamie. Ahead, in Boston, my job—and Joe—were waiting. And Jamie himself? I tried to push the thought away, determined not to think of him until the decision was made.

I felt a slight ruffling of my hair, and one lock brushed against my cheek, light as a lover's touch. But surely it was no more than the rush of air from the vent overhead, and my imagination that the stale smells of perfume and cigarettes were suddenly underlaid by the scents of wool and heather.

19

To Lay a Ghost

home at last, to the house on Furey Street, where I had lived with Frank and Brianna for nearly twenty years. The azaleas by the door were not quite dead, but their leaves hung in limp, shabby clusters, a thick layer of fallen leaves curling on the dry-baked bed underneath. It was a hot summer—there wasn't any other kind in Boston—and the August rains hadn't come, even though it was mid-September by now.

I set my bags by the front door and went to turn on the hose. It had been lying in the sun; the green rubber snake was hot enough to burn my hand, and I shifted it uneasily from palm to palm until the rumble of water brought it suddenly alive and cooled it with a burst of spray.

I didn't like azaleas all that much to start with. I would have pulled them out long since, but I had been reluctant to alter any detail of the house after Frank's death, for Brianna's sake. Enough of a shock, I thought, to begin university and have your father die in one year, without more changes. I had been ignoring the house for a long time; I could go on doing so.

"All right!" I said crossly to the azaleas, as I turned off the hose. "I hope you're happy, because that's all you get. I want to go have a drink myself. And a bath," I added, seeing their mud-spattered leaves.

I sat on the edge of the big sunken tub in my dressing gown, watching the water thunder in, churning the bubble bath into clouds of perfumed seafoam. Steam rose from the boiling surface; the water would be almost too hot.

I turned it off—one quick, neat twist of the tap—and sat for a moment, the house around me still save for the crackle of popping bath bubbles, faint as the sounds of a far-off battle. I realized perfectly well what I was doing. I had been doing it ever since I stepped aboard the Flying Scotsman in Inverness, and felt the thrum of the track come alive beneath my feet. I was testing myself.

I had been taking careful note of the machines—all the contrivances of modern daily life—and more important, of my own response to them. The train to Edinburgh, the plane to Boston, the taxicab from the airport, and all the dozens of tiny mechanical flourishes attending—vending machines, street lights, the plane's mile-high lavatory, with its swirl of nasty blue-green disinfectant, whisking waste and germs away with the push of a button. Restaurants, with their tidy certificates from the Department of Health, guaranteeing at least a better than even chance of escaping food poisoning when eating therein. Inside my own house, the omnipresent buttons that supplied light and heat and water and cooked food.

The question was—did I care? I dipped a hand into the steaming bathwater and swirled it to and fro, watching the shadows of the vortex dancing in the marble depths. Could I live without all the "conveniences," large and small, to which I was accustomed?

I had been asking myself that with each touch of a button, each rumble of a motor, and was quite sure that the answer was "yes." Time didn't make all the difference, after all; I could walk across the city and find people who lived without many of these conveniences—farther abroad and there were entire countries where people lived in reasonable content and complete ignorance of electricity.

For myself, I had never cared a lot. I had lived with my uncle Lamb, an eminent archaeologist, since my own parents' death when I was five. Consequently, I had grown up in conditions that could conservatively be called "primitive," as I accompanied him on all his field expeditions. Yes, hot baths and light bulbs were nice, but I had lived without them during several periods of my life—during the war, for instance—and never found the lack of them acute.

The water had cooled enough to be tolerable. I dropped the dressing gown on the floor and stepped in, feeling a pleasant shiver as the heat at my feet made my shoulders prickle in cool contrast.

I subsided into the tub and relaxed, stretching my legs. Eighteenth-century hip baths were barely more than large barrels; one normally bathed in segments, immersing the center of the body first, with the legs hanging outside, then stood up and rinsed the upper torso while soaking the feet. More frequently, one bathed from a pitcher and basin, with the aid of a cloth.

No, conveniences and comforts were merely that. Nothing essential, nothing I couldn't do without.

Not that conveniences were the only issue, by a long chalk. The past was a dangerous country. But even the advances of so-called civilization were no guarantee of safety. I had lived through two major "modern" wars—actually served on the battlefields of one of them—and could see another taking shape on the telly every evening.

"Civilized" warfare was, if anything, more horrifying than its older versions. Daily life might be safer, but only if one chose one's walk in it with care. Parts of Roxbury now were as dangerous as any alley I had walked in the Paris of two hundred years past.

I sighed and pulled up the plug with my toes. No use speculating about impersonal things like bathtubs, bombs, and rapists. Indoor plumbing was no more than a minor distraction. The real issue was the people involved, and always had been. Me, and Brianna, and Jamie.

The last of the water gurgled away. I stood up, feeling slightly light-headed, and wiped away the last of the bubbles. The big mirror was misted with steam, but clear enough to show me myself from the knees upward, pink as a boiled shrimp.

Dropping the towel, I looked myself over. Flexed my arms, raised them overhead, checking for bagginess. None; biceps and triceps all nicely defined, deltoids neatly rounded and sloping into the high curve of the pectoralis major. I turned slightly to one side, tensing and relaxing my abdominals—obliques in decent tone, the rectus abdominis flattening almost to concavity.

"Good thing the family doesn't run to fat," I murmured. Uncle Lamb had remained trim and taut to the day of his death at seventy-five. I supposed my father—Uncle Lamb's brother—had been constructed similarly, and wondered suddenly what my mother's backside had looked like. Women, after all, had a certain amount of excess adipose tissue to contend with.

I turned all the way round and peered back over my shoulder at the mirror. The long columnar muscles of my back gleamed wetly as I twisted; I still had a waist, and a good narrow one, too.

As for my own backside—"Well, no dimples, anyway," I said aloud. I turned around and stared at my reflection.

"It could be a lot worse," I said to it.

Feeling somewhat heartened, I put on my nightgown and went about the business of putting the house to bed. No cats to put out, no dogs to feed—Bozo, the last of our dogs, had died of old age the year before, and I had not wanted to get another, with Brianna off at school and my own hours at the hospital long and irregular.

Adjust the thermostat, check the locks of windows and doors, see that the burners of the stove were off. That was all there was to it. For eighteen years, the nightly route had included a stop in Brianna's room, but not since she had left for university.

Moved by a mixture of habit and compulsion, I pushed open the door to her room and clicked on the light. Some people have the knack of objects, and others haven't. Bree had it; scarcely an inch of wall space showed between the posters, photographs, dried flowers, scraps of tie-dyed fabric, framed certificates and other impedimenta on the walls.

Some people have a way of arranging everything about them, so the objects take on not only their own meaning, and a relation to the other things displayed with them, but something more besides—an indefinable aura that belongs as much to their invisible owner as to the objects themselves. *I am here because Brianna placed me here,* the things in the room seemed to say. *I am here because she is who she is.*

It was odd that she should have that, really, I thought. Frank had had it; when I had gone to empty his university office after his death, I had thought it like the fossilized cast of some extinct animal; books and papers and bits of rubbish holding exactly the shape and texture and vanished weight of the mind that had inhabited the space.

For some of Brianna's objects, the relation to her was obvious—pictures of me, of Frank, of Bozo, of friends. The scraps of fabric were ones she had made, her chosen patterns, the colors she liked—a brilliant turquoise, deep indigo, magenta, and clear yellow. But other things—why should the scatter of dried freshwater snail shells on the bureau say to me "Brianna"? Why that one lump of rounded pumice, taken from the beach at Truro, indistinguishable from a hundred thousand others—except for the fact that she had taken it?

I didn't have a way with objects. I had no impulse either to acquire or to decorate—Frank had often complained of the Spartan furnishings at home, until Brianna grew old enough to take a hand. Whether it was the fault of my nomadic upbringing, or only the way I was, I lived mostly inside my skin, with no impulse to alter my surroundings to reflect me.

Jamie was the same. He had had the few small objects, always carried in his sporran for utility or as talismans, and beyond that, had neither owned nor cared for things. Even during the short period when we had lived luxuriously in Paris, and the longer time of tranquillity at Lallybroch, he had never shown any disposition to acquire objects.

For him as well, it might have been the circumstances of his early manhood, when he had lived like a hunted animal, never owning anything beyond the weapons he depended on for survival. But perhaps it was natural to him also, this isolation from the world of things, this sense of self-sufficiency —one of the things that had made us seek completion in each other.

Odd all the same, that Brianna should have so much resembled both her fathers, in their very different ways. I said a silent good night to the ghost of my absent daughter, and put out the light.

The thought of Frank went with me into the bedroom. The sight of the big double bed, smooth and untroubled under its dark blue satin spread, brought him suddenly and vividly to mind, in a way I had not thought of him in many months.

I supposed it was the possibility of impending departure that made me think of him now. This room—this bed, in fact—was where I had said goodbye to him for the last time.

"Can't you come to bed, Claire? It's past midnight." Frank looked up at me over the edge of his book. He was already in bed himself, reading with the book propped upon his knees. The soft pool of light from the lamp made him look as though he were floating in a warm bubble, serenely isolated from the dark chilliness of the rest of the room. It was early January, and despite the furnace's best efforts, the only truly warm place at night was bed, under heavy blankets.

I smiled at him, and rose from my chair, dropping the heavy wool dressing gown from my shoulders.

"Am I keeping you up? Sorry. Just reliving this morning's surgery."

"Yes, I know," he said dryly. "I can tell by looking at you. Your eyes glaze over and your mouth hangs open."

"Sorry," I said again, matching his tone. "I can't be responsible for what my face is doing when I'm thinking."

"But what good does thinking do?" he asked, sticking a bookmark in his book. "You've done whatever you could—worrying about it now won't change . . . ah, well." He shrugged irritably and closed the book. "I've said it all before."

"You have," I said shortly.

I got into bed, shivering slightly, and tucked my gown down round my legs. Frank scooted automatically in my direction, and I slid down under the sheets beside him, huddling together to pool our warmth against the cold.

"Oh, wait; I've got to move the phone." I flung back the covers and scrambled out again, to move the phone from Frank's side of the bed to mine. He liked to sit in bed in the early evening, chatting with students and colleagues while I read or made surgical notes beside him, but he resented being wakened by the late calls that came from the hospital for me. Resented it enough that I had arranged for the hospital to call only for absolute emergencies, or when I left instructions to keep me informed of a specific patient's progress. Tonight I had left instructions; it was a tricky bowel resection. If things went wrong, I might have to go back in in a hurry.

Frank grunted as I turned out the light and slipped into bed again, but after a moment, he rolled toward me, throwing an arm across my middle. I rolled onto my side and curled against him, gradually relaxing as my chilled toes thawed.

I mentally replayed the details of the operation, feeling again the chill at my feet from the refrigeration in the operating room and the initial, unsettling feeling of the warmth in the patient's belly as my gloved fingers slid inside. The diseased bowel itself, coiled like a viper, patterned with the purple splotches of ecchymosis and the slow leakage of bright blood from tiny ruptures.

"I'd been thinking." Frank's voice came out of the darkness behind me, excessively casual.

"Mm?" I was still absorbed in the vision of the surgery, but struggled to pull myself back to the present. "About what?"

"My sabbatical." His leave from the university was due to start in a month.

He had planned to make a series of short trips through the northeastern United States, gathering material, then go to England for six months, returning to Boston to spend the last three months of the sabbatical writing.

"I'd thought of going to England straight off," he said carefully.

"Well, why not? The weather will be dreadful, but if you're going to spend most of the time in libraries . . ."

"I want to take Brianna with me."

I stopped dead, the cold in the room suddenly coalescing into a small lump of suspicion in the pit of my stomach.

"She can't go now; she's only a semester from graduation. Surely you can wait until we can join you in the summer? I've put in for a long vacation then, and perhaps . . ."

"I'm going now. For good. Without you."

I pulled away and sat up, turning on the light. Frank lay blinking up at me, dark hair disheveled. It had gone gray at the temples, giving him a distinguished air that seemed to have alarming effects on the more susceptible of his female students. I felt quite astonishingly composed.

"Why now, all of a sudden? The latest one putting pressure on you, is she?"

The look of alarm that flashed into his eyes was so pronounced as to be comical. I laughed, with a noticeable lack of humor.

"You actually thought I didn't know? God, Frank! You are the most . . . oblivious man!"

He sat up in bed, jaw tight.

"I thought I had been most discreet."

"You may have been at that," I said sardonically. "I counted six over the last ten years—if there were really a dozen or so, then you were quite the model of discretion."

His face seldom showed great emotion, but a whitening beside his mouth told me that he was very angry indeed.

"This one must be something special," I said, folding my arms and leaning back against the headboard in assumed casualness. "But still—why the rush to go to England now, and why take Bree?"

"She can go to boarding school for her last term," he said shortly. "Be a new experience for her."

"Not one I expect she wants," I said. "She won't want to leave her friends, especially not just before graduation. And certainly not to go to an English boarding school!" I shuddered at the thought. I had come within inches of being immured in just such a school as a child; the scent of the hospital cafeteria sometimes evoked memories of it, complete with the waves of terrified helplessness I had felt when Uncle Lamb had taken me to visit the place.

"A little discipline never hurt anyone," Frank said. He had recovered his temper, but the lines of his face were still tight. "Might have done you some good." He waved a hand, dismissing the topic. "Let that be. Still, I've decided

to go back to England permanently. I've a good position offered at Cambridge, and I mean to take it up. You won't leave the hospital, of course. But I don't mean to leave my daughter behind."

"Your daughter?" *I felt momentarily incapable of speech. So he had a new job all set, and a new mistress to go along. He'd been planning this for some time, then. A whole new life—but not with Brianna.*

"My daughter," *he said calmly.* "You can come to visit whenever you like, of course . . ."

"You . . . bloody . . . bastard!" *I said.*

"Do be reasonable, Claire." *He looked down his nose, giving me Treatment A, long-suffering patience, reserved for students appealing failing grades.* "You're scarcely ever home. If I'm gone, there will be no one to look after Bree properly."

"You talk as though she's eight, not almost eighteen! For heaven's sake, she's nearly grown."

"All the more reason she needs care and supervision," *he snapped.* "If you'd seen what I'd seen at the university—the drinking, the drugging, the . . ."

"I do see it," *I said through my teeth.* "At fairly close range in the emergency room. Bree is not likely to—"

"She damn well is! Girls have no sense at that age—she'll be off with the first fellow who—"

"Don't be idiotic! Bree's very sensible. Besides, all young people experiment, that's how they learn. You can't keep her swaddled in cotton wool all her life."

"Better swaddled than fucking a black man!" *he shot back. A mottled red showed faintly over his cheekbones.* "Like mother, like daughter, eh? But that's not how it's going to be, damn it, not if I've anything to say about it!"

I heaved out of bed and stood up, glaring down at him.

"You," *I said,* "have not got one bloody, filthy, stinking thing to say, about Bree or anything else!" *I was trembling with rage, and had to press my fists into the sides of my legs to keep from striking him.* "You have the absolute, unmitigated gall to tell me that you are leaving me to live with the latest of a succession of mistresses, and then imply that I have been having an affair with Joe Abernathy? That is what you mean, isn't it?"

He had the grace to lower his eyes slightly.

"Everyone thinks you have," *he muttered.* "You spend all your time with the man. It's the same thing, so far as Bree is concerned. Dragging her into . . . situations, where she's exposed to danger, and . . . and to those sorts of people . . ."

"Black people, I suppose you mean?"

"I damn well do," *he said, looking up at me with eyes flashing.* "It's bad enough to have the Abernathys to parties all the time, though at least he's educated. But that obese person I met at their house with the tribal tattoos and the mud in his hair? That repulsive lounge lizard with the oily voice? And* *young Abernathy's taken to hanging round Bree day and night, taking her to marches and rallies and orgies in low dives . . ."*

"I shouldn't think there are any high dives," I said, repressing an inappropriate urge to laugh at Frank's unkind but accurate assessment of two of Leonard Abernathy's more outré friends. "Did you know Lenny's taken to calling himself Muhammad Ishmael Shabazz now?"

"Yes, he told me," he said shortly, "and I am taking no risk of having my daughter become Mrs. Shabazz."

"I don't think Bree feels that way about Lenny," I assured him, struggling to suppress my irritation.

"She isn't going to, either. She's going to England with me."

"Not if she doesn't want to," I said, with great finality.

No doubt feeling that his position put him at a disadvantage, Frank climbed out of bed and began groping for his slippers.

"I don't need your permission to take my daughter to England," he said. "And Bree's still a minor; she'll go where I say. I'd appreciate it if you'd find her medical records; the new school will need them."

"Your daughter?" I said again. I vaguely noticed the chill in the room, but was so angry that I felt hot all over. "Bree's my daughter, and you'll take her bloody nowhere!"

"You can't stop me," he pointed out, with aggravating calmness, picking up his dressing gown from the foot of the bed.

"The hell I can't," I said. "You want to divorce me? Fine. Use any grounds you like—with the exception of adultery, which you can't prove, because it doesn't exist. But if you try to take Bree away with you, I'll have a thing or two to say about adultery. Do you want to know how many of your discarded mistresses have come to see me, to ask me to give you up?"

His mouth hung open in shock.

"I told them all that I'd give you up in a minute," I said, "if you asked." I folded my arms, tucking my hands into my armpits. I was beginning to feel the chilliness again. "I did wonder why you never asked—but I supposed it was because of Brianna."

His face had gone quite bloodless now, and showed white as a skull in the dimness on the other side of the bed.

"Well," he said, with a poor attempt at his usual self-possession, "I shouldn't have thought you minded. It's not as though you ever made a move to stop me."

I stared at him, completely taken aback.

"Stop you?" I said. "What should I have done? Steamed open your mail and waved the letters under your nose? Made a scene at the faculty Christmas party? Complained to the Dean?"

His lips pressed tight together for a moment, then relaxed.

"You might have behaved as though it mattered to you," he said quietly.

"It mattered." My voice sounded strangled.

He shook his head, still staring at me, his eyes dark in the lamplight.

"Not enough." He paused, face floating pale in the air above his dark dressing gown, then came round the bed to stand by me.

"Sometimes I wondered if I could rightfully blame you," he said, almost thoughtfully. "He looked like Bree, didn't he? He was like her?"

"Yes."

He breathed heavily, almost a snort.

"I could see it in your face—when you'd look at her, I could see you thinking of him. Damn you, Claire Beauchamp," he said, very softly. "Damn you and your face that can't hide a thing you think or feel."

There was a silence after this, of the sort that makes you hear all the tiny unhearable noises of creaking wood and breathing houses—only in an effort to pretend you haven't heard what was just said.

"I did love you," I said softly, at last. "Once."

"Once," he echoed. "Should I be grateful for that?"

The feeling was beginning to come back to my numb lips.

"I did tell you," I said. "And then, when you wouldn't go . . . Frank, I did try."

Whatever he heard in my voice stopped him for a moment.

"I did," I said, very softly.

He turned away and moved toward my dressing table, where he touched things restlessly, picking them up and putting them down at random.

"I couldn't leave you at the first—pregnant, alone. Only a cad would have done that. And then . . . Bree." He stared sightlessly at the lipstick he held in one hand, then set it gently back on the glassy tabletop. "I couldn't give her up," he said softly. He turned to look at me, eyes dark holes in a shadowed face.

"Did you know I couldn't sire a child? I . . . had myself tested, a few years ago. I'm sterile. Did you know?"

I shook my head, not trusting myself to speak.

"Bree is mine, my daughter," he said, as though to himself. "The only child I'll ever have. I couldn't give her up." He gave a short laugh. "I couldn't give her up, but you couldn't see her without thinking of him, could you? Without that constant memory, I wonder—would you have forgotten him, in time?"

"No." The whispered word seemed to go through him like an electric shock. He stood frozen for a moment, then whirled to the closet and began to jerk on his clothes over his pajamas. I stood, arms wrapped around my body, watching as he pulled on his overcoat and stamped out of the room, not looking at me. The collar of his blue silk pajamas stuck up over the astrakhan trim of his coat.

A moment later, I heard the closing of the front door—he had sufficient presence of mind not to slam it—and then the sound of a cold motor turning reluctantly over. The headlights swept across the bedroom ceiling as the car backed down the drive, and then were gone, leaving me shaking by the rumpled bed.

Frank didn't come back. I tried to sleep, but found myself lying rigid in the cold bed, mentally reliving the argument, listening for the crunch of his tires in the drive. At last, I got up and dressed, left a note for Bree, and went out myself.

The hospital hadn't called, but I might as well go and have a look at my patient; it was better than tossing and turning all night. And, to be honest, I would not have minded had Frank come home to find me gone.

The streets were slick as butter, black ice gleaming in the streetlights. The yellow phosphor glow lit whorls of falling snow; within an hour, the ice that lined the streets would be concealed beneath fresh powder, and twice as perilous to travel. The only consolation was that there was no one on the streets at 4:00 A.M. to be imperiled. No one but me, that is.

Inside the hospital, the usual warm, stuffy institutional smell wrapped itself round me like a blanket of familiarity, shutting out the snow-filled black night outside.

"He's okay," the nurse said to me softly, as though a raised voice might disturb the sleeping man. "All the vitals are stable, and the count's okay. No bleeding." I could see that it was true; the patient's face was pale, but with a faint undertone of pink, like the veining in a white rose petal, and the pulse in the hollow of his throat was strong and regular.

I let out the deep breath I hadn't realized I was holding. "That's good," I said. "Very good." The nurse smiled warmly at me, and I had to resist the impulse to lean against him and dissolve. The hospital surroundings suddenly seemed like my only refuge.

There was no point in going home. I checked briefly on my remaining patients, and went down to the cafeteria. It still smelled like a boarding school, but I sat down with a cup of coffee and sipped it slowly, wondering what I would tell Bree.

It might have been a half-hour later when one of the ER nurses hurried through the swinging doors and stopped dead at the sight of me. Then she came on, quite slowly.

I knew at once; I had seen doctors and nurses deliver the news of death too often to mistake the signs. Very calmly, feeling nothing whatever, I set down the almost full cup, realizing as I did so that for the rest of my life, I would remember that there was a chip in the rim, and that the "B" of the gold lettering on the side was almost worn away.

". . . said you were here. Identification in his wallet . . . police said . . . snow on black ice, a skid . . . DOA . . ." the nurse was talking, babbling, as I strode through the bright white halls, not looking at her, seeing the faces of the nurses at the station turn toward me in slow motion, not knowing, but seeing from a glance at me that something final had happened.

He was on a gurney in one of the emergency room cubicles; a spare, anony-

mous space. There was an ambulance parked outside—perhaps the one that had brought him here. The double doors at the end of the corridor were open to the icy dawn. The ambulance's red light was pulsing like an artery, bathing the corridor in blood.

I touched him briefly. His flesh had the inert, plastic feel of the recently dead, so at odds with the lifelike appearance. There was no wound visible; any damage was hidden beneath the blanket that covered him. His throat was smooth and brown; no pulse moved in its hollow.

I stood there, my hand on the motionless curve of his chest, looking at him, as I had not looked for some time. A strong and delicate profile, sensitive lips, and a chiseled nose and jaw. A handsome man, despite the lines that cut deep beside his mouth, lines of disappointment and unspoken anger, lines that even the relaxation of death could not wipe away.

I stood quite still, listening. I could hear the wail of a new ambulance approaching, voices in the corridor. The squeak of gurney wheels, the crackle of a police radio, and the soft hum of a fluorescent light somewhere. I realized with a start that I was listening for Frank, expecting . . . what? That his ghost would be hovering still nearby, anxious to complete our unfinished business?

I closed my eyes, to shut out the disturbing sight of that motionless profile, going red and white and red in turn as the light throbbed through the open doors.

"Frank," I said softly, to the unsettled, icy air, "if you're still close enough to hear me—I did love you. Once. I did."

Then Joe was there, pushing through the crowded corridor, face anxious over his green scrub suit. He had come straight from surgery; there was a small spray of blood across the lenses of his glasses, a smear of it on his chest.

"Claire," he said, "God, Claire!" and then I started to shake. In ten years, he had never called me anything but "Jane" or "L.J." If he was using my name, it must be real. My hand showed startlingly white in Joe's dark grasp, then red in the pulsing light, and then I had turned to him, solid as a tree trunk, rested my head on his shoulder, and—for the first time—wept for Frank.

＊

I leaned my face against the bedroom window of the house on Furey Street. It was hot and humid on this blue September evening, filled with the sound of crickets and lawn sprinklers. What I saw, though, was the uncompromising black and white of that winter's night two years before—black ice and the white of hospital linen, and then the blurring of all judgments in the pale gray dawn.

My eyes blurred now, remembering the anonymous bustle in the corridor and the pulsing red light of the ambulance that had washed the silent cubicle in bloody light, as I wept for Frank.

Now I wept for him for the last time, knowing even as the tears slid down my cheeks that we had parted, once and for all, twenty-odd years before, on the crest of a green Scottish hill.

My weeping done, I rose and laid a hand on the smooth blue coverlet, gently rounded over the pillow on the left—Frank's side.

"Goodbye, my dear," I whispered, and went out to sleep downstairs, away from the ghosts.

It was the doorbell that woke me in the morning, from my makeshift bed on the sofa.

"Telegram, ma'am," the messenger said, trying not to stare at my nightgown.

Those small yellow envelopes have probably been responsible for more heart attacks than anything besides fatty bacon for breakfast. My own heart squeezed like a fist, then went on beating in a heavy, uncomfortable manner.

I tipped the messenger and carried the telegram down the hall. It seemed important not to open it until I had reached the relative safety of the bathroom, as though it were an explosive device that must be defused under water.

My fingers shook and fumbled as I opened it, sitting on the edge of the tub, my back pressed against the tiled wall for reinforcement.

It was a brief message—of course, a Scot would be thrifty with words, I thought absurdly.

HAVE FOUND HIM STOP, it read. WILL YOU COME BACK QUERY ROGER.

I folded the telegram neatly and put it back into its envelope. I sat there and stared at it for quite a long time. Then I stood up and went to dress.

20

Diagnosis

Joe Abernathy was seated at his desk, frowning at a small rectangle of pale cardboard he held in both hands.

"What's that?" I said, sitting on the edge of his desk without ceremony.

"A business card." He handed the card to me, looking at once amused and irritated.

It was a pale gray laid-finish card; expensive stock, fastidiously printed in an elegant serif type. *Muhammad Ishmael Shabazz III*, the center line read, with address and phone number below.

"Lenny?" I asked, laughing. "Muhammad Ishmael Shabazz the *third*?"

"Uh-huh." Amusement seemed to be getting the upper hand. The gold tooth flashed briefly as he took the card back. "He says he's not going to take a white man's name, no slave name. He's going to reclaim his African heritage," he said sardonically. "All right, I say; I ask him, you gonna go round with a bone through your nose next thing? It's not enough he's got his hair out to *here*"—he gestured, fluffing his hands on either side of his own close-cropped head—"and he's going round in a thing down to his knees, looks like his sister made it in Home Ec class. No, Lenny—excuse me, Muhammad—he's got to be *African* all the way."

Joe waved a hand out the window, at his privileged vista over the park. "I tell him, look around, man, you see any lions? This look like Africa to you?" He leaned back in his padded chair, stretching out his legs. He shook his head in resignation. "There's no talkin' to a boy that age."

"True," I said. "But what's this 'third' about?"

A reluctant gleam of gold answered me. "Well, he was talking all about his 'lost tradition' and his 'missing history' and all. He says, 'How am I going to hold my head up, face-to-face with all these guys I meet at Yale named Cadwallader IV and Sewell Lodge, Jr., and I don't even know my own grandaddy's name, I don't know where I come from?'"

Joe snorted. "I told him, you want to know where you come from, kid, look in the mirror. Wasn't the *Mayflower*, huh?"

He picked up the card again, a reluctant grin on his face.

"So he says, if he's taking back his heritage, why not take it back all the way? If his grandaddy wouldn't give him a name, he'll give his grandaddy one. And the only trouble with *that*," he said, looking up at me under a cocked brow, "is that it kind of leaves me man in the middle. Now I have to be Muhammad Ishmael Shabazz, *Junior,* so Lenny can be a 'proud African-American'." He thrust himself back from the desk, chin on his chest, staring balefully at the pale gray card.

"You're lucky, L.J.," he said. "At least Bree isn't giving you grief about who her granddaddy was. All you have to worry about is will she be doing dope and getting pregnant by some draft dodger who takes off for Canada."

I laughed, with more than a touch of irony. "That's what *you* think," I told him.

"Yeah?" He cocked an interested eyebrow at me, then took off his gold-rimmed glasses and wiped them on the end of his tie. "So how was Scotland?" he asked, eyeing me. "Bree like it?"

"She's still there," I said. "Looking for *her* history."

Joe was opening his mouth to say something when a tentative knock on the door interrupted him.

"Dr. Abernathy?" A plump young man in a polo shirt peered doubtfully into the office, leaning over the top of a large cardboard box he held clutched to his substantial abdomen.

"Call me Ishmael," Joe said genially.

"What?" The young man's mouth hung slightly open, and he glanced at me in bewilderment, mingled with hope. "Are *you* Dr. Abernathy?"

"No," I said, "he is, when he puts his mind to it." I rose from the desk, brushing down my skirts. "I'll leave you to your appointment, Joe, but if you have time later—"

"No, stay a minute, L.J.," he interrupted, rising. He took the box from the young man, then shook his hand formally. "You'd be Mr. Thompson? John Wicklow called to tell me you'd be coming. Pleased to meet you."

"Horace Thompson, yes," the young man said, blinking slightly. "I brought, er, a specimen . . ." He waved vaguely at the cardboard box.

"Yes, that's right. I'd be happy to look at it for you, but I think Dr. Randall here might be of assistance, too." He glanced at me, the glint of mischief in his eyes. "I just want to see can you do it to a dead person, L.J."

"Do *what* to a dead—" I began, when he reached into the opened box and carefully lifted out a skull.

"Oh, pretty," he said in delight, turning the object gently to and fro.

"Pretty" was not the first adjective that struck me; the skull was stained and greatly discolored, the bone gone a deep streaky brown. Joe carried it to the window and held it in the light, his thumbs gently stroking the small bony ridges over the eye sockets.

"Pretty lady," he said softly, talking as much to the skull as to me or Horace Thompson. "Full-grown, mature. Maybe late forties, middle fifties. Do you have the legs?" he asked, turning abruptly to the plump young man.

"Yeah, right here," Horace Thompson assured him, reaching into the box. "We have the whole body, in fact."

Horace Thompson was probably someone from the coroner's office, I thought. Sometimes they brought bodies to Joe that had been found in the countryside, badly deteriorated, for an expert opinion as to the cause of death. This one looked considerably deteriorated.

"Here, Dr. Randall." Joe leaned over and carefully placed the skull in my hands. "Tell me whether this lady was in good health, while I check her legs."

"Me? I'm not a forensic scientist." Still, I glanced automatically down. It was either an old specimen, or had been weathered extensively; the bone was smooth, with a gloss that fresh specimens never had, stained and discolored by the leaching of pigments from the earth.

"Oh, all right." I turned the skull slowly in my hands, watching the bones, naming them each in my mind as I saw them. The smooth arch of the parietals, fused to the declivity of the temporal, with the small ridge where the jaw muscle originated, the jutting projection that meshed itself with the maxillary into the graceful curve of the squamosal arch. She had had lovely cheekbones, high and broad. The upper jaw had most of its teeth—straight and white.

Deep eyes. The scooped bone at the back of the orbits was dark with shadow; even by tilting the skull to the side, I couldn't get light to illuminate the whole cavity. The skull felt light in my hands, the bone fragile. I stroked her brow and my hand ran upward, and down behind the occiput, my fingers seeking the dark hole at the base, the foramen magnum, where all the messages of the nervous system pass to and from the busy brain.

Then I held it close against my stomach, eyes closed, and felt the shifting sadness, filling the cavity of the skull like running water. And an odd faint sense—of surprise?

"Someone killed her," I said. "She didn't want to die." I opened my eyes to find Horace Thompson staring at me, his own eyes wide in his round, pale face. I handed him the skull, very gingerly. "Where did you find her?" I asked.

Mr. Thompson exchanged glances with Joe, then looked back at me, both eyebrows still high.

"She's from a cave in the Caribbean," he said. "There were a lot of artifacts with her. We think she's maybe between a hundred-fifty and two hundred years old."

"She's *what*?"

Joe was grinning broadly, enjoying his joke.

"Our friend Mr. Thompson here is from the anthropology department at Harvard," he said. "His friend Wicklow knows me; asked me would I have a look at this skeleton, to tell them what I could about it."

"The nerve of you!" I said indignantly. "I thought she was some unidentified body the coroner's office dragged in."

"Well, she's unidentified," Joe pointed out. "And certainly liable to stay that way." He rooted about in the cardboard box like a terrier. The end flap said PICT-SWEET CORN.

"Now what have we got here?" he said, and very carefully drew out a plastic sack containing a jumble of vertebrae.

"She was in pieces when we got her," Horace explained.

"Oh, de headbone connected to de . . . neckbone," Joe sang softly, laying out the vertebrae along the edge of the desk. His stubby fingers darted skillfully among the bones, nudging them into alignment. "De neckbone connected to de . . . backbone . . ."

"Don't pay any attention to him," I told Horace. "You'll just encourage him."

"Now hear . . . de word . . . of de Lawd!" he finished triumphantly. "Jesus Christ, L.J., you're somethin' else! Look here." Horace Thompson and I bent obediently over the line of spiky vertebral bones. The wide body of the axis had a deep gouge; the posterior zygapophysis had broken clean off, and the fracture plane went completely through the centrum of the bone.

"A broken neck?" Thompson asked, peering interestedly.

"Yeah, but more than that, I think." Joe's finger moved over the line of the fracture plane. "See here? The bone's not just cracked, it's *gone* right there. Somebody tried to cut this lady's head clean off. With a dull blade," he concluded with relish.

Horace Thompson was looking at me queerly. "How did you know she'd been killed, Dr. Randall?" he asked.

I could feel the blood rising in my face. "I don't know," I said. "I—she—*felt* like it, that's all."

"Really?" He blinked a few times, but didn't press me further. "How odd."

"She does it all the time," Joe informed him, squinting at the femur he was measuring with a pair of calipers. "Mostly on live people, though. Best diagnostician I ever saw." He set down the calipers and picked up a small plastic ruler. "A *cave*, you said?"

"We think it was a . . . er, secret slave burial," Mr. Thompson explained, blushing, and I suddenly realized why he had seemed so abashed when he realized which of us was the Dr. Abernathy he had been sent to see. Joe shot him a sudden sharp glance, but then bent back to his work. He kept humming "Dem Dry Bones" faintly to himself as he measured the pelvic inlet, then went back to the legs, this time concentrating on the tibia. Finally he straightened up, shaking his head.

"Not a slave," he said.

Horace blinked. "But she must have been," he said. "The things we found with her . . . a clear African influence . . ."

"No," Joe said flatly. He tapped the long femur, where it rested on his desk. His fingernail clicked on the dry bone. "She wasn't black."

"You can tell that? From bones?" Horace Thompson was visibly agitated. "But I thought—that paper by Jensen, I mean—theories about racial physical differences—largely exploded—" He blushed scarlet, unable to finish.

"Oh, they're there," said Joe, very dryly indeed. "If you want to think blacks and whites are equal under the skin, be my guest, but it ain't scientifically so." He turned and pulled a book from the shelf behind him. *Tables of Skeletal Variance*, the title read.

"Take a look at this," Joe invited. "You can see the differences in a lot of bones, but especially in the leg bones. Blacks have a completely different femur-to-tibia ratio than whites do. And that lady"—he pointed to the skeleton on his desk—"was white. Caucasian. No question about it."

"Oh," Horace Thompson murmured. "Well. I'll have to think—I mean—it was very kind of you to look at her for me. Er, thank you," he added, with an awkward little bow. We silently watched him bundle his bones back into the PICT-SWEET box, and then he was gone, pausing at the door to give us both another brief bob of the head.

Joe gave a short laugh as the door closed behind him. "Want to bet he takes her down to Rutgers for a second opinion?"

"Academics don't give up theories easily," I said, shrugging. "I lived with one long enough to know that."

Joe snorted again. "So you did. Well, now that we've got Mr. Thompson and his dead white lady sorted out, what can I do for *you*, L.J.?"

I took a deep breath and turned to face him.

"I need an honest opinion, from somebody I can depend on to be objective. No," I amended, "I take that back. I need an opinion and then—depending on the opinion—maybe a favor."

"No problem," Joe assured me. "Especially the opinion. My specialty, opinions." He rocked back in his chair, unfolded his gold-rimmed glasses and set them firmly atop his broad nose. Then he folded his hands across his chest, fingers steepled, and nodded at me. "Shoot."

"Am I sexually attractive?" I demanded. His eyes always reminded me of toffee drops, with their warm golden-brown color. Now they went completely round, enhancing the resemblance.

Then they narrowed, but he didn't answer immediately. He looked me over carefully, head to toe.

"It's a trick question, right?" he said. "I give you an answer and one of those women's libbers jumps out from behind the door, yells 'Sexist pig!' and hits me over the head with a sign that says 'Castrate Male Chauvinists.' Huh?"

"No," I assured him. "A sexist male chauvinist answer is basically what I want."

"Oh, okay. As long as we're straight, then." He resumed his perusal, squinting closely as I stood up straight.

"Skinny white broad with too much hair, but a great ass," he said at last. "Nice tits, too," he added, with a cordial nod. "That what you want to know?"

"Yes," I said, relaxing my rigid posture. "That's exactly what I wanted to know. It isn't the sort of question you can ask just anybody."

He pursed his lips in a silent whistle, then threw back his head and roared with delight.

"Lady Jane! You've got you a *man*!"

I felt the blood rising in my cheeks, but tried to keep my dignity. "I don't know. Maybe. Just maybe."

"Maybe, hell! Jesus Christ on a piece of toast, L.J., it's about *time*!"

"Kindly quit cackling," I said, lowering myself into his visitor's chair. "It doesn't become a man of your years and station."

"My years? O*ho*," he said, peering shrewdly at me through the glasses. "He's younger than you? That's what you're worried about?"

"Not a lot," I said, the blush beginning to recede. "But I haven't seen him in twenty years. You're the only person I know who's known me for a long time; have I changed terribly since we met?" I looked at him straight on, demanding honesty.

He looked at me, took off his glasses and squinted, then replaced them.

"No," he said. "You wouldn't, though, unless you got fat."

"I wouldn't?"

"Nah. Ever been to your high school reunion?"

"I didn't go to a high school."

His sketchy brows flicked upward. "No? Well, I have. And I tell you what, L.J.; you see all these people you haven't seen for twenty years, and there's this split second when you meet somebody you used to know, when you think, 'My *God*, he's changed!,' and then all of a sudden, he hasn't—it's just like the twenty years weren't there. I mean"—he rubbed his head vigorously, struggling for meaning—"you see they've got some gray, and some lines, and maybe they aren't just the same as they were, but two minutes past that shock, and you don't see it anymore. They're just the same people they always were, and you have to make yourself stand back a ways to see that they aren't eighteen anymore.

"Now, if people get fat," he said meditatively, "*they* change some. It's harder to see who they were, because the faces change. But you"—he squinted at me again—"you're never going to be fat; you don't have the genes for it."

"I suppose not," I said. I looked down at my hands, clasped together in my lap. Slender wristbones; at least I wasn't fat yet. My rings gleamed in the autumn sun from the window.

"Is it Bree's daddy?" he asked softly.

I jerked my head up and stared at him. "How the hell did you know that?" I said.

He smiled slightly. "I've known Bree how long? Ten years, at least." He shook his head. "She's got a lot of you in her, L.J., but I've never seen anything of Frank. Daddy's got red hair, huh?" he asked. "And he's one big son of a bitch, or everything I learned in Genetics 101 was a damn lie."

"Yes," I said, and felt a kind of delirious excitement at that simple admission. Until I had told Bree herself and Roger about Jamie, I had said nothing about him for twenty years. The joy of suddenly being able to talk freely about him was intoxicating.

"Yes, he's big and red-haired, and he's Scottish," I said, making Joe's eyes go round once more.

"And Bree's in Scotland now?"

I nodded. "Bree is where the favor comes in."

Two hours later, I left the hospital for the last time, leaving behind me a letter of resignation, addressed to the Hospital Board, all the necessary documents for the handling of my property until Brianna should be of age, and another one, to be executed at that time, turning everything over to her. As I drove out of the parking lot, I experienced a feeling of mingled panic, regret, and elation. I was on my way.

21

Q.E.D.

"I found the deed of sasine." Roger's face was flushed with excitement. He had hardly been able to contain himself, waiting with open impatience at the train station in Inverness while Brianna hugged me and my bags were retrieved. He had barely got us stuffed into his tiny Morris and the car's ignition started before blurting out his news.

"What, for Lallybroch?" I leaned over the seat back between him and Brianna, in order to hear him over the noise of the motor.

"Yes, the one Jamie—your Jamie—wrote, deeding the property to his nephew, the younger Jamie."

"It's at the manse," Brianna put in, twisting to look at me. "We were afraid to bring it with us; Roger had to sign his name in blood to get it out of the SPA collection." Her fair skin was pinkened by excitement and the chilly day, raindrops in her ruddy hair. It was always a shock to me to see her again after an absence—mothers always think their children beautiful, but Bree really was.

I smiled at her, glowing with affection tinged with panic. Could I really be thinking of leaving her? Mistaking the smile for one of pleasure in the news, she went on, gripping the back of the seat in excitement.

"And you'll never guess what else we found!"

"What *you* found," Roger corrected, squeezing her knee with one hand as he negotiated the tiny orange car through a roundabout. She gave him a quick glance and a reciprocal touch with an air of intimacy about it that set off my maternal alarm bells on the spot. Like that already, was it?

I seemed to feel Frank's shade glaring accusingly over my shoulder. Well, at least Roger wasn't black. I coughed and said, "Really? What is it?"

They exchanged a glance and grinned widely at each other.

"Wait and see, Mama," said Bree, with irritating smugness.

"See?" she said, twenty minutes later, as I bent over the desk in the manse's study. On the battered surface of the late Reverend Wakefield's desk lay a sheaf of yellowed papers, foxed and browned at the edges. They were carefully enclosed in protective plastic covers now, but obviously had been carelessly used at one time; the edges were tattered, one sheet was torn roughly in half, and all the sheets had notes and annotations scribbled in the margins and inserted in the text. This was obviously someone's rough draft —of something.

"It's the text of an article," Roger told me, shuffling through a pile of huge folio volumes that lay on the sofa. "It was published in a sort of journal called *Forrester's,* put out by a printer called Alexander Malcolm, in Edinburgh, in 1765."

I swallowed, my shirtwaist dress feeling suddenly too tight under the arms; 1765 was almost twenty years past the time when I had left Jamie.

I stared at the scrawling letters, browned with age. They were written by someone of difficult penmanship, here cramped and there sprawling, with exaggerated loops on "g" and "y." Perhaps the writing of a left-handed man, who wrote most painfully with his right hand.

"See, here's the published version." Roger brought the opened folio to the desk and laid it before me, pointing. "See the date? It's 1765, and it matches this handwritten manuscript almost exactly; only a few of the marginal notes aren't included."

"Yes," I said. "And the deed of sasine . . ."

"Here it is." Brianna fumbled hastily in the top drawer and pulled out a much crumpled paper, likewise encased in protective plastic. Protection here was even more after the fact than with the manuscript; the paper was rainspattered, filthy and torn, many of the words blurred beyond recognition. But the three signatures at the bottom still showed plainly.

By my hand, read the difficult writing, here executed with such care that only the exaggerated loop of the "y" showed its kinship with the careless manuscript, *James Alexander Malcolm MacKenzie Fraser.* And below, the two lines where the witnesses had signed. In a thin, fine script, *Murtagh FitzGibbons Fraser,* and, below that, in my own large, round hand, *Claire Beauchamp Fraser.*

I sat down quite suddenly, putting my hand over the document instinctively, as though to deny its reality.

"That's it, isn't it?" said Roger quietly. His outward composure was belied by his hands, trembling slightly as he lifted the stack of manuscript pages to set them next to the deed. "You signed it. Proof positive—if we needed it," he added, with a quick glance at Bree.

She shook her head, letting her hair fall down to hide her face. They didn't need it, either of them. The vanishing of Geilie Duncan through the stones five months before had been all the evidence anyone could need as to the truth of my story.

Still, having it all laid out in black and white was rather staggering. I took my hand away and looked again at the deed, and then at the handwritten manuscript.

"Is it the same, Mama?" Bree bent anxiously over the pages, her hair brushing softly against my hand. "The article wasn't signed—or it was, but with a pseudonym." She smiled briefly. "The author signed himself 'Q.E.D.' It looked the same to us, but we aren't either of us handwriting experts and we didn't want to give these to an expert until you'd seen them."

"I think so." I felt breathless, but quite certain at the same time, with an upwelling of incredulous joy. "Yes, I'm almost sure. Jamie wrote this." Q.E.D., indeed! I had an absurd urge to tear the manuscript pages out of their plastic shrouds and clutch them in my hands, to feel the ink and paper he had touched; the certain evidence that he had survived.

"There's more. Internal evidence." Roger's voice betrayed his pride. "See there? It's an article against the Excise Act of 1764, advocating the repeal of the restrictions on export of liquor from the Scottish Highlands to England. Here it is"—his racing finger stopped suddenly on a phrase—" 'for as has been known for ages past, "Freedom and Whisky gang tegither." ' See how he's put that Scottish dialect phrase in quotes? He got it from somewhere else."

"He got it from me," I said softly. "I told him that—when he was setting out to steal Prince Charles's port."

"I remembered." Roger nodded, eyes shining with excitement. "But it's a quote from Burns," I said, frowning suddenly. "Perhaps the writer got it there—wasn't Burns alive then?"

"He was," said Bree smugly, forestalling Roger. "But Robert Burns was six years old in 1765."

"And Jamie would be forty-four." Suddenly, it all seemed real. He was alive—had been alive, I corrected myself, trying to keep my emotions in check. I laid my fingers flat against the manuscript pages, trembling.

"And if—" I said, and had to stop to swallow again.

"And if time goes on in parallel, as we think it does—" Roger stopped, too, looking at me. Then his eyes shifted to Brianna.

She had gone quite pale, but both lips and eyes were steady, and her fingers were warm when she touched my hand.

"Then you can go back, Mama," she said softly. "You can find him."

❧

The plastic hangers rattled against the steel tubing of the dress rack as I thumbed my way slowly through the available selection.

"Can I be helpin' ye at all, miss?" The salesgirl peered up at me like a helpful Pekingese, blue-ringed eyes barely visible through bangs that brushed the top of her nose.

"Have you got any more of these old-fashioned sorts of dresses?" I gestured at the rack before me, thick with examples of the current craze—laced-bodiced, long-skirted dresses in gingham cotton and velveteen.

The salesgirl's mouth was caked so thickly that I expected the white lipstick to crack when she smiled, but it didn't.

"Oh, aye," she said. "Got a new lot o' the Jessica Gutenburgs in just today. Aren't they the grooviest, these old-style gowns?" She ran an admiring finger over a brown velvet sleeve, then whirled on her ballet flats and pointed toward the center of the store. "Just there, aye? Where it says, on the sign."

The sign, stuck on the top of a circular rack, said CAPTURE THE CHARM OF THE EIGHTEENTH CENTURY in large white letters across the top. Just below, in curlicue script, was the signature, *Jessica Gutenburg*.

Reflecting on the basic improbability of anyone actually being named Jessica Gutenburg, I waded through the contents of the rack, pausing at a truly stunning number in cream velvet, with satin inserts and a good deal of lace.

"Look lovely on, that would." The Pekingese was back, pug nose sniffing hopefully for a sale.

"Maybe so," I said, "but not very practical. You'd get filthy just walking out of the store." I pushed the white dress away with some regret, proceeding to the next size ten.

"Oh, I just love the red ones!" The girl clasped her hands in ecstasy at the brilliant garnet fabric.

"So do I," I murmured, "but we don't want to look too garish. Wouldn't do to be taken for a prostitute, would it?" The Peke gave me a startled look through the thickets, then decided I was joking, and giggled appreciatively.

"Now, that one," she said decisively, reaching past me, "that's perfect, that is. That's your color, here."

Actually, it *was* almost perfect. Floor-length, with three-quarter sleeves edged with lace. A deep, tawny gold, with shimmers of brown and amber and sherry in the heavy silk.

I lifted it carefully off the rack and held it up to examine it. A trifle fancy, but it might do. The construction seemed halfway decent; no loose threads or unraveling seams. The machine-made lace on the bodice was just tacked on, but that would be easy enough to reinforce.

"Want to try it on? The dressing rooms are just over there." The Peke was frisking about near my elbow, encouraged by my interest. Taking a quick look at the price tag, I could see why; she must work on commission. I took a deep breath at the figure, which would cover a month's rent on a London flat, but then shrugged. After all, what did I need money for?

Still, I hesitated.

"I don't know . . ." I said doubtfully, "it is lovely. But . . ."

"Oh, don't worry a bit about it's being too young for you," the Pekingese reassured me earnestly. "You don't look a day over twenty-five! Well . . . maybe thirty," she concluded lamely, after a quick glance at my face.

"Thanks," I said dryly. "I wasn't worried about that, though. I don't suppose you have any without zippers, do you?"

"Zippers?" Her small round face went quite blank beneath the makeup. "Erm . . . no. Don't think we do."

"Well, not to worry," I said, taking the dress over my arm and turning toward the dressing room. "If I go through with this, zippers will be the least of it."

22

All Hallows' Eve

"Two golden guineas, six sovereigns, twenty-three shillings, eighteen florins ninepence, ten halfpence, and . . . twelve farthings." Roger dropped the last coin on the tinkling pile, then dug into his shirt pocket, lean face absorbed as he searched. "Oh, here." He brought out a small plastic bag and carefully poured a handful of tiny copper coins into a pile alongside the other money.

"Doits," he explained. "The smallest denomination of Scottish coinage of the time. I got as many as I could, because that's likely what you'd use most of the time. You wouldn't use the large coins unless you had to buy a horse or something."

"I know." I picked up a couple of sovereigns and tilted them in my hand, letting them clink together. They were heavy—gold coins, nearly an inch in diameter. It had taken Roger and Bree four days in London, going from one rare-coin dealer to the next, to assemble the small fortune gleaming in the lamplight before me.

"You know, it's funny; these coins are worth a lot more now than their face value," I said, picking up a golden guinea, "but in terms of what they'll buy, they were worth then just about as much as now. This is six months' income for a small farmer."

"I was forgetting," Roger said, "that you know all this already; what things were worth and how they were sold."

"It's easy to forget," I said, eyes still on the money. From the corner of my vision, I saw Bree draw suddenly close to Roger, and his hand go out to her automatically.

I took a deep breath and looked up from the tiny heaps of gold and silver. "Well, that's that. Shall we go and have some dinner?"

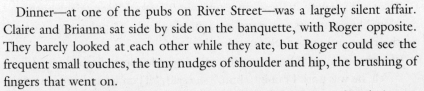

Dinner—at one of the pubs on River Street—was a largely silent affair. Claire and Brianna sat side by side on the banquette, with Roger opposite. They barely looked at each other while they ate, but Roger could see the frequent small touches, the tiny nudges of shoulder and hip, the brushing of fingers that went on.

How would he manage, he wondered to himself. If it were his choice, or his parent? Separation came to all families, but most often it was death that intervened, to sever the ties between parent and child. It was the element of choice here that made it so difficult—not that it could ever be easy, he thought, forking in a mouthful of hot shepherd's pie.

As they rose to leave after supper, he laid a hand on Claire's arm.

"Just for the sake of nothing," he said, "will you try something for me?"

"I expect so," she said, smiling. "What is it?"

He nodded at the door. "Close your eyes and step out of the door. When you're outside, open them. Then come in and tell me what's the first thing you saw."

Her mouth twitched with amusement. "All right. We'll hope the first thing I see isn't a policeman, or you'll have to come bail me out of jail for being drunk and disorderly."

"So long as it isn't a duck."

Claire gave him a queer look, but obediently turned toward the door of the pub and closed her eyes. Brianna watched her mother disappear through the door, hand extended to the paneling of the entry to keep her bearings. She turned to Roger, copper eyebrows raised.

"What are you up to, Roger? *Ducks?*"

"Nothing," he said, eyes still fixed on the empty entrance. "It's just an old custom. Samhain—Hallowe'en, you know?—that's one of the feasts when it was customary to try to divine the future. And one of the ways of divination was to walk to the end of the house, and then step outside with your eyes closed. The first thing you see when you open them is an omen for the near future."

"Ducks are bad omens?"

"Depends what they're doing," he said absently, still watching the entry. "If they have their heads under their wings, that's death. What's keeping her?"

"Maybe we'd better go see," Brianna said nervously. "I don't expect there are a lot of sleeping ducks in downtown Inverness, but with the river so close . . ."

Just as they reached the door, though, its stained-glass window darkened and it swung open to reveal Claire, looking mildly flustered.

"You'll never believe what's the first thing I saw," she said, laughing as she saw them.

"Not a duck with its head under its wing?" asked Brianna anxiously.

"No," her mother said, giving her a puzzled look. "A policeman. I turned to the right and ran smack into him."

"He was coming toward you, then?" Roger felt inexplicably relieved.

"Well, he was until I ran into him," she said. "Then we waltzed round the pavement a bit, clutching each other." She laughed, looking flushed and pretty, with her brown-sherry eyes sparkling in the amber pub lights. "Why?"

"That's good luck," Roger said, smiling. "To see a man coming toward you on Samhain means you'll find what you seek."

"Does it?" Her eyes rested on his, quizzical, then her face lit with a sudden smile. "Wonderful! Let's go home and celebrate, shall we?"

The anxious constraint that had lain on them over dinner seemed suddenly to have vanished, to be replaced with a sort of manic excitement, and they laughed and joked on the trip back to the manse, where they drank toasts to past and future—Loch Minneaig Scotch for Claire and Roger, Coca-Cola for Brianna—and talked excitedly about the plans for the next day. Brianna had insisted on carving a pumpkin into a jack-o'-lantern, which sat on the sideboard, grinning benevolently on the proceedings.

"You've got the money, now," Roger said, for the tenth time.

"And your cloak," Brianna chimed in.

"Yes, yes, yes," Claire said impatiently. "Everything I need—or everything I can manage, at least," she amended. She paused, then impulsively reached out and took both Bree and Roger by the hand.

"Thank you both," she said, squeezing their hands. Her eyes shone moist, and her voice was suddenly husky. "Thank you. I can't say what I feel. I can't. But—oh, my dears, I will miss you!"

Then she and Bree were in each other's arms, Claire's head tucked into her daughter's neck, the both of them hugged tight, as though simple force could somehow express the depth of feeling between them.

Then they broke apart, eyes wet, and Claire laid a hand on her daughter's cheek. "I'd better go up now," she whispered. "There are things to do, still. I'll see you in the morning, Baby." She rose on tiptoe to plant a kiss on her daughter's nose, then turned and hurried from the room.

After her mother's exit, Brianna sat down again with her glass of Coke, and heaved a deep sigh. She didn't speak, but sat looking into the fire, turning the glass slowly between her hands.

Roger busied himself, setting the room to rights for the night, closing the windows, tidying the desk, putting away the reference books he had used to help Claire prepare for her journey. He paused by the jack-o'-lantern, but it looked so jolly, with the candlelight streaming from its slanted eyes and jagged mouth, that he couldn't bring himself to blow it out.

"I shouldn't think it's likely to set anything on fire," he remarked. "Shall we leave it?"

There was no answer. When he glanced at Brianna, he found her sitting still as stone, eyes fixed on the hearth. She hadn't heard him. He sat down beside her and took her hand.

"She might be able to come back," he said gently. "We don't know."

Brianna shook her head slowly, not taking her eyes from the leaping flames.

"I don't think so," she said softly. "She told you what it was like. She may not even make it through." Long fingers drummed restlessly on a denimed thigh.

Roger glanced at the door, to be sure that Claire was safely upstairs, then sat down on the sofa next to Brianna.

"She belongs with him, Bree," he said. "Can ye not see it? When she speaks of him?"

"I see it. I know she needs him." The full lower lip trembled slightly. "But . . . I need *her*!" Brianna's hands clenched suddenly tight on her knees, and she bent forward, as though trying to contain some sudden pain.

Roger stroked her hair, marveling at the softness of the glowing strands that slid through his fingers. He wanted to take her into his arms, as much for the feel of her as to offer comfort, but she was rigid and unresponsive.

"You're grown, Bree," he said softly. "You live on your own now, don't you? You may love her, but you don't need her anymore—not the way you did when you were small. Has she no right to her own joy?"

"Yes. But . . . Roger, you don't understand!" she burst out. She pressed her lips tight together and swallowed hard, then turned to him, eyes dark with distress.

"She's all that's left, Roger! The only one who really *knows* me. She and Daddy—Frank"—she corrected herself—"they were the ones who knew me from the beginning, the ones who saw me learn to walk and were proud of me when I did something good in school, and who—" She broke off, and the tears overflowed, leaving gleaming tracks in the firelight.

"This sounds really *dumb,*" she said with sudden violence. "Really, really *dumb*! But it's—" she groped, helpless, then sprang to her feet, unable to stay still.

"It's like—there are all these things I don't even know!" she said, pacing with quick, angry steps. "Do you think I remember what I looked like, learning to walk, or what the first word I said was? No, but Mama does! And that's so *stupid,* because what difference does it make, it doesn't make any difference at all, but it's important, it matters because *she* thought it was, and . . . oh, Roger, if she's gone, there won't be a soul left in the world who cares what I'm like, or thinks I'm special not because of anything, but just because I'm me! She's the only person in the world who really, really cares I was born, and if she's gone . . ." She stood still on the hearthrug, hands clenched at her sides, and mouth twisted with the effort to control herself, tears wet on her cheeks. Then her shoulders slumped and the tension went out of her tall figure.

"And that's just really dumb and selfish," she said, in a quietly reasonable tone. "And you don't understand, and you think I'm awful."

"No," Roger said quietly. "I think maybe not." He stood and came behind her, putting his arms around her waist, urging her to lean back against him. She resisted at first, stiff in his arms, but then yielded to the need for physical comfort and relaxed, his chin propped on her shoulder, head tilted to touch her own.

"I never realized," he said. "Not 'til now. D'ye remember all those boxes in the garage?"

"Which ones?" she said, with a sniffling attempt at a laugh. "There are hundreds."

"The ones that say 'Roger' on them." He gave her a slight squeeze and brought his arms up, crisscrossed on her chest, holding her snug against himself.

"They're full of my parents' old clobber," he said. "Pictures and letters and baby clothes and books and old bits of rubbish. The Reverend packed them up when he took me to live with him. Treated them just like his most precious historical documents—double-boxing, and mothproofing and all that."

He rocked slowly back and forth, swaying from side to side, carrying her with him as he watched the fire over her shoulder.

"I asked him once why he bothered to keep them—I didn't want any of it, didn't care. But he said we'd keep it just the same; it was my history, he said —and everyone needs a history."

Brianna sighed, and her body seemed to relax still further, joining him in his rhythmic, half-unconscious sway.

"Did you ever look inside them?"

He shook his head. "It isn't important what's in them," he said. "Only that they're there."

He let go of her then, and stepped back so that she turned to face him. Her face was blotched and her long, elegant nose a little swollen.

"You're wrong, you know," he said softly, and held out his hand to her. "It isn't only your mother who cares."

Brianna had gone to bed long since, but Roger sat on in the study, watching the flames die down in the hearth. Hallowe'en had always seemed to him a restless night, alive with waking spirits. Tonight was even more so, with the knowledge of what would happen in the morning. The jack-o'-lantern on the desk grinned in anticipation, filling the room with the homely scent of baking pies.

The sound of a footfall on the stair roused him from his thoughts. He had thought it might be Brianna, unable to sleep, but the visitor was Claire.

"I thought you might still be awake," she said. She was in her nightdress, a pale glimmer of white satin against the dark hallway.

He smiled and stretched out a hand, inviting her in. "No. I never could sleep on All Hallows'. Not after all the stories my father told me; I always thought I could hear ghosts talking outside my window."

She smiled, coming into the firelight. "And what did they say?"

" 'See'st thou this great gray head, with jaws which have no meat?' " Roger quoted. "You know the story? The little tailor who spent the night in a haunted church, and met the hungry ghost?"

"I do. I think if I'd heard *that* outside my window, I'd have spent the rest of the night hiding under the bedclothes."

"Oh, I usually did," Roger assured her. "Though once, when I was seven or so, I got up my nerve, stood up on the bed and peed on the windowsill—the Reverend had just told me that pissing on the doorposts is supposed to keep a ghost from coming in the house."

Claire laughed delightedly, the firelight dancing in her eyes. "Did it work?"

"Well, it would have worked better had the window been open," Roger said, "but the ghosts didn't come in, no."

They laughed together, and then one of the small awkward silences that had punctuated the evening fell between them, the sudden realization of enormity gaping beneath the tightrope of conversation. Claire sat beside him, watching the fire, her hands moving restlessly among the folds of her gown. The light winked from her wedding rings, silver and gold, in sparks of fire.

"I'll take care of her, you know," Roger said quietly, at last. "You do know that, don't you?"

Claire nodded, not looking at him.

"I know," she said softly. He could see the tears, caught trembling at the edge of her lashes, glowing with firelight. She fumbled in the pocket of her gown, and drew out a long white envelope.

"You'll think me a dreadful coward," she said, "and I am. But I . . . I honestly don't think I can do it—say goodbye to Bree, I mean." She stopped, to bring her voice under control, and then held out the envelope to him.

"I wrote it all down for her—everything I could. Will you . . . ?"

Roger took the envelope. It was warm from resting next to her body. From some obscure feeling that it must not be allowed to grow cold before it reached her daughter, he thrust it into his own breast pocket, feeling the crackle of paper as the envelope bent.

"Yes," he said, hearing his own voice thicken. "Then you'll go . . ."

"Early," she said, taking a deep breath. "Before dawn. I've arranged for a car to pick me up." Her hands twisted together in her lap. "If I—" She bit her lip, then looked at Roger pleadingly. "I don't know, you see," she said.

"I don't know whether I can do it. I'm very much afraid. Afraid to go. Afraid not to go. Just—afraid."

"I would be, too." He held out his hand and she took it. He held it for a long time, feeling the pulse in her wrist, light and fast against his fingers.

After a long time, she squeezed his hand gently and let go.

"Thank you, Roger," she said. "For everything." She leaned over and kissed him lightly on the lips. Then she rose and went out, a white ghost in the darkness of the hall, borne on the Hallowe'en wind.

Roger sat on for some time alone, feeling her touch still warm on his skin. The jack-o'-lantern was nearly burned out. The smell of candle wax rose strongly in the restless air, and the pagan gods looked out for the last time, through eyes of guttering flame.

23

Craigh na Dun

The early morning air was cold and misty, and I was glad of the cloak. It had been twenty years since I'd worn one, but with the sorts of things people wore nowadays, the Inverness tailor who'd made it for me had not found an order for a woolen cloak with a hood at all odd.

I kept my eyes on the path. The crest of the hill had been invisible, wreathed in mist, when the car had left me on the road below.

"Here?" the driver had said, peering dubiously out of his window at the deserted countryside. "Sure, mum?"

"Yes," I'd said, half-choked with terror. "This is the place."

"Aye?" He looked dubious, in spite of the large note I put in his hand. "D'ye want me to wait, mum? Or to come later, to fetch ye back?"

I was sorely tempted to say yes. After all, what if I lost my nerve? At the moment, my grip on that slippery substance seemed remarkably feeble.

"No," I said, swallowing. "No, that won't be necessary." If I couldn't do it, I would just have to walk back to Inverness, that was all. Or perhaps Roger and Brianna would come; I thought that would be worse, to be ignominiously retrieved. Or would it be a relief?

The granite pebbles rolled beneath my feet and a clod of dirt fell in a small rushing shower, dislodged by my passage. I couldn't possibly really be doing this, I thought. The weight of the money in my reinforced pocket swung against my thigh, the heavy certainty of gold and silver a reminder of reality. I *was* doing it.

I couldn't. Thoughts of Bree as I had seen her late last night, peacefully asleep in her bed, assaulted me. The tendrils of remembered horror reached out from the hilltop above, as I began to sense the nearness of the stones. Screaming, chaos, the feeling of being torn in pieces. I couldn't.

I couldn't, but I kept on climbing, palms sweating, my feet moving as though no longer under my control.

It was full dawn by the time I reached the top of the hill. The mist lay below, and the stones stood clear and dark against a crystal sky. The sight of them left me wet-palmed with apprehension, but I walked forward, and passed into the circle.

They were standing on the grass in front of the cleft stone, facing each other. Brianna heard my footsteps and whirled around to face me.

I stared at her, speechless with astonishment. She was wearing a Jessica Gutenburg dress, very much like the one I had on, except that hers was a vivid lime green, with plastic jewels stitched across the bosom.

"That's a perfectly horrible color for you," I said.

"It's the only one they had in a size sixteen," she answered calmly.

"What in the name of goodness are you doing here?" I demanded, recovering some remnant of coherence.

"We came to see you off," she said, and a hint of a smile flickered on her lips. I looked at Roger, who shrugged slightly and gave me a lopsided smile of his own.

"Oh. Yes. Well," I said. The stone stood behind Brianna, twice the height of a man. I could look through the foot-wide crack, and see the faint morning sun shining on the grass outside the circle.

"You're going," she said firmly, "or I am."

"You! Are you out of your mind?"

"No." She glanced at the cleft stone and swallowed. It might have been the lime-green dress that made her face look chalk-white. "I can do it—go through, I mean. I know I can. When Geilie Duncan went through the stones, I heard them. Roger did too." She glanced at him as though for reassurance, then fixed her gaze firmly on me.

"I don't know whether I could find Jamie Fraser or not; maybe only you can. But if you won't try, then I will."

My mouth opened, but I couldn't find anything to say.

"Don't you see, Mama? He has to know—has to know he did it, he did what he meant to for us." Her lips quivered, and she pressed them together for a minute.

"We owe it to him, Mama," she said softly. "Somebody has to find him, and tell him." Her hand touched my face, briefly. "Tell him I was born."

"Oh, Bree," I said, my voice so choked I could barely speak. "Oh, Bree!"

She was holding my hands tight between her own, squeezing hard.

"He gave you to me," she said, so low I could hardly hear her. "Now I have to give you back to him, Mama."

The eyes that were so like Jamie's looked down at me, blurred by tears.

"If you find him," she whispered, "when you find my father—give him this." She bent and kissed me, fiercely, gently, then straightened and turned me toward the stone.

"Go, Mama," she said, breathless. "I love you. Go!"

From the corner of my eye, I saw Roger move toward her. I took one step, and then another. I heard a sound, a faint roaring. I took the last step, and the world disappeared.

PART SIX

Edinburgh

24

A. Malcolm, Printer

My first coherent thought was, "It's raining. This must be Scotland." My second thought was that this observation was no great improvement over the random images jumbling around inside my head, banging into each other and setting off small synaptic explosions of irrelevance.

I opened one eye, with some difficulty. The lid was stuck shut, and my entire face felt cold and puffy, like a submerged corpse's. I shuddered faintly at the thought, the slight movement making me aware of the sodden fabric all around me.

It was certainly raining—a soft, steady drum of rain that raised a faint mist of droplets above the green moor. I sat up, feeling like a hippopotamus emerging from a bog, and promptly fell over backward.

I blinked and closed my eyes against the downpour. Some small sense of who I was—and where I was—was beginning to come back to me. *Bree*. Her face emerged suddenly into memory, with a jolt that made me gasp as though I'd been punched in the stomach. Jagged images of loss and the rip of separation pulled at me, a faint echo of the chaos in the stone passage.

Jamie. There it was; the anchor point to which I had clung, my single hold on sanity. I breathed slow and deep, hands folded over my pounding heart, summoning Jamie's face. For a moment, I thought I had lost him, and then it came, clear and bold in my mind's eye.

Once again, I struggled upright, and this time stayed, propped by my outstretched hands. Yes, certainly it was Scotland. It could hardly by anything else, of course, but it was also the Scotland of the past. At least, I *hoped* it was the past. It wasn't the Scotland I'd left, at any rate. The trees and bushes grew in different patterns; there was a patch of maple saplings just below me that hadn't been there when I'd climbed the hill—when? That morning? Two days ago?

I had no idea how much time had passed since I had entered the standing stones, or how long I had lain unconscious on the hillside below the circle. Quite a while, judging from the sogginess of my clothing; I was soaked through to the skin, and small chilly rivulets ran down my sides under my gown.

One numbed cheek was beginning to tingle; putting my hand to it, I could feel a pattern of incised bumps. I looked down and saw a layer of fallen rowan berries, gleaming red and black among the grass. Very appropriate, I thought, vaguely amused. I had fallen down under a rowan—the Highland protection against witchcraft and enchantment.

I grasped the smooth trunk of the rowan tree, and laboriously hauled myself to my feet. Still holding onto the tree for support, I looked to the northeast. The rain had faded the horizon to a gray invisibility, but I knew that Inverness lay in that direction. No more than an hour's trip by car, along modern roads.

The road existed; I could see the outline of a rough track that led along the base of the hill, a dark, silvery line in the gleaming green wetness of the moor plants. However, forty-odd miles on foot was a far cry from the journey by car that had brought me here.

I was beginning to feel somewhat better, standing up. The weakness in my limbs was fading, along with the feeling of chaos and disruption in my mind. It had been as bad as I'd feared, this passage; perhaps worse. I could feel the terrible presence of the stones above me, and shuddered, my skin prickling with cold.

I was alive, though. Alive, and with a small feeling of certainty, like a tiny glowing sun beneath my ribs. *He was here.* I knew it now, though I hadn't known it when I threw myself between the stones; that had been a leap of faith. But I had cast out my thought of Jamie like a lifeline tossed into a raging torrent—and the line had tightened in my grasp, and pulled me free.

I was wet, cold, and felt battered, as though I had been washing about in the surf against a rocky shore. But I was here. And somewhere in this strange country of the past was the man I had come to find. The memories of grief and terror were receding, as I realized that my die was cast. I could not go back; a return trip would almost surely be fatal. As I realized that I was likely here to stay, all hesitations and terrors were superseded by a strange calm, almost exultant. I could not go back. There was nothing to do but go forward—to find him.

Cursing my carelessness in not having thought to tell the tailor to make my cloak with a waterproof layer between fabric and lining, I pulled the water-soaked garment closer. Even wet, the wool held some warmth. If I began to move, I would grow warmer. A quick pat reassured me that my bundle of sandwiches had made the trip with me. That was good; the thought of walking forty miles on an empty stomach was a daunting one.

With luck, I wouldn't have to. I might find a village or a house that had a horse I could buy. But if not, I was prepared. My plan was to go to Inverness —by whatever means offered itself—and there take a public coach to Edinburgh.

There was no telling where Jamie was at the moment. He might be in Edinburgh, where his article had been published, but he might easily be somewhere else. If I could not find him there, I could go to Lallybroch, his home. Surely his family would know where he was—if any of them were left. The sudden thought chilled me, and I shivered.

I thought of a small bookstore that I passed every morning on my way from the parking lot to the hospital. They had been having a sale on posters; I had seen the display of psychedelic examples when I left Joe's office for the last time.

"Today is the first day of the rest of your life," said one poster, above an illustration of a foolish-looking chick, absurdly poking its head out of an eggshell. In the other window, another poster showed a caterpillar, inching its way up a flower stalk. Above the stalk soared a brilliantly colored butterfly, and below was the motto "A journey of a thousand miles begins with a single step."

The most irritating thing about clichés, I decided, was how frequently they were true. I let go of the rowan tree, and started down the hill toward my future.

It was a long, jolting ride from Inverness to Edinburgh, crammed cheek by jowl into a large coach with two other ladies, the small and whiny son of one of the ladies, and four gentlemen of varying sizes and dispositions.

Mr. Graham, a small and vivacious gentleman of advanced years who was seated next to me, was wearing a bag of camphor and asafoetida about his neck, to the eyewatering discomfort of the rest of the coach.

"Capital for dispelling the evil humors of influenza," he explained to me, waving the bag gently under my nose like a censer. "I have worn this daily through the autumn and winter months, and haven't been sick a day in nearly thirty years!"

"Amazing!" I said politely, trying to hold my breath. I didn't doubt it; the fumes probably kept everyone at such a distance that germs couldn't reach him.

The effects on the little boy didn't seem nearly so beneficial. After a number of loud and injudicious remarks about the smell in the coach, Master Georgie had been muffled in his mother's bosom, from which he now peeped, looking rather green. I kept a close eye on him, as well as on the chamber pot beneath the seat opposite, in case quick action involving a conjunction of the two should be called for.

I gathered that the chamber pot was for use in inclement weather or other emergency, as normally the ladies' modesty required stops every hour or so, at which point the passengers would scatter into the roadside vegetation like a covey of quail, even those who did not require relief of bladder or bowels seeking some relief from the stench of Mr. Graham's asafoetida bag.

After one or two changes, Mr. Graham found his place beside me superseded by Mr. Wallace, a plump young lawyer, returning to Edinburgh after seeing to the disposition of the estate of an elderly relative in Inverness, as he explained to me.

I didn't find the details of his legal practice nearly as fascinating as he did, but under the circumstances, his evident attraction to me was mildly reassuring, and I passed several hours in playing with him upon a small chess set that he produced from a pocket and laid upon his knee.

My attention was distracted both from the discomforts of the journey and the intricacies of chess by anticipation of what I might find in Edinburgh. A. Malcolm. The name kept running through my mind like an anthem of hope. A. Malcolm. It had to be Jamie, it simply had to! James Alexander Malcolm MacKenzie Fraser.

"Considering the way the Highland rebels were treated after Culloden, it would be very reasonable for him to use an assumed name in a place like Edinburgh," Roger Wakefield had explained to me. "Particularly him—he was a convicted traitor, after all. Made rather a habit of it, too, it looks like," he had added critically, looking over the scrawled manuscript of the antitax diatribe. "For the times, this is bloody near sedition."

"Yes, that sounds like Jamie," I had said dryly, but my heart had leapt at the sight of that distinctively untidy scrawl, with its boldly worded sentiments. My Jamie. I touched the small hard rectangle in my skirt pocket, wondering how long it would be, before we reached Edinburgh.

The weather kept unseasonably fine, with no more than the occasional drizzle to hinder our passage, and we completed the journey in less than two days, stopping four times to change horses and refresh ourselves at posthouse taverns.

The coach debouched into a yard at the back of Boyd's Whitehorse tavern, near the foot of the Royal Mile in Edinburgh. The passengers emerged into the watery sunshine like newly hatched chrysalids, rumpled of wing and jerky in movement, unaccustomed to mobility. After the dimness of the coach, even the cloudy gray light of Edinburgh seemed blinding.

I had pins and needles in my feet from so long sitting, but hurried nonetheless, hoping to escape from the courtyard while my erstwhile companions were busy with the retrieval of their belongings. No such luck; Mr. Wallace caught up with me near the street.

"Mrs. Fraser!" he said. "Might I beg the pleasure of accompanying you to your destination? You will surely require some assistance in the removal of your luggage." He looked over his shoulder toward the coach, where the ostlers were heaving the bags and portmanteaux apparently at random into the crowd, to the accompaniment of incoherent grunts and shouts.

"Er . . ." I said. "Thank you, but I . . . er, I'm leaving my luggage in charge of the landlord. My . . . my . . ." I groped frantically. "My husband's servant will come fetch it later."

His plump face fell slightly at the word "husband," but he rallied gallantly, taking my hand and bowing low over it.

"I quite see. May I express my profound appreciation for the pleasure of your company on our journey, then, Mrs. Fraser? And perhaps we shall meet again." He straightened up, surveying the crowd that eddied past us. "Is your husband meeting you? I should be delighted to make his acquaintance."

While Mr. Wallace's interest in me had been rather flattering, it was rapidly becoming a nuisance.

"No, I shall be joining him later," I said. "So nice to have met you, Mr. Wallace; I'll hope to see you again sometime." I shook Mr. Wallace's hand enthusiastically, which disconcerted him enough for me to slither off through the throng of passengers, ostlers and food sellers.

I didn't dare pause near the coachyard for fear he would come out after me. I turned and darted up the slope of the Royal Mile, moving as quickly as my voluminous skirts would allow, jostling and bumping my way through the crowd. I had had the luck to pick a market day for my arrival, and I was soon lost to sight from the coachyard among the luckenbooths and oyster sellers who lined the street.

Panting like an escaped pickpocket, I stopped for breath halfway up the hill. There was a public fountain here, and I sat down on the rim to catch my breath.

I was here. Really here. Edinburgh sloped up behind me, to the glowering heights of Edinburgh Castle, and down before me, to the gracious majesty of Holyrood Palace at the foot of the city.

The last time I had stood by this fountain, Bonnie Prince Charlie had been addressing the gathered citizenry of Edinburgh, inspiring them with the sight of his royal presence. He had bounded exuberantly from the rim to the carved center finial of the fountain, one foot in the basin, clinging to one of the spouting heads for support, shouting "On to England!" The crowd had roared, pleased at this show of youthful high spirits and athletic prowess. I would myself have been more impressed had I not noticed that the water in the fountain had been turned off in anticipation of the gesture.

I wondered where Charlie was now. He had gone back to Italy after Culloden, I supposed, there to live whatever life was possible for royalty in permanent exile. What he was doing, I neither knew nor cared. He had passed from the pages of history, and from my life as well, leaving wreck and ruin in his wake. It remained to be seen what might be salvaged now.

I was very hungry; I had had nothing to eat since a hasty breakfast of rough parritch and boiled mutton, made soon after dawn at a posthouse in Dundaff. I had one last sandwich remaining in my pocket, but had been reluctant to eat it in the coach, under the curious gaze of my fellow travelers.

I pulled it out and carefully unwrapped it. Peanut butter and jelly on white bread, it was considerably the worse for wear, with the purple stains of the jelly seeping through the limp bread, and the whole thing mashed into a flattened wodge. It was delicious.

I ate it carefully, savoring the rich, oily taste of the peanut butter. How many mornings had I slathered peanut butter on bread, making sandwiches for Brianna's school lunches? Firmly suppressing the thought, I examined the passersby for distraction. They did look somewhat different from their modern equivalents; both men and women tended to be shorter, and the signs of poor nutrition were evident. Still, there was an overwhelming familiarity to them—these were people I knew, Scots and English for the most part, and hearing the rich burring babble of voices in the street, after so many years of the flat nasal tones of Boston, I had quite an extraordinary feeling of coming home.

I swallowed the last rich, sweet bite of my old life, and crumpled the wrapper in my hand. I glanced around, but no one was looking in my direction. I opened my hand, and let the bit of plastic film fall surreptitiously to the ground. Wadded up, it rolled a few inches on the cobbles, crinkling and unfolding itself as though alive. The light wind caught it, and the small transparent sheet took sudden wing, scudding over the gray stones like a leaf.

The draft of a set of passing wheels sucked it under a drayman's cart; it winked once with reflected light, and was gone, disappearing without notice from the passersby. I wondered whether my own anachronistic presence would cause as little harm.

"You are dithering, Beauchamp," I said to myself. "Time to get on." I took a deep breath and stood up.

"Excuse me," I said, catching the sleeve of a passing baker's boy. "I'm looking for a printer—a Mr. Malcolm. Alexander Malcolm." A feeling of mingled dread and excitement gurgled through my middle. What if there was no printshop run by Alexander Malcolm in Edinburgh?

There was, though; the boy's face screwed up in thought and then relaxed.

"Oh, aye, mum—just down the way and to your left. Carfax Close." And hitching his loaves up under his arm with a nod, he plunged back into the crowded street.

Carfax Close. I edged my way back into the crowd, pressing close to the buildings, to avoid the occasional shower of slops that splattered into the street from the windows high above. There were several thousand people in Edinburgh, and the sewage from all of them was running down the gutters of the cobbled street, depending on gravity and the frequent rain to keep the city habitable.

The low, dark opening to Carfax Close yawned just ahead, across the expanse of the Royal Mile. I stopped dead, looking at it, my heart beating hard enough to be heard a yard away, had anyone been listening.

It wasn't raining, but was just about to, and the dampness in the air made my hair curl. I pushed it off my forehead, tidying it as best I could without a mirror. Then I caught sight of a large plate-glass window up ahead, and hurried forward.

The glass was misty with condensation, but provided a dim reflection, in which my face looked flushed and wide-eyed, but otherwise presentable. My hair, however, had seized the opportunity to curl madly in all directions, and was writhing out of its hairpins in excellent imitation of Medusa's locks. I yanked the pins out impatiently, and began to twist up my curls.

There was a woman inside the shop, leaning across the counter. There were three small children with her, and I watched with half an eye as she turned from her business to address them impatiently, swatting with her reticule at the middle one, a boy who was fiddling with several stalks of fresh anise that stood in a pail of water on the floor.

It was an apothecary's shop; glancing up, I saw the name "Haugh" above the door, and felt a thrill of recognition. I had bought herbs here, during the brief time I had lived in Edinburgh. The decor of the window had been augmented sometime since by the addition of a large jar of colored water, in which floated something vaguely humanoid. A fetal pig, or perhaps an infant baboon; it had leering, flattened features that pressed against the rounded side of the jar in a disconcerting fashion.

"Well, at least I look better than *you*!" I muttered, shoving in a recalcitrant pin.

I looked better than the woman inside, too, I thought. Her business concluded, she was stuffing her purchase into the bag she carried, her thin face frowning as she did so. She had the rather pasty look of a city dweller, and her skin was deeply lined, with sharp creases running from nose to mouth, and a furrowed forehead.

"De'il tak' ye, ye wee ratten," she was saying crossly to the little boy as they all clattered out of the shop together. "Have I no told ye time and again to keep yer paws in yer pockets?"

"Excuse me." I stepped forward, interrupting, impelled by a sudden irresistible curiosity.

"Aye?" Distracted from maternal remonstration, she looked blankly at me. Up close, she looked even more harried. The corners of her mouth were pinched, and her lips folded in—no doubt because of missing teeth.

"I couldn't help admiring your children," I said, with as much pretense of admiration as I could manage on short notice. I beamed kindly at them. "Such pretty babies! Tell me, how old are they?"

Her jaw dropped, confirming the absence of several teeth. She blinked at me, then said, "Oh! Well, that's maist kind o' ye, mum. Ah . . . Maisri here is ten," she said, nodding at the eldest girl, who was in the act of wiping her nose on her sleeve, "Joey's eight—tak' yer finger out o' yer nose, ye clattie imp!" she hissed, then turned and proudly patted her youngest on the head. "And wee Polly's just turned six this May."

"Really!" I gazed at the woman, affecting astonishment. "You scarcely look old enough to have children of that age. You must have married very young."

She preened slightly, smirking.

"Och, no! Not so young as all that; why, I was all o' nineteen when Maisri was born."

"Amazing," I said, meaning it. I dug in my pocket and offered the children each a penny, which they took with shy bobs of thanks. "Good day to you—and congratulations on your lovely family," I said to the woman, and walked away with a smile and a wave.

Nineteen when the eldest was born, and Maisri was ten now. She was twenty-nine. And I, blessed by good nutrition, hygiene, and dentistry, not worn down by multiple pregnancies and hard physical labor, looked a good deal younger than she. I took a deep breath, pushed back my hair, and marched into the shadows of Carfax Close.

It was a longish, winding close, and the printshop was at the foot. There were thriving businesses and tenements on either side, but I had no attention to spare for anything beyond the neat white sign that hung by the door.

A. MALCOLM

PRINTER AND BOOKSELLER

it said, and beneath this, *Books, calling cards, pamphlets, broadsheets, letters, etc.*

I stretched out my hand and touched the black letters of the name. A. Malcolm. Alexander Malcolm. James Alexander Malcolm MacKenzie Fraser. Perhaps.

Another minute, and I would lose my nerve. I shoved open the door and walked in.

There was a broad counter across the front of the room, with an open flap in it, and a rack to one side that held several trays of type. Posters and notices of all sorts were tacked up on the opposite wall; samples, no doubt.

The door into the back room was open, showing the bulky angular frame of a printing press. Bent over it, his back turned to me, was Jamie.

"Is that you, Geordie?" he asked, not turning around. He was dressed in shirt and breeches, and had a small tool of some kind in his hand, with which he was doing something to the innards of the press. "Took ye long enough. Did ye get the—"

"It isn't Geordie," I said. My voice was higher than usual. "It's me," I said. "Claire."

He straightened up very slowly. He wore his hair long; a thick tail of a deep, rich auburn sparked with copper. I had time to see that the neat ribbon that tied it back was green, and then he turned around.

He stared at me without speaking. A tremor ran down the muscular throat as he swallowed, but still he didn't say anything.

It was the same broad, good-humored face, dark blue eyes aslant the high, flat cheekbones of a Viking, long mouth curling at the ends as though always on the verge of smiling. The lines surrounding eyes and mouth were deeper, of course. The nose had changed just a bit. The knife-edge bridge was slightly thickened near the base by the ridge of an old, healed fracture. It made him look fiercer, I thought, but lessened that air of aloof reserve, and lent his appearance a new rough charm.

I walked through the flap in the counter, seeing nothing but that unblinking stare. I cleared my throat.

"When did you break your nose?"

The corners of the wide mouth lifted slightly.

"About three minutes after I last saw ye—Sassenach."

There was a hesitation, almost a question in the name. There was no more than a foot between us. I reached out tentatively and touched the tiny line of the break, where the bone pressed white against the bronze of his skin.

He flinched backward as though an electric spark had arced between us, and the calm expression shattered.

"You're real," he whispered. I had thought him pale already. Now all vestiges of color drained from his face. His eyes rolled up and he slumped to the floor in a shower of papers and oddments that had been sitting on the press—he fell rather gracefully for such a large man, I thought abstractedly.

It was only a faint; his eyelids were beginning to flutter by the time I knelt beside him and loosened the stock at his throat. I had no doubts at all by now, but still I looked automatically as I pulled the heavy linen away. It was there, of course, the small triangular scar just above the collarbone, left by the knife of Captain Jonathan Randall, Esquire, of His Majesty's Eighth Dragoons.

His normal healthy color was returning. I sat cross-legged on the floor and hoisted his head onto my thigh. His hair felt thick and soft in my hand. His eyes opened.

"That bad, is it?" I said, smiling down at him with the same words he had used to me on the day of our wedding, holding my head in his lap, twenty-odd years before.

"That bad, and worse, Sassenach," he answered, mouth twitching with something almost a smile. He sat up abruptly, staring at me.

"God in heaven, you *are* real!"

"So are you." I lifted my chin to look up at him. "I th-thought you were dead." I had meant to speak lightly, but my voice betrayed me. The tears spilled down my cheeks, only to soak into the rough cloth of his shirt as he pulled me hard against him.

I shook so that it was some time before I realized that he was shaking, too, and for the same reason. I don't know how long we sat there on the dusty floor, crying in each other's arms with the longing of twenty years spilling down our faces.

His fingers twined hard in my hair, pulling it loose so that it tumbled down my neck. The dislodged pins cascaded over my shoulders and pinged on the floor like pellets of hail. My own fingers were clasped around his forearm, digging into the linen as though I were afraid he would disappear unless physically restrained.

As though gripped by the same fear, he suddenly grasped me by the shoulders and held me away from him, staring desperately into my face. He put his hand to my cheek, and traced the bones over and over again, oblivious to my tears and to my abundantly running nose.

I sniffed loudly, which seemed to bring him to his senses, for he let go and groped hastily in his sleeve for a handkerchief, which he used clumsily to swab first my face, then his own.

"Give me that." I grabbed the erratically waving swatch of cloth and blew my nose firmly. "Now you." I handed him the cloth and watched as he blew his nose with a noise like a strangled goose. I giggled, undone with emotion.

He smiled too, knuckling the tears away from his eyes, unable to stop staring at me.

Suddenly I couldn't bear not to be touching him. I lunged at him, and he got his arms up just in time to catch me. I squeezed until I could hear his ribs crack, and felt his hands roughly caressing my back as he said my name over and over.

At last I could let go, and sat back a little. He glanced down at the floor between his legs, frowning.

"Did you lose something?" I asked, surprised.

He looked up and smiled, a little shyly.

"I was afraid I'd lost hold altogether and pissed myself, but it's all right. I've just sat on the alepot."

Sure enough, a pool of aromatic brown liquid was spreading slowly beneath him. With a squeak of alarm, I scrambled to my feet and helped him up. After trying vainly to assess the damage behind, he shrugged and unfastened his breeches. He pushed the tight fabric down over his haunches, then stopped and looked at me, blushing slightly.

"It's all right," I said, feeling a rich blush stain my own cheeks. "We're married." I cast my eyes down, nonetheless, feeling a little breathless. "At least, I suppose we are."

He stared at me for a long moment, then a smile curved his wide, soft mouth.

"Aye, we are," he said. Kicking free of the stained breeches, he stepped toward me.

I stretched out a hand toward him, as much to stop as to welcome him. I wanted more than anything to touch him again, but was unaccountably shy. After so long, how were we to start again?

He felt the constraint of mingled shyness and intimacy as well. Stopping a few inches from me, he took my hand. He hesitated for a moment, then bent his head over it, his lips barely brushing my knuckles. His fingers touched the silver ring and stopped there, holding the metal lightly between thumb and forefinger.

"I never took it off," I blurted. It seemed important he should know that. He squeezed my hand lightly, but didn't let go.

"I want—" He stopped and swallowed, still holding my hand. His fingers found and touched the silver ring once more. "I want verra much to kiss you," he said softly. "May I do that?"

The tears were barely dammed. Two more welled up and overflowed; I felt them, full and round, roll down my cheeks.

"Yes," I whispered.

He drew me slowly close to him, holding our linked hands just under his breast.

"I havena done this for a verra long time," he said. I saw the hope and the fear dark in the blue of his eyes. I took the gift and gave it back to him.

"Neither have I," I said softly.

His hands cupped my face with exquisite gentleness, and he set his mouth on mine.

I didn't know quite what I had been expecting. A reprise of the pounding fury that had accompanied our final parting? I had remembered that so often, lived it over in memory, helpless to change the outcome. The half-rough, timeless hours of mutual possession in the darkness of our marriage bed? I had longed for that, wakened often sweating and trembling from the memory of it.

But we were strangers now, barely touching, each seeking the way toward joining, slowly, tentatively, seeking and giving unspoken permission with our silent lips. My eyes were closed, and I knew without looking that Jamie's were, as well. We were, quite simply, afraid to look at each other.

Without raising his head, he began to stroke me lightly, feeling my bones through my clothes, familiarizing himself again with the terrain of my body. At last his hand traveled down my arm and caught my right hand. His fingers traced my hand until they found the ring again, and circled it, feeling the interlaced silver of the Highland pattern, polished with long wear, but still distinct.

His lips moved from mine, across my cheeks and eyes. I gently stroked his back, feeling through his shirt the marks I couldn't see, the remnants of old scars, like my ring, worn but still distinct.

"I've seen ye so many times," he said, his voice whispering warm in my ear. "You've come to me so often. When I dreamed sometimes. When I lay in fever. When I was so afraid and so lonely I knew I must die. When I needed you, I would always see ye, smiling, with your hair curling up about your face. But ye never spoke. And ye never touched me."

"I can touch you now." I reached up and drew my hand gently down his temple, his ear, the cheek and jaw that I could see. My hand went to the nape of his neck, under the clubbed bronze hair, and he raised his head at last, and cupped my face between his hands, love glowing strong in the dark blue eyes.

"Dinna be afraid," he said softly. "There's the two of us now."

We might have gone on standing there gazing at each other indefinitely, had the shop bell over the door not rung. I let go of Jamie and looked around sharply, to see a small, wiry man with coarse dark hair standing in the door, mouth agape, holding a small parcel in one hand.

"Oh, there ye are, Geordie! What's kept ye?" Jamie said.

Geordie said nothing, but his eyes traveled dubiously over his employer, standing bare-legged in his shirt in the middle of the shop, his breeches, shoes, and stockings discarded on the floor, and me in his arms, with my gown all crumpled and my hair coming down. Geordie's narrow face creased into a censorious frown.

"I quit," he said, in the rich tones of the West Highlands. "The printing's one thing—I'm wi' ye there, and ye'll no think otherwise—but I'm Free Church and my daddy before me and my grandsire before him. Workin' for a Papist is one thing—the Pope's coin's as good as any, aye?—but workin' for an immoral Papist is another. Do as ye like wi' your own soul, man, but if it's come to orgies in the shop, it's come too far, that's what I say. I quit!"

He placed the package precisely in the center of the counter, spun on his heel and stalked toward the door. Outside, the Town Clock on the Tolbooth began to strike. Geordie turned in the doorway to glare accusingly at us.

"And it not even noon yet!" he said. The shop door slammed behind him.

Jamie stared after him for a moment, then sank slowly down onto the floor again, laughing so hard, the tears came to his eyes.

"And it's not even noon yet!" he repeated, wiping the tears off his cheeks. "Oh, God, Geordie!" He rocked back and forth, grasping his knees with both hands.

I couldn't help laughing myself, though I was rather worried.

"I didn't mean to cause you trouble," I said. "Will he come back, do you think?"

He sniffed and wiped his face carelessly on the tail of his shirt.

"Oh, aye. He lives just across the way, in Wickham Wynd. I'll go and see him in a bit, and . . . and explain," he said. He looked at me, realization dawning, and added, "God knows how!" It looked for a minute as though he might start laughing again, but he mastered the impulse and stood up.

"Have you got another pair of breeches?" I asked, picking up the discarded ones and draping them across the counter to dry.

"Aye, I have—upstairs. Wait a bit, though." He snaked a long arm into the cupboard beneath the counter, and came out with a neatly lettered notice that said GONE OUT. Attaching this to the outside of the door, and firmly bolting the inside, he turned to me.

"Will ye step upstairs wi' me?" he said. He crooked an arm invitingly, eyes sparkling. "If ye dinna think it immoral?"

"Why not?" I said. The impulse to explode in laughter was just below the surface, sparkling in my blood like champagne. "We're married, aren't we?"

The upstairs was divided into two rooms, one on either side of the landing, and a small privy closet just off the landing itself. The back room was plainly devoted to storage for the printing business; the door was propped open, and I could see wooden crates filled with books, towering bundles of pamphlets neatly tied with twine, barrels of alcohol and powdered ink, and a jumble of odd-looking hardware that I assumed must be spare parts for a printing press.

The front room was spare as a monk's cell. There was a chest of drawers with a pottery candlestick on it, a washstand, a stool, and a narrow cot, little more than a camp bed. I let out my breath when I saw it, only then realizing that I had been holding it. He slept alone.

A quick glance around confirmed that there was no sign of a feminine presence in the room, and my heart began to beat with a normal rhythm again. Plainly no one lived here but Jamie; he had pushed aside the curtain that blocked off a corner of the room, and the row of pegs revealed there supported no more than a couple of shirts, a coat and long waistcoat in sober gray, a gray wool cloak, and the spare pair of breeches he had come to fetch.

He had his back turned to me as he tucked in his shirt and fastened the new breeches, but I could see the self-consciousness in the tense line of his shoulders. I could feel a similar tension in the back of my own neck. Given a moment to recover from the shock of seeing each other, we were both stricken now with shyness. I saw his shoulders straighten and then he turned around to face me. The hysterical laughter had left us, and the tears, though his face still showed the marks of so much sudden feeling, and I knew mine did, too.

"It's verra fine to see ye, Claire," he said softly. "I thought I never . . .

well." He shrugged slightly, as though to ease the tightness of the linen shirt across his shoulders. He swallowed, then met my eyes directly.

"The child?" he said. Everything he felt was evident on his face; urgent hope, desperate fear, and the struggle to contain both.

I smiled at him, and put out my hand. "Come here."

I had thought long and hard about what I might bring with me, should my journey through the stones succeed. Given my previous brush with accusations of witchcraft, I had been very careful. But there was one thing I had had to bring, no matter what the consequences might be if anyone saw them.

I pulled him down to sit beside me on the cot, and pulled out of my pocket the small rectangular package I had done up with such care in Boston. I undid its waterproof wrapping, and thrust its contents into his hands. "There," I said.

He took them from me, gingerly, like one handling an unknown and possibly dangerous substance. His big hands framed the photographs for a moment, holding them confined. Brianna's round newborn face was oblivious between his fingers, tiny fists curled on her blanket, slanted eyes closed in the new exhaustion of existence, her small mouth slightly open in sleep.

I looked up at his face; it was absolutely blank with shock. He held the pictures close to his chest, unmoving, wide-eyed and staring as though he had just been transfixed by a crossbow bolt through the heart—as I supposed he had.

"Your daughter sent you this," I said. I turned his blank face toward me and gently kissed him on the mouth. That broke the trance; he blinked and his face came to life again.

"My . . . she . . ." His voice was hoarse with shock. "Daughter. My daughter. She . . . knows?"

"She does. Look at the rest." I slid the first picture from his grasp, revealing the snapshot of Brianna, uproariously festooned with the icing of her first birthday cake, a four-toothed smile of fiendish triumph on her face as she waved a new plush rabbit overhead.

Jamie made a small inarticulate sound, and his fingers loosened. I took the small stack of photographs from him and gave them back, one at a time.

Brianna at two, stubby in her snowsuit, cheeks round and flushed as apples, feathery hair wisping from under her hood.

Bree at four, hair a smooth bell-shaped gleam as she sat, one ankle propped on the opposite knee as she smiled for the photographer, proper and poised in a white pinafore.

At five, in proud possession of her first lunchbox, waiting to board the school bus to kindergarten.

"She wouldn't let me go with her; she wanted to go alone. She's very b-brave, not afraid of anything . . ." I felt half-choked as I explained, displayed, pointed to the changing images that fell from his hands and slid down to the floor as he began to snatch each new picture.

"Oh, God!" he said, at the picture of Bree at ten, sitting on the kitchen floor with her arms around Smoky, the big Newfoundland. That one was in color; her hair a brilliant shimmer against the dog's shiny black coat.

His hands were shaking so badly that he couldn't hold the pictures anymore; I had to show him the last few—Bree full-grown, laughing at a string of fish she'd caught; standing at a window in secretive contemplation; red-faced and tousled, leaning on the handle of the ax she had been using to split kindling. These showed her face in all the moods I could capture, always that face, long-nosed and wide-mouthed, with those high, broad, flat Viking cheekbones and slanted eyes—a finer-boned, more delicate version of her father's, of the man who sat on the cot beside me, mouth working wordlessly, and the tears running soundless down his own cheeks.

He splayed a hand out over the photographs, trembling fingers not quite touching the shiny surfaces, and then he turned and leaned toward me, slowly, with the improbable grace of a tall tree falling. He buried his face in my shoulder and went very quietly and thoroughly to pieces.

I held him to my breast, arms tight around the broad, shaking shoulders, and my own tears fell on his hair, making small dark patches in the ruddy waves. I pressed my cheek against the top of his head, and murmured small incoherent things to him as though he were Brianna. I thought to myself that perhaps it was like surgery—even when an operation is done to repair existing damage, the healing still is painful.

"Her name?" He raised his face at last, wiping his nose on the back of his hand. He picked up the pictures again, gently, as though they might disintegrate at his touch. "What did ye name her?"

"Brianna," I said proudly.

"Brianna?" he said, frowning at the pictures. "What an awful name for a wee lassie!"

I started back as though struck. "It is not awful!" I snapped. "It's a beautiful name, and besides you *told* me to name her that! What do you mean, it's an awful name?"

"*I* told ye to name her that?" He blinked.

"You most certainly did! When we—when we—the last time I saw you." I pressed my lips tightly together so I wouldn't cry again. After a moment, I had mastered my feelings enough to add, "You told me to name the baby for your father. His name was Brian, wasn't it?"

"Aye, it was." A smile seemed to be struggling for dominance of the other emotions on his face. "Aye," he said. "Aye, you're right, I did. It's only—well, I thought it would be a boy, is all."

"And you're sorry she wasn't?" I glared at him, and began snatching up the scattered photographs. His hands on my arms stopped me.

"No," he said. "No, I'm not sorry. Of course not!" His mouth twitched slightly. "But I willna deny she's the hell of a shock, Sassenach. So are you."

I sat still for a moment, looking at him. I had had months to prepare myself for this, and still my knees felt weak and my stomach was clenched in knots. He had been taken completely unawares by my appearance; little wonder if he was reeling a bit under the impact.

"I expect I am. Are you sorry I came?" I asked. I swallowed. "Do—do you want me to go?"

His hands clamped my arms so tightly that I let out a small yelp. Realizing that he was hurting me, he loosened his grip, but kept a firm hold nonetheless. His face had gone quite pale at the suggestion. He took a deep breath and let it out.

"No," he said, with an approximation of calmness. "I don't. I—" He broke off abruptly, jaw clamped. "No," he said again, very definitely.

His hand slid down to take hold of mine, and with the other he reached down to pick up the photographs. He laid them on his knee, looking at them with head bent, so I couldn't see his face.

"Brianna," he said softly. "Ye say it wrong, Sassenach. Her name is Brianna." He said it with an odd Highland lilt, so that the first syllable was accented, the second barely pronounced. *Bree*anah.

"*Bree*anah?" I said, amused. He nodded, eyes still fixed on the pictures.

"Brianna," he said. "It's a beautiful name."

"Glad you like it," I said.

He glanced up then, and met my eyes, with a smile hidden in the corner of his long mouth.

"Tell me about her." One forefinger traced the pudgy features of the baby in the snowsuit. "What was she like as a wee lassie? What did she first say, when she learned to speak?"

His hand drew me closer, and I nestled close to him. He was big, and solid, and smelled of clean linen and ink, with a warm male scent that was as exciting to me as it was familiar.

" 'Dog,' " I said. "That was her first word. The second one was 'No!' "

The smile widened across his face. "Aye, they all learn that one fast. She'll like dogs, then?" He fanned the pictures out like cards, searching out the one with Smoky. "That's a lovely dog with her there. What sort is that?"

"A Newfoundland." I bent forward to thumb through the pictures. "There's another one here with a puppy a friend of mine gave her . . ."

The dim gray daylight had begun to fade, and the rain had been pattering on the roof for some time, before our talk was interrupted by a fierce subterranean growl emanating from below the lace-trimmed bodice of my Jessica Gutenburg. It had been a long time since the peanut butter sandwich.

"Hungry, Sassenach?" Jamie asked, rather unnecessarily, I thought.

"Well, yes, now that you mention it. Do you still keep food in the top drawer?" When we were first married, I had developed the habit of keeping small bits of food on hand, to supply his constant appetite, and the top drawer of any chest of drawers where we lived generally provided a selection of rolls, small cakes, or bits of cheese.

He laughed and stretched. "Aye, I do. There's no much there just now, though, but a couple of stale bannocks. Better I take ye down to the tavern, and—" The look of happiness engendered by perusing the photographs of Brianna faded, to be replaced by a look of alarm. He glanced quickly at the window, where a soft purplish color was beginning to replace the pale gray, and the look of alarm deepened.

"The tavern! Christ! I've forgotten Mr. Willoughby!" He was on his feet and groping in the chest for fresh stockings before I could say anything. Coming out with the stockings in one hand and two bannocks in the other, he tossed the latter into my lap and sat down on the stool, hastily yanking on the former.

"Who's Mr. Willoughby?" I bit into a bannock, scattering crumbs.

"Damn," he said, more to himself than me, "I said I'd come for him at noon, but it went out o' my head entirely! It must be four o'clock by now!"

"It is; I heard the clock strike a little while ago."

"Damn!" he repeated. Thrusting his feet into a pair of pewter-buckled shoes, he rose, snatched his coat from the peg, and then paused at the door.

"You'll come wi' me?" he asked anxiously.

I licked my fingers and rose, pulling my cloak around me.

"Wild horses couldn't stop me," I assured him.

25

House of Joy

"Who is Mr. Willoughby?" I inquired, as we paused under the arch of Carfax Close to peer out at the cobbled street.

"Er . . . he's an associate of mine," Jamie replied, with a wary glance at me. "Best put up your hood, it's pouring."

It was in fact raining quite hard; sheets of water fell from the arch overhead and gurgled down the gutters, cleansing the streets of sewage and rubbish. I took a deep breath of the damp, clean air, feeling exhilarated by the wildness of the evening and the closeness of Jamie, tall and powerful by my side. I had found him. I had found him, and whatever unknowns life now held, they didn't seem to matter. I felt reckless and indestructible.

I took his hand and squeezed it; he looked down and smiled at me, squeezing back.

"Where are we going?"

"To The World's End." The roar of the water made conversation difficult. Without further speech, Jamie took me by the elbow to help me across the cobbles, and we plunged down the steep incline of the Royal Mile.

Luckily, the tavern called The World's End was no more than a hundred yards away; hard as the rain was, the shoulders of my cloak were scarcely more than dampened when we ducked beneath the low lintel and into the narrow entry-hall.

The main room was crowded, warm and smoky, a snug refuge from the storm outside. There were a few women seated on the benches that ran along the walls, but most of the patrons were men. Here and there was a man in the well-kept dress of a merchant, but most men with homes to go to were in them at this hour; the tavern hosted a mix of soldiers, wharf rats, laborers and apprentices, with here and there the odd drunkard for variety.

Heads looked up at our appearance, and there were shouts of greeting, and a general shuffling and pushing, to make room at one of the long tables. Clearly Jamie was well-known in The World's End. A few curious glances came my way, but no one said anything. I kept my cloak pulled close around me, and followed Jamie through the crush of the tavern.

"Nay, mistress, we'll no be stayin'," he said to the young barmaid who bustled forward with an eager smile. "I've only come for himself."

The girl rolled her eyes. "Oh, aye, and no before time, either! Mither's put him doon the stair."

"Aye, I'm late," Jamie said apologetically. "I had . . . business that kept me."

The girl looked curiously at me, but then shrugged and dimpled at Jamie.

"Och, it's no trouble, sir. Harry took him doon a stoup of brandy, and we've heard little more of him since."

"Brandy, eh?" Jamie sounded resigned. "Still awake, is he?" He reached into the pocket of his coat and brought out a small leather pouch, from which he extracted several coins, which he dropped into the girl's outstretched hand.

"I expect so," she said cheerfully, pocketing the money. "I heard him singin' a whiles since. Thankee, sir!"

With a nod, Jamie ducked under the lintel at the back of the room, motioning me to follow. A tiny, barrel-ceilinged kitchen lay behind the main taproom, with a huge kettle of what looked like oyster stew simmering in the hearth. It smelled delicious, and I could feel my mouth starting to water at the rich aroma. I hoped we could do our business with Mr. Willoughby over supper.

A fat woman in a grimy bodice and skirt knelt by the hearth, stuffing billets of wood into the fire. She glanced up at Jamie and nodded, but made no move to get up.

He lifted a hand in response, and headed for a small wooden door in the corner. He lifted the bolt and swung the door open to reveal a dark stairway leading down, apparently into the bowels of the earth. A light flickered somewhere far below, as though elves were mining diamonds beneath the tavern.

Jamie's shoulders filled the narrow stairwell, obstructing my view of whatever lay below us. When he stepped out into the open space below, I could see heavy oak rafters, and a row of huge casks, standing on a long plank set on hurdles against the stone wall.

Only a single torch burned at the foot of the stair. The cellar was shadowy, and its cavelike depths seemed quite deserted. I listened, but didn't hear anything but the muffled racket of the tavern upstairs. Certainly no singing.

"Are you sure he's down here?" I bent to peer beneath the row of casks, wondering whether perhaps the bibulous Mr. Willoughby had been overcome with an excess of brandy and sought some secluded spot to sleep it off.

"Oh, aye." Jamie sounded grim, but resigned. "The wee bugger's hiding, I expect. He knows I dinna like it when he drinks in public houses."

I raised an eyebrow at this, but he merely strode into the shadows, muttering under his breath. The cellar stretched some way, and I could hear him, shuffling cautiously in the dark, long after I lost sight of him. Left in the circle of torchlight near the stairs, I looked around with interest.

Besides the row of casks, there were a number of wooden crates stacked near the center of the room, against an odd little chunk of wall that stood by itself, rising some five feet out of the cellar floor, running back into the darkness.

I had heard of this feature of the tavern when we had stayed in Edinburgh twenty years before with His Highness Prince Charles, but what with one thing and another, I had never actually seen it before. It was the remnant of a wall constructed by the city fathers of Edinburgh, following the disastrous Battle of Flodden Field in 1513. Concluding—with some justice—that no good was likely to come of association with the English to the south, they had built a wall defining both the city limits and the limit of the civilized world of Scotland. Hence "The World's End," and the name had stuck through several versions of the tavern that had eventually been built upon the remnants of the old Scots' wishful thinking.

"Damned little bugger." Jamie emerged from the shadows, a cobweb stuck in his hair, and a frown on his face. "He must be back of the wall."

Turning, he put his hands to his mouth and shouted something. It sounded like incomprehensible gibberish—not even like Gaelic. I dug a finger dubiously into one ear, wondering whether the trip through the stones had deranged my hearing.

A sudden movement caught the corner of my eye, causing me to look up, just in time to see a ball of brilliant blue fly off the top of the ancient wall and smack Jamie squarely between the shoulderblades.

He hit the cellar floor with a frightful thump, and I dashed toward his fallen body.

"Jamie! Are you all right?"

The prone figure made a number of coarse remarks in Gaelic and sat up slowly, rubbing his forehead, which had struck the stone floor a glancing blow. The blue ball, meanwhile, had resolved itself into the figure of a very small Chinese, who was giggling in unhinged delight, sallow round face shining with glee and brandy.

"Mr. Willoughby, I presume?" I said to this apparition, keeping a wary eye out for further tricks.

He appeared to recognize his name, for he grinned and nodded madly at me, his eyes creased to gleaming slits. He pointed to himself, said something in Chinese, and then sprang into the air and executed several backflips in rapid succession, bobbing up on his feet in beaming triumph at the end.

"Bloody flea." Jamie got up, wiping the skinned palms of his hands gingerly on his coat. With a quick snatch, he caught hold of the Chinaman's collar and jerked him off his feet.

"Come on," he said, parking the little man on the stairway and prodding him firmly in the back. "We need to be going, and quick now." In response, the little blue-clad figure promptly sagged into limpness, looking like a bag of laundry resting on the step.

"He's all right when he's sober," Jamie explained apologetically to me, as he hoisted the Chinese over one shoulder. "But he really shouldna drink brandy. He's a terrible sot."

"So I see. Where on earth did you get him?" Fascinated, I followed Jamie up the stairs, watching Mr. Willoughby's pigtail swing back and forth like a metronome across the felted gray wool of Jamie's cloak.

"On the docks." But before he could explain further, the door above opened, and we were back in the tavern's kitchen. The stout proprietor saw us emerge, and came toward us, her fat cheeks puffed with disapproval.

"Now, Mr. Malcolm," she began, frowning, "ye ken verra weel as you're welcome here, and ye'll ken as weel that I'm no a fussy woman, such not bein' a convenient attitude when maintainin' a public hoose. But I've telt ye before, yon wee yellow mannie is no—"

"Aye, ye've mentioned it, Mrs. Patterson," Jamie interrupted. He dug in his pocket and came up with a coin, which he handed to the stout publican with a bow. "And your forbearance is much appreciated. It willna happen again. I hope," he added under his breath. He placed his hat on his head, bowed again to Mrs. Patterson, and ducked under the low lintel into the main tavern.

Our reentry caused another stir, but a negative one this time. People fell silent, or muttered half-heard curses under their breath. I gathered that Mr. Willoughby was perhaps not this local's most popular patron.

Jamie edged his way through the crowd, which gave way reluctantly. I followed as best I could, trying not to meet anyone's eyes, and trying not to breathe. Unused as I was to the unhygienic miasma of the eighteenth century, the stench of so many unwashed bodies in a small space was nearly overwhelming.

Near the door, though, we met trouble, in the person of a buxom young woman whose dress was a notch above the sober drab of the landlady and her daughter. Her neckline was a notch lower, and I hadn't much trouble in guessing her principal occupation. Absorbed in flirtatious conversation with a couple of apprentice lads when we emerged from the kitchen, she looked up as we passed, and sprang to her feet with a piercing scream, knocking over a cup of ale in the process.

"It's him!" she screeched, pointing a wavering finger at Jamie. "The foul fiend!" Her eyes seemed to have trouble focusing; I gathered that the spilled ale wasn't her first of the evening, early as it was.

Her companions stared at Jamie with interest, the more so when the young lady advanced, stabbing her finger in the air like one leading a chorus. "Him! The wee poolie I telt ye of—him that did the disgustin' thing to me!"

I joined the rest of the crowd in looking at Jamie with interest, but quickly realized, as did they, that the young woman was not talking to him, but rather to his burden.

"Ye neffit qurd!" she yelled, addressing her remarks to the seat of Mr. Willoughby's blue-silk trousers. "Hiddie-pyke! Slug!"

This spectacle of maidenly distress was rousing her companions; one, a tall, burly lad, stood up, fists clenched, and leaned on the table, eyes gleaming with ale and aggro.

"S'him, aye? Shall I knivvle him for ye, Maggie?"

"Dinna try, laddie," Jamie advised him shortly, shifting his burden for better balance. "Drink your drink, and we'll be gone."

"Oh, aye? And you're the little ked's pimpmaster, are ye?" The lad sneered unbecomingly, his flushed face turning in my direction. "At least your other whore's no yellow—le's ha' a look at her." He flung out a paw and grabbed the edge of my cloak, revealing the low bodice of the Jessica Gutenburg.

"Looks pink enough to me," said his friend, with obvious approval. "Is she like it all over?" Before I could move, he snatched at the bodice, catching the edge of the lace. Not designed for the rigors of eighteenth-century life, the flimsy fabric ripped halfway down the side, exposing quite a lot of pink.

"Leave off, ye whoreson!" Jamie swung about, eyes blazing, free fist doubled in threat.

"Who ye miscallin', ye skrae-shankit skoot?" The first youth, unable to get out from behind the table, leapt on top of it, and launched himself at Jamie, who neatly sidestepped the lad, allowing him to crash face-first into the wall.

Jamie took one giant step toward the table, brought his fist down hard on top of the other apprentice's head, making the lad's jaw go slack, then grabbed me by the hand and dragged me out the door.

"Come on!" he said, grunting as he shifted the Chinaman's slippery form for a better grip. "They'll be after us any moment!"

They were; I could hear the shouting as the more boisterous elements poured out of the tavern into the street behind us. Jamie took the first opening off the Royal Mile, into a narrow, dark wynd, and we splashed through mud and unidentifiable slops, ducked through an archway, and down another twisting alleyway that seemed to lead through the bowels of Edinburgh. Dark walls flashed past, and splintered wooden doors, and then we were round a corner, in a small courtyard, where we paused for breath.

"What . . . on earth . . . did he do?" I gasped. I couldn't imagine what the little Chinese could have done to a strapping young wench like the recent Maggie. From all appearances, she could have squashed him like a fly.

"Well, it's the feet, ye ken," Jamie explained, with a glance of resigned irritation at Mr. Willoughby.

"Feet?" I glanced involuntarily at the tiny Chinese man's feet, neat miniatures shod in felt-soled black satin.

"Not his," Jamie said, catching my glance. "The women's."

"*What* women?" I asked.

"Well, so far it's only been whores," he said, glancing through the arch-way in search of pursuit, "but ye canna tell what he may try. No judgment," he explained briefly. "He's a heathen."

"I see," I said, though so far, I didn't. "What—"

"There they are!" A shout at the far end of the alley interrupted my question.

"Damn, I thought they'd give it up. Come on, this way!"

We were off once more, down an alley, back onto the Royal Mile, a few steps down the hill, and back into a close. I could hear shouts and cries behind us on the main street, but Jamie grasped my arm and jerked me after him through an open doorway, into a yard full of casks, bundles, and crates. He looked frantically about, then heaved Mr. Willoughby's limp body into a large barrel filled with rubbish. Pausing only long enough to drop a piece of canvas on the Chinese's head for concealment, he dragged me behind a wagon loaded with crates, and pulled me down beside him.

I was gasping from the unaccustomed exertion, and my heart was racing from the adrenaline of fear. Jamie's face was flushed with cold and exercise, and his hair was sticking up in several directions, but he was scarcely breath-ing hard.

"Do you do this sort of thing all the time?" I asked, pressing a hand to my bosom in a vain effort to make my heart slow down.

"Not exactly," he said, peering warily over the top of the wagon in search of pursuit.

The echo of pounding feet came faintly, then disappeared, and everything was quiet, save for the patter of rain on the boxes above us.

"They've gone past. We'd best stay here a bit, to make sure, though." He lifted down a crate for me to sit on, procured another for himself, and sat down sighing, pushing the loose hair out of his face with one hand.

He gave me a lopsided smile. "I'm sorry, Sassenach. I didna think it would be quite so . . ."

"Eventful?" I finished for him. I smiled back and pulled out a handker-chief to wipe a drop of moisture from the end of my nose. "It's all right." I glanced at the large barrel, where stirrings and rustlings indicated that Mr. Willoughby was returning to a more or less conscious state. "Er . . . how do you know about the feet?"

"He told me; he's a taste for the drink, ye ken," he explained, with a glance at the barrel where his colleague lay concealed. "And when he's taken a drop too much, he starts talkin' about women's feet, and all the horrible things he wants to do wi' them."

"What sort of horrible things can you do with a foot?" I was fascinated. "Surely the possibilities are limited."

"No, they aren't," Jamie said grimly. "But it isna something I want to be talking about in the public street."

A faint singsong came from the depths of the barrel behind us. It was hard to tell, amid the natural inflections of the language, but I thought Mr. Willoughby was asking a question of some sort.

"Shut up, ye wee poutworm," Jamie said rudely. "Another word, and I'll walk on your damn face myself; see how ye like that." There was a high-pitched giggle, and the barrel fell silent.

"He wants someone to walk on his face?" I asked.

"Aye. You," Jamie said briefly. He shrugged apologetically, and his cheeks flushed a deeper red. "I hadna time to tell him who ye were."

"Does he speak English?"

"Oh, aye, in a way, but not many people understand him when he does. I mostly talk to him in Chinee."

I stared at him. "You speak Chinese?"

He shrugged, tilting his head with a faint smile. "Well, I speak Chinee about as well as Mr. Willoughby speaks English, but then, he hasna got all that much choice in who he talks to, so he puts up wi' me."

My heart showed signs of returning to normal, and I leaned back against the wagon bed, my hood farther forward against the drizzle.

"Where on earth did he get a name like Willoughby?" I asked. While I was curious about the Chinese, I was even more curious about what a respectable Edinburgh printer was doing with one, but I felt a certain hesitance in prying into Jamie's life. Freshly returned from the supposed dead—or its equivalent—I could hardly demand to know all the details of his life on the spot.

Jamie rubbed a hand across his nose. "Aye, well. It's only that his real name's Yi Tien Cho. He says it means 'Leans against heaven.' "

"Too hard for the local Scots to pronounce?" Knowing the insular nature of most Scots, I wasn't surprised that they were disinclined to venture into strange linguistic waters. Jamie, with his gift for tongues, was a genetic anomaly.

He smiled, teeth a white gleam in the gathering darkness. "Well, it's no that, so much. It's only, if ye say his name just a wee bit off, like, it sounds verra much like a coarse word in Gaelic. I thought Willoughby would maybe do better."

"I see." I thought perhaps under the circumstances, I shouldn't ask just what the indelicate Gaelic word was. I glanced over my shoulder, but the coast seemed clear.

Jamie caught the gesture and rose, nodding. "Aye, we can go now; the lads will ha' gone back to the tavern by now."

"Won't we have to pass by The World's End on the way back to the printshop?" I asked dubiously. "Or is there a back way?" It was full dark by now, and the thought of stumbling through the middens and muddy back passages of Edinburgh was unappealing.

"Ah . . . no. We willna be going to the printshop." I couldn't see his face, but there seemed a certain reserve in his manner. Perhaps he had a residence somewhere else in the city? I felt a certain hollowness at the prospect; the room above the printshop was very clearly a monk's cell; but perhaps he had an entire house somewhere else—with a family in it? There had been no time for any but the most essential exchange of information at the printshop. I had no way of knowing what he had done over the last twenty years, or what he might now be doing.

Still, he had plainly been glad—to say the least—to see me, and the air of frowning consideration he now bore might well have to do with his inebriated associate, rather than with me.

He bent over the barrel, saying something in Scots-accented Chinese. This was one of the odder sounds I had ever heard; rather like the squeaks of a bagpipe tuning up, I thought, vastly entertained by the performance.

Whatever he'd said, Mr. Willoughby replied to it volubly, interrupting himself with giggles and snorts. At last, the little Chinese climbed out of the barrel, his diminutive figure silhouetted by the light of a distant lantern in the alleyway. He sprang down with fair agility and promptly prostrated himself on the ground before me.

Bearing in mind what Jamie had told me about the feet, I took a quick step back, but Jamie laid a reassuring hand on my arm.

"Nay, it's all right, Sassenach," he said. "He's only makin' amends for his disrespect to ye earlier."

"Oh. Well." I looked dubiously at Mr. Willoughby, who was gabbling something to the ground under his face. At a loss for the proper etiquette, I stooped down and patted him on the head. Evidently that was all right, for he leapt to his feet and bowed to me several times, until Jamie told him impatiently to stop, and we made our way back to the Royal Mile.

The building Jamie led us to was discreetly hidden down a small close just above the Kirk of the Canongate, perhaps a quarter-mile above Holyrood Palace. I saw the lanterns mounted by the gates of the palace below, and shivered slightly at the sight. We had lived with Charles Stuart in the palace for nearly five weeks, in the early, victorious phase of his short career. Jamie's uncle, Colum MacKenzie, had died there.

The door opened to Jamie's knock, and all thoughts of the past vanished. The woman who stood peering out at us, candle in hand, was petite, dark-haired and elegant. Seeing Jamie, she drew him in with a glad cry, and kissed his cheek in greeting. My insides squeezed tight as a fist, but then relaxed again, as I heard him greet her as "Madame Jeanne." Not what one would call a wife—nor yet, I hoped, a mistress.

Still, there was something about the woman that made me uneasy. She was clearly French, though she spoke English well—not so odd; Edinburgh was a seaport, and a fairly cosmopolitan city. She was dressed soberly, but richly, in heavy silk cut with a flair, but she wore a good deal more rouge and powder than the average Scotswoman. What disturbed me was the way she was looking at me—frowning, with a palpable air of distaste.

"Monsieur Fraser," she said, touching Jamie on the shoulder with a possessive air that I didn't like at all, "if I might have a word in private with you?"

Jamie, handing his cloak to the maid who came to fetch it, took a quick look at me, and read the situation at once.

"Of course, Madame Jeanne," he said courteously, reaching out a hand to draw me forward. "But first—allow me to introduce my wife, Madame Fraser."

My heart stopped beating for a moment, then resumed, with a force that I was sure was audible to everyone in the small entry hall. Jamie's eyes met mine, and he smiled, the grip of his fingers tightening on my arm.

"Your . . . wife?" I couldn't tell whether astonishment or horror was more pronounced on Madame Jeanne's face. "But Monsieur Fraser . . . you bring her *here*? I thought . . . a woman . . . well enough, but to insult our own *jeune filles* is not good . . . but then . . . a *wife* . . ." Her mouth hung open unbecomingly, displaying several decayed molars. Then she shook herself suddenly back into an attitude of flustered poise, and inclined her head to me with an attempt at graciousness. *"Bonsoir* . . . Madame."

"Likewise, I'm sure," I said politely.

"Is my room ready, Madame?" Jamie said. Without waiting for an answer, he turned toward the stair, taking me with him. "We shall be spending the night."

He glanced back at Mr. Willoughby, who had come in with us. He had sat down at once on the floor, where he sat dripping rain, a dreamy expression on his small, flat face.

"Er . . . ?" Jamie made a small questioning motion toward Mr. Willoughby, his eyebrows raised at Madame Jeanne. She stared at the little Chinese for a moment as though wondering where he had come from, then, returned to herself, clapped her hands briskly for the maid.

"See if Mademoiselle Josie is at liberty, if you please, Pauline," she said. "And then fetch up hot water and fresh towels for Monsieur Fraser and his . . . wife." She spoke the word with a sort of stunned amazement, as though she still didn't quite believe it.

"Oh, and one more thing, if you would be so kind, Madame?" Jamie leaned over the banister, smiling down at her. "My wife will require a fresh gown; she has had an unfortunate accident to her wardrobe. If you could provide something suitable by morning? Thank you, Madame Jeanne. *Bonsoir*!"

I didn't speak, as I followed him up four flights of winding stairs to the top of the house. I was much too busy thinking, my mind in a whirl. "Pimpmaster," the lad in the pub had called him. But surely that was only an epithet—such a thing was absolutely impossible. For the Jamie Fraser I had known, it was impossible, I corrected myself, looking up at the broad shoulders under the dark gray serge coat. But for this man?

I didn't know quite what I had been expecting, but the room was quite ordinary, small and clean—though that was extraordinary, come to think of it—furnished with a stool, a simple bed and chest of drawers, upon which stood a basin and ewer and a clay candlestick with a beeswax candle, which Jamie lighted from the taper he had carried up.

He shucked off his wet coat and draped it carelessly on the stool, then sat down on the bed to remove his wet shoes.

"God," he said, "I'm starving. I hope the cook's not gone to bed yet."

"Jamie . . ." I said.

"Take off your cloak, Sassenach," he said, noticing me still standing against the door. "You're soaked."

"Yes. Well . . . yes." I swallowed, then went on. "There's just . . . er . . . Jamie, why have you got a regular room in a brothel?" I burst out.

He rubbed his chin, looking mildly embarrassed. "I'm sorry, Sassenach," he said. "I know it wasna right to bring ye here, but it was the only place I could think of where we might get your dress mended at short notice, besides finding a hot supper. And then I had to put Mr. Willoughby where he wouldna get in more trouble, and as we had to come here anyway . . . well"—he glanced at the bed—"it's a good deal more comfortable than my cot at the printshop. But perhaps it was a poor idea. We can leave, if ye feel it's not—"

"I don't mind about that," I interrupted. "The question is—why have you got a room in a brothel? Are you such a good customer that—"

"A customer?" He stared up at me, eyebrows raised. "Here? God, Sassenach, what d'ye think I am?"

"Damned if I know," I said. "That's why I'm asking. Are you going to answer my question?"

He stared at his stockinged feet for a moment, wiggling his toes on the floorboard. At last he looked up at me, and answered calmly, "I suppose so. I'm not a customer of Jeanne's, but she's a customer of mine—and a good one. She keeps a room for me because I'm often abroad late on business, and I'd as soon have a place I can come to where I can have food and a bed at any hour, and privacy. The room is part of my arrangement with her."

I had been holding my breath. Now I let out about half of it. "All right," I said. "Then I suppose the next question is, what business has the owner of a brothel got with a printer?" The absurd thought that perhaps he printed advertising circulars for Madame Jeanne flitted through my brain, to be instantly dismissed.

"Well," he said slowly. "No. I dinna think that's the question."

"It's not?"

"No." With one fluid move, he was off the bed and standing in front of me, close enough for me to have to look up into his face. I had a sudden urge to take a step backward, but didn't, largely because there wasn't room.

"The question is, Sassenach, why have ye come back?" he said softly.

"That's a hell of a question to ask me!" My palms pressed flat against the rough wood of the door. "Why do you *think* I came back, damn you?"

"I dinna ken." The soft Scottish voice was cool, but even in the dim light, I could see the pulse throbbing in the open throat of his shirt.

"Did ye come to be my wife again? Or only to bring me word of my daughter?" As though he sensed that his nearness unnerved me, he turned away suddenly, moving toward the window, where the shutters creaked in the wind.

"You are the mother of my child—for that alone, I owe ye my soul—for the knowledge that my life hasna been in vain—that my child is safe." He turned again to face me, blue eyes intent.

"But it has been a time, Sassenach, since you and I were one. You'll have had your life—then—and I have had mine here. You'll know nothing of what I've done, or been. Did ye come now because ye wanted to—or because ye felt ye must?"

My throat felt tight, but I met his eyes.

"I came now because before . . . I thought you were dead. I thought you'd died at Culloden."

His eyes dropped to the windowsill, where he picked at a splinter.

"Aye, I see," he said softly. "Well . . . I meant to be dead." He smiled, without humor, eyes intent on the splinter. "I tried hard enough." He looked up at me again.

"How did ye find out I hadna died? Or where I was, come to that?"

"I had help. A young historian named Roger Wakefield found the records; he tracked you to Edinburgh. And when I saw 'A. Malcolm,' I knew . . . I thought . . . it might be you," I ended lamely. Time enough for the details later.

"Aye, I see. And then ye came. But still . . . why?"

I stared at him without speaking for a moment. As though he felt the need of air, or perhaps only for something to do, he fumbled with the latch of the shutters and thrust them halfway open, flooding the room with the sound of rushing water, and the cold, fresh smell of rain.

"Are you trying to tell me you don't want me to stay?" I said, finally. "Because if so . . . I mean, I know you'll have a life now . . . maybe you have . . . other ties . . ." With unnaturally acute senses, I could hear the small sounds of activity throughout the house below, even above the rush of the storm, and the pounding of my own heart. My palms were damp, and I wiped them surreptitiously against my skirt.

He turned from the window to stare at me.

"Christ!" he said. "Not want ye?" His face was pale now, and his eyes unnaturally bright.

"I have burned for you for twenty years, Sassenach," he said softly. "Do ye not know that? Jesus!" The breeze stirred the loose wisps of hair around his face, and he brushed them back impatiently.

"But I'm no the man ye knew, twenty years past, am I?" He turned away, with a gesture of frustration. "We know each other now less than we did when we wed."

"Do you want me to go?" The blood was pounding thickly in my ears.

"No!" He swung quickly toward me, and gripped my shoulder tightly, making me pull back involuntarily. "No," he said, more quietly. "I dinna want ye to go. I told ye so, and I meant it. But . . . I must know." He bent his head toward me, his face alive with troubled question.

"Do ye want me?" he whispered. "Sassenach, will ye take me—and risk the man that I am, for the sake of the man ye knew?"

I felt a great wave of relief, mingled with fear. It ran from his hand on my shoulder to the tips of my toes, weakening my joints.

"It's a lot too late to ask that," I said, and reached to touch his cheek, where the rough beard was starting to show. It was soft under my fingers, like stiff plush. "Because I've already risked everything I had. But whoever you are now, Jamie Fraser—yes. Yes, I do want you."

The light of the candle flame glowed blue in his eyes, as he held out his hands to me, and I stepped wordless into his embrace. I rested my face against his chest, marveling at the feel of him in my arms; so big, so solid and warm. Real, after the years of longing for a ghost I could not touch.

Disentangling himself after a moment, he looked down at me, and touched my cheek, very gently. He smiled slightly.

"You've the devil's own courage, aye? But then, ye always did."

I tried to smile at him, but my lips trembled.

"What about you? How do you know what *I'm* like? You don't know what I've been doing for the last twenty years, either. I might be a horrible person, for all you know!"

The smile on his lips moved into his eyes, lighting them with humor. "I suppose ye might, at that. But, d'ye know, Sassenach—I dinna think I care?"

I stood looking at him for another minute, then heaved a deep sigh that popped a few more stitches in my gown.

"Neither do I."

It seemed absurd to be shy with him, but shy I was. The adventures of the evening, and his words to me, had opened up the chasm of reality—those twenty unshared years that gaped between us, and the unknown future that lay beyond. Now we had come to the place where we would begin to know each other again, and discover whether we were in fact the same two who had once existed as one flesh—and whether we might be one again.

A knock at the door broke the tension. It was a small servingmaid, with a tray of supper. She bobbed shyly to me, smiled at Jamie, and laid both supper—cold meat, hot broth, and warm oatbread with butter—and the fire with a quick and practiced hand, then left us with a murmured "Good e'en to ye."

We ate slowly, talking carefully only of neutral things; I told him how I had made my way from Craigh na Dun to Inverness, and made him laugh with stories of Mr. Graham and Master Georgie. He in turn told me about Mr. Willoughby; how he had found the little Chinese, half-starved and dead drunk, lying behind a row of casks on the docks at Burntisland, one of the shipping ports near Edinburgh.

We said nothing much of ourselves, but as we ate, I became increasingly conscious of his body, watching his fine, long hands as he poured wine and cut meat, seeing the twist of his powerful torso under his shirt, and the graceful line of neck and shoulder as he stooped to retrieve a fallen napkin. Once or twice, I thought I saw his gaze linger on me in the same way—a sort of hesitant avidity—but he quickly glanced away each time, hooding his eyes so that I could not tell what he saw or felt.

As the supper concluded, the same thought was uppermost in both our minds. It could scarcely be otherwise, considering the place in which we found ourselves. A tremor of mingled fear and anticipation shot through me.

At last, he drained his wineglass, set it down, and met my eyes directly.

"Will ye . . ." He stopped, the flush deepening on his features, but met my eyes, swallowed once, and went on. "Will ye come to bed wi' me, then? I mean," he hurried on, "it's cold, and we're both damp, and—"

"And there aren't any chairs," I finished for him. "All right." I pulled my hand loose from his, and turned toward the bed, feeling a queer mix of excitement and hesitance that made my breath come short.

He pulled off his breeches and stockings quickly, then glanced at me.

"I'm sorry, Sassenach; I should have thought ye'd need help wi' your laces."

So he didn't undress women often, I thought, before I could stop myself, and my lips curved in a smile at the thought.

"Well, it's not laces," I murmured, "but if you'd give a hand in the back there . . ." I laid aside my cloak, and turned my back to him, lifting my hair to expose the neck of the dress.

There was a puzzled silence. Then I felt a finger sliding slowly down the groove of my backbone.

"What's that?" he said, sounding startled.

"It's called a zipper," I said, smiling, though he couldn't see me. "See the little tab at the top? Just take hold of that, and pull it straight down."

The zipper teeth parted with a muted ripping noise, and the remnants of Jessica Gutenburg sagged free. I pulled my arms out of the sleeves and let the dress drop heavily around my feet, turning to face Jamie before I lost my nerve.

He jerked back, startled by this sudden chrysalis-shedding. Then he blinked, and stared at me.

I stood in front of him in nothing but my shoes and gartered rose-silk stockings. I had an overwhelming urge to snatch the dress back up, but I resisted it. I stiffened my spine, raised my chin, and waited.

He didn't say a word. His eyes gleamed in the candlelight as he moved his head slightly, but he still had that trick of hiding all his thoughts behind an inscrutable mask.

"Will you bloody say something?" I demanded at last, in a voice that shook only a little.

His mouth opened, but no words came out. He shook his head slowly from side to side.

"Jesus," he whispered at last. "Claire . . . you are the most beautiful woman I have ever seen."

"You," I said with conviction, "are losing your eyesight. It's probably glaucoma; you're too young for cataracts."

He laughed at that, a little unsteadily, and then I saw that he was in fact blinded—his eyes shone with moisture, even as he smiled. He blinked hard, and held out his hand.

"I," he said, with equal conviction, "ha' got eyes like a hawk, and always did. Come here to me."

A little reluctantly, I took his hand, and stepped out of the inadequate shelter of the remains of my dress. He drew me gently in, to stand between his knees as he sat on the bed. Then he kissed me softly, once on each breast, and laid his head between them, his breath coming warm on my bare skin.

"Your breast is like ivory," he said softly, the word almost "breest" in the Highland Scots that always grew broad when he was truly moved. His hand rose to cup one breast, his fingers tanned into darkness against my own pale glow.

"Only to see them, sae full and sae round—Christ, I could lay my head here forever. But to touch ye, my Sassenach . . . you wi' your skin like white velvet, and the sweet long lines of your body . . ." He paused, and I could feel the working of his throat muscles as he swallowed, his hand moving slowly down the curving slope of waist and hip, the swell and taper of buttock and thigh.

"Dear God," he said, still softly. "I couldna look at ye, Sassenach, and keep my hands from you, nor have ye near me, and not want ye." He lifted his head then, and planted a kiss over my heart, then let his hand float down the gentle curve of my belly, lightly tracing the small marks left there by Brianna's birth.

"You . . . really don't mind?" I said hesitantly, brushing my own fingers over my stomach.

He smiled up at me with something half-rueful in his expression. He hesitated for a moment, then drew up the hem of his shirt.

"Do you?" he asked.

The scar ran from midthigh nearly to his groin, an eight-inch length of twisted, whitish tissue. I couldn't repress a gasp at its appearance, and dropped to my knees beside him.

I laid my cheek on his thigh, holding tight to his leg, as though I would keep him now—as I had not been able to keep him then. I could feel the slow, deep pulse of the blood through his femoral artery under my fingers— a bare inch away from the ugly gully of that twisting scar.

"It doesna fright ye, nor sicken ye, Sassenach?" he asked, laying a hand on my hair. I lifted my head and stared up at him.

"Of course not!"

"Aye, well." He reached to touch my stomach, his eyes holding mine. "And if ye bear the scars of your own battles, Sassenach," he said softly, "they dinna trouble me, either."

He lifted me to the bed beside him then, and leaned to kiss me. I kicked off my shoes, and curled my legs up, feeling the warmth of him through his shirt. My hands found the button at the throat, fumbling to open it.

"I want to see you."

"Well, it's no much to see, Sassenach," he said, with an uncertain laugh. "But whatever it is, it's yours—if ye want it."

He pulled the shirt over his head and tossed it on the floor, then leaned back on the palms of his hands, displaying his body.

I didn't know quite what I had been expecting. In fact, the sight of his naked body took my breath away. He was still tall, of course, and beautifully made, the long bones of his body sleek with muscle, elegant with strength. He glowed in the candlelight, as though the light came from within him.

He had changed, of course, but the change was subtle; as though he had been put into an oven and baked to a hard finish. He looked as though both muscle and skin had drawn in just a bit, grown closer to the bone, so he was more tightly knit; he had never seemed gawky, but the last hint of boyish looseness had vanished.

His skin had darkened slightly, to a pale gold, burned to bronze on face and throat, paling down the length of his body to a pure white, tinged with blue veins, in the hollow of his thighs. His pubic hair stood out in a ferocious auburn bush, and it was quite obvious that he had not been lying; he did want me, and very badly.

My eyes met his, and his mouth quirked suddenly.

"I did say once I would be honest with ye, Sassenach."

I laughed, feeling tears sting my eyes at the same time, a rush of confused emotion surging up in me.

"So did I." I reached toward him, hesitant, and he took my hand. The strength and warmth of it were startling, and I jerked slightly. Then I tightened my grasp, and he rose to his feet, facing me.

We stood still then, awkwardly hesitating. We were intensely aware of each other—how could we not be? It was quite a small room, and the available atmosphere was completely filled with a charge like static electricity, almost strong enough to be visible. I had a feeling of empty-bellied terror, like the sort you get at the top of a roller coaster.

"Are you as scared as I am?" I finally said, sounding hoarse to my own ears.

He looked me over carefully, and raised one eyebrow.

"I dinna think I can be," he said. "You're covered wi' gooseflesh. Are ye scairt, Sassenach, or only cold?"

"Both," I said, and he laughed.

"Get in, then," he said. He released my hand and bent to turn back the quilt.

I didn't stop shaking when he slid under the quilt beside me, though the heat of his body was a physical shock.

"God, you're not cold!" I blurted. I turned toward him, and the warmth of him shimmered against my skin from head to toes. Instinctively drawn, I pressed close against him, shivering. I could feel my nipples tight and hard against his chest, and the sudden shock of his naked skin against my own.

He laughed a little uncertainly. "No, I'm not. I suppose I must be afraid, aye?" His arms came around me, gently, and I touched his chest, feeling hundreds of tiny goose bumps spring up under my fingertips, among the ruddy curling hairs.

"When we were afraid of each other before," I whispered, "on our wedding night—you held my hands. You said it would be easier if we touched."

He made a small sound as my fingertip found his nipple.

"Aye, I did," he said, sounding breathless. "Lord, touch me like that again." His hands tightened suddenly, holding me against him.

"Touch me," he said again softly, "and let me touch you, my Sassenach." His hand cupped me, stroking, touching, and my breast lay taut and heavy in his palm. I went on trembling, but now he was doing it, too.

"When we wed," he whispered, his breath warm against my cheek, "and I saw ye there, so bonny in your white dress—I couldna think of anything but when we'd be alone, and I could undo your laces and have ye naked, next to me in the bed."

"Do you want me now?" I whispered, and kissed the sunburned flesh in the hollow above his collarbone. His skin was faintly salty to the taste, and his hair smelled of woodsmoke and pungent maleness.

He didn't answer, but moved abruptly, so I felt the hardness of him, stiff against my belly.

It was terror as much as desire that pressed me close against him. I wanted him, all right; my breasts ached and my belly was tight with it, the unaccustomed rush of arousal slippery between my legs, opening me for him. But as strong as lust, was the desire simply to be taken, to have him master me, quell my doubts in a moment of rough usage, take me hard and swiftly enough to make me forget myself.

I could feel the urge to do it tremble in the hands that cupped my buttocks, in the involuntary jerk of his hips, brought up short as he stopped himself.

Do it, I thought, in an agony of apprehension. For God's sake, do it now and don't be gentle!

I couldn't say it. I saw the need of it on his face, but he couldn't say it, either; it was both too soon and too late for such words between us.

But we had shared another language, and my body still recalled it. I pressed my hips against him sharply, grasping his, the curves of his buttocks clenched hard under my hands. I turned my face upward, urgent to be kissed, at the same moment that he bent abruptly to kiss me.

My nose hit his forehead with a sickening crunch. My eyes watered profusely as I rolled away from him, clutching my face.

"Ow!"

"Christ, have I hurt ye, Claire?" Blinking away the tears, I could see his face, hovering anxiously over me.

"No," I said stupidly. "My nose is broken, though, I think."

"No, it isn't," he said, gently feeling the bridge of my nose. "When ye break your nose, it makes a nasty crunching sound, and ye bleed like a pig. It's all right."

I felt gingerly beneath my nostrils, but he was right; I wasn't bleeding. The pain had receded quickly, too. As I realized that, I also realized that he was lying on me, my legs sprawled wide beneath him, his cock just touching me, no more than a hairsbreadth from the moment of decision.

I saw the realization dawn in his eyes as well. Neither of us moved, barely breathing. Then his chest swelled as he took a deep breath, reached and took both my wrists in one hand. He pulled them up, over my head, and held me there, my body arched taut and helpless under him.

"Give me your mouth, Sassenach," he said softly, and bent to me. His head blotted out the candlelight, and I saw nothing but a dim glow and the darkness of his flesh as his mouth touched mine. Gently, brushing, then pressing, warm, and I opened to him with a little gasp, his tongue seeking mine.

I bit his lip, and he drew back a little, startled.

"Jamie," I said against his lips, my own breath warm between us. "Jamie!" That was all I could say, but my hips jerked against him, and jerked again, urging violence. I turned my head and fastened my teeth in the flesh of his shoulder.

He made a small sound deep in his throat and came into me hard. I was tight as any virgin and cried out, arching under him.

"Don't stop!" I said. "For God's sake, don't stop!"

His body heard me and answered in the same language, his grasp of my wrists tightening as he plunged hard into me, the force of it reaching my womb with each stroke.

Then he let go of my wrists and half-fell on me, the weight of him pinning me to the bed as he reached under, holding my hips hard, keeping me immobile.

I whimpered and writhed against him, and he bit my neck.

"Be still," he said in my ear. I was still, only because I couldn't move. We lay pressed tight together, shuddering. I could feel the pounding against my ribs, but didn't know whether it was my heart, or his.

Then he moved in me, very slightly, a question of the flesh. It was enough; I convulsed in answer, held helpless under him, and felt the spasms of my release stroke him, stroke him, seize and release him, urging him to join me.

He reared up on both hands, back arched and head thrown back, eyes closed and breathing hard. Then very slowly, he bent his head forward and opened his eyes. He looked down at me with unutterable tenderness, and the candlelight gleamed briefly on the wetness on his cheek, maybe sweat or maybe tears.

"Oh, Claire," he whispered. "Oh, God, Claire."

And his release began, deep inside me, without his moving, shivering through his body so that his arms trembled, the ruddy hairs quivering in the dim light, and he dropped his head with a sound like a sob, his hair hiding his face as he spilled himself, each jerk and pulse of his flesh between my legs rousing an echo in my own.

When it was over, he held himself over me, still as stone for a long moment. Then, very gently, he lowered himself, pressed his head against mine, and lay as if dead.

I stirred at last from a deep, contented stupor, lifting my hand to lay it over the spot where his pulse beat slow and strong, just at the base of his breastbone.

"It's like bicycle riding, I expect," I said. My head rested peacefully in the curve of his shoulder, my hand idly playing with the red-gold curls that sprang up in thickets across his chest. "Did you know you've got lots more hairs on your chest than you used to?"

"No," he said drowsily, "I dinna usually count them. Have bye-sickles got lots of hair, then?"

It caught me by surprise, and I laughed.

"No," I said. "I just meant that we seemed to recall what to do all right."

Jamie opened one eye and looked down at me consideringly. "It would take a real daftie to forget *that*, Sassenach," he said. "I may be lacking practice, but I havena lost all my faculties yet."

We were still for a long time, aware of each other's breathing, sensitive to each small twitch and shifting of position. We fitted well together, my head curled into the hollow of his shoulder, the territory of his body warm under my hand, both strange and familiar, awaiting rediscovery.

The building was a solid one, and the sound of the storm outside drowned most noises from within, but now and then the sounds of feet or voices were dimly audible below us; a low, masculine laugh, or the higher voice of a woman, raised in professional flirtation.

Hearing it, Jamie stirred a little uncomfortably.

"I should maybe have taken ye to a tavern," he said. "It's only—"

"It's all right," I assured him. "Though I must say, of all the places I'd imagined being with you again, I somehow never thought of a brothel." I hesitated, not wanting to pry, but curiosity got the best of me. "You . . . er . . . don't *own* this place, do you, Jamie?"

He pulled back a little, staring down at me.

"Me? God in heaven, Sassenach, what d'ye think I am?"

"Well, I don't know, do I?" I pointed out, with some asperity. "The first thing you do when I find you is faint, and as soon as I've got you back on your feet, you get me assaulted in a pub and chased through Edinburgh in company with a deviant Chinese, ending up in a brothel—whose madam seems to be on awfully familiar terms with you, I might add." The tips of his ears had gone pink, and he seemed to be struggling between laughter and indignation.

"You then take off your clothes, announce that you're a terrible person with a depraved past, and take me to bed. What did you *expect* me to think?"

Laughter won out.

"Well, I'm no a saint, Sassenach," he said. "But I'm no a pimp, either."

"Glad to hear it," I said. There was a momentary pause, and then I said, "Do you mean to tell me what you *are*, or shall I go on running down the disreputable possibilities until I come close?"

"Oh, aye?" he said, entertained by this suggestion. "What's your best guess?"

I looked him over carefully. He lay at ease amid the tumbled sheets, one arm behind his head, grinning at me.

"Well, I'd bet my shift you're not a printer," I said.

The grin widened.

"Why not?"

I poked him rudely in the ribs. "You're much too fit. Most men in their forties have begun to go soft round the middle, and you haven't a spare ounce on you."

"That's mostly because I havena got anyone to cook for me," he said ruefully. "If ye ate in taverns all the time, ye wouldna be fat, either. Luckily, it looks as though ye eat regularly." He patted my bottom familiarly, and then ducked, laughing, as I slapped at his hand.

"Don't try to distract me," I said, resuming my dignity. "At any rate, you didn't get muscles like that slaving over a printing press."

"Ever tried to work one, Sassenach?" He raised a derisive eyebrow.

"No." I furrowed my brow in thought. "I don't suppose you've taken up highway robbery?"

"No," he said, the grin widening. "Guess again."

"Embezzlement."

"No."

"Well, likely not kidnapping for ransom," I said, and began to tick other possibilities off on my fingers. "Petty thievery? No. Piracy? No, you couldn't possibly, unless you've got over being seasick. Usury? Hardly." I dropped my hand and stared at him.

"You were a traitor when I last knew you, but that scarcely seems a good way of making a living."

"Oh, I'm still a traitor," he assured me. "I just havena been convicted lately."

"*Lately?*"

"I spent several years in prison for treason, Sassenach," he said, rather grimly. "For the Rising. But that was some time back."

"Yes, I knew that."

His eyes widened. "Ye knew that?"

"That and a bit more," I said. "I'll tell you later. But putting that all aside for the present and returning to the point at issue—what *do* you do for a living these days?"

"I'm a printer," he said, grinning widely.

"*And* a traitor?"

"And a traitor," he confirmed, nodding. "I've been arrested for sedition six times in the last two years, and had my premises seized twice, but the court wasna able to prove anything."

"And what happens to you if they *do* prove it, one of these times?"

"Oh," he said airily, waving his free hand in the air, "the pillory. Ear-nailing. Flogging. Imprisonment. Transportation. That sort of thing. Likely not hanging."

"What a relief," I said dryly. I felt a trifle hollow. I hadn't even tried to imagine what his life might be like, if I found him. Now that I had, I was a little taken aback.

"I did warn ye," he said. The teasing was gone now, and the dark blue eyes were serious and watchful.

"You did," I said, and took a deep breath.

"Do ye want to leave now?" He spoke casually enough, but I saw his fingers clench and tighten on a fold of the quilt, so that the knuckles stood out white against the sunbronzed skin.

"No," I said. I smiled at him, as best I could manage. "I didn't come back just to make love with you once. I came to be with you—if you'll have me," I ended, a little hesitantly.

"If I'll have you!" He let out the breath he had been holding, and sat up to face me, cross-legged on the bed. He reached out and took my hands, engulfing them between his own.

"I—canna even say what I felt when I touched you today, Sassenach, and knew ye to be real," he said. His eyes traveled over me, and I felt the heat of him, yearning, and my own heat, melting toward him. "To find you again—and then to lose ye . . ." He stopped, throat working as he swallowed.

I touched his face, tracing the fine, clean line of cheekbone and jaw.

"You won't lose me," I said. "Not ever again." I smiled, smoothing back the thick ruff of ruddy hair behind his ear. "Not even if I find out you've been committing bigamy and public drunkenness."

He jerked sharply at that, and I dropped my hand, startled.

"What is it?"

"Well—" he said, and stopped. He pursed his lips and glanced at me quickly. "It's just—"

"Just what? Is there something else you haven't told me?"

"Well, printing seditious pamphlets isna all that profitable," he said, in explanation.

"I don't suppose so," I said, my heart starting to speed up again at the prospect of further revelations. "What else have you been doing?"

"Well, it's just that I do a wee bit of smuggling," he said apologetically. "On the side, like."

"A *smuggler*?" I stared. "Smuggling what?"

"Well, whisky mostly, but rum now and then, and a fair bit of French wine and cambric."

"So that's it!" I said. The pieces of the puzzle all settled into place—Mr. Willoughby, the Edinburgh docks, and the riddle of our present surroundings. "That's what your connection is with this place—what you meant by saying Madame Jeanne is a customer?"

"That's it." He nodded. "It works verra well; we store the liquor in one of the cellars below when it comes in from France. Some of it we sell directly to Jeanne; some she keeps for us until we can ship it on."

"Um. And as part of the arrangements . . ." I said delicately, "you, er . . ."

The blue eyes narrowed at me.

"The answer to what you're thinking, Sassenach, is no," he said very firmly.

"Oh, is it?" I said, feeling extremely pleased. "Mind reader, are you? And what am I thinking?"

"You were wondering do I take out my price in trade sometimes, aye?" He lifted one brow at me.

"Well, I was," I admitted. "Not that it's any of my business."

"Oh, isn't it, then?" He raised both ruddy brows and took me by both shoulders, leaning toward me.

"Is it?" he said, a moment later. He sounded a little breathless.

"Yes," I said, sounding equally breathless. "And you don't—"

"I don't. Come here."

He wrapped his arms around me, and pulled me close. The body's memory is different from the mind's. When I thought, and wondered, and worried, I was clumsy and awkward, fumbling my way. Without the interference of conscious thought, my body knew him, and answered him at once in tune, as though his touch had left me moments before, and not years.

"I was more afraid this time than on our wedding night," I murmured, my eyes fixed on the slow, strong pulsebeat in the hollow of his throat.

"Were ye, then?" His arm shifted and tightened round me. "Do I frighten ye, Sassenach?"

"No." I put my fingers on the tiny pulse, breathing the deep musk of his effort. "It's only . . . the first time . . . I didn't think it would be forever. I meant to go, then."

He snorted faintly, the sweat gleaming lightly in the small hollow in the center of his chest.

"And ye did go, and came again," he said. "You're here; there's no more that matters, than that."

I raised myself slightly to look at him. His eyes were closed, slanted and catlike, his lashes that striking color I remembered so well because I had seen it so often; deep auburn at the tips, fading to a red so pale as nearly to be blond at the roots.

"What did you think, the first time we lay together?" I asked. The dark blue eyes opened slowly, and rested on me.

"It has always been forever, for me, Sassenach," he said simply.

Sometime later, we fell asleep entwined, with the sound of the rain falling soft against the shutters, mingling with the muffled sounds of commerce below.

It was a restless night. Too tired to stay awake a moment longer, I was too happy to fall soundly asleep. Perhaps I was afraid he would vanish if I slept. Perhaps he felt the same. We lay close together, not awake, but too aware of each other to sleep deeply. I felt every small twitch of his muscles, every movement of his breathing, and knew he was likewise aware of me.

Half-dozing, we turned and moved together, always touching, in a sleepy, slow-motion ballet, learning again in silence the language of our bodies. Somewhere in the deep, quiet hours of the night, he turned to me without a word, and I to him, and we made love to each other in a slow, unspeaking tenderness that left us lying still at last, in possession of each other's secrets.

Soft as a moth flying in the dark, my hand skimmed his leg, and found the thin deep runnel of the scar. My fingers traced its invisible length and paused, with the barest of touches at its end, wordlessly asking, "How?"

His breathing changed with a sigh, and his hand lay over mine.

"Culloden," he said, the whispered word an evocation of tragedy. Death. Futility. And the terrible parting that had taken me from him.

"I'll never leave you," I whispered. "Not again."

His head turned on the pillow, his features lost in darkness, and his lips brushed mine, light as the touch of an insect's wing. He turned onto his back, shifting me next to him, his hand resting heavy on the curve of my thigh, keeping me close.

Sometime later, I felt him shift again, and turn the bedclothes back a little way. A cool draft played across my forearm; the tiny hairs prickled upright, and then flattened beneath the warmth of his touch. I opened my eyes, to find him turned on his side, absorbed in the sight of my hand. It lay still on the quilt, a carved white thing, all the bones and tendons chalked in gray as the room began its imperceptible shift from night to day.

"Draw her for me," he whispered, head bent as he gently traced the shapes of my fingers, long and ghostly beneath the darkness of his own touch.

"What has she of you, of me? Can ye tell me? Are her hands like yours, Claire, or mine? Draw her for me, let me see her." He laid his own hand down beside my own. It was his good hand, the fingers straight and flat-jointed, the nails clipped short, square and clean.

"Like mine," I said. My voice was low and hoarse with waking, barely loud enough to register above the drumming of the rain outside. The house beneath was silent. I raised the fingers of my immobile hand an inch in illustration.

"She has long, slim hands like mine—but bigger than mine, broad across the backs, and a deep curve at the outside, near the wrist—like that. Like yours; she has a pulse just there, where you do." I touched the spot where a vein crossed the curve of his radius, just where the wrist joins the hand. He was so still I could feel his heartbeat under my fingertip.

"Her nails are like yours; square, not oval like mine. But she has the crooked little finger on her right hand that I have," I said, lifting it. "My mother had it, too; Uncle Lambert told me." My own mother had died when I was five. I had no clear memory of her, but thought of her whenever I saw my own hand unexpectedly, caught in a moment of grace like this one. I laid the hand with the crooked finger on his, then lifted it to his face.

"She has this line," I said softly, tracing the bold sweep from temple to cheek. "Your eyes, exactly, and those lashes and brows. A Fraser nose. Her mouth is more like mine, with a full bottom lip, but it's wide, like yours. A pointed chin, like mine, but stronger. She's a big girl—nearly six feet tall." I felt his start of astonishment, and nudged him gently, knee to knee. "She has long legs, like yours, but very feminine."

"And has she that small blue vein just there?" His hand touched my own face, thumb tender in the hollow of my temple. "And ears like tiny wings, Sassenach?"

"She always complained about her ears—said they stuck out," I said, feeling the tears sting my eyes as Brianna came suddenly to life between us.

"They're pierced. You don't mind, do you?" I said, talking fast to keep the tears at bay. "Frank did; he said it looked cheap, and she shouldn't, but she wanted to do it, and I let her, when she was sixteen. Mine were; it didn't seem right to say she couldn't when I did, and her friends all did, and I didn't—didn't want—"

"Ye were right," he said, interrupting the flow of half-hysterical words. "Ye did fine," he repeated, softly but firmly, holding me close. "Ye were a wonderful mother, I know it."

I was crying again, quite soundlessly, shaking against him. He held me gently, stroking my back and murmuring. "Ye did well," he kept saying. "Ye did right." And after a little while, I stopped crying.

"Ye gave me a child, *mo nighean donn*," he said softly, into the cloud of my hair. "We are together for always. She is safe; and we will live forever now, you and I." He kissed me, very lightly, and laid his head upon the pillow next to me. "Brianna," he whispered, in that odd Highland way that made her name his own. He sighed deeply, and in an instant, was asleep. In another, I fell asleep myself, my last sight his wide, sweet mouth, relaxed in sleep, half-smiling.

26

Whore's Brunch

From years of answering the twin calls of motherhood and medicine, I had developed the ability to wake from even the soundest sleep at once and completely. I woke so now, immediately aware of the worn linen sheets around me, the dripping of the eaves outside, and the warm scent of Jamie's body mingling with the cold, sweet air that breathed through the crack of the shutters above me.

Jamie himself was not in bed; without reaching out or opening my eyes, I knew that the space beside me was empty. He was close by, though. There was a sound of stealthy movement, and a faint scraping noise nearby. I turned my head on the pillow and opened my eyes.

The room was filled with a gray light that washed the color from everything, but left the pale lines of his body clear in the dimness. He stood out against the darkness of the room, solid as ivory, vivid as though he were etched upon the air. He was naked, his back turned to me as he stood in front of the chamber pot he had just pulled from its resting place beneath the washstand.

I admired the squared roundness of his buttocks, the small muscular hollow that dented each one, and their pale vulnerability. The groove of his backbone, springing in a deep, smooth curve from hips to shoulders. As he moved slightly, the light caught the faint silver shine of the scars on his back, and the breath caught in my throat.

He turned around then, face calm and faintly abstracted. He saw me watching him, and looked slightly startled.

I smiled but stayed silent, unable to think of anything to say. I kept looking at him, though, and he at me, the same smile upon his lips. Without speaking, he moved toward me and sat on the bed, the mattress shifting under his weight. He laid his hand open on the quilt, and I put my own into it without hesitation.

"Sleep well?" I asked idiotically.

A grin broadened across his face. "No," he said. "Did you?"

"No." I could feel the heat of him, even at this distance, in spite of the chilly room. "Aren't you cold?"

"No."

We fell quiet again, but could not take our eyes away from each other. I looked him over carefully in the strengthening light, comparing memory to reality. A narrow blade of early sun knifed through the shutters' crack, lighting a lock of hair like polished bronze, gilding the curve of his shoulder, the smooth flat slope of his belly. He seemed slightly larger than I had remembered, and one hell of a lot more immediate.

"You're bigger than I remembered," I ventured. He tilted his head, looking down at me in amusement.

"You're a wee bit smaller, I think."

His hand engulfed mine, fingers delicately circling the bones of my wrist. My mouth was dry; I swallowed and licked my lips.

"A long time ago, you asked me if I knew what it was between us," I said.

His eyes rested on mine, so dark a blue as to be nearly black in a light like this.

"I remember," he said softly. His fingers tightened briefly on mine. "What it is—when I touch you; when ye lie wi' me."

"I said I didn't know."

"I didna ken either." The smile had faded a bit, but was still there, lurking in the corners of his mouth.

"I still don't," I said. "But—" and stopped to clear my throat.

"But it's still there," he finished for me, and the smile moved from his lips, lighting his eyes. "Aye?"

It was. I was still as aware of him as I might have been of a lighted stick of dynamite in my immediate vicinity, but the feeling between us had changed. We had fallen asleep as one flesh, linked by the love of the child we had made, and had waked as two people—bound by something different.

"Yes. Is it—I mean, it's not just because of Brianna, do you think?"

The pressure on my fingers increased.

"Do I want ye because you're the mother of my child?" He raised one ruddy eyebrow in incredulity. "Well, no. Not that I'm no grateful," he added hastily. "But—no." He bent his head to look down at me intently, and the sun lit the narrow bridge of his nose and sparked in his lashes.

"No," he said. "I think I could watch ye for hours, Sassenach, to see how you have changed, or how ye're the same. Just to see a wee thing, like the curve of your chin"—he touched my jaw gently, letting his hand slide up to cup my head, thumb stroking my earlobe—"or your ears, and the bittie holes for your earbobs. Those are all the same, just as they were. Your hair—I called ye *mo nighean donn*, d'ye recall? My brown one." His voice was little more than a whisper, his fingers threading my curls between them.

"I expect that's changed a bit," I said. I hadn't gone gray, but there were paler streaks where my normal light brown had faded to a softer gold, and here and there, the glint of a single silver strand.

"Like beechwood in the rain," he said, smiling and smoothing a lock with one forefinger, "and the drops coming down from the leaves across the bark."

I reached out and stroked his thigh, touching the long scar that ran down it.

"I wish I could have been there to take care of you," I said softly. "It was the most horrible thing I ever did—leaving you, knowing . . . that you meant to be killed." I could hardly bear to speak the word.

"Well, I tried hard enough," he said, with a wry grimace that made me laugh, in spite of my emotion. "It wasna my fault I didna succeed." He glanced dispassionately at the long, thick scar that ran down his thigh. "Not the fault of the Sassenach wi' the bayonet, either."

I heaved myself up on one elbow, squinting at the scar. "A *bayonet* did that?"

"Aye, well. It festered, ye see," he explained.

"I know; we found the journal of the Lord Melton who sent you home from the battlefield. He didn't think you'd make it." My hand tightened on his knee, as though to reassure myself that he was in fact here before me, alive.

He snorted. "Well, I damn nearly didn't. I was all but dead when they pulled me out of the wagon at Lallybroch." His face darkened with memory.

"God, sometimes I wake up in the night, dreaming of that wagon. It was two days' journey, and I was fevered or chilled, or both together. I was covered wi' hay, and the ends of it sticking in my eyes and my ears and through my shirt, and fleas hopping all through it and eating me alive, and my leg killing me at every jolt in the road. It was a verra bumpy road, too," he added broodingly.

"It sounds horrible," I said, feeling the word quite inadequate. He snorted briefly.

"Aye. I only stood it by imagining what I'd do to Melton if I ever met him again, to get back at him for not shooting me."

I laughed again, and he glanced down at me, a wry smile on his lips.

"I'm not laughing because it's funny," I said, gulping a little. "I'm laughing because otherwise I'll cry, and I don't want to—not now, when it's over."

"Aye, I know." He squeezed my hand.

I took a deep breath. "I—I didn't look back. I didn't think I could stand to find out—what happened." I bit my lip; the admission seemed a betrayal. "It wasn't that I tried—that I wanted—to forget," I said, groping clumsily for words. "I couldn't forget you; you shouldn't think that. Not ever. But I—"

"Dinna fash yourself, Sassenach," he interrupted. He patted my hand gently. "I ken what ye mean. I try not to look back myself, come to that."

"But if I had," I said, staring down at the smooth grain of the linen, "if I had—I might have found you sooner."

The words hung in the air between us like an accusation, a reminder of the bitter years of loss and separation. Finally he sighed, deeply, and put a finger under my chin, lifting my face to his.

"And if ye had?" he said. "Would ye have left the lassie there without her mother? Or come to me in the time after Culloden, when I couldna care for ye, but only watch ye suffer wi' the rest, and feel the guilt of bringing ye to such a fate? Maybe see ye die of the hunger and sickness, and know I'd killed ye?" He raised one eyebrow in question, then shook his head.

"No. I told ye to go, and I told ye to forget. Shall I blame ye for doing as I said, Sassenach? No."

"But we might have had more time!" I said. "We might have—" He stopped me by the simple expedient of bending and putting his mouth on mine. It was warm and very soft, and the stubble of his face was faintly scratchy on my skin.

After a moment he released me. The light was growing, putting color in his face. His skin glowed bronze, sparked with the copper of his beard. He took a deep breath.

"Aye, we might. But to think of that—we cannot." His eyes met mine steadily, searching. "I canna look back, Sassenach, and live," he said simply. "If we have no more than last night, and this moment, it is enough."

"Not for me, it isn't!" I said, and he laughed.

"Greedy wee thing, are ye no?"

"Yes," I said. The tension broken, I returned my attention to the scar on his leg, to keep away for the moment from the painful contemplation of lost time and opportunity.

"You were telling me how you got that."

"So I was." He rocked back a little, squinting down at the thin white line down the top of his thigh.

"Well, it was Jenny—my sister, ye ken?" I did indeed remember Jenny; half her brother's size, and dark as he was blazing fair, but a match and more for him in stubbornness.

"She said she wasna going to let me die," he said, with a rueful smile. "And she didn't. My opinion didna seem to have anything to do wi' the matter, so she didna bother to ask me."

"That sounds like Jenny." I felt a small glow of comfort at the thought of my sister-in-law. Jamie hadn't been alone as I feared, then; Jenny Murray would have fought the Devil himself to save her brother—and evidently had.

"She dosed me for the fever, and put poultices on my leg to draw the poison, but nothing worked, and it only got worse. It swelled and stank, and then began to go black and rotten, so they thought they must take the leg off, if I was to live."

He recounted this quite matter-of-factly, but I felt a little faint at the thought.

"Obviously they didn't," I said. "Why not?"

Jamie scratched his nose and rubbed a hand back through his hair, wiping the wild spill of it out of his eyes. "Well, that was Ian," he said. "He wouldna let her do it. He said he kent well enough what it was like to live wi' one leg, and while he didna mind it so much himself, he thought I wouldna like to—all things considered," he added, with a wave of the hand and a glance at me that encompassed everything—the loss of the battle, of the war, of me, of home and livelihood—of all the things of his normal life. I thought Ian might well have been right.

"So instead Jenny made three of the tenants come to sit on me and hold me still, and then she slit my leg to the bone wi' a kitchen knife and washed the wound wi' boiling water," he said casually.

"Jesus H. Christ!" I blurted, shocked into horror.

He smiled faintly at my expression. "Aye, well, it worked."

I swallowed heavily, tasting bile. "Jesus. I'd think you'd have been a cripple for life!"

"Well, she cleansed it as best she could, and stitched it up. She said she wasna going to let me die, and she wasna going to have me be a cripple, and she wasna going to have me lie about all the day feelin' sorry for myself, and—" He shrugged, resigned. "By the time she finished tellin' me all the things she wouldna let me do, it seemed the only thing left to me was to get well."

I echoed his laugh, and his smile broadened at the memory. "Once I could get up, she made Ian take me outside after dark and make me walk. Lord, we must ha' been a sight, Ian wi' his wooden leg, and me wi' my stick, limping up and down the road like a pair of lame cranes!"

I laughed again, but had to blink back tears; I could see all too well the two tall, limping figures, struggling stubbornly against darkness and pain, leaning on each other for support.

"You lived in a cave for a time, didn't you? We found the story of it."

His eyebrows went up in surprise. "A story about it? About me, ye mean?"

"You're a famous Highland legend," I told him dryly, "or you will be, at least."

"For living in a cave?" He looked half-pleased, half-embarrassed. "Well, that's a foolish thing to make a story about, aye?"

"Arranging to have yourself betrayed to the English for the price on your head was maybe a little more dramatic," I said, still more dryly. "Taking rather a risk there, weren't you?"

The end of his nose was pink, and he looked somewhat abashed.

"Well," he said awkwardly, "I didna think prison would be verra dreadful, and everything considered. . . ."

I spoke as calmly as I could, but I wanted to shake him, suddenly and ridiculously furious with him in retrospect.

"Prison, my arse! You knew perfectly well you might have been hanged, didn't you? And you bloody did it anyway!"

"I had to do something," he said, shrugging. "And if the English were fool enough to pay good money for my lousy carcass—well, there's nay law against takin' advantage of fools, is there?" One corner of his mouth quirked up, and I was torn between the urge to kiss him and the urge to slap him.

I did neither, but sat up in bed and began combing the tangles out of my hair with my fingers.

"I'd say it's open to question who the fool was," I said, not looking at him, "but even so, you should know that your daughter's very proud of you."

"She is?" He sounded thunderstruck, and I looked up at him, laughing despite my irritation.

"Well, of course she is. You're a bloody hero, aren't you?"

He went quite red in the face at this, and stood up, looking thoroughly disconcerted.

"Me? No!" He rubbed a hand through his hair, his habit when thinking or disturbed in his mind.

"No. I mean," he said slowly, "I wasna heroic at all about it. It was only . . . I couldna bear it any longer. To see them all starving, I mean, and not be able to care for them—Jenny, and Ian and the children; all the tenants and their families." He looked helplessly down at me. "I really didna care if the English hanged me or not," he said. "I didna think they would, because of what ye'd told me, but even if I'd known for sure it meant that—I would ha' done it, Sassenach, and not minded. But it wasna bravery—not at all." He threw up his hands in frustration, turning away. "There was nothing else I could do!"

"I see," I said softly, after a moment. "I understand." He was standing by the chiffonier, still naked, and at this, he turned half-round to face me.

"Do ye, then?" His face was serious.

"I know you, Jamie Fraser." I spoke with more certainty than I had felt at any time since the moment I stepped through the rock.

"Do ye, then?" he asked again, but a faint smile shadowed his mouth.

"I think so."

The smile on his lips widened, and he opened his mouth to reply. Before he could speak, though, there was a knock upon the chamber door.

I started as though I had touched a hot stove. Jamie laughed, and bent to pat my hip as he went to the door.

"I expect it's the chambermaid with our breakfast, Sassenach, not the constable. And we *are* marrit, aye?" One eyebrow rose quizzically.

"Even so, shouldn't you put something on?" I asked, as he reached for the doorknob.

He glanced down at himself.

"I shouldna think it's likely to come as a shock to anyone in this house, Sassenach. But to honor your sensibilities—" He grinned at me, and taking a linen towel from the washstand, wrapped it casually about his loins before pulling open the door.

I caught sight of a tall male figure standing in the hall, and promptly pulled the bedclothes over my head. This was a reaction of pure panic, for if it had been the Edinburgh constable or one of his minions, I could scarcely expect much protection from a couple of quilts. But then the visitor spoke, and I was glad that I was safely out of sight for the moment.

"Jamie?" The voice sounded rather startled. Despite the fact that I had not heard it in twenty years, I recognized it at once. Rolling over, I surreptitiously lifted a corner of the quilt and peeked out beneath it.

"Well, of course it's me," Jamie was saying, rather testily. "Have ye no got eyes, man?" He pulled his brother-in-law, Ian, into the room and shut the door.

"I see well enough it's you," Ian said, with a note of sharpness. "I just didna ken whether to believe my eyes!" His smooth brown hair showed threads of gray, and his face bore the lines of a good many years' hard work. But Joe Abernathy had been right; with his first words, the new vision merged with the old, and this was the Ian Murray I had known before.

"I came here because the lad at the printshop said ye'd no been there last night, and this was the address Jenny sends your letters to," he was saying. He looked round the room with wide, suspicious eyes, as though expecting something to leap out from behind the armoire. Then his gaze flicked back to his brother-in-law, who was making a perfunctory effort to secure his makeshift loincloth.

"I never thought to find ye in a kittle-hoosie, Jamie!" he said. "I wasna sure, when the . . . the lady answered the door downstairs, but then—"

"It's no what ye think, Ian," Jamie said shortly.

"Oh, it's not, aye? And Jenny worrying that ye'd make yourself ill, living without a woman so long!" Ian snorted. "I'll tell her she needna concern herself wi' your welfare. And where's my son, then, down the hall with another o' the harlots?"

"Your son?" Jamie's surprise was evident. "Which one?"

Ian stared at Jamie, the anger on his long, half-homely face fading into alarm.

"Ye havena got him? Wee Ian's not here?"

"Young Ian? Christ, man, d'ye think I'd bring a fourteen-year-old lad into a brothel?"

Ian opened his mouth, then shut it, and sat down on the stool.

"Tell ye the truth, Jamie, I canna say what ye'd do anymore," he said levelly. He looked up at his brother-in-law, jaw set. "Once I could. But not now."

"And what the hell d'ye mean by that?" I could see the angry flush rising in Jamie's face.

Ian glanced at the bed, and away again. The red flush didn't recede from Jamie's face, but I saw a small quiver at the corner of his mouth. He bowed elaborately to his brother-in-law.

"Your pardon, Ian, I was forgettin' my manners. Allow me to introduce ye to my companion." He stepped to the side of the bed and pulled back the quilts.

"No!" Ian cried, jumping to his feet and looking frantically at the floor, the wardrobe, anywhere but at the bed.

"What, will ye no give your regards to my wife, Ian?" Jamie said.

"Wife?" Forgetting to look away, Ian goggled at Jamie in horror. "Ye've marrit a whore?" he croaked.

"I wouldn't call it that, exactly," I said. Hearing my voice, Ian jerked his head in my direction.

"Hullo," I said, waving cheerily at him from my nest of bedclothes. "Been a long time, hasn't it?"

I'd always thought the descriptions of what people did when seeing ghosts rather exaggerated, but had been forced to revise my opinions in light of the responses I had been getting since my return to the past. Jamie had fainted dead away, and if Ian's hair was not literally standing on end, he assuredly looked as though he had been scared out of his wits.

Eyes bugging out, he opened and closed his mouth, making a small gobbling noise that seemed to entertain Jamie quite a lot.

"That'll teach ye to go about thinkin' the worst of my character," he said, with apparent satisfaction. Taking pity on his quivering brother-in-law, Jamie poured out a tot of brandy and handed him the glass. "Judge not, and ye'll no be judged, eh?"

I thought Ian was going to spill the drink on his breeches, but he managed to get the glass to his mouth and swallow.

"What—" he wheezed, eyes watering as he stared at me. "How—?"

"It's a long story," I said, with a glance at Jamie. He nodded briefly. We had had other things to think about in the last twenty-four hours besides how to explain me to people, and under the circumstances, I rather thought explanations could wait.

"I don't believe I know Young Ian. Is he missing?" I asked politely.

Ian nodded mechanically, not taking his eyes off me.

"He stole away from home last Friday week," he said, sounding rather dazed. "Left a note that he'd gone to his uncle." He took another swig of brandy, coughed and blinked several times, then wiped his eyes and sat up straighter, looking at me.

"It'll no be the first time, ye see," he said to me. He seemed to be regaining his self-confidence, seeing that I appeared to be flesh and blood, and showed no signs either of getting out of bed, or of putting my head under my arm and strolling round without it, in the accepted fashion of Highland ghosts.

Jamie sat down on the bed next to me, taking my hand in his.

"I've not seen Young Ian since I sent him home wi' Fergus six months ago," he said. He was beginning to look as worried as Ian. "You're sure he said he was coming to me?"

"Well, he hasna got any other uncles that I know of," Ian said, rather acerbically. He tossed back the rest of the brandy and set the cup down.

"Fergus?" I interrupted. "Is Fergus all right, then?" I felt a surge of joy at the mention of the French orphan whom Jamie had once hired in Paris as a pickpocket, and brought back to Scotland as a servant lad.

Distracted from his thoughts, Jamie looked down at me.

"Oh, aye, Fergus is a bonny man now. A bit changed, of course." A shadow seemed to cross his face, but it cleared as he smiled, pressing my hand. "He'll be fair daft at seein' you once more, Sassenach."

Uninterested in Fergus, Ian had risen and was pacing back and forth across the polished plank floor.

"He didna take a horse," he muttered. "So he'd have nothing anyone would rob him for." He swung round to Jamie. "How did ye come, last time ye brought the lad here? By the land round the Firth, or did ye cross by boat?"

Jamie rubbed his chin, frowning as he thought. "I didna come to Lallybroch for him. He and Fergus crossed through the Carryarrick Pass and met me just above Loch Laggan. Then we came down through Struan and Weem and . . . aye, now I remember. We didna want to cross the Campbell lands, so we came to the east, and crossed the Forth at Donibristle."

"D'ye think he'd do that again?" Ian asked. "If it's the only way he knows?"

Jamie shook his head doubtfully. "He might. But he kens the coast is dangerous."

Ian resumed his pacing, hands clasped behind his back. "I beat him 'til he could barely stand, let alone sit, the last time he ran off," Ian said, shaking his head. His lips were tight, and I gathered that Young Ian was perhaps rather a trial to his father. "Ye'd think the wee fool would think better o' such tricks, aye?"

Jamie snorted, but not without sympathy.

"Did a thrashing ever stop you from doing anything you'd set your mind on?"

Ian stopped his pacing and sat down on the stool again, sighing.

"No," he said frankly, "but I expect it was some relief to my father." His face cracked into a reluctant smile, as Jamie laughed.

"He'll be all right," Jamie declared confidently. He stood up and let the towel drop to the floor as he reached for his breeches. "I'll go and put about the word for him. If he's in Edinburgh, we'll hear of it by nightfall."

Ian cast a glance at me in the bed, and stood up hastily.

"I'll go wi' ye."

I thought I saw a shadow of doubt flicker across Jamie's face, but then he nodded and pulled the shirt over his head.

"All right," he said, as his head popped through the slit. He frowned at me.

"I'm afraid ye'll have to stay here, Sassenach," he said.

"I suppose I will," I said dryly. "Seeing that I haven't any clothes." The maid who brought our supper had removed my dress, and no replacement had as yet appeared.

Ian's feathery brows shot up to his hairline, but Jamie merely nodded.

"I'll tell Jeanne on the way out," he said. He frowned slightly, thinking. "It may be some time, Sassenach. There are things—well, I've business to take care of." He squeezed my hand, his expression softening as he looked at me.

"I dinna want to leave ye," he said softly. "But I must. You'll stay here until I come again?"

"Don't worry," I assured him, waving a hand at the linen towel he had just discarded. "I'm not likely to go anywhere in that."

The thud of their feet retreated down the hall and faded into the sounds of the stirring house. The brothel was rising, late and languid by the stern Scottish standards of Edinburgh. Below me I could hear the occasional slow muffled thump, the clatter of shutters thrust open nearby, a cry of "Gardy-loo!" and a second later, the splash of slops flung out to land on the street far below.

Voices somewhere far down the hall, a brief inaudible exchange, and the closing of a door. The building itself seemed to stretch and sigh, with a creaking of timbers and a squeaking of stairs, and a sudden puff of coal-smelling warm air came out from the back of the cold hearth, the exhalation of a fire lit on some lower floor, sharing my chimney.

I relaxed into the pillows, feeling drowsy and heavily content. I was slightly and pleasantly sore in several unaccustomed places, and while I had been reluctant to see Jamie go, there was no denying that it was nice to be alone for a bit to mull things over.

I felt much like one who has been handed a sealed casket containing a long-lost treasure. I could feel the satisfying weight and the shape of it, and know the great joy of its possession, but still did not know exactly what was contained therein.

I was dying to know everything he had done and said and thought and been, through all the days between us. I had of course known that if he had survived Culloden, he would have a life—and knowing what I did of Jamie Fraser, it was unlikely to be a simple one. But knowing that, and being confronted with the reality of it, were two different things.

He had been fixed in my memory for so long, glowing but static, like an insect frozen in amber. And then had come Roger's brief historical sightings, like peeks through a keyhole; separate pictures like punctuations, alterations; adjustments of memory, each showing the dragonfly's wings raised or lowered at a different angle, like the single frames of a motion picture. Now time had begun to run again for us, and the dragonfly was in flight before me, flickering from place to place, so I saw little more yet than the glitter of its wings.

There were so many questions neither of us had had a chance to ask yet— what of his family at Lallybroch, his sister Jenny and her children? Obviously Ian was alive, and well, wooden leg notwithstanding—but had the rest of the family and the tenants of the estate survived the destruction of the Highlands? If they had, why was Jamie here in Edinburgh?

And if they were alive—what would we tell them about my sudden reappearance? I bit my lip, wondering whether there was *any* explanation—short of the truth—which might make sense. It might depend on what Jamie had told them when I disappeared after Culloden; there had seemed no need to concoct a reason for my vanishing at the time; it would simply be assumed that I had perished in the aftermath of the Rising, one more of the nameless corpses lying starved on the rocks or slaughtered in a leafless glen.

Well, we'd manage that when we came to it, I supposed. I was more curious just now about the extent and the danger of Jamie's less legitimate activities. Smuggling and sedition, was it? I was aware that smuggling was nearly as honorable a profession in the Scottish Highlands as cattle-stealing had been twenty years before, and might be conducted with relatively little risk. Sedition was something else, and seemed like an occupation of dubious safety for a convicted ex-Jacobite traitor.

That, I supposed, was the reason for his assumed name—or one reason, at any rate. Disturbed and excited as I had been when we arrived at the brothel the night before, I had noticed that Madame Jeanne referred to him by his own name. So presumably he smuggled under his own identity, but carried out his publishing activities—legal and illegal—as Alex Malcolm.

I had seen, heard and felt enough, during the all too brief hours of the night, to be fairly sure that the Jamie Fraser I had known still existed. How many other men he might be now remained to be seen.

There was a tentative rap at the door, interrupting my thoughts. Breakfast, I thought, and not before time. I was ravenous.

"Come in," I called, and sat up in bed, pulling up the pillows to lean against.

The door opened very slowly, and after quite a long pause, a head poked its way through the opening, much in the manner of a snail emerging from its shell after a hailstorm.

It was topped with an ill-cut shag of dark brown hair so thick that the cropped edges stuck out like a shelf above a pair of large ears. The face beneath was long and bony; rather pleasantly homely, save for a pair of beautiful brown eyes, soft and huge as a deer's, that rested on me with a mingled expression of interest and hesitancy.

The head and I regarded each other for a moment.

"Are you Mr. Malcolm's . . . woman?" it asked.

"I suppose you could say so," I replied cautiously. This was obviously not the chambermaid with my breakfast. Neither was it likely to be one of the other employees of the establishment, being evidently male, though very young. He seemed vaguely familiar, though I was sure I hadn't seen him before. I pulled the sheet a bit higher over my breasts. "And who are you?" I inquired.

The head thought this over for some time, and finally answered, with equal caution, "Ian Murray."

"Ian Murray?" I shot up straight, rescuing the sheet at the last moment. "Come in here," I said peremptorily. "If you're who I think you are, why aren't you where you're supposed to be, and what are you doing here?" The face looked rather alarmed, and showed signs of withdrawal.

"Stop!" I called, and put a leg out of bed to pursue him. The big brown eyes widened at the sight of my bare limb, and he froze. "Come in, I said."

Slowly, I withdrew the leg beneath the quilts, and equally slowly, he followed it into the room.

He was tall and gangly as a fledgling stork, with perhaps nine stone spread sparsely over a six-foot frame. Now that I knew who he was, the resemblance to his father was clear. He had his mother's pale skin, though, which blushed furiously red as it occurred to him suddenly that he was standing next to a bed containing a naked woman.

"I . . . er . . . was looking for my . . . for Mr. Malcolm, I mean," he murmured, staring fixedly at the floorboards by his feet.

"If you mean your uncle Jamie, he's not here," I said.

"No. No, I suppose not." He seemed unable to think of anything to add to this, but remained staring at the floor, one foot twisted awkwardly to the side, as though he were about to draw it up under him, like the wading bird he so much resembled.

"Do ye ken where . . ." he began, lifting his eyes, then, as he caught a glimpse of me, lowered them, blushed again and fell silent.

"He's looking for you," I said. "With your father," I added. "They left here not half an hour ago."

His head snapped up on its skinny neck, goggling.

"My father?" he gasped. "My father was here? Ye know him?"

"Why, yes," I said, without thinking. "I've known Ian for quite a long time."

He might be Jamie's nephew, but he hadn't Jamie's trick of inscrutability. Everything he thought showed on his face, and I could easily trace the progression of his expressions. Raw shock at learning of his father's presence in Edinburgh, then a sort of awestruck horror at the revelation of his father's long-standing acquaintance with what appeared to be a woman of a certain occupation, and finally the beginnings of angry absorption, as the young man began an immediate revision of his opinions of his father's character.

"Er—" I said, mildly alarmed. "It isn't what you think. I mean, your father and I—it's really your uncle and I, I mean—" I was trying to figure out how to explain the situation to him without getting into even deeper waters, when he whirled on his heel and started for the door.

"Wait a minute," I said. He stopped, but didn't turn around. His well-scrubbed ears stood out like tiny wings, the morning light illuminating their delicate pinkness. "How old are you?" I asked.

He turned around to face me, with a certain painful dignity. "I'll be fifteen in three weeks," he said. The red was creeping up his cheeks again. "Dinna worry, I'm old enough to know—what sort of place this is, I mean." He jerked his head toward me in an attempt at a courtly bow.

"Meaning no offense to ye, mistress. If Uncle Jamie—I mean, I—" he groped for suitable words, failed to find any, and finally blurted, "verra pleased to meet ye, mum!" turned and bolted through the door, which shut hard enough to rattle in its frame.

I fell back against the pillows, torn between amusement and alarm. I did wonder what the elder Ian was going to say to his son when they met—and vice versa. As long as I was wondering, I wondered what had brought the younger Ian here in search of Jamie. Evidently, he knew where his uncle was likely to be found; yet judging from his diffident attitude, he had never before ventured into the brothel.

Had he extracted the information from Geordie at the printshop? That seemed unlikely. And yet, if he hadn't—then that meant he had learned of his uncle's connection with this place from some other source. And the most likely source was Jamie himself.

But in that case, I reasoned, Jamie likely already knew that his nephew was in Edinburgh, so why pretend he hadn't seen the boy? Ian was Jamie's oldest friend; they had grown up together. If whatever Jamie was up to was worth the cost of deceiving his brother-in-law, it was something serious.

I had got no further with my musings, when there came another knock on the door.

"Come in," I said, smoothing out the quilts in anticipation of the break-fast tray to be placed thereon.

When the door opened, I had directed my attention at a spot about five feet above the floor, where I expected the chambermaid's head to material-ize. Upon the last opening of the door, I had had to adjust my vision upward a foot, to accommodate the appearance of Young Ian. This time, I was obliged to drop it.

"What in the bloody hell are you doing here?" I demanded as the diminu-tive figure of Mr. Willoughby entered on hands and knees. I sat up and hastily tucked my feet underneath me, pulling not only sheet but quilts well up around my shoulders.

In answer, the Chinese advanced to within a foot of the bed, then let his head fall to the floor with a loud clunk. He raised it and repeated the process with great deliberation, making a horrid sound like a melon being cleaved with an ax.

"Stop that!" I exclaimed, as he prepared to do it a third time.

"Thousand apology," he explained, sitting up on his heels and blinking at me. He was quite a bit the worse for wear, and the dark red mark where his forehead had smacked the floor didn't add anything to his appearance. I trusted he didn't mean he'd been going to hit his head on the floor a thousand times, but I wasn't sure. He obviously had the hell of a hangover; for him to have attempted it even once was impressive.

"That's quite all right," I said, edging cautiously back against the wall. "There's nothing to apologize for."

"Yes, apology," he insisted. "Tsei-mi saying wife. Lady being most honor-able First Wife, not stinking whore."

"Thanks a lot," I said. "Tsei-mi? You mean Jamie? Jamie Fraser?"

The little man nodded, to the obvious detriment of his head. He clutched it with both hands and closed his eyes, which promptly disappeared into the creases of his cheeks.

"Tsei-mi," he affirmed, eyes still closed. "Tsei-mi saying apology to most honored First Wife. Yi Tien Cho most humble servant." He bowed deeply, still holding onto his head. "Yi Tien Cho," he added, opening his eyes and tapping his chest to indicate that that was his name, in case I should be confusing him with any other humble servants in the vicinity.

"That's quite all right," I said. "Er, pleased to meet you."

Evidently heartened by this, he slid bonelessly onto his face, prostrating himself before me.

"Yi Tien Cho lady's servant," he said. "First Wife please to walk on humble servant, if like."

"Ha," I said coldly. "I've heard about you. Walk on you, eh? Not bloody likely!"

A slit of gleaming black eye showed, and he giggled, so irrepressibly that I couldn't help laughing myself. He sat up again, smoothing down the spikes of dirt-stiffened black hair that sprang, porcupine-like, from his skull.

"I wash First Wife's feet?" he offered, grinning widely.

"Certainly not," I said. "If you really want to do something helpful, go and tell someone to bring me breakfast. No, wait a minute," I said, changing my mind. "First, tell me where you met Jamie. If you don't mind," I added, to be polite.

He sat back on his heels, head bobbing slightly. "Docks," he said. "Two year ago. I come China, long way, no food. Hiding barrel," he explained, reaching his arms in a circle, to demonstrate his means of transportation.

"A stowaway?"

"Trade ship," he nodded. "On docks here, stealing food. Stealing brandy one night, getting stinking drunk. Very cold to sleep; die soon, but Tsei-mi find." He jabbed a thumb at his chest once more. "Tsei-mi's humble servant. Humble servant First Wife." He bowed to me, swaying alarmingly in the process, but came upright again without mishap.

"Brandy seems to be your downfall," I observed. "I'm sorry I haven't anything to give you for your head; I don't have any medicines with me at the moment."

"Oh, not worry," he assured me. "I having healthy balls."

"How nice for you," I said, trying to decide whether he was gearing up for another attempt on my feet, or merely still too drunk to distinguish basic anatomy. Or perhaps there was some connection in Chinese philosophy, between the well-being of head and testicles? Just in case, I looked round for something that might be used as a weapon, in case he showed a disposition to begin burrowing under the bedclothes.

Instead, he reached into the depths of one baggy blue-silk sleeve and with the air of a conjuror, drew out a small white silk bag. He upended this, and two balls dropped out into his palm. They were larger than marbles and smaller than baseballs; about the size, in fact, of the average testicle. A good deal harder, though, being apparently made of some kind of polished stone, greenish in color.

"Healthy balls," Mr. Willoughby explained, rolling them together in his palm. They made a pleasant clicking noise. "Streaked jade, from Canton," he said. "Best kind of healthy balls."

"Really?" I said, fascinated. "And they're medicinal—good for you, that's what you're saying?"

He nodded vigorously, then stopped abruptly with a faint moan. After a pause, he spread out his hand, and rolled the balls to and fro, keeping them in movement with a dextrous circling of his fingers.

"All body one part; hand all parts," he said. He poked a finger toward his open palm, touching delicately here and there between the smooth green spheres. "Head there, stomach there, liver there," he said. "Balls make all good."

"Well, I suppose they're as portable as Alka-Seltzer," I said. Possibly it was the reference to stomach that caused my own to emit a loud growl at this point.

"First Wife wanting food," Mr. Willoughby observed shrewdly.

"Very astute of you," I said. "Yes, I do want food. Do you suppose you could go and tell someone?"

He dumped the healthy balls back into their bag at once, and springing to his feet, bowed deeply.

"Humble servant go now," he said, and went, crashing rather heavily into the door post on his way out.

This was becoming ridiculous, I thought. I harbored substantial doubt as to whether Mr. Willoughby's visit would result in food; he'd be lucky to make it to the bottom of the stair without falling on his head, if I was any judge of his condition.

Rather than go on sitting here in the nude, receiving random deputations from the outside world, I thought it time to take steps. Rising and carefully wrapping a quilt around my body, I took a few, out into the corridor.

The upper floor seemed deserted. Aside from the room I had left, there were only two other doors up here. Glancing up, I could see unadorned rafters overhead. We were in the attic then; chances were that the other rooms here were occupied by servants, who were presumably now employed downstairs.

I could hear faint noises drifting up the stairwell. Something else drifted up, as well—the scent of frying sausage. A loud gustatory rumble informed me that my stomach hadn't missed this, and furthermore, that my innards considered the consumption of one peanut butter sandwich and one bowl of soup in one twenty-four-hour period a wholly inadequate level of nutrition.

I tucked the ends of the quilt in, sarong-fashion, just above my breasts, and picking up my trailing skirts, followed the scent of food downstairs.

The smell—and the clinking, clattering, sloshing noises of a number of people eating—were coming from a closed door on the first floor above ground level. I pushed it open, and found myself at the end of a long room equipped as a refectory.

The table was surrounded by twenty-odd women, a few gowned for day, but most of them in a state of dishabille that made my quilt modest by comparison. A woman near the end of the table caught sight of me hovering in the doorway, and beckoned, companionably sliding over to make room for me on the end of the long bench.

"You'll be the new lass, aye?" she said, looking me over with interest. "You're a wee bit older than Madame usually takes on—she likes 'em no more than five and twenty. You're no bad at all, though," she assured me hastily. "I'm sure you'll do fine."

"Good skin and a pretty face," observed the dark-haired lady across from us, sizing me up with the detached air of one appraising horseflesh. "And nice bubbies, what I can see." She lifted her chin slightly, peering across the table at what could be seen of my cleavage.

"Madame doesna like us to take the kivvers off the beds," my original acquaintance said reprovingly. "Ye should wear your shift, if ye havena something pretty to show yourself in yet."

"Aye, be careful with the quilt," advised the dark-haired girl, still scrutinizing me. "Madame'll dock your wages, an' ye get spots on the bedclothes."

"What's your name, my dearie?" A short, rather plump girl with a round, friendly face leaned past the dark girl's elbow to smile at me. "Here we're all chatterin' at ye, and not welcomed ye proper at all. I'm Dorcas, this is Peggy"—she jerked a thumb at the dark-haired girl, then pointed across the table to the fair-haired woman beside me—"and that's Mollie."

"My name is Claire," I said, smiling and hitching the quilt a bit higher in self-consciousness. I wasn't sure how to correct their impression that I was Madame Jeanne's newest recruit; for the moment, that seemed less important than getting some breakfast.

Apparently divining my need, the friendly Dorcas reached to the sideboard behind her, passed me a wooden plate, and shoved a large dish of sausages in my direction.

The food was well-cooked and would have been good in any case; starved as I was, it was ambrosial. A hell of a lot better than the hospital cafeteria's breakfasts, I observed to myself, taking another ladle of fried potatoes.

"Had a rough one for your first, aye?" Millie, next to me, nodded at my bosom. Glancing down, I was mortified to see a large red patch peeking above the edge of my quilt. I couldn't see my neck, but the direction of Millie's interested gaze made it clear that the small tingling sensations there were evidence of further bite-marks.

"Your nose is a wee bit puffed, too," Peggy said, frowning at me critically. She reached across the table to touch it, disregarding the fact that the gesture caused her flimsy wrap to fall open to the waist. "Slap ye, did he? If they get too rough, ye should call out, ye know; Madame doesna allow the customers to mistreat us—give a good screech and Bruno will be in there in a moment."

"Bruno?" I said, a little faintly.

"The porter," Dorcas explained, busily spooning eggs into her mouth. "Big as a bear—that's why we call him Bruno. What's his name really?" she asked the table at large, "Horace?"

"Theobald," corrected Millie. She turned to call to a servingmaid at the end of the room, "Janie, will ye fetch in more ale? The new lassie's had none yet!"

"Aye, Peggy's right," she said, turning back to me. She wasn't at all pretty, but had a nicely shaped mouth and a pleasant expression. "If ye get a man likes to play a bit rough, that's one thing—and don't sic Bruno on a good customer, or there'll be hell to pay, and you'll do the paying. But if ye think ye might really be damaged, then just give a good skelloch. Bruno's never far away during the night. Oh, here's the ale," she added, taking a big pewter mug from the servingmaid and plonking it in front of me.

"She's no damaged," Dorcas said, having completed her survey of the visible aspects of my person. "A bit sore between the legs, though, aye?" she said shrewdly, grinning at me.

"Ooh, look, she's *blushing*," said Mollie, giggling with delight. "Ooh, you *are* a fresh one, aren't ye?"

I took a deep gulp of the ale. It was dark, rich, and extremely welcome, as much for the width of the cup rim that hid my face as for its taste.

"Never mind." Mollie patted my arm kindly. "After breakfast, I'll show ye where the tubs are. Ye can soak your parts in warm water, and they'll be good as new by tonight."

"Be sure to show her where the jars are, too," put in Dorcas. "Sweet herbs," she explained to me. "Put them in the water before ye sit in it. Madame likes us to smell sweet."

"Eef ze men want to lie wiz a feesh, zey would go to ze docks; eet ees more cheap," Peggy intoned, in what was patently meant to be an imitation of Madame Jeanne. The table erupted in giggles, which were rapidly quelled by the sudden appearance of Madame herself, who entered through a door at the end of the room.

Madame Jeanne was frowning in a worried fashion, and seemed too preoccupied to notice the smothered hilarity.

"*Tsk!*" murmured Mollie, seeing the proprietor. "An early customer. I hate it when they come in the middle o' breakfast," she grumbled. "Stop ye digesting your food proper, it does."

"Ye needn't worry, Mollie; it's Claire'll have to take him," Peggy said, tossing her dark plait out of the way. "Newest lass takes the ones no one wants," she informed me.

"Stick your finger up his bum," Dorcas advised me. "That brings 'em off faster than anything. I'll save ye a bannock for after, if ye like."

"Er . . . thanks," I said. Just then, Madame Jeanne's eye lit upon me, and her mouth dropped open in a horrified "O."

"What are *you* doing here?" she hissed, rushing up to grab me by the arm.

"Eating," I said, in no mood to be snatched at. I detached my arm from her grasp and picked up my ale cup.

"Merde!" she said. "Did no one bring you food this morning?"

"No," I said. "Nor yet clothes." I gestured at the quilt, which was in imminent danger of falling off.

"Nez de Cleopatre!" she said violently. She stood up and glanced around the room, eyes flashing daggers. "I will have the worthless scum of a maid flayed for this! A thousand apologies, Madame!"

"That's quite all right," I said graciously, aware of the looks of astonishment on the faces of my breakfast companions. "I've had a wonderful meal. Nice to have met you all, ladies," I said, rising and doing my best to bow graciously while clutching my quilt. "Now, Madame . . . about my gown?"

Amid Madame Jeanne's agitated protestations of apology, and reiterated hopes that I would not find it necessary to tell Monsieur Fraser that I had been exposed to an undesirable intimacy with the working members of the establishment, I made my clumsy way up two more flights of stairs, and into a small room draped with hanging garments in various stages of completion, with bolts of cloth stacked here and there in the corners of the chamber.

"A moment, please," Madame Jeanne said, and with a deep bow, left me to the company of a dressmaker's dummy, with a large number of pins protruding from its stuffed bosom.

Apparently this was where the costuming of the inmates took place. I walked around the room, quilt trailing, and observed several flimsy silk wrappers under construction, together with a couple of elaborate gowns with very low necks, and a number of rather imaginative variations on the basic shift and camisole. I removed one shift from its hook, and put it on.

It was made of fine cotton, with a low, gathered neck, and embroidery in the form of multiple hands that curled enticingly under the bosom and down the sides of the waist, spreading out into a rakish caress atop the hips. It hadn't been hemmed, but was otherwise complete, and gave me a great deal more freedom of movement than had the quilt.

I could hear voices in the next room, where Madame was apparently haranguing Bruno—or so I deduced the identity of the male rumble.

"I do not care *what* the miserable girl's sister has done," she was saying, "do you not realize that the wife of Monsieur Jamie was left naked and starving—"

"Are you sure she's his wife?" the deep male voice asked. "I had heard—"

"So had I. But if he says this woman is his wife, I am not disposed to argue, *n'est-ce pas?*" Madame sounded impatient. "Now, as to this wretched Madeleine—"

"It's not her fault, Madame," Bruno broke in. "Have you not heard the news this morning—about the Fiend?"

Madame gave a small gasp. "No! Not another?"

"Yes, Madame." Bruno's voice was grim. "No more than a few doors away—above the Green Owl tavern. The girl was Madeleine's sister; the priest brought the news just before breakfast. So you can see—"

"Yes, I see." Madame sounded a little breathless. "Yes, of course. Of course. Was it—the same?" Her voice quivered with distaste.

"Yes, Madame. A hatchet or a big knife of some sort." He lowered his voice, as people do when recounting horrid things. "The priest told me that her head had been completely severed. Her body was near the door of her room, and her head"—his voice dropped even lower, almost to a whisper— "her head was sitting on the mantelpiece, looking into the room. The landlord swooned when he found her."

A heavy thud from the next room suggested that Madame Jeanne had done likewise. Gooseflesh rippled up my arms, and my own knees felt a trifle watery. I was beginning to agree with Jamie's fear that his installing me in a house of prostitution had been injudicious.

At any rate, I was now clad, if not entirely dressed, and I went into the room next door, to find Madame Jeanne in semi-recline on the sofa of a small parlor, with a burly, unhappy-looking man sitting on the hassock near her feet.

Madame started up at the sight of me. "Madame Fraser! Oh, I am so sorry! I did not mean to leave you waiting, but I have had . . ." she hesitated, looking for some delicate expression ". . . some distressing news."

"I'd say so," I said. "What's this about a Fiend?"

"You heard?" She was already pale; now her complexion went a few shades whiter, and she wrung her hands. "What will he say? He will be furious!" she moaned.

"Who?" I asked. "Jamie, or the Fiend?"

"Your husband," she said. She looked about the parlor, distracted. "When he hears that his wife has been so shamefully neglected, mistaken for a *fille de joie* and exposed to—to—"

"I really don't think he'll mind," I said. "But I would like to hear about the Fiend."

"You would?" Bruno's heavy eyebrows rose. He was a big man, with sloping shoulders and long arms that made him look rather like a gorilla; a resemblance enhanced by a low brow and a receding chin. He looked eminently suited to the role of bouncer in a brothel.

"Well," he hesitated, glancing at Madame Jeanne for guidance, but the proprietor caught sight of the small enameled clock on the mantelpiece and jumped to her feet with an exclamation of shock.

"*Crottin!*" she exclaimed. "I must go!" And with no more than a perfunctory wave in my direction, she sped from the room, leaving Bruno and me looking after her in surprise.

"Oh," he said, recovering himself. "That's right, it was coming at ten o'clock." It was a quarter-past ten, by the enamel clock. Whatever "it" was, I hoped it would wait.

"Fiend," I prompted.

Like most people, Bruno was only too willing to reveal all the gory details, once past a pro forma demur for the sake of social delicacy.

The Edinburgh Fiend was—as I had deduced from the conversation thus far—a murderer. Like an early-day Jack the Ripper, he specialized in women of easy virtue, whom he killed with blows from a heavy-bladed instrument. In some cases, the bodies had been dismembered or otherwise "interfered with," as Bruno said, in lowered voice.

The killings—eight in all—had occurred at intervals over the last two years. With one exception, the women had been killed in their own rooms; most lived alone—two had been killed in brothels. Hence Madame's agitation, I supposed.

"What was the exception?" I asked.

Bruno crossed himself. "A nun," he whispered, the words evidently still a shock to him. "A French Sister of Mercy."

The Sister, coming ashore at Edinburgh with a group of nuns bound for London, had been abducted from the docks, without any of her companions noticing her absence in the confusion. By the time she was discovered in one of Edinburgh's wynds, after nightfall, it was far too late.

"Raped?" I asked, with clinical interest.

Bruno eyed me with considerable suspicion.

"I do not know," he said formally. He rose heavily to his feet, his simian shoulders drooping with fatigue. I supposed he had been on duty all night; it must be his bedtime now. "If you will excuse me, Madame," he said, with remote formality, and went out.

I sat back on the small velvet sofa, feeling mildly dazed. Somehow I hadn't realized that quite so much went on in brothels in the daytime.

There was a sudden loud hammering at the door. It didn't sound like knocking, but as though someone really were using a metal-headed hammer to demand admittance. I got to my feet to answer the summons, but without further warning, the door burst open, and a slender imperious figure strode into the room, speaking French in an accent so pronounced and an attitude so furious that I could not follow it all.

"Are you looking for Madame Jeanne?" I managed to put in, seizing a small pause when he stopped to draw breath for more invective. The visitor was a young man of about thirty, slightly built and strikingly handsome, with thick black hair and brows. He glared at me under these, and as he got a good look at me, an extraordinary change went across his face. The brows rose, his black eyes grew huge, and his face went white.

"Milady!" he exclaimed, and flung himself on his knees, embracing me about the thighs as he pressed his face into the cotton shift at crotch level.

"Let go!" I exclaimed, shoving at his shoulders to detach him. "I don't work here. Let go, I say!"

"Milady!" he was repeating in tones of rapture. "Milady! You have come back! A miracle! God has restored you!"

He looked up at me, smiling as tears streamed down his face. He had large white perfect teeth. Suddenly memory stirred and shifted, showing me the outlines of an urchin's face beneath the man's bold visage.

"Fergus!" I said. "Fergus, is that really you? Get up, for God's sake—let me see you!"

He rose to his feet, but didn't pause to let me inspect him. He gathered me into a rib-cracking hug, and I clutched him in return, pounding his back in the excitement of seeing him again. He had been ten or so when I last saw him, just before Culloden. Now he was a man, and the stubble of his beard rasped against my cheek.

"I thought I was seeing a ghost!" he exclaimed. "It is really you, then?"

"Yes, it's me," I assured him.

"You have seen milord?" he asked excitedly. "He knows you are here?"

"Yes."

"Oh!" He blinked and stepped back half a pace, as something occurred to him. "But—but what about—" He paused, clearly confused.

"What about what?"

"There ye are! What in the name of God are ye doing up here, Fergus?" Jamie's tall figure loomed suddenly in the doorway. His eyes widened at the sight of me in my embroidered shift. "Where are your clothes?" he asked. "Never mind," he said then, waving his hand impatiently as I opened my mouth to answer. "I havena time just now. Come along, Fergus, there's eighteen ankers of brandy in the alleyway, and the excisemen on my heels!"

And with a thunder of boots on the wooden staircase, they were gone, leaving me alone once more.

I wasn't sure whether I should join the party downstairs or not, but curiosity got the better of discretion. After a quick visit to the sewing room in search of more extensive covering, I made my way down, a large shawl half-embroidered with hollyhocks flung round my shoulders.

I had gathered only a vague impression of the layout of the house the night before, but the street noises that filtered through the windows made it clear which side of the building faced the High Street. I assumed the alley-way to which Jamie had referred must be on the other side, but wasn't sure. The houses of Edinburgh were frequently constructed with odd little wings and twisting walls, to take advantage of every inch of space.

I paused on the large landing at the foot of the stairs, listening for the sound of rolling casks as a guide. As I stood there, I felt a sudden draft on my bare feet, and turned to see a man standing in the open doorway from the kitchen.

He seemed as surprised as I, but after blinking at me, he smiled and stepped forward to grip me by the elbow.

"And a good morning to you, my dear. I didn't expect to find any of you ladies up and about so early in the morning."

"Well, you know what they say about early to bed and early to rise," I said, trying to extricate my elbow.

He laughed, showing rather badly stained teeth in a narrow jaw. "No, what do they say about it?"

"Well, it's something they say in America, come to think of it," I replied, suddenly realizing that Benjamin Franklin, even if currently publishing, probably didn't have a wide readership in Edinburgh.

"Got a wit about you, chuckie," he said, with a slight smile. "Send you down as a decoy, did she?"

"No. Who?" I said.

"The madam," he said, glancing around. "Where is she?"

"I have no idea," I said. "Let go!"

Instead, he tightened his grip, so that his fingers dug uncomfortably into the muscles of my upper arm. He leaned closer, whispering in my ear with a gust of stale tobacco fumes.

"There's a reward, you know," he murmured confidentially. "A percent-age of the value of the seized contraband. No one would need to know but you and me." He flicked one finger gently under my breast, making the nipple stand up under the thin cotton. "What d'ye say, chuck?"

I stared at him. "The excisemen are on my heels," Jamie had said. This must be one, then; an officer of the Crown, charged with the prevention of smuggling and the apprehension of smugglers. What had Jamie said? "The pillory, transportation, flogging, imprisonment, ear-nailing," waving an airy hand as though such penalties were the equivalent of a traffic ticket.

"Whatever are you talking about?" I said, trying to sound puzzled. "And for the last time, let go of me!" He couldn't be alone, I thought. How many others were there around the building?

"Yes, please let go," said a voice behind me. I saw the exciseman's eyes widen as he glanced over my shoulder.

Mr. Willoughby stood on the second stair in rumpled blue silk, a large pistol gripped in both hands. He bobbed his head politely at the excise officer.

"Not stinking whore," he explained, blinking owlishly. "Honorable wife."

The exciseman, clearly startled by the unexpected appearance of a Chinese, gawked from me to Mr. Willoughby and back again.

"Wife?" he said disbelievingly. "You say she's your *wife?*"

Mr. Willoughby, clearly catching only the salient word, nodded pleasantly.

"Wife," he said again. "Please letting go." His eyes were mere bloodshot slits, and it was apparent to me, if not to the exciseman, that his blood was still approximately 80 proof.

The exciseman pulled me toward himself and scowled at Mr. Willoughby. "Now, listen here—" he began. He got no further, for Mr. Willoughby, evidently assuming that he had given fair warning, raised the pistol and pulled the trigger.

There was a loud crack, an even louder shriek, which must have been mine, and the landing was filled with a cloud of gray powder-smoke. The exciseman staggered back against the paneling, a look of intense surprise on his face, and a spreading rosette of blood on the breast of his coat.

Moving by reflex, I leapt forward and grasped the man under the arms, easing him gently down to the floorboards of the landing. There was a flurry of noise from above, as the inhabitants of the house crowded chattering and exclaiming onto the upper landing, attracted by the shot. Bounding footsteps came up the lower stairs two at a time.

Fergus burst through what must be the cellar door, a pistol in his hand.

"Milady," he gasped, catching sight of me sitting in the corner with the exciseman's body sprawled across my lap. "What have you done?"

"Me?" I said indignantly. "*I* haven't done anything; it's Jamie's pet Chinaman." I nodded briefly toward the stair, where Mr. Willoughby, the pistol dropped unregarded by his feet, had sat down on the step and was now regarding the scene below with a benign and bloodshot eye.

Fergus said something in French that was too colloquial to translate, but sounded highly uncomplimentary to Mr. Willoughby. He strode across the landing, and reached out a hand to grasp the little Chinaman's shoulder—or so I assumed, until I saw that the arm he extended did not end in a hand, but in a hook of gleaming dark metal.

"Fergus!" I was so shocked at the sight that I stopped my attempts to stanch the exciseman's wound with my shawl. "What—what—" I said incoherently.

"What?" he said, glancing at me. Then, following the direction of my gaze, said, "Oh, that," and shrugged. "The English. Don't worry about it, milady, we haven't time. You, *canaille*, get downstairs!" He jerked Mr. Willoughby off the stairs, dragged him to the cellar door and shoved him through it, with a callous disregard for safety. I could hear a series of bumps, suggesting that the Chinese was rolling downstairs, his acrobatic skills having temporarily deserted him, but had no time to worry about it.

Fergus squatted next to me, and lifted the exciseman's head by the hair. "How many companions are with you?" he demanded. "Tell me quickly, *cochon,* or I slit your throat!"

From the evident signs, this was a superfluous threat. The man's eyes were already glazing over. With considerable effort, the corners of his mouth drew back in a smile.

"I'll see . . . you . . . burn . . . in . . . hell," he whispered, and with a last convulsion that fixed the smile in a hideous rictus upon his face, he coughed up a startling quantity of bright red foamy blood, and died in my lap.

More feet were coming up the stairs at a high rate of speed. Jamie charged through the cellar door and barely stopped himself before stepping on the excise officer's trailing legs. His eyes traveled up the body's length and rested on my face with horrified amazement.

"What have ye done, Sassenach?" he demanded.

"Not her—the yellow pox," Fergus put in, saving me the trouble. He thrust the pistol into his belt and offered me his real hand. "Come, milady, you must get downstairs!"

Jamie forestalled him, bending over me as he jerked his head in the direction of the front hall.

"I'll manage here," he said. "Guard the front, Fergus. The usual signal, and keep your pistol hidden unless there's need."

Fergus nodded and vanished at once through the door to the hall.

Jamie had succeeded in bundling the corpse awkwardly in the shawl; he lifted it off me, and I scrambled to my feet, greatly relieved to be rid of it, in spite of the blood and other objectionable substances soaking the front of my shift.

"Ooh! I think he's *dead*!" An awestruck voice floated down from above, and I looked up to see a dozen prostitutes peering down like cherubim from on high.

"Get back to your rooms!" Jamie barked. There was a chorus of frightened squeals, and they scattered like pigeons.

Jamie glanced around the landing for traces of the incident, but luckily there were none—the shawl and I had caught everything.

"Come on," he said.

The stairs were dim and the cellar at the foot pitch-black. I stopped at the bottom, waiting for Jamie. The exciseman had not been lightly built, and Jamie was breathing hard when he reached me.

"Across to the far side," he said, gasping. "A false wall. Hold my arm."

With the door above shut, I couldn't see a thing; luckily Jamie seemed able to steer by radar. He led me unerringly past large objects that I bumped in passing, and finally came to a halt. I could smell damp stone, and putting out a hand, felt a rough wall before me.

Jamie said something loudly in Gaelic. Apparently it was the Celtic equivalent of "Open Sesame," for there was a short silence, then a grating noise, and a faint glowing line appeared in the darkness before me. The line widened into a slit, and a section of the wall swung out, revealing a small doorway, made of a wooden framework, upon which cut stones were mounted so as to look like part of the wall.

The concealed cellar was a large room, at least thirty feet long. Several figures were moving about, and the air was ripely suffocating with the smell of brandy. Jamie dumped the body unceremoniously in a corner, then turned to me.

"God, Sassenach, are ye all right?" The cellar seemed to be lighted with candles, dotted here and there in the dimness. I could just see his face, skin drawn tight across his cheekbones.

"I'm a little cold," I said, trying not to let my teeth chatter. "My shift is soaked with blood. Otherwise I'm all right. I think."

"Jeanne!" He turned and called toward the far end of the cellar, and one of the figures came toward us, resolving itself into a very worried-looking madam. He explained the situation in a few words, causing the worried expression to grow considerably worse.

"Horreur!" she said. "Killed? On my premises? With *witnesses?*"

"Aye, I'm afraid so." Jamie sounded calm. "I'll manage about it. But in the meantime, ye must go up. He might not have been alone. You'll know what to do."

His voice held a tone of calm assurance, and he squeezed her arm. The touch seemed to calm her—I hoped that was why he had done it—and she turned to leave.

"Oh, and Jeanne," Jamie called after her. "When ye come back, can ye bring down some clothes for my wife? If her gown's not ready, I think Daphne is maybe the right size."

"Clothes?" Madame Jeanne squinted into the shadows where I stood. I helpfully stepped out into the light, displaying the results of my encounter with the exciseman.

Madame Jeanne blinked once or twice, crossed herself, and turned without a word, to disappear through the concealed doorway, which swung to behind her with a muffled thud.

I was beginning to shake, as much with reaction as with the cold. Accustomed as I was to emergency, blood, and even sudden death, the events of the morning had been more than a little harrowing. It was like a bad Saturday night in the emergency room.

"Come along, Sassenach," Jamie said, putting a hand gently on the small of my back. "We'll get ye washed." His touch worked on me as well as it had on Madame Jeanne; I felt instantly better, if still apprehensive.

"Washed? In what? Brandy?"

He gave a slight laugh at that. "No, water. I can offer ye a bathtub, but I'm afraid it will be cold."

It was extremely cold.

"Wh-wh-where did this water come from?" I asked, shivering. "Off a glacier?" The water gushed out of a pipe set in the wall, normally kept plugged with an insanitary-looking wad of rags, wrapped to form a rough seal around the chunk of wood that served as a plug.

I pulled my hand out of the chilly stream and wiped it on the shift, which was too far gone for anything to make much difference. Jamie shook his head as he maneuvered the big wooden tub closer to the spout.

"Off the roof," he answered. "There's a rainwater cistern up there. The guttering pipe runs down the side of the building, and the cistern pipe is hidden inside it." He looked absurdly proud of himself, and I laughed.

"Quite an arrangement," I said. "What do you use the water for?"

"To cut the liquor," he explained. He gestured at the far side of the room, where the shadowy figures were working with notable industry among a large array of casks and tubs. "It comes in a hundred and eighty degrees above proof. We mix it here wi' pure water, and recask it for sale to the taverns."

He shoved the rough plug back into the pipe, and bent to pull the big tub across the stone floor. "Here, we'll take it out of the way; they'll be needing the water." One of the men was in fact standing by with a small cask clasped in his arms; with no more than a curious glance at me, he nodded to Jamie and thrust the cask beneath the stream of water.

Behind a hastily arranged screen of empty barrels, I peered dubiously down into the depths of my makeshift tub. A single candle burned in a puddle of wax nearby, glimmering off the surface of the water and making it look black and bottomless. I stripped off, shivering violently, thinking that the comforts of hot water and modern plumbing had seemed a hell of a lot easier to renounce when they were close at hand.

Jamie groped in his sleeve and pulled out a large handkerchief, at which he squinted dubiously.

"Aye, well, it's maybe cleaner than your shift," he said, shrugging. He handed it to me, then excused himself to oversee operations at the other end of the room.

The water was freezing and so was the cellar, and as I gingerly sponged myself, the icy trickles running down my stomach and thighs brought on small fits of shivering.

Thoughts of what might be happening overhead did little to ease my feelings of chilly apprehension. Presumably, we were safe enough for the moment, so long as the false cellar wall deceived any searching excisemen.

But if the wall failed to hide us, our position was all but hopeless. There appeared to be no way out of this room but by the door in the false wall—and if that wall were breached, we would not only be caught red-handed in possession of quite a lot of contraband brandy, but also in custody of the body of a murdered King's Officer.

And surely the disappearance of that officer would provoke an intensive search? I had visions of excisemen combing the brothel, questioning and threatening the women, emerging with complete descriptions of myself, Jamie, and Mr. Willoughby, as well as several eyewitness accounts of the murder. Involuntarily, I glanced at the far corner, where the dead man lay beneath his bloodstained shroud, covered with pink and yellow hollyhocks. The Chinaman was nowhere to be seen, having apparently passed out behind the ankers of brandy.

"Here, Sassenach. Drink this; your teeth are chattering so, you're like to bite through your tongue." Jamie had reappeared by my seal hole like a St. Bernard dog, bearing a firkin of brandy.

"Th-thanks." I had to drop the washcloth and use both hands to steady the wooden cup so it wouldn't clack against my teeth, but the brandy helped; it dropped like a flaming coal into the pit of my stomach and sent small curling tendrils of warmth through my frigid extremities as I sipped.

"Oh, God, that's better," I said, stopping long enough to gasp for breath. "Is this the uncut version?"

"No, that would likely kill ye. This is maybe a little stronger than what we sell, though. Finish up and put something on; then ye can have a bit more." Jamie took the cup from my hand and gave me back the handkerchief washcloth. As I hurriedly finished my chilly ablutions, I watched him from the corner of my eye. He was frowning as he gazed at me, clearly deep in thought. I had imagined that his life was complicated; it hadn't escaped me that my presence was undoubtedly complicating it a good bit more. I would have given a lot to know what he was thinking.

"What are you thinking about, Jamie?" I said, watching him sidelong as I swabbed the last of the smudges from my thighs. The water swirled around my calves, disturbed by my movements, and the candlelight lit the waves with sparks, as though the dark blood I had washed from my body now glowed once more live and red in the water.

The frown vanished momentarily as his eyes cleared and fixed on my face.

"I am thinking that you're verra beautiful, Sassenach," he said softly.

"Maybe if one has a taste for gooseflesh on a large scale," I said tartly, stepping out of the tub and reaching for the cup.

He grinned suddenly at me, teeth flashing white in the dimness of the cellar.

"Oh, aye," he said. "Well, you're speaking to the only man in Scotland who has a terrible cockstand at sight of a plucked chicken."

I spluttered in my brandy and choked, half-hysterical from tension and terror.

Jamie quickly shrugged out of his coat and wrapped the garment around me, hugging me close against him as I shivered and coughed and gasped.

"Makes it hard to pass a poulterer's stall and stay decent," he murmured in my ear, briskly rubbing my back through the fabric. "Hush, Sassenach, hush now. It'll be fine."

I clung to him, shaking. "I'm sorry," I said. "I'm all right. It's my fault, though. Mr. Willoughby shot the exciseman because he thought he was making indecent advances to me."

Jamie snorted. "That doesna make it your fault, Sassenach," he said dryly. "And for what it's worth, it's no the first time the Chinaman's done something foolish, either. When he's drink taken, he'll do anything, and never mind how mad it is."

Suddenly Jamie's expression changed as he realized what I had said. He stared down at me, eyes wide. "Did ye say 'exciseman,' Sassenach?"

"Yes, why?"

He didn't answer, but let go my shoulders and whirled on his heel, snatching the candle off the cask in passing. Rather than be left in the dark, I followed him to the corner where the corpse lay under its shawl.

"Hold this." Jamie thrust the candle unceremoniously into my hand and knelt by the shrouded figure, pulling back the stained fabric that covered the face.

I had seen quite a few dead bodies; the sight was no shock, but it still wasn't pleasant. The eyes had rolled up beneath half-closed lids, which did nothing to help the generally ghastly effect. Jamie frowned at the dead face, drop-jawed and waxy in the candlelight, and muttered something under his breath.

"What's wrong?" I asked. I had thought I would never be warm again, but Jamie's coat was not only thick and well-made, it held the remnants of his own considerable body heat. I was still cold, but the shivering had eased.

"This isna an exciseman," Jamie said, still frowning. "I know all the Riding Officers in the district, and the superintending officers, too. But I've no seen this fellow before." With some distaste, he turned back the sodden flap of the coat and groped inside.

He felt about gingerly but thoroughly inside the man's clothing, emerging at last with a small penknife, and a small booklet bound in red paper.

" 'New Testament,' " I read, with some astonishment.

Jamie nodded, looking up at me with one brow raised. "Exciseman or no, it seems a peculiar thing to bring with ye to a kittle-hoosie." He wiped the little booklet on the shawl, then drew the folds of fabric quite gently back over the face, and rose to his feet, shaking his head.

"That's the only thing in his pockets. Any Customs inspector or exciseman must carry his warrant upon his person at all times, for otherwise he's no authority to carry out a search of premises or seize goods." He glanced up, eyebrows raised. "Why did ye think he was an exciseman?"

I hugged the folds of Jamie's coat around myself, trying to remember what the man had said to me on the landing. "He asked me whether I was a decoy, and where the madam was. Then he said that there was a reward—a percentage of seized contraband, that's what he said—and that no one would know but him and me. And you'd said there were excisemen after you," I added. "So naturally I thought he was one. Then Mr. Willoughby turned up and things rather went to pot."

Jamie nodded, still looking puzzled. "Aye, well. I havena got any idea who he is, but it's a good thing that he isna an exciseman. I thought at first something had come verra badly unstuck, but it's likely all right."

"Unstuck?"

He smiled briefly. "I've an arrangement with the Superintending Customs Officer for the district, Sassenach."

I gaped at him. "Arrangement?"

He shrugged. "Well, bribery then, if ye like to be straight out about it." He sounded faintly irritated.

"No doubt that's standard business procedure?" I said, trying to sound tactful. One corner of his mouth twitched slightly.

"Aye, it is. Well, in any case, there's an understanding, as ye might say, between Sir Percival Turner and myself, and to find him sending excise officers into this place would worry me considerably."

"All right," I said slowly, mentally juggling all the half-understood events of the morning, and trying to make a pattern of them. "But in that case, what did you mean by telling Fergus the excisemen were on your heels? And why has everyone been racing round like chickens with their heads off?"

"Oh, that." He smiled briefly, and took my arm, turning me away from the corpse at our feet. "Well, it's an arrangement, as I said. And part of it is that Sir Percival must satisfy his own masters in London, by seizing sufficient amounts of contraband now and again. So we see to it that he's given the opportunity. Wally and the lads brought down two wagonloads from the coast; one of the best brandy, and the other filled with spiled casks and the punked wine, topped off with a few ankers of cheap swill, just to give it all flavor.

"I met them just outside the city this morning, as we planned, and then we drove the wagons in, takin' care to attract the attention of the Riding Officer, who just happened to be passing with a small number of dragoons. They came along and we led them a canty chase through the alleyways, until the time for me and the good tubs to part company wi' Wally and his load of swill. Wally jumped off his wagon then, and made awa', and I drove like hell down here, wi' two or three dragoons following, just for show, like. Looks well in a report, ye ken." He grinned at me, quoting, " *'The smugglers escaped in spite of industrious pursuit, but His Majesty's valiant soldiers succeeded in capturing an entire wagonload of spirits, valued at sixty pounds, ten shillings.'* You'll know the sort of thing?"

"I expect so," I said. "Then it was you and the good liquor that was arriving at ten? Madame Jeanne said—"

"Aye," he said, frowning. "She was meant to have the cellar door open and the ramp in place at ten sharp—we havena got long to get everything unloaded. She was bloody late this morning; I had to circle round twice to keep from bringing the dragoons straight to the door."

"She was a bit distracted," I said, remembering suddenly about the Fiend. I told Jamie about the murder at the Green Owl, and he grimaced, crossing himself.

"Poor lass," he said.

I shuddered briefly at the memory of Bruno's description, and moved closer to Jamie, who put an arm about my shoulders. He kissed me absently on the forehead, glancing again at the shawl-covered shape on the ground.

"Well, whoever he was, if he wasna an exciseman, there are likely no more of them upstairs. We should be able to get out of here soon."

"That's good." Jamie's coat covered me to the knees, but I felt the covert glances cast from the far end of the room at my bare calves, and was all too uncomfortably aware that I was naked under it. "Will we be going back to the printshop?" What with one thing and another, I didn't think I wanted to take advantage of Madame Jeanne's hospitality any longer than necessary.

"Maybe for a bit. I'll have to think." Jamie's tone was abstracted, and I could see that his brow was furrowed in thought. With a brief hug, he released me, and began to walk about the cellar, staring meditatively at the stones underfoot.

"Er . . . what did you do with Ian?"

He glanced up, looking blank; then his face cleared.

"Oh, Ian. I left him making inquiries at the taverns above the Market Cross. I'll need to remember to meet him, later," he muttered, as though making a note to himself.

"I met Young Ian, by the way," I said conversationally.

Jamie looked startled. "He came here?"

"He did. Looking for you—about a quarter of an hour after you left, in fact."

"Thank God for small mercies!" He rubbed a hand through his hair, looking simultaneously amused and worried. "I'd have had the devil of a time explaining to Ian what his son was doing here."

"You *know* what he was doing here?" I asked curiously.

"No, I don't! He was supposed to be—ah, well, let it be. I canna be worrit about it just now." He relapsed into thought, emerging momentarily to ask, "Did Young Ian say where he was going, when he left ye?"

I shook my head, gathering the coat around myself, and he nodded, sighed, and took up his slow pacing once more.

I sat down on an upturned tub and watched him. In spite of the general atmosphere of discomfort and danger, I felt absurdly happy simply to be near him. Feeling that there was little I could do to help the situation at present, I settled myself with the coat wrapped round me, and abandoned myself to the momentary pleasure of looking at him—something I had had no chance to do, in the tumult of events.

In spite of his preoccupation, he moved with the surefooted grace of a swordsman, a man so aware of his body as to be able to forget it entirely. The men by the casks worked by torchlight; it gleamed on his hair as he turned, lighting it like a tiger's fur, with stripes of gold and dark.

I caught the faint twitch as two fingers of his right hand flickered together against the fabric of his breeches, and felt a strange little lurch of recognition in the gesture. I had seen him do that a thousand times as he was thinking, and seeing it now again, felt as though all the time that had passed in our separation was no more than the rising and setting of a single sun.

As though catching my thought, he paused in his strolling and smiled at me.

"You'll be warm enough, Sassenach?" he asked.

"No, but it doesn't matter." I got off my tub and went to join him in his peregrinations, slipping a hand through his arm. "Making any progress with the thinking?"

He laughed ruefully. "No. I'm thinking of maybe half a dozen things together, and half of them things I canna do anything about. Like whether Young Ian's where he should be."

I stared up at him. "Where he should be? Where do you think he should be?"

"He *should* be at the printshop," Jamie said, with some emphasis. "But he *should* ha' been with Wally this morning, and he wasn't."

"With Wally? You mean you knew he wasn't at home, when his father came looking for him this morning?"

He rubbed his nose with a finger, looking at once irritated and amused. "Oh, aye. I'd promised Young Ian I wouldna say anything to his Da, though, until he'd a chance to explain himself. Not that an explanation is likely to save his arse," he added.

Young Ian had, as his father said, come to join his uncle in Edinburgh without the preliminary bother of asking his parents' leave. Jamie had discovered this dereliction fairly quickly, but had not wanted to send his nephew alone back to Lallybroch, and had not yet had time to escort him personally.

"It's not that he canna look out for himself," Jamie explained, amusement winning in the struggle of expressions on his face. "He's a nice capable lad. It's just—well, ye ken how things just happen around some folk, without them seeming to have anything much to do wi' it?"

"Now that you mention it, yes," I said wryly. "I'm one of them."

He laughed out loud at that. "God, you're right, Sassenach! Maybe that's why I like Young Ian so well; he 'minds me of you."

"He reminded me a bit of *you*," I said.

Jamie snorted briefly. "God, Jenny will maim me, and she hears her baby son's been loitering about a house of ill repute. I hope the wee bugger has the sense to keep his mouth shut, once he's home."

"I hope he *gets* home," I said, thinking of the gawky almost-fifteen-year-old I had seen that morning, adrift in an Edinburgh filled with prostitutes, excisemen, smugglers, and hatchet-wielding Fiends. "At least he isn't a girl," I added, thinking of this last item. "The Fiend doesn't seem to have a taste for young boys."

"Aye, well, there are plenty of others who have," Jamie said sourly. "Between Young Ian and you, Sassenach, I shall be lucky if my hair's not gone white by the time we get out of this stinking cellar."

"Me?" I said in surprise. "You don't need to worry about me."

"I don't?" He dropped my arm and rounded on me, glaring. "I dinna need to worry about ye? Is that what ye said? Christ! I leave ye safely in bed waiting for your breakfast, and not an hour later, I find ye downstairs in your shift, clutching a corpse to your bosom! And now you're standing in front of me bare as an egg, with fifteen men over there wondering who in hell ye are —and how d'ye think I'm going to explain ye to them, Sassenach? Tell me that, eh?" He shoved a hand through his hair in exasperation.

"Sweet bleeding Jesus! And I've to go up the coast in two days without fail, but I canna leave ye in Edinburgh, not wi' Fiends creepin' about with hatchets, and half the people who've seen ye thinking you're a prostitute, and . . . and . . ." The lacing around his pigtail broke abruptly under the pressure, and his hair fluffed out round his head like a lion's mane. I laughed. He glared for a moment longer, but then a reluctant grin made its way slowly through the frown.

"Aye, well," he said, resigned. "I suppose I'll manage."

"I suppose you will," I said, and stood on tiptoe to brush his hair back behind his ears. Working on the same principle that causes magnets of opposing polarities to snap together when placed in close proximimtry, he bent his head and kissed me.

"I had forgotten," he said, a moment later.

"Forgotten what?" His back was warm through the thin shirt.

"Everything." He spoke very softly, mouth against my hair. "Joy. Fear. Fear, most of all." His hand came up and smoothed my curls away from his nose.

"I havena been afraid for a verra long time, Sassenach," he whispered. "But now I think I am. For there is something to be lost, now."

I drew back a little, to look up at him. His arms were locked tight around my waist, his eyes dark as bottomless water in the dimness. Then his face changed and he kissed me quickly on the forehead.

"Come along, Sassenach," he said, taking me by the arm. "I'll tell the men you're my wife. The rest of it will just have to bide."

27

Up in Flames

The dress was a trifle lower-cut than necessary, and a bit tight in the bosom, but on the whole, not a bad fit.

"And how did you know Daphne would be the right size?" I asked, spooning up my soup.

"I said I didna bed wi' the lasses," Jamie replied circumspectly. "I never said I didna look at them." He blinked at me like a large red owl—some congenital tic made him incapable of closing one eye in a wink—and I laughed.

"That gown becomes ye a good deal more than it did Daphne, though." He cast a glance of general approval at my bosom and waved at a servingmaid carrying a platter of fresh bannocks.

Moubray's tavern was doing a thriving dinner business. Several cuts above the snug, smoky atmosphere to be found in The World's End and similar serious drinking establishments, Moubray's was a large and elegant place, with an outside stair that ran up to the second floor, where a commodious dining room accommodated the appetites of Edinburgh's prosperous tradesmen and public officials.

"Who are you at the moment?" I asked. "I heard Madame Jeanne call you 'Monsieur Fraser'—are you Fraser in public, though?"

He shook his head and broke a bannock into his soup bowl. "No, at the moment, I'm Sawney Malcolm, Printer and Publisher."

"Sawney? That's a nickname for Alexander, is it? I should have thought 'Sandy' was more like it, especially considering your hair." Not that his hair was sandy-colored in the least, I reflected, looking at it. It was like Bree's hair—very thick, with a slight wave to it, and all the colors of red and gold mixed; copper and cinnamon, auburn and amber, red and roan and rufous, all mingled together.

I felt a sudden wave of longing for Bree; at the same time, I longed to untie Jamie's hair from its formal plait and run my hands up under it, to feel the solid curve of his skull, and the soft strands tangled in my fingers. I could still recall the tickle of it, spilling loose and rich across my breasts in the morning light.

My breath coming a little short, I bent my head to my oyster stew.

Jamie appeared not to have noticed; he added a large pat of butter to his bowl, shaking his head as he did so.

"Sawney's what they say in the Highlands," he informed me. "And in the Isles, too. Sandy's more what ye'd hear in the Lowlands—or from an ignorant Sassenach." He lifted one eyebrow at me, smiling, and raised a spoonful of the rich, fragrant stew to his mouth.

"All right," I said. "I suppose more to the point, though—who am I?"

He had noticed, after all. I felt one large foot nudge mine, and he smiled at me over the rim of his cup.

"You're my wife, Sassenach," he said gruffly. "Always. No matter who I may be—you're my wife."

I could feel the flush of pleasure rise in my face, and see the memories of the night before reflected in his own. The tips of his ears were faintly pink.

"You don't suppose there's too much pepper in this stew?" I asked, swallowing another spoonful. "Are you sure, Jamie?"

"Aye," he said. "Aye, I'm sure," he amended, "and no, the pepper's fine. I like a wee bit of pepper." The foot moved slightly against mine, the toe of his shoe barely brushing my ankle.

"So I'm Mrs. Malcolm," I said, trying out the name on my tongue. The mere fact of saying "Mrs." gave me an absurd little thrill, like a new bride. Involuntarily, I glanced down at the silver ring on my right fourth finger.

Jamie caught the glance, and raised his cup to me.

"To Mrs. Malcolm," he said softly, and the breathless feeling came back.

He set down the cup and took my hand; his own was big and so warm that a general feeling of glowing heat spread rapidly through my fingers. I could feel the silver ring, separate from my flesh, its metal heated by his touch.

"To have and to hold," he said, smiling.

"From this day forward," I said, not caring in the least that we were attracting interested glances from the other diners.

Jamie bent his head and pressed his lips against the back of my hand, an action that turned the interested glances into frank stares. A clergyman was seated across the room; he glared at us and said something to his companions, who turned round to stare. One was a small, elderly man; the other, I was surprised to see, was Mr. Wallace, my companion from the Inverness coach.

"There are private rooms upstairs," Jamie murmured, blue eyes dancing over my knuckles, and I lost interest in Mr. Wallace.

"How interesting," I said. "You haven't finished your stew."

"Damn the stew."

"Here comes the servingmaid with the ale."

"Devil take her." Sharp white teeth closed gently on my knuckle, making me jerk slightly in my seat.

"People are watching you."

"Let them, and I trust they've a fine day for it."

His tongue flicked gently between my fingers.

"There's a man in a green coat coming this way."

"To hell—" Jamie began, when the shadow of the visitor fell upon the table.

"A good day to you, Mr. Malcolm," said the visitor, bowing politely. "I trust I do not intrude?"

"You do," said Jamie, straightening up but keeping his grip on my hand. He turned a cool gaze on the newcomer. "I think I do not know ye, sir?"

The gentleman, an Englishman of maybe thirty-five, quietly dressed, bowed again, not intimidated by this marked lack of hospitality.

"I have not had the pleasure of your acquaintance as yet, sir," he said deferentially. "My master, however, bade me greet you, and inquire whether you—and your companion—might be so agreeable as to take a little wine with him."

The tiny pause before the word "companion" was barely discernible, but Jamie caught it. His eyes narrowed.

"My wife and I," he said, with precisely the same sort of pause before "wife," "are otherwise engaged at the moment. Should your master wish to speak wi' me—"

"It is Sir Percival Turner who sends to ask, sir," the secretary—for so he must be—put in quickly. Well-bred as he was, he couldn't resist a tiny flick of one eyebrow, as one who uses a name he expects to conjure with.

"Indeed," said Jamie dryly. "Well, with all respect to Sir Percival, I am preoccupied at present. If you will convey him my regrets?" He bowed, with a politeness so pointed as to come within a hair of rudeness, and turned his back on the secretary. That gentleman stood for a moment, his mouth slightly open, then pivoted smartly on his heel and made his way through the scatter of tables to a door on the far side of the dining room.

"Where was I?" Jamie demanded. "Oh, aye—to hell wi' gentlemen in green coats. Now, about these private rooms—"

"How are you going to explain me to people?" I asked.

He raised one eyebrow.

"Explain what?" He looked me up and down. "Why must I make excuses for ye? You're no missing any limbs; you're not poxed, hunchbacked, toothless or lame—"

"You know what I mean," I said, kicking him lightly under the table. The lady sitting near the wall nudged her companion and widened her eyes disapprovingly at us. I smiled nonchalantly at them.

"Aye, I do," he said, grinning. "However, what wi' Mr. Willoughby's activities this morning, and one thing and another, I havena had much chance to think about the matter. Perhaps I'll just say—"

"My dear fellow, so you are married! Capital news! Simply capital! My deepest congratulations, and may I be—dare I hope to be?—the first to extend my felicitations and best wishes to your lady?"

A small, elderly gentleman in a tidy wig leaned heavily on a gold-knobbed stick, beaming genially at us both. It was the little gentleman who had been sitting with Mr. Wallace and the clergyman.

"You will pardon the minor discourtesy of my sending Johnson to fetch you earlier, I am sure," he said deprecatingly. "It is only that my wretched infirmity prevents rapid movement, as you see."

Jamie had risen to his feet at the appearance of the visitor, and with a polite gesture, now drew out a chair.

"You'll join us, Sir Percival?" he said.

"Oh, no, no indeed! Shouldn't dream of intruding on your new happiness, my dear sir. Truly, I had no idea—" Still protesting gracefully, he sank down into the proffered chair, wincing as he extended his foot beneath the table.

"I am a martyr to gout, my dear," he confided, leaning close enough for me to smell his foul old-man's breath beneath the wintergreen that spiced his linen.

He didn't look corrupt, I thought—breath notwithstanding—but then appearances could be deceiving; it was only about four hours since I had been mistaken for a prostitute.

Making the best of it, Jamie called for wine, and accepted Sir Percival's continued effusions with some grace.

"It is rather fortunate that I should have encountered you here, my dear fellow," the elderly gentleman said, breaking off his flowery compliments at last. He laid a small, manicured hand on Jamie's sleeve. "I had something particular to say to you. In fact, I had sent a note to the printshop, but my messenger failed to find you there."

"Ah?" Jamie cocked an eyebrow in question.

"Yes," Sir Percival went on. "I believe you had spoken to me—some weeks ago, I scarce recall the occasion—of your intention to travel north on business. A matter of a new press, or something of the sort?" Sir Percival had quite a sweet face, I thought, handsomely patrician despite his years, with large, guileless blue eyes.

"Aye, that's so," Jamie agreed courteously. "I am invited by Mr. McLeod of Perth, to see a new style of letterpress he's recently put in use."

"Quite." Sir Percival paused to remove a snuffbox from his pocket, a pretty thing enameled in green and gold, with cherubs on the lid.

"I really should not advise a trip to the north just now," he said, opening the box and concentrating on its contents. "Really I should not. The weather is like to be inclement at this season; I am sure it would not suit Mrs. Malcolm." Smiling at me like an elderly angel, he inhaled a large pinch of snuff and paused, linen handkerchief at the ready.

Jamie sipped at his wine, his face blandly composed.

"I am grateful for your advice, Sir Percival," he said. "You'll perhaps have received word from your agents of recent storms to the north?"

Sir Percival sneezed, a small, neat sound, like a mouse with a cold. He was rather like a white mouse altogether, I thought, seeing him dab daintily at his pointed pink nose.

"Quite," he said again, putting away the kerchief and blinking benevolently at Jamie. "No, I would—as a particular friend with your welfare at heart—most strongly advise that you remain in Edinburgh. After all," he added, turning the beam of his benevolence on me, "you surely have an inducement to remain comfortably at home now, do you not? And now, my dear young people, I am afraid I must take my leave; I must not detain you any longer from what must be your wedding breakfast."

With a little assistance from the hovering Johnson, Sir Percival got up and tottered off, his gold-knobbed stick tap-tapping on the floor.

"He seems a nice old gent," I remarked, when I was sure he was far enough away not to hear me.

Jamie snorted. "Rotten as a worm-riddled board," he said. He picked up his glass and drained it. "Ye'd think otherwise," he said meditatively, putting it down and staring after the wizened figure, now cautiously negotiating the head of the stairs. "A man as close as Sir Percival is to Judgment Day, I mean. Ye'd think fear o' the Devil would prevent him, but not a bit."

"I suppose he's like everyone else," I said cynically. "Most people think they're going to live forever."

Jamie laughed, his exuberant spirits returning with a rush.

"Aye, that's true," he said. He pushed my wineglass toward me. "And now you're here, Sassenach, I'm convinced of it. Drink up, *mo nighean donn,* and we'll go upstairs."

———◆———

"Post coitum omne animalium triste est," I remarked, with my eyes closed.

There was no response from the warm, heavy weight on my chest, save the gentle sigh of his breathing. After a moment, though, I felt a sort of subterranean vibration, which I interpreted as amusement.

"That's a verra peculiar sentiment, Sassenach," Jamie said, his voice blurred with drowsiness. "Not your own, I hope?"

"No." I stroked the damp bright hair back from his forehead, and he turned his face into the curve of my shoulder, with a small contented snuffle.

The private rooms at Moubray's left a bit to be desired in the way of amorous accommodation. Still, the sofa at least offered a padded horizontal surface, which, if you came right down to it, was all that was necessary. While I had decided that I was not past wanting to commit passionate acts after all, I was still too old to want to commit them on the bare floorboards.

"I don't know who said it—some ancient philosopher or other. It was quoted in one of my medical textbooks; in the chapter on the human reproductive system."

The vibration made itself audible as a small chuckle.

"Ye'd seem to have applied yourself to your lessons to good purpose, Sassenach," he said. His hand passed down my side and wormed its way slowly underneath to cup my bottom. He sighed with contentment, squeezing slightly.

"I canna think when I have felt less *triste*," he said.

"Me either," I said, tracing the whorl of the small cowlick that lifted the hair from the center of his forehead. "That's what made me think of it—I rather wondered what led the ancient philosopher to that conclusion."

"I suppose it depends on the sorts of *animaliae* he'd been fornicating with," Jamie observed. "Maybe it was just that none o' them took to him, but he must ha' tried a fair number, to make such a sweeping statement."

He held tighter to his anchor as the tide of my laughter bounced him gently up and down.

"Mind ye, dogs sometimes do look a trifle sheepish when they've done wi' mating," he said.

"Mm. And how do sheep look, then?"

"Aye, well, female sheep just go on lookin' like sheep—not havin' a great deal of choice in the matter, ye ken."

"Oh? And what do the male sheep look like?"

"Oh, they look fair depraved. Let their tongues hang out, drooling, and their eyes roll back, while they make disgusting noises. Like most male animals, aye?" I could feel the curve of his grin against my shoulder. He squeezed again, and I pulled gently on the ear closest to hand.

"I didn't notice your tongue hanging out."

"Ye werena noticing; your eyes were closed."

"I didn't hear any disgusting noises, either."

"Well, I couldna just think of any on the spur of the moment," he admitted. "Perhaps I'll do better next time."

We laughed softly together, and then were quiet, listening to each other breathe.

"Jamie," I said softly at last, smoothing the back of his head, "I don't think I've ever been so happy."

He rolled to one side, shifting his weight carefully so as not to squash me, and lifted himself to lie face-to-face with me.

"Nor me, my Sassenach," he said, and kissed me, very lightly, but lingering, so that I had time just to close my lips in a tiny bite on the fullness of his lower lip.

"It's no just the bedding, ye ken," he said, drawing back a little at last. His eyes looked down at me, a soft deep blue like the warm tropic sea.

"No," I said, touching his cheek. "It isn't."

"To have ye with me again—to talk wi' you—to know I can say anything, not guard my words or hide my thoughts—God, Sassenach," he said, "the Lord knows I am lust-crazed as a lad, and I canna keep my hands from you—or anything else—" he added, wryly, "but I would count that all well lost, had I no more than the pleasure of havin' ye by me, and to tell ye all my heart."

"It was lonely without you," I whispered. "So lonely."

"And me," he said. He looked down, long lashes hiding his eyes, and hesitated for a moment.

"I willna say that I have lived a monk," he said quietly. "When I had to—when I felt that I must or go mad—"

I laid my fingers against his lips, to stop him.

"Neither did I," I said. "Frank—"

His own hand pressed gently against my mouth. Both dumb, we looked at each other, and I could feel the smile growing behind my hand, and my own under his, to match it. I took my hand away.

"It doesna signify," he said. He took his hand off my mouth.

"No," I said. "It doesn't matter." I traced the line of his lips with my finger.

"So tell me all your heart," I said. "If there's time."

He glanced at the window to gauge the light—we were to meet Ian at the print shop at five o'clock, to check the progress of the search for Young Ian —and then rolled carefully off me.

"There's two hours, at least, before we must go. Sit up and put your clothes on, and I'll have them bring some wine and biscuits."

This sounded wonderful. I seemed to have been starving ever since I found him. I sat up and began to rummage through the pile of discarded clothes on the floor, looking for the set of stays the low-necked gown required.

"I'm no ways sad, but I do maybe feel a bit ashamed," Jamie observed, wriggling long, slender toes into a silk stocking. "Or I should, at least."

"Why is that?"

"Well, here I am, in paradise, so to speak, wi' you and wine and biscuits, while Ian's out tramping the pavements and worrying for his son."

"Are you worried about Young Ian?" I asked, concentrating on my laces.

He frowned slightly, pulling on the other stocking.

"Not so much worried for him, as afraid he may not turn up before tomorrow."

"What happens tomorrow?" I asked, and then belatedly recalled the encounter with Sir Percival Turner. "Oh, your trip to the north—that was supposed to be tomorrow?"

He nodded. "Aye, there's a rendezvous set at Mullin's Cove, tomorrow being the dark of the moon. A lugger from France, wi' a load of wine and cambric."

"And Sir Percival was warning you not to make that rendezvous?"

"So it seems. What's happened, I canna say, though I expect I'll find out. Could be as there's a visiting Customs Officer in the district, or he's had word of some activity on the coast there that has nothing to do wi' us, but could interfere." He shrugged and finished his last garter.

He spread out his hands upon his knees then, palm up, and slowly curled the fingers inward. The left curled at once into a fist, compact and neat, a blunt instrument ready for battle. The fingers of his right hand curled more slowly; the middle finger was crooked, and would not lie along the second. The fourth finger would not curl at all, but stuck out straight, holding the little finger at an awkward angle beside it.

He looked from his hands to me, smiling.

"D'ye remember the night when ye set my hand?"

"Sometimes, in my more horrible moments." That night was one to re-member—only because it couldn't be forgotten. Against all odds, I had rescued him from Wentworth Prison and a death sentence—but not in time to prevent his being cruelly tortured and abused by Black Jack Randall.

I picked up his right hand and transferred it to my own knee. He let it lie there, warm, heavy and inert, and didn't object as I felt each finger, pulling gently to stretch the tendons and twisting to see the range of motion in the joints.

"My first orthopedic surgery, that was," I said wryly.

"Have ye done a great many things like that since?" he asked curiously, looking down at me.

"Yes, a few. I'm a surgeon—but it doesn't mean then what it means now," I added hastily. "Surgeons in my time don't pull teeth and let blood. They're more like what's meant now by the word 'physician'—a doctor with training in all the fields of medicine, but with a specialty."

"Special, are ye? Well, ye've always been that," he said, grinning. The crippled fingers slid into my palm and his thumb stroked my knuckles. "What is it a surgeon does that's special, then?"

I frowned, trying to think of the right phrasing. "Well, as best I can put it —a surgeon tries to effect healing . . . by means of a knife."

His long mouth curled upward at the notion.

"A nice contradiction, that; but it suits ye, Sassenach."

"It does?" I said, startled.

He nodded, never taking his eyes off my face. I could see him studying me closely, and wondered self-consciously what I must look like, flushed from lovemaking, with my hair in wild disorder.

"Ye havena been lovelier, Sassenach," he said, smile growing wider as I reached up to smooth my hair. He caught my hand, and kissed it gently. "Leave your curls be.

"No," he said, holding my hands trapped while he looked me over, "no, a knife is verra much what you are, now I think of it. A clever-worked scabbard, and most gorgeous to see, Sassenach"—he traced the line of my lips with a finger, provoking a smile—"but tempered steel for a core . . . and a wicked sharp edge, I do think."

"Wicked?" I said, surprised.

"Not heartless, I don't mean," he assured me. His eyes rested on my face, intent and curious. A smile touched his lips. "No, never that. But you can be ruthless strong, Sassenach, when the need is on ye."

I smiled, a little wryly. "I can," I said.

"I have seen that in ye before, aye?" His voice grew softer and his grasp on my hand tightened. "But now I think ye have it much more than when ye were younger. You'll have needed it often since, no?"

I realized quite suddenly why he saw so clearly what Frank had never seen at all.

"You have it too," I said. "And you've needed it. Often." Unconsciously, my fingers touched the jagged scar that crossed his middle finger, twisting the distal joints.

He nodded.

"I have wondered," he said, so low I could scarcely hear him. "Wondered often, if I could call that edge to my service, and sheathe it safe again. For I have seen a great many men grow hard in that calling, and their steel decay to dull iron. And I have wondered often, was I master in my soul, or did I become the slave of my own blade?

"I have thought again and again," he went on, looking down at our linked hands . . . "that I had drawn my blade too often, and spent so long in the service of strife that I wasna fit any longer for human intercourse."

My lips twitched with the urge to make a remark, but I bit them instead. He saw it, and smiled, a little wryly.

"I didna think I should ever laugh again in a woman's bed, Sassenach," he said. "Or even come to a woman, save as a brute, blind with need." A note of bitterness came into his voice.

I lifted his hand, and kissed the small scar on the back of it.

"I can't see you as a brute," I said. I meant it lightly, but his face softened as he looked at me, and he answered seriously.

"I know that, Sassenach. And it is that ye canna see me so that gives me hope. For I am—and know it—and yet perhaps . . ." He trailed off, watching me intently.

"You have that—the strength. Ye have it, and your soul as well. So perhaps my own may be saved."

I had no notion what to say to this, and said nothing for a while, but only held his hand, caressing the twisted fingers and the large, hard knuckles. It was a warrior's hand—but he was not a warrior, now.

I turned the hand over and smoothed it on my knee, palm up. Slowly, I traced the deep lines and rising hillocks, and the tiny letter "C" at the base of his thumb; the brand that marked him mine.

"I knew an old lady in the Highlands once, who said the lines in your hand don't predict your life; they reflect it."

"Is that so, then?" His fingers twitched slightly, but his palm lay still and open.

"I don't know. She said you're born with the lines of your hand—with a life—but then the lines change, with the things you do, and the person you are." I knew nothing about palmistry, but I could see one deep line that ran from wrist to midpalm, forking several times.

"I think that might be the one they call a life-line," I said. "See all the forks? I suppose that would mean you'd changed your life a lot, made a lot of choices."

He snorted briefly, but with amusement rather than derision.

"Oh, aye? Well, that's safe enough to say." He peered into his palm, leaning over my knee. "I suppose the first fork would be when I met Jack Randall, and the second when I wed you—see, they're close together, there."

"So they are." I ran my finger slowly along the line, making his fingers twitch slightly as it tickled. "And Culloden maybe would be another?"

"Perhaps." But he did not wish to talk of Culloden. His own finger moved on. "And when I went to prison, and came back again, and came to Edinburgh."

"And became a printer." I stopped and looked up at him, brows raised. "How on earth *did* you come to be a printer? It's the last thing I would have thought of."

"Oh, that." His mouth widened in a smile. "Well—it was an accident, aye?"

To start with he had only been looking for a business that would help to conceal and facilitate the smuggling. Possessed of a sizable sum from a recent profitable venture, he had determined to purchase a business whose normal operations involved a large wagon and team of horses, and some discreet premises that could be used for the temporary storage of goods in transit.

Carting suggested itself, but was rejected precisely because the operations of that business made its practitioners subject to more or less constant scrutiny from the Customs. Likewise, the ownership of a tavern or inn, while superficially desirable because of the large quantities of supplies brought in, was too vulnerable in its legitimate operation to hide an illegitimate one; tax collectors and Customs agents hung about taverns like fleas on a fat dog.

"I thought of printing, when I went to a place to have some notices made up," he explained. "As I was waiting to put in my order, I saw the wagon come rumbling up, all loaded wi' boxes of paper and casks of alcohol for the ink powder, and I thought, by God, that's it! For excisemen would never be troubling a place like that."

It was only after purchasing the shop in Carfax Close, hiring Geordie to run the press, and actually beginning to fill orders for posters, pamphlets, folios, and books, that the other possibilities of his new business had occurred to him.

"It was a man named Tom Gage," he explained. He loosed his hand from my grasp, growing eager in the telling, gesturing and rubbing his hands through his hair as he talked, disheveling himself with enthusiasm.

"He brought in small orders for this or that—innocent stuff, all of it—but often, and stayed to talk over it, taking trouble to talk to me as well as to Geordie, though he must have seen I knew less about the business than he did himself."

He smiled at me wryly.

"I didna ken much about printing, Sassenach, but I do ken men."

It was obvious that Gage was exploring the sympathies of Alexander Malcolm; hearing the faint sibilance of Jamie's Highland speech, he had prodded delicately, mentioning this acquaintance and that whose Jacobite sympathies had led them into trouble after the Rising, picking up the threads of mutual acquaintance, skillfully directing the conversation, stalking his prey. Until at last, the amused prey had bluntly told him to bring what he wanted made; no King's man would hear of it.

"And he trusted you." It wasn't a question; the only man who had ever trusted Jamie Fraser in error was Charles Stuart—and in that case, the error was Jamie's.

"He did." And so, an association was begun, strictly business in the beginning, but deepening into friendship as time went on. Jamie had printed all the materials generated by Gage's small group of radical political writers—from publicly acknowledged articles to anonymous broadsheets and pamphlets filled with material incriminating enough to get the authors summarily jailed or hanged.

"We'd go to the tavern down the street and talk, after the printing was done. I met a few of Tom's friends, and finally Tom said I should write a small piece myself. I laughed and told him that with my hand, by the time I'd penned anything that could be read, we'd all be dead—of old age, not hanging.

"I was standing by the press as we were talking, setting the type wi' my left hand, not even thinking. He just stared at me, and then he started to laugh.

He pointed at the tray, and at my hand, and went on laughing, 'til he had to sit down on the floor to stop."

He stretched out his arms in front of him, flexing his hands and studying them dispassionately. He curled one hand into a fist and bent it slowly up toward his face, making the muscles of his arm ripple and swell under the linen.

"I'm hale enough," he said. "And with luck, may be so for a good many years yet—but not forever, Sassenach. I ha' fought wi' sword and dirk many times, but to every warrior comes the day when his strength will fail him." He shook his head and stretched out a hand toward his coat, which lay on the floor.

"I took these, that day wi' Tom Gage, to remind me of it," he said.

He took my hand and put into it the things he had taken from his pocket. They were cool, and hard to the touch, small heavy oblongs of lead. I didn't need to feel the incised ends to know what the letters on the type slugs were.

"Q.E.D.," I said.

"The English took my sword and dirk away," he said softly. His finger touched the slugs that lay in my palm. "But Tom Gage put a weapon into my hands again, and I think I shall not lay it down."

We walked arm in arm down the cobbled slope of the Royal Mile at a quarter to five, suffused with a glow engendered by several bowls of well-peppered oyster stew and a bottle of wine, shared at intervals during our "private communications."

The city glowed all around us, as though sharing our happiness. Edinburgh lay under a haze that would soon thicken to rain again, but for now, the light of the setting sun hung gold and pink and red in the clouds, and shone in the wet patina of the cobbled street, so that the gray stones of the buildings softened and streamed with reflected light, echoing the glow that warmed my cheeks and shone in Jamie's eyes when he looked at me.

Drifting down the street in this state of softheaded self-absorption, it was several minutes before I noticed anything amiss. A man, impatient of our meandering progress, stepped briskly around us, and then came to a dead stop just in front of me, making me trip on the wet stones and throw a shoe.

He flung up his head and stared skyward for a moment, then hurried off down the street, not running, but walking as fast as he could go.

"What's the matter with him?" I said, stooping to retrieve my shoe. Suddenly I noticed that all around us, folk were stopping, staring up, and then starting to rush down the street.

"What do you think—?" I began, but when I turned to Jamie, he too was staring intently upward. I looked up, too, and it took only a moment to see that the red glow in the clouds above was a good deal deeper than the general color of the sunset sky, and seemed to flicker in an uneasy fashion most uncharacteristic of sunsets.

"Fire," he said. "God, I think it's in Leith Wynd!"

At the same moment, someone farther down the street raised the cry of "Fire!" and as though this official diagnosis had given them leave to run at last, the hurrying figures below broke loose and cascaded down the street like a herd of lemmings, anxious to fling themselves into the pyre.

A few saner souls ran upwards, past us, also shouting "Fire!" but presumably with the intent of alerting whatever passed for a fire department.

Jamie was already in motion, tugging me along as I hopped awkwardly on one foot. Rather than stop, I kicked the other shoe off, and followed him, slipping and stubbing my toes on the cold wet cobbles as I ran.

The fire was not in Leith Wynd, but next door, in Carfax Close. The mouth of the close was choked with excited onlookers, shoving and craning in an effort to see, shouting incoherent questions at one another. The smell of smoke struck hot and pungent through the damp evening air, and waves of crackling heat beat against my face as I ducked into the close.

Jamie didn't hesitate, but plunged into the crowd, making a path by main force. I pressed close behind him before the human waves could close again, and elbowed my way through, unable to see anything but Jamie's broad back ahead of me.

Then we popped out in the front of the crowd, and I could see all too well. Dense clouds of gray smoke rolled out of both the printshop's lower windows, and I could hear a whispering, crackling noise that rose above the noise of the spectators as though the fire were talking to itself.

"My press!" With a cry of anguish, Jamie darted up the front step and kicked in the door. A cloud of smoke rolled out of the open doorway and engulfed him like a hungry beast. I caught a brief glimpse of him, staggering from the impact of the smoke; then he dropped to his knees and crawled into the building.

Inspired by this example, several men from the crowd ran up the steps of the printshop, and likewise disappeared into the smoke-filled interior. The heat was so intense that I felt my skirts blow against my legs with the wind of it, and wondered how the men could stand it, there inside.

A fresh outbreak of shouting in the crowd behind me announced the arrival of the Town Guard, armed with buckets. Obviously accustomed to this task, the men flung off their wine-red uniform coats and began at once to attack the fire, smashing the windows and flinging pails of water through them with a fierce abandon. Meanwhile, the crowd swelled, its noise augmented by a constant cascade of pattering feet down the many staircases of the close, as families on the upper floors of the surrounding buildings hastily ushered hordes of excited children down to safety.

I couldn't think that the efforts of the bucket brigade, valiant as they were, would have much effect on what was obviously a fire well underway. I was edging back and forth on the pavement, trying vainly to see anything moving within, when the lead man in the bucket line uttered a startled cry and leaped back, just in time to avoid being crowned by a tray of lead type that whizzed through the broken window and landed on the cobbles with a crash, scattering slugs in all directions.

Two or three urchins wriggled through the crowd and snatched at the slugs, only to be cuffed and driven off by indignant neighbors. One plump lady in a kertch and apron darted forward, risking life and limb, and took custody of the heavy type-tray, dragging it back to the curb, where she crouched protectively over it like a hen on a nest.

Before her companions could scoop up the fallen type, though, they were driven back by a hail of objects that rained from both windows: more type trays, roller bars, inking pads, and bottles of ink, which broke on the pavement, leaving big spidery blotches that ran into the puddles spilled by the fire fighters.

Encouraged by the draft from the open door and windows, the voice of the fire had grown from a whisper into a self-satisfied, chuckling roar. Prevented from flinging water through the windows by the rain of objects being thrown out of them, the leader of the Town Guard shouted to his men, and holding a soaked handkerchief over his nose, ducked and ran into the building, followed by a half-dozen of his fellows.

The line quickly re-formed, full buckets coming hand to hand round the corner from the nearest pump and up the stoop, excited lads snatching the empty buckets that bounced down the step, to race back with them to the pump for refilling. Edinburgh is a stone city, but with so many buildings crammed cheek by jowl, all equipped with multiple hearths and chimneys, fire must be still a frequent occurrence.

Evidently so, for a fresh commotion behind me betokened the belated arrival of the fire engine. The waves of people parted like the Red Sea, to allow passage of the engine, drawn by a team of men rather than horses, which could not have negotiated the tight quarters of the wynds.

The engine was a marvel of brass, glowing like a coal itself in the reflected flames. The heat was becoming more intense; I could feel my lungs dry and labor with each gulp of hot air, and was terrified for Jamie. How long could he breathe, in that hellish fog of smoke and heat, let alone the danger of the flames themselves?

"Jesus, Mary, and Joseph!" Ian, forcing his way through the crowd despite his wooden leg, had appeared suddenly by my elbow. He grabbed my arm to keep his balance as another rain of objects forced the people around us back again.

"Where's Jamie?" he shouted in my ear.

"In there!" I bellowed back, pointing.

There was a sudden bustle and commotion at the door of the printshop, with a confused shouting that rose even over the sound of the fire. Several sets of legs appeared, shuffling to and fro beneath the emergent plume of smoke that billowed from the door. Six men emerged, Jamie among them, staggering under the weight of a huge piece of bulky machinery—Jamie's precious printing press. They eased it down the step and pushed it well into the crowd, then turned back to the printshop.

Too late for any more rescue maneuvers; there was a crash from inside, a fresh blast of heat that sent the crowd scuttling backward, and suddenly the windows of the upper story were lit with dancing flames inside. A small stream of men issued from the building, coughing and choking, some of them crawling, blackened with soot and dampened with the sweat of their efforts. The engine crew pumped madly, but the thick stream of water from their hose made not the slightest impression on the fire.

Ian's hand clamped down on my arm like the jaws of a trap.

"Ian!" he shrieked, loud enough to be heard above the noises of crowd and fire alike.

I looked up in the direction of his gaze, and saw a wraithlike shape at the second-story window. It seemed to struggle briefly with the sash, and then to fall back or be enveloped in the smoke.

My heart leapt into my mouth. There was no telling whether the shape was indeed Young Ian, but it was certainly a human form. Ian had lost no time in gaping, but was stumping toward the door of the printshop with all the speed his leg would allow.

"Wait!" I shouted, running after him.

Jamie was leaning on the printing press, chest heaving as he tried to catch his breath and thank his assistants at the same time.

"Jamie!" I snatched at his sleeve, ruthlessly jerking him away from a red-faced barber, who kept excitedly wiping sooty hands on his apron, leaving long black streaks among the smears of dried soap and the spots of blood.

"Up there!" I shouted, pointing. "Young Ian's upstairs!"

Jamie stepped back, swiping a sleeve across his blackened face, and stared wildly at the upper windows. Nothing was to be seen but the roiling shimmer of the fire against the panes.

Ian was struggling in the hands of several neighbors who sought to prevent his entering the shop.

"No, man, ye canna go in!" the Guard captain cried, trying to grasp Ian's flailing hands. "The staircase has fallen, and the roof will go next!"

Despite his stringy build and the handicap of his leg, Ian was tall and vigorous, and the feeble grasp of his well-meaning Town Guard captors— mostly retired pensioners from the Highland regiments—was no match for his mountain-hardened strength, reinforced as it was by parental desperation. Slowly but surely, the whole confused mass jerked by inches up the steps of the printshop as Ian dragged his would-be rescuers with him toward the flames.

I felt Jamie draw breath, gulping air as deep as he could with his seared lungs, and then he was up the steps as well, and had Ian round the waist, dragging him back.

"Come down, man!" he shouted hoarsely. "Ye'll no manage—the stair is gone!" He glanced round, saw me, and thrust Ian bodily backward, off-balance and staggering, into my arms. "Hold him," he shouted, over the roar of the flames. "I'll fetch down the lad!"

With that, he turned and dashed up the steps of the adjoining building, pushing his way through the patrons of the ground-floor chocolate shop, who had emerged onto the pavement to gawk at the excitement, pewter cups still clutched in their hands.

Following Jamie's example, I locked my arms tight around Ian's waist and didn't let go. He made an abortive attempt to follow Jamie, but then stopped and stood rigid in my arms, his heart beating wildly just under my cheek.

"Don't worry," I said, pointlessly. "He'll do it; he'll get him out. He will. I know he will."

Ian didn't answer—might not have heard—but stood still and stiff as a statue in my grasp, breath coming harshly with a sound like a sob. When I released my hold on his waist, he didn't move or turn, but when I stood beside him, he snatched my hand and held it hard. My bones would have ground together, had I not been squeezing back just as hard.

It was no more than a minute before the window above the chocolate shop opened and Jamie's head and shoulders appeared, red hair glowing like a stray tongue of flame escaped from the main fire. He climbed out onto the sill, and cautiously turned, squatting, until he faced the building.

Rising to his stockinged feet, he grasped the gutter of the roof overhead and pulled, slowly raising himself by the strength of his arms, long toes scrabbling for a grip in the crevices between the mortared stones of the housefront. With a grunt audible even over the sound of fire and crowd, he eeled over the edge of the roof and disappeared behind the gable.

A shorter man could not have managed. Neither could Ian, with his wooden leg. I heard Ian say something under his breath; a prayer I thought, but when I glanced at him, his jaw was clenched, face set in lines of fear.

"What in hell is he going to do up there?" I thought, and was unaware that I had spoken aloud until the barber, shading his eyes next to me, replied.

"There's a trapdoor built in the roof o' the printshop, ma'am. Nay doubt Mr. Malcolm means to gain access to the upper story so. Is it his 'prentice up there, d'ye know?"

"No!" Ian snapped, hearing this. "It's my son!"

The barber shrank back before Ian's glare, murmuring "Oh, aye, just so, sir, just so!" and crossing himself. A shout from the crowd grew into a roar as two figures appeared on the roof of the chocolate shop, and Ian dropped my hand, springing forward.

Jamie had his arm round Young Ian, who was bent and reeling from the smoke he had swallowed. It was reasonably obvious that neither of them was going to be able to negotiate a return through the adjoining building in his present condition.

Just then, Jamie spotted Ian below. Cupping his hand around his mouth, he bellowed "Rope!"

Rope there was; the Town Guard had come equipped. Ian snatched the coil from an approaching Guardsman, leaving that worthy blinking in indignation, and turned to face the house.

I caught the gleam of Jamie's teeth as he grinned down at his brother-in-law, and the look of answering wryness on Ian's face. How many times had they thrown a rope between them, to raise hay to the barn loft, or bind a load to the wagon for carrying?

The crowd fell back from the whirl of Ian's arm, and the heavy coil flew up in a smooth parabola, unwinding as it went, landing on Jamie's outstretched arm with the precision of a bumblebee lighting on a flower. Jamie hauled in the dangling tail, and disappeared momentarily, to anchor the rope about the base of the building's chimney.

A few precarious moments' work, and the two smoke-blackened figures had come to a safe landing on the pavement below. Young Ian, rope slung under his arms and round his chest, stood upright for a moment, then, as the tension of the rope slackened, his knees buckled and he slid into a gangling heap on the cobbles.

"Are ye all right? *A bhalaich,* speak to me!" Ian fell to his knees beside his son, anxiously trying to unknot the rope round Young Ian's chest, while simultaneously trying to lift up the lad's lolling head.

Jamie was leaning against the railing of the chocolate shop, black in the face and coughing his lungs out, but otherwise apparently unharmed. I sat down on the boy's other side, and took his head on my lap.

I wasn't sure whether to laugh or cry at the sight of him. When I had seen him in the morning, he had been an appealing-looking lad, if no great beauty, with something of his father's homely, good-natured looks. Now, at evening, the thick hair over one side of his forehead had been singed to a bleached red stubble, and his eyebrows and lashes had been burned off entirely. The skin beneath was the soot-smeared bright pink of a suckling pig just off the spit.

I felt for a pulse in the spindly neck and found it, reassuringly strong. His breathing was hoarse and irregular, and no wonder; I hoped the lining of his lungs had not been burned. He coughed, long and rackingly, and the thin body convulsed on my lap.

"Is he all right?" Ian's hands instinctively grabbed his son beneath the armpits and sat him up. His head wobbled to and fro, and he pitched forward into my arms.

"I think so; I can't tell for sure." The boy was still coughing, but not fully conscious; I held him against my shoulder like an enormous baby, patting his back futilely as he retched and gagged.

"Is he all right?" This time it was Jamie, squatting breathless alongside me. His voice was so hoarse I wouldn't have recognized it, roughened as it was by smoke.

"I think so. What about you? You look like Malcolm X," I said, peering at him over Young Ian's heaving shoulder.

"I do?" He put a hand to his face, looking startled, then grinned reassuringly. "Nay, I canna say how I look, but I'm no an ex-Malcolm yet; only a wee bit singed round the edges."

"Get back, get back!" The Guard captain was at my side, gray beard bristling with anxiety, plucking at my sleeve. "Move yourself, ma'am, the roof's going!"

Sure enough, as we scrambled to safety, the roof of the printshop fell in, and an awed sound rose from the watching crowd as an enormous fountain of sparks whirled skyward, brilliant against the darkening sky.

As though heaven resented this intrusion, the spume of fiery ash was answered by the first pattering of raindrops, plopping heavily on the cobbles all around us. The Edinburghians, who surely ought to have been accustomed to rain by now, made noises of consternation and began to scuttle back into the surrounding buildings like a herd of cockroaches, leaving nature to complete the fire engine's work.

A moment later, Ian and I were alone with Young Ian. Jamie, having dispensed money liberally to the Guard and other assistants, and having arranged for his press and its fittings to be housed in the barber's storeroom, trudged wearily toward us.

"How's the lad?" he asked, wiping a hand down his face. The rain had begun to come down more heavily, and the effect on his soot-blackened countenance was picturesque in the extreme. Ian looked at him, and for the first time, the anger, worry and fear faded somewhat from his countenance. He gave Jamie a lopsided smile.

"He doesna look a great deal better than ye do yourself, man—but I think he'll do now. Give us a hand, aye?"

Murmuring small Gaelic endearments suitable for babies, Ian bent over his son, who was by this time sitting up groggily on the curbstone, swaying to and fro like a heron in a high wind.

By the time we reached Madame Jeanne's establishment, Young Ian could walk, though still supported on either side by his father and uncle. Bruno, who opened the door, blinked incredulously at the sight, and then swung the door open, laughing so hard he could barely close it after us.

I had to admit that we were nothing much to look at, wet through and streaming with rain. Jamie and I were both barefoot, and Jamie's clothes were in rags, singed and torn and covered with streaks of soot. Ian's dark hair straggled in his eyes, making him look like a drowned rat with a wooden leg.

Young Ian, though, was the focus of attention, as multiple heads came popping out of the drawing room in response to the noise Bruno was making. With his singed hair, swollen red face, beaky nose, and lashless, blinking eyes, he strongly resembled the fledgling young of some exotic bird species —a newly hatched flamingo, perhaps. His face could scarcely grow redder, but the back of his neck flamed crimson, as the sound of feminine giggles followed us up the stairs.

Safely ensconced in the small upstairs sitting room, with the door closed, Ian turned to face his hapless offspring.

"Going to live, are ye, ye wee bugger?" he demanded.

"Aye, sir," Young Ian replied in a dismal croak, looking rather as though he wished the answer were "No."

"Good," his father said grimly. "D'ye want to explain yourself, or shall I just belt hell out of ye now and save us both time?"

"Ye canna thrash someone who's just had his eyebrows burnt off, Ian," Jamie protested hoarsely, pouring out a glass of porter from the decanter on the table. "It wouldna be humane." He grinned at his nephew and handed him the glass, which the boy clutched with alacrity.

"Aye, well. Perhaps not," Ian agreed, surveying his son. One corner of his mouth twitched. Young Ian was a pitiable sight; he was also an extremely funny one. "That doesna mean ye aren't going to get your arse blistered later, mind," he warned the boy, "and that's besides whatever your mother means to do to ye when she sees ye again. But for now, lad, take your ease."

Not noticeably reassured by the magnanimous tone of this last statement, Young Ian didn't answer, but sought refuge in the depths of his glass of porter.

I took my own glass with a good deal of pleasure. I had realized belatedly just why the citizens of Edinburgh reacted to rain with such repugnance; once one was wet through, it was the devil to get dry again in the damp confines of a stone house, with no change of clothes and no heat available but a small hearthfire.

I plucked the damp bodice away from my breasts, caught Young Ian's interested glance, and decided regretfully that I really couldn't take it off with the boy in the room. Jamie seemed to have been corrupting the lad to quite a sufficient extent already. I gulped the porter instead, feeling the rich flavor purl warmingly through my innards.

"D'ye feel well enough to talk a bit, lad?" Jamie sat down opposite his nephew, next to Ian on the hassock.

"Aye . . . I think so," Young Ian croaked cautiously. He cleared his throat like a bullfrog and repeated more firmly, "Aye, I can."

"Good. Well, then. First, how did ye come to be in the printshop, and then, how did it come to be on fire?"

Young Ian pondered that one for a minute, then took another gulp of his porter for courage and said, "I set it."

Jamie and Ian both sat up straight at that. I could see Jamie revising his opinion as to the advisability of thrashing people without eyebrows, but he mastered his temper with an obvious effort, and said merely, "Why?"

The boy took another gulp of porter, coughed, and drank again, apparently trying to decide what to say.

"Well," he began uncertainly, "there was a man," and came to a dead stop.

"A man," Jamie prompted patiently when his nephew showed signs of having become suddenly deaf and dumb. "What man?"

Young Ian clutched his glass in both hands, looking deeply unhappy.

"Answer your uncle this minute, clot," Ian said sharply. "Or I'll take ye across my knee and tan ye right here."

With a mixture of similar threats and promptings, the two men managed to extract a more or less coherent story from the boy.

Young Ian had been at the tavern at Kerse that morning, where he had been told to meet Wally, who would come down from the rendezvous with the wagons of brandy, there to load the punked casks and spoiled wine to be used as subterfuge.

"Told?" Ian asked sharply. "Who told ye?"

"I did," Jamie said, before Young Ian could speak. He waved a hand at his brother-in-law, urging silence. "Aye, I kent he was here. We'll talk about it later, Ian, if ye please. It's important we know what happened today."

Ian glared at Jamie and opened his mouth to disagree, then shut it with a snap. He nodded to his son to go on.

"I was hungry, ye see," Young Ian said.

"When are ye not?" his father and uncle said together, in perfect unison. They looked at each other, snorted with sudden laughter, and the strained atmosphere in the room eased slightly.

"So ye went into the tavern to have a bite," Jamie said. "That's all right, lad, no harm done. And what happened while ye were there?"

That, it transpired, was where he had seen the man. A small, ratty-looking fellow, with a seaman's pigtail, and a blind eye, talking to the landlord.

"He was askin' for you, Uncle Jamie," Young Ian said, growing easier in his speech with repeated applications of porter. "By your own name."

Jamie started, looking surprised. "Jamie Fraser, ye mean?" Young Ian nodded, sipping. "Aye. But he knew your other name as well—Jamie Roy, I mean."

"Jamie Roy?" Ian turned a puzzled glance on his brother-in-law, who shrugged impatiently.

"It's how I'm known on the docks. Christ, Ian, ye know what I do!"

"Aye, I do, but I didna ken the wee laddie was helpin' ye to do it." Ian's thin lips pressed tight together, and he turned his attention back to his son. "Go on, lad. I willna interrupt ye again."

The seaman had asked the tavernkeeper how best an old seadog, down on his luck and looking for employment, might find one Jamie Fraser, who was known to have a use for able men. The landlord pleading ignorance of that name, the seaman had leaned closer, pushed a coin across the table, and in a lowered voice asked whether the name "Jamie Roy" was more familiar.

The landlord remaining deaf as an adder, the seaman had soon left the tavern, with Young Ian right behind him.

"I thought as how maybe it would be good to know who he was, and what he meant," the lad explained, blinking.

"Ye might have thought to leave word wi' the publican for Wally," Jamie said. "Still, that's neither here nor there. Where did he go?"

Down the road at a brisk walk, but not so brisk that a healthy boy could not follow at a careful distance. An accomplished walker, the seaman had made his way into Edinburgh, a distance of some five miles, in less than an hour, and arrived at last at the Green Owl tavern, followed by Young Ian, near wilted with thirst from the walk.

I started at the name, but didn't say anything, not wanting to interrupt the story.

"It was terrible crowded," the lad reported. "Something happened in the morning, and everyone was talking of it—but they shut up whenever they saw me. Anyway, it was the same there." He paused to cough and clear his throat. "The seaman ordered drink—brandy—then asked the landlord was he acquainted wi' a supplier of brandy named Jamie Roy or Jamie Fraser."

"Did he, then?" Jamie murmured. His gaze was intent on his nephew, but I could see the thoughts working behind his high forehead, making a small crease between his thick brows.

The man had gone methodically from tavern to tavern, dogged by his faithful shadow, and in each establishment had ordered brandy and repeated his question.

"He must have a rare head, to be drinkin' that much brandy," Ian remarked.

Young Ian shook his head. "He didna drink it. He only smelt it."

His father clicked his tongue at such a scandalous waste of good spirit, but Jamie's red brows climbed still higher.

"Did he taste any of it?" he asked sharply.

"Aye. At the Dog and Gun, and again at the Blue Boar. He had nay more than a wee taste, though, and then left the glass untouched. He didna drink at all at the other places, and we went to five o' them, before . . ." He trailed off, and took another drink.

Jamie's face underwent an astonishing transformation. From an expression of frowning puzzlement, his face went completely blank, and then resolved itself into an expression of revelation.

"Is that so, now," he said softly to himself. "Indeed." His attention came back to his nephew. "And then what happened, lad?"

Young Ian was beginning to look unhappy again. He gulped, the tremor visible all the way down his skinny neck.

"Well, it was a terrible long way from Kerse to Edinburgh," he began, "and a terrible dry walk, too . . ."

His father and uncle exchanged jaundiced glances.

"Ye drank too much," Jamie said, resigned.

"Well, I didna ken he was going to so many taverns, now, did I?" Young Ian cried in self-defense, going pink in the ears.

"No, of course not, lad," Jamie said kindly, smothering the beginning of Ian's more censorious remarks. "How long did ye last?"

Until midway down the Royal Mile, it turned out, where Young Ian, overcome by the cumulation of early rising, a five-mile walk, and the effects of something like two quarts of ale, had dozed off in a corner, waking an hour later to find his quarry long gone.

"So I came here," he explained. "I thought as how Uncle Jamie should know about it. But he wasna here." The boy glanced at me, and his ears grew still pinker.

"And just why did ye think he *should* be here?" Ian favored his offspring with a gimlet eye, which then swiveled to his brother-in-law. The simmering anger Ian had been holding in check since the morning suddenly erupted. "The filthy gall of ye, Jamie Fraser, takin' my son to a bawdy house!"

"A fine one you are to talk, Da!" Young Ian was on his feet, swaying a bit, but with his big, bony hands clenched at his sides.

"Me? And what d'ye mean by that, ye wee gomerel?" Ian cried, his eyes going wide with outrage.

"I mean you're a damned hypocrite!" his son shouted hoarsely. "Preachin' to me and Michael about purity and keepin' to one woman, and all the time ye're slinkin' about the city, sniffin' after whores!"

"What?" Ian's face had gone entirely purple. I looked in some alarm to Jamie, who appeared to be finding something funny in the present situation.

"You're a . . . a . . . goddamned whited sepulchre!" Young Ian came up with the simile triumphantly, then paused as though trying to think of another to equal it. His mouth opened, though nothing emerged but a soft belch.

"That boy is rather drunk," I said to Jamie.

He picked up the decanter of porter, eyed the level within, and set it down.

"You're right," he said. "I should ha' noticed sooner, but it's hard to tell, scorched as he is."

The elder Ian wasn't drunk, but his expression strongly resembled his offspring's, what with the suffused countenance, popping eyes, and straining neck cords.

"What the bloody, stinking hell d'ye mean by that, ye whelp?" he shouted. He moved menacingly toward Young Ian, who took an involuntary step backward and sat down quite suddenly as his calves met the edge of the sofa.

"Her," he said, startled into monosyllables. He pointed at me, to make it clear. "Her! You deceivin' my Mam wi' this filthy whore, that's what I mean!"

Ian fetched his son a clout over the ear that knocked him sprawling on the sofa.

"Ye great clot!" he said, scandalized. "A fine way to speak o' your auntie Claire, to say nothing o' me and your Mam!"

"Aunt?" Young Ian gawped at me from the cushions, looking so like a nestling begging for food that I burst out laughing despite myself.

"You left before I could introduce myself this morning," I said.

"But you're dead," he said stupidly.

"Not yet," I assured him. "Unless I've caught pneumonia from sitting here in a damp dress."

His eyes had grown perfectly round as he stared at me. Now a fugitive gleam of excitement came into them.

"Some o' the auld women at Lallybroch say ye were a wisewoman—a white lady, or maybe even a fairy. When Uncle Jamie came home from Culloden without ye, they said as how ye'd maybe gone back to the fairies, where ye maybe came from. Is that true? D'ye live in a dun?"

I exchanged a glance with Jamie, who rolled his eyes toward the ceiling.

"No," I said. "I . . . er, I . . ."

"She escaped to France after Culloden," Ian broke in suddenly, with great firmness. "She thought your uncle Jamie was killed in the battle, so she went to her kin in France. She'd been one of Prince *Tearlach*'s particular friends—she couldna come back to Scotland after the war without puttin' herself in sore danger. But then she heard of your uncle, and as soon as she kent that her husband wasna deid after all, she took ship at once and came to find him."

Young Ian's mouth hung open slightly. So did mine.

"Er, yes," I said, closing it. "That's what happened."

The lad turned large, shining eyes from me to his uncle.

"So ye've come back to him," he said happily. "God, that's romantic!"

The tension of the moment was broken. Ian hesitated, but his eyes softened as he looked from Jamie to me.

"Aye," he said, and smiled reluctantly. "Aye, I suppose it is."

"I didna expect to be doing this for him for a good two or three years yet," Jamie remarked, holding his nephew's head with an expert hand as Young Ian retched painfully into the spittoon I was holding.

"Aye, well, he's always been forward," Ian answered resignedly. "Learnt to walk before he could stand, and was forever tumblin' into the fire or the washpot or the pigpen or the cowbyre." He patted the skinny, heaving back. "There, lad, let it come."

A little more, and the lad was deposited in a wilted heap on the sofa, there to recover from the effects of smoke, emotion, and too much porter under the censoriously mingled gaze of uncle and father.

"Where's that damn tea I sent for?" Jamie reached impatiently for the bell, but I stopped him. The brothel's domestic arrangements were evidently still disarranged from the excitements of the morning.

"Don't bother," I said. "I'll go down and fetch it." I scooped up the spittoon and carried it out with me at arm's length, hearing Ian say behind me, in a reasonable tone of voice, "Look, fool—"

I found my way to the kitchen with no difficulty, and obtained the necessary supplies. I hoped Jamie and Ian would give the boy a few minutes' respite; not only for his own sake, but so that I would miss nothing of his story.

I had clearly missed *something;* when I returned to the small sitting room, an air of constraint hung over the room like a cloud, and Young Ian glanced up and then quickly away to avoid my eye. Jamie was his usual imperturbable self, but the elder Ian looked almost as flushed and uneasy as his son. He hurried forward to take the tray from me, murmuring thanks, but would not meet my eye.

I raised one eyebrow at Jamie, who gave me a slight smile and a shrug. I shrugged back and picked up one of the bowls on the tray.

"Bread and milk," I said, handing it to Young Ian, who at once looked happier.

"Hot tea," I said, handing the pot to his father.

"Whisky," I said, handing the bottle to Jamie, "and cold tea for the burns." I whisked the lid off the last bowl, in which a number of napkins were soaking in cold tea.

"Cold tea?" Jamie's ruddy brows lifted. "Did the cook have no butter?"

"You don't put butter on burns," I told him. "Aloe juice, or the juice of a plantain or plantago, but the cook didn't have any of that. Cold tea is the best we could manage."

I poulticed Young Ian's blistered hands and forearms and blotted his scarlet face gently with the tea-soaked napkins while Jamie and Ian did the honors with teapot and whisky bottle, after which we all sat down, somewhat restored, to hear the rest of Ian's story.

"Well," he began, "I walked about the city for a bit, tryin' to think what best to do. And finally my head cleared a bit, and I reasoned that if the man I'd been following was goin' from tavern to tavern down the High Street, if I went to the other end and started *up* the street, I could maybe find him that way."

"That was a bright thought," Jamie said, and Ian nodded approvingly, the frown lifting a bit from his face. "Did ye find him?"

Young Ian nodded, slurping a bit. "I did, then."

Running down the Royal Mile nearly to the Palace of Holyrood at the foot, he had toiled his way painstakingly up the street, stopping at each tavern to inquire for the man with the pigtail and one eye. There was no word of his quarry anywhere below the Canongate, and he was beginning to despair of his idea, when suddenly he had seen the man himself, sitting in the taproom of the Holyrood Brewery.

Presumably this stop was for respite, rather than information, for the seaman was sitting at his ease, drinking beer. Young Ian had darted behind a hogshead in the yard, and remained there, watching, until at length the man rose, paid his score, and made his leisurely way outside.

"He didna go to any more taverns," the boy reported, wiping a stray drop of milk off his chin. "He went straight to Carfax Close, to the printshop."

Jamie said something in Gaelic under his breath. "Did he? And what then?"

"Well, he found the shop shut up, of course. When he saw the door was locked, he looked careful like, up at the windows, as though he was maybe thinking of breaking in. But then I saw him look about, at all the folk coming and going—it was a busy time of day, wi' all the folk coming to the chocolate shop. So he stood on the stoop a moment, thinking, and then he set off back up the close—I had to duck into the tailor's shop on the corner so as not to be seen."

The man had paused at the entrance of the close, then, making up his mind, had turned to the right, gone down a few paces, and disappeared into a small alley.

"I kent as how the alley led up to the court at the back of the close," Young Ian explained. "So I saw at once what he meant to be doing."

"There's a wee court at the back of the close," Jamie explained, seeing my puzzled look. "It's for rubbish and deliveries and such—but there's a back door out of the printshop opens onto it."

Young Ian nodded, putting down his empty bowl. "Aye. I thought it must be that he meant to get into the place. And I thought of the new pamphlets."

"Jesus," Jamie said. He looked a little pale.

"Pamphlets?" Ian raised his brows at Jamie. "What kind of pamphlets?"

"The new printing for Mr. Gage," Young Ian explained.

Ian still looked as blank as I felt.

"Politics," Jamie said bluntly. "An argument for repeal of the last Stamp Act—with an exhortation to civil opposition—by violence, if necessary. Five thousand of them, fresh-printed, stacked in the back room. Gage was to come round and get them in the morning, tomorrow."

"Jesus," Ian said. He had gone even paler than Jamie, at whom he stared in a sort of mingled horror and awe. "Have ye gone straight out o' your mind?" he inquired. "You, wi' not an inch on your back unscarred? Wi' the ink scarce dry on your pardon for treason? You're mixed up wi' Tom Gage and his seditious society, and got my son involved as well?"

His voice had been rising throughout, and now he sprang to his feet, fists clenched.

"How could ye do such a thing, Jamie—how? Have we not suffered enough for your actions, Jenny and me? All through the war and after—Christ, I'd think you'd have your fill of prisons and blood and violence!"

"I have," Jamie said shortly. "I'm no part of Gage's group. But my business is printing, aye? He paid for those pamphlets."

Ian threw up his hands in a gesture of vast irritation. "Oh, aye! And that will mean a great deal when the Crown's agents arrest ye and take ye to London to be hangit! If those things were to be found on your premises—" Struck by a sudden thought, he stopped and turned to his son.

"Oh, that was it?" he asked. "Ye kent what those pamphlets were—that's why ye set them on fire?"

Young Ian nodded, solemn as a young owl.

"I couldna move them in time," he said. "Not five thousand. The man—the seaman—he'd broke out the back window, and he was reachin' in for the doorlatch."

Ian whirled back to face Jamie.

"Damn you!" he said violently. "Damn ye for a reckless, harebrained fool, Jamie Fraser! First the Jacobites, and now this!"

Jamie had flushed up at once at Ian's words, and his face grew darker at this.

"Am I to blame for Charles Stuart?" he said. His eyes flashed angrily and he set his teacup down with a thump that sloshed tea and whisky over the polished tabletop. "Did I not try all I could to stop the wee fool? Did I not give up everything in that fight—*everything*, Ian! My land, my freedom, my wife—to try to save us all?" He glanced at me briefly as he spoke, and I caught one very small quick glimpse of just what the last twenty years had cost him.

He turned back to Ian, his brows lowering as he went on, voice growing hard.

"And as for what I've cost your family—what have ye profited, Ian? Lallybroch belongs to wee James now, no? To *your* son, not mine!"

Ian flinched at that. "I never asked—" he began.

"No, ye didn't. I'm no accusing ye, for God's sake! But the fact's there—Lallybroch's no mine anymore, is it? My father left it to me, and I cared for it as best I could—took care o' the land and the tenants—and ye helped me, Ian." His voice softened a bit. "I couldna have managed without you and Jenny. I dinna begrudge deeding it to Young Jamie—it had to be done. But still . . ." He turned away for a moment, head bowed, broad shoulders knotted tight beneath the linen of his shirt.

I was afraid to move or speak, but I caught Young Ian's eye, filled with infinite distress. I put a hand on his skinny shoulder for mutual reassurance, and felt the steady pounding of the pulse in the tender flesh above his collarbone. He set his big, bony paw on my hand and held on tight.

Jamie turned back to his brother-in-law, struggling to keep his voice and temper under control. "I swear to ye, Ian, I didna let the lad be put in danger. I kept him out of the way so much as I possibly could—didna let the shoremen see him, or let him go out on the boats wi' Fergus, hard as he begged me." He glanced at Young Ian and his expression changed, to an odd mixture of affection and irritation.

"I didna ask him to come to me, Ian, and I told him he must go home again."

"Ye didna *make* him go, though, did you?" The angry color was fading from Ian's face, but his soft brown eyes were still narrow and bright with fury. "And ye didna send word, either. For God's sake, Jamie, Jenny hasna slept at night anytime this month!"

Jamie's lips pressed tight. "No," he said, letting the words escape one at a time. "No. I didn't. I—" He glanced at the boy again, and shrugged uncomfortably, as though his shirt had grown suddenly too tight.

"No," he said again. "I meant to take him home myself."

"He's old enough to travel by himself," Ian said shortly. "He got here alone, no?"

"Aye. It wasna that." Jamie turned aside restlessly, picking up a teacup and rolling it to and fro between his palms. "No, I meant to take him, so that I could ask your permission—yours and Jenny's—for the lad to come live wi' me for a time."

Ian uttered a short, sarcastic laugh. "Oh, aye! Give our permission for him to be hangit or transported alongside you, eh?"

The anger flashed across Jamie's features again as he looked up from the cup in his hands.

"Ye know I wouldna let any harm come to him," he said. "For Christ's sake, Ian, I care for the lad as though he were my own son, and well ye ken it, too!"

Ian's breath was coming fast; I could hear it from my place behind the sofa. "Oh, I ken it well enough," he said, staring hard into Jamie's face. "But he's not your son, aye? He's mine."

Jamie stared back for a long moment, then reached out and gently set the teacup back on the table. "Aye," he said quietly. "He is."

Ian stood for a moment, breathing hard, then wiped a hand carelessly across his forehead, pushing back the thick dark hair.

"Well, then," he said. He took one or two deep breaths, and turned to his son.

"Come along, then," he said. "I've a room at Halliday's."

Young Ian's bony fingers tightened on mine. His throat worked, but he didn't move to rise from his seat.

"No, Da," he said. His voice quivered, and he blinked hard, not to cry. "I'm no going wi' ye."

Ian's face went quite pale, with a deep red patch over the angular cheekbones, as though someone had slapped him hard on both cheeks.

"Is that so?" he said.

Young Ian nodded, swallowing. "I—I'll go wi' ye in the morning, Da; I'll go home wi' ye. But not now."

Ian looked at his son for a long moment without speaking. Then his shoulders slumped, and all the tension went out of his body.

"I see," he said quietly. "Well, then. Well."

Without another word, he turned and left, closing the door very carefully behind him. I could hear the awkward thump of his wooden leg on each step, as he made his way down the stair. There was a brief sound of shuffling as he reached the bottom, then Bruno's voice in farewell, and the thud of the main door shutting. And then there was no sound in the room but the hiss of the hearthfire behind me.

The boy's shoulder was shaking under my hand, and he was holding tighter than ever to my fingers, crying without making a sound.

Jamie came slowly to sit beside him, his face full of troubled helplessness.

"Ian, oh, wee Ian," he said. "Christ, laddie, ye shouldna have done that."

"I had to." Ian gasped and gave a sudden snuffle, and I realized that he had been holding his breath. He turned a scorched countenance on his uncle, raw features contorted in anguish.

"I didna want to hurt Da," he said. "I didn't!"

Jamie patted his knee absently. "I know, laddie," he said, "but to say such a thing to him—"

"I couldna tell him, though, and I had to tell you, Uncle Jamie!"

Jamie glanced up, suddenly alert at his nephew's tone.

"Tell me? Tell me what?"

"The man. The man wi' the pigtail."

"What about him?"

Young Ian licked his lips, steeling himself.

"I think I kilt him," he whispered.

Startled, Jamie glanced at me, then back at Young Ian.

"How?" he asked.

"Well . . . I lied a bit," Ian began, voice trembling. The tears were still welling in his eyes, but he brushed them aside. "When I went into the printshop—I had the key ye gave me—the man was already inside."

The seaman had been in the backmost room of the shop, where the stacks of newly printed orders were kept, along with the stocks of fresh ink, the blotting papers used to clean the press, and the small forge where worn slugs were melted down and recast into fresh type.

"He was taking some o' the pamphlets from the stack, and putting them inside his jacket," Ian said, gulping. "When I saw him, I screeched at him to put them back, and he whirled round at me wi' a pistol in his hand."

The pistol had discharged, scaring Young Ian badly, but the ball had gone wild. Little daunted, the seaman had rushed at the boy, raising the pistol to club him instead.

"There was no time to run, or to think," he said. He had let go my hand by now, and his fingers twisted together upon his knee. "I reached out for the first thing to hand and threw it."

The first thing to hand had been the lead-dipper, the long-handled copper ladle used to pour molten lead from the melting pot into the casting molds. The forge had been still alight, though well-banked, and while the melting pot held no more than a small puddle, the scalding drops of lead had flown from the dipper into the seaman's face.

"God, how he screamed!" A strong shudder ran through Young Ian's slender frame, and I came round the end of the sofa to sit next to him and take both his hands.

The seaman had reeled backward, clawing at his face, and upset the small forge, knocking live coals everywhere.

"That was what started the fire," the boy said. "I tried to beat it out, but it caught the edge of the fresh paper, and all of a sudden, something went *whoosh!* in my face, and it was as though the whole room was alight."

"The barrels of ink, I suppose," Jamie said, as though to himself. "The powder's dissolved in alcohol."

The sliding piles of flaming paper fell between Young Ian and the back door, a wall of flame that billowed black smoke and threatened to collapse upon him. The seaman, blinded and screaming like a banshee, had been on his hands and knees between the boy and the door into the front room of the printshop and safety.

"I—I couldna bear to touch him, to push him out o' the way," he said, shuddering again.

Losing his head completely, he had run up the stairs instead, but then found himself trapped as the flames, racing through the back room and drawing up the stair like a chimney, rapidly filled the upper room with blinding smoke.

"Did ye not think to climb out the trapdoor onto the roof?" Jamie asked.

Young Ian shook his head miserably. "I didna ken it was there."

"Why *was* it there?" I asked curiously.

Jamie gave me the flicker of a smile. "In case of need. It's a foolish fox has but one exit to his bolthole. Though I must say, it wasna fire I was thinking of when I had it made." He shook his head, ridding himself of the distraction.

"But ye think the man didna escape the fire?" he asked.

"I dinna see how he could," Young Ian answered, beginning to sniffle again. "And if he's dead, then I killed him. I couldna tell Da I was a m-mur —mur—" He was crying again, too hard to get the word out.

"You're no a murderer, Ian," Jamie said firmly. He patted his nephew's shaking shoulder. "Stop now, it's all right—ye havena done wrong, laddie. Ye haven't, d'ye hear?"

The boy gulped and nodded, but couldn't stop crying or shaking. At last I put my arms around him, turned him and pulled his head down onto my shoulder, patting his back and making the sort of small soothing noises one makes to little children.

He felt very odd in my arms; nearly as big as a full-grown man, but with fine, light bones, and so little flesh on them that it was like holding a skeleton. He was talking into the depths of my bosom, his voice so disjointed by emotion and muffled by fabric that it was difficult to make out the words.

". . . mortal sin . . ." he seemed to be saying, ". . . damned to hell . . . couldna tell Da . . . afraid . . . canna go home ever . . ."

Jamie raised his brows at me, but I only shrugged helplessly, smoothing the thick, bushy hair on the back of the boy's head. At last Jamie leaned forward, took him firmly by the shoulders and sat him up.

"Look ye, Ian," he said. "No, look—look at me!"

By dint of supreme effort, the boy straightened his drooping neck and fixed brimming, red-rimmed eyes on his uncle's face.

"Now then." Jamie took hold of his nephew's hands and squeezed them lightly. "First—it's no a sin to kill a man that's trying to kill you. The Church allows ye to kill if ye must, in defense of yourself, your family, or your country. So ye havena committed mortal sin, and you're no damned."

"I'm not?" Young Ian sniffed mightily, and mopped at his face with a sleeve.

"No, you're not." Jamie let the hint of a smile show in his eyes. "We'll go together and call on Father Hayes in the morning, and ye'll make your confession and be absolved then, but he'll tell ye the same as I have."

"Oh." The syllable held profound relief, and Young Ian's scrawny shoulders rose perceptibly, as though a burden had rolled off of them.

Jamie patted his nephew's knee again. "For the second thing, ye needna fear telling your father."

"No?" Young Ian had accepted Jamie's word on the state of his soul without hesitation, but sounded profoundly dubious about this secular opinion.

"Well, I'll not say he'll no be upset," Jamie added fairly. "In fact, I expect it will turn the rest of his hair white on the spot. But he'll understand. He isna going to cast ye out or disown ye, if that's what you're scairt of."

"You think he'll understand?" Young Ian looked at Jamie with eyes in which hope battled with doubt. "I—I didna think he . . . has my Da ever killed a man?" he asked suddenly.

Jamie blinked, taken aback by the question. "Well," he said slowly, "I suppose—I mean, he's fought in battle, but I—to tell ye the truth, Ian, I dinna ken." He looked a little helplessly at his nephew.

"It's no the sort of thing men talk much about, aye? Except sometimes soldiers, when they're deep in drink."

Young Ian nodded, absorbing this, and sniffed again, with a horrid gurgling noise. Jamie, groping hastily in his sleeve for a handkerchief, looked up suddenly, struck by a thought.

"That's why ye said ye must tell me, but not your Da? Because ye knew I've killed men before?"

His nephew nodded, searching Jamie's face with troubled, trusting eyes. "Aye. I thought . . . I thought ye'd know what to do."

"Ah." Jamie drew a deep breath, and exchanged a glance with me. "Well . . ." His shoulders braced and broadened, and I could see him accept the burden Young Ian had laid down. He sighed.

"What ye do," he said, "is first to ask yourself if ye had a choice. You didn't, so put your mind at ease. Then ye go to confession, if ye can; if not, say a good Act of Contrition—that's good enough, when it's no a mortal sin. Ye harbor no fault, mind," he said earnestly, "but the contrition is because ye greatly regret the necessity that fell on ye. It does sometimes, and there's no preventing it.

"And then say a prayer for the soul of the one you've killed," he went on, "that he may find rest, and not haunt ye. Ye ken the prayer called Soul Peace? Use that one, if ye have leisure to think of it. In a battle, when there is no time, use Soul Leading—'Be this soul on Thine arm, O Christ, Thou King of the City of Heaven, Amen.' "

"Be this soul on Thine arm, O Christ, Thou King of the City of Heaven, Amen," Young Ian repeated under his breath. He nodded slowly. "Aye, all right. And then?"

Jamie reached out and touched his nephew's cheek with great gentleness. "Then ye live with it, laddie," he said softly. "That's all."

28

Virtue's Guardian

"You think the man Young Ian followed has something to do with Sir Percival's warning?" I lifted a cover on the supper tray that had just been delivered and sniffed appreciatively; it seemed a very long time since Moubray's stew.

Jamie nodded, picking up a sort of hot stuffed roll.

"I should be surprised if he had not," he said dryly. "While there's likely more than one man willing to do me harm, I canna think it likely that gangs o' them are roaming about Edinburgh." He took a bite and chewed industriously, shaking his head.

"Nay, that's clear enough, and nothing to be greatly worrit over."

"It's not?" I took a small bite of my own roll, then a bigger one. "This is delicious. What is it?"

Jamie lowered the roll he had been about to take a bite of, and squinted at it. "Pigeon minced wi' truffles," he said, and stuffed it into his mouth whole.

"No," he said, and paused to swallow. "No," he said again, more clearly. "That's likely just a matter of a rival smuggler. There are two gangs that I've had a wee bit of difficulty with now and then." He waved a hand, scattering crumbs, and reached for another roll.

"The way the man behaved—smellin' the brandy, but seldom tasting it— he may be a *dégustateur de vin*; someone that can tell from a sniff where a wine was made, and from a taste, which year it was bottled. A verra valuable fellow," he added thoughtfully, "and a choice hound to set on my trail."

Wine had come along with the supper. I poured out a glass and passed it under my own nose.

"He could track you—you, personally—through the brandy?" I asked curiously.

"More or less. You'll remember my cousin Jared?"

"Of course I do. You mean he's still alive?" After the slaughter of Culloden and the erosions of its aftermath, it was wonderfully heartening to hear that Jared, a wealthy Scottish émigré with a prosperous wine business in Paris, was still among the quick, and not the dead.

"I expect they'll have to head him up in a cask and toss him into the Seine to get rid of him," Jamie said, teeth gleaming white in his soot-stained countenance. "Aye, he's not only alive, but enjoying it. Where d'ye think I get the French brandy I bring into Scotland?"

The obvious answer was "France," but I refrained from saying so. "Jared, I suppose?" I said instead.

Jamie nodded, mouth full of another roll. "Hey!" He leaned forward and snatched the plate out from under the tentative reach of Young Ian's skinny fingers. "You're no supposed to be eating rich stuff like that when your wame's curdled," he said, frowning and chewing. He swallowed and licked his lips. "I'll call for more bread and milk for ye."

"But Uncle," said Young Ian, looking longingly at the savory rolls. "I'm awfully hungry." Purged by confession, the boy had recovered his spirits considerably, and evidently, his appetite as well.

Jamie looked at his nephew and sighed. "Aye well. Ye swear you're no going to vomit on me?"

"No, Uncle," Young Ian said meekly.

"All right, then." Jamie shoved the plate in the boy's direction, and returned to his explanation.

"Jared sends me mostly the second-quality bottling from his own vineyards in the Moselle, keepin' the first quality for sale in France, where they can tell the difference."

"So the stuff you bring into Scotland is identifiable?"

He shrugged, reaching for the wine. "Only to a *nez*, a *dégustateur*, that is. But the fact is, that wee Ian here saw the man taste the wine at the Dog and Gun and at the Blue Boar, and those are the two taverns on the High Street that buy brandy from me exclusively. Several others buy from me, but from others as well.

"In any case, as I say, I'm none so concerned at havin' someone look for Jamie Roy at a tavern." He lifted his wineglass and passed it under his own nose by reflex, made a slight, unconscious face, and drank. "No," he said, lowering the glass, "what worries me is that the man should have found his way to the printshop. For I've taken considerable pains to make sure that the folk who see Jamie Roy on the docks at Burntisland are not the same ones who pass the time o' day in the High Street with Mr. Alec Malcolm, the printer."

I knitted my brows, trying to work it out.

"But Sir Percival called you Malcolm, and he knows you're a smuggler," I protested.

Jamie nodded patiently. "Half the men in the ports near Edinburgh are smugglers, Sassenach," he said. "Aye, Sir Percival kens fine I'm a smuggler, but he doesna ken I'm Jamie Roy—let alone James Fraser. He thinks I bring in bolts of undeclared silk and velvet from Holland—because that's what I pay him in." He smiled wryly. "I trade brandy for them, to the tailor on the corner. Sir Percival's an eye for fine cloth, and his lady even more. But he doesna ken I've to do wi' the liquor—let alone how much—or he'd be wanting a great deal more than the odd bit of lace and yardage, I'll tell ye."

"Could one of the tavern owners have told the seaman about you? Surely they've seen you."

He ruffled a hand through his hair, as he did when thinking, making a few short hairs on the crown stand up in a whorl of tiny spikes.

"Aye, they've seen me," he said slowly, "but only as a customer. Fergus handles the business dealings wi' the taverns—and Fergus is careful never to go near the printshop. He always meets me here, in private." He gave me a crooked grin. "No one questions a man's reasons for visiting a brothel, aye?"

"Could that be it?" I asked, struck by a sudden thought. "Any man can come here without question. Could the seaman Young Ian followed have seen you here—you and Fergus? Or heard your description from one of the girls? After all, you're not the most inconspicuous man I've ever seen." He wasn't, either. While there might be any number of redheaded men in Edinburgh, few of them towered to Jamie's height, and fewer still strode the streets with the unconscious arrogance of a disarmed warrior.

"That's a verra useful thought, Sassenach," he said, giving me a nod. "It will be easy enough to find out whether a pigtailed seaman with one eye has been here recently; I'll have Jeanne ask among her lassies."

He stood up, and stretched rackingly, his hands nearly touching the wooden rafters.

"And then, Sassenach, perhaps we'll go to bed, aye?" He lowered his arms and blinked at me with a smile. "What wi' one thing and another, it's been the bloody hell of a day, no?"

"It has, rather," I said, smiling back.

Jeanne, summoned for instructions, arrived together with Fergus, who opened the door for the madam with the easy familiarity of a brother or cousin. Little wonder if he felt at home, I supposed; he had been born in a Paris brothel, and spent the first ten years of his life there, sleeping in a cupboard beneath the stairs, when not making a living by picking pockets on the street.

"The brandy is gone," he reported to Jamie. "I have sold it to MacAlpine —at a small sacrifice in price, I regret, milord. I thought a quick sale the best."

"Better to have it off the premises," Jamie said, nodding. "What have ye done wi' the body?"

Fergus smiled briefly, his lean face and dark forelock lending him a distinctly piratical air.

"Our intruder also has gone to MacAlpine's tavern, milord—suitably disguised."

"As what?" I demanded.

The pirate's grin turned on me; Fergus had turned out a very handsome man, the disfigurement of his hook notwithstanding.

"As a cask of crème de menthe, milady," he said.

"I do not suppose anyone has drunk crème de menthe in Edinburgh any time in the last hundred years," observed Madame Jeanne. "The heathen Scots are not accustomed to the use of civilized liqueurs; I have never seen a customer here take anything beyond whisky, beer, or brandywine."

"Exactly, Madame," Fergus said, nodding. "We do not want Mr. Mac-Alpine's tapmen broaching the cask, do we?"

"Surely somebody's going to look in that cask sooner or later," I said. "Not to be indelicate, but—"

"Exactly, milady," Fergus said, with a respectful bow to me. "Though crème de menthe has a very high content of alcohol. The tavern's cellar is but a temporary resting place on our unknown friend's journey to his eternal rest. He goes to the docks tomorrow, and thence to somewhere quite far away. It is only that I did not want him cluttering up Madame Jeanne's premises in the meantime."

Jeanne addressed a remark in French to St. Agnes that I didn't quite catch, but then shrugged and turned to go.

"I will make inquiries of *les filles* concerning this seaman tomorrow, Monsieur, when they are at leisure. For now—"

"For now, speaking of leisure," Fergus interrupted, "might Mademoiselle Sophie find herself unemployed this evening?"

The madam favored him with a look of ironic amusement. "Since she saw you come in, *mon petit saucisse,* I expect that she has kept herself available." She glanced at Young Ian, slouched against the cushions like a scarecrow from which all the straw stuffing has been removed. "And will I find a place for the young gentleman to sleep?"

"Oh, aye." Jamie looked consideringly at his nephew. "I suppose ye can lay a pallet in my room."

"Oh, no!" Young Ian blurted. "You'll want to be alone wi' your wife, will ye not, Uncle?"

"What?" Jamie stared at him uncomprehendingly.

"Well, I mean . . ." Young Ian hesitated, glancing at me, and then hastily away. "I mean, nay doubt you'll be wanting to . . . er . . . mmphm?" A Highlander born, he managed to infuse this last noise with an amazing wealth of implied indelicacy.

Jamie rubbed his knuckles hard across his upper lip.

"Well, that's verra thoughtful of ye, Ian," he said. His voice quivered slightly with the effort of not laughing. "And I'm flattered that ye have such a high opinion of my virility as to think I'm capable of anything but sleeping in bed after a day like this. But I think perhaps I can forgo the satisfaction of my carnal desires for one night—fond as I am of your auntie," he added, giving me a faint grin.

"But Bruno tells me the establishment is not busy tonight," Fergus put in, glancing round in some bewilderment. "Why does the boy not—"

"Because he's no but fourteen, for God's sake!" Jamie said, scandalized.

"Almost fifteen!" Young Ian corrected, sitting up and looking interested.

"Well, that is certainly sufficient," Fergus said, with a glance at Madame Jeanne for confirmation. "Your brothers were no older when I first brought them here, and they acquitted themselves honorably."

"You *what*?" Jamie goggled at his protégé.

"Well, someone had to," Fergus said, with slight impatience. "Normally, a boy's father—but of course, le Monsieur is not—meaning no disrespect to your esteemed father, of course," he added, with a nod to Young Ian, who nodded back like a mechanical toy, "but it is a matter for experienced judgment, you understand?"

"Now"—he turned to Madame Jeanne, with the air of a gourmand consulting the wine steward—"Dorcas, do you think, or Penelope?"

"No, no," she said, shaking her head decidedly, "it should be the second Mary, absolutely. The small one."

"Oh, with the yellow hair? Yes, I think you are right," Fergus said approvingly. "Fetch her, then."

Jeanne was off before Jamie could manage more than a strangled croak in protest.

"But—but—the lad canna—" he began.

"Yes, I can," Young Ian said. "At least, I think I can." It wasn't possible for his face to grow any redder, but his ears were crimson with excitement, the traumatic events of the day completely forgotten.

"But it's—that is to say—I canna be letting ye—" Jamie broke off and stood glaring at his nephew for a long moment. Finally, he threw his hands up in the air in exasperated defeat.

"And what am I to say to your mother?" he demanded, as the door opened behind him.

Framed in the door stood a very short young girl, plump and soft as a partridge in her blue silk chemise, her round sweet face beaming beneath a loose cloud of yellow hair. At the sight of her, Young Ian froze, scarcely breathing.

When at last he must draw breath or die, he drew it, and turned to Jamie. With a smile of surpassing sweetness, he said, "Well, Uncle Jamie, if I were you"—his voice soared up in a sudden alarming soprano, and he stopped, clearing his throat before resuming in a respectable baritone—"I wouldna tell her. Good night to ye, Auntie," he said, and walked purposefully forward.

"I canna decide whether I must kill Fergus or thank him." Jamie was sitting on the bed in our attic room, slowly unbuttoning his shirt.

I laid the damp dress over the stool and knelt down in front of him to unbuckle the knee buckles of his breeches.

"I suppose he was trying to do his best for Young Ian."

"Aye—in his bloody immoral French way." Jamie reached back to untie the lace that held his hair back. He had not plaited it again when we left Moubray's, and it fell soft and loose on his shoulders, framing the broad cheekbones and long straight nose, so that he looked like one of the fiercer Italian angels of the Renaissance.

"Was it the Archangel Michael who drove Adam and Eve out of the Garden of Eden?" I asked, stripping off his stockings.

He gave a slight chuckle. "Do I strike ye so—as the guardian o' virtue? And Fergus as the wicked serpent?" His hands came under my elbows as he bent to lift me up. "Get up, Sassenach; ye shouldna be on your knees, serving me."

"You've had rather a time of it today yourself," I answered, making him stand up with me. "Even if you didn't have to kill anyone." There were large blisters on his hands, and while he had wiped away most of the soot, there was still a streak down the side of his jaw.

"Mm." My hands went around his waist to help with the waistband of his breeches, but he held them there, resting his cheek for a moment against the top of my head.

"I wasna quite honest wi' the lad, ye ken," he said.

"No? I thought you did wonderfully with him. He felt better after he talked to you, at least."

"Aye, I hope so. And may be the prayers and such will help—they canna hurt him, at least. But I didna tell him everything."

"What else is there?" I tilted up my face to his, touching his lips softly with my own. He smelled of smoke and sweat.

"What a man most often does, when he's soul-sick wi' killing, is to find a woman, Sassenach," he answered softly. "His own, if he can; another, if he must. For she can do what he cannot—and heal him."

My fingers found the lacing of his fly; it came loose with a tug.

"That's why you let him go with the second Mary?"

He shrugged, and stepping back a pace, pushed the breeches down and off. "I couldna stop him. And I think perhaps I was right to let him, young as he is." He smiled crookedly at me. "At least he'll not be fashing and fretting himself over that seaman tonight."

"I don't imagine so. And what about you?" I pulled the chemise off over my head.

"Me?" He stared down at me, eyebrows raised, the grimy linen shirt hanging loose upon his shoulders.

I glanced behind him at the bed.

"Yes. You haven't killed anyone, but do you want to . . . mmphm?" I met his gaze, raising my own brows in question.

The smile broadened across his face, and any resemblance to Michael, stern guardian of virtue, vanished. He lifted one shoulder, then the other, and let them fall, and the shirt slid down his arms to the floor.

"I expect I do," he said. "But you'll be gentle wi' me, aye?"

29

Culloden's Last Victim

In the morning, I saw Jamie and Ian off on their pious errand, and then set off myself, stopping to purchase a large wicker basket from a vendor in the street. It was time I began to equip myself again, with whatever I could find in the way of medical supplies. After the events of the preceding day, I was beginning to fear I would have need of them before long.

Haugh's apothecary shop hadn't changed at all, through English occupation, Scottish Rising, and the Stuart's fall, and my heart rose in delight as I stepped through the door into the rich, familiar smells of hartshorn, peppermint, almond oil, and anise.

The man behind the counter was Haugh, but a much younger Haugh than the middle-aged man I had dealt with twenty years before, when I had patronized this shop for tidbits of military intelligence, as well as for nostrums and herbs.

The younger Haugh did not know me, of course, but went courteously about the business of finding the herbs I wanted, among the neatly ranged jars on his shelves. A good many were common—rosemary, tansy, marigold —but a few on my list made the young Haugh's ginger eyebrows rise, and his lips purse in thoughtfulness as he looked over the jars.

There was another customer in the shop, hovering near the counter, where tonics were dispensed and compounds ground to order. He strode back and forth, hands clasped behind his back, obviously impatient. After a moment, he came up to the counter.

"How long?" he snapped at Mr. Haugh's back.

"I canna just say, Reverend," the apothecary's voice was apologetic. "Louisa did say as 'twould need to be boiled."

The only reply to this was a snort, and the man, tall and narrow-shouldered in black, resumed his pacing, glancing from time to time at the doorway to the back room, where the invisible Louisa was presumably at work. The man looked slightly familiar, but I had no time to think where I had seen him before.

Mr. Haugh was squinting dubiously at the list I had given him. "Aconite, now," he muttered. "Aconite. And what might that be, I wonder?"

"Well, it's poison, for one thing," I said. Mr. Haugh's mouth dropped open momentarily.

"It's a medicine, too," I assured him. "But you have to be careful in the use of it. Externally, it's good for rheumatism, but a very tiny amount taken by mouth will lower the rate of the pulse. Good for some kinds of heart trouble."

"Really," Mr. Haugh said, blinking. He turned to his shelves, looking rather helpless. "Er, do ye ken what it smells like, maybe?"

Taking this for invitation, I came round the counter and began to sort through the jars. They were all carefully labeled, but the labels of some were clearly old, the ink faded, and the paper peeling at the edges.

"I'm afraid I'm none so canny wi' the medicines as my Da yet," young Mr. Haugh was saying at my elbow. "He'd taught me a good bit, but then he passed on a year ago, and there's things here as I dinna ken the use of, I'm afraid."

"Well, that one's good for cough," I said, taking down a jar of elecampane with a glance at the impatient Reverend, who had taken out a handkerchief and was wheezing asthmatically into it. "Particularly sticky-sounding coughs."

I frowned at the crowded shelves. Everything was dusted and immaculate, but evidently not filed according either to alphabetical or botanical order. Had old Mr. Haugh merely remembered where things were, or had he a system of some kind? I closed my eyes and tried to remember the last time I had been in the shop.

To my surprise, the image came back easily. I had come for foxglove then, to make the infusions for Alex Randall, younger brother of Black Jack Randall—and Frank's six-times great-grandfather. Poor boy, he had been dead now twenty years, though he had lived long enough to sire a son. I felt a twinge of curiosity at the thought of that son, and of his mother, who had been my friend, but I forced my mind away from them, back to the image of Mr. Haugh, standing on tiptoe to reach up to his shelves, over near the right-hand side . . .

"There." Sure enough, my hand rested near the jar labeled FOXGLOVE. To one side of it was a jar labeled HORSETAIL, to the other, LILY OF THE VALLY ROOT. I hesitated, looking at them, running over in my mind the possible uses of those herbs. Cardiac herbs, all of them. If aconite was to be found, it would be close by, then.

It was. I found it quickly, in a jar labeled AULD WIVES HUID.

"Be careful with it." I handed the jar gingerly to Mr. Haugh. "Even a bit of it will make your skin go numb. Perhaps I'd better have a glass bottle for it." Most of the herbs I'd bought had been wrapped up in squares of gauze or twisted in screws of paper, but the young Mr. Haugh nodded and carried the jar of aconite into the back room, held at arm's length, as though he expected it to explode in his face.

"Ye'd seem to know a good deal more about the medicines than the lad," said a deep, hoarse voice behind me.

"Well, I've somewhat more experience than he has, likely." I turned to find the minister leaning on the counter, watching me under thick brows with pale blue eyes. I realized with a start where I had seen him; in Moubray's, the day before. He gave no sign of recognizing me; perhaps because my cloak covered Daphne's dress. I had noticed that many men took relatively little notice of the face of a woman *en décolletage,* though it seemed a regrettable habit in a clergyman. He cleared his throat.

"Mmphm. And d'ye ken what to do for a nervous complaint, then?"

"What sort of nervous complaint?"

He pursed his lips and frowned, as though unsure whether to trust me. The upper lip came to a slight point, like an owl's beak, but the lower was thick and pendulous.

"Well . . . 'tis a complicated case. But to speak generally, now"—he eyed me carefully—"what would ye give for a sort of . . . fit?"

"Epileptic seizure? Where the person falls down and twitches?"

He shook his head, showing a reddened band about his neck, where the high white stock had chafed it.

"No, a different kind of fit. Screaming and staring."

"Screaming *and* staring?"

"Not at once, ye ken," he added hastily. "First the one, and then the other—or rather, roundabout. First she'll do naught but stare for days on end, not speaking, and then of a sudden, she'll scream fit to wake the deid."

"That sounds very trying." It did; if he had a wife so afflicted, it could easily explain the deep lines of strain that bracketed his mouth and eyes, and the blue circles of exhaustion beneath his eyes.

I tapped a finger on the counter, considering. "I don't know; I'd have to see the patient."

The minister's tongue touched his lower lip. "Perhaps . . . would ye be willing maybe, to come and see her? It isn't far," he added, rather stiffly. Pleading didn't come naturally to him, but the urgency of his request communicated itself despite the stiffness of his figure.

"I can't, just now," I told him. "I have to meet my husband. But perhaps this afternoon—"

"Two o'clock," he said promptly. "Henderson's, in Carrubber's Close. Campbell is the name, the Reverend Archibald Campbell."

Before I could say yes or no, the curtain between the front room and the back twitched aside, and Mr. Haugh appeared with two bottles, one of which he handed to each of us.

The Reverend eyed his with suspicion, as he groped in his pocket for a coin.

"Weel, and there's your price," he said ungraciously, slapping it on the counter. "And we'll hope as you've given me the right one, and no the lady's poison."

The curtain rustled again and a woman looked out after the departing form of the minister.

"Good riddance," she remarked. "Happence for an hour's work, and insult on the top of it! The Lord might ha' chosen better, is all I can say!"

"Do you know him?" I asked, curious whether Louisa might have any helpful information about the afflicted wife.

"Not to say I ken him weel, no," Louisa said, staring at me in frank curiosity. "He's one o' they Free Church meenisters, as is always rantin' on the corner by the Market Cross, tellin' folk as their behavior's of nay consequence at all, and all that's needful for salvation is that they shall 'come to grips wi' Jesus'—like as if Our Lord was to be a fair-day wrestler!" She sniffed disdainfully at this heretical viewpoint, crossing herself against contamination.

"I'm surprised the likes of the Reverend Campbell should come in our shop, hearin' what he thinks o' Papists by and large." Her eyes sharpened at me.

"But you'll maybe be Free Church yoursel', ma'am; meanin' no offense to ye, if so."

"No, I'm a Catholic—er, a Papist, too," I assured her. "I was only wondering whether you knew anything about the Reverend's wife, and her condition."

Louisa shook her head, turning to deal with a new customer.

"Nay, I've ne'er seen the lady. But whatever's the matter with her," she added, frowning after the departed Reverend, "I'm sure that livin' wi' *him* doesna improve it any!"

The weather was chill but clear, and only a faint hint of smoke lingered in the Rectory garden as a reminder of the fire. Jamie and I sat on a bench against the wall, absorbing the pale winter sunshine as we waited for Young Ian to finish his confession.

"Did you tell Ian that load of rubbish he gave Young Ian yesterday? About where I'd been all this time?"

"Oh, aye," he said. "Ian's a good deal too canny to believe it, but it's a likely enough story, and he's too good a friend to insist on the truth."

"I suppose it will do, for general consumption," I agreed. "But shouldn't you have told it to Sir Percival, instead of letting him think we were newly-weds?"

He shook his head decidedly. "Och, no. For the one thing, Sir Percival has no notion of my real name, though I'll lay a year's takings he knows it isna Malcolm. I dinna want him to be thinking of me and Culloden together, by any means. And for another, a story like the one I gave Ian would cause the devil of a lot more talk than the news that the printer's taken a wife."

" 'Oh, what a tangled web we weave,' " I intoned, " 'when first we practice to deceive.' "

He gave me a quick blue glance, and the corner of his mouth lifted slightly.

"It gets a bit easier with practice, Sassenach," he said. "Try living wi' me for a time, and ye'll find yourself spinning silk out of your arse easy as sh—, er, easy as kiss-my-hand."

I burst out laughing.

"I want to see you do that," I said.

"You already have." He stood up and craned his neck, trying to see over the wall into the Rectory garden.

"Young Ian's being the devil of a time," he remarked, sitting down again. "How can a lad not yet fifteen have that much to confess?"

"After the day and night he had yesterday? I suppose it depends how much detail Father Hayes wants to hear," I said, with a vivid recollection of my breakfast with the prostitutes. "Has he been in there all this time?"

"Er, no." The tips of Jamie's ears grew slightly pinker in the morning light. "I, er, I had to go first. As an example, ye ken."

"No wonder it took some time," I said, teasing. "How long has it been since you've been to confession?"

"I told Father Hayes it was six months."

"And was it?"

"No, but I supposed if he was going to shrive me for thieving, assault, and profane language, he might as well shrive me for lying, too."

"What, no fornication or impure thoughts?"

"Certainly not," he said austerely. "Ye can think any manner of horrible things without sin, and it's to do wi' your wife. It's only if you're thinking it about other ladies, it's impure."

"I had no idea I was coming back to save your soul," I said primly, "but it's nice to be useful."

He laughed, bent and kissed me thoroughly.

"I wonder if that counts as an indulgence," he said, pausing for breath. "It ought to, no? It does a great deal more to keep a man from the fires of hell than saying the rosary does. Speaking of which," he added, digging into his pocket and coming out with a rather chewed-looking wooden rosary, "remind me that I must say my penance sometime today. I was about to start on it, when ye came up."

"How many Hail Marys are you supposed to say?" I asked, fingering the beads. The chewed appearance wasn't illusion; there were definite small toothmarks on most of the beads.

"I met a Jew last year," he said, ignoring the question. "A natural philosopher, who'd sailed round the world six times. He told me that in both the Musselman faith and the Jewish teachings, it was considered an act of virtue for a man and his wife to lie wi' each other.

"I wonder if that has anything to do wi' both Jews and Musselmen being circumcised?" he added thoughtfully. "I never thought to ask him that—though perhaps he would ha' found it indelicate to say."

"I shouldn't think a foreskin more or less would impair the virtue," I assured him.

"Oh, good," he said, and kissed me once more.

"What happened to your rosary?" I asked, picking up the string where it had fallen on the grass. "It looks like the rats have been at it."

"Not rats," he said. "Bairns."

"What bairns?"

"Oh, any that might be about." He shrugged, tucking the beads back in his pocket. "Young Jamie has three now, and Maggie and Kitty two each. Wee Michael's just married, but his wife's breeding." The sun was behind him, darkening his face, so that his teeth flashed suddenly white when he smiled. "Ye didna ken ye were a great-aunt seven times over, aye?"

"A great-aunt?" I said, staggered.

"Well, I'm a great-uncle," he said cheerfully, "and I havena found it a terrible trial, except for having my beads gnawed when the weans are cutting teeth—that, and bein' expected to answer to 'Nunkie' a lot."

Sometimes twenty years seemed like an instant, and sometimes it seemed like a very long time indeed.

"Er . . . there isn't a feminine equivalent of 'Nunkie,' I hope?"

"Oh, no," he assured me. "They'll all call ye Great-Auntie Claire, and treat ye wi' the utmost respect."

"Thanks a lot," I muttered, with visions of the hospital's geriatric wing fresh in my mind.

Jamie laughed, and with a lightness of heart no doubt engendered by being newly freed from sin, grasped me around the waist and lifted me onto his lap.

"I've never before seen a great-auntie wi' a lovely plump arse like that," he said with approval, bouncing me slightly on his knees. His breath tickled the back of my neck as he leaned forward. I let out a small shriek as his teeth closed lightly on my ear.

"Are ye all right, Auntie?" said Young Ian's voice just behind us, full of concern.

Jamie started convulsively, nearly unshipping me from his lap, then tightened his hold on my waist.

"Oh, aye," he said. "It's just your auntie saw a spider."

"Where?" said Young Ian, peering interestedly over the bench.

"Up there." Jamie rose, standing me on my feet, and pointed to the lime tree, where—sure enough—the web of an orb weaver stretched across the crook of two branches, sparkling with damp. The weaver herself sat in the center, round as a cherry, wearing a gaudy pattern of green and yellow on her back.

"I was telling your auntie," Jamie said, as Young Ian examined the web in lashless fascination, "about a Jew I met, a natural philosopher. He'd made a study of spiders, it seems; in fact, he was in Edinburgh to deliver a learned paper to the Royal Society, in spite of being a Jew."

"Really? Did he tell ye a lot about spiders?" Young Ian asked eagerly.

"A lot more than I cared to know," Jamie informed his nephew. "There are times and places for talkin' of spiders that lay eggs in caterpillars so the young hatch out and devour the poor beast while it's still alive, but during supper isna one of them. He did say one thing I thought verra interesting, though," he added, squinting at the web. He blew gently on it, and the spider scuttled briskly into hiding.

"He said that spiders spin two kinds of silk, and if ye have a lens—and can make the spider sit still for it, I suppose—ye can see the two places where the silk comes out; spinnerets, he called them. In any case, the one kind of silk is sticky, and if a wee bug touches it, he's done for. But the other kind is dry silk, like the sort ye'd embroider with, but finer."

The orb weaver was advancing cautiously toward the center of her web again.

"See where she walks?" Jamie pointed to the web, anchored by a number of spokes, supporting the intricate netlike whorl. "The spokes there, those are spun of the dry silk, so the spider can walk over it herself wi' no trouble. But the rest o' the web is the sticky kind of silk—or mostly so—and if ye watch a spider careful for quite a long time, you'll see that she goes only on the dry strands, for if she walked on the sticky stuff, she'd be stuck herself."

"Is that so?" Ian breathed reverently on the web, watching intently as the spider moved away along her nonskid road to safety.

"I suppose there's a moral there for web weavers," Jamie observed to me, sotto voce. "Be sure ye know which of your strands are sticky."

"I suppose it helps even more if you have the kind of luck that will conjure up a handy spider when you need one," I said dryly.

He laughed and took my arm.

"That's not luck, Sassenach," he told me. "It's watchfulness. Ian, are ye coming?"

"Oh, aye." Young Ian abandoned the web with obvious reluctance and followed us to the kirkyard gate.

"Oh, Uncle Jamie, I meant to ask, can I borrow your rosary?" he said, as we emerged onto the cobbles of the Royal Mile. "The priest told me I must say five decades for my penance, and that's too many to keep count of on my fingers."

"Surely." Jamie stopped and fished in his pocket for the rosary. "Be sure to give it back, though."

Young Ian grinned. "Aye, I reckon you'll be needing it yourself, Uncle Jamie. The priest told me he was verra wicked," Young Ian confided to me, with a lashless wink, "and told me not to be like him."

"Mmphm." Jamie glanced up and down the road, gauging the speed of an approaching handcart, edging its way down the steep incline. Freshly shaved that morning, his cheeks had a rosy glow about them.

"How many decades of the rosary are you supposed to say as penance?" I asked curiously.

"Eighty-five," he muttered. The rosiness of his freshly shaved cheeks deepened.

Young Ian's mouth dropped open in awe.

"How long has it been since ye went to confession, Uncle?" he asked.

"A long time," Jamie said tersely. "Come on!"

Jamie had an appointment after dinner to meet with a Mr. Harding, representative of the Hand in Hand Assurance Society, which had insured the premises of the printshop, to inspect the ashy remains with him and verify the loss.

"I willna need ye, laddie," he said reassuringly to Young Ian, who looked less than enthusiastic about the notion of revisiting the scene of his adventures. "You go wi' your auntie to see this madwoman."

"I canna tell how ye do it," he added to me, raising one brow. "You're in the city less than two days, and all the afflicted folk for miles about are clutching at your hems."

"Hardly all of them," I said dryly. "It's only one woman, after all, and I haven't even seen her yet."

"Aye, well. At least madness isna catching—I hope." He kissed me briefly, then turned to go, clapping Young Ian companionably on the shoulder. "Look after your auntie, Ian."

Young Ian paused for a moment, looking after the tall form of his departing uncle.

"Do you want to go with him, Ian?" I asked. "I can manage alone, if you—"

"Oh, no, Auntie!" He turned back to me, looking rather abashed. "I dinna want to go, at all. It's only—I was wondering—well, what if they . . . find anything? In the ashes?"

"A body, you mean," I said bluntly. I had realized, of course, that the distinct possibility that Jamie and Mr. Harding *would* find the body of the one-eyed seaman was the reason Jamie had told Ian to accompany me.

The boy nodded, looking ill at ease. His skin had faded to a sort of rosy tan, but was still too dark to show any paleness due to emotion.

"I don't know," I said. "If the fire was a very hot one, there may be nothing much left to find. But don't worry about it." I touched his arm in reassurance. "Your uncle will know what to do."

"Aye, that's so." His face brightened, full of faith in his uncle's ability to handle any situation whatever. I smiled when I saw his expression, then realized with a small start of surprise that I had that faith, too. Be it drunken Chinese, corrupt Customs agents, or Mr. Harding of the Hand in Hand Assurance Society, I hadn't any doubt that Jamie would manage.

"Come on, then," I said, as the bell in the Canongate Kirk began to ring. "It's just on two now."

Despite his visit to Father Hayes, Ian had retained a certain air of dreamy bliss, which returned to him now, and there was little conversation as we made our way up the slope of the Royal Mile to Henderson's lodging house, in Carrubber's Close.

It was a quiet hotel, but luxurious by Edinburgh standards, with a patterned carpet on the stairs and colored glass in the street window. It seemed rather rich surroundings for a Free Church minister, but then I knew little about Free Churchmen; perhaps they took no vow of poverty as the Catholic clergy did.

Showed up to the third floor by a young boy, we found the door opened to us at once by a heavyset woman wearing an apron and a worried expression. I thought she might be in her mid-twenties, though she had already lost several of her front teeth.

"You'll be the lady as the Reverend said would call?" she asked. Her expression lightened a bit at my nod, and she swung the door wider.

"Mr. Campbell's had to go oot the noo," she said in a broad Lowland accent, "but he said as how he'd be most obliged to hae yer advice regardin' his sister, mum."

Sister, not wife. "Well, I'll do my best," I said. "May I see Miss Campbell?"

Leaving Ian to his memories in the sitting room, I accompanied the woman, who introduced herself as Nellie Cowden, to the back bedroom.

Miss Campbell was, as advertised, staring. Her pale blue eyes were wide open, but didn't seem to be looking at anything—certainly not at me.

She sat in the sort of wide, low chair called a nursing chair, with her back to the fire. The room was dim, and the backlighting made her features indistinct, except for the unblinking eyes. Seen closer to, her features were still indistinct; she had a soft, round face, undistinguished by any apparent bone structure, and baby-fine brown hair, neatly brushed. Her nose was small and snub, her chin double, and her mouth hung pinkly open, so slack as to obscure its natural lines.

"Miss Campbell?" I said cautiously. There was no response from the plump figure in the chair. Her eyes did blink, I saw, though much less frequently than normal.

"She'll nae answer ye, whilst she's in this state," Nellie Cowden said behind me. She shook her head, wiping her hands upon her apron. "Nay, not a word."

"How long has she been like this?" I picked up a limp, pudgy hand and felt for the pulse. It was there, slow and quite strong.

"Oh, for twa days so far, this time." Becoming interested, Miss Cowden leaned forward, peering into her charge's face. "Usually she stays like that for a week or more—thirteen days is the longest she's done it."

Moving slowly—though Miss Campbell seemed unlikely to be alarmed—I began to examine the unresisting figure, meanwhile asking questions of her attendant. Miss Margaret Campbell was thirty-seven, Miss Cowden told me, the only relative of the Reverend Archibald Campbell, with whom she had lived for the past twenty years, since the death of their parents.

"What starts her doing this? Do you know?"

Miss Cowden shook her head. "No tellin', Mum. Nothin' seems to start it. One minute she'll be lookin' aboot, talkin' and laughin', eatin' her dinner like the sweet child she is, and the next—wheesht!" She snapped her fingers, then, for effect, leaned forward and snapped them again, deliberately, just under Miss Campbell's nose.

"See?" she said. "I could hae six men wi' trumpets pass through the room, and she'd pay it nay more mind."

I was reasonably sure that Miss Campbell's trouble was mental, not physical, but I made a complete examination, anyway—or as complete as could be managed without undressing that clumsy, inert form.

"It's when she comes oot of it that's the worst, though," Miss Cowden assured me, squatting next to me as I knelt on the floor to check Miss Campbell's plantar reflexes. Her feet, loosed from shoes and stockings, were damp and smelled musty.

I drew a fingernail firmly down the sole of each foot in turn, checking for a Babinski reflex that might indicate the presence of a brain lesion. Nothing, though; her toes curled under, in normal startlement.

"What happens then? Is that the screaming the Reverend mentioned?" I rose to my feet. "Will you bring me a lighted candle, please?"

"Oh, aye, the screamin'." Miss Cowden hastened to oblige, lighting a wax taper from the fire. "She do shriek somethin' awful then, on and on 'til she's worn herself oot. Then she'll fall asleep—sleep the clock around, she will—and wake as though nothin' had happened."

"And she's quite all right when she wakes?" I asked. I moved the candle flame slowly back and forth, a few inches before the patient's eyes. The pupils shrank in automatic response to the light, but the irises stayed fixed, not following the flame. My hand itched for the solid handle of an ophthal-moscope, to examine the retinas, but no such luck.

"Well, not to say all right," Miss Cowden said slowly. I turned from the patient to look at her and she shrugged, massive shoulders powerful under the linen of her blouse.

"She's saft in the heid, puir dear," she said, matter-of-factly. "Has been for nigh on twenty year."

"You haven't been taking care of her all that time, surely?"

"Oh, no! Mr. Campbell had a woman as cared for her where they lived, in Burntisland, but the woman was none so young, and didna wish to leave her home. So when the Reverend made up his mind to take up the Missionary Society's offer, and to take his sister wi' him to the West Indies—why, he advertised for a strong woman o' good character who wouldna mind travel to be an abigail for her . . . and here I am." Miss Cowden gave me a gap-toothed smile in testimony to her own virtues.

"The West Indies? He's planning to take Miss Campbell on a ship to the West Indies?" I was staggered; I knew just enough of sailing conditions to think that any such trip would be a major ordeal to a woman in good health. This woman—but then I reconsidered. All things concerned, Margaret Campbell might endure such a trip better than a normal woman—at least if she remained in her trance.

"He thought as the change of climate might be good for her," Miss Cowden was explaining. "Get her away from Scotland, and all the dreadful memories. Ought to ha' done it long since, is what I say."

"What sort of dreadful memories?" I asked. I could see by the gleam in Miss Cowden's eye that she was only too ready to tell me. I had finished the examination by this time, and concluded that there was little physically wrong with Miss Campbell save inactivity and poor diet, but there was the chance that something in her history might suggest some treatment.

"Weel," she began, sidling toward the table, where a decanter and several glasses stood on a tray, "it's only what Tilly Lawson told me, her as looked after Miss Campbell for sae long, but she did swear it was the truth, and her a godly woman. If ye'd care to take a drop of cordial, mum, for the sake o' the Reverend's hospitality?"

The chair Miss Campbell sat on was the only one in the room, so Miss Cowden and I perched inelegantly on the bed, side by side, and watched the silent figure before us, as we sipped our blackberry cordial, and she told me Margaret Campbell's story.

Margaret Campbell had been born in Burntisland, no more than five miles from Edinburgh, across the Firth of Forth. At the time of the '45, when Charles Stuart had marched into Edinburgh to reclaim his father's throne, she had been seventeen.

"Her father was a Royalist, o' course, and her brother in a government regiment, marching north to put down the wicked rebels," said Miss Cowden, taking a tiny sip of the cordial to make it last. "But not Miss Margaret. Nay, she was for the Bonnie Prince, and the Hielan' men that followed him."

One, in particular, though Miss Cowden did not know his name. But a fine man he must have been, for Miss Margaret stole away from her home to meet him, and told him all the bits of information that she gleaned from listening to her father and his friends, and from her brother's letters home.

But then had come Falkirk; a victory, but a costly one, followed by retreat. Rumor had attended the flight of the Prince's army to the north, and not a soul doubted but that their flight led to destruction. Miss Margaret, desperate at the rumors, left her home at dead of night in the cold March spring, and went to find the man she loved.

Now here the account had been uncertain—whether it was that she had found the man and he had spurned her, or that she had not found him in time, and been forced to turn back from Culloden Moor—but in any case, turn back she did, and the day after the battle, she had fallen into the hands of a band of English soldiers.

"Dreadful, what they did to her," Miss Cowden said, lowering her voice as though the figure in the chair could hear. "Dreadful!" The English soldiers, blind with the lust of the hunt and the kill, pursuing the fugitives of Culloden, had not stopped to ask her name or the sympathies of her family. They had known by her speech that she was a Scot, and that knowledge had been enough.

They had left her for dead in a ditch half full of freezing water, and only the fortuitous presence of a family of tinkers, hiding in the nearby brambles for fear of the soldiers, had saved her.

"I canna help but think it a pity they did save her, un-Christian thing it is to say," Miss Cowden whispered. "If not, the puir lamb might ha' slippit her earthly bonds and gone happy to God. But as it is—" She gestured clumsily at the silent figure, and drank down the last drops of her cordial.

Margaret had lived, but did not speak. Somewhat recovered, but silent, she traveled with the tinkers, moving south with them to avoid the pillaging of the Highlands that took place in the wake of Culloden. And then one day, sitting in the yard of a pothouse, holding the tin to collect coppers as the tinkers busked and sang, she had been found by her brother, who had stopped with his Campbell regiment to refresh themselves on the way back to their quarters at Edinburgh.

"She kent him, and him her, and the shock o' their meeting gave her back her voice, but not her mind, puir thing. He took her home, o' course, but she was always as though she was in the past—sometime before she met the Hielan' man. Her father was dead then, from the influenza, and Tilly Lawson said as the shock o' seeing her like that kilt her mother, but could be as that were the influenza, too, for there was a great deal of it about that year."

The whole affair had left Archibald Campbell deeply embittered against both Highland Scots and the English army, and he had resigned his commission. With his parents dead, he found himself middling well-to-do, but the sole support of his damaged sister.

"He couldna marry," Miss Cowden explained, "for what woman would have him, and she"—with a nod toward the fire—"was thrown into the bargain?"

In his difficulties, he had turned to God, and become a minister. Unable to leave his sister, or to bear the confinement of the family house at Burntisland with her, he had purchased a coach, hired a woman to look after Margaret, and begun to make brief journeys into the surrounding countryside to preach, often taking her with him.

In his preaching he had found success, and this year had been asked by the Society of Presbyterian Missionaries if he would undertake his longest journey yet, to the West Indies, there to organize churches and appoint elders on the colonies of Barbados and Jamaica. Prayer had given him his answer, and he had sold the family property in Burntisland and moved his sister to Edinburgh while he made preparations for the journey.

I glanced once more at the figure by the fire. The heated air from the hearth stirred the skirts about her feet, but beyond that small movement, she might have been a statue.

"Well," I said with a sigh, "there's not a great deal I can do for her, I'm afraid. But I'll give you some prescriptions—receipts, I mean—to have made up at the apothecary's before you go."

If they didn't help, they couldn't hurt, I reflected, as I copied down the short lists of ingredients. Chamomile, hops, rue, tansy, and verbena, with a strong pinch of peppermint, for a soothing tonic. Tea of rose hips, to help correct the slight nutritional deficiency I had noted—spongy, bleeding gums, and a pale, bloated look about the face.

"Once you reach the Indies," I said, handing Miss Cowden the paper, "you must see that she eats a great deal of fruit—oranges, grapefruit, and lemons, particularly. You should do the same," I added, causing a look of profound suspicion to flit across the maid's wide face. I doubted she ate any vegetable matter beyond the occasional onion or potato, save her daily parritch.

The Reverend Campbell had not returned, and I saw no real reason to wait for him. Bidding Miss Campbell adieu, I pulled open the door of the bedroom, to find Young Ian standing on the other side of it.

"Oh!" he said, startled. "I was just comin' to find ye, Auntie. It's nearly half-past three, and Uncle Jamie said—"

"Jamie?" The voice came from behind me, from the chair beside the fire.

Miss Cowden and I whirled to find Miss Campbell sitting bolt upright, eyes still wide but focused now. They were focused on the doorway, and as Young Ian stepped inside, Miss Campbell began to scream.

Rather unsettled by the encounter with Miss Campbell, Young Ian and I made our way thankfully back to the refuge of the brothel, where we were greeted matter-of-factly by Bruno and taken to the rear parlor. There we found Jamie and Fergus deep in conversation.

"True, we do not trust Sir Percival," Fergus was saying, "but in this case, what point is there to his telling you of an ambush, save that such an ambush is in fact to occur?"

"Damned if I ken why," Jamie said frankly, leaning back and stretching in his chair. "And that being so, we do, as ye say, conclude that there's meant to be an ambush by the excisemen. Two days, he said. That would be Mullen's Cove." Then, catching sight of me and Ian, he half-rose, motioning us to take seats.

"Will it be the rocks below Balcarres, then?" Fergus asked.

Jamie frowned in thought, the two stiff fingers of his right hand drumming slowly on the tabletop.

"No," he said at last. "Let it be Arbroath; the wee cove under the abbey there. Just to be sure, aye?"

"All right." Fergus pushed back the half-empty plate of oatcakes from which he had been refreshing himself, and rose. "I shall spread the word, milord. Arbroath, in four days." With a nod to me, he swirled his cloak about his shoulders and went out.

"Is it the smuggling, Uncle?" Young Ian asked eagerly. "Is there a French lugger coming?" He picked up an oatcake and bit into it, scattering crumbs over the table.

Jamie's eyes were still abstracted, thinking, but they cleared as he glanced sharply at his nephew. "Aye, it is. And *you*, Young Ian, are having nothing to do with it."

"But I could help!" the boy protested. "You'll need someone to hold the mules, at least!"

"After all your Da said to you and me yesterday, wee Ian?" Jamie raised his brows. "Christ, ye've a short memory, lad!"

Ian looked mildly abashed at this, and took another oatcake to cover his confusion. Seeing him momentarily silent, I took the opportunity to ask my own questions.

"You're going to Arbroath to meet a French ship that's bringing in smuggled liquor?" I asked. "You don't think that's dangerous, after Sir Percival's warning?"

Jamie glanced at me with one brow still raised, but answered patiently enough.

"No; Sir Percival was warning me that the rendezvous in two days' time is known. That was to take place at Mullen's Cove. I've an arrangement wi' Jared and his captains, though. If a rendezvous canna be kept for some reason, the lugger will stand offshore and come in again the next night—but to a different place. And there's a third fallback as well, should the second meeting not come off."

"But if Sir Percival knows the first rendezvous, won't he know the others, too?" I persisted.

Jamie shook his head and poured out a cup of wine. He quirked a brow at me to ask whether I wanted any, and upon my shaking my head, sipped it himself.

"No," he said. "The rendezvous points are arranged in sets of three, between me and Jared, sent by sealed letter inside a packet addressed to Jeanne, here. Once I've read the letter, I burn it. The men who'll help meet the lugger will all know the first point, of course—I suppose one o' them will have let something slip," he added, frowning into his cup. "But no one— not even Fergus—kens the other two points unless we need to make use of one. And when we do, all the men ken well enough to guard their tongues."

"But then it's bound to be safe, Uncle!" Young Ian burst out. "Please let me come! I'll keep well back out o' the way," he promised.

Jamie gave his nephew a slightly jaundiced look.

"Aye, ye will," he said. "You'll come wi' me to Arbroath, but you and your auntie will stay at the inn on the road above the abbey until we've finished. I've got to take the laddie home to Lallybroch, Claire," he explained, turning to me. "And mend things as best I can with his parents." The elder Ian had left Halliday's that morning before Jamie and Young Ian arrived, leaving no message, but presumably bound for home. "Ye willna mind the journey? I wouldna ask it, and you just over your travel from Inverness"—his eyes met mine with a small, conspiratorial smile—"but I must take him back as soon as may be."

"I don't mind at all," I assured him. "It will be good to see Jenny and the rest of your family again."

"But Uncle—" Young Ian blurted. "What about—"

"Be still!" Jamie snapped. "That will be all from you, laddie. Not another word, aye?"

Young Ian looked wounded, but took another oatcake and inserted it into his mouth in a marked manner, signifying his intention to remain completely silent.

Jamie relaxed then, and smiled at me.

"Well, and how was your visit to the madwoman?"

"Very interesting," I said. "Jamie, do you know any people named Campbell?"

"Not above three or four hundred of them," he said, a smile twitching his long mouth. "Had ye a particular Campbell in mind?"

"A couple of them." I told him the story of Archibald Campbell and his sister, Margaret, as related to me by Nellie Cowden.

He shook his head at the tale, and sighed. For the first time, he looked truly older, his face tightened and lined by memory.

"It's no the worst tale I've heard, of the things that happened after Culloden," he said. "But I dinna think—wait." He stopped, and looked at me, eyes narrowed in thought. "Margaret Campbell. Margaret. Would she be a bonny wee lass—perhaps the size o' the second Mary? And wi' soft brown hair like a wren's feather, and a verra sweet face?"

"She probably was, twenty years ago," I said, thinking of that still, plump figure sitting by the fire. "Why, do you know her after all?"

"Aye, I think I do." His brow was furrowed in thought, and he looked down at the table, drawing a random line through the spilled crumbs. "Aye, if I'm right, she was Ewan Cameron's sweetheart. You'll mind Ewan?"

"Of course." Ewan had been a tall, handsome joker of a man, who had worked with Jamie at Holyrood, gathering bits of intelligence that filtered through from England. "What's become of Ewan? Or should I not ask?" I said, seeing the shadow come over Jamie's face.

"The English shot him," he said quietly. "Two days after Culloden." He closed his eyes for a moment, then opened them and smiled tiredly at me.

"Well, then, may God bless the Reverend Archie Campbell. I'd heard of him, a time or two, during the Rising. He was a bold soldier, folk said, and a brave one—and I suppose he'll need to be now, poor man." He sat a moment longer, then stood up with decision.

"Aye, well, there's a great deal to be done before we leave Edinburgh. Ian, you'll find the list of the printshop customers upstairs on the table; fetch it down to me and I'll mark off for ye the ones with orders outstanding. Ye must go to see each one and offer back their money. Unless they choose to wait until I've found new premises and laid in new stock—that might take as much as two months, though, tell them."

He patted his coat, where something made a small jingling sound.

"Luckily the assurance money will pay back the customers, and have a bit left over. Speaking of which"—he turned and smiled at me—"your job, Sassenach, is to find a dressmaker who will manage ye a decent gown in two days' time. For I expect Daphne would like her dress back, and I canna take ye home to Lallybroch naked."

30

Rendezvous

The chief entertainment of the ride north to Arbroath was watching the conflict of wills between Jamie and Young Ian. I knew from long experience that stubbornness was one of the major components of a Fraser's character. Ian seemed not unduly handicapped in that respect, though only half a Fraser; either the Murrays were no slouches with regard to stubbornness, or the Fraser genes were strong ones.

Having had the opportunity to observe Brianna at close range for many years, I had my own opinion about that, but kept quiet, merely enjoying the spectacle of Jamie having for once met his match. By the time we passed Balfour, he was wearing a distinctly hunted look.

This contest between immovable object and irresistible force continued until early evening of the fourth day, when we reached Arbroath to find that the inn where Jamie had intended to leave Ian and myself no longer existed. No more than a tumbled-down stone wall and one or two charred roof-beams remained to mark the spot; otherwise, the road was deserted for miles in either direction.

Jamie looked at the heap of stones in silence for some time. It was reasonably obvious that he could not just leave us in the middle of a desolate, muddy road. Ian, wise enough not to press the advantage, kept also silent, though his skinny frame fairly vibrated with eagerness.

"All right, then," Jamie said at last, resigned. "Ye'll come. But only so far as the cliff's edge, Ian—d'ye hear? You'll take care of your auntie."

"I hear, Uncle Jamie," Young Ian replied, with deceptive meekness. I caught Jamie's wry glance, though, and understood that if Ian was to take care of auntie, auntie was also to take care of Ian. I hid a smile, nodding obediently.

The rest of the men were timely, arriving at the rendezvous point on the cliffside just after dark. A couple of the men seemed vaguely familiar, but most were just muffled shapes; it was two days past the dark of the moon, but the tiny sliver rising over the horizon made conditions here little more illuminating than those obtaining in the brothel's cellars. No introductions were made, the men greeting Jamie with unintelligible mutters and grunts.

There was one unmistakable figure, though. A large mule-drawn wagon appeared, rattling its way down the road, driven by Fergus and a diminutive object that could only be Mr. Willoughby, whom I had not seen since he had shot the mysterious man on the stairs of the brothel.

"He hasn't a pistol with him tonight, I hope," I murmured to Jamie.

"Who?" he said, squinting into the gathering gloom. "Oh, the Chinee? No, none of them have." Before I could ask why not, he had gone forward, to help back the wagon around, ready to make a getaway toward Edinburgh, so soon as the contraband should be loaded. Young Ian pressed his way forward, and I, mindful of my job as custodian, followed him.

Mr. Willoughby stood on tiptoe to reach into the back of the wagon, emerging with an odd-looking lantern, fitted with a pierced metal top and sliding metal sides.

"Is that a dark lantern?" I asked, fascinated.

"Aye, it is," said Young Ian, importantly. "Ye keep the slides shut until we see the signal out at sea." He reached for the lantern. "Here, give it me; I'll take it—I ken the signal."

Mr. Willoughby merely shook his head, pulling the lantern out of Young Ian's grasp. "Too tall, too young," he said. "Tsei-mi say so," he added, as though that settled the matter once and for all.

"What?" Young Ian was indignant. "What d'ye mean too tall and too young, ye wee—"

"He means," said a level voice behind us, "that whoever's holding the lantern is a bonny target, should we have visitors. Mr. Willoughby kindly takes the risk of it, because he's the smallest man among us. You're tall enough to see against the sky, wee Ian, and young enough to have nay sense yet. Stay out o' the way, aye?"

Jamie gave his nephew a light cuff over the ear, and passed by to kneel on the rocks by Mr. Willoughby. He said something low-voiced in Chinese, and there was the ghost of a laugh from the Chinaman. Mr. Willoughby opened the side of the lantern, holding it conveniently to Jamie's cupped hands. A sharp click, repeated twice, and I caught the flicker of sparks struck from a flint.

It was a wild piece of coast—not surprising, most of Scotland's coast was wild and rocky—and I wondered how and where the French ship would anchor. There was no natural bay, only a curving of the coastline behind a jutting cliff that sheltered this spot from observation from the road.

Dark as it was, I could see the white lines of the surf purling in across the small half-moon beach. No smooth tourist beach this—small pockets of sand lay ruffled and churned between heaps of seaweed and pebbles and juts of rock. Not an easy footing for men carrying casks, but convenient to the crevices in the surrounding rocks, where the casks could be hidden.

Another black figure loomed up suddenly beside me.

"Everyone's settled, sir," it said softly. "Up in the rocks."

"Good, Joey." A sudden flare lit Jamie's profile, intent on the newly caught wick. He held his breath as the flame steadied and grew, taking up oil from the lantern's reservoir, then let it out with a sigh as he gently closed the metal slide.

"Fine, then," he said, standing up. He glanced up at the cliff to the south, observing the stars over it, and said, "Nearly nine o'clock. They'll be in soon. Mind ye, Joey—no one's to move 'til I call out, aye?"

"Aye, sir." The casual tone of the answer made it apparent that this was a customary exchange, and Joey was plainly surprised when Jamie gripped his arm.

"Be sure of it," Jamie said. "Tell them all again—no one moves 'til I give the word."

"Aye, sir," Joey said again, but this time with more respect. He faded back into the night, making no sound on the rocks.

"Is something wrong?" I asked, pitching my voice barely loud enough to be heard over the breakers. Though the beach and cliffs were evidently deserted, the dark setting and the secretive conduct of my companions compelled caution.

Jamie shook his head briefly; he'd been right about Young Ian, I thought —his own dark silhouette was clear against the paler black of the sky behind him.

"I dinna ken." He hesitated for a moment, then said, "Tell me, Sassenach —d'ye smell anything?"

Surprised, I obligingly took a deep sniff, held it for a moment, and let it out. I smelled any number of things, including rotted seaweed, the thick smell of burning oil from the dark lantern, and the pungent body odor of Young Ian, standing close beside me, sweating with a mix of excitement and fear.

"Nothing odd, I don't think," I said. "Do you?"

The silhouette's shoulders rose and dropped in a shrug. "Not now. A moment ago, I could ha' sworn I smelt gunpowder."

"I dinna smell anything," Young Ian said. His voice broke from excitement, and he hastily cleared his throat, embarrassed. "Willie MacLeod and Alec Hays searched the rocks. They didna find any sign of excisemen."

"Aye, well." Jamie's voice sounded uneasy. He turned to Young Ian, grasping him by the shoulder.

"Ian, you're to take charge of your auntie, now. The two of ye get back of the gorse bushes there. Keep well away from the wagon. If anything should happen—"

The beginnings of Young Ian's protest were cut off, apparently by a tightening of Jamie's hand, for the boy jerked back with a small grunt, rubbing his shoulder.

"*If* anything should happen," Jamie continued, with emphasis, "you're to take your auntie and go straight home to Lallybroch. Dinna linger."

"But—" I said.

"Uncle!" Young Ian said.

"Do it," said Jamie, in tones of steel, and turned aside, the discussion concluded.

Young Ian was grim on the trip up the cliff trail, but did as he was told, dutifully escorting me some distance past the gorse bushes and finding a small promontory where we might see out some way over the water.

"We can see from here," he whispered unnecessarily.

We could indeed. The rocks fell away in a shallow bowl beneath us, a broken cup filled with darkness, the light of the water spilling from the broken edge where the sea hissed in. Once I caught a tiny movement, as a metal buckle caught the faint light, but for the most part, the ten men below were completely invisible.

I squinted, trying to pick out the location of Mr. Willoughby with his lantern, but saw no sign of light, and concluded that he must be standing behind the lantern, shielding it from sight from the cliff.

Young Ian stiffened suddenly next to me.

"Someone's coming!" he whispered. "Quick, get behind me!" Stepping courageously out in front of me, he plunged a hand under his shirt, into the band of his breeches, and withdrew a pistol; dark as it was, I could see the faint gleam of starlight along the barrel.

He braced himself, peering into the dark, slightly hunched over the gun with both hands clamped on the weapon.

"Don't shoot, for God's sake!" I hissed in his ear. I didn't dare grab his arm for fear of setting off the pistol, but was terrified lest he make any noise that might attract attention to the men below.

"I'd be obliged if ye'd heed your auntie, Ian," came Jamie's soft, ironic tones from the blackness below the cliff edge. "I'd as soon not have ye blow my head off, aye?"

Ian lowered the pistol, shoulders slumping with what might have been a sigh either of relief or disappointment. The gorse bushes quivered, and then Jamie was before us, brushing gorse prickles from the sleeve of his coat.

"Did no one tell ye not to come armed?" Jamie's voice was mild, with no more than a note of academic interest. "It's a hanging offense to draw a weapon against an officer of the King's Customs," he explained, turning to me. "None o' the men are armed, even wi' so much as a fish knife, in case they're taken."

"Aye, well, Fergus said they wouldna hang me, because my beard's not grown yet," Ian said awkwardly. "I'd only be transported, he said."

There was a soft hiss as Jamie drew in his breath through his teeth in exasperation.

"Oh, aye, and I'm sure your mother will be verra pleased to hear ye've been shipped off to the Colonies, even if Fergus was right!" He put out his hand. "Give me that, fool.

"Where did ye get it, anyway?" he asked, turning the pistol over in his hand. "Already primed, too. I knew I smelt gunpowder. Lucky ye didna blow your cock off, carrying it in your breeches."

Before Young Ian could answer, I interrupted, pointing out to sea. "Look!"

The French ship was little more than a blot on the face of the sea, but its sails shone pale in the glimmer of starlight. A two-masted ketch, it glided slowly past the cliff and stood off, silent as one of the scattered clouds behind it.

Jamie was not watching the ship, but looking downward, toward a point where the rock face broke in a tumble of boulders, just above the sand. Looking where he was looking, I could just make out a tiny prickle of light. Mr. Willoughby, with the lantern.

There was a brief flash of light that glistened across the wet rocks and was gone. Young Ian's hand was tense on my arm. We waited, breaths held, to the count of thirty. Ian's hand squeezed my arm, just as another flash lit the foam on the sand.

"What was that?" I said.

"What?" Jamie wasn't looking at me, but out at the ship.

"On the shore; when the light flashed, I thought I saw something half-buried in the sand. It looked like—"

The third flash came, and a moment later, an answering light shone from the ship—a blue lantern, an eerie dot that hung from the mast, doubling itself in reflection in the dark water below.

I forgot the glimpse of what appeared to be a rumpled heap of clothing, carelessly buried in the sand, in the excitement of watching the ship. Some movement was evident now, and a faint splash reached our ears as something was thrown over the side.

"The tide's coming in," Jamie muttered in my ear. "The ankers float; the current will carry them ashore in a few minutes."

That solved the problem of the ship's anchorage—it didn't need one. But how then was the payment made? I was about to ask when there was a sudden shout, and all hell broke loose below.

Jamie thrust his way at once through the gorse bushes, followed in short order by me and Young Ian. Little could be seen distinctly, but there was a considerable turmoil taking place on the sandy beach. Dark shapes were stumbling and rolling over the sand, to the accompaniment of shouting. I caught the words "Halt, in the King's name!" and my blood froze.

"Excisemen!" Young Ian had caught it, too.

Jamie said something crude in Gaelic, then threw back his head and shouted himself, his voice carrying easily across the beach below.

"Éirich 'illean!" he bellowed. *"Suas am bearrach is teich!"*

Then he turned to Young Ian and me. "Go!" he said.

The noise suddenly increased as the clatter of falling rocks joined the shouting. Suddenly a dark figure shot out of the gorse by my feet and made off through the dark at high speed. Another followed, a few feet away.

A high-pitched scream came from the dark below, high enough to be heard over the other noises.

"That's Willoughby!" Young Ian exclaimed. "They've got him!"

Ignoring Jamie's order to go, we both crowded forward to peer through the screen of gorse. The dark-lantern had fallen atilt and the slide had come open, shooting a beam of light like a spotlight over the beach, where the shallow graves in which the Customs men had buried themselves gaped in the sand. Black figures swayed and struggled and shouted through the wet heaps of seaweed. A dim glow of light around the lantern was sufficient to show two figures clasped together, the smaller kicking wildly as it was lifted off its feet.

"I'll get him!" Young Ian sprang forward, only to be pulled up with a jerk as Jamie caught him by the collar.

"Do as you're told and see my wife safe!"

Gasping for breath, Young Ian turned to me, but I wasn't going anywhere, and set my feet firmly in the dirt, resisting his tug on my arm.

Ignoring us both, Jamie turned and ran along the clifftop, stopping several yards away. I could see him clearly in silhouette against the sky, as he dropped to one knee and readied the pistol, bracing it on his forearm to sight downward.

The sound of the shot was no more than a small cracking noise, lost amid the tumult. The result of it, though, was spectacular. The lantern exploded in a shower of burning oil, abruptly darkening the beach and silencing the shouting.

The silence was broken within seconds by a howl of mingled pain and indignation. My eyes, momentarily blinded by the flash of the lantern, adapted quickly, and I saw another glow—the light of several small flames, which seemed to be moving erratically up and down. As my night vision cleared, I saw that the flames rose from the coat sleeve of a man, who was dancing up and down as he howled, beating ineffectually at the fire started by the burning oil that had splashed him.

The gorse bushes quivered violently as Jamie plunged over the cliffside and was lost to view below.

"Jamie!"

Roused by my cry, Young Ian yanked harder, pulling me half off my feet and forcibly dragging me away from the cliff.

"Come on, Auntie! They'll be up here, next thing!"

This was undeniably true; I could hear the shouts on the beach coming closer, as the men swarmed up the rocks. I picked up my skirts and went, following the boy as fast as we could go through the rough marrow-grass of the clifftop.

I didn't know where we were going, but Young Ian seemed to. He had taken off his coat and the white of his shirt was easily visible before me, floating like a ghost through the thickets of alder and birch that grew farther inland.

"Where are we?" I panted, coming up alongside him when he slowed at the bank of a tiny stream.

"The road to Arbroath's just ahead," he said. He was breathing heavily, and a dark smudge of mud showed down the side of his shirt. "It'll be easier going in a moment. Are ye all right, Auntie? Shall I carry ye across?"

I politely declined this gallant offer, privately noting that I undoubtedly weighed as much as he did. I took off my shoes and stockings, and splashed my way knee-deep across the streamlet, feeling icy mud well up between my toes.

I was shivering violently when I emerged, and did accept Ian's offer of his coat—excited as he was, and heated by the exercise, he was clearly in no need of it. I was chilled not only by the water and the cold November wind, but by fear of what might be happening behind us.

We emerged panting onto the road, the wind blowing cold in our faces. My nose and lips were numb in no time, and my hair blew loose behind me, heavy on my neck. It's an ill wind that blows nobody good, though; it carried the sound of voices to us, moments before we would have walked into them.

"Any signal from the cliff?" a deep male voice asked. Ian stopped so abruptly in his tracks that I bumped into him.

"Not yet," came the reply. "I thought I heard a bit of shouting that way, but then the wind turned."

"Well, get up that tree again then, heavy-arse," the first voice said impatiently. "If any o' the whoresons get past the beach, we'll nibble 'em here. Better us get the headmoney than the buggers on the beach."

"It's cold," grumbled the second voice. "Out in the open where the wind gnaws your bones. Wish we'd drawn the watch at the abbey—at least it would be warm there."

Young Ian's hand was clutching my upper arm tight enough to leave bruises. I pulled, trying to loosen his grip, but he paid no attention.

"Aye, but less chance o' catching the big fish," the first voice said. "Ah, and what I might do with fifty pound!"

"Awright," said the second voice, resigned. "Though how we're to see red hair in the dark, I've no notion."

"Just lay 'em by the heels, Oakie; we'll look at their heads later."

Young Ian was finally roused from his trance by my tugging, and stumbled after me off the road and into the bushes.

"What do they mean by the watch at the abbey?" I demanded, as soon as I thought we were out of earshot of the watchers on the road. "Do you know?"

Young Ian's dark thatch bobbed up and down. "I think so, Auntie. It must be Arbroath abbey. That's the meeting point, aye?"

"Meeting point?"

"If something should go wrong," he explained. "Then it's every man for himself, all to meet at the abbey as soon as they can."

"Well, it couldn't go more wrong," I observed. "What was it your uncle shouted when the Customs men popped up?"

Young Ian had half-turned to listen for pursuit from the road; now the pale oval of his face turned back to me. "Oh—he said, 'Up, lads! Over the cliff and run!'"

"Sound advice," I said dryly. "So if they followed it, most of the men may have gotten away."

"Except Uncle Jamie and Mr. Willoughby." Young Ian was running one hand nervously through his hair; it reminded me forcibly of Jamie, and I wished he would stop.

"Yes." I took a deep breath. "Well, there's nothing we can do about them just now. The other men, though—if they're headed for the abbey—"

"Aye," he broke in, "that's what I was tryin' to decide; ought I do as Uncle Jamie said, and take ye to Lallybroch, or had I best try to get to the abbey quick and warn the others as they come?"

"Get to the abbey," I said, "as fast as you can."

"Well, but—I shouldna like to leave ye out here by yourself, Auntie, and Uncle Jamie said—"

"There's a time to follow orders, Young Ian, and a time to think for yourself," I said firmly, tactfully ignoring the fact that I was in fact doing the thinking for him. "Does this road lead to the abbey?"

"Aye, it does. No more than a mile and a quarter." Already he was shifting to and fro on the balls of his feet, eager to be gone.

"Good. You cut round the road and head for the abbey. I'll walk straight along the road, and see if I can distract the excisemen until you're safely past. I'll meet you at the abbey. Oh, wait—you'd best take your coat."

I surrendered the coat reluctantly; besides being loath to part with its warmth, it felt like giving up my last link with a friendly human presence. Once Young Ian was away, I would be completely alone in the cold dark of the Scottish night.

"Ian?" I held his arm, to keep him a moment longer.

"Aye?"

"Be careful, won't you?" On impulse, I stood on tiptoe and kissed his cold cheek. I was near enough to see his brows arch in surprise. He smiled, and then he was gone, an alder branch snapping back into place behind him.

It was very cold. The only sounds were the *whish* of the wind through the bushes and the distant murmur of the surf. I pulled the woolen shawl tightly round my shoulders, shivering, and headed back toward the road.

Ought I to make a noise? I wondered. If not, I might be attacked without warning, since the waiting men might hear my footsteps but couldn't see that I wasn't an escaping smuggler. On the other hand, if I strolled through singing a jaunty tune to indicate that I was a harmless woman, they might just lie hidden in silence, not wanting to give away their presence—and giving away their presence was exactly what I had in mind. I bent and picked up a rock from the side of the road. Then, feeling even colder than before, I stepped out onto the road and walked straight on, without a word.

31

Smugglers' Moon

The wind was high enough to keep the trees and bushes in a constant stir, masking the sound of my footsteps on the road—and those of anyone who might be stalking me, too. Less than a fortnight past the feast of Samhain, it was the sort of wild night that made one easily believe that spirits and evil might well be abroad.

It wasn't a spirit that grabbed me suddenly from behind, hand clamped tight across my mouth. Had I not been prepared for just such an eventuality, I would have been startled senseless. As it was, my heart gave a great leap and I jerked convulsively in my captor's grasp.

He had grabbed me from the left, pinning my left arm tight against my side, his right hand over my mouth. *My* right arm was free, though. I drove the heel of my shoe into his kneecap, buckling his leg, and then, taking advantage of his momentary stagger, leaned forward and smashed backward at his head with the rock in my hand.

It was of necessity a glancing blow, but it struck hard enough that he grunted with surprise, and his grip loosened. I kicked and squirmed, and as his hand slipped across my mouth, I got my teeth onto a finger and bit down as hard as I could.

"The maxillary muscles run from the sagittal crest at the top of the skull to an insertion on the mandible," I thought, dimly recalling the description from *Grey's Anatomy*. "This gives the jaw and teeth considerable crushing power; in fact, the average human jaw is capable of exerting over three hundred pounds of force."

I didn't know whether I was bettering the average, but I was undeniably having an effect. My assailant was thrashing frantically to and fro in a futile effort to dislodge the death grip I had on his finger.

His hold on my arm had loosened in the struggle, and he was forced to lower me. As soon as my feet touched the dirt once more, I let go of his hand, whirled about, and gave him as hearty a root in the stones with my knee as I could manage, given my skirts.

Kicking men in the testicles is vastly overrated as a means of defense. That is to say, it does work—and spectacularly well—but it's a more difficult maneuver to carry out than one might think, particularly when one is wearing heavy skirts. Men are extremely careful of those particular appendages, and thoroughly wary of any attempt on them.

In this case, though, my attacker was off guard, his legs wide apart to keep his balance, and I caught him fairly. He made a hideous wheezing noise like a strangled rabbit and doubled up in the roadway.

"Is that you, Sassenach?" The words were hissed out of the darkness to my left. I leaped like a startled gazelle, and uttered an involuntary scream.

For the second time within as many minutes, a hand clapped itself over my mouth.

"For God's sake, Sassenach!" Jamie muttered in my ear. "It's me."

I didn't bite him, though I was strongly tempted to.

"I know," I said, through my teeth, when he released me. "Who's the other fellow that grabbed me, though?"

"Fergus, I expect." The amorphous dark shape moved away a few feet and seemed to be prodding another shape that lay on the road, moaning faintly. "Is it you, Fergus?" he whispered. Receiving a sort of choked noise in response, he bent and hauled the second shape to its feet.

"Don't talk!" I urged them in a whisper. "There are excisemen just ahead!"

"Is that so?" said Jamie, in a normal voice. "They're no verra curious about the noise we're making, are they?"

He paused, as though waiting for an answer, but no sound came but the low keening of the wind through the alders. He laid a hand on my arm and shouted into the night.

"MacLeod! Raeburn!"

"Aye, Roy," said a mildly testy voice in the shrubbery. "We're here. Innes, too, and Meldrum, is it?"

"Aye, it's me."

Shuffling and talking in low voices, more shapes emerged from the bushes and trees.

". . . four, five, six," Jamie counted. "Where are Hays and the Gordons?"

"I saw Hays go intae the water," one of the shapes volunteered. "He'll ha' gone awa' round the point. Likely the Gordons and Kennedy did, too. I didna hear anything as though they'd been taken."

"Well enough," Jamie said. "Now, then, Sassenach. What's this about excisemen?"

Given the nonappearance of Oakie and his companion, I was beginning to feel rather foolish, but I recounted what Ian and I had heard.

"Aye?" Jamie sounded interested. "Can ye stand yet, Fergus? Ye can? Good lad. Well, then, perhaps we'll have a look. Meldrum, have ye a flint about ye?"

A few moments later, a small torch struggling to stay alight in his hand, he strode down the road, and around the bend. The smugglers and I waited in tense silence, ready either to run or to rush to his assistance, but there were no noises of ambush. After what seemed like an eternity, Jamie's voice floated back along the road.

"Come along, then," he said, sounding calm and collected.

He was standing in the middle of the road, near a large alder. The torch-light fell round him in a flickering circle, and at first I saw nothing but Jamie. Then there was a gasp from the man beside me, and a choked sound of horror from another.

Another face appeared, dimly lit, hanging in the air just behind Jamie's left shoulder. A horrible, congested face, black in the torchlight that robbed everything of color, with bulging eyes and tongue protruding. The hair, fair as dry straw, rose stirring in the wind. I felt a fresh scream rise in my throat, and choked it off.

"Ye were right, Sassenach," Jamie said. "There *was* an exciseman." He tossed something to the ground, where it landed with a small plop! "A warrant," he said, nodding toward the object. "His name was Thomas Oakie. Will any of ye ken him?"

"Not like he is now," a voice muttered behind me. "Christ, his mither wouldna ken him!" There was a general mutter of negation, with a nervous shuffling of feet. Clearly, everyone was as anxious to get away from the place as I was.

"All right, then." Jamie stopped the retreat with a jerk of his head. "The cargo's lost, so there'll be no shares, aye? Will anyone need money for the present?" He reached for his pocket. "I can provide enough to live on for a bit—for I doubt we'll be workin' the coast for a time."

One or two of the men reluctantly advanced within clear sight of the thing hanging from the tree to receive their money, but the rest of the smugglers melted quietly away into the night. Within a few minutes, only Fergus—still white, but standing on his own—Jamie, and I were left.

"*Jesu!*" Fergus whispered, looking up at the hanged man. "Who will have done it?"

"I did—or so I expect the tale will be told, aye?" Jamie gazed upward, his face harsh in the sputtering torchlight. "We'll no tarry longer, shall we?"

"What about Ian?" I said, suddenly remembering the boy. "He went to the abbey, to warn you!"

"He did?" Jamie's voice sharpened. "I came from that direction, and didna meet him. Which way did he go, Sassenach?"

"That way," I said, pointing.

Fergus made a small sound that might have been laughter.

"The abbey's the other way," Jamie said, sounding amused. "Come on, then; we'll catch him up when he realizes his mistake and comes back."

"Wait," said Fergus, holding up a hand. There was a cautious rustling in the shrubbery, and Young Ian's voice said, "Uncle Jamie?"

"Aye, Ian," his uncle said dryly. "It's me."

The boy emerged from the bushes, leaves stuck in his hair, eyes wide with excitement.

"I saw the light, and thought I must come back to see that Auntie Claire was all right," he explained. "Uncle Jamie, ye mustna linger about wi' a torch—there are excisemen about!"

Jamie put an arm about his nephew's shoulders and turned him, before he should notice the thing hanging from the alder tree.

"Dinna trouble yourself, Ian," he said evenly. "They've gone."

Swinging the torch through the wet shrubbery, he extinguished it with a hiss.

"Let's go," he said, his voice calm in the dark. "Mr. Willoughby's down the road wi' the horses; we'll be in the Highlands by dawn."

PART SEVEN

Home Again

32

The Prodigal's Return

It was a four-day journey on horseback to Lallybroch from Arbroath, and there was little conversation for most of it. Both Young Ian and Jamie were preoccupied, presumably for different reasons. For myself, I was kept busy wondering, not only about the recent past, but about the immediate future.

Ian must have told Jamie's sister, Jenny, about me. How would she take my reappearance?

Jenny Murray had been the nearest thing I had ever had to a sister, and by far the closest woman friend of my life. Owing to circumstance, most of my close friends in the last fifteen years had been men; there were no other female doctors, and the natural gulf between nursing staff and medical staff prevented more than casual acquaintance with other women working at the hospital. As for the women in Frank's circle, the departmental secretaries and university wives . . .

More than any of that, though, was the knowledge that of all the people in the world, Jenny was the one who might love Jamie Fraser as much—if not more—than I did. I was eager to see Jenny again, but could not help wondering how she would take the story of my supposed escape to France, and my apparent desertion of her brother.

The horses had to follow each other in single file down the narrow track. My own bay slowed obligingly as Jamie's chestnut paused, then turned aside at his urging into a clearing, half-hidden by an overhang of alder branches.

A gray stone cliff rose up at the edge of the clearing, its cracks and bumps and ridges so furred with moss and lichen that it looked like the face of an ancient man, all spotted with whiskers and freckled with warts. Young Ian slid down from his pony with a sigh of relief; we had been in the saddle since dawn.

"Oof!" he said, frankly rubbing his backside. "I've gone all numb."

"So have I," I said, doing the same. "I suppose it's better than being saddlesore, though." Unaccustomed to riding for long stretches, both Young Ian and I had suffered considerably during the first two days of the journey; in fact, too stiff to dismount by myself the first night, I had had to be ignominiously hoisted off my horse and carried into the inn by Jamie, much to his amusement.

"How does Uncle Jamie do it?" Ian asked me. "His arse must be made of leather."

"Not to look at," I replied absently. "Where's he gone, though?" The chestnut, already hobbled, was nibbling at the grass under an oak to one side of the clearing, but of Jamie himself, there was no sign.

Young Ian and I looked blankly at each other; I shrugged, and went over to the cliff face, where a trickle of water ran down the rock. I cupped my hands beneath it and drank, grateful for the cold liquid sliding down my dry throat, in spite of the autumn air that reddened my cheeks and numbed my nose.

This tiny glen clearing, invisible from the road, was characteristic of most of the Highland scenery, I thought. Deceptively barren and severe, the crags and moors were full of secrets. If you didn't know where you were going, you could walk within inches of a deer, a grouse, or a hiding man, and never know it. Small wonder that many of those who had taken to the heather after Culloden had managed to escape, their knowledge of the hidden places making them invisible to the blind eyes and clumsy feet of the pursuing English.

Thirst slaked, I turned from the cliff face and nearly ran into Jamie, who had appeared as though sprung out of the earth by magic. He was putting his tinderbox back into the pocket of his coat, and the faint smell of smoke clung to his coat. He dropped a small burnt stick to the grass and ground it to dust with his foot.

"Where did you come from?" I said, blinking at this apparition. "And where have you been?"

"There's a wee cave just there," he explained, jerking a thumb behind him. "I only wanted to see whether anyone's been in it."

"Have they?" Looking closely, I could see the edge of the outcrop that concealed the cave's entrance. Blending as it did with the other deep cracks in the rock face, it wouldn't be visible unless you were deliberately looking for it.

"Aye, they have," he said. His brows were slightly furrowed, not in worry, but as though he were thinking about something. "There's charcoal mixed wi' the earth; someone's had a fire there."

"Who do you think it was?" I asked. I stuck my head around the outcrop, but saw nothing but a narrow bar of darkness, a small rift in the face of the mountain. It looked thoroughly uninviting.

I wondered whether any of his smuggling connections might have traced him all the way from the coast to Lallybroch. Was he worried about pursuit, or an ambush? Despite myself, I looked over my shoulder, but saw nothing but the alders, dry leaves rustling in the autumn breeze.

"I dinna ken," he said absently. "A hunter, I suppose; there are grouse bones scattered about, too."

Jamie didn't seem perturbed by the unknown person's possible identity, and I relaxed, the feeling of security engendered by the Highlands wrapping itself about me once more. Both Edinburgh and the smugglers' cove seemed a long way away.

Young Ian, fascinated by the revelation of the invisible cave, had disappeared through the crevice. Now he reappeared, brushing a cobweb out of his hair.

"Is this like Cluny's Cage, Uncle?" he asked, eyes bright.

"None so big, Ian," Jamie answered with a smile. "Poor Cluny would scarce fit through the entrance o' this one; he was a stout big fellow, forbye, near twice my girth." He touched his chest ruefully, where a button had been torn loose by squeezing through the narrow entrance.

"What's Cluny's Cage?" I asked, shaking the last drops of icy water from my hands and thrusting them under my armpits to thaw out.

"Oh—that's Cluny MacPherson," Jamie replied. He bent his head, and splashed the chilly water up into his face. Lifting his head, he blinked the sparkling drops from his lashes and smiled at me. "A verra ingenious man, Cluny. The English burnt his house, and pulled down the foundation, but Cluny himself escaped. He built himself a wee snuggery in a nearby cavern, and sealed over the entrance wi' willow branches all woven together and chinked wi' mud. Folk said ye could stand three feet away, and no notion that the cave was there, save the smell of the smoke from Cluny's pipe."

"Prince Charles stayed there too, for a bit, when he was hunted by the English," Young Ian informed me. "Cluny hid him for days. The English bastards hunted high and low, but never found His Highness—or Cluny, either!" he concluded, with considerable satisfaction.

"Come here and wash yourself, Ian," Jamie said, with a hint of sharpness that made Young Ian blink. "Ye canna face your parents covered wi' filth."

Ian sighed, but obediently bent his head over the trickle of water, sputtering and gasping as he splashed his face, which while not strictly speaking filthy, undeniably bore one or two small stains of travel.

I turned to Jamie, who stood watching his nephew's ablutions with an air of abstraction. Did he look ahead, I wondered, to what promised to be an awkward meeting at Lallybroch, or back to Edinburgh, with the smoldering remains of his printshop and the dead man in the basement of the brothel? Or back further still, to Charles Edward Stuart, and the days of the Rising?

"What do you tell your nieces and nephews about him?" I asked quietly, under the noise of Ian's snorting. "About Charles?"

Jamie's gaze sharpened and focused on me; I had been right, then. His eyes warmed slightly, and the hint of a smile acknowledged the success of my mind-reading, but then both warmth and smile disappeared.

"I never speak of him," he said, just as quietly, and turned away to catch the horses.

Three hours later, we came through the last of the windswept passes, and out onto the final slope that led down to Lallybroch. Jamie, in the lead, drew up his horse and waited for me and Young Ian to come up beside him.

"There it is," he said. He glanced at me, smiling, one eyebrow raised. "Much changed, is it?"

I shook my head, rapt. From this distance, the house seemed completely unchanged. Built of white harled stone, its three stories gleamed immaculately amid its cluster of shabby outbuildings and the spread of stone-dyked brown fields. On the small rise behind the house stood the remains of the ancient broch, the circular stone tower that gave the place its name.

On closer inspection, I could see that the outbuildings had changed a bit; Jamie had told me that the English soldiery had burned the dovecote and the chapel the year after Culloden, and I could see the gaps where they had been. A space where the wall of the kailyard had been broken through had been repaired with stone of a different color, and a new shed built of stone and scrap lumber was evidently serving as a dovecote, judging from the row of plump feathered bodies lined up on the rooftree, enjoying the late autumn sun.

The rose brier planted by Jamie's mother, Ellen, had grown up into a great, sprawling tangle latticed to the wall of the house, only now losing the last of its leaves.

A plume of smoke rose from the western chimney, carrying away toward the south on a wind from the sea. I had a sudden vision of the fire in the hearth of the sitting room, its light rosy on Jenny's clear-cut face in the evening as she sat in her chair, reading aloud from a novel or book of poems while Jamie and Ian sat absorbed in a game of chess, listening with half an ear. How many evenings had we spent that way, the children upstairs in their beds, and me sitting at the rosewood secretary, writing down receipts for medicines or doing some of the interminable domestic mending?

"Will we live here again, do you think?" I asked Jamie, careful to keep any trace of longing from my voice. More than any other place, the house at Lallybroch had been home to me, but that had been a long time ago—and any number of things had changed since then.

He paused for a long minute, considering. Finally he shook his head, gathering up the reins in his hand. "I canna say, Sassenach," he said. "It would be pleasant, but—I dinna ken how things may be, aye?" There was a small frown on his face, as he looked down at the house.

"It's all right. If we live in Edinburgh—or even in France—it's all right, Jamie." I looked up into his face and touched his hand in reassurance. "As long as we're together."

The faint look of worry lifted momentarily, lightening his features. He took my hand, raised it to his lips, and kissed it gently.

"I dinna mind much else myself, Sassenach, so long as ye'll stay by me."

We sat gazing into each other's eyes, until a loud, self-conscious cough from behind alerted us to Young Ian's presence. Scrupulously careful of our privacy, he had been embarrassingly circumspect on the trip from Edinburgh, crashing off through the heather to a great distance when we camped, and taking remarkable pains so as not inadvertently to surprise us in an indiscreet embrace.

Jamie grinned and squeezed my hand before letting it go and turning to his nephew.

"Almost there, Ian," he said, as the boy negotiated his pony up beside us. "We'll be there well before supper if it doesna rain," he added, squinting under his hand to gauge the possibilities of the clouds drifting slowly over the Monadhliath Mountains.

"Mmphm." Young Ian didn't sound thrilled at the prospect, and I glanced at him sympathetically.

" 'Home is the place where, when you have to go there, they have to take you in,' " I quoted.

Young Ian gave me a wry look. "Aye, that's what I'm afraid of, Auntie."

Jamie, hearing this exchange, glanced back at Young Ian, and blinked solemnly—his own version of an encouraging wink.

"Dinna be downhearted, Ian. Remember the story o' the Prodigal Son, aye? Your Mam will be glad to see ye safe back."

Young Ian cast him a glance of profound disillusion.

"If ye expect it's the fatted calf that's like to be kilt, Uncle Jamie, ye dinna ken my mother so well as ye think."

The lad sat gnawing his lower lip for a moment, then drew himself up in the saddle with a deep breath.

"Best get it over, aye?" he said.

"Will his parents really be hard on him?" I asked, watching Young Ian pick his way carefully down the rocky slope.

Jamie shrugged.

"Well, they'll forgive him, of course, but he's like to get a rare ballocking and his backside tanned before that. I'll be lucky to get off wi' the same," he added wryly. "Jenny and Ian are no going to be verra pleased wi' me, either, I'm afraid." He kicked up his mount, and started down the slope.

"Come along, Sassenach. Best get it over, aye?"

———◆———

I wasn't sure what to expect in terms of a reception at Lallybroch, but in the event, it was reassuring. As on all previous arrivals, our presence was heralded by the barking of a miscellaneous swarm of dogs, who galloped out of hedge and field and kailyard, yapping first with alarm, and then with joy.

Young Ian dropped his reins and slid down into the furry sea of welcome, dropping into a crouch to greet the dogs who leapt on him and licked his face. He stood up smiling with a half-grown puppy in his arms, which he brought over to show me.

"This is Jocky," he said, holding up the squirming brown and white body. "He's mine; Da gave him to me."

"Nice doggie," I told Jocky, scratching his floppy ears. The dog barked and squirmed ecstatically, trying to lick me and Ian simultaneously.

"You're getting covered wi' dog hairs, Ian," said a clear, high voice, in tones of marked disapproval. Looking up from the dog, I saw a tall, slim girl of seventeen or so, rising from her seat by the side of the road.

"Well, you're covered wi' foxtails, so there!" Young Ian retorted, swinging about to address the speaker.

The girl tossed a headful of dark brown curls and bent to brush at her skirt, which did indeed sport a number of the bushy grass-heads, stuck to the homespun fabric.

"Da says ye dinna deserve to have a dog," she remarked. "Running off and leaving him like ye did."

Young Ian's face tightened defensively. "I did think o' taking him," he said, voice cracking slightly. "But I didna think he'd be safe in the city." He hugged the dog tighter, chin resting between the furry ears. "He's grown a bit; I suppose he's been eating all right?"

"Come to greet us, have ye, wee Janet? That's kind." Jamie's voice spoke pleasantly from behind me, but with a cynical note that made the girl glance up sharply and blush at the sight of him.

"Uncle Jamie! Oh, and . . ." Her gaze shifted to me, and she ducked her head, blushing more furiously.

"Aye, this is your auntie Claire." Jamie's hand was firm under my elbow as he nodded toward the girl. "Wee Janet wasna born yet, last ye were here, Sassenach. Your mother will be to home, I expect?" he said, addressing Janet.

The girl nodded, wide-eyed, not taking her fascinated gaze from my face. I leaned down from my horse and extended a hand, smiling.

"I'm pleased to meet you," I said.

She stared for a long moment, then suddenly remembered her manners, and dropped into a curtsy. She rose and took my hand gingerly, as though afraid it might come off in her grasp. I squeezed hers, and she looked faintly reassured at finding me merely flesh and blood.

"I'm . . . pleased, mum," she murmured.

"Are Mam and Da verra angry, Jen?" Young Ian gently put the puppy on the ground near her feet, breaking her trance. She glanced at her younger brother, her expression of impatience tinged with some sympathy.

"Well, and why wouldn't they be, clot-heid?" she said. "Mam thought ye'd maybe met a boar in the wood, or been taken by gypsies. She scarcely slept until they found out where ye'd gone," she added, frowning at her brother.

Ian pressed his lips tight together, looking down at the ground, but didn't answer.

She moved closer, and picked disapprovingly at the damp yellow leaves adhering to the sleeves of his coat. Tall as she was, he topped her by a good six inches, gangly and rawboned next to her trim competence, the resemblance between them limited to the rich darkness of their hair and a fugitive similarity of expression.

"You're a sight, Ian. Have ye been sleepin' in your clothes?"

"Well, of course I have," he said impatiently. "What d'ye think, I ran away wi' a nightshirt and changed into it every night on the moor?"

She gave a brief snort of laughter at this picture, and his expression of annoyance faded a bit.

"Oh, come on, then, gowk," she said, taking pity on him. "Come into the scullery wi' me, and we'll get ye brushed and combed before Mam and Da see ye."

He glared at her, then turned to look up at me, with an expression of mingled bewilderment and annoyance. "Why in the name o' heaven," he demanded, his voice cracking with strain, "does everyone think bein' *clean* will help?"

Jamie grinned at him, and dismounting, clapped him on the shoulder, raising a small cloud of dust.

"It canna hurt anything, Ian. Go along wi' ye; I think perhaps it's as well if your parents havena got so many things to deal with all at once—and they'll be wanting to see your auntie first of all."

"Mmphm." With a morose nod of assent, Young Ian moved reluctantly off toward the back of the house, towed by his determined sister.

"What have ye been eating?" I heard her say, squinting up at him as they went. "You've a great smudge of filth all round your mouth."

"It isna filth, it's whiskers!" he hissed furiously under his breath, with a quick backward glance to see whether Jamie and I had heard this exchange. His sister stopped dead, peering up at him.

"Whiskers?" she said loudly and incredulously. *"You?"*

"Come on!" Grabbing her by the elbow, he hustled her off through the kailyard gate, his shoulders hunched in self-consciousness.

Jamie lowered his head against my thigh, face buried in my skirts. To the casual observer, he might have been occupied in loosening the saddlebags, but the casual observer couldn't have seen his shoulders shaking or felt the vibration of his soundless laughter.

"It's all right, they're gone," I said, a moment later, gasping for breath myself from the strain of silent mirth.

Jamie raised his face, red and breathless, from my skirts, and used a fold of the cloth to dab his eyes.

"Whiskers? *You?*" he croaked in imitation of his niece, setting us both off again. He shook his head, gulping for air. "Christ, she's like her mother! That's just what Jenny said to me, in just that voice, when she caught me shavin' for the first time. I nearly cut my throat." He wiped his eyes again on the back of his hand, and rubbed a palm tenderly across the thick, soft stubble that coated his own jaws and throat with an auburn haze.

"Do you want to go and shave yourself before we meet Jenny and Ian?" I asked, but he shook his head.

"No," he said, smoothing back the hair that had escaped from its lacing. "Young Ian's right; bein' clean won't help."

They must have heard the dogs outside; both Ian and Jenny were in the sitting room when we came in, she on the sofa knitting woolen stockings, while he stood before the fire in plain brown coat and breeks, warming the backs of his legs. A tray of small cakes with a bottle of home-brewed ale was set out, plainly in readiness for our arrival.

It was a very cozy, welcoming scene, and I felt the tiredness of the journey drop away as we entered the room. Ian turned at once as we came in, self-conscious but smiling, but it was Jenny that I looked for.

She was looking for me, too. She sat still on the couch, her eyes wide, turned to the door. My first impression was that she was quite different, the second, that she had not changed at all. The black curls were still there, thick and lively, but blanched and streaked with a deep, rich silver. The bones, too, were the same—the broad, high cheekbones, strong jaw, and long nose that she shared with Jamie. It was the flickering firelight and the shadows of the gathering afternoon that gave the strange impression of change, one moment deepening the lines beside her eyes and mouth 'til she looked like a crone; the next erasing them with the ruddy glow of girlhood, like a 3-D picture in a box of Cracker Jack.

On our first meeting in the brothel, Ian had acted as if I were a ghost. Jenny did much the same now, blinking slightly, her mouth slightly open, but not otherwise changing expression as I crossed the room toward her.

Jamie was just behind me, his hand at my elbow. He squeezed it lightly as we reached the sofa, then let go. I felt rather as though I were being presented at Court, and resisted the impulse to curtsy.

"We're home, Jenny," he said. His hand rested reassuringly on my back.

She glanced quickly at her brother, then stared at me again.

"It's you, then, Claire?" Her voice was soft and tentative, familiar, but not the strong voice of the woman I remembered.

"Yes, it's me," I said. I smiled and reached out my hands to her. "It's good to see you, Jenny."

She took my hands, lightly. Then her grip strengthened and she rose to her feet. "Christ, it *is* you!" she said, a little breathless, and suddenly the woman I had known was back, dark blue eyes alive and dancing, searching my face with curiosity.

"Well, of course it is," Jamie said gruffly. "Surely Ian told ye; did ye think he was lying?"

"You'll scarce have changed," she said, ignoring her brother as she touched my face wonderingly. "Your hair's a bit lighter, but my God, ye look the same!" Her fingers were cool; her hands smelled of herbs and red-currant jam, and the faint hint of ammonia and lanolin from the dyed wool she was knitting.

The long-forgotten smell of the wool brought everything back at once—so many memories of the place, and the happiness of the time I had lived here—and my eyes blurred with tears.

She saw it, and hugged me hard, her hair smooth and soft against my face. She was much shorter than I, fine-boned and delicate to look at, but still I had the feeling of being enveloped, warmly supported and strongly held, as though by someone larger than myself.

She released me after a moment, and stood back, half-laughing. "God, ye even smell the same!" she exclaimed, and I burst out laughing, too.

Ian had come up; he leaned down and embraced me gently, brushing his lips against my cheek. He smelled faintly of dried hay and cabbage leaves, with the ghost of peat smoke laid over his own deep, musky scent.

"It's good to see ye back again, Claire," he said. His soft brown eyes smiled at me, and the sense of homecoming deepened. He stood back a little awkwardly, smiling. "Will ye eat something, maybe?" He gestured toward the tray on the table.

I hesitated a moment, but Jamie moved toward it with alacrity.

"A drop wouldna come amiss, Ian, thank ye kindly," he said. "You'll have some, Claire?"

Glasses were filled, the biscuits passed, and small spoken pleasantries murmured through mouthfuls as we sat down around the fire. Despite the outward cordiality, I was strongly aware of an underlying tension, not all of it to do with my sudden reappearance.

Jamie, seated beside me on the oak settle, took no more than a sip of his ale, and the oatcake sat untasted on his knee. I knew he hadn't accepted the refreshments out of hunger, but in order to mask the fact that neither his sister nor his brother-in-law had offered him a welcoming embrace.

I caught a quick glance passing between Ian and Jenny; and a longer stare, unreadable, exchanged between Jenny and Jamie. A stranger here in more ways than one, I kept my own eyes cast down, observing under the shelter of my lashes. Jamie sat to my left; I could feel the tiny movement between us as the two stiff fingers of his right hand drummed their small tattoo against his thigh.

The conversation, what there was of it, petered out, and the room fell into an uncomfortable silence. Through the faint hissing of the peat fire, I could hear a few distant thumps in the direction of the kitchen, but nothing like the sounds I remembered in this house, of constant activity and bustling movement, feet always pounding on the stair, and the shouts of children and squalling of babies splitting the air in the nursery overhead.

"How are all of your children?" I asked Jenny, to break the silence. She started, and I realized that I had inadvertently asked the wrong question.

"Oh, they're well enough," she replied hesitantly. "All verra bonny. And the grandchildren, too," she added, breaking into a sudden smile at the thought of them.

"They've mostly gone to Young Jamie's house," Ian put in, answering my real question. "His wife's had a new babe just the week past, so the three girls have gone to help a bit. And Michael's up in Inverness just now, to fetch down some things come in from France."

Another glance flicked across the room, this one between Ian and Jamie. I felt the small tilt of Jamie's head, and saw Ian's not-quite-nod in response. And what in hell was *that* about? I wondered. There were so many invisible cross-currents of emotion in the room that I had a sudden impulse to stand up and call the meeting to order, just to break the tension.

Apparently Jamie felt the same. He cleared his throat, looking directly at Ian, and addressed the main point on the agenda, saying, "We've brought the lad home with us."

Ian took a deep breath, his long, homely face hardening slightly. "Have ye, then?" The thin layer of pleasantry spread over the occasion vanished suddenly, like morning dew.

I could feel Jamie beside me, tensing slightly as he prepared to defend his nephew as best he might.

"He's a good lad, Ian," he said.

"Is he, so?" It was Jenny who answered, her fine black brows drawn down in a frown. "Ye couldna tell, the way he acts at home. But perhaps he's different wi' you, Jamie." There was a strong note of accusation in her words, and I felt Jamie tense at my side.

"It's kind of ye to speak up for the lad, Jamie," Ian put in, with a cool nod in his brother-in-law's direction. "But I think we'd best hear from Young Ian himself, if ye please. Will he be upstairs?"

A muscle near Jamie's mouth twitched, but he answered noncommittally.

"In the scullery, I expect; he wanted to tidy himself a bit before seein' ye." His right hand slid down and pressed against my leg in warning. He hadn't mentioned meeting Janet, and I understood; she had been sent away with her siblings, so that Jenny and Ian could deal with the matters of my appearance and their prodigal son in some privacy, but had crept back unbeknownst to her parents, wanting either to catch a glimpse of her notorious aunt Claire, or to offer succor to her brother.

I lowered my eyelids, indicating that I understood. No point in mentioning the girl's presence, in a situation already so fraught with tension.

The sound of feet and the regular thump of Ian's wooden leg sounded in the uncarpeted passage. Ian had left the room in the direction of the scullery; now he returned, grimly ushering Young Ian before him.

The prodigal was as presentable as soap, water, and razor could make him. His bony jaws were reddened with scraping and the hair on his neck was clotted in wet spikes, most of the dust beaten from his coat, and the round neck of his shirt neatly buttoned to the collarbone. There was little to be done about the singed half of his head, but the other side was neatly combed. He had no stock, and there was a large rip in the leg of his breeks, but all things considered, he looked as well as someone could who expects momentarily to be shot.

"Mam," he said, ducking his head awkwardly in his mother's direction.

"Ian," she said softly, and he looked up at her, clearly startled at the gentleness of her tone. A slight smile curved her lips as she saw his face. "I'm glad you're safe home, *mo chridhe*," she said.

The boy's face cleared abruptly, as though he had just heard the reprieve read to the firing squad. Then he caught a glimpse of his father's face, and stiffened. He swallowed hard, and bent his head again, staring hard at the floorboards.

"Mmphm," Ian said. He sounded sternly Scotch; much more like the Reverend Campbell than the easygoing man I had known before. "Now then, I want to hear what ye've got to say for yourself, laddie."

"Oh. Well . . . I . . ." Young Ian trailed off miserably, then cleared his throat and had another try. "Well . . . nothing, really, Father," he murmured.

"Look at me!" Ian said sharply. His son reluctantly raised his head and looked at his father, but his gaze kept flicking away, as though afraid to rest very long on the stern countenance before him.

"D'ye ken what ye did to your mother?" Ian demanded. "Disappeared and left her thinkin' ye dead or hurt? Gone off without a word, and not a smell of ye for three days, until Joe Fraser brought down the letter ye left? Can ye even think what those three days were like for her?"

Either Ian's expression or his words seemed to have a strong effect on his errant offspring; Young Ian bowed his head again, eyes fixed on the floor.

"Aye, well, I thought Joe would bring the letter sooner," he muttered.

"Aye, that letter!" Ian's face was growing more flushed as he talked. " 'Gone to Edinburgh,' it said, cool as dammit." He slapped a hand flat on the table, with a smack that made everyone jump. "Gone to Edinburgh! Not a 'by your leave,' not an 'I'll send word,' not a thing but 'Dear Mother, I have gone to Edinburgh. Ian'!"

Young Ian's head snapped up, eyes bright with anger.

"That's not true! I said 'Don't worry for me,' and I said *Love,* Ian'! I did! Did I no, Mother?" For the first time, he looked at Jenny, appealing.

She had been still as a stone since her husband began to talk, her face smooth and blank. Now her eyes softened, and the hint of a curve touched her wide, full mouth again.

"Ye did, Ian," she said softly. "It was kind to say—but I did worry, aye?"

His eyes fell, and I could see the oversized Adam's apple bobble in his lean throat as he swallowed.

"I'm sorry, Mam," he said, so low I could scarcely hear him. "I—I didna mean . . ." his words trailed off, ending in a small shrug.

Jenny made an impulsive movement, as though to extend a hand to him, but Ian caught her eye, and she let the hand fall to her lap.

"The thing is," Ian said, speaking slowly and precisely, "it's no the first time, is it, Ian?"

The boy didn't answer, but made a small twitching movement that might have been assent. Ian took a step closer to his son. Close as they were in height, the differences between them were obvious. Ian was tall and lanky, but firmly muscled for all that, and a powerful man, wooden leg or no. By comparison, his son seemed almost frail, fledgling-boned and gawky.

"No, it's not as though ye had no idea what ye were doing; not like we'd never told ye the dangers, not like we'd no forbidden ye to go past Broch Mordha—not like ye didna ken we'd worry, aye? Ye kent all that—and ye did it anyway."

This merciless analysis of his behavior caused a sort of indefinite quiver, like an internal squirm, to go through Young Ian, but he kept up a stubborn silence.

"Look at me, laddie, when I'm speakin' to ye!" The boy's head rose slowly. He looked sullen now, but resigned; evidently he had been through scenes like this before, and knew where they were heading.

"I'm not even going to ask your uncle what ye've been doing," Ian said. "I can only hope ye weren't such a fool in Edinburgh as ye've been here. But ye've disobeyed me outright, and broken your mother's heart, whatever else ye've done."

Jenny moved again, as though to speak, but a brusque movement of Ian's hand stopped her.

"And what did I tell ye the last time, wee Ian? What did I say when I gave ye your whipping? You tell me that, Ian!"

The bones in Young Ian's face stood out, but he kept his mouth shut, sealed in a stubborn line.

"Tell me!" Ian roared, slamming his hand on the table again.

Young Ian blinked in reflex, and his shoulder blades drew together, then apart, as though he were trying to alter his size, and unsure whether to grow larger or try to be smaller. He swallowed hard, and blinked once more.

"Ye said—ye said ye'd skin me. Next time." His voice broke in a ridiculous squeak on the last word, and he clamped his mouth hard shut on it.

Ian shook his head in heavy disapproval. "Aye. And I thought ye'd have enough sense to see there was no next time, but I was wrong about that, hm?" He breathed in heavily and let it out with a snort.

"I'm fair disgusted wi' ye, Ian, and that's the truth." He jerked his head toward the doorway. "Go outside. I'll see ye by the gate, presently."

There was a tense silence in the sitting room, as the sound of the miscreant's dragging footsteps disappeared down the passage. I kept my own eyes carefully on my hands, folded in my lap. Beside me, Jamie drew a slow, deep breath and sat up straighter, steeling himself.

"Ian." Jamie spoke mildly to his brother-in-law. "I wish ye wouldna do that."

"What?" Ian's brow was still furrowed with anger as he turned toward Jamie. "Thrash the lad? And what have you to say about it, aye?"

Jamie's jaw tensed, but his voice stayed calm.

"I've nothing to say about it, Ian—he's your son; you'll do as ye like. But maybe you'll let me speak for the way he's acted?"

"How he's acted?" Jenny cried, starting suddenly to life. She might leave dealing with her son to Ian, but when it came to her brother, no one was likely to speak for her. "Sneakin' away in the night like a thief, ye mean? Or perhaps ye'll mean consorting wi' criminals, and risking his neck for a cask of brandy!"

Ian silenced her with a quick gesture. He hesitated, still frowning, but then nodded abruptly at Jamie, giving permission.

"Consorting wi' criminals like me?" Jamie asked his sister, a definite edge to his voice. His eyes met hers straight on, matching slits of blue.

"D'ye ken where the money comes from, Jenny, that keeps you and your bairns and everyone here in food, and the roof from fallin' in over your head? It's not from me printing up copies o' the Psalms in Edinburgh!"

"And did I think it was?" she flared at him. "Did I ask ye what ye did?"

"No, ye didn't," he flashed back. "I think ye'd rather not know—but ye do know, don't you?"

"And will ye blame me for what ye do? It's *my* fault that I've children, and that they must eat?" She didn't flush red like Jamie did; when Jenny lost her temper, she went dead white with fury.

I could see him struggling to keep his own temper. "Blame ye? No, of course I dinna blame ye—but is it right for you to blame me, that Ian and I canna keep ye all just working the land?"

Jenny too was making an effort to subdue her rising temper. "No," she said. "Ye do what ye must, Jamie. Ye ken verra well I didna mean you when I said 'criminals,' but—"

"So ye mean the men who work for me? I do the same things, Jenny. If they're criminals, what am I, then?" He glared at her, eyes hot with resentment.

"You're my brother," she said shortly, "little pleased as I am to say so, sometimes. Damn your eyes, Jamie Fraser! Ye ken quite well I dinna mean to quarrel wi' whatever ye see fit to do! If ye robbed folk on the highway, or kept a whorehouse in Edinburgh, 'twould be because there was no help for it. That doesna mean I want ye takin' my son to be part of it!"

Jamie's eyes tightened slightly at the corners at the mention of whorehouses in Edinburgh, and he darted a quick glance of accusation at Ian, who shook his head. He looked mildly stunned at his wife's ferocity.

"I've said not a word," he said briefly. "Ye ken how she is."

Jamie took a deep breath and turned back to Jenny, obviously determined to be reasonable.

"Aye, I see that. But ye canna think I would take Young Ian into danger— God, Jenny, I care for him as though he were my own son!"

"Aye?" Her skepticism was pronounced. "So that's why ye encouraged him to run off from his home, and kept him with ye, wi' no word to ease our minds about where he was?"

Jamie had the grace to look abashed at this.

"Aye, well, I'm sorry for that," he muttered. "I meant to—" He broke off with an impatient gesture. "Well, it doesna matter what I meant; I should have sent word, and I didna. But as for encouraging him to run off—"

"No, I dinna suppose ye did," Ian interrupted. "Not directly, anyway." The anger had faded from his long face. He looked tired now, and a little sad. The bones in his face were more pronounced, leaving him hollow-cheeked in the waning afternoon light.

"It's only that the lad loves ye, Jamie," he said quietly. "I see him listen when ye visit, and talk of what ye do; I can see his face. He thinks it's all excitement and adventure, how ye live, and a good long way from shoveling goat-shit for his mother's garden." He smiled briefly, despite himself.

Jamie gave his brother-in-law a quick smile in return, and a lifted shoulder. "Well, but it's usual for a lad of that age to want a bit of adventure, no? You and I were the same."

"Whether he wants it or no, he shouldna be having the sort of adventures he'll get with you," Jenny interrupted sharply. She shook her head, the line between her brows growing deeper as she looked disapprovingly at her brother. "The good Lord kens as there's a charm on your life, Jamie, or ye'd ha' been dead a dozen times."

"Aye, well. I suppose He had something in mind to preserve me for." Jamie glanced at me with a brief smile, and his hand sought mine. Jenny darted a glance at me, too, her face unreadable, then returned to the subject at hand.

"Well, that's as may be," she said. "But I canna say as the same's true for Young Ian." Her expression softened slightly as she looked at Jamie.

"I dinna ken everything about the way ye live, Jamie—but I ken *you* well enough to say it's likely not the way a wee laddie should live."

"Mmphm." Jamie rubbed a hand over his stubbled jaw, and tried again. "Aye, well, that's what I mean about Young Ian. He's carried himself like a man this last week. I dinna think it right for ye to thrash him like a wee laddie, Ian."

Jenny's eyebrows rose, graceful wings of scorn.

"A man, now, is he? Why, he's but a baby, Jamie—he's not but fourteen!"

Despite his annoyance, one side of Jamie's mouth curled slightly.

"I was a man at fourteen, Jenny," he said softly.

She snorted, but a film of moisture shone suddenly over her eyes.

"Ye thought ye were." She stood and turned away abruptly, blinking. "Aye, I mind ye then," she said, face turned to the bookshelf. She reached out a hand as though to support herself, grasping the edge.

"Ye were a bonny lad, Jamie, riding off wi' Dougal to your first raid, and your dirk all bright on your thigh. I was sixteen, and I thought I'd never seen a sight so fair as you on your pony, so straight and tall. And I mind ye coming back, too, all covered in mud, and a scratch down the side of your face from falling in brambles, and Dougal boasting to Da how brawly ye'd done—driven off six kine by yourself, and had a dunt on the head from the flat of a broadsword, and not made a squeak about it." Her face once more under control, she turned back from her contemplation of the books to face her brother. "That's what a man is, aye?"

A hint of humor stole back into Jamie's face as he met her gaze.

"Aye, well, there's maybe a bit more to it than that," he said.

"Is there," she said, more dryly still. "And what will that be? To be able to bed a girl? Or to kill a man?"

I had always thought Janet Fraser had something of the Sight, particularly where her brother was concerned. Evidently the talent extended to her son, as well. The flush over Jamie's cheekbones deepened, but his expression didn't change.

She shook her head slowly, looking steadily at her brother. "Nay, Young

Ian's not a man yet—but you are, Jamie; and ye ken the difference verra well."

Ian, who had been watching the fireworks between the two Frasers with the same fascination as I had, now coughed briefly.

"Be that as it may," he said dryly. "Young Ian's been waiting for his whipping for the last quarter-hour. Whether or not it's suitable to beat him, to make him wait any longer for it is a bit cruel, aye?"

"Have ye really got to do it, Ian?" Jamie made one last effort, turning to appeal to his brother-in-law.

"Well," said Ian slowly, "as I've told the lad he's going to be thrashed, and he kens verra well he's earned it, I canna just go back on my word. But as for me doing it—no, I dinna think I will." A faint gleam of humor showed in the soft brown eyes. He reached into a drawer of the sideboard, drew out a thick leather strap, and thrust it into Jamie's hand. "You do it."

"Me?" Jamie was horror-struck. He made a futile attempt to shove the strap back into Ian's hand, but his brother-in-law ignored it. "I canna thrash the lad!"

"Oh, I think ye can," Ian said calmly, folding his arms. "Ye've said often enough ye care for him as though he were your son." He tilted his head to one side, and while his expression stayed mild, the brown eyes were implacable. "Well, I'll tell ye, Jamie—it's no that easy to be his Da; best ye go and find that out now, aye?"

Jamie stared at Ian for a long moment, then looked to his sister. She raised one eyebrow, staring him down.

"You deserve it as much as he does, Jamie. Get ye gone."

Jamie's lips pressed tight together and his nostrils flared white. Then he whirled on his heel and was gone without speaking. Rapid steps sounded on the boards, and a muffled slam came from the far end of the passage.

Jenny cast a quick glance at Ian, a quicker one at me, and then turned to the window. Ian and I, both a good deal taller, came to stand behind her. The light outside was failing rapidly, but there was still enough to see the wilting figure of Young Ian, leaning dispiritedly against a wooden gate, some twenty yards from the house.

Looking around in trepidation at the sound of footsteps, he saw his uncle approaching and straightened up in surprise.

"Uncle Jamie!" His eye fell on the strap then, and he straightened a bit more. "Are . . . are *you* goin' to whip me?"

It was a still evening, and I could hear the sharp hiss of air through Jamie's teeth.

"I suppose I'll have to," he said frankly. "But first I must apologize to ye, Ian."

"To me?" Young Ian sounded mildly dazed. Clearly he wasn't used to having his elders think they owed him an apology, especially before beating him. "Ye dinna need to do that, Uncle Jamie."

The taller figure leaned against the gate, facing the smaller one, head bent.

"Aye, I do. It was wrong of me, Ian, to let ye stay in Edinburgh, and it was maybe wrong, too, to tell ye stories and make ye think of running away to start with. I took ye to places I shouldna, and might have put ye in danger, and I've caused more of a moil wi' your parents than maybe ye should be in by yourself. I'm sorry for it, Ian, and I'll ask ye to forgive me."

"Oh." The smaller figure rubbed a hand through his hair, plainly at a loss for words. "Well . . . aye. Of course I do, Uncle."

"Thank ye, Ian."

They stood in silence for a moment, then Young Ian heaved a sigh and straightened his drooping shoulders.

"I suppose we'd best do it, then?"

"I expect so." Jamie sounded at least as reluctant as his nephew, and I heard Ian, next to me, snort slightly, whether with indignation or amusement, I couldn't tell.

Resigned, Young Ian turned and faced the gate without hesitation. Jamie followed more slowly. The light was nearly gone and we could see no more than the outlines of figures at this distance, but we could hear clearly from our position at the window. Jamie was standing behind his nephew, shifting uncertainly, as though unsure what to do next.

"Mmphm. Ah, what does your father . . ."

"It's usually ten, Uncle." Young Ian had shed his coat, and tugged at his waist now, speaking over his shoulder. "Twelve if it's pretty bad, and fifteen if it's really awful."

"Was this only bad, would ye say, or pretty bad?"

There was a brief, unwilling laugh from the boy.

"If Father's makin' *you* do it, Uncle Jamie, it's really awful, but I'll settle for pretty bad. Ye'd better give me twelve."

There was another snort from Ian at my elbow. This time, it was definitely amusement. "Honest lad," he murmured.

"All right, then." Jamie drew in his breath and pulled his arm back, but was interrupted by Young Ian.

"Wait, Uncle, I'm no quite ready."

"Och, ye've got to do that?" Jamie's voice sounded a bit strangled.

"Aye. Father says only girls are whipped wi' their skirts down," Young Ian explained. "Men must take it bare-arsed."

"He's damn well right about *that* one," Jamie muttered, his quarrel with Jenny obviously still rankling. "Ready now?"

The necessary adjustments made, the larger figure stepped back and swung. There was a loud crack, and Jenny winced in sympathy with her son.

Beyond a sudden intake of breath, though, the lad was silent, and stayed so through the rest of the ordeal, though I blanched a bit myself.

Finally Jamie dropped his arm, and wiped his brow. He held out a hand to Ian, slumped over the fence. "All right, lad?" Young Ian straightened up, with a little difficulty this time, and pulled up his breeks. "Aye, Uncle. Thank ye." The boy's voice was a little thick, but calm and steady. He took Jamie's outstretched hand. To my surprise, though, instead of leading the boy back to the house, Jamie thrust the strap into Ian's other hand.

"Your turn," he announced, striding over to the gate and bending over. Young Ian was as shocked as those of us in the house.

"What!" he said, stunned.

"I said it's your turn," his uncle said in a firm voice. "I punished you; now you've got to punish me."

"I canna do that, Uncle!" Young Ian was as scandalized as though his uncle had suggested he commit some public indecency.

"Aye, ye can," said Jamie, straightening up to look his nephew in the eye. "Ye heard what I said when I apologized to ye, did ye no?" Ian nodded in a dazed fashion. "Weel, then. I've done wrong just as much as you, and I've to pay for it, too. I didna like whipping you, and ye're no goin' to like whipping me, but we're both goin' through wi' it. Understand?"

"A-Aye, Uncle," the boy stammered.

"All right, then." Jamie tugged down his breeches, tucked up his shirttail, and bent over once more, clutching the top rail. He waited a second, then spoke again, as Ian stood paralyzed, strap dangling from his nerveless hand.

"Go on." His voice was steel; the one he used with the whisky smugglers; not to obey was unthinkable. Ian moved timidly to do as he was ordered. Standing back, he took a halfhearted swing. There was a dull thwacking sound.

"That one didna count," Jamie said firmly. "Look, man, it was just as hard for me to do it to you. Make a proper job of it, now."

The thin figure squared its shoulders with sudden determination and the leather whistled through the air. It landed with a crack like lightning. There was a startled yelp from the figure on the fence, and a suppressed giggle, at least half shock, from Jenny.

Jamie cleared his throat. "Aye, that'll do. Finish it, then."

We could hear Young Ian counting carefully to himself under his breath between strokes of the leather, but aside from a smothered "Christ!" at number nine, there was no further sound from his uncle.

With a general sigh of relief from inside the house, Jamie rose off the fence after the last stroke, and tucked his shirt into his breeks. He inclined his head formally to his nephew. "Thank ye, Ian." Dropping the formality, he then rubbed his backside, saying in a tone of rueful admiration, "Christ, man, ye've an arm on ye!"

"So've you, Uncle," said Ian, matching his uncle's wry tones. The two figures, barely visible now, stood laughing and rubbing themselves for a moment. Jamie flung an arm about his nephew's shoulders and turned him toward the house. "If it's all the same to you, Ian, I dinna want to have to do that again, aye?" he said, confidentially.

"It's a bargain, Uncle Jamie."

A moment later, the door opened at the end of the passage, and with a look at each other, Jenny and Ian turned as one to greet the returning prodigals.

33

Buried Treasure

"You look rather like a baboon," I observed.

"Oh, aye? And what's one of those?" In spite of the freezing November air pouring in through the half-open window, Jamie showed no signs of discomfort as he dropped his shirt onto the small pile of clothing.

He stretched luxuriously, completely naked. His joints made little popping noises as he arched his back and stretched upward, fists resting easily on the smoke-dark beams overhead.

"Oh, God, it feels good not to be on a horse!"

"Mm. To say nothing of having a real bed to sleep in, instead of wet heather." I rolled over, luxuriating in the warmth of the heavy quilts, and the relaxation of sore muscles into the ineffable softness of the goose-down mattress.

"D'ye mean to tell me what's a baboon, then?" Jamie inquired, "Or are ye just makin' observations for the pleasure of it?" He turned to pick up a frayed willow twig from the washstand, and began to clean his teeth. I smiled at the sight; if I had had no other impact during my earlier sojourn in the past, I had at least been instrumental in seeing that virtually all of the Frasers and Murrays of Lallybroch retained their teeth, unlike most Highlanders—unlike most Englishmen, for that matter.

"A baboon," I said, enjoying the sight of his muscular back flexing as he scrubbed, "is a sort of very large monkey with a red behind."

He snorted with laughter and choked on the willow twig. "Well," he said, removing it from his mouth, "I canna fault your observations, Sassenach." He grinned at me, showing brilliant white teeth, and tossed the twig aside. "It's been thirty years since anyone took a tawse to me," he added, passing his hands tenderly over the still-glowing surfaces of his rear. "I'd forgot how much it stings."

"And here Young Ian was speculating that your arse was tough as saddle leather," I said, amused. "Was it worth it, do you think?"

"Oh, aye," he said, matter-of-factly, sliding into bed beside me. His body was hard and cold as marble, and I squeaked but didn't protest as he gathered me firmly against his chest. "Christ, you're warm," he murmured.

"Come closer, hm?" His legs insinuated themselves between mine, and he cupped my bottom, drawing me in.

He gave a sigh of pure content, and I relaxed against him, feeling our temperatures start to equalize through the thin cotton of the nightdress Jenny had lent me. The peat fire in the hearth had been lit, but hadn't been able to do much yet toward dispelling the chill. Body heat was much more effective.

"Oh, aye, it was worth it," he said. "I could have beaten Young Ian half-senseless—his father has, once or twice—and it would ha' done nothing but make him more determined to run off, once he got the chance. But he'll walk through hot coals before he risks havin' to do something like that again."

He spoke with certainty, and I thought he was undoubtedly right. Young Ian, looking bemused, had received absolution from his parents, in the form of a kiss from his mother and a swift hug from his father, and then retired to his bed with a handful of cakes, there no doubt to ponder the curious consequences of disobedience.

Jamie too had been absolved with kisses, and I suspected that this was more important to him than the effects of his performance on Young Ian.

"At least Jenny and Ian aren't angry with you any longer," I said.

"No. It's no really that they were angry so much, I think; it's only that they dinna ken what to do wi' the lad," he explained. "They've raised two sons already, and Young Jamie and Michael are fine lads both; but both of them are more like Ian—soft-spoke, and easy in their manner. Young Ian's quiet enough, but he's a great deal more like his mother—and me."

"Frasers are stubborn, eh?" I said, smiling. This bit of clan doctrine was one of the first things I had learned when I met Jamie, and nothing in my subsequent experience had suggested that it might be in error.

He chuckled, soft and deep in his chest.

"Aye, that's so. Young Ian may look like a Murray, but he's a Fraser born, all right. And it's no use to shout at a stubborn man, or beat him, either; it only makes him more set on having his way."

"I'll bear that in mind," I said dryly. One hand was stroking my thigh, gradually inching the cotton nightdress upward. Jamie's internal furnace had resumed its operations, and his bare legs were warm and hard against mine. One knee nudged gently, seeking an entrance between my thighs. I cupped his buttocks and squeezed gently.

"Dorcas told me that a number of gentlemen pay very well for the privilege of being smacked at the brothel. She says they find it . . . arousing."

Jamie snorted briefly, tensing his buttocks, then relaxing as I stroked them lightly.

"Do they, then? I suppose it's true, if Dorcas says so, but I canna see it, myself. There are a great many more pleasant ways to get a cockstand, if ye ask me. On the other hand," he added fairly, "perhaps it makes a difference if it's a bonny wee lassie in her shift on the other end o' the strap, and not your father—or your nephew, come to that."

"Perhaps it does. Shall I try sometime?" The hollow of his throat lay just by my face, sunburned and delicate, showing the faint white triangle of a scar just above the wide arch of his collarbone. I set my lips on the pulsebeat there, and he shivered, though neither of us was cold any longer.

"No," he said, a little breathless. His hand fumbled at the neck of my shift, pulling loose the ribbons. He rolled onto his back then, lifting me suddenly above him as though I weighed nothing at all. A flick of his finger brought the loosened chemise down over my shoulders, and my nipples rose at once as the cold air struck them.

His eyes were more slanted than usual as he smiled up at me, half-lidded as a drowsing cat, and the warmth of his palms encircled both breasts.

"I said I could think of more pleasant ways, aye?"

The candle had guttered and gone out, the fire on the hearth burned low, and a pale November starlight shone through the misted window. Dim as it was, my eyes were so adapted to the dark that I could pick out all the details of the room; the thick white porcelain jug and basin, its blue band black in the starlight, the small embroidered sampler on the wall, and the rumpled heap of Jamie's clothes on the stool by the bed.

Jamie was clearly visible, too; covers thrown back, chest gleaming faintly from exertion. I admired the long slope of his belly, where small whorls of dark auburn hair spiraled up across the pale, fresh skin. I couldn't keep my fingers from touching him, tracing the lines of the powerfully sprung ribs that shaped his torso.

"It's so good," I said dreamily. "So good to have a man's body to touch."

"D'ye like it still, then?" He sounded half-shy, half-pleased, as I fondled him. His own arm came around my shoulder, stroking my hair.

"Mm-hm." It wasn't a thing I had consciously missed, but having it now reminded me of the joy of it; that drowsy intimacy in which a man's body is as accessible to you as your own, the strange shapes and textures of it like a sudden extension of your own limbs.

I ran my hand down the flat slope of his belly, over the smooth jut of hipbone and the swell of muscled thigh. The remnants of firelight caught the red-gold fuzz on arms and legs, and glowed in the auburn thicket nested between his thighs.

"God, you are a wonderful hairy creature," I said. "Even there." I slid my hand down the smooth crease of his thigh and he spread his legs obligingly, letting me touch the thick, springy curls in the crease of his buttocks.

"Aye, well, no one's hunted me yet for my pelt," he said comfortably. His hand cupped my own rear firmly, and a large thumb passed gently over the rounded surface. He propped one arm behind his head, and looked lazily down the length of my body.

"You're even less worth the skinning than I am, Sassenach."

"I should hope so." I moved slightly to accommodate his touch as he extended his explorations, enjoying the warmth of his hand on my naked back.

"Ever seen a smooth branch that's been in still water a long time?" he asked. A finger passed lightly up my spine, raising a ripple of gooseflesh in its wake. "There are tiny wee bubbles on it, hundreds and thousands and millions of them, so it looks as though it's furred all about wi' a silver frost." His fingers brushed my ribs, my arms, my back, and the tiny down-hairs rose everywhere in the wake of his touch, tingling.

"That's what ye look like, my Sassenach," he said, almost whispering. "All smooth and naked, dipped in silver."

Then we lay quiet for a time, listening to the drip of rain outside. A cold autumn air drifted through the room, mingling with the fire's smoky warmth. He rolled onto his side, facing away from me, and drew the quilts up to cover us.

I curled up behind him, knees fitting neatly behind his own. The firelight shone dully from behind me now, gleaming over the smooth round of his shoulder and dimly illuminating his back. I could see the faint lines of the scars that webbed his shoulders, thin streaks of silver on his flesh. At one time, I had known those scars so intimately, I could have traced them with my fingers, blindfolded. Now there was a thin half-moon curve I didn't know; a diagonal slash that hadn't been there before, the remnants of a violent past I hadn't shared.

I touched the half-moon, tracing its length.

"No one's hunted you for your pelt," I said softly, "but they've hunted you, haven't they?"

His shoulder moved slightly, not quite a shrug. "Now and then," he said.

"Now?" I asked.

He breathed slowly for a moment or two before answering.

"Aye," he said. "I think so."

My fingers moved down to the diagonal slash. It had been a deep cut; old and well-healed as the damage was, the line was sharp and clear beneath my fingertips.

"Do you know who?"

"No." He was quiet for a moment; then his hand closed over my own, where it lay across his stomach. "But I maybe ken why."

The house was very quiet. With most of the children and grandchildren gone, there were only the far-off servants in their quarters behind the kitchen, Ian and Jenny in their room at the far end of the hall, and Young Ian somewhere upstairs—all asleep. We could have been alone at the end of the world; both Edinburgh and the smugglers' cove seemed very far away.

"Do ye recall, after the fall of Stirling, not so long before Culloden, when all of a sudden there was gossip from everywhere, about gold being sent from France?"

"From Louis? Yes—but he never sent it." Jamie's words summoned up those brief frantic days of Charles Stuart's reckless rise and precipitous fall, when rumor had been the common currency of conversation. "There was always gossip—about gold from France, ships from Spain, weapons from Holland—but nothing came of most of it."

"Oh, something came—though not from Louis—but no one kent it, then."

He told me then of his meeting with the dying Duncan Kerr, and the wanderer's whispered words, heard in the inn's attic under the watchful eye of an English officer.

"He was fevered, Duncan, but not crazed wi' it. He kent he was dying, and he kent me, too. It was his only chance to tell someone he thought he could trust—so he told me."

"White witches and seals?" I repeated. "I must say, it sounds like gibberish. But you understood it?"

"Well, not all of it," Jamie admitted. He rolled over to face me, frowning slightly. "I've no notion who the white witch might be. At the first, I thought he meant you, Sassenach, and my heart nearly stopped when he said it." He smiled ruefully, and his hand tightened on mine, clasped between us.

"I thought all at once that perhaps something had gone wrong—maybe ye'd not been able to go back to Frank and the place ye came from—maybe ye'd somehow ended in France, maybe ye were there right then—all kinds o' fancies went through my head."

"I wish it had been true," I whispered.

He gave me a lopsided smile, but shook his head.

"And me in prison? And Brianna would be what—just ten or so? No, dinna waste your time in regretting, Sassenach. You're here now, and ye'll never leave me again." He kissed me gently on the forehead, then resumed his tale.

"I didna have any idea where the gold had come from, but I kent his telling me where it was, and why it was there. It was Prince *Tearlach*'s, sent for him. And the bit about the silkies—" He raised his head a little and nodded toward the window, where the rose brier cast its shadows on the glass.

"Folk said when my mother ran away from Leoch that she'd gone to live wi' the silkies; only because the maid that saw my father when he took her said as he looked like a great silkie who'd shed his skin and come to walk on the land like a man. And he did." Jamie smiled and passed a hand through his own thick hair, remembering. "He had hair thick as mine, but a black like jet. It would shine in some lights, as though it was wet, and he moved quick and sleekit, like a seal through the water." He shrugged suddenly, shaking off the recollection of his father.

"Well, so. When Duncan Kerr said the name Ellen, I kent it was my mother he meant—as a sign that he knew my name and my family, kent who I was; that he wasna raving, no matter how it sounded. And knowin' that—" He shrugged again. "The Englishman had told me where they found Duncan, near the coast. There are hundreds of bittie isles and rocks all down that coast, but only one place where the silkies live, at the ends of the MacKenzie lands, off Coigach."

"So you went there?"

"Aye, I did." He sighed deeply, his free hand drifting to the hollow of my waist. "I wouldna have done it—left the prison, I mean—had I not still thought it maybe had something to do wi' you, Sassenach."

Escape had been an enterprise of no great difficulty; prisoners were often taken outside in small gangs, to cut the peats that burned on the prison's hearths, or to cut and haul stone for the ongoing work of repairing the walls.

For a man to whom the heather was home, disappearing had been easy. He had risen from his work and turned aside by a hummock of grass, unfastening his breeches as though to relieve himself. The guard had looked politely away, and looking back a moment later, beheld nothing but an empty moor, holding no trace of Jamie Fraser.

"See, it was little trouble to slip off, but men seldom did," he explained. "None of us were from near Ardsmuir—and had we been, there was little left for most o' the men to gang to."

The Duke of Cumberland's men had done their work well. As one contemporary had put it, evaluating the Duke's achievement later, "He created a desert and called it peace." This modern approach to diplomacy had left some parts of the Highlands all but deserted; the men killed, imprisoned, or transported, crops and houses burned, the women and children turned out to starve or seek refuge elsewhere as best they might. No, a prisoner escaping from Ardsmuir would have been truly alone, without kin or clan to turn to for succor.

Jamie had known there would be little time before the English commander realized where he must be heading and organized a party of pursuit. On the other hand, there were no real roads in this remote part of the kingdom, and a man who knew the country was at a greater advantage on foot than were the pursuing outlanders on horseback.

He had made his escape in midafternoon. Taking his bearings by the stars, he had walked through the night, arriving at the coast near dawn the next day.

"See, I kent the silkies' place; it's well known amongst the MacKenzies, and I'd been there once before, wi' Dougal."

The tide had been high, and the seals mostly out in the water, hunting crabs and fish among the fronds of floating kelp, but the dark streaks of their droppings and the indolent forms of a few idlers marked the seals' three islands, ranged in a line just inside the lip of a small bay, guarded by a clifflike headland.

By Jamie's interpretation of Duncan's instructions, the treasure lay on the third island, the farthest away from the shore. It was nearly a mile out, a long swim even for a strong man, and his own strength was sapped from the hard prison labor and the long walk without food. He had stood on the clifftop, wondering whether this was a wild-goose chase, and whether the treasure—if there was one—was worth the risk of his life.

"The rock was all split and broken there; when I came too close to the edge, chunks would fall awa' from my feet and plummet down the cliff. I didna see how I'd ever reach the water, let alone the seals' isle. But then I was minded what Duncan said about Ellen's tower," Jamie said. His eyes were open, fixed not on me, but on that distant shore where the crash of falling rock was lost in the smashing of the waves.

The "tower" was there; a small spike of granite that stuck up no more than five feet from the tip of the headland. But below that spike, hidden by the rocks, was a narrow crack, a small chimney that ran from top to bottom of the eighty-foot cliff, providing a possible passage, if not an easy one, for a determined man.

From the base of Ellen's tower to the third island was still over a quarter-mile of heaving green water. Undressing, he had crossed himself, and commending his soul to the keeping of his mother, he had dived naked into the waves.

He made his way slowly out from the cliff, floundering and choking as the waves broke over his head. No place in Scotland is that far from the sea, but Jamie had been raised inland, his experience of swimming limited to the placid depths of lochs and the pools of trout streams.

Blinded by salt and deafened by the roaring surf, he had fought the waves for what seemed hours, then thrust his head and shoulders free, gasping for breath, only to see the headland looming—not behind, as he had thought, but to his right.

"The tide was goin' out, and I was goin' with it," he said wryly. "I thought, well, that's it, then, I'm gone, for I knew I could never make my way back. I hadna eaten anything in two days, and hadn't much strength left."

He ceased swimming then, and simply spread himself on his back, giving himself to the embrace of the sea. Light-headed from hunger and effort, he had closed his eyes against the light and searched his mind for the words of the old Celtic prayer against drowning.

He paused for a moment then, and was quiet for so long that I wondered whether something was wrong. But at last he drew breath and said shyly, "I expect ye'll think I'm daft, Sassenach. I havena told anyone about it—not even Jenny. But—I heard my mother call me, then, right in the middle of praying." He shrugged, uncomfortable.

"It was maybe only that I'd been thinking of her when I left the shore," he said. "And yet—" He fell silent, until I touched his face.

"What did she say?" I asked quietly.

"She said, 'Come here to me, Jamie—come to me, laddie!' " He drew a deep breath and let it out slowly. "I could hear her plain as day, but I couldna see anything; there was no one there, not even a silkie. I thought perhaps she was callin' me from Heaven—and I was so tired I really would not ha' minded dying then, but I rolled myself over and struck out toward where I'd heard her voice. I thought I would swim ten strokes and then stop again to rest—or to sink."

But on the eighth stroke, the current had taken him.

"It was just as though someone had picked me up," he said, sounding still surprised at the memory of it. "I could feel it under me and all around; the water was a bit warmer than it had been, and it carried me with it. I didna have to do anything but paddle a bit, to keep my head above water."

A strong, curling current, eddying between headland and islands, it had taken him to the edge of the third islet, where no more than a few strokes brought him within reach of its rocks.

It was a small lump of granite, fissured and creviced like all the ancient rocks of Scotland, and slimed with seaweed and seal droppings to boot, but he crawled on shore with all the thankfulness of a shipwrecked sailor for a land of palm trees and white-sand beaches. He fell down upon his face on the rocky shelf and lay there, grateful for breath, half-dozing with exhaustion.

"Then I felt something looming over me, and there was a terrible stink o' dead fish," he said. "I got up onto my knees at once, and there he was—a great bull seal, all sleek and wet, and his black eyes starin' at me, no more than a yard away."

Neither fisher nor seaman himself, Jamie had heard enough stories to know that bull seals were dangerous, particularly when threatened by intrusions upon their territory. Looking at the open mouth, with its fine display of sharp, peglike teeth, and the burly rolls of hard fat that girdled the enormous body, he was not disposed to doubt it.

"He weighed more than twenty stone, Sassenach," he said. "If he wasna inclined to rip the flesh off my bones, still he could ha' knocked me into the sea wi' one swipe, or dragged me under to drown."

"Obviously he didn't, though," I said dryly. "What happened?"

He laughed. "I think I was too mazed from tiredness to do anything sensible," he said. "I just looked at him for a moment, and then I said, 'It's all right; it's only me.' "

"And what did the seal do?"

Jamie shrugged slightly. "He looked me over for a bit longer—silkies dinna blink much, did ye know that? It's verra unnerving to have one look at ye for long—then he gave a sort of a grunt and slid off the rock into the water."

Left in sole possession of the tiny islet, Jamie had sat blankly for a time, recovering his strength, and then at last began a methodical search of the crevices. Small as the area was, it took little time to find a deep split in the rock that led down to a wide hollow space, a foot below the rocky surface. Floored with dry sand and located in the center of the island, the hollow would be safe from flooding in all but the worst storms.

"Well, don't keep me in suspense," I said, poking him in the stomach. "Was the French gold there?"

"Well, it was and it wasn't, Sassenach," he answered, neatly sucking in his stomach. "I'd been expecting gold bullion; that's what the rumor said that Louis would send. And thirty thousand pounds' worth of gold bullion would make a good-sized hoard. But all there was in the hollow was a box, less than a foot long, and a small leather pouch. The box did have gold in it, though—and silver, too."

Gold and silver indeed. The wooden box had contained two hundred and five coins, gold ones and silver ones, some as sharply cut as though new-minted, some with their markings worn nearly to blankness.

"Ancient coins, Sassenach."

"Ancient? What, you mean very old—"

"Greek, Sassenach, and Roman. Verra old indeed."

We lay staring at each other in the dim light for a moment, not speaking.

"That's incredible," I said at last. "It's treasure, all right, but not—"

"Not what Louis would send, to help feed an army, no," he finished for me. "No, whoever put this treasure there, it wasna Louis or any of his ministers."

"What about the bag?" I said, suddenly remembering. "What was in the pouch you found?"

"Stones, Sassenach. Gemstones. Diamonds and pearls and emeralds and sapphires. Not many, but nicely cut and big enough." He smiled, a little grimly. "Aye, big enough."

He had sat on a rock under the dim gray sky, turning the coins and the jewels over and over between his fingers, stunned into bewilderment. At last, roused by a sensation of being watched, he had looked up to find himself surrounded by a circle of curious seals. The tide was out, the females had come back from their fishing, and twenty pairs of round black eyes surveyed him cautiously.

The huge black male, emboldened by the presence of his harem, had come back too. He barked loudly, darting his head threateningly from side to side, and advanced on Jamie, sliding his three-hundred-pound bulk a few feet closer with each booming exclamation, propelling himself with his flippers across the slick rock.

"I thought I'd best leave, then," he said. "I'd found what I came to find, after all. So I put the box and the pouch back where I'd found them—I couldna carry them ashore, after all, and if I did—what then? So I put them back, and crawled down into the water, half-frozen wi' cold."

A few strokes from the island had taken him again into the current heading landward; it was a circular current, like most eddies, and the gyre had carried him to the foot of the headland within half an hour, where he crawled ashore, dressed, and fell asleep in a nest of marrow grass.

He paused then, and I could see that while his eyes were open and fixed on me, it wasn't me they saw.

"I woke at dawn," he said softly. "I have seen a great many dawns, Sassenach, but never one like that one.

"I could feel the earth turn beneath me, and my own breath coming wi' the breathing of the wind. It was as though I had no skin nor bone, but only the light of the rising sun inside me."

His eyes softened, as he left the moor and came back to me.

"So then the sun came up higher," he said, matter-of-factly. "And when it warmed me enough to stand, I got up and went inland toward the road, to meet the English."

"But why did you go back?" I demanded. "You were free! You had money! And—"

"And where would I spend such money as that, Sassenach?" he asked. "Walk into a cottar's hearth and offer him a gold denarius, or a wee emerald?" He smiled at my indignation and shook his head.

"Nay," he said gently, "I had to go back. Aye, I could ha' lived on the moor for a time—half-starved and naked, but I might have managed. But they were hunting me, Sassenach, and hunting hard, for thinking that I might know where the gold was hid. No cot near Ardsmuir would be safe from the English, so long as I was free, and might be thought to seek refuge there.

"I've seen the English hunting, ye ken," he added, a harder note creeping into his voice. "Ye'll have seen the panel in the entry hall?"

I had; one panel of the glowing oak that lined the hall below had been smashed in, perhaps by a heavy boot, and the crisscross scars of saber slashes marred the paneling from door to stairs.

"We keep it so to remember," he said. "To show to the weans, and tell them when they ask—this is what the English are."

The suppressed hate in his voice struck me low in the pit of the stomach. Knowing what I knew of what the English army had done in the Highlands, there was bloody little I could say in argument. I said nothing, and he continued after a moment.

"I wouldna expose the folk near Ardsmuir to that kind of attention, Sassenach." At the word "Sassenach," his hand squeezed mine and a small smile curved the corner of his mouth. Sassenach I might be to him, but not English.

"For that matter," he went on, "were I not taken, the hunt would likely come here again—to Lallybroch. If I would risk the folk near Ardsmuir, I would not risk my own. And even without that—" He stopped, seeming to struggle to find words.

"I had to go back," he said slowly. "For the sake of the men there, if for nothing else."

"The men in the prison?" I said, surprised. "Were some of the Lallybroch men arrested with you?"

He shook his head. The small vertical line that appeared between his brows when he thought hard was visible, even by starlight.

"No. There were men there from all over the Highlands—from every clan, almost. Only a few men from each clan—remnants and ragtag. But the more in need of a chief, for all that."

"And that's what you were to them?" I spoke gently, restraining the urge to smooth the line away with my fingers.

"For lack of any better," he said, with the flicker of a smile.

He had come from the bosom of family and tenants, from a strength that had sustained him for seven years, to find a lack of hope and a loneliness that would kill a man faster than the damp and the filth and the quaking ague of the prison.

And so, quite simply, he had taken the ragtag and remnants, the castoff survivors of the field of Culloden, and made them his own, that they and he might survive the stones of Ardsmuir as well. Reasoning, charming, and cajoling where he could, fighting where he must, he had forced them to band together, to face their captors as one, to put aside ancient clan rivalries and allegiances, and take him as their chieftain.

"They were mine," he said softly. "And the having of them kept me alive." But then they had been taken from him and from each other— wrenched apart and sent into indenture in a foreign land. And he had not been able to save them.

"You did your best for them. But it's over now," I said softly.

We lay in each other's arms in silence for a long time, letting the small noises of the house wash over us. Different from the comfortable commercial bustle of the brothel, the tiny creaks and sighing spoke of quiet, and home, and safety. For the first time, we were truly alone together, removed from danger and distraction.

There was time, now. Time to hear the rest of the story of the gold, to hear what he had done with it, to find out what had happened to the men of Ardsmuir, to speculate about the burning of the printshop, Young Ian's one-eyed seaman, the encounter with His Majesty's Customs on the shore by Arbroath, to decide what to do next. And since there was time, there was no need to speak of any of that, now.

The last peat broke and fell apart on the hearth, its glowing interior hissing red in the cold. I snuggled closer to Jamie, burying my face in the side of his neck. He tasted faintly of grass and sweat, with a whiff of brandy.

He shifted his body in response, bringing us together all down our naked lengths.

"What, again?" I murmured, amused. "Men your age aren't supposed to do it again so soon."

His teeth nibbled gently on my earlobe. "Well, you're doing it too, Sassenach," he pointed out. "And you're older than I am."

"That's different," I said, gasping a little as he moved suddenly over me, his shoulders blotting out the starlit window. "I'm a woman."

"And if ye weren't a woman, Sassenach," he assured me, settling to his work, "I wouldna be doing it either. Hush, now."

I woke just past dawn to the scratching of the rose brier against the window, and the muffled thump and clang of breakfast fixing in the kitchen below. Peering over Jamie's sleeping form, I saw that the fire was dead out. I slid out of bed, quietly so as not to wake him. The floorboards were icy under my feet and I reached, shivering, for the first available garment.

Swathed in the folds of Jamie's shirt, I knelt on the hearth and went about the laborious business of rekindling the fire, thinking rather wistfully that I might have included a box of safety matches in the short list of items I had thought worthwhile to bring. Striking sparks from a flint to catch kindling does work, but not usually on the first try. Or the second. Or . . .

Somewhere around the dozenth attempt, I was rewarded by a tiny black spot on the twist of tow I was using for kindling. It grew at once and blossomed into a tiny flame. I thrust it hastily but carefully beneath the little tent of twigs I had prepared, to shelter the blooming flame from the cold breeze.

I had left the window ajar the night before, to insure not being suffocated by the smoke—peat fires burned hot, but dully, with a lot of smoke, as the blackened beams overhead attested. Just now, though, I thought we could dispense with fresh air—at least until I got the fire thoroughly under way.

The pane was rimed at the bottom with a light frost; winter was not far off. The air was so crisp and fresh that I paused before shutting the window, breathing in great gulps of dead leaf, dried apples, cold earth, and damp, sweet grass. The scene outside was perfect in its still clarity, stone walls and dark pines drawn sharp as black quillstrokes against the gray overcast of the morning.

A movement drew my eye to the top of the hill, where the rough track led to the village of Broch Mordha, ten miles distant. One by one, three small Highland ponies came up over the rise, and started down the hill toward the farmhouse.

They were too far away for me to make out the faces, but I could see by the billowing skirts that all three riders were women. Perhaps it was the girls —Maggie, Kitty, and Janet—coming back from Young Jamie's house. My own Jamie would be glad to see them.

I pulled the shirt, redolent of Jamie, around me against the chill, deciding to take advantage of what privacy might remain to us this morning by thawing out in bed. I shut the window, and paused to lift several of the light peat bricks from the basket by the hearth and feed them carefully to my fledgling fire, before shedding the shirt and crawling under the covers, numb toes tingling with delight at the luxurious warmth.

Jamie felt the chill of my return, and rolled instinctively toward me, gathering me neatly in and curling round me spoon-fashion. He sleepily rubbed his face against my shoulder.

"Sleep well, Sassenach?" he muttered.

"Never better," I assured him, snuggling my cold bottom into the warm hollow of his thighs. "You?"

"Mmmmm." He responded with a blissful groan, wrapping his arms about me. "Dreamed like a fiend."

"What about?"

"Naked women, mostly," he said, and set his teeth gently in the flesh of my shoulder. "That, and food." His stomach rumbled softly. The scent of biscuits and fried bacon in the air was faint but unmistakable.

"So long as you don't confuse the two," I said, twitching my shoulder out of his reach.

"I can tell a hawk from a handsaw, when the wind sets north by nor'west," he assured me, "and a sweet, plump lassie from a salt-cured ham, too, appearances notwithstanding." He grabbed my buttocks with both hands and squeezed, making me yelp and kick him in the shins.

"Beast!"

"Oh, a beast, is it?" he said, laughing. "Well, then . . ." Growling deep in his throat, he dived under the quilt and proceeded to nip and nibble his way up the insides of my thighs, blithely ignoring my squeaks and the hail of kicks on his back and shoulders. Dislodged by our struggles, the quilt slid off onto the floor, revealing the tousled mass of his hair, flying wild over my thighs.

"Perhaps there's less difference than I thought," he said, his head popping up between my legs as he paused for breath. He pressed my thighs flat against the mattress and grinned up at me, spikes of red hair standing on end like a porcupine's quills. "Ye do taste a bit salty, come to try it. What do ye—"

He was interrupted by a sudden bang as the door flew open and rebounded from the wall. Startled, we turned to look. In the doorway stood a young girl I had never seen before. She was perhaps fifteen or sixteen, with long flaxen hair and big blue eyes. The eyes were somewhat bigger than normal, and filled with an expression of horrified shock as she stared at me. Her gaze moved slowly from my tangled hair to my bare breasts, and down the slopes of my naked body, until it encountered Jamie, lying prone between my thighs, white-faced with a shock equal to hers.

"Daddy!" she said, in tones of total outrage. "*Who* is that woman?"

34

Daddy

"Oaddy?" I said blankly. *"Daddy?"*

Jamie had turned to stone when the door opened. Now he shot bolt upright, snatching at the fallen quilt. He shoved the disheveled hair out of his face, and glared at the girl.

"What in the name of bloody hell are you doing here?" he demanded. Red-bearded, naked, and hoarse with fury, he was a formidable sight, and the girl took a step backward, looking uncertain. Then her chin firmed and she glared back at him.

"I came with Mother!"

The effect on Jamie could not have been greater had she shot him through the heart. He jerked violently, and all the color went out of his face.

It came flooding back, as the sound of rapid footsteps sounded on the wooden staircase. He leapt out of bed, tossing the quilt hastily in my direction, and grabbed his breeks.

He had barely pulled them on when another female figure burst into the room, skidded to a halt, and stood staring, bug-eyed, at the bed.

"It's true!" She whirled toward Jamie, fists clenched against the cloak she still wore. "It's true! It's the Sassenach witch! How could ye do such a thing to me, Jamie Fraser?"

"Be still, Laoghaire!" he snapped. "I've done nothing to ye!"

I sat up against the wall, clutching the quilt to my bosom and staring. It was only when he spoke her name that I recognized her. Twenty-odd years ago, Laoghaire MacKenzie had been a slender sixteen-year-old, with rose-petal skin, moonbeam hair, and a violent—and unrequited—passion for Jamie Fraser. Evidently, a few things had changed.

She was nearing forty and no longer slender, having thickened considerably. The skin was still fair, but weathered, and stretched plumply over cheeks flushed with anger. Strands of ashy hair straggled out from under her respectable white kertch. The pale blue eyes were the same, though—they turned on me again, with the same expression of hatred I had seen in them long ago.

"He's mine!" she hissed. She stamped her foot. "Get ye back to the hell that ye came from, and leave him to me! Go, I say!"

As I made no move to obey, she glanced wildly about in search of a weapon. Catching sight of the blue-banded ewer, she seized it and drew back her arm to fling it at me. Jamie plucked it neatly from her hand, set it back on the bureau, and grasped her by the upper arm, hard enough to make her squeal.

He turned her and shoved her roughly toward the door. "Get ye downstairs," he ordered. "I'll speak wi' ye presently, Laoghaire."

"You'll speak wi' me? Speak wi' me, is it!" she cried. Face contorted, she swung her free hand at him, raking his face from eye to chin with her nails.

He grunted, grabbed her other wrist, and dragging her to the door, pushed her out into the passage and slammed the door to and turned the key.

By the time he turned around again, I was sitting on the edge of the bed, fumbling with shaking hands as I tried to pull my stockings on.

"I can explain it to ye, Claire," he said.

"I d-don't think so," I said. My lips were numb, along with the rest of me, and it was hard to form words. I kept my eyes fixed on my feet as I tried—and failed—to tie my garters.

"Listen to me!" he said violently, bringing his fist down on the table with a crash that made me jump. I jerked my head up, and caught a glimpse of him towering over me. With his red hair tumbled loose about his shoulders, his face unshaven, bare-chested, and the raw marks of Laoghaire's nails down his cheek, he looked like a Viking raider, bent on mayhem. I turned away to look for my shift.

It was lost in the bedclothes; I scrabbled about among the sheets. A considerable pounding had started up on the other side of the door, accompanied by shouts and shrieks, as the commotion attracted the other inhabitants of the house.

"You'd best go and explain things to your daughter," I said, pulling the crumpled cotton over my head.

"She's not my daughter!"

"No?" My head popped out of the neck of the shift, and I lifted my chin to stare up at him. "And I suppose you aren't married to Laoghaire, either?"

"I'm married to you, damn it!" he bellowed, striking his fist on the table again.

"I don't think so." I felt very cold. My stiff fingers couldn't manage the lacing of the stays; I threw them aside, and stood up to look for my gown, which was somewhere on the other side of the room—behind Jamie.

"I need my dress."

"You're no going anywhere, Sassenach. Not until—"

"Don't call me that!" I shrieked it, surprising both of us. He stared at me for a moment, then nodded.

"All right," he said quietly. He glanced at the door, now reverberating under the force of the pounding. He drew a deep breath and straightened, squaring his shoulders.

"I'll go and settle things. Then we'll talk, the two of us. Stay here, Sass—Claire." He picked up his shirt and yanked it over his head. Unlocking the door, he stepped out into the suddenly silent corridor and closed it behind him.

I managed to pick up the dress, then collapsed on the bed and sat shaking all over, the green wool crumpled across my knees.

I couldn't think in a straight line. My mind spun in small circles around the central fact; he was married. Married to Laoghaire! And he had a family. And yet he had wept for Brianna.

"Oh, Bree!" I said aloud. "Oh, God, Bree!" and began to cry—partly from shock, partly at the thought of Brianna. It wasn't logical, but this discovery seemed a betrayal of her, as much as of me—or of Laoghaire.

The thought of Laoghaire turned shock and sorrow to rage in a moment. I rubbed a fold of green wool savagely across my face, leaving the skin red and prickly.

Damn him! How dare he? If he had married again, thinking me dead, that was one thing. I had half-expected, half-feared it. But to marry that woman —that spiteful, sneaking little bitch who had tried to murder me at Castle Leoch . . . but he likely didn't know that, a small voice of reason in my head pointed out.

"Well, he *should* have known!" I said. "Damn him to hell, how could he take her, anyway?" The tears were rolling heedlessly down my face, hot spurts of loss and fury, and my nose was running. I groped for a handkerchief, found none, and in desperation, blew my nose at last on a corner of the sheet.

It smelled of Jamie. Worse, it smelled of the two of us, and the faint, musky lingerings of our pleasure. There was a small tingling spot on the inside of my thigh, where Jamie had nipped me, a few minutes before. I brought the flat of my hand down hard on the spot in a vicious slap, to kill the feeling.

"Liar!" I screamed. I grabbed the pitcher Laoghaire had tried to throw at me, and hurled it myself. It crashed against the door in an explosion of splinters.

I stood in the middle of the room, listening. It was quiet. There was no sound from below; no one was coming to see what had made the crash. I imagined they were all much too concerned with soothing Laoghaire to worry about me.

Did they live here, at Lallybroch? I recalled Jamie, taking Fergus aside, sending him ahead, ostensibly to tell Ian and Jenny we were coming. And, presumably, to warn them about me, and get Laoghaire out of the way before I arrived.

What in the name of God did Jenny and Ian think about this? Clearly they must know about Laoghaire—and yet they had received me last night, with no sign of it on their faces. But if Laoghaire had been sent away—why did she come back? Even trying to think about it made my temples throb.

The act of violence had drained enough rage for me to be able once more to control my shaking fingers. I kicked the stays into a corner and pulled the green gown over my head.

I had to get out of there. That was the only half-coherent thought in my head, and I clung to it. I had to leave. I couldn't stay, not with Laoghaire and her daughters in the house. They belonged there—I didn't.

I managed to tie up the garters this time, do up the laces of the dress, fasten the multiple hooks of the overskirt, and find my shoes. One was under the washstand, the other by the massive oak armoire, where I had kicked them the night before, dropping my clothes carelessly anywhere in my eagerness to crawl into the welcoming bed and nestle warmly in Jamie's arms.

I shivered. The fire had gone out again, and there was an icy draft from the window. I felt chilled to the bone, despite my clothes.

I wasted some time in searching for my cloak before realizing that it was downstairs; I had left it in the parlor the day before. I pushed my fingers through my hair, but was too upset to look for a comb. The strands crackled with electricity from having the woolen dress pulled over my head, and I slapped irritably at the floating hairs that stuck to my face.

Ready. Ready as I'd be, at least. I paused for one last look around, then heard footsteps coming up the stair.

Not fast and light, like the last ones. These were heavier, and slow, deliberate. I knew without seeing him that it was Jamie coming—and that he wasn't anxious to see me.

Fine. I didn't want to see him, either. Better just to leave at once, without speaking. What was there to say?

I backed away as the door opened, unaware that I was moving, until my legs hit the edge of the bed. I lost my balance and sat down. Jamie paused in the doorway, looking down at me.

He had shaved. That was the first thing I noticed. In echo of Young Ian the day before, he had hastily shaved, brushed his hair back and tidied himself before facing trouble. He seemed to know what I was thinking; the ghost of a smile passed over his face, as he rubbed his freshly scraped chin.

"D'ye think it will help?" he asked.

I swallowed, and licked dry lips, but didn't answer. He sighed, and answered himself.

"No, I suppose not." He stepped into the room and closed the door. He stood awkwardly for a moment, then moved toward the bed, one hand extended toward me. "Claire—"

"Don't touch me!" I leapt to my feet and backed away, circling toward the door. His hand fell to his side, but he stepped in front of me, blocking the way.

"Will ye no let me explain, Claire?"

"It seems to be a little late for that," I said, in what I meant to be a cold, disdainful tone. Unfortunately, my voice shook.

He pushed the door shut behind him.

"Ye never used to be unreasonable," he said quietly.

"And don't tell me what I used to be!" The tears were much too near the surface, and I bit my lip to hold them back.

"All right." His face was very pale; the scratches Laoghaire had given him showed as three red lines, livid down his cheek.

"I dinna live with her," he said. "She and the girls live at Balriggan, over near Broch Mordha." He watched me closely, but I said nothing. He shrugged a little, settling the shirt on his shoulders, and went on.

"It was a great mistake—the marriage between us."

"With two children? Took you a while to realize, didn't it?" I burst out.

His lips pressed tight together.

"The lassies aren't mine; Laoghaire was a widow wi' the two bairns when I wed her."

"Oh." It didn't make any real difference, but still, I felt a small wave of something like relief, on Brianna's behalf. She was the sole child of Jamie's heart, at least, even if I—

"I've not lived wi' them for some time; I live in Edinburgh, and send money to them, but—"

"You don't need to tell me," I interrupted. "It doesn't make any difference. Let me by, please—I'm going."

The thick, ruddy brows drew sharply together.

"Going where?"

"Back. Away. I don't know—let me by!"

"You aren't going anywhere," he said definitely.

"You can't stop me!"

He reached out and grabbed me by both arms.

"Aye, I can," he said. He could; I jerked furiously, but couldn't budge the iron grip on my biceps.

"Let go of me this minute!"

"No, I won't!" He glared at me, eyes narrowed, and I suddenly realized that calm as he might seem outwardly, he was very nearly as upset as I was. I saw the muscles of his throat move as he swallowed, controlling himself enough to speak again.

"I willna let ye go until I've explained to ye, why . . ."

"What is there to explain?" I demanded furiously. "You married again! What else is there?"

The color was rising in his face; the tips of his ears were already red, a sure sign of impending fury.

"And have you lived a nun for twenty years?" he demanded, shaking me slightly. "Have ye?"

"No!" I flung the word at his face, and he flinched slightly. "No, I bloody haven't! And I don't think you've been a monk, either—I never did!"

"Then—" he began, but I was much too furious to listen anymore.

"You lied to me, damn you!"

"I never did!" The skin was stretched tight over his cheekbones, as it was when he was very angry indeed.

"You did, you bastard! You know you did! Let go!" I kicked him sharply in the shin, hard enough to numb my toes. He exclaimed in pain, but didn't let go. Instead, he squeezed harder, making me yelp.

"I never said a thing to ye—"

"No, you didn't! But you lied, anyway! You let me think you weren't married, that there wasn't anyone, that you—that you—" I was half-sobbing with rage, gasping between words. "You should have told me, the minute I came! Why in hell didn't you tell me?" His grip on my arms slackened, and I managed to wrench myself free. He took a step toward me, eyes glittering with fury. I wasn't afraid of him; I drew back my fist and hit him in the chest.

"Why?" I shrieked, hitting him again and again and again, the sound of the blows thudding against his chest. "Why, why, *why*!"

"Because I was afraid!" He got hold of my wrists and threw me backward, so I fell across the bed. He stood over me, fists clenched, breathing hard.

"I am a coward, damn you! I couldna tell ye, for fear ye would leave me, and unmanly thing that I am, I thought I couldna bear that!"

"Unmanly? With two wives? Ha!"

I really thought he would slap me; he raised his arm, but then his open palm clenched into a fist.

"Am I a man? To want you so badly that nothing else matters? To see you, and know I would sacrifice honor or family or life itself to lie wi' you, even though ye'd left me?"

"You have the filthy, unmitigated, bleeding gall to say such a thing to me?" My voice was so high, it came out as a thin and vicious whisper. "You'll blame *me*?"

He stopped then, chest heaving as he caught his breath.

"No. No, I canna blame you." He turned aside, blindly. "How could it have been your fault? Ye wanted to stay wi' me, to die with me."

"I did, the more fool I," I said. "*You* sent me back, you made me go! And now you want to blame me for going?"

He turned back to me, eyes dark with desperation.

"I had to send ye away! I had to, for the bairn's sake!" His eyes went involuntarily to the hook where his coat hung, the pictures of Brianna in its pocket. He took one deep, quivering breath, and calmed himself with a visible effort.

"No," he said, much more quietly. "I canna regret that, whatever the cost. I would have given my life, for her and for you. If it took my heart and soul, too . . ."

He drew a long, quivering breath, mastering the passion that shook him. "I canna blame ye for going."

"You blame me for coming back, though."

He shook his head as though to clear it.

"No, God no!"

He grabbed my hands tight between his own, the strength of his grip grinding the bones together.

"Do ye know what it is to live twenty years without a heart? To live half a man, and accustom yourself to living in the bit that's left, filling in the cracks wi' what mortar comes handy?"

"Do I know?" I echoed. I struggled to loose myself, to little effect. "Yes, you bloody bastard, I know that! What did you think, I'd gone straight back to Frank and lived happy ever after?" I kicked at him as hard as I could. He flinched, but didn't let go.

"Sometimes I hoped ye did," he said, speaking through clenched teeth. "And then sometimes I could see it—him with you, day and night, lyin' with ye, taking your body, holding my child! And God, I could kill ye for it!"

Suddenly, he dropped my hands, whirled, and smashed his fist through the side of the oak armoire. It was an impressive blow; the armoire was a sturdy piece of furniture. It must have bruised his knuckles considerably, but without hesitation, he drove the other fist into the oak boards as well, as though the shining wood were Frank's face—or mine.

"Feel like that about it, do you?" I said coldly, as he stepped back, panting. "I don't even have to imagine you with Laoghaire—I've bloody *seen* her!"

"I dinna care a fig for Laoghaire, and never have!"

"Bastard!" I said again. "You'd marry a woman without wanting her, and then throw her aside the minute—"

"Shut up!" he roared. "Hold your tongue, ye wicked wee bitch!" He slammed a fist down on the washstand, glaring at me. "I'm damned the one way or the other, no? If I felt anything for her, I'm a faithless womanizer, and if I didn't, I'm a heartless beast."

"You should have told me!"

"And if I had?" He grabbed my hand and jerked me to my feet, holding me eye to eye with him. "You'd have turned on your heel and gone without a word. And having seen ye again—I tell ye, I would ha' done far worse than lie to keep you!"

He pressed me tight against his body and kissed me, long and hard. My knees turned to water, and I fought to keep my feet, buttressed by the vision of Laoghaire's angry eyes, and her voice, echoing shrill in my ears. *He's mine!*

"This is senseless," I said, pulling away. Fury had its own intoxication, but the hangover was setting in fast, a black dizzy vortex. My head swam so that I could hardly keep my balance. "I can't think straight. I'm leaving."

I lurched toward the door, but he caught me by the waist, yanking me back.

He whirled me toward himself and kissed me again, hard enough to leave a quicksilver taste of blood in my mouth. It was neither affection nor desire, but a blind passion, a determination to possess me. He was through talking.

So was I. I pulled my mouth away and slapped him hard across the face, fingers curved to rake his flesh.

He jerked back, cheek scraped raw, then twisted his fingers tight in my hair, bent and took my mouth again, deliberate and savage, ignoring the kicks and blows I rained on him.

He bit my lower lip, hard, and when I opened my lips, gasping, thrust his tongue into my mouth, stealing breath and words together.

He threw me bodily onto the bed where we had lain laughing an hour before, and pinned me there at once with the weight of his body.

He was most mightily roused.

So was I.

Mine, he said, without uttering a word. *Mine!*

I fought him with boundless fury and no little skill, and *Yours,* my body echoed back. *Yours, and may you be damned for it!*

I didn't feel him rip my gown, but I felt the heat of his body on my bare breasts, through the thin linen of his shirt, the long, hard muscle of his thigh straining against my own. He took his hand off my arm to tear at his breeches, and I clawed him from ear to breast, striping his skin with pale red.

We were doing our level best to kill each other, fueled by the rage of years apart—mine for his sending me away, his for my going, mine for Laoghaire, his for Frank.

"Bitch!" he panted. "Whore!"

"Damn you!" I got a hand in his own long hair, and yanked, pulling his face down to me again. We rolled off the bed and landed on the floor in a tangled heap, rolling to and fro in a welter of half-uttered curses and broken words.

I didn't hear the door open. I didn't hear anything, though she must have called out, more than once. Blind and deaf, I knew nothing but Jamie until the shower of cold water struck us, sudden as an electric shock. Jamie froze. All the color left his face, leaving the bones jutting stark beneath the skin.

I lay dazed, drops of water dripping from the ends of his hair onto my breasts. Just behind him, I could see Jenny, her face as white as his, holding an empty pan in her hands.

"Stop it!" she said. Her eyes were slanted with a horrified anger. "How could ye, Jamie? Rutting like a wild beast, and not carin' if all the house hears ye!"

He moved off me, slowly, clumsy as a bear. Jenny snatched a quilt from the bed and flung it over my body.

On all fours, he shook his head like a dog, sending droplets of water flying. Then, very slowly, he got to his feet, and pulled his ripped breeches back into place.

"Are ye no ashamed?" she cried, scandalized.

Jamie stood looking down at her as though he had never seen any creature quite like her, and was making up his mind what she might be. The wet ends of his hair dripped over his bare chest.

"Yes," he said at last, quite mildly. "I am."

He seemed dazed. He closed his eyes and a brief, deep shudder went over him. Without a word, he turned and went out.

35

Flight from Eden

Jenny helped me to the bed, making small clucking noises; whether of shock or concern, I couldn't tell. I was vaguely conscious of hovering figures in the doorway—servants, I supposed—but wasn't disposed to pay much attention.

"I'll find ye something to put on," she murmured, fluffing a pillow and pushing me back onto it. "And perhaps a bit of a drink. You're all right?"

"Where's Jamie?"

She glanced at me quickly, sympathy mixed with a gleam of curiosity.

"Dinna be afraid; I'll no let him at ye again." She spoke firmly, then pressed her lips tight together, frowning as she tucked the quilt around me. "How he could do such a thing!"

"It wasn't his fault—not this." I ran a hand through my tangled hair, indicating my general dishevelment. "I mean—I did it, as much as he did. It was both of us. He—I—" I let my hand fall, helpless to explain. I was bruised and shaken, and my lips were swollen.

"I see," was all Jenny said, but she gave me a long, assessing look, and I thought it quite possible that she did see.

I didn't want to talk about the recent happenings, and she seemed to sense this, for she kept quiet for a bit, giving a soft-voiced order to someone in the hall, then moving about the room, straightening furniture and tidying things. I saw her pause for a moment as she saw the holes in the armoire, then she stooped to pick up the larger pieces of the shattered ewer.

As she dumped them into the basin, there was a faint thud from the house below; the slam of the big main door. She stepped to the window and pushed the curtain aside.

"It's Jamie," she said. She glanced at me, and let the curtain fall. "He'll be going up to the hill; he goes there, if he's troubled. That, or he gets drunk wi' Ian. The hill's better."

I gave a small snort.

"Yes, I expect he's troubled, all right."

There was a light step in the hallway, and the younger Janet appeared, carefully balancing a tray of biscuits, whisky, and water. She looked pale and scared.

"Are ye . . . well, Aunt?" she asked tentatively, setting down the tray.

"I'm fine," I assured her, pushing myself upright and reaching for the whisky decanter.

A sharp glance having assured Jenny of the same, she patted her daughter's arm and turned toward the door.

"Stay wi' your auntie," she ordered. "I'll go and find a dress." Janet nodded obediently, and sat down by the bed on a stool, watching me as I ate and drank.

I began to feel physically much stronger with a little food inside me. Internally, I felt quite numb; the recent events seemed at once dreamlike and yet completely clear in my mind. I could recall the smallest details; the blue calico bows on the dress of Laoghaire's daughter, the tiny broken veins in Laoghaire's cheeks, a rough-torn fingernail on Jamie's fourth finger.

"Do you know where Laoghaire is?" I asked Janet. The girl had her head down, apparently studying her own hands. At my question, she jerked upright, blinking.

"Oh!" she said. "Oh. Aye, she and Marsali and Joan went back to Balriggan, where they live. Uncle Jamie made them go."

"Did he," I said flatly.

Janet bit her lip, twisting her hands in her apron. Suddenly she looked up at me.

"Aunt—I'm so awfully sorry!" Her eyes were a warm brown, like her father's, but swimming now with tears.

"It's all right," I said, having no idea what she meant, but trying to be soothing.

"But it was me!" she burst out. She looked thoroughly miserable, but determined to confess. "I—I told Laoghaire ye were here. That's why she came."

"Oh." Well, that explained that, I supposed. I finished the whisky and set the glass carefully back on the tray.

"I didna think—I mean, I didna have it in mind to cause a kebbie-lebbie, truly not. I didna ken that you—that she—"

"It's all right," I said again. "One of us would have found out sooner or later." It made no difference, but I glanced at her with some curiosity. "Why did you tell her, though?"

The girl glanced cautiously over her shoulder, hearing steps start up from below. She leaned close to me.

"Mother told me to," she whispered. And with that, she rose and hastily left the room, brushing past her mother in the doorway.

I didn't ask. Jenny had found a dress for me—one of the elder girls'—and there was no conversation beyond the necessary as she helped me into it.

When I was dressed and shod, my hair combed and put up, I turned to her.

"I want to go," I said. "Now."

She didn't argue, but only looked me over, to see that I was strong enough. She nodded then, dark lashes covering the slanted blue eyes so like her brother's.

"I think that's best," she said quietly.

It was late morning when I left Lallybroch for what I knew would be the last time. I had a dagger at my waist, for protection, though it was unlikely I would need it. My horse's saddlebags held food and several bottles of ale; enough to see me back to the stone circle. I had thought of taking back the pictures of Brianna from Jamie's coat, but after a moment's hesitation, had left them. She belonged to him forever, even if I didn't.

It was a cold autumn day, the morning's gray promise fulfilled with a mourning drizzle. No one was in sight near the house, as Jenny led the horse out of the stable, and held the bridle for me to mount.

I pulled the hood of my cloak farther forward, and nodded to her. Last time, we had parted with tears and embraces, as sisters. She let go the reins, and stood back, as I turned the horse's head toward the road.

"Godspeed!" I heard her call behind me. I didn't answer, nor did I look back.

I rode most of the day, without really noticing where I was going; taking heed only for the general direction, and letting the gelding pick his own way through the mountain passes.

I stopped when the light began to go; hobbled the horse to graze, lay down wrapped in my cloak, and dropped straight asleep, unwilling to stay awake for fear I might think, and remember. Numbness was my only refuge. I knew it would go, but I clung to its gray comfort so long as I might.

It was hunger that brought me unwillingly back to life the next day. I had not paused to eat through all the day before, nor when rising in the morning, but by noon my stomach had begun to register loud protests, and I stopped in a small glen beside a sparkling burn, and unwrapped the food that Jenny had slipped into my saddlebag.

There were oatcakes and ale, and several small loaves of fresh-baked bread, slit down the middle, stuffed with sheepmilk cheese and homemade pickle. Highland sandwiches, the hearty fare of shepherds and warriors, as characteristic of Lallybroch as peanut butter had been of Boston. Very suitable, that my quest should end with one of these.

I ate a sandwich, drank one of the stone bottles of ale, and swung back into the saddle, turning the horse's head to the northeast once more. Unfortunately, while the food had brought fresh strength to my body, it had given fresh life to my feelings as well. As we climbed higher and higher into the clouds, my spirits fell lower—and they hadn't been high to begin with.

The horse was willing enough, but I wasn't. Near midafternoon, I felt that I simply couldn't go on. Leading the horse far enough into a small thicket that it wouldn't be noticeable from the road, I hobbled it loosely, and walked farther under the trees myself, 'til I came to the trunk of a fallen aspen, smooth-skinned, stained green with moss.

I sat slumped over, elbows on my knees and head on my hands. I ached in every joint. Not really from the encounter of the day before, or from the rigors of riding; from grief.

Constraint and judgment had been a great deal of my life. I had learned at some pains the art of healing; to give and to care, but always stopping short of that danger point where too much was given to make me effective. I had learned detachment and disengagement, to my cost.

With Frank, too, I had learned the balancing act of civility; kindness and respect that did not pass those unseen boundaries into passion. And Brianna? Love for a child cannot be free; from the first signs of movement in the womb, a devotion springs up as powerful as it is mindless, irresistible as the process of birth itself. But powerful as it is, it is a love always of control; one is in charge, the protector, the watcher, the guardian—there is great passion in it, to be sure, but never abandon.

Always, always, I had had to balance compassion with wisdom, love with judgment, humanity with ruthlessness.

Only with Jamie had I given everything I had, risked it all. I had thrown away caution and judgment and wisdom, along with the comforts and constraints of a hard-won career. I had brought him nothing but myself, been nothing but myself with him, given him soul as well as body, let him see me naked, trusted him to see me whole and cherish my frailties—because he once had.

I had feared he couldn't, again. Or wouldn't. And then had known those few days of perfect joy, thinking that what had once been true was true once more; I was free to love him, with everything I had and was, and be loved with an honesty that matched my own.

The tears slid hot and wet between my fingers. I mourned for Jamie, and for what I had been, with him.

Do you know, his voice said, whispering, *what it means, to say again "I love you," and to mean it?*

I knew. And with my head in my hands beneath the pine trees, I knew I would never mean it again.

Sunk as I was in miserable contemplation, I didn't hear the footsteps until he was nearly upon me. Startled by the crack of a branch nearby, I rocketed off the fallen tree like a rising pheasant and whirled to face the attacker, heart in my mouth and dagger in hand.

"Christ!" My stalker shied back from the open blade, clearly as startled as I was.

"What the hell are you doing here?" I demanded. I pressed my free hand to my chest. My heart was pounding like a kettledrum and I was sure I was as white as he was.

"Jesus, Auntie Claire! Where'd ye learn to pull a knife like that? Ye scairt hell out of me." Young Ian passed a hand over his brow, Adam's apple bobbing as he swallowed.

"The feeling is mutual," I assured him. I tried to sheathe the dagger, but my hand was shaking too much with reaction to manage it. Knees wobbling, I sank back on the aspen trunk and laid the knife on my thigh.

"I repeat," I said, trying to gain mastery of myself, "what are you doing here?" I had a bloody good idea what he was doing there, and I wasn't having any. On the other hand, I needed a moment's recovery from the fright before I could reliably stand up.

Young Ian bit his lip, glanced around, and at my nod of permission, sat down awkwardly on the trunk beside me.

"Uncle Jamie sent me—" he began. I didn't pause to hear more, but got up at once, knees or no knees, thrusting the dagger into my belt as I turned away.

"Wait, Aunt! Please!" He grabbed at my arm, but I jerked loose, pulling away from him.

"I'm not interested," I said, kicking the fronds of bracken aside. "Go home, wee Ian. I've places to go." I hoped I had, at least.

"But it isn't what you think!" Unable to stop me leaving the clearing, he was following me, arguing as he ducked low branches. "He needs you, Aunt, really he does! Ye must come back wi' me!"

I didn't answer him; I had reached my horse, and bent to undo the hobbles.

"Auntie Claire! Will ye no listen to me?" He loomed up on the far side of the horse, gawky height peering at me over the saddle. He looked very much like his father, his good-natured, half-homely face creased with anxiety.

"No," I said briefly. I stuffed the hobbles into the saddlebag, and put my foot into the stirrup, swinging up with a satisfyingly majestic swish of skirts and petticoats. My dignified departure was hampered at this point by the fact that Young Ian had the horse's reins in a death grip.

"Let go," I said peremptorily.

"Not until ye hear me out," he said. He glared up at me, jaw clenched with stubbornness, soft brown eyes ablaze. I glared back at him. Gangling as he was, he had Ian's skinny muscularity; unless I was prepared to ride him down, there seemed little choice but to listen to him.

All right, I decided. Fat lot of good it would do, to him or his double-dealing uncle, but I'd listen.

"Talk," I said, mustering what patience I could.

He drew a deep breath, eyeing me warily to see whether I meant it. Deciding that I did, he blew his breath out, making the soft brown hair over his brow flutter, and squared his shoulders to begin.

"Well," he started, seeming suddenly unsure. "It . . . I . . . he . . ."

I made a low sound of exasperation in my throat. "Start at the beginning," I said. "But don't make a song and dance of it, hm?"

He nodded, teeth set in his upper lip as he concentrated.

"Well, there was the hell of a stramash broke out at the house, after ye left, when Uncle Jamie came back," he began.

"I'll just bet there was," I said. Despite myself, I was conscious of a small stirring of curiosity, but fought it down, assuming an expression of complete indifference.

"I've never seen Uncle Jamie sae furious," he said, watching my face carefully. "Nor Mother, either. They went at it hammer and tongs, the two o' them. Father tried to quiet them, but it was like they didna even hear him. Uncle Jamie called Mother a meddling besom, and a *lang-nebbit* . . . and . . . and a lot of worse names," he added, flushing.

"He shouldn't have been angry with Jenny," I said. "She was only trying to help—I think." I felt sick with the knowledge that I had caused this rift, too. Jenny had been Jamie's mainstay since the death of their mother when both were children. Was there no end to the damage I had caused by coming back?

To my surprise, Jenny's son smiled briefly. "Well, it wasna all one-sided," he said dryly. "My mother's no the person to be taking abuse lying down, ye ken. Uncle Jamie had a few toothmarks on him before the end of it." He swallowed, remembering.

"In fact, I thought they'd damage each other, surely; Mother went for Uncle Jamie wi' an iron girdle, and he snatched it from her and threw it through the kitchen window. Scairt the chickens out o' the yard," he added, with a feeble grin.

"Less about chickens, Young Ian," I said, looking down at him coldly. "Get on with it; I want to leave."

"Well, then Uncle Jamie knocked over the bookshelf in the parlor—I dinna think he did it on purpose," the lad added hastily, "he was just too fashed to see straight—and went out the door. Father stuck his head out the window and shouted at him where was he going, and he said he was going to find you."

"Then why are you here, and not him?" I was leaning forward slightly, watching his hand on the reins; if his fingers showed signs of relaxation, perhaps I could twitch the rein out of his grasp.

Young Ian sighed. "Well, just as Uncle Jamie was setting out on his horse,

Aunt . . . er . . . I mean his wi—" He blushed miserably. "Laoghaire. She . . . she came down the hill and into the dooryard."

At this point, I gave up pretending indifference.

"And what happened then?"

He frowned. "There was an awful collieshangie, but I couldna hear much. Auntie . . . I mean Laoghaire—she doesna seem to know how to fight properly, like my Mam and Uncle Jamie. She just weeps and wails a lot. Mam says she snivels," he added.

"Mmphm," I said. "And so?"

Laoghaire had slid off her own mount, clutched Jamie by the leg, and more or less dragged him off as well, according to Young Ian. She had then subsided into a puddle in the dooryard, clutching Jamie about the knees, weeping and wailing as was her usual habit.

Unable to escape, Jamie had at last hauled Laoghaire to her feet, flung her bodily over his shoulder, and carried her into the house and up the stairs, ignoring the fascinated gazes of his family and servants.

"Right," I said. I realized that I had been clenching my jaw, and consciously unclenched it. "So he sent you after me because he was too occupied with his *wife*. Bastard! The gall of him! He thinks he can just send someone to fetch me back, like a hired girl, because it doesn't suit his convenience to come himself? He thinks he can have his cake and eat it, does he? Bloody arrogant, selfish, overbearing . . . Scot!" Distracted as I was by the picture of Jamie carrying Laoghaire upstairs, "Scot" was the worst epithet I could come up with on short notice.

My knuckles were white where my hand clutched the edge of the saddle. Not caring about subtlety any more, I leaned down, snatching for the reins.

"Let go!"

"But Auntie Claire, it's not that!"

"What's not that?" Caught by his tone of desperation, I glanced up. His long, narrow face was tight with the anguished need to make me understand.

"Uncle Jamie didna stay to tend Laoghaire!"

"Then why did he send you?"

He took a deep breath, renewing his grip on my reins.

"She shot him. He sent me to find ye, because he's dying."

"If you're lying to me, Ian Murray," I said, for the dozenth time, "you'll regret it to the end of your life—which will be short!"

I had to raise my voice to be heard. The rising wind came whooshing past me, lifting my hair in streamers off my shoulders, whipping my skirts tight around my legs. The weather was suitably dramatic; great black clouds choked the mountain passes, boiling over the crags like seafoam, with a faint distant rumble of thunder, like far-off surf on packed sand.

Lacking breath, Young Ian merely shook his bowed head as he leaned into the wind. He was afoot, leading both ponies across a treacherously boggy stretch of ground near the edge of a tiny loch. I glanced instinctively at my wrist, missing my Rolex.

It was difficult to tell where the sun was, with the in-rolling storm filling half the western sky, but the upper edge of the dark-tinged clouds glowed a brilliant white that was almost gold. I had lost the knack of telling time by sun and sky, but thought it was no more than midafternoon.

Lallybroch lay several hours ahead; I doubted we would reach it by dark. Meaching my way reluctantly toward Craigh na Dun, I had taken nearly two days to reach the small wood where Young Ian had caught up with me. He had, he said, spent only one day in the pursuit; he had known roughly where I was headed, and he himself had shod the pony I rode; my tracks had been plain to him, where they showed in the mud-patches among the heather on the open moor.

Two days since I had left, and one—or more—on the journey back. Three days, then, since Jamie had been shot.

I could get few useful details from Young Ian; having succeeded in his mission, he wanted only to return to Lallybroch as fast as possible, and saw no point in further conversation. Jamie's gunshot wound was in the left arm, he said. That was good, so far as it went. The ball had penetrated into Jamie's side, as well. That wasn't good. Jamie was conscious when last seen —that was good—but was starting a fever. Not good at all. As to the possible effects of shock, the type or severity of the fever, or what treatment had so far been administered, Young Ian merely shrugged.

So perhaps Jamie was dying; perhaps he wasn't. It wasn't a chance I could take, as Jamie himself would know perfectly well. I wondered momentarily whether he might conceivably have shot himself, as a means of forcing me to return. Our last interview could have left him in little doubt as to my response had he come after me, or used force to make me return.

It was beginning to rain, in soft spatters that caught in my hair and lashes, blurring my sight like tears. Past the boggy spot, Young Ian had mounted again, leading the way upward to the final pass that led to Lallybroch.

Jamie was devious enough to have thought of such a plan, all right, and certainly courageous enough to have carried it out. On the other hand, I had never known him to be reckless. He had taken plenty of bold risks—marrying me being one of them, I thought ruefully—but never without an estimation of the cost, and a willingness to pay it. Would he have thought drawing me back to Lallybroch worth the chance of actually dying? That hardly seemed logical, and Jamie Fraser was a very logical man.

I pulled the hood of my cloak further over my head, to keep the increasing downpour out of my face. Young Ian's shoulders and thighs were dark with wet, and the rain dripped from the brim of his slouch hat, but he sat straight in the saddle, ignoring the weather with the stoic nonchalance of a trueborn Scot.

Very well. Given that Jamie likely hadn't shot himself, was he shot at all? He might have made up the story, and sent his nephew to tell it. On consideration, though, I thought it highly unlikely that Young Ian could have delivered the news so convincingly, were it false.

I shrugged, the movement sending a cold rivulet down inside the front of my cloak, and set myself to wait with what patience I could for the journey to be ended. Years in the practice of medicine had taught me not to anticipate; the reality of each case was bound to be unique, and so must be my response to it. My emotions, however, were much harder to control than my professional reactions.

Each time I had left Lallybroch, I had thought I would never return. Now here I was, going back once more. Twice now, I had left Jamie, knowing with certainty that I would never see him again. And yet here I was, going back to him like a bloody homing pigeon to its loft.

"I'll tell you one thing, Jamie Fraser," I muttered under my breath. "If you aren't at death's door when I get there, you'll live to regret it!"

36

Practical and Applied Witchcraft

It was several hours past dark when we arrived at last, soaked to the skin. The house was silent, and dark, save for two dimly lighted windows downstairs in the parlor. There was a single warning bark from one of the dogs, but Young Ian shushed the animal, and after a quick, curious nosing at my stirrup, the black-and-white shape faded back into the darkness of the dooryard.

The warning had been enough to alert someone; as Young Ian led me into the hall, the door to the parlor opened. Jenny poked her head out, her face drawn with worry.

At the sight of Young Ian, she popped out into the hallway, her expression transformed to one of joyous relief, at once superseded by the righteous anger of a mother confronted by an errant offspring.

"Ian, ye wee wretch!" she said. "Where have ye been all this time? Your Da and I ha' been worrit sick for ye!" She paused long enough to look him over anxiously. "You're all right?"

At his nod, her lips grew tight again. "Aye, well. You're for it now, laddie, I'll tell ye! And just where the devil *have* ye been, anyway?"

Gangling, knob-jointed, and dripping wet, Young Ian looked like nothing so much as a drowned scarecrow, but he was still large enough to block me from his mother's view. He didn't answer Jenny's scolding, but shrugged awkwardly and stepped aside, exposing me to his mother's startled gaze.

If my resurrection from the dead had disconcerted her, this second reappearance stunned her. Her deep blue eyes, normally as slanted as her brother's, opened so wide, they looked round. She stared at me for a long moment, without saying anything, then her gaze swiveled once more to her son.

"A cuckoo," she said, almost conversationally. "That's what ye are, laddie —a great cuckoo in the nest. God knows whose son ye were meant to be; it wasna mine."

Young Ian flushed hotly, dropping his eyes as the red burned in his cheeks. He pushed the feathery damp hair out of his eyes with the back of one hand.

"I—well, I just . . ." he began, eyes on his boots, "I couldna just . . ."

"Oh, never mind about it now!" his mother snapped. "Get ye upstairs to your bed; your Da will deal wi' ye in the morning."

Ian glanced helplessly at the parlor door, then at me. He shrugged once more, looked at the sodden hat in his hands as though wondering how it had got there, and shuffled slowly down the hall.

Jenny stood quite still, eyes fixed on me, until the padded door at the end of the hallway closed with a soft thump behind Young Ian. Her face showed lines of strain, and the shadows of sleeplessness smudged her eyes. Still fine-boned and erect, for once she looked her age, and more.

"So you're back," she said flatly.

Seeing no point in answering the obvious, I nodded briefly. The house was quiet around us, and full of shadows, the hallway lighted only by a three-pronged candlestick set on the table.

"Never mind about it now," I said, softly, so as not to disturb the house's slumber. There was, after all, only one thing of importance at the moment. "Where's Jamie?"

After a small hesitation, she nodded as well, accepting my presence for the moment. "In there," she said, waving toward the parlor door.

I started toward the door, then paused. There was the one thing more. "Where's Laoghaire?" I asked.

"Gone," she said. Her eyes were flat and dark in the candlelight, unreadable.

I nodded in response, and stepped through the door, closing it gently but firmly behind me.

Too long to be laid on the sofa, Jamie lay on a camp bed set up before the fire. Asleep or unconscious, his profile rose dark and sharp-edged against the light of the glowing coals, unmoving.

Whatever he was, he wasn't dead—at least not yet. My eyes growing accustomed to the dim light of the fire, I could see the slow rise and fall of his chest beneath nightshirt and quilt. A flask of water and a brandy bottle sat on the small table by the bed. The padded chair by the fire had a shawl thrown over its back; Jenny had been sitting there, watching over her brother.

There seemed no need now for haste. I untied the strings at the neck of my cloak, and spread the soggy garment over the chairback, taking the shawl in substitute. My hands were cold; I put them under my arms, hugging myself, to bring them to something like a normal temperature before I touched him.

When I did venture to place a thawed hand on his forehead, I nearly jerked it back. He was hot as a just-fired pistol, and he twitched and moaned at my touch. Fever, indeed. I stood looking down at him for a moment, then carefully moved to the side of the bed and sat down in Jenny's chair. I didn't think he would sleep long, with a temperature like that, and it seemed a shame to wake him needlessly soon, merely to examine him.

The cloak behind me dripped water on the floor, a slow, arrhythmic patting. It reminded me unpleasantly of an old Highland superstition—the "death-drop." Just before a death occurs, the story goes, the sound of water dripping is heard in the house, by those sensitive to such things.

I wasn't, thank heaven, subject to noticing supernatural phenomena of that sort. No, I thought wryly, it takes something like a crack through time to get *your* attention. The thought made me smile, if only briefly, and dispelled the frisson I had felt at the thought of the death-drop.

As the rain chill left me, though, I still felt uneasy, and for obvious reasons. It wasn't that long ago that I had stood by another makeshift bed, deep in the night-watches, and contemplated death, and the waste of a marriage. The thoughts I had begun in the wood hadn't stopped on the hasty journey back to Lallybroch, and they continued now, without my conscious volition.

Honor had led Frank to his decision—to keep me as his wife, and raise Brianna as his own. Honor, and an unwillingness to decline a responsibility he felt was his. Well, here before me lay another honorable man.

Laoghaire and her daughters, Jenny and her family, the Scots prisoners, the smugglers, Mr. Willoughby and Geordie, Fergus and the tenants—how many other responsibilities had Jamie shouldered, through our years apart?

Frank's death had absolved me of one of my own obligations; Brianna herself of another. The Hospital Board, in their eternal wisdom, had severed the single great remaining tie that bound me to that life. I had had time, with Joe Abernathy's help, to relieve myself of the smaller responsibilities, to depute and delegate, divest and resolve.

Jamie had had neither warning nor choice about my reappearance in his life; no time to make decisions or resolve conflicts. And he was not one to abandon his responsibilities, even for the sake of love.

Yes, he'd lied to me. Hadn't trusted me to recognize his responsibilities, to stand by him—or to leave him—as his circumstances demanded. He'd been afraid. So had I; afraid that he wouldn't choose me, confronted with the struggle between a twenty-year-old love and a present-day family. So I'd run away.

"Who you jiving, L.J.?" I heard Joe Abernathy's voice say, derisive and affectionate. I had fled toward Craigh na Dun with all the speed and decision of a condemned felon approaching the steps of the gallows. Nothing had slowed my journey but the hope that Jamie would come after me.

True, the pangs of conscience and wounded pride had spurred me on, but the one moment when Young Ian had said, "He's dying," had shown those up for the flimsy things they were.

My marriage to Jamie had been for me like the turning of a great key, each small turn setting in play the intricate fall of tumblers within me. Bree had been able to turn that key as well, edging closer to the unlocking of the door of myself. But the final turn of the lock was frozen—until I had walked into the printshop in Edinburgh, and the mechanism had sprung free with a final, decisive click. The door now was ajar, the light of an unknown future shining through its crack. But it would take more strength than I had alone to push it open.

I watched the rise and fall of his breath, and the play of light and shadow on the strong, clean lines of his face, and knew that nothing truly mattered between us but the fact that we both still lived. So here I was. Again. And whatever the cost of it might be to him or me, here I stayed.

I didn't realize that his eyes had opened until he spoke.

"Ye came back, then," he said softly. "I knew ye would."

I opened my mouth to reply, but he was still talking, eyes fixed on my face, pupils dilated to pools of darkness.

"My love," he said, almost whispering. "God, ye do look so lovely, wi' your great eyes all gold, and your hair so soft round your face." He brushed his tongue across dry lips. "I knew ye must forgive me, Sassenach, once ye knew."

Once I knew? My brows shot up, but I didn't speak; he had more to say.

"I was so afraid to lose ye again, *mo chridhe,*" he murmured. "So afraid. I havena loved anyone but you, my Sassenach, never since the day I saw ye— but I couldna . . . I couldna bear . . ." His voice drifted off in an unintelligible mumble, and his eyes closed again, lashes lying dark against the high curve of his cheek.

I sat still, wondering what I should do. As I watched, his eyes opened suddenly once again. Heavy and drowsy with fever, they sought my face.

"It willna be long, Sassenach," he said, as though reassuring me. One corner of his mouth twitched in an attempt at a smile. "Not long. Then I shall touch ye once more. I do long to touch you."

"Oh, Jamie," I said. Moved by tenderness, I reached out and laid my hand along his burning cheek.

His eyes snapped wide with shock, and he jerked bolt upright in bed, letting out a bloodcurdling yell of anguish as the movement jarred his wounded arm.

"Oh God, oh Christ, oh Jesus Lord God Almighty!" he said, bent half-breathless and clutching at his left arm. "You're real! Bloody stinking filthy pig-swiving hell! Oh, Christ!"

"Are you all right?" I said, rather inanely. I could hear startled exclamations from the floor above, muffled by the thick planks, and the thump of feet as one after another of Lallybroch's inhabitants leapt from their beds to investigate the uproar.

Jenny's head, eyes even wider than before, poked through the parlor door. Jamie saw her, and somehow found sufficient breath to roar "Get *out*!" before doubling up again with an agonized groan.

"Je-sus," he said between clenched teeth. "What in God's holy name are ye doing here, Sassenach?"

"What do you mean, what am I doing here?" I said. "You sent for me. And what do you mean, I'm real?"

He unclenched his jaw and tentatively loosened his grip on his left arm. The resultant sensation proving unsatisfactory, he promptly grabbed it again and said several things in French involving the reproductive organs of assorted saints and animals.

"For God's sake, lie down!" I said. I took him by the shoulders and eased him back onto the pillows, noting with some alarm how close his bones were to the surface of his heated skin.

"I thought ye were a fever dream, 'til you touched me," he said, gasping. "What the hell d'ye mean, popping up by my bed and scarin' me to death?" He grimaced in pain. "Christ, it feels like my damn arm's come off at the shoulder. Och, bugger it!" he exclaimed, as I firmly detached the fingers of his right hand from his left arm.

"Didn't you send Young Ian to tell me you were dying?" I said, deftly rolling back the sleeve of his nightshirt. The arm was wound in a huge bandage above the elbow, and I groped for the end of the linen strip.

"Me? No! Ow, that hurts!"

"It'll hurt worse before I'm through with you," I said, carefully unwrapping. "You mean the little bastard came after me on his own? You didn't *want* me to come back?"

"Want ye back? No! Want ye to come back to me for nothing but pity, the same as ye might show for a dog in a ditch? Bloody hell! No! I forbade the little bugger to go after ye!" He scowled furiously at me, ruddy brows knitting together.

"I'm a doctor," I said coldly, "not a veterinarian. And if you didn't want me back, what was all that you were saying before you realized I was real, hm? Bite the blanket or something; the end's stuck, and I'm going to pull it loose."

He bit his lip instead, and made no noise but a swift intake of air through his nose. It was impossible to judge his color in the firelight, but his eyes closed briefly, and small beads of sweat popped out on his forehead.

I turned away for a moment, groping in the drawer of Jenny's desk where the extra candles were kept. I needed more light before I did anything.

"I suppose Young Ian told me you were dying just to get me back here. He must have thought I wouldn't come otherwise." The candles were there; fine beeswax, from the Lallybroch hives.

"For what it's worth, I am dying." His voice came from behind me, dry and blunt, despite his breathlessness.

I turned back to him in some surprise. His eyes rested on my face quite calmly, now that the pain in his arm had lessened a bit, but his breath was still coming unevenly, and his eyes were heavy and bright with fever. I didn't respond at once, but lit the candles I had found, placing them in the big candelabra that usually decorated the sideboard, unused save for great occasions. The flames of five additional candles brightened the room as though in preparation for a party. I bent over the bed, noncommital.

"Let's have a look at it."

The wound itself was a ragged dark hole, scabbed at the edges and faintly blue-tinged. I pressed the flesh on either side of the wound; it was red and angry-looking, and there was a considerable seepage of pus. Jamie stirred uneasily as I drew my fingertips gently but firmly down the length of the muscle.

"You have the makings of a very fine little infection there, my lad," I said. "Young Ian said it went into your side; a second shot, or did it go through your arm?"

"It went through. Jenny dug the ball out of my side. That wasna so bad, though. Just an inch or so in." He spoke in brief spurts, lips tightening involuntarily between sentences.

"Let me see where it went through."

Moving very slowly, he turned his hand to the outside, letting the arm fall away from his side. I could see that even that small movement was intensely painful. The exit wound was just above the elbow joint, on the inside of the upper arm. Not directly opposite the entrance wound, though; the ball had been deflected in its passage.

"Hit the bone," I said, trying not to imagine what that must have felt like. "Do you know if the bone's broken? I don't want to poke you more than I need to."

"Thanks for small mercies," he said, with an attempt at a smile. The muscles of his face trembled, though, and went slack with exhaustion.

"No, I think it's not broken," he said. "I've broken my collarbone and my hand before, and it's no like that, though it hurts a bit."

"I expect it does." I felt my way carefully up the swell of his biceps, testing for tenderness. "How far up does the pain go?"

He glanced at his wounded arm, almost casually. "Feels like I've a hot poker in my arm, not a bone. But it's no just the arm pains me now; my whole side's gone stiff and sore." He swallowed, licking his lips again. "Will ye give me a taste of the brandy?" he asked. "It hurts to feel my heart beating," he added apologetically.

Without comment, I poured a cup of water from the flask on the table, and held it to his lips. He raised one brow, but drank thirstily, then let his head fall back against the pillow. He breathed deeply for a moment, eyes closed, then opened them and looked directly at me.

"I've had two fevers in my life that near killed me," he said. "I think this one likely will. I wouldna send for ye, but . . . I'm glad you're here." He swallowed once, then went on. "I . . . wanted to say to ye that I'm sorry.

And to bid ye a proper farewell. I wouldna ask ye to stay 'til the end, but . . . would ye . . . would ye stay wi' me—just for a bit?"

His right hand was pressed flat against the mattress, steadying him. I could see that he was fighting hard to keep any note of pleading from his voice or eyes, to make it a simple request, one that could be refused.

I sat down on the bed beside him, careful not to jar him. The firelight glowed on one side of his face, sparking the red-gold stubble of his beard, picking up the small flickers of silver here and there, leaving the other side masked in shadow. He met my eyes, not blinking. I hoped the yearning that showed in his face was not quite so apparent on my own.

I reached out and ran a hand gently down the side of his face, feeling the soft scratchiness of beard stubble.

"I'll stay for a bit," I said. "But you're not going to die."

He raised one eyebrow. "You brought me through one bad fever, using what I still think was witchcraft. And Jenny got me through the next, wi' naught but plain stubbornness. I suppose wi' the both of ye here, ye might just manage it, but I'm no at all sure I want to go through such an ordeal again. I think I'd rather just die and ha' done with it, if it's all the same to you."

"Ingrate," I said. "Coward." Torn between exasperation and tenderness, I patted his cheek and stood up, groping in the deep pocket of my skirt. There was one item I had carried on my person at all times, not trusting it to the vagaries of travel.

I laid the small, flat case on the table and flipped the latch. "I'm not going to let you die this time either," I informed him, "greatly as I may be tempted." I carefully extracted the roll of gray flannel and laid it on the table with a soft clinking noise. I unrolled the flannel, displaying the gleaming row of syringes, and rummaged in the box for the small bottle of penicillin tablets.

"What in God's name are those?" Jamie asked, eyeing the syringes with interest. "They look wicked sharp."

I didn't answer, occupied in dissolving the penicillin tablets in the vial of sterile water. I selected a glass barrel, fitted a needle, and pressed the tip through the rubber covering the mouth of the bottle. Holding it up to the light, I pulled back slowly on the plunger, watching the thick white liquid fill the barrel, checking for bubbles. Then pulling the needle free, I depressed the plunger slightly until a drop of liquid pearled from the point and rolled slowly down the length of the spike.

"Roll onto your good side," I said, turning to Jamie, "and pull up your shirt."

He eyed the needle in my hand with keen suspicion, but reluctantly obeyed. I surveyed the terrain with approval.

"Your bottom hasn't changed a bit in twenty years," I remarked, admiring the muscular curves.

"Neither has yours," he replied courteously, "but I'm no insisting you expose it. Are ye suffering a sudden attack of lustfulness?"

"Not just at present," I said evenly, swabbing a patch of skin with a cloth soaked in brandy.

"That's a verra nice make of brandy," he said, peering back over his shoulder, "but I'm more accustomed to apply it at the other end."

"It's also the best source of alcohol available. Hold still now, and relax." I jabbed deftly and pressed the plunger slowly in.

"Ouch!" Jamie rubbed his posterior resentfully.

"It'll stop stinging in a minute." I poured an inch of brandy into the cup. "Now you can have a bit to drink—a very little bit."

He drained the cup without comment, watching me roll up the collection of syringes. Finally he said, "I thought ye stuck pins in ill-wish dolls when ye meant to witch someone; not in the people themselves."

"It's not a pin, it's a hypodermic syringe."

"I dinna care what ye call it; it felt like a bloody horseshoe nail. Would ye care to tell me why jabbing pins in my arse is going to help my arm?"

I took a deep breath. "Well, do you remember my once telling you about germs?"

He looked quite blank.

"Little beasts too small to see," I elaborated. "They can get into your body through bad food or water, or through open wounds, and if they do, they can make you ill."

He stared at his arm with interest. "I've germs in my arm, have I?"

"You very definitely have." I tapped a finger on the small flat box. "The medicine I just shot into your backside kills germs, though. You get another shot every four hours 'til this time tomorrow, and then we'll see how you're doing."

I paused. Jamie was staring at me, shaking his head.

"Do you understand?" I asked. He nodded slowly.

"Aye, I do. I should ha' let them burn ye, twenty years ago."

37

What's in a Name

After giving him a shot and settling him comfortably, I sat watching until he fell asleep again, allowing him to hold my hand until his own grip relaxed in sleep and the big hand dropped slack by his side.

I sat by his bed for the rest of the night, dozing sometimes, and rousing myself by means of the internal clock all doctors have, geared to the rhythms of a hospital's shift changes. Two more shots, the last at daybreak, and by then the fever had loosed its hold perceptibly. He was still very warm to the touch, but his flesh no longer burned, and he rested easier, falling asleep after the last shot with no more than a few grumbles and a faint moan as his arm twinged.

"Bloody eighteenth-century germs are no match for penicillin," I told his sleeping form. "No resistance. Even if you had syphilis, I'd have it cleaned up in no time."

And what then? I wondered, as I staggered off to the kitchen in search of hot tea and food. A strange woman, presumably the cook or the housemaid, was firing up the brick oven, ready to receive the daily loaves that lay rising in their pans on the table. She didn't seem surprised to see me, but cleared away a small space for me to sit down, and brought me tea and fresh girdle-cakes with no more than a quick "Good mornin' to ye, mum" before returning to her work.

Evidently, Jenny had informed the household of my presence. Did that mean she accepted it herself? I doubted it. Clearly, she had wanted me to go, and wasn't best pleased to have me back. If I was going to stay, there was plainly going to be a certain amount of explanation about Laoghaire, from both Jenny and Jamie. And I *was* going to stay.

"Thank you," I said politely to the cook, and taking a fresh cup of tea with me, went back to the parlor to wait until Jamie saw fit to wake up again.

People passed by the door during the morning, pausing now and then to peep through, but always went on hurriedly when I looked up. At last, Jamie showed signs of waking, just before noon; he stirred, sighed, groaned as the movement jarred his arm, and subsided once more.

I gave him a few moments to realize that I was there, but his eyes stayed shut. He wasn't asleep, though; the lines of his body were slightly tensed, not relaxed in slumber. I had watched him sleep all night; I knew the difference.

"All right," I said. I leaned back in the chair, settling myself comfortably, well out of his reach. "Let's hear it, then."

A small slit of blue showed under the long auburn lashes, then disappeared again.

"Mmmm?" he said, pretending to wake slowly. The lashes fluttered against his cheeks.

"Don't stall," I said crisply. "I know perfectly well you're awake. Open your eyes and tell me about Laoghaire."

The blue eyes opened and rested on me with an expression of some disfavor.

"You're no afraid of giving me a relapse?" he inquired. "I've always heard sick folk shouldna be troubled owermuch. It sets them back."

"You have a doctor right here," I assured him. "If you pass out from the strain, I'll know what to do about it."

"That's what I'm afraid of." His narrowed gaze flicked to the little case of drugs and hypodermics on the table, then back to me. "My arse feels like I've sat in a gorse bush wi' no breeks on."

"Good," I said pleasantly. "You'll get another one in an hour. Right now, you're going to talk."

His lips pressed tight together, but then relaxed as he sighed. He pushed himself laboriously upright against the pillows, one-handed. I didn't help him.

"All right," he said at last. He didn't look at me, but down at the quilt, where his finger traced the edge of the starred design.

"Well, it was when I'd come back from England."

He had come up from the Lake District and over the Carter's Bar, that great ridge of high ground that divides England from Scotland, on whose broad back the ancient courts and markets of the Borders had been held.

"There's a stone there to mark the border, maybe you'll know; it looks the sort of stone to last a while." He glanced at me, questioning, and I nodded. I did know it; a huge menhir, some ten feet tall. In my time, someone had carved on its one face ENGLAND, and on the other, SCOTLAND.

There he stopped to rest, as thousands of travelers had stopped over the years, his exiled past behind him, the future—and home—below and beyond, past the hazy green hollows of the Lowlands, up into the gray crags of the Highlands, hidden by fog.

His good hand ran back and forth through his hair, as it always did when he thought, leaving the cowlicks on top standing up in small, bright whorls.

"You'll not know how it is, to live among strangers for so long."

"Won't I?" I said, with some sharpness. He glanced up at me, startled, then smiled faintly, looking down at the coverlet.

"Aye, maybe ye will," he said. "Ye change, no? Much as ye want to keep the memories of home, and who ye are—you're changed. Not one of the strangers; ye could never be that, even if ye wanted to. But different from who ye were, too."

I thought of myself, standing silent beside Frank, a bit of flotsam in the eddies of university parties, pushing a pram through the chilly parks of Boston, playing bridge and talking with other wives and mothers, speaking the foreign language of middle-class domesticity. Strangers indeed.

"Yes," I said. "I know. Get on."

He sighed, rubbing his nose with a forefinger. "So I came back," he said. He looked up, a smile hidden in the corner of his mouth. "What is it ye told wee Ian? 'Home is the place where, when ye have to go there, they have to take ye in'?"

"That's it," I said. "It's a quotation from a poet called Frost. But what do you mean? Surely your family was glad to see you!"

He frowned, fingering the quilt. "Aye, they were," he said slowly. "It's not that—I dinna mean they made me feel unwelcome, not at all. But I had been away so long—Michael and wee Janet and Ian didna even remember me." He smiled ruefully. "They'd heard about me, though. When I came into the kitchen, they'd squash back against the walls and stare at me, wi' their eyes gone round."

He leaned forward a little, intent on making me understand.

"See, it was different, when I hid in the cave. I wasna in the house, and they seldom saw me, but I was always *here,* I was always part of them. I hunted for them; I kent when they were hungry, or cold, or when the goats were ill or the kail crop poor, or a new draft under the kitchen door.

"Then I went to prison," he said abruptly. "And to England. I wrote to them—and they to me—but it canna be the same, to see a few black words on the paper, telling things that happened months before.

"And when I came back—" He shrugged, wincing as the movement jarred his arm. "It was different. Ian would ask me what I thought of fencing in auld Kirby's pasture, but I'd know he'd already set Young Jamie to do it. I'd walk through the fields, and folk would squint at me, suspicious, thinking me a stranger. Then their eyes would go big as they'd seen a ghost, when they knew me."

He stopped, looking out at the window, where the brambles of his mother's rose beat against the glass as the wind changed. "I *was* a ghost, I think." He glanced at me shyly. "If ye ken what I mean."

"Maybe," I said. Rain was streaking the glass, with drops the same gray as the sky outside.

"You feel like your ties to the earth are broken," I said softly. "Floating through rooms without feeling your footsteps. Hearing people speak to you, and not making sense of it. I remember that—before Bree was born." But I had had one tie then; I had her, to anchor me to life.

He nodded, not looking at me, and then was quiet for a minute. The peat fire hissed on the hearth behind me, smelling of the Highlands, and the rich scent of cock-a-leekie and baking bread spread through the house, warm and comforting as a blanket.

"I was here," he said softly, "but not home."

I could feel the pull of it around me—the house, the family, the place itself. I, who couldn't remember a childhood home, felt the urge to sit down here and stay forever, enmeshed in the thousand strands of daily life, bound securely to this bit of earth. What would it have meant to him, who had lived all his life in the strength of that bond, endured his exile in the hope of coming back to it, and then arrived to find himself still rootless?

"And I suppose I was lonely," he said quietly. He lay still on the pillow, eyes closed.

"I suppose you were," I said, careful to let no tone either of sympathy or condemnation show. I knew something of loneliness, too.

He opened his eyes then, and met my gaze with a naked honesty. "Aye, there was that too," he said. "Not the main thing, no—but aye, that too."

Jenny had tried, with varying degrees of gentleness and insistence, to persuade him to marry again. She had tried intermittently since the days after Culloden, presenting first one and then another personable young widow, this and that sweet-tempered virgin, all to no avail. Now, bereft of the feelings that had sustained him so far, desperately seeking some sense of connection—he had listened.

"Laoghaire was married to Hugh MacKenzie, one of Colum's tacksmen," he said, eyes closed once more. "Hugh was killed at Culloden, though, and two years later, Laoghaire married Simon MacKimmie of clan Fraser. The two lassies—Marsali and Joan—they're his. The English arrested him a few years later, and took him to prison in Edinburgh." He opened his eyes, looking up at the dark ceiling beams overhead. "He had a good house, and property worth seizing. That was enough to make a Highland man a traitor, then, whether he'd fought for the Stuarts openly or not." His voice was growing hoarse, and he stopped to clear his throat.

"Simon wasn't as lucky as I was. He died in prison, before they could bring him to trial. The Crown tried for some time to take the estate, but Ned Gowan went to Edinburgh, and spoke for Laoghaire, and he managed to save the main house and a little money, claiming it was her dower right."

"Ned Gowan?" I spoke with mingled surprise and pleasure. "He can't still be alive, surely?" It was Ned Gowan, a small and elderly solicitor who advised the MacKenzie clan on legal matters, who had saved me from being burned as a witch, twenty years before. I had thought him quite ancient then.

Jamie smiled, seeing my pleasure. "Oh, aye. I expect they'll have to knock him on the head wi' an ax to kill him. He looks just the same as he always did, though he must be past seventy now."

"Does he still live at Castle Leoch?"

He nodded, reaching to the table for the tumbler of water. He drank awkwardly, right-handed, and set it back.

"What's left of it. Aye, though he's traveled a great deal these last years, appealing treason cases and filing lawsuits to recover property." Jamie's smile had a bitter edge. "There's a saying, aye? 'After a war, first come the corbies to eat the flesh; and then the lawyers, to pick the bones.' "

His right hand went to his left shoulder, massaging it unconsciously.

"No, he's a good man, is Ned, in spite of his profession. He goes back and forth to Inverness, to Edinburgh—sometimes even to London or Paris. And he stops here from time to time, to break his journey."

It was Ned Gowan who had mentioned Laoghaire to Jenny, returning from Balriggan to Edinburgh. Pricking up her ears, Jenny had inquired for further details, and finding these satisfactory, had at once sent an invitation to Balriggan, for Laoghaire and her two daughters to come to Lallybroch for Hogmanay, which was near.

> *The house was bright that night, with candles lit in the windows, and bunches of holly and ivy fixed to the staircase and the doorposts. There were not so many pipers in the Highlands as there had been before Culloden, but one had been found, and a fiddler as well, and music floated up the stairwell, mixed with the heady scent of rum punch, plum cake, almond squirts, and Savoy biscuits.*
>
> *Jamie had come down late and hesitant. Many people here he had not seen in nearly ten years, and he was not eager to see them now, feeling changed and distant as he did. But Jenny had made him a new shirt, brushed and mended his coat, and combed his hair smooth and plaited it for him before going downstairs to see to the cooking. He had no excuse to linger, and at last had come down, into the noise and swirl of the gathering.*
>
> *"Mister Fraser!" Peggy Gibbons was the first to see him; she hurried across the room, face glowing, and threw her arms about him, quite unabashed. Taken by surprise, he hugged her back, and within moments was surrounded by a small crowd of women, exclaiming over him, holding up small children born since his departure, kissing his cheeks and patting his hands.*
>
> *The men were shyer, greeting him with a gruff word of welcome or a slap on the back as he made his way slowly through the rooms, until, quite overwhelmed, he had escaped temporarily into the laird's study.*

Once his father's room, and then his own, it now belonged to his brother-in-law, who had run Lallybroch through the years of his absence. The ledgers and stockbooks and accounts were all lined up neatly on the edge of the battered desk; he ran a finger along the leather spines, feeling a sense of comfort at the touch. It was all in here; the planting and the harvests, the careful purchases and acquisitions, the slow accumulations and dispersals that were the rhythm of life to the tenants of Lallybroch.

On the small bookshelf, he found his wooden snake. Along with everything else of value, he had left it behind when he went to prison. A small icon carved of cherrywood, it had been the gift of his elder brother, dead in childhood. He was sitting in the chair behind the desk, stroking the snake's well-worn curves, when the door of the study opened.

"Jamie?" she had said, hanging shyly back. He had not bothered to light a lamp in the study; she was silhouetted by the candles burning in the hall. She wore her pale hair loose, like a maid, and the light shone through it, haloing her unseen face.

"You'll remember me, maybe?" she had said, tentative, reluctant to come into the room without invitation.

"Aye," he said, after a pause. "Aye, of course I do."

"The music's starting," she said. It was; he could hear the whine of the fiddle and the stamp of feet from the front parlor, along with an occasional shout of merriment. It showed signs of being a good party already; most of the guests would be asleep on the floor come morning.

"Your sister says you're a bonny dancer," she said, still shy, but determined.

"It will ha' been some time since I tried," he said, feeling shy himself, and painfully awkward, though the fiddle music ached in his bones and his feet twitched at the sound of it.

"It's 'Tha mo Leabaidh 'san Fhraoch'—'In the Heather's my Bed'—you'll ken that one. Will ye come and try wi' me?" She had held out a hand to him, small and graceful in the half-dark. And he had risen, clasped her outstretched hand in his own, and taken his first steps in pursuit of himself.

"It was in here," he said, waving his good hand at the room where we sat. "Jenny had had the furniture cleared away, all but one table wi' the food and the whisky, and the fiddler stood by the window there, wi' a new moon over his shoulder." He nodded at the window, where the rose vine trembled. Something of the light of that Hogmanay feast lingered on his face, and I felt a small pang, seeing it.

"We danced all that night, sometimes wi' others, but mostly with each other. And at the dawn, when those still awake went to the end o' the house to see what omens the New Year might bring, the two of us went, too. The single women took it in turns to spin about, and walk through the door wi' their eyes closed, then spin again and open their eyes to see what the first thing they might see would be—for that tells them about the man they'll marry, ye ken."

There had been a lot of laughter, as the guests, heated by whisky and dancing, pushed and shoved at the door. Laoghaire had held back, flushed and laughing, saying it was a game for young girls, and not for a matron of thirty-four, but the others had insisted, and try she had. Spun three times clockwise and opened the door, stepped out into the cold dawnlight and spun again. And when she opened her eyes, they had rested on Jamie's face, wide with expectation.

"So . . . there she was, a widow wi' two bairns. She needed a man, that was plain enough. I needed . . . something." He gazed into the fire, where the low flame glimmered through the red mass of the peat; heat without much light. "I supposed that we might help each other."

They had married quietly at Balriggan, and he had moved his few possessions there. Less than a year later, he had moved out again, and gone to Edinburgh.

"What on earth happened?" I asked, more than curious.

He looked up at me, helpless.

"I canna say. It wasna that anything was wrong, exactly—only that nothing was right." He rubbed a hand tiredly between his brows. "It was me, I think; my fault. I always disappointed her somehow. We'd sit down to supper and all of a sudden the tears would well up in her eyes, and she'd leave the table sobbing, and me sitting there wi' not a notion what I'd done or said wrong."

His fist clenched on the coverlet, then relaxed. "God, I *never* knew what to do for her, or what to say! Anything I said just made it worse, and there would be days—nay, weeks!—when she'd not speak to me, but only turn away when I came near her, and stand staring out the window until I went away again."

His fingers went to the parallel scratches down the side of his neck. They were nearly healed now, but the marks of my nails still showed on his fair skin. He looked at me wryly.

"You never did that to me, Sassenach."

"Not my style," I agreed, smiling faintly. "If I'm mad at you, you'll bloody know why, at least."

He snorted briefly and lay back on his pillows. Neither of us spoke for a bit. Then he said, staring up at the ceiling, "I thought I didna want to hear anything about what it was like—wi' Frank, I mean. I was maybe wrong about that.''

"I'll tell you anything you want to know," I said. "But not just now. It's still your turn."

He sighed and closed his eyes.

"She was afraid of me," he said softly, a minute later. "I tried to be gentle wi' her—God, I tried again and again, everything I knew to please a woman. But it was no use."

His head turned restlessly, making a hollow in the feather pillow.

"Maybe it was Hugh, or maybe Simon. I kent them both, and they were good men, but there's no telling what goes on in a marriage bed. Maybe it was bearing the children; not all women can stand it. But something hurt her, sometime, and I couldna heal it for all my trying. She shrank away when I touched her, and I could see the sickness and the fear in her eyes." There were lines of sorrow around his own closed eyes, and I reached impulsively for his hand.

He squeezed it gently and opened his eyes. "That's why I left, finally," he said softly. "I couldna bear it anymore."

I didn't say anything, but went on holding his hand, putting a finger on his pulse to check it. His heartbeat was reassuringly slow and steady.

He shifted slightly in the bed, moving his shoulders and making a grimace of discomfort as he did so.

"Arm hurt a lot?" I asked.

"A bit."

I bent over him, feeling his brow. He was very warm, but not feverish. There was a line between the thick ruddy brows, and I smoothed it with a knuckle.

"Head ache?"

"Yes."

"I'll go and make you some willow-bark tea." I made to rise, but his hand on my arm stopped me.

"I dinna need tea," he said. "It would ease me, though, if maybe I could lay my head in your lap, and have ye rub my temples a bit?" Blue eyes looked up at me, limpid as a spring sky.

"You don't fool me a bit, Jamie Fraser," I said. "I'm not going to forget about your next shot." Nonetheless, I was already moving the chair out of the way, and sitting down beside him on the bed.

He made a small grunting sound of content as I moved his head into my lap and began to stroke it, rubbing his temples, smoothing back the thick wavy mass of his hair. The back of his neck was damp; I lifted the hair away and blew softly on it, seeing the smooth fair skin prickle into gooseflesh at the nape of his neck.

"Oh, that feels good," he murmured. Despite my resolve not to touch him beyond the demands of caretaking until everything between us was resolved, I found my hands molding themselves to the clean, bold lines of his neck and shoulders, seeking the hard knobs of his vertebrae and the broad, flat planes of his shoulder blades.

He was firm and solid under my hands, his breath a warm caress on my thigh, and it was with some reluctance that I at last eased him back onto the pillow and reached for the ampule of penicillin.

"All right," I said, turning back the sheet and reaching for the hem of his shirt. "A quick stick, and you'll—" My hand brushed over the front of his nightshirt, and I broke off, startled.

"Jamie!" I said, amused. "You can't possibly!"

"I dinna suppose I can," he agreed comfortably. He curled up on his side like a shrimp, his lashes dark against his cheek. "But a man can dream, no?"

I didn't go upstairs to bed that night, either. We didn't talk much, just lay close together in the narrow bed, scarcely moving, so as not to jar his injured arm. The rest of the house was quiet, everyone safely in bed, and there was no sound but the hissing of the fire, the sigh of the wind, and the scratch of Ellen's rosebush at the window, insistent as the demands of love.

"Do ye know?" he said softly, somewhere in the black, small hours of the night. "Do ye know what it's like to be with someone that way? To try all ye can, and seem never to have the secret of them?"

"Yes," I said, thinking of Frank. "Yes, I do know."

"I thought perhaps ye did." He was quiet for a moment, and then his hand touched my hair lightly, a shadowy blur in the firelight.

"And then . . . ," he whispered, "then to have it back again, that knowing. To be free in all ye say or do, and know that it is right."

"To say 'I love you,' and mean it with all your heart," I said softly to the dark.

"Aye," he answered, barely audible. "To say that."

His hand rested on my hair, and without knowing quite how it happened, I found myself curled against him, my head just fitting in the hollow of his shoulder.

"For so many years," he said, "for so long, I have been so many things, so many different men." I felt him swallow, and he shifted slightly, the linen of his nightshirt rustling with starch.

"I was Uncle to Jenny's children, and Brother to her and Ian. 'Milord' to Fergus, and 'Sir' to my tenants. 'Mac Dubh' to the men of Ardsmuir and 'MacKenzie' to the other servants at Helwater. 'Malcolm the printer,' then, and 'Jamie Roy' at the docks." The hand stroked my hair, slowly, with a whispering sound like the wind outside. "But here," he said, so softly I could barely hear him, "here in the dark, with you . . . I have no name."

I lifted my face toward his, and took the warm breath of him between my own lips.

"I love you," I said, and did not need to tell him how I meant it.

38

I Meet a Lawyer

As I had predicted, eighteenth-century germs were no match for a modern antibiotic. Jamie's fever had virtually disappeared within twenty-four hours, and within the next two days the inflammation in his arm began to subside as well, leaving no more than a reddening about the wound itself and a very slight oozing of pus when pressed.

On the fourth day, after satisfying myself that he was mending nicely, I dressed the wound lightly with coneflower salve, bandaged it again, and left to dress and make my own toilet upstairs.

Ian, Janet, Young Ian, and the servants had all put their heads in at intervals over the last few days, to see how Jamie progressed. Jenny had been conspicuously absent from these inquiries, but I knew that she was still entirely aware of everything that happened in her house. I hadn't announced my intention of coming upstairs, yet when I opened the door to my bedroom, there was a large pitcher of hot water standing by the ewer, gently steaming, and a fresh cake of soap laid alongside it.

I picked it up and sniffed. Fine-milled French soap, perfumed with lily of the valley, it was a delicate comment on my status in the household—honored guest, to be sure; but not one of the family, who would all make do as a matter of course with the usual coarse soap made of tallow and lye.

"Right," I muttered. "Well, we'll see, won't we?" and lathered the cloth for washing.

As I was arranging my hair in the glass a half-hour later, I heard the sounds below of someone arriving. Several someones, in fact, from the sounds of it. I came down the stairs to find a small mob of children in residence, streaming in and out of the kitchen and front parlor, with here and there a strange adult visible in the midst of them, who stared curiously at me as I came down the stairs.

Entering the parlor, I found the camp bed put away and Jamie, shaved and in a fresh nightshirt, neatly propped up on the sofa under a quilt with his left arm in a sling, surrounded by four or five children. These were shepherded by Janet, Young Ian, and a smiling young man who was a Fraser of sorts by the shape of his nose, but otherwise bore only the faintest resemblances to the tiny boy I had seen last at Lallybroch twenty years before.

"There she is!" Jamie exclaimed with pleasure at my appearance, and the entire roomful of people turned to look at me, with expressions ranging from pleasant greeting to gape-mouthed awe.

"You'll remember Young Jamie?" the elder Jamie said, nodding to the tall, broad-shouldered young man with curly black hair and a squirming bundle in his arms.

"I remember the curls," I said, smiling. "The rest has changed a bit."

Young Jamie grinned down at me. "I remember ye well, Auntie," he said, in a deep-brown voice like well-aged ale. "Ye held me on your knee and played Ten Wee Piggies wi' my toes."

"I can't possibly have," I said, looking up at him in some dismay. While it seemed to be true that people really didn't change markedly in appearance between their twenties and their forties, they most assuredly did so between four and twenty-four.

"Perhaps ye can have a go wi' wee Benjamin here," Young Jamie suggested with a smile. "Maybe the knack of it will come back to ye." He bent and carefully laid his bundle in my arms.

A very round face looked up at me with that air of befuddlement so common to new babies. Benjamin appeared mildly confused at having me suddenly exchanged for his father, but didn't object. Instead, he opened his small pink mouth very wide, inserted his fist and began to gnaw on it in a thoughtful manner.

A small blond boy in homespun breeks leaned on Jamie's knee, staring up at me in wonder. "Who's that, Nunkie?" he asked in a loud whisper.

"That's your great-auntie Claire," Jamie said gravely. "Ye'll have heard about her, I expect?"

"Oh, aye," the little boy said, nodding madly. "Is she as old as Grannie?"

"Even older," Jamie said, nodding back solemnly. The lad gawked up at me for a moment, then turned back to Jamie, face screwed up in scorn.

"Get on wi' ye, Nunkie! She doesna look anything like as old as Grannie! Why, there's scarce a bit o' silver in her hair!"

"Thank you, child," I said, beaming at him.

"Are ye sure that's our great-auntie Claire?" the boy went on, looking doubtfully at me. "Mam says Great-Auntie Claire was maybe a witch, but this lady doesna look much like it. She hasna got a single wart on her nose that *I* can see!"

"Thanks," I said again, a little more dryly. "And what's your name?"

He turned suddenly shy at being thus directly addressed, and buried his head in Jamie's sleeve, refusing to speak.

"This is Angus Walter Edwin Murray Carmichael," Jamie answered for him, ruffling the silky blond hair. "Maggie's eldest son, and most commonly known as Wally."

"*We* call him Snot-rag," a small red-haired girl standing by my knee informed me. " 'Cause his neb is always clotted wi' gook."

Angus Walter jerked his face out of his uncle's shirt and glared at his female relation, his features beet-red with fury.

"Is *not*!" he shouted. "Take it back!" Not waiting to see whether she would or not, he flung himself at her, fists clenched, but was jerked off his feet by his great-uncle's hand, attached to his collar.

"Ye dinna hit girls," Jamie informed him firmly. "It's not manly."

"But she said I was snotty!" Angus Walter wailed. "I *must* hit her!"

"And it's no verra civil to pass remarks about someone's personal appearance, Mistress Abigail," Jamie said severely to the little girl. "Ye should apologize to your cousin."

"Well, but he *is* . . ." Abigail persisted, but then caught Jamie's stern eyes and dropped her own, flushing scarlet. "Sorry, Wally," she murmured.

Wally seemed at first indisposed to consider this adequate compensation for the insult he had suffered, but was at last prevailed upon to cease trying to hit his cousin by his uncle promising him a story.

"Tell the one about the kelpie and the horseman!" my red-haired acquaintance exclaimed, pushing forward to be in on it.

"No, the one about the Devil's chess game!" chimed in one of the other children. Jamie seemed to be a sort of magnet for them; two boys were plucking at his coverlet, while a tiny brown-haired girl had climbed up onto the sofa back by his head, and begun intently plaiting strands of his hair.

"Pretty, Nunkie," she murmured, taking no part in the hail of suggestions.

"It's Wally's story," Jamie said firmly, quelling the incipient riot with a gesture. "He can choose as he likes." He drew a clean handkerchief out from under the pillow and held it to Wally's nose, which was in fact rather unsightly.

"Blow," he said in an undertone, and then, louder, "and then tell me which you'll have, Wally."

Wally snuffled obligingly, then said, "St. Bride and the geese, please, Nunkie."

Jamie's eyes sought me, resting on my face with a thoughtful expression.

"All right," he said, after a pause. "Well, then. Ye'll ken that the greylag mate for life? If ye kill a grown goose, hunting, ye must always wait, for the mate will come to mourn. Then ye must try to kill the second, too, for otherwise it will grieve itself to death, calling through the skies for the lost one."

Little Benjamin shifted in his wrappings, squirming in my arms. Jamie smiled and shifted his attention back to Wally, hanging open-mouthed on his great-uncle's knee.

"So," he said, "it was a time, more hundreds of years past than you could ken or dream of, that Bride first set foot on the stone of the Highlands, along with Michael the Blessed . . ."

Benjamin let out a small squawk at this point, and began to rootle at the front of my dress. Young Jamie and his siblings seemed to have disappeared, and after a moment's patting and joggling had proved vain, I left the room in search of Benjamin's mother, leaving the story in progress behind me.

I found the lady in question in the kitchen, embedded in a large company of girls and women, and after turning Benjamin over to her, spent some time in introductions, greeting, and the sort of ritual by which women appraise each other, openly and otherwise.

The women were all very friendly; evidently everyone knew or had been told who I was, for while they introduced me from one to another, there was no apparent surprise at the return of Jamie's first wife—either from the dead or from France, depending on what they'd been told.

Still, there were very odd undercurrents passing through the gathering. They scrupulously avoided asking me questions; in another place, this might be mere politeness, but not in the Highlands, where any stranger's life history was customarily extracted in the course of a casual visit.

And while they treated me with great courtesy and kindness, there were small looks from the corner of the eye, the passing of glances exchanged behind my back, and casual remarks made quietly in Gaelic.

But strangest of all was Jenny's absence. She was the hearthfire of Lallybroch; I had never been in the house when it was not suffused with her presence, all the inhabitants in orbit about her like planets about the sun. I could think of nothing less like her than that she should leave her kitchen with such a mob of company in the house.

Her presence was as strong now as the perfume of the fresh pine boughs that lay in a large pile in the back pantry, their presence beginning to scent the house; but of Jenny herself, not a hair was to be seen.

She had avoided me since the night of my return with Young Ian—natural enough, I supposed, under the circumstances. Neither had I sought an interview with her. Both of us knew there was a reckoning to be made, but neither of us would seek it then.

It was warm and cozy in the kitchen—too warm. The intermingled scents of drying cloth, hot starch, wet diapers, sweating bodies, oatcake frying in lard, and bread baking were becoming a bit too heady, and when Katherine mentioned the need of a pitcher of cream for the scones, I seized the opportunity to escape, volunteering to fetch it down from the dairy shed.

After the press of heated bodies in the kitchen, the cold, damp air outside was so refreshing that I stood still for a minute, shaking the kitchen smells out of my petticoats and hair before making my way to the dairy shed. This shed was some distance away from the main house, convenient to the milking shed, which in turn was built to adjoin the two small paddocks in which sheep and goats were kept. Cattle were kept in the Highlands, but normally for beef, rather than milk, cow's milk being thought suitable only for invalids.

To my surprise, as I came out of the dairy shed, I saw Fergus leaning on the paddock fence, staring moodily at the mass of milling wooly backs below. I had not expected to see him here, and wondered whether Jamie knew he had returned.

Jenny's prized Merino sheep—imported, hand-fed and a great deal more spoilt than any of her grandchildren—spotted me as I passed, and rushed en masse for the side of their pen, blatting frenziedly in hope of tidbits. Fergus looked up, startled at the racket, then waved halfheartedly. He called something, but it was impossible to hear him over the uproar.

There was a large bin of frost-blasted cabbage heads near the pen; I pulled out a large, limp green head, and doled out leaves to a dozen or so pairs of eagerly grasping lips, in hopes of shutting them up.

The ram, a huge wooly creature named Hughie, with testicles that hung nearly to the ground like wool-covered footballs, shouldered his massive way into the front rank with a loud and autocratic *Bahh!* Fergus, who had reached my side by this time, picked up a whole cabbage and hurled it at Hughie with considerable force and fair accuracy.

"Tais-toi!" he said irritably.

Hughie shied and let out an astonished, high-pitched *Beh!* as the cabbage bounced off his padded back. Then, shaking himself back into some semblance of dignity, he trotted off, testes swinging with offended majesty. His flock, sheeplike, trailed after him, uttering a low chorus of discontented *bahs* in his wake.

Fergus glowered malevolently after them.

"Useless, noisy, smelly beasts," he said. Rather ungratefully, I thought, given that the scarf and stockings he was wearing had almost certainly been woven from their wool.

"Nice to see you again, Fergus," I said, ignoring his mood. "Does Jamie know you're back yet?" I wondered just how much Fergus knew of recent events, if he had just arrived at Lallybroch.

"No," he said, rather listlessly. "I suppose I should tell him I am here." In spite of this, he made no move toward the house, but continued staring into the churned mud of the paddock. Something was obviously eating at him; I hoped nothing had gone wrong with his errand.

"Did you find Mr. Gage all right?" I asked.

He looked blank for a moment, then a spark of animation came back into his lean face.

"Oh, yes. Milord was right; I went with Gage to warn the other members of the Society, and then we went together to the tavern where they were to meet. Sure enough, there was a nest of Customs men there waiting, disguised. And may they be waiting as long as their fellow in the cask, ha ha!"

The gleam of savage amusement died out of his eyes then, and he sighed.

"We cannot expect to be paid for the pamphlets, of course. And even though the press was saved, God knows how long it may be until milord's business is reestablished."

He spoke with such mournfulness that I was surprised.

"You don't help with the printing business, do you?" I asked.

He raised one shoulder and let it fall. "Not to say help, milady. But milord was kind enough to allow me to invest a part of my share of the profits from the brandy in the printing business. In time, I should have become a full partner."

"I see," I said sympathetically. "Do you need money? Perhaps I can—"

He shot me a glance of surprise, and then a smile that displayed his perfect, square white teeth.

"Thank you, milady, but no. I myself need very little, and I have enough." He patted the side pocket of his coat, which jingled reassuringly.

He paused, frowning, and thrust both wrists deep into the pockets of his coat.

"Noo . . ." he said slowly. "It is only—well, the printing business is most respectable, milady."

"I suppose so," I said, slightly puzzled. He caught my tone and smiled, rather grimly.

"The difficulty, milady, is that while a smuggler may be in possession of an income more than sufficient for the support of a wife, smuggling as a sole profession is not likely to appeal to the parents of a respectable young lady."

"Oho," I said, everything becoming clear. "You want to get married? To a respectable young lady?"

He nodded, a little shyly.

"Yes, Madame. But her mother does not favor me."

I couldn't say I blamed the young lady's mother, all things considered. While Fergus was possessed of dark good looks and a dashing manner that might well win a young girl's heart, he lacked a few of the things that might appeal somewhat more to conservative Scottish parents, such as property, income, a left hand, and a last name.

Likewise, while smuggling, cattle-lifting, and other forms of practical communism had a long and illustrious history in the Highlands, the French did not. And no matter how long Fergus himself had lived at Lallybroch, he remained as French as Notre Dame. He would, like me, always be an outlander.

"If I were a partner in a profitable printing firm, you see, perhaps the good lady might be induced to consider my suit," he explained. "But as it is . . ." He shook his head disconsolately.

I patted his arm sympathetically. "Don't worry about it," I said. "We'll think of something. Does Jamie know about this girl? I'm sure he'd be willing to speak to her mother for you."

To my surprise, he looked quite alarmed.

"Oh, no, milady! Please, say nothing to him—he has a great many things of more importance to think of just now."

On the whole, I thought this was probably true, but I was surprised at his vehemence. Still, I agreed to say nothing to Jamie. My feet were growing chilly from standing in the frozen mud, and I suggested that we go inside.

"Perhaps a little later, milady," he said. "For now, I believe I am not suitable company even for sheep." With a heavy sigh, he turned and trudged off toward the dovecote, shoulders slumped.

To my surprise, Jenny was in the parlor with Jamie. She had been outside; her cheeks and the end of her long, straight nose were pink with the cold, and the scent of winter mist lingered in her clothes.

"I've sent Young Ian to saddle Donas," she said. She frowned at her brother. "Can ye stand to walk to the barn, Jamie, or had he best bring the beast round for ye?"

Jamie stared up at her, one eyebrow raised.

"I can walk wherever it's needful to go, but I'm no going anywhere just now."

"Did I not tell ye he'd be coming?" Jenny said impatiently. "Amyas Kettrick stopped by here late last night, and said he'd just come from Kinwallis. Hobart's meaning to come today, he said." She glanced at the pretty enameled clock on the mantel. "If he left after breakfast, he'll be here within the hour."

Jamie frowned at his sister, tilting his head back against the sofa.

"I told ye, Jenny, I'm no afraid of Hobart MacKenzie," he said shortly. "Damned if I'll run from him!"

Jenny's brows rose as she looked coldly at her brother.

"Oh, aye?" she said. "Ye weren't afraid of Laoghaire, either, and look where that got ye!" She jerked her head at the sling on his arm.

Despite himself, Jamie's mouth curled up on one side.

"Aye, well, it's a point," he said. "On the other hand, Jenny, ye ken guns are scarcer than hen's teeth in the Highlands. I dinna think Hobart's going to come and ask to borrow my own pistol to shoot me with."

"I shouldna think he'd bother; he'll just walk in and spit ye through the gizzard like the silly gander ye are!" she snapped.

Jamie laughed, and she glared at him. I seized the moment to interrupt.

"Who," I inquired, "is Hobart MacKenzie, and why exactly does he want to spit you like a gander?"

Jamie turned his head to me, the light of amusement still in his eyes.

"Hobart is Laoghaire's brother, Sassenach," he explained. "As for spitting me or otherwise—"

"Laoghaire's sent for him from Kinwallis, where he lives," Jenny interrupted, "and told him about . . . all this." A slight, impatient gesture encompassed me, Jamie, and the awkward situation in general.

"The notion being that Hobart's meant to come round and expunge the slight upon his sister's honor by expunging me," Jamie explained. He seemed to find the idea entertaining. I wasn't so sure about it, and neither was Jenny.

"You're not worried about this Hobart?" I asked.

"Of course not," he said, a little irritably. He turned to his sister. "For God's sake, Jenny, ye ken Hobart MacKenzie! The man couldna stick a pig without cutting off his own foot!"

She looked him up and down, evidently gauging his ability to defend himself against an incompetent pigsticker, and reluctantly concluding that he might manage, even one-handed.

"Mmphm," she said. "Well, and what if he comes for ye and ye kill him, aye? What then?"

"Then he'll be dead, I expect," Jamie said dryly.

"And ye'll be hangit for murder," she shot back, "or on the run, wi' all the rest of Laoghaire's kin after ye. Want to start a blood feud, do ye?"

Jamie narrowed his eyes at his sister, emphasizing the already marked resemblance between them.

"What I want," he said, with exaggerated patience, "is my breakfast. D'ye mean to feed me, or d'ye mean to wait until I faint from hunger, and then hide me in the priest hole 'til Hobart leaves?"

Annoyance struggled with humor on Jenny's fine-boned face as she glared at her brother. As usual with both Frasers, humor won out.

"It's a thought," she said, teeth flashing in a brief, reluctant smile. "If I could drag your stubborn carcass that far, I'd club ye myself." She shook her head and sighed.

"All right, Jamie, ye'll have it your way. But ye'll try not to make a mess on my good Turkey carpet, aye?"

He looked up at her, long mouth curling up on one side.

"It's a promise, Jenny," he said. "Nay bloodshed in the parlor."

She snorted. "Clot," she said, but without rancor. "I'll send Janet wi' your parritch." And she was gone, in a swirl of skirts and petticoats.

"Did she say Donas?" I asked, looking after her in bemusement. "Surely it isn't the same horse you took from Leoch!"

"Och, no." Jamie tilted his head back, smiling up at me. "This is Donas's grandson—or one of them. We give the name to the sorrel colts in his honor."

I leaned over the back of the sofa, gently feeling down the length of the injured arm from the shoulder.

"Sore?" I asked, seeing him wince as I pressed a few inches above the wound. It was better; the day before, the area of soreness had started higher.

"Not bad," he said. He removed the sling and tried gingerly extending the arm, grimacing. "I dinna think I'll turn handsprings awhile yet, though."

I laughed.

"No, I don't suppose so." I hesitated. "Jamie—this Hobart. You really don't think—"

"I don't," he said firmly. "And if I did, I'd still want my breakfast first. I dinna mean to be killed on an empty stomach."

I laughed again, somewhat reassured.

"I'll go and get it for you," I promised.

As I stepped out into the hall, though, I caught sight of a flutter through one of the windows, and stopped to look. It was Jenny, cloaked and hooded against the cold, headed up the slope to the barn. Seized by a sudden impulse, I snatched a cloak from the hall tree and darted out after her. I had things to say to Jenny Murray, and this might be the best chance of catching her alone.

I caught up with her just outside the barn; she heard my step behind her and turned, startled. She glanced about quickly, but saw we were alone. Realizing that there was no way of putting off a confrontation, she squared her shoulders under the woolen cloak and lifted her head, meeting my eyes straight on.

"I thought I'd best tell Young Ian to unsaddle the horse," she said. "Then I'm going to the root cellar to fetch up some onions for a tart. Will ye come with me?"

"I will." Pulling my cloak tight around me against the winter wind, I followed her into the barn.

It was warm inside, at least by contrast with the chill outdoors, dark, and filled with the pleasant scent of horses, hay, and manure. I paused a moment to let my eyes adapt to the dimness, but Jenny walked directly down the central aisle, footsteps light on the stone floor.

Young Ian was sprawled at length on a pile of fresh straw; he sat up, blinking at the sound.

Jenny glanced from her son to the stall, where a soft-eyed sorrel was peacefully munching hay from its manger, unburdened by saddle or bridle.

"Did I not tell ye to ready Donas?" she asked the boy, her voice sharp.

Young Ian scratched his head, looking a little sheepish, and stood up.

"Aye, mam, ye did," he said. "But I didna think it worth the time to saddle him, only to have to unsaddle him again."

Jenny stared up at him.

"Oh, aye?" she said. "And what made ye so certain he wouldna be needed?"

Young Ian shrugged, and smiled down at her.

"Mam, ye ken as well as I do that Uncle Jamie wouldna run away from anything, let alone Uncle Hobart. Don't ye?" he added, gently.

Jenny looked up at her son and sighed. Then a reluctant smile lighted her face and she reached up, smoothing the thick, untidy hair away from his face.

"Aye, wee Ian. I do." Her hand lingered along his ruddy cheek, then dropped away.

"Go along to the house, then, and have second breakfast wi' your uncle," she said. "Your auntie and I are goin' to the root cellar. But ye come and fetch me smartly, if Mr. Hobart MacKenzie should come, aye?"

"Right away, Mam," he promised, and shot for the house, impelled by the thought of food.

Jenny watched him go, moving with the clumsy grace of a young whooping crane, and shook her head, the smile still on her lips.

"Sweet laddie," she murmured. Then, recalled to the present circumstances, she turned to me with decision.

"Come along, then," she said. "I expect ye want to talk to me, aye?"

Neither of us said anything until we reached the quiet sanctuary of the root cellar. It was a small room dug under the house, pungent with the scent of the long braided strings of onions and garlic that hung from the rafters, the sweet, spicy scent of dried apples, and the moist, earthy smell of potatoes, spread in lumpy brown blankets over the shelves that lined the cellar.

"D'ye remember telling me to plant potatoes?" Jenny asked, passing a hand lightly over the clustered tubers. "That was a lucky thing; 'twas the potato crop kept us alive, more than one winter after Culloden."

I remembered, all right. I had told her as we stood together on a cold autumn night, about to part—she to return to a newborn baby, I to hunt for Jamie, an outlaw in the Highlands, under sentence of death. I had found him, and saved him—and Lallybroch, evidently. And she had tried to give them both to Laoghaire.

"Why?" I said softly, at last. I spoke to the top of her head, bent over her task. Her hand went out with the regularity of clockwork, pulling an onion from the long hanging braid, breaking the tough, withered stems from the plait and tossing it into the basket she carried.

"Why did you do it?" I said. I broke off an onion from another braid, but instead of putting it in the basket, held it in my hands, rolling it back and forth like a baseball, hearing the papery skin rustle between my palms.

"Why did I do what?" Her voice was perfectly controlled again; only someone who knew her well could have heard the note of strain in it. I knew her well—or had, at one time.

"Why did I make the match between my brother and Laoghaire, d'ye mean?" She glanced up quickly, smooth black brows raised in question, but then bent back to the braid of onions. "You're right; he wouldna have done it, without I made him."

"So you did make him do it," I said. The wind rattled the door of the root cellar, sending a small sifting of dirt down upon the cut-stone steps.

"He was lonely," she said, softly. "So lonely. I couldna bear to see him so. He was wretched for so long, ye ken, mourning for you."

"I thought he was dead," I said quietly, answering the unspoken accusation.

"He might as well have been," she said, sharply, then raised her head and sighed, pushing back a lock of dark hair.

"Aye, maybe ye truly didna ken he'd lived; there were a great many who didn't, after Culloden—and it's sure he thought *you* were dead and gone then. But he was sair wounded, and not only his leg. And when he came home from England—" She shook her head, and reached for another onion. "He was whole enough to look at, but not—" She gave me a look, straight on, with those slanted blue eyes, so disturbingly like her brother's. "He's no the sort of man should sleep alone, aye?"

"Granted," I said shortly. "But we did live, the both of us. Why did you send for Laoghaire when we came back with Young Ian?"

Jenny didn't answer at first, but only went on reaching for onions, breaking, reaching, breaking, reaching.

"I liked you," she said at last, so low I could barely hear her. "Loved ye, maybe, when ye lived here with Jamie, before."

"I liked you, too," I said, just as softly. "Then why?"

Her hands stilled at last and she looked up at me, fists balled at her sides.

"When Ian told me ye'd come back," she said slowly, eyes fastened on the onions, "ye could have knocked me flat wi' a down-feather. At first, I was excited, wanting to see ye—wanting to know where ye'd been—" she added, arching her brows slightly in inquiry. I didn't answer, and she went on.

"But then I was afraid," she said softly. Her eyes slid away, shadowed by their thick fringe of black lashes.

"I saw ye, ye ken," she said, still looking off into some unseeable distance. "When he wed Laoghaire, and them standing by the altar—ye were there wi' them, standing at his left hand, betwixt him and Laoghaire. And I kent that meant ye would take him back."

The hair prickled slightly on the nape of my neck. She shook her head slowly, and I saw she had gone pale with the memory. She sat down on a barrel, the cloak spreading out around her like a flower.

"I'm not one of those born wi' the Sight, nor one who has it regular. I've never had it before, and hope never to have it again. But I saw ye there, as clear as I see ye now, and it scairt me so that I had to leave the room, right in the midst o' the vows." She swallowed, looking at me directly.

"I dinna ken who ye are," she said softly. "Or . . . or . . . what. We didna ken your people, or your place. I never asked ye, did I? Jamie chose ye, that was enough. But then ye were gone, and after so long—I thought he might have forgot ye enough to wed again, and be happy."

"He wasn't, though," I said, hoping for confirmation from Jenny.

She gave it, shaking her head.

"No," she said quietly. "But Jamie's a faithful man, aye? No matter how it was between the two of them, him and Laoghaire, if he'd sworn to be her man, he wouldna leave her altogether. It didna matter that he spent most of his time in Edinburgh; I kent he'd always come back here—he'd be bound here, to the Highlands. But then you came back."

Her hands lay still in her lap, a rare sight. They were still finely shaped, long-fingered and deft, but the knuckles were red and rough with years of work, and the veins stood out blue beneath the thin white skin.

"D'ye ken," she said, looking into her lap, "I have never been further than ten miles from Lallybroch, in all my life?"

"No," I said, slightly startled. She shook her head slowly, then looked up at me.

"You have, though," she said. "You've traveled a great deal, I expect." Her gaze searched my face, looking for clues.

"I have."

She nodded, as though thinking to herself.

"You'll go again," she said, nearly whispering. "I kent ye would go again. You're not bound here, not like Laoghaire—not like me. And he would go with ye. And I should never see him again." She closed her eyes briefly, then opened them, looking at me under her fine dark brows.

"That's why," she said. "I thought if ye kent about Laoghaire, ye'd go again at once—you did—" she added, with a faint grimace, "and Jamie would stay. But ye came back." Her shoulders rose in a faint, helpless shrug. "And I see it's no good; he's bound to ye, for good or ill. It's you that's his wife. And if ye leave again, he will go with ye."

I searched helplessly for words to reassure her. "But I won't. I won't go again. I only want to stay here with him—always."

I laid a hand on her arm and she stiffened slightly. After a moment, she laid her own hand over mine. It was chilled, and the tip of her long, straight nose was red with cold.

"Folk say different things of the Sight, aye?" she said after a moment.

"Some say it's doomed; whatever ye see that way must come to pass. But others say nay, it's no but a warning; take heed and ye can change things. What d'ye think, yourself?" She looked sideways at me, curiously.

I took a deep breath, the smell of onions stinging the back of my nose. This was hitting home in no uncertain terms.

"I don't know," I said, and my voice shook slightly. "I'd always thought that of course you could change things if you knew about them. But now . . . I don't know," I ended softly, thinking of Culloden.

Jenny watched me, her eyes so deep a blue as almost to be black in the dim light. I wondered again just how much Jamie had told her—and how much she knew without the telling.

"But ye must try, even so," she said, with certainty. "Ye couldna just leave it, could ye?"

I didn't know whether she meant this personally, but I shook my head.

"No," I said. "You couldn't. You're right; you have to try."

We smiled at each other, a little shyly.

"You'll take good care of him?" Jenny said suddenly. "Even if ye go? Ye will, aye?"

I squeezed her cold fingers, feeling the bones of her hand light and fragile-seeming in my grasp.

"I will," I said.

"Then that's all right," she said softly, and squeezed back.

We sat for a moment, holding each other's hands, until the door of the root cellar swung open, admitting a blast of rain and wind down the stairs.

"Mam?" Young Ian's head poked in, eyes bright with excitement. "Hobart MacKenzie's come! Da says to come quick!"

Jenny sprang to her feet, barely remembering to snatch up the basket of onions.

"Has he come armed, then?" she asked anxiously. "Has he brought a pistol or a sword?"

Ian shook his head, his dark hair lifting wildly in the wind.

"Oh, no, Mam!" he said. "It's worse. He's brought a lawyer!"

Anything less resembling vengeance incarnate than Hobart MacKenzie could scarcely be imagined. A small, light-boned man of about thirty, he had pale blue, pale-lashed eyes with a tendency to water, and indeterminate features that began with a receding hairline and dwindled down into a similarly receding chin that seemed to be trying to escape into the folds of his stock.

He was smoothing his hair at the mirror in the hall when we came in the front door, a neatly curled bob wig sitting on the table beside him. He blinked at us in alarm, then snatched up the wig and crammed it on his head, bowing in the same motion.

"Mrs. Jenny," he said. His small, rabbity eyes flicked in my direction, away, then back again, as though he hoped I really wasn't there, but was very much afraid I was.

Jenny glanced from him to me, sighed deeply, and took the bull by the horns.

"Mr. MacKenzie," she said, dropping him a formal curtsy. "Might I present my good-sister, Claire? Claire, Mr. Hobart MacKenzie of Kinwallis."

His mouth dropped open and he simply gawked at me. I started to extend a hand to him, but thought better of it. I would have liked to know what Emily Post had to recommend in a situation like this, but as Miss Post wasn't present, I was forced to improvise.

"How nice to meet you," I said, smiling as cordially as possible.

"Ah . . ." he said. He bobbed his head tentatively at me. "Um . . . your . . . servant, ma'am."

Fortunately, at this point in the proceedings, the door to the parlor opened. I looked at the small, neat figure framed in the doorway, and let out a cry of delighted recognition.

"Ned! Ned Gowan!"

It was indeed Ned Gowan, the elderly Edinburgh lawyer who had once saved me from burning as a witch. He was noticeably more elderly now, shrunken with age and so heavily wrinkled as to look like one of the dried apples I had seen in the root cellar.

The bright black eyes were the same, though, and they fastened on me at once with an expression of joy.

"My dear!" he exclaimed, hastening forward at a rapid hobble. He seized my hand, beaming, and pressed it to his withered lips in fervent gallantry.

"I had heard that you—"

"How did you come to be—"

"—so delightful to see you!"

"—so happy to see you again, but—"

A cough from Hobart MacKenzie interrupted this rapturous exchange, and Mr. Gowan looked up, startled, then nodded.

"Oh, aye, of course. Business first, my dear," he said, with a gallant bow to me, "and then if ye will, I should be most charmed to hear the tale of your adventures."

"Ah . . . I'll do my best," I said, wondering just how much he would insist on hearing.

"Splendid, splendid." He glanced about the hall, bright little eyes taking in Hobart and Jenny, who had hung up her cloak and was smoothing her hair. "Mr. Fraser and Mr. Murray are already in the parlor. Mr. MacKenzie, if you and the ladies would consent to join us, perhaps we can settle your affairs expeditiously, and proceed to more congenial matters. If you will allow me, my dear?" He crooked a bony arm to me invitingly.

Jamie was still on the sofa where I had left him, and in approximately the same condition—that is, alive. The children were gone, with the exception of one chubby youngster who was curled up on Jamie's lap, fast asleep. Jamie's hair now sported several small plaits on either side, with silk ribbons woven gaily through them, which gave him an incongruously festive air.

"You look like the Cowardly Lion of Oz," I told him in an undertone, sitting down on a hassock behind his sofa. I didn't think it likely that Hobart MacKenzie intended any outright mischief, but if anything happened, I meant to be in close reach of Jamie.

He looked startled, and put a hand to his head.

"I do?"

"Shh," I said, "I'll tell you later."

The other participants had now arranged themselves around the parlor, Jenny sitting down by Ian on the other love seat, and Hobart and Mr. Gowan taking two velvet chairs.

"We are assembled?" Mr. Gowan inquired, glancing around the room. "All interested parties are present? Excellent. Well, to begin with, I must declare my own interest. I am here in the capacity of solicitor to Mr. Hobart MacKenzie, representing the interests of Mrs. James Fraser"—he saw me start, and added, with precision—"that is, the *second* Mrs. James Fraser, née Laoghaire MacKenzie. That is understood?"

He glanced inquiringly at Jamie, who nodded.

"It is."

"Good." Mr. Gowan picked up a glass from the table next to him and took a tiny sip. "My clients, the MacKenzies, have accepted my proposal to seek a legal solution to the imbroglio which I understand has resulted from the sudden and unexpected—though of course altogether happy and fortuitous—" he added, with a bow to me, "return of the first Mrs. Fraser."

He shook his head reprovingly at Jamie.

"You, my dear young man, have contrived to entangle yourself in considerable legal difficulties, I am sorry to say."

Jamie raised one eyebrow and looked at his sister.

"Aye, well, I had help," he said dryly. "Just what difficulties are we speakin' of?"

"Well, to begin with," Ned Gowan said cheerily, his sparkling black eyes sinking into nets of wrinkles as he smiled at me, "the first Mrs. Fraser would be well within her rights to bring a civil suit against ye for adultery, and criminal fornication, forbye. Penalties for which include—"

Jamie glanced back at me, with a quick blue gleam.

"I think I'm no so worrit by that possibility," he told the lawyer. "What else?"

Ned Gowan nodded obligingly and held up one withered hand, folding down the fingers as he ticked off his points.

"With respect to the second Mrs. Fraser—née Laoghaire MacKenzie—ye could, of course, be charged wi' bigamous misconduct, intent to defraud, actual fraud committed—whether wi' intent or no, which is a separate question—felonious misrepresentation"—he happily folded down his fourth finger and drew breath for more—"and . . ."

Jamie had been listening patiently to this catalogue. Now he interrupted, leaning forward.

"Ned," he said gently, "what the hell does the bloody woman want?"

The small lawyer blinked behind his spectacles, lowered his hand, and cast up his eyes to the beams overhead.

"Weel, the lady's chief desire as stated," he said circumspectly, "is to see ye castrated and disemboweled in the market square at Broch Mordha, and your head mounted on a stake over her gate."

Jamie's shoulders vibrated briefly, and he winced as the movement jarred his arm.

"I see," he said, his mouth twitching.

A smile gathered up the wrinkles by Ned's ancient mouth.

"I was obliged to inform Mrs.—that is, the lady—" he amended, with a glance at me and a slight cough, "that her remedies under the law were somewhat more limited than would accommodate her desires."

"Quite," Jamie said dryly. "But I assume the general idea is that she doesna particularly want me back as a husband?"

"No," Hobart put in unexpectedly. "Crow's bait, maybe, but not a husband."

Ned cast a cold glance at his client.

"Ye willna compromise your case by admitting things in advance of settlement, aye?" he said reprovingly. "Or what are ye payin' me for?" He turned back to Jamie, professional dignity unimpaired.

"While Miss MacKenzie does not wish to resume a marital position wi' regard to you—an action which would be impossible in any case," he added fairly, "unless ye should wish to divorce the present Mrs. Fraser, and remarry—"

"No, I dinna want to do that," Jamie assured him hurriedly, with another glance at me.

"Well, in such case," Ned went on, unruffled, "I should advise my clients that it is more desirable where possible to avoid the cost—and the publicity—" he added, cocking an invisible eyebrow in admonition to Hobart, who nodded hastily, "of a suit at law, with a public trial and its consequent exposure of facts. That being the case—"

"How much?" Jamie interrupted.

"Mr. Fraser!" Ned Gowan looked shocked. "I havena mentioned anything in the nature of a pecuniary settlement as yet—"

"Only because ye're too busy enjoying yourself, ye wicked auld rascal," Jamie said. He was irritated—a red patch burned over each cheekbone—but amused, too. "Get to it, aye?"

Ned Gowan inclined his head ceremoniously.

"Weel, ye must understand," he began, "that a successful suit brought under the charges as described might result in Miss MacKenzie and her brother mulcting ye in substantial damages—verra substantial indeed," he added, with a faint lawyerly gloating at the prospect.

"After all, Miss MacKenzie has not only been subject to public humiliation and ridicule leading to acute distress of mind, but is also threatened with loss of her chief means of support—"

"She isna threatened wi' any such thing," Jamie interrupted heatedly. "I told her I should go on supporting her and the two lassies! What does she think I am?"

Ned exchanged a glance with Hobart, who shook his head.

"Ye dinna want to know what she thinks ye are," Hobart assured Jamie. "I wouldna have thought she kent such words, myself. But ye do mean to pay?"

Jamie nodded impatiently, rubbing his good hand through his hair.

"Aye, I will."

"Only until she's marrit again, though." Everyone's head turned in surprise toward Jenny, who nodded firmly to Ned Gowan.

"If Jamie's married to Claire, the marriage between him and Laoghaire wasna valid, aye?"

The lawyer bowed.

"That is true, Mrs. Murray."

"Well, then," Jenny said, in a decided manner. "She's free to marry again at once, is she no? And once she does, my brother shouldna be providing for her household."

"An excellent point, Mrs. Murray." Ned Gowan took up his quill and scratched industriously. "Well, we make progress," he declared, laying it down again and beaming at the company. "Now, the next point to be covered . . ."

An hour later, the decanter of whisky was empty, the sheets of foolscap on the table were filled with Ned Gowan's chicken-scratchings, and everyone lay limp and exhausted—except Ned himself, spry and bright-eyed as ever.

"Excellent, excellent," he declared again, gathering up the sheets and tapping them neatly into order. "So—the main provisions of the settlement are as follows: Mr. Fraser agrees to pay to Miss MacKenzie the sum of five hundred pounds in compensation for distress, inconvenience, and the loss of his conjugal services"—Jamie snorted slightly at this, but Ned affected not to hear him, continuing his synopsis—"and in addition, agrees to maintain her household at the rate of one hundred pounds per annum, until such time as the aforesaid Miss MacKenzie may marry again, at which time such payment shall cease. Mr. Fraser agrees also to provide a bride-portion for each of Miss MacKenzie's daughters, of an additional three hundred pounds, and as a final provision, agrees not to pursue a prosecution against Miss MacKenzie for assault with intent to commit murder. In return, Miss MacKenzie acquits Mr. Fraser of any and all other claims. This is in accordance with your understanding and consent, Mr. Fraser?" He quirked a brow at Jamie.

"Aye, it is," Jamie said. He was pale from sitting up too long, and there was a fine dew of sweat at his hairline, but he sat straight and tall, the child still asleep in his lap, thumb firmly embedded in her mouth.

"Excellent," Ned said again. He rose, beaming, and bowed to the company. "As our friend Dr. John Arbuthnot says, 'Law is a bottomless pit.' But not more so at the moment than my stomach. Is that delectable aroma indicative of a saddle of mutton in our vicinity, Mrs. Jenny?"

At table, I sat to one side of Jamie, Hobart MacKenzie to the other, now looking pink and relaxed. Mary MacNab brought in the joint, and by ancient custom, set it down in front of Jamie. Her gaze lingered on him a moment too long. He picked up the long, wicked carving knife with his good hand and offered it politely to Hobart.

"Will ye have a go at it, Hobart?" he said.

"Och, no," Hobart said, waving it away. "Better let your wife carve it. I'm no hand wi' a knife—likely cut my finger off instead. You know me, Jamie," he said comfortably.

Jamie gave his erstwhile brother-in-law a long look over the saltcellar.

"Once I would ha' thought, so, Hobart," he said. "Pass me the whisky, aye?"

"The thing to do is to get her married at once," Jenny declared. The children and grandchildren had all retired, and Ned and Hobart had departed for Kinwallis, leaving the four of us to take stock over brandy and cream cakes in the laird's study.

Jamie turned to his sister. "The matchmaking's more in your line, aye?" he said, with a noticeable edge to his voice. "I expect you can think of a suitable man or two for the job, if ye put your mind to it?"

"I expect I can," she said, matching his edge with one of her own. She was embroidering; the needle stabbed through the linen fabric, flashing in the lamplight. It had begun to sleet heavily outside, but the study was cozy, with a small fire on the hearth and the pool of lamplight spilling warmth over the battered desk and its burden of books and ledgers.

"There's the one thing about it," she said, eyes on her work. "Where d'ye mean to get twelve hundred pounds, Jamie?"

I had been wondering that myself. The insurance settlement on the print-shop had fallen far short of that amount, and I doubted that Jamie's share of the smuggling proceeds amounted to anything near that magnitude. Certainly Lallybroch itself could not supply the money; survival in the Highlands was a chancy business, and even several good years in a row would provide only the barest surplus.

"Well, there's only the one place, isn't there?" Ian looked from his sister to his brother-in-law and back. After a short silence, Jamie nodded.

"I suppose so," he said reluctantly. He glanced at the window, where the rain was slashing across the glass in slanting streaks. "A vicious time of year for it, though."

Ian shrugged, and sat forward a bit in his chair. "The spring tide will be in a week."

Jamie frowned, looking troubled.

"Aye, that's so, but . . ."

"There's no one has a better right to it, Jamie," Ian said. He reached out and squeezed his friend's good arm, smiling. "It was meant for Prince Charles' followers, aye? And ye were one of those, whether ye wanted to be or no."

Jamie gave him back a rueful half-smile.

"Aye, I suppose that's true." He sighed. "In any case, it's the only thing I can see to do." He glanced back and forth between Ian and Jenny, evidently debating whether to add something else. His sister knew him even better than I did. She lifted her head from her work and looked at him sharply.

"What is it, Jamie?" she said.

He took a deep breath.

"I want to take Young Ian," he said.

"No," she said instantly. The needle had stopped, stuck halfway through a brilliant red bud in the pattern, the color of blood against the white smock.

"He's old enough, Jenny," Jamie said quietly.

"He's not!" she objected. "He's but barely fifteen; Michael and Jamie were both sixteen at least, and better grown."

"Aye, but wee Ian's a better swimmer than either of his brothers," Ian said judiciously. His forehead was furrowed with thought. "It will have to be one of the lads, after all," he pointed out to Jenny. He jerked his head toward Jamie, cradling his arm in its sling. "Jamie canna very well be swimming himself, in his present condition. Or Claire, for that matter," he added, with a smile at me.

"Swim?" I said, utterly bewildered. "Swim *where*?"

Ian looked taken aback for a moment; then he glanced at Jamie, brows lifted.

"Oh. Ye hadna told her?"

Jamie shook his head. "I had, but not all of it." He turned to me. "It's the treasure, Sassenach—the seals' gold."

Unable to take the treasure with him, he had concealed it in its place and returned to Ardsmuir.

"I didna ken what best to do about it," he explained. "Duncan Kerr gave the care of it to me, but I had no notion who it belonged to, or who put it there, or what I was to do with it. 'The white witch' was all Duncan said, and that meant nothing to me but you, Sassenach."

Reluctant to make use of the treasure himself, and yet feeling that someone should know about it, lest he die in prison, he had sent a carefully coded letter to Jenny and Ian at Lallybroch, giving the location of the cache, and the use for which it had—presumably—been meant.

Times had been hard for Jacobites then, sometimes even more so for those who had escaped to France—leaving lands and fortunes behind—than for those who remained to face English persecution in the Highlands. At about the same time, Lallybroch had experienced two bad crops in a row, and letters had reached them from France, asking for any help possible to succor erstwhile companions there, in danger of starvation.

"We had nothing to send; in fact, we were damn close to starving here," Ian explained. "I sent word to Jamie, and he said as he thought perhaps it wouldna be wrong to use a small bit of the treasure to help feed Prince *Tearlach*'s followers."

"It seemed likely it was put there by one of the Stuarts' supporters," Jamie chimed in. He cocked a ruddy brow at me, and his mouth quirked up at one corner. "I thought I wouldna send it to Prince Charles, though."

"Good thinking," I said dryly. Any money given to Charles Stuart would have been wasted, squandered within weeks, and anyone who had known Charles intimately, as Jamie had, would know that very well.

Ian had taken his eldest son, Jamie, and made his way across Scotland to the seals' cove near Coigach. Fearful of any word of the treasure getting out, they had not sought a fisherman's boat, but instead Young Jamie had swum to the seals' rock as his uncle had several years before. He had found the treasure in its place, abstracted two gold coins and three of the smaller gemstones, and secreting these in a bag tied securely round his neck, had replaced the rest of the treasure and made his way back through the surf, arriving exhausted.

They had made their way to Inverness then, and taken ship to France, where their cousin Jared Fraser, a successful expatriate wine merchant, had helped them to change the coins and jewels discreetly into cash, and taken the responsibility of distributing it among the Jacobites in need.

Three times since, Ian had made the laborious trip to the coast with one of his sons, each time to abstract a small part of the hidden fortune to supply a need. Twice the money had gone to friends in need in France; once it had been needed to purchase fresh planting-stock for Lallybroch and provide the food to see its tenants through a long winter when the potato crop failed.

Only Jenny, Ian, and the two elder boys, Jamie and Michael, knew of the treasure. Ian's wooden leg prevented his swimming to the seals' island, so one of his sons must always make the trip with him. I gathered that it had been something of a rite of passage for both Young Jamie and Michael, entrusted with such a great secret. Now it might be Young Ian's turn.

"No," Jenny said again, but I thought her heart wasn't in it. Ian was already nodding thoughtfully.

"Would ye take him with ye to France, too, Jamie?"

Jamie nodded.

"Aye, that's the thing. I shall have to leave Lallybroch, and stay away for a good bit, for Laoghaire's sake—I canna be living here with you, under her nose," he said apologetically to me, "at least not until she's suitably wed to someone else." He switched his attention back to Ian.

"I havena told ye everything that's happened in Edinburgh, Ian, but all things considered, I think it likely best I stay away from there for a time, too."

I sat quiet, trying to digest this news. I hadn't realized that Jamie meant to leave Lallybroch—leave Scotland altogether, it sounded like.

"So what d'ye mean to do, Jamie?" Jenny had given up any pretense of sewing, and sat with her hands in her lap.

He rubbed his nose, looking tired. This was the first day he had been up; I privately thought he should have been back in bed hours ago, but he had insisted upon staying up to preside over dinner and visit with everyone.

"Well," he said slowly, "Jared's offered more than once to take me into his firm. Perhaps I shall stay in France, at least for a year. I was thinking Young Ian could go with us, and be schooled in Paris."

Jenny and Ian exchanged a long look, one of those in which long-married couples are capable of carrying out complete conversations in the space of a few heartbeats. At last, Jenny tilted her head a bit to one side. Ian smiled and took her hand.

"It'll be all right, *mo nighean dubh*," he said to her in a low, tender voice. Then he turned to Jamie.

"Aye, take him. It'll be a great chance for the lad."

"You're sure?" Jamie hesitated, speaking to his sister, rather than Ian. Jenny nodded. Her blue eyes glistened in the lamplight, and the end of her nose was slightly red.

"I suppose it's best we give him his freedom while he still thinks it's ours to give," she said. She looked at Jamie, then at me, straight and steady. "But you'll take good care of him, aye?"

39

Lost, and by the Wind Grieved

This part of Scotland was as unlike the leafy glens and lochs near Lallybroch as the North Yorkshire moors. Here there were virtually no trees; only long sweeps of rock-strewn heather, rising into crags that touched the lowering sky and disappeared abruptly into curtains of mist.

As we got nearer to the seacoast, the mist became heavier, setting in earlier in the afternoon, lingering longer in the morning, so that only for a couple of hours in the middle of the day did we have anything like clear riding. The going was consequently slow, but none of us minded greatly, except Young Ian, who was beside himself with excitement, impatient to arrive.

"How far is it from the shore to the seals' island?" he asked Jamie for the tenth time.

"A quarter mile, I make it," his uncle replied.

"I can swim that far," Young Ian repeated, for the tenth time. His hands were clenched tightly on the reins, and his bony jaw set with determination.

"Aye, I know ye can," Jamie assured him patiently. He glanced at me, the hint of a smile hidden in the corner of his mouth. "Ye willna need to, though; just swim straight for the island, and the current will carry ye."

The boy nodded, and lapsed into silence, but his eyes were bright with anticipation.

The headland above the cove was mist-shrouded and deserted. Our voices echoed oddly in the fog, and we soon stopped talking, out of an abiding sense of eeriness. I could hear the seals barking far below, the sound wavering and mixing with the crash of the surf, so that now and then it sounded like sailors hallooing to one another over the sound of the sea.

Jamie pointed out the rock chimney of Ellen's tower to Young Ian, and taking a coil of rope from his saddle, picked his way over the broken rock of the headland to the entrance.

"Keep your shirt on 'til you're down," he told the lad, shouting to be heard above the wave. "Else the rock will tear your back to shreds."

Ian nodded understanding, then, the rope tied securely round his middle, gave me a nervous grin, took two jerky steps, and disappeared into the earth.

Jamie had the other end of the rope wrapped round his own waist, paying out the length of it carefully with his sound hand as the boy descended.

Crawling on hands and knees, I made my way over the short turf and pebbles to the crumbling edge of the cliff, where I could look over to the half-moon beach below.

It seemed a very long time, but finally I saw Ian emerge from the bottom of the chimney, a small, antlike figure. He untied his rope, peered around, spotted us at the top of the cliff, and waved enthusiastically. I waved back, but Jamie merely muttered, "All right, get on, then," under his breath.

I could feel him tense beside me as the boy stripped off to his breeks and scrambled down the rocks to the water, and I felt his flinch as the small figure dived headlong into the gray-blue waves.

"Brrr!" I said, watching. "The water must be freezing!"

"It is," Jamie said with feeling. "Ian's right; it's a vicious time of year to be swimming."

His face was pale and set. I didn't think it was the result of discomfort from his wounded arm, though the long ride and the exercise with the rope couldn't have done it any good. While he had shown nothing but encouraging confidence while Ian was making his descent, he wasn't making any effort to hide his worry now. The fact was that there was no way for us to reach Ian, should anything go wrong.

"Maybe we should have waited for the mist to lift," I said, more to distract him than because I thought so.

"If we had 'til next Easter, we might," he agreed ironically. "Though I'll grant ye, I've seen it clearer than this," he added, squinting into the swirling murk below.

The three islands were only intermittently visible from the cliff as the fog swept across them. I had been able to see the bobbing dot of Ian's head for the first twenty yards as he left the shore, but now he had disappeared into the mist.

"Do you think he's all right?" Jamie bent to help me scramble upright. The cloth of his coat was damp and rough under my fingers, soaked with mist and the fine droplets of ocean spray.

"Aye, he'll do. He's a bonny swimmer; and it's none so difficult a swim, either, once he's into the current." Still, he stared into the mist as though sheer effort could pierce its veils.

On Jamie's advice, Young Ian had timed his descent to begin when the tide began to go out, so as to have as much assistance as possible from the tide-race. Looking over the edge, I could see a floating mass of bladder wrack, half-stranded on the widening strip of beach.

"Perhaps two hours before he comes back." Jamie answered my unspoken question. He turned reluctantly from his vain perusal of the mist-hidden cove. "Damn, I wish I'd gone myself, arm or no arm."

"Both Young Jamie and Michael have done it," I reminded him. He gave me a rueful smile.

"Oh, aye. Ian will do fine. It's only that it's a good deal easier to do something that's a bit dangerous than it is to wait and worry while someone else does it."

"Ha," I told him. "So now you know what's it like being married to *you*."

He laughed.

"Oh, aye, I suppose so. Besides, it would be a shame to cheat Young Ian of his adventure. Come on, then, let's get out of the wind."

We moved inland a bit, away from the crumbling edge of the cliff, and sat down to wait, using the horses' bodies as shelter. Rough, shaggy Highland ponies, they appeared unmoved by the unpleasant weather, merely standing together, heads down, tails turned against the wind.

The wind was too high for easy conversation. We sat quietly, leaning together like the horses, with our backs to the windy shore.

"What's that?" Jamie raised his head, listening.

"What?"

"I thought I heard shouting."

"I expect it's the seals," I said, but before the words were out of my mouth, he was up and striding toward the cliff's edge.

The cove was still full of curling mist, but the wind had uncovered the seals' island, and it was clearly visible, at least for the moment. There were no seals on it now, though.

A small boat was drawn up on a sloping rock shelf at one side of the island. Not a fisherman's boat; this one was longer and more pointed at the prow, with one set of oars.

As I stared, a man appeared from the center of the island. He carried something under one arm, the size and shape of the box Jamie had described. I didn't have long to speculate as to the nature of this object, though, for just then a second man came up the far slope of the island and into sight.

This one was carrying Young Ian. He had the boy's half-naked body slung carelessly over one shoulder. It swung head down, arms dangling with a limpness that made it clear the boy was unconscious or dead.

"Ian!" Jamie's hand clamped over my mouth before I could shout again.

"Hush!" He dragged me to my knees to keep me out of sight. We watched, helpless, as the second man heaved Ian carelessly into the boat, then took hold of the gunwales to run it back into the water. There wasn't a chance of making the descent down the chimney and the swim to the island before they succeeded in making their escape. But escape to where?

"Where did they come from?" I gasped. Nothing else stirred in the cove below, save the mist and the shifting kelp-beds, turning in the tide.

"A ship. It's a ship's boat." Jamie added something low and heartfelt in Gaelic, and then was gone. I turned to see him fling himself on one of the horses and wrench its head around. Then he was off, riding hell-for-leather across the headland, away from the cove.

Rough as the footing across the headland was, the horses were shod for it better than I was. I hastily mounted and followed Jamie, a high-pitched whinny of protest from Ian's hobbled mount ringing in my ears.

It was less than a quarter of a mile to the ocean side of the headland, but it seemed to take forever to reach it. I saw Jamie ahead of me, his hair flying loose in the wind, and beyond him, the ship, lying to offshore.

The ground broke away in a tumble of rock that fell down to the ocean, not so steep as the cliffs of the cove, but much too rough to take a horse down. By the time I had reined up, Jamie was off his horse, and picking his way down the rubble toward the water.

To the left, I could see the longboat from the island, pulling round the curve of the headland. Someone on the ship must have been looking out for them, for I heard a faint hail from the direction of the ship, and saw small figures suddenly appear in the rigging.

One of these must also have seen us, for there was a sudden agitation aboard, with heads popping up above the rail and more yelling. The ship was blue, with a broad black band painted all around it. There was a line of gunports set in this band, and as I watched, the forward one opened, and the round black eye of the gun peeked out.

"Jamie!" I shrieked, as loudly as I could. He looked up from the rocks at his feet, saw where I was pointing, and hurled himself flat in the rubble as the gun went off.

The report wasn't terribly loud, but there was a sort of whistling noise past my head that made me duck instinctively. Several of the rocks around me exploded in puffs of flying rock chips, and it occurred to me, rather belatedly, that the horses and I were a great deal more visible there at the top of the headland than Jamie was on the cliff below.

The horses, having grasped this essential fact long before I did, were on their way back to where we had left their hobbled fellow well before the dust had settled. I flung myself bodily over the edge of the headland, slid several feet in a shower of gravel, and wedged myself into a deep crevice in the cliff.

There was another explosion somewhere above my head, and I pressed myself even closer into the rock. Evidently the people on board the ship were satisfied with the effect of their last shot, for relative silence now descended.

My heart was hammering against my ribs, and the air around my face was full of a fine gray dust that gave me an irresistible urge to cough. I risked a look over my shoulder, and was in time to see the longboat being hoisted aboard ship. Of Ian and his two captors, there was no sign.

The gunport closed silently as I watched, and the rope that held the anchor slithered up, streaming water. The ship turned slowly, seeking wind. The air was light and the sails barely puffed, but even that was enough.

Slowly, then faster, she was moving toward the open sea. By the time Jamie had reached my roosting place, the ship had all but vanished in the thick cloudbank that obscured the horizon.

"Jesus" was all he said when he reached me, but he clutched me hard for a moment. "Jesus."

He let go then, and turned to look out over the sea. Nothing moved save a few tendrils of slow-floating mist. The whole world seemed stricken with silence; even the occasional cries of the murres and shearwaters had been cut off by the cannon's boom.

The gray rock near my foot showed a fresh patch of lighter gray, where shot had struck off a wide flake of stone. It was no more than three feet above the crevice where I had taken refuge.

"What shall we do?" I felt numbed, both by the shock of the afternoon, and by the sheer enormity of what had happened. Impossible to believe that in less than an hour, Ian had disappeared from us as completely as though he had been wiped off the face of the earth. The fogbank loomed thick and impenetrable, a little way off the coast before us, a barrier as impassible as the curtain between earth and the underworld.

My mind kept replaying images: the mist, drifting over the outlines of the silkies' island, the sudden appearance of the boat, the men coming over the rocks, Ian's lanky, teenaged body, white-skinned as the mist, skinny limbs dangling like a disjointed doll's. I had seen everything with that clarity that attends tragedy; every detail fixed in my mind's eye, to be shown again and again, always with that half-conscious feeling that this time, I should be able to alter it.

Jamie's face was set in rigid lines, the furrows cut deep from nose to mouth.

"I don't know," he said. "Damn me to hell, I don't *know* what to do!" His hands flexed suddenly into fists at his sides. He shut his eyes, breathing heavily.

I felt even more frightened at this admission. In the brief time I had been back with him, I had grown once more accustomed to having Jamie always know what to do, even in the direst circumstances. This confession seemed more upsetting than anything that had yet happened.

A sense of helplessness swirled round me like the mist. Every nerve cried out to do *something*. But what?

I saw the streak of blood on his cuff, then; he had gashed his hand, climbing down the rocks. That, I could help, and I felt a sense of thankfulness that there was, after all, one thing I could do, however small.

"You've cut yourself," I said. I touched his injured hand. "Let me see; I'll wrap it for you."

"No," he said. He turned away, face strained, still looking desperately out into the fog. When I reached for him again, he jerked away.

"No, I said! Leave it be!"

I swallowed hard and wrapped my arms about myself under my cloak. There was little wind now, even on the headland, but it was cold and clammy nonetheless.

He rubbed his hand carelessly against the front of his coat, leaving a rusty smear. He was still staring out to sea, toward the spot where the ship had vanished. He closed his eyes, and pressed his lips tight together. Then he opened them, made a small gesture of apology toward me, and turned toward the headland.

"I suppose we must catch the horses," he said quietly. "Come on."

We walked back across the thick, short turf and strewn rocks without speaking, silent with shock and grief. I could see the horses, small stick-legged figures in the distance, clustered together with their hobbled companion. It seemed to have taken hours to run from the headland to the outer shore; going back seemed much longer.

"I don't think he was dead," I said, after what seemed like a year. I laid a hand tentatively on Jamie's arm, meaning to be comforting, but he wouldn't have noticed if I had struck him with a blackjack. He walked on slowly, head down.

"No," he said, and I saw him swallow hard. "No, he wasn't dead, or they'd not have taken him."

"*Did* they take him aboard the ship?" I pressed. "Did you see them?" I thought it might be better for him if he would talk.

He nodded. "Aye, they passed him aboard; I saw it clear. I suppose that's some hope," he muttered, as though to himself. "If they didna knock him on the head at once, maybe they won't." Suddenly remembering that I was there, he turned and looked at me, eyes searching my face.

"You're all right, Sassenach?"

I was scraped raw in several places, covered with filth, and shaky-kneed with fright, but basically sound.

"I'm fine." I put my hand on his arm again. This time he let it stay.

"That's good," he said softly, after a moment. He tucked my hand into the crook of his elbow, and we went on.

"Have you any idea who they were?" I had to raise my voice slightly to be heard above the wash of the surf behind us, but I wanted to keep him talking if I could.

He shook his head, frowning. The effort of talking seemed to be bringing him slowly out of his own shock.

"I heard one of the sailors shout to the men in the boat, and he spoke in French. But that proves nothing—sailors come from everywhere. Still, I have seen enough of ships at the docks to think that this one didna have quite the look of a merchant—nor the look of an English ship at all," he added, "though I couldna say why, exactly. The way the sails were rigged, maybe."

"It was blue, with a black line painted round it," I said. "That was all I had time to see, before the guns started firing."

Was it possible to trace a ship? The germ of the idea gave me hope; perhaps the situation was not so hopeless as I had first thought. If Ian was not dead, and we could find out where the ship was going . . .

"Did you see a name on it?" I asked.

"A name?" He looked faintly surprised at the notion. "What, *on* the ship?"

"Do ships not usually have their names painted on the sides?" I asked.

"No, what for?" He sounded honestly puzzled.

"So you could bloody tell who they are!" I said, exasperated. Taken by surprise by my tone, he actually smiled a little.

"Aye, well, I should expect that perhaps they dinna much want anyone telling who they are, given their business," he said dryly.

We paced on together for a few moments, thinking. Then I said curiously, "Well, but how do legitimate ships tell who each other is, if they haven't got names painted on?"

He glanced at me, one eyebrow raised.

"I should know you from another woman," he pointed out, "and ye havena got your name stitched upon your bosom."

"Not so much as a letter 'A,' " I said, flippantly, but seeing his blank look, added, "You mean ships look different enough—and there are few enough of them—that you can tell one from another just by looking?"

"Not me," he said honestly. "I know a few; ships where I ken the captain, and have been aboard to do business, or a few like the packet boats, that go back and forth so often that I've seen them in port dozens of times. But a sailing man would ken a great deal more."

"Then it *might* be possible to find out what the ship that took Ian is called?"

He nodded, looking at me curiously. "Aye, I think so. I have been trying to call to mind everything about it as we walked, so as to tell Jared. He'll know a great many ships, and a great many more captains—and perhaps one of them will know a blue ship, wide in the beam, with three masts, twelve guns, and a scowling figurehead."

My heart bounded upward. "So you *do* have a plan!"

"I wouldna call it so much a plan," he said. "It's only I canna think of anything else to do." He shrugged, and wiped a hand over his face. Tiny droplets of moisture were condensing on us as we walked, glistening in the ruddy hairs of his eyebrows and coating his cheeks with a wetness like tears. He sighed.

"The passage is arranged from Inverness. The best I can see to do is to go; Jared will be expecting us in Le Havre. When we see him, perhaps he can help us to find out what the blue ship is called, and maybe where it's bound. Aye," he said dryly, anticipating my question, "ships have home ports, and if they dinna belong to the navy, they have runs they commonly make, and papers for the harbormaster, too, showing where they're bound."

I began to feel better than I had since Ian had descended Ellen's tower.

"If they're not pirates or privateers, that is," he added, with a warning look which put an immediate damper on my rising spirits.

"And if they are?"

"Then God knows, but I don't," he said briefly, and would not say any more until we reached the horses.

They were grazing on the headland near the tower where we had left Ian's mount, behaving as though nothing had happened, pretending to find the tough sea grass delicious.

"Tcha!" Jamie viewed them disapprovingly. "Silly beasts." He grabbed the coil of rope and wrapped it twice round a projecting stone. Handing me the end, with a terse instruction to hold it, he dropped the free end down the chimney, shed his coat and shoes, and disappeared down the rope himself without further remark.

Sometime later, he came back up, sweating profusely, with a small bundle tucked under his arm. Young Ian's shirt, coat, shoes and stockings, with his knife and the small leather pouch in which the lad kept such valuables as he had.

"Do you mean to take them home to Jenny?" I asked. I tried to imagine what Jenny might think, say, or do at the news, and succeeded all too well. I felt a little sick, knowing that the hollow, aching sense of loss I felt was as nothing to what hers would be.

Jamie's face was flushed from the climb, but at my words, the blood drained from his cheeks. His hands tightened on the bundle.

"Oh, aye," he said, very softly, with great bitterness. "Aye, I shall go home and tell my sister that I have lost her youngest son? She didna want him to come wi' me, but I insisted. I'll take care of him, I said. And now he is hurt and maybe dead—but here are his clothes, to remember him by?" His jaw clenched, and he swallowed convulsively.

"I'd rather be dead myself," he said.

He knelt on the ground then, shaking out the articles of clothing, folding them carefully, and laying them together in a pile. He folded the coat carefully around the other things, stood up, and stuffed the bundle into his saddlebag.

"Ian will be needing them, I expect, when we find him," I said, trying to sound convinced.

Jamie looked at me, but after a moment, he nodded.

"Aye," he said softly. "I expect he will."

It was too late in the day to begin the ride to Inverness. The sun was setting, announcing the fact with a dull reddish glow that barely penetrated the gathering mist. Without speaking, we began to make camp. There was cold food in the saddlebags, but neither of us had the heart to eat. Instead, we rolled ourselves up in cloaks and blankets and lay down to sleep, cradled in small hollows that Jamie had scooped in the earth.

I couldn't sleep. The ground was hard and stony beneath my hips and shoulders, and the thunder of the surf below would have been sufficient to keep me awake, even had my mind not been filled with thoughts of Ian.

Was he badly hurt? The limpness of his body had bespoken some damage, but I had seen no blood. Presumably, he had merely been hit on the head. If so, what would he feel when he woke, to find himself abducted, and being carried farther from home and family with each passing minute?

And how were we ever to find him? When Jamie had first mentioned Jared, I had felt hopeful, but the more I thought of it, the slimmer seemed the prospects of actually finding a single ship, which might now be sailing in any direction at all, to anyplace in the world. And would his captors bother to keep Ian, or would they, on second thoughts, conclude that he was a dangerous nuisance, and pitch him overboard?

I didn't think I slept, but I must have dozed, my dreams full of trouble. I woke shivering with cold, and edged out a hand, reaching for Jamie. He wasn't there. When I sat up, I found that he had spread his blanket over me while I dozed, but it was a poor substitute for the heat of his body.

He was sitting some distance away, with his back to me. The offshore wind had risen with the setting of the sun, and blown some of the mist away; a half-moon shed enough light through the clouds to show me his hunched figure clearly.

I got up and walked over to him, folding my cloak tight about me against the chill. My steps made a light crunching sound on the crumbled granite, but the sound was drowned in the sighing rumble of the sea below. Still, he must have heard me; he didn't turn around, but gave no sign of surprise when I sank down beside him.

He sat with his chin in his hands, his elbows on his knees, eyes wide and sightless as he gazed out into the dark water of the cove. If the seals were awake, they were quiet tonight.

"Are you all right?" I said quietly. "It's beastly cold." He was wearing nothing but his coat, and in the small, chilled hours of the night, in the wet, cold air above the sea, that was far from enough. I could feel the tiny, constant shiver that ran through him when I set my hand on his arm.

"Aye, I'm fine," he said, with a marked lack of conviction.

I merely snorted at this piece of prevarication, and sat down next to him on another chunk of granite.

"It wasn't your fault," I said, after we had sat in silence for some time, listening to the sea.

"Ye should go and sleep, Sassenach." His voice was even, but with an undertone of hopelessness that made me move closer to him, trying to embrace him. He was clearly reluctant to touch me, but I was shivering very obviously myself by this time.

"I'm not going anywhere."

He sighed deeply and pulled me closer, settling me upon his knee, so that his arms came inside my cloak, holding tight. Little by little, the shivering eased.

"What are you doing out here?" I asked at last.

"Praying," he said softly. "Or trying to."

"I shouldn't have interrupted you." I made as though to move away, but his hold on me tightened.

"No, stay," he said. We stayed clasped close; I could feel the warmth of his breathing in my ear. He drew in his breath as though about to speak, but then let it out without saying anything. I turned and touched his face.

"What is it, Jamie?"

"Is it wrong for me to have ye?" he whispered. His face was bone-white, his eyes no more than dark pits in the dim light. "I keep thinking—is it my fault? Have I sinned so greatly, wanting you so much, needing ye more than life itself?"

"Do you?" I took his face between my hands, feeling the wide bones cold under my palms. "And if you do—how can that be wrong? I'm your wife." In spite of everything, the simple word "wife" made my heart lighten.

He turned his face slightly, so his lips lay against my palm, and his hand came up, groping for mine. His fingers were cold, too, and hard as driftwood soaked in seawater.

"I tell myself so. God has given ye to me; how can I not love you? And yet —I keep thinking, and canna stop."

He looked down at me then, brow furrowed with trouble.

"The treasure—it was all right to use it when there was need, to feed the hungry, or to rescue folk from prison. But to try to buy my freedom from guilt—to use it only so that I might live free at Lallybroch with you, and not trouble myself over Laoghaire—I think maybe that was wrong to do."

I drew his hand down around my waist, and pulled him close. He came, eager for comfort, and laid his head on my shoulder.

"Hush," I said to him, though he hadn't spoken again. "Be still. Jamie, have you ever done something for yourself alone—not with any thought of anyone else?"

His hand rested gently on my back, tracing the seam of my bodice, and his breathing held the hint of a smile.

"Oh, many and many a time," he whispered. "When I saw you. When I took ye, not caring did ye want me or no, did ye have somewhere else to be, someone else to love."

"Bloody man," I whispered in his ear, rocking him as best I could. "You're an awful fool, Jamie Fraser. And what about Brianna? That wasn't wrong, was it?"

"No." He swallowed; I could hear the sound of it clearly, and feel the pulse beat in his neck where I held him. "But now I have taken ye back from her, as well. I love you—and I love Ian, like he was my own. And I am thinking maybe I cannot have ye both."

"Jamie Fraser," I said again, with as much conviction as I could put into my voice, "you're a terrible fool." I smoothed the hair back from his forehead and twisted my fist in the thick tail at his nape, pulling his head back to make him look at me.

I thought my face must look to him as his did to me; the bleached bones of a skull, with the lips and eyes dark as blood.

"You didn't force me to come to you, or snatch me away from Brianna. I came, because I wanted to—because I wanted *you*, as much as you did me— and my being here has nothing to do with what's happened. We're *married,* blast you, by any standard you care to name—before God, man, Neptune, or what-have-you."

"Neptune?" he said, sounding a little stunned.

"Be quiet," I said. "We're married, I say, and it isn't wicked for you to want me, or to have me, and no God worth his salt would take your nephew away from you because you wanted to be happy. So there!"

"Besides," I added, pulling back and looking up at him a moment later, "I'm not bloody going back, so what could you do about it, anyway?"

The small vibration in his chest this time was laughter, not cold.

"Take ye and be damned for it, I expect," he said. He kissed my forehead gently. "Loving you has put me through hell more than once, Sassenach; I'll risk it again, if need be."

"Bah," I said. "And you think loving *you*'s been a bed of roses, do you?" This time he laughed out loud.

"No," he said, "but you'll maybe keep doing it?"

"Maybe I will, at that."

"You're a verra stubborn woman," he said, the smile clear in his voice.

"It bloody takes one to know one," I said, and then we were both quiet for quite some time.

It was very late—perhaps four o'clock in the morning. The half-moon was low in the sky, seen only now and then through the moving clouds. The clouds themselves were moving faster; the wind was shifting and the mist breaking up, in the turning hour between dark and dawn. Somewhere below, one of the seals barked loudly, once.

"Do ye think perhaps ye could stand to go now?" Jamie said suddenly.

"Not wait for the daylight? Once off the headland, the going's none so bad that the horses canna manage in the dark."

My whole body ached from weariness, and I was starving, but I stood up at once, and brushed the hair out of my face.

"Let's go," I said.

PART EIGHT

On the Water

40

I Shall Go Down to the Sea

"It will have to be the *Artemis*." Jared flipped shut the cover of his portable writing desk and rubbed his brow, frowning. Jamie's cousin had been in his fifties when I knew him before, and was now well past seventy, but the snub-nosed hatchet face, the spare, narrow frame, and the tireless capacity for work were just the same. Only his hair marked his age, gone from lank darkness to a scanty, pure and gleaming white, jauntily tied with a red silk ribbon.

"She's no more than a midsized sloop, with a crew of forty or so," he remarked. "But it's late in the season, and we'll not likely do better—all of the Indiamen will have gone a month since. *Artemis* would have gone with the convoy to Jamaica, was she not laid up for repair."

"I'd sooner have a ship of yours—and one of your captains," Jamie assured him. "The size doesna matter."

Jared cocked a skeptical eyebrow at his cousin. "Oh? Well, and ye may find it matter more than ye think, out at sea. It's like to be squally, this late in the season, and a sloop will be bobbin' like a cork. Might I ask how ye weathered the Channel crossing in the packet boat, cousin?"

Jamie's face, already drawn and grim, grew somewhat grimmer at this question. The completest of landlubbers, he was not just prone to seasickness, but prostrated by it. He had been violently ill all the way from Inverness to Le Havre, though sea and weather had been quite calm. Now, some six hours later, safe ashore in Jared's warehouse by the quay, there was still a pale tinge to his lips and dark circles beneath his eyes.

"I'll manage," he said shortly.

Jared eyed him dubiously, well aware of his response to seagoing craft of any kind. Jamie could scarcely set foot on a ship at anchor without going green; the prospect of his crossing the Atlantic, sealed inescapably in a small and constantly tossing ship for two or three months, was enough to boggle the stoutest mind. It had been troubling mine for some time.

"Well, I suppose there's no help for it," Jared said with a sigh, echoing my thought. "And at least you'll have a physician to hand," he added, with a smile at me. "That is, I suppose you intend accompanying him, my dear?"

"Yes indeed," I assured him. "How long will it be before the ship is ready?

I'd like to find a good apothecary's, to stock my medicine chest before the voyage.''

Jared pursed his lips in concentration. "A week, God willing," he said. "*Artemis* is in Bilbao at the moment; she's to carry a cargo of tanned Spanish hides, with a load of copper from Italy—she'll ship that here, once she arrives, which should be day after tomorrow, with a fair wind. I've no captain signed on for the voyage yet, but a good man in mind; I may have to go to Paris to fetch him, though, and that will be two days there and two back. Add a day to complete stores, fill the water casks, add all the bits and pieces, and she should be ready to leave at dawn tomorrow week.''

"How long to the West Indies?" Jamie asked. The tension in him showed in the lines of his body, little affected either by our journey or by the brief rest. He was strung taut as a bow, and likely to remain so until we had found Young Ian.

"Two months, in the season," Jared replied, the small frown still lining his forehead. "But you're a month past the season now; hit the winter gales and it could be three. Or more.''

Or never, but Jared, ex-seaman that he was, was too superstitious—or too tactful—to voice this possibility. Still, I saw him touch the wood of his desk surreptitiously for luck.

Neither would he voice the other thought that occupied my mind; we had no positive proof that the blue ship was headed for the West Indies. We had only the records Jared had obtained for us from the Le Havre harbormaster, showing two visits by the ship—aptly named *Bruja*—within the last five years, each time giving her home port as Bridgetown, on the island of Barbados.

"Tell me about her again—the ship that took Young Ian," Jared said. "How did she ride? High in the water, or sunk low, as if she were loaded heavy for a voyage?''

Jamie closed his eyes for a moment, concentrating, then opened them with a nod. "Heavy-laden, I could swear it. Her gunports were no more than six feet from the water.''

Jared nodded, satisfied. "Then she was leaving port, not coming in. I've messengers out to all the major ports in France, Portugal and Spain. With luck, they'll find the port she shipped from, and then we'll know her destination for sure from her papers." His thin lips quirked suddenly downward. "Unless she's turned pirate, and sailing under false papers, that is.''

The old wine merchant carefully set aside the lap desk, its carved mahogany richly darkened by years of use, and rose to his feet, moving stiffly.

"Well, that's the most that can be done for the moment. Let's go to the house, now; Mathilde will have supper waiting. Tomorrow I'll take ye over the manifests and orders, and your wife can find her bits of herbs.''

It was nearly five o'clock, and full dark at this time of year, but Jared had two linksmen waiting to escort us the short distance to his house, equipped with torches to light the way and armed with stout clubs. Le Havre was a thriving port city, and the quay district was no place to walk alone after dark, particularly if one was known as a prosperous wine merchant.

Despite the exhaustion of the Channel crossing, the oppressive clamminess and pervasive fish-smell of Le Havre, and a gnawing hunger, I felt my spirits rise as we followed the torches through the dark, narrow streets. Thanks to Jared, we had at least a chance of finding Young Ian.

Jared had concurred with Jamie's opinion that if the pirates of the *Bruja*—for so I thought of them—had not killed Young Ian on the spot, they were likely to keep him unharmed. A healthy young male of any race could be sold as a slave or indentured servant in the West Indies for upward of two hundred pounds; a respectable sum by current standards.

If they did intend so to dispose of Young Ian profitably, *and* if we knew the port to which they were sailing, it should be a reasonably easy matter to find and recover the boy. A gust of wind and a few chilly drops from the hovering clouds dampened my optimism slightly, reminding me that while it might be no great matter to find Ian once we had reached the West Indies, both the *Bruja* and the *Artemis* had to reach the islands first. And the winter storms were beginning.

The rain increased through the night, drumming insistently on the slate roof above our heads. I would normally have found the sound soothing and soporific; under the circumstances, the low thrum seemed threatening, not peaceful.

Despite Jared's substantial dinner and the excellent wines that accompanied it, I found myself unable to sleep, my mind summoning images of rain-soaked canvas and the swell of heavy seas. At least my morbid imaginings were keeping only myself awake; Jamie had not come up with me but had stayed to talk with Jared about the arrangements for the upcoming voyage.

Jared was willing to risk a ship and a captain to help in the search. In return, Jamie would sail as supercargo.

"As *what*?" I had said, hearing this proposal.

"The supercargo," Jared had explained patiently. "That's the man whose duty it is to oversee the loading, the unloading, and the sale and disposition of the cargo. The captain and the crew merely sail the ship; someone's got to look after the contents. In a case where the welfare of the cargo will be affected, the supercargo's orders may override even the captain's authority."

And so it was arranged. While Jared was more than willing to go to some risk in order to help a kinsman, he saw no reason not to profit from the arrangement. He had therefore made quick provision for a miscellaneous cargo to be loaded from Bilbao and Le Havre; we would sail to Jamaica to unload the bulk of it, and would arrange for the reloading of the *Artemis* with rum produced by the sugarcane plantation of Fraser et Cie on Jamaica, for the return trip.

The return trip, however, would not occur until good sailing weather returned, in late April or early May. For the time between arrival on Jamaica in February and return to Scotland in May, Jamie would have disposal of the *Artemis* and her crew, to travel to Barbados—or other places—in search of Young Ian. Three months. I hoped it would be enough.

It was a generous arrangement. Still, Jared, who had been an expatriate wine-seller for many years in France, was wealthy enough that the loss of a ship, while distressing, would not cripple him. The fact did not escape me that while Jared was risking a small portion of his fortune, we were risking our lives.

The wind seemed to be dying; it no longer howled down the chimney with quite such force. Sleep proving still elusive, I got out of bed, and with a quilt wrapped round my shoulders for warmth, went to the window.

The sky was a deep, mottled gray, the scudding rain clouds edged with brilliant light from the moon that hid behind them, and the glass was streaked with rain. Still, enough light seeped through the clouds for me to make out the masts of the ships moored at the quay, less than a quarter of a mile away. They swayed to and fro, their sails furled tight against the storm, rising and falling in uneasy rhythm as the waves rocked the boats at anchor. In a week's time, I would be on one.

I had not dared to think what life might be like once I had found Jamie, lest I not find him after all. Then I *had* found him, and in quick succession, had contemplated life as a printer's wife among the political and literary worlds of Edinburgh, a dangerous and fugitive existence as a smuggler's lady, and finally, the busy, settled life of a Highland farm, which I had known before and loved.

Now, in equally quick succession, all these possibilities had been jerked away, and I faced an unknown future once more.

Oddly enough, I was not so much distressed by this as excited by it. I had been settled for twenty years, rooted as a barnacle by my attachments to Brianna, to Frank, to my patients. Now fate—and my own actions—had ripped me loose from all those things, and I felt as though I were tumbling free in the surf, at the mercy of forces a great deal stronger than myself.

My breath had misted the glass. I traced a small heart in the cloudiness, as I had used to do for Brianna on cold mornings. Then, I would put her initials inside the heart—B.E.R., for Brianna Ellen Randall. Would she still call herself Randall? I wondered, or Fraser, now? I hesitated, then drew two letters inside the outline of the heart—a "J" and a "C."

I was still standing before the window when the door opened and Jamie came in.

"Are ye awake still?" he asked, rather unnecessarily.

"The rain kept me from sleeping." I went and embraced him, glad of his warm solidness to dispel the cold gloom of the night.

He hugged me, resting his cheek against my hair. He smelt faintly of seasickness, much more strongly of candlewax and ink.

"Have you been writing?" I asked.

He looked down at me in astonishment. "I have, but how did ye know that?"

"You smell of ink."

He smiled slightly, stepping back and running his hand through his hair. "You've a nose as keen as a truffle pig's, Sassenach."

"Why, thank you, what a graceful compliment," I said. "What were you writing?"

The smile disappeared from his face, leaving him looking strained and tired.

"A letter to Jenny," he said. He went to the table, where he shed his coat and began to unfasten his stock and jabot. "I didna want to write her until we'd seen Jared, and I could tell her what plans we had, and what the prospects were for bringing Ian home safe." He grimaced, and pulled the shirt over his head. "God knows what she'll do when she gets it—and thank God, I'll be at sea when she does," he added wryly, emerging from the folds of linen.

It couldn't have been an easy piece of composition, but I thought he seemed easier for the writing of it. He sat down to take off his shoes and stockings, and I came behind him to undo the clubbed queue of his hair.

"I'm glad the writing's over, at least," he said, echoing my thought. "I'd been dreading telling her, more than anything else."

"You told her the truth?"

He shrugged. "I always have."

Except about me. I didn't voice the thought, though, but began to rub his shoulders, kneading the knotted muscles.

"What did Jared do with Mr. Willoughby?" I asked, massage bringing the Chinese to mind. He had accompanied us on the Channel crossing, sticking to Jamie like a small blue-silk shadow. Jared, used to seeing everything on the docks, had taken Mr. Willoughby in stride, bowing gravely to him and addressing him with a few words of Mandarin, but his housekeeper had viewed this unusual guest with considerably more suspicion.

"I believe he's gone to sleep in the stable." Jamie yawned, and stretched himself luxuriously. "Mathilde said she wasna accustomed to have heathens in the house and didna mean to start now. She was sprinkling the kitchen wi' holy water after he ate supper there." Glancing up, he caught sight of the heart I had traced on the windowpane, black against the misted glass, and smiled.

"What's that?"

"Just silliness," I said.

He reached up and took my right hand, the ball of his thumb caressing the small scar at the base of my own thumb, the letter "J" he had made with the point of his knife, just before I left him, before Culloden.

"I didna ask," he said, "whether ye wished to come with me. I could leave ye here; Jared would have ye stay wi' him and welcome, here or in Paris. Or ye could go back to Lallybroch, if ye wished."

"No, you didn't ask," I said. "Because you knew bloody well what the answer would be."

We looked at each other and smiled. The lines of heartsickness and weariness had lifted from his face. The candlelight glowed softly on the burnished crown of his head as he bent and gently kissed the palm of my hand.

The wind still whistled in the chimney, and the rain ran down the glass like tears outside, but it no longer mattered. Now I could sleep.

The sky had cleared by morning. A brisk, cold breeze rattled the window-panes of Jared's study, but couldn't penetrate to the cozy room inside. The house at Le Havre was much smaller than his lavish Paris residence, but still boasted three stories of solid, half-timbered comfort.

I pushed my feet farther toward the crackling fire, and dipped my quill into the inkwell. I was making up a list of all the things I thought might be needed in the medical way for a two-month voyage. Distilled alcohol was both the most important and the easiest to obtain; Jared had promised to get me a cask in Paris.

"We'd best label it something else, though," he'd told me. "Or the sailors will have drunk it before you've left port."

Purified lard, I wrote slowly, *St.-John's-wort; garlic, ten pounds; yarrow.* I wrote *borage,* then shook my head and crossed it out, replacing it with the older name by which it was more likely known now, *bugloss.*

It was slow work. At one time, I had known the medicinal uses of all the common herbs, and not a few uncommon ones. I had had to; they were all that was available.

At that, many of them were surprisingly effective. Despite the skepticism—and outspoken horror—of my supervisors and colleagues at the hospital in Boston, I had used them occasionally on my modern patients to good effect. ("Did you *see* what Dr. Randall did?" a shocked intern's cry echoed in memory, making me smile as I wrote. "She fed the stomach in 134B *boiled flowers!*")

The fact remained that one wouldn't use yarrow and comfrey on a wound if iodine were available, nor treat a systemic infection with bladderwort in preference to penicillin.

I had forgotten a lot, but as I wrote the names of the herbs, the look and the smell of each one began to come back to me—the dark, bituminous look and pleasant light smell of birch oil, the sharp tang of the mint family, the dusty sweet smell of chamomile and the astringency of bistort.

Across the table, Jamie was struggling with his own lists. A poor penman, he wrote laboriously with his crippled right hand, pausing now and then to rub the healing wound above his left elbow and mutter curses under his breath.

"Have ye lime juice on your list, Sassenach?" he inquired, looking up.

"No. Ought I to have?"

He brushed a strand of hair out of his face and frowned at the sheet of paper in front of him.

"It depends. Customarily, it would be the ship's surgeon who provides the lime juice, but in a ship the size of the *Artemis,* there generally isn't a surgeon, and the provision of foodstuffs falls to the purser. But there isn't a purser, either; there's no time to find a dependable man, so I shall fill that office, too."

"Well, if you'll be purser and supercargo, I expect I'll be the closest thing to a ship's surgeon," I said, smiling slightly. "I'll get the lime juice."

"All right." We returned to a companionable scratching, unbroken until the entrance of Josephine, the parlormaid, to announce the arrival of a person. Her long nose wrinkled in unconscious disapproval at the information.

"He waits upon the doorstep. The butler tried to send him away, but he insists that he has an appointment with you, Monsieur James?" The questioning tone of this last implied that nothing could seem more unlikely, but duty compelled her to relay the improbable suggestion.

Jamie's eyebrows rose. "A person? What sort of person?" Josephine's lips primmed together as though she really could not bring herself to say. I was becoming curious to see this person, and ventured over to the window. Sticking my head far out, I could see the top of a very dusty black slouch hat on the doorstep, and not much more.

"He looks like a peddler; he's got a bundle of some kind on his back," I reported, craning out still farther, hands on the sill. Jamie clutched me by the waist and drew me back, thrusting his own head out in turn.

"Och, it's the coin dealer Jared mentioned!" he exclaimed. "Bring him up, then."

With an eloquent expression on her narrow face, Josephine departed, returning in short order with a tall, gangling youth of perhaps twenty, dressed in a badly outmoded style of coat, wide unbuckled breeches that flapped limply about his skinny shanks, drooping stockings and the cheapest of wooden sabots.

The filthy black hat, courteously removed indoors, revealed a thin face with an intelligent expression, adorned with a vigorous, if scanty, brown beard. Since virtually no one in Le Havre other than a few seamen wore a beard, it hardly needed the small shiny black skullcap on the newcomer's head to tell me he was a Jew.

The boy bowed awkwardly to me, then to Jamie, struggling with the straps of his peddler's pack.

"Madame," he said, with a bob that made his curly sidelocks dance, "Monsieur. It is most good of you to receive me." He spoke French oddly, with a singsong intonation that made him hard to follow.

While I entirely understood Josephine's reservations about this . . . person, still, he had wide, guileless blue eyes that made me smile at him despite his generally unprepossessing appearance.

"It's we who should be grateful to you," Jamie was saying. "I had not expected you to come so promptly. My cousin tells me your name is Mayer?"

The coin dealer nodded, a shy smile breaking out amid the sprigs of his youthful beard.

"Yes, Mayer. It is no trouble; I was in the city already."

"Yet you come from Frankfort, no? A long way," Jamie said politely. He smiled as he looked over Mayer's costume, which looked as though he had retrieved it from a rubbish tip. "And a dusty one, too, I expect," he added. "Will you take wine?"

Mayer looked flustered at this offer, but after opening and closing his mouth a few times, finally settled on a silent nod of acceptance.

His shyness vanished, though, once the pack was opened. Though from the outside the shapeless bundle looked as though it might contain, at best, a change of ragged linen and Mayer's midday meal, once opened it revealed several small wooden racks, cleverly fitted into a framework inside the pack, each rack packed carefully with tiny leather bags, cuddling together like eggs in a nest.

Mayer removed a folded square of fabric from beneath the racks, whipped it open, and spread it with something of a flourish on Jamie's desk. Then one by one, Mayer opened the bags and drew out the contents, placing each gleaming round reverently on the deep blue velvet of the cloth.

"An Aquilia Severa aureus," he said, touching one small coin that glowed with the deep mellowness of ancient gold from the velvet. "And here, a Sestercius of the Calpurnia family." His voice was soft and his hands sure, stroking the edge of a silver coin only slightly worn, or cradling one in his palm to demonstrate the weight of it.

He looked up from the coins, eyes bright with the reflections of the precious metal.

"Monsieur Fraser tells me that you desire to inspect as many of the Greek and Roman rarities as possible. I have not my whole stock with me, of course, but I have quite a few—and I could send to Frankfort for others, if you desire."

Jamie smiled, shaking his head. "I'm afraid we haven't time, Mr. Mayer. We—"

"Just Mayer, Monsieur Fraser," the young man interrupted, perfectly polite, but with a slight edge in his voice.

"Indeed." Jamie bowed slightly. "I hope my cousin shall not have misled you. I shall be most happy to pay the cost of your journey, and something for your time, but I am not wishful to purchase any of your stock myself . . . Mayer."

The young man's eyebrows rose in inquiry, along with one shoulder.

"What I wish," Jamie said slowly, leaning forward to look closely at the coins on display, "is to compare your stock with my recollection of several ancient coins I have seen, and then—should I see any that are similar—to inquire whether you—or your family, I should say, for I expect you are too young yourself—should be familiar with anyone who might have purchased such coins twenty years ago."

He glanced up at the young Jew, who was looking justifiably astonished, and smiled.

"That may be asking a bit much of you, I know. But my cousin tells me that your family is one of the few who deals in such matters, and is by far the most knowledgeable. If you can acquaint me likewise with any persons in the West Indies with interests in this area, I should be deeply obliged to you."

Mayer sat looking at him for a moment, then inclined his head, the sunlight winking from the border of small jet beads that adorned his skullcap. It was plain that he was intensely curious, but he merely touched his pack and said, "My father or my uncle would have sold such coins, not me; but I have here the catalogue and record of every coin that has passed through our hands in thirty years. I will tell you what I can."

He drew the velvet cloth toward Jamie and sat back.

"Do you see anything here like the coins you remember?"

Jamie studied the rows of coins with close attention, then gently nudged a silver piece, about the size of an American quarter. Three leaping porpoises circled its edge, surrounding a charioteer in the center.

"This one," he said. "There were several like it—small differences, but several with these porpoises." He looked again, picked out a worn gold disc with an indistinct profile, then a silver one, somewhat larger and in better condition, with a man's head shown both full-face and in profile.

"These," he said. "Fourteen of the gold ones, and ten of the ones with two heads."

"Ten!" Mayer's bright eyes popped wide with astonishment. "I should not have thought there were so many in Europe."

Jamie nodded. "I'm quite certain—I saw them closely; handled them, even."

"These are the twin heads of Alexander," Mayer said, touching the coin with reverence. "Very rare indeed. It is a tetradrachm, struck to commemorate the battle fought at Amphipolos, and the founding of a city on the site of the battlefield."

Jamie listened with attention, a slight smile on his lips. While he had no great interest in ancient money himself, he did have a great appreciation for a man with a passion.

A quarter of an hour more, another consultation of the catalogue, and the business was complete. Four Greek drachmas of a type Jamie recognized had been added to the collection, several small gold and silver coins, and a thing called a quintinarius, a Roman coin in heavy gold.

Mayer bent and reached into his pack once more, this time pulling out a sheaf of foolscap pages furled into a roll and tied with ribbon. Untied, they showed row upon row of what looked from a distance like bird tracks; on closer inspection, they proved to be Hebraic writing, inked small and precise.

He thumbed slowly through the pages, stopping here and there with a murmured "Um," then passing on. At last he laid the pages on his shabby knee and looked up at Jamie, head cocked to one side.

"Our transactions are naturally carried out in confidence, Monsieur," he said, "and so while I could tell you, for example, that certainly we had sold such and such a coin, in such and such a year, I should not be able to tell you the name of the purchaser." He paused, evidently thinking, then went on.

"We did in fact sell coins of your description—three drachmas, two each of the heads of Egalabalus and the double head of Alexander, and no fewer than six of the gold Calpurnian aurei in the year 1745." He hesitated.

"Normally, that is all I could tell you. However . . . in this case, Monsieur, I happen to know that the original buyer of these coins is dead—has been dead for some years, in fact. Really, I cannot see that under the circumstances . . ." He shrugged, making up his mind.

"The purchaser was an Englishman, Monsieur. His name was Clarence Marylebone, Duke of Sandringham."

"Sandringham!" I exclaimed, startled into speech.

Mayer looked curiously at me, then at Jamie, whose face betrayed nothing beyond polite interest.

"Yes, Madame," he said. "I know that the Duke is dead, for he possessed an extensive collection of ancient coins, which my uncle bought from his heirs in 1746—the transaction is listed here." He raised the catalogue slightly, and let it fall.

I knew the Duke of Sandringham was dead, too, and by more immediate experience. Jamie's godfather, Murtagh, had killed him, on a dark night in March 1746, soon before the battle of Culloden brought an end to the Jacobite rebellion. I swallowed briefly, recalling my last sight of the Duke's face, its blueberry eyes fixed in an expression of intense surprise.

Mayer's eyes went back and forth between us, then he added hesitantly, "I can tell you also this; when my uncle purchased the Duke's collection after his death, there were no tetradrachms in it."

"No," Jamie murmured, to himself. "There wouldn't have been." Then, recollecting himself, he stood and reached for the decanter that stood on the sideboard.

"I thank you, Mayer," he said formally. "And now, let us drink to you and your wee book, there."

A few minutes later, Mayer was kneeling on the floor, doing up the fastenings of his ragged pack. The small pouch filled with silver livres that Jamie had given him in payment was in his pocket. He rose and bowed in turn to Jamie and to me before straightening and putting on his disreputable hat.

"I bid you goodbye, Madame," he said.

"Goodbye to you, too, Mayer," I replied. Then I asked, somewhat hesitantly, "Is 'Mayer' really your only name?"

Something flickered in the wide blue eyes, but he answered politely, heaving the heavy sack onto his back, "Yes, Madame. The Jews of Frankfort are not allowed to use family names." He looked up and smiled lopsidedly. "For the sake of convenience, the neighbors call us after an old red shield that was painted on the front of our house, many years ago. But beyond that . . . no, Madame. We have no name."

Josephine came then to conduct our visitor to the kitchen, taking care to walk several paces in front of him, her nostrils pinched white as though smelling something foul. Mayer stumbled after her, his clumsy sabots clattering on the polished floor.

Jamie relaxed in his chair, eyes abstracted in deep thought.

I heard the door close downstairs a few minutes later, with what was almost a slam, and the click of sabots on the stone steps below. Jamie heard it too, and turned toward the window.

"Well, Godspeed to ye, Mayer Red-Shield," he said, smiling.

"Jamie," I said, suddenly thinking of something, "do you speak German?"

"Eh? Oh, aye," he said vaguely, his attention still fixed on the window and the noises outside.

"What is 'red shield' in German?" I asked.

He looked blank for a moment, then his eyes cleared as his brain made the proper connection.

"*Rothschild*, Sassenach," he said. "Why?"

"Just a thought," I said. I looked toward the window, where the clatter of wooden shoes was long since lost in the noises of the street. "I suppose everyone has to start somewhere."

"Fifteen men on a dead man's chest," I observed. "Yo-ho-ho, and a bottle of rum."

Jamie gave me a look.

"Oh, aye?" he said.

"The Duke being the dead man," I explained. "Do you think the seals' treasure was really his?"

"I couldna say for sure, but it seems at least likely." Jamie's two stiff fingers tapped briefly on the table in a meditative rhythm. "When Jared mentioned Mayer the coin dealer to me, I thought it worth inquiring—for surely the most likely person to have sent the *Bruja* to retrieve the treasure was the person who put it there."

"Good reasoning," I said, "but evidently it wasn't the same person, if it was the Duke who put it there. Do you think the whole treasure amounted to fifty thousand pounds?"

Jamie squinted at his reflection in the rounded side of the decanter, considering. Then he picked it up and refilled his glass, to assist thought.

"Not as metal, no. But did ye notice the prices that some of those coins in Mayer's catalogue have sold for?"

"I did."

"As much as a thousand pound—sterling!—for a moldy bit of metal!" he said, marveling.

"I don't think metal molds," I said, "but I take your point. Anyway," I said, dismissing the question with a wave of my hand, "the point here is this; do you suppose the seals' treasure could have been the fifty thousand pounds that the Duke had promised to the Stuarts?"

In the early days of 1744, when Charles Stuart had been in France, trying to persuade his royal cousin Louis to grant him some sort of support, he had received a ciphered offer from the Duke of Sandringham, of fifty thousand pounds—enough to hire a small army—on condition that he enter England to retake the throne of his ancestors.

Whether it had been this offer that finally convinced the vacillating Prince Charles to undertake his doomed excursion, we would never know. It might as easily have been a challenge from someone he was drinking with, or a slight—real or imagined—by his mistress, that had sent him to Scotland with nothing more than six companions, two thousand Dutch broadswords, and several casks of brandywine with which to charm the Highland chieftains.

In any case, the fifty thousand pounds had never been received, because the Duke had died before Charles reached England. Another of the speculations that troubled me on sleepless nights was the question of whether that money would have made a difference. If Charles Stuart had received it, would he have taken his ragged Highland army all the way to London, retaken the throne and regained his father's crown?

If he had—well, if he had, the Jacobite rebellion might have succeeded,

Culloden might not have happened, I should never have gone back through the circle of stone . . . and I and Brianna would likely both have died in childbed and been dust these many years past. Surely twenty years should have been enough to teach me the futility of "if."

Jamie had been considering, meditatively rubbing the bridge of his nose.

"It might have been," he said at last. "Given a proper market for the coins and gems—ye ken such things take time to sell; if ye must dispose of them quickly, you'll get but a fraction of the price. But given long enough to search out good buyers—aye, it might reach fifty thousand."

"Duncan Kerr was a Jacobite, wasn't he?"

Jamie frowned, nodding. "He was. Aye, it could be—though God knows it's an awkward kind of fortune to be handing to the commander of an army to pay his troops!"

"Yes, but it's also small, portable, and easy to hide," I pointed out. "And if you were the Duke, and busy committing treason by dealing with the Stuarts, that might be important to you. Sending fifty thousand pounds in sterling, with strongboxes and carriages and guards, would attract the hell of a lot more attention than sending one man secretly across the Channel with a small wooden box."

Jamie nodded again. "Likewise, if ye had a collection of such rarities already, it would attract no attention to be acquiring more, and no one would likely notice what coins ye had. It would be a simple matter to take out the most valuable, replace them with cheap ones, and no one the wiser. No banker who might talk, were ye to shift money or land." He shook his head admiringly.

"It's a clever scheme, aye, whoever made it." He looked up inquiringly at me.

"But then, why did Duncan Kerr come, nearly ten years after Culloden? And what happened to him? Did he come to leave the fortune on the silkies' isle then, or to take it away?"

"And who sent the *Bruja* now?" I finished for him. I shook my head, too.

"Damned if I know. Perhaps the Duke had a confederate of some sort? But if he did, we don't know who it was."

Jamie sighed, and impatient with sitting for so long, stood up and stretched. He glanced out the window, estimating the height of the sun, his usual method of telling time, whether a clock was handy or not.

"Aye, well, we'll have time for speculation once we're at sea. It's near on noon, now, and the Paris coach leaves at three o'clock."

The apothecary's shop in the Rue de Varennes was gone. In its place were a thriving tavern, a pawnbroker's, and a small goldsmith's shop, crammed companionably cheek by jowl.

"Master Raymond?" The pawnbroker knitted grizzled brows. "I have heard of him, Madame"—he darted a wary glance at me, suggesting that whatever he had heard had not been very admirable—"but he has been gone for several years. If you are requiring a good apothecary, though, Krasner in the Place d'Aloes, or perhaps Madame Verrue, near the Tuileries . . ." He stared with interest at Mr. Willoughby, who accompanied me, then leaned over the counter to address me confidentially.

"Might you be interested in selling your Chinaman, Madame? I have a client with a marked taste for the Orient. I could get you a very good price—with no more than the usual commission, I assure you."

Mr. Willoughby, who did not speak French, was peering with marked contempt at a porcelain jar painted with pheasants, done in an Oriental style.

"Thank you," I said, "but I think not. I'll try Krasner."

Mr. Willoughby had attracted relatively little attention in Le Havre, a port city teeming with foreigners of every description. On the streets of Paris, wearing a padded jacket over his blue-silk pajamas, and with his queue wrapped several times around his head for convenience, he caused considerable comment. He did, however, prove surprisingly knowledgeable about herbs and medicinal substances.

"*Bai jei ai,*" he told me, picking up a pinch of mustard seed from an open box in Krasner's emporium. "Good for *shen-yen*—kidneys."

"Yes, it is," I said, surprised. "How did you know?"

He allowed his head to roll slightly from side to side, as I had learned was his habit when pleased at being able to astonish someone.

"I know healers one time," was all he said, though, before turning to point at a basket containing what looked like balls of dried mud.

"*Shan-yü,*" he said authoritatively. "Good—*very* good—cleanse blood, liver he work good, no dry skin, help see. You buy."

I stepped closer to examine the objects in question and found them to be a particularly homely sort of dried eel, rolled into balls and liberally coated with mud. The price was quite reasonable, though, so to please him, I added two of the nasty things to the basket over my arm.

The weather was mild for early December, and we walked back toward Jared's house in the Rue Tremoulins. The streets were bright with winter sunshine, and lively with vendors, beggars, prostitutes, shopgirls, and the other denizens of the poorer part of Paris, all taking advantage of the temporary thaw.

At the corner of the Rue du Nord and the Allée des Canards, though, I saw something quite out of the ordinary; a tall, slope-shouldered figure in black frock coat and a round black hat.

"Reverend Campbell!" I exclaimed.

He whirled about at being so addressed, then, recognizing me, bowed and removed his hat.

"Mistress Malcolm!" he said. "How most agreeable to see you again." His eye fell on Mr. Willoughby, and he blinked, features hardening in a stare of disapproval.

"Er . . . this is Mr. Willoughby," I introduced him. "He's an . . . associate of my husband's. Mr. Willoughby, the Reverend Archibald Campbell."

"Indeed." The Reverend Campbell normally looked quite austere, but contrived now to look as though he had breakfasted on barbed wire, and found it untasty.

"I thought that you were sailing from Edinburgh to the West Indies," I said, in hopes of taking his gelid eye off the Chinaman. It worked; his gaze shifted to me, and thawed slightly.

"I thank you for your kind inquiries, Madame," he said. "I still harbor such intentions. However, I had urgent business to transact first in France. I shall be departing from Edinburgh on Thursday week."

"And how is your sister?" I asked. He glanced at Mr. Willoughby with dislike, then taking a step to one side so as to be out of the Chinaman's direct sight, lowered his voice.

"She is somewhat improved, I thank you. The draughts you prescribed have been most helpful. She is much calmer, and sleeps quite regularly now. I must thank you again for your kind attentions."

"That's quite all right," I said. "I hope the voyage will agree with her." We parted with the usual expressions of good will, and Mr. Willoughby and I walked down the Rue du Nord, back toward Jared's house.

"Reverend meaning most holy fella, not true?" Mr. Willoughby said, after a short silence. He had the usual Oriental difficulty in pronouncing the letter "r," which made the word "Reverend" more than slightly picturesque, but I gathered his meaning well enough.

"True," I said, glancing down at him curiously. He pursed his lips and pushed them in and out, then grunted in a distinctly amused manner.

"Not so holy, *that* Reverend fella," he said.

"What makes you say so?"

He gave me a bright-eyed glance, full of shrewdness.

"I see him one time, Madame Jeanne's. Not loud talking then. Very quiet then, Reverend fella."

"Oh, really?" I turned to look back, but the Reverend's tall figure had disappeared into the crowd.

"Stinking whores," Mr. Willoughby amplified, making an extremely rude gesture in the vicinity of his crotch in illustration.

"Yes, I gathered," I said. "Well, I suppose the flesh is weak now and then, even for Scottish Free Church ministers."

At dinner that night, I mentioned seeing the Reverend, though without adding Mr. Willoughby's remarks about the Reverend's extracurricular activities.

"I ought to have asked him where in the West Indies he was going," I said. "Not that he's a particularly scintillating companion, but it might be useful to know someone there."

Jared, who was consuming veal patties in a businesslike way, paused to swallow, then said, "Dinna trouble yourself about that, my dear. I've made up a list for you of useful acquaintances. I've written letters for ye to carry to several friends there, who will certainly lend ye assistance."

He cut another sizable chunk of veal, wiped it through a puddle of wine sauce, and chewed it, while looking thoughtfully at Jamie.

Having evidently come to a decision of some kind, he swallowed, took a sip of wine, and said in a conversational voice, "We met on the level, Cousin."

I stared at him in bewilderment, but Jamie, after a moment's pause, replied, "And we parted on the square."

Jared's narrow face broke into a wide smile.

"Ah, that's a help!" he said. "I wasna just sure, aye? but I thought it worth the trial. Where were ye made?"

"In prison," Jamie replied briefly. "It will be the Inverness lodge, though."

Jared nodded in satisfaction. "Aye, well enough. There are lodges on Jamaica and Barbados—I'll have letters for ye to the Masters there. But the largest lodge is on Trinidad—better than two thousand members there. If ye should need great help in finding the lad, that's where ye must ask. Word of everything that happens in the islands comes through that lodge, sooner or later."

"Would you care to tell me what you're talking about?" I interrupted.

Jamie glanced at me and smiled.

"Freemasons, Sassenach."

"You're a Mason?" I blurted. "You didn't tell me that!"

"He's not meant to," Jared said, a bit sharply. "The rites of Freemasonry are secret, known only to the members. I wouldna have been able to give Jamie an introduction to the Trinidad lodge, had he not been one of us already."

The conversation became general again, as Jamie and Jared fell to discussing the provisioning of the *Artemis,* but I was quiet, concentrating on my own veal. The incident, small as it was, had reminded me of all the things I didn't know about Jamie. At one time, I should have said I knew him as well as one person can know another.

Now, there would be moments, talking intimately together, falling asleep in the curve of his shoulder, holding him close in the act of love, when I felt I knew him still, his mind and heart as clear to me as the lead crystal of the wineglasses on Jared's table.

And others, like now, when I would stumble suddenly over some unsuspected bit of his past, or see him standing still, eyes shrouded with recollections I didn't share. I felt suddenly unsure and alone, hesitating on the brink of the gap between us.

Jamie's foot pressed against mine under the table, and he looked across at me with a smile hidden in his eyes. He raised his glass a little, in a silent toast, and I smiled back, feeling obscurely comforted. The gesture brought back a sudden memory of our wedding night, when we had sat beside each other sipping wine, strangers frightened of each other, with nothing between us but a marriage contract—and the promise of honesty.

There are things ye maybe canna tell me, he had said. *I willna ask ye, or force ye. But when ye do tell me something, let it be the truth. There is nothing between us now but respect, and respect has room for secrets, I think—but not for lies.*

I drank deeply from my own glass, feeling the strong bouquet of the wine billow up inside my head, and a warm flush heat my cheeks. Jamie's eyes were still fixed on me, ignoring Jared's soliloquy about ship's biscuit and candles. His foot nudged mine in silent inquiry, and I pressed back in answer.

"Aye, I'll see to it in the morning," he said, in reply to a question from Jared. "But for now, Cousin, I think I shall retire. It's been a long day." He pushed back his chair, stood up, and held out his arm to me.

"Will ye join me, Claire?"

I stood up, the wine rushing through my limbs, making me feel warm all over and slightly giddy. Our eyes met with a perfect understanding. There was more than respect between us now, and room for all our secrets to be known, in good time.

In the morning, Jamie and Mr. Willoughby went with Jared, to complete their errands. I had another errand of my own—one that I preferred to do alone. Twenty years ago, there had been two people in Paris whom I cared for deeply. Master Raymond was gone; dead or disappeared. The chances that the other might still be living were slim, but still, I had to see, before I left Europe for what might be the last time. With my heart beating erratically, I stepped into Jared's coach, and told the coachman to drive to the Hôpital des Anges.

The grave was set in the small cemetery reserved for the convent, under the buttresses of the nearby cathedral. Even though the air from the Seine was damp and cold, and the day cloudy, the walled cemetery held a soft light, reflected from the blocks of pale limestone that sheltered the small plot from wind. In the winter, there were no shrubs or flowers growing, but leafless aspens and larches spread a delicate tracery against the sky, and a deep green moss cradled the stones, thriving despite the cold.

It was a small stone, made of a soft white marble. A pair of cherub's wings spread out across the top, sheltering the single word that was the stone's only other decoration. "Faith," it read.

I stood looking down at it until my vision blurred. I had brought a flower; a pink tulip—not the easiest thing to find in Paris in December, but Jared kept a conservatory. I knelt down and laid it on the stone, stroking the soft curve of the petal with a finger, as though it were a baby's cheek.

"I thought I wouldn't cry," I said a little later.

I felt the weight of Mother Hildegarde's hand on my head.

"Le Bon Dieu orders things as He thinks best," she said softly. "But He seldom tells us why."

I took a deep breath and wiped my cheeks with a corner of my cloak. "It was a long time ago, though." I rose slowly to my feet and turned to find Mother Hildegarde watching me with an expression of deep sympathy and interest.

"I have noticed," she said slowly, "that time does not really exist for mothers, with regard to their children. It does not matter greatly how old the child is—in the blink of an eye, the mother can see the child again as it was when it was born, when it learned to walk, as it was at any age—at any time, even when the child is fully grown and a parent itself."

"Especially when they're asleep," I said, looking down again at the little white stone. "You can always see the baby then."

"Ah." Mother nodded, satisfied. "I thought you had had more children; you have the look, somehow." ·

"One more." I glanced at her. "And how do you know so much about mothers and children?"

The small black eyes shone shrewdly under heavy brow ridges whose sparse hairs had gone quite white.

"The old require very little sleep," she said, with a deprecatory shrug. "I walk the wards at night, sometimes. The patients talk to me."

She had shrunk somewhat with advancing age, and the wide shoulders were slightly bowed, thin as a wire hanger beneath the black serge of her habit. Even so, she was still taller than I, and towered over most of the nuns, more scarecrow-like, but imposing as ever. She carried a walking stick but strode erect, firm of tread and with the same piercing eye, using the stick more frequently to prod idlers or direct underlings than to lean on.

I blew my nose and we turned back along the path to the convent. As we walked slowly back, I noticed other small stones set here and there among the larger ones.

"Are those all children?" I asked, a little surprised.

"The children of the nuns," she said matter-of-factly. I gaped at her in astonishment, and she shrugged, elegant and wry as always.

"It happens," she said. She walked a few steps farther, then added, "Not often, of course." She gestured with her stick around the confines of the cemetery.

"This place is reserved for the sisters, a few benefactors of the Hôpital— and those they love."

"The sisters or the benefactors?"

"The sisters. Here, you lump!"

Mother Hildegarde paused in her progress, spotting an orderly leaning idly against the church wall, smoking a pipe. As she berated him in the elegantly vicious Court French of her girlhood, I stood back, looking around the tiny cemetery.

Against the far wall, but still in consecrated ground, was a row of small stone tablets, each with a single name, "Bouton." Below each name was a Roman numeral, I through XV. Mother Hildegarde's beloved dogs. I glanced at her current companion, the sixteenth holder of that name. This one was coal-black, and curly as a Persian lamb. He sat bolt upright at her feet, round eyes fixed on the delinquent orderly, a silent echo of Mother Hildegarde's outspoken disapproval.

The sisters, and those they love.

Mother Hildegarde came back, her fierce expression altering at once to the smile that transformed her strong gargoyle features into beauty.

"I am so pleased that you have come again, *ma chère*," she said. "Come inside; I shall find things that may be useful to you on your journey." Tucking the stick in the crook of her arm, she instead took my forearm for support, grasping it with a warm bony hand whose skin had grown paper-thin. I had the odd feeling that it was not I who supported her, but the other way around.

As we turned into the small yew alley that led to the entrance to the Hôpital, I glanced up at her.

"I hope you won't think me rude, Mother," I said hesitantly, "but there is one question I wanted to ask you . . ."

"Eighty-three," she replied promptly. She grinned broadly, showing her long yellow horse's teeth. "Everyone wants to know," she said complacently. She looked back over her shoulder toward the tiny graveyard, and lifted one shoulder in a dismissive Gallic shrug.

"Not yet," she said confidently. "*Le Bon Dieu* knows how much work there is still to do."

41

We Set Sail

It was a cold, gray day—there is no other kind in Scotland in December—when the *Artemis* touched at Cape Wrath, on the northwest coast.

I peered out of the tavern window into a solid gray murk that hid the cliffs along the shore. The place was depressingly reminiscent of the landscape near the silkies' isle, with the smell of dead seaweed strong in the air, and the crashing of waves so loud as to inhibit conversation, even inside the small pothouse by the wharf. Young Ian had been taken nearly a month before. Now it was past Christmas, and here we were, still in Scotland, no more than a few miles from the seals' island.

Jamie was striding up and down the dock outside, in spite of the cold rain, too restless to stay indoors by the fire. The sea journey from France back to Scotland had been no better for him than the first Channel crossing, and I knew the prospect of two or three months aboard the *Artemis* filled him with dread. At the same time, his impatience to be in pursuit of the kidnappers was so acute that any delay filled him with frustration. More than once I had awakened in the middle of the night to find him gone, walking the streets of Le Havre alone.

Ironically, this final delay was of his own making. We had touched at Cape Wrath to retrieve Fergus, and with him, the small group of smugglers whom Jamie had sent him to fetch, before leaving ourselves for Le Havre.

"There's no telling what we shall find in the Indies, Sassenach," Jamie had explained to me. "I dinna mean to go up against a shipload of pirates single-handed, nor yet to fight wi' men I dinna ken alongside me." The smugglers were all men of the shore, accustomed to boats and the ocean, if not to ships; they would be hired on as part of the *Artemis*'s crew, shorthanded in consequence of the late season in which we sailed.

Cape Wrath was a small port, with little traffic at this time of year. Besides the *Artemis,* only a few fishing boats and a ketch were tied up at the wooden wharf. There was a small pothouse, though, in which the crew of the *Artemis* cheerfully passed their time while waiting, the men who would not fit inside the house crouching under the eaves, swilling pots of ale passed through the windows by their comrades indoors. Jamie walked on the shore, coming in only for meals, when he would sit before the fire, the wisps of steam rising from his soggy garments symptomatic of his increasing aggravation of soul.

Fergus was late. No one seemed to mind the wait but Jamie and Jared's captain. Captain Raines, a small, plump, elderly man, spent most of his time on the deck of his ship, keeping one weather eye on the overcast sky, and the other on his barometer.

"That's verra strong-smelling stuff, Sassenach," Jamie observed, during one of his brief visits to the taproom. "What is it?"

"Fresh ginger," I answered, holding up the remains of the root I was grating. "It's the thing most of my herbals say is best for nausea."

"Oh, aye?" He picked up the bowl, sniffed at the contents, and sneezed explosively, to the vast amusement of the onlookers. I snatched back the bowl before he could spill it.

"You don't take it like snuff," I said. "You drink it in tea. And I hope to heaven it works, because if it doesn't, we'll be scooping you out of the bilges, if bilges are what I think they are."

"Oh, not to worry, missus," one of the older hands assured me, overhearing. "Lots o' green hands feel a bit queerlike the first day or two. But usually they comes round soon enough; by the third day, they've got used to the pitch and roll, and they're up in the rigging, happy as larks."

I glanced at Jamie, who was markedly unlarklike at the moment. Still, this comment seemed to give him some hope, for he brightened a bit, and waved to the harassed servingmaid for a glass of ale.

"It may be so," he said. "Jared said the same; that seasickness doesna generally last more than a few days, provided the seas aren't too heavy." He took a small sip of his ale, and then, with growing confidence, a deeper swallow. "I can stand three days of it, I suppose."

Late in the afternoon of the second day, six men appeared, winding their way along the stony shore on shaggy Highland ponies.

"There's Raeburn in the lead," Jamie said, shading his eyes and squinting to distinguish the identities of the six small dots. "Kennedy after him, then Innes—he's missing the left arm, see?—and Meldrum, and that'll be Mac-Leod with him, they always ride together like that. Is the last man Gordon, then, or Fergus?"

"It must be Gordon," I said, peering over his shoulder at the approaching men, "because it's much too fat to be Fergus."

"Where the devil is Fergus, then?" Jamie asked Raeburn, once the smugglers had been greeted, introduced to their new shipmates, and sat down to a hot supper and a cheerful glass.

Raeburn bobbed his head in response, hastily swallowing the remains of his pasty.

"Weel, he said to me as how he'd some business to see to, and would I see to the hiring of the horses, and speak to Meldrum and MacLeod about coming, for they were out wi' their own boat at the time, and not expected back for a day or twa more, and . . ."

"What business?" Jamie said sharply, but got no more than a shrug in reply. Jamie muttered something under his breath in Gaelic, but returned to his own supper without further comment.

The crew being now complete—save Fergus—preparations began in the morning for getting under way. The deck was a scene of organized confusion, with bodies darting to and fro, popping up through hatchways, and dropping suddenly out of the rigging like dead flies. Jamie stood near the wheel, keeping out of the way, but lending a hand whenever a matter requiring muscle rather than skill arose. For the most part, though, he simply stood, eyes fixed on the road along the shore.

"We shall have to sail by midafternoon, or miss the tide." Captain Raines spoke kindly, but firmly. "We'll have surly weather in twenty-four hours; the glass is falling, and I feel it in my neck." The Captain tenderly massaged the part in question, and nodded at the sky, which had gone from pewter to lead-gray since early morning. "I'll not set sail in a storm if I can help it, and if we mean to make the Indies as soon as possible—"

"Aye, I understand, Captain," Jamie interrupted him. "Of course; ye must do as seems best." He stood back to let a bustling seaman go past, and the Captain disappeared, issuing orders as he went.

As the day wore on, Jamie seemed composed as usual, but I noticed that the stiff fingers fluttered against his thigh more and more often, the only outward sign of worry. And worried he was. Fergus had been with him since the day twenty years before, when Jamie had found him in a Paris brothel, and hired him to steal Charles Stuart's letters.

More than that; Fergus had lived at Lallybroch since before Young Ian was born. The boy had been a younger brother to Fergus, and Jamie the closest thing to a father that Fergus had ever known. I could not imagine any business so urgent that it would have kept him from Jamie's side. Neither could Jamie, and his fingers beat a silent tattoo on the wood of the rail.

Then it was time, and Jamie turned reluctantly away, tearing his eyes from the empty shore. The hatches were battened, the lines coiled, and several seamen leapt ashore to cast free the mooring hawsers; there were six of them, each a rope as thick around as my wrist.

I put a hand on Jamie's arm in silent sympathy.

"You'd better come down below," I said. "I've got a spirit lamp. I'll brew you some hot ginger tea, and then you—"

The sound of a galloping horse echoed along the shore, the scrunch of hoofbeats on gravel echoing from the cliffside well in advance of its appearance.

"There he is, the wee fool," Jamie said, his relief evident in voice and body. He turned to Captain Raines, one brow raised in question. "There's enough of the tide left? Aye, then, let's go."

"Cast off!" the Captain bellowed, and the waiting hands sprang into action. The last of the lines tethering us to the piling was slipped free and neatly coiled, and all around us, lines tightened and sails snapped overhead, as the bosun ran up and down the deck, bawling orders in a voice like rusty iron.

"She moves! She stirs! 'She seems to feel / the thrill of life along her keel'!" I declaimed, delighted to feel the deck quiver beneath my feet as the ship came alive, the energy of all the crew poured into its inanimate hulk, transmuted by the power of the wind-catching sails.

"Oh, God," said Jamie hollowly, feeling the same thing. He grasped the rail, closed his eyes and swallowed.

"Mr. Willoughby says he has a cure for seasickness," I said, watching him sympathetically.

"Ha," he said, opening his eyes. "I ken what he means, and if he thinks I'll let him—what the bloody hell!"

I whirled to look, and saw what had caused him to break off. Fergus was on deck, reaching up to help down a girl perched awkwardly above him on the railing, her long blond hair whipping in the wind. Laoghaire's daughter —Marsali MacKimmie.

Before I could speak, Jamie was past me and striding toward the pair.

"What in the name of holy God d'ye mean by this, ye wee coofs?" he was demanding, by the time I made my way into earshot through the obstacle course of lines and seamen. He loomed menacingly over the pair, a foot taller than either of them.

"We are married," Fergus said, bravely moving in front of Marsali. He looked both scared and excited, his face pale beneath the shock of black hair.

"Married!" Jamie's hands clenched at his sides, and Fergus took an involuntary step backward, nearly treading on Marsali's toes. "What d'ye mean, 'married'?"

I assumed this was a rhetorical question, but it wasn't; Jamie's appreciation of the situation had, as usual, outstripped mine by yards and seized at once upon the salient point.

"Have ye bedded her?" he demanded bluntly. Standing behind him, I couldn't see his face, but I knew what it must look like, if only because I could see the effect of his expression on Fergus. The Frenchman turned a couple of shades paler and licked his lips.

"Er . . . no, milord," he said, just as Marsali, eyes blazing, thrust her chin up and said defiantly, "Yes, he has!"

Jamie glanced briefly back and forth between the two of them, snorted loudly, and turned away.

"Mr. Warren!" he called down the deck to the ship's sailing master. "Put back to the shore, if ye please!"

Mr. Warren stopped, openmouthed, in the middle of an order addressed to the rigging, and stared, first at Jamie, then—quite elaborately—at the receding shoreline. In the few moments since the appearance of the putative newlyweds, the *Artemis* had moved more than a thousand yards from the shore, and the rocks of the cliffs were slipping by with increasing speed.

"I don't believe he can," I said. "I think we're already in the tide-race."

No sailor himself, Jamie had spent sufficient time in the company of seamen at least to understand the notion that time and tide wait for no one. He breathed through his teeth for a moment, then jerked his head toward the ladder that led belowdecks.

"Come down, then, the both of ye."

Fergus and Marsali sat together in the tiny cabin, huddled on one berth, hands clutched tight. Jamie waved me to a seat on the other berth, then turned to the pair, hands on his hips.

"Now, then," he said. "What's this nonsense of bein' married?"

"It is true, milord," Fergus said. He was quite pale, but his dark eyes were bright with excitement. His one hand tightened on Marsali's, his hook resting across his thigh.

"Aye?" Jamie said, with the maximum of skepticism. "And who married ye?"

The two glanced at each other, and Fergus licked his lips briefly before replying.

"We—we are handfast."

"Before witnesses," Marsali put in. In contrast to Fergus's paleness, a high color burned in her cheeks. She had her mother's roseleaf skin, but the stubborn set of her jaw had likely come from somewhere else. She put a hand to her bosom, where something crackled under the fabric. "I ha' the contract, and the signatures, here."

Jamie made a low growling noise in his throat. By the laws of Scotland, two people could in fact be legally married by clasping hands before witnesses—handfasting—and declaring themselves to be man and wife.

"Aye, well," he said. "But ye're no bedded, yet, and a contract's not enough, in the eyes o' the Church." He glanced out of the stern casement, where the cliffs were just visible through the ragged mist, then nodded with decision.

"We'll stop at Lewes for the last provisions. Marsali will go ashore there; I'll send two seamen to see her home to her mother."

"Ye'll do no such thing!" Marsali cried. She sat up straight, glaring at her stepfather. "I'm going wi' Fergus!"

"Oh, no, you're not, my lassie!" Jamie snapped. "D'ye have no feeling for your mother? To run off, wi' no word, and leave her to be worrit—"

"I left word." Marsali's square chin was high. "I sent a letter from Inverness, saying I'd married Fergus and was off to sail wi' you."

"Sweet bleeding Jesus! She'll think I kent all about it!" Jamie looked horror-stricken.

"We—I—did ask the lady Laoghaire for the honor of her daughter's hand, milord," Fergus put in. "Last month, when I came to Lallybroch."

"Aye. Well, ye needna tell me what she said," Jamie said dryly, seeing the sudden flush on Fergus's cheeks. "Since I gather the general answer was no."

"She said he was a bastard!" Marsali burst out indignantly. "And a criminal, and—and—"

"He is a bastard and a criminal," Jamie pointed out. "And a cripple wi' no property, either, as I'm sure your mother noticed."

"I dinna care!" Marsali gripped Fergus's hand and looked at him with fierce affection. "I want him."

Taken aback, Jamie rubbed a finger across his lips. Then he took a deep breath and returned to the attack.

"Be that as it may," he said, "ye're too young to be married."

"I'm fifteen; that's plenty old enough!"

"Aye, and he's thirty!" Jamie snapped. He shook his head, "Nay, lassie, I'm sorry about it, but I canna let ye do it. If it were nothing else, the voyage is too dangerous—"

"You're taking *her*!" Marsali's chin jerked contemptuously in my direction.

"You'll leave Claire out of this," Jamie said evenly. "She's none of your concern, and—"

"Oh, she's not? You leave my mother for this English whore, and make her a laughingstock for the whole countryside, and it's no my concern, is it?" Marsali leapt up and stamped her foot on the deck. "And you ha' the hellish nerve to tell me what *I* shall do?"

"I have," Jamie said, keeping hold of his temper with some difficulty. "My private affairs are not your concern—"

"And mine aren't any of yours!"

Fergus, looking alarmed, was on his feet, trying to calm the girl.

"Marsali, *ma chère*, you must not speak to milord in such a way. He is only—"

"I'll speak to him any way I want!"

"No, you will not!" Surprised at the sudden harshness in Fergus's tone, Marsali blinked. Only an inch or two taller than his new wife, the Frenchman had a certain wiry authority that made him seem much bigger than he was.

"No," he said more softly. "Sit down, *ma p'tite*." He pressed her back down on the berth, and stood before her.

"Milord has been to me more than a father," he said gently to the girl. "I owe him my life a thousand times. He is also your stepfather. However your mother may regard him, he has without doubt supported and sheltered her and you and your sister. You owe him respect, at the least."

Marsali bit her lip, her eyes bright. Finally she ducked her head awkwardly at Jamie.

"I'm sorry," she murmured, and the air of tension in the cabin lessened slightly.

"It's all right, lassie," Jamie said gruffly. He looked at her and sighed. "But still, Marsali, we must send ye back to your mother."

"I won't go." The girl was calmer now, but the set of her pointed chin was the same. She glanced at Fergus, then at Jamie. "He says we havena bedded together, but we have. Or at any rate, I shall say we have. If ye send me home, I'll tell everyone that he's had me; so ye see—I shall either be married or ruined." Her tone was reasonable and determined. Jamie closed his eyes.

"May the Lord deliver me from women," he said between his teeth. He opened his eyes and glared at her.

"All right!" he said. "You're married. But you'll do it right, before a priest. We'll find one in the Indies, when we land. And until ye've been blessed, Fergus doesna touch you. Aye?" He turned a ferocious gaze on both of them.

"Yes, milord," said Fergus, his features suffused with joy. *"Merci beaucoup!"* Marsali narrowed her eyes at Jamie, but seeing that he wasn't to be moved, she bowed her head demurely, with a sidelong glance at me.

"Yes, Daddy," she said.

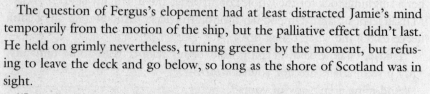

The question of Fergus's elopement had at least distracted Jamie's mind temporarily from the motion of the ship, but the palliative effect didn't last. He held on grimly nevertheless, turning greener by the moment, but refusing to leave the deck and go below, so long as the shore of Scotland was in sight.

"I may never see it again," he said gloomily, when I tried to persuade him to go below and lie down. He leaned heavily on the rail he had just been vomiting over, eyes resting longingly on the unprepossessingly bleak coast behind us.

"No, you'll see it," I said, with an unthinking surety. "You're coming back. I don't know when, but I know you'll come back."

He turned his head to look up at me, puzzled. Then the ghost of a smile crossed his face.

"You've seen my grave," he said softly. "Haven't ye?"

I hesitated, but he didn't seem upset, and I nodded.

"It's all right," he said. He closed his eyes, breathing heavily. "Don't . . . don't tell me when, though, if ye dinna mind."

"I can't," I said. "There weren't any dates on it. Just your name—and mine."

"Yours?" His eyes popped open.

I nodded again, feeling my throat tighten at the memory of that granite slab. It had been what they call a "marriage stone," a quarter-circle carved to fit with another in a complete arch. I had, of course, seen only the one half.

"It had all your names on it. That's how I knew it was you. And underneath, it said, 'Beloved husband of Claire.' At the time, I didn't see how— but now, of course, I do."

He nodded slowly, absorbing it. "Aye, I see. Aye well, I suppose if I shall be in Scotland, and still married to you—then maybe 'when' doesna matter so much." He gave me a shadow of his usual grin, and added wryly, "It also means we'll find Young Ian safe, for I'll tell ye, Sassenach, I willna set foot in Scotland again without him."

"We'll find him," I said, with an assurance I didn't altogether feel. I put a hand on his shoulder and stood beside him, watching Scotland slowly recede in the distance.

———

By the time evening set in, the rocks of Scotland had disappeared in the sea mists, and Jamie, chilled to the bone and pale as a sheet, suffered himself to be led below and put to bed. At this point, the unforeseen consequences of his ultimatum to Fergus became apparent.

There were only two small private cabins, besides the Captain's; if Fergus and Marsali were forbidden to share one until their union was formally blessed, then clearly Jamie and Fergus would have to take one, and Marsali and I the other. It seemed destined to be a rough voyage, in more ways than one.

I had hoped that the sickness might ease, if Jamie couldn't see the slow heave and fall of the horizon, but no such luck.

"Again?" said Fergus, sleepily rousing on one elbow in his berth, in the middle of the night. "How can he? He has eaten nothing all day!"

"Tell *him* that," I said, trying to breathe through my mouth as I sidled toward the door, a basin in my hands, making my way with difficulty through the tiny, cramped quarters. The deck rose and fell beneath my unaccustomed feet, making it hard to keep my balance.

"Here, milady, allow me." Fergus swung bare feet out of bed and stood up beside me, staggering and nearly bumping into me as he reached for the basin.

"You should go and sleep now, milady," he said, taking it from my hands. "I will see to him, be assured."

"Well . . ." The thought of my berth was undeniably tempting. It had been a long day.

"Go, Sassenach," Jamie said. His face was a ghastly white, sheened with sweat in the dim light of the small oil light that burned on the wall. "I'll be all right."

This was patently untrue; at the same time, it was unlikely that my presence would help particularly. Fergus could do the little that could be done; there was no known cure for seasickness, after all. One could only hope that Jared was right, and that it would ease of itself as the *Artemis* made its way out into the longer swells of the Atlantic.

"All right," I said, giving in. "Perhaps you'll feel better in the morning."

Jamie opened one eye for a moment, then groaned, and shivering, closed it again.

"Or perhaps I'll be dead," he suggested.

On that cheery note, I made my way out into the dark companionway, only to stumble over the prostrate form of Mr. Willoughby, curled up against the door of the cabin. He grunted in surprise, then, seeing that it was only me, rolled slowly onto all fours and crawled into the cabin, swaying with the rolling of the ship. Ignoring Fergus's exclamation of distate, he curled himself about the pedestal of the table, and fell promptly back asleep, an expression of beatific content on his small round face.

My own cabin was just across the companionway, but I paused for a moment, to breathe in the fresh air coming down from the deck above. There was an extraordinary variety of noises, from the creak and crack of timbers all around, to the snap of sails and the whine of rigging above, and the faint echo of a shout somewhere on deck.

Despite the racket and the cold air pouring in down the companionway, Marsali was sound asleep, a humped black shape in one of the two berths. Just as well; at least I needn't try to make awkward conversation with her.

Despite myself, I felt a pang of sympathy for her; this was likely not what she had expected of her wedding night. It was too cold to undress; fully clothed, I crawled into my small box-berth and lay listening to the sounds of the ship around me. I could hear the hissing of the water passing the hull, only a foot or two beyond my head. It was an oddly comforting sound. To the accompaniment of the song of the wind and the faint sound of retching across the corridor, I fell peacefully asleep.

The *Artemis* was a tidy ship, as ships go, but when you cram thirty-two men—and two women—into a space eighty feet long and twenty-five wide, together with six tons of rough-cured hides, forty-two barrels of sulfur, and enough sheets of copper and tin to sheathe the *Queen Mary,* basic hygiene is bound to suffer.

By the second day, I had already flushed a rat—a small rat, as Fergus pointed out, but still a rat—in the hold where I went to retrieve my large medicine box, packed away there by mistake during the loading. There was a soft shuffling noise in my cabin at night, which when the lantern was lit proved to be the footsteps of several dozen middling-size cockroaches, all fleeing frantically for the shelter of the shadows.

The heads, two small quarter-galleries on either side of the ship toward the bow, were nothing more than a pair of boards—with a strategic slot between them—suspended over the bounding waves eight feet below, so that the user was likely to get an unexpected dash of cold seawater at some highly inopportune moment. I suspected that this, coupled with a diet of salt pork and hardtack, likely caused constipation to be epidemic among seamen.

Mr. Warren, the ship's master, proudly informed me that the decks were swabbed regularly every morning, the brass polished, and everything generally made shipshape, which seemed a desirable state of affairs, given that we were in fact aboard a ship. Still, all the holystoning in the world could not disguise the fact that thirty-four human beings occupied this limited space, and only one of us bathed.

Given such circumstances, I was more than startled when I opened the door of the galley on the second morning, in search of boiling water.

I had expected the same dim and grubby conditions that obtained in the cabins and holds, and was dazzled by the glitter of sunlight through the overhead lattice on a rank of copper pans, so scrubbed that the metal of their bottoms shone pink. I blinked against the dazzle, my eyes adjusting, and saw that the walls of the galley were solid with built-in racks and cupboards, so constructed as to be proof against the roughest seas.

Blue and green glass bottles of spice, each tenderly jacketed in felt against injury, vibrated softly in their rack above the pots. Knives, cleavers, and skewers gleamed in deadly array, in a quantity sufficient to deal with a whale carcass, should one present itself. A rimmed double shelf hung from the bulkhead, thick with bulb glasses and shallow plates, on which a quantity of fresh-cut turnip tops were set to sprout for greens. An enormous pot bubbled softly over the stove, emitting a fragrant steam. And in the midst of all this spotless splendor stood the cook, surveying me with baleful eye.

"Out," he said.

"Good morning," I said, as cordially as possible. "My name is Claire Fraser."

"Out," he repeated, in the same graveled tones.

"I am Mrs. Fraser, the wife of the supercargo, and ship's surgeon for this voyage," I said, giving him eyeball for eyeball. "I require six gallons of boiling water, when convenient, for cleaning of the head."

His small, bright blue eyes grew somewhat smaller and brighter, the black pupils of them training on me like gunbarrels.

"I am Aloysius O'Shaughnessy Murphy," he said. "Ship's cook. And I require ye to take yer feet off my fresh-washed deck. I do not allow women in my galley." He glowered at me under the edge of the black cotton kerchief that swathed his head. He was several inches shorter than I, but made up for it by measuring about three feet more in circumference, with a wrestler's shoulders and a head like a cannonball, set upon them without apparent benefit of an intervening neck. A wooden leg completed the ensemble.

I took one step back, with dignity, and spoke to him from the relative safety of the passageway.

"In that case," I said, "you may send up the hot water by the messboy."

"I may," he agreed. "And then again, I may not." He turned his broad back on me in dismissal, busying himself with a chopping block, a cleaver, and a joint of mutton.

I stood in the passageway for a moment, thinking. The thud of the cleaver sounded regularly against the wood. Mr. Murphy reached up to his spice rack, grasped a bottle without looking, and sprinkled a good quantity of the contents over the diced meat. The dusty scent of sage filled the air, superseded at once by the pungency of an onion, whacked in two with a casual swipe of the cleaver and tossed into the mixture.

Evidently the crew of the *Artemis* did not subsist entirely upon salt pork and hardtack, then. I began to understand the reasons for Captain Raines's rather pear-shaped physique. I poked my head back through the door, taking care to stand outside.

"Cardamom," I said firmly. "Nutmeg, whole. Dried this year. Fresh extract of anise. Ginger root, two large ones, with no blemishes." I paused. Mr. Murphy had stopped chopping, cleaver poised motionless above the block.

"And," I added, "half a dozen whole vanilla beans. From Ceylon."

He turned slowly, wiping his hands upon his leather apron. Unlike his surroundings, neither the apron nor his other apparel was spotless.

He had a broad, florid face, edged with stiff sandy whiskers like a scrubbing brush, which quivered slightly as he looked at me, like the antennae of some large insect. His tongue darted out to lick pursed lips.

"Saffron?" he asked hoarsely.

"Half an ounce," I said promptly, taking care to conceal any trace of triumph in my manner.

He breathed in deeply, lust gleaming bright in his small blue eyes.

"Ye'll find a mat just outside, ma'am, should ye care to wipe yer boots and come in."

One head sterilized within the limits of boiling water and Fergus's tolerance, I made my way back to my cabin to clean up for luncheon. Marsali was not there; she was undoubtedly attending to Fergus, whose labors at my insistence had been little short of heroic.

I rinsed my own hands with alcohol, brushed my hair, and then went across the passage to see whether—by some wild chance—Jamie wanted anything to eat or drink. One glance disabused me of this notion.

Marsali and I had been given the largest cabin, which meant that each of us had approximately six square feet of space, not including the beds. These were box-berths, a sort of enclosed bed built into the wall, about five and a half feet long. Marsali fitted neatly into hers, but I was forced to adopt a slightly curled position, like a caper on toast, which caused me to wake up with pins and needles in my feet.

Jamie and Fergus had similar berths. Jamie was lying on his side, wedged into one of these like a snail into its shell; one of which beasts he strongly resembled at the moment, being a pale and viscid gray in color, with streaks of green and yellow that contrasted nastily with his red hair. He opened one eye when he heard me come in, regarded me dimly for a moment, and closed it again.

"Not so good, hm?" I said sympathetically.

The eye opened again, and he seemed to be preparing to say something. He opened his mouth, changed his mind, and closed it again.

"No," he said, and shut the eye once more.

I tentatively smoothed his hair, but he seemed too sunk in misery to notice.

"Captain Raines says it will likely be calmer by tomorrow," I offered. The sea wasn't terribly rough as it was, but there was a noticeable rise and fall.

"It doesna matter," he said, not opening his eyes. "I shall be dead by then —or at least I hope so."

"Afraid not," I said, shaking my head. "Nobody dies of seasickness; though I must say it seems a wonder that they don't, looking at you."

"Not that." He opened his eyes, and struggled up on one elbow, an effort that left him clammy with sweat and white to the lips.

"Claire. Be careful. I should have told ye before—but I didna want to worry ye, and I thought—" His face changed. Familiar as I was with expressions of bodily infirmity, I had the basin there just in time.

"Oh, God." He lay limp and exhausted, pale as the sheet.

"What should you have told me?" I asked, wrinkling my nose as I put the basin on the floor near the door. "Whatever it was, you should have told me before we sailed, but it's too late to think of that."

"I didna think it would be so bad," he murmured.

"You never do," I said, rather tartly. "What did you want to tell me, though?"

"Ask Fergus," he said. "Say I said he must tell ye. And tell him Innes is all right."

"What are you talking about?" I was mildly alarmed; delirium wasn't a common effect of seasickness.

His eyes opened, and fixed on mine with great effort. Beads of sweat stood out on his brow and upper lip.

"Innes," he said. "He canna be the one. He doesna mean to kill me."

A small shiver ran up my spine.

"Are you quite all right, Jamie?" I asked. I bent and wiped his face, and he gave me the ghost of an exhausted smile. He had no fever, and his eyes were clear.

"Who?" I said carefully, with a sudden feeling that there were eyes fixed on my back. "Who *does* mean to kill you?"

"I don't know." A passing spasm contorted his features, but he clamped his lips tight, and managed to subdue it.

"Ask Fergus," he whispered, when he could talk again. "In private. He'll tell ye."

I felt exceedingly helpless. I had no notion what he was talking about, but if there was any danger, I wasn't about to leave him alone.

"I'll wait until he comes down," I said.

One hand was curled near his nose. It straightened slowly and slid under the pillow, coming out with his dirk, which he clasped to his chest.

"I shall be all right," he said. "Go on, then, Sassenach. I shouldna think they'd try anything in daylight. If at all."

I didn't find this reassuring in the slightest, but there seemed nothing else to do. He lay quite still, the dirk held to his chest like a stone tomb-figure.

"Go," he murmured again, his lips barely moving.

Just outside the cabin door, something stirred in the shadows at the end of the passage. Peering sharply, I made out the crouched silk shape of Mr. Willoughby, chin resting on his knees. He spread his knees apart, and bowed his head politely between them.

"Not worry, honorable First Wife," he assured me in a sibilant whisper. "I watch."

"Good," I said, "keep doing it." And went, in considerable distress of mind, to find Fergus.

Fergus, found with Marsali on the after deck, peering into the ship's wake at several large white birds, was somewhat more reassuring.

"We are not sure that anyone intends actually to kill milord," he explained. "The casks in the warehouse might have been an accident—I have seen such things happen more than once—and likewise the fire in the shed, but—"

"Wait one minute, young Fergus," I said, gripping him by the sleeve. "*What* casks, and *what* fire?"

"Oh," he said, looking surprised. "Milord did not tell you?"

"Milord is sick as a dog, and incapable of telling me anything more than that I should ask you."

Fergus shook his head, clicking his tongue in a censorious French way.

"He never thinks he will be so ill," he said. "He always is, and yet every time he must set foot on a ship, he insists that it is only a matter of will; his mind will be master, and he will not allow his stomach to be dictating his actions. Then within ten feet of the dock, he has turned green."

"He never told me that," I said, amused at this description. "Stubborn little fool."

Marsali had been hanging back behind Fergus with an air of haughty reserve, pretending that I wasn't there. At this unexpected description of Jamie, though, she was surprised into a brief snort of laughter. She caught my eye and turned hastily away, cheeks flaming, to stare out to sea.

Fergus smiled and shrugged. "You know what he is like, milady," he said, with tolerant affection. "He could be dying, and one would never know."

"You'd know if you went down and looked at him now," I said tartly. At the same time, I was conscious of surprise, accompanied by a faint feeling of warmth in the pit of my stomach. Fergus had been with Jamie almost daily for twenty years, and still Jamie would not admit to him the weakness that he would readily let me see. Were he dying, *I* would know about it, all right.

"Men," I said, shaking my head.

"Milady?"

"Never mind," I said. "You were telling me about casks and fires."

"Oh, indeed, yes." Fergus brushed back his thick shock of black hair with his hook. "It was the day before I met you again, milady, at Madame Jeanne's."

The day I had returned to Edinburgh, no more than a few hours before I had found Jamie at the printshop. He had been at the Burntisland docks with Fergus and a gang of six men during the night, taking advantage of the late dawn of winter to retrieve several casks of unbonded Madeira, smuggled in among a shipment of innocent flour.

"Madeira does not soak through the wood so quickly as some other wines do," Fergus explained. "You cannot bring in brandy under the noses of the Customs like that, for the dogs will smell it at once, even if their masters do not. But not Madeira, provided it has been freshly casked."

"Dogs?"

"Some of the Customs inspectors have dogs, milady, trained to smell out such contraband as tobacco and brandy." He waved away the interruption, squinting his eyes against the brisk sea wind.

"We had removed the Madeira safely, and brought it to the warehouse—

one of those belonging apparently to Lord Dundas, but in fact it belongs jointly to milord and Madame Jeanne."

"Indeed," I said, again with that minor dip of the stomach I had felt when Jamie opened the door of the brothel on Queen Street. "Partners, are they?"

"Well, of a sort." Fergus sounded regretful. "Milord has only a five percent share, in return for his finding the place, and making the arrangements. Printing as an occupation is much less profitable than keeping a *hôtel de joie*." Marsali didn't look round, but I thought her shoulders stiffened further.

"I daresay," I said. Edinburgh and Madame Jeanne were a long way behind us, after all. "Get on with the story. Someone may cut Jamie's throat before I find out why."

"Of course, milady." Fergus bobbed his head apologetically.

The contraband had been safely hidden, awaiting disguise and sale, and the smugglers had paused to refresh themselves with a drink in lieu of breakfast, before making their way home in the brightening dawn. Two of the men had asked for their shares at once, needing the money to pay gaming debts and buy food for their families. Jamie agreeing to this, he had gone across to the warehouse office, where some gold was kept.

As the men relaxed over their whisky in a corner of the warehouse, their joking and laughter was interrupted by a sudden vibration that shook the floor beneath their feet.

"Come-down!" shouted MacLeod, an experienced warehouseman, and the men had dived for cover, even before they had seen the great rack of hogsheads near the office quiver and rumble, one two-ton cask rolling down the stack with ponderous grace, to smash in an aromatic lake of ale, followed within seconds by a cascade of its monstrous fellows.

"Milord was crossing in front of the rank," Fergus said, shaking his head. "It was only by the grace of the Blessed Virgin herself that he was not crushed." A bounding cask had missed him by inches, in fact, and he had escaped another only by diving headfirst out of its way and under an empty wine-rack that had deflected its course.

"As I say, such things happen often," Fergus said, shrugging. "A dozen men are killed each year in such accidents, in the warehouses near Edinburgh alone. But with the other things . . . ."

The week before the incident of the casks, a small shed full of packing straw had burst into flames while Jamie was working in it. A lantern placed between him and the door had apparently fallen over, setting the straw alight and trapping Jamie in the windowless shed, behind a sudden wall of flame.

"The shed was fortunately of a most flimsy construction, and the boards half-rotted. It went up like matchwood, but milord was able to kick a hole in the back wall and crawl out, with no injury. We thought at first that the lantern had merely fallen of its own accord, and were most grateful for his escape. It was only later that milord told me he thought that he had heard a noise—perhaps a shot, perhaps only the cracking noises an old warehouse makes as its boards settle—and when he turned to see, found the flames shooting up before him."

Fergus sighed. He looked rather tired, and I wondered whether perhaps he had stayed awake to stand watch over Jamie during the night.

"So," he said, shrugging once more. "We do not know. Such incidents may have been no more than accident—they may not. But taking such occurrences together with what happened at Arbroath—"

"You may have a traitor among the smugglers," I said.

"Just so, milady." Fergus scratched his head. "But what is more disturbing to milord is the man whom the Chinaman shot at Madame Jeanne's."

"Because you think he was a Customs agent, who'd tracked Jamie from the docks to the brothel? Jamie said he couldn't be, because he had no warrant."

"Not proof," Fergus noted. "But worse, the booklet he had in his pocket."

"The New Testament?" I saw no particular relevance to that, and said so.

"Oh, but there is, milady—or might be, I should say," Fergus corrected himself. "You see, the booklet was one that milord himself had printed."

"I see," I said slowly, "or at least I'm beginning to."

Fergus nodded gravely. "To have the Customs trace brandy from the points of delivery to the brothel would be bad, of course, but not fatal—another hiding place could be found; in fact, milord has arrangements with the owners of two taverns that . . . but that is of no matter." He waved it away. "But to have the agents of the Crown connect the notorious smuggler Jamie Roy with the respectable Mr. Malcolm of Carfax Close . . ." He spread his hands wide. "You see?"

I did. Were the Customs to get too close to his smuggling operations, Jamie could merely disperse his assistants, cease frequenting his smugglers' haunts, and disappear for a time, retreating into his guise as a printer until it seemed safe to resume his illegal activities. But to have his two identities both detected and merged was not only to deprive him of both his sources of income, but to arouse such suspicion as might lead to discovery of his real name, his seditious activities, and thence to Lallybroch and his history as rebel and convicted traitor. They would have evidence to hang him a dozen times—and once was enough.

"I certainly do see. So Jamie wasn't only worried about Laoghaire and Hobart MacKenzie, when he told Ian he thought it would be as well for us to skip to France for a bit."

Paradoxically, I felt somewhat relieved by Fergus's revelations. At least I hadn't been single-handedly responsible for Jamie's exile. My reappearance might have precipitated the crisis with Laoghaire, but I had had nothing to do with any of this.

"Exactly, milady. And still, we do not know for certain that one of the men has betrayed us—or whether, even if there should be a traitor among them, he should wish to kill milord."

"That's a point." It was, but not a large one. If one of the smugglers had undertaken to betray Jamie for money, that was one thing. If it was for some motive of personal vengeance, though, the man might well feel compelled to take matters into his own hands, now that we were—temporarily, at least—out of reach of the King's Customs.

"If so," Fergus was continuing, "it will be one of six men—the six milord sent me to collect, to sail with us. These six were present both when the casks fell, and when the shed caught fire; all have been to the brothel." He paused. "And all of them were present on the road at Arbroath, when we were ambushed, and found the exciseman hanged."

"Do they all know about the printshop?"

"Oh, no, milady! Milord has always been most careful to let none of the smuggling men know of that—but it is always possible that one of them shall have seen him on the streets in Edinburgh, followed him to Carfax Close, and so learned of A. Malcolm." He smiled wryly. "Milord is not the most inconspicuous of men, milady."

"Very true," I said, matching his tone. "But now all of them know Jamie's real name—Captain Raines calls him Fraser."

"Yes," he said, with a faint, grim smile. "That is why we must discover whether we do indeed sail with a traitor—and who it is."

Looking at him, it occurred to me for the first time that Fergus was indeed a grown man now—and a dangerous one. I had known him as an eager, squirrel-toothed boy of ten, and to me, something of that boy would always remain in his face. But some time had passed since he had been a Paris street urchin.

Marsali had remained staring out to sea during most of this discussion, preferring to take no risk of having to converse with me. She had obviously been listening, though, and now I saw a shiver pass through her thin shoulders—whether of cold or apprehension, I couldn't tell. She likely hadn't planned on shipping with a potential murderer when she had agreed to elope with Fergus.

"You'd better take Marsali below," I said to Fergus. "She's going blue round the edges. Don't worry," I said to Marsali, in a cool voice, "I shan't be in the cabin for some time."

"Where are you going, milady?" Fergus was squinting at me, slightly suspicious. "Milord will not wish you to be—"

"I don't mean to," I assured him. "I'm going to the galley."

"The galley?" His fine black brows shot up.

"To see whether Aloysius O'Shaughnessy Murphy has anything to suggest for seasickness," I said. "If we don't get Jamie back on his feet, he isn't going to care whether anyone cuts his throat or not."

Murphy, sweetened by an ounce of dried orange peel and a bottle of Jared's best claret, was quite willing to oblige. In fact, he seemed to consider the problem of keeping food in Jamie's stomach something of a professional challenge, and spent hours in mystic contemplation of his spice rack and pantries—all to no avail.

We encountered no storms, but the winter winds drove a heavy swell before them, and the *Artemis* rose and fell ten feet at a time, laboring up and down the great glassy peaks of the waves. There were times, watching the hypnotic rise and lurch of the taffrail against the horizon, when I felt a few interior qualms of my own, and turned hastily away.

Jamie showed no signs of being about to fulfill Jared's heartening prophecy and spring to his feet, suddenly accustomed to the motion. He remained in his berth, the color of rancid custard, moving only to stagger to the head, and guarded in turns day and night by Mr. Willoughby and Fergus.

On the positive side of things, none of the six smugglers made any move that might be considered threatening. All expressed a sympathetic concern for Jamie's welfare, and—carefully watched—all had visited him briefly in his cabin, with no suspicious circumstances attending.

For my part, I spent the days in exploring the ship, attending to such small medical emergencies as arose from the daily business of sailing—a smashed finger, a cracked rib, bleeding gums and an abscessed tooth—and pounding herbs and making medicines in a corner of the galley, allowed to work there by Murphy's grace.

Marsali was absent from our shared cabin when I rose, already asleep when I returned to it, and silently hostile when the cramped confines of shipboard forced us to meet on deck or over meals. I assumed that the hostility was in part the result of her natural feelings for her mother, and in part the result of frustration over passing her night hours in my company, rather than Fergus's.

For that matter, if she remained untouched—and judging from her sullen demeanor, I was reasonably sure she did—it was owing entirely to Fergus's respect for Jamie's dictates. In terms of his role as guardian of his stepdaughter's virtue, Jamie himself was a negligible force at the moment.

"Wot, not the broth, too?" Murphy said. The cook's broad red face lowered menacingly. "Which I've had folk rise from their deathbeds after a sup of that broth!"

He took the pannikin of broth from Fergus, sniffed at it critically, and thrust it under my nose.

"Here, smell that, missus. Marrow bones, garlic, caraway seed, and a lump o' pork fat to flavor, all strained careful through muslin, same as some folks bein' poorly to their stomachs can't abide chunks, but chunks you'll not find there, not a one!"

The broth was in fact a clear golden brown, with an appetizing smell that made my own mouth water, despite the excellent breakfast I had made less than an hour before. Captain Raines had a delicate stomach, and in consequence had taken some pains both in the procurement of a cook and the provisioning of the galley, to the benefit of the officers' table.

Murphy, with a wooden leg and the general dimensions of a rum cask, looked the picture of a thoroughgoing pirate, but in fact had a reputation as the best sea-cook in Le Havre—as he had told me himself, without the least boastfulness. He considered cases of seasickness a challenge to his skill, and Jamie, still prostrate after four days, was a particular affront to him.

"I'm sure it's wonderful broth," I assured him. "It's just that he can't keep *anything* down."

Murphy grunted dubiously, but turned and carefully poured the remains of the broth into one of the numerous kettles that steamed day and night over the galley fire.

Scowling horribly and running one hand through the wisps of his scanty blond hair, he opened a cupboard and closed it, then bent to rummage through a chest of provisions, muttering under his breath.

"A bit o' hardtack, maybe?" he muttered. "Dry, that's what's wanted. Maybe a whiff o' vinegar, though; tart pickle, say . . ."

I watched in fascination as the cook's huge, sausage-fingered hands flicked deftly through the stock of provisions, plucking dainties and assembling them swiftly on a tray.

" 'Ere, let's try this, then," he said, handing me the finished tray. "Let 'im suck on the pickled gherkins, but don't let 'im bite 'em yet. Then follow on with a bite of the plain hardtack—there ain't no weevils in it yet, I don't think—but see as he don't drink water with it. Then a bite of gherkin, well-chewed, to make the spittle flow, a bite of hardtack, and so to go on with. That much stayin' down, then, we can proceed to the custard, which it's fresh-made last evening for the Captain's supper. Then if that sticks . . ." His voice followed me out of the galley, continuing the catalogue of available nourishment. ". . . milk toast, which it's made with goat's milk, and fresh-milked, too . . .

". . . syllabub beat up well with whisky and a nice *egg* . . ." boomed down the passageway as I negotiated the narrow turn with the loaded tray, carefully stepping over Mr. Willoughby, who was as usual crouched in a corner of the passage by Jamie's door like a small blue lapdog.

One step inside the cabin, though, I could see that the exercise of Murphy's culinary skill was going to be once again in vain. In the usual fashion of a man feeling unwell, Jamie had managed to arrange his surroundings to be as depressing and uncomfortable as possible. The tiny cabin was dank and squalid, the cramped berth covered with a cloth so as to exclude both light and air, and half-piled with a tangle of clammy blankets and unwashed clothes.

"Rise and shine," I said cheerfully. I set down the tray and pulled off the makeshift curtain, which appeared to be one of Fergus's shirts. What light there was came from a large prism embedded in the deck overhead. It struck the berth, illuminating a countenance of ghastly pallor and baleful mien.

He opened one eye an eighth of an inch.

"Go away," he said, and shut it again.

"I've brought you some breakfast," I said firmly.

The eye opened again, coldly blue and gelid.

"Dinna mention the word 'breakfast' to me," he said.

"Call it luncheon then," I said. "It's late enough." I pulled up a stool next to him, picked a gherkin from the tray, and held it invitingly under his nose. "You're supposed to suck on it," I told him.

Slowly, the other eye opened. He said nothing, but the pair of blue orbs swiveled around, resting on me with an expression of such ferocious eloquence that I hastily withdrew the pickle.

The eyelids drooped slowly shut once more.

I surveyed the wreckage, frowning. He lay on his back, his knees drawn up. While the built-in berth provided more stability for the sleeper than the crews' swinging hammocks, it was designed to accommodate the usual run of passengers, who—judging from the size of the berth—were assumed to be no more than a modest five feet three or so.

"You can't be at all comfortable in there," I said.

"I am not."

"Would you like to try a hammock instead? At least you could stretch—"

"I would not."

"The captain says he requires a list of the cargo from you—at your convenience."

He made a brief and unrepeatable suggestion as to what Captain Raines might do with his list, not bothering to open his eyes.

I sighed, and picked up his unresisting hand. It was cold and damp, and his pulse was fast.

"Well," I said after a pause. "Perhaps we could try something I used to do with surgical patients. It seemed to help sometimes."

He gave a low groan, but didn't object. I pulled up a stool and sat down, still holding his hand.

I had developed the habit of talking with the patients for a few minutes before they were taken to surgery. My presence seemed to reassure them, and I had found that if I could fix their attention on something beyond the impending ordeal, they seemed to do better—there was less bleeding, the postanesthetic nausea was less, and they seemed to heal better. I had seen it happen often enough to believe that it was not imagination; Jamie hadn't been altogether wrong when assuring Fergus that the power of mind over flesh was possible.

"Let's think of something pleasant," I said, pitching my voice to be as low and soothing as possible. "Think of Lallybroch, of the hillside above the house. Think of the pine trees there—can you smell the needles? Think of the smoke coming up from the kitchen chimney on a clear day, and an apple in your hand. Think about how it feels in your hand, all hard and smooth, and then—"

"Sassenach?" Both Jamie's eyes were open, and fixed on me in intense concentration. Sweat gleamed in the hollow of his temples.

"Yes?"

"Go away."

"What?"

"Go away," he repeated, very gently, "or I shall break your neck. Go away *now*."

I rose with dignity and went out.

Mr. Willoughby was leaning against an upright in the passage, peering thoughtfully into the cabin.

"Don't have those stone balls with you, do you?" I asked.

"Yes," he answered, looking surprised. "Wanting healthy balls for Tsei-mi?" He began to fumble in his sleeve, but I stopped him with a gesture.

"What I want to do is bash him on the head with them, but I suppose Hippocrates would frown on that."

Mr. Willoughby smiled uncertainly and bobbed his head several times in an effort to express appreciation of whatever I thought I meant.

"Never mind," I said. I glared back over my shoulder at the heap of reeking bedclothes. It stirred slightly, and a groping hand emerged, patting gingerly around the floor until it found the basin that stood there. Grasping this, the hand disappeared into the murky depths of the berth, from which presently emerged the sound of dry retching.

"Bloody man!" I said, exasperation mingled with pity—and a slight feeling of alarm. The ten hours of a Channel crossing were one thing; what would his state be like after two months of this?

"Head of pig," Mr. Willoughby agreed, with a lugubrious nod. "He is rat, you think, or maybe dragon?"

"He smells like a whole zoo," I said. "Why dragon, though?"

"One is born in Year of Dragon, Year of Rat, Year of Sheep, Year of Horse," Mr. Willoughby explained. "Being different, each year, different people. You are knowing is Tsei-mi rat, or dragon?"

"You mean which year was he born in?" I had vague memories of the menus in Chinese restaurants, decorated with the animals of the Chinese zodiac, with explanations of the supposed character traits of those born in each year. "It was 1721, but I don't know offhand which animal that was the year of."

"I am thinking rat," said Mr. Willoughby, looking thoughtfully at the tangle of bedclothes, which were heaving in a mildly agitated manner. "Rat very clever, very lucky. But dragon, too, could be. He is most lusty in bed, Tsei-mi? Dragons most passionate people."

"Not so as you would notice lately," I said, watching the heap of bed-clothes out of the corner of my eye. It heaved upward and fell back, as though the contents had turned over suddenly.

"I have Chinese medicine," Mr. Willoughby said, observing this phenom-enon thoughtfully. "Good for vomit, stomach, head, all making most peace-ful and serene."

I looked at him with interest. "Really? I'd like to see that. Have you tried it on Jamie yet?"

The little Chinese shook his head regretfully.

"Not want," he replied. "Say damn-all, throwing overboard if I am come near."

Mr. Willoughby and I looked at each other with a perfect understanding.

"You know," I said, raising my voice a decibel or two, "prolonged dry retching is very bad for a person."

"Oh, most bad, yes." Mr. Willoughby had shaved the forward part of his skull that morning; the bald curve shone as he nodded vigorously.

"It erodes the stomach tissues, and irritates the esophagus."

"This is so?"

"Quite so. It raises the blood pressure and strains the abdominal muscles, too. Can even tear them, and cause a hernia."

"Ah."

"And," I continued, raising my voice just a trifle, "it can cause the testicles to become tangled round each other inside the scrotum, and cuts off the circulation there."

"Ooh!" Mr. Willoughby's eyes went round.

"If *that* happens," I said ominously, "the only thing to do, usually, is to amputate before gangrene sets in."

Mr. Willoughby made a hissing sound indicative of understanding and deep shock. The heap of bedclothes, which had been tossing to and fro in a restless manner during this conversation, was quite still.

I looked at Mr. Willoughby. He shrugged. I folded my arms and waited. After a minute, a long foot, elegantly bare, was extruded from the bed-clothes. A moment later, its fellow joined it, resting on the floor.

"Damn the pair of ye," said a deep Scottish voice, in tones of extreme malevolence. "Come in, then."

Fergus and Marsali were leaning over the aft rail, cozily shoulder to shoulder, Fergus's arm about the girl's waist, her long fair hair fluttering in the wind.

Hearing approaching footsteps, Fergus glanced back over his shoulder. Then he gasped, whirled round, and crossed himself, eyes bulging.

"Not . . . one . . . word, if ye please," Jamie said between clenched teeth.

Fergus opened his mouth, but nothing came out. Marsali, turning to look too, emitted a shrill scream.

"Da! What's happened to ye?"

The obvious fright and concern in her face stopped Jamie from whatever acerbic remark he had been about to make. His face relaxed slightly, making the slender gold needles that protruded from behind his ears twitch like ant's feelers.

"It's all right," he said gruffly. "It's only some rubbish of the Chinee's, to cure the puking."

Wide-eyed, Marsali came up to him, gingerly extending a finger to touch the needles embedded in the flesh of his wrist below the palm. Three more flashed from the inside of his leg, a few inches above the ankle.

"Does—does it work?" she asked. "How does it feel?"

Jamie's mouth twitched, his normal sense of humor beginning to reassert itself.

"I feel like a bloody ill-wish doll that someone's been poking full o' pins," he said. "But then I havena vomited in the last quarter-hour, so I suppose it must work." He shot a quick glare at me and Mr. Willoughby, standing side by side near the rail.

"Mind ye," he said, "I dinna feel like sucking on gherkins just yet, but I could maybe go so far as to relish a glass of ale, if ye mind where some might be found, Fergus."

"Oh. Oh, yes, milord. If you will come with me?" Unable to refrain from staring, Fergus reached out a tentative hand to take Jamie's arm, but thinking better of it, turned in the direction of the after gangway.

"Shall I tell Murphy to start cooking your luncheon?" I called after Jamie as he turned to follow Fergus. He gave me a long, level look over one shoulder. The golden needles sprouted through his hair in twin bunches, gleaming in the morning light like a pair of devil's horns.

"Dinna try me too high, Sassenach," he said. "I'm no going to forget, ye ken. Tangled testicles—pah!"

Mr. Willoughby had been ignoring this exchange, squatting on his heels in the shadow of the aft-deck scuttlebutt, a large barrel filled with water for refreshment of the deck watch. He was counting on his fingers, evidently absorbed in some kind of calculation. As Jamie stalked away, he looked up.

"Not rat," he said, shaking his head. "Not dragon, too. Tsei-mi born in Year of Ox."

"Really?" I said, looking after the broad shoulders and red head, lowered stubbornly against the wind. "How appropriate."

42

The Man in the Moon

s his title suggested, Jamie's job as supercargo was not onerous. Beyond checking the contents of the hold against the bills of lading to insure that the *Artemis* was in fact carrying the requisite quantities of hides, tin, and sulfur, there was nothing for him to do while at sea. His duties would begin once we reached Jamaica, when the cargo must be unloaded, rechecked, and sold, with the requisite taxes paid, commissions deducted, and paperwork filed.

In the meantime, there was little for him—or me—to do. While Mr. Picard, the bosun, eyed Jamie's powerful frame covetously, it was obvious that he would never make a seaman. Quick and agile as any of the crew, his ignorance of ropes and sails made him useless for anything beyond the occasional situation where sheer strength was required. It was plain he was a soldier, not a sailor.

He did assist with enthusiasm at the gunnery practice that was held every other day, helping to run the four huge guns on their carriages in and out with a tremendous racket, and spending hours in rapt discussion of esoteric cannon lore with Tom Sturgis, the gunner. During these thunderous exercises, Marsali, Mr. Willoughby, and I sat safely out of the way under the care of Fergus, who was excluded from the fireworks because of his missing hand.

Somewhat to my surprise, I had been accepted as the ship's surgeon with little question from the crew. It was Fergus who explained that in small merchant ships, even barber-surgeons were uncommon. It was commonly the gunner's wife—if he had one—who dealt with the small injuries and illnesses of the crew.

I saw the normal run of crushed fingers, burnt hands, skin infections, abscessed teeth, and digestive ills, but in a crew of only thirty-two men, there was seldom enough work to keep me busy beyond the hour of sick call each morning.

In consequence, both Jamie and I had a great deal of free time. And, as the *Artemis* drew gradually south into the great gyre of the Atlantic, we began to spend most of this time with each other.

For the first time since my return to Edinburgh, there was time to talk; to relearn all the half-forgotten things we knew of each other, to find out the new facets that experience had polished, and simply to take pleasure in each other's presence, without the distractions of danger and daily life.

We strolled the deck constantly, up and down, marking off miles as we conversed of everything and nothing, pointing out to each other the phenomena of a sea voyage; the spectacular sunrises and sunsets, schools of strange green and silver fish, enormous islands of floating seaweed, harboring thousands of tiny crabs and jellyfish, the sleek dolphins that appeared for several days in a row, swimming parallel with the ship, leaping out of the water now and then, as though to get a look at the curious creatures above the water.

The moon rose huge and fast and golden, a great glowing disc that slid upward, out of the water and into the sky like a phoenix rising. The water was dark now, and the dolphins invisible, but I thought somehow that they were still there, keeping pace with the ship on her flight through the dark.

It was a scene breathtaking enough even for the sailors, who had seen it a thousand times, to stop and sigh with pleasure at the sight, as the huge orb rose to hang just over the edge of the world, seeming almost near enough to touch.

Jamie and I stood close together by the rail, admiring it. It seemed so close that we could make out with ease the dark spots and shadows on its surface.

"It seems so close ye could speak to the Man in the Moon," he said, smiling, and waved a hand in greeting to the dreaming golden face above.

" 'The weeping Pleiads wester / and the moon is under seas,' " I quoted. "And look, it is, down there, too." I pointed over the rail, to where the trail of moonlight deepened, glowing in the water as though a twin of the moon itself were sunken there.

"When I left," I said, "men were getting ready to fly to the moon. I wonder whether they'll make it."

"Do the flying machines go so high, then?" Jamie asked. He squinted at the moon. "I should say it's a great way, for all it looks so close just now. I read a book by an astronomer—he said it was perhaps three hundred leagues from the earth to the moon. Is he wrong, then, or is it only that the— airplanes, was it?—will fly so far?"

"It takes a special kind, called a rocket," I said. "Actually, it's a lot farther than that to the moon, and once you get far away from the earth, there's no air to breathe in space. They'll have to carry air with them on the voyage, like food and water. They put it in sort of canisters."

"Really?" He gazed up, face full of light and wonder. "What will it look like there, I wonder?"

"I know that," I said. "I've seen pictures. It's rocky, and barren, with no life at all—but very beautiful, with cliffs and mountains and craters—you can see the craters from here; the dark spots." I nodded toward the smiling moon, then smiled at Jamie myself. "It's not unlike Scotland—except that it isn't green."

He laughed, then evidently reminded by the word "pictures," reached into his coat and drew out the little packet of photographs. He was cautious about them, never taking them out where they might be seen by anyone, even Fergus, but we were alone back here, with little chance of interruption.

The moon was bright enough to see Brianna's face, glowing and mutable, as he thumbed slowly through the pictures. The edges were becoming frayed, I saw.

"Will she walk about on the moon, d'ye think?" he asked softly, pausing at a shot of Bree looking out a window, secretly dreaming, unaware of being photographed. He glanced up again at the orb above us, and I realized that for him, a voyage to the moon seemed very little more difficult or farfetched than the one in which we were engaged. The moon, after all, was only another distant, unknown place.

"I don't know," I said, smiling a bit.

He thumbed through the pictures slowly, absorbed as he always was by the sight of his daughter's face, so like his own. I watched him quietly, sharing his silent joy at this promise of our immortality.

I thought briefly of that stone in Scotland, engraved with his name, and took comfort from its distance. Whenever our parting might come, chances were it would not be soon. And even when and where it did—Brianna would still be left of us.

More of Housman's lines drifted through my head—*Halt by the headstone naming / The heart no longer stirred, / And say the lad that loved you / Was one that kept his word.*

I drew close to him, feeling the heat of his body through coat and shirt, and rested my head against his arm as he turned slowly through the small stack of photographs.

"She is beautiful," he murmured, as he did every time he saw the pictures. "And clever, too, did ye not say?"

"Just like her father," I told him, and felt him chuckle softly.

I felt him stiffen slightly as he turned one picture over, and lifted my head to see which one he was looking at. It was one taken at the beach, when Brianna was about sixteen. It showed her standing thigh-deep in the surf, hair in a sandy tangle, kicking water at her friend, a boy named Rodney, who was backing away, laughing too, hands held up against the spray of water.

Jamie frowned slightly, lips pursed.

"That—" he began. "Do they—" He paused and cleared his throat. "I wouldna venture to criticize, Claire," he said, very carefully, "but do ye not think this is a wee bit . . . indecent?"

I suppressed an urge to laugh.

"No," I said, composedly. "That's really quite a modest bathing suit—for the time." While the suit in question *was* a bikini, it was by no means skimpy, rising to at least an inch below Bree's navel. "I chose this picture because I thought you'd want to er . . . see as much of her as possible."

He looked mildly scandalized at this thought, but his eyes returned to the picture, drawn irresistibly. His face softened as he looked at her.

"Aye, well," he said. "Aye, she's verra lovely, and I'm glad to know it." He lifted the picture, studying it carefully. "No, it's no the thing she's wearing I meant; most women who bathe outside do it naked, and their skins are no shame to them. It's only—this lad. Surely she shouldna be standing almost naked before a man?" He scowled at the hapless Rodney, and I bit my lip at the thought of the scrawny little boy, whom I knew very well, as a masculine threat to maidenly purity.

"Well," I said, drawing a deep breath. We were on slightly delicate ground here. "No. I mean, boys and girls do play together—like that. You know people dress differently then; I've told you. No one's really covered up a great deal except when the weather's cold."

"Mmphm," he said. "Aye, ye've told me." He managed to convey the distinct impression that on the basis of what I'd told him, he was not impressed with the moral conditions under which his daughter was living.

He scowled at the picture again, and I thought it was fortunate that neither Bree nor Rodney was present. I had seen Jamie as lover, husband, brother, uncle, laird, and warrior, but never before in his guise as a ferocious Scottish father. He was quite formidable.

For the first time, I thought that perhaps it was not altogether a bad thing that he wasn't able to oversee Bree's life personally; he would have frightened the living daylights out of any lad bold enough to try to court her.

Jamie blinked at the picture once or twice, then took a deep breath, and I could feel him brace himself to ask.

"D'ye think she is—a virgin?" The halt in his voice was barely perceptible, but I caught it.

"Of course she is," I said firmly. I thought it very likely, in fact, but this wasn't a situation in which to admit the possibility of doubt. There were things I could explain to Jamie about my own time, but the idea of sexual freedom wasn't one of them.

"Oh." The relief in his voice was inexpressible, and I bit my lip to keep from laughing. "Aye, well, I was sure of it, only I—that is—" He stopped and swallowed.

"Bree's a very good girl," I said. I squeezed his arm lightly. "Frank and I may not have got on so well together, but we were both good parents to her, if I do say so."

"Aye, I know ye were. I didna mean to say otherwise." He had the grace to look abashed, and tucked the beach picture carefully back into the packet.

He put the pictures back into his pocket, patting them to be sure they were safe.

He stood looking up at the moon, then, his brows drew together in a slight frown. The sea wind lifted strands of his hair, tugging them loose from the ribbon that bound it, and he brushed them back absentmindedly. Clearly there was still something on his mind.

"Do ye think," he began slowly, not looking at me. "Do ye think that it was quite wise to come to me now, Claire? Not that I dinna want ye," he added hastily, feeling me stiffen beside him. He caught my hand, preventing my turning away.

"No, I didna mean that at all! Christ, I do want ye!" He drew me closer, pressing my hand in his against his heart. "I want ye so badly that sometimes I think my heart will burst wi' the joy of having ye," he added more softly. "It's only—Brianna's alone now. Frank is gone, and you. She has no husband to protect her, no men of her family to see her safely wed. Will she not have need of ye awhile yet? Should ye no have waited a bit, I mean?"

I paused before answering, trying to get my own feelings under control.

"I don't know," I said at last; my voice quivered, in spite of my struggle to control it. "Look—things aren't the same then."

"I know that!"

"You don't!" I pulled my hand loose, and glared at him. "You don't know, Jamie, and there isn't any way for me to tell you, because you won't believe me. But Bree's a grown woman; she'll marry when and as she likes, not when someone arranges it for her. She doesn't *need* to marry, for that matter. She's having a good education; she can earn her own living—women do that. She won't have to have a man to protect her—"

"And if there's no need for a man to protect a woman, and care for her, then I think it will be a verra poor time!" He glared back at me.

I drew a deep breath, trying to be calm.

"I didn't say there's no need for it." I placed a hand on his shoulder, and spoke in a softer tone. "I said, she can choose. She needn't take a man out of necessity; she can take one for love."

His face began to relax, just slightly.

"You took me from need," he said. "When we wed."

"And I came back for love," I said. "Do you think I needed you any less, only because I could feed myself?"

The lines of his face eased, and the shoulder under my hand relaxed a bit as he searched my face.

"No," he said softly. "I dinna think that."

He put his arm around me and drew me close. I put my arms around his waist and held him, feeling the small flat patch of Brianna's pictures in his pocket under my cheek.

"I did worry about leaving her," I whispered, a little later. "She made me go; we were afraid that if I waited longer, I might not be able to find you. But I did worry."

"I know. I shouldna ha' said anything." He brushed my curls away from his chin, smoothing them down.

"I left her a letter," I said. "It was all I could think to do—knowing I might . . . might not see her again." I pressed my lips tight together and swallowed hard.

His fingertips stroked my back, very softly.

"Aye? That was good, Sassenach. What did ye say to her?"

I laughed, a little shakily.

"Everything I could think of. Motherly advice and wisdom—what I had of it. All the practical things—where the deed to the house and the family papers were. And everything I knew or could think of, about how to live. I expect she'll ignore it all, and have a wonderful life—but at least she'll know I thought about her."

It had taken me nearly a week, going through the cupboards and desk drawers of the house in Boston, finding all of the business papers, the bankbooks and mortgage papers and the family things. There were a good many bits and pieces of Frank's family lying about; huge scrapbooks and dozens of genealogy charts, albums of photographs, cartons of saved letters. My side of the family was a good deal simpler to sum up.

I lifted down the box I kept on the shelf of my closet. It was a small box. Uncle Lambert was a saver, as all scholars are, but there had been little to save. The essential documents of a small family—birth certificates, mine and my parents', their marriage lines, the registration for the car that had killed them—what ironic whim had prompted Uncle Lamb to save that? More likely he had never opened the box, but only kept it, in a scholar's blind faith that information must never be destroyed, for who knew what use it might be, and to whom?

I had seen its contents before, of course. There had been a period in my teens when I opened it nightly to look at the few photos it contained. I remembered the bone-deep longing for the mother I didn't remember, and the vain effort to imagine her, to bring her back to life from the small dim images in the box.

The best of them was a close-up photograph of her, face turned toward the camera, warm eyes and a delicate mouth, smiling under the brim of a felt cloche hat. The photograph had been hand-tinted; the cheeks and lips were an unnatural rose-pink, the eyes soft brown. Uncle Lamb said that that was wrong; her eyes had been gold, he said, like mine.

I thought perhaps that time of deep need had passed for Brianna, but was not sure. I had had a studio portrait made of myself the week before; I placed it carefully in the box and closed it, and put the box in the center of my desk, where she would find it. Then I sat down to write.

My dear Bree— I wrote, and stopped. I couldn't. Couldn't possibly be contemplating abandoning my child. To see those three black words stark on the page brought the whole mad idea into a cold clarity that struck me to the bone.

My hand shook, and the tip of the pen made small wavering circles in the air above the paper. I put it down, and clasped my hands between my thighs, eyes closed.

"Get a grip on yourself, Beauchamp," I muttered. "Write the bloody thing and have done. If she doesn't need it, it will do no harm, and if she does, it will be there." I picked up the pen and began again.

> *I don't know if you will ever read this, but perhaps it's as well to set it down. This is what I know of your grandparents (your real ones), your great-grandparents, and your medical history . . .*

I wrote for some time, covering page after page. My mind grew calmer with the effort of recall, and the necessity of setting down the information clearly, and then I stopped, thinking.

What could I tell her, beyond those few bare bloodless facts? How to impart what sparse wisdom I had gained in forty-eight years of a fairly eventful life? My mouth twisted wryly in consideration of that. Did any daughter listen? Would I, had my mother been there to tell me?

It made no difference, though; I would just have to set it down, to be of use if it could.

But what was true, that would last forever, in spite of changing times and ways, what would stand her in good stead? Most of all, how could I tell her just how much I loved her?

The enormity of what I was about to do gaped before me, and my fingers clenched tight on the pen. I couldn't think—not and do this. I could only set the pen to the paper and hope.

Baby— I wrote, and stopped. Then swallowed hard, and started again.

> *You are my baby, and always will be. You won't know what that means until you have a child of your own, but I tell you now, anyway— you'll always be as much a part of me as when you shared my body and I felt you move inside. Always.*
>
> *I can look at you, asleep, and think of all the nights I tucked you in, coming in the dark to listen to your breathing, lay my hand on you and feel your chest rise and fall, knowing that no matter what happens, everything is right with the world because you are alive.*
>
> *All the names I've called you through the years—my chick, my pumpkin, precious dove, darling, sweetheart, dinky, smudge . . . I know*

why the Jews and Muslims have nine hundred names for God; one small word is not enough for love.

I blinked hard to clear my vision, and went on writing, fast; I didn't dare take time to choose my words, or I would never write them.

I remember everything about you, from the tiny line of golden down that zigged across your forehead when you were hours old to the bumpy toenail on the big toe you broke last year, when you had that fight with Jeremy and kicked the door of his pickup truck.

God, it breaks my heart to think it will stop now—that watching you, seeing all the tiny changes—I won't know when you stop biting your nails, if you ever do—seeing you grow suddenly taller than I, and your face take its shape. I always will remember, Bree, I always will.

There's probably no one else on earth, Bree, who knows what the back of your ears looked like when you were three years old. I used to sit beside you, reading "One Fish, Two Fish, Red Fish, Blue Fish," or "The Three Billy Goats Gruff," and see those ears turn pink with happiness. Your skin was so clear and fragile, I thought a touch would leave fingerprints on you.

You look like Jamie, I told you. You have something from me, too, though—look at the picture of my mother, in the box, and the little black-and-white one of her mother and grandmother. You have that broad clear brow they have; so do I. I've seen a good many of the Frasers, too—I think you'll age well, if you take care of your skin.

Take care of everything, Bree—oh, I wish—well, I have wished I could take care of you and protect you from everything all your life, but I can't, whether I stay or go. Take care of yourself, though—for me.

The tears were puckering the paper now; I had to stop to blot them, lest they smear the ink beyond reading. I wiped my face, and resumed, slower now.

You should know, Bree—I don't regret it. In spite of everything, I don't regret it. You'll know something now, of how lonely I was for so long, without Jamie. It doesn't matter. If the price of that separation was your life, neither Jamie nor I can regret it—I know he wouldn't mind my speaking for him.

Bree . . . you are my joy. You're perfect, and wonderful—and I hear you saying now, in that tone of exasperation, "But of course you think that—you're my mother!" Yes, that's how I know.

Bree, you are worth everything—and more. I've done a great many things in my life so far, but the most important of them all was to love your father and you.

I blew my nose and reached for another fresh sheet of paper. That was the most important thing; I could never say all I felt, but this was the best I could do. What might I add, to be of aid in living well, in growing up and growing old? What had I learned, that I might pass on to her?

Choose a man like your father, I wrote. *Either of them.* I shook my head over that—could there be two men more different?—but left it, thinking of Roger Wakefield. *Once you've chosen a man, don't try to change him,* I wrote, with more confidence. *It can't be done. More important—don't let him try to change you. He can't do it either, but men always try.*

I bit the end of the pen, tasting the bitter tang of India ink. And finally I put down the last and the best advice I knew, on growing older.

> *Stand up straight and try not to get fat.*
> *With All My Love Always,*
> *Mama*

Jamie's shoulders shook as he leaned against the rail, whether with laughter or some other emotion, I couldn't tell. His linen glowed white with moonlight, and his head was dark against the moon. At last he turned and pulled me to him.

"I think she will do verra well," he whispered. "For no matter what poor gowk has fathered her, no lass has ever had a better mother. Kiss me, Sassenach, for believe me—I wouldna change ye for the world."

43

Phantom Limbs

Fergus, Mr. Willoughby, Jamie, and I had all kept careful watch upon the six Scottish smugglers since our departure from Scotland, but there was not the slightest hint of suspicious behavior from any of them, and after a time, I found myself relaxing my wariness around them. Still, I felt some reserve toward most of them, save Innes. I had finally realized why neither Fergus nor Jamie thought him a possible traitor; with but one arm, Innes was the only smuggler who could not have strung up the exciseman on the Arbroath road.

Innes was a quiet man. None of the Scots was what one might call garrulous, but even by their high standards of taciturnity, he was reserved. I was therefore not surprised to see him grimacing silently one morning, bent over behind a hatch cover, evidently engaged in some silent internal battle.

"Have you a pain, Innes?" I asked, stopping.

"Och!" He straightened, startled, but then fell back into his half-crouched position, his one arm locked across his belly. "Mmphm," he muttered, his thin face flushing at being so discovered.

"Come along with me," I said, taking him by the elbow. He looked frantically about for salvation, but I towed him, resisting but not audibly protesting, back to my cabin, where I forced him to sit upon the table and removed his shirt so that I could examine him.

I palpated his lean and hairy abdomen, feeling the firm, smooth mass of the liver on one side, and the mildly distended curve of the stomach on the other. The intermittent way in which the pains came on, causing him to writhe like a worm on a hook, then passing off, gave me a good idea that what troubled him was simple flatulence, but best to be thorough.

I probed for the gallbladder, just in case, wondering as I did so just what I would do, should it prove to be an acute attack of cholecystitis or an inflamed appendix. I could envision the cavity of the belly in my mind, as though it lay open in fact before me, my fingers translating the soft, lumpy shapes beneath the skin into vision—the intricate folds of the intestines, softly shielded by their yellow quilting of fat-padded membrane, the slick, smooth lobes of the liver, deep purple-red, so much darker than the vivid scarlet of the heart's pericardium above. Opening that cavity was a risky thing to do, even equipped with modern anesthetics and antibiotics. Sooner or later, I knew, I would be faced with the necessity of doing it, but I sincerely hoped it would be later.

"Breathe in," I said, hands on his chest, and saw in my mind the pink-flushed grainy surface of a healthy lung. "Breathe out, now," and felt the color fade to soft blue. No rales, no halting, a nice clear flow. I reached for one of the thick sheets of vellum paper I used for stethoscopes.

"When did you last move your bowels?" I inquired, rolling the paper into a tube. The Scot's thin face turned the color of fresh liver. Fixed with my gimlet eye, he mumbled something incoherent, in which the word "four" was just distinguishable.

"Four *days*?" I said, forestalling his attempts to escape by putting a hand on his chest and pinning him flat to the table. "Hold still, I'll just have a listen here, to be sure."

The heart sounds were reassuringly normal; I could hear the valves open and close with their soft, meaty clicks, all in the right places. I was quite sure of the diagnosis—had been virtually from the moment I had looked at him—but by now there was an audience of heads peering curiously round the doorway; Innes's mates, watching. For effect, I moved the end of my tubular stethoscope down farther, listening for belly sounds.

Just as I thought, the rumble of trapped gas was clearly audible in the upper curve of the large intestine. The lower sigmoid colon was blocked, though; no sound at all down there.

"You have belly gas," I said, "and constipation."

"Aye, I ken that fine," Innes muttered, looking frantically for his shirt.

I put my hand on the garment in question, preventing him from leaving while I catechized him about his diet of late. Not surprisingly, this consisted almost entirely of salt pork and hardtack.

"What about the dried peas and the oatmeal?" I asked, surprised. Having inquired as to the normal fare aboard ship, I had taken the precaution of stowing—along with my surgeon's cask of lime juice and the collection of medicinal herbs—three hundred pounds of dried peas and a similar quantity of oatmeal, intending that this should be used to supplement the seamen's normal diet.

Innes remained tongue-tied, but this inquiry unleashed a flood of revelation and grievance from the onlookers in the doorway.

Jamie, Fergus, Marsali, and I all dined daily with Captain Raines, feasting on Murphy's ambrosia, so I was unaware of the deficiencies of the crew's mess. Evidently the difficulty was Murphy himself, who, while holding the highest culinary standards for the captain's table, considered the crew's dinner to be a chore rather than a challenge. He had mastered the routine of producing the crew's meals quickly and competently, and was highly resistant to any suggestions for an improved menu that might require further time or trouble. He declined absolutely to trouble with such nuisances as soaking peas or boiling oatmeal.

Compounding the difficulty was Murphy's ingrained prejudice against oatmeal, a crude Scottish mess that offended his aesthetic sense. I knew what he thought about that, having heard him muttering things about "dog's vomit" over the trays of breakfast that included the bowls of parritch to which Jamie, Marsali, and Fergus were addicted.

"Mr. Murphy says as how salt pork and hardtack is good enough for every crew he's had to feed for thirty year—given figgy-dowdy or plum duff for pudding, and beef on Sundays, too—though if that's beef, I'm a Chinaman —and it's good enough for us," Gordon burst in.

Accustomed to polyglot crews of French, Italian, Spanish, and Norwegian sailors, Murphy was also accustomed to having his meals accepted and consumed with a voracious indifference that transcended nationalities. The Scots' stubborn insistence on oatmeal roused all his own Irish intransigence, and the matter, at first a small, simmering disagreement, was now beginning to rise to a boil.

"We knew as there was meant to be parritch," MacLeod explained, "for Fergus did say so, when he asked us to come. But it's been nothing but the meat and biscuit since we left Scotland, which is a wee bit griping to the belly if ye're not used to it."

"We didna like to trouble Jamie Roy ower such a thing," Raeburn put in. "Geordie's got his girdle, and we've been makin' our own oatcake ower the lamps in the crew quarters. But we've run through what corn we brought in our bags, and Mr. Murphy's got the keys to the pantry store." He glanced shyly at me under his sandy blond lashes. "We didna like to ask, knowin' what he thought of us."

"Ye wouldna ken what's meant by the term 'spalpeens,' would ye, Mistress Fraser?" MacRae asked, raising one bushy brow.

While listening to this outpouring of woe, I had been selecting assorted herbs from my box—anise and angelica, two large pinches of horehound, and a few sprigs of peppermint. Tying these into a square of gauze, I closed the box and handed Innes his shirt, into which he burrowed at once, in search of refuge.

"I'll speak to Mr. Murphy," I promised the Scots. "Meanwhile," I said to Innes, handing him the gauze bundle, "brew you a good pot of tea from that, and drink a cupful at every watch change. If we've had no results by tomorrow, we'll try stronger measures."

As if in answer to this, a high, squeaking fart emerged from under Innes, to an ironic cheer from his colleagues.

"Aye, that's right, Mistress Fraser; maybe ye can scare the shit out o' him," MacLeod said, a broad grin splitting his face.

Innes, scarlet as a ruptured artery, took the bundle, bobbed his head in inarticulate thanks, and fled precipitously, followed in more leisurely fashion by the other smugglers.

A rather acrimonious debate with Murphy followed, terminating without bloodshed, but with the compromise that *I* would be responsible for the preparation of the Scots' morning parritch, permitted to do so under provision that I confined myself to a single pot and spoon, did not sing while cooking, and was careful not to make a mess in the precincts of the sacred galley.

It was only that night, tossing restlessly in the cramped and chilly confines of my berth, that it occurred to me how odd the morning's incident had been. Were this Lallybroch, and the Scots Jamie's tenants, not only would they have had no hesitation in approaching him about the matter, they would have had no need to. He would have known already what was wrong, and taken steps to remedy the situation. Accustomed as I had always been to the intimacy and unquestioning loyalty of Jamie's own men, I found this distance troubling.

Jamie was not at the captain's table next morning, having gone out in the small boat with two of the sailors to catch whitebait, but I met him on his return at noon, sunburned, cheerful, and covered with scales and fish blood.

"What have ye done to Innes, Sassenach?" he said, grinning. "He's hiding in the starboard head, and says ye told him he mustna come out at all until he'd shit."

"I didn't tell him *that,* exactly," I explained. "I just said if he hadn't moved his bowels by tonight, I'd give him an enema of slippery elm."

Jamie glanced over his shoulder in the direction of the head.

"Well, I suppose we will hope that Innes's bowels cooperate, or I doubt but he'll spend the rest of the voyage in the head, wi' a threat like that hangin' ower him."

"Well, I shouldn't worry; now that he and the others have their parritch back, their bowels ought to take care of themselves without undue interference from me."

Jamie glanced down at me, surprised.

"Got their parritch back? Whatever d'ye mean, Sassenach?"

I explained the genesis of the Oatmeal War, and its outcome, as he fetched a basin of water to clean his hands. A small frown drew his brows close together as he pushed his sleeves up his arms.

"They ought to have come to me about it," he said.

"I expect they would have, sooner or later," I said. "I only happened to find out by accident, when I found Innes grunting behind a hatch cover."

"Mmphm." He set about scouring the bloodstains off his fingers, rubbing the clinging scales free with a small pumice stone.

"These men aren't like your tenants at Lallybroch, are they?" I said, voicing the thought I had had.

"No," he said quietly. He dipped his fingers in the basin, leaving tiny shimmering circles where the fish scales floated. "I'm no their laird; only the man who pays them."

"They like you, though," I protested, then remembered Fergus's story and amended this rather weakly to, "or at least five of them do."

I handed him the towel. He took it with a brief nod, and dried his hands. Looking down at the strip of cloth, he shook his head.

"Aye, MacLeod and the rest like me well enough—or five of them do," he repeated ironically. "And they'll stand by me if it's needful—five of them. But they dinna ken me much, nor me them, save Innes."

He tossed the dirty water over the side, and tucking the empty basin under his arm, turned to go below, offering me his arm.

"There was more died at Culloden than the Stuart cause, Sassenach," he said. "You'll be coming for your dinner now?"

I did not find out why Innes was different, until the next week. Perhaps emboldened by the success of the purgative I had given him, Innes came voluntarily to call upon me in my cabin a week later.

"I am wondering, mistress," he said politely, "whether there might be a medicine for something as isna there."

"What?" I must have looked puzzled at this description, for he lifted the empty sleeve of his shirt in illustration.

"My arm," he explained. "It's no there, as ye can plainly see. And yet it pains me something terrible sometimes." He blushed slightly.

"I did wonder for some years was I only a bit mad," he confided, in lowered tones. "But I spoke a bit wi' Mr. Murphy, and he tells me it's the same with his leg that got lost, and Fergus says he wakes sometimes, feeling his missing hand slide into someone's pocket." He smiled briefly, teeth a flash under his drooping mustache. "So I thought maybe if it was a common thing, to feel a limb that wasn't there, perhaps there was something that might be done about it."

"I see." I rubbed my chin, pondering. "Yes, it is common; it's called a phantom limb, when you still have feelings in a part that's been lost. As for what to do about it. . . ." I frowned, trying to think whether I had ever heard of anything therapeutic for such a situation. To gain time, I asked, "How did you happen to lose the arm?"

"Oh, 'twas the blood poison," he said, casually. "I tore a small hole in my hand wi' a nail one day, and it festered."

I stared at the sleeve, empty from the shoulder.

"I suppose it did," I said faintly.

"Oh, aye. It was a lucky thing, though; it was that stopped me bein' transported wi' the rest."

"The rest of whom?"

He looked at me, surprised. "Why, the other prisoners from Ardsmuir. Did Mac Dubh not tell ye about that? When they stopped the fortress from being a prison, they sent off all of the Scottish prisoners to be indenture men in the Colonies—all but Mac Dubh, for he was a great man, and they didna want him out o' their sight, and me, for I'd lost the arm, and was no good for hard labor. So Mac Dubh was taken somewhere else, and I was let go—pardoned and set free. So ye see, it was a most fortunate accident, save only for the pain that comes on sometimes at night." He grimaced, and made as though to rub the nonexistent arm, stopping and shrugging at me in illustration of the problem.

"I see. So you were with Jamie in prison. I didn't know that." I was turning through the contents of my medicine chest, wondering whether a general pain reliever like willow-bark tea or horehound with fennel would work on a phantom pain.

"Oh, aye." Innes was losing his shyness, and beginning to speak more freely. "I should have been dead of starvation by now, had Mac Dubh not come to find me, when he was released himself."

"He went looking for you?" Out of the corner of my eye, I spotted a flash of blue, and beckoned to Mr. Willoughby, who was passing by.

"Aye. When he was released from his parole, he came to inquire, to see whether he could trace any of the men who'd been taken to America—to see whether any might have returned." He shrugged, the missing arm exaggerating the gesture. "But there were none in Scotland, save me."

"I see. Mr. Willoughby, have you a notion what might be done about this?" Motioning to the Chinese to come and look, I explained the problem, and was pleased to hear that he did indeed have a notion. We stripped Innes of his shirt once again, and I watched, taking careful notes, as Mr. Willoughby pressed hard with his fingers at certain spots on the neck and torso, explaining as best he might what he was doing.

"Arm is in the ghost world," he explained. "Body not; here in upper world. Arm tries to come back, for it does not like to be away from body. This—*An-mo*—press-press—this stops pain. But also we tell arm not come back."

"And how d'ye do that?" Innes was becoming interested in the procedure. Most of the crew would not let Mr. Willoughby touch them, regarding him as heathen, unclean, and a pervert to boot, but Innes had known and worked with the Chinese for the last two years.

Mr. Willoughby shook his head, lacking words, and burrowed in my medicine box. He came up with the bottle of dried hot peppers, and shaking out a careful handful, put it into a small dish.

"Have fire?" he inquired. I had a flint and steel, and with these he succeeded in kindling a spark to ignite the dried herb. The pungent smell filled the cabin, and we all watched as a small plume of white rose up from the dish and formed a small, hovering cloud over the dish.

"Send smoke of *fan jiao* messenger to ghost world, speak arm," Mr. Willoughby explained. Inflating his lungs and puffing out his cheeks like a blowfish, he blew lustily at the cloud, dispersing it. Then, without pausing, he turned and spat copiously on Innes's stump.

"Why, ye heathen bugger!" Innes cried, eyes bulging with fury. "D'ye dare spit on me?"

"Spit on ghost," Mr. Willoughby explained, taking three quick steps backward, toward the door. "Ghost afraid spittle. Not come back now right away."

I laid a restraining hand on Innes's remaining arm.

"Does your missing arm hurt now?" I asked.

The rage began to fade from his face as he thought about it.

"Well . . . no," he admitted. Then he scowled at Mr. Willoughby. "But that doesna mean I'll have ye spit on me whenever the fancy takes ye, ye wee poutworm!"

"Oh, no," Mr. Willoughby said, quite cool. "I not spit. You spit now. Scare you own ghost."

Innes scratched his head, not sure whether to be angry or amused.

"Well, I will be damned," he said finally. He shook his head, and picking up his shirt, pulled it on. "Still," he said, "I think perhaps next time, I'll try your tea, Mistress Fraser."

44

Forces of Nature

"I," said Jamie, "am a fool." He spoke broodingly, watching Fergus and Marsali, who were absorbed in close conversation by the rail on the opposite side of the ship.

"What makes you think so?" I asked, though I had a reasonably good idea. The fact that all four of the married persons aboard were living in unwilling celibacy had given rise to a certain air of suppressed amusement among the members of the crew, whose celibacy was involuntary.

"I have spent twenty years longing to have ye in my bed," he said, verifying my assumption, "and within a month of having ye back again, I've arranged matters so that I canna even kiss ye without sneakin' behind a hatch cover, and even then, half the time I look round to find Fergus looking cross-eyed down his nose at me, the little bastard! And no one to blame for it but my own foolishness. What did I think I was doing?" he demanded rhetorically, glaring at the pair across the way, who were nuzzling each other with open affection.

"Well, Marsali *is* only fifteen," I said mildly. "I expect you thought you were being fatherly—or stepfatherly."

"Aye, I did." He looked down at me with a grudging smile. "The reward for my tender concern being that I canna even touch my own wife!"

"Oh, you can touch me," I said. I took one of his hands, caressing the palm gently with my thumb. "You just can't engage in acts of unbridled carnality."

We had had a few abortive attempts along those lines, all frustrated by either the inopportune arrival of a crew member or the sheer uncongeniality of any nook aboard the *Artemis* sufficiently secluded as to be private. One late-night foray into the after hold had ended abruptly when a large rat had leapt from a stack of hides onto Jamie's bare shoulder, sending me into hysterics and depriving Jamie abruptly of any desire to continue what he was doing.

He glanced down at our linked hands, where my thumb continued to make secret love to his palm, and narrowed his eyes at me, but let me continue. He closed his fingers gently round my hand, his own thumb feather-light on my pulse. The simple fact was that we couldn't keep our hands off each other—no more than Fergus and Marsali could—despite the fact that we knew very well such behavior would lead only to greater frustration.

"Aye, well, in my own defense, I meant well," he said ruefully, smiling down into my eyes.

"Well, you know what they say about good intentions."

"What do they say?" His thumb was stroking gently up and down my wrist, sending small fluttering sensations through the pit of my stomach. I thought it must be true what Mr. Willoughby said, about sensations on one part of the body affecting another.

"They pave the road to Hell." I gave his hand a squeeze, and tried to take mine away, but he wouldn't let go.

"Mmphm." His eyes were on Fergus, who was teasing Marsali with an albatross's feather, holding her by one arm and tickling her beneath the chin as she struggled ineffectually to get away.

"Verra true," he said. "I meant to make sure the lass had a chance to think what she was about before the matter was too late for mending. The end result of my interference being that I lie awake half the night trying not to think about you, and listening to Fergus lust across the cabin, and come up in the morning to find the crew all grinning in their beards whenever they see me." He aimed a vicious glare at Maitland, who was passing by. The beardless cabin boy looked startled, and edged carefully away, glancing nervously back over his shoulder.

"How do you hear someone lust?" I asked, fascinated.

He glanced down at me, looking mildly flustered.

"Oh! Well . . . it's only . . ."

He paused for a moment, then rubbed the bridge of his nose, which was beginning to redden in the sharp breeze.

"Have ye any idea what men in a prison do, Sassenach, having no women for a verra long time?"

"I could guess," I said, thinking that perhaps I didn't really want to hear, firsthand. He hadn't spoken to me before about his time in Ardsmuir.

"I imagine ye could," he said dryly. "And ye'd be right, too. There's the three choices; use each other, go a bit mad, or deal with the matter by yourself, aye?"

He turned to look out to sea, and bent his head slightly to look down at me, a slight smile visible on his lips. "D'ye think me mad, Sassenach?"

"Not most of the time," I replied honestly, turning round beside him. He laughed and shook his head ruefully.

"No, I dinna seem able to manage it. I now and then wished I *could* go mad"—he said thoughtfully "—it seemed a great deal easier than having always to think what to do next—but it doesna seem to come natural to me. Nor does buggery," he added, with a wry twist of his mouth.

"No, I shouldn't think so." Men who might in the ordinary way recoil in horror from the thought of using another man could still bring themselves to the act, out of desperate need. Not Jamie. Knowing what I did of his experiences at the hands of Jack Randall, I suspected that he very likely *would* have gone mad before seeking such resort himself.

He shrugged slightly, and stood silent, looking out to sea. Then he glanced down at his hands, spread before him, clutching the rail.

"I fought them—the soldiers who took me. I'd promised Jenny I wouldn't—she thought they'd hurt me—but when the time came, I couldna seem to help it." He shrugged again, and slowly opened and closed his right hand. It was his crippled hand, the third finger marked by a thick scar that ran the length of the first two joints, the fourth finger's second joint fused into stiffness, so that the finger stuck out awkwardly, even when he made a fist.

"I broke this again then, against a dragoon's jaw," he said ruefully, waggling the finger slightly. "That was the third time; the second was at Culloden. I didna mind it much. But they put me in chains, and I minded that a great deal."

"I'd think you would." It was hard—not difficult, but surprisingly painful—to think of that lithe, powerful body subdued by metal, bound and humbled.

"There's nay privacy in prison," he said. "I minded that more than the fetters, I think. Day and night, always in sight of someone, wi' no guard for your thoughts but to feign sleep. As for the other . . ." He snorted briefly, and shoved the loose hair back behind his ear. "Well, ye wait for the light to go, for the only modesty there is, is darkness."

The cells were not large, and the men lay close together for warmth in the night. With no modesty save darkness, and no privacy save silence, it was impossible to remain unaware of the accommodation each man made to his own needs.

"I was in irons for more than a year, Sassenach," he said. He lifted his arms, spread them eighteen inches apart, and stopped abruptly, as though reaching some invisible limit. "I could move that far—and nay more," he said, staring at his immobile hands. "And I couldna move my hands at all without the chain makin' a sound."

Torn between shame and need, he would wait in the dark, breathing in the stale and brutish scent of the surrounding men, listening to the murmurous breath of his companions, until the stealthy sounds nearby told him that the telltale clinking of his irons would be ignored.

"If there's one thing I ken verra well, Sassenach," he said quietly, with a brief glance at Fergus, "it's the sound of a man makin' love to a woman who's not there."

He shrugged and jerked his hands suddenly, spreading them wide on the rail, bursting his invisible chains. He looked down at me then with a half-smile, and I saw the dark memories at the back of his eyes, under the mocking humor.

I saw too the terrible need there, the desire strong enough to have endured loneliness and degradation, squalor and separation.

We stood quite still, looking at each other, oblivious of the deck traffic passing by. He knew better than any man how to hide his thoughts, but he wasn't hiding them from me.

The hunger in him went bone-deep, and my own bones seemed to dissolve in recognition of it. His hand was an inch from mine, resting on the wooden rail, long-fingered and powerful. . . . If I touched him, I thought suddenly, he would turn and take me, here, on the deck boards.

As though hearing my thought, he took my hand suddenly, pressing it tight against the hard muscle of his thigh.

"How many times have we lain together, since ye came back to me?" he whispered. "Once, twice, in the brothel. Three times in the heather. And then at Lallybroch, again in Paris." His fingers tapped lightly against my wrist, one after the other, in time with my pulse.

"Each time, I left your bed as hungry as ever I came to it. It takes no more to ready me now than the scent of your hair brushing past my face, or the feel of your thigh against mine when we sit to eat. And to see ye stand on deck, wi' the wind pressing your gown tight to your body . . ."

The corner of his mouth twitched slightly as he looked at me. I could see the pulse beat strong in the hollow of his throat, his skin flushed with wind and desire.

"There are moments, Sassenach, when for one copper penny, I'd have ye on the spot, back against the mast and your skirts about your waist, and devil take the bloody crew!"

My fingers convulsed against his palm, and he tightened his grasp, nodding pleasantly in response to the greeting of the gunner, coming past on his way toward the quarter-gallery.

The bell for the Captain's dinner sounded beneath my feet, a sweet metallic vibration that traveled up through the soles of my feet and melted the marrow of my bones. Fergus and Marsali left their play and went below, and the crew began preparations for the changing of the watch, but we stayed standing by the rail, fixed in each other's eyes, burning.

"The Captain's compliments, Mr. Fraser, and will you be joining him for dinner?" It was Maitland, the cabin boy, keeping a cautious distance as he relayed this message.

Jamie took a deep breath, and pulled his eyes away from mine.

"Aye, Mr. Maitland, we'll be there directly." He took another breath, settled his coat on his shoulders, and offered me his arm.

"Shall we go below, Sassenach?"

"Just a minute." I drew my hand out of my pocket, having found what I was looking for. I took his hand and pressed the object into his palm.

He stared down at the image of King George III in his hand, then up at me.

"On account," I said. "Let's go and eat."

The next day found us on deck again; though the air was still chilly, the cold was far preferable to the stuffiness of the cabins. We took our usual path, down one side of the ship and up the other, but then Jamie stopped, pausing to lean against the rail as he told me some anecdote about the printing business.

A few feet away, Mr. Willoughby sat cross-legged in the protection of the mainmast, a small cake of wet black ink by the toe of his slipper and a large sheet of white paper on the deck before him. The tip of his brush touched the paper lightly as a butterfly, leaving surprising strong shapes behind.

As I watched, fascinated, he began again at the top of the page. He worked rapidly, with a sureness of stroke that was like watching a dancer or a fencer, sure of his ground.

One of the deckhands passed dangerously close to the edge of the paper, almost—but not quite—placing a large dirty foot on the snowy white. A few moments later, another man did the same thing, though there was plenty of room to pass by. Then the first man came back, this time careless enough to kick over the small cake of black ink as he passed.

"Tck!" the seaman exclaimed in annoyance. He scuffed at the black splotch on the otherwise immaculate deck. "Filthy heathen! Look 'ere, wot he's done!"

The second man, returning from his brief errand, paused in interest. "On the clean deck? Captain Raines won't be pleased, will he?" He nodded at Mr. Willoughby, mock-jovial. "Best hurry and lick it up, little fella, before the Captain comes."

"Aye, that'll do; lick it up. Quick, now!" The first man moved a step nearer the seated figure, his shadow falling on the page like a blot. Mr. Willoughby's lips tightened just a shade, but he didn't look up. He completed the second column, righted the ink cake and dipped his brush without taking his eyes from the page, and began a third column, hand moving steadily.

"I *said*," began the first seaman, loudly, but stopped in surprise as a large white handkerchief fluttered down on the deck in front of him, covering the inkblot.

"Your pardon, gentlemen," said Jamie. "I seem to have dropped something." With a cordial nod to the seamen, he bent down and swept up the handkerchief, leaving nothing but a faint smear on the decking. The seamen glanced at each other, uncertain, then at Jamie. One man caught sight of the blue eyes over the blandly smiling mouth, and blanched visibly. He turned hastily away, tugging at his mate's arm.

"Norratall, sir," he mumbled. "C'mon, Joe, we're wanted aft."

Jamie didn't look either at the departing seamen or at Mr. Willoughby, but came toward me, tucking his handkerchief back in his sleeve.

"A verra pleasant day, is it not, Sassenach?" he said. He threw back his head, inhaling deeply. "Refreshing air, aye?"

"More so for some than for others, I expect," I said, amused. The air at this particular spot on deck smelled rather strongly of the alum-tanned hides in the hold below.

"That was kind of you," I said as he leaned back against the rail next to me. "Do you think I should offer Mr. Willoughby the use of my cabin to write?"

Jamie snorted briefly. "No. I've told him he can use my cabin, or the table in the mess between meals, but he'd rather be here—stubborn wee fool that he is."

"Well, I suppose the light's better," I said dubiously, eyeing the small hunched figure, crouched doggedly against the mast. As I watched, a gust of wind lifted the edge of the paper; Mr. Willoughby pinned it at once, holding it still with one hand while continuing his short, sure brushstrokes with the other. "It doesn't look comfortable, though."

"It's not." Jamie ran his fingers through his hair in mild exasperation. "He does it on purpose, to provoke the crew."

"Well, if that's what he's after, he's doing a good job," I observed. "What on earth for, though?"

Jamie leaned back against the rail beside me, and snorted once more.

"Aye, well, that's complicated. Ever met a Chinaman before, have ye?"

"A few, but I suspect they're a bit different in my time," I said dryly. "They tend not to wear pigtails and silk pajamas, for one thing, nor do they have obsessions about ladies' feet—or if they did, they didn't tell me about it," I added, to be fair.

Jamie laughed and moved a few inches closer, so that his hand on the rail brushed mine.

"Well, it's to do wi' the feet," he said. "Or that's the start of it, anyway. See, Josie, who's one of the whores at Madame Jeanne's, told Gordon about it, and of course he's told everyone now."

"What on earth is it about the feet?" I demanded, curiosity becoming overwhelming. "What does he *do* to them?"

Jamie coughed, and a faint flush rose in his cheeks. "Well, it's a bit . . ."

"You couldn't possibly tell me anything that would shock me," I assured him. "I *have* seen quite a lot of things in my life, you know—and a good many of them with you, come to that."

"I suppose ye have, at that," he said, grinning. "Aye, well, it's no so much what he does, but—well, in China, the highborn ladies have their feet bound."

"I've heard of that," I said, wondering what all the fuss was about. "It's supposed to make their feet small and graceful."

Jamie snorted again. "Graceful, aye? D'ye know how it's done?" And proceeded to tell me.

"They take a tiny lassie—nay more than a year old, aye?—and turn under the toes of her feet until they touch her heel, then tie bandages about the foot to hold it so."

"Ouch!" I said involuntarily.

"Yes, indeed," he said dryly. "Her nanny will take the bandages off now and then to clean the foot, but puts them back directly. After some time, her wee toes rot and fall off. And by the time she's grown, the poor lassie's little more at the end of her legs than a crumple of bones and skin, smaller than the size o' my fist." His closed fist knocked softly against the wood of the rail in illustration. "But she's considered verra beautiful, then," he ended. "Graceful, as ye say."

"That's perfectly disgusting!" I said. "But what has that got to do with—" I glanced at Mr. Willoughby, but he gave no sign of hearing us; the wind was blowing from him toward us, carrying our words out to sea.

"Say this was a lassie's foot, Sassenach," he said, stretching his right hand out flat before him. "Curl the toes under to touch the heel, and what have ye in the middle?" He curled his fingers loosely into a fist in illustration.

"What?" I said, bewildered. Jamie extended the middle finger of his left hand, and thrust it abruptly through the center of his fist in an unmistakably graphic gesture.

"A hole," he said succinctly.

"You're kidding! *That's* why they do it?"

His forehead furrowed slightly, then relaxed. "Oh, am I jesting? By no means, Sassenach. He says"—he nodded delicately at Mr. Willoughby— "that it's a most remarkable sensation. To a man."

"Why, that perverted little beast!"

Jamie laughed at my indignation.

"Aye, well, that's about what the crew thinks, too. Of course, he canna get quite the same effect wi' a European woman, but I gather he . . . tries, now and then."

I began to understand the general feeling of hostility toward the little Chinese. Even a short acquaintance with the crew of the *Artemis* had taught me that seamen on the whole tended to be gallant creatures, with a strong romantic streak where women were concerned—no doubt because they did without female company for a good part of the year.

"Hm," I said, with a glance of suspicion at Mr. Willoughby. "Well, that explains them, all right, but what about him?"

"That's what's a wee bit complicated." Jamie's mouth curled upward in a wry smile. "See, to Mr. Yi Tien Cho, late of the Heavenly Kingdom of China, *we're* the barbarians."

"Is that so?" I glanced up at Brodie Cooper, coming down the ratlines above, the filthy, calloused soles of his feet all that was visible from below. I rather thought both sides had a point. "Even you?"

"Oh, aye. I'm a filthy, bad-smelling *gwao-fe*—that means a foreign devil, ye ken—wi' the stink of a weasel—I think that's what *huang-shu-lang* means —and a face like a gargoyle," he finished cheerfully.

"He *told* you all that?" It seemed an odd recompense for saving some- one's life. Jamie glanced down at me, cocking one eyebrow.

"Have ye noticed, maybe, that verra small men will say *anything* to ye, when they've drink taken?" he asked. "I think brandy makes them forget their size; they think they're great hairy brutes, and swagger something fierce."

He nodded at Mr. Willoughby, industriously painting. "He's a bit more circumspect when he's sober, but it doesna change what he thinks. It fair galls him, aye? Especially knowing that if it wasna for me, someone would likely knock him on the head or put him through the window into the sea some quiet night."

He spoke with simple matter-of-factness, but I hadn't missed the sideways looks directed at us by the passing seamen, and had already realized just why Jamie was passing time in idle conversation by the rail with me. If anyone had been in doubt about Mr. Willoughby's being under Jamie's protection, they would be rapidly disabused of the notion.

"So you saved his life, gave him work, and keep him out of trouble, and he insults you and thinks you're an ignorant barbarian," I said dryly. "Sweet little fellow."

"Aye, well." The wind had shifted slightly, blowing a lock of Jamie's hair free across his face. He thumbed it back behind his ear and leaned farther toward me, our shoulders nearly touching. "Let him say what he likes; I'm the only one who understands him."

"Really?" I laid a hand over Jamie's where it rested on the rail.

"Well, maybe not to say understand him," he admitted. He looked down at the deck between his feet. "But I do remember," he said softly, "what it's like to have nothing but your pride—and a friend."

I remembered what Innes had said, and wondered whether it was the one- armed man who had been his friend in time of need. I knew what he meant; I had had Joe Abernathy, and knew what a difference it made.

"Yes, I had a friend at the hospital . . ." I began, but was interrupted by loud exclamations of disgust emanating from under my feet.

"Damn! Blazing Hades! That filth-eating son of a pig-fart!"

I looked down, startled, then realized, from the muffled Irish oaths proceeding from below, that we were standing directly over the galley. The shouting was loud enough to attract attention from the hands forward, and a small group of sailors gathered with us, watching in fascination as the cook's black-kerchiefed head poked out of the hatchway, glaring ferociously at the crowd.

"Burry-arsed swabs!" he shouted. "What're ye lookin' at? Two of yer idle barsteds tumble arse down here and toss this muck over the side! D'ye mean me to be climbin' ladders all day, and me with half a leg?" The head disappeared abruptly, and with a good-natured shrug, Picard motioned to one of the younger sailors to come along below.

Shortly there was a confusion of voices and a bumping of some large object down below, and a terrible smell assaulted my nostrils.

"Jesus Christ on a piece of toast!" I snatched a handkerchief from my pocket and clapped it to my nose; this wasn't the first smell I had encountered afloat, and I usually kept a linen square soaked in wintergreen in my pocket, as a precaution. "What's that?"

"By the smell of it, dead horse. A verra old horse, at that, and a long time dead." Jamie's long, thin nose looked a trifle pinched around the nostrils, and all around, sailors were gagging, holding their noses, and generally commenting unfavorably on the smell.

Maitland and Grosman, faces averted from their burden, but slightly green nonetheless, manhandled a large cask through the hatchway and onto the deck. The top had been split, and I caught a brief glimpse of a yellowish-white mass in the opening, glistening faintly in the sun. It seemed to be moving. Maggots, in profusion.

"Eew!" The exclamation was jerked from me involuntarily. The two sailors said nothing, their lips being pressed tightly together, but both of them looked as though they agreed with me. Together, they manhandled the cask to the rail and heaved it up and over.

Such of the crew as were not otherwise employed gathered at the rail to watch the cask bobbing in the wake, and be entertained by Murphy's outspokenly blasphemous opinion of the ship's chandler who had sold it to him. Manzetti, a small Italian seaman with a thick russet pigtail, was standing by the rail, loading a musket.

"Shark," he explained with a gleam of teeth beneath his mustache, seeing me watching him. "Very good to eat."

"Ar," said Sturgis approvingly.

Such of the crew as were not presently occupied gathered at the stern, watching. There were sharks, I knew; Maitland had pointed out to me two dark, flexible shapes hovering in the shadow of the hull the evening before, keeping pace with the ship with no apparent effort save a small and steady oscillation of sickled tails.

"There!" A shout went up from several throats as the cask jerked suddenly in the water. A pause, and Manzetti fixed his aim carefully in the vicinity of the floating cask. Another jerk, as though something had bumped it violently, and another.

The water was a muddy gray, but clear enough for me to catch a glimpse of something moving under the surface, fast. Another jerk, the cask heeled to one side, and suddenly the sharp edge of a fin creased the surface of the water, and a gray back showed briefly, tiny waves purling off it.

The musket discharged next to me with a small roar and a cloud of black-powder smoke that left my eyes stinging. There was a universal shout from the observers, and when the watering of my eyes subsided, I could see a small brownish stain spreading round the cask.

"Did he hit the shark, or the horsemeat?" I asked Jamie, in a low-voiced aside.

"The cask," he said with a smile. "Still, it's fine shooting."

Several more shots went wild, while the cask began to dance an agitated jig, the frenzied sharks striking it repeatedly. Bits of white and brown flew from the broken cask, and a large circle of grease, rotten blood, and debris spread round the shark's feast. As though by magic, seabirds began to appear, one and two at a time, diving for tidbits.

"No good," said Manzetti at last, lowering the musket and wiping his face with his sleeve. "Too far." He was sweating and stained from neck to hairline with black powder; the wiping left a streak of white across his eyes, like a raccoon's mask.

"I could relish a slab of shark," said the Captain's voice near my ear. I turned to see him peering thoughtfully over the rail at the scene of carnage. "Perhaps we might lower a boat, Mr. Picard."

The bosun turned with an obliging roar, and the *Artemis* hauled her wind, coming round in a small circle to draw near the remains of the floating cask. A small boat was launched, containing Manzetti, with musket, and three seamen armed with gaffs and rope.

By the time they reached the spot, there was nothing left of the cask but a few shattered bits of wood. There was still plenty of activity, though; the water roiled with the sharks' thrashing beneath the surface, and the scene was nearly obscured by a raucous cloud of seabirds. As I watched, I saw a pointed snout rise suddenly from the water, mouth open, seize one of the birds and disappear beneath the waves, all in the flick of an eyelash.

"Did you see that?" I said, awed. I was aware, in a general way, that sharks were well-equipped with teeth, but this practical demonstration was more striking than any number of *National Geographic* photographs.

"Why, Grandmother dear, what big teeth ye have!" said Jamie, sounding suitably impressed.

"Oh, they do indeed," said a genial voice nearby. I glanced aside to find Murphy grinning at my elbow, broad face shining with a savage glee. "Little good it will do the buggers, with a ball blown clean through their fucking brains!" He pounded a hamlike fist on the rail, and shouted, "Get me one of them jagged buggers, Manzetti! There's a bottle o' cookin' brandy waitin' if ye do!"

"Is it a personal matter to ye, Mr. Murphy?" Jamie asked politely. "Or professional concern?"

"Both, Mr. Fraser, both," the cook replied, watching the hunt with a fierce attention. He kicked his wooden leg against the side, with a hollow clunk. "They've had a taste o' me," he said with grim relish, "but I've tasted a good many more o' them!"

The boat was barely visible through the flapping screen of birds, and their screams made it hard to hear anything other than Murphy's war cries.

"Shark steak with mustard!" Murphy was bellowing, eyes mere slits in an ecstasy of revenge. "Stewed liver wi' piccalilli! I'll make soup o' yer fins, and jelly yer eyeballs in sherry wine, ye wicked barsted!"

I saw Manzetti, kneeling in the bows, take aim with his musket, and the puff of black smoke as he fired. And then I saw Mr. Willoughby.

I hadn't seen him jump from the rail; no one had, with all eyes fixed on the hunt. But there he was, some distance away from the melee surrounding the boat, his shaven head glistening like a fishing float as he wrestled in the water with an enormous bird, its wings churning the water like an eggbeater.

Alerted by my cry, Jamie tore his eyes from the hunt, goggled for an instant, and before I could move or speak, was perched on the rail himself.

My shout of horror coincided with a surprised roar from Murphy, but Jamie was gone, too, lancing into the water near the Chinaman with barely a splash.

There were shouts and cries from the deck—and a shrill screech from Marsali—as everyone realized what had happened. Jamie's wet red head emerged next to Mr. Willoughby, and in seconds, he had an arm tight about the Chinaman's throat. Mr. Willoughby clung tightly to the bird, and I wasn't sure, just for the moment, whether Jamie intended rescue or throttling, but then he kicked strongly, and began to tow the struggling mass of bird and man back toward the ship.

Triumphant shouts from the boat, and a spreading circle of deep red in the water. There was a tremendous thrashing as one shark was gaffed and hauled behind the small boat by a rope about its tail. Then everything was confusion, as the men in the boat noticed what else was going on in the water nearby.

Lines were thrown over one side and then the other, and crewmen rushed back and forth in high excitement, undecided whether to help with rescue or shark, but at last Jamie and his burdens were hauled in to starboard, and dumped dripping on the deck, while the captured shark—several large bites taken out of its body by its hungry companions—was drawn in, still feebly snapping, to port.

"Je . . . sus . . . Christ," Jamie said, chest heaving. He lay flat on the deck, gasping like a landed fish.

"Are you all right?" I knelt beside him, and wiped the water off his face with the hem of my skirt. He gave me a lopsided smile and nodded, still gasping.

"Jesus," he said at last, sitting up. He shook his head and sneezed. "I thought I was eaten, sure. Those fools in the boat started toward us, and there were sharks all round them, under the water, bitin' at the gaffed one." He tenderly massaged his calves. "It's nay doubt oversensitive of me, Sassenach, but I've always dreaded the thought of losing a leg. It seems almost worse than bein' killed outright."

"I'd as soon you didn't do either," I said dryly. He was beginning to shiver; I pulled off my shawl and wrapped it around his shoulders, then looked about for Mr. Willoughby.

The little Chinese, still clinging stubbornly to his prize, a young pelican nearly as big as he was, ignored both Jamie and the considerable abuse flung in his direction. He squelched below, dripping, protected from physical castigation by the clacking bill of his captive, which discouraged anyone from getting too close to him.

A nasty chunking sound and a crow of triumph from the other side of the deck announced Murphy's use of an ax to dispatch his erstwhile nemesis. The seamen clustered round the corpse, knives drawn, to get pieces of the skin. Further enthusiastic chopping, and Murphy came strolling past, beaming, a choice section of tail under his arm, the huge yellow liver hanging from one hand in a bag of netting, and the bloody ax slung over his shoulder.

"Not drowned, are ye?" he said, ruffling Jamie's damp hair with his spare hand. "I can't see why ye'd bother wi' the little bugger, myself, but I'll say 'twas bravely done. I'll brew ye up a fine broth from the tail, to keep off the chill," he promised, and stumped off, planning menus aloud.

"Why did he do it?" I asked. "Mr. Willoughby, I mean."

Jamie shook his head and blew his nose on his shirttail.

"Damned if I know. He wanted the bird, I expect, but I couldna say why. To eat, maybe?"

Murphy overheard this and swung round at the head of the galley ladder, frowning.

"Ye can't eat pelicans," he said, shaking his head in disapproval. "Fishytasting, no matter how ye cook 'em. And God knows what one's doing out here anyway; they're shorebirds, pelicans. Blown out by a storm I suppose. Awkward buggers." His bald head disappeared into his realm, murmuring happily of dried parsley and cayenne.

Jamie laughed and stood up.

"Aye, well, perhaps it's only he wants the feathers to make quills of. Come along below, Sassenach. Ye can help me dry my back."

He had spoken jokingly, but as soon as the words were out of his mouth, his face went blank. He glanced quickly to port, where the crew was arguing and jostling over the remains of the shark, while Fergus and Marsali cautiously examined the severed head, lying gape-jawed on the deck. Then his eyes met mine, with a perfect understanding.

Thirty seconds later, we were below in his cabin. Cold drops from his wet hair rained over my shoulders and slid down my bosom, but his mouth was hot and urgent. The hard curves of his back glowed warm through the soaked fabric of the shirt that stuck to them.

"Ifrinn!" he said breathlessly, breaking loose long enough to yank at his breeches. "Christ, they're stuck to me! I canna get them off!"

Snorting with laughter, he jerked at the laces, but the water had soaked them into a hopeless knot.

"A knife!" I said. "Where's a knife?" Snorting myself at the sight of him, struggling frantically to get his drenched shirttail out of his breeches, I began to rummage through the drawers of the desk, tossing out bits of paper, bottle of ink, a snuffbox—everything but a knife. The closest thing was an ivory letter opener, made in the shape of a hand with a pointing finger.

I seized upon this and grasped him by the waistband, trying to saw at the tangled laces.

He yelped in alarm and backed away.

"Christ, be careful wi' that, Sassenach! It's no going to do ye any good to get my breeks off, and ye geld me in the process!"

Half-crazed with lust as we were, that seemed funny enough to double us both up laughing.

"Here!" Rummaging in the chaos of his berth, he snatched up his dirk and brandished it triumphantly. An instant later, the laces were severed and the sopping breeks lay puddled on the floor.

He seized me, picked me up bodily, and laid me on the desk, heedless of crumpled papers and scattered quills. Tossing my skirts up past my waist, he grabbed my hips and half-lay on me, his hard thighs forcing my legs apart.

It was like grasping a salamander; a blaze of heat in a chilly shroud. I gasped as the tail of his sopping shirt touched my bare belly, then gasped again as I heard footsteps in the passage.

"Stop!" I hissed in his ear. "Someone's coming!"

"Too late," he said, with breathless certainty. "I must have ye, or die."

He took me, with one quick, ruthless thrust, and I bit his shoulder hard, tasting salt and wet linen, but he made no sound. Two strokes, three, and I had my legs locked tight around his buttocks, my cry muffled in his shirt, not caring either who else might be coming.

He had me, quickly and thoroughly, and thrust himself home, and home, and home again, with a deep sound of triumph in his throat, shuddering and shaking in my arms.

Two minutes later, the cabin door swung open. Innes looked slowly round the wreckage of the room. His soft brown gaze traveled from the ravaged desk to me, sitting damp and disheveled, but respectably clothed, upon the berth, and rested at last on Jamie, who sat collapsed on a stool, still clad in his wet shirt, chest heaving and the deep red color fading slowly from his face.

Innes's nostrils flared delicately, but he said nothing. He walked into the cabin, nodding at me, and bent to reach under Fergus's berth, whence he pulled out a bottle of brandywine.

"For the Chinee," he said to me. "So as he mightn't take a chill." He turned toward the door and paused, squinting thoughtfully at Jamie.

"Ye might should have Mr. Murphy make ye some broth on that same account, Mac Dubh. They do say as 'tis dangerous to get chilled after hard work, aye? Ye dinna want to take the ague." There was a faint twinkle in the mournful brown depths.

Jamie brushed back the salty tangle of his hair, a slow smile spreading across his face.

"Aye, well, and if it should come to that, Innes, at least I shall die a happy man."

We found out the next day what Mr. Willoughby wanted the pelican for. I found him on the afterdeck, the bird perched on a sail-chest beside him, its wings bound tight to its body by means of strips of cloth. It glared at me with round yellow eyes, and clacked its bill in warning.

Mr. Willoughby was pulling in a line, on the end of which was a small, wriggling purple squid. Detaching this, he held it up in front of the pelican and said something in Chinese. The bird regarded him with deep suspicion, but didn't move. Quickly, he seized the upper bill in his hand, pulled it up, and tossed the squid into the bird's pouch. The pelican, looking surprised, gulped convulsively and swallowed it.

"*Hao-liao*," Mr. Willoughby said approvingly, stroking the bird's head. He saw me watching, and beckoned me to come closer. Keeping a cautious eye on the wicked bill, I did so.

"Ping An," he said, indicating the pelican. "Peaceful one." The bird erected a small crest of white feathers, for all the world as though it were pricking up its ears at its name, and I laughed.

"Really? What are you going to do with him?"

"I teach him hunt for me," the little Chinese said matter-of-factly. "You watch."

I did. After several more squid and a couple of small fish had been caught and fed to the pelican, Mr. Willoughby removed another strip of soft cloth from the recesses of his costume, and wrapped this snugly round the bird's neck.

"Not want choke," he explained. "Not swallow fish." He then tied a length of light line tightly to this collar, motioned to me to stand back, and with a swift jerk, released the bindings that held the bird's wings.

Surprised at the sudden freedom, the pelican waddled back and forth on the locker, flapped its huge bony wings once or twice, and then shot into the sky in an explosion of feathers.

A pelican on the ground is a comical thing, all awkward angles, splayed feet, and gawky bill. A soaring pelican, circling over water, is a thing of wonder, graceful and primitive, startling as a pterodactyl among the sleeker forms of gulls and petrels.

Ping An, the peaceful one, soared to the limit of his line, struggled to go higher, then, as though resigned, began to circle. Mr. Willoughby, eyes squinted nearly shut against the sun, spun slowly round and round on the deck below, playing the pelican like a kite. All the hands in the rigging and on deck nearby stopped what they were doing to watch in fascination.

Sudden as a bolt from a crossbow, the pelican folded its wings and dived, cleaving the water with scarcely a splash. As it popped to the surface, looking mildly surprised, Mr. Willoughby began to tow it in. Aboard once more, the pelican was persuaded with some difficulty to give up its catch, but at last suffered its captor to reach cautiously into the leathery subgular pouch and extract a fine, fat sea bream.

Mr. Willoughby smiled pleasantly at a gawking Picard, took out a small knife, and slit the still-living fish down the back. Pinioning the bird in one wiry arm, he loosened the collar with his other hand, and offered it a flapping piece of bream, which Ping An eagerly snatched from his fingers and gulped.

"His," Mr. Willoughby explained, wiping blood and scales carelessly on the leg of his trousers. "Mine," nodding toward the half-fish still sitting on the locker, now motionless.

Within a week, the pelican was entirely tame, able to fly free, collared, but without the tethering line, returning to his master to regurgitate a pouchful of shining fish at his feet. When not fishing, Ping An either took up a position on the crosstrees, much to the displeasure of the crewmen responsible for swabbing the deck beneath, or followed Mr. Willoughby around the deck, waddling absurdly from side to side, eight-foot wings half-spread for balance.

The crew, both impressed by the fishing and wary of Ping An's great snapping bill, steered clear of Mr. Willoughby, who made his words each day beside the mast, weather permitting, secure under the benign yellow eye of his new friend.

I paused one day to watch Mr. Willoughby at his work, staying out of sight behind the shelter of the mast. He sat for a moment, a look of quiet satisfaction on his face, contemplating the finished page. I couldn't read the characters, of course, but the shape of the whole thing was somehow very pleasing to look at.

Then he glanced quickly around, as though checking to see that no one was coming, picked up the brush, and with great care, added a final character, in the upper left corner of the page. Without asking, I knew it was his signature.

He sighed then, and lifted his face to look out over the rail. Not inscrutable, by any means, his expression was filled with a dreaming delight, and I knew that whatever he saw, it was neither the ship, nor the heaving ocean beyond.

At last, he sighed again and shook his head, as though to himself. He laid hands on the paper, and quickly, gently, folded it, once, and twice, and again. Then rising to his feet, he went to the rail, extended his hands over the water, and let the folded white shape fall.

It tumbled toward the water. Then the wind caught it and whirled it upward, a bit of white receding in the distance, looking much like the gulls and terns who squawked behind the ship in search of scraps.

Mr. Willoughby didn't stay to watch it, but turned away from the rail and went below, the dream still stamped on his small, round face.

45

Mr. Willoughby's Tale

As we passed the center of the Atlantic gyre and headed south, the days and evenings became warm, and the off-duty crew began to congregate on the forecastle for a time after supper, to sing songs, dance to Brodie Cooper's fiddle, or listen to stories. With the same instinct that makes children camping in the wood tell ghost stories, the men seemed particularly fond of horrible tales of shipwreck and the perils of the sea.

As we passed farther south, and out the realm of Kraken and sea serpent, the mood for monsters passed, and the men began instead to tell stories of their homes.

It was after most of these had been exhausted that Maitland, the cabin boy, turned to Mr. Willoughby, crouched as usual against the foot of the mast, with his cup cradled to his chest.

"How was it that you came from China, Willoughby?" Maitland asked curiously. "I've not seen more than a handful of Chinese sailors, though folk do say as there's a great many people in China. Is it such a fine place that the inhabitants don't care to take leave of it, perhaps?"

At first demurring, the little Chinese seemed mildly flattered at the interest provoked by this question. With a bit more urging, he consented to tell of his departure from his homeland—requiring only that Jamie should translate for him, his own English being inadequate to the task. Jamie readily agreeing, he sat down beside Mr. Willoughby, and cocked his head to listen.

"I was a Mandarin," Mr. Willoughby began, in Jamie's voice, "a Mandarin of letters, one gifted in composition. I wore a silk gown, embroidered in very many colors, and over this, the scholar's blue silk gown, with the badge of my office embroidered upon breast and back—the figure of a *feng-huang* —a bird of fire."

"I think he means a phoenix," Jamie added, turning to me for a moment before directing his attention back to the patiently waiting Mr. Willoughby, who began speaking again at once.

"I was born in Pekin, the Imperial City of the Son of Heaven—"

"That is how they call their emperor," Fergus whispered to me. "Such presumption, to equate their king with the Lord Jesus!"

"Shh," hissed several people, turning indignant faces toward Fergus. He made a rude gesture at Maxwell Gordon, but fell silent, turning back to the small figure sitting crouched against the mast.

"I was found early to have some skill in composition, and while I was not at first adept in the use of brush and ink, I learned at last with great effort to make the representations of my brush resemble the ideas that danced like cranes within my mind. And so I came to the notice of Wu-Xien, a Mandarin of the Imperial Household, who took me to live with him, and oversaw my training.

"I rose rapidly in merit and eminence, so that before my twenty-sixth birthday, I had attained a globe of red coral upon my hat. And then came an evil wind, that blew the seeds of misfortune into my garden. It may be that I was cursed by an enemy, or perhaps that in my arrogance I had omitted to make proper sacrifice—for surely I was not lacking in reverence to my ancestors, being careful always to visit my family's tomb each year, and to have joss sticks always burning in the Hall of Ancestors—"

"If his compositions were always so long-winded, no doubt the Son of Heaven lost patience and tossed him in the river," Fergus muttered cynically.

"—but whatever the cause," Jamie's voice continued, "my poetry came before the eyes of Wan-Mei, the Emperor's Second Wife. Second Wife was a woman of great power, having borne no less than four sons, and when she asked that I might become part of her own household, the request was granted at once."

"And what was wrong wi' that?" demanded Gordon, leaning forward in interest. "A chance to get on in the world, surely?"

Mr. Willoughby evidently understood the question, for he nodded in Gordon's direction as he continued, and Jamie's voice took up the story.

"Oh, the honor was inestimable; I should have had a large house of my own within the walls of the palace, and a guard of soldiers to escort my palanquin, with a triple umbrella borne before me in symbol of my office, and perhaps even a peacock feather for my hat. My name would have been inscribed in letters of gold in the Book of Merit."

The little Chinaman paused, scratching at his scalp. The hair had begun to sprout from the shaved part, making him look rather like a tennis ball.

"However, there is a condition of service within the Imperial Household; all the servants of the royal wives must be eunuchs."

A gasp of horror greeted this, followed by a babble of agitated comment, in which the remarks "Bloody heathen!" and "Yellow bastards!" were heard to predominate.

"What is a eunuch?" Marsali asked, looking bewildered.

"Nothing you need ever concern yourself with, *chèrie*," Fergus assured her, slipping an arm about her shoulders. "So you ran, *mon ami?*" he addressed Mr. Willoughby in tones of deepest sympathy. "I should do the same, without doubt!"

A deep murmur of heartfelt approbation reinforced this sentiment. Mr. Willoughby seemed somewhat heartened by such evident approval; he bobbed his head once or twice at his listeners before resuming his story.

"It was most dishonorable of me to refuse the Emperor's gift. And yet—it is a grievous weakness—I had fallen in love with a woman."

There was a sympathetic sigh at this, most sailors being wildly romantic souls, but Mr. Willoughby stopped, jerking at Jamie's sleeve and saying something to him.

"Oh, I'm wrong," Jamie corrected himself. "He says it was not '*a* woman'—just 'Woman'—all women, or the idea of women in general, he means. That's it?" he asked, looking down at Mr. Willoughby.

The Chinaman nodded, satisfied, and sat back. The moon was full up by now, three-quarters full, and bright enough to show the little Mandarin's face as he talked.

"Yes," he said, through Jamie, "I thought much of women; their grace and beauty, blooming like lotus flowers, floating like milkweed on the wind. And the myriad sounds of them, sometimes like the chatter of ricebirds, or the song of nightingales; sometimes the cawing of crows," he added with a smile that creased his eyes to slits and brought his hearers to laughter, "but even then I loved them.

"I wrote all my poems to Woman—sometimes they were addressed to one lady or another, but most often to Woman alone. To the taste of breasts like apricots, the warm scent of a woman's navel when she wakens in the winter, the warmth of a mound that fills your hand like a peach, split with ripeness."

Fergus, scandalized, put his hands over Marsali's ears, but the rest of his hearers were most receptive.

"No wonder the wee fellow was an esteemed poet," Raeburn said with approval. "It's verra heathen, but I like it!"

"Worth a red knob on your hat, anyday," Maitland agreed.

"Almost worth learning a bit of Chinee for," the master's mate chimed in, eyeing Mr. Willoughby with fresh interest. "Does he have a lot of those poems?"

Jamie waved the audience—by now augmented by most of the off-duty hands—to silence and said, "Go on, then," to Mr. Willoughby.

"I fled on the Night of Lanterns," the Chinaman said. "A great festival, and one when people would be thronging the streets; there would be no danger of being noticed by the watchmen. Just after dark, as the processions were assembling throughout the city, I put on the garments of a traveler—"

"That's like a pilgrim," Jamie interjected, "they go to visit their ancestors' tombs far away, and wear white clothes—that's for mourning, ye ken?"

"—and I left my house. I made my way through the crowds without difficulty, carrying a small anonymous lantern I had bought—one without my name and place of residence painted on it. The watchmen were hammering upon their bamboo drums, the servants of the great households beating gongs, and from the roof of the palace, fireworks were being set off in great profusion."

The small round face was marked by nostalgia, as he remembered.

"It was in a way a most appropriate farewell for a poet," he said. "Fleeing nameless, to the sound of great applause. As I passed the soldiers' garrison at the city gate, I looked back, to see the many roofs of the Palace outlined by bursting flowers of red and gold. It looked like a magic garden—and a forbidden one, for me."

Yi Tien Cho had made his way without incident through the night, but had nearly been caught the next day.

"I had forgotten my fingernails," he said. He spread out a hand, small and short-fingered, the nails bitten to the quicks. "For a Mandarin has long nails, as symbol that he is not obliged to work with his hands, and my own were the length of one of my finger joints."

A servant at the house where he had stopped for refreshment next day saw them, and ran to tell the guard. Yi Tien Cho ran, too, and succeeded at last in eluding his pursuers by sliding into a wet ditch and lying hidden in the bushes.

"While lying there, I destroyed my nails, of course," he said. He waggled the little finger of his right hand. "I was obliged to tear that nail out, for it had a golden *da zi* inlaid in it, which I could not dislodge."

He had stolen a peasant's clothes from a bush where they had been hung to dry, leaving the torn-out nail with its golden character in exchange, and made his way slowly across country toward the coast. At first he paid for his food with the small store of money he had brought away, but outside Lulong he met with a band of robbers, who took his money but left him his life.

"And after that," he said simply, "I stole food when I could, and starved when I could not. And at last the wind of fortune changed a little, and I met with a group of traveling apothecaries, on their way to the physicians' fair near the coast. In return for my skill at drawing banners for their booth and composing labels extolling the virtues of their medicines, they carried me along with them."

Once reaching the coast, he had made his way to the waterfront, and tried there to pass himself off as a seaman, but failed utterly, as his fingers, so skillful with brush and ink, knew nothing of the art of knots and lines. There were several foreign ships in port; he had chosen the one whose sailors looked the most barbarous as being likely to carry him farthest away, and seizing his chance, had slipped past the deck guard and into the hold of the *Serafina,* bound for Edinburgh.

"You had always meant to leave the country altogether?" Fergus asked, interested. "It seems a desperate choice."

"Emperor's reach very long," Mr. Willoughby said softly in English, not waiting for translation. "I am exile, or I am dead."

His listeners gave a collective sigh at the awesome contemplation of such bloodthirsty power, and there was a moment of silence, with only the whine of the rigging overhead, while Mr. Willoughby picked up his neglected cup and drained the last drops of his grog.

He set it down, licking his lips, and laid his hand once more on Jamie's arm.

"It is strange," Mr. Willoughby said, and the air of reflection in his voice was echoed exactly by Jamie's, "but it was my joy of women that Second Wife saw and loved in my words. Yet by desiring to possess me—and my poems—she would have forever destroyed what she admired."

Mr. Willoughby uttered a small chuckle, whose irony was unmistakable.

"Nor is that the end of the contradiction my life has become. Because I could not bring myself to surrender my manhood, I have lost all else—honor, livelihood, country. By that, I mean not only the land itself, with the slopes of noble fir trees where I spent my summers in Tartary, and the great plains of the south, the flowing of rivers filled with fish, but also the loss of myself. My parents are dishonored, the tombs of my ancestors fall into ruin, and no joss burns before their images.

"All order, all beauty is lost. I am come to a place where the golden words of my poems are taken for the clucking of hens, and my brushstrokes for their scratchings. I am taken as less than the meanest beggar, who swallows serpents for the entertainment of the crowds, allowing passersby to draw the serpent from my mouth by its tail for the tiny payment that will let me live another day."

Mr. Willoughby glared round at his hearers, making his parallel evident.

"I am come to a country of women coarse and rank as bears." The Chinaman's voice rose passionately, though Jamie kept to an even tone, reciting the words, but stripping them of feeling. "They are creatures of no grace, no learning, ignorant, bad-smelling, their bodies gross with sprouting hair, like dogs! And these—these! disdain me as a yellow worm, so that even the lowest whores will not lie with me.

"For the love of Woman, I am come to a place where no woman is worthy of love!" At this point, seeing the dark looks on the seamen's faces, Jamie ceased translating, and instead tried to calm the Chinaman, laying a big hand on the blue-silk shoulder.

"Aye, man, I quite see. And I'm sure there's no a man present would have done otherwise, given the choice. Is that not so, lads?" he asked, glancing over his shoulder with eyebrows raised significantly.

His moral force was sufficient to extort a grudging murmur of agreement, but the crowd's sympathy with the tale of Mr. Willoughby's travails had been quite dissipated by his insulting conclusion. Pointed remarks were made about licentious, ungrateful heathen, and a great many extravagantly admiring compliments paid to Marsali and me, as the men dispersed aft.

Fergus and Marsali left then, too, Fergus pausing en route to inform Mr. Willoughby that any further remarks about European women would cause him, Fergus, to be obliged to wrap his, Willoughby's, queue about his neck and strangle him with it.

Mr. Willoughby ignored remarks and threats alike, merely staring straight ahead, his black eyes shining with memory and grog. Jamie at last stood up, too, and held out a hand to help me down from my cask.

It was as we were turning to leave that the Chinaman reached down between his legs. Completely without lewdness, he cupped his testicles, so that the rounded mass pressed against the silk. He rolled them slowly in the palm of his hand, staring at the bulge in deep meditation.

"Sometime," he said, as though to himself, "I think not worth it."

46

We Meet a Porpoise

I had been conscious for some time that Marsali was trying to get up the nerve to speak to me. I had thought she would, sooner or later; whatever her feelings toward me, I was the only other woman aboard. I did my best to help, smiling kindly and saying "Good morning," but the first move would have to be hers.

She made it, finally, in the middle of the Atlantic Ocean, a month after we had left Scotland.

I was writing in our shared cabin, making surgical notes on a minor amputation—two smashed toes on one of the foredeck hands. I had just completed a drawing of the surgical site, when a shadow darkened the doorway of the cabin, and I looked up to see Marsali standing there, chin thrust out pugnaciously.

"I need to know something," she said firmly. "I dinna like ye, and I reckon ye ken that, but Da says you're a wisewoman, and I think you're maybe an honest woman, even if ye are a whore, so you'll maybe tell me."

There were any number of possible responses to this remarkable statement, but I refrained from making any of them.

"Maybe I will," I said, putting down the pen. "What is it you need to know?"

Seeing that I wasn't angry, she slid into the cabin and sat down on the stool, the only available spot.

"Weel, it's to do wi' bairns," she explained. "And how ye get them."

I raised one eyebrow. "Your mother didn't tell you where babies come from?"

She snorted impatiently, her small blond brows knotted in fierce scorn. "O' course I ken where they come from! Any fool knows that much. Ye let a man put his prick between your legs, and there's the devil to pay, nine months later. What I want to know is how ye *don't* get them."

"I see." I regarded her with considerable interest. "You don't want a child? Er . . . once you're properly married, I mean? Most young women seem to."

"Well," she said slowly, twisting a handful of her dress. "I think I maybe would like a babe sometime. For itself, I mean. If it maybe had dark hair, like

Fergus." A hint of dreaminess flitted across her face, but then her expression hardened once more.

"But I can't," she said.

"Why not?"

She pushed out her lips, thinking, then pulled them in again. "Well, because of Fergus. We havena lain together yet. We havena been able to do more than kiss each other now and again behind the hatch covers—thanks to Da and his bloody-minded notions," she added bitterly.

"Amen," I said, with some wryness.

"Eh?"

"Never mind." I waved a hand, dismissing it. "What has that got to do with not wanting babies?"

"I want to like it," she said matter-of-factly. "When we get to the prick part."

I bit the inside of my lower lip.

"I . . . er . . . imagine that has something to do with Fergus, but I'm afraid I don't quite see what it has to do with babies."

Marsali eyed me warily. Without hostility for once, more as though she were estimating me in some fashion.

"Fergus likes ye," she said.

"I'm fond of him, too," I answered cautiously, not sure where the conversation was heading. "I've known him for quite a long time, ever since he was a boy."

She relaxed suddenly, some of the tension going out of the slender shoulders.

"Oh. You'll know about it, then—where he was born?"

Suddenly I understood her wariness.

"The brothel in Paris? Yes, I know about that. He told you, then?"

She nodded. "Aye, he did. A long time ago, last Hogmanay." Well, I supposed a year was a long time to a fifteen-year-old.

"That's when I told him I loved him," she went on. Her eyes were fixed on her skirt, and a faint tinge of pink showed in her cheeks. "And he said he loved me, too, but my mother wasna going to ever agree to the match. And I said why not, there was nothing so awful about bein' French, not everybody could be Scots, and I didna think his hand mattered a bit either—after all, there was Mr. Murray wi' his wooden leg, and Mother liked *him* well enough—but then he said, no, it was none of those things, and then he told me—about Paris, I mean, and being born in a brothel and being a pickpocket until he met Da."

She raised her eyes, a look of incredulity in the light blue depths. "I think he thought I'd *mind*," she said, wonderingly. "He tried to go away, and said he wouldna see me anymore. Well—" she shrugged, tossing her fair hair out of the way, "I soon took care of that." She looked at me straight on, then, hands clasped in her lap.

"It's just I didna want to mention it, in case ye didn't know already. But since ye do . . . well, it's no Fergus I'm worried about. He says he knows what to do, and I'll like it fine, once we're past the first time or two. But that's not what my Mam told me."

"What *did* she tell you?" I asked, fascinated.

A small line showed between the light brows. "Well . . ." Marsali said slowly, "it wasna so much she said it—though she did say, when I told her about Fergus and me, that he'd do terrible things to me because of living wi' whores and having one for a mother—it was more she . . . she acted like it."

Her face was a rosy pink now, and she kept her eyes in her lap, where her fingers twisted themselves in the folds of her skirt. The wind seemed to be picking up; small strands of blond hair rose gently from her head, wafted by the breeze from the window.

"When I started to bleed the first time, she told me what to do, and about how it was part o' the curse of Eve, and I must just put up wi' it. And I said, what was the curse of Eve? And she read me from the Bible all about how St. Paul said women were terrible, filthy sinners because of what Eve did, but they could still be saved by suffering and bearing children."

"I never did think a lot of St. Paul," I observed, and she looked up, startled.

"But he's in the Bible!" she said, shocked.

"So are a lot of other things," I said dryly. "Heard that story about Gideon and his daughter, have you? Or the fellow who sent his lady out to be raped to death by a crowd of ruffians, so they wouldn't get *him?* God's chosen men, just like Paul. But go on, do."

She gaped at me for a minute, but then closed her mouth and nodded, a little stunned.

"Aye, well. Mother said as how it meant I was nearly old enough to be wed, and when I did marry, I must be sure to remember it was a woman's duty to do as her husband wanted, whether she liked it or no. And she looked so sad when she told me that . . . I thought whatever a woman's duty was, it must be awful, and from what St. Paul said about suffering and bearing children . . ."

She stopped and sighed. I sat quietly, waiting. When she resumed, it was haltingly, as though she had trouble choosing her words.

"I canna remember my father. I was only three when the English took him away. But I was old enough when my mother wed—wed Jamie—to see how it was between them." She bit her lip; she wasn't used to calling Jamie by his name.

"Da—Jamie, I mean—he's kind, I think; he always was to Joan and me.

But I'd see, when he'd lay his hand on my mother's waist and try to draw her close—she'd shrink away from him." She gnawed her lip some more, then continued.

"I could see she was afraid; she didna like him to touch her. But I couldna see that he ever did anything to be afraid *of,* not where we could see—so I thought it must be something he did when they were in their bed, alone. Joan and I used to wonder what it could be; Mam never had marks on her face or her arms, and she didna limp when she walked—not like Magdalen Wallace, whose husband always beats her when he's drunk on market day— so we didna think Da hit her."

Marsali licked her lips, dried by the warm salt air, and I pushed the jug of water toward her. She nodded in thanks and poured a cupful.

"So I thought," she said, eyes fixed on the stream of water, "that it must be because Mam had had children—had us—and she knew it would be terrible again and so she didna want to go to bed with—with Jamie for fear of it."

She took a drink, then set down the cup and looked at me directly, firming her chin in challenge.

"I saw ye with my Da," she said. "Just that minute, before he saw me. I— I think ye liked what he was doing to you in the bed."

I opened my mouth, and closed it again.

"Well . . . yes," I said, a little weakly. "I did."

She grunted in satisfaction. "Mmphm. And ye like it when he touches ye; I've seen. Well, then. Ye havena got any children. And I'd heard there are ways not to have them, only nobody seems to know just how, but you must, bein' a wisewoman and all."

She tilted her head to one side, studying me.

"I'd like a babe," she admitted, "but if it's got to be a babe or liking Fergus, then it's Fergus. So it won't be a babe—if you'll tell me how."

I brushed the curls back behind my ear, wondering where on earth to start.

"Well," I said, drawing a deep breath, "to begin with, I have had children."

Her eyes sprang wide and round at this.

"Ye do? Does Da—does Jamie know?"

"Well, of course he does," I replied testily. "They were his."

"I never heard Da had any bairns at all." The pale eyes narrowed with suspicion.

"I don't imagine he thought it was any of your business," I said, perhaps a trifle more sharply than necessary. "And it's not, either," I added, but she just raised her brows and went on looking suspicious.

"The first baby died," I said, capitulating. "In France. She's buried there. My—our second daughter is grown now; she was born after Culloden."

"So he's never seen her? The grown one?" Marsali spoke slowly, frowning.

I shook my head, unable to speak for a moment. There seemed to be something stuck in my throat, and I reached for the water. Marsali pushed the jug absently in my direction, leaning against the swing of the ship.

"That's verra sad," she said softly, to herself. Then she glanced up at me, frowning once more in concentration as she tried to work it all out.

"So ye've had children, and it didna make a difference to you? Mmphm. But it's been a long while, then—did ye have other men whilst ye were away in France?" Her lower lip came up over the upper one, making her look very much like a small and stubborn bulldog.

"That," I said firmly, putting the cup down, "is definitely none of your business. As to whether childbirth makes a difference, possibly it does to some women, but not all of them. But whether it does or not, there are good reasons why you might not want to have a child right away."

She withdrew the pouting underlip and sat up straight, interested.

"So there is a way?"

"There are a lot of ways, and unfortunately most of them don't work," I told her, with a pang of regret for my prescription pad and the reliability of contraceptive pills. Still, I remembered well enough the advice of the *maîtresses sage-femme,* the experienced midwives of the Hôpital des Anges, where I had worked in Paris twenty years before.

"Hand me the small box in the cupboard over there," I said, pointing to the doors above her head. "Yes, that one.

"Some of the French midwives make a tea of bayberry and valerian," I said, rummaging in my medicine box. "But it's rather dangerous, and not all that dependable, I don't think."

"D'ye miss her?" Marsali asked abruptly. I glanced up, startled. "Your daughter?" Her face was abnormally expressionless, and I suspected the question had more to do with Laoghaire than with me.

"Yes," I said simply. "But she's grown; she has her own life." The lump in my throat was back, and I bent my head over the medicine box, hiding my face. The chances of Laoghaire ever seeing Marsali again were just about as good as the chances that I would ever see Brianna; it wasn't a thought I wanted to dwell on.

"Here," I said, pulling out a large chunk of cleaned sponge. I took one of the thin surgical knives from the fitted slots in the lid of the box and carefully sliced off several thin pieces, about three inches square. I searched through the box again and found the small bottle of tansy oil, with which I carefully saturated one square under Marsali's fascinated gaze.

"All right," I said. "That's about how much oil to use. If you haven't any oil, you can dip the sponge in vinegar—even wine will work, in a pinch. You put the bit of sponge well up inside you before you go to bed with a man—mind you do it even the first time; you can get with child from even once."

Marsali nodded, her eyes wide, and touched the sponge gently with a forefinger. "Aye? And—and after? Do I take it out again, or—"

An urgent shout from above, coupled with a sudden heeling of the *Artemis* as she backed her mainsails, put an abrupt end to the conversation. Something was happening up above.

"I'll tell you later," I said, pushing the sponge and bottle toward her, and headed for the passage.

Jamie was standing with the Captain on the afterdeck, watching the approach of a large ship behind us. She was perhaps three times the size of the *Artemis,* three-masted, with a perfect forest of rigging and sail, through which small black figures hopped like fleas on a bedsheet. A puff of white smoke floated in her wake, token of a cannon recently fired.

"Is she firing on us?" I asked in amazement.

"No," Jamie said grimly. "A warning shot only. She means to board us."

"Can they?" I addressed the question to Captain Raines, who was looking even more glum than usual, the downturned corners of his mouth sunk in his beard.

"They can," he said. "We'll not outrun her in a stiff breeze like this, on the open sea."

"What is she?" Her ensign flew at the masthead, but seen against the sun at this distance, it looked completely black.

Jamie glanced down at me, expressionless. "A British man-o-war, Sassenach. Seventy-four guns. Perhaps ye'd best go below."

This was bad news. While Britain was no longer at war with France, relations between the two countries were by no means cordial. And while the *Artemis* was armed, she had only four twelve-pound guns; sufficient to deter small pirates, but no match for a man-of-war.

"What can they want of us?" Jamie asked the Captain. Raines shook his head, his soft, plump face set grimly.

"Likely pressing," he answered. "She's shorthanded; you can see by her rigging—and her foredeck all ahoo," he noted disapprovingly, eyes fixed on the man-of-war, now looming as she drew alongside. He glanced at Jamie. "They can press any of our hands who look to be British—which is something like half the crew. And yourself, Mr. Fraser—unless you wish to pass for French?"

"Damn," Jamie said softly. He glanced at me and frowned. "Did I not tell ye to get below?"

"You did," I said, not going. I drew closer to him, my eyes fixed on the man-of-war, where a small boat was now being lowered. One officer, in a gilded coat and laced hat, was climbing down the side.

"If they press the British hands," I asked Captain Raines, "what will happen to them?"

"They'll serve aboard the *Porpoise*—that's her," he nodded at the man-of-war, which sported a puff-lipped fish as the figurehead, "as members of the Royal Navy. She may release the pressed hands when she reaches port—or she may not."

"What? You mean they can just kidnap men and make them serve as sailors for as long as they please?" A thrill of fear shot through me, at the thought of Jamie's being abruptly taken away.

"They can," the Captain said shortly. "And if they do, we'll have a job of it to reach Jamaica ourselves, with half a crew." He turned abruptly and went forward, to greet the arriving boat.

Jamie gripped my elbow and squeezed.

"They'll not take Innes or Fergus," he said. "They'll help ye to hunt for Young Ian. If they take us"— I noted the "us" with a sharp pang —"you'll go on to Jared's place at Sugar Bay, and search from there." He looked down and gave me a brief smile. "I'll meet ye there," he said, and gave my elbow a reassuring squeeze. "I canna say how long it might be, but I'll come to ye there."

"But you could pass as a Frenchman!" I protested. "You know you could!"

He looked at me for a moment, and shook his head, smiling faintly.

"No," he said softly. "I canna let them take my men, and stay behind, hiding under a Frenchman's name."

"But—" I started to protest that the Scottish smugglers were *not* his men, had no claim on his loyalty, and then stopped, realizing that it was useless. The Scots might not be his tenants or his kin, and one of them might well be a traitor. But he had brought them here, and if they went, he would go with them.

"Dinna mind it, Sassenach," he said softly. "I shall be all right, one way or the other. But I think it is best if our name is Malcolm, for the moment."

He patted my hand, then released it and went forward, shoulders braced to meet whatever was coming. I followed, more slowly. As the gig pulled alongside, I saw Captain Raines's eyebrows rise in astonishment.

"God save us, what is this?" he murmured under his breath, as a head appeared above the *Artemis*'s rail.

It was a young man, evidently in his late twenties, but with his face drawn and shoulders slumping with fatigue. A uniform coat that was too big for him had been tugged on over a filthy shirt, and he staggered slightly as the deck of the *Artemis* rose beneath him.

"You are the captain of this ship?" The Englishman's eyes were red-rimmed from tiredness, but he picked Raines from the crowd of grim-faced hands at a glance. "I am acting captain Thomas Leonard, of His Majesty's ship *Porpoise*. For the love of God," he said, speaking hoarsely, "have you a surgeon aboard?"

Over a warily offered glass of port below, Captain Leonard explained that the *Porpoise* had suffered an outbreak of some infectious plague, beginning some four weeks before.

"Half the crew are down with it," he said, wiping a crimson drop from his stubbled chin. "We've lost thirty men so far, and look fair to lose a lot more."

"You lost your captain?" Raines asked.

Leonard's thin face flushed slightly. "The—the captain and the two senior lieutenants died last week, and the surgeon and the surgeon's mate, as well. I was third lieutenant." That explained both his surprising youth and his nervous state; to be landed suddenly in sole command of a large ship, a crew of six hundred men, and a rampant infection aboard, was enough to rattle anyone.

"If you have anyone aboard with some medical experience . . ." He looked hopefully from Captain Raines to Jamie, who stood by the desk, frowning slightly.

"I'm the *Artemis*'s surgeon, Captain Leonard," I said, from my place in the doorway. "What symptoms do your men have?"

"You?" The young captain's head swiveled to stare at me. His jaw hung slackly open, showing the furred tongue and stained teeth of a tobacco-chewer.

"My wife's a rare healer, Captain," Jamie said mildly. "If it's help ye came for, I'd advise ye to answer her questions, and do as she tells ye."

Leonard blinked once, but then took a deep breath and nodded. "Yes. Well, it seems to start with griping pains in the belly, and a terrible flux and vomiting. The afflicted men complain of headache, and they have considerable fever. They . . ."

"Do some of them have a rash on their bellies?" I interrupted.

He nodded eagerly. "They do. And some of them bleed from the arse as well. Oh, I beg pardon, ma'am," he said, suddenly flustered. "I meant no offense, only that—"

"I think I know what that might be," I interrupted his apologies. A feeling of excitement began to grow in me; the feeling of a diagnosis just under my hands, and the sure knowledge of how to proceed with it. The call of trumpets to a warhorse, I thought with wry amusement. "I'd need to look at them, to be sure, but—"

"My wife would be pleased to advise ye, Captain," Jamie said firmly. "But I'm afraid she canna go aboard your ship."

"Are you sure?" Captain Leonard looked from one to the other of us, eyes desperate with disappointment. "If she could only look at my crew . . ."

"No," Jamie said, at the same moment I replied, "Yes, of course!"

There was an awkward silence for a moment. Then Jamie rose to his feet, said politely, "You'll excuse us, Captain Leonard?" and dragged me bodily out of the cabin, down the passage to the afterhold.

"Are ye daft?" he hissed, still clutching me by one arm. "Ye canna be thinking of setting foot on a ship wi' the plague! Risk your life and the crew and Young Ian, all for the sake of a pack of Englishmen?"

"It isn't plague," I said, struggling to get free. "And I wouldn't be risking my life. Let go of my arm, you bloody Scot!"

He let go, but stood blocking the ladder, glowering at me.

"Listen," I said, striving for patience. "It isn't plague; I'm almost sure it's typhoid fever—the rash sounds like it. I can't catch that, I've been vaccinated for it."

Momentary doubt flitted across his face. Despite my explanations, he was still inclined to consider germs and vaccines in the same league with black magic.

"Aye?" he said skeptically. "Well, perhaps that's so, but still . . ."

"Look," I said, groping for words. "I'm a doctor. They're sick, and I can do something about it. I . . . it's . . . well, I have to, that's all!"

Judging from its effect, this statement appeared to lack something in eloquence. Jamie raised one eyebrow, inviting me to go on.

I took a deep breath. How should I explain it—the need to touch, the compulsion to heal? In his own way, Frank had understood. Surely there was a way to make it clear to Jamie.

"I took an oath," I said. "When I became a physician."

Both eyebrows went up. "An oath?" he echoed. "What sort of oath?"

I had said it aloud only the one time. Still, I had had a framed copy in my office; Frank had given it to me, a gift when I graduated from medical school. I swallowed a small thickening in my throat, closed my eyes, and read what I could remember from the scroll before my mind's eye.

"I swear by Apollo the physician, by Aesculapius, Hygeia, and Panacea, and I take to witness all the gods, all the goddesses, to keep according to my ability and my judgment the following Oath:

I will prescribe regimen for the good of my patients according to my ability and my judgment and never do harm to anyone. To please no one will I prescribe a deadly drug, nor give advice which may cause his death. But I will preserve the purity of my life and my art. In every house where I come I will enter only for the good of my patients, keeping myself far from all intentional ill-doing and all seduction, and especially from the pleasures of love with women or with men, be they free or slaves. All that may come to my knowledge in the exercise of my profession or outside of my profession or in daily commerce with men, which ought not to be spread abroad, I will keep secret and will never reveal. If I keep this oath faithfully, may I enjoy my life and practice my art, respected by all men and in all times; but if I swerve from it or violate it, may the reverse be my lot."

I opened my eyes, to find him looking down at me thoughtfully. "Er . . . parts of it are just for tradition," I explained.

The corner of his mouth twitched slightly. "I see," he said. "Well, the first part sounds a wee bit pagan, but I like the part about how ye willna seduce anyone."

"I thought you'd like that one," I said dryly. "Captain Leonard's virtue is safe with me."

He gave a small snort and leaned back against the ladder, running one hand slowly through his hair.

"Is that how it's done, then, in the company of physicians?" he asked. "Ye hold yourself bound to help whoever calls for it, even an enemy?"

"It doesn't make a great difference, you know, if they're ill or hurt." I looked up, searching his face for understanding.

"Aye, well," he said slowly. "I've taken an oath now and then, myself— and none of them lightly." He reached out and took my right hand, his fingers resting on my silver ring. "Some weigh heavier than others, though," he said, watching my face in turn.

He was very close to me, the sun from the hatchway overhead striping the linen of his sleeve, the skin of his hand a deep ruddy bronze where it cradled my own white fingers, and the glinting silver of my wedding ring.

"It does," I said softly, speaking to his thought. "You know it does." I laid my other hand against his chest, its gold ring glowing in a bar of sunlight. "But where one vow can be kept, without damage to another . . . ?"

He sighed, deeply enough to move the hand on my chest, then bent and kissed me, very gently.

"Aye, well, I wouldna have ye be forsworn," he said, straightening up with a wry twist to his mouth. "You're sure of this vaccination of yours? It does work?"

"It works," I assured him.

"Perhaps I should go with ye," he said, frowning slightly.

"You can't—you haven't been vaccinated, and typhoid's awfully contagious."

"You're only thinking it's typhoid, from what Leonard says," he pointed out. "Ye dinna ken for sure that it's that."

"No," I admitted. "But there's only one way to find out."

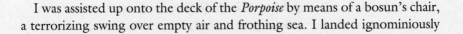

I was assisted up onto the deck of the *Porpoise* by means of a bosun's chair, a terrorizing swing over empty air and frothing sea. I landed ignominiously in a sprawl on the deck. Once I regained my feet, I was astonished to find how solid the deck of the man-of-war felt, compared to the tiny, pitching quarterdeck of the *Artemis,* far below. It was like standing on the Rock of Gibraltar.

My hair had blown loose during the trip between the ships; I twisted it up and repinned it as best I could, then reached to take the medicine box I had brought from the midshipman who held it.

"You'd best show me where they are," I said. The wind was brisk, and I was aware that it was taking a certain amount of work on the part of both crews to keep the two ships close together, even as both drifted leeward.

It was dark in the tween-decks, the confined space lit by small oil lamps that hung from the ceiling, swaying gently with the rise and fall of the ship, so that the ranks of hammocked men lay in deep shadow, blotched with dim patches of light from above. They looked like pods of whales, or sleeping sea beasts, lying humped and black, side by side, swaying with the movement of the sea beneath.

The stench was overpowering. What air there was came down through crude ventilator shafts that reached the upper deck, but that wasn't a lot. Worse than unwashed seamen was the reek of vomitus and the ripe, throat-clogging smell of blood-streaked diarrhea, which liberally spattered the decking beneath the hammocks, where sufferers had been too ill to reach the few available chamber pots. My shoes stuck to the deck, coming away with a nasty sucking noise as I made my way cautiously into the area.

"Give me a better light," I said peremptorily to the apprehensive-looking young midshipman who had been told off to accompany me. He was holding a kerchief to his face and looked both scared and miserable, but he obeyed, holding up the lantern he carried so that I could peer into the nearest hammock.

The occupant groaned and turned away his face as the light struck him. He was flushed with fever, and his skin hot to the touch. I pulled his shirt up and felt his stomach; it too was hot, the skin distended and hard. As I prodded gently here and there, the man writhed like a worm on a hook, uttering piteous groans.

"It's all right," I said soothingly, urging him to flatten out again. "Yes, I'll help you; it will feel better soon. Let me look into your eyes, now. Yes, that's right."

I pulled back the eyelid; his pupil shrank in the light, leaving his eyes brown and red-rimmed with suffering.

"Christ, take away the light!" he gasped, jerking his head away. "It splits my head!" Fever, vomiting, abdominal cramps, headache.

"Do you have chills?" I asked, waving back the midshipman's lantern.

The answer was more a moan than a word, but in the affirmative. Even in the shadows, I could see that many of the men in the hammocks were wrapped in their blankets, though it was stifling hot here below.

If not for the headache, it could be simple gastroenteritis—but not with this many men stricken. Something very contagious indeed, and I was fairly sure what. Not malaria, coming *from* Europe to the Caribbean. Typhus was a possibility; spread by the common body louse, it was prone to rapid spread in close quarters like these, and the symptoms were similar to those I saw around me—with one distinctive difference.

That seaman didn't have the characteristic belly rash, nor the next, but the third one did. The light red rosettes were plain on the clammy white skin. I pressed firmly on one, and it disappeared, blinking back into existence a moment later, as the blood returned to the skin. I squeezed my way between the hammocks, the heavy, sweating bodies pressing in on me from either side, and made my way back to the companionway where Captain Leonard and two more of his midshipmen waited for me.

"It's typhoid," I told the Captain. I was as sure as I could be, lacking a microscope and blood culture.

"Oh?" His drawn face remained apprehensive. "Do you know what to do for it, Mrs. Malcolm?"

"Yes, but it won't be easy. The sick men need to be taken above, washed thoroughly, and laid where they can have fresh air to breathe. Beyond that, it's a matter of nursing; they'll need to have a liquid diet—and lots of water —*boiled* water, that's very important!—and sponging to bring down the fever. The most important thing is to avoid infecting any more of your crew, though. There are several things that need to be done—"

"Do them," he interrupted. "I shall give orders to have as many of the healthy men as can be spared to attend you; order them as you will."

"Well," I said, with a dubious glance at the surroundings. "I can make a start, and tell you how to be going on, but it's going to be a big job. Captain Raines and my husband will be anxious to be on our way."

"Mrs. Malcolm," the Captain said earnestly, "I shall be eternally grateful for any assistance you can render us. We are most urgently bound for Jamaica, and unless the remainder of my crew can be saved from this wicked illness, we will never reach that island." He spoke with profound seriousness, and I felt a twinge of pity for him.

"All right," I said with a sigh. "Send me a dozen healthy crewmen, for a start."

Climbing to the quarterdeck, I went to the rail and waved at Jamie, who was standing by the *Artemis's* wheel, looking upward. I could see his face clearly, despite the distance; it was worried, but relaxed into a broad smile when he saw me.

"Are ye comin' down now?" he shouted, cupping his hands.

"Not yet!" I shouted back. "I need two hours!" Holding up two fingers to make my meaning clear in case he hadn't heard, I stepped back from the rail, but not before I saw the smile fade from his face. He'd heard.

I saw the sick men removed to the afterdeck, and a crew of hands set to strip them of their filthy clothes, and hose and sponge them with seawater from the pumps. I was in the galley, instructing the cook and galley crew in food-handling precautions, when I felt the movement of the deck under my feet.

The cook to whom I was talking snaked out a hand and snapped shut the latch of the cupboard behind him. With the utmost dispatch, he grabbed a loose pot that leapt off its shelf, thrust a large ham on a spit into the lower cupboard, and whirled to clap a lid on the boiling pot hung over the galley fire.

I stared at him in astonishment. I had seen Murphy perform this same odd ballet, whenever the *Artemis* cast off or changed course abruptly.

"What—" I said, but then abandoned the question, and headed for the quarterdeck, as fast as I could go. We were under way; big and solid as the *Porpoise* was, I could feel the vibration that ran through the keel as she took the wind.

I burst onto the deck to find a cloud of sails overhead, set and drawing, and the *Artemis* falling rapidly behind us. Captain Leonard was standing by the helmsman, looking back to the *Artemis,* as the master bawled commands to the men overhead.

"What are you doing?" I shouted. "You bloody little bastard, what's going on here?"

The Captain glanced at me, plainly embarrassed, but with his jaw set stubbornly.

"We must get to Jamaica with the utmost dispatch," he said. His cheeks were chapped red with the rushing sea wind, or he might have blushed. "I am sorry, Mrs. Malcolm—indeed I regret the necessity, but—"

"But nothing!" I said, furious. "Put about! Heave to! Drop the bloody anchor! You can't take me away like this!"

"I regret the necessity," he said again, doggedly. "But I believe that we require your continuing services most urgently, Mrs. Malcolm. Don't worry," he said, striving for a reassurance that he didn't achieve. He reached out as though to pat my shoulder, but then thought better of it. His hand dropped to his side.

"I have promised your husband that the navy will provide you accommodation in Jamaica until the *Artemis* arrives there."

He flinched backward at the look on my face, evidently afraid that I might attack him—and not without reason.

"What do you *mean* you promised my husband?" I said, through gritted teeth. "Do you mean that J—that Mr. Malcolm *permitted* you to abduct me?"

"Er . . . no. No, he didn't." The Captain appeared to be finding the interview a strain. He dragged a filthy handkerchief from his pocket and wiped his brow and the back of his neck. "He was most intransigent, I'm afraid."

"Intransigent, eh? Well, so am I!" I stamped my foot on the deck, aiming for his toes, and missing only because he leapt agilely backward. "If you expect me to help you, you bloody kidnapper, just bloody think again!"

The Captain tucked his handkerchief away and set his jaw. "Mrs. Malcolm. You compel me to tell you what I told your husband. The *Artemis* sails under a French flag, and with French papers, but more than half her crew are Englishmen or Scots. I could have pressed these men to service here—and I badly need them. Instead, I have agreed to leave them unmolested, in return for the gift of your medical knowledge."

"So you've decided to press me instead. And my husband *agreed* to this . . . this *bargain*?"

"No, he didn't," the young man said, rather dryly. "The captain of the *Artemis,* however, perceived the force of my argument." He blinked down at me, his eyes swollen from days without sleep, the too-big jacket flapping around his slender torso. Despite his youth and his slovenly appearance, he had considerable dignity.

"I must beg your pardon for what must seem the height of ungentlemanly behavior, Mrs. Malcolm—but the truth is that I am desperate," he said simply. "You may be our only chance. I must take it."

I opened my mouth to reply, but then closed it. Despite my fury—and my profound unease about what Jamie was going to say when I saw him again—I felt some sympathy for his position. It was quite true that he stood in danger of losing most of his crew, without help. Even with my help, we would lose some—but that wasn't a prospect I cared to dwell on.

"All right," I said, through my teeth. "All . . . *right*!" I looked out over the rail, at the dwindling sails of the *Artemis.* I wasn't prone to seasickness, but I felt a distinct hollowing in the pit of my stomach as the ship—and Jamie—fell far behind. "I wouldn't appear to have a lot of choice in the matter. If you can spare as many men as possible to scrub down the tween-decks—oh, and have you any alcohol on board?"

He looked mildly surprised. "Alcohol? Well, there is the rum for the hands' grog, and possibly some wine from the gun room locker. Will that do?"

"If that's what you have, it will have to do." I tried to push aside my own emotions, long enough to deal with the situation. "I suppose I must speak to the purser, then."

"Yes, of course. Come with me." Leonard started toward the companion-way that led belowdecks, then, flushing, stood back and gestured awkwardly to let me go first—lest my descent expose my lower limbs indelicately, I supposed. Biting my lip with a mixture of anger and amusement, I went.

I had just reached the bottom of the ladder when I heard a confusion of voices above.

"No, I tell 'ee, the captain's not to be disturbed! Whatever you have to say will—"

"Leave go! I tell *you*, if you don't let me speak to him now, it will be too late!"

And then Leonard's voice, suddenly sharp as he turned to the interlopers. "Stevens? What is this? What's the matter?"

"No matter, sir," said the first voice, suddenly obsequious. "Only that Tompkins here is sure as he knows the cove what was on that ship—the big 'un, with the red hair. He says—"

"I haven't time," the captain said shortly. "Tell the mate, Tompkins, and I shall attend to it later."

I was, naturally, halfway back up the ladder by the time these words were spoken, and listening for all I was worth.

The hatchway darkened as Leonard began the backward descent down the ladder. The young man glanced at me sharply, but I kept my face carefully blank, saying only, "Have you many food stores left, Captain? The sick men will need to be fed very carefully. I don't suppose there would be any milk aboard, but—"

"Oh, there's milk," he said, suddenly more cheerful. "We have six milch goats, in fact. The gunner's wife, Mrs. Johansen, does quite wonderfully with them. I'll send her to talk with you, after we've seen the purser."

Captain Leonard introduced me briefly to Mr. Overholt, the purser, and then left, with the injunction that I should be afforded every possible service. Mr. Overholt, a small, plump man with a bald and shining head, peered at me out of the deep collar of his coat like an undersized Humpty-Dumpty, murmuring unhappily about the scarcity of everything near the end of a cruise, and how unfortunate everything was, but I scarcely attended to him. I was much too agitated, thinking of what I had overheard.

Who was this Tompkins? The voice was entirely unfamiliar, and I was sure I had never heard the name before. More important, what did he know about Jamie? And what was Captain Leonard likely to do with the information? As it was, there was nothing I could do now, save contain my impatience, and with the half of my mind not busy with fruitless speculation, work out with Mr. Overholt what supplies were available for use in sickroom feeding.

Not a great deal, as it turned out.

"No, they certainly can't eat salt beef," I said firmly. "Nor yet hardtack, though if we soak the biscuit in boiled milk, perhaps we can manage that as they begin to recover. If you knock the weevils out first," I added, as an afterthought.

"Fish," Mr. Overholt suggested, in a hopeless sort of way. "We often encounter substantial schools of mackerel or even bonita, as we approach the Caribbean. Sometimes the crew will have luck with baited lines."

"Maybe that would do," I said, absently. "Boiled milk and water will be enough in the early stages, but as the men begin to recover, they should have something light and nourishing—soup, for instance. I suppose we could make a fish soup? Unless you have something else that might be suitable?"

"Well . . ." Mr. Overholt looked profoundly uneasy. "There *is* a small quantity of dried figs, ten pound of sugar, some coffee, a quantity of Naples biscuit, and a large cask of Madeira wine, but of course we cannot use that."

"Why not?" I stared at him, and he shuffled his feet uneasily.

"Why, those supplies are intended for the use of our passenger," he said.

"What sort of passenger?" I asked blankly.

Mr. Overholt looked surprised. "The Captain did not tell you? We are carrying the new governor for the island of Jamaica. That is the cause—well, *one* cause"—he corrected himself, dabbing nervously at his bald head with a handkerchief—"of our haste."

"If he's not sick, the Governor can eat salt beef," I said firmly. "Be good for him, I shouldn't wonder. Now, if you'll have the wine taken to the galley, I've work to do."

Aided by one of the remaining midshipmen, a short, stocky youth named Pound, I made a rapid tour of the ship, ruthlessly dragooning supplies and hands. Pound, trotting beside me like a small, ferocious bulldog, firmly informed surprised and resentful cooks, carpenters, sweepers, swabbers, sailmakers, and holdsmen that all my wishes—no matter how unreasonable—must be gratified instantly, by the captain's orders.

Quarantine was the most important thing. As soon as the tween-decks had been scrubbed and aired, the patients would have to be carried down again, but the hammocks restrung with plenty of space between—the unaffected crew would have to sleep on deck—and provided with adequate toilet facilities. I had seen a pair of large kettles in the galley that I thought might do. I made a quick note on the mental list I was keeping, and hoped the chief cook was not as possessive of his receptacles as Murphy was.

I followed Pound's round head, covered with close-clipped brown curls, down toward the hold in search of worn sails that might be used for cloths. Only half my mind was on my list; with the other half, I was contemplating the possible source of the typhoid outbreak. Caused by a bacillus of the *Salmonella* genus, it was normally spread by ingestion of the bacillus, carried on hands contaminated by urine or feces.

Given the sanitary habits of seamen, any one of the crew could be the carrier of the disease. The most likely culprit was one of the food handlers, though, given the widespread and sudden nature of the outbreak—the cook or one of his two mates, or possibly one of the stewards. I would have to find out how many of these there were, which messes they served, and whether anyone had changed duties four weeks ago—no, five, I corrected myself. The outbreak had begun four weeks ago, but there was an incubation period for the disease to be considered, too.

"Mr. Pound," I called, and a round face peered up at me from the foot of the ladder.

"Yes, ma'am?"

"Mr. Pound—what's your first name, by the way?" I asked.

"Elias, ma'am," he said, looking mildly bewildered.

"Do you mind if I call you so?" I dropped off the foot of the ladder and smiled at him. He smiled hesitantly back.

"Er . . . no, ma'am. The Captain might mind, though," he added cautiously. " 'Tisn't really naval, you know."

Elias Pound couldn't be more than seventeen or eighteen; I doubted that Captain Leonard was more than five or six years older. Still, protocol was protocol.

"I'll be very naval in public," I assured him, suppressing a smile. "But if you're going to work with me, it will be easier to call you by name." I knew, as he didn't, what lay ahead—hours and days and possibly weeks of labor and exhaustion, when the senses would blur, and only bodily habit and blind instinct—and the leadership of a tireless chief—would keep those caring for the sick on their feet.

I was far from tireless, but the illusion would have to be kept up. This could be done with the help of two or three others, whom I could train; substitutes for my own hands and eyes, who could carry on when I must rest. Fate—and Captain Leonard—had designated Elias Pound as my new right hand; best to be on comfortable terms with him at once.

"How long have you been at sea, Elias?" I asked, stopping to peer after him as he ducked under a low platform that held enormous loops of a huge, evil-smelling chain, each link more than twice the size of my fist. The anchor chain? I wondered, touching it curiously. It looked strong enough to moor the *Queen Elizabeth,* which seemed a comforting thought.

"Since I was seven, ma'am," he said, working his way out backward, dragging a large chest. He stood up puffing slightly from the exertion, and wiped his round, ingenuous face. "My uncle's commander in *Triton,* so he was able to get me a berth in her. I come to join the *Porpoise* just this voyage, though, out of Edinburgh." He flipped open the chest, revealing an assortment of rust-smeared surgical implements—at least I hoped it was rust—and a jumbled collection of stoppered bottles and jugs. One of the jars had cracked, and a fine white dust like plaster of Paris lay over everything in the chest.

"This is what Mr. Hunter, the surgeon, had with him, ma'am," he said. "Will you have use for it?"

"God knows," I said, peering into the chest. "But I'll have a look. Have someone else fetch it up to the sickbay, though, Elias. I need you to come and speak firmly to the cook."

As I oversaw the scrubbing of the tween-decks with boiling seawater, my mind was occupied with several distinct trains of thought.

First, I was mentally charting the necessary steps to take in combating the disease. Two men, far gone from dehydration and malaise, had died during the removal from the tween-decks, and now lay at the far end of the after-deck, where the sailmaker was industriously stitching them into their hammocks for burial, a pair of round shot sewn in at their feet. Four more weren't going to make it through the night. The remaining forty-five had chances ranging from excellent to slim; with luck and skill, I might save most of them. But how many new cases were brewing, undetected, among the remaining crew?

Huge quantities of water were boiling in the galley at my order; hot seawater for cleansing, boiled fresh water for drinking. I made another tick on my mental list; I must see Mrs. Johansen, she of the milch goats, and arrange for the milk to be sterilized as well.

I must interview the galley hands about their duties; if a single source of infection could be found and isolated, it would do a lot to halt the spread of the disease. Tick.

All of the available alcohol on the ship was being gathered in the sickbay, to the profound horror of Mr. Overholt. It could be used in its present form, but it would be better to have purified alcohol. Could a means be found of distilling it? Check with the purser. Tick.

All the hammocks must be boiled and dried before the healthy hands slept in them. That would have to be done quickly, before the next watch went to its rest. Send Elias for a crew of swabbers and sweepers; laundry duty seemed most in their line. Tick.

Under the growing mental list of necessities were vague but continuing thoughts of the mysterious Tompkins and his unknown information. Whatever it was, it had not resulted in our changing course to return to the *Artemis*. Either Captain Leonard had not taken it seriously, or he was simply too eager to get to Jamaica to allow anything to hinder his progress.

I had paused for a moment by the rail, to organize my thoughts. I pushed back the hair from my forehead, and lifted my face to the cleansing wind, letting it blow away the stench of sickness. Puffs of ill-smelling steam rose from the nearby hatchway, from the hot-water cleansing going on below. It would be better down there when they had finished, but a long way from fresh air.

I looked out over the rail, hoping vainly for the glimpse of a sail, but the *Porpoise* was alone, the *Artemis*—and Jamie—left far behind.

I pushed away the sudden rush of loneliness and panic. I must speak soon with Captain Leonard. Answers to two, at least, of the problems that concerned me lay with him; the possible source of the typhoid outbreak—and the role of the unknown Mr. Tompkins in Jamie's affairs. But for the moment, there were more pressing matters.

"Elias!" I called, knowing he would be somewhere within reach of my voice. "Take me to Mrs. Johansen and the goats, please."

47

Plague Ship

Two days later, I had still not found time to speak to Captain Leonard. Twice, I had gone to his cabin, but found the young Captain gone or unavailable—taking position, I was told, or consulting charts, or otherwise engaged in some bit of sailing arcana.

Mr. Overholt had taken to avoiding me and my insatiable demands, locking himself in his cabin with a pomander of dried sage and hyssop tied round his neck to ward off plague. The able-bodied crewmen assigned to the work of cleaning and shifting had been lethargic and dubious at first, but I had chivvied and scolded, glared and shouted, stamped my foot and shrieked, and got them gradually moving. I felt more like a sheepdog than a doctor—snapping and growling at their heels, and hoarse now with the effort.

It was working, though; there was a new feeling of hope and purpose among the crew—I could feel it. Four new deaths today, and ten new cases reporting, but the sounds of groaning distress from the tween-decks were much less, and the faces of the still-healthy showed the relief that comes of doing something—anything. I had so far failed to find the source of the contagion. If I could do that, and prevent any fresh outbreaks, I might—just possibly—halt the devastation within a week, while the *Porpoise* still had hands enough to sail her.

A quick canvass of the surviving crew had turned up two men pressed from a county gaol where they had been imprisoned for brewing illicit liquor. I had seized on these gratefully and put them to work building a still in which—to the horror of the crew—half the ship's store of rum was being distilled into pure alcohol for disinfection.

I had posted one of the surviving midshipmen by the entrance to the sickbay and another by the galley, each armed with a basin of pure alcohol and instructions to see that no one went in or came out without dipping their hands. Beside each midshipman stood a marine with his rifle, charged with the duty of seeing that no one should drink the grimy contents of the barrel into which the used alcohol was emptied when it became too filthy to be used any longer.

In Mrs. Johansen, the gunner's wife, I had found an unexpected ally. An intelligent woman in her thirties, she had understood—despite her having only a few words of broken English, and my having no Swedish at all—what I wanted done, and had done it.

If Elias was my right hand, Annekje Johansen was the left. She had single-handedly taken over the responsibility of scalding the goats' milk, patiently pounding hard biscuit—removing the weevils as she did so—to be mixed with it, and feeding the resulting mixture to those hands strong enough to digest it.

Her own husband, the chief gunner, was one of the victims of the typhoid, but he fortunately seemed one of the lighter cases, and I had every hope that he might recover—as much because of his wife's devoted nursing as because of his own hardy constitution.

"Ma'am, Ruthven says as somebody's been a-drinking of the pure alcohol again." Elias Pound popped up at my elbow, his round pink face looking drawn and wan, substantially thinned by the pressures of the last few days.

I said something extremely bad, and his brown eyes widened.

"Sorry," I said. I wiped the back of a hand across my brow, trying to get my hair out of my eyes. "Don't mean to offend your tender ears, Elias."

"Oh, I've heard it before, ma'am," Elias assured me. "Just not from a lady, like."

"I'm not a lady, Elias," I said tiredly. "I'm a doctor. Have someone go and search the ship for whoever it was; they'll likely be unconscious by now." He nodded and whirled on one foot.

"I'll look in the cable tier," he said. "That's where they usually hide when they're drunk."

This was the fourth in the last three days. Despite all guards set over the still and the purified alcohol, the hands, living on half their usual daily ration of grog, were so desperate for drink that they contrived somehow to get at the pure grain alcohol meant for sterilization.

"Goodness, Mrs. Malcolm," the purser had said, shaking his bald head when I complained about the problem. "Seamen will drink *anything,* ma'am! Spoilt plum brandy, peaches mashed inside a rubber boot and left to ferment—why, I've even known a hand caught stealing the old bandages from the surgeon's quarters and soaking them, in hopes of getting a whiff of alcohol. No, ma'am, telling them that drinking it will kill them certainly won't stop them."

Kill them it did. One of the four men who had drunk it had died; two more were in their own boarded-off section of the sickbay, deeply comatose. If they survived, they were likely to be permanently brain-damaged.

"Not that being on a bloody floating hellhole like this isn't likely to brain-damage anyone," I remarked bitterly to a tern who alighted on the rail nearby. "As if it isn't enough, trying to save half the miserable lot from typhoid, now the other half is trying to kill themselves with my alcohol! Damn the bloody lot of them!"

The tern cocked its head, decided I was not edible, and flew away. The ocean stretched empty all around—before us, where the unknown West Indies concealed Young Ian's fate, and behind, where Jamie and the *Artemis* had long since vanished. And me in the middle, with six hundred drink-mad English sailors and a hold full of inflamed bowels.

I stood fuming for a moment, then turned with decision toward the forward gangway. I didn't care if Captain Leonard was personally pumping the bilges, he was going to talk to me.

I stopped just inside the door of the cabin. It was not yet noon, but the Captain was asleep, head pillowed on his forearms, on top of an outspread book. The quill had fallen from his fingers, and the glass inkstand, cleverly held in its anchored bracket, swayed gently with the motion of the ship. His face was turned to the side, cheek pressed flat on his arm. Despite the heavy beard stubble, he looked absurdly young.

I turned, meaning to come back later, but in moving, brushed against the locker, where a stack of books was precariously balanced amid a rubble of papers, navigational instruments, and half-rolled charts. The top volume fell with a thump to the deck.

The sound was scarcely audible above the general sounds of creaking, flapping, whining rigging, and shouting that made up the background of life on shipboard, but it brought him awake, blinking and looking startled.

"Mrs. Fra—Mrs. Malcolm!" he said. He rubbed a hand over his face, and shook his head quickly, trying to wake himself. "What—that is—you required something?"

"I didn't mean to wake you," I said. "But I do need more alcohol—if necessary, I can use straight rum—and you really must speak to the hands, to see if there is some way of stopping them trying to drink the distilled alcohol. We've had another that's poisoned himself today. And if there's any way of bringing more fresh air down to the sickbay . . ." I stopped, seeing that I was overwhelming him.

He blinked and scratched, slowly pulling his thoughts into order. The buttons on his sleeve had left two round red imprints on his cheek, and his hair was flattened on that side.

"I see," he said, rather stupidly. Then, as he began to wake, his expression cleared. "Yes. Of course. I will give orders to have a windsail rigged, to bring more air below. As for the alcohol—I must beg leave to consult the purser, as I do not myself know our present capacities in that regard." He turned and took a breath, as though to shout, but then remembered that his steward was no longer within earshot, being now below in the sickbay. Just then, the *ting* of the ship's bell came faintly from above.

"I beg your pardon, Mrs. Malcolm," he said, politeness recovered. "It is nearly noon; I must go and take our position. I will send the purser to you, should you care to remain here for a moment."

"Thank you." I sat down in the chair he had just vacated. He turned to go, making an attempt to straighten the too-large braided coat over his shoulders.

"Captain Leonard?" I said, moved by a sudden impulse. He turned back, questioning.

"If you don't mind my asking—how old are you?"

He blinked and his face tightened, but he answered me.

"I am nineteen, ma'am. Your servant, ma'am." And with that, he vanished through the door. I could hear him in the companionway, calling out in a voice half-cracked with fatigue.

Nineteen! I sat quite still, paralyzed with shock. I had thought him very young, but not nearly that young. His face weathered from exposure and lined with strain and sleeplessness, he had looked to be at least in his mid-twenties. *My God!* I thought, appalled. *He's no more than a baby!*

Nineteen. Just Brianna's age. And to be suddenly thrust into command not only of a ship—and not just a ship, but an English man-of-war—and not merely a man-of-war, but one with a plague aboard that had deprived her suddenly of a quarter of her crew and virtually all her command—I felt the fright and fury that had bubbled inside me for the last few days begin to ebb, as I realized that the high-handedness that had led him to kidnap me was in fact not arrogance or ill-judgment, but the result of sheer desperation.

He had to have help, he had said. Well, he was right, and I was it. I took a deep breath, visualizing the mess I had left behind in the sickbay. That was mine, and mine alone, to do the best I could with.

Captain Leonard had left the logbook open on the desk, his entry half-complete. There was a small damp spot on the page; he had drooled slightly in his sleep. In a spasm of irritated pity, I flipped over the page, wishing to hide this further evidence of his vulnerability.

My eye caught a word on the new page, and I stopped, a chill snaking down from the nape of my neck as I remembered something. When I had wakened him unexpectedly, the captain had started up, seen me, and said, "Mrs. Fra—" before catching himself. And the name on the page before me, the word that had caught my attention, was "Fraser." He knew who I was—and who Jamie was.

I rose quickly and shut the door, dropping the bolt. At least I would have warning if anyone came. Then I sat down at the captain's desk, pressed flat the pages, and began to read.

I flipped back to find the record of the meeting with the *Artemis,* three days before. Captain Leonard's entries were distinct from those of his predecessor, and mostly quite brief—not surprising, considering how much he had had to deal with of late. Most entries contained only the usual navigational information, with a brief note of the names of those men who had died since the previous day. The meeting with the *Artemis* was noted, though, and my own presence.

> 3 February 1767. Met near eight bells with *Artemis,* a small two-masted brig under French colors. Hailed her and requested the assistance of her surgeon, C. Malcolm, who was taken on board and remains with us to assist with the sick.

C. Malcolm, eh? No mention of my being a woman; perhaps he thought it irrelevant, or wished to avoid any inquiries over the propriety of his actions. I went on to the next entry.

> 4 February 1767. I have rec'd information this day from Harry Tompkins, able seaman, that the supercargo of the brig *Artemis* is known to him as a criminal by the name of James Fraser, known also by the names of Jamie Roy and of Alexandr Malcolm. This Fraser is a seditionist, and a notorious smuggler, for whose capture a substantial reward is offered by the King's Customs. Information was received from Tompkins after we had parted company with *Artemis;* I thought it not expeditious to pursue *Artemis,* as we are ordered with all possible dispatch for Jamaica, because of our passenger. However, as I have promised to return the *Artemis*'s surgeon to them there, Fraser may be arrested at that time.
>
> Two men dead of the plague—which the *Artemis*'s surgeon informs me is the Typhoide. Jno. Jaspers, able seaman, DD, Harty Kepple, cook's mate, DD.

That was all; the next day's entry was confined entirely to navigation and the recording of the death of six men, all with "DD" written beside their names. I wondered what it meant, but was too distracted to worry about it.

I heard steps coming down the passageway, and barely got the bolt lifted before the purser's knock sounded on the door. I scarcely heard Mr. Overholt's apologies; my mind was too busy trying to make sense of this new revelation.

Who in blinking, bloody hell was this man Tompkins? No one I had ever seen or heard about, I was sure, and yet he obviously knew a dangerous amount about Jamie's activities. Which led to two questions: How had an English seaman come by such information—and who else knew it?

". . . cut the grog rations further, to give you an additional cask of rum," Mr. Overholt was saying dubiously. "The hands won't like it, but we might manage; we're only two weeks out of Jamaica now."

"Whether they like it or not, I need the alcohol more than they need grog," I answered brusquely. "If they complain too much, tell them if I don't have the rum, none of them may *make* it to Jamaica."

Mr. Overholt sighed, and wiped small beads of sweat from his shiny brow. "I'll tell them, ma'am," he said, too beaten down to object.

"Fine. Oh, Mr. Overholt?" He turned back, questioning. "What does the legend 'DD' mean? I saw the Captain write it in his log."

A small flicker of humor lighted in the purser's deep-sunk eyes.

"It means 'Discharged, Dead,' ma'am," he replied. "The only sure way for most of us, of leaving His Majesty's Navy."

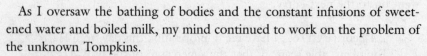

As I oversaw the bathing of bodies and the constant infusions of sweetened water and boiled milk, my mind continued to work on the problem of the unknown Tompkins.

I knew nothing of the man, save his voice. He might be one of the faceless horde overhead, the silhouettes that I saw in the rigging when I came up on deck for air, or one of the hurrying anonymous bodies, hurtling up and down the decks in a vain effort to do the work of three men.

I would meet him, of course, if he became infected; I knew the names of each patient in the sickbay. But I could hardly allow the matter to wait, in the rather ghoulish hope that Tompkins would contract typhoid. At last I made up my mind to ask; the man presumably knew who I was, anyway. Even if he found out that I had been asking about him, it was unlikely to do any harm.

Elias was the natural place to begin. I waited until the end of the day to ask, trusting to fatigue to dull his natural curiosity.

"Tompkins?" The boy's round face drew together in a brief frown, then cleared. "Oh, yes, ma'am. One o' the forecastle hands."

"Where did he come aboard, do you know?" There was no good way of accounting for this sudden interest in a man I had never met, but luckily, Elias was much too tired to wonder about it.

"Oh," he said vaguely, "at Spithead, I think. Or—no! I remember now, 'twas Edinburgh." He rubbed his knuckles under his nose to stifle a yawn. "That's it, Edinburgh. I wouldn' remember, only he was a pressed man, and a unholy fuss he made about it, claimin' as how they couldn' press him, he was protected, account of he worked for Sir Percival Turner, in the Customs." The yawn got the better of him and he gaped widely, then subsided. "But he didn' have no written protection from Sir Percival," he concluded, blinking, "so there wasn' nothing to be done."

"A Customs agent, was he?" *That* went quite some way toward explaining things, all right.

"Mm-hm. Yes, mum, I mean." Elias was trying manfully to stay awake, but his glazing eyes were fixed on the swaying lantern at the end of the sickbay, and he was swaying with it.

"You go on to bed, Elias," I said, taking pity on him. "I'll finish here."

He shook his head quickly, trying to shake off sleep.

"Oh, no, ma'am! I ain't sleepy, not a bit!" He reached clumsily for the cup and bottle I held. "You give me that, mum, and go to rest yourself." He would not be moved, but stubbornly insisted on helping to administer the last round of water before staggering off to his cot.

I was nearly as tired as Elias by the time we finished, but sleep would not come. I lay in the dead surgeon's cabin, staring up at the shadowy beam above my head, listening to the creak and rumble of the ship about me, wondering.

So Tompkins worked for Sir Percival. And Sir Percival assuredly knew that Jamie was a smuggler. But was there more to it than that? Tompkins knew Jamie by sight. How? And if Sir Percival had been willing to tolerate Jamie's clandestine activities in return for bribes, then—well, perhaps none of those bribes had made it to Tompkins's pockets. But in that case . . . and what about the ambush at Arbroath cove? Was there a traitor among the smugglers? And if so . . .

My thoughts were losing coherence, spinning in circles like the revolutions of a dying top. The powdered white face of Sir Percival faded into the purple mask of the hanged Customs agent on the Arbroath road, and the gold and red flames of an exploding lantern lit the crevices of my mind. I rolled onto my stomach, clutching the pillow to my chest, the last thought in my mind that I must find Tompkins.

As it was, Tompkins found me. For more than two days, the situation in the sickbay was too pressing for me to leave for more than the barest space of time. On the third day, though, matters seemed easier, and I retired to the surgeon's cabin, intending to wash myself and rest briefly before the midday drum beat for the noon meal.

I was lying on the cot, a cool cloth over my tired eyes, when I heard the sound of bumping and voices in the passage outside my door. A tentative knock sounded on my door, and an unfamiliar voice said, "Mrs. Malcolm? There's been a h'accident, if you please, ma'am."

I swung open the door to find two seamen supporting a third, who stood storklike on one leg, his face white with shock and pain.

It took no more than a single glance for me to know whom I was looking at. The man's face was ridged down one side with the livid scars of a bad burn, and the twisted eyelid on that side exposed the milky lens of a blind eye, had I needed any further confirmation that here stood the one-eyed seaman Young Ian had thought he'd killed, lank brown hair grew back from

a balding brow to a scrawny pigtail that drooped over one shoulder, exposing a pair of large, transparent ears.

"Mr. Tompkins," I said with certainty, and his remaining eye widened in
surprise. "Put him down over there, please."

The men deposited Tompkins on a stool by the wall, and went back to
their work; the ship was too shorthanded to allow for distraction. Heart
beating heavily, I knelt down to examine the wounded leg.

He knew who I was, all right; I had seen it in his face when I opened the
door. There was a great deal of tension in the leg under my hand. The injury
was gory, but not serious, given suitable care; a deep gash scored down the
calf of the leg. It had bled substantially, but there were no deep arteries cut;
it had been well-wrapped with a piece of someone's shirt, and the bleeding
had nearly stopped when I unwound the homemade bandage.

"How did you do this, Mr. Tompkins?" I asked, standing up and reaching
for the bottle of alcohol. He glanced up, his single eye alert and wary.

"Splinter wound, ma'am," he answered, in the nasal tones I had heard
once before. "A spar broke as I was a-standing on it." The tip of his tongue
stole out, furtively wetting his lower lip.

"I see." I turned and flipped open the lid of my empty medicine box,
pretending to survey the available remedies. I studied him out of the corner
of one eye, while I tried to think how best to approach him. He was on his
guard; tricking him into revelations or winning his trust were clearly out of
the question.

My eyes flicked over the tabletop, seeking inspiration. And found it. With
a mental apology to the shade of Aesculapius the physician, I picked up the
late surgeon's bone-saw, a wicked thing some eighteen inches long, of rust-
flecked steel. I looked at this thoughtfully, turned, and laid the toothed edge
of the instrument gently against the injured leg, just above the knee. I smiled
charmingly into the seaman's terrified single eye.

"Mr. Tompkins," I said, "let us talk frankly."

◄━━━━━►

An hour later, able-bodied seaman Tompkins had been restored to his
hammock, stitched and bandaged, shaking in every limb, but able-bodied
still. For my part, I felt a little shaky as well.

Tompkins was, as he had insisted to the press-gang in Edinburgh, an agent
of Sir Percival Turner. In that capacity, he went about the docks and warehouses of all the shipping ports in the Firth of Forth, from Culross and
Donibristle to Restalrig and Musselburgh, picking up gossip and keeping his
beady eye sharp-peeled to catch any evidence of unlawful activity.

The attitude of Scots toward English tax laws being what it was, there was
no lack of such activity to report. What was done with such reports, though,
varied. Small smugglers, caught red-handed with a bottle or two of un-

bonded rum or whisky, might be summarily arrested, tried and convicted, and sentenced to anything from penal servitude to transportation, with forfeiture of all their property to the Crown.

The bigger fish, though, were reserved to Sir Percival's private judgment. In other words, allowed to pay substantial bribes for the privilege of continuing their operations under the blind eye (here Tompkins laughed sardonically, touching the ruined side of his face) of the King's agents.

"Sir Percival's got ambitions, see?" While not noticeably relaxed, Tompkins had at least unbent enough to lean forward, one eye narrowing as he gestured in explanation. "He's in with Dundas and all them. Everything goes right, and he might have a peerage, not just a knighthood, eh? But that'll take more than money."

One thing that could help was some spectacular demonstration of competence and service to the Crown.

"As in the sort of arrest that might make 'em sit up and take notice, eh? Ooh! That smarts, missus. You sure of what you're a-doing of, there?" Tompkins squinted dubiously downward, to where I was sponging the site of the injury with dilute alcohol.

"I'm sure," I said. "Go on, then. I suppose a simple smuggler wouldn't have been good enough, no matter how big?"

Evidently not. However, when word had reached Sir Percival that there might just possibly be a major political criminal within his grasp, the old gentleman had nearly blown a gasket with excitement.

"But sedition's a harder thing to prove than smuggling, eh? You catch one of the little fish with the goods, and they're saying not a thing will lead you further on. Idealists, them seditionists," Tompkins said, shaking his head with disgust. "Never rat on each other, they don't."

"So you didn't know who you were looking for?" I stood and took one of my cat-gut sutures from its jar, threading it through a needle. I caught Tompkins's apprehensive look, but did nothing to allay his anxiety. I wanted him anxious—and voluble.

"No, we didn't know who the big fish was—not until another of Sir Percival's agents had the luck to tumble to one of Fraser's associates, what gave 'em the tip he was Malcolm the printer, and told his real name. Then it all come clear, o' course."

My heart skipped a beat.

"Who was the associate?" I asked. The names and faces of the six smugglers darted through my mind—little fish. Not idealists, any of them. But to which of them was loyalty no bar?

"I don't know. No, it's true, missus, I swear! Ow!" he said frantically as I jabbed the needle under the skin.

"I'm not trying to hurt you," I assured him, in as false a voice as I could muster. "I have to stitch the wound, though."

"Oh! Ow! I don't know, to be sure I don't! I'd tell, if I did, as God's my witness!"

"I'm sure you would," I said, intent on my stitching.

"Oh! Please, missus! Stop! Just for a moment! All I know is it was an Englishman! That's all!"

I stopped, and stared up at him. "An Englishman?" I said blankly.

"Yes, missus. That's what Sir Percival said." He looked down at me, tears trembling on the lashes of both his eyes. I took the final stitch, as gently as I could, and tied the suture knot. Without speaking, I got up, poured a small tot of brandy from my private bottle, and handed it to him.

He gulped it gratefully, and seemed much restored in consequence. Whether out of gratitude, or sheer relief for the end of the ordeal, he told me the rest of the story. In search of evidence to support a charge of sedition, he had gone to the printshop in Carfax Close.

"I know what happened there," I assured him. I turned his face toward the light, examining the burn scars. "Is it still painful?"

"No, Missus, but it hurt precious bad for some time," he said. Being incapacitated by his injuries, Tompkins had taken no part in the ambush at Arbroath cove, but he had heard—"not direct-like, but I heard, you know," he said, with a shrewd nod of the head—what had happened.

Sir Percival had given Jamie warning of an ambush, to lessen the chances of Jamie's thinking him involved in the affair, and possibly revealing the details of their financial arrangements in quarters where such revelations would be detrimental to Sir Percival's interests.

At the same time, Sir Percival had learned—from the associate, the mysterious Englishman—of the fallback arrangement with the French delivery vessel, and had arranged the grave-ambush on the beach at Arbroath.

"But what about the Customs officer who was killed on the road?" I asked sharply. I couldn't repress a small shudder, at memory of that dreadful face. "Who did that? There were only five men among the smugglers who could possibly have done it, and none of them are Englishmen!"

Tompkins rubbed a hand over his mouth; he seemed to be debating the wisdom of telling me or not. I picked up the brandy bottle and set it by his elbow.

"Why, I'm much obliged, Missus Fraser! You're a true Christian, missus, and so I shall tell anyone who asks!"

"Skip the testimonials," I said dryly. "Just tell me what you know about the Customs officer."

He filled the cup and drained it, sipping slowly. Then, with a sigh of satisfaction, he set it down and licked his lips.

"It wasn't none of the smugglers done him in, missus. It was his own mate."

"What!" I jerked back, startled, but he nodded, blinking his good eye in token of sincerity.

"That's right, missus. There was two of 'em, wasn't there? Well, the one of them had his instructions, didn't he?"

The instructions had been to wait until whatever smugglers escaped the ambush on the beach had reached the road, whereupon the Customs officer was to drop a noose over his partner's head in the dark and strangle him swiftly, then string him up and leave him, as evidence of the smugglers' murderous wrath.

"But why?" I said, bewildered and horrified. "What was the point of doing that?"

"Do you not see?" Tompkins looked surprised, as though the logic of the situation should be obvious. "We'd failed to get the evidence from the printshop that would have proved the case of sedition against Fraser, and with the shop burnt to the ground, no possibility of another chance. Nor had we ever caught Fraser red-handed with the goods himself, only some of the small fish who worked for him. One of the other agents thought he'd a clue where the stuff was kept, but something happened to him—perhaps Fraser caught him or bought him off, for he disappeared one day in November, and wasn't heard of again, nor the hiding place for the contraband, neither."

"I see." I swallowed, thinking of the man who had accosted me on the stairs of the brothel. What had become of that cask of crème de menthe? "But—"

"Well, I'm telling you, missus, just you wait." Tompkins raised a monitory hand. "So—here's Sir Percival, knowing as he's got a rare case, with a man's not only one of the biggest smugglers on the Firth, *and* the author of some of the most first-rate seditious material it's been my privilege to see, *but* is also a pardoned Jacobite traitor, whose name will make the trial a sensation from one end of the kingdom to the other. The only trouble being"—he shrugged—"as there's no evidence."

It began to make a hideous sort of sense, as Tompkins explained the plan. The murder of a Customs officer killed in pursuit of duty would not only make any smuggler arrested for the crime subject to a capital charge, but was the sort of heinous crime that would cause a major public outcry. The matter-of-fact acceptance that smugglers enjoyed from the populace would not protect them in a matter of such callous villainy.

"Your Sir Percival has got the makings of a really first-class son of a bitch," I observed. Tompkins nodded meditatively, blinking into his cup.

"Well, you've the right of it there, missus, I'll not say you're wrong."

"And the Customs officer who was killed—I suppose he was just a convenience?"

Tompkins sniggered, with a fine spray of brandy. His one eye seemed to be having some trouble focusing.

"Oh, very convenient, Missus, more ways than one. Don't you grieve none on his account. There was a good many folk glad enough to see Tom Oakie swing—and not the least of 'em, Sir Percival."

"I see." I finished fastening the bandage about his calf. It was getting late; I would have to get back to the sickbay soon.

"I'd better call someone to take you to your hammock," I said, taking the nearly empty bottle from his unresisting hand. "You should rest your leg for at least three days; tell your officer I said you can't go aloft until I've taken out the stitches."

"I'll do that, missus, and I thank you for your kindness to a poor unfortunate sailor." Tompkins made an abortive attempt to stand, looking surprised when he failed. I got a hand under his armpit and heaved, getting him on his feet, and—he declining my offer to summon him assistance—helped him to the door.

"You needn't worry about Harry Tompkins, missus," he said, weaving unsteadily into the corridor. He turned and gave me an exaggerated wink. "Old Harry always ends up all right, no matter what." Looking at him, with his long nose, pink-tipped from liquor, his large, transparent ears, and his single sly brown eye, it came to me suddenly what he reminded me of.

"When were you born, Mr. Tompkins?" I asked.

He blinked for a moment, uncomprehending, but then said, "The Year of our Lord 1713, missus. Why?"

"No reason," I said, and waved him off, watching as he caromed slowly down the corridor, dropping out of sight at the ladder like a bag of oats. I would have to check with Mr. Willoughby to be sure, but at the moment, I would have wagered my chemise that 1713 had been a Year of the Rat.

48

Moment of Grace

Over the next few days, a routine set in, as it does in even the most desperate circumstances, provided that they continue long enough. The hours after a battle are urgent and chaotic, with men's lives hanging on a second's action. Here a doctor can be heroic, knowing for certain that the wound just stanched has saved a life, that the quick intervention will save a limb. But in an epidemic, there is none of that.

Then come the long days of constant watching and battles fought on the field of germs—and with no weapons suited to that field, it can be no more than a battle of delay, doing the small things that may not help but must be done, over and over and over again, fighting the invisible enemy of disease, in the tenuous hope that the body can be supported long enough to outlast its attacker.

To fight disease without medicine is to push against a shadow; a darkness that spreads as inexorably as night. I had been fighting for nine days, and forty-six more men were dead.

Still, I rose each day at dawn, splashed water into my grainy eyes, and went once more to the field of war, unarmed with anything save persistence—and a barrel of alcohol.

There were some victories, but even these left a bitter taste in my mouth. I found the likely source of infection—one of the messmates, a man named Howard. First serving on board as a member of one of the gun crews, Howard had been transferred to galley duty six weeks before, the result of an accident with a recoiling gun-carriage that had crushed several fingers.

Howard had served the gun room, and the first known case of the disease —taken from the incomplete records of the dead surgeon, Mr. Hunter—was one of the marines who messed there. Four more cases, all from the gun room, and then it had begun to spread, as infected but still ambulatory men left the deadly contamination smeared in the ship's heads, to be picked up there and passed to the crew at large.

Howard's admission that he had seen sickness like this before, on other ships where he had served, was enough to clinch the matter. However, the cook, shorthanded as everyone else aboard, had declined absolutely to part with a valuable hand, only because of "a goddamned female's silly notion!"

Elias could not persuade him, and I had been obliged to summon the captain himself, who—misunderstanding the nature of the disturbance, had arrived with several armed marines. There was a most unpleasant scene in the galley, and Howard was removed to the brig—the only place of certain quarantine—protesting in bewilderment, and demanding to know his crime.

As I came up from the galley, the sun was going down into the ocean in a blaze that paved the western sea with gold like the streets of Heaven. I stopped for a moment, just a moment, transfixed by the sight.

It had happened many times before, but it always took me by surprise. Always in the midst of great stress, wading waist-deep in trouble and sorrow, as doctors do, I would glance out a window, open a door, look into a face, and there it would be, unexpected and unmistakable. A moment of peace.

The light spread from the sky to the ship, and the great horizon was no longer a blank threat of emptiness, but the habitation of joy. For a moment, I lived in the center of the sun, warmed and cleansed, and the smell and sight of sickness fell away; the bitterness lifted from my heart.

I never looked for it, gave it no name; yet I knew it always, when the gift of peace came. I stood quite still for the moment that it lasted, thinking it strange and not strange that grace should find me here, too.

Then the light shifted slightly and the moment passed, leaving me as it always did, with the lasting echo of its presence. In a reflex of acknowledgment, I crossed myself and went below, my tarnished armor faintly gleaming.

<hr>

Elias Pound died of the typhoid four days later. It was a virulent infection; he came to the sickbay heavy-eyed with fever and wincing at the light; six hours later he was delirious and unable to rise. The next dawn he pressed his cropped round head against my bosom, called me "Mother," and died in my arms.

I did what had to be done throughout the day, and stood by Captain Leonard at sunset, when he read the burial service. The body of Midshipman Pound was consigned to the sea, wrapped in his hammock.

I declined the Captain's invitation to dinner, and went instead to sit in a remote corner of the afterdeck, next to one of the great guns, where I could look out over the water, showing my face to no one. The sun went down in gold and glory, succeeded by a night of starred velvet, but there was no moment of grace, no peace in either sight for me.

As the darkness settled over the ship, all her movements began to slow. I leaned my head against the gun, the polished metal cool under my cheek. A seaman passed me at a fast walk, intent on his duties, and then I was alone.

I ached desperately; my head throbbed, my back was stiff and my feet swollen, but none of these was of any significance, compared to the deeper ache that knotted my heart.

Any doctor hates to lose a patient. Death is the enemy, and to lose someone in your care to the clutch of the dark angel is to be vanquished yourself, to feel the rage of betrayal and impotence, beyond the common, human grief of loss and the horror of death's finality. I had lost twenty-three men between dawn and sunset of this day. Elias was only the first.

Several had died as I sponged their bodies or held their hands; others, alone in their hammocks, had died uncomforted even by a touch, because I could not reach them in time. I thought I had resigned myself to the realities of this time, but knowing—even as I held the twitching body of an eighteen-year-old seaman as his bowels dissolved in blood and water—that penicillin would have saved most of them, and I had none, was galling as an ulcer, eating at my soul.

The box of syringes and ampules had been left behind on the *Artemis,* in the pocket of my spare skirt. If I had had it, I could not have used it. If I had used it, I could have saved no more than one or two. But even knowing that, I raged at the futility of it all, clenching my teeth until my jaw ached as I went from man to man, armed with nothing but boiled milk and biscuit, and my two empty hands.

My mind followed the same dizzying lines my feet had traveled earlier, seeing faces—faces contorted in anguish or smoothing slowly in the slackness of death, but all of them looking at me. At me. I lifted my futile hand and slammed it hard against the rail. I did it again, and again, scarcely feeling the sting of the blows, in a frenzy of furious rage and grief.

"Stop that!" a voice spoke behind me, and a hand seized my wrist, preventing me from slapping the rail yet again.

"Let go!" I struggled, but his grip was too strong.

"Stop," he said again, firmly. His other arm came around my waist, and he pulled me back, away from the rail. "You mustn't do that," he said. "You'll hurt yourself."

"I don't bloody care!" I wrenched against his grasp, but then slumped, defeated. What did it matter?

He let go of me then, and I turned to find myself facing a man I had never seen before. He wasn't a sailor; while his clothes were crumpled and stale with long wear, they had originally been very fine; the dove-gray coat and waistcoat had been tailored to flatter his slender frame, and the wilted lace at his throat had come from Brussels.

"Who the hell are you?" I said in astonishment. I brushed at my wet cheeks, sniffed, and made an instinctive effort to smooth down my hair. I hoped the shadows hid my face.

He smiled slightly, and handed me a handkerchief, crumpled, but clean.

"My name is Grey," he said, with a small, courtly bow. "I expect that you must be the famous Mrs. Malcolm, whose heroism Captain Leonard has been so strongly praising." I grimaced at that, and he paused.

"I am sorry," he said. "Have I said something amiss? My apologies, Madame, I had no notion of offering you offense." He looked anxious at the thought, and I shook my head.

"It is not heroic to watch men die," I said. My words were thick, and I stopped to blow my nose. "I'm just here, that's all. Thank you for the handkerchief." I hesitated, not wanting to hand the used handkerchief back to him, but not wanting simply to pocket it, either. He solved the dilemma with a dismissive wave of his hand.

"Might I do anything else for you?" He hesitated, irresolute. "A cup of water? Some brandy, perhaps?" He fumbled in his coat, drawing out a small silver pocket flask engraved with a coat of arms, which he offered to me.

I took it, with a nod of thanks, and took a swallow deep enough to make me cough. It burned down the back of my throat, but I sipped again, more cautiously this time, and felt it warm me, easing and strengthening. I breathed deeply and drank again. It helped.

"Thank you," I said, a little hoarsely, handing back the flask. That seemed somewhat abrupt, and I added, "I'd forgotten that brandy is good to drink; I've been using it to wash people in the sickbay." The statement brought back the events of the day to me with crushing vividness, and I sagged back onto the powder box where I had been sitting.

"I take it the plague continues unabated?" he asked quietly. He stood in front of me, the glow of a nearby lantern shining on his dark blond hair.

"Not unabated, no." I closed my eyes, feeling unutterably bleak. "There was only one new case today. There were four the day before, and six the day before that."

"That sounds hopeful," he observed. "As though you are defeating the disease."

I shook my head slowly. It felt dense and heavy as one of the cannonballs piled in the shallow bins by the guns.

"No. All we're doing is to stop more men being infected. There isn't a bloody thing I can do for the ones who already have it."

"Indeed." He stooped and picked up one of my hands. Surprised, I let him have it. He ran a thumb lightly over the blister where I had burned myself scalding milk, and touched my knuckles, reddened and cracked from the constant immersion in alcohol.

"You would appear to have been very active, Madame, for someone who is doing nothing," he said dryly.

"Of course I'm doing something!" I snapped, yanking my hand back. "It doesn't do any good!"

"I'm sure—" he began.

"It doesn't!" I slammed my fist on the gun, the noiseless blow seeming to symbolize the pain-filled futility of the day. "Do you know how many men I lost today? Twenty-three! I've been on my feet since dawn, elbow-deep in filth and vomit and my clothes stuck to me, and none of it's been any good! I couldn't help! Do you hear me? I couldn't help!"

His face was turned away, in shadow, but his shoulders were stiff.

"I hear you," he said quietly. "You shame me, Madam. I had kept to my cabin at the Captain's orders, but I had no idea that the circumstances were such as you describe, or I assure you that I should have come to help, in spite of them."

"Why?" I said blankly. "It isn't your job."

"Is it yours?" He swung around to face me, and I saw that he was handsome, in his late thirties, perhaps, with sensitive, fine-cut features, and large blue eyes, open in astonishment.

"Yes," I said.

He studied my face for a moment, and his own expression changed, fading from surprise to thoughtfulness.

"I see."

"No, you don't, but it doesn't matter." I pressed my fingertips hard against my brow, in the spot Mr. Willoughby had shown me, to relieve headache. "If the Captain means you to keep to your cabin, then you likely should. There are enough hands to help in the sickbay; it's just that . . . nothing helps," I ended, dropping my hands.

He walked over to the rail, a few feet away from me, and stood looking out over the expanse of dark water, sparked here and there as a random wave caught the starlight.

"I do see," he repeated, as though talking to the waves. "I had thought your distress due only to a woman's natural compassion, but I see it is something quite different." He paused, hands gripping the rail, an indistinct figure in the starlight.

"I have been a soldier, an officer," he said. "I know what it is, to hold men's lives in your hand—and to lose them."

I was quiet, and so was he. The usual shipboard sounds went on in the distance, muted by night and the lack of men to make them. At last he sighed and turned toward me again.

"What it comes to, I think, is the knowledge that you are not God." He paused, then added, softly, "And the very real regret that you cannot be."

I sighed, feeling some of the tension drain out of me. The cool wind lifted the weight of my hair from my neck, and the curling ends drifted across my face, gentle as a touch.

"Yes," I said.

He hesitated a moment, as though not knowing what to say next, then bent, picked up my hand, and kissed it, very simply, without affectation.

"Good night, Mrs. Malcolm," he said, and turned away, the sound of his footsteps loud on the deck.

He was no more than a few yards past me when a seaman, hurrying by, spotted him and stopped with a cry. It was Jones, one of the stewards.

"My Lord! You shouldn't ought to be out of your cabin, sir! The night air's mortal, and the plague loose on board—and the Captain's orders—whatever is your servant a-thinking of, sir, to let you walk about like this?"

My acquaintance nodded apologetically.

"Yes, yes, I know. I shouldn't have come up; but I thought that if I stayed in the cabin a moment longer I should be stifled altogether."

"Better stifled than dead o' the bloody flux, sir, and you'll pardon of my saying so," Jones replied sternly. My acquaintance made no remonstrance to this, but merely murmured something and disappeared in the shadows of the afterdeck.

I reached out a hand and grasped Jones by the sleeve as he passed, causing him to start, with a wordless yelp of alarm.

"Oh! Mrs. Malcolm," he said, coming to earth, a bony hand splayed across his chest. "Christ, I did think you was a ghost, mum, begging your pardon."

"I beg yours," I said, politely. "I only wanted to ask—who was the man you were just talking to?"

"Oh, him?" Jones twisted about to look over his shoulder, but the aptly named Mr. Grey had long since vanished. "Why, that's Lord John Grey, mum, him as is the new governor of Jamaica." He frowned censoriously in the direction taken by my acquaintance. "He ain't supposed to be up here; the Captain's give strict orders he's to stay safe below, out o' harm's way. All we need's to come into port with a dead political aboard, and there'll be the devil to pay, mum, savin' your presence."

He shook his head disapprovingly, then turned to me with a bob of the head.

"You'll be retiring, mum? Shall I bring you down a nice cup of tea and maybe a bit o' biscuit?"

"No, thank you, Jones," I said. "I'll go and check the sickbay again before I go to bed. I don't need anything."

"Well, you do, mum, and you just say. Anytime. Good night to you, mum." He touched his forelock briefly and hurried off.

I stood at the rail alone for a moment before going below, drawing in deep breaths of the clean, fresh air. It would be a good many hours yet until dawn; the stars burned bright and clear over my head, and I realized, quite suddenly, that the moment of grace I had wordlessly prayed for had come, after all.

"You're right," I said at last, aloud, to the sea and sky. "A sunset wouldn't have been enough. Thank you," I added, and went below.

49

Land Ho!

It's true, what the sailors say. You can smell land, a long time before you see it.

Despite the long voyage, the goat pen in the hold was a surprisingly pleasant place. By now, the fresh straw had been exhausted, and the goats' hooves clicked restlessly to and fro on bare boards. Still, the heaps of manure were swept up daily, and neatly piled in baskets to be heaved overboard, and Annekje Johansen brought dry armloads of hay to the manger each morning. There was a strong smell of goat, but it was a clean, animal scent, and quite pleasant by contrast with the stench of unwashed sailors.

"*Komma, komma, komma, dyr get,*" she crooned, luring a yearling within reach with a twiddled handful of hay. The animal stretched out cautious lips, and was promptly seized by the neck and pulled forward, its head secured under Annekje's brawny arm.

"Ticks, is it?" I asked, coming forward to help. Annekje looked up and gave me her broad, gap-toothed smile.

"*Guten Morgen,* Mrs. Claire," she said. "*Ja,* tick. Here." She took the young goat's drooping ear in one hand and turned up the silky edge to show me the blueberry bulge of a blood-gorged tick, burrowed deep in the tender skin.

She clutched the goat to hold it still, and dug into the ear, pinching the tick viciously between her nails. She pulled it free with a twist, and the goat blatted and kicked, a tiny spot of blood welling from its ear where the tick had been detached.

"Wait," I said, when she would have released the animal. She glanced at me, curious, but kept her hold and nodded. I took the bottle of alcohol I wore slung at my belt like a sidearm, and poured a few drops on the ear. It was soft and tender, the tiny veins clearly visible beneath the satin skin. The goat's square-pupilled eyes bulged farther and its tongue stuck out in agitation as it bleated.

"No sore ear," I said, in explanation, and Annekje nodded in approval.

Then the goatling was free, and went plunging back into the herd, to butt its head against its mother's side in a frantic search for milky reassurance. Annekje looked about for the discarded tick and found it lying on the deck, tiny legs helpless to move its swollen body. She smashed it casually under the heel of her shoe, leaving a tiny dark blotch on the board.

"We come to land?" I asked, and she nodded, with a wide, happy smile. She waved expansively upward, where sunlight fell through the grating overhead.

"*Ja.* Smell?" she said, sniffing vigorously in illustration. She beamed. "Land, *ja*! Water, grass. Is goot, goot!"

"I need to go to land," I said, watching her carefully. "Go quiet. Secret. Not tell."

"Ah?" Annekje's eyes widened, and she looked at me speculatively. "Not tell Captain, *ja*?"

"Not tell anyone," I said, nodding hard. "You can help?"

She was quiet for a moment, thinking. A big, placid woman, she reminded me of her own goats, adapting cheerfully to the queer life of shipboard, enjoying the pleasures of hay and warm company, thriving despite the lurching deck and stuffy shadows of the hold.

With that same air of capable adaptation, she looked up at me and nodded calmly.

"*Ja,* I help."

It was past midday when we anchored off what one of the midshipmen told me was Watlings Island.

I looked over the rail with considerable curiosity. This flat island, with its wide white beaches and lines of low palms, had once been called San Salvador. Renamed for the present in honor of a notorious buccaneer of the last century, this dot of land was presumably Christopher Columbus's first sight of the New World.

I had the substantial advantage over Columbus of having known for a fact that the land was here, but still I felt a faint echo of the joy and relief that the sailors of those tiny wooden caravels had felt at that first landfall.

Long enough on a rolling ship, and you forget what it is to walk on land. Getting sea legs, they call it. It's a metamorphosis, this leg-getting, like the change from tadpole to frog, a painless shift from one element to another. But the smell and sight of land makes you remember that you were born to the earth, and your feet ache suddenly for the touch of solid ground.

The problem at the moment was actually getting my feet *on* solid ground. Watlings Island was no more than a pause, to replenish our severely depleted water supply before the run through the Windward Isles down to Jamaica. It would be at least another week's sail, and the presence of so many invalids aboard requiring vast infusions of liquid had run the great water casks in the hold nearly dry.

San Salvador was a small island, but I had learned from careful questioning of my patients that there was a fair amount of shipping traffic through its main port in Cockburn Town. It might not be the ideal place to escape, but it looked as though there would be little other choice; I had no intention of enjoying the navy's "hospitality" on Jamaica, serving as the bait that would lure Jamie to arrest.

Starved as the crew was for the sight and feel of land, no one was allowed to go ashore save the watering party, now busy with their casks and sledges up Pigeon Creek, at whose foot we were anchored. One of the marines stood at the head of the gangway, blocking any attempt at leaving.

Such members of the crew as were not involved in watering or on watch stood by the rail, talking and joking or merely gazing at the island, the dream of hope fulfilled. Some way down the deck, I caught sight of a long, blond tail of hair, flying in the shore breeze. The Governor too had emerged from seclusion, pale face upturned to the tropic sun.

I would have gone to speak to him, but there was no time. Annekje had already gone below for the goat. I wiped my hands on my skirt, making my final estimations. It was no more than two hundred yards to the thick growth of palms and underbrush. If I could get down the gangway and into the jungle, I thought I had a good chance of getting away.

Anxious as he was to be on his way to Jamaica, Captain Leonard was unlikely to waste much time in trying to catch me. And if they did catch me —well, the Captain could hardly punish me for trying to leave the ship; I was neither a seaman nor a formal captive, after all.

The sun shone on Annekje's blond head as she made her way carefully up the ladder, a young goat cozily nestled against her wide bosom. A quick glance, to see that I was in place, and she headed for the gangway.

Annekje spoke to the sentry in her queer mixture of English and Swedish, pointing to the goat and then ashore, insisting that it must have fresh grass. The marine appeared to understand her, but stood firm.

"No, ma'am," he said, respectfully enough, "no one is to go ashore save the watering party; captain's orders."

Standing just out of sight, I watched as she went on arguing, thrusting her goatling urgently in his face, forcing him a step back, a step to the side, maneuvering him artfully just far enough that I could slip past behind him. No more than a moment, now; he was almost in place. When she had drawn him away from the head of the gangplank, she would drop the goat and cause sufficient confusion in the catching of it that I would have a minute or two to make my escape.

I shifted nervously from foot to foot. My feet were bare; it would be easier to run on the sandy beach. The sentry moved, his red-coated back fully turned to me. A foot more, I thought, just a foot more.

"Such a fine day, is it not, Mrs. Malcolm?"

I bit my tongue.

"Very fine, Captain Leonard," I said, with some difficulty. My heart seemed to have stopped dead when he spoke. It now resumed beating much faster than usual, to make up for lost time.

The Captain stepped up beside me and looked over the rail, his young face shining with Columbus's joy. Despite my strong desire to push him overboard, I felt myself smile grudgingly at the sight of him.

"This landfall is as much your victory as mine, Mrs. Malcolm," he said. "Without you, I doubt we should ever have brought the *Porpoise* to land." He very shyly touched my hand, and I smiled again, a little less grudgingly.

"I'm sure you would have managed, Captain," I said. "You seem to be a most competent sailor."

He laughed, and blushed. He had shaved in honor of the land, and his smooth cheeks glowed pink and raw.

"Well, it is mostly the hands, ma'am; I may say they have done nobly. And their efforts, of course, are due in turn to your skill as a physician." He looked at me, brown eyes shining earnestly.

"Indeed, Mrs. Malcolm—I cannot say what your skill and kindness have meant to us. I—I mean to say so, too, to the Governor and to Sir Greville— you know, the King's Commissioner on Antigua. I shall write a letter, a most sincere testimonial to you and to your efforts on our behalf. Perhaps— perhaps it will help." He dropped his eyes.

"Help with what, Captain?" My heart was still beating fast.

Captain Leonard bit his lip, then looked up.

"I had not meant to say anything to you, ma'am. But I—really I cannot in honor keep silence. Mrs. Fraser, I know your name, and I know what your husband is."

"Really?" I said, trying to keep control of my own emotions. "What is he?"

The boy looked surprised at that. "Why, ma'am, he is a criminal." He paled a little. "You mean—you did not know?"

"Yes, I knew that," I said dryly. "Why are you telling me, though?"

He licked his lips, but met my eyes bravely enough. "When I discovered your husband's identity, I wrote it in the ship's log. I regret that action now, but it is too late; the information is official. Once I reach Jamaica, I must report his name and destination to the authorities there, and likewise to the commander at the naval barracks on Antigua. He will be taken when the *Artemis* docks." He swallowed. "And if he is taken—"

"He'll be hanged," I said, finishing what he could not. The boy nodded, wordless. His mouth opened and closed, seeking words.

"I have seen men hanged," he said at last. "Mrs. Fraser, I just—I—" He stopped then, fighting for control, and found it. He drew himself up straight and looked at me straight on, the joy of his landing drowned in sudden misery.

"I am sorry," he said softly. "I cannot ask you to forgive me; I can only say that I am most terribly sorry."

He turned on his heel and walked away. Directly before him stood Annekje Johansen and her goat, still in heated conversation with the sentry.

"What is this?" Captain Leonard demanded angrily. "Remove this animal from the deck at once! Mr. Holford, what are you thinking of?"

Annekje's eyes flicked from the captain to my face, instantly divining what had gone wrong. She stood still, head bowed to the captain's scolding, then marched away toward the hatchway to the goats' hold, clutching her yearling. As she passed, one big blue eye winked solemnly. We would try again. But how?

Racked by guilt and bedeviled by contrary winds, Captain Leonard avoided me, seeking refuge on his quarterdeck as we made our cautious way past Acklin Island and Samana Cay. The weather aided him in this evasion; it stayed bright, but with odd, light breezes alternating with sudden gusts, so that constant adjustment of the sails was required—no easy task, in a ship so shorthanded.

It was four days later, as we shifted course to enter the Caicos Passage, that a sudden booming gust of wind struck the ship out of nowhere, catching her ill-rigged and unprepared.

I was on deck when the gust struck. There was a sudden *whoosh* that sent my skirts billowing and propelled me flying down the deck, followed by a sharp, loud *crack!* somewhere overhead. I crashed head-on into Ramsdell Hodges, one of the forecastle crew, and we whirled together in a mad pirouette before falling entangled to the deck.

There was confusion all around, with hands running and orders shouted. I sat up, trying to collect my scattered wits.

"What is it?" I demanded of Hodges, who staggered to his feet and reached down to lift me up. "What's happened?"

"The fucking mainmast's split," he said succinctly. "Saving your presence, ma'am, but it has. And now there'll be hell to pay."

The *Porpoise* limped slowly south, not daring to risk the banks and shoals of the passage without a mainmast. Instead, Captain Leonard put in for repairs at the nearest convenient anchorage, Bottle Creek, on the shore of North Caicos Island.

This time, we were allowed ashore, but no great good did it do me. Tiny and dry, with few sources of fresh water, the Turks and Caicos provided little more than numerous tiny bays that might shelter passing ships caught in storms. And the idea of hiding on a foodless, waterless island, waiting for a convenient hurricane to blow me a ship, did not appeal.

To Annekje, though, our change of course suggested a new plan.

"I know these island," she said, nodding wisely. "We go round now, Grand Turk, Mouchoir. Not Caicos."

I looked askance, and she squatted, drawing with a blunt forefinger in the yellow sand of the beach.

"See—Caicos Passage," she said, sketching a pair of lines. At the top, between the lines, she sketched the small triangle of a sail. "Go through," she said, indicating the Caicos Passage, "but mast is gone. Now—" She quickly drew several irregular circles, to the right of the passage. "North Caicos, South Caicos, Caicos, Grand Turk," she said, stabbing a finger at each circle in turn. Go round now—reefs. Mouchoir." And she drew another pair of lines, indicating a passage to the southeast of Grand Turk Island.

"Mouchoir Passage?" I had heard the sailors mention it, but had no idea how it applied to my potential escape from the *Porpoise.*

Annekje nodded, beaming, then drew a long, wavy line, some way below her previous illustrations. She pointed at it proudly. "Hispaniola. St. Domingue. Big island, is there towns, lots ships."

I raised my eyebrows, still baffled. She sighed, seeing that I didn't understand. She thought a moment, then stood up, dusting her heavy thighs. We had been gathering whelks from the rocks in a shallow pan. She seized this, dumped out the whelks, and filled it with seawater. Then, laying it on the sand, she motioned to me to watch.

She stirred the water carefully, in a circular motion, then lifted her finger out, stained dark with the purple blood of the whelks. The water continued to move, swirling past the tin sides.

Annekje pulled a thread from the raveling hem of her skirt, bit off a short piece, and spat it into the water. It floated, following the swirl of the water in lazy circles round the pan.

"You," she said, pointing at it. "Vater move you." She pointed back to her drawing in the sand. A new triangle, in the Mouchoir Passage. A line, curving from the tiny sail down to the left, indicating the ship's course. And now, the blue thread representing me, rescued from its immersion. She placed it by the tiny sail representing the *Porpoise,* then dragged it off, down the Passage toward the coast of Hispaniola.

"Jump," she said simply.

"You're crazy!" I said in horror.

She chuckled in deep satisfaction at my understanding. "*Ja,*" she said. "But it vork. Vater move you." She pointed to the end of the Mouchoir Passage, to the coast of Hispaniola, and stirred the water in the pan once more. We stood side by side, watching the ripples of her manufactured current die away.

Annekje glanced thoughtfully sideways at me. "You try not drown, *ja?*"

I took a deep breath and brushed the hair out of my eyes.

"*Ja,*" I said. "I'll try."

50

I Meet a Priest

The sea was remarkably warm, as seas go, and like a warm bath as compared to the icy surf off Scotland. On the other hand, it was extremely wet. After two or three hours of immersion, my feet were numb and my fingers chilled where they gripped the ropes of my makeshift life preserver, made of two empty casks.

The gunner's wife was as good as her word, though. The long, dim shape I had glimpsed from the *Porpoise* grew steadily nearer, its low hills dark as black velvet against a silver sky. Hispaniola—Haiti.

I had no way of telling time, and yet two months on shipboard, with its constant bells and watch-changes, had given me a rough feeling for the passage of the night hours. I thought it must have been near midnight when I left the *Porpoise;* now it was likely near 4:00 A.M., and still over a mile to the shore. Ocean currents are strong, but they take their time.

Worn out from work and worry, I twisted the rope awkwardly about one wrist to prevent my slipping out of the harness, laid my forehead on one cask, and drifted off to sleep with the scent of rum strong in my nostrils.

The brush of something solid beneath my feet woke me to an opal dawn, the sea and sky both glowing with the colors found inside a shell. With my feet planted in cold sand, I could feel the strength of the current flowing past me, tugging on the casks. I disentangled myself from the rope harness and with considerable relief, let the unwieldy things go bobbing toward the shore.

There were deep red indentations on my shoulders. The wrist I had twisted through the wet rope was rubbed raw; I was chilled, exhausted, and very thirsty, and my legs were rubbery as boiled squid.

On the other hand, the sea behind me was empty, the *Porpoise* nowhere in sight. I had escaped.

Now, all that remained to be done was to get ashore, find water, find some means of quick transport to Jamaica, and find Jamie and the *Artemis,* preferably before the Royal Navy did. I thought I could just about manage the first item on the agenda.

Such little as I knew of the Caribbean from postcards and tourist brochures had led me to think in terms of white-sand beaches and crystal lagoons. In fact, prevailing conditions ran more toward a lot of dense and ugly vegetation, embedded in extremely sticky dark-brown mud.

The thick bushlike plants must be mangroves. They stretched as far as I could see in either direction; there was no alternative but to clamber through them. Their roots rose out of the mud in big loops like croquet wickets, which I tripped over regularly, and the pale, smooth gray twigs grew in bunches like finger bones, snatching at my hair as I passed.

Squads of tiny purple crabs ran off in profound agitation at my approach. My feet sank into the mud to the ankles, and I thought better of putting on my shoes, wet as they were. I rolled them up in my wet skirt, kirtling it up above my knees and took out the fish knife Annekje had given me, just in case. I saw nothing threatening, but felt better with a weapon in my hand.

The rising sun on my shoulders at first was welcome, as it thawed my chilled flesh and dried my clothes. Within an hour, though, I wished that it would go behind a cloud. I was sweating heavily as the sun rose higher, caked to the knees with drying mud, and growing thirstier by the moment.

I tried to see how far the mangroves extended, but they rose above my head, and tossing waves of narrow, gray-green leaves were all I could see.

"The whole bloody island can't be mangroves," I muttered, slogging on. "There has to be solid land *someplace*." And water, I hoped.

A noise like a small cannon going off nearby startled me so that I dropped the fish knife. I groped frantically in the mud for it, then dived forward onto my face as something large whizzed past my head, missing me by inches.

There was a loud rattling of leaves, and then a sort of conversational-sounding *"Kwark?"*

"What?" I croaked. I sat up cautiously, knife in one hand, and wiped the wet, muddy curls out of my face with the other. Six feet away, a large black bird was sitting on a mangrove, regarding me with a critical eye.

He bent his head, delicately preening his sleek black feathers, as though to contrast his immaculate appearance with my own dishevelment.

"Well, la-di-dah," I said sarcastically. "You've got wings, mate."

The bird stopped preening and eyed me censoriously. Then he lifted his beak into the air, puffed his chest, and as though to further establish his sartorial superiority, suddenly inflated a large pouch of brilliant red skin that ran from the base of his neck halfway down his body.

"Bwoom!" he said, repeating the cannon-like noise that had startled me before. It startled me again, but not so much.

"Don't *do* that," I said irritably. Paying no attention, the bird slowly flapped its wings, settled back on its branch, and boomed again.

There was a sudden harsh cry from above, and with a loud flapping of wings, two more large black birds plopped down, landing in a mangrove a few feet away. Encouraged by the audience, the first bird went on booming at regular intervals, the skin of his pouch flaming with excitement. Within moments, three more black shapes had appeared overhead.

I was reasonably sure they weren't vultures, but I still wasn't inclined to stay. I had miles to go before I slept—or found Jamie. The chances of finding him in time were something I preferred not to dwell on.

A half-hour later, I had made so little progress that I could still hear the intermittent booming of my fastidious acquaintance, now joined by a number of similarly vocal friends. Panting with exertion, I picked a thickish root and sat down to rest.

My lips were cracked and dry, and the thought of water was occupying my mind to the exclusion of virtually everything else, even Jamie. I had been struggling through the mangroves for what seemed like forever, yet I could still hear the sound of the ocean. In fact, the tide must have been following me, for as I sat, a thin sheet of foaming, dirty seawater came purling through the mangrove roots to touch my toes briefly before receding.

"Water, water everywhere," I said ruefully, watching it, "nor any drop to drink."

A small movement on the damp mud caught my eye. Bending down, I saw several small fishes, of a sort I had never seen before. So far from flopping about, gasping for breath, these fish were sitting upright, propped on their pectoral fins, looking as though the fact that they were out of water was of no concern at all.

Fascinated, I bent closer to inspect them. One or two shifted on their fins, but they seemed not to mind being looked at. They goggled solemnly back at me, eyes bulging. It was only as I looked closer that I realized that the goggling appearance was caused by the fact that each fish appeared to have four eyes, not two.

I stared at one for a long minute, feeling the sweat trickle down between my breasts.

"Either I'm hallucinating," I told it conversationally, "or *you* are."

The fish didn't answer, but hopped suddenly, landing on a branch several inches above the ground. Perhaps it sensed something, for a moment later, another wave washed through, this one splashing up to my ankles.

A sudden welcome coolness fell on me. The sun had obligingly gone behind a cloud, and with its vanishing, the whole feel of the mangrove forest changed.

The gray leaves rattled as a sudden wind came up, and all the tiny crabs and fish and sand fleas disappeared as though by magic. They obviously knew something I didn't, and I found their going rather sinister.

I glanced up at the cloud where the sun had vanished, and gasped. A huge purple mass of boiling cloud was coming up behind the hills, so fast that I could actually see the leading edge of the mass, blazing white with shielded sunlight, moving forward toward me.

The next wave came through, two inches higher than the last, and taking longer to recede. I was neither a fish nor a crab, but by this time I had tumbled to the fact that a storm was on its way, and moving with amazing speed.

I glanced around, but saw nothing more than the seemingly infinite stretch of mangroves before me. Nothing that could be used for shelter. Still, being caught out in a rainstorm was hardly the worst that could happen, under the circumstances. My tongue felt dry and sticky, and I licked my lips at the thought of cool, sweet rain falling on my face.

The swish of another wave halfway up my shins brought me to a sudden awareness that I was in danger of more than getting wet. A quick glance into the upper branches of the mangroves showed me dried tufts of seaweed tangled in the twigs and crotches—high-tide level—and well above my head.

I felt a moment's panic, and tried to calm myself. If I lost my bearings in this place, I was done for. "Hold on, Beauchamp," I muttered to myself. I remembered a bit of advice I'd learned as an intern—"The first thing to do in a cardiac arrest is take your own pulse." I smiled at the memory, feeling panic ebb at once. As a gesture, I did take my pulse; a little fast, but strong and steady.

All right, then, which way? Toward the mountain; it was the only thing I could see above the sea of mangroves. I pushed my way through the branches as fast as I could, ignoring the ripping of my skirts and the increasing pull of each wave on my legs. The wind was coming from the sea behind me, pushing the waves higher. It blew my hair constantly into my eyes and mouth, and I wiped it back again and again, cursing out loud for the comfort of hearing a voice, but my throat was soon so dry that it hurt to talk.

I squelched on. My skirt kept pulling loose from my belt, and somewhere I dropped my shoes, which disappeared at once in the boiling foam that now washed well above my knees. It didn't seem to matter.

The tide was midthigh when the rain hit. With a roar that drowned the rattle of the leaves, it fell in drenching sheets that soaked me to the skin in moments. At first I wasted time vainly tilting my head back, trying to direct the rivulets that ran down my face into my open mouth. Then sense reasserted itself; I took off the kerchief tucked around my shoulders, let the rain soak it and wrung it out several times, to remove the vestiges of salt. Then I let it soak in the rain once more, lifted the wadded fabric to my mouth, and sucked the water from it. It tasted of sweat and seaweed and coarse cotton. It was delicious.

I had kept going, but was still in the clutches of the mangroves. The incoming tide was nearly waist-deep, and the walking getting much harder. Thirst slaked momentarily, I put my head down and pushed forward as fast as I could.

Lightning flashed over the mountains, and a moment later came the growl of thunder. The wash of the tide was so strong now that I could move forward only as each wave came in, half-running as the water shoved me along, then clinging to the nearest mangrove stem as the wash sucked back, dragging my trailing legs.

I was beginning to think that I had been over-hasty in abandoning Captain Leonard and the *Porpoise.* The wind was rising still further, dashing rain into my face so that I could barely see. Sailors say every seventh wave is higher. I found myself counting, as I slogged forward. It was the ninth wave, in fact, that struck me between the shoulder blades and knocked me flat before I could grasp a branch.

I floundered, helpless and choking in a blur of sand and water, then found my feet and stood upright again. The wave had half-drowned me, but had also altered my direction. I was no longer facing the mountain. I was, however, facing a large tree, no more than twenty feet away.

Four more waves, four more surging rushes forward, four more grim clutchings as the tide-race sought to pull me back, and I was on the muddy bank of a small inlet, where a tiny stream ran through the mangroves and out to sea. I crawled up it, slipping and staggering as I clambered into the welcoming embrace of the tree.

From a perch twelve feet up, I could see the stretch of the mangrove swamp behind me, and beyond that, the open sea. I changed my mind once more about the wisdom of my leaving the *Porpoise;* no matter how awful things were on land, they were a good deal worse out there.

Lightning shattered over a surface of boiling water, as wind and tide-race fought for control of the waves. Farther out, in the Mouchoir Passage, the swell was so high, it looked like rolling hills. The wind was high enough now to make a thin, whistling scream as it passed by, chilling me to the skin in my wet clothes. Thunder cracked together with the lightning flashes now, as the storm moved over me.

The *Artemis* was slower than the man-of-war; slow enough, I hoped, to be still safe, far out in the Atlantic.

I saw one clump of mangroves struck, a hundred feet away; the water hissed back, boiled away, and the dry land showed for a moment, before the waves rolled back, drowning the black wire of the blasted stems. I wrapped my arms about the trunk of the tree, pressed my face against the bark, and prayed. For Jamie, and the *Artemis.* For the *Porpoise,* Annekje Johansen and Tom Leonard and the Governor. And for me.

It was full daylight when I woke, my leg wedged between two branches, and numb from the knee down. I half-climbed, half-fell from my perch, landing in the shallow water of the inlet. I scooped up a handful of the water, tasted it, and spat it out. Not salt, but too brackish to drink.

My clothes were damp, but I was parched. The storm was long gone; everything around me was peaceful and normal, with the exception of the blackened mangroves. In the distance, I could hear the booming of the big black birds.

Brackish water here promised fresher water farther up the inlet. I rubbed my leg, trying to work out the pins-and-needles, then limped up the bank.

The vegetation began to change from the gray-green mangroves to a lusher green, with a thick undergrowth of grass and mossy plants that obliged me to walk in the water. Tired and thirsty as I was, I could go only a short distance before having to sit down and rest. As I did so, several of the odd little fish hopped up onto the bank beside me, goggling as though in curiosity.

"Well, I think you look rather peculiar, too," I told one.

"Are you English?" said the fish incredulously. The impression of Alice in Wonderland was so pronounced that I merely blinked stupidly at it for a moment. Then my head snapped up, and I stared into the face of the man who had spoken.

His face was weathered and sunburned to the color of mahogany, but the black hair that curled back from his brow was thick and ungrizzled. He stepped out from behind the mangrove, moving cautiously, as though afraid to startle me.

He was a bit above middle height and burly, thick through the shoulder, with a broad, boldly carved face, whose naturally friendly expression was tinged with wariness. He was dressed shabbily, with a heavy canvas bag slung across his shoulder—and a canteen made of goatskin hung from his belt.

"Vous êtes Anglaise?" he asked, repeating his original question in French. *"Comment ça va?"*

"Yes, I'm English," I said, croaking. "May I have some water, please?"

His eyes popped wide open—they were a light hazel—but he didn't say anything, just took the skin bag from his belt and handed it to me.

I laid the fish knife on my knee, close within reach, and drank deeply, scarcely able to gulp fast enough.

"Careful," he said. "It's dangerous to drink too fast."

"I know," I said, slightly breathless as I lowered the bag. "I'm a doctor." I lifted the canteen and drank again, but forced myself to swallow more slowly this time.

My rescuer was regarding me quizzically—and little wonder, I supposed. Sea-soaked and sun-dried, mud-caked and sweat-stained, with my hair straggling down over my face, I looked like a beggar, and probably a demented one at that.

"A doctor?" he said in English, showing that his thoughts had been traveling in the direction I suspected. He eyed me closely, in a way strongly reminiscent of the big black bird I had met earlier. "A doctor of *what,* if I might ask?"

"Medicine," I said, pausing briefly between gulps.

He had strongly drawn black brows. These rose nearly to his hairline.

"Indeed," he said, after a noticeable pause.

"Indeed," I said in the same tone of voice, and he laughed.

He inclined his head toward me in a formal bow. "In that case, Madame Physician, allow me to introduce myself. Lawrence Stern, Doctor of Natural Philosophy, of the Gesellschaft von Naturwissenschaft Philosophieren, Munich."

I blinked at him.

"A naturalist," he elaborated, gesturing at the canvas bag over his shoulder. "I was making my way toward those frigate birds in hopes of observing their breeding display, when I happened to overhear you, er . . ."

"Talking to a fish," I finished. "Yes, well . . . have they really got four eyes?" I asked, in hopes of changing the subject.

"Yes—or so it seems." He glanced down at the fish, who appeared to be following the conversation with rapt attention. "They seem to employ their oddly shaped optics when submerged, so that the upper pair of eyes observes events above the surface of the water, and the lower pair similarly takes note of happenings below it."

He looked then at me, with a hint of a smile. "Might I perhaps have the honor of knowing your name, Madame Physician?"

I hesitated, unsure what to tell him. I pondered the assortment of available aliases and decided on the truth.

"Fraser," I said. "Claire Fraser. Mrs. James Fraser," I added for good measure, feeling vaguely that marital status might make me seem slightly more respectable, appearances notwithstanding. I fingered back the curl hanging in my left eye.

"Your servant, Madame," he said with a gracious bow. He rubbed the bridge of his nose thoughtfully, looking at me.

"You have been shipwrecked, perhaps?" he ventured. It seemed the most logical—if not the only—explanation of my presence, and I nodded.

"I need to find a way to get to Jamaica," I said. "Do you think you can help me?"

He stared at me, frowning slightly, as though I were a specimen he couldn't quite decide how to classify, but then he nodded. He had a broad mouth that looked made for smiling; one corner turned up, and he extended a hand to help me up.

"Yes," he said. "I can help. But I think maybe first we find you some food, and maybe clothes, eh? I have a friend, who lives not so far away. I will take you there, shall I?"

What with parching thirst and the general press of events, I had paid little attention to the demands of my stomach. At the mention of food, however, it came immediately and vociferously to life.

"That," I said loudly, in hopes of drowning it out, "would be very nice indeed." I brushed back the tangle of my hair as well as I could, and ducking under a branch, followed my rescuer into the trees.

As we emerged from a palmetto grove, the ground opened out into a meadow-like space, then rose up in a broad hill before us. At the top of the hill, I could see a house—or at least a ruin. Its yellow plaster walls were cracked and overrun by pink bougainvillaeas and straggling guavas, the tin roof sported several visible holes, and the whole place gave off an air of mournful dilapidation.

"Hacienda de la Fuente," my new acquaintance said, with a nod toward it. "Can you stand the walk up the hill, or—" He hesitated, eyeing me as though estimating my weight. "I could carry you, I suppose," he said, with a not altogether flattering tone of doubt in his voice.

"I can manage," I assured him. My feet were bruised and sore, and punctured by fallen palmetto fronds, but the path before us looked relatively smooth.

The hillside leading up to the house was crisscrossed with the faint lines of sheep trails. There were a number of these animals present, peacefully grazing under the hot Hispaniola sun. As we stepped out of the trees, one sheep spotted us and uttered a short bleat of surprise. Like clockwork, every sheep on the hillside lifted its head in unison and stared at us.

Feeling rather self-conscious under this unblinking phalanx of suspicious eyes, I picked up my muddy skirts and followed Dr. Stern toward the main path—trodden by more than sheep, to judge from its width—that led up and over the hill.

It was a fine, bright day, and flocks of orange and white butterflies flickered through the grass. They lighted on the scattered blooms with here and there a brilliant yellow butterfly shining like a tiny sun.

I breathed in deeply, a lovely smell of grass and flowers, with minor notes of sheep and sun-warmed dust. A brown speck lighted for a moment on my sleeve and clung, long enough for me to see the velvet scales on its wing, and the tiny curled hose of its proboscis. The slender abdomen pulsed, breathing to its wing-beats, and then it was gone.

It might have been the promise of help, the water, the butterflies, or all three, but the burden of fear and fatigue under which I had labored for so long began to lift. True, I still had to face the problem of finding transport to Jamaica, but with thirst assuaged, a friend at hand, and the possibility of lunch just ahead, that no longer appeared the impossible task it had seemed in the mangroves.

"There he is!" Lawrence stopped, waiting for me to come up alongside him on the path. He gestured upward, toward a slight, wiry figure, picking its way carefully down the hillside toward us. I squinted at the figure as it wandered through the sheep, who took no apparent notice of his passage.

"Jesus!" I said. "It's St. Francis of Assisi."

Lawrence glanced at me in surprise.

"No, neither one. I told you he's English." He raised an arm and shouted, "*¡Hola!* Señor Fogden!"

The gray-robed figure paused suspiciously, one hand twined protectively in the wool of a passing ewe.

"*¿Quien es?*"

"Stern!" called Lawrence. "Lawrence Stern! Come along," he said, and extended a hand to pull me up the steep hillside onto the sheep path above.

The ewe was making determined efforts to escape her protector, which distracted him from our approach. A slender man a bit taller than I, he had a lean face that might have been handsome if not disfigured by a reddish beard that straggled dust-mop-like round the edges of his chin. His long and straying hair had gone to gray in streaks and runnels, and fell forward into his eyes with some frequency. An orange butterfly took wing from his head as we reached him.

"Stern?" he said, brushing back the hair with his free hand and blinking owlishly in the sunlight. "I don't know any . . . oh, it's you!" His thin face brightened. "Why didn't you say it was the shitworm man; I should have known you at once!"

Stern looked mildly embarrassed at this, and glanced at me apologetically. "I . . . ah . . . collected several interesting parasites from the excrement of Mr. Fogden's sheep, upon the occasion of my last visit," he explained.

"Horrible great worms!" Father Fogden said, shuddering violently in recollection. "A foot long, some of them, at least!"

"No more than eight inches," Stern corrected, smiling. He glanced at the nearest sheep, his hand resting on his collecting bag as though in anticipation of further imminent contributions to science. "Was the remedy I suggested effective?"

Father Fogden looked vaguely doubtful, as though trying to remember quite what the remedy had been.

"The turpentine drench," the naturalist prompted.

"Oh, yes!" The sun broke out on the priest's lean countenance, and he beamed fondly upon us. "Of course, of course! Yes, it worked splendidly. A few of them died, but the rest were quite cured. Capital, entirely capital!"

Suddenly it seemed to dawn on Father Fogden that he was being less than hospitable.

"But you must come in!" he said. "I was just about to partake of the midday meal; I insist you must join me." The priest turned to me. "This will be Mrs. Stern, will it?"

Mention of eight-inch intestinal worms had momentarily suppressed my hunger pangs, but at the mention of food, they came gurgling back in full force.

"No, but we should be delighted to partake of your hospitality," Stern answered politely. "Pray allow me to introduce my companion—a Mrs. Fraser, a countrywoman of yours."

Fogden's eyes grew quite round at this. A pale blue, with a tendency to water in bright sun, they fixed wonderingly upon me.

"An Englishwoman?" he said, disbelieving. "Here?" The round eyes took in the mud and salt stains on my crumpled dress, and my general air of disarray. He blinked for a moment, then stepped forward, and with the utmost dignity, bowed low over my hand.

"Your most obedient servant, Madame," he said. He rose and gestured grandly at the ruin on the hill. *"Mi casa es su casa."* He whistled sharply, and a small King Charles cavalier spaniel poked its face inquiringly out of the weeds.

"We have a guest, Ludo," the priest said, beaming. "Isn't that nice?" Tucking my hand firmly under one elbow, he took the sheep by its topknot of wool and towed us both toward the Hacienda de la Fuente, leaving Stern to follow.

The reason for the name became clear as we entered the dilapidated courtyard; a tiny cloud of dragonflies hovered like blinking lights over an algae-filled pool in one corner; it looked like a natural spring that someone had curbed in when the house was built. At least a dozen jungle fowl sprang up from the shattered pavement and flapped madly past our feet, leaving a small cloud of dust and feathers behind them. From other evidences left behind, I deduced that the trees overhanging the patio were their customary roost, and had been for some time.

"And so I was fortunate enough to encounter Mrs. Fraser among the mangroves this morning," Stern concluded. "I thought that perhaps you might . . . oh, look at that beauty! A magnificent Odonata!"

A tone of amazed delight accompanied this last statement, and he pushed unceremoniously past us to peer up into the shadows of the palm-thatched patio roof, where an enormous dragonfly, at least four inches across, was darting to and fro, blue body catching fire when it crossed one of the errant rays of sunshine poking through the tattered roof.

"Oh, do you want it? Be my guest." Our host waved a gracious hand at the dragonfly. "Here, Becky, trot in there and I'll see to your hoof in a bit." He shooed the ewe into the patio with a slap on the rump. It snorted and galloped off a few feet, then fell at once to browsing on the scattered fruit of a huge guava that overhung the ancient wall.

In fact, the trees around the patio had grown up to such an extent that the branches at many points interlaced. The whole of the courtyard seemed roofed with them, a sort of leafy tunnel, leading down the length of the patio into the gaping cavern of the house's entrance.

Drifts of dust and the pink paper leaves of bougainvillaea lay heaped against the sill, but just beyond, the dark wood floor gleamed with polish, bare and immaculate. It was dark inside, after the brilliance of the sunlight, but my eyes quickly adapted to the surroundings, and I looked around curiously.

It was a very plain room, dark and cool, furnished with no more than a long table, a few stools and chairs, and a small sideboard, over which hung a hideous painting in the Spanish style—an emaciated Christ, goateed and pallid in the gloom, indicating with one skeletal hand the bleeding heart that throbbed in his chest.

This ghastly object so struck my eye that it was a moment before I realized there was someone else in the room. The shadows in one corner of the room coalesced, and a small round face emerged, wearing an expression of remarkable malignity. I blinked and took a step back. The woman—for so she was—took a step forward, black eyes fixed on me, unblinking as the sheep.

She was no more than four feet tall, and so thick through the body as to seem like a solid block, without joint or indentation. Her head was a small round knob atop her body, with the smaller knob of a sparse gray bun scraped tightly back behind it. She was a light mahogany color—whether from the sun or naturally, I couldn't tell—and looked like nothing so much as a carved wooden doll. An ill-wish doll.

"Mamacita," said the priest, speaking Spanish to the graven image, "what good fortune! We have guests who will eat with us. You remember Señor Stern?" he added, gesturing at Lawrence.

"*Sí, claro,*" said the image, through invisible wooden lips. "The Christ-killer. And who is the *puta alba?*"

"And this is Señora Fraser," Father Fogden went on, beaming as though she had not spoken. "The poor lady has had the misfortune to be ship-wrecked; we must assist her as much as we can."

Mamacita looked me over slowly from top to toe. She said nothing, but the wide nostrils flared with infinite contempt.

"Your food's ready," she said, and turned away.

"Splendid!" the priest said happily. "Mamacita welcomes you; she'll bring us some food. Won't you sit down?"

The table was already laid with a large cracked plate and a wooden spoon. The priest took two more plates and spoons from the sideboard, and distributed them haphazardly about the table, gesturing hospitably at us to be seated.

A large brown coconut sat on the chair at the head of the table. Fogden tenderly picked this up and set it alongside his plate. The fibrous husk was darkened with age, and the hair was worn off it in patches, showing an almost polished appearance; I thought he must have had it for some time.

"Hallo there," he said, patting it affectionately. "And how are you keeping this fine day, Coco?"

I glanced at Stern, but he was studying the portrait of Christ, a small frown between his thick black brows. I supposed it was up to me to open a conversation.

"You live alone here, Mr.—ah, Father Fogden?" I inquired of our host. "You, and—er, Mamacita?"

"Yes, I'm afraid so. That's why I'm so pleased to see you. I haven't any real company but Ludo and Coco, you know," he explained, patting the hairy nut once more.

"Coco?" I said politely, thinking that on the evidence to hand so far, Coco wasn't the only nut among those present. I darted another glance at Stern, who looked mildly amused, but not alarmed.

"Spanish for bugbear—*coco*," the priest explained. "A hobgoblin. See him there, wee button nose and his dark little eyes?" Fogden jabbed two long, slender fingers suddenly into the depressions in the end of the coconut and jerked them back, chortling.

"Ah-ah!" he cried. "Mustn't stare, Coco, it's rude, you know!"

The pale blue eyes darted a piercing glance at me, and with some difficulty, I removed my teeth from my lower lip.

"Such a pretty lady," he said, as though to himself. "Not like my Ermenegilda, but very pretty nonetheless—isn't she, Ludo?"

The dog, thus addressed, ignored me, but bounded joyfully at its master, shoving its head under his hand and barking. He scratched its ears affectionately, then turned his attention back to me.

"Would one of Ermenegilda's dresses fit you, I wonder?"

I didn't know whether to answer this or not. Instead, I merely smiled politely, and hoped what I was thinking didn't show on my face. Fortunately, at this point Mamacita came back, carrying a steaming clay pot wrapped in towels. She slapped a ladleful of the contents on each plate, then went out, her feet—if she had any—moving invisibly beneath the shapeless skirt.

I stirred the mess on my plate, which appeared to be vegetable in nature. I took a cautious bite, and found it surprisingly good.

"Fried plantain, mixed with manioc and red beans," Lawrence explained, seeing my hesitation. He took a large spoonful of the steaming pulp himself and ate it without pausing for it to cool.

I had expected something of an inquisition about my presence, identity, and prospects. Instead, Father Fogden was singing softly under his breath, keeping time on the table with his spoon between bites.

I darted a glance at Lawrence, eyebrows up. He merely smiled, raised one shoulder in a slight shrug, and bent to his own food.

No real conversation occurred until the conclusion of the meal, when Mamacita—"unsmiling" seemed an understatement of her expression—removed the plates, replacing them with a platter of fruit, three cups, and a gigantic clay pitcher.

"Have you ever drunk sangria, Mrs. Fraser?"

I opened my mouth to say "Yes," thought better of it, and said, "No, what is it?" Sangria had been a popular drink in the 1960s, and I had had it many times at faculty parties and hospital social events. But for now, I was sure that it was unknown in England and Scotland; Mrs. Fraser of Edinburgh would never have heard of sangria.

"A mixture of red wine and the juices of orange and lemon," Lawrence Stern was explaining. "Mulled with spices, and served hot or cold, depending upon the weather. A most comforting and healthful beverage, is it not, Fogden?"

"Oh, yes. Oh, yes. Most comforting." Not waiting for me to find out for myself, the priest drained his cup, and reached for the pitcher before I had taken the first sip.

It was the same; the same sweet, throat-rasping taste, and I suffered the momentary illusion that I was back at the party where I had first tasted it, in company with a marijuana-smoking graduate student and a professor of botany.

This illusion was fostered by Stern's conversation, which dealt with his collections, and by Father Fogden's behavior. After several cups of sangria, he had risen, rummaged through the sideboard, and emerged with a large clay pipe. This he packed full of a strong-smelling herb shaken out of a paper twist, and proceeded to smoke.

"Hemp?" Stern asked, seeing this. "Tell me, do you find it settling to the digestive processes? I have heard it is so, but the herb is unobtainable in most European cities, and I have no firsthand observations of its effect."

"Oh, it is most genial and comforting to the stomach," Father Fogden assured him. He drew in a huge breath, held it, then exhaled long and dreamily, blowing a stream of soft white smoke that floated in streamers of haze near the room's low ceiling. "I shall send a packet home with you, dear fellow. Do say, now, what do you mean doing, you and this shipwrecked lady you have rescued?"

Stern explained his plan; after a night's rest, we intended to walk as far as the village of St. Luis du Nord, and from there see whether a fishing boat might carry us to Cap-Haïtien, thirty miles distant. If not, we would have to make our way overland to Le Cap, the nearest port of any size.

The priest's sketchy brows drew close together, frowning against the smoke.

"Mm? Well, I suppose there isn't much choice, is there? Still, you must go careful, particularly if you go overland to Le Cap. Maroons, you know."

"Maroons?" I glanced quizzically at Stern, who nodded, frowning.

"That's true. I did meet with two or three small bands as I came north through the valley of the Artibonite. They didn't molest me, though—I daresay I looked little better off than they, poor wretches. The Maroons are escaped slaves," he explained to me. "Having fled the cruelty of their masters, they take refuge in the remote hills, where the jungle hides them."

"They might not trouble you," Father Fogden said. He sucked deeply on his pipe, with a low, slurping noise, held his breath for a long count and then let it out reluctantly. His eyes were becoming markedly bloodshot. He closed one of them and examined me rather blearily with the other. "She doesn't look worth robbing, really."

Stern smiled broadly, looking at me, then quickly erased the smile, as though feeling he had been less than tactful. He coughed and took another cup of sangria. The priest's eyes gleamed over the pipe, red as a ferret's.

"I believe I need a little fresh air," I said, pushing back my chair. "And perhaps a little water, to wash with?"

"Oh, of course, of course!" Father Fogden cried. He rose, swaying unsteadily, and thumped the coals from his pipe carelessly out onto the sideboard. "Come with me."

The air in the patio seemed fresh and invigorating by comparison, despite its mugginess. I inhaled deeply, looking on with interest as Father Fogden fumbled with a bucket by the fountain in the corner.

"Where does the water come from?" I asked. "Is it a spring?" The stone trough was lined with soft tendrils of green algae, and I could see these moving lazily; evidently there was a current of some kind.

It was Stern who answered.

"Yes, there are hundreds of such springs. Some of them are said to have spirits living in them—but I do not suppose you subscribe to such superstition, sir?"

Father Fogden seemed to have to think about this. He set the half-filled bucket down on the coping and squinted into the water, trying to fix his gaze on one of the small silver fish that swam there.

"Ah?" he said vaguely. "Well, no. Spirits, no. Still—oh, yes, I had forgotten. I had something to show you." Going to a cupboard set into the wall, he pulled open the cracked wooden door and removed a small bundle of coarse unbleached muslin, which he put gingerly into Stern's hands.

"It came up in the spring one day last month," he said. "It died when the noon sun struck it, and I took it out. I'm afraid the other fish nibbled it a bit," he said apologetically, "but you can still see."

Lying in the center of the cloth was a small dried fish, much like those darting about in the spring, save that this one was pure white. It was also blind. On either side of the blunt head, there was a small swelling where an eye should have been, but that was all.

"Do you think it is a ghost fish?" the priest inquired. "I thought of it when you mentioned spirits. Still, I can't think what sort of sin a fish might have committed, so as to be doomed to roam about like that—eyeless, I mean. I mean"—he closed one eye again in his favorite expression—"one doesn't think of fish as having souls, and yet, if they don't, how can they become ghosts?"

"I shouldn't think they do, myself," I assured him. I peered more closely at the fish, which Stern was examining with the rapt joy of the born natural-ist. The skin was very thin, and so transparent that the shadows of the internal organs and the knobbly line of the vertebrae were clearly visible, yet it did have scales, tiny and translucent, though dulled by dryness.

"It is a blind cave fish," Stern said, reverently stroking the tiny blunt head. "I have seen one only once before, in a pool deep inside a cave, at a place called Abandawe. And that one escaped before I could examine it closely. My dear fellow—" He turned to the priest, eyes shining with excitement. "Might I have it?"

"Of course, of course." The priest fluttered his fingers in offhand generos-ity. "No use to me. Too small to eat, you know, even if Mamacita would think of cooking it, which she wouldn't." He glanced around the patio, kicking absently at a passing hen. "Where *is* Mamacita?"

"Here, *cabrón,* where else?" I hadn't seen her come out of the house, but there she was, a dusty, sunbrowned little figure stooping to fill another bucket from the spring.

A faintly musty, unpleasant smell reached my nostrils, and they twitched uneasily. The priest must have noticed, for he said, "Oh, you mustn't mind, it's only poor Arabella."

"Arabella?"

"Yes, in here." The priest held aside a ragged curtain of burlap that screened off a corner of the patio, and I glanced behind it.

A ledge jutted out of the stone wall at waist-height. On it were ranged a long row of sheep's skulls, pure white and polished.

"I can't bear to part with them, you see." Father Fogden gently stroked the heavy curve of a skull. "This was Beatriz—so sweet and gentle. She died in lambing, poor thing." He indicated two much smaller skulls nearby, shaped and polished like the rest.

"Arabella is a—a sheep, too?" I asked. The smell was much stronger here, and I thought I really didn't want to know where it was coming from at all.

"A member of my flock, yes, certainly." The priest turned his oddly bright blue eyes on me, looking quite fierce. "She was murdered! Poor Arabella, such a gentle, trusting soul. How they can have had the wickedness to betray such innocence for the sake of carnal lusts!"

"Oh, dear," I said, rather inadequately. "I'm terribly sorry to hear that. Ah—who murdered her?"

"The sailors, the wicked heathen! Killed her on the beach and roasted her poor body over a gridiron, just like St. Lawrence the Martyr."

"Heavens," I said.

The priest sighed, and his spindly beard appeared to droop with mourning.

"Yes, I must not forget the hope of Heaven. For if Our Lord observes the fall of every sparrow, He can scarcely have failed to observe Arabella. She must have weighed near on ninety pounds, at least, such a good grazer as she was, poor child."

"Ah," I said, trying to infuse the remark with a suitable sympathy and horror. It then occurred to me what the priest had said.

"Sailors?" I asked. "When did you say this—this sad occurrence took place?" It couldn't be the *Porpoise,* I thought. Surely, Captain Leonard would not have thought me so important that he had risked bringing his ship in so close to the island, in order to pursue me? But my hands grew damp at the thought, and I wiped them unobtrusively on my robe.

"This morning," Father Fogden replied, setting back the lamb's skull he had picked up to fondle. "But," he added, his manner brightening a bit, "I must say they're making wonderful progress with her. It usually takes more than a week, and already you can quite see . . ."

He opened the cupboard again, revealing a large lump, covered with several layers of damp burlap. The smell was markedly stronger now, and a number of small brown beetles scuttled away from the light.

"Are those members of the Dermestidae you have there, Fogden?" Lawrence Stern, having tenderly committed the corpse of his cave fish to a jar of alcoholic spirits, had come to join us. He peered over my shoulder, sunburned features creased in interest.

Inside the cupboard, the white maggot larvae of dermestid beetles were hard at work, polishing the skull of Arabella the sheep. They had made a good start on the eyes. The manioc shifted heavily in my stomach.

"Is that what they are? I suppose so; dear voracious little fellows." The priest swayed alarmingly, catching himself on the edge of the cupboard. As he did so, he finally noticed the old woman, standing glaring at him, a bucket in either hand.

"Oh, I had quite forgotten! You will be needing a change of clothing, will you not, Mrs. Fraser?"

I looked down at myself. The dress and shift I was wearing were ripped in so many places that they were barely decent, and so soaked and sodden with water and swamp-mud that I was scarcely tolerable, even in such undemanding company as that of Father Fogden and Lawrence Stern.

Father Fogden turned to the graven image. "Have we not something this unfortunate lady might wear, Mamacita?" he asked in Spanish. He seemed to hesitate, swaying gently. "Perhaps, one of the dresses in—"

The woman bared her teeth at me. "They are much too small for such a cow," she said, also in Spanish. "Give her your old robe, if you must." She cast an eye of scorn on my tangled hair and mud-streaked face. "Come," she said in English, turning her back on me. "You wash."

She led me to a smaller patio at the back of the house, where she provided me with two buckets of cold, fresh water, a worn linen towel, and a small pot of soft soap, smelling strongly of lye. Adding a shabby gray robe with a rope belt, she bared her teeth at me again and left, remarking genially in Spanish, "Wash away the blood on your hands, Christ-killing whore."

I shut the patio gate after her with a considerable feeling of relief, stripped off my sticky, filthy clothes with even more relief, and made my toilet as well as might be managed with cold water and no comb.

Clad decently, if oddly, in Father Fogden's extra robe, I combed out my wet hair with my fingers, contemplating my peculiar host. I wasn't sure whether the priest's excursions into oddness were some form of dementia, or only the side effects of long-term alcoholism and cannabis intoxication, but he seemed a gentle, kindly soul, in spite of it. His servant—if that's what she was—was another question altogether.

Mamacita made me more than slightly nervous. Mr. Stern had announced his intention of going down to the seaside to bathe, and I was reluctant to go back into the house until he returned. There had been quite a lot of sangria left, and I suspected that Father Fogden—if he was still conscious—would be little protection by this time against that basilisk glare.

Still, I couldn't stay outside all afternoon; I was very tired, and wanted to sit down at least, though I would have preferred to find a bed and sleep for a week. There was a door opening into the house from my small patio; I pushed it open and stepped into the dark interior.

I was in a small bedroom. I looked around, amazed; it didn't seem part of the same house as the Spartan main room and the shabby patios. The bed was made up with feather pillows and a coverlet of soft red wool. Four huge patterned fans were spread like bright wings across the whitewashed walls, and wax candles in a branched brass candelabrum sat on the table.

The furniture was simply but carefully made, and polished with oil to a soft, deep gloss. A curtain of striped cotton hung across the end of the room. It was pushed partway back, and I could see a row of dresses hung on hooks behind it, in a rainbow of silken color.

These must be Ermenegilda's dresses, the ones that Father Fogden had mentioned. I walked forward to look at them, my bare feet quiet on the floor. The room was dustless and clean, but very quiet, without the scent or vibration of human occupancy. No one lived in this room anymore.

The dresses were beautiful; all of silk and velvet, moiré and satin, mousseline and panne. Even hanging lifeless here from their hooks, they had the sheen and beauty of an animal's pelt, where some essence of life lingers in the fur.

I touched one bodice, purple velvet, heavy with embroidered silver pansies, centered with pearls. She had been small, this Ermenegilda, and slightly built—several of the dresses had ruffles and pads cleverly sewn inside the bodices, to add to the illusion of a bust. The room was comfortable, though not luxurious; the dresses were splendid—things that might have been worn at Court in Madrid.

Ermenegilda was gone, but the room still seemed inhabited. I touched a sleeve of peacock blue in farewell and tiptoed away, leaving the dresses to their dreams.

I found Lawrence Stern on the veranda at the back of the house, overlooking a precipitous slope of aloe and guava. In the distance, a small humped island sat cradled in a sea of glimmering turquoise. He rose in courtesy, giving me a small bow and a look of surprise.

"Mrs. Fraser! You are in greatly improved looks, I must say. The Father's robe suits you somewhat more than it does him." He smiled at me, hazel eyes creasing in a flattering expression of admiration.

"I expect the absence of dirt has more to do with it," I said, sitting down in the chair he offered me. "Is that something to drink?" There was a pitcher on the rickety wooden table between the chairs; moisture had condensed in a heavy dew on the sides and droplets ran enticingly down the sides. I had been thirsty so long that the sight of anything liquid automatically made my cheeks draw in with longing.

"More sangria," Stern said. He poured out a small cupful for each of us, and sipped his own, sighing with enjoyment. "I hope you will not think me intemperate, Mrs. Fraser, but after months of tramping country, drinking nothing but water and the slaves' crude rum—" He closed his eyes in bliss. "Ambrosia."

I was rather disposed to agree.

"Er . . . is Father Fogden . . . ?" I hesitated, looking for some tactful way of inquiring after our host's state. I needn't have bothered.

"Drunk," Stern said frankly. "Limp as a worm, laid out on the table in the *sala*. He nearly always is, by the time the sun's gone down," he added.

"I see." I settled back in the chair, sipping my own sangria. "Have you known Father Fogden long?"

Stern rubbed a hand over his forehead, thinking. "Oh, for a few years." He glanced at me. "I was wondering—do you by chance know a James Fraser, from Edinburgh? I realize it is a common name, but—oh, you do?"

I hadn't spoken, but my face had given me away, as it always did, unless I was carefully prepared to lie.

"My husband's name is James Fraser," I said.

Stern's face lighted with interest. "Indeed!" he exclaimed. "And is he a very large fellow, with—"

"Red hair," I agreed. "Yes, that's Jamie." Something occurred to me. "He told me he'd met a natural philosopher in Edinburgh, and had a most interesting conversation about . . . various things." What I was wondering was where Stern had learned Jamie's real name. Most people in Edinburgh would have known him only as "Jamie Roy," the smuggler, or as Alexander Malcolm, the respectable printer of Carfax Close. Surely Dr. Stern, with his distinct German accent, couldn't be the "Englishman" Tompkins had spoken of?

"Spiders," Stern said promptly. "Yes, I recall perfectly. Spiders and caves. We met in a—a—" His face went blank for a moment. Then he coughed, masterfully covering the lapse. "In a, um, drinking establishment. One of the —ah—female employees happened to encounter a large specimen of *Arachnida* hanging from the ceiling in her—that is, from the ceiling as she was engaged in . . . ah, conversation with me. Being somewhat frightened in consequence, she burst into the passageway, shrieking incoherently." Stern took a large gulp of sangria as a restorative, evidently finding the memory stressful.

"I had just succeeded in capturing the animal and securing it in a specimen jar when Mr. Fraser burst into the room, pointed a species of firearm at me, and said—" Here Stern developed a prolonged coughing fit, pounding himself vigorously on the chest.

"Eheu! Do you not find this particular pitcher perhaps a trifle strong, Mrs. Fraser? I suspect that the old woman has added too many sliced lemons."

I suspected that Mamacita would have added cyanide, had she any to hand, but in fact the sangria was excellent.

"I hadn't noticed," I said, sipping. "But do go on. Jamie came in with a pistol and said—?"

"Oh. Well, in fact, I cannot say I recall precisely what was said. There appeared to have been a slight misapprehension, owing to his impression that the lady's outcry was occasioned by some inopportune motion or speech of my own, rather than by the arachnid. Fortunately, I was able to display the beast to him, whereupon the lady was induced to come so far as the door—we could not persuade her to enter the room again—and identify it as the cause of her distress."

"I see," I said. I could envision the scene very well indeed, save for one point of paramount interest. "Do you happen to recall what he was wearing? Jamie?"

Lawrence Stern looked blank. "Wearing? Why . . . no. My impression is that he was clad for the street, rather than in dishabille, but—"

"That's quite all right," I assured him. "I only wondered." "Clad," after all, was the operative word. "So he introduced himself to you?"

Stern frowned, running a hand through his thick black curls. "I don't believe he did. As I recall, the lady referred to him as Mr. Fraser; sometime later in the conversation—we availed ourselves of suitable refreshment and remained conversing nearly until the dawn, finding considerable interest in each other's company, you see. At some point, he invited me to address him by his given name." He raised one eyebrow sardonically. "I trust you do not think it overfamiliar of me to have done so, upon such brief acquaintance?"

"No, no. Of course not." Wanting to change the subject, I continued, "You said you talked about spiders and caves? Why caves?"

"By way of Robert the Bruce and the story—which your husband was inclined to think apocryphal—regarding his inspiration to persevere in his quest for the throne of Scotland. Presumably, the Bruce was in hiding in a cave, pursued by his enemies, and—"

"Yes, I know the story," I interrupted.

"It was James's opinion that spiders do not frequent caves in which humans dwell; an opinion with which I basically concurred, though pointing out that in the larger type of cave, such as occurs on this island—"

"There are caves here?" I was surprised, and then felt foolish. "But of course, there must be, if there are cave fish, like the one in the spring. I always thought Caribbean islands were made of coral, though. I shouldn't have thought you'd find caves in coral."

"Well, it is possible, though not highly likely," Stern said judiciously. "However, the island of Hispaniola is not a coral atoll but is basically volcanic in origin—with the addition of crystalline schists, fossiliferous sedimentary deposits of a considerable antiquity, and widespread deposits of limestone. The limestone is particularly karstic in spots."

"You don't say." I poured a fresh cup of spiced wine.

"Oh, yes." Lawrence leaned over to pick up his bag from the floor of the veranda. Pulling out a notebook, he tore a sheet of paper from it and crumpled it in his fist.

"There," he said, holding out his hand. The paper slowly unfolded itself, leaving a mazed topography of creases and crumpled peaks. "That is what this island is like—you remember what Father Fogden was saying about the Maroons? The runaway slaves who have taken refuge in these hills? It is not lack of pursuit on the part of their masters that allows them to vanish with such ease. There are many parts of this island where no man—white or black, I daresay—has yet set foot. And in the lost hills, there are caves still more lost, whose existence no one knows save perhaps the aboriginal inhabitants of this place—and they are long gone, Mrs. Fraser.

"I have seen one such cave," he added reflectively. "Abandawe, the Maroons call it. They consider it a most sinister and sacred spot, though I do not know why."

Encouraged by my close attention, he took another gulp of sangria and continued his natural history lecture.

"Now that small island"—he nodded at the floating island visible in the sea beyond—"that is the Ile de la Tortue—Tortuga. That one is in fact a coral atoll, its lagoon long since filled in by the actions of the coral animalculae. Did you know it was once the haunt of pirates?" he asked, apparently feeling that he ought to infuse his lecture with something of more general interest than karstic formations and crystalline schists.

"Real pirates? Buccaneers, you mean?" I viewed the little island with more interest. "That's rather romantic."

Stern laughed, and I glanced at him in surprise.

"I am not laughing at you, Mrs. Fraser," he assured me. A smile lingered on his lips as he gestured at the Ile de la Tortue. "It is merely that I had occasion once to talk with an elderly resident of Kingston, regarding the habits of the buccaneers who had at one point made their headquarters in the nearby village of Port Royal."

He pursed his lips, decided to speak, decided otherwise, then, with a sideways glance at me, decided to risk it. "You will pardon the indelicacy, Mrs. Fraser, but as you are a married woman, and as I understand, have some familiarity with the practice of medicine—" He paused, and might have stopped there, but he had drunk nearly two-thirds of the pitcher; the broad, pleasant face was deeply flushed.

"You have perhaps heard of the abominable practices of sodomy?" he asked, looking at me sideways.

"I have," I said. "Do you mean—"

"I assure you," he said, with a magisterial nod. "My informant was most discursive upon the habits of the buccaneers. Sodomites to a man," he said, shaking his head.

"What?"

"It was a matter of public knowledge," he said. "My informant told me that when Port Royal fell into the sea some sixty years ago, it was widely assumed to be an act of divine vengeance upon these wicked persons in retribution for their vile and unnatural usages."

"Gracious," I said. I wondered what the voluptuous Tessa of *The Impetuous Pirate* would have thought about this.

He nodded, solemn as an owl.

"They say you can hear the bells of the drowned churches of Port Royal when a storm is coming, ringing for the souls of the damned pirates."

I thought of inquiring further into the precise nature of the vile and unnatural usages, but at this point in the proceedings, Mamacita stumped out onto the veranda, said curtly, "Food," and disappeared again.

"I wonder which cave Father Fogden found *her* in," I said, shoving back my chair.

Stern glanced at me in surprise. "Found her? But I forgot," he said, face clearing, "you don't know." He peered at the open door where the old woman had vanished, but the interior of the house was quiet and dark as a cave.

"He found her in Habana," he said, and told me the rest of the story.

Father Fogden had been a priest for ten years, a missionary of the order of St. Anselm, when he had come to Cuba fifteen years before. Devoted to the needs of the poor, he had worked among the slums and stews of Habana for several years, thinking of nothing more than the relief of suffering and the love of God—until the day he met Ermenegilda Ruiz Alcantara y Meroz in the marketplace.

"I don't suppose he knows, even now, how it happened," Stern said. He wiped away a drop of wine that ran down the side of his cup, and drank again. "Perhaps she didn't know, either, or perhaps she planned it from the moment she saw him."

In any case, six months later the city of Habana was agog at the news that the young wife of Don Armando Alcantara had run away—with a priest.

"And her mother," I said, under my breath, but he heard me, and smiled slightly.

"Ermenegilda would never leave Mamacita behind," he said. "Nor her dog Ludo."

They would never have succeeded in escaping—for the reach of Don Armando was long and powerful—save for the fact that the English conveniently chose the day of their elopement to invade the island of Cuba, and Don Armando had many things more important to worry him than the whereabouts of his runaway young wife.

The fugitives rode to Bayamo—much hampered by Ermenegilda's dresses, with which she would not part—and there hired a fishing boat, which carried them to safety on Hispaniola.

"She died two years later," Stern said abruptly. He set down his cup, and refilled it from the sweating pitcher. "He buried her himself, under the bougainvillaea."

"And here they've stayed since," I said. "The priest, and Ludo and Mamacita."

"Oh, yes." Stern closed his eyes, his profile dark against the setting sun. "Ermenegilda would not leave Mamacita, and Mamacita will never leave Ermenegilda."

He tossed back the rest of his cup of sangria.

"No one comes here," he said. "The villagers won't set foot on the hill. They're afraid of Ermenegilda's ghost. A damned sinner, buried by a reprobate priest in unhallowed ground—of course she will not lie quiet."

The sea breeze was cool on the back of my neck. Behind us, even the chickens in the patio had grown quiet with falling twilight. The Hacienda de la Fuente lay still.

"You come," I said, and he smiled. The scent of oranges rose up from the empty cup in my hands, sweet as bridal flowers.

"Ah, well," he said. "I am a scientist. I don't believe in ghosts." He extended a hand to me, somewhat unsteadily. "Shall we dine, Mrs. Fraser?"

After breakfast the next morning, Stern was ready to set off for St. Luis. Before leaving, though, I had a question or two about the ship the priest had mentioned; if it were the *Porpoise,* I wanted to steer clear of it.

"What sort of ship was it?" I asked, pouring a cup of goat's milk to go with the breakfast of fried plantain.

Father Fogden, apparently little the worse for his excesses of the day before, was stroking his coconut, humming dreamily to himself.

"Ah?" he said, startled out of his reverie by Stern's poking him in the ribs. I patiently repeated my query.

"Oh." He squinted in deep thought, then his face relaxed. "A wooden one."

Lawrence bent his broad face over his plate, hiding a smile. I took a breath and tried again.

"The sailors who killed Arabella—did you see them?"

His narrow brows rose.

"Well, of course I saw them. How else would I know they had done it?"

I seized on this evidence of logical thought.

"Naturally. And did you see what they were wearing? I mean"—I saw him opening his mouth to say "clothes," and hastily forestalled him —"did they seem to be wearing any sort of uniform?" The crew of the *Porpoise* commonly wore "slops" when not performing any ceremonial duty, but even these rough clothes bore the semblance of a uniform, being mostly all of a dirty white and similar in cut.

Father Fogden laid down his cup, leaving a milky mustache across his upper lip. He brushed at this with the back of his hand, frowning and shaking his head.

"No, I think not. All I recall of them, though, is that the leader wore a hook—missing a hand, I mean." He waggled his own long fingers at me in illustration.

I dropped my cup, which exploded on the tabletop. Stern sprang up with an exclamation, but the priest sat still, watching in surprise as a thin white stream ran across the table and into his lap.

"Whatever did you do that for?" he said reproachfully.

"I'm sorry," I said. My hands were trembling so that I couldn't even manage to pick up the shards of the shattered cup. I was afraid to ask the next question. "Father—has the ship sailed away?"

"Why no," he said, looking up in surprise from his damp robe. "How could it? It's on the beach."

Father Fogden led the way, his skinny shanks a gleaming white as he kirtled his cassock about his thighs. I was obliged to do the same, for the hillside above the house was thick with grass and thorny shrubs that caught at the coarse wool skirts of my borrowed robe.

The hill was crisscrossed with sheep paths, but these were narrow and faint, losing themselves under the trees and disappearing abruptly in thick grass. The priest seemed confident about his destination, though, and scampered briskly through the vegetation, never looking back.

I was breathing hard by the time we reached the crest of the hill, even though Lawrence Stern had gallantly assisted me, pushing branches out of my way, and taking my arm to haul me up the steeper slopes.

"Do you think there really is a ship?" I said to him, low-voiced, as we approached the top of the hill. Given our host's behavior so far, I wasn't so sure he might not have imagined it, just to be sociable.

Stern shrugged, wiping a trickle of sweat that ran down his bronzed cheek.

"I suppose there will be *something* there," he replied. "After all, there is a dead sheep."

A qualm ran over me in memory of the late departed Arabella. Someone *had* killed the sheep, and I walked as quietly as I could, as we approached the top of the hill. It couldn't be the *Porpoise;* none of her officers or men wore a hook. I tried to tell myself that it likely wasn't the *Artemis,* either, but my heart beat still faster as we came to a stand of giant agave on the crest of the hill.

I could see the Caribbean glowing blue through the succulent's branches, and a narrow strip of white beach. Father Fogden had come to a halt, beckoning us to his side.

"There they are, the wicked creatures," he muttered. His blue eyes glittered bright with fury, and his scanty hair fairly bristled, like a moth-eaten porcupine. "Butchers!" he said, hushed but vehement, as though talking to himself. "Cannibals!"

I gave him a startled look, but then Lawrence Stern grasped my arm, drawing me to a wider opening between two trees.

"Oy! There *is* a ship," he said.

There was. It was lying tilted on its side, drawn up on the beach, its masts unstepped, untidy piles of cargo, sails, rigging, and water casks scattered all about it. Men crawled over the beached carcass like ants. Shouts and hammer blows rang out like gunshots, and the smell of hot pitch was thick on the air.

The unloaded cargo gleamed dully in the sun; copper and tin, slightly tarnished by the sea air. Tanned hides had been laid flat on the sand, brown stiff blotches drying in the sun.

"It *is* them! It's the *Artemis!*" The matter was settled by the appearance near the hull of a squat, one-legged figure, head shaded from the sun by a gaudy kerchief of yellow silk.

"Murphy!" I shouted. "Fergus! *Jamie!*" I broke from Stern's grasp and ran down the far side of the hill, his cry of caution disregarded in the excitement of seeing the *Artemis.*

Murphy whirled at my shout, but was unable to get out of my way. Carried by momentum and moving like a runaway freight, I crashed straight into him, knocking him flat.

"Murphy!" I said, and kissed him, caught up in the joy of the moment.

"Hoy!" he said, shocked. He wriggled madly, trying to get out from under me.

"Milady!" Fergus appeared at my side, crumpled and vivid, his beautiful smile dazzling in a sun-dark face. "Milady!" He helped me off the grunting Murphy, then grabbed me to him in a rib-cracking hug. Marsali appeared behind him, a broad smile on her face.

"Merci aux les saints!" he said in my ear. "I was afraid we would never see you again!" He kissed me heartily himself, on both cheeks and the mouth, then released me at last.

I glanced at the *Artemis,* lying on her side on the beach like a stranded beetle. "What on earth happened?"

Fergus and Marsali exchanged a glance. It was the sort of look in which questions are asked and answered, and it rather startled me to see the depths of intimacy between them. Fergus drew a deep breath and turned to me.

"Captain Raines is dead," he said.

The storm that had come upon me during my night in the mangrove swamp had also struck the *Artemis.* Carried far off her path by the howling wind, she had been forced over a reef, tearing a sizable hole in her bottom.

Still, she had remained afloat. The aft hold filling rapidly, she had limped toward the small inlet that opened so near, offering shelter.

"We were no more than three hundred yards from the shore when the accident happened," Fergus said, his face drawn by the memory. The ship had heeled suddenly over, as the contents of the aft hold had shifted, beginning to float. And just then, an enormous wave, coming from the sea, had struck the leaning ship, washing across the tilting quarterdeck, and carrying away Captain Raines, and four seamen with him.

"The shore was so near!" Marsali said, her face twisted with distress. "We were aground ten minutes later! If only—"

Fergus stopped her with a hand on her arm.

"We cannot guess God's ways," he said. "It would have been the same, if we had been a thousand miles at sea, save that we would not have been able to give them decent burial." He nodded toward the far edge of the beach, near the jungle, where five small mounds, topped with crude wooden crosses, marked the final resting places of the drowned men.

"I had some holy water that Da brought me from Notre Dame in Paris," Marsali said. Her lips were cracked, and she licked them. "In a little bottle. I said a prayer, and sprinkled it on the graves. D'ye—d'ye think they would have l-liked that?"

I caught the quaver in her voice, and realized that for all her self-possession, the last two days had been a terrifying ordeal for the girl. Her face was grimy, her hair coming down, and the sharpness was gone from her eyes, softened by tears.

"I'm sure they would," I said gently, patting her arm. I glanced at the faces crowding around, searching for Jamie's great height and fiery head, even as the realization dawned that he was not there.

"Where *is* Jamie?" I said. My face was flushed from the run down the hill. I felt the blood begin to drain from my cheeks, as a trickle of fear rose in my veins.

Fergus was staring at me, lean face mirroring mine.

"He is not with you?" he said.

"No. How could he be?" The sun was blinding, but my skin felt cold. I could feel the heat shimmer over me, but to no effect. My lips were so chilled, I could scarcely form the question.

"Where is he?"

Fergus shook his head slowly back and forth, like an ox stunned by the slaughterer's blow.

"I don't know."

51

In Which Jamie Smells a Rat

Jamie Fraser lay in the shadows under the *Porpoise*'s jolly boat, chest heaving with effort. Getting aboard the man-of-war without being seen had been no small task; his right side was bruised from being slammed against the side of the ship as he hung from the boarding nets, struggling to pull himself up to the rail. His arms felt as though they had been jerked from their sockets and there was a large splinter in one hand. But he was here, and so far unseen.

He chewed delicately at his palm, groping for the end of the splinter with his teeth, as he got his bearings. Russo and Stone, *Artemis* hands who had served aboard men-of-war, had spent hours describing to him the structure of a large ship, the compartments and decks, and the probable location of the surgeon's quarters. Hearing something described and being able to find your way about in it were two different things, though. At least the miserable thing rocked less than the *Artemis,* though he could still feel the subtle, nauseating heave of the deck beneath him.

The end of the splinter worked free; nipping it between his teeth, he drew it slowly out and spat it on the deck. He sucked the tiny wound, tasting blood, and slid cautiously out from under the jolly boat, ears pricked to catch the sound of an approaching footstep.

The deck below this one, down the forward companionway. The officers' quarters would be there, and with luck, the surgeon's cabin as well. Not that she was likely to be in her quarters; not her. She'd cared enough to come tend the sick—she would be with them.

He had waited until dark to have Robbie MacRae row him out. Raines had told him that the *Porpoise* would likely weigh anchor with the evening tide, two hours from now. If he could find Claire and escape over the side before that—he could swim ashore with her, easily—the *Artemis* would be waiting for them, concealed in a small cove on the other side of Caicos Island. If he couldn't—well, he would deal with that when he came to it.

Fresh from the cramped small world of the *Artemis,* the belowdecks of the *Porpoise* seemed huge and sprawling; a shadowed warren. He stood still, nostrils flaring as he deliberately drew the fetid air deep into his lungs. There were all the nasty stenches associated with a ship at sea for a long time, overlaid with the faint floating stink of feces and vomit.

He turned to the left and began to walk softly, long nose twitching. Where the smell of sickness was the strongest; that was where he would find her.

Four hours later, in mounting desperation, he made his way aft for the third time. He had covered the entire ship—keeping out of sight with some difficulty—and Claire was nowhere to be found.

"Bloody woman!" he said under his breath. "Where have ye gone, ye fashious wee hidee?"

A small worm of fear gnawed at the base of his heart. She had said her vaccine would protect her from the sickness, but what if she had been wrong? He could see for himself that the man-of-war's crew had been badly diminished by the deadly sickness—knee-deep in it, the germs might have attacked her too, vaccine or not.

He thought of germs as small blind things, about the size of maggots, but equipped with vicious razor teeth, like tiny sharks. He could all too easily imagine a swarm of the things fastening onto her, killing her, draining her flesh of life. It was just such a vision that had made him pursue the *Porpoise*— that, and a murderous rage toward the English buggerer who had had the filth-eating insolence to steal away his wife beneath his very nose, with a vague promise to return her, once they'd made use of her.

Leave her to the Sassenachs, unprotected?

"Not bloody likely," he muttered under his breath, dropping down into a dark cargo space. She wouldn't be in such a place, of course, but he must think a moment, what to do. Was this the cable tier, the aft cargo hatch, the forward stinking God knew what? Christ, he hated boats!

He drew in a deep breath and stopped, surprised. There were animals here; goats. He could smell them plainly. There was also a light, dimly visible around the edge of a bulkhead, and the murmur of voices. Was one of them a woman's voice?

He edged forward, listening. There were feet on the deck above, a patter and thump that he recognized; bodies dropping from the rigging. Had someone above seen him? Well, and if they had? It was no crime, so far as he knew, for a man to come seeking his wife.

The *Porpoise* was asail; he had felt the thrum of the sails, passing through the wood all the way to the keel as she took the wind. They had long since missed the rendezvous with the *Artemis*.

That being so, there was likely nothing to lose by appearing boldly before the captain and demanding to see Claire. But perhaps she was here—it *was* a woman's voice.

It was a woman's figure, too, silhouetted against the lantern's light, but the woman wasn't Claire. His heart leapt convulsively at the gleam of light on her hair, but then fell at once as he saw the thick, square shape of the woman by the goat pen. There was a man with her; as Jamie watched, the man bent and picked up a basket. He turned and came toward Jamie.

He stepped into the narrow aisle between the bulkheads, blocking the seaman's way.

"Here, what do you mean—" the man began, and then, raising his eyes to Jamie's face, stopped, gasping. One eye was fixed on him in horrified recognition; the other showed only as a bluish-white crescent beneath the withered lid.

"God preserve us!" the seaman said. "What are *you* doing here?" The seaman's face gleamed pale and jaundiced in the dim light.

"Ye ken me, do ye?" Jamie's heart was hammering against his ribs, but he kept his voice level and low. "I have not the honor to know your own name, I think?"

"I should prefer to leave that particular circumstance unchanged, your honor, if you've no objection." The one-eyed seaman began to edge backward, but was forestalled as Jamie gripped his arm, hard enough to elicit a small yelp.

"Not quite so fast, if ye please. Where is Mrs. Malcolm, the surgeon?"

It would have been difficult for the seaman to look more alarmed, but at this question, he managed it.

"I don't know!" he said.

"You do," Jamie said sharply. "And ye'll tell me this minute, or I shall break your neck."

"Well, now, I can't be tellin' you anything if you break my neck, can I?" the seaman pointed out, beginning to recover his nerve. He lifted his chin pugnaciously over his basket of manure. "Now, you leave go of me, or I'll call—" The rest was lost in a squawk as a large hand fastened about his neck and began inexorably to squeeze. The basket fell to the deck, and balls of goat manure exploded out of it like shrapnel.

"Ak!" Harry Tompkins's legs thrashed wildly, scattering goat dung in every direction. His face turned the color of a beetroot as he clawed ineffectually at Jamie's arm. Judging the results clinically, Jamie let go as the man's eye began to bulge. He wiped his hand on his breeches, disliking the greasy feel of the man's sweat on his palm.

Tompkins lay on the deck in a sprawl of limbs, wheezing faintly.

"Ye're quite right," Jamie said. "On the other hand, if I break your arm, I expect you'll still be able to speak to me, aye?" He bent, grasped the man by one skinny arm and jerked him to his feet, twisting the arm roughly behind his back.

"I'll tell you, I'll tell you!" The seaman wriggled madly, panicked. "Damn you, you're as wicked cruel as she was!"

"Was? What do you mean, 'was'?" Jamie's heart squeezed tight in his chest, and he jerked the arm, more roughly than he had meant to do. Tompkins let out a screech of pain, and Jamie slackened the pressure slightly.

"Let go! I'll tell you, but for pity's sake, let go!" Jamie lessened his grasp, but didn't let go.

"Tell me where my wife is!" he said, in a tone that had made stronger men than Harry Tompkins fall over their feet to obey.

"She's lost!" the man blurted. "Gone overboard!"

"What!" He was so stunned that he let go his hold. Overboard. Gone overboard. Lost.

"When?" he demanded. "How? Damn you, tell me what happened!" He advanced on the seaman, fists clenched.

The seaman was backing away, rubbing his arm and panting, a look of furtive satisfaction in his one eye.

"Don't worry, your honor," he said, a queer, jeering tone in his voice. "You won't be lonesome long. You'll join her in hell in a few days—dancing from the yardarm over Kingston Harbor!"

Too late, Jamie heard the footfall on the boards behind him. He had no time even to turn his head before the blow fell.

He had been struck in the head frequently enough to know that the sensible thing was to lie still until the giddiness and the lights that pulsed behind your eyelids with each heartbeat stopped. Sit up too soon and the pain made you vomit.

The deck was rising and falling, rising and falling under him, in the horrible way of ships. He kept his eyes tight closed, concentrating on the knotted ache at the base of his skull in order not to think of his stomach.

Ship. He should be on a ship. Yes, but the surface under his cheek was wrong—hard wood, not the linen of his berth's bedding. And the smell, the smell was wrong, it was—

He shot bolt upright, memory shooting through him with a vividness that made the pain in his head pale by comparison. The darkness moved queasily around him, blinking with colored lights, and his stomach heaved. He closed his eyes and swallowed hard, trying to gather his scattered wits about the single appalling thought that had lanced through his brain like a spit through mutton.

Claire. Lost. Drowned. Dead.

He leaned to the side and threw up. He retched and coughed, as though his body was trying forcibly to expel the thought. It didn't work; when he finally stopped, leaning against the bulkhead in exhaustion, it was still with him. It hurt to breathe, and he clenched his fists on his thighs, trembling.

There was the sound of a door opening, and bright light struck him in the eyes with the force of a blow. He winced, closing his eyes against the glare of the lantern.

"Mr. Fraser," a soft, well-bred voice said. "I am—truly sorry. I wish you to know that, at least."

Through a cracked eyelid, he saw the drawn, harried face of young Leonard—the man who had taken Claire. The man wore a look of regret. Regret! Regret, for killing her.

Fury pulled him up against the weakness, and sent him lunging across the slanted deck in an instant. There was an outcry as he hit Leonard and bore him backward into the passage, and a good, juicy *thunk!* as the bugger's head hit the boards. People were shouting, and shadows leapt crazily all round him as the lanterns swayed, but he paid no attention.

He smashed Leonard's jaw with one great blow, his nose with the next. The weakness mattered nothing. He would spend all his strength and die here glad, but let him batter and maim now, feel the bones crack and the blood hot and slick on his fists. Blessed Michael, let him avenge her first!

There were hands on him, snatching and jerking, but they didn't matter. They would kill him now, he thought dimly, and that didn't matter, either. The body under him jerked and twitched between his legs, and lay still.

When the next blow came, he went willingly into the dark.

The light touch of fingers on his face awakened him. He reached drowsily up to take her hand, and his palm touched . . .

"Aaaah!"

With an instinctive revulsion, he was on his feet, clawing at his face. The big spider, nearly as frightened as he was, made off toward the shrubbery at high speed, long hairy legs no more than a blur.

There was an outburst of giggling behind him. He turned around, his heart pounding like a drum, and found six children, roosting in the branches of a big green tree, all grinning down at him with tobacco-stained teeth.

He bowed to them, feeling dizzy and rubber-legged, the start of fright that had got him up now dying in his blood.

"Mesdemoiselles, messieurs," he said, croaking, and in the half-awake recesses of his brain wondered what had made him speak to them in French? Had he half-heard them speaking, as he lay asleep?

French they were, for they answered him in that language, strongly laced with a gutteral sort of creole accent that he had never heard before.

"*Vous êtes matelot?*" the biggest boy asked, eyeing him with interest.

His knees gave way and he sat down on the ground, suddenly enough to make the children laugh again.

"*Non,*" he replied, struggling to make his tongue work. "*Je suis guerrier.*"

His mouth was dry and his head ached like a fiend. Faint memories swam about in the parritch that filled his head, too vague to grasp.

"A soldier!" exclaimed one of the smaller children. His eyes were round and dark as sloes. "Where is your sword and *pistola*, eh?"

"Don't be silly," an older girl told him loftily. "How could he swim with a *pistola*? It would be ruined. Don't you know any better, guava-head?"

"Don't call me that!" the smaller boy shouted, face contorting in rage. "Shitface!"

"Frog-guts!"

"Caca-brains!"

The children were scrabbling through the branches like monkeys, screaming and chasing each other. Jamie rubbed a hand hard over his face, trying to think.

"Mademoiselle!" He caught the eye of the older girl and beckoned to her. She hesitated for a moment, then dropped from her branch like a ripe fruit, landing on the ground before him in a puff of yellow dust. She was barefoot, wearing nothing but a muslin shift and a colored kerchief round her dark, curly hair.

"Monsieur?"

"You seem a woman of some knowledge, Mademoiselle," he said. "Tell me, please, what is the name of this place?"

"Cap-Haïtien," she replied promptly. She eyed him with considerable curiosity. "You talk funny," she said.

"I am thirsty. Is there water nearby?" Cap-Haïtien. So he was on the island of Hispaniola. His mind was slowly beginning to function again; he had a vague memory of terrible effort, of swimming for his life in a frothing cauldron of heaving waves, and rain pelting his face so hard that it made little difference whether his head was above or below the surface. And what else?

"This way, this way!" The other children had dropped out of the tree, and a little girl was tugging his hand, urging him to follow.

He knelt by the little stream, splashing water over his head, gulping delicious cool handfuls, while the children scampered over the rocks, pelting each other with mud.

Now he remembered—the rat-faced seaman, and Leonard's surprised young face, the deep-red rage and the satisfying feel of flesh crushed against bone under his fist.

And Claire. The memory came back suddenly, with a sense of confused emotion—loss and terror, succeeded by relief. What had happened? He stopped what he was doing, not hearing the questions the children were flinging at him.

"Are you a deserter?" one of the boys asked again. "Have you been in a fight?" The boy's eyes rested curiously on his hands. His knuckles were cut and swollen, and his hands ached badly; the fourth finger felt as though he had cracked it again.

"Yes," he said absently, his mind occupied. Everything was coming back; the dark, stuffy confines of the brig where they had left him to wake, and the dreadful waking, to the thought that Claire was dead. He had huddled there on the bare boards, too shaken with grief to notice at first the increasing heave and roll of the ship, or the high-pitched whine of the rigging, loud enough to filter down even to his oubliette.

But after a time, the motion and noise were great enough to penetrate even the cloud of grief. He had heard the sounds of the growing storm, and the shouts and running overhead, and then was much too occupied to think of anything.

There was nothing in the small room with him, nothing to hold to. He had bounced from wall to wall like a dried pea in a wean's rattle, unable to tell up from down, right from left in the heaving dark, and not much caring, either, as waves of seasickness rolled through his body. He had thought then of nothing but death, and that with a fervor of longing.

He had been nearly unconscious, in fact, when the door to his prison had opened, and a strong smell of goat assailed his nostrils. He had no idea how the woman had got him up the ladder to the afterdeck, or why. He had only a confused memory of her babbling urgently to him in broken English as she pulled him along, half-supporting his weight as he stumbled and slid on the rain-wet decking.

He remembered the last thing she had said, though, as she pushed him toward the tilting taffrail.

"She is not dead," the woman had said. "She go there"—pointing at the rolling sea—"you go, too. Find her!" and then she had bent, got a hand in his crutch and a sturdy shoulder under his rump, and heaved him neatly over the rail and into the churning water.

"You are not an Englishman," the boy was saying. "It's an English ship, though, isn't it?"

He turned automatically, to look where the boy pointed, and saw the *Porpoise,* riding at anchor far out in the shallow bay. Other ships were scattered throughout the harbor, all clearly visible from this vantage point on a hill just outside the town.

"Yes," he said to the boy. "An English ship."

"One for me!" the boy exclaimed happily. He turned to shout to another lad. "Jacques! I was right! English! That's four for me, and only two for you this month!"

"Three!" Jacques corrected indignantly. "I get Spanish *and* Portuguese. *Bruja* was Portuguese, so I can count that, too!"

Jamie reached out and caught the older boy's arm.

"*Pardon,* Monsieur," he said. "Your friend said *Bruja?*"

"Yes, she was in last week," the boy answered. "Is *Bruja* a Portuguese name, though? We weren't sure whether to count it Spanish or Portuguese."

"Some of the sailors were in my *maman*'s taverna," one of the little girls chimed in. "They sounded like they were talking Spanish, but it wasn't like Uncle Geraldo talks."

"I think I should like to talk to your *maman, chèrie*," he said to the little girl. "Do any of you know, perhaps, where this *Bruja* was going when she left?"

"Bridgetown," the oldest girl put in promptly, trying to regain his attention. "I heard the clerk at the garrison say so."

"The garrison?"

"The barracks are next door to my *maman*'s taverna," the smaller girl chimed in, tugging at his sleeve. "The ship captains all go there with their papers, while the sailors get drunk. Come, come! *Maman* will feed you if I tell her to."

"I think your *maman* will throw me out the door," he told her, rubbing a hand across the heavy stubble on his chin. "I look like a vagabond." He did. There were stains of blood and vomit on his clothes despite the swim, and he knew by the feel of his face that it was bruised and bloodshot.

"*Maman* has seen much worse than you," the little girl assured him. "Come on!"

He smiled and thanked her, and allowed them to lead him down the hill, staggering slightly, as his land legs had not yet returned. He found it odd but somehow comforting that the children should not be frightened of him, horrible as he no doubt looked.

Was this what the goat-woman had meant? That Claire had swum ashore on this island? He felt a welling of hope that was as refreshing to his heart as the water had been to his parched throat. Claire was stubborn, reckless, and had a great deal more courage than was safe for a woman, but she was by no means such a fool as to fall off a man-of-war by accident.

And the *Bruja*—and Ian—were nearby! He would find them both, then. The fact that he was barefoot, penniless, and a fugitive from the Royal Navy seemed of no consequence. He had his wits and his hands, and with dry land once more beneath his feet, all things seemed possible.

52

A Wedding Takes Place

There was nothing to be done, but to repair the *Artemis* as quickly as possible, and make sail for Jamaica. I did my best to put aside my fear for Jamie, but I scarcely ate for the next two days, my appetite impeded by the large ball of ice that had taken up residence in my stomach.

For distraction, I took Marsali up to the house on the hill, where she succeeded in charming Father Fogden by recalling—and mixing for him—a Scottish receipt for a sheep-dip guaranteed to destroy ticks.

Stern helpfully pitched in with the labor of repair, delegating to me the guardianship of his specimen bag, and charging me with the task of searching the nearby jungle for any curious specimens of *Arachnida* that might come to hand as I looked for medicinal plants. While thinking privately that I would prefer to meet any of the larger specimens of *Arachnida* with a good stout boot, rather than my bare hands, I accepted the charge, peering into the internal water-filled cups of bromeliads in search of the bright-colored frogs and spiders who inhabited these tiny worlds.

I returned from one of these expeditions on the afternoon of the third day, with several large lily-roots, some shelf fungus of a vivid orange, and an unusual moss, together with a live tarantula—carefully trapped in one of the sailor's stocking caps and held at arm's length—large and hairy enough to send Lawrence into paroxysms of delight.

When I emerged from the jungle's edge, I saw that we had reached a new stage of progress; the *Artemis* was no longer canted on her side, but was slowly regaining an upright position on the sand, assisted by ropes, wedges, and a great deal of shouting.

"It's nearly finished, then?" I asked Fergus, who was standing near the stern, doing a good bit of the shouting as he instructed his crew in the placement of wedges. He turned to me, grinning and wiping the sweat from his forehead.

"Yes, milady! The caulking is complete. Mr. Warren gives it as his opinion that we may launch the ship near evening, when the day is grown cool, so the tar is hardened."

"That's marvelous!" I craned my neck back, looking up at the naked mast that towered high above. "Have we got sails?"

"Oh, yes," he assured me. "In fact, we have everything except—"

A shout of alarm from MacLeod interrupted whatever he had been about to say. I whirled to look toward the distant road out of the palmettos, where the sun winked off the glint of metal.

"Soldiers!" Fergus reacted faster than anyone, leaping from the scaffolding to land in a thudding spray of sand beside me. "Quick, milady! To the wood! Marsali!" he shouted, looking wildly about for the girl.

He licked sweat from his upper lip, eyes darting from the jungle to the approaching soldiers. "Marsali!" he shouted, once more.

Marsali appeared round the edge of the hull, pale and startled. Fergus grasped her by the arm and shoved her toward me. "Go with milady! Run!"

I snatched Marsali's hand and ran for the forest, sand spurting beneath our feet. There were shouts from the road behind us, and a shot cracked overhead, followed by another.

Ten steps, five, and then we were in the shadow of the trees. I collapsed behind the shelter of a thorny bush, gasping for breath against the stabbing pain of a stitch in my side. Marsali knelt on the earth beside me, her cheeks streaked with tears.

"What?" she gasped, struggling for breath. "Who are they? What—will they—do? To Fergus. What?"

"I don't know." Still breathing heavily, I grasped a cedar sapling and pulled myself to my knees. Peering through the underbrush on all fours, I could see that the soldiers had reached the ship.

It was cool and damp under the trees, but the lining of my mouth was dry as cotton. I bit the inside of my cheek, trying to encourage a little saliva to flow.

"I think it will be all right." I patted Marsali's shoulder, trying to be reassuring. "Look, there are only ten of them," I whispered, counting as the last soldier trotted out of the palmetto grove. "They're French; the *Artemis* has French papers. It may be all right."

And then again, it might not. I was well aware that a ship aground and abandoned was legal salvage. It was a deserted beach. And all that stood between these soldiers and a rich prize were the lives of the *Artemis*'s crew.

A few of the seamen had pistols to hand; most had knives. But the soldiers were armed to the teeth, each man with musket, sword, and pistols. If it came to a fight, it would be a bloody one, but the odds were heavily on the mounted soldiers.

The men near the ship were silent, grouped close together behind Fergus, who stood out, straight-backed and grim, as the spokesman. I saw him push back his shock of hair with his hook, and plant his feet solidly in the sand, ready for whatever might come. The creak and jingle of harness seemed muted in the damp, hot air, and the horses moved slowly, hooves muffled in the sand.

The soldiers came to a halt ten feet away from the little knot of seamen. A big man who seemed to be in command raised one hand in an order to stay, and swung down from his horse.

I was watching Fergus, rather than the soldiers. I saw his face change, then freeze, white under his tan. I glanced quickly at the soldier coming toward him across the sand, and my own blood froze.

"*Silence, mes amis,*" said the big man, in a voice of pleasant command. "*Silence, et restez, s'il vous plaît.*" Silence, my friends, and do not move, if you please.

I would have fallen, were I not already on my knees. I closed my eyes in a wordless prayer of thanksgiving.

Next to me, Marsali gasped. I opened my eyes and clapped a hand over her open mouth.

The commander took off his hat, and shook out a thick mass of sweat-soaked auburn hair. He grinned at Fergus, teeth white and wolfish in a short, curly red beard.

"You are in charge here?" Jamie said in French. "You, come with me. The rest"—he nodded at the crew, several of whom were goggling at him in open amazement—"you stay where you are. Don't talk," he added, off-handedly.

Marsali jerked at my arm, and I realized how tightly I had been holding her.

"Sorry," I whispered, letting go, but not taking my eyes from the beach.

"What is he doing?" Marsali hissed in my ear. Her face was pale with excitement, and the little freckles left by the sun stood out on her nose in contrast. "How did he get here?"

"I don't know! Be quiet, for God's sake!"

The crew of the *Artemis* exchanged glances, waggled their eyebrows, and nudged each other in the ribs, but fortunately also obeyed orders and didn't speak. I hoped to heaven that their obvious excitement would be construed merely as consternation over their impending fate.

Jamie and Fergus had walked over toward the shore, conferring in low voices. Now they separated, Fergus coming back toward the hull with an expression of grim determination, Jamie calling the soldiers to dismount and gather round him.

I couldn't tell what Jamie was saying to the soldiers, but Fergus was close enough for us to hear.

"These are soldiers from the garrison at Cap-Haïtien," he announced to the crew members. "Their commander—Captain Alessandro—" he said, lifting his eyebrows and grimacing hideously to emphasize the name, "says that they will assist us in launching the *Artemis*." This announcement was greeted with faint cheers from some of the men, and looks of bewilderment from others.

"But how did Mr. Fraser—" began Royce, a rather slow-witted seaman, his heavy brows drawn together in a puzzled frown. Fergus allowed no time for questions, but plunged into the midst of the crew, putting an arm about Royce's shoulders and dragging him toward the scaffolding, talking loudly to drown out any untoward remarks.

"Yes, is it not a most fortunate accident?" he said loudly. I could see that he was twisting Royce's ear with his sound hand. "Most fortunate indeed! Captain Alessandro says that a *habitant* on his way from his plantation saw the ship aground, and reported it to the garrison. With so much help, we will have the *Artemis* aswim in no time at all." He let go of Royce and clapped his hand sharply against his thigh.

"Come, come, let us set to work at once! Manzetti—up you go! Mac-Leod, MacGregor, seize your hammers! Maitland—" He spotted Maitland, standing on the sand gawking at Jamie. Fergus whirled and clapped the cabin boy on the back hard enough to make him stagger.

"Maitland, *mon enfant!* Give us a song to speed our efforts!" Looking rather dazed, Maitland began a tentative rendition of "The Nut-Brown Maid." A few of the seamen began to climb back onto the scaffolding, glancing suspiciously over their shoulders.

"Sing!" Fergus bellowed, glaring up at them. Murphy, who appeared to be finding something extremely funny, mopped his sweating red face and obligingly joined in the song, his wheezing bass reinforcing Maitland's pure tenor.

Fergus stalked up and down beside the hull, exhorting, directing, urging —and making such a spectacle of himself that few telltale glances went in Jamie's direction. The uncertain tap of hammers started up again.

Meanwhile, Jamie was giving careful directions to his soldiers. I saw more than one Frenchman glance at the *Artemis* as he talked, with a look of dimly concealed greed that suggested that a selfless desire to help their fellow beings was perhaps not the motive uppermost in the soldiers' minds, no matter what Fergus had announced.

Still, the soldiers went to work willingly enough, stripping off their leather jerkins and laying aside most of their arms. Three of the soldiers, I noticed, did not join the work party, but remained on guard, fully armed, eyes sharp on the sailors' every move. Jamie alone remained aloof, watching everything.

"Should we come out?" Marsali murmured in my ear. "It seems safe, now."

"No," I said. My eyes were fixed on Jamie. He stood in the shade of a tall palmetto, at ease, but erect. Behind the unfamiliar beard, his expression was unreadable, but I caught the faint movement at his side, as the two stiff fingers flickered once against his thigh.

"No," I said again. "It isn't over yet."

The work went on through the afternoon. The stack of wooden rollers mounted, cut ends scenting the air with the tang of fresh sap. Fergus's voice was hoarse, and his shirt clung wetly to his lean torso. The horses, hobbled, wandered slowly under the edge of the forest, browsing. The sailors had given up singing now, and had settled to work, with no more than an occasional glance toward the palmetto where Captain Alessandro stood in the shade, arms folded.

The sentry near the trees paced slowly up and down, musket carried at the ready, a wistful eye on the cool green shadows. He passed close enough on one circuit for me to see the dark, greasy curls dangling down his neck, and the pockmarks on his plump cheeks. He creaked and jingled as he walked. The rowel was missing from one of his spurs. He looked hot, and fairly cross.

It was a long wait, and the inquisitiveness of the forest midges made it longer still. After what seemed forever, though, I saw Jamie give a nod to one of the guards, and come from the beach toward the trees. I signed to Marsali to wait, and ducking under branches, ignoring the thick brush, I dodged madly toward the place where he had disappeared.

I popped breathlessly out from behind a bush, just as he was doing up the laces of his flies. His head jerked up at the sound, his eyes widened, and he let out a yell that would have summoned Arabella the sheep back from the dead, let alone the waiting sentry.

I dodged back into hiding, as crashing boots and shouts of inquiry headed in our direction.

"*C'est bien!*" Jamie shouted. He sounded a trifle shaken. "*Ce n'est qu'un serpent!*"

The sentry spoke an odd dialect of French, but appeared to be asking rather nervously whether the serpent was dangerous.

"*Non, c'est innocent,*" Jamie answered. He waved at the sentry, whose inquiring head I could just see, peering reluctantly over the bush. The sentry, who seemed unenthusiastic about snakes, however innocent, disappeared promptly back to his duty.

Without hesitation, Jamie plunged into the bush.

"Claire!" He crushed me tight against his chest. Then he grabbed me by the shoulders and shook me, hard.

"Damn you!" he said, in a piercing whisper. "I thought ye were dead for sure! How dare ye do something harebrained like jump off a ship in the middle of the night! Have ye no sense at all?"

"Let go!" I hissed. The shaking had made me bite my lip. "Let go, I say! What do you mean, how dare *I* do something harebrained? You idiot, what possessed you to follow me?"

His face was darkened by the sun; now a deep red began to darken it further, washing up from the edges of his new beard.

"What possessed me?" he repeated. "You're my wife, for the Lord's sake! Of course I would follow ye; why did ye not wait for me? Christ, if I had time, I'd—" The mention of time evidently reminded him that we hadn't much, and with a noticeable effort, he choked back any further remarks, which was just as well, because I had a number of things to say in that vein myself. I swallowed them, with some difficulty.

"What in bloody hell are you doing here?" I asked instead.

The deep flush subsided slightly, succeeded by the merest hint of a smile amid the unfamiliar foliage.

"I'm the captain," he said. "Did ye not notice?"

"Yes, I noticed! Captain Alessandro, my foot! What do you mean to do?"

Instead of answering, he gave me a final, gentle shake and divided a glare between me and Marsali, who had poked an inquiring head out.

"Stay here, the both of ye, and dinna stir a foot or I swear I'll beat ye senseless."

Without pausing for a response, he whirled and strode back through the trees, toward the beach.

Marsali and I exchanged stares, which were interrupted a second later, when Jamie, breathless, hurtled back into the small clearing. He grabbed me by both arms, and kissed me briefly but thoroughly.

"I forgot. I love you," he said, giving me another shake for emphasis. "And I'm glad you're no dead. Dinna do that again!" Letting go, he crashed back into the brush and disappeared.

I felt breathless, myself, and more than a little rattled, but undeniably happy.

Marsali's eyes were round as saucers.

"What shall we do?" she asked. "What's Da going to do?"

"I don't know," I said. My cheeks were flushed, and I could still feel the touch of his mouth on mine, and the unfamiliar tingling left by the brush of beard and mustache. My tongue touched the small stinging place where I had bitten my lip. "I don't know what he's going to do," I repeated. "I suppose we'll have to wait and see."

It was a long wait. I was dozing against the trunk of a huge tree, near dusk, when Marsali's hand on my shoulder brought me awake.

"They're launching the ship!" she said in an excited whisper.

They were; under the eyes of the sentries, the remaining soldiers and the crew of the *Artemis* were all manning the ropes and rollers that would move her down the beach into the waters of the inlet. Even Fergus, Innes, and Murphy joined in the labor, missing limbs notwithstanding.

The sun was going down; its disc shone huge and orange-gold, blinding above a sea gone the purple of whelks. The men were no more than black silhouettes against the light, anonymous as the slaves of an Egyptian wall-painting, tethered by ropes to their massive burden.

The monotonous "Heave!" of the bosun's shout was succeeded by a weak cheer as the hull slid the last few feet, drawn away from the shore by tow-ropes from the *Artemis*'s jolly boat and cutter.

I saw the flash of red hair as Jamie moved up the side and swung aboard, then the gleam of metal as one of the soldiers followed him. They stood guard together, red hair and black no more than dots at the head of the rope ladder, as the crew of the *Artemis* entered the jolly boat, rowed out and came up the ladder, interspersed with the rest of the French soldiers.

The last man disappeared up the ladder. The men in the boats sat on their oars, looking up, tense and alert. Nothing happened.

Next to me, I heard Marsali exhale noisily, and realized I had been holding my own breath much too long.

"What are they *doing*?" she said, in exasperation.

As though in answer to this, there was one loud, angry shout from the *Artemis*. The men in the boats jerked up, ready to lunge aboard. No other signal came, though. The *Artemis* floated serenely on the rising waters of the inlet, perfect as an oil painting.

"I've had enough," I said suddenly to Marsali. "Whatever those bloody men are doing, they've done it. Come on."

I drew in a fresh gulp of the cool evening air, and walked out of the trees, Marsali behind me. As we came down the beach, a slim black figure dropped over the ship's side and galloped through the shallows, gleaming gouts of green and purple seawater spouting from his footsteps.

"*Mo chridhe chèrie!*" Fergus ran dripping toward us, face beaming, and seizing Marsali, swung her off her feet with exuberance and whirled her round.

"Done!" he crowed. "Done without a shot fired! Trussed like geese and packed like salted herrings in the hold!" He kissed Marsali heartily, then set her down on the sand, and turning to me, bowed ceremoniously, with the elaborate flourish of an imaginary hat.

"Milady, the captain of the *Artemis* desires you will honor him with your company over supper."

The new captain of the *Artemis* was standing in the middle of his cabin, eyes closed and completely naked, blissfully scratching his testicles.

"Er," I said, confronted with this sight. His eyes popped open and his face lit with joy. The next moment, I was enfolded in his embrace, face pressed against the red-gold curls of his chest.

We didn't say anything for quite some time. I could hear the thrum of footsteps on the deck overhead, the shouts of the crew, ringing with joy at the imminence of escape, and the creak and flap of sails being rigged. The *Artemis* was coming back to life around us.

My face was warm, tingling from the rasp of his beard. I felt suddenly strange and shy holding him, he naked as a jay and myself as bare under the remnants of Father Fogden's tattered robe.

The body that pressed against my own with mounting urgency was the same from the neck down, but the face was a stranger's, a Viking marauder's. Besides the beard that transformed his face, he smelled unfamiliar, his own sweat overlaid with rancid cooking oil, spilled beer, and the reek of harsh perfume and unfamiliar spices.

I let go, and took a step back.

"Shouldn't you dress?" I asked. "Not that I don't enjoy the scenery," I added, blushing despite myself. "I—er . . . I think I like the beard. Maybe," I added doubtfully, scrutinizing him.

"I don't," he said frankly, scratching his jaw. "I'm crawling wi' lice, and it itches like a fiend."

"Eew!" While I was entirely familiar with *Pediculus humanus,* the common body louse, acquaintance had not endeared me. I rubbed a hand nervously through my own hair, already imagining the prickle of feet on my scalp, as tiny sestets gamboled through the thickets of my curls.

He grinned at me, white teeth startling in the auburn beard.

"Dinna fash yourself, Sassenach," he assured me. "I've already sent for a razor and hot water."

"Really? It seems rather a pity to shave it off right away." Despite the lice, I leaned forward to peer at his hirsute adornment. "It's like your hair, all different colors. Rather pretty, really."

I touched it, warily. The hairs were odd; thick and wiry, very curly, in contrast to the soft thick smoothness of the hair on his head. They sprang exuberantly from his skin in a profusion of colors; copper, gold, amber, cinnamon, a roan so deep as almost to be black. Most startling of all was a thick streak of silver that ran from his lower lip to the line of his jaw.

"That's funny," I said, tracing it. "You haven't any white hairs on your head, but you have right here."

"I have?" He put a hand to his jaw, looking startled, and I suddenly realized that he likely had no idea what he looked like. Then he smiled wryly, and bent to pick up the pile of discarded clothes from the floor.

"Aye, well, little wonder if I have; I wonder I've not gone white-haired altogether from the things I've been through this month." He paused, eyeing me over the wadded white breeches.

"And speaking of that, Sassenach, as I was saying to ye in the trees—"

"Yes, speaking of that," I interrupted. "What in the name of God did you *do*?"

"Oh, the soldiers, ye mean?" He scratched his chin meditatively. "Well, it was simple enough. I told the soldiers that as soon as the ship was launched, we'd gather everyone on deck, and at my signal, they were to fall on the crew and push them into the hold." A broad grin blossomed through the foliage. "Only Fergus had mentioned it to the crew, ye see; so when each soldier came aboard, two of the crewmen snatched him by the arms while a third gagged him, bound his arms, and took away his weapons. Then we pushed all of *them* into the hold. That's all." He shrugged, modestly nonchalant.

"Right," I said, exhaling. "And as for just how you happened to be here in the first place . . . ."

At this juncture we were interrupted by a discreet knock on the cabin's door.

"Mr. Fraser? Er . . . Captain, I mean?" Maitland's angular young face peered round the jamb, cautious over a steaming bowl. "Mr. Murphy's got the galley fire going, and here's your hot water, with his compliments."

"Mr. Fraser will do," Jamie assured him, taking the tray with bowl and razor in one hand. "A less seaworthy captain doesna bear thinking of." He paused, listening to the thump of feet above our heads.

"Though since I *am* the captain," he said slowly, "I suppose that means I shall say when we sail and when we stop?"

"Yes, sir, that's one thing a captain does," Maitland said. He added helpfully, "The captain also says when the hands are to have extra rations of food and grog."

"I see." The upward curl of Jamie's mouth was still visible, beard notwithstanding. "Tell me, Maitland—how much d'ye think the hands can drink and still sail the ship?"

"Oh, quite a lot, sir," Maitland said earnestly. His brow wrinkled in thought. "Maybe—an extra double ration all round?"

Jamie lifted one eyebrow. "Of brandy?"

"Oh, no, sir!" Maitland looked shocked. "Grog. If it was to be brandy, only an extra half-ration, or they'd be rolling in the bilges."

"Double grog, then." Jamie bowed ceremoniously to Maitland, unhampered by the fact that he was still completely unclad. "Make it so, Mr. Maitland. And the ship will not lift anchor until I have finished my supper."

"Yes, sir!" Maitland bowed back; Jamie's manners were catching. "And shall I desire the Chinee to attend you directly after the anchor is weighed?"

"Somewhat before that, Mr. Maitland, thank ye kindly."

Maitland was turning to leave, with a last admiring glance at Jamie's scars, but I stopped him.

"One more thing, Maitland," I said.

"Oh, yes, mum?"

"Will you go down to the galley and ask Mr. Murphy to send up a bottle of his strongest vinegar? And then find where the men have put some of my medicines, and fetch them as well?"

His narrow forehead creased in puzzlement, but he nodded obligingly. "Oh, yes, mum. This directly minute."

"Just what d'ye mean to do wi' the vinegar Sassenach?" Jamie observed me narrowly, as Maitland vanished into the corridor.

"Souse you in it to kill the lice," I said. "I don't intend to sleep with a seething nest of vermin."

"Oh," he said. He scratched the side of his neck meditatively. "Ye mean to sleep with me, do you?" He glanced at the berth, an uninviting hole in the wall.

"I don't know where, precisely, but yes, I do," I said firmly. "And I wish you wouldn't shave your beard just yet," I added, as he bent to set down the tray he was holding.

"Why not?" He glanced curiously over his shoulder at me, and I felt the heat rising in my cheeks.

"Er . . . well. It's a bit . . . different."

"Oh, aye?" He stood up and took a step toward me. In the cramped confines of the cabin, he seemed even bigger—and a lot more naked—than he ever had on deck.

The dark blue eyes had slanted into triangles of amusement.

"How, different?" he asked.

"Well, it . . . um . . ." I brushed my fingers vaguely past my burning cheeks. "It feels different. When you kiss me. On my . . . skin."

His eyes locked on mine. He hadn't moved, but he seemed much closer.

"Ye have verra fine skin, Sassenach," he said softly. "Like pearls and opals." He reached out a finger and very gently traced the line of my jaw. And then my neck, and the wide flare of collarbone and back, and down, in a slow-moving serpentine that brushed the tops of my breasts, hidden in the deep cowl neck of the priest's robe. "Ye have a *lot* of verra fine skin, Sassenach," he added. One eyebrow quirked up. "If that's what ye were thinking?"

I swallowed and licked my lips, but didn't look away.

"That's more or less what I was thinking, yes."

He took his finger away and glanced at the bowl of steaming water.

"Aye, well. It seems a shame to waste the water. Shall I send it back to Murphy to make soup, or shall I drink it?"

I laughed, both tension and strangeness dissolving at once.

"You shall sit down," I said, "and wash with it. You smell like a brothel."

"I expect I do," he said, scratching. "There's one upstairs in the tavern where the soldiers go to drink and gamble." He took up the soap and dropped it in the hot water.

"Upstairs, eh?" I said.

"Well, the girls come down, betweentimes," he explained. "It wouldna be mannerly to stop them sitting on your lap, after all."

"And your mother brought you up to have nice manners, I expect," I said, very dryly.

"Upon second thoughts, I think perhaps we shall anchor here for the night," he said thoughtfully, looking at me.

"Shall we?"

"And sleep ashore, where there's room."

"Room for *what?*" I asked, regarding him with suspicion.

"Well, I have it planned, aye?" he said, sloshing water over his face with both hands.

"You have *what* planned?" I asked. He snorted and shook the excess water from his beard before replying.

"I have been thinking of this for months, now," he said, with keen antici-pation. "Every night, folded up in that godforsaken nutshell of a berth, listening to Fergus grunt and fart across the cabin. I thought it all out, just what I would do, did I have ye naked and willing, no one in hearing, and room enough to serve ye suitably." He lathered the cake of soap vigorously between his palms, and applied it to his face.

"Well, I'm willing enough," I said, intrigued. "And there's room, cer-tainly. As for naked . . ."

"I'll see to that," he assured me. "That's part o' the plan, aye? I shall take ye to a private spot, spread out a quilt to lie on, and commence by sitting down beside you."

"Well, that's a start, all right," I said. "What then?" I sat down next to him on the berth. He leaned close and bit my earlobe very delicately.

"As for what next, then I shall take ye on my knee and kiss ye." He paused to illustrate, holding my arms so I couldn't move. He let go a minute later, leaving my lips slightly swollen, tasting of ale, soap, and Jamie.

"So much for step one," I said, wiping soapsuds from my mouth. "What then?"

"Then I shall lay ye down upon the quilt, twist your hair up in my hand and taste your face and throat and ears and bosom wi' my lips," he said. "I thought I would do that until ye start to make squeaking noises."

"I don't make squeaking noises!"

"Aye, ye do," he said. "Here, hand me the towel, aye?"

"Then," he went on cheerfully, "I thought I would begin at the other end. I shall lift up your skirt and—" His face disappeared into the folds of the linen towel.

"And what?" I asked, thoroughly intrigued.

"And kiss the insides of your thighs, where the skin's so soft. The beard might help there, aye?" He stroked his jaw, considering.

"It might," I said, a little faintly. "What am I supposed to be doing while you do this?"

"Well, ye might moan a bit, if ye like, to encourage me, but otherwise, ye just lie still."

He didn't sound as though he needed any encouragement whatever. One of his hands was resting on my thigh as he used the other to swab his chest with the damp towel. As he finished, the hand slid behind me, and squeezed.

"My beloved's arm is under me," I quoted. "And his hand behind my head. Comfort me with apples, and stay me with flagons, For I am sick of love."

There was a flash of white teeth in his beard.

"More like grapefruit," he said, one hand cupping my behind. "Or possibly gourds. Grapefruit are too small."

"Gourds?" I said indignantly.

"Well, wild gourds get that big sometimes," he said. "But aye, that's next." He squeezed once more, then removed the hand in order to wash the armpit on that side. "I lie upon my back and have ye stretched at length upon me, so that I can get hold of your buttocks and fondle them properly." He stopped washing to give me a quick example of what he thought proper, and I let out an involuntary gasp.

"Now," he went on, resuming his ablutions, "should ye wish to kick your legs a bit, or make lewd motions wi' your hips and pant in my ear at that point in the proceedings, I should have no great objection."

"I do not pant!"

"Aye, ye do. Now, about your breasts—"

"Oh, I thought you'd forgotten those."

"Never in life," he assured me. "No," he went blithely on, "that's when I take off your gown, leaving ye in naught but your shift."

"I'm not wearing a shift."

"Oh? Well, no matter," he said, dismissing this. "I meant to suckle ye through the thin cotton, 'til your nipples stood up hard in my mouth, and then take it off, but it's no great concern; I'll manage without. So, allowing for the absence of your shift, I shall attend to your breasts until ye make that wee bleating noise—"

"I don't—"

"And then," he said, interrupting, "since ye will, according to the plan, be naked, and—provided I've done it right so far—possibly willing as well—"

"Oh, just possibly," I said. My lips were still tingling from step one.

"—then I shall spread open your thighs, take down my breeks, and—" He paused, waiting.

"And?" I said, obligingly.

The grin widened substantially.

"And we'll see what sort of noise it is ye don't make then, Sassenach."

There was a slight cough in the doorway behind me.

"Oh, your pardon, Mr. Willoughby," Jamie said apologetically. "I wasna expecting ye so soon. Perhaps ye'd care to go and have a bit of supper? And if ye would, take those things along and ask Murphy will he burn them in the galley fire." He tossed the remains of his uniform to Mr. Willoughby, and bent to rummage in a sealocker for fresh clothing.

"I never thought to meet Lawrence Stern again," he remarked, burrowing through the tangled linen. "How does he come to be here?"

"Oh, he *is* the Jewish natural philosopher you told me about?"

"He is. Though I shouldna think there are so many Jewish philosophers about as to cause great confusion."

I explained how I had come to meet Stern in the mangroves. ". . . and then he brought me up to the priest's house," I said, and stopped, suddenly reminded. "Oh, I almost forgot! You owe the priest two pounds sterling, on account of Arabella."

"I do?" Jamie glanced at me, startled, a shirt in his hand.

"You do. Maybe you'd best ask Lawrence if he'll act as ambassador; the priest seems to get on with him."

"All right. What's happened to this Arabella, though? Has one of the crew debauched her?"

"I suppose you might say that." I drew breath to explain further, but before I could speak, another knock sounded on the door.

"Can a man not dress in peace?" Jamie demanded irritably. "Come, then!"

The door swung open, revealing Marsali, who blinked at the sight of her nude stepfather. Jamie hastily swathed his midsection in the shirt he was holding, and nodded to her, sangfroid only slightly impaired.

"Marsali, lass. I'm glad to see ye unhurt. Did ye require something?"

The girl edged into the room, taking up a position between the table and a sea chest.

"Aye, I do," she said. She was sunburned, and her nose was peeling, but I thought she seemed pale nonetheless. Her fists were clenched at her sides, and her chin lifted as for battle.

"I require ye to keep your promise," she said.

"Aye?" Jamie looked wary.

"Your promise to let me and Fergus be married, so soon as we came to the Indies." A small wrinkle appeared between her fair eyebrows. "Hispaniola *is* in the Indies, no? The Jew said so."

Jamie scratched at his beard, looking reluctant.

"It is," he said. "And aye, I suppose if I . . . well, aye. I did promise. But —you're still sure of yourselves, the two of ye?" She lifted her chin higher, jaw set firmly.

"We are."

Jamie lifted one eyebrow.

"Where's Fergus?"

"Helping stow the cargo. I kent we'd be under way soon, so I thought I'd best come and ask now."

"Aye. Well." Jamie frowned, then sighed with resignation. "Aye, I said. But I did say as ye must be blessed by a priest, did I no? There's no priest closer than Bayamo, and that's three days' ride. But perhaps in Jamaica . . ."

"Nay, you're forgetting!" Marsali said triumphantly. "We've a priest right here. Father Fogden can marry us."

I felt my jaw drop, and hastily closed it. Jamie was scowling at her.

"We sail first thing in the morning!"

"It won't take long," she said. "It's only a few words, after all. We're already married, by law; it's only to be blessed by the Church, aye?" Her hand flattened on her abdomen where her marriage contract presumably resided beneath her stays.

"But your mother . . ." Jamie glanced helplessly at me for reinforcement. I shrugged, equally helpless. The task of trying either to explain Father Fogden to Jamie or to dissuade Marsali was well beyond me.

"He likely won't do it, though." Jamie came up with this objection with a palpable air of relief. "The crew have been trifling with one of his parishioners named Arabella. He willna want anything to do wi' us, I'm afraid."

"Yes, he will! He'll do it for me—he likes me!" Marsali was almost dancing on her toes with eagerness.

Jamie looked at her for a long moment, eyes fixed on hers, reading her face. She was very young.

"You're sure, then, lassie?" he said at last, very gently. "Ye want this?"

She took a deep breath, a glow spreading over her face.

"I am, Da. I truly am. I want Fergus! I love him!"

Jamie hesitated a moment, then rubbed a hand through his hair and nodded.

"Aye, then. Go and send Mr. Stern to me, then fetch Fergus and tell him to make ready."

"Oh, Da! Thank you, thank you!" Marsali flung herself at him and kissed him. He held her with one arm, clutching the shirt about his middle with the other. Then he kissed her on the forehead and pushed her gently away.

"Take care," he said, smiling. "Ye dinna want to go to your bridal covered wi' lice."

"Oh!" This seemed to remind her of something. She glanced at me and blushed, putting up a hand to her own pale locks, which were matted with sweat and straggling down her neck from a careless knot.

"Mother Claire," she said shyly, "I wonder—would ye—could ye lend me a bit of the special soap ye make wi' the chamomile? I—if there's time—" she added, with a hasty glance at Jamie, "I should like to wash my hair."

"Of course," I said, and smiled at her. "Come along and we'll make you pretty for your wedding." I looked her over appraisingly, from glowing round face to dirty bare feet. The crumpled muslin of her sea-shrunk gown stretched tight over her bosom, slight as it was, and the grubby hem hovered several inches above her sandy ankles.

A thought struck me, and I turned to Jamie. "She should have a nice dress to be married in," I said.

"Sassenach," he said, with obviously waning patience, "we havena—"

"No, but the priest does," I interrupted. "Tell Lawrence to ask Father Fogden whether we might borrow one of his gowns; Ermenegilda's, I mean. I think they're almost the right size."

Jamie's face went blank with surprise above his beard.

"Ermenegilda?" he said. "Arabella? Gowns?" He narrowed his eyes at me. "What sort of priest *is* this man, Sassenach?"

I paused in the doorway, Marsali hovering impatiently in the passage beyond.

"Well," I said, "he drinks a bit. And he's rather fond of sheep. But he might remember the words to the wedding ceremony."

━━◆━━

It was one of the more unusual weddings I had attended. The sun had long since sunk into the sea by the time all arrangements were made. To the disgruntlement of Mr. Warren, the ship's master, Jamie had declared that we would not leave until the next day, so as to allow the newlyweds one night of privacy ashore.

"Damned if I'd care to consummate a marriage in one of those godforsaken pesthole berths," he told me privately. "If they got coupled in there to start wi', we'd never pry them out. And the thought of takin' a maidenhead in a hammock—"

"Quite," I said. I poured more vinegar on his head, smiling to myself. "Very thoughtful of you."

Now Jamie stood by me on the beach, smelling rather strongly of vinegar, but handsome and dignified in blue coat, clean stock and linen, and gray serge breeks, with his hair clubbed back and ribboned. The wild red beard was a bit incongruous above his otherwise sober garb, but it had been neatly trimmed and fine-combed with vinegar, and stockinged feet notwithstanding, he made a fine picture as father of the bride.

Murphy, as one chief witness, and Maitland, as the other, were somewhat less prepossessing, though Murphy had washed his hands and Maitland his face. Fergus would have preferred Lawrence Stern as a witness, and Marsali had asked for me, but both were dissuaded; first on grounds that Stern was not a Christian, let alone a Catholic, and then, by consideration that while I was religiously qualified, that fact was unlikely to weigh heavily with Laoghaire, once she found out about it.

"I've told Marsali she must write to her mother to say she's wed," Jamie murmured to me as we watched the preparations on the beach go forward. "But perhaps I shall suggest she doesna say much more about it than that."

I saw his point; Laoghaire was not going to be pleased at hearing that her eldest daughter had eloped with a one-handed ex-pickpocket twice her age. Her maternal feelings were unlikely to be assuaged by hearing that the marriage had been performed in the middle of the night on a West Indian beach by a disgraced—if not actually defrocked—priest, witnessed by twenty-five seamen, ten French horses, a small flock of sheep—all gaily beribboned in honor of the occasion—and a King Charles spaniel, who added to the generally festive feeling by attempting to copulate with Murphy's wooden leg at every opportunity. The only thing that could make things worse, in Laoghaire's view, would be to hear that I had participated in the ceremony.

Several torches were lit, bound to stakes pounded into the sand, and the flames streamed seaward in tails of red and orange, bright against the black velvet night. The brilliant stars of the Caribbean shone overhead like the lights of heaven. While it was not a church, few brides had had a more beautiful setting for their nuptials.

I didn't know what prodigies of persuasion had been required on Lawrence's part, but Father Fogden was there, frail and insubstantial as a ghost, the blue sparks of his eyes the only real signs of life. His skin was gray as his robe, and his hands trembled on the worn leather of his prayer book.

Jamie glanced sharply at him, and appeared to be about to say something, but then merely muttered under his breath in Gaelic and pressed his lips tightly together. The spicy scent of sangria wafted from Father Fogden's vicinity, but at least he had reached the beach under his own power. He stood swaying between two torches, laboriously trying to turn the pages of his book as the light offshore wind jerked them fluttering from his fingers.

At last he gave up, and dropped the book on the sand with a little *plop*!

"Um," he said, and belched. He looked about and gave us a small, saintlike smile. "Dearly beloved of God."

It was several moments before the throng of shuffling, murmuring spectators realized that the ceremony had started, and began to poke each other and straighten to attention.

"Wilt thou take this woman?" Father Fogden demanded, suddenly rounding ferociously on Murphy.

"No!" said the cook, startled. "I don't hold wi' women. Messy things."

"You don't?" Father Fogden closed one eye, the remaining orb bright and accusing. He looked at Maitland.

"Do *you* take this woman?"

"Not me, sir, no. Not that anyone wouldn't be pleased," he added hastily. "Him, please." Maitland pointed at Fergus, who stood next to the cabin boy, glowering at the priest.

"Him? You're sure? He hasn't a hand," Father Fogden said doubtfully. "Won't she mind?"

"I will not!" Marsali, imperious in one of Ermenegilda's gowns, blue silk encrusted with gold embroidery along the low, square neckline and puffed sleeves, stood beside Fergus. She looked lovely, with her hair clean and bright as fresh straw, brushed to a gloss and floating loose round her shoulders, as became a maiden. She also looked angry.

"Go on!" She stamped her foot, which made no noise on the sand, but seemed to startle the priest.

"Oh, yes," he said nervously, taking one step back. "Well, I don't suppose it's an impt—impeddy—impediment, after all. Not as though he'd lost his cock, I mean. He hasn't, has he?" the priest inquired anxiously, as the possibility occurred to him. "I can't marry you if he has. It's not allowed."

Marsali's face was already bathed in red by torchlight. The expression on it at this point reminded me strongly of how her mother had looked upon finding me at Lallybroch. A visible tremor ran through Fergus's shoulders, whether of rage or laughter, I couldn't tell.

Jamie quelled the incipient riot by striding firmly into the middle of the wedding and placing a hand on the shoulders of Fergus and Marsali.

"This man," he said, with a nod toward Fergus, "and this woman," with another toward Marsali. "Marry them, Father. Now. Please," he added, as an obvious afterthought, and stood back a pace, restoring order among the audience by dint of dark glances from side to side.

"Oh, quite. Quite," Father Fogden repeated, swaying gently. "Quite, quite." A long pause followed, during which the priest squinted at Marsali.

"Name," he said abruptly. "I have to have a name. Can't get married without a name. Just like a cock. Can't get married without a name; can't get married without a c—"

"Marsali Jane MacKimmie Joyce!" Marsali spoke up loudly, drowning him out.

"Yes, yes," he said hurriedly. "Of course it is. Marsali. Mar-sa-lee. Just so. Well, then, do you Mar-sa-lee take this man—even though he's missing a hand and possibly other parts not visible—to be your lawful husband? To have and to hold, from this day forward, forsaking . . ." At this point he trailed off, his attention fixed on one of the sheep that had wandered into the light and was chewing industriously on a discarded stocking of striped wool.

"I do!"

Father Fogden blinked, brought back to attention. He made an unsuccessful attempt to stifle another belch, and transferred his bright blue gaze to Fergus.

"You have a name, too? *And* a cock?"

"Yes," said Fergus, wisely choosing not to be more specific. "Fergus."

The priest frowned slightly at this. "Fergus?" he said. "Fergus. Fergus. Yes, Fergus, got that. That's all? No more name? Need more names, surely."

"Fergus," Fergus repeated, with a note of strain in his voice. Fergus was the only name he had ever had—bar his original French name of Claudel. Jamie had given him the name Fergus in Paris, when they had met, twenty years before. But naturally a brothel-born bastard would have no last name to give a wife.

"Fraser," said a deep, sure voice beside me. Fergus and Marsali both glanced back in surprise, and Jamie nodded. His eyes met Fergus's, and he smiled faintly.

"Fergus Claudel Fraser," he said, slowly and clearly. One eyebrow lifted as he looked at Fergus.

Fergus himself looked transfixed. His mouth hung open, eyes wide black pools in the dim light. Then he nodded slightly, and a glow rose in his face, as though he contained a candle that had just been lit.

"Fraser," he said to the priest. His voice was husky, and he cleared his throat. "Fergus Claudel Fraser."

Father Fogden had his head tilted back, watching the sky, where a crescent of light floated over the trees, holding the black orb of the moon in its cup. He lowered his head to face Fergus, looking dreamy.

"Well, that's good," he said. "Isn't it?"

A small poke in the ribs from Maitland brought him back to an awareness of his responsibilities.

"Oh! Um. Well. Man and wife. Yes, I pronounce you man—no, that's not right, you haven't said whether you'd take her. She has both hands," he added helpfully.

"I will," Fergus said. He had been holding Marsali's hand; now he let go and dug hastily in his pocket, coming out with a small gold ring. He must have bought it in Scotland, I realized, and kept it ever since, not wanting to make the marriage official until it had been blessed. Not by a priest—by Jamie.

The beach was silent as he slid the ring on her finger, all eyes fixed on the small gold circle and the two heads bent close together over it, one bright, one dark.

So she had done it. One fifteen-year-old girl, with nothing but stubbornness as a weapon. "I want him," she had said. And kept saying it, through her mother's objections and Jamie's arguments, through Fergus's scruples and her own fears, through three thousand miles of homesickness, hardship, ocean storm, and shipwreck.

She raised her face, shining, and found her mirror in Fergus's eyes. I saw them look at each other, and felt the tears prickle behind my lids.

"I want him." I had not said that to Jamie at our marriage; I had not wanted him, then. But I had said it since, three times; in two moments of choice at Craigh na Dun, and once again at Lallybroch.

"I want him." I wanted him still, and nothing whatever could stand between us.

He was looking down at me; I could feel the weight of his gaze, dark blue and tender as the sea at dawn.

"What are ye thinking, *mo chridhe*?" he asked softly.

I blinked back the tears and smiled at him. His hands were large and warm on mine.

"What I tell you three times is true," I said. And standing on tiptoe, I kissed him as the sailor's cheer went up.

PART NINE

Worlds Unknown

53

Bat Guano

Bat guano is a slimy blackish green when fresh, a powdery light brown when dried. In both states, it emits an eye-watering reek of musk, ammonia, and decay.

"*How* much of this stuff did you say we're taking?" I asked, through the cloth I had wrapped about my lower face.

"Ten tons," Jamie replied, his words similarly muffled. We were standing on the upper deck, watching as the slaves trundled barrowloads of the reeking stuff down the gangplank and over to the open hatchway of the after hold.

Tiny particles of the dried guano blew from the barrows and filled the air around us with a deceptively beautiful cloud of gold, that sparked and glimmered in the late afternoon sun. The men's bodies were coated with the stuff as well; the runnels of sweat carved dark channels in the dust on their bare torsos, and the constant tears ran down their faces and chests, so that they were striped in black and gold like exotic zebras.

Jamie dabbed at his own streaming eyes as the wind veered slightly toward us. "D'ye ken how to keelhaul someone, Sassenach?"

"No, but if it's Fergus you have in mind as a candidate, I'm with you. How far is it to Jamaica?" It was Fergus, making inquiries in the marketplace on King's Street in Bridgetown, who had gained the *Artemis* her first commission as a trading and hauling vessel; the shipment of ten cubic tons of bat guano from Barbados to Jamaica, for use as fertilizer on the sugar plantation of one Mr. Grey, planter.

Fergus himself was rather self-consciously overseeing the loading of the huge quarried blocks of dried guano, which were tipped from their barrows and handed down one by one into the hold. Marsali, never far from his side, had in this case moved as far as the forecastle, where she sat on a barrel filled with oranges, the lovely new shawl Fergus had bought her in the market wrapped over her face.

"We are meant to be traders, no?" Fergus had argued. "We have an empty hold to fill. Besides," he had added logically, clinching the argument, "Monsieur Grey will pay us more than adequately."

"How far, Sassenach?" Jamie squinted at the horizon, as though hoping to see land rising from the sparkling waves. Mr. Willoughby's magic needles

rendered him seaworthy, but he submitted to the process with no real enthusiasm. "Three or four days' sail, Warren says," he admitted with a sigh, "and
the weather holds fair."

"Maybe the smell will be better at sea," I said.

"Oh, yes, milady," Fergus assured me, overhearing as he passed. "The
owner tells me that the stench dissipates itself significantly, once the dried
material is removed from the caves where it accumulates." He leapt into the
rigging and went up, climbing like a monkey despite his hook. Reaching the
top rigging, Fergus tied the red kerchief that was the signal to hands on
shore to come aboard, and slid down again, pausing to say something rude
to Ping An, who was perched on the lowest crosstrees, keeping a bright
yellow eye on the proceedings below.

"Fergus seems to be taking quite a proprietary interest in this cargo," I
observed.

"Aye, well, he's a partner," Jamie said. "I told him if he'd a wife to
support, he must think of how to do it. And as it may be some time before
we're in the printing business again, he must turn his hand to what offers.
He and Marsali have half the profit on this cargo—against the dowry I
promised her," he added wryly, and I laughed.

"You know," I said, "I really would like to read the letter Marsali's sending to her mother. First Fergus, I mean, then Father Fogden and Mamacita,
and now a dowry of ten tons of bat shit."

"I shall never be able to set foot in Scotland again, once Laoghaire reads
it," said Jamie, but he smiled nonetheless. "Have ye thought yet what to do
wi' your new acquisition?"

"Don't remind me," I said, a little grimly. "Where is he?"

"Somewhere below," Jamie said, his attention distracted by a man coming
down the wharf toward us. "Murphy's fed him, and Innes will find a place
for him. Your pardon, Sassenach; I think this will be someone looking for
me." He swung down from the rail and went down the gangplank, neatly
skipping around a slave coming up with a barrowload of guano.

I watched with interest as he greeted the man, a tall colonial in the dress of
a prosperous planter, with a weathered red face that spoke of long years in
the islands. He extended a hand toward Jamie, who took it in a firm clasp.
Jamie said something, and the man replied, his expression of wariness changing to an instant cordiality.

This must be the result of Jamie's visit to the Masonic lodge in Bridgetown, where he had gone immediately upon landing the day before, mindful
of Jared's suggestion. He had identified himself as a member of the brother-
hood, and spoken to the Master of the lodge, describing Young Ian and
asking for any news of either the boy or the ship *Bruja*. The Master had
promised to spread the word among such Freemasons as might have occa-

sion to frequent the slave market and the shipping docks. With luck, this was the fruit of that promise.

I watched eagerly as the planter reached into his coat and withdrew a paper, which he unfolded and showed to Jamie, apparently explaining something. Jamie's face was intent, his ruddy brows drawn together with concentration, but showed neither exultation nor disappointment. Maybe it was not news of Ian at all. After our visit to the slave market the day before, I was half-inclined to hope not.

Lawrence, Fergus, Marsali, and I had gone to the slave market under the cranky chaperonage of Murphy, while Jamie called on the Masonic Master. The slave market was near the docks, down a dusty road lined with sellers of fruit and coffee, dried fish and coconuts, yams and red cochineal bugs, sold for dye in small, corked glass bottles.

Murphy, with his passion for order and propriety, had insisted that Marsali and I must each have a parasol, and had forced Fergus to buy two from a roadside vendor.

"All the white women in Bridgetown carry parasols," he said firmly, trying to hand me one.

"I don't need a parasol," I said, impatient at talk of something so inconsequential as my complexion, when we might be near to finding Ian at last. "The sun isn't that hot. Let's go!"

Murphy glowered at me, scandalized.

"Ye don't want folk to think ye ain't respectable, that ye don't care enough to keep yer skin fine!"

"I wasn't planning to take up residence here," I said tartly. "I don't care *what* they think." Not pausing to argue further, I began walking down the road, toward a distant murmur of noise that I took to be the slave market.

"Yer face will . . . get . . . red!" Murphy said, huffing indignantly alongside me, attempting to open the parasol as he stumped along.

"Oh, a fate worse than death, I'm sure!" I snapped. My nerves were strung tight, in anticipation of what we might find. "All right, then, give me the bloody thing!" I snatched it from him, snapped it open, and set it over my shoulder with an irritable twirl.

As it was, within minutes I was grateful for Murphy's intransigence. While the road was shaded by tall palms and cecropia trees, the slave market itself was held in a large, stone-paved space without the grace of any shade, save that provided by ramshackle open booths roofed with sheets of tin or palm fronds, in which the slave-dealers and auctioneers sought occasional refuge from the sun. The slaves themselves were mostly held in large pens at the side of the square, open to the elements.

The sun *was* fierce in the open, and the light bouncing off the pale stones was blinding after the green shade of the road. I blinked, eyes watering, and hastily adjusted my parasol over my head.

So shaded, I could see a bewildering array of bodies, naked or nearly so, gleaming in every shade from pale café au lait to a deep blue-black. Bouquets of color blossomed in front of the auction blocks, where the plantation owners and their servants gathered to inspect the wares, vivid amid the stark blacks and whites.

The stink of the place was staggering, even to one accustomed to the stenches of Edinburgh and the reeking tween-decks of the *Porpoise*. Heaps of wet human excrement lay in the corners of the slave pens, buzzing with flies, and a thick oily reek floated on the air, but the major component of the smell was the unpleasantly intimate scent of acres of hot bare flesh, baking in the sun.

"Jesu," Fergus muttered next to me. His dark eyes flicked right and left in shocked disapproval. "It's worse than the slums in Montmartre." Marsali didn't say a word, but drew closer to his side, her nostrils pinched.

Lawrence was more matter-of-fact; I supposed he must have seen slave markets before during his explorations of the islands.

"The whites are at that end," he said, gesturing toward the far side of the square. "Come; we'll ask for news of any young men sold recently." He placed a large square hand in the center of my back and urged me gently forward through the crowd.

Near the edge of the market, an old black woman squatted on the ground, feeding charcoal to a small brazier. As we drew near, a little group of people approached her: a planter, accompanied by two black men dressed in rough cotton shirts and trousers, evidently his servants. One of them was holding the arm of a newly purchased female slave; two other girls, naked but for small strips of cloth wrapped about their middles, were led by ropes around their necks.

The planter bent and handed the old woman a coin. She turned and drew several short brass rods from the ground behind her, holding them up for the man's inspection. He studied them for a moment, picked out two, and straightened up. He handed the branding irons to one of his servants, who thrust the ends into the old woman's brazier.

The other servant stepped behind the girl and pinioned her arms. The first man then pulled the irons from the fire and planted both together on the upper slope of her right breast. She shrieked, a high steam-whistle sound loud enough to turn a few heads nearby. The irons pulled away, leaving the letters HB in raw pink flesh.

I had stopped dead at the sight of this. Not realizing that I was no longer with them, the others had gone on. I turned round and round, looking vainly for any trace of Lawrence or Fergus. I never had any difficulty finding Jamie in crowds; his bright head was always visible above everyone else's. But

Fergus was a small man, Murphy, no taller, and Lawrence, no more than middle height; even Marsali's yellow parasol was lost among the many others in the square.

I turned away from the brazier with a shudder, hearing screams and whimpers behind me, but not wanting to look back. I hurried past several auction blocks, eyes averted, but then was slowed and finally stopped by a thickening of the crowd around me.

The men and women blocking my way were listening to an auctioneer who was touting the virtues of a one-armed slave who stood naked on the block for inspection. He was a short man, but broadly built, with massive thighs and a strong chest. The missing arm had been crudely amputated above the elbow; sweat dripped from the end of the stump.

"No good for field work, that's true," the auctioneer was admitting. "But a sound investment for breeding. Look at those legs!" He carried a long rattan cane, which he flicked against the slave's calves, then grinned fatly at the crowd.

"Will you give a guarantee of virility?" the man standing behind me said, with a distinct tone of skepticism. "I had a buck three year past, big as a mule, and not a foal dropped on his account; couldn't do a thing, the juba-girls said."

The crowd tittered at that, and the auctioneer pretended to be offended.

"Guarantee?" he said. He wiped a hand theatrically over his jowls, gathering oily sweat on the palm. "See for yourselves, O ye of little faith!" Bending slightly, he grasped the slave's penis and began to massage it vigorously.

The man grunted in surprise and tried to draw back, but was prevented by the auctioneer's assistant, who clutched him firmly by his single arm. There was an outburst of laughter from the crowd, and a few scattered cheers as the soft black flesh hardened and began to swell.

Some small thing inside me suddenly snapped; I heard it, distinctly. Outraged by the market, the branding, the nakedness, the crude talk and casual indignity, outraged most of all by my own presence here, I could not even think what I was doing, but began to do it, all the same. I felt very oddly detached, as though I stood outside myself, watching.

"Stop it!" I said, very loudly, hardly recognizing my own voice. The auctioneer looked up, startled, and smiled ingratiatingly at me. He looked directly into my eyes, with a knowing leer.

"Sound breeding stock, ma'am," he said. "Guaranteed, as you see."

I folded my parasol, lowered it, and stabbed the pointed end of it as hard as I could into his fat stomach. He jerked back, eyes bulging in surprise. I yanked the parasol back and smashed it on his head, then dropped it and kicked him, hard.

Somewhere deep inside, I knew it would make no difference, would not help in any way, would do nothing but harm. And yet I could not stand here, consenting by silence. It was not for the branded girls, the man on the block, not for any of them that I did it; it was for myself.

There was a good deal of noise around me, and hands snatched at me, pulling me off the auctioneer. This worthy, recovered sufficiently from his initial shock, grinned nastily at me, took aim, and slapped the slave hard across the face.

I looked around for reinforcements, and caught a quick glimpse of Fergus, face contorted in rage, lunging through the crowd toward the auctioneer. There was a shout, and several men turned in his direction. People began to push and shove. Someone tripped me and I sat down hard on the stones.

Through a haze of dust, I saw Murphy, six feet away. With a resigned expression on his broad red face, he bent, detached his wooden leg, straightened up, and hopping gracefully forward, brought it down with great force on the auctioneer's head. The man tottered and fell, as the crowd surged back, trying to get out of the way.

Fergus, baffled of his prey, skidded to a halt by the fallen man and glared ferociously round. Lawrence, dark, grim, and bulky, came striding through the crowd from the other direction, hand on the cane-knife at his belt.

I sat on the ground, shaken. I no longer felt detached. I felt sick, and terrified, realizing that I had just committed an act of folly that was likely to result in Fergus, Lawrence, and Murphy being badly beaten, if nothing worse.

And then Jamie was there.

"Stand up, Sassenach," he said quietly, stooping over me and giving me his hands. I managed it, knees shaking. I saw Raeburn's long mustache twitching at one side, MacLeod behind him, and realized that his Scots were with him. Then my knees gave way, but Jamie's arms held me up.

"Do something," I said in a choked voice into his chest. "Please. Do something."

He had. With his usual presence of mind, he had done the only thing that would quell the riot and prevent harm. He had bought the one-armed man. And as the ironic result of my little outburst of sensibilities, I was now the appalled owner of a genuine male Guinea slave, one-armed, but in glowing health and of guaranteed virility.

I sighed, trying not to think of the man, presumably now somewhere under my feet, fed, and—I hoped—clad. The papers of ownership, which I had refused even to touch, said that he was a full-blooded Gold Coast Negro, a Yoruba, sold by a French planter from Barbuda, one-armed, bearing a brand on the left shoulder of a fleur-de-lys and the initial "A," and known by the name Temeraire. The Bold One. The papers did not suggest what in the name of God I was to do with him.

Jamie had finished looking at the papers his Masonic acquaintance had brought—they were very like the ones I had received for Temeraire, so far as I could see from the rail of the ship. He handed them back with a bow of thanks, a slight frown on his face. The men exchanged a few more words, and parted with another handshake.

"Is everyone aboard?" Jamie asked, stepping off the gangplank. There was a light breeze; it fluttered the dark blue ribbon that tied back the thick tail of his hair.

"Aye, sir," said Mr. Warren, with the casual jerk of the head that passed for a salute in a merchant ship. "Shall we make sail?"

"We shall, if ye please. Thank ye, Mr. Warren." With a small bow, Jamie passed him and came to stand beside me.

"No," he said quietly. His face was calm, but I could feel the depths of his disappointment. Interviews the day before with the two men who dealt in white indentured labor at the slave market had provided no useful information—the Masonic planter had been a beacon of last-minute hope.

There wasn't anything helpful to be said. I put my hand over his where it lay on the rail, and squeezed lightly. Jamie looked down and gave me a faint smile. He took a deep breath and straightened his shoulders, shrugging to settle his coat over them.

"Aye, well. I've learned something, at least. That was a Mr. Villiers, who owns a large sugar plantation here. He bought six slaves from the captain of the ship *Bruja*, three days ago—but none of them Ian."

"Three days?" I was startled. "But—the *Bruja* left Hispaniola more than two weeks ago!"

He nodded, rubbing his cheek. He had shaved, a necessity before making public inquiries, and his skin glowed fresh and ruddy above the snowy linen of his stock.

"She did. And she arrived here on Wednesday—five days ago."

"So she'd been somewhere else, before coming to Barbados! Do we know where?"

He shook his head.

"Villiers didna ken. He said he had spoken some time wi' the captain of the *Bruja*, and the man seemed verra secretive about where he'd been and what he'd been doing. Villiers thought no great thing of it, knowin' as the *Bruja* has a reputation as a crook ship—and seein' as how the captain was willing to sell the slaves for a good price."

"Still"—he brightened slightly—"Villiers did show me the papers for the slaves he'd bought. Ye'll have seen those for your slave?"

"I wish you wouldn't call him that," I said. "But yes. Were the ones you saw the same?"

"Not quite. Three o' the papers gave no previous owner—though Villiers says they were none of them fresh from Africa; all of them have a few words of English, at least. One listed a previous owner, but the name had been scratched out; I couldna read it. The other two gave a Mrs. Abernathy of Rose Hall, Jamaica, as the previous owner."

"Jamaica? How far—"

"I dinna ken," he interrupted. "But Mr. Warren will know. It may be right. In any case, I think we must go to Jamaica next—if only to dispose of our cargo before we all die o' disgust." He wrinkled his long nose fastidiously and I laughed.

"You look like an anteater when you do that," I told him.

The attempt to distract him was successful; the wide mouth curved upward slightly.

"Oh, aye? There's a beastie eats ants, is there?" He did his best to respond to the teasing, turning his back on the Barbados docks. He leaned against the rail and smiled down at me. "I shouldna think they'd be verra filling."

"I suppose it must eat a lot of them. They can't be any worse than haggis, after all." I took a breath before going on, and let it out quickly, coughing. "God, what's that?"

The *Artemis* had by now slid free of the loading wharf and out into the harbor. As we came about into the wind, a deep, pungent smell struck the ship, a lower and more sinister note in the olfactory dockside symphony of dead barnacles, wet wood, fish, rotted seaweed, and the constant warm breath of the tropical vegetation on shore.

I pressed my handkerchief hard over my nose and mouth. "What is it?"

"We're passing the burning ground, mum, at the foot o' the slave market," Maitland explained, overhearing my question. He pointed toward the shore, where a plume of white smoke rose from behind a screen of bayberry bushes. "They burn the bodies of the slaves who don't survive their passage from Africa," he explained. "First they unload the living cargo, and then, as the ship is swabbed out, the bodies are removed and thrown onto the pyre here, to prevent sickness spreading into the town."

I looked at Jamie, and found the same fear in his face that showed in my own.

"How often do they burn bodies?" I asked. "Every day?"

"Don't know, mum, but I don't think so. Maybe once a week?" Maitland shrugged and went on about his duties.

"We have to look," I said. My voice sounded strange to my own ears, calm and clear. I didn't feel that way.

Jamie had gone very pale. He had turned round again, and his eyes were fixed on the plume of smoke, rising thick and white from behind the palm trees.

His lips pressed tight, then, and his jaw set hard.

"Aye," was all he said, and turned to tell Mr. Warren to put about.

The keeper of the flames, a wizened little creature of indistinguishable color and accent, was vociferously shocked at the notion that a lady should enter the burning ground, but Jamie elbowed him brusquely aside. He didn't try to prevent me following him, or turn to see that I did; he knew I would not leave him alone here.

It was a small hollow, set behind a screen of trees, convenient to a small wharf that extended into the river. Black-smeared pitch barrels and piles of dry wood stood in grim sticky clumps amid the brilliant greens of tree-ferns and dwarf poinciana. To the right, a huge pyre had been built, with a platform of wood, onto which the bodies had been thrown, dribbled with pitch.

This had been lit only a short time before; a good blaze had started at one side of the heap, but only small tongues of flame licked up from the rest. It was smoke that obscured the bodies, rolling up over the heap in a wavering thick veil that gave the outflung limbs a horrid illusion of movement.

Jamie had stopped, staring at the heap. Then he sprang onto the platform, heedless of smoke and scorching, and began jerking bodies loose, grimly pawing through the grisly remains.

A smaller heap of gray ashes and shards of pure white friable bone lay nearby. The curve of an occiput lay on top of the heap, fragile and perfect as an eggshell.

"Makee fine crop." The soot-smeared little creature who tended the fire was at my elbow, offering information in evident hopes of reward. He—or she—pointed at the ashes. "Put on crop; makee grow-grow."

"No, thank you," I said faintly. The smoke obscured Jamie's figure for a moment, and I had the terrible feeling that he had fallen, was burning in the pyre. The horrible, jolly smell of roasting meat rose on the air, and I thought I would be sick.

"Jamie!" I called. *"Jamie!"*

He didn't answer, but I heard a deep, racking cough from the heart of the fire. Several long minutes later, the veil of smoke parted, and he staggered out, choking.

He made his way down the platform and stood bent over, coughing his lungs out. He was covered with an oily soot, his hands and clothes smeared with pitch. He was blind with the smoke; tears poured down his cheeks, making runnels in the soot.

I threw several coins to the keeper of the pyre, and taking Jamie by the arm, led him, blind and choking, out of the valley of death. Under the palms, he sank to his knees and threw up.

"Don't touch me," he gasped, when I tried to help him. He retched over and over again, but finally stopped, swaying on his knees. Then he slowly staggered to his feet.

"Don't touch me," he said again. His voice, roughened by smoke and sickness, was that of a stranger.

He walked to the edge of the dock, removed his coat and shoes, and dived into the water, fully clothed. I waited for a moment, then stooped and picked up the coat and shoes, holding them gingerly at arm's length. I could see in the inner pocket the faint rectangular bulge of Brianna's pictures.

I waited until he came back and hoisted himself out of the water, dripping. The pitch smears were still there, but most of the soot and the smell of the fire were gone. He sat on the wharf, head on his knees, breathing hard. A row of curious faces edged the *Artemis*'s rail above us.

Not knowing what else to do, I leaned down and laid a hand on his shoulder. Without raising his head, he reached up a hand and grasped mine.

"He wasn't there," he said, in his muffled, rasping stranger's voice.

The breeze was freshening; it stirred the tendrils of wet hair that lay across his shoulders. I looked back, to see that the plume of smoke rising from the little valley had changed to black. It flattened and began to drift out over the sea, the ashes of the dead slaves fleeing on the wind, back toward Africa.

54

"The Impetuous Pirate"

"I can't own anyone, Jamie," I said, looking in dismay at the papers spread out in the lamplight before me. "I just *can't*. It isn't right."

"Well, I'm inclined to agree wi' ye, Sassenach. But what are we to do with the fellow?" Jamie sat on the berth next to me, close enough to see the ownership documents over my shoulder. He rubbed a hand through his hair, frowning.

"We could set him free—that would seem the right thing—and yet, if we do—what will happen to him then?" He hunched forward, squinting down his nose to read the papers. "He's no more than a bit of French and English; no skills to speak of. If we were to set him free, or even give him a bit of money—can he manage to live, on his own?"

I nibbled thoughtfully on one of Murphy's cheese rolls. It was good, but the smell of the burning oil in the lamp blended oddly with the aromatic cheese, underlaid—as everything was—with the insidious scent of bat guano that permeated the ship.

"I don't know," I said. "Lawrence told me there are a lot of free blacks on Hispaniola. Lots of Creoles and mixed-race people, and a good many who own their own businesses. Is it like that on Jamaica, too?"

He shook his head, and reached for a roll from the tray.

"I dinna think so. It's true, there are some free blacks who earn a living for themselves, but those are the ones who have some skill—sempstresses and fishers and such. I spoke to this Temeraire a bit. He was a cane-cutter until he lost his arm, and doesna ken how to do anything else much."

I laid the roll down, barely tasted, and frowned unhappily at the papers. The mere idea of owning a slave frightened and disgusted me, but it was beginning to dawn on me that it might not be so simple to divest myself of the responsibility.

The man had been taken from a barracoon on the Guinea coast, five years before. My original impulse, to return him to his home, was clearly impossible; even had it been possible to find a ship headed for Africa that would agree to take him as a passenger, the overwhelming likelihood was that he would be immediately enslaved again, either by the ship that accepted him, or by another slaver in the West African ports.

Traveling alone, one-armed and ignorant, he would have no protection at all. And even if he should by some miracle reach Africa safely and keep himself out of the hands of both European and African slavers, there was virtually no chance of his ever finding his way back to his village. Should he do so, Lawrence had kindly explained, he would likely be killed or driven away, as his own people would regard him now as a ghost, and a danger to them.

"I dinna suppose ye would consider selling him?" Jamie put the question delicately, raising one eyebrow. "To someone we could be sure would treat him kindly?"

I rubbed two fingers between my brows, trying to soothe the growing headache.

"I can't see that that's any better than owning him ourselves," I protested. "Worse, probably, because we couldn't be sure what the new owners would do with him."

Jamie sighed. He had spent most of the day climbing through the dark, reeking cargo holds with Fergus, making up inventories against our arrival in Jamaica, and he was tired.

"Aye, I see that," he said. "But it's no kindness to free him to starve, that I can see."

"No." I fought back the uncharitable wish that I had never seen the one-armed slave. It would have been a great deal easier for me if I had not—but possibly not for him.

Jamie rose from the berth and stretched himself, leaning on the desk and flexing his shoulders to ease them. He bent and kissed me on the forehead, between the brows.

"Dinna fash, Sassenach. I'll speak to the manager at Jared's plantation. Perhaps he can find the man some employment, or else—"

A warning shout from above interrupted him.

"Ship ahoy! Look alive, below! Off the port bow, ahoy!" The lookout's cry was urgent, and there was a sudden rush and stir, as hands began to turn out. Then there was a lot more shouting, and a jerk and shudder as the *Artemis* backed her sails.

"What in the name of God—" Jamie began. A rending crash drowned his words, and he pitched sideways, eyes wide with alarm, as the cabin tilted. The stool I was on fell over, throwing me onto the floor. The oil lamp had shot from its bracket, luckily extinguishing itself before hitting the floor, and the place was in darkness.

"Sassenach! Are ye all right?" Jamie's voice came out of the murk close at hand, sharp with anxiety.

"Yes," I said, scrambling out from under the table. "Are you? What happened? Did someone hit us?"

Not pausing to answer any of these questions, Jamie had reached the door and opened it. A babel of shouts and thumps came down from the deck above, punctuated by the sudden popcorn-sound of small-arms fire.

"Pirates," he said briefly. "We've been boarded." My eyes were becoming accustomed to the dim light; I saw his shadow lunge for the desk, reaching for the pistol in the drawer. He paused to snatch the dirk from under the pillow of his berth, and made for the door, issuing instructions as he went.

"Take Marsali, Sassenach, and get below. Go aft as far as ye can get—the big hold where the guano blocks are. Get behind them, and stay there." Then he was gone.

I spent a moment feeling my way through the cupboard over my berth, in search of the morocco box Mother Hildegarde had given me when I saw her in Paris. A scalpel might be little use against pirates, but I would feel better with a weapon of some kind in my hand, no matter how small.

"Mother Claire?" Marsali's voice came from the door, high and scared.

"I'm here," I said. I caught the gleam of pale cotton as she moved, and pressed the ivory letter-opener into her hand. "Here, take this, just in case. Come on; we're to go below."

With a long-handled amputation blade in one hand, and a cluster of scalpels in the other, I led the way through the ship to the after hold. Feet thundered on the deck overhead, and curses and shouts rang through the night, overlaid with a dreadful groaning, scraping noise that I thought must be caused by the rubbing of the *Artemis*'s timbers against those of the unknown ship that had rammed us.

The hold was black as pitch and thick with dusty fumes. We made our way slowly, coughing, toward the back of the hold.

"Who are they?" Marsali asked. Her voice had a strangely muffled sound, the echoes of the hold deadened by the blocks of guano stacked around us. "Pirates, d'ye think?"

"I expect they must be." Lawrence had told us that the Caribbean was a rich hunting ground for pirate luggers and unscrupulous craft of all kinds, but we had expected no trouble, as our cargo was not particularly valuable. "I suppose they must not have much sense of smell."

"Eh?"

"Never mind," I said. "Come sit down; there's nothing we can do but wait."

I knew from experience that waiting while men fought was one of the most difficult things in life to do, but in this case, there wasn't any sensible alternative.

Down here, the sounds of the battle were muted to a distant thumping, though the constant rending groan of the scraping timbers echoed through the whole ship.

"Oh, God, Fergus," Marsali whispered, listening, her voice filled with agony. "Blessed Mary, save him!"

I silently echoed the prayer, thinking of Jamie, somewhere in the chaos overhead. I crossed myself in the dark, touching the small spot between my brows that he had kissed a few minutes before, not wanting to think that it could so easily be the last touch of him I would ever know.

Suddenly, there was an explosion overhead, a roar that sent vibrations through the jutting timbers we were sitting on.

"They're blowing up the ship!" Marsali jumped to her feet, panicked. "They'll sink us! We must get out! We'll drown down here!"

"Wait!" I called. "It's only the guns!" but she had not waited to hear. I could hear her, blundering about in a blind panic, whimpering among the blocks of guano.

"Marsali! Come back!" There was no light at all in the hold; I took a few steps through the smothering atmosphere, trying to locate her by sound, but the deadening effect of the crumbling blocks hid her movements from me. There was another booming explosion overhead, and a third close on its heels. The air was filled with dust loosed from the vibrations, and I choked, eyes watering.

I wiped at my eyes with a sleeve, and blinked. I was not imagining it; there was a light in the hold, a dim glow that limned the edge of the nearest block.

"Marsali?" I called. "Where are you?"

The answer was a terrified shriek, from the direction of the light. I dashed around the edge of the block, dodged between two others, and emerged into the space by the ladder, to find Marsali in the clutches of a large, half-naked man.

He was hugely obese, the rolling layers of his fat decorated with a stipple of tattoos, a jangling necklace of coins and buttons hung round his neck. Marsali slapped at him, shrieking, and he jerked his face away, impatient.

Then he caught sight of me, and his eyes widened. He had a wide, flat face, and a tarred topknot of black hair. He grinned nastily at me, showing a marked lack of teeth, and said something that sounded like slurred Spanish.

"Let her go!" I said loudly. *"Basta, cabrón!"* That was as much Spanish as I could summon; he seemed to think it funny, for he grinned more widely, let go of Marsali, and turned toward me. I threw one of my scalpels at him.

It bounced off his head, startling him, and he ducked wildly. Marsali dodged past him, and sprang for the ladder.

The pirate waffled for a moment, torn between us, but then turned to the ladder, leaping up several rungs with an agility that belied his weight. He caught Marsali by the foot as she dived through the hatch, and she screamed.

Cursing incoherently under my breath, I ran to the bottom of the ladder, and reaching up, swung the long-handled amputation knife at his foot, as hard as I could. There was a high-pitched screech from the pirate. Something flew past my head, and a spray of blood spattered across my cheek, wet-hot on my skin.

Startled, I dropped back, looking down by reflex to see what had fallen. It was a small brown toe, calloused and black-nailed, smudged with dirt.

The pirate hit the deck beside me with a thud that shivered the floor-boards, and lunged. I ducked, but he caught a handful of my sleeve. I yanked away, ripping fabric, and jabbed at his face with the blade in my hand.

Jerking back in surprise, he slipped on his own blood and fell. I jumped for the ladder and climbed for my life, dropping the blade.

He was so close behind me that he succeeded in catching hold of the hem of my skirt, but I pulled it from his grasp and lunged upward, lungs burning from the dust of the choking hold. The man was shouting, a language I didn't know. Some dim recess of my brain, not occupied with immediate survival, speculated that it might be Portuguese.

I burst out of the hold onto the deck, into the midst of a surging chaos. The air was thick with black-powder smoke, and small knots of men were pushing and shoving, cursing and stumbling all over the deck.

I couldn't take time to look around; there was a hoarse bellow from the hatchway behind me, and I dived for the rail. I hesitated for a moment, balanced on the narrow wooden strip. The sea spun past in a dizzy churn of black below. I grasped the rigging and began to climb.

It was a mistake; I knew that almost at once. He was a sailor, I was not. Neither was he hampered by wearing a dress. The ropes danced and jerked in my hands, vibrating under the impact of his weight as he hit the lines below me.

He was coming up the underside of the lines, climbing like a gibbon, even as I made my slower way across the upper slope of the rigging. He drew even with me, and spat in my face. I kept climbing, propelled by desperation; there was nothing else to do. He kept pace with me, easily, hissing words through an evil, half-toothed grin. It didn't matter what language he was speaking; his meaning was perfectly clear. Hanging by one hand, he drew the cutlass from his sash, and swung it in a vicious cut that barely missed me.

I was too frightened even to scream. There was nowhere to go, nothing to do. I squeezed my eyes tight shut, and hoped it would be quick.

It was. There was a sort of thump, a sharp grunt, and a strong smell of fish.

I opened my eyes. The pirate was gone. Ping An was sitting on the cross-trees, three feet away, crest erect with irritation, wings half-spread to keep his balance.

"Gwa!" he said crossly. He turned a beady little yellow eye on me, and clacked his bill in warning. Ping An hated noise and commotion. Evidently, he didn't like Portuguese pirates, either.

There were spots before my eyes, and I felt light-headed. I clung tight to the rope, shaking, until I thought I could move again. The noise below had slackened now, and the tenor of the shouting had changed. Something had happened; I thought it was over.

There was a new noise, a sudden flap of sails, and a long, grinding sound, with a vibration that made the line I was holding sing in my hand. It *was* over; the pirate ship was moving away. On the far side of the *Artemis,* I saw the web of the pirate's mast and rigging begin to move, black against the silver Caribbean sky. Very, very slowly, I began the long trip back down.

The lanterns were still lit below. A haze of black-powder smoke lay over everything, and bodies lay here and there about the deck. My glance flickered over them as I lowered myself, searching for red hair. I found it, and my heart leapt.

Jamie was sitting on a cask near the wheel, with his head tilted back, eyes closed, a cloth pressed to his brow, and a cup of whisky in his hand. Mr. Willoughby was on his knees alongside, administering first aid—in the form of more whisky—to Willie MacLeod, who sat against the foremast, looking sick.

I was shaking all over from exertion and reaction. I felt giddy and slightly cold. Shock, I supposed, and no wonder. I could do with a bit of that whisky as well.

I grasped the smaller lines above the rail, and slid the rest of the way to the deck, not caring that my palms were skinned raw. I was sweating and cold at the same time, and the down-hairs on my face were prickling unpleasantly.

I landed clumsily, with a thump that made Jamie straighten up and open his eyes. The look of relief in them pulled me the few feet to him. I felt better, with the warm solid flesh of his shoulder under my hand.

"Are you all right?" I said, leaning over him to look.

"Aye, it's no more than a wee dunt," he said, smiling up at me. There was a small gash at his hairline, where something like a pistol butt had caught him, but the blood had clotted already. There were stains of dark, drying blood on the front of his shirt, but the sleeve of his shirt was also bloody. In fact, it was nearly soaked, with fresh bright red.

"Jamie!" I clutched at his shoulder, my vision going white at the edges. "You aren't all right—look, you're bleeding!"

My hands and feet were numb, and I only half-felt his hands grasp my arms as he rose from the cask in sudden alarm. The last thing I saw, amid flashes of light, was his face, gone white beneath the tan.

"My God!" said his frightened voice, out of the whirling blackness. "It's no my blood, Sassenach, it's yours!"

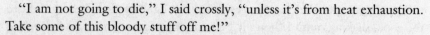

"I am not going to die," I said crossly, "unless it's from heat exhaustion. Take some of this bloody stuff off me!"

Marsali, who had been tearfully pleading with me not to expire, looked rather relieved at this outburst. She stopped crying and sniffed hopefully, but

made no move to remove any of the cloaks, coats, blankets, and other impedimenta in which I was swaddled.

"Oh, I canna do that, Mother Claire!" she said. "Da says ye must be kept
warm!"

"Warm? I'm being boiled alive!" I was in the captain's cabin, and even
with the stern windows wide open, the atmosphere belowdecks was stifling,
hot with sun and acrid with the fumes of the cargo.

I tried to struggle out from under my wrappings, but got no more than a
few inches before a bolt of lightning struck me in the right arm. The world
went dark, with small bright flashes zigging through my vision.

"Lie still," said a stern Scots voice, through a wave of giddy sickness. An
arm was under my shoulders, a large hand cradling my head. "Aye, that's
right, lie back on my arm. All right now, Sassenach?"

"No," I said, looking at the colored pinwheels inside my eyelids. "I'm
going to be sick."

I was, and a most unpleasant process it was, too, with fiery knives being
jabbed into my right arm with each spasm.

"Jesus H. Roosevelt Christ," I said at last, gasping.

"Finished, are ye?" Jamie lowered me carefully and eased my head back
onto the pillow.

"If you mean am I dead, the answer is unfortunately no." I cracked one
eyelid open. He was kneeling by my berth, looking no end piratical himself,
with a bloodstained strip of cloth bound round his head, and still wearing his
blood-soaked shirt.

He stayed still, and so did the cabin, so I cautiously opened the other eye.
He smiled faintly at me.

"No, you're no dead; Fergus will be glad to hear it."

As though this had been a signal, the Frenchman's head poked anxiously
into the cabin. Seeing me awake, his face broke into a dazzling smile and
disappeared. I could hear his voice overhead, loudly informing the crew of
my survival. To my profound embarrassment, the news was greeted with a
rousing cheer from the upper deck.

"What happened?" I asked.

"What *happened?*" Jamie, pouring water into a cup, stopped and stared
over the rim at me. He knelt down again beside me, snorting, and raised my
head for a sip of water.

"What happened, she says! Aye, what indeed? I tell ye to stay all snug
below wi' Marsali, and next thing I ken, ye've dropped out of the sky and
landed at my feet, sopping wi' blood!"

He shoved his face into the berth and glared at me. Sufficiently impressive
when clean-shaven and unhurt, he was considerably more ferocious when
viewed, stubbled, bloodstained, and angry, at a distance of six inches. I
promptly shut my eyes again.

"Look at me!" he said peremptorily, and I did, against my better judgment.

Blue eyes bored into mine, narrowed with fury.

"D'ye ken ye came damn close to dying?" he demanded. "Ye've a bone-deep slash down your arm from oxter to elbow, and had I not got a cloth round it in time, ye'd be feeding the sharks this minute!"

One big fist crashed down on the side of the berth next to me, making me start. The movement hurt my arm, but I didn't make a sound.

"Damn ye, woman! Will ye never do as you're told?"

"Probably not," I said meekly.

He turned a black scowl on me, but I could see the corner of his mouth twitching under the copper stubble.

"God," he said longingly. "What I wouldna give to have ye tied facedown over a gun, and me wi' a rope's end in my hand." He snorted again, and pulled his face out of the berth.

"Willoughby!" he bellowed. In short order, Mr. Willoughby trotted in, beaming, with a steaming pot of tea and a bottle of brandy on a tray.

"Tea!" I breathed, struggling to sit up. "Ambrosia." In spite of the stifling atmosphere of the cabin, the hot tea was just what I needed. The delightful, brandy-laced stuff slid down my throat and glowed peacefully in the pit of my quivering stomach.

"Nobody makes tea better than the English," I said, inhaling the aroma, "except the Chinese."

Mr. Willoughby beamed in gratification and bowed ceremoniously. Jamie snorted again, bringing his total up to three for the afternoon.

"Aye? Well, enjoy it while ye can."

This sounded more or less sinister, and I stared at him over the rim of the cup. "And just what do you mean by that?" I demanded.

"I'm going to doctor your arm when you're finished," he informed me. He picked up the pot and peered into it.

"How much blood did ye tell me a person has in his body?" he asked.

"About eight quarts," I said, bewildered. "Why?"

He lowered the pot and glared at me.

"Because," he said precisely, "judging from the amount ye left on the deck, you've maybe four of them left. Here, have some more." He refilled the cup, set down the pot, and stalked out.

"I'm afraid Jamie's rather annoyed with me," I observed ruefully to Mr. Willoughby.

"Not angry," he said comfortingly. "Tsei-mi scared very bad." The little Chinaman laid a hand on my right shoulder, delicate as a resting butterfly. "This hurts?"

I sighed. "To be perfectly honest," I said, "yes, it does."

Mr. Willoughby smiled and patted me gently. "I help," he said consolingly. "Later."

In spite of the throbbing in my arm, I was feeling sufficiently restored to inquire about the rest of the crew, whose injuries, as reported by Mr. Willoughby, were limited to cuts and bruises, plus one concussion and a minor arm fracture.

A clatter in the passage heralded Jamie's return, accompanied by Fergus, who carried my medicine box under one arm, and yet another bottle of brandy in his hand.

"All right," I said, resigned. "Let's have a look at it."

I was no stranger to horrible wounds, and this one—technically speaking —was not all that bad. On the other hand, it was my own personal flesh involved here, and I was not disposed to be technical.

"Ooh," I said rather faintly. While being a bit picturesque about the nature of the wound, Jamie had also been quite accurate. It was a long, clean-edged slash, running at a slight angle across the front of my biceps, from the shoulder to an inch or so above the elbow joint. And while I couldn't actually see the bone of my humerus, it was without doubt a very deep wound, gaping widely at the edges.

It was still bleeding, in spite of the cloth that had been wrapped tightly round it, but the seepage was slow; no major vessels seemed to have been severed.

Jamie had flipped open my medical box and was rootling meditatively through it with one large forefinger.

"You'll need sutures and a needle," I said, feeling a sudden jolt of alarm as it occurred to me that I was about to have thirty or forty stitches taken in my arm, with no anesthesia bar brandy.

"No laudanum?" Jamie asked, frowning into the box. Evidently, he had been thinking along the same lines.

"No. I used it all on the *Porpoise*." Controlling the shaking of my left hand, I poured a sizable tot of straight brandy into my empty teacup, and took a healthy mouthful.

"That was thoughtful of you, Fergus," I said, nodding at the fresh brandy bottle as I sipped, "but I don't think it's going to take *two* bottles." Given the potency of Jared's French brandy, it was unlikely to take more than a teacupful.

I was wondering whether it was more advisable to get dead drunk at once, or to stay at least half-sober in order to supervise operations; there wasn't a chance in hell that I could do the suturing myself, left-handed and shaking like a leaf. Neither could Fergus do it one-handed. True, Jamie's big hands could move with amazing lightness over some tasks, but . . .

Jamie interrupted my apprehensions, shaking his head and picking up the second bottle.

"This one's no for drinking, Sassenach, that's for washing out the wound."

"What!" In my state of shock, I had forgotten the necessity for disinfection. Lacking anything better, I normally washed out wounds with distilled grain alcohol, cut half and half with water, but I had used my supply of that as well, in our encounter with the man-of-war.

I felt my lips go slightly numb, and not just because the internal brandy was taking effect. Highlanders were among the most stoic and courageous of warriors, and seamen as a class weren't far behind. I had seen such men lie uncomplaining while I set broken bones, did minor surgery, sewed up terrible wounds, and put them through hell generally, but when it came to disinfection with alcohol, it was a different story—the screams could be heard for miles.

"Er . . . wait a minute," I said. "Maybe just a little boiled water. . . ."

Jamie was watching me, not without sympathy.

"It willna get easier wi' waiting, Sassenach," he said. "Fergus, take the bottle." And before I could protest, he had lifted me out of the berth and sat down with me on his lap, holding me tight about the body, pinning my left arm so I couldn't struggle, while he took my right wrist in a firm grip and held my wounded arm out to the side.

I believe it was bloody old Ernest Hemingway who said you're supposed to pass out from pain, but unfortunately you never do. All I can say in response to that is that either Ernest had a fine distinction for states of consciousness, or else no one ever poured brandy on several cubic inches of *his* raw flesh.

To be fair, I suppose I must not absolutely have lost consciousness myself, since when I began noticing things again, Fergus was saying, "Please, milady! You must not scream like that; it upsets the men."

Clearly it upset Fergus; his lean face was pale, and droplets of sweat ran down his jaw. He was right about the men, too—several faces were peering into the cabin from door and window, wearing expressions of horror and concern.

I summoned the presence of mind to nod weakly at them. Jamie's arm was still locked about my middle; I couldn't tell which of us was shaking; both, I thought.

I made it into the wide captain's chair, with considerable assistance, and lay back palpitating, the fire in my arm still sizzling. Jamie was holding one of my curved suture needles and a length of sterilized cat-gut, looking as dubious over the prospects as I felt.

It was Mr. Willoughby who intervened, quietly taking the needle from Jamie's hands.

"I can do this," he said, in tones of authority. "A moment." And he disappeared aft, presumably to fetch something.

Jamie didn't protest, and neither did I. We heaved twin sighs of relief, in fact, which made me laugh.

"And to think," I said, "I once told Bree that big men were kind and gentle, and the short ones tended to be nasty."

"Well, I suppose there's always the exception that proves the rule, no?" He mopped my streaming face with a wet cloth, quite gently.

"I dinna want to know how ye did this," he said, with a sigh, "but for God's sake, Sassenach, don't do it again!"

"Well, I didn't *intend* to do anything . . ." I began crossly, when I was interrupted by the return of Mr. Willoughby. He was carrying the little roll of green silk I had seen when he cured Jamie's seasickness.

"Oh, ye've got the wee stabbers?" Jamie peered interestedly at the small gold needles, then smiled at me. "Dinna fash yourself, Sassenach, they don't hurt . . . or not much, anyway," he added.

Mr. Willoughby's fingers probed the palm of my right hand, prodding here and there. Then he grasped each of my fingers, wiggled it, and pulled it gently, so that I felt the joints pop slightly. Then he laid two fingers at the base of my wrist, pressing down in the space between the radius and the ulna.

"This is the Inner Gate," he said softly. "Here is quiet. Here is peace." I sincerely hoped he was right. Picking up one of the tiny gold needles, he placed the point over the spot he had marked, and with a dexterous twirl of thumb and forefinger, pierced the skin.

The prick made me jump, but he kept a tight, warm hold on my hand, and I relaxed again.

He placed three needles in each wrist, and a rakish, porcupine-like spray on the crest of my right shoulder. I was getting interested, despite my guinea pig status. Beyond an initial prick at placement, the needles caused no discomfort. Mr. Willoughby was humming, in a low, soothing sort of way, tapping and pressing places on my neck and shoulder.

I couldn't honestly tell whether my right arm was numbed, or whether I was simply distracted by the goings-on, but it did feel somewhat less agonized—at least until he picked up the suture needle and began.

Jamie was sitting on a stool by my left side, holding my left hand as he watched my face. After a moment, he said, rather gruffly, "Let your breath out, Sassenach; it's no going to get any worse than that."

I let go of the breath I hadn't realized I was holding, and realized as well what he was telling me. It was dread of being hurt that had me rigid as a board in the chair. The actual pain of the stitches was unpleasant, all right, but nothing I couldn't stand.

I let my breath out cautiously, and gave him a rough approximation of a smile. Mr. Willoughby was singing under his breath in Chinese. Jamie had translated the words for me a week earlier; it was a pillow-song, in which a young man catalogued the physical charms of his partner, one by one. I hoped he would finish the stitching before he got to her feet.

"That's a verra wicked slash," Jamie said, eyes on Mr. Willoughby's work. I preferred not to look myself. "A parang, was it, or a cutlass, I wonder?"

"I think it was a cutlass," I said. "In fact, I know it was. He came after . . ."

"I wonder what led them to attack us," Jamie said, not paying any attention to me. His brows were drawn in speculation. "It canna ha' been the cargo, after all."

"I shouldn't think so," I said. "But maybe they didn't know what we were carrying?" This seemed grossly unlikely; any ship that came within a hundred yards of us would have known—the ammoniac reek of bat guano hovered round us like a miasma.

"Perhaps it's only they thought the ship small enough to take. The *Artemis* itself would bring a fair price, cargo or no."

I blinked as Mr. Willoughby paused in his song to tie a knot. I thought he was down to the navel by now, but wasn't paying close attention.

"Do we know the name of the pirate ship?" I asked. "Granted, there's likely a lot of pirates in these waters, but we do know that the *Bruja* was in this area three days ago, and—"

"That's what I'm wondering," he said. "I couldna see a great deal in the darkness, but she was the right size, wi' that wide Spanish beam."

"Well, the pirate that was after me spoke—" I started, but the sound of voices in the corridor made me stop.

Fergus edged in, shy of interrupting, but obviously bursting with excitement. He held something shiny and jingling in one hand.

"Milord," he said, "Maitland has found a dead pirate on the forward deck."

Jamie's red brows went up, and he looked from Fergus to me.

"Dead?"

"Very dead, milord," said Fergus, with a small shudder. Maitland was peeking over his shoulder, anxious to claim his share of the glory. "Oh, yes, sir," he assured Jamie earnestly. "Dead as a doornail; his poor head's bashed in something shocking!"

All three men turned and stared at me. I gave them a modest little smile.

Jamie rubbed a hand over his face. His eyes were bloodshot, and a trickle of blood had dried in front of his ear.

"Sassenach," he began, in measured tones.

"I tried to tell you," I said virtuously. Between shock, brandy, acupuncture, and the dawning realization of survival, I was beginning to feel quite pleasantly light-headed. I scarcely noticed Mr. Willoughby's final efforts.

"He was wearing this, milord." Fergus stepped forward and laid the pirate's necklace on the table in front of us. It had the silver buttons from a military uniform, polished *kona* nuts, several large shark's teeth, pieces of polished abalone shell and chunks of mother of pearl, and a large number of jingling coins, all pierced for stringing on a leather thong.

"I thought you should see this at once, milord," Fergus continued. He reached out a hand and lifted one of the shimmering coins. It was silver, untarnished, and through the gathering brandy haze, I could see on its face the twin heads of Alexander. A tetradrachm, of the fourth century B.C. Mint condition.

Thoroughly worn out by the events of the afternoon, I had fallen asleep at once, the pain in my arm dulled by brandy. Now it was full dark, and the brandy had worn off. My arm seemed to swell and throb with each beat of my heart, and any small movement sent tiny jabs of a sharper pain whipping through my arm, like warning flicks of a scorpion's tail.

The moon was three-quarters full, a huge lopsided shape like a golden teardrop, hanging just above the horizon. The ship heeled slightly, and the moon slid slowly out of sight, the Man in the Moon leering rather unpleasantly as he went. I was hot, and possibly a trifle feverish.

There was a jug of water in the cupboard on the far side of the cabin. I felt weak and giddy as I swung my feet over the edge of the berth, and my arm registered a strong protest against being disturbed. I must have made some sound, for the darkness on the floor of the cabin stirred suddenly, and Jamie's voice came drowsily from the region of my feet.

"Are ye hurting, Sassenach?"

"A little," I said, not wanting to be dramatic about it. I set my lips and rose unsteadily to my feet, cradling my right elbow in my left hand.

"That's good," he said.

"That's *good*?" I said, my voice rising indignantly.

There was a soft chuckle from the darkness, and he sat up, his head popping suddenly into sight as it rose above the shadows into the moonlight.

"Aye, it is," he said. "When a wound begins to hurt ye, it means it's healing. Ye didna feel it when it happened, did you?"

"No," I admitted. I certainly felt it now. The air was a good deal cooler out on the open sea, and the salt wind coming through the window felt good on my face. I was damp and sticky with sweat, and the thin chemise clung to my breasts.

"I could see ye didn't. That's what frightened me. Ye never feel a fatal wound, Sassenach," he said softly.

I laughed shortly, but cut it off as the movement jarred my arm.

"And how do you know that?" I asked, fumbling left-handed to pour water into a cup. "Not the sort of thing you'd learn firsthand, I mean."

"Murtagh told me."

The water seemed to purl soundlessly into the cup, the sound of its pouring lost in the hiss of the bow-wave outside. I set down the jug and lifted the cup, the surface of the water black in the moonlight. Jamie had never mentioned Murtagh to me, in the months of our reunion. I had asked Fergus, who told me that the wiry little Scot had died at Culloden, but he knew no more than the bare fact.

"At Culloden." Jamie's voice was barely loud enough to be heard above the creak of timber and the whirring of the wind that bore us along. "Did ye ken they burnt the bodies there? I wondered, listening to them do it—what it would be like inside the fire when it came my turn." I could hear him swallow, above the creaking of the ship. "I found that out, this morning."

The moonlight robbed his face of depth and color; he looked like a skull, with the broad, clean planes of cheek and jawbone white and his eyes black empty pits.

"I went to Culloden meaning to die," he said, his voice scarcely more than a whisper. "Not the rest of them. I should have been happy to stop a musket ball at once, and yet I cut my way across the field and halfway back, while men on either side o' me were blown to bloody bits." He stood up, then, looking down at me.

"Why?" he said. "Why, Claire? Why am I alive, and they are not?"

"I don't know," I said softly. "For your sister, and your family, maybe? For me?"

"They had families," he said. "Wives, and sweethearts; children to mourn them. And yet they are gone. And I am still here."

"I don't know, Jamie," I said at last. I touched his cheek, already roughened by newly sprouting beard, irrepressible evidence of life. "You aren't ever going to know."

He sighed, his cheekbone pressed against my palm for a moment.

"Aye, I ken that well enough. But I canna help the asking, when I think of them—especially Murtagh." He turned restlessly away, his eyes empty shadows, and I knew he walked Drumossie Moor again, with the ghosts.

"We should have gone sooner; the men had been standing for hours, starved and half-frozen. But they waited for His Highness to give the order to charge."

And Charles Stuart, perched safely on a rock, well behind the line of battle, having seized personal command of his troops for the first time, had dithered and delayed. And the English cannon had had time to bear squarely on the lines of ragged Highlanders, and opened fire.

"It was a relief, I think," Jamie said softly. "Every man on the field knew the cause was lost, and we were dead. And still we stood there, watching the English guns come up, and the cannon mouths open black before us. No one spoke. I couldna hear anything but the wind, and the English soldiers shouting, on the other side of the field."

And then the guns had roared, and men had fallen, and those still standing, rallied by a late and ragged order, had seized their swords and charged the enemy, the sound of their Gaelic shrieking drowned by the guns, lost in the wind.

"The smoke was so thick, I couldna see more than a few feet before me. I kicked off my shoon and ran into it, shouting." The bloodless line of his lips turned up slightly.

"I was happy," he said, sounding a bit surprised. "Not scairt at all. I meant to die, after all; there was nothing to fear except that I might be wounded and not die at once. But I would die, and then it would be all over, and I would find ye again, and it would be all right."

I moved closer to him, and his hand rose up from the shadows to take mine.

"Men fell to either side of me, and I could hear the grapeshot and the musket balls hum past my head like bumblebees. But I wasna touched."

He had reached the British lines unscathed, one of very few Highlanders to have completed the charge across Culloden Moor. An English gun crew looked up, startled, at the tall Highlander who burst from the smoke like a demon, the blade of his broadsword gleaming with rain and then dull with blood.

"There was a small part of my mind that asked why I should be killin' them," he said reflectively. "For surely I knew that we were lost; there was no gain to it. But there is a lust to killing—you'll know that?" His fingers tightened on mine, questioning, and I squeezed back in affirmation.

"I couldna stop—or I would not." His voice was quiet, without bitterness or recrimination. "It's a verra old feeling, I think; the wish to take an enemy with ye to the grave. I could feel it there, a hot red thing in my chest and belly, and . . . I gave myself to it," he ended simply.

There were four men tending the cannon, none armed with more than a pistol and knife, none expecting attack at such close quarters. They stood helpless against the berserk strength of his despair, and he killed them all.

"The ground shook under my feet," he said, "and I was near deafened by the noise. I couldna think. And then it came to me that I was behind the English guns." A soft chuckle came from below. "A verra poor place to try to be killed, no?"

So he had started back across the moor, to join the Highland dead.

"He was sitting against a tussock near the middle of the field—Murtagh. He'd been struck a dozen times at least, and there was a dreadful wound in his head—I knew he was dead."

He hadn't been, though; when Jamie had fallen to his knees beside his godfather and taken the small body in his arms, Murtagh's eyes had opened.

"He saw me. And he smiled." And then the older man's hand had touched his cheek briefly. "Dinna be afraid, *a bhalaich*," Murtagh had said, using the endearment for a small, beloved boy. "It doesna hurt a bit to die."

I stood quietly for a long time, holding Jamie's hand. Then he sighed, and his other hand closed very, very gently about my wounded arm.

"Too many folk have died, Sassenach, because they knew me—or suffered for the knowing. I would give my own body to save ye a moment's pain— and yet I could wish to close my hand just now, that I might hear ye cry out and know for sure that I havena killed you, too."

I leaned forward, pressing a kiss on the skin of his chest. He slept naked in the heat.

"You haven't killed me. You didn't kill Murtagh. And we'll find Ian. Take me back to bed, Jamie."

Sometime later, as I drowsed on the edge of sleep, he spoke from the floor beside my bed.

"Ye know, I seldom wanted to go home to Laoghaire," he said contemplatively. "And yet, at least when I did, I'd find her where I'd left her."

I turned my head to the side, where his soft breathing came from the darkened floor. "Oh? And is that the kind of wife you want? The sort who stays put?"

He made a small sound between a chuckle and a cough, but didn't answer, and after a few moments, the sound of his breathing changed to a soft, rhythmic snore.

55

Ishmael

I slept restlessly, and woke up late and feverish, with a throbbing headache just behind my eyes. I felt ill enough not to protest when Marsali insisted on bathing my forehead, but relaxed gratefully, eyes closed, enjoying the cool touch of the vinegar-soaked cloth on my pounding temples.

It was so soothing, in fact, that I drifted off to sleep again after she left. I was dreaming uneasily of dark mine shafts and the chalk of charred bones, when I was suddenly roused by a crash that brought me bolt upright and sent a shaft of pure white pain ripping through my head.

"What?" I exclaimed, clutching my head in both hands, as though this might prevent it falling off. "What is it?" The window had been covered to keep the light from disturbing me, and it took a moment for my stunned vision to adapt to the dimness.

On the opposite side of the cabin, a large figure was mimicking me, clutching its own head in apparent agony. Then it spoke, releasing a volley of very bad language, in a mixture of Chinese, French, and Gaelic.

"Damn!" it said, the exclamations tapering off into milder English. "God-damn it to hell!" Jamie staggered to the window, still rubbing the head he had smashed on the edge of my cupboard. He shoved aside the covering and pushed the window open, bringing a welcome draft of fresh air in along with a dazzle of light.

"What in the name of bloody hell do you think you're doing?" I demanded, with considerable asperity. The light jabbed my tender eyeballs like needles, and the movement involved in clutching my head had done the stitches in my arm no good at all.

"I was looking for your medicine box," he replied, wincing as he felt the crown of his head. "Damn, I've caved in my skull. Look at that!" He thrust two fingers, slightly smeared with blood, under my nose. I dropped the vinegar-soaked cloth over the fingers and collapsed back on my pillow.

"Why do you need the medicine box, and why didn't you ask me in the first place, instead of bumping around like a bee in a bottle?" I said irritably.

"I didna want to wake ye from your sleep," he said, sheepishly enough that I laughed, despite the various throbbings going on in my anatomy.

"That's all right; I wasn't enjoying it," I assured him. "Why do you need the box? Is someone hurt?"

"Aye. I am," he said, dabbing gingerly at the top of his head with the cloth and scowling at the result. "Ye dinna want to look at my head?"

The answer to this was "Not especially," but I obligingly motioned to him to bend over, presenting the top of his head for inspection. There was a reasonably impressive lump under the thick hair, with a small cut from the edge of the shelf, but the damage seemed a bit short of concussion.

"It's not fractured," I assured him. "You have the thickest skull I've ever seen." Moved by an instinct as old as motherhood, I leaned forward and kissed the bump gently. He lifted his head, eyes wide with surprise.

"That's supposed to make it feel better," I explained. A smile tugged at the corner of his mouth.

"Oh. Well, then." He bent down and gently kissed the bandage on my wounded arm.

"Better?" he inquired, straightening up.

"Lots."

He laughed, and reaching for the decanter, poured out a tot of whisky, which he handed to me.

"I wanted that stuff ye use to wash out scrapes and such," he explained, pouring another for himself.

"Hawthorn lotion. I haven't got any ready-made, because it doesn't keep," I said, pushing myself upright. "If it's urgent, though, I can brew some; it doesn't take long." The thought of getting up and walking to the galley was daunting, but perhaps I'd feel better once I was moving.

"Not urgent," he assured me. "It's only there's a prisoner in the hold who's a bit bashed about."

I lowered my cup, blinking at him.

"A prisoner? Where did we get a prisoner?"

"From the pirate ship." He frowned at his whisky. "Though I dinna think he's a pirate."

"What is he?"

He tossed off the whisky neatly, in one gulp, and shook his head.

"Damned if I know. From the scars on his back, likely a runaway slave, but in that case, I canna think why he did what he did."

"What did he do?"

"Dived off the *Bruja* into the sea. MacGregor saw him go, and then after the *Bruja* made sail, he saw the man bobbing about in the waves and threw him a rope."

"Well, that is funny; why should he do that?" I asked. I was becoming interested, and the throbbing in my head seemed to be lessening as I sipped my whisky.

Jamie ran his fingers through his hair, and stopped, wincing.

"I dinna ken, Sassenach," he said, gingerly smoothing the hair on his crown flat. "It wouldna be likely for a crew like ours to try to board the pirate—any merchant would just fight them off; there's no reason to try to take them. But if he didna mean to escape from us—perhaps he meant to escape from them, aye?"

The last golden drops of the whisky ran down my throat. It was Jared's special blend, the next-to-last bottle, and thoroughly justified the name he had given it—*Ceò Gheasacach*. "Magic Mist." Feeling somewhat restored, I pushed myself upright.

"If he's hurt, perhaps I should take a look at him," I suggested, swinging my feet out of the berth.

Given Jamie's behavior of the day before, I fully expected him to press me flat and call for Marsali to come and sit on my chest. Instead, he looked at me thoughtfully, and nodded.

"Aye, well. If ye're sure ye can stand, Sassenach?"

I wasn't all that sure, but gave it a try. The room tilted when I stood up, and black and yellow spots danced before my eyes, but I stayed upright, clinging to Jamie's arm. After a moment, a small amount of blood reluctantly consented to reenter my head, and the spots went away, showing Jamie's face looking anxiously down at me.

"All right," I said, taking a deep breath. "Carry on."

The prisoner was below in what the crew called the orlop, a lower-deck space full of miscellaneous cargo. There was a small timbered area, walled off at the bow of the ship, that sometimes housed drunk or unruly seamen, and here he had been secured.

It was dark and airless down in the bowels of the ship, and I felt myself becoming dizzy again as I made my way slowly along the companionway behind Jamie and the glow of his lantern.

When he unlocked the door, at first I saw nothing at all in the makeshift brig. Then, as Jamie stooped to enter with his lantern, the shine of the man's eyes betrayed his presence. "Black as the ace of spades" was the first thought that popped into my slightly addled mind, as the edges of face and form took shape against the darkness of the timbers.

No wonder Jamie had thought him a runaway slave. The man looked African, not island-born. Besides the deep red-black of his skin, his demeanor wasn't that of a man raised as a slave. He was sitting on a cask, hands bound behind his back and feet tied together, but I saw his head rise and his shoulders straighten as Jamie ducked under the lintel of the tiny space. He was very thin, but very muscular, clad in nothing but a ragged pair of trousers. The lines of his body were clear; he was tensed for attack or defense, but not submission.

Jamie saw it, too, and motioned me to stay well back against the wall. He placed the lantern on a cask, and squatted down before the captive, at eye-level.

"*Amiki,*" he said, spreading out his empty hands, palm up. "*Amiki. Bene-*

bene." Friend. Is good. It was taki-taki, the all-purpose pidgin polyglot that the traders from Barbados to Trinidad spoke in the ports.

The man stared impassively at Jamie for a moment, eyes still as tide pools. Then one eyebrow flicked up and he extended his bound feet before him.

"*Bene-bene, amiki?*" he said, with an ironic intonation that couldn't be missed, whatever the language. Is good, friend?

Jamie snorted briefly, amused, and rubbed a finger under his nose.

"It's a point," he said in English.

"Does he speak English, or French?" I moved a little closer. The captive's eyes rested on me for a moment, then passed away, indifferent.

"If he does, he'll no admit it. Picard and Fergus tried talking to him last night. He willna say a word, just stares at them. What he just said is the first he's spoken since he came aboard. *¿Habla Español?*" he said suddenly to the prisoner. There was no response. The man didn't even look at Jamie; just went on staring impassively at the square of open doorway behind me.

"Er, *sprechen sie Deutsche?*" I said tentatively. He didn't answer, which was just as well, as the question had exhausted my own supply of German. "*Nicht* Hollander, either, I don't suppose."

Jamie shot me a sardonic look. "I canna tell much about him, Sassenach, but I'm fairly sure he's no a Dutchman."

"They have slaves on Eleuthera, don't they? That's a Dutch island," I said irritably. "Or St. Croix—that's Danish, isn't it?" Slowly as my mind was working this morning, it hadn't escaped me that the captive was our only clue to the pirates' whereabouts—and the only frail link to Ian. "Do you know enough taki-taki to ask him about Ian?"

Jamie shook his head, eyes intent on the prisoner. "No. Besides what I said to him already, I ken how to say '*not* good,' 'how much?' 'give it to me,' and 'drop that, ye bastard,' none of which seems a great deal to the point at present."

Stymied for the moment, we stared at the prisoner, who stared impassively back.

"To hell with it," Jamie said suddenly. He drew the dirk from his belt, went behind the cask, and sawed through the thongs around the prisoner's wrists.

He cut the ankle bindings as well, then sat back on his heels, the knife laid across his thigh.

"Friend," he said firmly in taki-taki. "Is good?"

The prisoner didn't say anything, but after a moment, he nodded slightly, his expression warily quizzical.

"There's a chamber pot in the corner," Jamie said in English, rising and sheathing his dirk. "Use it, and then my wife will tend your wounds."

A very faint flicker of amusement crossed the man's face. He nodded once more, this time in acceptance of defeat. He rose slowly from the cask and turned, stiff hands fumbling at his trousers. I looked askance at Jamie.

"It's one of the worst things about being bound that way," he explained matter-of-factly. "Ye canna take a piss by yourself."

"I see," I said, not wanting to think about how he knew that.

"That, and the pain in your shoulders," he said. "Be careful touching him, Sassenach." The note of warning in his voice was clear, and I nodded. It wasn't the man's shoulders he was concerned about.

I still felt light-headed, and the stuffiness of the surroundings had made my headache throb again, but I was less battered than the prisoner, who had indeed been "bashed about" at some stage of the proceedings.

Bashed though he was, his injuries seemed largely superficial. A swollen knot rose on the man's forehead, and a deep scrape had left a crusted reddish patch on one shoulder. He was undoubtedly bruised in a number of places, but given the remarkably deep shade of his skin and the darkness of the surroundings, I couldn't tell where.

There were deep bands of rawness on ankles and wrists, where he had pulled against the thongs. I hadn't made any of the hawthorn lotion, but I had brought the jar of gentian salve. I eased myself down on the deck next to him, but he took no more notice of me than of the deck beneath his feet, even when I began to spread the cool blue cream on his wounds.

What was more interesting than the fresh injuries, though, were the healed ones. At close range, I could see the faint white lines of three parallel slashes, running across the slope of each cheekbone, and a series of three short vertical lines on the high, narrow forehead, just between his brows. Tribal scars. African-born for sure, then; such scars were made during manhood rituals, or so Murphy had told me.

His flesh was warm and smooth under my fingers, slicked with sweat. I felt warm, too; sweaty and unwell. The deck rose gently beneath me, and I put my hand on his back to keep my balance. The thin, tough lines of healed whipstrokes webbed his shoulders, like the furrows of tiny worms beneath his skin. The feel of them was unexpected; so much like the feel of the marks on Jamie's own back. I swallowed, feeling queasy, but went on with my doctoring.

The man ignored me completely, even when I touched spots I knew must be painful. His eyes were fixed on Jamie, who was watching the prisoner with equal intentness.

The problem was plain. The man was almost certainly a runaway slave. He hadn't wanted to speak to us, for fear that his speech would give away his owner's island, and that we would then find out his original owner and return him to captivity.

Now we knew that he spoke—or at least understood—English, it was bound to increase his wariness. Even if we assured him that it was not our intention either to return him to an owner or to enslave him ourselves, he was unlikely to trust us. I couldn't say that I blamed him, under the circumstances.

On the other hand, this man was our best—and possibly the only—chance of finding out what had happened to Ian Murray aboard the *Bruja*.

When at length I had bandaged the man's wrists and ankles, Jamie gave me a hand to rise, then spoke to the prisoner.

"You'll be hungry, I expect," he said. "Come along to the cabin, and we'll eat." Not waiting for a response, he took my good arm and turned to the door. There was silence behind us as we moved into the corridor, but when I looked back, the slave was there, following a few feet behind.

Jamie led us to my cabin, disregarding the curious glances of the sailors we passed, only stopping by Fergus long enough to order food to be sent from the galley.

"Back to bed with ye, Sassenach," he said firmly, when we reached the cabin. I didn't argue. My arm hurt, my head hurt, and I could feel little waves of heat flickering behind my eyes. It looked as though I would have to break down and use a little of the precious penicillin on myself, after all. There was still a chance that my body could throw off the infection, but I couldn't afford to wait too long.

Jamie had poured out a glass of whisky for me, and another for our guest. Still wary, the man accepted it, and took a sip, eyes widening in surprise. I supposed Scotch whisky must be a novelty to him.

Jamie took a glass for himself and sat down, motioning the slave to the other seat, across the small table.

"My name is Fraser," he said. "I am captain here. My wife," he added, with a nod toward my berth.

The prisoner hesitated, but then set down his glass with an air of decision.

"They be callin' me Ishmael," he said, in a voice like honey poured over coal. "I ain't no pirate. I be a cook."

"Murphy's going to like that," I remarked, but Jamie ignored me. There was a faint line between the ruddy brows, as he felt his way into the conversation.

"A ship's cook?" he asked, taking care to make his voice sound casual. Only the tap of his two stiff fingers against his thigh betrayed him—and that, only to me.

"No, mon, I don't got nothin' to do with that ship!" Ishmael was vehement. "They taken me off the shore, say they kill me, I don' go long by them, be easy. I ain't no pirate!" he repeated, and it dawned on me belatedly that of course he wouldn't wish to be taken for a pirate—whether he was one or not. Piracy was punishable by hanging, and he could have no way of knowing that we were as eager as he to stay clear of the Royal Navy.

"Aye, I see." Jamie hit the right balance, between soothing and skeptical.

He leaned back slightly in the big wheel-backed chair. "And how did the *Bruja* come to take ye prisoner, then? Not where," he added quickly, as a look of alarm flitted across the prisoner's face.

"Ye needna tell me where ye came from; that's of no concern to me. Only I should care to know how ye came to fall into their hands, and how long ye've been with them. Since, as ye say, ye werena one of them." The hint was broad enough to spread butter on. We didn't mean to return him to his owner; however, if he didn't oblige with information, we might just turn him over to the Crown as a pirate.

The prisoner's eyes darkened; no fool, he had grasped the point at once. His head twitched briefly sideways, and his eyes narrowed.

"I be catchin' fish by the river," he said. "Big ship, he come sailin' up the river slow, little boats be pullin' him. Men in the little boat, they see me, holler out. I drop the fish, be runnin', but they close by. They men jump out, kotch me by the cane field, figure they take me to sell. Tha's all, mon." He shrugged, signaling the conclusion of his story.

"Aye, I see." Jamie's eyes were intent on the prisoner. He hesitated, wanting to ask where the river was, but not quite daring to, for fear the man would clam up again. "While ye were on the ship—did ye see any boys among the crew, or as prisoners, too? Boys, young men?"

The man's eyes widened slightly; he hadn't been expecting that. He paused warily, but then nodded, with a faintly derisive glint in his eye.

"Yes, mon, they have boys. Why? You be wantin' one?" His glance flicked to me and then back to Jamie, one eyebrow raised.

Jamie's head jerked, and a slight flush rose on his cheekbones at the implication.

"I do," he said levelly. "I am looking for a young kinsman who was taken by pirates. I should feel myself greatly obliged to anyone who might assist me in finding him." He lifted one eyebrow significantly.

The prisoner grunted slightly, his nostrils flaring.

"That so? What you be doin' for me, I be helpin' you fin' this boy?"

"I should set you ashore at any port of your choosing, with a fair sum in gold," Jamie replied. "But of course I should require proof that ye did have knowledge of my nephew's whereabouts, aye?"

"Huh." The prisoner was still wary, but beginning to relax. "You tell me, mon—what this boy be like?"

Jamie hesitated for a moment, studying the prisoner, but then shook his head.

"No," he said thoughtfully. "I dinna think that will work. *You* describe to *me* such lads as ye saw on the pirate vessel."

The prisoner eyed Jamie for a moment, then broke out in a low, rich laugh.

"You no particular fool, mon," he said. "You know that?"

"I know that," Jamie said dryly. "So long as ye know it as well. Tell me, then."

Ishmael snorted briefly, but complied, pausing only to refresh himself from the tray of food Fergus had brought. Fergus himself lounged against the door, watching the prisoner through half-lidded eyes.

"They be twelve boys talkin' strange, like you."

Jamie's eyebrows shot up, and he exchanged a glance of astonishment with me. Twelve?

"Like me?" He said. "White boys, English? Or Scots, d'ye mean?"

Ishmael shook his head in incomprehension; "Scot" was not in his vocabulary.

"Talkin' like dogs fightin'," he explained. "Grrrr! Wuff!" He growled, shaking his head in illustration like a dog worrying a rat, and I saw Fergus's shoulders shake in suppressed hilarity.

"Scots for sure," I said, trying not to laugh. Jamie shot me a brief dirty look, then returned his attention to Ishmael.

"Verra well, then," he said, exaggerating his natural soft burr. "Twelve Scottish lads. What did they look like?"

Ishmael squinted dubiously, chewing a piece of mango from the tray. He wiped the juice from the corner of his mouth and shook his head.

"I only see them once, mon. Tell you all I see, though." He closed his eyes and frowned, the vertical lines on his forehead drawing close together.

"Four boys be yellow-haired, six brown, two with black hair. Two shorter than me, one maybe the size that *griffone* there"—he nodded toward Fergus, who stiffened in outrage at the insult—"one big, not so big as you . . ."

"Aye, and how will they have been dressed?" Slowly, carefully, Jamie drew him through the descriptions, asking for details, demanding comparisons—how tall? how fat? what color eyes?—carefully concealing the direction of his interest as he drew the man further into conversation.

My head had stopped spinning, but the fatigue was still there, weighting my senses. I let my eyes close, obscurely soothed by the deep, murmuring voices. Jamie *did* sound rather like a big, fierce dog, I thought, with his soft growling burr and the abrupt, clipped sound of his consonants.

"Wuff," I murmured under my breath, and my belly muscles quivered slightly under my folded hands.

Ishmael's voice was just as deep, but smooth and low, rich as hot chocolate made with cream. I began to drift, lulled by the sound of it.

He sounded like Joe Abernathy, I thought drowsily, dictating an autopsy report—unvarnished and unappetizing physical details, related in a voice like a deep golden lullaby.

I could see Joe's hands in memory, dark on the pale skin of an accident victim, moving swiftly as he made his verbal notes to the tape recorder.

"Deceased is a tall man, approximately six feet in height, and slender in build. . . ."

A tall man, slender.

"—that one, he bein' tall, bein' thin . . ."

I came awake suddenly, heart pounding, hearing the echo of Joe's voice coming from the table a few feet away.

"No!" I said, quite suddenly, and all three men stopped and looked at me in surprise. I pushed back the weight of my damp hair and waved weakly at them.

"Don't mind me; I was dreaming, I think."

They returned to their conversation, and I lay still, eyes half-closed, but no longer sleepy.

There was no physical resemblance. Joe was stocky and bearlike; this Ishmael slender and lean, though the swell of muscle over the curve of his shoulder suggested considerable strength.

Joe's face was broad and amiable; this man's narrow and wary-eyed, with a high forehead that made his tribal scars the more striking. Joe's skin was the color of fresh coffee, Ishmael's the deep red-black of a burning ember, which Stern had told me was characteristic of slaves from the Guinea coast—not so highly prized as the blue-black Senegalese, but more valuable than the yellow-brown Yaga and Congolese.

But if I closed my eyes entirely, I could hear Joe's voice speaking, even allowing for the faint Caribbean lilt of slave-English. I cracked my eyelids and looked carefully, searching for any signs of resemblance. There were none, but I did see what I had seen before, and not noticed, among the other scars and marks on the man's battered torso. What I had thought merely a scrape was in fact a deep abrasion that overlay a wide, flat scar, cut in the form of a rough square just below the point of the shoulder. The mark was raw and pink, newly healed. I should have seen it at once, if not for the darkness of the orlop, and the scrape that obscured it.

I lay quite still, trying to remember. "No *slave* name," Joe had said derisively, referring to his son's self-christening. Clearly, Ishmael had cut away an owner's brand, to prevent identification, should he be recaptured. But whose? And surely the name Ishmael was no more than coincidence.

Maybe not so farfetched a one, though; "Ishmael" almost certainly wasn't the man's real name. "They be *callin'* me Ishmael," he had said. That, too, was a slave name, given him by one owner or another. And if young Lenny had been climbing his family tree, as it seemed, what more likely than that he should have chosen one of his ancestors' given names in symbol? If. But if he was . . .

I lay looking up at the claustrophobic ceiling of the berth, suppositions spinning through my head. Whether this man had any link with Joe or not, the possibility had reminded me of something.

Jamie was catechizing the man about the personnel and structure of the *Bruja*—for so the ship that had attacked us had been—but I was paying no attention. I sat up, cautiously, so as not to make the dizziness worse, and signaled to Fergus.

"I need air," I said. "Help me up on deck, will you?" Jamie glanced at me with a hint of worry, but I smiled reassuringly at him, and took Fergus's arm.

"Where are the papers for that slave we bought on Barbados?" I demanded, as soon as we were out of earshot of the cabin. "And where's the slave, for that matter?"

Fergus looked at me curiously, but obligingly rummaged in his coat.

"I have the papers here, milady," he said, handing them to me. "As for the slave, I believe he is in the crew's quarters. Why?" he added, unable to restrain his curiosity.

I ignored the question, fumbling through the grubby, repellent bits of paper.

"There it is," I said, finding the bit I remembered Jamie reading to me. "Abernathy! It *was* Abernathy! Branded on the left shoulder with a fleur-de-lys. Did you notice that mark, Fergus?"

He shook his head, looking mildly bewildered.

"No, milady."

"Then come with me," I said, turning toward the crew's quarters. "I want to see how big it is."

The mark was about three inches long and three wide; a flower, surmounting the initial "A," burned into the skin a few inches below the point of the shoulder. It was the right size, and in the right place, to match the scar on the man Ishmael. It wasn't, however, a fleur-de-lys; that had been the mistake of a careless transcriber. It was a sixteen-petaled rose—the Jacobite emblem of Charles Stuart. I blinked at it in amazement; what patriotic exile had chosen this bizarre method of maintaining allegiance to the vanquished Stuarts?

"Milady, I think you should return to your bed," Fergus said. He was frowning at me as I stooped over Temeraire, who bore this inspection as stolidly as everything else. "You are the color of goose turds, and milord will not like it at all if I allow you to fall down on the deck."

"I won't fall down," I assured him. "And I don't care what color I am. I think we've just had a stroke of luck. Listen, Fergus, I want you to do something for me."

"Anything, milady," he said, grabbing me by the elbow as a shift in the wind sent me staggering across the suddenly tilting deck. "But not," he added firmly, "until you are safely back in your bed."

I allowed him to lead me back to the cabin, for I really didn't feel at all well, but not before giving him my instructions. As we entered the cabin, Jamie stood up from the table to greet us.

"There ye are, Sassenach! Are ye all right?" he asked, frowning down at me. "Ye've gone a nasty color, like a spoilt custard."

"I am perfectly fine," I said, through my teeth, easing myself down on the bunk to avoid jarring my arm. "Have you and Mr. Ishmael finished your conversation?"

Jamie glanced at the prisoner, and I saw the flat black gaze that locked with his. The atmosphere between them was not hostile, but it was charged in some way. Jamie nodded in dismissal.

"We've finished—for the moment," he said. He turned to Fergus. "See our guest below, will ye, Fergus, and see to it that he's fed and clothed?" He remained standing until Ishmael had left under Fergus's wing. Then he sat down beside my berth and squinted into the darkness at me.

"Ye look awful," he said. "Had I best fetch your kit and be feeding ye a wee tonic or somesuch?"

"No," I said. "Jamie, listen—I think I know where our friend Ishmael came from."

He lifted one brow.

"You do?"

I explained about the scar on Ishmael, and the almost matching brand on the slave Temeraire, without mentioning what had given me the idea in the first place.

"Five will get you ten that they came from the same place—from this Mrs. Abernathy's, on Jamaica." I said.

"Five will . . . ? Och," he said, waving away my confusing reference in the interests of continuing the discussion. "Well, ye could be right, Sassenach, and I hope so. The wily black bastard wouldna say where he was from. Not that I can blame him," he added fairly. "God, if I'd got away from such a life, there's no power on earth would take me back!" He spoke with a surprising vehemence.

"No, I wouldn't blame him either," I said. "But what did he tell you, about the boys? Has he seen Young Ian?"

The frowning lines of his face relaxed.

"Aye, I'm almost sure he has." One fist curled on his knee in anticipation. "Two of the lads he described could be Ian. And knowin' it was the *Bruja*, I canna think otherwise. And if you're right about where he's come from, Sassenach, we might have him—we may find him at last!" Ishmael, while refusing to give any clue as to where the *Bruja* had picked him up, had gone so far as to say that the twelve boys—all prisoners—had been taken off the ship together, soon after his own capture.

"Twelve lads," Jamie repeated, his momentary look of excitement fading back into a frown. "What in the name of God would someone be wanting, to kidnap twelve lads from Scotland?"

"Perhaps he's a collector," I said, feeling more light-headed by the moment. "Coins, and gems, and Scottish boys."

"Ye think whoever's got Ian has the treasure as well?" He glanced curiously at me.

"I don't know," I said, feeling suddenly very tired. I yawned rackingly. "We may know for sure about Ishmael, though. I told Fergus to see that Temeraire gets a look at him. If they are from the same place . . ." I yawned again, my body seeking the oxygen that loss of blood had deprived me of.

"That's verra sensible of ye, Sassenach," Jamie said, sounding faintly surprised that I was capable of sense. For that matter, I was a little surprised myself; my thoughts were becoming more fragmented by the moment, and it was an effort to keep talking logically.

Jamie saw it; he patted my hand and stood up.

"Ye dinna trouble yourself about it now, Sassenach. Rest, and I'll send Marsali down wi' some tea."

"Whisky," I said, and he laughed.

"All right, then, whisky," he agreed. He smoothed my hair back, and leaning into the berth, kissed my hot forehead.

"Better?" he asked, smiling.

"Lots." I smiled back and closed my eyes.

56

Turtle Soup

When I woke again, in the late afternoon, I ached all over. I had thrown off the covers in my sleep, and lay sprawled in my shift, my skin hot and dry in the soft air. My arm ached abominably, and I could feel each of Mr. Willoughby's forty-three elegant stitches like red-hot safety pins stuck through my flesh.

No help for it; I was going to have to use the penicillin. I might be proof against smallpox, typhoid, and the common cold in its eighteenth-century incarnation, but I wasn't immortal, and God only knew what insanitary substances the Portuguese had been employing his cutlass on before applying it to me.

The short trip across the room to the cupboard where my clothes hung left me sweating and shivering, and I had to sit down quite suddenly, the skirt clutched to my bosom, in order to avoid falling.

"Sassenach! Are ye all right?" Jamie poked his head through the low doorway, looking worried.

"No," I said. "Come here a minute, will you? I need you to do something."

"Wine? A biscuit? Murphy's made a wee broth for ye, special." He was beside me in a moment, the back of his hand cool against my flushed cheek. "God, you're burning!"

"Yes, I know," I said. "Don't worry, though; I have medicine for it."

I fumbled one-handed in the pocket of the skirt, and pulled out the case containing the syringes and ampules. My right arm was sore enough that any movement made me clench my teeth.

"Your turn," I said wryly, shoving the case across the table toward Jamie. "Here's your chance for revenge, if you want it."

He looked blankly at the case, then at me.

"What?" he said. "Ye want me to stab ye with one of these spikes?"

"I wish you wouldn't put it quite that way, but yes," I said.

"In the bum?" His lips twitched.

"Yes, damn you!"

He looked at me for a moment, one corner of his mouth curling slightly upward. Then he bowed his head over the case, red hair glowing in the shaft of sun from the window.

"Tell me what to do, then," he said.

I directed him carefully, guiding him through the preparation and filling of the syringe, and then took it myself, checking for air bubbles, clumsily left-handed. By the time I had given it back to him and arranged myself on the berth, he had ceased to find anything faintly funny about the situation.

"Are ye sure ye want me to do it?" he said doubtfully. "I'm no verra good with my hands."

That made me laugh, in spite of my throbbing arm. I had seen him do everything with those hands, from delivering foals and building walls, to skinning deer and setting type, all with the same light and dextrous touch.

"Well, aye," he said, when I said as much. "But it's no quite the same, is it? The closest thing I've done to this is to dirk a man in the wame, and it feels a bit strange to think of doin' such a thing to you, Sassenach."

I glanced back over my shoulder, to find him gnawing dubiously on his lower lip, the brandy-soaked pad in one hand, the syringe held gingerly in the other.

"Look," I said. "I did it to you; you *know* what it feels like. It wasn't that bad, was it?" He was beginning to make me rather nervous.

"Mmphm." Pressing his lips together, he knelt down by the bed and gently wiped a spot on my backside with the cool, wet pad. "Is this all right?"

"That's fine. Press the point in at a bit of an angle, not straight in—you see how the point of the needle's cut at an angle? Push it in about a quarter-inch—don't be afraid to jab a bit, skin's tougher than you think to get through—and then push down the plunger very slowly, you don't want to do it too fast."

I closed my eyes and waited. After a moment, I opened them and looked back. He was pale, and a faint sheen of sweat glimmered over his cheekbones.

"Never mind." I heaved myself upright, bracing against the wave of dizziness. "Here, give me that." I snatched the pad from his hand and swiped a patch across the top of my thigh. My hand trembled slightly from the fever.

"But—"

"Shut up!" I took the syringe and aimed it as well as I could, left-handed, then plunged it into the muscle. It hurt. It hurt more when I pressed down on the plunger, and my thumb slipped off.

Then Jamie's hands were there, one steadying my leg, the other on the needle, slowly pressing down until the last of the white liquid had vanished from the tube. I took one quick, deep breath when he pulled it out.

"Thanks," I said, after a moment.

"I'm sorry," he said softly, a minute later. His hand came behind my back, easing me down.

"It's all right." My eyes were closed, and there were little colored patterns on the inside of my eyelids. They reminded me of the lining of a doll's suitcase I had had as a child; tiny pink and silver stars on a dark background. "I'd forgotten; it's hard to do it the first few times. I suppose sticking a dirk in someone *is* easier," I added. "You aren't worried about hurting them, after all."

He didn't say anything, but exhaled rather strongly through his nose. I could hear him moving about the room, putting the case of syringes away and hanging up my skirt. The site of the injection felt like a knot under my skin.

"I'm sorry," I said. "I didn't mean it that way."

"Well, ye should," he said evenly. "It *is* easier to kill someone to save your own life than it is to hurt someone to save theirs. Ye're a deal braver than I am, and I dinna mind your saying so."

I opened my eyes and looked at him.

"The hell you don't."

He stared down at me, blue eyes narrowed. The corner of his mouth turned up.

"The hell I don't," he agreed.

I laughed, but it hurt my arm.

"I'm not, and you aren't, and I didn't mean it that way, anyway," I said, and closed my eyes again.

"Mmphm."

I could hear the thump of feet on the deck above, and Mr. Warren's voice, raised in organized impatience. We had passed Great Abaco and Eleuthera in the night, and were now headed south toward Jamaica, with the wind behind us.

"*I* wouldn't risk being shot and hacked at, and arrested and hanged, if there were any choice about it," I said.

"Neither would I," he said dryly.

"But you—" I began, and then stopped. I looked at him curiously. "You really think that," I said slowly. "That you don't have a choice about it. Don't you?"

He was turned slightly away from me, eyes fixed on the port. The sun shone on the bridge of his long, straight nose and he rubbed a finger slowly up and down it. The broad shoulders rose slightly, and fell.

"I'm a man, Sassenach," he said, very softly. "If I thought there was a choice . . . then I maybe couldna do it. Ye dinna need to be so brave about things if ye ken ye canna help it, aye?" He looked at me then, with a faint smile. "Like a woman in childbirth, aye? Ye must do it, and it makes no difference if you're afraid—ye'll do it. It's only when ye ken ye can say no that it takes courage."

I lay quiet for a bit, watching him. He had closed his eyes and leaned back in the chair, auburn lashes long and absurdly childish against his cheeks.

They contrasted strangely with the smudges beneath his eyes and the deeper lines at the corners. He was tired; he'd barely slept since the sighting of the pirate vessel.

"I haven't told you about Graham Menzies, have I?" I said at last. The blue eyes opened at once.

"No. Who was he?"

"A patient. At the hospital in Boston."

Graham had been in his late sixties when I knew him; a Scottish immigrant who hadn't lost his burr, despite nearly forty years in Boston. He was a fisherman, or had been; when I knew him he owned several lobster boats, and let others do the fishing for him.

He was a lot like the Scottish soldiers I had known at Prestonpans and Falkirk; stoic and humorous at once, willing to joke about anything that was too painful to suffer in silence.

"You'll be careful, now, lassie," was the last thing he said to me as I watched the anesthetist set up the intravenous drip that would maintain him while I amputated his cancerous left leg. "Be sure ye're takin' off the right one, now."

"Don't worry," I assured him, patting the weathered hand that lay on the sheet. "I'll get the right one."

"Ye will?" His eyes widened in simulated horror. "I thought 'twas the *left* one was bad!" He was still chuckling asthmatically as the gas mask came down over his face.

The amputation had gone well, and Graham had recovered and gone home, but I was not really surprised to see him back again, six months later. The lab report on the original tumor had been dubious, and the doubts were now substantiated; metastasis to the lymph nodes in the groin.

I removed the cancerous nodes. Radiation treatment was applied. Cobalt. I removed the spleen, to which the disease had spread, knowing that the surgery was entirely in vain, but not willing to give up.

"It's a lot easier not to give up, when it isn't you that's sick," I said, staring up at the timbers overhead.

"Did he give up, then?" Jamie asked.

"I don't think I'd call it that, exactly."

> "I have been thinking," *Graham announced. The sound of his voice echoed tinnily through the earpieces of my stethoscope.*
>
> "Have you?" *I said.* "Well, don't do it out loud 'til I've finished here, that's a good lad."
>
> *He gave a brief snort of laughter, but lay quietly as I auscultated his chest, moving the disc of the stethoscope swiftly from ribs to sternum.*
>
> "All right," *I said at last, slipping the tubes out of my ears and*

letting them fall over my shoulders. "What have you been thinking about?"

"Killing myself."

His eyes met mine straight on, with just a hint of challenge. I glanced behind me, to be sure that the nurse had left, then pulled up the blue plastic visitor's chair and sat down next to him.

"Pain getting bad?" I asked. "There are things we can do, you know. You only need to ask." I hesitated before adding the last; he never had asked. Even when it was obvious that he needed medication, he never mentioned his discomfort. To mention it myself seemed an invasion of his privacy; I saw the small tightening at the corners of his mouth.

"I've a daughter," he said. "And two grandsons; bonny lads. But I'm forgetting; you'll have seen them last week, aye?"

I had. They came at least twice a week to see him, bringing scribbled school papers and autographed baseballs to show their grandpa.

"And there's my mother, living up to the rest home on Canterbury," he said thoughtfully. "It costs dearly, that place, but it's clean, and the food's good enough she enjoys complainin' about it while she eats."

He glanced dispassionately at the flat bedsheet, and lifted his stump.

"A month, d'ye think? Four? Three?"

"Maybe three," I said. "With luck," I added idiotically.

He snorted at me, and jerked his head at the IV drip above him.

"Tcha! And worse luck I wouldna wish on a beggar." He looked around at all the paraphernalia; the automatic respirator, the blinking cardiac monitor, the litter of medical technology. "Nearly a hundred dollars a day it's costing, to keep me here," he said. "Three months, that would be—great heavens, ten thousand dollars!" He shook his head, frowning.

"A bad bargain, I call that. Not worth it." His pale gray eyes twinkled suddenly up at me. "I'm Scots, ye know. Born thrifty, and not likely to get over it now."

"So I did it for him," I said, still staring upward. "Or rather, we did it together. He was prescribed morphia for the pain—that's like laudanum, only much stronger. I drew off half of each ampule and replaced the missing bit with water. It meant he didn't get the relief of a full dose for nearly twenty-four hours, but that was the safest way to get a big dose with no risk of being found out.

"We talked about using one of the botanical medicines I was studying; I knew enough to make up something fatal, but I wasn't sure of it being painless, and he didn't want to risk me being accused, if anyone got suspicious and did a forensic examination." I saw Jamie's eyebrow lift, and flapped a hand. "It doesn't matter; it's a way of finding out how someone died."

"Ah. Like a coroner's court?"

"A bit. Anyway, he'd be supposed to have morphia in his blood; that wouldn't prove anything. So that's what we did."

I drew a deep breath.

"There would have been no trouble, if I'd given him the injection, and left. That's what he'd asked me to do."

Jamie was quiet, eyes fixed intently on me.

"I couldn't do it, though." I looked at my left hand, seeing not my own smooth flesh, but the big, swollen knuckles of a commercial fisherman, and the fat green veins that crossed his wrist.

"I got the needle in," I said. I rubbed a finger over the spot on the wrist, where a large vein crosses the distal head of the radius. "But I couldn't press down the plunger."

In memory, I saw Graham Menzies's other hand rise from his side, trailing tubes, and close over my own. He hadn't much strength, then, but enough.

"I sat there until he was gone, holding his hand." I felt it still, the steady beat of the wrist-pulse under my thumb, growing slower, and slower still, as I held his hand, and then waiting for a beat that did not come.

I looked up at Jamie, shaking off the memory.

"And then a nurse came in." It had been one of the younger nurses—an excitable girl, with no discretion. She wasn't very experienced, but knew enough to tell a dead man when she saw one. And me just sitting there, doing nothing—most undoctorlike conduct. And the empty morphia syringe, lying on the table beside me.

"She talked, of course," I said.

"I expect she would."

"I had the presence of mind to drop the syringe into the incinerator chute after she left, though. It was her word against mine, and the whole matter was just dismissed."

My mouth twisted wryly. "Except that the next week, they offered me a job as head of the whole department. Very important. A lovely office on the sixth floor of the hospital—safely away from the patients, where I couldn't murder anyone else."

My finger was still rubbing absently across my wrist. Jamie reached out and stopped it by laying his own hand over mine.

"When was this, Sassenach?" he asked, his voice very gentle.

"Just before I took Bree and went to Scotland. That's why I went, in fact;

they gave me an extended leave—said I'd been working too hard, and deserved a nice vacation." I didn't try to keep the irony out of my voice.

"I see." His hand was warm on mine, despite the heat of my fever. "If it hadna been for that, for losing your work—would ye have come, Sassenach? Not just to Scotland. To me?"

I looked up at him and squeezed his hand, taking a deep breath.

"I don't know," I said. "I really don't. If I hadn't come to Scotland, met Roger Wakefield, found out that you—" I stopped and swallowed, overwhelmed. "It was Graham who sent me to Scotland," I said at last, feeling slightly choked. "He asked me to go someday—and say hello to Aberdeen for him." I glanced up at Jamie suddenly.

"I didn't! I never did go to Aberdeen."

"Dinna trouble yourself, Sassenach." Jamie squeezed my hand. "I'll take ye there myself—when we go back. Not," he added practically, "that there's anything to see there."

It was growing stuffy in the cabin. He rose and went to open one of the stern windows.

"Jamie," I said, watching his back, "what do you want?"

He glanced around, frowning slightly in thought.

"Oh—an orange would be good," he said. "There's some in the desk, aye?" Without waiting for a reply, he rolled back the lid of the desk, revealing a small bowl of oranges, bright among the litter of quills and papers. "D'ye want one, too?"

"All right," I said, smiling. "That wasn't really what I meant, though. I meant—what do you want to do, once we've found Ian?"

"Oh." He sat down by the berth, an orange in his hands, and stared at it for a moment.

"D'ye know," he said at last, "I dinna think anyone has ever asked me that —what it was I wanted to do." He sounded mildly surprised.

"Not as though you very often had a choice about it, is it?" I said dryly. "Now you do, though."

"Aye, that's true." He rolled the orange between his palms, head bent over the dimpled sphere. "I suppose it's come to ye that we likely canna go back to Scotland—at least for a time?" he said. I had told him of Tompkins's revelations about Sir Percival and his machinations, of course, but we had had little time to discuss the matter—or its implications.

"It has," I said. "That's why I asked."

I was quiet then, letting him come to terms with it. He had lived as an outlaw for a good many years, hiding first physically, and then by means of secrecy and aliases, eluding the law by slipping from one identity to another.

But now all these were known; there was no way for him to resume any of his former activities—or even to appear in public in Scotland.

His final refuge had always been Lallybroch. But even that avenue of retreat was lost to him now. Lallybroch would always be his home, but it was no longer his; there was a new laird now. I knew he would not begrudge the fact that Jenny's family possessed the estate—but he must, if he were human, regret the loss of his heritage.

I could hear his faint snort, and thought he had probably reached the same point in his thinking that I had in mine.

"Not Jamaica or the English-owned islands, either," he observed ruefully. "Tom Leonard and the Royal Navy may think us both dead for the moment, but they'll be quick enough to notice otherwise if we stay for any length of time."

"Have you thought of America?" I asked this delicately. "The Colonies, I mean."

He rubbed his nose doubtfully.

"Well, no. I hadna really thought of it. It's true we'd likely be safe from the Crown there, but . . ." He trailed off, frowning. He picked up his dirk and scored the orange, quickly and neatly, then began to peel it.

"No one would be hunting you there," I pointed out. "Sir Percival hasn't got any interest in you, unless you're in Scotland, where arresting you would do him some good. The British Navy can't very well follow you ashore, and the West Indian governors haven't anything to say about what goes on in the Colonies, either."

"That's true," he said slowly. "But the Colonies . . ." He took the peeled orange in one hand, and began to toss it lightly, a few inches in the air. "It's verra primitive, Sassenach," he said. "A wilderness, aye? I shouldna like to take ye into danger."

That made me laugh, and he glanced sharply at me, then, catching my thought, relaxed into a half-rueful smile.

"Aye, well, I suppose draggin' ye off to sea and letting ye be kidnapped and locked up in a plague ship is dangerous enough. But at least I havena let ye be eaten by cannibals, yet."

I wanted to laugh again, but there was a bitter note to his voice that made me bite my lip instead.

"There aren't any cannibals in America," I said.

"There are!" he said heatedly. "I printed a book for a society of Catholic missionaries, that told all about the heathen Iroquois in the north. They tie up their captives and chop bits off of them, and then rip out their hearts and eat them before their eyes!"

"Eat the hearts first and then the eyes, do they?" I said, laughing in spite of myself. "All right," I said, seeing his scowl, "I'm sorry. But for one thing, you can't believe everything you read, and for another—"

I didn't get to finish. He leaned forward and grasped my good arm, tight enough to make me squeak with surprise.

"Damn you, listen to me!" he said. "It's no light matter!"

"Well . . . no, I suppose not," I said, tentatively. "I didn't mean to make fun of you—but, Jamie, I *did* live in Boston for nearly twenty years. You've never set foot in America!"

"That's true," he said evenly. "And d'ye think the place ye lived in is anything like what it's like now, Sassenach?"

"Well—" I began, then paused. While I had seen any number of historic buildings near Boston Common, sporting little brass plaques attesting to their antiquity, the majority of them had been built later than 1770; many a lot later. And beyond a few buildings . . .

"Well, no," I admitted. "It's not; I know it's not. But I don't think it's a complete wilderness. There *are* cities and towns now; I know that much."

He let go of my arm and sat back. He still held the orange in his other hand.

"I suppose that's so," he said slowly. "Ye dinna hear so much of the towns —only that it's such a wild savage place, though verra beautiful. But I'm no a fool, Sassenach." His voice sharpened slightly, and he dug his thumb savagely into the orange, splitting it in half.

"I dinna believe something only because someone's set words down in a book—for God's sake, I print the damn things! I ken verra well just what charlatans and fools some writers are—I see them! And surely I ken the difference between a romance and a fact set down in cold blood!"

"All right," I said. "Though I'm not sure it's all that easy to tell the difference between romance and fact in print. But even if it's dead true about the Iroquois, the whole continent isn't swarming with bloodthirsty savages. I *do* know that much. It's a very big place, you know," I added, gently.

"Mmphm," he said, plainly unconvinced. Still, he bent his attention to the orange, and began to divide it into segments.

"This is very funny," I said ruefully. "When I made up my mind to come back, I read everything I could find about England and Scotland and France about this time, so I'd know as much as I could about what to expect. And here we end up in a place I know nothing about, because it never dawned on me we'd cross the ocean, with you being so seasick."

That made him laugh, a little grudgingly.

"Aye, well, ye never ken what ye can do 'til ye have to. Believe me, Sassenach, once I've got Ian safely back, I shall never set foot on a filthy, godforsaken floating plank in my life again—except to go home to Scotland, when it's safe," he added, as an afterthought. He offered me an orange segment and I took it, token of a peace offering.

"Speaking of Scotland, you still have your printing press there, safe in

Edinburgh," I said. "We could have it sent over, maybe—if we settled in one of the larger American cities."

He looked up at that, startled.

"D'ye think it would be possible to earn a living, printing? There are that many people? It takes a fair-sized city, ye ken, to need a printer or bookseller."

"I'm sure you could. Boston, Philadelphia . . . not New York yet, I don't think. Williamsburg, maybe? I don't know which ones, but there are several places big enough to need printing—the shipping ports, certainly." I remembered the flapping posters, advertising dates of embarkation and arrival, sales of goods and recruitment of seamen, that decorated the walls of every seaside tavern in Le Havre.

"Mmphm." This one was a thoughtful noise. "Aye, well, if we might do that . . ."

He poked a piece of fruit into his mouth and ate it slowly.

"What about you?" he said abruptly.

I glanced at him, startled.

"What about me?"

His eyes were fixed intently on me, reading my face.

"Would it suit ye to go to such a place?" He looked down then, carefully separating the other half of the fruit. "I mean—you've your work to do as well, aye?" He looked up and smiled, wryly.

"I learned in Paris that I couldna stop ye doing it. And ye said yourself, ye might not have come, had Menzies's death not stopped you, where ye were. Can ye be a healer in the Colonies, d'ye think?"

"I expect I can," I said slowly. "There are people sick and injured, almost anywhere you go, after all." I looked at him, curious.

"You're a very odd man, Jamie Fraser."

He laughed at that, and swallowed the rest of his orange.

"Oh, I am, aye? And what d'ye mean by that?"

"Frank loved me," I said slowly. "But there were . . . pieces of me, that he didn't know what to do with. Things about me that he didn't understand, or maybe that frightened him." I glanced at Jamie. "Not you."

His head was bent over a second orange, hands moving swiftly as he scored it with his dirk, but I could see the faint smile in the corner of his mouth.

"No, Sassenach, ye dinna frighten me. Or rather ye do, but only when I think ye may kill yourself from carelessness."

I snorted briefly.

"You scare me, for the same reason, but I don't suppose there's anything I can do about it."

His chuckle was deep and easy.

"And ye think I canna do anything about it, either, so I shouldna be worrit?"

"I didn't say you shouldn't worry—do you think I don't worry? But no, you probably can't do anything about me."

I saw him opening his mouth to disagree. Then he changed his mind, and laughed again. He reached out and popped an orange segment into my mouth.

"Well, maybe no, Sassenach, and maybe so. But I've lived a long enough time now to think it maybe doesna matter so much—so long as I can love you."

Speechless with orange juice, I stared at him in surprise.

"And I do," he said softly. He leaned into the berth and kissed me, his mouth warm and sweet. Then he drew back, and gently touched my cheek.

"Rest now," he said firmly. "I'll bring ye some broth, in a bit."

I slept for several hours, and woke up still feverish, but hungry. Jamie brought me some of Murphy's broth—a rich green concoction, swimming in butter and reeking with sherry—and insisted, despite my protests, on feeding it to me with a spoon.

"I have a perfectly good hand," I said crossly.

"Aye, and I've seen ye use it, too," he replied, deftly gagging me with the spoon. "If ye're clumsy with a spoon as wi' that needle, you'll have this all spilt down your bosom and wasted, and Murphy will brain me wi' the ladle. Here, open up."

I did, my resentment gradually melting into a sort of warm and glowing stupor as I ate. I hadn't taken anything for the pain in my arm, but as my empty stomach expanded in grateful relief, I more or less quit noticing it.

"Will ye have another bowl?" Jamie asked, as I swallowed the last spoonful. "Ye'll need your strength kept up." Not waiting for an answer, he uncovered the small tureen Murphy had sent, and refilled the bowl.

"Where's Ishmael?" I asked, during the brief hiatus.

"On the after deck. He didna seem comfortable belowdecks—and I canna say I blame him, having seen the slavers at Bridgetown. I had Maitland sling him a hammock."

"Do you think it's safe to leave him loose like that? What kind of soup is this?" The last spoonful had left a delightful, lingering taste on my tongue; the next revived the full flavor.

"Turtle; Stern took a big hawksbill last night. He sent word he's saving ye the shell to make combs of, for your hair." Jamie frowned slightly, whether at the thought of Lawrence Stern's gallantry or Ishmael's presence, I couldn't tell. "As for the black, he's not loose—Fergus is watching him."

"Fergus is on his honeymoon," I protested. "You shouldn't make him do it. Is this really turtle soup? I've never had it before. It's marvelous."

Jamie was unmoved by contemplation of Fergus's tender state.

"Aye, well, he'll be wed a long time," he said callously. "Do him no harm to keep his breeches on for one night. And they do say that abstinence makes the heart grow firmer, no?"

"Absence," I said, dodging the spoon for a moment. "And fonder. If anything's growing firmer from abstinence, it wouldn't be his heart."

"That's verra bawdy talk for a respectable marrit woman," Jamie said reprovingly, sticking the spoon in my mouth. "And inconsiderate, forbye."

I swallowed. "Inconsiderate?"

"I'm a wee bit firm myself at the moment," he replied evenly, dipping and spooning. "What wi' you sitting there wi' your hair loose and your nipples starin' me in the eye, the size of cherries."

I glanced down involuntarily, and the next spoonful bumped my nose. Jamie clicked his tongue, and picking up a cloth, briskly blotted my bosom with it. It was quite true that my shift was made of thin cotton, and even when dry, reasonably easy to see through.

"It's not as though you haven't seen them before," I said, amused.

He laid down the cloth and raised his brows.

"I have drunk water every day since I was weaned," he pointed out. "It doesna mean I canna be thirsty, still." He picked up the spoon. "You'll have a wee bit more?"

"No, thanks," I said, dodging the oncoming spoon. "I want to hear more about this firmness of yours."

"No, ye don't; you're ill."

"I feel much better," I assured him. "Shall I have a look at it?" He was wearing the loose petticoat breeches the sailors wore, in which he could easily have concealed three or four dead mullet, let alone a fugitive firmness.

"You shall not," he said, looking slightly shocked. "Someone might come in. And I canna think your looking at it would help a bit."

"Well, you can't tell that until I *have* looked at it, can you?" I said. "Besides, you can bolt the door."

"Bolt the door? What d'ye think I'm going to do? Do I look the sort of man would take advantage of a woman who's not only wounded and boiling wi' fever, but drunk as well?" he demanded. He stood up, nonetheless.

"I am not drunk," I said indignantly. "You can't get drunk on turtle soup!" Nonetheless, I was conscious that the glowing warmth in my stomach seemed to have migrated somewhat lower, taking up residence between my thighs, and there was undeniably a slight lightness of head not strictly attributable to fever.

"You can if ye've been drinking turtle soup as made by Aloysius

O'Shaughnessy Murphy," he said. "By the smell of it, he's put at least a full bottle o' the sherry in it. A verra intemperate race, the Irish."

"Well, I'm still not drunk." I straightened up against the pillows as best I could. "You told me once that if you could still stand up, you weren't drunk."

"You aren't standing up," he pointed out.

"You are. And I could if I wanted to. Stop trying to change the subject. We were talking about your firmness."

"Well, ye can just stop talking about it, because—" He broke off with a small yelp, as I made a fortunate grab with my left hand.

"Clumsy, am I?" I said, with considerable satisfaction. "Oh, my. Heavens, you *do* have a problem, don't you?"

"Will ye leave go of me?" he hissed, looking frantically over his shoulder at the door. "Someone could come in any moment!"

"I told you you should have bolted the door," I said, not letting go. Far from being a dead mullet, the object in my hand was exhibiting considerable liveliness.

He eyed me narrowly, breathing through his nose.

"I wouldna use force on a sick woman," he said through his teeth, "but you've a damn healthy grip for someone with a fever, Sassenach. If you—"

"I told you I felt better," I interrupted, "but I'll make you a bargain; you bolt the door and I'll prove I'm not drunk." I rather regretfully let go, to indicate good faith. He stood staring at me for a moment, absentmindedly rubbing the site of my recent assault on his virtue. Then he lifted one ruddy eyebrow, turned, and went to bolt the door.

By the time he turned back, I had made it out of the berth and was standing—a trifle shakily, but still upright—against the frame. He eyed me critically.

"It's no going to work, Sassenach," he said, shaking his head. He looked rather regretful, himself. "We'll never stay upright, wi' a swell like there is underfoot tonight, and ye know I'll not fit in that berth by myself, let alone wi' you."

There was a considerable swell; the lantern on its swivel-bracket hung steady and level, but the shelf above it tilted visibly back and forth as the *Artemis* rode the waves. I could feel the faint shudder of the boards under my bare feet, and knew Jamie was right. At least he was too absorbed in the discussion to be seasick.

"There's always the floor," I suggested hopefully. He glanced down at the limited floor space and frowned. "Aye, well. There is, but we'd have to do it like snakes, Sassenach, all twined round each other amongst the table legs."

"I don't mind."

"No," he said, shaking his head, "it would hurt your arm." He rubbed a knuckle across his lower lip, thinking. His eyes passed absently across my body at about hip level, returned, fixed, and lost their focus. I thought the bloody shift must be more transparent than I realized.

Deciding to take matters into my own hands, I let go my hold on the frame of the berth and lurched the two paces necessary to reach him. The roll of the ship threw me into his arms, and he barely managed to keep his own balance, clutching me tightly round the waist.

"Jesus!" he said, staggered, and then, as much from reflex as from desire, bent his head and kissed me.

It was startling. I was accustomed to be surrounded by the warmth of his embrace; now it was I who was hot to the touch and he who was cool. From his reaction, he was enjoying the novelty as much as I was.

Light-headed, and reckless with it, I nipped the side of his neck with my teeth, feeling the waves of heat from my face pulsate against the column of his throat. He felt it, too.

"God, you're like holding a hot coal!" His hands dropped lower and pressed me hard against him.

"Firm is it? Ha," I said, getting my mouth free for a moment. "Take those baggy things off." I slid down his length and onto my knees in front of him, fumbling mazily at his flies. He freed the laces with a quick jerk, and the petticoat breeches ballooned to the floor with a whiff of wind.

I didn't wait for him to remove his shirt; just lifted it and took him. He made a strangled sound and his hands came down on my head as though he wanted to restrain me, but hadn't the strength.

"Oh, Lord!" he said. His hands tightened in my hair, but he wasn't trying to push me away. "This must be what it's like to make love in Hell," he whispered. "With a burning she-devil."

I laughed, which was extremely difficult under the circumstances. I choked, and pulled back a moment, breathless.

"Is this what a succubus does, do you think?"

"I wouldna doubt it for a moment," he assured me. His hands were still in my hair, urging me back.

A knock sounded on the door, and he froze. Confident that the door was indeed bolted, I didn't.

"Aye? What is it?" he said, with a calmness rather remarkable for a man in his position.

"Fraser?" Lawrence Stern's voice came through the door. "The Frenchman says the black is asleep, and may he have leave to go to bed now?"

"No," said Jamie shortly. "Tell him to stay where he is; I'll come along and relieve him in a bit."

"Oh." Stern's voice sounded a little hesitant. "Surely. His . . . um, his wife seems . . . eager for him to come now."

Jamie inhaled sharply.

"Tell her," he said, a small note of strain becoming evident in his voice, "that he'll be there . . . presently."

"I will say so." Stern sounded dubious about Marsali's reception of this news, but then his voice brightened. "Ah . . . is Mrs. Fraser feeling somewhat improved?"

"Verra much," said Jamie, with feeling.

"She enjoyed the turtle soup?"

"Greatly. I thank ye." His hands on my head were trembling.

"Did you tell her that I've put aside the shell for her? It was a fine hawksbill turtle; a most elegant beast."

"Aye. Aye, I did." With an audible gasp, Jamie pulled away and reaching down, lifted me to my feet.

"Good night, Mr. Stern!" he called. He pulled me toward the berth; we struggled four-legged to keep from crashing into tables and chairs as the floor rose and fell beneath us.

"Oh." Lawrence sounded faintly disappointed. "I suppose Mrs. Fraser is asleep, then?"

"Laugh, and I'll throttle ye," Jamie whispered fiercely in my ear. "She is, Mr. Stern," he called through the door. "I shall give her your respects in the morning, aye?"

"I trust she will rest well. There seems to be a certain roughness to the sea this evening."

"I . . . have noticed, Mr. Stern." Pushing me to my knees in front of the berth, he knelt behind me, groping for the hem of my shift. A cool breeze from the open stern window blew over my naked buttocks, and a shiver ran down the backs of my thighs.

"Should you or Mrs. Fraser find yourselves discommoded by the motion, I have a most capital remedy to hand—a compound of mugwort, bat dung, and the fruit of the mangrove. You have only to ask, you know."

Jamie didn't answer for a moment.

"Oh, Christ!" he whispered. I took a sizable bite of the bedclothes.

"Mr. Fraser?"

"I said, 'Thank you'!" Jamie replied, raising his voice.

"Well, I shall bid you a good evening, then."

Jamie let out his breath in a long shudder that was not quite a moan.

"Mr. Fraser?"

"Good evening, Mr. Stern!" Jamie bellowed.

"Oh! Er . . . good evening."

Stern's footsteps receded down the companionway, lost in the sound of the waves that were now crashing loudly against the hull. I spit out the mouthful of quilt.

"Oh . . . my . . . God!"

His hands were large and hard and cool on my heated flesh.

"You've the roundest arse I've ever seen!"

A lurch by the *Artemis* here aiding his efforts to an untoward degree, I uttered a loud shriek.

"Shh!" He clasped a hand over my mouth, bending over me so that he lay over my back, the billowing linen of his shirt falling around me and the weight of him pressing me to the bed. My skin, crazed with fever, was sensitive to the slightest touch, and I shook in his arms, the heat inside me rushing outward as he moved within me.

His hands were under me then, clutching my breasts, the only anchor as I lost my boundaries and dissolved, conscious thought a displaced element in the chaos of sensations—the warm damp of tangled quilts beneath me, the cold sea wind and misty spray that wafted over us from the rough sea outside, the gasp and brush of Jamie's warm breath on the back of my neck, and the sudden prickle and flood of cold and heat, as my fever broke in a dew of satisfied desire.

Jamie's weight rested on my back, his thighs behind mine. It was warm, and comforting. After a long time, his breathing eased, and he rose off me. The thin cotton of my shift was damp, and the wind plucked it away from my skin, making me shiver.

Jamie closed the window with a snap, then bent and picked me up like a rag doll. He lowered me into the berth, and pulled the quilt up over me.

"How is your arm?" he said.

"What arm?" I murmured drowsily. I felt as though I had been melted and poured into a mold to set.

"Good," he said, a smile in his voice. "Can ye stand up?"

"Not for all the tea in China."

"I'll tell Murphy ye liked the soup." His hand rested for a moment on my cool forehead, passed down the curve of my cheek in a light caress, and then was gone. I didn't hear him leave.

57

Promised Land

"It's persecution!" Jamie said indignantly. He stood behind me, looking over the rail of the *Artemis*. Kingston Harbor stretched to our left, glowing like liquid sapphires in the morning light, the town above half-sunk in jungle green, cubes of yellowed ivory and pink rose-quartz in a lush setting of emerald and malachite. And on the cerulean bosom of the water below floated the majestic sight of a great three-masted ship, furled canvas white as gull wings, gun decks proud and brass gleaming in the sun. His Majesty's man-of-war *Porpoise*.

"The filthy boat's pursuing me," he said, glaring at it as we sailed past at a discreet distance, well outside the harbor mouth. "Everywhere I go, there it is again!"

I laughed, though in truth, the sight of the *Porpoise* made me slightly nervous, too.

"I don't suppose it's personal," I told him. "Captain Leonard did say they were bound for Jamaica."

"Aye, but why would they no head straight to Antigua, where the naval barracks and the navy shipyards are, and them in such straits as ye left them?" He shaded his eyes, peering at the *Porpoise*. Even at this distance, small figures were visible in the rigging, making repairs.

"They had to come here first," I explained. "They were carrying a new governor for the colony." I felt an absurd urge to duck below the rail, though I knew that even Jamie's red hair would be indistinguishable at this distance.

"Aye? I wonder who's that?" Jamie spoke absently; we were no more than an hour away from arrival at Jared's plantation on Sugar Bay, and I knew his mind was busy with plans for finding Young Ian.

"A chap named Grey," I said, turning away from the rail. "Nice man; I met him on the ship, just briefly."

"Grey?" Startled, Jamie looked down at me. "Not Lord John Grey, by chance?"

"Yes, that was his name? Why?" I glanced up at him, curious. He was staring at the *Porpoise* with renewed interest.

"Why?" He heard me when I repeated the question a second time, and glanced down at me, smiling. "Oh. It's only that I ken Lord John; he's a friend of mine."

"Really?" I was no more than mildly surprised. Jamie's friends had once included the French minister of finance and Charles Stuart, as well as Scottish beggars and French pickpockets. I supposed it was not remarkable that he should now count English aristocrats among his acquaintance, as well as Highland smugglers and Irish seacooks.

"Well, that's luck," I said. "Or at least I suppose it is. Where do you know Lord John from?"

"He was the Governor of Ardsmuir prison," he replied, surprising me after all. His eyes were still fixed on the *Porpoise,* narrowed in speculation.

"And he's a *friend* of yours?" I shook my head. "I'll never understand men."

He turned and smiled at me, taking his attention at last from the English ship.

"Well, friends are where ye find them, Sassenach," he said. He squinted toward the shore, shading his eyes with his hand. "Let us hope this Mrs. Abernathy proves to be one."

As we rounded the tip of the headland, a lithe black figure materialized next to the rail. Now clothed in spare seaman's clothes, with his scars hidden, Ishmael looked less like a slave and a good deal more like a pirate. Not for the first time, I wondered just how much of what he had told us was the truth.

"I be leavin' now," he announced abruptly.

Jamie lifted one eyebrow and glanced over the rail, into the soft blue depths.

"Dinna let me prevent ye," he said politely. "But would ye not rather have a boat?"

Something that might have been humor flickered briefly in the black man's eyes, but didn't disturb the severe outlines of his face.

"You say you put me ashore where I want, I be tellin' you 'bout those boys," he said. He nodded toward the island, where a riotous growth of jungle spilled down the slope of a hill to meet its own green shadow in the shallow water. "That be where I want."

Jamie looked thoughtfully from the uninhabited shore to Ishmael, and then nodded.

"I'll have a boat lowered." He turned to go to the cabin. "I promised ye gold as well, no?"

"Don't be wantin' gold, mon." Ishmael's tone, as well as his words, stopped Jamie in his tracks. He looked at the black man with interest, mingled with a certain reserve.

"Ye'll have something else in mind?"

Ishmael jerked his head in a short nod. He didn't seem outwardly nervous, but I noticed the faint gleam of sweat on his temples, despite the mild noon breeze.

"I be wantin' that one-arm nigger." He stared boldly at Jamie as he spoke, but there was a diffidence under the confident facade.

"Temeraire?" I blurted out in astonishment. "Why?"

Ishmael flicked a glance at me, but addressed his words to Jamie, half-bold, half-cajoling.

"He ain't no good to you, mon; can't be doin' field work or ship work neither, ain't got but one arm."

Jamie didn't reply directly, but stared at Ishmael for a moment. Then he turned and called for Fergus to bring up the one-armed slave.

Temeraire, brought up on deck, stood expressionless as a block of wood, barely blinking in the sun. He too had been provided with seaman's clothes, but he lacked Ishmael's raffish elegance in them. He looked like a stump upon which someone had spread out washing to dry.

"This man wants you to go with him, to the island there," Jamie said to Temeraire, in slow, careful French. "Do you want to do this thing?"

Temeraire did blink at that, and a brief look of startlement widened his eyes. I supposed that no one had asked him what he wanted in many years—if ever. He glanced warily from Jamie to Ishmael and back again, but didn't say anything.

Jamie tried again.

"You do not have to go with this man," he assured the slave. "You may come with us, and we will take care of you. No one will hurt you. But you can go with him, if you like."

Still the slave hesitated, eyes flicking right and left, clearly startled and disturbed by the unexpected choice. It was Ishmael who decided the matter. He said something, in a strange tongue full of liquid vowels and syllables that repeated like a drumbeat.

Temeraire let out a gasp, fell to his knees, and pressed his forehead to the deck at Ishmael's feet. Everyone on deck stared at him, then looked at Ishmael, who stood with arms folded with a sort of wary defiance.

"He be goin' with me," he said.

And so it was. Picard rowed the two blacks ashore in the dinghy, and left them on the rocks at the edge of the jungle, supplied with a small bag of provisions, each equipped with a knife.

"Why there?" I wondered aloud, watching the two small figures make their way slowly up the wooded slope. "There aren't any towns nearby, are there? Or any plantations?" To the eye, the shore presented an unbroken expanse of jungle.

"Oh, there are plantations," Lawrence assured me. "Far up in the hills;

that's where they grow the coffee and indigo—the sugarcane grows better near the coast." He squinted toward the shore, where the two dark figures had disappeared. "It is more likely that they have gone to join a band of Maroons, though," he said.

"There are Maroons on Jamaica as well as on Hispaniola?" Fergus asked, interested.

Lawrence smiled, a little grimly.

"There are Maroons wherever there are slaves, my friend," he said. "There are always men who prefer to take the chance of dying like animals, rather than live as captives."

Jamie turned his head sharply to look at Lawrence, but said nothing.

Jared's plantation at Sugar Bay was called Blue Mountain House, presumably for the sake of the low, hazy peak that rose inland a mile behind it, blue with pines and distance. The house itself was set near the shore, in the shallow curve of the bay. In fact, the veranda that ran along one side of the house overhung a small lagoon, the building set on sturdy silvered-wood pilings that rose from the water, crusted with a spongy growth of tunicates and mussels and the fine green seaweed called mermaid's hair.

We were expected; Jared had sent a letter by a ship that left Le Havre a week before the *Artemis*. Owing to our delay on Hispaniola, the letter had arrived nearly a month in advance of ourselves, and the overseer and his wife —a portly, comfortable Scottish couple named MacIvers—were relieved to see us.

"I thought surely the winter storms had got ye," Kenneth MacIver said for the fourth time, shaking his head. He was bald, the top of his head scaly and freckled from long years' exposure to the tropic sun. His wife was a plump, genial, grandmotherly soul—who, I realized to my shock, was roughly five years younger than myself. She herded Marsali and me off for a quick wash, brush, and nap before supper, while Fergus and Jamie went with Mr. MacIver to direct the partial unloading of the *Artemis*'s cargo and the disposition of her crew.

I was more than willing to go; while my arm had healed sufficiently to need no more than a light bandage, it had prevented me from bathing in the sea as was my usual habit. After a week aboard the *Artemis*, unbathed, I looked forward to fresh water and clean sheets with a longing that was almost hunger.

I had no landlegs yet; the worn wooden floorboards of the plantation house gave the disconcerting illusion of seeming to rise and fall beneath my feet, and I staggered down the hallway after Mrs. MacIver, bumping into walls.

The house had an actual bathtub in a small porch; wooden, but filled—

mirabile dictu!—with hot water, by the good offices of two black slave women who heated kettles over a fire in the yard and carried them in. I should have felt much too guilty at this exploitation to enjoy my bath, but I didn't. I wallowed luxuriously, scrubbing the salt and grime from my skin with a loofah sponge and lathering my hair with a shampoo made from chamomile, geranium oil, fat-soap shavings, and the yolk of an egg, graciously supplied by Mrs. MacIver.

Smelling sweet, shiny-haired, and languid with warmth, I collapsed gratefully into the bed I was given. I had time only to think how delightful it was to stretch out at full length, before I fell asleep.

When I woke, the shadows of dusk were gathering on the veranda outside the open French doors of my bedroom, and Jamie lay naked beside me, hands folded on his belly, breathing deep and slow.

He felt me stir, and opened his eyes. He smiled sleepily and reaching up a hand, pulled me down to his mouth. He had had a bath, too; he smelled of soap and cedar needles. I kissed him at length, slowly and thoroughly, running my tongue across the wide curve of his lip, finding his tongue with mine in a soft, dark joust of greeting and invitation.

I broke loose, finally, and came up for air. The room was filled with a wavering green light, reflections from the lagoon outside, as though the room itself were underwater. The air was at once warm and fresh, smelling of sea and rain, with tiny currents of breeze that caressed the skin.

"Ye smell sweet, Sassenach," he murmured, voice husky with sleep. He smiled, reaching up to twine his fingers into my hair. "Come here to me, curly-wig."

Freed from pins and freshly washed, my hair was clouding over my shoulders in a perfect explosion of Medusa-like curls. I reached up to smooth it back, but he tugged gently, bending me forward so the veil of brown and gold and silver fell loose over his face.

I kissed him, half-smothered in clouds of hair, and lowered myself to lie on top of him, letting the fullness of my breasts squash gently against his chest. He moved slightly, rubbing, and sighed with pleasure.

His hands cupped my buttocks, trying to move me upward enough to enter me.

"Not bloody yet," I whispered. I pressed my hips down, rolling them, enjoying the feel of the silky stiffness trapped beneath my belly. He made a small breathless sound.

"We haven't had room or time to make love properly in months," I told him. "So we're taking our time about it now, right?"

"Ye take me at something of a disadvantage, Sassenach," he murmured into my hair. He squirmed under me, pressing upward urgently. "Ye dinna think we could take our time next time?"

"No, we couldn't," I said firmly. "Now. Slow. Don't move."

He made a sort of rumbling noise in his throat, but sighed and relaxed, letting his hands fall away to the sides. I squirmed lower on his body, making him inhale sharply, and set my mouth on his nipple.

I ran my tongue delicately round the tiny nub, making it stand up stiff, enjoying the coarse feel of the curly auburn hairs that surrounded it. I felt him tense under me, and put my hands on his upper arms to hold him still while I went on with it, biting gently, sucking and flicking with my tongue.

A few minutes later, I raised my head, brushed my hair back with one hand, and asked, "What's that you're saying?"

He opened one eye.

"The rosary," he informed me. "It's the only way I'm going to stand it." He closed his eyes and resumed murmuring in Latin. *"Ave Maria, gratia plena . . ."*

I snorted and went to work on the other one.

"You're losing your place," I said, next time I came up for air. "You've said the Lord's Prayer three times in a row."

"I'm surprised to hear I'm still makin' any sense at all." His eyes were closed, and a dew of moisture gleamed on his cheekbones. He moved his hips with increasing restiveness. "Now?"

"Not yet." I dipped my head lower and seized by impulse, went *Pffft!* into his navel. He convulsed, and taken by surprise, emitted a noise that could only be described as a giggle.

"Don't do that!" he said.

"Will if I want to," I said, and did it again. "You sound just like Bree," I told him. "I used to do that to her when she was a baby; she loved it."

"Well, I'm no a wee bairn, if ye hadna noticed the difference," he said a little testily. "If ye must do that, at least try it a bit lower, aye?"

I did.

"You don't have any hair at all at the tops of your thighs," I said, admiring the smooth white skin there. "Why is that, do you think?"

"The cow licked it all off last time she milked me," he said between his teeth. "For God's sake, Sassenach!"

I laughed, and returned to my work. At last I stopped and raised myself on my elbows.

"I think you've had enough," I said, brushing hair out of my eyes. "You haven't said anything but 'Jesus Christ' over and over again for the last few minutes."

Given the cue, he surged upward, and flipped me onto my back, pinning me with the solid weight of his body.

"You're going to live to regret this, Sassenach," he said with a grim satisfaction.

I grinned at him, unrepentant.

"Am I?"

He looked down at me, eyes narrowed. "Take my time, was it? You'll beg for it, before I've done wi' ye."

I tugged experimentally at my wrists, held tight in his grasp, and wriggled slightly under him with anticipation.

"Ooh, mercy," I said. "You beast."

He snorted briefly, and bent his head to the curve of my breast, white as pearl in the dim green water-light.

I closed my eyes and lay back against the pillows.

"Pater noster, qui es in coelis . . ." I whispered.

We were very late to supper.

Jamie lost no time over supper in asking about Mrs. Abernathy of Rose Hall.

"Abernathy?" MacIver frowned, tapping his knife on the table to assist thought. "Aye, seems I've heard the name, though I canna just charge my memory."

"Och, ye ken Abernathy's fine," his wife interrupted, pausing in her instructions to a servant for the preparation of the hot pudding. "It's that place up the Yallahs River, in the mountains. Cane, mostly, but a wee bit of coffee, too."

"Oh, aye, to be sure!" her husband exclaimed. "What a memory ye've got, Rosie!" He beamed fondly at his wife.

"Well, I might not ha' brought it to mind mysel'," she said modestly, "only as how that minister over to New Grace kirk last week was askin' after Mrs. Abernathy, too."

"What minister is this, ma'am?" Jamie asked, taking a split roast chicken from the huge platter presented to him by a black servant.

"Such a fine braw appetite as ye have, Mr. Fraser!" Mrs. MacIver exclaimed admiringly, seeing his loaded plate. "It's the island air does it, I expect."

The tips of Jamie's ears turned pink.

"I expect it is," he said, carefully not looking at me. "This minister . . . ?"

"Och, aye. Campbell, his name was, Archie Campbell." I started, and she glanced quizzically at me. "You'll know him?"

I shook my head, swallowing a pickled mushroom. "I've met him once, in Edinburgh."

"Oh. Well, he's come to be a missionary, and bring the heathen blacks to the salvation of Our Lord Jesus." She spoke with admiration, and glared at her husband when he snorted. "Now, ye'll no be makin' your Papist remarks, Kenny! The Reverend Campbell's a fine holy man, and a great scholar, forbye. I'm Free Church mysel'," she said, leaning toward me confidingly. "My parents disowned me when I wed Kenny, but I told them I was sure he'd come to see the light sooner or later."

"A lot later," her husband remarked, spooning jam onto his plate. He grinned at his wife, who sniffed and returned to her story.

"So, 'twas on account of the Reverend's bein' a great scholar that Mrs. Abernathy had written him, whilst he was still in Edinburgh, to ask him questions. And now that he's come here, he had it in mind to go and see her. Though after all Myra Dalrymple and the Reverend Davis telt him, I should be surprised he'd set foot on her place," she added primly.

Kenny MacIver grunted, motioning to a servant in the doorway with another huge platter.

"I wouldna put a great deal of stock in anything the Reverend Davis says, myself," he said. "The man's too godly to shit. But Myra Dalrymple's a sensible woman. Ouch!" He snatched back the fingers his wife had just cracked with a spoon, and sucked them.

"What did Miss Dalrymple have to say of Mrs. Abernathy?" Jamie inquired, hastily intervening before full-scale marital warfare could break out.

Mrs. MacIver's color was high, but she smoothed the frown from her brow as she turned to answer him.

"Well, a great deal of it was no more than ill-natured gossip," she admitted. "The sorts of things folk will always say about a woman as lives alone. That she's owerfond of the company of her men-slaves, aye?"

"But there was the talk when her husband died," Kenny interrupted. He slid several small, rainbow-striped fish off the platter the stooping servant held for him. "I mind it well, now I come to think on the name."

Barnabas Abernathy had come from Scotland, and had purchased Rose Hall five years before. He had run the place decently, turning a small profit in sugar and coffee, causing no comment among his neighbors. Then, two years ago, he had married a woman no one knew, bringing her home from a trip to Guadeloupe.

"And six months later, he was dead," Mrs. MacIver concluded with grim relish.

"And the talk is that Mrs. Abernathy had something to do with it?" Having some idea of the plethora of tropical parasites and diseases that attacked Europeans in the West Indies, I was inclined to doubt it, myself. Barnabas Abernathy could easily have died of anything from malaria to elephantiasis, but Rosie MacIver was right—folk were partial to ill-natured gossip.

"Poison," Rosie said, low-voiced, with a quick glance at the door to the kitchen. "The doctor who saw him said so. Mind, it could ha' been the slave-women. There was talk about Barnabas and his female slaves, and it's more common than folk like to say for a plantation cook-girl to be slipping something into the stew, but—" She broke off as another servant came in, carrying a cut-glass relish pot. Everyone was silent as the woman placed it on the table and left, curtsying to her mistress.

"You needn't worry," Mrs. MacIver said reassuringly, seeing me look after the woman. "We've a boy who tastes everything, before it's served. It's all quite safe."

I swallowed the mouthful of fish I had taken, with some difficulty.

"Did the Reverend Campbell go to see Mrs. Abernathy, then?" Jamie put in.

Rosie took the distraction gratefully. She shook her head, agitating the lace ruffles on her cap.

"No, I'm sure not, for 'twas the very next day there was the stramash about his sister."

In the excitement of tracking Ian and the *Bruja*, I had nearly forgotten Margaret Jane Campbell.

"What happened to his sister?" I asked, curious.

"Why, she's disappeared!" Mrs. MacIver's blue eyes went wide with importance. Blue Mountain House was remote, some ten miles out of Kingston by land, and our presence provided an unparalleled opportunity for gossip.

"What?" Fergus had been addressing himself to his plate with single-minded devotion, but now looked up, blinking. "Disappeared? Where?"

"The whole island's talking of it," Kenny put in, snatching the conversational ball from his wife. "Seems the Reverend had a woman engaged as abigail to his sister, but the woman died of a fever on the voyage."

"Oh, that's too bad!" I felt a real pang for Nellie Cowden, with her broad, pleasant face.

"Aye." Kenny nodded offhandedly. "Well, and so the Reverend found a place for his sister to lodge. Feebleminded, I understand?" He lifted a brow at me.

"Something like that."

"Aye, well, the lass seemed quiet and biddable, and Mrs. Forrest, who had the house where she lodged, would take her to sit on the veranda in the cool part of the day. So Tuesday last, a boy comes to say as Mrs. Forrest is wanted quicklike to come to her sister, who's having a child. And Mrs. Forrest got flustered and went straight off, forgetting Miss Campbell on the veranda. And when she thought of it, and sent someone back to see—why Miss Campbell was gone. And not a smell of her since, in spite of the Reverend raising heaven and earth, ye might say." MacIver rocked back on his chair, puffing out his sun-mottled cheeks.

Mrs. MacIver wagged her head, *tsk*ing mournfully.

"Myra Dalrymple told the Reverend as how he should go to the Governor for help to find her," she said. "But the Governor's scarce settled, and not yet ready to receive anyone. He's having a great reception this coming

Thursday, for to meet all the important folk o' the island. Myra said as the Reverend must go, and speak to the Governor there, but he's no of a mind to do that, it bein' such a worldly occasion, aye?"

"A reception?" Jamie set down his spoon, looking at Mrs. MacIver with interest. "Is it by invitation, d'ye know?"

"Oh, no," she said, shaking her head. "Anyone may come as likes to, or so I've heard."

"Is that so?" Jamie glanced at me, smiling. "What d'ye think, Sassenach— would ye care to step out wi' me at the Governor's Residence?"

I stared at him in astonishment. I should have thought that the last thing he would wish to do was show himself in public. I was also surprised that he would let anything at all stop his visiting Rose Hall at the earliest opportunity.

"It's a good opportunity to ask about Ian, no?" he explained. "After all, he might not be at Rose Hall, but someplace else on the island."

"Well, aside from the fact that I've nothing to wear . . ." I temporized, trying to figure out what he was really up to.

"Och, that's no trouble," Rosie MacIver assured me. "I've one of the cleverest sempstresses on the island; she'll have ye tricked out in no time."

Jamie was nodding thoughtfully. He smiled, eyes slanting as he looked at me over the candle flame.

"Violet silk, I think," he said. He plucked the bones delicately from his fish and set them aside. "And as for the other—dinna fash, Sassenach. I've something in mind. You'll see."

58

Masque of the Red Death

"Oh who is that young sinner with the handcuffs on his wrists?
And what has he been after that they groan and shake their fists?
And wherefore is he wearing such a conscience-stricken air?
Oh they're taking him to prison for the colour of his hair."

Jamie put down the wig in his hand and raised one eyebrow at me in the mirror. I grinned at him and went on, declaiming with gestures:

" 'Tis a shame to human nature, such a head of hair as his;
In the good old time 'twas hanging for the colour that it is;
Though hanging isn't bad enough and flaying would be fair
For the nameless and abominable colour of his hair!"

"Did ye not tell me ye'd studied for a doctor, Sassenach?" he inquired. "Or was it a poet, after all?"

"Not me," I assured him, coming to straighten his stock. "Those sentiments are by one A. E. Housman."

"Surely one of him is sufficient," Jamie said dryly. "Given the quality of his opinions." He picked up the wig and fitted it carefully on his head, raising little puffs of scented powder as he poked it here and there. "Is Mr. Housman an acquaintance of yours, then?"

"You might say so." I sat down on the bed to watch. "It's only that the doctors' lounge at the hospital I worked at had a copy of Housman's collected works that someone had left there. There isn't time between calls to read most novels, but poems are ideal. I expect I know most of Housman by heart, now."

He looked warily at me, as though expecting another outburst of poetry, but I merely smiled at him, and he returned to his work. I watched the transformation in fascination.

Red-heeled shoes and silk stockings clocked in black. Gray satin breeches with silver knee buckles. Snowy linen, with Brussels lace six inches deep at cuff and jabot. The coat, a masterpiece in heavy gray with blue satin cuffs and crested silver buttons, hung behind the door, awaiting its turn.

He finished the careful powdering of his face, and licking the end of one finger, picked up a false beauty mark, dabbed it in gum arabic, and affixed it neatly near the corner of his mouth.

"There," he said, swinging about on the dressing stool to face me. "Do I look like a red-heided Scottish smuggler?"

I inspected him carefully, from full-bottomed wig to morocco-heeled shoes.

"You look like a gargoyle," I said. His face flowered in a wide grin. Outlined in white powder, his lips seemed abnormally red, his mouth even wider and more expressive than it usually was.

"Non!" said Fergus indignantly, coming in in time to hear this. "He looks like a Frenchman."

"Much the same thing," Jamie said, and sneezed. Wiping his nose on a handkerchief, he assured the young man, "Begging your pardon, Fergus."

He stood up and reached for the coat, shrugging it over his shoulders and settling the edges. In three-inch heels, he towered to a height of six feet seven; his head nearly brushed the plastered ceiling.

"I don't know," I said, looking up at him dubiously. "I've never seen a Frenchman that size."

Jamie shrugged, his coat rustling like autumn leaves. "Aye, well, there's no hiding my height. But so long as my hair is hidden, I think it will be all right. Besides," he added, gazing with approval at me, "folk willna be looking at me. Stand up and let me see, aye?"

I obliged, rotating slowly to show off the deep flare of the violet silk skirt. Cut low in the front, the décolletage was filled with a froth of lace that rippled down the front of the bodice in a series of V's. Matching lace cascaded from the elbow-length sleeves in graceful white falls that left my wrists bare.

"Rather a pity I don't have your mother's pearls," I remarked. I didn't regret their lack; I had left them for Brianna, in the box with the photographs and family documents. Still, with the deep décolletage and my hair twisted up in a knot, the mirror showed a long expanse of bare neck and bosom, rising whitely out of the violet silk.

"I thought of that." With the air of a conjuror, Jamie produced a small box from his inside pocket and presented it to me, making a leg in his best Versailles fashion.

Inside was a small, gleaming fish, carved in a dense black material, the edges of its scales touched with gold.

"It's a pin," he explained. "Ye could maybe wear it fastened to a white ribbon round your neck?"

"It's beautiful!" I said, delighted. "What's it made of? Ebony?"

"Black coral," he said. "I got it yesterday, when Fergus and I were in Montego Bay." He and Fergus had taken the *Artemis* round the island, disposing at last of the cargo of bat guano, delivered to its purchaser.

I found a length of white satin ribbon, and Jamie obligingly tied it about my neck, bending to peer over my shoulder at the reflection in the mirror.

"No, they won't be looking at me," he said. "Half o' them will be lookin' at you, Sassenach, and the other half at Mr. Willoughby."

"Mr. Willoughby? Is that safe? I mean—" I stole a look at the little Chinese, sitting patiently cross-legged on a stool, gleaming in clean blue silk, and lowered my voice. "I mean, they'll have wine, won't they?"

Jamie nodded. "And whisky, and cambric, and claret cup, and port, and champagne punch—and a wee cask of the finest French brandy—contributed by the courtesy of Monsieur Etienne Marcel de Provac Alexandre." He put a hand on his chest and bowed again, in an exaggerated pantomime that made me laugh. "Nay worry," he said, straightening up. "He'll behave, or I'll have his coral globe back—will I no, ye wee heathen?" he added with a grin to Mr. Willoughby.

The Chinese scholar nodded with considerable dignity. The embroidered black silk of his round cap was decorated with a small carved knob of red coral—the badge of his calling, restored to him by the chance encounter with a coral trader on the docks at Montego, and Jamie's good nature.

"You're quite sure we have to go?" The palpitations I was experiencing were due in part to the tightness of the stays I was wearing, but in greater degree to recurring visions of Jamie's wig falling off and the reception coming to a complete stop as the entire assemblage paused to stare at his hair before calling en masse for the Royal Navy.

"Aye, we do." He smiled at me reassuringly. "Dinna worry, Sassenach; if anyone's there from the *Porpoise,* it's not likely they'll recognize me—not like this."

"I hope not. Do you think anyone from the ship *will* be there tonight?"

"I doubt it." He scratched viciously at the wig above his left ear. "Where did ye get this thing, Fergus? I believe it's got lice."

"Oh, no, milord," Fergus assured him. "The wigmaker from whom I rented it assured me that it had been well dusted with hyssop and horse nettle to prevent any such infestations." Fergus himself was wearing his own hair, thickly powdered, and was handsome—if less startling than Jamie—in a new suit of dark blue velvet.

There was a tentative knock at the door, and Marsali stepped in. She too had had her wardrobe refurbished, and glowed in a dress of soft pink, with a deep rose sash.

She glowed somewhat more than I thought the dress accounted for, in fact, and as we made our way down the narrow corridor to the carriage, pulling in our skirts to keep them from brushing the walls, I managed to lean forward and murmur in her ear.

"Are you using the tansy oil?"

"Mm?" she said absently, her eyes on Fergus as he bowed and held open the carriage door for her. "What did ye say?"

"Never mind," I said, resigned. That was the least of our worries at the moment.

The Governor's mansion was ablaze with lights. Lanterns were perched along the low wall of the veranda, and hung from the trees along the paths of the ornamental garden. Gaily dressed people were emerging from their carriages on the crushed-shell drive, passing into the house through a pair of huge French doors.

We dismissed our own—or, rather, Jared's—carriage, but stood for a moment on the drive, waiting for a brief lull in the arrivals. Jamie seemed mildly nervous—for him; his fingers twitched now and then against the gray satin, but his manner was outwardly as calm as ever.

There was a short reception line in the foyer; several of the minor dignitaries of the island had been invited to assist the new governor in welcoming his guests. I passed ahead of Jamie down the line, smiling and nodding to the Mayor of Kingston and his wife. I quailed a bit at the sight of a fully decorated admiral next in line, resplendent in gilded coat and epaulettes, but no sign of anything beyond a mild amazement crossed his features as he shook hands with the gigantic Frenchman and the tiny Chinese who accompanied me.

There was my acquaintance from the *Porpoise;* Lord John's blond hair was hidden under a formal wig tonight, but I recognized the fine, clear features and slight, muscular body at once. He stood a little apart from the other dignitaries, alone. Rumor had it that his wife had refused to leave England to accompany him to this posting.

He turned to greet me, his face fixed in an expression of formal politeness. He looked, blinked, and then broke into a smile of extraordinary warmth and pleasure.

"Mrs. Malcolm!" he exclaimed, seizing my hands. "I am vastly pleased to see you!"

"The feeling is entirely mutual," I said, smiling back at him. "I didn't know you were the Governor, last time we met. I'm afraid I was a bit informal."

He laughed, his face glowing with the light of the candles in the wall sconces. Seen clearly in the light for the first time, I realized what a remarkably handsome man he was.

"You might be thought to have had an excellent excuse," he said. He looked me over carefully. "May I say that you are in remarkable fine looks this evening? Clearly the island air must agree with you somewhat more than the miasmas of shipboard. I had hoped to meet you again before leaving the

Porpoise, but when I inquired for you, I was told by Mr. Leonard that you were unwell. I trust you are entirely recovered?"

"Oh, entirely," I told him, amused. Unwell, eh? Evidently Tom Leonard was not about to admit to losing me overboard. I wondered whether he had put my disappearance in the log.

"May I introduce my husband?" I turned to wave at Jamie, who had been detained in animated conversation with the admiral, but who was now advancing toward us, accompanied by Mr. Willoughby.

I turned back to find the Governor gone green as a gooseberry. He stared from Jamie to me, and back again, pale as though confronted by twin specters.

Jamie came to a stop beside me, and inclined his head graciously toward the Governor.

"John," he said softly. "It's good to see ye, man."

The Governor's mouth opened and shut without making a sound.

"Let us make an opportunity to speak, a bit later," Jamie murmured. "But for now—my name is Etienne Alexandre." He took my arm, and bowed formally. "And may I have the pleasure to present to you my wife, Claire?" he said aloud, shifting effortlessly into French.

"Claire?" The Governor looked wildly at me. *"Claire?"*

"Er, yes," I said, hoping he wasn't going to faint. He looked very much as though he might, though I had no idea why the revelation of my Christian name ought to affect him so strongly.

The next arrivals were waiting impatiently for us to move out of the way. I bowed, fluttering my fan, and we walked into the main salon of the Residence. I glanced back over my shoulder to see the Governor, shaking hands mechanically with the new arrival, staring after us with a face like white paper.

The salon was a huge room, low-ceilinged and filled with people, noisy and bright as a cageful of parrots. I felt some relief at the sight. Among this crowd, Jamie wouldn't be terribly conspicuous, despite his size.

A small orchestra played at one side of the room, near a pair of doors thrown open to the terrace outside. I saw a number of people strolling there, evidently seeking either a breath of air, or sufficient quiet to hold a private conversation. At the other side of the room, yet another pair of doors opened into a short hallway, where the retiring rooms were.

We knew no one, and had no social sponsor to make introductions. However, due to Jamie's foresight, we had no need of one. Within moments of our arrival, women had begun to cluster around us, fascinated by Mr. Willoughby.

"My acquaintance, Mr. Yi Tien Cho," Jamie introduced him to a stout young woman in tight yellow satin. "Late of the Celestial Kingdom of China, Madame."

"Ooh!" The young lady fluttered her fan before her face, impressed. "Really from China? But what an unthinkable distance you must have come! Do let me welcome you to our small island, Mr.—Mr. Cho?" She extended a hand to him, clearly expecting it to be kissed.

Mr. Willoughby bowed deeply, hands in his sleeves, and obligingly said something in Chinese. The young woman looked thrilled. Jamie looked momentarily startled, and then the mask of urbanity dropped back over his face. I saw Mr. Willoughby's shining black eyes fix on the tips of the lady's shoes, protruding from under the hem of her dress, and wondered just what he had said to her.

Jamie seized the opportunity—and the lady's hand—bowing over it with extreme politeness.

"Your servant, Madame," he said in thickly accented English. "Etienne Alexandre. And might I present to you my wife, Claire?"

"Oh, yes, so pleased to meet you!" The young woman, flushed with excitement, took my hand and squeezed it. "I'm Marcelline Williams; perhaps you'll be acquainted with my brother, Judah? He owns Twelvetrees—you know, the large coffee plantation? I've come to stay with him for the season, and I'm having ever so marvelous a time!"

"No, I'm afraid we don't know anyone here," I said apologetically. "We've only just arrived ourselves—from Martinique, where my husband's sugar business is."

"Oh," Miss Williams cried, her eyes flying wide open. "But you must allow me to make you acquainted with my particular friends, the Stephenses! I believe they once visited Martinique, and Georgina Stephens is such a charming person—you will like her at once, I promise!"

And that was all there was to it. Within an hour, I had been introduced to dozens of people, and was being carried slowly round the room, eddying from one group to the next, passed hand to hand by the current of introductions launched by Miss Williams.

Across the room, I could see Jamie, standing head and shoulders above his companions, the picture of aristocratic dignity. He was conversing cordially with a group of men, all eager to make the acquaintance of a prosperous businessman who might offer useful contacts with the French sugar trade. I caught his eye once, in passing, and he gave me a brilliant smile and a gallant French bow. I still wondered what in the name of God he thought he was up to, but shrugged mentally. He would tell me when he was ready.

Fergus and Marsali, as usual needing no one's company but each other's, were dancing at one end of the floor, her glowing pink face smiling into his. For the sake of the occasion, Fergus had forgone his useful hook, replacing it with a black leather glove filled with bran, pinned to the sleeve of his coat. This rested against the back of Marsali's gown, a trifle stiff-looking, but not so unnatural as to provoke comment.

I danced past them, revolving sedately in the arms of a short, tubby English planter named Carstairs, who wheezed pleasantries into my bosom, red face streaming sweat.

As for Mr. Willoughby, he was enjoying an unparalleled social triumph, the center of attention of a cluster of ladies who vied with each other in pressing dainties and refreshments on him. His eyes were bright, and a faint flush shone on his sallow cheeks.

Mr. Carstairs deposited me among a group of ladies at the end of the dance, and gallantly went to fetch a cup of claret. I at once returned to the business of the evening, asking the ladies whether they might be familiar with people to whose acquaintance I had been recommended, named Abernathy.

"Abernathy?" Mrs. Hall, a youngish matron, fluttered her fan and looked blank. "No, I cannot say I am acquainted with them. Do they take a great part in society, do you know?"

"Oh, no, Joan!" Her friend, Mrs. Yoakum, looked shocked, with the particular kind of enjoyable shock that precedes some juicy revelation. "You've heard of the Abernathys! You remember, the man who bought Rose Hall, up on the Yallahs River?"

"Oh, yes!" Mrs. Hall's blue eyes widened. "The one who died so soon after buying it?"

"Yes, that's the one," another lady chimed in, overhearing. "Malaria, they *said* it was, but *I* spoke to the doctor who attended him—he had come to dress Mama's bad leg, you know she is such a martyr to the dropsy—and *he* told me—in strictest confidence, of course . . . ."

The tongues wagged merrily. Rosie MacIver had been a faithful reporter; all the stories she had conveyed were here, and more. I caught hold of the conversational thread and gave it a jerk in the desired direction.

"Does Mrs. Abernathy have indentured labor, as well as slaves?"

Here opinion was more confused. Some thought that she had several indentured servants, some thought only one or two—no one present had actually set foot in Rose Hall, but of course people *said* . . .

A few minutes later, the gossip had turned to fresh meat, and the *incredible* behavior of the new curate, Mr. Jones, with the widowed Mrs. Mina Alcott, but then, what could be expected of a woman with *her* reputation, and surely it was not entirely the young man's fault, and she so much older, though of course, one in Holy Orders might be expected to be held to a higher standard . . . I made an excuse and slipped away to the ladies' retiring room, my ears ringing.

I saw Jamie as I went, standing near the refreshment table. He was talking to a tall, red-haired girl in embroidered cotton, a trace of unguarded tenderness lingering in his eyes as he looked at her. She was smiling eagerly up at him, flattered by his attention. I smiled at the sight, wondering what the young lady would think, did she realize that he was not really looking at her at all, but imagining her as the daughter he had never seen.

I stood in front of the looking glass in the outer retiring room, tucking in stray curls loosened by the exertion of dancing, and took pleasure in the temporary silence. The retiring room was luxuriously appointed, being in fact three separate chambers, with the privy facilities and a room for the storage of hats, shawls, and extraneous clothing opening off the main room, where I stood. This had not only a long pier-glass and a fully appointed dressing table, but also a chaise longue, covered in red velvet. I eyed it with some wistfulness—the slippers I was wearing were pinching my feet badly—but duty called.

So far, I had learned nothing beyond what we already knew about the Abernathy plantation, though I had compiled a useful list of several other plantations near Kingston that employed indentured labor. I wondered whether Jamie intended to call upon his friend the Governor to help in the search for Ian—that might possibly justify risking an appearance here to-night.

But Lord John's response to the revelation of my identity was both puzzling and disturbing; you would think the man had seen a ghost. I squinted at my violet reflection, admiring the glitter of the black-and-gold fish at my throat, but failed to see anything unsettling in my appearance. My hair was tucked up with pins decorated with seed pearls and brilliants, and discreet use of Mrs. MacIver's cosmetics had darkened my lids and blushed my cheeks quite becomingly, if I did say so myself.

I shrugged, fluttered my lashes seductively at my image, then patted my hair and returned to the salon.

I made my way toward the long tables of refreshments, where a huge array of cakes, pastries, savories, fruits, candies, stuffed rolls, and a number of objects I couldn't put a name to but presumed edible were displayed. As I turned absentmindedly from the refreshment table with a plate of fruit, I collided headlong with a dark-hued waistcoat. Apologizing to its owner in confusion, I found myself looking up into the dour face of the Reverend Archibald Campbell.

"Mrs. Malcolm!" he exclaimed in astonishment.

"Er . . . Reverend Campbell," I replied, rather weakly. "What a surprise." I dabbed tentatively at a smear of mango on his abdomen, but he took a marked step backward, and I desisted.

He looked rather coldly at my décolletage.

"I trust I find you well, Mrs. Malcolm?" he said.

"Yes, thank you," I said. I wished he would stop calling me Mrs. Malcolm before someone to whom I had been introduced as Madame Alexandre heard him.

"I was so sorry to hear about your sister," I said, hoping to distract him. "Have you any word of her yet?"

He bent his head stiffly, accepting my sympathy.

"No. My own attempts at instigating a search have of course been limited," he said. "It was at the suggestion of one of my parishioners that I accompanied him and his wife here tonight, with the intention of putting my case before the Governor, and begging his assistance in locating my sister. I assure you, Mrs. Malcolm, no less weighty a consideration would have impelled my attendance at a function such as this."

He cast a glance of profound dislike at a laughing group nearby, where three young men were competing with each other in the composition of witty toasts to a group of young ladies, who received these attentions with much giggling and energetic fan-fluttering.

"I'm truly sorry for your misfortune, Reverend," I said, edging aside. "Miss Cowden told me a bit about your sister's tragedy. If I should be able to be of help . . ."

"No one can help," he interrupted. His eyes were bleak. "It was the fault of the Papist Stuarts, with their wicked attempt upon the throne, and the licentious Highlanders who followed them. No, no one can help, save God. He has destroyed the house of Stuart; he will destroy the man Fraser as well, and on that day, my sister will be healed."

"Fraser?" The trend of the conversation was making me distinctly uneasy. I glanced quickly across the room, but luckily Jamie was nowhere in sight.

"That is the name of the man who seduced Margaret from her family and her proper loyalties. His may not have been the hand that struck her down, but it was on his account that she had left her home and safety, and placed herself in danger. Aye, God will requite James Fraser fairly," he said with a sort of grim satisfaction at the thought.

"Yes, I'm sure he will," I murmured. "If you will excuse me, I believe I see a friend . . ." I tried to escape, but a passing procession of footmen bearing dishes of meat blocked my way.

"God will not suffer lewdness to endure forever," the Reverend went on, evidently feeling that the Almighty's opinions coincided largely with his own. His small gray eyes rested with icy disapproval on a group nearby, where several ladies fluttered around Mr. Willoughby like bright moths about a Chinese lantern.

Mr. Willoughby was brightly lit, too, in more than one sense of the word. His high-pitched giggle rose above the laughter of the ladies, and I saw him lurch heavily against a passing servant, nearly upsetting a tray of sorbet cups.

"Let the women learn with all sobriety," the Reverend was intoning, "avoiding all gaudiness of clothing and broided hair." He seemed to be hitting his stride; no doubt Sodom and Gomorrah would be up next. "A woman who has no husband should devote herself to the service of the Lord, not be disporting herself with abandon in public places. Do you see Mrs. Alcott? And she a widow, who should be engaged in pious works!"

I followed the direction of his frown and saw that he was looking at a chubby, jolly-looking woman in her thirties, with light brown hair done in gathered ringlets, who was giggling at Mr. Willoughby. I looked at her with interest. So this was the infamous merry widow of Kingston!

The little Chinese had now got down upon his hands and knees and was crawling around on the floor, pretending to look for a lost earring, while Mrs. Alcott squeaked in mock alarm at his forays toward her feet. I thought perhaps I had better find Fergus without delay, and have him detach Mr. Willoughby from his new acquaintance before matters went too far.

Evidently offended beyond bearing by the sight, the Reverend abruptly put down the cup of lemon squash he had been holding, turned and made his way through the crowd toward the terrace, vigorously elbowing people out of his way.

I breathed a sigh of relief; conversation with the Reverend Campbell was a lot like exchanging frivolities with the public hangman—though, in fact, the only hangman with whom I had been personally acquainted was much better company than the Reverend.

Suddenly I saw Jamie's tall figure, heading for a door on the far side of the room, where I assumed the Governor's private quarters to be. He must be going to talk to Lord John now. Moved by curiosity, I decided to join him.

The floor was by now so crowded that it was difficult to make my way across it. By the time I reached the door through which Jamie had gone, he had long since disappeared, but I pushed my way through.

I was in a long hallway, dimly lighted by candles in sconces, and pierced at intervals by long casement windows, through which red light from the torches on the terrace outside flickered, picking up the gleam of metal from the decorations on the walls. These were largely military, consisting of ornamental sprays of pistols, knives, shields and swords. Lord John's personal souvenirs? I wondered, or had they come with the house?

Away from the clamor of the salon, it was remarkably quiet. I walked down the hallway, my steps muffled by the long Turkey carpet that covered the parquet.

There was an indistinguishable murmur of male voices ahead. I turned a corner into a shorter corridor and saw a door ahead from which light spilled —that must be the Governor's private office. Inside, I heard Jamie's voice.

"Oh, God, John!" he said.

I stopped dead, halted much more by the tone of that voice than by the words—it was broken with an emotion I had seldom heard from him.

Walking very quietly, I drew closer. Framed in the half-open door was Jamie, head bowed as he pressed Lord John Grey tight in a fervent embrace.

I stood still, completely incapable of movement or speech. As I watched, they broke apart. Jamie's back was turned to me, but Lord John faced the hallway; he could have seen me easily, had he looked. He wasn't looking toward the hallway, though. He was staring at Jamie, and on his face was a look of such naked hunger that the blood rushed to my own cheeks when I saw it.

I dropped my fan. I saw the Governor's head turn, startled at the sound. Then I was running down the hall, back toward the salon, my heartbeat drumming in my ears.

I shot through the door into the salon and came to a halt behind a potted palm, heart pounding. The wrought-iron chandeliers were thick with beeswax candles, and pine torches burned brightly on the walls, but even so, the corners of the room were dark. I stood in the shadows, trembling.

My hands were cold, and I felt slightly sick. What in the name of God was going on?

The Governor's shock at learning that I was Jamie's wife was now at least partially explained; that one glimpse of unguarded, painful yearning had told me exactly how matters stood on his side. Jamie was another question altogether.

He was the Governor of Ardsmuir prison, he had said, casually. And less casually, on another occasion, *D'ye ken what men in prison do?*

I did know, but I would have sworn on Brianna's head that Jamie didn't; hadn't, couldn't, under any circumstances whatever. At least I would have sworn that before tonight. I closed my eyes, chest heaving, and tried not to think of what I had seen.

I couldn't, of course. And yet, the more I thought of it, the more impossible it seemed. The memories of Jack Randall might have faded with the physical scars he had left, but I could not believe that they would ever fade sufficiently for Jamie to tolerate the physical attentions of another man, let alone to welcome them.

But if he knew Grey so intimately as to make what I had witnessed plausible in the name of friendship alone, then why had he not told me of him before? Why go to such lengths to see the man, as soon as he learned that Grey was in Jamaica? My stomach dropped once more, and the feeling of sickness returned. I wanted badly to sit down.

As I leaned against the wall, trembling in the shadows, the door to the Governor's quarters opened, and the Governor came out, returning to his party. His face was flushed and his eyes shone. I could at that moment easily have murdered him, had I anything more lethal than a hairpin to hand.

The door opened again a few minutes later, and Jamie emerged, no more than six feet away. His mask of cool reserve was in place, but I knew him well enough to see the marks of a strong emotion under it. But while I could see it, I couldn't interpret it. Excitement? Apprehension? Fear and joy mingled? Something else? I had simply never seen him look that way before.

He didn't seek conversation or refreshments, but instead began to stroll about the room, obviously looking for someone. For me.

I swallowed heavily. I couldn't face him—not in front of a crowd. I stayed where I was, watching him, until he finally went out onto the terrace. Then I left my hiding place, and crossed the room as quickly as I could, heading for the refuge of the retiring room. At least there I would be able to sit down for a moment.

I pushed open the heavy door and stepped inside, relaxing at once as the warm, comforting scents of women's perfume and powder surrounded me. Then the other smell struck me. It too was a familiar scent—one of the smells of my profession. But not expected here.

The retiring room was still quiet; the loud rumble from the salon had dropped abruptly to a faint murmur, like a far-off thunderstorm. It was, however, no longer a place of refuge.

Mina Alcott lay sprawled across the red velvet chaise, her head hanging backward over the edge, her skirts in disarray about her neck. Her eyes were open, fixed in upside-down surprise. The blood from her severed throat had turned the velvet black beneath her, and dripped down into a large pool beneath her head. Her light brown hair had come loose from its dressing, the matted ends of her ringlets dangling in the puddle.

I stood frozen, too paralyzed even to call for help. Then I heard the sound of gay voices in the hallway outside, and the door pushed open. There was a moment's silence as the women behind me saw it too.

Light from the corridor spilled through the door and across the floor, and in the moment before the screaming began, I saw the footprints leading toward the window—the small neat prints of a felt-soled foot, outlined in blood.

59

In Which Much Is Revealed

They had taken Jamie somewhere. I, shaking and incoherent, had been put—with a certain amount of irony—in the Governor's private office with Marsali, who insisted on trying to bathe my face with a damp towel, in spite of my resistance.

"They canna think Da had anything to do with it!" she said, for the fifth time.

"They don't." I finally pulled myself together enough to talk to her. "But they think Mr. Willoughby did—and Jamie brought him here."

She stared at me, wide-eyed with horror.

"Mr. Willoughby? But he couldn't!"

"I wouldn't have thought so." I felt as though someone had been beating me with a club; everything ached. I sat slumped on a small velvet love seat, aimlessly twirling a glass of brandy between my hands, unable to drink it.

I couldn't even decide what I *ought* to feel, let alone sort out the conflicting events and emotions of the evening. My mind kept jumping between the grisly scene in the retiring room, and the tableau I had seen a half-hour earlier, in this very room.

I sat looking at the Governor's big desk. I could still see the two of them, Jamie and Lord John, as though they had been painted on the wall before me.

"I just don't believe it," I said out loud, and felt slightly better for the saying.

"Neither do I," said Marsali. She was pacing the floor, her footsteps changing from the click of heels on parquet to a muffled thump as she hit the flowered carpet. "He can't have! I ken he's a heathen, but we've lived wi' the man! We *know* him!"

Did we? Did I know Jamie? I would have sworn I did, and yet . . . I kept remembering what he had said to me at the brothel, during our first night together. *Will ye take me, and risk the man that I am, for the sake of the man ye knew?* I had thought then—and since—that there was not so much difference between them. But if I were wrong?

"I'm not wrong!" I muttered, clutching my glass fiercely. "I'm not!" If Jamie could take Lord John Grey as a lover, and hide it from me, he wasn't remotely the man I thought he was. There had to be some other explanation.

He didn't tell you about Laoghaire, said an insidious little voice inside my head.

"That's different," I said to it stoutly.

"What's different?" Marsali was looking at me in surprise.

"I don't know; don't mind me." I brushed a hand across my face, trying to wipe away confusion and weariness. "It's taking them a long time."

The walnut case-clock had struck two o'clock in the morning before the door of the office opened and Fergus came in, accompanied by a grim-looking militiaman.

Fergus was somewhat the worse for wear; most of the powder had gone from his hair, shaken onto the shoulders of his dark blue coat like dandruff. What was left gave his hair a grayish cast, as though he had aged twenty years overnight. No surprise; I felt as though I had.

"We can go now, *chèrie,*" he said quietly to Marsali. He turned to me. "Will you come with us, milady, or wait for milord?"

"I'll wait," I said. I wasn't going to bed until I had seen Jamie, no matter how long it took.

"I will have the carriage return for you, then," he said, and put a hand on Marsali's back to usher her out.

The militiaman said something under his breath as they passed him. I didn't catch it, but evidently Fergus did. He stiffened, eyes narrowing, and turned back toward the man. The militiaman rocked up onto the balls of his feet, smiling evilly and looking expectant. Clearly he would like nothing better than an excuse to hit Fergus.

To his surprise, Fergus smiled charmingly at him, square white teeth gleaming.

"My thanks, *mon ami,*" he said, "for your assistance in this most trying situation." He thrust out a black-gloved hand, which the militiaman accepted in surprise.

Then Fergus jerked his arm suddenly backward. There was a brief rip, and a pattering sound, as a small stream of bran struck the parquet floor.

"Keep it," he told the militiaman graciously. "A small token of my appreciation." And then they were gone, leaving the man slack-jawed, staring down in horror at the apparently severed hand in his grasp.

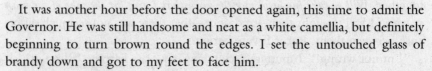

It was another hour before the door opened again, this time to admit the Governor. He was still handsome and neat as a white camellia, but definitely beginning to turn brown round the edges. I set the untouched glass of brandy down and got to my feet to face him.

"Where is Jamie?"

"Still being questioned by Captain Jacobs, the militia commander." He sank into his chair, looking bemused. "I had no notion he spoke French so remarkably well."

"I don't suppose you know him all that well," I said, deliberately baiting. What I wanted badly to know was just how well he *did* know Jamie. He didn't rise to it, though; merely took off his formal wig and laid it aside, running a hand through his damp blond hair with relief.

"Can he keep up such an impersonation, do you think?" he asked, frowning, and I realized that he was so occupied with thoughts of the murder and of Jamie that he was paying little, if any, attention to me.

"Yes," I said shortly. "Where do they have him?" I got up, heading for the door.

"In the formal parlor," he said. "But I don't think you should—"

Not pausing to listen, I yanked open the door and poked my head into the hall, then hastily drew it back and slammed the door.

Coming down the hall was the Admiral I had met in the receiving line, face set in lines of gravity suitable to the situation. Admirals I could deal with. However, he was accompanied by a flotilla of junior officers, and among the entourage I had spotted a face I knew, though he was now wearing the uniform of a first lieutenant, instead of an oversized captain's coat.

He was shaved and rested, but his face was puffy and discolored; someone had beaten him up in the not too distant past. Despite the differences in his appearance, I had not the slightest difficulty in recognizing Thomas Leonard. I had the distinct feeling that he wouldn't have any trouble recognizing me, either, violet silk notwithstanding.

I looked frantically about the office for someplace to hide, but short of crawling into the kneehole of the desk, there was no place at all. The Governor was watching me, fair brows raised in astonishment.

"What—" he began, but I rounded on him, finger to my lips.

"Don't give me away, if you value Jamie's life!" I hissed melodramatically, and so saying, flung myself onto the velvet love seat, snatched up the damp towel and dropped it on my face, and—with a superhuman effort of will— forced all my limbs to go limp.

I heard the door open, and the Admiral's high, querulous voice.

"Lord John—" he began, and then evidently noticed my supine form, for he broke off and resumed in a slightly lower voice, "Oh! I collect you are engaged?"

"Not precisely engaged, Admiral, no." Grey had fast reflexes, I would say that for him; he sounded perfectly self-possessed, as though he were quite used to being found in custody of unconscious females. "The lady was overcome by the shock of discovering the body."

"Oh!" said the Admiral again, this time dripping with sympathy. "I quite see that. Beastly shock for a lady, to be sure." He hesitated, then dropping his voice to a sort of hoarse whisper, said, "D'you think she's asleep?"

"I should think so," the Governor assured him. "She's had enough brandy to fell a horse." My fingers twitched, but I managed to lie still.

"Oh, quite. Best thing for shock, brandy." The Admiral went on whispering, sounding like a rusted hinge. "Meant to tell you I have sent to Antigua for additional troops—quite at your disposal—guards, search the town—if the militia don't find the fellow first," he added.

"I hope they may not," said a viciously determined voice among the officers. "I'd like to catch the yellow bugger myself. There wouldn't be enough of him left to hang, believe me!"

A deep murmur of approval at this sentiment went through the men, to be sternly quelled by the Admiral.

"Your sentiments do you credit, gentlemen," he said, "but the law will be observed in all respects. You will make that clear to the troops in your command; when the miscreant is taken, he is to be brought to the Governor, and justice will be properly executed, I assure you." I didn't like the way he emphasized the word "executed," but he got a grudging chorus of assent from his officers.

The Admiral, having delivered this order in his ordinary voice, dropped back into a whisper to take his leave.

"I shall be staying in the town, at MacAdams' Hotel," he croaked. "Do not hesitate to send to me for any assistance, Your Excellency."

There was a general shuffle and murmur as the naval officers took their leave, observing discretion for the sake of my slumbers. Then came the sound of a single pair of footsteps, and then the *whoosh* and creak of someone settling heavily into a chair. There was silence for a moment.

Then Lord John said "You can get up now, if you wish. I am supposing that you are not in fact prostrate with shock," he added, ironically. "Somehow I suspect that a mere murder would not be sufficient to discompose a woman who could deal single-handedly with a typhoid epidemic."

I removed the towel from my face and swung my feet off the chaise, sitting up to face him. He was leaning on his desk, chin in his hands, staring at me.

"There are shocks," I said precisely, smoothing back my damp curls and giving him an eyeball, "and then there are shocks. If you know what I mean."

He looked surprised; then a flicker of understanding came into his expression. He reached into the drawer of his desk, and pulled out my fan, white silk embroidered with violets.

"This is yours, I suppose? I found it in the corridor." His mouth twisted wryly as he looked at me. "I see. I suppose, then, you will have some notion of how your appearance earlier this evening affected *me*."

"I doubt it very much," I said. My fingers were still icy, and I felt as though I had swallowed some large, cold object that pressed uncomfortably under my breastbone. I breathed deeply, trying to force it down, to no avail. "You didn't know that Jamie was married?"

He blinked, but not in time to keep me from seeing a small grimace of pain, as though someone had struck him suddenly across the face.

"I knew he *had* been married," he corrected. He dropped his hands, fiddling aimlessly with the small objects that littered his desk. "He told me— or gave me to understand, at least—that you were dead."

Grey picked up a small silver paperweight, and turned it over and over in his hands, eyes fixed on the gleaming surface. A large sapphire was set in it, winking blue in the candlelight.

"Has he never mentioned me?" he asked softly. I wasn't sure whether the undertone in his voice was pain or anger. Despite myself, I felt some small sense of pity for him.

"Yes, he did," I said. "He said you were his friend." He glanced up, the fine-cut face lightening a bit.

"Did he?"

"You have to understand," I said. "He—I—we were separated by the war, the Rising. Each of us thought the other was dead. I found him again only— my God, was it only four months ago?" I felt staggered, and not only by the events of the evening. I felt as though I had lived several lifetimes since the day I had opened the door of the printshop in Edinburgh, to find A. Malcolm bending over his press.

The lines of stress in Grey's face eased a little.

"I see," he said slowly. "So—you have not seen him since—my God, that's twenty years!" He stared at me, dumbfounded. "And four months? Why—how—" He shook his head, brushing away the questions.

"Well, that's of no consequence just now. But he did not tell you—that is —has he not told you about Willie?"

I stared at him blankly.

"Who's Willie?"

Instead of explaining, he bent and opened the drawer of his desk. He pulled out a small object and laid it on the desk, motioning me to come closer.

It was a portrait, an oval miniature, set in a carved frame of some fine-grained dark wood. I looked at the face, and sat down abruptly, my knees gone to water. I was only dimly aware of Grey's face, floating above the desk like a cloud on the horizon, as I picked up the miniature to look at it more closely.

He might have been Bree's brother, was my first thought. The second, coming with the force of a blow to the solar plexus, was "My God in heaven, he *is* Bree's brother!"

There couldn't be much doubt about it. The boy in the portrait was perhaps nine or ten, with a childish tenderness still lingering about his face, and his hair was a soft chestnut brown, not red. But the slanted blue eyes looked out boldly over a straight nose a fraction of an inch too long, and the high Viking cheekbones pressed tight against smooth skin. The tilt of the head held the same confident carriage as that of the man who had given him that face.

My hands trembled so violently that I nearly dropped it. I set it back on the desk, but kept my hand over it, as though it might leap up and bite me. Grey was watching me, not without sympathy.

"You didn't know?" he said.

"Who—" My voice was hoarse with shock, and I had to stop and clear my throat. "Who is his mother?"

Grey hesitated, eyeing me closely, then shrugged slightly.

"Was. She's dead."

"Who was she?" The ripples of shock were still spreading from an epicenter in my stomach, making the crown of my head tingle and my toes go numb, but at least my vocal cords were coming back under my control. I could hear Jenny saying, *He's no the sort of man should sleep alone, aye?* Evidently he wasn't.

"Her name was Geneva Dunsany," Grey said. "My wife's sister."

My mind was reeling, in an effort to make sense of all this, and I suppose I was less than tactful.

"Your *wife?*" I said, goggling at him. He flushed deeply and looked away. If I had been in any doubt about the nature of the look I had seen him give Jamie, I wasn't any longer.

"I think you had better bloody well explain to me just what you have to do with Jamie, and this Geneva, and this boy," I said, picking up the portrait once more.

He raised one brow, cool and reserved; he had been shocked, too, but the shock was wearing off.

"I cannot see that I am under any particular obligation to do so," he said.

I fought back the urge to rake my nails down his face, but the impulse must have shown on my face, for he pushed back his chair and got his feet under him, ready to move quickly. He eyed me warily across the expanse of dark wood.

I took several deep breaths, unclenched my fists, and spoke as calmly as I could.

"Right. You're not. But I would appreciate it very much if you did. And why did you show me the picture if you didn't mean me to know?" I added. "Since I know that much, I'll certainly find out the rest from Jamie. You might as well tell me your side of it now." I glanced at the window; the slice of sky that showed between the half-open shutters was still a velvet black, with no sign of dawn. "There's time."

He breathed deeply, and laid down the paperweight. "I suppose there is." He jerked his head abruptly at the decanter. "Will you have brandy?"

"I will," I said promptly, "and I strongly suggest you have some, too. I expect you need it as much as I do."

A slight smile showed briefly at the corner of his mouth.

"Is that a medical opinion, Mrs. Malcolm?" he asked dryly.

"Absolutely," I said.

This small truce established, he sat back, rolling his beaker of brandy slowly between his hands.

"You said Jamie mentioned me to you," he said. I must have flinched slightly at his use of Jamie's name, for he frowned at me. "Would you prefer that I referred to him by his surname?" he said, coldly. "I should scarcely know which to use, under the circumstances."

"No." I waved it away, and took a sip of brandy. "Yes, he mentioned you. He said you had been the Governor of the prison at Ardsmuir, and that you were a friend—and that he could trust you," I added reluctantly. Possibly Jamie felt he could trust Lord John Grey, but I was not so sanguine.

The smile this time was not quite so brief.

"I am glad to hear that," Grey said softly. He looked down into the amber liquid in his cup, swirling it gently to release its heady bouquet. He took a sip, then set the cup down with decision.

"I met him at Ardsmuir, as he said," he began. "And when the prison was shut down and the other prisoners sold to indenture in America, I arranged that Jamie should be paroled instead to a place in England, called Helwater, owned by friends of my family." He looked at me, hesitating, then added simply, "I could not bear the thought of never seeing him again, you see."

In a few brief words, he acquainted me with the bare facts of Geneva's death and Willie's birth.

"Was he in love with her?" I asked. The brandy was doing its bit to warm my hands and feet, but it didn't touch the large cold object in my stomach.

"He has never spoken to me of Geneva," Grey said. He gulped the last of his brandy, coughed, and reached to pour another cup. It was only when he finished this operation that he looked at me again, and added, "But I doubt it, having known her." His mouth twisted wryly.

"He never told me about Willie, either, but there was a certain amount of gossip about Geneva and old Lord Ellesmere, and by the time the boy was four or five, the resemblance made it quite clear who his father was—to anyone who cared to look." He took another deep swallow of brandy. "I suspect that my mother-in-law knows, but of course she would never breathe a word."

"She wouldn't?"

He stared at me over the rim of his cup.

"No, would you? If it were a choice of your only grandchild being either the ninth Earl of Ellesmere, and heir to one of the wealthiest estates in England, or the penniless bastard of a Scottish criminal?"

"I see." I drank some more of my own brandy, trying to imagine Jamie with a young English girl named Geneva—and succeeding all too well.

"Quite," Grey said dryly. "Jamie saw, too. And very wisely arranged to leave Helwater before it became obvious to everyone."

"And that's where you come back into the story, is it?" I asked.

He nodded, eyes closed. The Residence was quiet, though there was a certain distant stir that made me aware that people were still about.

"That's right," he said. "Jamie gave the boy to me."

The stable at Ellesmere was well-built; cozy in the winter, it was a cool haven in summer. The big bay stallion flicked its ears lazily at a passing fly, but stood stolidly content, enjoying the attentions of his groom.

"Isobel is most displeased with you," Grey said.

"Is she?" Jamie's voice was indifferent. There was no need any longer to worry about displeasing any of the Dunsanys.

"She said you had told Willie you were leaving, which upset him dreadfully. He's been howling all day."

Jamie's face was turned away, but Grey saw the faint tightening at the side of his throat. He rocked backward, leaning against the stable wall as he watched the curry comb come down and down and down in hard, even strokes that left dark trails across the shimmering coat.

"Surely it would have been easier to say nothing to the boy?" Grey said quietly.

"I suppose it would—for Lady Isobel." Fraser turned to put up the curry comb, and slapped a hand on the stallion's rump in dismissal. Grey thought there was an air of finality in the gesture; tomorrow Jamie would be gone. He felt a slight thickening in his own throat, but swallowed it. He rose and followed Fraser toward the door of the stall.

"Jamie—" he said, putting his hand on Fraser's shoulder. The Scot swung round, his features hastily readjusting themselves, but not fast enough to hide the misery in his eyes. He stood still, looking down at the Englishman.

"You're right to go," Grey said. Alarm flared in Fraser's eyes, quickly supplanted by wariness.

"Am I?" he said.

"Anyone with half an eye could see it," Grey said dryly. "If anyone ever actually looked at a groom, someone would have noticed long before now." He glanced back at the bay stallion, and

cocked one brow. "Some sires stamp their get. I have the distinct impression that any offspring of yours would be unmistakable."

Jamie said nothing, but Grey fancied that he had grown a shade paler than usual.

"Surely you can see—well, no, perhaps not," he corrected himself, "I don't suppose you have a looking glass, have you?"

Jamie shook his head mechanically. "No," he said absently. "I shave in the reflection from the trough." He drew in a deep breath, and let it out slowly.

"Aye, well," he said. He glanced toward the house, where the French doors were standing open onto the lawn. Willie was accustomed to play there after lunch on fine days.

Fraser turned to him with sudden decision. "Will ye walk with me?" he said.

Not pausing for an answer, he set off past the stable, turning down the lane that led from the paddock to the lower pasture. It was nearly a quarter-mile before he came to a halt, in a sunny clearing by a clump of willows, near the edge of the mere.

Grey found himself puffing slightly from the quick pace—too much soft living in London, he chided himself. Fraser, of course, was not even sweating, despite the warmth of the day.

Without preamble, turning to face Grey, he said, "I wish to ask a favor of ye." The slanted blue eyes were direct as the man himself.

"If you think I would tell anyone . . ." Grey began, then shook his head. "Surely you don't think I could do such a thing. After all, I have known—or at least suspected—for some time."

"No." A faint smile lifted Jamie's mouth. "No, I dinna think ye would. But I would ask ye . . ."

"Yes," Grey said promptly. The corner of Jamie's mouth twitched.

"Ye dinna wish to know what it is first?"

"I should imagine that I know; you wish me to look out for Willie; perhaps to send you word of his welfare."

Jamie nodded.

"Aye, that's it." He glanced up the slope, to where the house lay half-hidden in its nest of fiery maples. "It's an imposition, maybe, to ask ye to come all the way from London to see him now and then."

"Not at all," Grey interrupted. "I came this afternoon to give you some news of my own; I am to be married."

"Married?" The shock was plain on Fraser's face. "To a woman?"

"I think there are not many alternatives," Grey replied dryly. "But yes, since you ask, to a woman. To the Lady Isobel."

"Christ, man! Ye canna do that!"

"I can," Grey assured him. He grimaced. "I made trial of my capacity in London; be assured that I shall make her an adequate husband. You needn't necessarily enjoy the act in order to perform it —or perhaps you were aware of that?"

There was a small reflexive twitch at the corner of Jamie's eye; not quite a flinch, but enough for Grey to notice. Jamie opened his mouth, then closed it again and shook his head, obviously thinking better of what he had been about to say.

"Dunsany is growing too old to take a hand in the running of the estate," Grey pointed out. "Gordon is dead, and Isobel and her mother cannot manage the place alone. Our families have known each other for decades. It is an entirely suitable match."

"Is it, then?" The sardonic skepticism in Jamie's voice was clear. Grey turned to him, fair skin flushing as he answered sharply.

"It is. There is more to a marriage than carnal love. A great deal more."

Fraser swung sharply away. He strode to the edge of the mere, and stood, boots sunk in the reedy mud, looking over the ruffled waves for some time. Grey waited patiently, taking the time to unribbon his hair and reorder the thick blond mass.

At long last, Fraser came back, walking slowly, head down as though still thinking. Face-to-face with Grey he looked up again.

"You are right," he said quietly. "I have no right to think ill of you, if ye mean no dishonor to the lady."

"Certainly not," Grey said. "Besides," he added more cheerfully, "it means I will be here permanently, to see to Willie."

"You mean to resign your commission, then?" One copper eyebrow flicked upward.

"Yes," Grey said. He smiled, a little ruefully. "It will be a relief, in a way. I was not meant for army life, I think."

Fraser seemed to be thinking. "I should be . . . grateful, then," he said, "if you would stand as stepfather to—to my son." He had likely never spoken the word aloud before, and the sound of it seemed to shock him. "I . . . would be obliged to you." Jamie sounded as though his collar were too tight, though in fact his shirt was open at the throat. Grey looked curiously at him, and saw that his countenance was slowly turning a dark and painful red.

"In return . . . If you want . . . I mean, I would be willing to . . . that is . . ."

Grey suppressed the sudden desire to laugh. He laid a light hand on the big Scot's arm, and saw Jamie brace himself not to flinch at the touch.

"My dear Jamie," he said, torn between laughter and exaspera-

tion. "Are you actually offering me your body in payment for my promise to look after Willie?"

Fraser's face was red to the roots of his hair.

"Aye, I am," he snapped, tight-lipped. "D'ye want it, or no?"

At this, Grey did laugh, in long gasping whoops, finally having to sit down on the grassy bank in order to recover himself.

"Oh, dear God," he said at last, wiping his eyes. "That I should live to hear an offer like that!"

Fraser stood above him, looking down, the morning light silhouetting him, lighting his hair in flames against the pale blue sky. Grey thought he could see a slight twitch of the wide mouth in the darkened face—humor, tempered with a profound relief.

"Ye dinna want me, then?"

Grey got to his feet, dusting the seat of his breeches. "I shall probably want you to the day I die," he said matter-of-factly. "But tempted as I am—" He shook his head, brushing wet grass from his hands.

"Do you really think that I would demand—or accept—any payment for such a service?" he asked. "Really, I should feel my honor most grossly insulted by that offer, save that I know the depth of feeling which prompted it."

"Aye, well," Jamie muttered. "I didna mean to insult ye."

Grey was not sure at this point whether to laugh or cry. Instead, he reached a hand up and gently touched Jamie's cheek, fading now to its normal pale bronze. More quietly, he said, "Besides, you cannot give me what you do not have."

Grey felt, rather than saw, the slight relaxation of tension in the tall body facing him.

"You shall have my friendship," Jamie said softly, "if that has any value to ye."

"A very great value indeed." The two men stood silent together for a moment, then Grey sighed and turned to look up at the sun. "It's getting late. I suppose you will have a great many things to do today?"

Jamie cleared his throat. "Aye, I have. I suppose I should be about my business."

"Yes, I suppose so."

Grey tugged down the points of his waistcoat, ready to go. But Jamie lingered awkwardly a moment, and then, as though suddenly making up his mind to it, stepped forward and bending down, cupped Grey's face between his hands.

Grey felt the big hands warm on the skin of his face, light and strong as the brush of an eagle's feather, and then Jamie Fraser's

soft wide mouth touched his own. There was a fleeting impression of
tenderness and strength held in check, the faint taste of ale and
fresh-baked bread. Then it was gone, and John Grey stood blinking
in the brilliant sun.

"Oh," he said.

Jamie gave him a shy, crooked smile.

"Aye, well," he said. "I suppose I'm maybe not poisoned." He
turned then, and disappeared into the screen of willows, leaving
Lord John Grey alone by the mere.

The Governor was quiet for a moment. Then he looked up with a bleak smile.

"That was the first time that he ever touched me willingly," he said quietly. "And the last—until this evening, when I gave him the other copy of that miniature."

I sat completely motionless, the brandy glass unregarded in my hands. I wasn't sure *what* I felt; shock, fury, horror, jealousy, and pity all washed through me in successive waves, mingling in eddies of confused emotion.

A woman had been violently done to death nearby, within the last few hours. And yet the scene in the retiring room seemed unreal by comparison with that miniature; a small and unimportant picture, painted in tones of red. For the moment, neither Lord John nor I was concerned with crime or justice—or with anything beyond what lay between us.

The Governor was examining my face, with considerable absorption.

"I suppose I should have recognized you on the ship," he said. "But of course, at the time, I had thought you long dead."

"Well, it was dark," I said, rather stupidly. I shoved a hand through my curls, feeling dizzy from brandy and sleeplessness. Then I realized what he had said.

"Recognized me? But you'd never met me!"

He hesitated, then nodded.

"Do you recall a dark wood, near Carryarrick in the Scottish Highlands, twenty years ago? And a young boy with a broken arm? You set it for me." He lifted one arm in demonstration.

"Jesus H. Roosevelt Christ." I picked up the brandy and took a swallow that made me cough and gasp. I blinked at him, eyes watering. Knowing now who he was, I could make out the fine, light bones and see the slighter, softer outline of the boy he had been.

"Yours were the first woman's breasts I had ever seen," he said wryly. "It was a considerable shock."

"From which you appear to have recovered," I said, rather coldly. "You seem to have forgiven Jamie for breaking your arm and threatening to shoot you, at least."

He flushed slightly, and set down his beaker.

"I—well—yes," he said, abruptly.

We sat there for quite some time, neither of us having any idea what to say. He took a breath once or twice, as though about to say something, but then abandoned it. At last, he closed his eyes as though commending his soul to God, opened them and looked at me.

"Do you know—" he began, then stopped. He looked down at his clenched hands, then, not at me. A blue stone winked on one knuckle, bright as a teardrop.

"Do you know," he said again, softly, addressing his hands, "what it is to love someone, and never—never!—be able to give them peace, or joy, or happiness?"

He looked up then, eyes filled with pain. "To know that you cannot give them happiness, not through any fault of yours or theirs, but only because you were not born the right person for them?"

I sat quiet, seeing not his, but another handsome face; dark, not fair. Not feeling the warm breath of the tropical night, but the icy hand of a Boston winter. Seeing the pulse of light like heart's blood, spilling across the cold snow of hospital linens.

. . . only because you were not born the right person for them.

"I know," I whispered, hands clenched in my lap. I had told Frank— Leave me. But he could not, no more than I could love him rightly, having found my match elsewhere.

Oh, Frank, I said, silently. Forgive me.

"I suppose I am asking whether you believe in fate," Lord John went on. The ghost of a smile wavered on his face. "You, of all people, would seem best suited to say."

"You'd think so, wouldn't you?" I said bleakly. "But I don't know, any more than you."

He shook his head, then reached out and picked up the miniature.

"I have been more fortunate than most, I suppose," he said quietly. "There was the one thing he would take from me." His expression softened as he looked down into the face of the boy in the palm of his hand. "And he has given me something most precious in return."

Without thinking, my hand spread out across my belly. Jamie had given me that same precious gift—and at the same great cost to himself.

The sound of footsteps came down the hall, muffled by the carpet. There was a sharp rap at the door, and a militiaman stuck his head into the office.

"Is the lady recovered yet?" he asked. "Captain Jacobs has finished his questions, and Monsieur Alexandre's carriage has returned."

I got hastily to my feet.

"Yes, I'm fine." I turned to the Governor, not knowing what to say to him. "I—thank you for—that is—"

He bowed formally to me, coming around the desk to see me out.

"I regret extremely that you should have been subjected to such a shocking experience, ma'am," he said, with no trace of anything but diplomatic regret in his voice. He had resumed his official manner, smooth and polished as his parquet floors.

I followed the militiaman, but at the door I turned impulsively.

"When we met, that night aboard the *Porpoise*—I'm glad you didn't know who I was. I . . . liked you. Then."

He stood for a second, polite, remote. Then the mask dropped away.

"I liked you, too," he said quietly. "Then."

I felt as though I were riding next to a stranger. The light was beginning to gray toward dawn, and even in the dimness of the coach, I could see Jamie sitting opposite me, his face drawn with weariness. He had taken off the ridiculous wig as soon as we drove away from Government House, discarding the facade of the polished Frenchman to let the disheveled Scot beneath show through. His unbound hair lay in waves over his shoulders, dark in that predawn light that robs everything of color.

"Do you think he did it?" I asked at last, only for something to say.

His eyes were closed. At this, they opened and he shrugged slightly.

"I don't know," he said. He sounded exhausted. "I have asked myself that a thousand times tonight—and been asked it even more." He rubbed his knuckles hard over his forehead.

"I canna imagine a man I know to do such a thing. And yet . . . well, ye ken he'll do anything when he's drink taken. And he's killed before, drunk— you'll mind the Customs man at the brothel?" I nodded, and he leaned forward, elbows on his knees, sinking his head into his hands.

"This is different, though," he said. "I canna think—but maybe so. Ye ken what he said about women on the ship. And if this Mrs. Alcott was to have toyed wi' him—"

"She did," I said. "I saw her."

He nodded without looking up. "So did any number of other people. But if she led him to think she meant more than she maybe did, and then perhaps she put him off, maybe laughed at him . . . and him fu' as a puggie wi' drink, and knives to hand on every wall of the place . . ." He sighed and sat up.

"God knows," he said bleakly. "I don't." He ran a hand backward through his hair, smoothing it.

"There's something else about it. I had to tell them that I scarcely knew Willoughby—that we'd met him on the packet boat from Martinique, and thought it kindly to introduce him about, but didna ken a thing of where he came from, or the sort of fellow he truly was."

"Did they believe it?"

He glanced at me wryly.

"So far. But the packet boat comes in again in six days—at which point, they'll question the captain and discover that he's never laid eyes on Monsieur Etienne Alexandre and his wife, let alone a wee yellow murdering fiend."

"That might be a trifle awkward," I observed, thinking of Fergus and the militiaman. "We're already rather unpopular on Mr. Willoughby's account."

"Nothing to what we will be, if six days pass and they havena found him," he assured me. "Six days is also maybe as long as it will take for gossip to spread from Blue Mountain House to Kingston about the MacIvers' visitors —for ye ken the servants there all know who we are."

"Damn."

He smiled briefly at that, and my heart turned over to see it.

"You've a nice way wi' words, Sassenach. Aye, well, all it means is that we must find Ian within six days. I shall go to Rose Hall at once, but I think I must just have a wee rest before setting out." He yawned widely behind his hand and shook his head, blinking.

We didn't speak again until after we had arrived at Blue Mountain House and made our way on tiptoe through the slumbering house to our room.

I changed in the dressing room, dropping the heavy stays on the floor with relief, and taking out the pins to let my hair fall free. Wearing only a silk chemise, I came into the bedroom, to see Jamie standing by the French door in his shirt, looking out over the lagoon.

He turned when he heard me, and beckoned, putting a finger to his lips.

"Come see," he whispered.

There was a small herd of manatees in the lagoon, big gray bodies gliding under the dark crystal water, rising gleaming like smooth, wet rocks. Birds were beginning to call in the trees near the house; besides this, the only sound was the frequent *whoosh* of the manatees' breath as they rose for air, and now and then an eerie sound like a hollow, distant wail, as they called to each other.

We watched them in silence, side by side. The lagoon began to turn green as the first rays of sun touched its surface. In that state of extreme fatigue where every sense is preternaturally heightened, I was as aware of Jamie as though I were touching him.

John Grey's revelations had relieved me of most of my fears and doubts— and yet there remained the fact that Jamie had not told me about his son. Of course he had reasons—and good ones—for his secrecy, but did he not think he could trust me to keep his secret? It occurred to me suddenly that perhaps he had kept quiet because of the boy's mother. Perhaps he had loved her, in spite of Grey's impressions.

She was dead; could it matter if he had? The answer was that it did. I had thought Jamie dead for twenty years, and it had made no difference at all in what I felt for him. What if he had loved this young English girl in such a way? I swallowed a small lump in my throat, trying to find the courage to ask him.

His face was abstracted, a small frown creasing his forehead, despite the dawning beauty of the lagoon.

"What are you thinking?" I asked at last, unable to ask for reassurance, fearing to ask for the truth.

"It's only that I had a thought," he answered, still staring out at the manatees. "About Willoughby, aye?"

The events of the night seemed far away and unimportant. Yet murder had been done.

"What was that?"

"Well, I couldna think at first that Willoughby could do such a thing— how could any man?" He paused, drawing a finger through the light mist of condensation that formed on the windowpanes as the sun rose. "And yet . . ." He turned to face me.

"Perhaps I can see." His face was troubled. "He was alone—verra much alone."

"A stranger, in a strange land," I said quietly, remembering the poems, painted in the open secrecy of bold black ink, sent flying toward a long-lost home, committed to the sea on wings of white paper.

"Aye, that's it." He stopped to think, rubbing a hand slowly through his hair, gleaming copper in the new daylight. "And when a man is alone that way—well, it's maybe no decent to say it, but making love to a woman is maybe the only thing will make him forget it for a time."

He looked down, turning his hands over, stroking the length of his scarred middle finger with the index finger of his left hand.

"That's what made me wed Laoghaire," he said quietly. "Not Jenny's nagging. Not pity for her or the wee lassies. Not even a pair of aching balls." His mouth turned up briefly at one corner, then relaxed. "Only needing to forget I was alone," he finished softly.

He turned restlessly, back to the window.

"So I am thinking that if the Chinee came to her, wanting that—needing that—and she wouldna take him . . ." He shrugged, staring out across the cool green of the lagoon. "Aye, maybe he could have done it," he said.

I stood beside him. Out in the center of the lagoon, a single manatee drifted lazily to the surface, turning on her back to hold the infant on her chest toward the sunlight.

He was silent for several minutes, and I was as well, not knowing how to take the conversation back to what I had seen and heard at Government House.

I felt rather than saw him swallow, and he turned from the window to face me. There were lines of tiredness in his face, but his expression was filled with a sort of determination—the sort of look he wore facing battle.

"Claire," he said, and at once I stiffened. He called me by my name only when he was most serious. "Claire, I must tell ye something."

"What?" I had been trying to think how to ask, but suddenly I didn't want to hear. I took half a step back, away from him, but he grabbed my arm.

He had something hidden in his fist. He took my unresisting hand and put the object into it. Without looking, I knew what it was; I could feel the carving of the delicate oval frame and the slight roughness of the painted surface.

"Claire." I could see the slight tremor at the side of his throat as he swallowed. "Claire—I must tell ye. I have a son."

I didn't say anything, but opened my hand. There it was; the same face I had seen in Grey's office, a childish, cocky version of the man before me.

"I should ha' told ye before." He was searching my face for some clue to my feelings, but for once, my giveaway countenance must have been perfectly blank. "I would have—only—" He took a deep breath for strength to go on.

"I havena ever told anyone about him," he said. "Not even Jenny."

That startled me enough to speak.

"Jenny doesn't know?"

He shook his head, and turned away to watch the manatees. Alarmed by our voices, they had retreated a short distance, but then had settled down again, feeding on the water weed at the edge of the lagoon.

"It was in England. It's—he's—I couldna say he was mine. He's a bastard, aye?" It might have been the rising sun that flushed his cheeks. He bit his lip and went on.

"I havena seen him since he was a wee lad. I never will see him again—except it might be in a wee painting like this." He took the small picture from me, cradling it in the palm of his hand like a baby's head. He blinked, head bent over it.

"I was afraid to tell ye," he said, low-voiced. "For fear ye would think that perhaps I'd gone about spawning a dozen bastards . . . for fear ye'd think that I wouldna care for Brianna so much, if ye kent I had another child. But I do care, Claire—a great deal more than I can tell ye." He lifted his head and looked directly at me.

"Will ye forgive me?"

"Did you—" The words almost choked me, but I had to say them. "Did you love her?"

An extraordinary expression of sadness crossed his face, but he didn't look away.

"No," he said softly. "She . . . wanted me. I should have found a way—

should have stopped her, but I could not. She wished me to lie wi' her. And I did, and . . . she died of it." He did look down then, long lashes hiding his eyes. "I am guilty of her death, before God; perhaps the more guilty—because I did not love her."

I didn't say anything, but put up a hand to touch his cheek. He pressed his own hand over it, hard, and closed his eyes. There was a gecko on the wall beside us, nearly the same color as the yellow plaster behind it, beginning to glow in the gathering daylight.

"What is he like?" I asked softly. "Your son?"

He smiled slightly, without opening his eyes.

"He's spoilt and stubborn," he said softly. "Ill-mannered. Loud. Wi' a wicked temper." He swallowed. "And braw and bonny and canty and strong," he said, so softly I could barely hear him.

"And yours," I said. His hand tightened on mine, holding it against the soft stubble of his cheek.

"And mine," he said. He took a deep breath, and I could see the glitter of tears under his closed lids.

"You should have trusted me," I said at last. He nodded, slowly, then opened his eyes, still holding my hand.

"Perhaps I should," he said quietly. "And yet I kept thinking—how should I tell ye everything, about Geneva, and Willie, and John—will ye know about John?" He frowned slightly, then relaxed as I nodded.

"He told me. About everything." His brows rose, but he went on.

"Especially after ye found out about Laoghaire. How could I tell ye, and expect ye to know the difference?"

"What difference?"

"Geneva—Willie's mother—she wanted my body," he said softly, watching the gecko's pulsing sides. "Laoghaire needed my name, and the work of my hands to keep her and her bairns." He turned his head then, dark blue eyes fixed on mine. "John—well." He lifted his shoulders and let them drop. "I couldna give him what he wanted—and he is friend enough not to ask it.

"But how shall I tell ye all these things," he said, the line of his mouth twisting. "And then say to you—it is only you I have ever loved? How should you believe me?"

The question hung in the air between us, shimmering like the reflection from the water below.

"If you say it," I said, "I'll believe you."

"You will?" He sounded faintly astonished. "Why?"

"Because you're an honest man, Jamie Fraser," I said, smiling so that I wouldn't cry. "And may the Lord have mercy on you for it."

"Only you," he said, so softly I could barely hear him. "To worship ye with my body, give ye all the service of my hands. To give ye my name, and all my heart and soul with it. Only you. Because ye will not let me lie—and yet ye love me."

I did touch him then.

"Jamie," I said softly, and laid my hand on his arm. "You aren't alone anymore."

He turned then and took me by the arms, searching my face.

"I swore to you," I said. "When we married. I didn't mean it then, but I swore—and now I mean it." I turned his hand over in both mine, feeling the thin, smooth skin at the base of his wrist, where the pulse beat under my fingers, where the blade of his dirk had cut his flesh once, and spilled his blood to mingle with mine forever.

I pressed my own wrist against his, pulse to pulse, heartbeat to heartbeat.

"Blood of my blood . . ." I whispered.

"Bone of my bone." His whisper was deep and husky. He knelt quite suddenly before me, and put his folded hands in mine; the gesture a Highlander makes when swearing loyalty to his chieftain.

"I give ye my spirit," he said, head bent over our hands.

" 'Til our life shall be done," I said softly. "But it isn't done yet, Jamie, is it?"

Then he rose and took the shift from me, and I lay back on the narrow bed naked, pulled him down to me through the soft yellow light, and took him home, and home, and home again, and we were neither one of us alone.

60

The Scent of Gemstones

Rose Hall was ten miles out of Kingston, up a steep and winding road of reddish dust that led into blue mountains. The road was overgrown, so narrow that we must ride in single file most of the way. I followed Jamie through the dark, sweet-scented caverns of cedar boughs, under trees nearly a hundred feet high. Huge ferns grew in the shade below, the fiddleheads nearly the size of real violin necks.

Everything was quiet, save for the calling of birds in the shrubbery—and even that fell silent as we passed. Jamie's horse stopped dead, once, and backed up, snorting; we waited as a tiny green snake wriggled across the path and into the undergrowth. I looked after it, but could see no farther than ten feet from the edge of the road; everything beyond was cool green shadow. I half-hoped that Mr. Willoughby had come this way—no one would ever find him, in a place like this.

The Chinaman had not been found in spite of an intensive search of the town by the island militia. The special detachment of marines from the barracks on Antigua was expected to arrive tomorrow. In the meantime, every house in Kingston was shut up like a bank vault, the owners armed to the teeth.

The mood of the town was thoroughly dangerous. Like the naval officers; it was the militia colonel's opinion that if the Chinaman were found, he would be lucky to survive long enough to be hanged.

"Be torn to pieces, I expect," Colonel Jacobs had said as he escorted us from the Residence on the night of the murder. "Have his balls ripped off and thrust down his stinking throat, I daresay," he added, with obvious grim satisfaction at the thought.

"I daresay," Jamie had murmured in French, assisting me into the carriage. I knew that the question of Mr. Willoughby was still troubling him; he had been quiet and thoughtful on the ride through the mountains. And yet there was nothing we could do. If the little Chinese was innocent, we could not save him; if he was guilty, we could not give him up. The best we might hope for was that he would not be found.

And in the meantime, we had five days to find Young Ian. If he were indeed at Rose Hall, all might be well. If he were not . . .

A fence and small gate marked the division of the plantation from the surrounding forest. Inside, the ground had been cleared, and planted in sugarcane and coffee. Some distance from the house, on a separate rise, a large, plain, mud-daub building stood, roofed with palm thatch. Dark-skinned people were going in and out, and the faint, cloying scent of burnt sugar hung over the place.

Below the refinery—or so I assumed the building to be—stood a large sugar press. A primitive-looking affair, this consisted of a pair of huge timbers crossed in the shape of an X, set on an enormous spindle, surmounting the boxlike body of the press. Two or three men were clambering over the press, but it was not working at present; the oxen who drove it were hobbled some distance away, grazing.

"How do they ever get the sugar down from here?" I asked curiously, thinking of the narrow trail we had come up. "On mules?" I brushed cedar needles off the shoulders of my coat, making myself presentable.

"No," Jamie answered absently. "They send it down the river on barges. The river's just over there, down the wee pass ye can see beyond the house." He pointed with his chin, reining up with one hand, and using the other to beat the dust of travel from the skirts of his coat.

"Ready, Sassenach?"

"As I'll ever be."

Rose Hall was a two-storied house; long and graciously proportioned, with a roof laid in expensive slates, rather than in the sheets of tin that covered most of the planters' residences. A long veranda ran all along one side of the house, with long windows and French doors opening on to it.

A great yellow rosebush grew by the front door, climbing on a trellis and spilling over the edge of the roof. The scent of its perfume was so heady that it made breathing difficult; or perhaps it was only excitement that made my breath come short and stick in my throat. I glanced around as we waited for the door to be answered, trying to catch a glimpse of any white-skinned figure near the sugar refinery above.

"Yes, sah?" A middle-aged slave woman opened the door, looking out curiously at us. She was wide-bodied, dressed in a white cotton smock, with a red turban wrapped round her head, and her skin was the deep, rich gold in the heart of the flowers on the trellis.

"Mr. and Mrs. Malcolm, to call upon Mrs. Abernathy, if ye please," Jamie said politely. The woman looked rather taken aback, as though callers were not a common occurrence, but after a moment's indecision, she nodded and stepped back, swinging the door wide.

"You be waitin' in the salon, please, sah," she said, in a soft lilt that made it "*sall*ong." "I be askin' the mistress will she see you."

It was a large room, long and graciously proportioned, lit by huge case-ment windows all down one side. At the far end of the room was the fire-place, an enormous structure with a stone overmantel and a hearth of pol-ished slates that occupied nearly the whole wall. You could have roasted an ox in it without the slightest difficulty, and the presence of a large spit suggested that the owner of the house did so on occasion.

The slave had shown us to a wicker sofa and invited us to be seated. I sat, looking about, but Jamie strolled restlessly about the room, peering through the windows that gave a view of the cane fields below the house.

It was an odd room; comfortably furnished with wicker and rattan furni-ture, well-equipped with fat, soft cushions, but ornamented with small, un-common curios. On one window ledge sat a row of silver handbells, gradu-ated from small to large. Several squat figures of stone and terra-cotta sat together on the table by my elbow; some sort of primitive fetishes or idols.

All of them were in the shape of women, hugely pregnant, or with enor-mous, rounded breasts and exaggerated hips, and all with a vivid and mildly disturbing sexuality about them. It was not a prudish age, by any means, but I wouldn't have expected to find such objects in a drawing room in any age.

Somewhat more orthodox were the Jacobite relics. A silver snuffbox, a glass flagon, a decorated fan, a large serving platter—even the large woven rug on the floor; all decorated with the square white rose of the Stuarts. That wasn't so odd—a great many Jacobites who had fled Scotland after Culloden had come to the West Indies to seek the repair of their fortunes. I found the sight encouraging. A householder with Jacobite sympathies might be wel-coming to a fellow Scot, and willing to oblige in the matter of Ian. *If he's here,* a small voice in my head warned.

Steps sounded in the inner part of the house, and there was a flutter at the door by the hearth. Jamie made a small grunting sound, as though someone had hit him, and I looked up, to see the mistress of the house step into the room.

I rose to my feet, and the small silver cup I had picked up fell to the floor with a clank.

"Kept your girlish figure, I see, Claire." Her head was tilted to one side, green eyes gleaming with amusement.

I was too paralyzed with surprise to respond aloud, but the thought drifted through my stunned mind that I couldn't say the same for her.

Geillis Duncan had always had a voluptuous abundance of creamy bosom and a generous swell of rounded hip. While still creamy-skinned, she was considerably more abundant and generous, in every dimension visible. She wore a loose muslin gown, under which the soft, thick flesh wobbled and swayed as she moved. The delicate bones of her face had long since been submerged in swelling plumpness, but the brilliant green eyes were the same, filled with malice and humor.

I took a deep breath, and got my voice back.

"I trust you won't take this the wrong way," I said, sinking slowly back onto the wicker sofa, "but why aren't you dead?"

She laughed, the silver in her voice as clear as a young girl's.

"Think I should have been, do you? Well, you're no the first—and I daresay you'll not be the last to think so, either."

Eyes creased to bright green triangles by amusement, she sank into her own chair, nodded casually to Jamie, and clapped her hands sharply to summon a servant. "Shall we have a dish of tea?" she asked me. "Do, and I'll read the leaves in your cup for ye, after. I've a reputation as a reader, after all; a fine teller o' the future, to be sure—and why not?" She laughed again, plump cheeks pinkening with mirth. If she had been as shocked by my appearance as I was at hers, she disguised it masterfully.

"Tea," she said, to the black maidservant who appeared in response to the summons. "The special kind in the blue tin, aye? And the bittie cakes wi' the nuts in, too."

"You'll take a bite?" she asked, turning back to me. " 'Tis something of an occasion, after all. I did wonder," she said, tilting her head to one side, like a gull judging the chances of snatching a fish, "whether our paths might cross again, after that day at Cranesmuir."

My heart was beginning to slow, the shock overcome in a great wave of curiosity. I could feel the questions bubbling up by the dozens, and picked one off the top at random.

"Did you know me?" I asked. "When you met me in Cranesmuir?"

She shook her head, the strands of cream-white hair coming loose from their pins and sliding down her neck. She poked haphazardly at her knot, still surveying me with interest.

"Not at the first, no. Though sure and I thought there was a great strangeness about ye—not that I was the only one to think that. Ye didna come through the stones prepared, did ye? Not on purpose, I mean?"

I bit back the words, "Not that time," and said instead, "No, it was an accident. You came on purpose, though—from 1967?"

She nodded, studying me intently. The thickened flesh between her brows was creased, and the crease deepened slightly as she looked at me.

"Aye—to help Prince *Tearlach*." Her mouth twisted to one side, as though she tasted something bad, and quite suddenly, she turned her head and spat. The globule of saliva hit the polished wooden floor with an audible *plop*.

"*An gealtaire salach Atailteach!*" she said. "Filthy Italian coward!" Her eyes darkened and shone with no pleasant light. "Had I known, I should have made my way to Rome and killed him, while there was time. His brother Henry might ha' been no better, though—a ballock-less, sniveling priest, that one. Not that it made a difference. After Culloden, any Stuart would be as useless as another."

She sighed, and shifted her bulk, the rattan of the chair creaking beneath her. She waved a hand impatiently, dismissing the Stuarts.

"Still, that's done with for now. Ye came by accident—walked through the stones near the date of a Fire Feast, did ye? That's how it usually happens."

"Yes," I said, startled. "I came through on Beltane. But what do you mean, 'usually happens'? Have you met a great many others—like . . . us?" I ended hesitantly.

She shook her head rather absently. "Not many." She seemed to be pondering something, though perhaps it was only the absence of her refreshments; she picked up the silver bell and rang it violently.

"Damn that Clotilda! Like us?" she said, returning to the question at hand. "No, I haven't. Only one besides you, that I ken. Ye could ha' knocked me over wi' a feather, when I saw the wee scar on your arm, and kent ye for one like myself." She touched the great swell of her own upper arm, where the small vaccination scar lay hidden beneath the puff of white muslin. She tilted her head in that bird-like way again, surveying me with one bright green eye.

"No, when I said that's how it usually happens, I meant, judging from the stories. Folk who disappear in fairy rings and the stone circles, I mean. They usually walk through near Beltane or Samhain; a few near the Sun Feasts— Midsummer's Day or the winter solstice."

"That's what the list was!" I said suddenly, reminded of the gray notebook I had left with Roger Wakefield. "You had a list of dates and initials— nearly two hundred of them. I didn't know what they were, but I saw that the dates were mostly in late April or early May, or near the end of October."

"Aye, that's right." She nodded, eyes still fixed on me in speculation. "So ye found my wee book? Is that how ye knew to come and look for me on Craigh na Dun? It *was* you, no? That shouted my name, just before I stepped through the stones?"

"Gillian," I said, and saw her pupils widen at the name that had once been hers, though her face stayed smooth. "Gillian Edgars. Yes, it was me. I didn't know if you saw me in the dark." I could see in memory the night-black circle of stones—and in the center, the blazing bonfire, and the figure of a slim girl standing by it, pale hair flying in the heat of the fire.

"I didn't see ye," she said. " 'Twas only later, when I heard ye call out at the witch trial and thought I'd heard your voice before. And then, when I saw the mark on your arm . . ." She shrugged massively, the muslin tight across her shoulders as she settled back. "Who was with ye, that night?" she asked curiously. "There were two I saw—a bonnie dark lad, and a girl."

She closed her eyes, concentrating, then opened them again to stare at me.

"Later on, I thought I kent her—but I couldna put a name to her, though I could swear I'd seen the face. Who was she?"

"Mistress Duncan? Or is it Mistress Abernathy, now?" Jamie interrupted, stepping forward and bowing to her formally. The first shock of her appearance was fading, but he was still pale, his cheekbones prominent under the stretched skin of his face.

She glanced at him, then looked again, as though noticing him for the first time.

"Well, and if it's no the wee fox cub!" she said, looking amused. She looked him carefully up and down, noting every detail of his appearance with interest.

"Grown to a bonny man, have ye no?" she said. She leaned back in the chair, which creaked loudly under her weight, and squinted appraisingly at him. "You've the look of the MacKenzies about ye, laddie. Ye always did, but now you're older, you've the look of both your uncles in your face."

"I am sure both Dougal and Colum would be pleased ye'd remember them so well." Jamie's eyes were fixed on her as intently as hers on him. He had never liked her—and was unlikely to change his opinion now—but he could not afford to antagonize her; not if she had Ian here somewhere.

The arrival of the tea interrupted whatever reply she might have made. Jamie moved to my side, and sat with me on the sofa, while Geilie carefully poured the tea and handed us each a cup, behaving exactly like a conventional hostess at a tea party. As though wishing to preserve this illusion, she offered the sugar bowl and milk jug, and sat back to make light conversation.

"If ye dinna mind my asking, Mrs. Abernathy," Jamie said, "how did ye come to this place?" Politely left unspoken was the larger question–*How did you escape being burned as a witch?*

She laughed, lowering her long lashes coquettishly over her eyes.

"Well, and ye'll maybe recall I was wi' child, back at Cranesmuir?"

"I seem to recall something of the sort." Jamie took a sip of his tea, the tips of his ears turning slightly pink. He had cause to remember that, all right; she had torn off her clothes in the midst of the witch trial, disclosing the secret bulge that would save her life—at least temporarily.

A small pink tongue poked out and delicately skimmed the tea droplets from her upper lip.

"Have ye had children yourself?" she asked, cocking an eyebrow at me.

"I have."

"Terrible chore, isn't it? Dragging about like a mud-caked sow, and then being ripped apart for the sake of something looks like a drowned rat." She shook her head, making a low noise of disgust in her throat. "The beauty o' motherhood, is it? Still, I should not complain, I suppose—the wee ratling saved my life for me. And wretched as childbirth is, it's better than being burnt at the stake."

"I'd suppose so," I said, "though not having tried the latter, I couldn't say for sure."

Geillis choked in her tea, spraying brown droplets over the front of her dress. She mopped at them carelessly, eyeing me with amusement.

"Well, I've not done it either, but I've seen them burn, poppet. And I think perhaps even lyin' in a muddy hole watching your belly grow is better than that."

"They kept you in the thieves' hole all the time?" The silver spoon was cool in my hand, but my palm grew sweaty at the memory of the thieves' hole in Cranesmuir. I had spent three days there with Geillis Duncan, accused as a witch. How long had she stayed there?

"Three months," she said, staring meditatively into her tea. "Three mortal months of frozen feet and crawling vermin, stinking scraps of food and the grave-smell clinging to my skin day and night."

She looked up then, mouth twisting in bitter amusement. "But I bore the child in style, at the end. When my pains began, they took me from the hole —little chance I'd run then, aye?—and the babe was born in my own old bedroom; in the fiscal's house."

Her eyes were slightly clouded, and I wondered whether the liquid in her glass was entirely tea.

"I had diamond-paned windows, do ye recall? All in shades of purple and green and white—the finest house in the village." She smiled reminiscently. "They gave me the bairn to hold, and the green light fell over his face. He looked as though he was drowned indeed. I thought he should be cold to the touch, like a corpse, but he wasn't; he was warm. Warm as his father's balls." She laughed suddenly, an ugly sound.

"Why are men such fools? Ye can lead them anywhere by the cock—for a while. Then give them a son and ye have them by the balls again. But it's all ye are to them, whether they're coming in or going out—a cunt."

She was leaning back in her chair. At this, she spread her thighs wide, and hoisted her glass in ironic toast above her pubic bone, squinting down across the swelling bulge of belly.

"Well, here's to it, I say! Most powerful thing in the world. The niggers know that, at least." She took a deep, careless swig of her drink. "They carve wee idols, all belly and cunt and breasts. Same as men do where we came from—you and I." She squinted at me, teeth bared in amusement. "Seen the dirty mags men buy under the counters then, aye?"

The bloodshot green eyes swiveled to Jamie. "And you'll know the pictures and the books the men pass about among themselves in Paris now, won't ye, fox? It's all the same." She waved a hand and drank again, deeply. "The only difference is the niggers have the decency to worship it."

"Verra perceptive of them," Jamie said calmly. He was sitting back in his chair, long legs stretched out in apparent relaxation, but I could see the tension in the fingers of the hand that gripped his own cup. "And how d'ye ken the pictures men look at in Paris, Mistress—Abernathy, is it now?"

She might be tipsy, but was by no means fuddled. She looked up sharply at the tone of his voice, and gave him a twisted smile.

"Oh, Mistress Abernathy will do well enough. When I lived in Paris, I had another name—Madame Melisande Robicheaux. Like that one? I thought it a bit grand, but your uncle Dougal gave it me, so I kept it—out of sentiment."

My free hand curled into a fist, out of sight in the folds of my skirt. I had heard of Madame Melisande, when we lived in Paris. Not a part of society, she had had some fame as a seer of the future; ladies of the court consulted her in deepest secrecy, for advice on their love lives, their investments, and their pregnancies.

"I imagine you could have told the ladies some interesting things," I said dryly.

Her laugh this time was truly amused. "Oh, I could, indeed! Seldom did, though. Folk don't usually pay for the truth, ye know. Sometimes, though— did ye ken that Jean-Paul Marat's mother meant to name her bairn Rudolphe? I told her I thought Rudolphe was ill-omened. I wondered now and then about that—would he grow up a revolutionary with a name like Rudolphe, or would he take it all out in writing poems, instead? Ever think that, fox—that a name might make a difference?" Her eyes were fixed on Jamie, green glass.

"Often," he said, and set down his cup. "It was Dougal got ye away from Cranesmuir, then?"

She nodded, stifling a small belch. "Aye. He came to take the babe— alone, for fear someone would find out he was the father, aye? I wouldna let it go, though. And when he came near to wrest it from me—why, I snatched the dirk from his belt and pressed it to the child's throat." A small smile of satisfaction at the memory curved her lovely lips.

"Told him I'd kill it, sure, unless he swore on his brother's life and his own soul to get me safe away."

"And he believed you?" I felt mildly ill at the thought of any mother holding a knife to the throat of her newborn child, even in pretense.

Her gaze swiveled back to me. "Oh, yes," she said softly, and the smile widened. "He knew me, did Dougal."

Sweating, even in the chill of December, and unable to take his eyes off the tiny face of his sleeping son, Dougal had agreed.

"When he leaned over me to take the child, I thought of plunging the dirk into his own throat instead," she said, reminiscently. "But it would have been a good deal harder to get away by myself, so I didn't."

Jamie's expression didn't change, but he picked up his tea and took a deep swallow.

Dougal had summoned the locksman, John MacRae, and the church sexton, and by means of discreet bribery, insured that the hooded figure dragged on a hurdle to the pitch barrel next morning would not be that of Geillis Duncan.

"I thought they'd use straw, maybe," she said, "but he was a cleverer man than that. Auld Grannie Joan MacKenzie had died three days before, and was meant to be burying that same afternoon. A few rocks in the coffin and the lid nailed down tight, and Bob's your uncle, eh? A real body, fine for burning." She laughed, and gulped the last swallow of her drink.

"Not everyone's seen their own funeral; fewer still ha' seen their own execution, aye?"

It had been the dead of winter, and the small grove of rowan trees outside the village stood bare, drifted with their own dead leaves, the dried red berries showing here and there on the ground like spots of blood.

It was a cloudy day, with the promise of sleet or snow, but the whole village turned out nonetheless; a witch-burning was not an event to be missed. The village priest, Father Bain, had died himself three months before, of fever brought on by a festering sore, but a new priest had been imported for the occasion from a village nearby. Perfuming his way with a censer held before him, the priest had come down the path to the grove, chanting the service for the dead. Behind him came the locksman and his two assistants, dragging the hurdle and its black-robed burden.

"I expect Grannie Joan would have been pleased," Geilie said, white teeth gleaming at the vision. "She couldna have expected more nor four or five people to her burying—as it was, she had the whole village, and the incense and special prayers to boot!"

MacRae had untied the body and carried it, lolling, to the barrel of pitch ready waiting.

"The court granted me the mercy to be weirrit before the burning," Geillis explained ironically. "So they expected the body to be dead—no difficulty there, if I was strangled already. The only thing anyone might ha' seen was that Grannie Joan weighed half what I did, newly delivered as I was, but no one seemed to notice she was light in MacRae's arms."

"You were *there*?" I said.

She nodded smugly. "Oh, aye. Well muffled in a cloak—everyone was, because o' the weather—but I wouldna have missed it."

As the priest finished his last prayer against the evils of enchantment, MacRae had taken the pine torch from his assistant and stepped forward.

"God, omit not this woman from Thy covenant, and the many evils that she in the body committed," he had said, and flung the fire into the pitch.

"It was faster than I thought it would be," Geillis said, sounding mildly surprised. "A great *whoosh!* of fire—there was a blast of hot air and a cheer from the crowd, and naught to be seen but the flames, shooting up high enough to singe the rowan branches overhead."

The fire had subsided within a minute, though, and the dark figure within was clear enough to be seen through the pale daylight flames. The hood and the hair had burned away with the first scorching rush, and the face itself was burned beyond recognition. A few moments more, and the clean dark shapes of the bones emerged from the melted flesh, an airy superstructure rising above the charring barrel.

"Only great empty holes where her eyes had been," she said. The moss-green eyes turned toward me, clouded by memory. "I thought perhaps she was looking at me. But then the skull exploded, and it was all over, and folk began to come away—all except a few who stayed in hopes of picking up a bit of bone as a keepsake."

She rose and went unsteadily to the small table near the window. She picked up the silver bell and rang it, hard.

"Aye," she said, her back turned to us. "Childbirth is maybe easier."

"So Dougal got ye away to France," Jamie said. The fingers of his right hand twitched slightly. "How came ye here to the West Indies?"

"Oh, that was later," she said carelessly. "After Culloden." She turned then, and smiled from Jamie to me.

"And what might bring the two of ye here to this place? Surely not the pleasure of my company?"

I glanced at Jamie, seeing the slight tensing of his back as he sat up straighter. His face stayed calm, though, only his eyes bright with wariness.

"We've come to seek a young kinsman of mine," he said. "My nephew, Ian Murray. We've some reason to think he is indentured here."

Geilie's pale brows rose high, making soft ridges in her forehead.

"Ian Murray?" she said, and shook her head in puzzlement. "I've no indentured whites at all, here. No whites, come to that. The only free man on the place is the overseer, and he's what they call a *griffone;* one-quarter black."

Unlike me, Geillis Duncan was a very good liar. Impossible to tell, from her expression of mild interest, whether she had ever heard the name Ian Murray before. But lying she was, and I knew it.

Jamie knew it, too; the expression that flashed through his eyes was not disappointment, but fury, quickly suppressed.

"Indeed?" he said politely. "And are ye not fearful, then, alone wi' your slaves here, so far from town?"

"Oh, no. Not at all."

She smiled broadly at him, then lifted her double chin and waggled it gently in the direction of the terrace behind him. I turned my head, and saw that the French door was filled from jamb to doorpost with an immense black man, several inches taller than Jamie, from whose rolled-up shirt sleeves protruded arms like tree trunks, knotted with muscle.

"Meet Hercules," Geilie said, with a tiny laugh. "He has a twin brother, too."

"Named Atlas, by chance?" I asked, with an edge to my voice.

"You guessed! Is she no the clever one, eh, fox?" She winked conspiratorially at Jamie, the rounded flesh of her cheek wobbling with the movement. The light caught her from the side as she turned her head, and I saw the red spiderwebs of tiny broken capillaries that netted her jowls.

Hercule took no note of this, or of anything else. His broad face was slack and dull, and there was no life in the deep-sunk eyes beneath the bony brow ridge. It gave me a very uneasy feeling to look at him, and not only because of his threatening size; looking at him was like passing by a haunted house, where something lurks behind blind windows.

"That will do, Hercule; ye can go back to work now." Geilie picked up the silver bell and tinkled it gently, once. Without a word, the giant turned and lumbered off the veranda. "I have no fear o' the slaves," she explained. "They're afraid o' me, for they think I'm a witch. Verra funny, considering, is it not?" Her eyes twinkled behind little pouches of fat.

"Geilie—that man." I hesitated, feeling ridiculous in asking such a question. "He's not a—a zombie?"

She laughed delightedly at that, clapping her hands together.

"Christ, a zombie? Jesus, Claire!" She chortled with glee, a bright pink rising from throat to hair roots.

"Well, I'll tell ye, he's no verra bright," she said at last, still gasping and wheezing. "But he's no dead, either!" and went off into further gales of laughter.

Jamie stared at me, puzzled.

"Zombie?"

"Never mind," I said, my face nearly as pink as Geilie's. "How many slaves have you got here?" I asked, wanting to change the subject.

"Hee hee," she said, winding down into giggles. "Oh, a hundred or so. It's no such a big place. Only three hundred acres in cane, and a wee bit of coffee on the upper slopes."

She pulled a lace-trimmed handkerchief from her pocket and patted her damp face, sniffing a bit as she regained her composure. I could feel, rather than see, Jamie's tension. I was sure he was as convinced as I that Geilie knew something about Ian Murray—if nothing else, she had betrayed no surprise whatever at our appearance. Someone had told her about us, and that someone could only be Ian.

The thought of threatening a woman to extract information wasn't one that would come naturally to Jamie, but it would to me. Unfortunately, the presence of the twin pillars of Hercules had put a stop to that line of thought. The next best idea seemed to be to search the house and grounds for any trace of the boy. Three hundred acres was a fair piece of ground, but if he was on the property, he would likely be in or near the buildings—the house, the sugar refinery, or the slave quarters.

I came out of my thoughts to realize that Geilie had asked me a question. "What's that?"

"I said," she repeated patiently, "that ye had a great deal of talent for the healing when I knew ye in Scotland; you'll maybe know more now?"

"I expect I might." I looked her over cautiously. Did she want my skill for herself? She wasn't healthy; a glance at her mottled complexion and the dark circles beneath her eyes was enough to show that. But was she actively ill?

"Not for me," she said, seeing my look. "Not just now, anyway. I've two slaves gone sick. Maybe ye'd be so kind as to look at them?"

I glanced at Jamie, who gave me the shadow of a nod. It was a chance to get into the slave quarters and look for Ian.

"I saw when we came in as ye had a bit of trouble wi' your sugar press," he said, rising abruptly. He gave Geilie a cool nod. "Perhaps I shall have a look at it, whilst you and my wife tend the sick." Without waiting for an answer, he took off his coat and hung it on the peg by the door. He went out by the veranda, rolling up the sleeves of his shirt, sunlight glinting on his hair.

"A handy sort, is he?" Geilie looked after him, amused. "My husband Barnabas was that sort—couldna keep his hands off any kind of machine. Or off the slave girls, either," she added. "Come along, the sick ones are back o' the kitchen."

The kitchen was in a separate small building of its own, connected to the house by a breezeway covered with blooming jasmine. Walking through it was like floating through a cloud of perfume, surrounded by a hum of bees loud enough to be felt on the skin, like the low drone of a bagpipe.

"Ever been stung?" Geillis swiped casually at a low-flying furry body, batting it out of the air.

"Now and then."

"So have I," she said. "Any number of times, and nothing worse than a red welt on my skin to show for it. One of these wee buggers stung one o' the kitchen slaves last spring, though, and the wench swelled up like a toad and died, right before my eyes!" She glanced at me, eyes wide and mocking. "Did wonders for my reputation, I can tell ye. The rest o' the slaves put it about I'd witched the lass; put a spell on her to kill her for burning the sponge cake. I havena had so much as a scorched pot, since." Shaking her head, she waved away another bee.

While appalled at her callousness, I was somewhat relieved by the story. Perhaps the other gossip I had heard at the Governor's ball had as little foundation in fact.

I paused, looking out through the jasmine's lacy leaves at the cane fields below. Jamie was in the clearing by the sugar press, looking up at the gigan-tic crossbars of the machine while a man I assumed to be the overseer pointed and explained. As I watched, he said something, gesturing, and the overseer nodded emphatically, waving his hands in voluble reply. If I didn't find any trace of Ian in the kitchen quarters, perhaps Jamie would learn something from the overseer. Despite Geilie's denials, every instinct I had insisted that the boy was here—somewhere.

There was no sign of him in the kitchen itself; only three or four women, kneading bread and snapping peas, who looked up curiously as we came through. I caught the eye of one young woman, and nodded and smiled at her; perhaps I would have a chance to come back and talk, later. Her eyes widened in surprise, and she bent her head at once, eyes on the bowl of peapods in her lap. I saw her steal a quick glance at me as we crossed the long room, and noticed that she balanced the bowl in front of the small bulge of an early pregnancy.

The first sick slave was in a small pantry off the kitchen itself, lying on a pallet laid under shelves stacked high with gauze-wrapped cheeses. The pa-tient, a young man in his twenties, sat up blinking at the sudden ray of light when I opened the door.

"What's the trouble with him?" I knelt down beside the man and touched his skin. Warm, damp, no apparent fever. He didn't seem in any particular distress, merely blinking sleepily as I examined him.

"He has a worm."

I glanced at Geilie in surprise. From what I had seen and heard so far in the islands, I thought it likely that at least three-quarters of the black popula-tion—and not a few of the whites—suffered from internal parasites. Nasty and debilitating as these could be, though, most were actively threatening only to the very young and the very old.

"Probably a lot more than one," I said. I pushed the slave gently onto his back and began to palpate his stomach. The spleen was tender and slightly enlarged—also a common finding here—but I felt no suspicious masses in the abdomen that might indicate a major intestinal infestation. "He seems moderately healthy; why have you got him in here in the dark?"

As though in answer to my question, the slave suddenly wrenched himself away from my hand, let out a piercing scream, and rolled up into a ball. Rolling and unrolling himself like a yo-yo, he reached the wall and began to bang his head against it, still screaming. Then, as suddenly as the fit had come on, it passed off, and the young man sank back onto the pallet, panting heavily and soaked with sweat.

"Jesus H. Roosevelt Christ," I said. "What was *that*?"

"A *loa-loa* worm," Geilie said, looking amused at my reaction. "They live in the eyeballs, just under the lining. They cross back and forth, from one eye to the other, and when they go across the bridge o' the nose, I'm told it's rather painful." She nodded at the slave, still quivering slightly on his pallet.

"The dark keeps them from moving so much," she explained. "The fellow from Andros who told me about them says ye must catch them when they've just come in one eye, for they're right near the surface, and ye can lift them out with a big darning needle. If ye wait, they go deeper, and ye canna get them." She turned back to the kitchen and shouted for a light.

"Here, I brought the needle, just in case." She groped in the bag at her waist and drew out a square of felt, with a three-inch steel needle thrust through it, which she extended helpfully to me.

"Are you out of your mind?" I stared at her, appalled.

"No. Did ye not say ye were a good healer?" she asked reasonably.

"I am, but—" I glanced at the slave, hesitated, then took the candle one of the kitchenmaids was holding out to me.

"Bring me some brandy, and a small sharp knife," I said. "Dip the knife—and the needle—in the brandy, then hold the tip in a flame for a moment. Let it cool, but don't touch it." As I spoke, I was gently pulling up one eyelid. The man's eye looked up at me, an oddly irregular, blotched brown iris in a bloodshot sclera the yellow of heavy cream. I searched carefully, bringing the candle flame close enough to shrink the pupil, then drawing it away, but saw nothing there.

I tried the other eye, and nearly dropped the candle. Sure enough, there was a small, transparent filament, *moving* under the conjunctiva. I gagged slightly at the sight, but controlled myself, and reached for the freshly sterilized knife, still holding back the eyelid.

"Take him by the shoulders," I said to Geilie. "Don't let him move, or I may blind him."

The surgery itself was horrifying to contemplate, but surprisingly simple to perform. I made one quick, small incision along the inside corner of the conjunctiva, lifted it slightly with the tip of the needle, and as the worm undulated lazily across the open field, I slipped the tip of the needle under the body and drew it out, neat as a loop of yarn.

Repressing a shudder of distaste, I flicked the worm away. It hit the wall with a tiny wet splat! and vanished in the shadows under the cheese.

There was no blood; after a brief debate with myself, I decided to leave it to the man's own tear ducts to irrigate the incision. That would have to be left to heal by itself; I had no fine sutures, and the wound was small enough not to need more than a stitch or two in any case.

I tied a clean pad of cloth over the closed eye with a bandage round the head, and sat back, reasonably pleased with my first foray into tropical medicine.

"Fine," I said, pushing back my hair. "Where's the other one?"

The next patient was in a shed outside the kitchen, dead. I squatted next to the body, that of a middle-aged man with grizzled hair, feeling both pity and outrage.

The cause of death was more than obvious: a strangulated hernia. The loop of twisted, gangrenous bowel protruded from one side of the belly, the stretched skin over it already tinged with green, though the body itself was still nearly as warm as life. An expression of agony was fixed on the broad features, and the limbs were still contorted, giving an unfortunately accurate witness to just what sort of death it had been.

"Why did you wait?" I stood up, glaring at Geilie. "For God's sake, you kept me drinking tea and chatting, while *this* was going on? He's been dead less than an hour, but he must have been in trouble a long time since—days! Why didn't you bring me out here at once?"

"He seemed pretty far gone this morning," she said, not at all disturbed by my agitation. She shrugged. "I've seen them so before; I didna think you could do anything much. It didna seem worth hurrying."

I choked back further recrimination. She was right; I could have operated, had I come sooner, but the chances of it doing any good were slim to nonexistent. The hernia repair was something I might have managed, even with such difficult conditions; after all, that was nothing more than pushing back the bowel protrusion and pulling the ruptured layers of abdominal muscle back together with sutures; infection was the only real danger. But once the loop of escaped intestine had twisted, so that the blood supply was cut off and the contents began to putrefy, the man was doomed.

But to allow the man to die here in this stuffy shed, alone . . . well, perhaps he would not have found the presence of one white woman more or less a comfort, in any case. Still, I felt an obscure sense of failure; the same I always felt in the presence of death. I wiped my hands slowly on a brandy-soaked cloth, mastering my feelings.

One to the good, one to the bad—and Ian still to be found.

"Since I'm here now, perhaps I'd best have a look at the rest of your slaves," I suggested. "An ounce of prevention, you know."

"Oh, they're well enough." Geilie waved a careless hand. "Still, if ye want to take the time, you're welcome. Later, though; I've a visitor coming this afternoon, and I want to talk more with ye, first. Come back to the house, now—someone will take care o' this." A brief nod disposed of "this," the slave's contorted body. She linked her arm in mine, urging me out of the shed and back toward the kitchen with soft thrustings of her weight.

In the kitchen, I detached myself, motioning toward the pregnant slave, now on her hands and knees, scrubbing the hearthstones.

"You go along; I want to have a quick look at this girl. She looks a bit toxic to me—you don't want her to miscarry."

Geilie gave me a curious glance, but then shrugged.

"She's foaled twice with no trouble, but you're the doctor. Aye, if that's your notion of fun, go ahead. Don't take too long, though; that parson said he'd come at four o'clock."

I made some pretense of examining the bewildered woman, until Geilie's draperies had disappeared into the breezeway.

"Look," I said. "I'm looking for a young white boy named Ian; I'm his aunt. Do you know where he might be?"

The girl—she couldn't be more than seventeen or eighteen—looked startled. She blinked, and darted a glance at one of the older women, who had quit her own work and come across the room to see what was going on.

"No, ma'am," the older woman said, shaking her head. "No white boys here. None at all."

"No, ma'am," the girl obediently echoed. "We don' know nothin' 'bout your boy." But she hadn't said that at first, and her eyes wouldn't meet mine.

The older woman had been joined now by the other two kitchenmaids, coming to buttress her. I was surrounded by an impenetrable wall of bland ignorance, and no way to break through it. At the same time, I was aware of a current running among the women—a feeling of mutual warning; of wariness and secrecy. It might be only the natural reaction to the sudden appearance of a white stranger in their domain—or it might be something more.

I couldn't take longer; Geilie would be coming back to look for me. I fumbled quickly in my pocket, and pulled out a silver florin, which I pressed into the girl's hand.

"If you should see Ian, tell him that his uncle is here to find him." Not waiting for an answer, I turned and hurried out of the kitchen.

I glanced down toward the sugar mill as I passed through the breezeway. The sugar press stood abandoned, the oxen grazing placidly in the long grass at the edge of the clearing. There was no sign of Jamie or the overseer; had he come back to the house?

I came through the French windows into the salon, and stopped short. Geilie sat in her wicker chair, Jamie's coat across the arm, and the photographs of Brianna spread over her lap. She heard my step and looked up, one pale brow arched over an acid smile.

"What a pretty lassie, to be sure. What's her name?"

"Brianna." My lips felt stiff. I walked slowly toward her, fighting the urge to snatch the pictures from her hands and run.

"Looks a great deal like her father, doesn't she? I thought she seemed familiar, that tall red-haired lass I saw that night on Craigh na Dun. He *is* her father, no?" She inclined her head toward the door where Jamie had vanished.

"Yes. Give them to me." It made no difference; she had seen the pictures already. Still, I couldn't stand to see her thick white fingers cupping Brianna's face.

Her mouth twitched as though she meant to refuse, but she tapped them neatly into a square and handed them to me without demur. I held them against my chest for a moment, not knowing what to do with them, then thrust them back into the pocket of my skirt.

"Sit ye down, Claire. The coffee's come." She nodded toward the small table, and the chair alongside. Her eyes followed me as I moved to it, alive with calculation.

She gestured for me to pour the coffee for both of us, and took her own cup without words. We sipped silently for a few moments. The cup trembled in my hands, spilling hot liquid across my wrist. I put it down, wiping my hand on my skirt, wondering in some dim recess of my mind why I should be afraid.

"Twice," she said suddenly. She looked at me with something akin to awe. "Sweet Christ Jesus, ye went through *twice*! Or no—*three* times, it must have been, for here ye are now." She shook her head, marveling, never taking her bright green eyes from my face.

"How?" she asked. "How could ye do it so many times, and live?"

"I don't know." I saw the look of hard skepticism flash across her face, and answered it, defensively. "I don't! I just—went."

"Was it not the same for you?" The green eyes had narrowed into slits of concentration. "What was it like, there between? Did ye not feel the terror? And the noise, fit to split your skull and spill your brains?"

"Yes, it was like that." I didn't want to talk to about it; didn't even like to think of the time-passage. I had blocked it deliberately from my mind, the roar of death and dissolution and the voices of chaos that urged me to join them.

"Did ye have blood to protect you, or stones? I wouldna think ye'd the nerve for blood—but maybe I'm wrong. For surely ye're stronger than I thought, to have done it three times, and lived through it."

"Blood?" I shook my head, confused. "No. Nothing. I told you—I . . . went. That's all." Then I remembered the night she had gone through the stones in 1968; the blaze of fire on Craigh na Dun, and the twisted, blackened shape in the center of that fire. "Greg Edgars," I said. The name of her first husband. "You didn't just kill him because he found you and tried to stop you, did you? He was—"

"The blood, aye." She was watching me, intent. "I didna think it could be done at all, the crossing—not without the blood." She sounded faintly amazed. "The auld ones—they always used the blood. That and the fire. They built great wicker cages, filled wi' their captives, and set them alight in the circles. I thought that was how they opened the passage."

My hands and my lips felt cold, and I picked up the cup to warm them. Where in the name of God was Jamie?

"And ye didna use stones, either?"

I shook my head. "What stones?"

She looked at me for a moment, debating whether to tell me. Her little pink tongue flicked over her lip, and then she nodded, deciding. With a small grunt, she heaved herself up from the chair and went toward the great hearth at the far end of the room, beckoning me to follow.

She knelt, with surprising grace for one of her figure, and pressed a greenish stone set into the mantelpiece, a foot or so above the hearth. It moved slightly, and there was a soft *click!* as one of the hearth slates rose smoothly out of its mortared setting.

"Spring mechanism," Geilie explained, lifting the slate carefully and setting it aside. "A Danish fellow named Leiven from St. Croix made it for me."

She reached into the cavity beneath and drew out a wooden box, about a foot long. There were pale brown stains on the smooth wood, and it looked swollen and split, as though it had been immersed in seawater at some time. I bit my lip hard at its appearance, and hoped my face didn't give anything away. If I had had any doubts about Ian being here, they had vanished—for here, unless I was very much mistaken, was the silkies' treasure. Fortunately, Geilie wasn't looking at me, but at the box.

"I learned about the stones from an Indian—not a red Indian, a Hindoo from Calcutta," she explained. "He came to me, looking for thornapple, and he told me about how to make medicines from the gemstones."

I looked over my shoulder for Jamie, but there was no sign of him. Where the hell was he? Had he found Ian, somewhere on the plantation?

"Ye can get the powdered stones from a London apothecary," she was saying, frowning slightly as she pushed at the sliding lid. "But they're mostly poor quality, and the *bhasmas* doesn't work so well. Best to have a stone at least of the second quality—what they call a *nagina* stone. That's a goodish-sized stone that's been polished. A stone of the first quality is faceted, and unflawed for preference, but most folk canna afford to burn those to ash. The ashes of the stone are the *bhasmas,*" she explained, turning to look up at me. "That's what ye use in the medicines. Here, can ye pry this damn thing loose? It's been spoilt in seawater, and the locking bit swells whenever the weather's damp—which it is all the time, this season of the year," she added, making a face over her shoulder at the clouds rolling in over the bay, far below.

She thrust the box into my hands and rose heavily to her feet, grunting with the effort.

It was a Chinese puzzle-box, I saw; a fairly simple one, with a small sliding panel that unlocked the main lid. The problem was that the smaller panel had swollen, sticking in its slot.

"It's bad luck to break one," Geilie observed, watching my attempts. "Else I'd just smash the thing and be done with it. Here, maybe this will help." She produced a small mother-of-pearl penknife from the recesses of her gown and handed it to me, then went to the window ledge and rang another of her silver bells.

I pried gently upward with the blade of the knife. I felt it catch in the wood, and wiggled it gingerly. Little by little, the small rectangle of wood edged out of its place, until I could get hold of it between thumb and forefinger and pull it all the way loose.

"There you go," I said, handing her back the box with some reluctance. It felt heavy, and there was an unmistakable metallic chinking as I tilted it.

"Thanks." As she took it, the black servingmaid came in through the far door. Geilie turned to order the girl to bring a tray of fresh tarts, and I saw that she had slipped the box between the folds of her skirts, hiding it.

"Nosy creatures," she said, frowning toward the departing maid's back as the girl passed through the door. "One of the difficulties wi' slaves; it's hard to have secrets." She put the box on the table, and pushed at the top; with a small, sharp *skreek!* of protest, the lid slid back.

She reached into the box and drew out her closed hand. She smiled mischievously at me, saying, "Little Jackie Horner sat in the corner, eating her Christmas pie. She put in her thumb, and pulled out a plum"—she opened her hand with a flourish—"and said 'What a good girl am I!' "

I had been expecting them, of course, but had no difficulty in looking impressed anyway. The reality of a gem is both more immediate and more startling than its description. Six or seven of them flashed and glimmered in her palm, flaming fire and frozen ice, the gleam of blue water in the sun, and a great gold stone like the eye of a lurking tiger.

Without meaning to, I drew near enough to look down into the well of her hand, staring with fascination. "Big enough," Jamie had described them as being, with a characteristic Scottish talent for understatement. Well, smaller than a breadbox, I supposed.

"I got them for the money, to start," Geilie was saying, prodding the stones with satisfaction. "Because they were easier to carry than a great weight of gold or silver, I mean; I didna think then what other use they might have."

"What, as *bhasmas?*" The idea of burning any of those glowing things to ash seemed a sacrilege.

"Oh, no, not these." Her hand closed on the stones, dipped into her pocket, and back into the box for more. A small shower of liquid fire dropped into her pocket, and she patted it affectionately. "No, I've a lot o' the smaller stones for that. These are for something else."

She eyed me speculatively, then jerked her head toward the door at the end of the room.

"Come along up to my workroom," she said. "I've a few things there you'll maybe be interested to see."

"Interested" was putting it mildly, I thought.

It was a long, light-filled room, with a counter down one side. Bunches of drying herbs hung from hooks overhead and lay on gauze-covered drying racks along the inner wall. Drawered cabinets and cupboards covered the rest of the wall space, and there was a small glass-fronted bookcase at the end of the room.

The room gave me a mild sense of déjà-vu; after a moment, I realized that it was because it strongly resembled Geilie's workroom in the village of Cranesmuir, in the house of her first husband—no, second, I corrected myself, remember the flaming body of Greg Edgars.

"How many times have you been married?" I asked curiously. She had begun building her fortune with her second husband, procurator fiscal of the district where they lived, forging his signature in order to divert money to her own use, and then murdering him. Successful with this modus operandi, I imagined she had tried it again; she was a creature of habit, was Geilie Duncan.

She paused a moment to count up. "Oh, five, I think. Since I came here," she added casually.

"Five?" I said, a little faintly. Not just a habit, it seemed; a positive addiction.

"A verra unhealthy atmosphere for Englishmen it is in the tropics," she said, and smiled slyly at me. "Fevers, ulcers, festering stomachs; any little thing will carry them off." She had evidently been mindful of her oral hygiene; her teeth were still very good.

She reached out and lightly caressed a small bottle that stood on the lowest shelf. It wasn't labeled, but I had seen crude white arsenic before. On the whole, I was glad I hadn't taken any food.

"Oh, you'll be interested in this," she said, spying a jar on an upper shelf. Grunting slightly as she stood on tiptoe, she reached it down and handed it to me.

It contained a very coarse powder, evidently a mixture of several substances, brown, yellow, and black, flecked with shreds of a semitranslucent material.

"What's this?"

"Zombie poison," she said, and laughed. "I thought ye'd like to see."

"Oh?" I said coldly. "I thought you told me there was no such thing."

"No," she corrected, still smiling. "I told ye Hercule wasn't dead; and he's not." She took the jar from me and replaced it on the shelf. "But there's no denying that he's a good bit more manageable if he's had a dose of this stuff once a week, mixed with his grain."

"What the hell is it?"

She shrugged, offhanded. "A bit of this and a bit of that. The main thing seems to be a kind of fish—a little square thing wi' spots; verra funny-looking. Ye take the skin and dry it, and the liver as well. But there are a few other things ye put in with it—I wish I kent what," she added.

"You don't know what's in it?" I stared at her. "Didn't you make it?"

"No. I had a cook," Geilie said, "or at least they sold him to me as a cook, but damned if I'd feel safe eating a thing he turned out of the kitchen, the sly black devil. He was a *houngan*, though."

"A what?"

"*Houngan* is what the blacks call one of their medicine-priests; though to be quite right about it, I believe Ishmael said his sort of black called him an *oniseegun*, or somesuch."

"Ishmael, hm?" I licked my dry lips. "Did he come with that name?"

"Oh, no. He had some heathen name wi' six syllables, and the man who sold him called him 'Jimmy'—the auctioneers call all the bucks Jimmy. I named him Ishmael, because of the story the seller told me about him."

Ishmael had been taken from a barracoon on the Gold Coast of Africa, one of a shipment of six hundred slaves from the villages of Nigeria and Ghana, stowed between decks of the slave ship *Persephone*, bound for Antigua. Coming through the Caicos Passage, the *Persephone* had run into a sudden squall, and been run aground on Hogsty Reef, off the island of Great Inagua. The ship had broken up, with barely time for the crew to escape in the ship's boats.

The slaves, chained and helpless betweendecks, had all drowned. All but one man who had earlier been taken from the hold to assist as a galley mate, both messboys having died of the pox en route from Africa. This man, left behind by the ship's crew, had nonetheless survived the wreck by clinging to a cask of spirits, which floated ashore on Great Inagua two days later.

The fishermen who discovered the castaway were more interested in his means of salvation than in the slave himself. Breaking open the cask, however, they were shocked and appalled to find inside the body of a man, somewhat imperfectly preserved by the spirits in which he had been soaking.

"I wonder if they drank the crème de menthe anyway," I murmured, having observed for myself that Mr. Overholt's assessment of the alcoholic affinities of sailors was largely correct.

"I daresay," said Geilie, mildly annoyed at having her story interrupted. "In any case, when I heard of it, I named him Ishmael straight off. Because of the floating coffin, aye?"

"Very clever," I congratulated her. "Er . . . did they find out who the man in the cask was?"

"I don't think so." She shrugged carelessly. "They gave him to the Governor of Jamaica, who had him put in a glass case, wi' fresh spirits, as a curiosity."

"*What?*" I said incredulously.

"Well, not so much the man himself, but some odd fungi that were growing on him," Geilie explained. "The Governor's got a passion for such things. The old Governor, I mean; I hear there's a new one, now."

"Quite," I said, feeling a bit queasy. I thought the ex-governor was more likely to qualify as a curiosity than the dead man, on the whole.

Her back was turned, as she pulled out drawers and rummaged through them. I took a deep breath, hoping to keep my voice casual.

"This Ishmael sounds an interesting sort; do you still have him?"

"No," she said indifferently. "The black bastard ran off. He's the one who made the zombie poison for me, though. Wouldn't tell me how, no matter what I did to him," she added, with a short, humorless laugh, and I had a sudden vivid memory of the weals across Ishmael's back. "He said it wasn't proper for women to make medicine, only men could do it. Or the verra auld women, once they'd quit bleeding. Hmph!"

She snorted, and reached into her pocket, pulling out a handful of stones.

"Anyway, that's not what I brought ye up to show ye."

Carefully, she laid five of the stones in a rough circle on the countertop. Then she took down from a shelf a thick book, bound in worn leather.

"Can ye read German?" she asked, opening it carefully.

"Not much, no," I said. I moved closer, to look over her shoulder. *Hexenhammer,* it said, in a fine, handwritten script.

"Witches' Hammer?" I asked. I raised one eyebrow. "Spells? Magic?"

The skepticism in my voice must have been obvious, for she glared at me over one shoulder.

"Look, fool," she said. "Who are ye? Or what, rather?"

"What am I?" I said, startled.

"That's right." She turned and leaned against the counter, studying me through narrowed eyes. "What are ye? Or me, come to that? What are we?"

I opened my mouth to reply, then closed it again.

"That's right," she said softly, watching. "It's not everyone can go through the stones, is it? Why us?"

"I don't know," I said. "And neither do you, I'll be bound. It doesn't mean we're witches, surely!"

"Doesn't it?" She lifted one brow, and turned several pages of the book.

"Some people can leave their bodies and travel miles away," she said, staring meditatively at the page. "Other people see them out wandering, and recognize them, and ye can bloody *prove* they were really tucked up safe in bed at the time. I've seen the records, all the eyewitness testimony. Some people have stigmata ye can see and touch—I've seen one. But not everybody. Only certain people."

She turned another page. "If everyone can do it, it's science. If only a few can, then it's witchcraft, or superstition, or whatever you like to call it," she said. "But it's real." She looked up at me, green eyes bright as a snake's over the crumbling book. "*We're* real, Claire—you and me. And special. Have ye never asked yourself why?"

I had. Any number of times. I had never gotten a reasonable answer to the question, though. Evidently, Geilie thought she had one.

She turned back to the stones she had laid on the counter, and pointed at them each in turn. "Stones of protection; amethyst, emerald, turquoise, lapis lazuli, and a male ruby."

"A *male* ruby?"

"Pliny says rubies have a sex to them; who am I to argue?" she said impatiently. "The male stones are what ye use, though; the female ones don't work."

I suppressed the urge to ask precisely how one distinguished the sex of rubies, in favor of asking, "Work for *what*?"

"For the travel," she said, glancing curiously at me. "Through the stones. They protect ye from the . . . whatever it is, out there." Her eyes grew slightly shadowed at the thought of the time-passage, and I realized that she was deathly afraid of it. Little wonder; so was I.

"When did ye come? The first time?" Her eyes were intent on mine.

"From 1945," I said slowly. "I came to 1743, if that's what you mean." I was reluctant to tell her too much; still, my own curiosity was overwhelming. She was right about one thing; she and I were different. I might never again have the chance to talk to another person who knew what she did. For that matter, the longer I could keep her talking, the longer Jamie would have to look for Ian.

"Hm." She grunted in a satisfied manner. "Near enough. It's two hundred year, in the Highland tales—when folk fall asleep on fairy duns and end up dancing all night wi' the Auld Folk; it's usually two hundred year later when they come back to their own place."

"You didn't, though. You came from 1968, but you'd been in Cranesmuir several years before I came there."

"Five years, aye." She nodded, abstracted. "Aye, well, that was the blood."

"Blood?"

"The sacrifice," she said, suddenly impatient. "It gives ye a greater range. And at least a bit of control, so ye have some notion how far ye're going. How did ye get to and fro three times, without blood?" she demanded.

"I . . . just came." The need to find out as much as I could made me add the little else I knew. "I think—I think it has something to do with being able to fix your mind on a certain person who's in the time you go to."

Her eyes were nearly round with interest.

"Really," she said softly. "Think o' that, now." She shook her head slowly, thinking. "Hm. That might be so. Still, the stones should work as well; there's patterns ye make, wi' the different gems, ye ken."

She pulled another fistful of shining stones from her pocket and spread them on the wooden surface, pawing through them.

"The protection stones are the points of the pentacle," she explained, intent on her rummaging, "but inside that, ye lay the pattern wi' different stones, depending which way ye mean to go, and how far. And ye lay a line of quicksilver between them, and fire it when ye speak the spells. And of course ye draw the pentacle wi' diamond dust."

"Of course," I murmured, fascinated.

"Smell it?" she asked, looking up for a moment and sniffing. "Ye wouldna think stones had a scent, aye? But they do, when ye grind them to powder."

I inhaled deeply, and did seem to find a faint, unfamiliar scent among the smell of dried herbs. It was a dry scent, pleasant but indescribable—the scent of gemstones.

She held up one stone with a small cry of triumph.

"This one! This is the one I needed; couldna find one anywhere in the islands, and finally I thought o' the box I'd left in Scotland." The stone she held was a black crystal of some kind; the light from the window passed through it, and yet it glittered like a piece of jet between her white fingers.

"What is it?"

"An adamant; a black diamond. The auld alchemists used them. The books say that to wear an adamant brings ye the knowledge of the joy in all things." She laughed, a short, sharp sound, devoid of her usual girlish charm. "If anything can bring knowledge o' joy in that passage through the stones, I want one!"

Something was beginning to dawn on me, rather belatedly. In defense of my slowness, I can only argue that I was simultaneously listening to Geilie and keeping an ear out for any sign of Jamie returning below.

"You mean to go back, then?" I asked, as casually as I could.

"I might." A small smile played around the corners of her mouth. "Now that I've got the things I need. I tell ye, Claire, I wouldna risk it, without." She stared at me, shaking her head. "Three times, wi' no blood," she murmured. "So it can be done.

"Well, best we go down now," she said, suddenly brisk, sweeping the stones up and dumping them back into her pocket. "The fox will be back— Fraser is his name, is it no? I thought Clotilda said something else, but the stupid bitch likely got it wrong."

As we made our way down the long workroom, something small and brown darted across the floor in front of me. Geilie was quick, despite her size; her small foot stamped on the centipede before I could react.

She watched the half-crushed beast wriggling on the floor for a moment, then stooped and slid a sheet of paper under it. Scooping it up, she decanted the thing thriftily into a glass jar.

"Ye dinna want to believe in witches and zombies and things that go bump in the night?" she said, with a small, sly smile at me. She nodded at the centipede, struggling round and round in frenzied, lopsided circles. "Well, legends are many-legged beasties, aye? But they generally have at least one foot on the truth."

She took down a clear brown-glass jug and poured the liquid into the centipede's bottle. The pungent scent of alcohol rose in the air. The centipede, washed up by the wave, kicked frantically for a moment, then sank to the bottom of the bottle, legs moving spasmodically. She corked the bottle neatly, and turned to go.

"You asked me why I thought we can pass through the stones," I said to her back. "Do you know why, Geilie?" She glanced over her shoulder at me.

"Why, to change things," she said, sounding surprised. "Why else? Come along; I hear your man down there."

Whatever Jamie had been doing, it had been hard work; his shirt was dampened with sweat, and clung to his shoulders. He swung around as we entered the room, and I saw that he had been looking at the wooden puzzle-box that Geilie had left on the table. It was obvious from his expression that I had been correct in my surmise—it was the box he had found on the silkies' isle.

"I believe I have succeeded in mending your sugar press, mistress," he said, bowing politely to Geilie. "A matter of a cracked cylinder, which your overseer and I contrived to stuff with wedges. Still, I fear ye may be needing another soon."

Geilie quirked her eyebrows, amused.

"Well, and I'm obliged to ye, Mr. Fraser. Can I not offer ye some refreshment after your labor?" Her hand hovered over the row of bells, but Jamie shook his head, picking up his coat from the sofa.

"I thank ye, mistress, but I fear we must take our leave. It's quite some way back to Kingston, and we must be on our way, if we mean to reach it before dark." His face went suddenly blank, and I knew he must have felt the pocket of his coat and realized that the photographs were missing.

He glanced quickly at me, and I gave him a brief nod, touching the side of my skirt where they lay.

"Thank you for your hospitality," I said, snatching up my hat, and moving toward the door with alacrity. Now that Jamie was back, I wanted nothing so much as to get quickly away from Rose Hall and its owner. Jamie hung back a moment, though.

"I wondered, Mistress Abernathy—since ye mentioned having lived in Paris for a time—whether ye might have been acquainted there wi' a gentleman of my own acquaintance. Did ye by chance ken the Duke of Sandringham?"

She cocked her cream-blond head at him inquisitively, but as he said no more, she nodded.

"Aye, I kent him. Why?"

Jamie gave her his most charming smile. "No particular reason, mistress; only a curiosity, ye might say."

The sky was completely overcast by the time we passed the gate, and it was clear that we weren't going to make it back to Kingston without getting soaked. Under the circumstances, I didn't care.

"Ye've got Brianna's pictures?" was the first thing Jamie asked, reining up for a moment.

"Right here." I patted my pocket. "Did you find any sign of Ian?"

He glanced back over his shoulder, as though fearing we might be pursued.

"I couldna get anything out of the overseer or any o' the slaves—they're bone-scairt of that woman, and I canna say I blame them a bit. But I know where he is." He spoke with considerable satisfaction.

"Where? Can we sneak back and get him?" I rose slightly in my saddle, looking back; the slates of Rose Hall were all that was visible through the treetops. I would have been most reluctant to set foot on the place again for any reason—except for Ian.

"Not now." Jamie caught at my bridle, turning the horse's head back to the trail. "I'll need help."

Under the pretext of finding material to repair the damaged sugar press, Jamie had managed to see most of the plantation within a quarter-mile of the house, including a cluster of slave huts, the stables, a disused drying shed for tobacco, and the building that housed the sugar refinery. Everyplace he went, he suffered no interference beyond curious or hostile glances—except near the refinery.

"That big black bugger who came up onto the porch was sitting on the ground outside," he said. "When I got too close to him, it made the overseer verra nervous indeed; he kept calling me away, warning me not to get too close to the fellow."

"That sounds like a really excellent idea," I said, shuddering slightly. "Not getting close to him, I mean. But you think he has something to do with Ian?"

"He was sitting in front of a wee door fixed into the ground, Sassenach." Jamie guided his horse adroitly around a fallen log in the path. "It must lead to a cellar beneath the refinery." The man had not moved an inch, in all the time that Jamie contrived to spend around the refinery. "If Ian's there, that's where he is."

"I'm fairly sure he's there, all right." I told him quickly the details of my visit, including my brief conversation with the kitchenmaids. "But what are we going to do?" I concluded. "We can't just leave him there! After all, we don't know what Geillis wants with him, but it can't be innocent, if she wouldn't admit he was there, can it?"

"Not innocent at all," he agreed, grim-faced. "The overseer wouldna speak to me of Ian, but he told me other things that would curl your hair, if it wasna already curled up like sheep's wool." He glanced at me, and a half-smile lit his face, in spite of his obvious perturbation.

"Judging by the state of your hair, Sassenach, I should say that it's going to rain verra soon now."

"How observant of you," I said sarcastically, vainly trying to tuck in the curls and tendrils that were escaping from under my hat. "The fact that the sky's black as pitch and the air smells like lightning wouldn't have a thing to do with your conclusions, of course."

The leaves of the trees all round us were fluttering like tethered butterflies, as the edge of the storm rose toward us up the slope of the mountain. From the small rise where we stood, I could see the storm clouds sweep in across the bay below, with a dark curtain of rain hanging beneath it like a veil.

Jamie rose in his saddle, looking over the terrain. To my unpracticed eye, our surroundings looked like solid, impenetrable jungle, but other possibilities were visible to a man who had lived in the heather for seven years.

"We'd best find a bit of shelter while we can, Sassenach," he said. "Follow me."

On foot, leading the horses, we left the narrow path and pressed into the forest, following what Jamie said was a wild pigs' trail. Within a few moments, he had found what he was looking for; a small stream that cut deep through the forest floor, with a steep bank, overgrown with ferns and dark, glossy bushes, interspersed with stands of slender saplings.

He set me to gathering ferns, each frond the length of my arm, and by the time I had returned with as many as I could carry, he had the framework of a tidy snug, formed by the arch of the bent saplings, tied to a fallen log, and covered over with branches cut from the nearby bushes. Hastily roofed with the spread ferns, it was not quite waterproof, but a great deal better than being caught in the open. Ten minutes later, we were safe inside.

There was a moment of absolute quiet as the wind on the edge of the storm passed by us. No birds chattered, no insects sang; they were as well equipped as we were to predict the rain. A few large drops fell, splattering on the foliage with an explosive sound like snapping twigs. Then the storm broke.

Caribbean rainstorms are abrupt and vigorous. None of the misty mousing about of an Edinburgh drizzle. The heavens blacken and split, dropping gallons of water within a minute. For as long as the rain lasts, speech is impossible, and a light fog rises from the ground like steam, vapor raised by the force of the raindrops striking the ground.

The rain pelted the ferns above us, and a faint mist filled the green shadows of our shelter. Between the clatter of the rain and the constant thunder that boomed among the hills, it was impossible to talk.

It wasn't cold, but there was a leak overhead, which dripped steadily on my neck. There was no room to move away; Jamie took off his coat and wrapped it around me, then put his arm around me to wait out the storm. In spite of the terrible racket outside, I felt suddenly safe, and peaceful, relieved of the strain of the last few hours, the last few days. Ian was as good as found, and nothing could touch us, here.

I squeezed his free hand; he smiled at me, then bent and kissed me gently. He smelled fresh and earthy, scented with the sap of the branches he had cut and the smell of his own healthy sweat.

It was nearly over, I thought. We had found Ian, and God willing, would get him back safely, very soon. And then what? We would have to leave Jamaica, but there were other places, and the world was wide. There were the French colonies of Martinique and Grenada, the Dutch-held island of Eleuthera; perhaps we would even venture as far as the continent—cannibals notwithstanding. So long as I had Jamie, I was not afraid of anything.

The rain ceased as abruptly as it had started. Drops fell singly from the shrubs and trees, with a pit-a-pat drip that echoed the ringing left in my ears by the storm's roar. A soft, fresh breeze came up the stream bed, carrying away humidity, lifting the damp curls from my neck with delicious coolness. The birds and the insects began again, quietly, and then in full voice, and the air itself seemed to dance with green life.

I stirred and sighed, pushing myself upright and shrugging off Jamie's coat.

"You know, Geilie showed me a special stone, a black diamond called an adamant," I said. "She said it's a stone the alchemists used; it gives a knowledge of the joy in all things. I think there might be one under this spot."

Jamie smiled at me.

"I shouldna be surprised at all, Sassenach," he said. "Here, ye've water all down your face."

He reached into his coat for a handkerchief, then stopped.

"Brianna's pictures," he said suddenly.

"Oh, I forgot." I dug in my pocket, and handed him back the pictures. He took them and thumbed rapidly through them, stopped, then went through them again, more slowly.

"What's wrong?" I asked, suddenly alarmed.

"One of them's gone," he said quietly. I felt an inexpressible feeling of dread begin to grow in the pit of my stomach, and the joy of a moment before began to ebb away.

"Are you sure?"

"I know them as well as I know your face, Sassenach," he said. "Aye, I'm sure. It's the one of her by the fire."

I remembered the picture in question well; it showed Brianna as an adult, sitting on a rock, outdoors by a campfire. Her knees were drawn up, her elbows resting on them, and she was looking directly into the camera, but with no knowledge of its presence, her face filled with firelit dreams, her hair blown back away from her face.

"Geilie must have taken it. She found the pictures in your coat while I was in the kitchen, and I took them away from her. She must have stolen it then."

"Damn the woman!" Jamie turned sharply to look toward the road, eyes dark with anger. His hand was tight on the remaining photographs. "What does she want with it?"

"Perhaps it's only curiosity," I said, but the feeling of dread would not go away. "What *could* she do with it, after all? She isn't likely to show it to anyone—who would come here?"

As though in answer to this question, Jamie's head lifted suddenly, and he grasped my arm in adjuration to be still. Some distance below, a loop of the road was visible through the overgrowth, a thin ribbon of yellowish mud. Along this ribbon came a plodding figure on horseback, a man dressed in black, small and dark as an ant at this distance.

Then I remembered what Geilie had said. *I'm expecting a visitor.* And later, *That parson said he'd come at four o'clock.*

"It's a parson, a minister of some kind," I said. "She said she was expecting him."

"It's Archie Campbell, is who it is," Jamie said, with some grimness. "What the devil—or perhaps I shouldna use that particular expression, wi' respect to Mistress Duncan."

"Perhaps he's come to exorcise her," I suggested, with a nervous laugh.

"He's his work cut out for him, if so." The angular figure disappeared into the trees, but it was several minutes before Jamie deemed him safely past us.

"What do you plan to do about Ian?" I asked, once we had made our way back to the path.

"I'll need help," he answered briskly. "I mean to come up the river with Innes and MacLeod and the rest. There's a landing there, no great distance from the refinery. We'll leave the boat there, go ashore and deal wi' Hercules —and Atlas, too, if he's a mind to be troublesome—break open the cellar, snatch Ian, and make off again. The dark o' the moon's in two days—I wish it could be sooner, but it will likely take that long to get a suitable boat and what arms we'll need."

"Using what for money?" I inquired bluntly. The expenditure for new clothes and shoes had taken a substantial portion of Jamie's share of profit from the bat guano. What was left would feed us for several weeks, and possibly be sufficient to rent a boat for a day or two, but it wouldn't stretch to buying large quantities of weapons.

Neither pistols nor swords were manufactured on the island; all weapons were imported from Europe and were in consequence expensive. Jamie himself had Captain Raines's two pistols; the Scots had nothing but their fish knives and the odd cutlass—insufficient for an armed raid.

He grimaced slightly, then glanced at me sidelong.

"I must ask John for help," he said simply. "Must I not?"

I rode silently for a moment, then nodded in acquiescence.

"I suppose you'll have to." I didn't like it, but it wasn't a question of my liking; it was Ian's life. "One thing, though, Jamie—"

"Aye, I know," he said, resigned. "Ye mean to come with me, no?"

"Yes," I said, smiling. "After all, what if Ian's hurt, or sick, or—"

"Aye, ye can come!" he said, rather testily. "Only do me the one wee favor, Sassenach. Try verra hard not to be killed or cut to pieces, aye? It's hard on a man's sensibilities."

"I'll try," I said, circumspectly. And nudging my horse closer to his, rode side by side down toward Kingston, through the dripping trees.

61

The Crocodile's Fire

There was a surprising amount of traffic on the river at night. Lawrence Stern, who had insisted on accompanying the expedition, told me that most of the plantations up in the hills used the river as their main linkage with Kingston and the harbor; roads were either atrocious or nonexistent, swallowed by lush growth with each new rainy season.

I had expected the river to be deserted, but we passed two small craft and a barge headed downstream as we tacked laboriously up the broad waterway, under sail. The barge, an immense dark shape stacked high with casks and bales, passed us like a black iceberg, huge, humped, and threatening. The low voices of the slaves poling it carried across the water, talking softly in a foreign tongue.

"It was kind of ye to come, Lawrence," Jamie said. We had a small, single-masted open boat, which barely held Jamie, myself, the six Scottish smugglers, and Stern. Despite the crowded quarters, I too was grateful for Stern's company; he had a stolid, phlegmatic quality about him that was very comforting under the circumstances.

"Well, I confess to some curiosity," Stern said, flapping the front of his shirt to cool his sweating body. In the dark, all I could see of him was a moving blotch of white. "I have met the lady before, you see."

"Mrs. Abernathy?" I paused, then asked delicately, "Er . . . what did you think of her?"

"Oh . . . she was a very pleasant lady; most . . . gracious."

Dark as it was, I couldn't see his face, but his voice held an odd note, half-pleased, half-embarrassed, that told me he had found the widow Abernathy quite attractive indeed. From which I concluded that Geilie had wanted something from the naturalist; I had never known her treat a man with any regard, save for her own ends.

"Where did you meet her? At her own house?" According to the attendees at the Governor's ball, Mrs. Abernathy seldom or never left her plantation.

"Yes, at Rose Hall. I had stopped to ask permission to collect a rare type of beetle—one of the Cucurlionidae—that I had found near a spring on the plantation. She invited me in, and . . . made me most welcome." This time there was a definite note of self-satisfaction in his voice. Jamie, handling the tiller next to me, heard it and snorted briefly.

"What did she want of ye?" he asked, no doubt having formed conclusions similar to mine about Geilie's motives and behavior.

"Oh, she was most gratifyingly interested in the specimens of flora and fauna I had collected on the island; she asked me about the locations and virtues of several different herbs. Ah, and about the other places I had been. She was particularly interested in my stories of Hispaniola." He sighed, momentarily regretful. "It is difficult to believe that such a lovely woman might engage in such reprehensible behavior as you describe, James."

"Lovely, aye?" Jamie's voice was dryly amused. "A bit smitten, were ye, Lawrence?"

Lawrence's voice echoed Jamie's smile. "There is a sort of carnivorous fly I have observed, friend James. The male fly, choosing a female to court, takes pains to bring her a bit of meat or other prey, tidily wrapped in a small silk package. While the female is engaged in unwrapping her tidbit, he leaps upon her, performs his copulatory duties, and hastens away. For if she should finish her meal before he has finished his own activities, or should he be so careless as not to bring her a tasty present—she eats him." There was a soft laugh in the darkness. "No, it was an interesting experience, but I think I shall not call upon Mrs. Abernathy again."

"Not if we're lucky about it, no," Jamie agreed.

———➤———

The men left me by the riverbank to mind the boat, and melted into the darkness, with instructions from Jamie to stay put. I had a primed pistol, given to me with the stern injunction not to shoot myself in the foot. The weight of it was comforting, but as the minutes dragged by in black silence, I found the dark and the solitude more and more oppressive.

From where I stood, I could see the house, a dark oblong with only the lower three windows lighted; that would be the salon, I thought, and wondered why there was no sign of any activity by the slaves. As I watched, though, I saw a shadow cross one of the lighted windows, and my heart jumped into my throat.

It wasn't Geilie's shadow, by any conceivable stretch of the imagination. It was tall, thin, and gawkily angular.

I looked wildly around, wanting to call out; but it was too late. The men were all out of earshot, headed for the refinery. I hesitated for a moment, but there was really nothing else to do. I kilted up my skirts and stepped into the dark.

By the time I stepped onto the veranda, I was damp with perspiration, and my heart was beating loudly enough to drown out all other sounds. I edged silently next to the nearest window, trying to peer in without being seen from within.

Everything was quiet and orderly within. There was a small fire on the hearth, and the glow of the flames gleamed on the polished floor. Geilie's rosewood secretary was unfolded, the desk shelf covered with piles of hand-written papers and what looked like very old books. I couldn't see anyone inside, but I couldn't see the whole room, either.

My skin prickled with imagination, thinking of the dead-eyed Hercules, silently stalking me in the dark. I edged farther down the veranda, looking over my shoulder with every other step.

There was an odd sense of desertion about the place this evening. There were none of the subdued voices of slaves that had attended my earlier visit, muttering to one another as they went about their tasks. But that might mean nothing, I told myself. Most of the slaves would stop work and go to their own quarters at sundown. Still, ought there not to be house servants, to tend the fire and fetch food from the kitchen?

The front door stood open. Spilled petals from the yellow rose lay across the doorstep, glowing like ancient gold coins in the faint light from the entryway.

I paused, listening. I thought I heard a faint rustle from inside the salon, as of someone turning the pages of a book, but I couldn't be sure. Taking my courage in both hands, I stepped across the threshold.

The feeling of desertion was more pronounced in here. There were unmis-takable signs of neglect visible; a vase of wilted flowers on the polished surface of a chest, a teacup and saucer left to sit on an occasional table, the dregs dried to a brown stain in the bottom of the cup. Where the hell was everybody?

I stopped at the door into the salon and listened again. I heard the quiet crackle of the fire, and again, that soft rustle, as of turning pages. By poking my head around the jamb, I could just see that there was someone seated in front of the secretary now. Someone undeniably male, tall and thin-shoul-dered, dark head bent over something before him.

"Ian!" I hissed, as loudly as I dared. "Ian!"

The figure started, pushed back the chair, and stood up quickly, blinking toward the shadows.

"Jesus!" I said.

"Mrs. Malcolm?" said the Reverend Archibald Campbell, astonished.

I swallowed, trying to force my heart down out of my throat. The Rever-end looked nearly as startled as I, but it lasted only a moment. Then his features hardened, and he took a step toward the door.

"What are you doing here?" he demanded.

"I'm looking for my husband's nephew," I said; there was no point in lying, and perhaps he knew where Ian was. I glanced quickly round the room, but it was empty, save for the Reverend, and the one small lighted lamp he had been using. "Where's Mrs. Abernathy?"

"I have no idea," he said, frowning. "She appears to have left. What do you mean, your husband's nephew?"

"Left?" I blinked at him. "Where has she gone?"

"I don't know." He scowled, his pointed upper lip clamped beaklike over the lower one. "She was gone when I rose this morning—and all of the servants with her, apparently. A fine way to treat an invited guest!"

I relaxed slightly, despite my alarm. At least I was in no danger of running into Geilie. I thought I could deal with the Reverend Campbell.

"Oh," I said. "Well, that does seem a bit inhospitable, I admit. I suppose you haven't seen a boy of about fifteen, very tall and thin, with thick dark brown hair? No, I didn't think you had. In that case, I expect I should be go—"

"Stop!" He grabbed me by the upper arm, and I stopped, surprised and unsettled by the strength of his grip.

"What is your husband's true name?" he demanded.

"Why—Alexander Malcolm," I said, tugging at my captive arm. "You know that."

"Indeed. And how is it, then, that when I described you and your husband to Mrs. Abernathy, she told me that your family name is Fraser—that your husband in fact is James Fraser?"

"Oh." I took a deep breath, trying to think of something plausible, but failed. I never had been good at lying on short notice.

"Where is your husband, woman?" he demanded.

"Look," I said, trying to extract myself from his grasp, "you're quite wrong about Jamie. He had nothing to do with your sister, he told me. He—"

"You've spoken to him about Margaret?" His grip tightened. I gave a small grunt of discomfort and yanked a bit harder.

"Yes. He says that it wasn't him—he wasn't the man she went to Culloden to see. It was a friend of his, Ewan Cameron."

"Ye're lying," he said flatly. "Or he is. It makes little difference. Where is he?" He gave me a small shake, and I jerked hard, managing to detach my arm from his grip.

"I tell you, he had nothing to do with what happened to your sister!" I was backing away, wondering how to get away from him without setting him loose to blunder about the grounds in search of Jamie, making noise and drawing unwelcome attention to the rescue effort. Eight men were enough to overcome the pillars of Hercules, but not enough to withstand a hundred roused slaves.

"Where?" The Reverend was advancing on me, eyes boring into mine.

"He's in Kingston!" I said. I glanced to one side; I was near a pair of

French doors opening onto the veranda. I thought I could get out without his catching me, but then what? Having him chase me through the grounds would be worse than keeping him talking in here.

I looked back at the Reverend, who was scowling at me in disbelief, and then what I had seen on the terrace registered in my mind's eye, and I jerked my head back around, staring.

I *had* seen it. There was a large white pelican perched on the veranda railing, head turned back, beak buried comfortably in its feathers. Ping An's plumage glinted silver against the night in the dim light from the doorway.

"What is it?" Reverend Campbell demanded. "Who is it? Who's out there?"

"Just a bird," I said, turning back to him. My heart was beating in a jerky rhythm. Mr. Willoughby must surely be nearby. Pelicans were common, near the mouths of rivers, near the shore, but I had never seen one so far inland. But if Mr. Willoughby was in fact lurking nearby, what ought I to do about it?

"I doubt very much that your husband is in Kingston," the Reverend was saying, narrowed eyes fixed on me with suspicion. "However, if he is, he will presumably be coming here, to retrieve you."

"Oh, no!" I said.

"No," I repeated, with as much assurance as I could manage. "Jamie isn't coming here. I came by myself, to visit Geillis—Mrs. Abernathy. My husband isn't expecting me back until next month."

He didn't believe me, but there was nothing he could do about it, either. His mouth pursed up in a tiny rosette, then unpuckered enough to ask, "So you are staying here?"

"Yes," I said, pleased that I knew enough about the geography of the place to pretend to be a guest. If the servants were gone, there was no one to say I wasn't, after all.

He stood still, regarding me narrowly for a long moment. Then his jaw tightened and he nodded grudgingly.

"Indeed. Then I suppose ye'll have some notion as to where our hostess has taken herself, and when she proposes to return?"

I was beginning to have a rather unsettling notion of where—if not exactly *when*—Geillis Abernathy might have gone, but the Reverend Campbell didn't seem the proper person with whom to share it.

"No, I'm afraid not," I said. "I . . . ah, I've been out visiting since yesterday, at the neighboring plantation. Just came back this minute."

The Reverend eyed me closely, but I was in fact wearing a riding habit—because it was the only decent set of clothes I owned, besides the violet ball dress and two wash-muslin gowns—and my story passed unchallenged.

"I see," he said. "Mmphm. Well, then." He fidgeted restlessly, his big bony hands clenching and unclenching themselves, as though he were not certain what to do with them.

"Don't let me disturb you," I said, with a charming smile and a nod at the desk. "I'm sure you must have important work to do."

He pursed his lips again, in that objectionable way that made him look like an owl contemplating a juicy mouse. "The work has been completed. I was only preparing copies of some documents that Mrs. Abernathy had requested."

"How interesting," I said automatically, thinking that with luck, after a few moments' small talk, I could escape under the pretext of retiring to my theoretical room—all the first-floor rooms opened onto the veranda, and it would be a simple matter to slip off into the night to meet Jamie.

"Perhaps you share our hostess's—and my own—interest in Scottish history and scholarship?" His gaze had sharpened, and with a sinking heart I recognized the fanatical gleam of the passionate researcher in his eyes. I knew it well.

"Well, it's very interesting, I'm sure," I said, edging toward the door, "but I must say, I really don't know very much about—" I caught sight of the top sheet on his pile of documents, and stopped dead.

It was a genealogy chart. I had seen plenty of those, living with Frank, but I recognized this particular one. It was a chart of the Fraser family—the bloody thing was even *headed* "Fraser of Lovat"—beginning somewhere around the 1400s, so far as I could see, and running down to the present. I could see Simon, the late—and not so lamented, in some quarters—Jacobite lord, who had been executed for his part in Charles Stuart's Rising, and his descendants, whose names I recognized. And down in one corner, with the sort of notation indicating illegitimacy, was Brian Fraser—Jamie's father. And beneath him, written in a precise black hand, *James A. Fraser.*

I felt a chill ripple up my back. The Reverend had noticed my reaction, and was watching with a sort of dry amusement.

"Yes, it is interesting that it should be the Frasers, isn't it?"

"That . . . *what* should be the Frasers?" I said. Despite myself, I moved slowly toward the desk.

"The subject of the prophecy, of course," he said, looking faintly surprised. "Do ye not know of it? But perhaps, your husband being an illegitimate descendant . . ."

"I don't know of it, no."

"Ah." The Reverend was beginning to enjoy himself, seizing the opportunity to inform me. "I thought perhaps Mrs. Abernathy had spoken of it to you; she being so interested as to have written to me in Edinburgh regarding the matter." He thumbed through the stack, extracting one paper that appeared to be written in Gaelic.

"This is the original language of the prophecy," he said, shoving Exhibit

A under my nose. "By the Brahan Seer; you'll have heard of the Brahan Seer, surely?" His tone held out little hope, but in fact, I had heard of the Brahan Seer, a sixteenth-century prophet along the lines of a Scottish Nostradamus.

"I have. It's a prophecy concerning the Frasers?"

"The Frasers of Lovat, aye. The language is poetic, as I pointed out to Mistress Abernathy, but the meaning is clear enough." He was gathering enthusiasm as he went along, notwithstanding his suspicions of me. "The prophecy states that a new ruler of Scotland will spring from Lovat's lineage. This is to come to pass following the eclipse of 'the kings of the white rose'— a clear reference to the Papist Stuarts, of course." He nodded at the white roses woven into the carpet. "There are somewhat more cryptic references included in the prophecy, of course; the time in which this ruler will appear, and whether it is to be a king or a queen—there is some difficulty in interpretation, owing to mishandling of the original . . ."

He went on, but I wasn't listening. If I had had any doubt about where Geilie had gone, it was fast disappearing. Obsessed with the rulers of Scotland, she had spent the better part of ten years in working for the restoration of a Stuart Throne. That attempt had failed most definitively at Culloden, and she had then expressed nothing but contempt for all extant Stuarts. And little wonder, if she thought she knew what was coming next.

But where would she go? Back to Scotland, perhaps, to involve herself with Lovat's heir? No, she was thinking of making the leap through time again; that much was clear from her conversation with me. She was preparing herself, gathering her resources—retrieving the treasure from the silkies' isle —and completing her researches.

I stared at the paper in a kind of fascinated horror. The genealogy, of course, was only recorded to the present. Did Geilie know who Lovat's descendants would be, in the future?

I looked up to ask the Reverend Campbell a question, but the words froze on my lips. Standing in the door to the veranda was Mr. Willoughby.

The little Chinese had evidently been having a rough time; his silk pajamas were torn and stained, and his round face was beginning to show the hollows of hunger and fatigue. His eyes passed over me with only a remote flicker of acknowledgment; all his attention was for the Reverend Campbell.

"Most holy fella," he said, and his voice held a tone I had never heard in him before; an ugly taunting note.

The Reverend whirled, so quickly that his elbow knocked against a vase; water and yellow roses cascaded over the rosewood desk, soaking the papers. The Reverend gave a cry of rage, and snatched the papers from the flood, shaking them frantically to remove the water before the ink should run.

"See what ye've done, ye wicked, murdering heathen!"

Mr. Willoughby laughed. Not his usual high giggle, but a low chuckle. It didn't sound at all amused.

"I murdering?" He shook his head slowly back and forth, eyes fixed on the Reverend. "Not me, holy fella. Is you, murderer."

"Begone, fellow," Campbell said coldly. "You should know better than to enter a lady's house."

"I know you." The Chinaman's voice was low and even, his gaze unwavering. "I see you. See you in red room, with the woman who laughs. See you too with stinking whores, in Scotland." Very slowly, he lifted his hand to his throat and drew it across, precise as a blade. "You kill pretty often, holy fella, I think."

The Reverend Campbell had gone pale, whether from shock or rage, I couldn't tell. I was pale, too—from fear. I wet my dry lips and forced myself to speak.

"Mr. Willoughby—"

"Not Willoughby." He didn't look at me; the correction was almost indifferent. "I am Yi Tien Cho."

Seeking escape from the present situation, my mind wondered absurdly whether the proper form of address would be Mr. Yi, or Mr. Cho?

"Get out at once!" The Reverend's paleness came from rage. He advanced on the little Chinese, massive fists clenched. Mr. Willoughby didn't move, seemingly indifferent to the looming minister.

"Better you leave, First Wife," he said, softly. "Holy fella liking women—not with cock. With knife."

I wasn't wearing a corset, but felt as though I were. I couldn't get enough breath to form words.

"Nonsense!" the Reverend said sharply. "I tell you again—get out! Or I shall—"

"Just stand still, please, Reverend Campbell," I said. Hands shaking, I drew the pistol Jamie had given me out of the pocket of my habit and pointed it at him. Rather to my surprise, he did stand still, staring at me as though I had just grown two heads.

I had never held anyone at gunpoint before; the sensation was quite oddly intoxicating, in spite of the way the pistol's barrel wavered. At the same time, I had no real idea what to do.

"Mr.—" I gave up, and used all his names. "Yi Tien Cho. Did you see the Reverend at the Governor's ball with Mrs. Alcott?"

"I see him kill her," Yi Tien Cho said flatly. "Better shoot, First Wife."

"Don't be ridiculous! My dear Mrs. Fraser, surely you cannot believe the word of a savage, who is himself—" The Reverend turned toward me, trying for a superior expression, which was rather impaired by the small beads of sweat that had formed at the edge of his receding hairline.

"But I think I do," I said. "You were there. I saw you. And you were in Edinburgh when the last prostitute was killed there. Nellie Cowden said you'd lived in Edinburgh for two years; that's how long the Fiend was killing girls there." The trigger was slippery under my forefinger.

"That's how long *he* had lived there, too!" The Reverend's face was losing its paleness, becoming more flushed by the moment. He jerked his head toward the Chinese.

"Will you take the word of the man who betrayed your husband?"

"Who?"

"Him!" The Reverend's exasperation roughened his voice. "It is this wicked creature who betrayed Fraser to Sir Percival Turner. Sir Percival told me!"

I nearly dropped the gun. Things were happening a lot too fast for me. I hoped desperately that Jamie and his men had found Ian and returned to the river—surely they would come to the house, if I was not at the rendezvous.

I lifted the pistol a little, meaning to tell the Reverend to go down the breezeway to the kitchen; locking him in one of the storage pantries was the best thing I could think of to do.

"I think you'd better—" I began, and then he lunged at me.

My finger squeezed the trigger in reflex. Simultaneously, there was a loud report, the weapon kicked in my hand, and a small cloud of black-powder smoke rolled past my face, making my eyes water.

I hadn't hit him. The explosion had startled him, but now his face settled into new lines of satisfaction. Without speaking, he reached into his coat and drew out a chased-metal case, six inches long. From one end of this protruded a handle of white staghorn.

With the horrible clarity that attends crisis of all kinds, I noted everything, from the nick in the edge of the blade as he drew it from the case, to the scent of the rose he crushed beneath one foot as he came toward me.

There was nowhere to run. I braced myself to fight, knowing fight was useless. The fresh scar of the cutlass slash burned on my arm, a reminder of what was coming that made my flesh shrink. There was a flash of blue in the corner of my vision, and a juicy *thunk*! as though someone had dropped a melon from some height. The Reverend turned very slowly on one shoe, eyes wide open and quite, quite blank. For that one moment, he looked like Margaret. Then he fell.

He fell all of a piece, not putting out a hand to save himself. One of the satinwood tables went flying, scattering potpourri and polished stones. The Reverend's head hit the floor at my feet, bounced slightly and lay still. I took one convulsive step back and stood trapped, back against the wall.

There was a dreadful contused depression in his temple. As I watched, his face changed color, fading before my eyes from the red of choler to a pasty white. His chest rose, fell, paused, rose again. His eyes were open; so was his mouth.

"Tsei-mi is here, First Wife?" The Chinese was putting the bag that held the stone balls back into his sleeve.

"Yes, he's here—out there." I waved vaguely toward the veranda. "What —he—did you really—?" I felt the waves of shock creeping over me and fought them back, closing my eyes and drawing in a breath as deep as I could manage.

"Was it you?" I said, my eyes still closed. If he was going to cave in my head as well, I didn't want to watch. "Did he tell the truth? Was it you who gave away the meeting place at Arbroath to Sir Percival? Who told him about Malcolm, and the printshop?"

There was neither answer nor movement, and after a moment, I opened my eyes. He was standing there, watching the Reverend Campbell.

Archibald Campbell lay still as death, but was not yet dead. The dark angel was coming, though; his skin had taken on the faint green tinge I had seen before in dying men. Still, his lungs moved, taking air with a high wheezing sound.

"It wasn't an Englishman, then," I said. My hands were wet, and I wiped them on my skirt. "An English *name*. Willoughby."

"Not Willoughby," he said sharply. "I am Yi Tien Cho!"

"Why!" I said, almost shouting. "Look at me, damn you! *Why?*"

He did look at me then. His eyes were black and round as marbles, but they had lost their shine.

"In China," he said, "there are . . . stories. Prophecy. That one day the ghosts will come. Everyone fear ghost." He nodded once, twice, then glanced again at the figure on the floor.

"I leave China to save my life. Waking up long time—I see ghosts. All round me, ghosts," he said softly.

"A big ghost comes—horrible white face, most horrible, hair on fire. I think he will eat my soul." His eyes had been fixed on the Reverend; now they rose to my face, remote and still as standing water.

"I am right," he said simply, and nodded again. He had not shaved his head recently, but the scalp beneath the black fuzz gleamed in the light from the window.

"He eat my soul, Tsei-mi. I am no more, Yi Tien Cho."

"He saved your life," I said. He nodded once more.

"I know. Better I die. Better die than be Willoughby. Willoughby! Ptah!" He turned his head and spat. His face contorted, suddenly angry.

"He talks my words, Tsei-mi! He eats my soul!" The fit of anger seemed to pass as quickly as it had come on. He was sweating, though the room was not terribly warm. He passed a trembling hand over his face, wiping away the moisture.

"There is a man I see in tavern. Ask for Mac-Doo. I am drunk," he said dispassionately. "Wanting woman, no woman come with me—laugh, saying yellow worm, point . . ." He waved a hand vaguely toward the front of his trousers. He shook his head, his queue rustling softly against the silk.

"No matter what *gwao-fei* do; all same to me. I am drunk," he said again. "Ghost-man wants Mac-Doo, ask I am knowing. Say yes, I know Mac-Doo." He shrugged. "It is not important what I say."

He was staring at the minister again. I saw the narrow black chest rise slowly, fall . . . rise once more, fall . . . and remain still. There was no sound in the room; the wheezing had stopped.

"It is a debt," Yi Tien Cho said. He nodded toward the still body. "I am dishonored. I am stranger. But I pay. Your life for mine, First Wife. You tell Tsei-mi."

He nodded once more, and turned toward the door. There was a faint rustling of feathers from the dark veranda. On the threshold he turned back.

"When I wake on dock, I am thinking ghosts have come, are all around me," Yi Tien Cho said softly. His eyes were dark and flat, with no depth to them. "But I am wrong. It is me; I am the ghost."

There was a stir of breeze at the French windows, and he was gone. The quick soft sound of felt-shod feet passed down the veranda, followed by the rustle of spread wings, and a soft, plaintive *Gwaaa!* that faded into the night-sounds of the plantation.

I made it to the sofa before my knees gave way. I bent down and laid my head on my knees, praying that I would not faint. The blood hammered in my ears. I thought I heard a wheezing breath, and jerked up my head in panic, but the Reverend Campbell lay quite still.

I could not stay in the same room with him. I got up, circling as far around the body as I could get, but before I reached the veranda door, I had changed my mind. All the events of the evening were colliding in my head like the bits of glass in a kaleidoscope.

I could not stop now to think, to make sense of it all. But I remembered the Reverend's words, before Yi Tien Cho had come. If there was any clue here to where Geillis Abernathy had gone, it would be upstairs. I took a candle from the table, lighted it, and made my way through the dark house to the staircase, resisting the urge to look behind me. I felt very cold.

◄━━━►

The workroom was dark, but a faint, eerie violet glow hovered over the far end of the counter. There was an odd burnt smell in the room, that stung the back of my nose and made me sneeze. The faint metallic aftertaste in the back of my throat reminded me of a long-ago chemistry class.

Quicksilver. Burning mercury. The vapor it gave off was not only eerily beautiful, but highly toxic as well. I snatched out a handkerchief and plastered it over my nose and mouth as I went toward the site of the violet glow.

The lines of the pentacle had been charred into the wood of the counter.

If she had used stones to mark a pattern, she had taken them with her, but she had left something else behind.

The photograph was heavily singed at the edges, but the center was untouched. My heart gave a thump of shock. I seized the picture, clutching Brianna's face to my chest with a mingled feeling of fury and panic.

What did she mean by this—this desecration? It couldn't have been meant as a gesture toward me or Jamie, for she could not have expected either of us ever to have seen it.

It must be magic—or Geilie's version of it. I tried frantically to recall our conversation in this room; what had she said? She had been curious about how I had traveled through the stones—that was the main thing. And what had I said? Only something vague, about fixing my attention on a person—yes, that was it—I said I had fixed my attention on a specific person inhabiting the time to which I was drawn.

I drew a deep breath, and discovered that I was trembling, both with delayed reaction from the scene in the salon, and from a dreadful, growing apprehension. It might be only that Geilie had decided to try my technique —if one could dignify it with such a word—as well as her own, and use the image of Brianna as a point of fixation for her travel. Or—I thought of the Reverend's piles of neat, handwritten papers, the carefully drawn genealogies, and thought I might just faint.

"One of the Brahan Seer's prophecies," he had said. "Concerning the Frasers of Lovat. Scotland's ruler will come from that lineage." But thanks to Roger Wakefield's researches, I knew—what Geilie almost certainly knew as well, obsessed as she was with Scottish history—that Lovat's direct line had failed in the 1800s. To all visible intents and purposes, that is. There was in fact one survivor of that line living in 1968—Brianna.

It took a moment for me to realize that the low, growling sound I heard was coming from my own throat, and a moment more of conscious effort to unclench my jaws.

I stuffed the mutilated photograph into the pocket of my skirt and whirled, running for the door as though the workroom were inhabited by demons. I had to find Jamie—now.

They were not there. The boat floated silently, empty in the shadows of the big cecropia where we had left it, but of Jamie and the rest, there was no sign at all.

One of the cane fields lay a short distance to my right, between me and the looming rectangle of the refinery beyond. The faint caramel smell of burnt sugar lingered over the field. Then the wind changed, and I smelled the clean, damp scent of moss and wet rocks from the stream, with all the tiny pungencies of the water plants intermingled.

The stream bank rose sharply here, going up in a mounded ridge that ended at the edge of the cane field. I scrambled up the slope, my palm slipping in soft sticky mud. I shook it off with a muffled exclamation of disgust and wiped my hand on my skirt. A thrill of anxiety ran through me. Bloody *hell,* where was Jamie? He should have been back long since.

Two torches burned by the front gate of Rose Hall, small dots of flickering light at this distance. There was a closer light as well; a glow from the left of the refinery. Had Jamie and his men met trouble there? I could hear a faint singing from that direction, and see a deeper glow that bespoke a large open fire. It seemed peaceful, but something about the night—or the place— made me very uneasy.

Suddenly I became aware of another scent, above the tang of watercress and burnt sugar—a strong putrid-sweet smell that I recognized at once as the smell of rotten meat. I took a cautious step, and all hell promptly broke loose underfoot.

It was as though a piece of the night had suddenly detached itself from the rest and sprung into action at about the level of my knees. A very large object exploded into movement close to me, and there was a stunning blow across my lower legs that knocked me off my feet.

My involuntary shriek coincided with a truly awful sound—a sort of loud, grunting hiss that confirmed my impression that I was in close juxtaposition to something large, alive, and reeking of carrion. I didn't know what it was, but I wanted no part of it.

I had landed very hard on my bottom. I didn't pause to see what was happening, but flipped over and made off through the mud and leaves on all fours, followed by a repetition of the grunting hiss, only louder, and a scrab-bling, sliding sort of rush. Something hit my foot a glancing blow, and I stumbled to my feet, running.

I was so panicked that I didn't realize that I suddenly could see, until the man loomed up before me. I crashed into him, and the torch he was carrying dropped to the ground, hissing as it struck the wet leaves.

Hands grabbed my shoulders, and there were shouts behind me. My face was pressed against a hairless chest with a strong musky smell about it. I regained my balance, gasping, and leaned back to look into the face of a tall black slave, who was gaping down at me in perplexed dismay.

"Missus, what you be doin' here?" he said. Before I could answer, though, his attention was distracted from me to what was going on behind me. His grip on my shoulders relaxed, and I turned to see.

Six men surrounded the beast. Two carried torches, which they held aloft to light the other four, dressed only in loin cloths, who cautiously circled, holding sharpened wooden poles at the ready.

My legs were still stinging and wobbly from the blow they had taken; when I saw what had struck me, they nearly gave way again. The thing was nearly twelve feet long, with an armored body the size of a rum cask. The great tail whipped suddenly to one side; the man nearest leapt aside, shouting in alarm, and the saurian's head turned, jaws opening slightly to emit another hiss.

The jaws clicked shut with an audible snap, and I saw the telltale carnassial tooth, jutting up from the lower jaw in an expression of grim and spurious pleasantry.

"Never smile at a crocodile," I said stupidly.

"No, ma'am, I surely won't," the slave said, leaving me and edging cautiously toward the scene of action.

The men with the poles were poking at the beast, evidently trying to irritate it. In this endeavor, they appeared to be succeeding. The fat, splayed limbs dug hard into the ground, and the crocodile charged, roaring. It lunged with astonishing speed; the man before it yelped and jumped back, lost his footing on the slippery mud and fell.

The man who had collided with me launched himself through the air and landed on the crocodile's back. The men with the torches danced back and forth, yelling encouragement, and one of the pole men, bolder than the others, dashed forward and whacked his pole across the broad, plated head to distract it, while the fallen slave scrabbled backward, bare heels scooping trenches in the black mud.

The man on the crocodile's back was groping—with what seemed to me suicidal mania—for the beast's mouth. Getting a hold with one arm about the thick neck, he managed to grab the end of the snout with one hand, and holding the mouth shut, screamed something to his companions.

Suddenly a figure I hadn't noticed before stepped out of the shadow of the cane. It went down on one knee before the struggling pair, and without hesitation, slipped a rope noose around the lizard's jaws. The shouting rose in a yell of triumph, cut off by a sharp word from the kneeling figure.

He rose and motioned violently, shouting commands. He wasn't speaking English, but his concern was obvious; the great tail was still free, lashing from side to side with a force that would have felled any man who came within range of it. Seeing the power of that stroke, I could only marvel that my own legs were merely bruised, and not broken.

The pole men dashed in closer, in response to the commands of their leader. I could feel the half-pleasant numbness of shock stealing over me, and in that state of unreality, it somehow seemed no surprise to see that the leader was the man called Ishmael.

"*Huwe!*" he said, making violent upward gestures with his palms that made his meaning obvious. Two of the pole men had gotten their poles shoved under the belly; a third now managed a lucky strike past the tossing head, and lodged his pole under the chest.

"*Huwe!*" Ishmael said again, and all three threw themselves hard upon their poles. With a sucking *splat*! the reptile flipped over and landed thrashing on its back, its underside a sudden gleaming white in the torchlight.

The torchbearers were shouting again; the noise rang in my ears. Then Ishmael stopped them with a word, his hand thrown out in demand, palm up. I couldn't tell what the word was, but it could as easily have been "Scalpel!" The intonation—and the result—were the same.

One of the torchbearers hastily tugged the cane-knife from his loincloth, and slapped it into his leader's hand. Ishmael turned on his heel and in the same movement, drove the point of the knife deep into the crocodile's throat, just where the scales of the jaw joined those of the neck.

The blood welled black in the torchlight. All the men stepped back then, and stood at a safe distance, watching the dying frenzy of the great reptile with a respect mingled with deep satisfaction. Ishmael straightened, shirt a pale blur against the dark canes; unlike the other men, he was fully dressed, save for bare feet, and a number of small leather bags swung at his belt.

Owing to some freak of the nervous system, I had kept standing all this time. The increasingly urgent messages from my legs made it through to my brain at this point, and I sat down quite suddenly, my skirts billowing on the muddy ground.

The movement attracted Ishmael's notice; the narrow head turned in my direction, and his eyes widened. The other men, seeing him, turned also, and a certain amount of incredulous comment in several languages followed.

I wasn't paying much attention. The crocodile was still breathing, in stertorous, bubbling gasps. So was I. My eyes were fixed on the long scaled head, its eye with a slit pupil glowing the greenish gold of tourmaline, its oddly indifferent gaze seeming fixed in turn on me. The crocodile's grin was upside down, but still in place.

The mud was cool and smooth beneath my cheek, black as the thick stream that flowed between the lizard's scales. The tone of the questions and comments had changed to concern, but I was no longer listening.

❦

I hadn't actually lost consciousness; I had a vague impression of jostling bodies and flickering light, and then I was lifted into the air, clutched tight in someone's arms. They were talking excitedly, but I caught only a word now and then. I dimly thought I should tell them to lay me down and cover me with something, but my tongue wasn't working.

Leaves brushed my face as my escort ruthlessly shouldered the canes aside; it was like pushing through a cornfield that had no ears, all stalks and rustling leaves. There was no conversation among the men now; the susurrus of our passage drowned even the sound of footsteps.

By the time we entered the clearing by the slave huts, both sight and wits had returned to me. Bar scrapes and bruises, I wasn't hurt, but I saw no point in advertising the fact. I kept my eyes closed and stayed limp as I was carried into one of the huts, fighting back panic, and hoping to come up with some sensible plan before I was obliged to wake up officially.

Where in bloody hell were Jamie and the others? If all went well—or worse, if it didn't—what were they going to do when they arrived at the landing place and found me gone, with traces—traces? the place was a bloody wallow!—of a struggle where I had been?

And what about friend Ishmael? What in the name of all merciful God was *he* doing here? I knew one thing—he wasn't bloody well cooking.

There was a good deal of festive noise outside the open door of the hut, and the scent of something alcoholic—not rum, something raw and pungent —floated in, a high note in the fuggy air of the hut, redolent of sweat and boiled yams. I cracked an eye and saw the reflected glimmer of firelight on the beaten earth. Shadows moved back and forth in front of the open door; I couldn't leave without being seen.

There was a general shout of triumph, and all the figures disappeared abruptly, in what I assumed was the direction of the fire. Presumably they were doing something to the crocodile, who had arrived when I did, swinging upside-down from the hunters' poles.

I rolled cautiously up onto my knees. Could I steal away while they were occupied with whatever they were doing? If I could make it to the nearest cane field, I was fairly sure they couldn't find me, but I was by no means so sure that I could find the river again, alone in the pitch-dark.

Ought I to make for the main house, instead, in hopes of running into Jamie and his rescue party? I shuddered slightly at the thought of the house, and the long, silent black form on the floor of the salon. But if I didn't go to either house or boat, how was I to find them, on a moonless night black as the Devil's armpit?

My planning was interrupted by a shadow in the doorway that momentarily blocked the light. I risked a peek, then sat bolt upright and screamed.

The figure came swiftly in and knelt by my pallet.

"Don' you be makin' that noise, woman," Ishmael said. "It ain't but me."

"Right," I said. Cold sweat prickled on my jaws and I could feel my heart pounding like a triphammer. "Knew it all the time."

They had cut off the crocodile's head and sliced out the tongue and the floor of the mouth. He wore the huge, cold-eyed thing like a hat, his eyes no more than a gleam in the depths beneath the portcullised teeth. The empty lower jaw sagged, fat-jowled and grimly jovial, hiding the lower half of his face.

"The *egungun*, he didn't hurt you none?" he asked.

"No," I said. "Thanks to the men. Er . . . you wouldn't consider taking that off, would you?"

He ignored the request and sat back on his heels, evidently considering me. I couldn't see his face, but every line of his body expressed the most profound indecision.

"Why you bein' here?" he asked at last.

For lack of any better idea, I told him. He didn't mean to bash me on the head, or he would have done it already, when I collapsed below the cane field.

"Ah," he said, when I had finished. The reptile's snout dipped slightly toward me as he thought. A drop of moisture fell from the valved nostril onto my bare hand, and I wiped it quickly on my skirt, shuddering.

"The missus not here tonight," he said, at last, as though wondering whether it was safe to trust me with the information.

"Yes, I know," I said. I gathered my feet under me, preparing to rise. "Can you—or one of the men—take me back to the big tree by the river? My husband will be looking for me," I added pointedly.

"Likely she be takin' the boy with her," Ishmael went on, ignoring me.

My heart had lifted when he had verified that Geilie was gone; now it fell, with a distinct thud in my chest.

"She's taken Ian? Why?"

I couldn't see his face, but the eyes inside the crocodile mask shone with a gleam of something that was partly amusement—but only partly.

"Missus likes boys," he said, the malicious tone making his meaning quite clear.

"Does she," I said flatly. "Do you know when she'll be coming back?"

The long, toothy snout turned suddenly up, but before he could reply, I sensed someone standing behind me, and swung around on the pallet.

"I know you," she said, a small frown puckering the wide, smooth forehead as she looked down at me. "Do I not?"

"We've met," I said, trying to swallow the heart that had leapt into my mouth in startlement. "How—how do you do, Miss Campbell?"

Better than when last seen, evidently, in spite of the fact that her neat wool challis gown had been replaced with a loose smock of coarse white cotton, sashed with a broad, raggedly torn strip of the same, stained dark blue with indigo. Both face and figure had grown more slender, though, and she had lost the pasty, sagging look of too many months spent indoors.

"I am well, I thank ye, ma'am," she said politely. The pale blue eyes had still that distant, unfocused look to them, and despite the new sun-glow on her skin, it was clear that Miss Margaret Campbell was still not altogether in the here and now.

This impression was borne out by the fact that she appeared not to have noticed Ishmael's unconventional attire. Or to have noticed Ishmael himself, for that matter. She went on looking at me, a vague interest passing across her snub features.

"It is most civil in ye to call upon me, ma'am," she said. "Might I offer ye refreshment of some kind? A dish of tea, perhaps? We keep no claret, for my brother holds that strong spirits are a temptation to the lusts of the flesh."

"I daresay they are," I said, feeling that I could do with a brisk spot of temptation at the moment.

Ishmael had risen, and now bowed deeply to Miss Campbell, the great head slipping precariously.

"You ready, *bébé*?" he asked softly. "The fire is waiting."

"Fire," she said. "Yes, of course," and turned to me.

"Will ye not join me, Mrs. Malcolm?" she asked graciously. "Tea will be served shortly. I do so enjoy looking into a nice fire," she confided, taking my arm as I rose. "Do you not find yourself sometimes imagining that you see things in the flames?"

"Now and again," I said. I glanced at Ishmael, who was standing in the doorway. His indecision was apparent in his stance, but as Miss Campbell moved inexorably toward him, towing me after her, he shrugged very slightly, and stepped aside.

Outside, a small bonfire burned brightly in the center of the clearing before the row of huts. The crocodile had already been skinned; the raw hide was stretched on a frame near one of the huts, throwing a headless shadow on the wooden wall. Several sharpened sticks were thrust into the ground around the fire, each strung with chunks of meat, sizzling with an appetizing smell that nonetheless made my stomach clench.

Perhaps three dozen people, men, women and children, were gathered near the fire, laughing and talking. One man was still singing softly, curled over a battered guitar.

As we appeared, one man caught sight of us, and turned sharply, saying something that sounded like "Hau!" At once, the talk and laughter stopped, and a respectful silence fell upon the crowd.

Ishmael walked slowly toward them, the crocodile's head grinning in apparent delight. The firelight shone off faces and bodies like polished jet and melted caramel, all with deep black eyes that watched us come.

There was a small bench near the fire, set on a sort of dais made of stacked planks. This was evidently the seat of honor, for Miss Campbell made for it directly, and gestured politely for me to sit down next to her.

I could feel the weight of eyes upon me, with expressions ranging from hostility to guarded curiosity, but most of the attention was for Miss Campbell. Glancing covertly around the circle of faces, I was struck by their strangeness. These were the faces of Africa, and alien to me; not faces like Joe's, that bore only the faint stamp of his ancestors, diluted by centuries of European blood. Black or not, Joe Abernathy was a great deal more like me than like these people—different to the marrow of their bones.

The man with the guitar had put it aside, and drawn out a small drum that he set between his knees. The sides were covered with the hide of some spotted animal; goat, perhaps. He began to tap it softly with the palms of his hands, in a half-halting rhythm like the beating of a heart.

I glanced at Miss Campbell, sitting tranquil beside me, hands carefully folded in her lap. She was gazing straight ahead, into the leaping flames, with a small, dreaming smile on her lips.

The swaying crowd of slaves parted, and two little girls came out, carrying a large basket between them. The handle of the basket was twined with white roses, and the lid jerked up and down, agitated by the movements of something inside.

The girls set the basket at Ishmael's feet, casting awed glances up at his grotesque headdress. He rested a hand on each of their heads, murmured a few words, and then dismissed them, his upraised palms a startling flash of yellow-pink, like butterflies rising from the girls' knotted hair.

The attitude of the spectators had so far been quiet and respectful. It continued so, but now they crowded closer, necks craning to see what would happen next, and the drum began to beat faster, still softly. One of the women was holding a stone bottle, she took one step forward, handed it to Ishmael, and melted back into the crowd.

Ishmael took up the bottle of liquor and poured a small amount on the ground, moving carefully in a circle around the basket. The basket, momentarily quiescent, heaved to and fro, evidently disturbed by the movement or the pungent scent of alcohol.

A man holding a stick wrapped in rags stepped forward, and held the stick in the bonfire until the rags blazed up, bright red. At a word from Ishmael, he dipped his torch to the ground where the liquor had been poured. There was a collective "Ah!" from the watchers as a ring of flame sprang up, burned blue and died away at once, as quickly as it came. From the basket came a loud "Cock-a-doodle-dooo!"

Miss Campbell stirred beside me, eyeing the basket with suspicion.

As though the crowing had been a signal—perhaps it was—a flute began to play, and the humming of the crowd rose to a higher pitch.

Ishmael came toward the makeshift dais where we sat, holding a red headrag between his hands. This he tied about Margaret's wrist, placing her hand gently back in her lap when he had finished.

"Oh, there is my handkerchief!" she exclaimed, and quite unselfconsciously raised her wrist and wiped her nose.

No one but me seemed to notice. The attention was on Ishmael, who was standing before the crowd, speaking in a language I didn't recognize. The cock in the basket crowed again, and the white roses on the handle quivered violently with its struggles.

"I do wish it wouldn't do that," said Margaret Campbell, rather petulantly. "If it does again, it will be three times, and that's bad luck, isn't it?"

"Is it?" Ishmael was now pouring the rest of the liquor in a circle round the dais. I hoped the flame wouldn't startle her.

"Oh, yes, Archie says so. 'Before the cock crows thrice, thou wilt betray me.' Archie says women are always betrayers. Is that so, do you think?"

"Depends on your point of view, I suppose," I murmured, watching the proceedings. Miss Campbell seemed oblivious to the swaying, humming slaves, the music, the twitching basket, and Ishmael, who was collecting small objects handed to him out of the crowd.

"I'm hungry," she said. "I do hope the tea will be ready soon."

Ishmael heard this. To my amazement, he reached into one of the bags at his waist and unwrapped a small bundle, which proved to hold a cup of chipped and battered porcelain, the remnants of gold leaf still visible on the rim. This he placed ceremoniously on her lap.

"Oh, goody," Margaret said happily, clapping her hands together. "Perhaps there'll be biscuits."

I rather thought not. Ishmael had placed the objects given him by the crowd along the edge of the dais. A few small bones, with lines carved across them, a spray of jasmine, and two or three crude little figures made of wood, each one wrapped in a scrap of cloth, with little shocks of hair glued to the head-nubbins with clay.

Ishmael spoke again, the torch dipped, and a sudden whiff of blue flame shot up around the dais. As it died away, leaving the scent of scorched earth and burnt brandy heavy in the cool night air, he opened the basket and brought out the cock.

It was a large, healthy bird, black feathers glistening in the torchlight. It struggled madly, uttering piercing squawks, but it was firmly trussed, its feet wrapped in cloth to prevent scratching. Ishmael bowed low, saying something, and handed the bird to Margaret.

"Oh, thank you," she said graciously.

The cock stretched out its neck, wattles bright red with agitation, and crowed piercingly. Margaret shook it.

"Naughty bird!" she said crossly, and raising it to her mouth, bit it just behind the head.

I heard the soft crack of the neck bones and the little grunt of effort as she flung her head up, wrenching off the head of the hapless cock.

She clutched the gurgling, struggling trussed carcass tight against her bosom, crooning, "Now, then, now, then, it's all right, darling," as the blood spurted and sprayed into the teacup and all over her dress.

The crowd had cried out at first, but now was quite still, watching. The flute, too, had fallen silent, but the drum beat on, sounding much louder than before.

Margaret dropped the drained carcass carelessly to one side, where a boy darted out of the crowd to retrieve it. She brushed absently at the blood on her skirt, picking up the teacup with her red-swathed hand.

"Guests first," she said politely. "Will you have one lump, Mrs. Malcolm, or two?"

I was fortunately saved from answering by Ishmael, who thrust a crude horn cup into my hands, indicating that I should drink from it. Considering the alternative, I raised it to my mouth without hesitation.

It was fresh-distilled rum, sharp and raw enough to strip the throat, and I choked, wheezing. The tang of some herb rose up the back of my throat and into my nose; something had been mixed with the liquor, or soaked in it. It was faintly tart, but not unpleasant.

Other cups like mine were making their way from hand to hand through the crowd. Ishmael made a sharp gesture, indicating that I should drink more. I obediently raised the cup to my lips, but let the fiery liquid lap against my mouth without swallowing. Whatever was happening here, I thought I might need such wits as I had.

Beside me, Miss Campbell was drinking from her teetotal cup with genteel sips. The feeling of expectancy among the crowd was rising; they were swaying now, and a woman had begun to sing, low and husky, her voice an offbeat counterpoint to the thump of the drum.

The shadow of Ishmael's headdress fell across my face, and I looked up. He too was swaying slowly, back and forth. The collarless white shirt he wore was speckled over the shoulders with black dots of blood, and stuck to his breast with sweat. I thought suddenly that the raw crocodile's head must weigh thirty pounds at least, a terrible weight to support; the muscles of his neck and shoulders were taut with effort.

He raised his hands and began to sing as well. I felt a shiver run down my back and coil at the base of my spine, where my tail would have been. With his face masked, the voice could have been Joe's; deep and honeyed, with a power that commanded attention. If I closed my eyes, it *was* Joe, with the light glinting off his spectacles, and catching the gold tooth far back as he smiled.

Then I opened my eyes again, half-shocked to see instead the crocodile's sinister yawn, and the fire gold-green in the cold, cruel eyes. My mouth was dry and there was a faint buzzing in my ears, weaving around the strong, sweet words.

He was getting attention, all right; the night by the fire was full of eyes, black-wide and shiny, and small moans and shouts marked the pauses in the song.

I closed my eyes and shook my head hard. I grabbed the edge of the wooden bench, clinging to its rough reality. I wasn't drunk, I knew; what-ever herb had been mixed with the rum was potent. I could feel it creeping snakelike through my blood, and kept my eyes tight closed, fighting its progress.

I couldn't block my ears, though, or the sound of that voice, rising and falling.

I didn't know how much time had passed. I came back to myself with a start, suddenly aware that the drum and the singing had stopped.

There was an absolute silence around the fire. I could hear the small rush of flame, and the rustle of cane leaves in the night wind; the quick darting scuttle of a rat in the palm-frond roof of the hut behind me.

The drug was still in my bloodstream, but the effects were dying; I could feel clarity coming back to my thoughts. Not so for the crowd; the eyes were fixed in a single, unblinking stare, like a wall of mirrors, and I thought suddenly of the voodoo legends of my time—of zombies and the *houngans* who made them. What had Geilie said? *Every legend has one foot on the truth*.

Ishmael spoke. He had taken off the crocodile's head. It lay on the ground at our feet, eyes gone dark in the shadow.

"*Ils sont arrivées,*" Ishmael said quietly. *They have come*. He lifted his wet face, lined with exhaustion, and turned to the crowd.

"Who asks?"

As though in response, a young woman in a turban moved out of the crowd, still swaying, half-dazed, and sank down on the ground before the dais. She put her hand on one of the carved images, a crude wooden icon in the shape of a pregnant woman.

Her eyes looked up with hope, and while I didn't recognize the words she spoke, it was clear what she asked.

"*Aya, gado.*" The voice spoke from beside me, but it wasn't Margaret Campbell's. It was the voice of an old woman, cracked and high, but confident, answering in the affirmative.

The young woman gasped with joy, and prostrated herself on the ground. Ishmael nudged her gently with a foot; she got up quickly and backed into the crowd, clutching the small image and bobbing her head, murmuring "*Mana, mana,*" over and over.

Next was a young man, by his face the brother of the first young woman, who squatted respectfully upon his haunches, touching his head before he spoke.

"*Grandmère,*" he began, in high, nasal French. Grandmother? I thought.

He asked his question looking shyly down at the ground. "Does the woman I love return my love?" His was the jasmine spray; he held it so that it brushed the top of a bare, dusty foot.

The woman beside me laughed, her ancient voice ironic but not unkind. "*Certainement,*" she answered. "She returns it; and that of three other men, besides. Find another; less generous, but more worthy."

The young man retired, crestfallen, to be replaced by an older man. This one spoke in an African language I did not know, a tone of bitterness in his voice as he touched one of the clay figures.

"*Setato hoye,*" said—who? The voice had changed. The voice of a man this time, full-grown but not elderly, answering in the same language with an angry tone.

I stole a look to the side, and despite the heat of the fire, felt the chill ripple up my forearms. It was Margaret's face no longer. The outlines were the same, but the eyes were bright, alert and focused on the petitioner, the mouth set in grim command, and the pale throat swelled like a frog's with the effort of strong speech as whoever-it-was argued with the man.

"They are here," Ishmael had said. "They," indeed. He stood to one side, silent but watchful, and I saw his eyes rest on me for a second before coming back to Margaret. Or whatever had been Margaret.

"They." One by one the people came forward, to kneel and ask. Some spoke in English, some French, or the slave patois, some in the African speech of their vanished homes. I couldn't understand all that was said, but when the questions were in French or English, they were often prefaced by a respectful "Grandfather," or "Grandmother," once by "Aunt."

Both the face and the voice of the oracle beside me changed, as "they" came to answer their call; male and female, mostly middle-aged or old, their shadows dancing on her face with the flicker of the fire.

Do you not sometimes imagine that you see things in the fire? The echo of her own small voice came back to me, thin and childish.

Listening, I felt the hair rise on the back of my neck, and understood for the first time what had brought Ishmael back to this place, risking recapture and renewed slavery. Not friendship, not love, nor any loyalty to his fellow slaves, but power.

What price is there for the power to tell the future? Any price, was the answer I saw, looking out at the rapt faces of the congregation. He had come back for Margaret.

It went on for some time. I didn't know how long the drug would last, but I saw people here and there sink down to the ground, and nod to sleep; others melted silently back to the darkness of the huts, and after a time, we were almost alone. Only a few remained around the fire, all men.

They were all husky and confident, and from their attitude, accustomed to command some respect, among slaves at least. They had hung back, together as a group, watching the proceedings, until at last one, clearly the leader, stepped forward.

"They be done, mon," he said to Ishmael, with a jerk of his head toward the sleeping forms around the fire. "Now you ask."

Ishmael's face showed nothing but a slight smile, yet he seemed suddenly nervous. Perhaps it was the closing in of the other men. There was nothing overtly menacing about them, but they seemed both serious and intent—not upon Margaret, for a change, but upon Ishmael.

At last he nodded, and turned to face Margaret. During the hiatus, her face had gone blank; no one at home.

"Bouassa," he said to her. "Come you, Bouassa."

I shrank involuntarily away, as far as I could get on the bench without falling into the fire. Whoever Bouassa was, he had come promptly.

"I be hearin'." It was a voice as deep as Ishmael's, and should have been as pleasant. It wasn't. One of the men took an involuntary step backward.

Ishmael stood alone; the other men seemed to shrink away from him, as though he suffered some contamination.

"Tell me what I want to know, you Bouassa," he said.

Margaret's head tilted slightly, a light of amusement in the pale blue eyes.

"What you want to know?" the deep voice said, with mild scorn. "For why, mon? You be goin', I tell you anything or not."

The small smile on Ishmael's face echoed that on Bouassa's.

"You say true," he said softly. "But these—" He jerked his head toward his companions, not taking his eyes from the face. "They be goin' with me?"

"Might as well," the deep voice said. It chuckled, rather unpleasantly. "The Maggot dies in three days. Won't be nothin' for them here. That all you be wantin' with me?" Not waiting for an answer, Bouassa yawned widely, and a loud belch erupted from Margaret's dainty mouth.

Her mouth closed, and her eyes resumed their vacant stare, but the men weren't noticing. An excited chatter erupted from them, to be hushed by Ishmael, with a significant glance at me. Abruptly quiet, they moved away, still muttering, glancing at me as they went.

Ishmael closed his eyes as the last man left the clearing, and his shoulders sagged. I felt a trifle drained myself.

"What—" I began, and then stopped. Across the fire, a man had stepped from the shelter of the sugarcane. Jamie, tall as the cane itself, with the dying fire staining shirt and face as red as his hair.

He raised a finger to his lips, and I nodded. I gathered my feet cautiously beneath me, picking up my stained skirt in one hand. I could be up, past the fire, and into the cane with him before Ishmael could reach me. But Margaret?

I hesitated, turned to look at her, and saw that her face had come alive once again. It was lifted, eager, lips parted and shining eyes narrowed so that they seemed slightly slanted, as she stared across the fire.

"Daddy?" said Brianna's voice beside me.

The hairs rippled softly erect on my forearms. It was Brianna's voice, Brianna's face, blue eyes dark and slanting with eagerness.

"Bree?" I whispered, and the face turned to me.

"Mama," said my daughter's voice, from the throat of the oracle.

"Brianna," said Jamie, and she turned her head sharply to look at him.

"Daddy," she said, with great certainty. "I knew it was you. I've been dreaming about you."

Jamie's face was white with shock. I saw his lips form the word "Jesus," without sound, and his hand moved instinctively to cross himself.

"Don't let Mama go alone," said the voice with great certainty. "You go with her. I'll keep you safe."

There was no sound save the crackling of the fire. Ishmael stood transfixed, staring at the woman beside me. Then she spoke again, in Brianna's soft, husky tones.

"I love you, Daddy. You too, Mama." She leaned toward me, and I smelled the fresh blood. Then her lips touched mine, and I screamed.

I was not conscious of leaping to my feet, or of crossing the clearing. All I knew was that I was clinging to Jamie, my face buried in the cloth of his coat, shaking.

His heart was pounding under my cheek, and I thought that he was shaking, too. I felt his hand trace the sign of the cross upon my back, and his arm lock tight about my shoulders.

"It's all right," he said, and I could feel his ribs swell and brace with the effort of keeping his voice steady. "She's gone."

I didn't want to look, but forced myself to turn my head toward the fire.

It was a peaceful scene. Margaret Campbell sat quietly on her bench, humming to herself, twiddling a long black tailfeather upon her knee. Ishmael stood behind her, one hand smoothing her hair in what looked like tenderness. He murmured something to her in a low, liquid tongue—a question—and she smiled placidly.

"Oh, I'm not a scrap tired!" she assured him, turning to look fondly up into the scarred face that hovered in the darkness above her. "Such a nice party, wasn't it?"

"Yes, *bébé*," he said gently. "But you rest now, eh?" He turned and clicked his tongue loudly. Suddenly two of the turbaned women materialized out of the night; they must have been waiting, just within call. Ishmael said something to them, and they came at once to tend Margaret, lifting her to her feet and leading her away between them, murmuring soft endearments in African and French.

Ishmael remained, watching us across the fire. He was still as one of Geilie's idols, carved out of night.

"I did not come alone," Jamie said. He gestured casually over his shoulder toward the cane field behind him, implying armed regiments.

"Oh, you be alone, mon," Ishmael said, with a slight smile. "No matter.

The *loa* speak to you; you be safe from me." He glanced back and forth between us, appraising.

"Huh," he said, in a tone of interest. "Never did hear a *loa* speak to *buckra*." He shook his head then, dismissing the matter.

"You be going now," he said, quietly but with considerable authority.

"Not yet." Jamie's arm dropped from my shoulder, and he straightened up beside me. "I have come for the boy Ian; I will not go without him."

Ishmael's brows went up, compressing the three vertical scars between them.

"Huh," he said again. "You forget that boy; he be gone."

"Gone where?" Jamie asked sharply.

The narrow head tilted to one side, as Ishmael looked him over carefully.

"Gone with the Maggot, mon," he said. "And where she go, you don' be going. That boy gone, mon," he said again, with finality. "You leave too, you a wise man." He paused, listening. A drum was talking, somewhere far away, the pulse of it little more than a disturbance of the night air.

"The rest be comin' soon," he remarked. "You safe from me, mon, not from them."

"Who are the rest?" I asked. The terror of the encounter with the *loa* was ebbing, and I was able to talk once more, though my spine still rippled with fear of the dark cane field at my back.

"Maroons, I expect," Jamie said. He raised a brow at Ishmael. "Or ye will be?"

The priest nodded, one formal bob of the head.

"That be true," he said. "You hear Bouassa speak? His *loa* bless us, we go." He gestured toward the huts and the dark hills behind them. "The drum callin' them down from the hills, those strong enough to go."

He turned away, the conversation obviously at an end.

"Wait!" Jamie said. "Tell us where she has gone—Mrs. Abernathy and the boy!"

Ishmael turned back, shoulders mantled in the crocodile's blood.

"To Abandawe," he said.

"And where's that?" Jamie demanded impatiently. I put a hand on his arm.

"I know where it is," I said, and Ishmael's eyes widened in astonishment. "At least—I know it's on Hispaniola. Lawrence told me. That was what Geilie wanted from him—to find out where it was."

"*What* is it? A town, a village? Where?" I could feel Jamie's arm tense under my hand, vibrating with the urgency to be gone.

"It's a cave," I said, feeling cold in spite of the balmy air and the nearness of the fire. "An old cave."

"Abandawe a magic place," Ishmael put in, deep voice soft, as though he feared to speak of it out loud. He looked at me hard, reassessing. "Clotilda say the Maggot take you to the room upstairs. You maybe be knowin' what she do there?"

"A little." My mouth felt dry. I remembered Geilie's hands, soft and plump and white, laying out the gems in their patterns, talking lightly of blood.

As though he caught the echo of this thought, Ishmael took a sudden step toward me.

"I ask you, woman—you still bleed?"

Jamie jerked under my hand, but I squeezed his arm to be still.

"Yes," I said. "Why? What has that to do with it?"

The *oniseegun* was plainly uneasy; he glanced from me back toward the huts. A stir was perceptible in the dark behind him; many bodies were moving to and fro, with a mutter of voices like the whisper of the cane fields. They were getting ready to go.

"A woman bleeds, she kill magic. You bleed, got your woman-power, the magic don't work for you. It the old women do magic; witch someone, call the *loas*, make sick, make well." He gave me a long, appraising look, and shook his head.

"You ain' gone do the magic, what the Maggot do. That magic kill her, sure, but it kill you, too." He gestured behind him, toward the empty bench. "You hear Bouassa speak? He say the Maggot die, three days. She taken the boy, he die. You go follow them, mon, you die, too, sure."

He stared at Jamie, and raised his hands in front of him, wrists crossed as though bound together. "I tell you, *amiki*," he said. He let his hands fall, jerking them apart, breaking the invisible bond. He turned abruptly, and vanished into the darkness, where the shuffle of feet was growing louder, punctuated with bumps as heavy objects were shifted.

"Holy Michael defend us," muttered Jamie. He ran a hand hard through his hair, making fiery wisps stand out in the flickering light. The fire was dying fast, with no one left to tend it.

"D'ye ken this place, Sassenach? Where Geillis has gone wi' Ian?"

"No, all I know is that it's somewhere up in the far hills on Hispaniola, and that a stream runs through it."

"Then we must take Stern," he said with decision. "Come on; the lads are by the river wi' the boat."

I turned to follow him, but paused on the edge of the cane field to look back.

"Jamie! Look!" Behind us lay the embers of the *egungun*'s fire, and the shadowy ring of slave huts. Farther away, the bulk of Rose Hall made a light patch against the hillside. But farther still, beyond the shoulder of the hill, the sky glowed faintly red.

"That will be Howe's place, burning," he said. He sounded oddly calm, without emotion. He pointed to the left, toward the flank of the mountain, where a small orange dot glowed, no more at this distance than a pinprick of light. "And that will be Twelvetrees, I expect."

The drum-voice whispered through the night, up and down the river. What had Ishmael said? *The drum callin' them down from the hills—those strong enough to go.*

A small line of slaves was coming down from the huts, women carrying babies and bundles, cooking pots slung over their shoulders, heads turbaned in white. Next to one young woman, who held her arm with careful respect, walked Margaret Campbell, likewise turbaned.

Jamie saw her, and stepped forward.

"Miss Campbell!" he said sharply. "Margaret!"

Margaret and her attendant stopped; the young woman moved as though to step between her charge and Jamie, but he held up both hands as he came, to show he meant no harm, and she reluctantly stepped back.

"Margaret," he said. "Margaret, do ye not know me?"

She stared vacantly at him. Very slowly, he touched her, holding her face between his hands.

"Margaret," he said to her, low-voiced, urgent. "Margaret, hear me! D'ye ken me, Margaret?"

She blinked once, then twice, and the smooth round face melted and thawed into life. It was not like the sudden possession of the *loas;* this was a slow, tentative coming, of something shy and fearful.

"Aye, I ken ye, Jamie," she said at last. Her voice was rich and pure, a young girl's voice. Her lips curled up, and her eyes came alive once more, her face still held in the hollow of his hands.

"It's been lang since I saw ye, Jamie," she said, looking up into his eyes. "Will ye have word of Ewan, then? Is he well?"

He stood very still for a minute, his face that careful blank mask that hid strong feeling.

"He is well," he whispered at last. "Verra well, Margaret. He gave me this, to keep until I saw ye." He bent his head and kissed her gently.

Several of the women had stopped, standing silently by to watch. At this, they moved and began to murmur, glancing uneasily at each other. When he released Margaret Campbell and stepped back, they closed in around her, protective and wary, nodding him back.

Margaret seemed oblivious; her eyes were still on Jamie's face, the smile on her lips.

"I thank ye, Jamie!" she called, as her attendant took her arm and began to urge her away. "Tell Ewan I'll be with him soon!" The little band of white-clothed women moved away, disappearing like ghosts into the darkness by the cane field.

Jamie made an impulsive move in their direction, but I stopped him with a hand on his arm.

"Let her go," I whispered, mindful of what lay on the floor in the salon of the plantation house. "Jamie, let her go. You can't stop her; she's better with them."

He closed his eyes briefly, then nodded.

"Aye, you're right." He turned, then stopped suddenly, and I whirled about to see what he had seen. There were lights in Rose Hall now. Torch-light, flickering behind the windows, upstairs and down. As we watched, a surly glow began to swell in the windows of the secret workroom on the second floor.

"It's past time to go," Jamie said. He seized my hand and we went quickly, diving into the dark rustle of the canes, fleeing through air suddenly thick with the smell of burning sugar.

62

Abandawe

"You can take the Governor's pinnace; that's small, but it's seawor-thy." Grey fumbled through the drawer of his desk. "I'll write an order for the dockers to hand it over to you."

"Aye, we'll need the boat—I canna risk the *Artemis;* as she's Jared's—but I think we'd best steal it, John." Jamie's brows were drawn together in a frown. "I wouldna have ye be involved wi' me in any visible way, aye? You'll be having trouble enough with things, without that."

Grey smiled unhappily. "Trouble? Yes, you might call it trouble, with four plantation houses burnt, and over two hundred slaves gone—God knows where! But I vastly doubt that anyone will take notice of my social acquain-tance, under the circumstances. Between fear of the Maroons and fear of the Chinaman, the whole island is in such a panic that a mere smuggler is the most negligible of trivialities."

"It's a great relief to me to be thought trivial," Jamie said, very dryly. "Still, we'll steal the boat. And if we're taken, ye've never heard my name or seen my face, aye?"

Grey stared at him, a welter of emotions fighting for mastery of his fea-tures, amusement, fear, and anger among them.

"Is that right?" he said at last. "Let you be taken, watch them hang you, and keep quiet about it—for fear of smirching my reputation? For God's sake, Jamie, what do you take me for?"

Jamie's mouth twitched slightly.

"For a friend, John," he said. "And if I'll take your friendship—and your damned boat!—then you'll take mine, and keep quiet. Aye?"

The Governor glared at him for a moment, lips pressed tight, but then his shoulders sagged in defeat.

"I will," he said shortly. "But I should regard it as a great personal favor if you would endeavor not to be captured."

Jamie rubbed a knuckle across his mouth, hiding a smile.

"I'll try verra hard, John."

The Governor sat down, wearily. There were deep circles under his eyes, and his impeccable linen was wilted; obviously he had not changed his clothes from the day before.

"All right. I don't know where you're going, and it's likely better I don't.

But if you can, keep out of the sealanes north of Antigua. I sent a boat this morning, to ask for as many men as the barracks there can supply, marines and sailors both. They'll be heading this way by the day after tomorrow at the latest, to guard the town and harbor against the escaped Maroons in case of an outright rebellion."

I caught Jamie's eye, and raised one brow in question, but he shook his head, almost imperceptibly. We had told the Governor of the uprising on the Yallahs River, and the escape of the slaves—something he had heard about from other sources, anyway. We had not told him what we had seen later that night, lying to under cover of a tiny cove, sails taken down to hide their whiteness.

The river was dark as onyx, but with a fugitive gleam from the broad expanse of water. We had heard them coming, and had time to hide before the ship came down upon us; the beating of drums and a savage exultation of many voices echoing through the river valley as the *Bruja* sailed past us, carried by the downward current. The bodies of the pirates no doubt lay somewhere upriver, left to rot peacefully among the frangipani and cedar.

The escaped slaves of the Yallahs River had not gone into the mountains of Jamaica, but out to sea, presumably to join Bouassa's followers on Hispaniola. The townsfolk of Kingston had nothing to fear from the escaped slaves —but it was a good deal better that the Royal Navy should concentrate their attention here than on Hispaniola, where we were bound.

Jamie rose to take our leave, but Grey stopped him.

"Wait. Will you not require a safe place for your—for Mrs. Fraser?" He didn't look at me, but at Jamie, eyes steady. "I should be honored if you would entrust her to my protection. She could stay here, in the Residence, until you return. No one would trouble her—or even need to know she was here."

Jamie hesitated, but there was no gentle way to phrase it.

"She must go with me, John," he said. "There is no choice about it; she must."

Grey's glance flickered to me, then away, but not before I had seen the look of jealousy in his eyes. I felt sorry for him, but there was nothing I could say; no way to tell him the truth.

"Yes," he said, and swallowed noticeably. "I see. Quite."

Jamie held out a hand to him. He hesitated for a moment, but then took it.

"Good luck, Jamie," he said, voice a little husky. "God go with you."

＜━━◆━━＞

Fergus had been somewhat more difficult to deal with. He had insisted absolutely on accompanying us, offering argument after argument, and arguing the more vehemently when he found that the Scottish smugglers would sail with us.

"You take them, but you will go without *me*?" Fergus's face was alive with indignation.

"I will," Jamie said firmly. "The smugglers are widowers or bachelors, all, but you're a marrit man." He glanced pointedly at Marsali, who stood watching the discussion, her face drawn with anxiety. "I thought she was oweryoung to be wed, and I was wrong; but I *know* she's oweryoung to be widowed. You'll stay." And he turned aside, the matter settled.

It was full dark when we set sail in Grey's pinnace, a thirty-foot, single-decked sloop, leaving two docksmen bound and gagged in the boathouse behind us. It was a small, single-masted ship, bigger than the fishing boat in which we had traveled up the Yallahs River, but barely large enough to qualify for the designation "ship."

Nonetheless, she seemed seaworthy enough, and we were soon out of Kingston Harbor, heeling over in a brisk evening breeze, on our way toward Hispaniola.

The smugglers handled the sailing among them, leaving Jamie, Lawrence and I to sit on one of the long benches along the rail. We chatted desultorily of this and that, but after a time, fell silent, absorbed in our own thoughts.

Jamie yawned repeatedly, and finally, at my urging, consented to lie down upon the bench, his head resting in my lap. I was myself strung too tightly to want to sleep.

Lawrence too was wakeful, staring upward into the sky, hands folded behind his head.

"There is moisture in the air tonight," he said, nodding upward toward the silver sliver of the crescent moon. "See the haze about the moon? It may rain before dawn; unusual for this time of year."

Talk about the weather seemed sufficiently boring to soothe my jangled nerves. I stroked Jamie's hair, thick and soft under my hand.

"Is that so?" I said. "You and Jamie both seem able to read the weather from the sky. All I know is the old bit about 'Red sky at night, sailor's delight; red sky at morning, sailor take warning.' I didn't notice what color the sky was tonight, did you?"

Lawrence laughed comfortably. "Rather a light purple," he said. "I cannot say whether it will be red in the morning, but it is surprising how frequently such signs are reliable. But of course there is a scientific principle involved—the refraction of light from the moisture in the air, just as I observed presently of the moon."

I lifted my chin, enjoying the breeze that lifted the heavy hair that fell on my neck.

"But what about odd phenomena? Supernatural things?" I asked him. "What about things where the rules of science seem not to apply?" *I am a scientist,* I heard him say in memory, his slight accent seeming only to reinforce his matter-of-factness. *I don't believe in ghosts.*

"Such as what, these phenomena?"

"Well—" I groped for a moment, then fell back on Geilie's own examples. "People who have bleeding stigmata, for example? Astral travel? Visions, supernatural manifestations . . . odd things, that can't be explained rationally."

Lawrence grunted, and settled his bulk more comfortably on the bench beside me.

"Well, I say it is the place of science only to observe," he said. "To seek cause where it may be found, but to realize that there are many things in the world for which no cause shall *be* found; not because it does not exist, but because we know too little to find it. It is not the place of science to insist on explanation—but only to observe, in hopes that the explanation will manifest itself."

"That may be science, but it isn't human nature," I objected. "People go on wanting explanations."

"They do." He was becoming interested in the discussion; he leaned back, folding his hands across his slight paunch, in a lecturer's attitude. "It is for this reason that a scientist constructs hypotheses—suggestions for the cause of an observation. But a hypothesis must never be confused with an explanation—with proof.

"I have seen a great many things which might be described as peculiar. Fish-falls, for instance, where a great many fish—all of the same species, mind you, all the same size—fall suddenly from a clear sky, over dry land. There would appear to be no rational cause for this—and yet, is it therefore suitable to attribute the phenomenon to supernatural interference? On the face of it, does it seem more likely that some celestial intelligence should amuse itself by flinging shoals of fish at us from the sky, or that there is some meteorological phenomenon—a waterspout, a tornado, something of the kind?—that while not visible to us, is still in operation? And yet"—his voice became more pensive—"why—and how!—might a natural phenomenon such as a waterspout remove the heads—and only the heads—of all the fish?"

"Have you seen such a thing yourself?" I asked, interested, and he laughed.

"There speaks a scientific mind!" he said, chuckling. "The first thing a scientist asks—how do you know? Who has seen it? Can I see it myself? Yes, I have seen such a thing—three times, in fact, though in one case the precipitation was of frogs, rather than fish.

"Were you near a seashore or a lake?"

"Once near a shore, once near a lake—that was the frogs—but the third time, it took place far inland; some twenty miles from the nearest body of water. And yet the fish were of a kind I have seen only in the deep ocean. In none of the cases did I see any sort of disturbance of the upper air—no clouds, no great wind, none of the fabled spouts of water that rise from the sea into the sky, assuredly. And yet the fish fell; so much is a fact, for I have seen them."

"And it isn't a fact if you haven't seen it?" I asked dryly.

He laughed in delight, and Jamie stirred, murmuring against my thigh. I smoothed his hair, and he relaxed into sleep again.

"It may be so; it may not. But a scientist could not say, could he? What is it the Christian Bible says—'Blest are they who have not seen, but have believed'?"

"That's what it says, yes."

"Some things must be accepted as fact without provable cause." He laughed again, this time without much humor. "As a scientist who is also a Jew, I have perhaps a different perspective on such phenomena as stigmata—and the idea of resurrection of the dead, which a very great proportion of the civilized world accepts as fact beyond question. And yet, this skeptical view is not one I could even breathe, to anyone save yourself, without grave danger of personal harm."

"Doubting Thomas was a Jew, after all," I said, smiling. "To begin with."

"Yes; and only when he ceased to doubt, did he become a Christian—and a martyr. One could argue that it was surety that killed him, no?" His voice was heavy with irony. "There is a great difference between those phenomena which are accepted on faith, and those which are proved by objective determination, though the cause of both may be equally 'rational' once known. And the chief difference is this: that people will treat with disdain such phenomena as are proved by the evidence of the senses, and commonly experienced—while they will defend to the death the reality of a phenomenon which they have neither seen nor experienced.

"Faith is as powerful a force as science," he concluded, voice soft in the darkness, "—but far more dangerous."

We sat quietly for a time, looking over the bow of the tiny ship, toward the thin slice of darkness that divided the night, darker than the purple glow of the sky, or the silver-gray sea. The black island of Hispaniola, drawing inexorably closer.

"Where did you see the headless fish?" I asked suddenly, and was not surprised to see the faint inclination of his head toward the bow.

"There," he said. "I have seen a good many odd things among these islands—but perhaps more there than anywhere else. Some places are like that."

I didn't speak for several minutes, pondering what might lie ahead—and hoping that Ishmael had been right in saying that it was Ian whom Geillis had taken with her to Abandawe. A thought occurred to me—one that had been lost or pushed aside during the events of the last twenty-four hours.

"Lawrence—the other Scottish boys. Ishmael told us he saw twelve of them, including Ian. When you were searching the plantation . . . did you find any trace of the others?"

He drew in his breath sharply, but did not answer at once. I could feel him, turning over words in his mind, trying to decide how to say what the chill in my bones had already told me.

The answer, when it came, was not from Lawrence, but from Jamie.

"We found them," he said softly, from the darkness. His hand rested on my knee, and squeezed gently. "Dinna ask more, Sassenach—for I willna tell ye."

I understood. Ishmael had to have been right; it must be Ian with Geilie, for Jamie could bear no other possibility. I laid a hand on his head, and he stirred slightly, turning so that his breath touched my hand.

"Blest are they who have not seen," I whispered under my breath, *"but have believed."*

We dropped anchor near dawn, in a small, nameless bay on the northern coast of Hispaniola. There was a narrow beach, faced with cliffs, and through a split in the rock, a narrow, sandy trail was visible, leading into the interior of the island.

Jamie carried me the few steps to shore, set me down, and then turned to Innes, who had splashed ashore with one of the parcels of food.

"I thank ye, *a charaid*," he said formally. "We shall part here; with the Virgin's blessing, we will meet here again in four days' time."

Innes's narrow face contracted in surprised disappointment; then resignation settled on his features.

"Aye," he said. "I'll mind the boatie then, 'til ye all come back."

Jamie saw the expression, and shook his head, smiling.

"Not just you, man; did I need a strong arm, it would be yours I should call on first. No, all of ye shall stay, save my wife and the Jew."

Resignation was replaced by sheer surprise.

"Stay here? All of us? But will ye not have need of us, Mac Dubh?" He squinted anxiously at the cliffs, with their burden of flowering vines. "It looks a fearsome place to venture into, without friends."

"I shall count it the act of greatest friendship for ye to wait here, as I say, Duncan," Jamie said, and I realized with a slight shock that I had never known Innes's given name.

Innes glanced again at the cliffs, his lean face troubled, then bent his head in acquiescence.

"Well, it's you as shall say, Mac Dubh. But ye ken we are willing—all of us."

Jamie nodded, his face turned away.

"Aye, I ken that fine, Duncan," he said softly. Then he turned back, held out an arm, and Innes embraced him, his one arm awkwardly thumping Jamie's back.

"If a ship should come," Jamie said, letting go, "then I wish ye to take heed for yourselves. The Royal Navy will be looking for that pinnace, aye? I doubt they shall come here, looking, but if they should—or if anything else at all should threaten ye—then leave. Sail away at once."

"And leave ye here? Nay, ye can order me to do a great many things, Mac Dubh, and do them I shall—but not that."

Jamie frowned and shook his head; the rising sun struck sparks from his hair and the stubble of his beard, wreathing his head in fire.

"It will do me and my wife no good to have ye killed, Duncan. Mind what I say. If a ship comes—go." He turned aside then, and went to take leave of the other Scots.

Innes sighed deeply, his face etched with disapproval, but he made no further protest.

It was hot and damp in the jungle, and there was little talk among the three of us as we made our way inland. There was nothing to say, after all; Jamie and I could not speak of Brianna before Lawrence, and there were no plans to be made until we reached Abandawe, and saw what was there. I dozed fitfully at night, waking several times to see Jamie, back against a tree near me, eyes fixed sightless on the fire.

At noon of the second day, we reached the place. A steep and rocky hillside of gray limestone rose before us, sprouted over with spiky aloes and a ruffle of coarse grass. And on the crest of the hill, I could see them. Great standing stones, megaliths, in a rough circle about the crown of the hill.

"You didn't say there was a stone circle," I said. I felt faint, and not only from the heat and damp.

"Are you quite well, Mrs. Fraser?" Lawrence peered at me in some alarm, his genial face flushed beneath its tan.

"Yes," I said, but my face must as usual have given me away, for Jamie was there in a moment, taking my arm and steadying me with a hand about my waist.

"For God's sake, be careful, Sassenach!" he muttered. "Dinna go near those things!"

"We have to know if Geilie's there, with Ian," I said. "Come on." I forced my reluctant feet into motion, and he came with me, still muttering under his breath in Gaelic—I thought it was a prayer.

"They were put up a very long time ago," Lawrence said, as we came up onto the crest of the hill, within a few feet of the stones. "Not by slaves—by the aboriginal inhabitants of the islands."

The circle was empty, and innocent-looking. No more than a staggered circle of large stones, set on end, motionless under the sun. Jamie was watching my face anxiously.

"Can ye hear them, Claire?" he said. Lawrence looked startled, but said nothing as I advanced carefully toward the nearest stone.

"I don't know," I said. "It isn't one of the proper days—not a Sun Feast, or a Fire Feast, I mean. It may not be open now; I don't know."

Holding tightly to Jamie's hand, I edged forward, listening. There seemed a faint hum in the air, but it might be no more than the usual sound of the jungle insects. Very gently, I laid the palm of my hand against the nearest stone.

I was dimly conscious of Jamie calling my name. Somewhere, my mind was struggling on a physical level, making the conscious effort to lift and lower my diaphragm, to squeeze and release the chambers of my heart. My ears were filled with a pulsating hum, a vibration too deep for sound, that throbbed in the marrow of my bones. And in some small, still place in the center of the chaos was Geilie Duncan, green eyes smiling into mine.

"Claire!"

I was lying on the ground, Jamie and Lawrence bending over me, faces dark and anxious against the sky. There was dampness on my cheeks, and a trickle of water ran down my neck. I blinked, cautiously moving my extremities, to be sure I still possessed them.

Jamie put down the handkerchief with which he had been bathing my face, and lifted me to a sitting position.

"Are ye all right, Sassenach?"

"Yes," I said, still mildly confused. "Jamie—she's here!"

"Who? Mrs. Abernathy?" Lawrence's heavy eyebrows shot up, and he glanced hastily behind him, as though expecting her to materialize on the spot.

"I heard her—saw her—whatever." My wits were coming slowly back. "She's here. Not in the circle; close by."

"Can ye tell where?" Jamie's hand was resting on his dirk, as he darted quick glances all around us.

I shook my head, and closed my eyes, trying—reluctantly—to recapture that moment of seeing. There was an impression of darkness, of damp coolness, and the flicker of red torchlight.

"I think she's in a cave," I said, amazed. "Is it close by, Lawrence?"

"It is," he said, watching my face with intense curiosity. "The entrance is not far from here."

"Take us there." Jamie was on his feet, lifting me to mine.

"Jamie." I stopped him with a hand on his arm.

"Aye?"

"Jamie—she knows I'm here, too."

That stopped him, all right. He paused, and I saw him swallow. Then his jaw tightened, and he nodded.

"A Mhìcheal bheannaichte, dìon sinn bho dheamhainnean," he said softly, and turned toward the edge of the hill. Blessed Michael, defend us from demons.

The blackness was absolute. I brought my hand to my face; felt my palm brush my nose, but saw nothing. It wasn't an empty blackness, though. The floor of the passage was uneven, with small sharp particles that crunched underfoot, and the walls in some places grew so close together that I wondered how Geilie had ever managed to squeeze through.

Even in the places where the passage grew wider, and the stone walls were too far away for my outstretched hands to brush against, I could feel them. It was like being in a dark room with another person—someone who kept quite silent, but whose presence I could feel, never more than an arm's length away.

Jamie's hand was tight on my shoulder, and I could feel his presence behind me, a warm disturbance in the cool void of the cave.

"Are we headed right?" he asked, when I stopped for a moment to catch my breath. "There are passages to the sides; I feel them as we pass. How can ye tell where we're going?"

"I can hear. Hear them. It. Don't you hear?" It was a struggle to speak, to form coherent thoughts. The call here was different; not the beehive sound of Craigh na Dun, but a hum like the vibration of the air following the striking of a great bell. I could feel it ringing in the long bones of my arms, echoing through pectoral girdle and spine.

Jamie gripped my arm hard.

"Stay with me!" he said. "Sassenach—don't let it take ye; stay!"

I reached blindly out and he caught me tight against his chest. The thump of his heart against my temple was louder than the hum.

"Jamie. Jamie, hold on to me." I had never been more frightened. "Don't let me go. If it takes me—Jamie, I can't come back again. It's worse every time. It will kill me, Jamie!"

His arms tightened round me 'til I felt my ribs crack, and gasped for breath. After a moment, he let go, and putting me gently aside, moved past me into the passage, taking care to keep his hand always on me.

"I'll go first," he said. "Put your hand in my belt, and dinna let go for anything."

Linked together, we moved slowly down, farther into the dark. Lawrence had wanted to come, but Jamie would not let him. We had left him at the mouth of the cave, waiting. If we should not return, he was to go back to the beach, to keep the rendezvous with Innes and the other Scots.

If we should not return . . .

He must have felt my grip tighten, for he stopped, and drew me alongside him.

"Claire," he said softly. "I must say something."

I knew already, and groped for his mouth to stop him, but my hand brushed by his face in the dark. He gripped my wrist, and held tight.

"If it will be a choice between her and one of us—then it must be me. Ye know that, aye?"

I knew that. If Geilie should be there, still, and one of us might be killed in stopping her, it must be Jamie to take the risk. For with Jamie dead, I would be left—and I could follow her through the stone, which he could not.

"I know," I whispered at last. I knew also what he did not say, and what he knew as well; that should Geilie have gone through already, then I must go as well.

"Then kiss me, Claire," he whispered. "And know that you are more to me than life, and I have no regret."

I couldn't answer, but kissed him, first his hand, its crooked fingers warm and firm, and the brawny wrist of a sword-wielder, and then his mouth, haven and promise and anguish all mingled, and the salt of tears in the taste of him.

Then I let go, and turned toward the left-hand tunnel.

"This way," I said. Within ten paces, I saw the light.

It was no more than a faint glow on the rocks of the passage, but it was enough to restore the gift of sight. Suddenly, I could see my hands and feet, though dimly. My breath came out in something like a sob, of relief and fear. I felt like a ghost taking shape as I walked toward the light and the soft bell-hum before me.

The light was stronger, now, then dimmed again as Jamie slid in front of me, and his back blocked my view. Then he bent and stepped through a low archway. I followed, and stood up in light.

It was a good-sized chamber, the walls farthest from the torch still cold and black with the slumber of the cave. The wall before us had wakened, though. It flickered and gleamed, particles of embedded mineral reflecting the flames of a pine torch, fixed in a crevice.

"So ye came, did you?" Geillis was on her knees, eyes fixed on a glittering stream of white powder that fell from her folded fist, drawing a line on the dark floor.

I heard a small sound from Jamie, half relief, half horror, as he saw Ian. The boy lay in the middle of the pentacle on his side, hands bound behind him, gagged with a strip of white cloth. Next to him lay an ax. It was made of a shiny dark stone, like obsidian, with a sharp, chipped edge. The handle was covered with gaudy beadwork, in an African pattern of stripes and zigzags.

"Don't come any closer, fox." Geilie sat back on her heels, showing her teeth to Jamie in an expression that was not a smile. She held a pistol in one hand; its fellow, charged and cocked, was thrust through the leather belt she wore about her waist.

Eyes fixed on Jamie, she reached into the pouch suspended from the belt and withdrew another handful of diamond dust. I could see beads of sweat standing on her broad white brow; the bell-hum from the time-passage must be reaching her as it reached me. I felt sick, and the sweat ran down my body in trickles under my clothes.

The pattern was almost finished. With the pistol carefully trained, she dribbled out the thin, shining stream until she had completed the penta-gram. The stones were already laid inside it—they glinted from the floor in sparks of color, connected by a gleaming line of poured quicksilver.

"There, then." She sat back on her heels with a sigh of relief, and wiped the thick, creamy hair back with one hand. "Safe. The diamond dust keeps out the noise," she explained to me. "Nasty, isn't it?"

She patted Ian, who lay bound and gagged on the ground in front of her, his eyes wide with fear above the white cloth of the gag. "There, there, *mo chridhe*. Dinna fret, it will be soon over."

"Take your hand off him, ye wicked bitch!" Jamie took an impulsive step forward, hand on his dirk, then stopped, as she lifted the barrel of the pistol an inch.

"Ye mind me o' your uncle Dougal, *a sionnach*," she said, tilting her head to one side coquettishly. "He was older when I met him than you are now, but you've the look of him about ye, aye? Like ye'd take what ye pleased and damn anyone who stands in your way."

Jamie looked at Ian, curled on the floor, then up at Geilie.

"I'll take what's mine," he said softly.

"But ye can't, now, can ye?" she said, pleasantly. "One more step, and I kill ye dead. I spare ye now, only because Claire seems fond of ye." Her eyes shifted to me, standing in the shadows behind Jamie. She nodded to me.

"A life for a life, sweet Claire. Ye tried to save me once, on Craigh na Dun; I saved you from the witch-trial at Cranesmuir. We're quits now, aye?"

Geilie picked up a small bottle, uncorked it, and poured the contents carefully over Ian's clothes. The smell of brandy rose up, strong and heady, and the torch flared brighter as the fumes of alcohol reached it. Ian bucked and kicked, making a strained noise of protest, and she kicked him sharply in the ribs.

"Be still!" she said.

"Don't do it, Geilie," I said, knowing that words would do no good.

"I have to," she said calmly. "I'm meant to. I'm sorry I shall have to take the girl, but I'll leave ye the man."

"What girl?" Jamie's fists were clenched tight at his side, knuckles white even in the dim torchlight.

"Brianna? That's the name, isn't it?" She shook back her heavy hair, smoothing it out of her face. "The last of Lovat's line." She smiled at me. "What luck ye should have come to see me, aye? I'd never ha' kent it, otherwise. I thought they'd all died out before 1900."

A thrill of horror shot through me. I could feel the same tremor run through Jamie as his muscles tightened.

It must have shown on his face. Geilie cried out sharply and leapt back. She fired as he lunged at her. His head snapped back, and his body twisted, hands still reaching for her throat. Then he fell, his body limp across the edge of the glittering pentagram. There was a strangled moan from Ian.

I felt rather than heard a sound rise in my throat. I didn't know what I had said, but Geilie turned her face in my direction, startled.

When Brianna was two, a car had carelessly sideswiped mine, hitting the back door next to where she was sitting. I slowed to a stop, checked briefly to see that she was unhurt, and then bounded out, headed for the other car, which had pulled over a little way ahead.

The other driver was a man in his thirties, quite large, and probably entirely self-assured in his dealings with the world. He looked over his shoulder, saw me coming, and hastily rolled up his window, shrinking back in his seat.

I had no consciousness of rage or any other emotion; I simply *knew,* with no shadow of doubt, that I could—and would—shatter the window with my hand, and drag the man out through it. He knew it, too.

I thought no further than that, and didn't have to; the arrival of a police car had recalled me to my normal state of mind, and then I started to shake. But the memory of the look on that man's face stayed with me.

Fire is a poor illuminator, but it would have taken total darkness to conceal that look on Geilie's face; the sudden realization of what was coming toward her.

She jerked the other pistol from her belt and swung it to bear on me; I saw the round hole of the muzzle clearly—and didn't care. The roar of the discharge caromed through the cave, the echoes sending down showers of rocks and dirt, but by then I had seized the ax from the floor.

I noted quite clearly the leather binding, ornamented with a beaded pattern. It was red, with yellow zigzags and black dots. The dots echoed the shiny obsidian of the blade, and the red and yellow picked up the hues of the flaming torch behind her.

I heard a noise behind me, but didn't turn. Reflections of the fire burned red in the pupils of her eyes. *The red thing,* Jamie had called it. *I gave myself to it,* he had said.

I didn't need to give myself; it had taken me.

There was no fear, no rage, no doubt. Only the stroke of the swinging ax.

The shock of it echoed up my arm, and I let go, my fingers numbed. I stood quite still, not even moving when she staggered toward me.

Blood in firelight is black, not red.

She took one blind step forward and fell, all her muscles gone limp, making no attempt to save herself. The last I saw of her face was her eyes; set wide, beautiful as gemstones, a green water-clear and faceted with the knowledge of death.

Someone was speaking, but the words made no sense. The cleft in the rock buzzed loudly, filling my ears. The torch flickered, flaring sudden yellow in a draft; the beating of the dark angel's wings, I thought.

The sound came again, behind me.

I turned and saw Jamie. He had risen to his knees, swaying. Blood was pouring from his scalp, dyeing one side of his face red-black. The other side was white as a harlequin's mask.

Stop the bleeding, said some remnant of instinct in my brain, and I fumbled for a handkerchief. But by then he had crawled to where Ian lay, and was groping at the boy's bonds, jerking loose the leather straps, drops of his blood pattering on the lad's shirt. Ian squirmed to his feet, his face ghastly pale, and put out a hand to help his uncle.

Then Jamie's hand was on my arm. I looked up, numbly offering the cloth. He took it and wiped it roughly over his face, then jerked at my arm, pulling me toward the tunnel mouth. I stumbled and nearly fell, caught myself, and came back to the present.

"Come!" he was saying. "Can ye not hear the wind? There is a storm coming, above."

Wind? I thought. In a cave? But he was right; the draft had not been my imagination; the faint exhalation from the crack near the entrance had changed to a steady, whining wind, almost a keening that rang in the narrow passage.

I turned to look over my shoulder, but Jamie grasped my arm hard and pushed me forward. My last sight of the cave was a blurred impression of jet and rubies, with a still white shape in the middle of the floor. Then the draft came in with a roar, and the torch went out.

"Jesus!" It was Young Ian's voice, filled with terror, somewhere close by. "Uncle Jamie!"

"Here." Jamie's voice came out of the darkness just in front of me, surprisingly calm, raised to be heard above the noise. "Here, lad. Come here to me, Ian. Dinna be afraid; it's only the cave breathing."

It was the wrong thing to say. When he said it, I could *feel* the cold breath of the rock touch my neck, and the hairs there rose up prickling. The image of the cave as a living thing, breathing all around us, blind and malevolent, struck me cold with horror.

Apparently the notion was as terrifying to Ian as it was to me, for I heard a faint gasp, and then his groping hand struck me and clung for dear life to my arm.

I clutched his hand with one of mine and probed the dark ahead with the other, finding Jamie's reassuringly large shape almost at once.

"I've got Ian," I said. "For God's sake, let's get out of here!"

He gripped my hand in answer, and linked together, we began to make our way back down the winding tunnel, stumbling through the pitch dark and stepping on each other's heels. And all the time, that ghostly wind whined at our backs.

I could see nothing; no hint of Jamie's shirt in front of my face, snowy white as I knew it to be, not even a flicker of the movement of my own light-colored skirts, though I heard them swish about my feet as I walked, the sound blending with that of the wind.

The thin rush of air rose and fell in pitch, whispering and wailing. I tried to force my mind away from the memory of what lay behind us, away from the morbid fancy that the wind held sighing voices, whispering secrets just past hearing.

"I can hear her," Ian said suddenly behind me. His voice rose, cracking with panic. "I can hear her! God, oh God, she's coming!"

I froze in my tracks, a scream wedged in my throat. The cool observer in my head knew quite well it was not so—only the wind and Ian's fright—but that made no difference to the spurt of sheer terror that rose from the pit of my stomach and turned my bowels to water. I knew she was coming, too, and screamed out loud.

Then Jamie had me, and Ian too, gripped tight against him, one in each arm, our ears muffled against his chest. He smelled of pine smoke and sweat and brandy, and I nearly sobbed in relief at the closeness of him.

"Hush!" he said fiercely. "Hush, the both of ye! I willna let her touch ye. Never!" He pressed us to him, hard; I felt his heart beating fast beneath my cheek and Ian's bony shoulder, squeezed against mine, and then the pressure relaxed.

"Come along now," Jamie said, more quietly. "It's but wind. Caves blow through their cracks when the weather changes aboveground. I've heard it before. There is a storm coming, outside. Come, now."

The storm was a brief one. By the time we had stumbled to the surface, blinking against the shock of sunlight, the rain had passed, leaving the world reborn in its wake.

Lawrence was sheltering under a dripping palm near the cave's entrance. When he saw us, he sprang to his feet, a look of relief relaxing the creases of his face.

"It is all right?" he said, looking from me to a blood-stained Jamie.

Jamie gave him half a smile, nodding.

"It is all right," he said. He turned and motioned to Ian. "May I present my nephew, Ian Murray? Ian, this is Dr. Stern, who's been of great assistance to us in looking for ye."

"I'm much obliged to ye, Doctor," Ian said, with a bob of his head. He wiped a sleeve across his streaked face, and glanced at Jamie.

"I knew ye'd come, Uncle Jamie," he said, with a tremulous smile, "but ye left it a bit late, aye?" The smile widened, then broke, and he began to tremble. He blinked hard, fighting back tears.

"I did then, and I'm sorry, Ian. Come here, *a bhalaich*." Jamie reached out and took him in a close embrace, patting his back and murmuring to him in Gaelic.

I watched for a moment, before I realized that Lawrence was speaking to me.

"Are you quite well, Mrs. Fraser?" he was asking. Without waiting for an answer, he took my arm.

"I don't quite know." I felt completely empty. Exhausted as though by childbirth, but without the exultation of spirit. Nothing seemed quite real; Jamie, Ian, Lawrence, all seemed like toy figures that moved and talked at a distance, making noises that I had to strain to understand.

"I think perhaps we should leave this place," Lawrence said, with a glance at the cave mouth from which we had just emerged. He looked slightly uneasy. He didn't ask about Mrs. Abernathy.

"I think you are right." The picture of the cave we had left was vivid in my mind—but just as unreal as the vivid green jungle and gray stones around us. Not waiting for the men to follow, I turned and walked away.

The feeling of remoteness increased as we walked. I felt like an automaton, built around an iron core, walking by clockwork. I followed Jamie's broad back through branches and clearings, shadow and sun, not noticing where we were going. Sweat ran down my sides and into my eyes, but I barely stirred to wipe it away. At length, toward sunset, we stopped in a small clearing near a stream, and made our primitive camp.

I had already discovered that Lawrence was a most useful person to have along on a camping trip. He was not only as good at finding or building shelter as was Jamie, but was sufficiently familiar with the flora and fauna of the area to be able to plunge into the jungle and return within half an hour bearing handfuls of edible roots, fungi, and fruit with which to augment the Spartan rations in our packs.

Ian was set to gather firewood while Lawrence foraged, and I sat Jamie down with a pan of water, to tend the damage to his head. I washed away the blood from face and hair, to find to my surprise that the ball had in fact not plowed a furrow through his scalp as I had thought. Instead, it had pierced the skin just above his hairline and—evidently—vanished into his head. There was no sign of an exit wound. Unnerved by this, I prodded his scalp with increasing agitation, until a sudden cry from the patient announced that I had discovered the bullet.

There was a large, tender lump on the back of his head. The pistol ball had traveled under the skin, skimming the curve of his skull, and come to rest just over his occiput.

"Jesus H. Christ!" I exclaimed. I felt it again, unbelieving, but there it was. "You always said your head was solid bone, and I'll be damned if you weren't right. She shot you point-blank, and the bloody ball bounced off your skull!"

Jamie, supporting his head in his hands as I examined him, made a sound somewhere between a snort and a groan.

"Aye, well," he said, his voice somewhat muffled in his hands, "I'll no say I'm not thick-heided, but if Mistress Abernathy had used a full charge of powder, it wouldna have been nearly thick enough."

"Does it hurt a lot?"

"Not the wound, no, though it's sore. I've a terrible headache, though."

"I shouldn't wonder. Hold on a bit; I'm going to take the ball out."

Not knowing in what condition we might find Ian, I had brought the smallest of my medical boxes, which fortunately contained a bottle of alcohol and a small scalpel. I shaved away a little of Jamie's abundant mane, just below the swelling, and soused the area with alcohol for disinfection. My fingers were chilled from the alcohol, but his head was warm and comfortingly live to the touch.

"Three deep breaths and hold on tight," I murmured. "I'm going to cut you, but it will be fast."

"All right." The back of his neck looked a little pale, but the pulse was steady. He obligingly drew in his breath deeply, and exhaled, sighing. I held the area of scalp taut between the index and third fingers of my left hand. On the third breath, I said, "Right now," and drew the blade hard and quick across the scalp. He grunted slightly, but didn't cry out. I pressed gently with my right thumb against the swelling, slightly harder—and the ball popped out of the incision I had made, falling into my left hand like a grape.

"Got it," I said, and only then realized that I had been holding my breath. I dropped the little pellet—somewhat flattened by its contact with his skull— into his hand, and smiled, a little shakily. "Souvenir," I said. I pressed a pad of cloth against the small wound, wound a strip of cloth round his head to hold it, and then quite suddenly, with no warning whatever, began to cry.

I could feel the tears rolling down my face, and my shoulders shaking, but

I felt still detached; somehow outside my body. I was conscious mostly of a mild amazement.

"Sassenach? Are ye all right?" Jamie was peering up at me, eyes worried under the rakish bandage.

"Yes," I said, stuttering from the force of my crying. "I d-don't k-know why I'm c-crying. I d-don't know!"

"Come here." He took my hand and drew me down onto his knee. He wrapped his arms around me and held me tight, resting his cheek on the top of my head.

"It will be all right," he whispered. "It's fine now, *mo chridhe,* it's fine." He rocked me gently, one hand stroking my hair and neck, and murmured small unimportant things in my ear. Just as suddenly as I had been detached, I was back inside my body, warm and shaking, feeling the iron core dissolve in my tears.

Gradually I stopped weeping, and lay still against his chest, hiccuping now and then, feeling nothing but peace and the comfort of his presence.

I was dimly aware that Lawrence and Ian had returned, but paid no attention to them. At one point, I heard Ian say, with more curiosity than alarm, "You're bleeding all down the back of your neck, Uncle Jamie."

"Perhaps you'll fix me a new bandage, then, Ian," Jamie said. His voice was soft and unconcerned. "I must just hold your auntie now." And sometime later I went to sleep, still held tight in the circle of his arms.

I woke up later, curled on a blanket next to Jamie. He was leaning against a tree, one hand resting on my shoulder. He felt me wake, and squeezed gently. It was dark, and I could hear a rhythmic snoring somewhere close at hand. It must be Lawrence, I thought drowsily, for I could hear Young Ian's voice, on the other side of Jamie.

"No," he was saying slowly, "it wasna really so bad, on the ship. We were all kept together, so there was company from the other lads, and they fed us decently, and let us out two at a time to walk about the deck. Of course, we were all scairt, for we'd no notion why we'd been taken—and none of the sailors would tell us anything—but we were not mistreated."

The *Bruja* had sailed up the Yallahs River, and delivered her human cargo directly to Rose Hall. Here the bewildered boys had been warmly welcomed by Mrs. Abernathy, and promptly popped into a new prison.

The basement beneath the sugar mill had been fitted up comfortably enough, with beds and chamber pots, and aside from the noise of the sugar-making above during the days, it was comfortable enough. Still, none of the boys could think why they were there, though any number of suggestions were made, each more improbable than the last.

"And every now and then, a great black fellow would come down into the place with Mrs. Abernathy. We always begged to know what it was we were there for, and would she not be letting us go, for mercy's sake? but she only smiled and patted us and said we would see, in good time. Then she would choose a lad, and the black fellow would clamp onto the lad's arm and take him awa' wi' them." Ian's voice sounded distressed, and little wonder.

"Did the lads come back again?" Jamie asked. His hand patted me softly, and I reached up and pressed it.

"No—or not usually. And that scairt us all something dreadful."

Ian's turn had come eight weeks after his arrival. Three lads had gone and not returned by then, and when Mistress Abernathy's bright green eyes rested on him, he was not disposed to cooperate.

"I kicked the black fellow, and hit him—I even bit his hand," Ian said ruefully, "and verra nasty he tasted, too—all over some kind of grease, he was. But it made nay difference; he only clouted me over the head, hard enough to make my ears ring, then picked me up and carried me off in his arms, as though I was no more than a wee bairn."

Ian had been taken into the kitchen, where he was stripped, bathed, dressed in a clean shirt—but nothing else—and taken to the main house.

"It was just at night," he said wistfully, "and all the windows lighted. It looked verra much like Lallybroch, when ye come down from the hills just at dark, and Mam's just lit the lamps—it almost broke my heart to see it, and think of home."

He had had little opportunity to feel homesick, though. Hercules—or Atlas—had marched him up the stairs into what was obviously Mistress Abernathy's bedroom. Mrs. Abernathy was waiting for him, dressed in a soft, loose sort of gown with odd-looking figures embroidered round the hem of it in red and silver thread.

She had been cordial and welcoming, and had offered him a drink. It smelled strange, but not nasty, and as he had little choice in the matter, he had drunk it.

There were two comfortable chairs in the room, on either side of a long, low table, and a great bed at one side, swagged and canopied like a king's. He had sat in one chair, Mrs. Abernathy in the other, and she had asked him questions.

"What sorts of questions?" Jamie asked, prompting as Ian seemed hesitant.

"Well, all about my home, and my family—she asked the names of all my sisters and brothers, and my aunts and uncles"— I jerked a bit. So that *was* why Geilie had betrayed no surprise at our appearance! —"and all sorts of things, Uncle. Then she—she asked me had I—had I ever lain wi' a lassie. Just as though she were asking did I have parritch to my breakfast!" Ian sounded shocked at the memory.

"I didna want to answer her, but I couldna seem to help myself. I felt verra warm, like I was fevered, and I couldna seem to move easy. But I answered all her questions, and her just sitting there, pleasant as might be, watching me close wi' those big green eyes."

"So ye told her the truth?"

"Aye. Aye, I did." Ian spoke slowly, reliving the scene. "I said I had, and I told her about—about Edinburgh, and the printshop, and the seaman, and the brothel, and Mary, and—everything."

For the first time, Geilie had seemed displeased with one of his answers. Her face had grown hard and her eyes narrowed, and for a moment, Ian was seriously afraid. He would have run, then, but for the heaviness in his limbs, and the presence of the giant who stood against the door, unmoving.

"She got up and stamped about a bit, and said I was ruined, then, as I wasna a virgin, and what business did a bittie wee lad like me have, to be goin' wi' the lassies and spoiling myself?"

Then she had stopped her ranting, poured a glass of wine and drank it off, and her temper had seemed to cool.

"She laughed then, and looked at me careful, and said as how I might not be such a loss, after all. If I was no good for what she had in mind, perhaps I might have other uses." Ian's voice sounded faintly constricted, as though his collar were too tight. Jamie made a soothing interrogatory sound, though, and he took a deep breath, determined to go on.

"Well, she—she took my hand and made me stand up. Then she took off the shirt I was wearing, and she—I swear it's true, Uncle!—she knelt on the floor in front of me, and took my cock into her mouth!"

Jamie's hand tightened on my shoulder, but his voice betrayed no more than a mild interest.

"Aye, I believe ye, Ian. She made love to ye, then?"

"Love?" Ian sounded dazed. "No—I mean, I dinna ken. It—she—well, she got my cock to stand up, and then she made me come to the bed and lie down and she did things. But it wasna at all like it was with wee Mary!"

"No, I shouldna suppose it was," his uncle said dryly.

"God, it felt queer!" I could sense Ian's shudder from the tone of his voice. "I looked up in the middle, and there was the black man, standing right by the bed, holding a candlestick. She told him to lift it higher, so that she could see better." He paused, and I heard a small glugging noise as he drank from one of the bottles. He let out a long, quivering breath.

"Uncle. Have ye ever—lain wi' a woman, when ye didna want to do it?"

Jamie hesitated a moment, his hand tight on my shoulder, but then he said quietly, "Aye, Ian. I have."

"Oh." The boy was quiet, and I heard him scratch his head. "D'ye ken how it can be, Uncle? How ye can do it, and not want to a bit, and hate doing it, and—and still it—it feels good?"

Jamie gave a small, dry laugh.

"Well, what it comes to, Ian, is that your cock hasna got a conscience, and you have." His hand left my shoulder as he turned toward his nephew. "Dinna trouble yourself, Ian," he said. "Ye couldna help it, and it's likely that it saved your life for ye. The other lads—the ones who didna come back to the cellar—d'ye ken if they were virgins?"

"Well—a few I know were for sure—for we had a great deal of time to talk, aye? and after a time we kent a lot about one another. Some o' the lads boasted of havin' gone wi' a lassie, but I thought—from what they said about it, ye ken—that they hadna done it, really." He paused for a moment, as though reluctant to ask what he knew he must.

"Uncle—d'ye ken what happened to them? The rest of the lads with me?"

"No, Ian," Jamie said, evenly. "I've no notion." He leaned back against the tree, sighing deeply. "D'ye think ye can sleep, wee Ian? If ye can, ye should, for it will be a weary walk to the shore tomorrow."

"Oh, I can sleep, Uncle," Ian assured him. "But should I not keep watch? It's you should be resting, after bein' shot and all that." He paused and then added, rather shyly, "I didna say thank ye, Uncle Jamie."

Jamie laughed, freely this time.

"You're verra welcome, Ian," he said, the smile still in his voice. "Lay your head and sleep, laddie. I'll wake ye if there's need."

Ian obligingly curled up and within moments, was breathing heavily. Jamie sighed and leaned back against the tree.

"Do you want to sleep too, Jamie?" I pushed myself up to sit beside him. "I'm awake; I can keep an eye out."

His eyes were closed, the dying firelight dancing on the lids. He smiled without opening them and groped for my hand.

"No. If ye dinna mind sitting with me for a bit, though, you can watch. The headache's better if I close my eyes."

We sat in contented silence for some time, hand in hand. An occasional odd noise or far-off scream from some jungle animal came from the dark, but nothing seemed threatening now.

"Will we go back to Jamaica?" I asked at last. "For Fergus and Marsali?"

Jamie started to shake his head, then stopped, with a stifled groan.

"No," he said, "I think we shall sail for Eleuthera. That's Dutch-owned, and neutral. We can send Innes back wi' John's boatie, and he can take a message to Fergus to come and join us. I would as soon not set foot on Jamaica again, all things considered."

"No, I suppose not." I was quiet for a moment, then said, "I wonder how Mr. Willoughby—Yi Tien Cho, I mean—will manage. I don't suppose anyone will find him, if he stays in the mountains, but—"

"Oh, he may manage brawly," Jamie interrupted. "He's the pelican to fish for him, after all." One side of his mouth turned up in a smile. "For that matter, if he's canny, he'll find a way south, to Martinique. There's a small colony there of Chinese traders. I'd told him of it; said I'd take him there, once our business on Jamaica was finished."

"You aren't angry at him now?" I looked at him curiously, but his face was smooth and peaceful, almost unlined in the firelight.

This time he was careful not to move his head, but lifted one shoulder in a shrug, and grimaced.

"Och, no." He sighed and settled himself more comfortably. "I dinna suppose he had much thought for what he did, or understood at all what might be the end of it. And it would be foolish to hate a man for not giving ye something he hasna got in the first place." He opened his eyes then, with a faint smile, and I knew he was thinking of John Grey.

Ian twitched in his sleep, snorted loudly, and rolled over onto his back, arms flung wide. Jamie glanced at his nephew, and the smile grew wider.

"Thank God," he said. "*He* goes back to his mother by the first ship headed for Scotland."

"I don't know," I said, smiling. "He might not want to go back to Lallybroch, after all this adventure."

"I dinna care whether he wants to or not," Jamie said firmly. "He's going, if I must pack him up in a crate. Are ye looking for something, Sassenach?" he added, seeing me groping in the dark.

"I've got it," I said, pulling the flat hypodermic case out of my pocket. I flipped it open to check the contents, squinting to see by the waning light. "Oh, good; there's enough left for one whopping dose."

Jamie sat up a little straighter.

"I'm not fevered a bit," he said, eyeing me warily. "And if ye have it in mind to shove that filthy spike into my head, ye can just think again, Sasse-nach!"

"Not you," I said. "Ian. Unless you mean to send him home to Jenny riddled with syphilis and other interesting forms of the clap."

Jamie's eyebrows rose toward his hairline, and he winced at the resultant sensation.

"Ow. Syphilis? Ye think so?"

"I shouldn't be a bit surprised. Pronounced dementia is one of the symptoms of the advanced disease—though I must say it would be hard to tell in her case. Still, better safe than sorry, hm?"

Jamie snorted briefly with amusement.

"Well, that may teach Young Ian the price o' dalliance. I'd best distract Stern while ye take the lad behind a bush for his penance, though; Lawrence is a bonny man for a Jew, but he's curious. I dinna want ye burnt at the stake in Kingston, after all."

"I expect that would be awkward for the Governor," I said dryly. "Much as he might enjoy it, personally."

"I shouldna think he would, Sassenach." His dryness matched my own. "Is my coat within reach?"

"Yes." I found the garment folded on the ground near me, and handed it to him. "Are you cold?"

"No." He leaned back, the coat laid across his knees. "It's only that I wanted to feel the bairns all close to me while I sleep." He smiled at me, folded his hands gently atop the coat and its pictures, and closed his eyes again. "Good night, Sassenach."

63

Out of the Depths

In the morning, buoyed by rest and a breakfast of biscuit and plantain, we pressed on toward the shore in good heart—even Ian, who ceased to limp ostentatiously after the first quarter-mile. As we came down the defile that led onto the beach, though, a remarkable sight met our eyes.

"Jesus God, it's them!" Ian blurted. "The pirates!" He turned, ready to flee back into the hills, but Jamie grasped him by the arm.

"Not pirates," he said. "It's the slaves. Look!"

Unskilled in the seamanship of large vessels, the escaped slaves of the Yallahs River plantations had evidently made a slow and blundering passage toward Hispaniola, and having somehow arrived at that island, had promptly run the ship aground. The *Bruja* lay canted on her side in the shallows, her keel sunk deep in the sandy mud. A very agitated group of slaves surrounded her, some rushing up and down the beach shouting, others dashing off toward the refuge of the jungle, a few remaining to help the last of their number off the beached hulk.

A quick glance out to sea showed the cause of their agitation. A patch of white showed on the horizon, growing in size even as we watched.

"A man-of-war," Lawrence said, sounding interested.

Jamie said something under his breath in Gaelic, and Ian glanced at him, shocked.

"Out of here," Jamie said tersely. He pulled Ian about and gave him a shove up the defile, then grabbed my hand.

"Wait!" said Lawrence, shading his eyes. "There's another ship coming. A little one."

The Governor of Jamaica's private pinnace, to be exact, leaning at a perilous angle as she shot round the curve of the bay, her canvas bellied by the wind on her quarter.

Jamie stood for a split second, weighing the possibilities, then grabbed my hand again.

"Let's go!" he said.

By the time we reached the edge of the beach, the pinnace's small boat was plowing through the shallows, Raeburn and MacLeod pulling hard at the oars. I was wheezing and gulping air, my knees rubbery from the run.

Jamie snatched me up bodily into his arms and ran into the surf, followed by Lawrence and Ian, gasping like whales.

I saw Gordon, a hundred yards out in the pinnace's bow, aim a gun at the shore, and knew we were followed. The musket discharged with a puff of smoke, and Meldrum, behind him, promptly raised his own weapon and fired. Taking it in turns, the two of them covered our splashing advance, until friendly hands could pull us over the side and raise the boat.

"Come about!" Innes, manning the wheel, barked the order, and the boom swung across, the sails filling at once. Jamie hauled me to my feet and deposited me on a bench, then flung himself down beside me, panting.

"Holy God," he wheezed. "Did I no—tell ye to—stay away—Duncan?"

"Save your breath, Mac Dubh," Innes said, a wide grin spreading under his mustache. "Ye havena enough to be wasting it." He shouted something to MacLeod, who nodded and did something to the lines. The pinnace heeled over, changed her course, and came about, headed straight out of the tiny cove—and straight toward the man-of-war, now close enough for me to see the fat-lipped porpoise grinning beneath its bowsprit.

MacLeod bellowed something in Gaelic, accompanied by a gesture that left the meaning of what he had said in no doubt. To a triumphant yodel from Innes, we shot past the *Porpoise,* directly under her bow and close enough to see surprised-looking heads poking out from the rail above.

I looked back as we left the cove, to see the *Porpoise* still heading in, massive under her three great masts. The pinnace could never outrace her on the open sea, but in close quarters, the little sloop was light and maneuverable as a feather by comparison to the leviathan man-of-war.

"It's the slave ship they'll be after," Meldrum said, turning to look alongside me. "We saw the man-o'-war pick her up, three miles off the island. We thought whilst they were otherwise occupied, we might as well nip in and pick ye all off the beach."

"Good enough," Jamie said with a smile. His chest was still heaving, but he had recovered his breath. "I hope the *Porpoise* will be sufficiently occupied for the time being."

A warning shout from Raeburn indicated that this was not to be, however. Looking back, I could see the gleam of brass on the *Porpoise*'s deck as the pair of long guns called stern chasers were uncovered and began their process of aiming.

Now it was us at gunpoint, and I found the sensation very objectionable. Still, we were moving, and fast, at that. Innes put the wheel hard over, then hard again, tacking a zigzag path past the headland.

The stern chasers boomed together. There was a splash off the port bow, twenty yards away, but a good deal too close for comfort, given the fact that a twenty-four pound ball through the floor of the pinnace would sink us like a rock.

Innes cursed and hunched his shoulders over the wheel, his missing arm giving him an odd, lopsided appearance. Our course became still more erratic, and the next three tries came nowhere near. Then came a louder boom, and I looked back to see the side of the canted *Bruja* erupt in splinters, as the *Porpoise* came in range and trained her forward guns on the grounded ship.

A rain of grapeshot hit the beach, striking dead in the center of a group of fleeing slaves. Bodies—and parts of bodies—flew into the air like black stick-figures and fell to the sand, staining it with red blotches. Severed limbs were scattered over the beach like driftwood.

"Holy Mary, Mother of God." Ian, white to the lips, crossed himself, staring in horror at the beach as the shelling went on. Two more shots struck the *Bruja*, opening up a great hole in her side. Several landed harmlessly in the sand, and two more found their mark among the fleeing people. Then we were round the edge of the headland, and heading into the open sea, the beach and its carnage lost to view.

"Pray for us sinners, now and at the hour of our death." Ian finished his prayer in a whisper, and crossed himself again.

There was little conversation in the boat, beyond Jamie's giving Innes instructions for Eleuthera, and a conference between Innes and MacLeod as to the proper heading. The rest of us were too appalled by what we had just seen—and too relieved at our own escape—to want to talk.

The weather was fair, with a bright, brisk breeze, and we made good way. By sundown, the island of Hispaniola had dropped below the horizon, and Grand Turk Island was rising to the left.

I ate my small share of the available biscuit, drank a cup of water, and curled myself in the bottom of the boat, lying down between Ian and Jamie to sleep. Innes, yawning, took his own rest in the bow, while MacLeod and Meldrum took it in turns to man the helm through the night.

A shout woke me in the morning. I rose on one elbow, blinking with sleep and stiff from a night spent on bare, damp boards. Jamie was standing by me, his hair blowing back in the morning breeze.

"What?" I asked Jamie. "What is it?"

"I dinna believe it," he said, staring aft over the rail. "It's that bloody boat again!"

I scrambled to my feet, to find that it was true; far astern were tiny white sails.

"Are you sure?" I said, squinting. "Can you tell at this distance?"

"I can't, no," Jamie said frankly, "but Innes and MacLeod can, and they say it's the bloodsucking English, right enough. They'll have guessed our heading, maybe, and come after us, as soon as they'd dealt with those poor black buggers on Hispaniola." He turned away from the rail, shrugging.

"Damned little to be done about it, save to hope we stay ahead of them.

Innes says there's a hope of giving them the slip off Cat Island, if we reach there by dark."

As the day wore on, we kept just out of firing distance, but Innes looked more and more worried.

The sea between Cat Island and Eleuthera was shallow, and filled with coral heads. A man-of-war could never follow us into the maze—but neither could we move swiftly enough through it to avoid being sunk by the *Porpoise*'s long guns. Once in those treacherous shoals and channels, we would be sitting ducks.

At last, reluctantly, the decision was made to head east, out to sea; we could not risk slowing, and there was a slight chance of giving the man-of-war the slip in the dark.

When dawn came, all sight of land had disappeared. The *Porpoise,* unfortunately, had not. She was no closer, but as the wind rose along with the sun, she shook out more sail, and began to gain. With every scrap of sail already hoisted, and nowhere to hide, there was nothing we could do but run—and wait.

All through the long hours of the morning, the *Porpoise* grew steadily larger astern. The sky had begun to cloud over, and the wind had risen considerably, but this helped the *Porpoise,* with her huge spread of canvas, a great deal more than it did us.

By ten o'clock, she was close enough to risk a shot. It fell far astern, but was frightening, nonetheless. Innes squinted back over his shoulder, judging the distance, then shook his head and settled grimly to his course. There was nothing to be gained by tacking now; we must head straight on, as long as we could, taking evasive action only when it was too late for anything else.

By eleven, the *Porpoise* had drawn within a quarter-mile, and the monotonous boom of her forward guns had begun to sound every ten minutes, as her gunner tried the range. If I closed my eyes, I could imagine Erik Johansen, bent sweating and powder-stained over his gun, the smoking slow-match in his hand. I hoped that Annekje had been left on Antigua with her goats.

By eleven-thirty, it had begun to rain, and a heavy sea was running. A sudden gust of wind struck us sideways, and the boat heeled over far enough to bring the port rail within a foot of the water. Dumped onto the deck by the motion, we disentangled ourselves as Innes and MacLeod skillfully righted the pinnace. I glanced back, as I did every few minutes, despite myself, and saw the seamen scampering aloft in the *Porpoise,* reefing the topsails.

"That's luck!" MacGregor shouted in my ear, nodding where I was looking. "That'll slow them."

By twelve-thirty, the sky had gone a peculiar purple-green, and the wind had risen to an eerie whine. The *Porpoise* had taken in yet more canvas, and in spite of the action, had had a staysail carried away, the scrap of canvas jerked from the mast and whipped away, flapping like an albatross. She had long since stopped firing on us, unable to aim at such a small target in the heavy swell.

With the sun gone from sight, I could no longer estimate time. The storm caught us squarely, perhaps an hour later. There was no possibility of hearing anything; by sign language and grimaces, Innes made the men lower the sails; to keep canvas flying, or even reefed, was to risk having the mast ripped from the floorboards.

I clung tight to the rail with one hand, to Ian's hand with the other. Jamie crouched behind us, arms spread to give us the shelter of his back. The rain lashed past, hard enough to sting the skin, driven almost horizontal by the wind, and so thick that I barely saw the faint shape on the horizon that I thought was Eleuthera.

The sea had risen to terrifying heights, with swells rolling forty feet high. The pinnace rode them lightly, carried up and up and up to dizzy heights, then dropped abruptly into a trough. Jamie's face was dead white in the storm-light, his sodden hair pasted against his scalp.

It was near dark that it happened. The sky was nearly black, but there was an eerie green glow all across the horizon that silhouetted the skeletal shape of the *Porpoise* behind us. Another of the rain squalls slammed us sideways, lurching and swaying atop a huge wave.

As we picked ourselves up from yet another bruising spill, Jamie grabbed my arm, and pointed behind us. The *Porpoise*'s foremast was oddly bent, the top of it leaning far to one side. Before I had time to realize what was happening, the top fifteen feet of the mast had split off and pitched into the sea, carrying with it rigging and spars.

The man-of-war swung heavily round this impromptu anchor, and came sliding sideways down the face of a wave. The wall of water towered over the ship, and came crashing down, catching her broadside. The *Porpoise* heeled, spun around once. The next wave rose, and took her stern first, pulling the high aft deck below the water, whipping the masts through the air like snapping twigs.

It took three more waves to sink her; no time for escape for her hapless crew, but plenty for those of us watching to share their terror. There was a great bubbling flurry in the trough of a wave, and the man-of-war was gone.

Jamie's arm was rigid as iron beneath my hand. All the men stared back, faces gone empty with horror. All save Innes, who crouched doggedly over the wheel, meeting each wave as it came.

A new wave rose up beside the rail and seemed to hover there, looming above me. The great wall of water was glassy clear; I could see suspended in

it the debris and the men of the wrecked *Porpoise,* limbs outflung in grotesque ballet. The body of Thomas Leonard hung no more than ten feet
from me, drowned mouth open in surprise, his long soft hair aswirl above
the gilded collar of his coat.

Then the wave struck. I was snatched off the deck, and at once engulfed in
chaos. Blind and deaf, unable to breathe, I was tumbled through space, my
arms and legs wrenched awry by the force of the water.

Everything was dark; there was nothing but sensation, and all of that
intense but indistinguishable. Pressure and noise and overwhelming cold. I
couldn't feel the pull of my clothing, or the jerk of the rope—if it was still
there—around my waist. A sudden faint warmth swathed my legs, distinct in
the surrounding cold as a cloud in a clear sky. Urine, I thought, but didn't
know whether it was my own, or the last touch of another human body,
swallowed as I was in the belly of the wave.

My head hit something with a sickening crack, and suddenly I was coughing my lungs out on the deck of the pinnace, still miraculously afloat. I sat up
slowly, choking and wheezing. My rope was still in place, yanked so tight
about my waist that I was sure my lower ribs were broken. I jerked feebly at
it, trying to breathe, and then Jamie was there, one arm around me, the
other groping at his belt for a knife.

"Are ye all right?" he bellowed, his voice barely audible above the shrieking wind.

"No!" I tried to shout back, but it came out as no more than a wheeze. I
shook my head, fumbling at my waist.

The sky was a queer purple-green, a color I had never seen before. Jamie
sawed at the rope, his bent head spray-soaked and the color of mahogany,
hair whipped across his face by the fury of the wind.

The rope popped and I gulped in air, ignoring a stabbing pain in my side
and the stinging of raw skin about my waist. The ship was pitching wildly,
the deck swinging up and down like a lawn glider. Jamie fell down on the
deck, pulling me with him, and began to work his way on hands and knees
toward the mast, some six feet away, dragging me.

My garments had been drenched through, plastered to me from my immersion in the wave. Now the blast of the wind was so great that it plucked
my skirts away from my legs and flung them up, half-dried, to beat about my
face like goose wings.

Jamie's arm was tight as an iron bar across my chest. I clung to him, trying
to aid our progress by shoving with my feet on the slippery deckboards.
Smaller waves washed over the rail, sousing us intermittently, but no more
huge monsters followed them.

Reaching hands grasped us and hauled us the last few feet, into the nomi-
nal shelter of the mast. Innes had tied the wheel over long since; as I looked

forward, I saw lightning strike the sea ahead, making the spokes of the wheel spring out black, leaving an image like a spider's web printed on my retina.

Speech was impossible—and unnecessary. Raeburn, Ian, Meldrum, and Lawrence were huddled against the mast, all tied; frightful as it was on deck, no one wanted to go below, to be tossed to and fro in bruising darkness, with no notion of what was happening overhead.

I was sitting on the deck, legs splayed, with the mast at my back and the line passed across my chest. The sky had gone lead-gray on one side, a deep, lucent green on the other, and lightning was striking at random over the surface of the sea, bright jags of brilliance across the dark. The wind was so loud that even the thunderclaps reached us only now and then, as muffled booms, like ships' guns firing at a distance.

Then a bolt crashed down beside the ship, lightning and thunder together, close enough to hear the hiss of boiling water in the ringing aftermath of the thunderclap. The sharp reek of ozone flooded the air. Innes turned from the light, his tall, thin figure so sharply cut against the flash that he looked momentarily like a skeleton, black bones against the sky.

The momentary dazzle and his movement made it seem for an instant that he stood whole once more, two arms swinging, as though his missing limb had emerged from the ghost world to join him, here on the brink of eternity.

Oh, de headbone connected to de . . . neckbone. Joe Abernathy's voice sang softly in memory. *And de neckbone connected to de . . . backbone . . .* I had a sudden hideous vision of the scattered limbs I had seen on the beach by the corpse of the *Bruja,* animated by the lightning, squirming and wriggling to reunite.

> *Dem bones, dem bones, are gonna walk around.*
> *Now, hear de word of de Lawd!*

Another clap of thunder and I screamed, not at the sound, but at the lightning bolt of memory. A skull in my hands, with empty eyes that had once been the green of the hurricane sky.

Jamie shouted something in my ear, but I couldn't hear him. I could only shake my head in speechless shock, my skin rippling with horror.

My hair, like my skirts, was drying in the wind; the strands of it danced on my head, pulling at the roots. As it dried, I felt the crackle of static electricity where my hair brushed my cheek. There was a sudden movement among the sailors around me and I looked up, to see the spars and rigging above coated in the blue phosphorescence of St. Elmo's fire.

A fireball dropped to the deck and rolled toward us, streaming phosphorescence. Jamie struck at it and it hopped delicately into the air and rolled away along the rail, leaving a scent of burning in its wake.

I looked up at Jamie to see if he was all right, and saw the loose ends of his hair standing out from his head, coated with fire and streaming backward like a demon's. Streaks of vivid blue outlined the fingers of his hand when he brushed the hair from his face. Then he looked down, saw me, and grasped my hand. A jolt of electricity shot through us both with the touch, but he didn't let go.

I couldn't say how long it lasted; hours or days. Our mouths dried from the wind, and grew sticky with thirst. The sky went from gray to black, but there was no telling whether it was night, or only the coming of rain.

The rain, when it did come, was welcome. It came with the drenching roar of a tropical shower, a drumming audible even above the wind. Better yet, it was hail, not rain; the hailstones hit my skull like pebbles, but I didn't care. I gathered the icy globules in both hands, and swallowed them half-melted, a cool benison to my tortured throat.

Meldrum and MacLeod crawled about the deck on hands and knees, scooping the hailstones into buckets and pots, anything that would hold water.

I slept intermittently, head lolling on Jamie's shoulder, and woke to find the wind still screaming. Numb to terror now, I only waited. Whether we lived or died seemed of little consequence, if only the dreadful noise would stop.

There was no telling day from night, no way to keep time, while the sun hid its face. The darkness seemed a little lighter now and then, but whether it was by virtue of daylight or moonlight, I couldn't tell. I slept, and woke, and slept again.

Then I woke, to find the wind a little quieter. The seas still heaved, and the tiny boat pitched like a cockleshell, throwing us up and dropping us with stomach-churning regularity. But the noise was less; I could hear, when MacGregor shouted to Ian to pass a cup of water. The men's faces were chapped and raw, their lips cracked to bleeding by the whistling wind, but they were smiling.

"It's gone by." Jamie's voice was low and husky in my ear, rusted by weather. "The storm's past."

It was; there were breaks in the lead-gray sky, and small flashes of a pale, fresh blue. I thought it must be early morning, sometime just past dawn, but couldn't tell for sure.

While the hurricane had ceased to blow, there was still a strong wind, and the storm surge carried us at an amazing speed. Meldrum took the wheel from Innes, and bending to check the compass, gave a cry of surprise. The fireball that had come aboard during the storm had harmed no one, but the compass was now a melted mass of silver metal, the wooden casing around it untouched.

"Amazing!" said Lawrence, touching it reverently with one finger.

"Aye, and inconvenient, forbye," said Innes dryly. He looked upward, toward the ragged remnants of the dashing clouds. "Much of a hand at celestial navigation, are ye, Mr. Stern?"

After much squinting at the rising sun and the remnants of the morning stars, Jamie, Innes, and Stern determined that our heading was roughly northeast.

"We must turn to the west," Stern said, leaning over the crude chart with Jamie and Innes. "We do not know where we are, but any land must surely be to the west."

Innes nodded, peering soberly at the chart, which showed a sprinkle of islands like coarse-ground pepper, floating on the waters of the Caribbean.

"Aye, that's so," he said. "We've been headed out to sea for God knows how long. The hull's in one piece, but that's all I'd say for it. As for the mast and sails—well, they'll maybe hold for a time." He sounded dubious in the extreme. "God knows where we may fetch up, though."

Jamie grinned at him, dabbing at a trickle of blood from his cracked lip.

"So long as it's land, Duncan, I'm no verra choosy about where."

Innes quirked an eyebrow at him, a slight smile on his lips.

"Aye? And here I thought ye'd settled for sure on a sailor's life, Mac Dubh; ye're sae canty on deck. Why, ye havena puked once in the last twa days!"

"That's because I havena eaten anything in the last twa days," Jamie said wryly. "I dinna much care if the island we find first is English, French, Spanish, or Dutch, but I should be obliged if ye'd find one with food, Duncan."

Innes wiped a hand across his mouth and swallowed painfully; the mention of food made everyone salivate, despite dry mouths.

"I'll do my best, Mac Dubh," he promised.

———————◆———————

"Land! It's land!" The call came at last, five days later, in a voice rendered so hoarse by wind and thirst that it was no more than a faint croak, but full of joy, nonetheless. I dashed up on deck to see, my feet slipping on the ladder rungs. Everyone was hanging over the rail, looking at the humped black shape on the horizon. It was far off, but undeniably land, solid and distinct.

"Where do you think we are?" I tried to say, but my voice was so hoarse, the words came out in a tiny whisper, and no one heard. It didn't matter; if we were headed straight for the naval barracks at Antigua, I didn't care.

The waves were running in huge, smooth swells, like the backs of whales. The wind was gusting now, and Innes called for the helmsman to bring the bow another point nearer the wind.

I could see a line of large birds flying, a stately procession skimming down the distant shoreline. Pelicans, searching the shallows for fish, with the sun gleaming on their wings.

I tugged at Jamie's sleeve and pointed at them.

"Look—" I began, but got no further. There was a sharp *crack!* and the world exploded in black and fire. I came to in the water. Dazed and half-choked, I floundered and fought in a world of dark green. Something was wrapped about my legs, dragging me down.

I flailed wildly, kicking to free my leg of the deadly grip. Something floated past my head, and I grabbed for it. Wood, blessed wood, something to hold onto in the surging waves.

A dark shape sleeked by like a seal beneath the water, and a red head bobbed up six feet away, gasping.

"Hold on!" Jamie said. He reached me with two strokes, and ducking under the piece of wood I held, dived down. I felt a tugging at my leg, a sharp pain, and then the dragging tension eased. Jamie's head popped up again, across the spar. He grasped my wrists and hung there, gulping air, as the rolling swell carried us, up and down.

I couldn't see the ship anywhere; had it sunk? A wave broke over my head, and Jamie disappeared temporarily. I shook my head, blinking, and he was there again. He smiled at me, a savage grin of effort, and his grip on my wrists tightened harder.

"Hold on!" he rasped again, and I did. The wood was harsh and splintery under my hands, but I clung for all I was worth. We drifted, half-blinded by spray, spinning like a bit of flotsam, so that sometimes I saw the distant shore, sometimes nothing but the open sea from which we had come. And when the waves washed over us, I saw nothing but water.

There was something wrong with my leg; a strange numbness, punctuated with flashes of sharp pain. The vision of Murphy's peg and the razor-grin of an openmouthed shark drifted through my mind; had my leg been taken by some toothy beast? I thought of my tiny hoard of warm blood, streaming from the stump of a bitten limb, draining away into the cold vastness of the sea, and I panicked, trying to snatch my hand from Jamie's grasp in order to reach down and see for myself.

He snarled something unintelligible at me and held on to my wrists like grim death. After a moment of frenzied thrashing, reason returned, and I calmed myself, thinking that if my leg were indeed gone, I would have lost consciousness by now.

At that, I *was* beginning to lose consciousness. My vision was growing gray at the edges, and floating bright spots covered Jamie's face. Was I really bleeding to death, or was it only cold and shock? It hardly seemed to matter, I thought muzzily; the effect was the same.

A sense of lassitude and utter peace stole gradually over me. I couldn't feel my feet or legs, and only Jamie's crushing grip on my hands reminded me of their existence. My head went under water, and I had to remind myself to hold my breath.

The wave subsided and the wood rose slightly, bringing my nose above water. I breathed, and my vision cleared slightly. A foot away was the face of Jamie Fraser, hair plastered to his head, wet features contorted against the spray.

"Hold on!" he roared. "Hold on, God damn you!"

I smiled gently, barely hearing him. The sense of great peace was lifting me, carrying me beyond the noise and chaos. There was no more pain. Nothing mattered. Another wave washed over me, and this time I forgot to hold my breath.

The choking sensation roused me briefly, long enough to see the flash of terror in Jamie's eyes. Then my vision went dark again.

"Damn you, Sassenach!" his voice said, from a very great distance. His voice was choked with passion. "Damn you! I swear if ye die on me, I'll *kill* you!"

I was dead. Everything around me was a blinding white, and there was a soft, rushing noise like the wings of angels. I felt peaceful and bodiless, free of terror, free of rage, filled with quiet happiness. Then I coughed.

I wasn't bodiless, after all. My leg hurt. It hurt a lot. I became gradually aware that a good many other things hurt, too, but my left shin took precedence in no uncertain terms. I had the distinct impression that the bone had been removed and replaced with a red-hot poker.

At least the leg was demonstrably there. When I cracked my eyes open to look, the haze of pain that floated over my leg seemed almost visible, though perhaps that was only a product of the general fuzziness in my head. Whether mental or physical in origin, the general effect was of a sort of whirling whiteness, shot with flickers of a brighter light. Watching it hurt my eyes, so I shut them again.

"Thank God, you're awake!" said a relieved-sounding Scottish voice near my ear.

"No I'm not," I said. My own voice emerged as a salt-crusted croak, rusty with swallowed seawater. I could feel seawater in my sinuses, too, which gave my head an unpleasant gurgling feel. I coughed again, and my nose began to run profusely. Then I sneezed.

"Eugh!" I said, in complete revulsion at the resultant cascade of slime over my upper lip. My hand seemed far off and insubstantial, but I made the effort to raise it, swiping clumsily at my face.

"Be still, Sassenach; I'll take care of ye." There was a definite note of amusement in the voice, which irritated me enough to open my eyes again. I caught a brief glimpse of Jamie's face, intent on mine, before vision vanished once again in the folds of an immense white handkerchief.

He wiped my face thoroughly, ignoring my strangled noises of protest and impending suffocation, then held the cloth to my nose.

"Blow," he said.

I did as he said. Rather to my surprise, it helped quite a lot. I could think more or less coherently, now that my head was unclogged.

Jamie smiled down at me. His hair was rumpled and stiff with dried salt, and there was a wide abrasion on his temple, an angry dark red against the bronzed skin. He seemed not to be wearing a shirt, but had a blanket of some kind draped about his shoulders.

"Do ye feel verra bad?" he asked.

"Horrible," I croaked in reply. I was also beginning to be annoyed at being alive, after all, and being required to take notice of things again. Hearing the rasp in my voice, Jamie reached for a jug of water on the table by my bed.

I blinked in confusion, but it really was a bed, not a berth or a hammock. The linen sheets contributed to the overwhelming impression of whiteness that had first engulfed me. This was reinforced by the whitewashed walls and ceiling, and the long white muslin draperies that bellied in like sails, rustling in the breeze from the open windows.

The flickering light came from reflections that shimmered over the ceiling; apparently there was water close by outside, and sun shining on it. It seemed altogether cozier than Davy Jones's locker. Still, I felt a brief moment of intense regret for the sense of infinite peace I had experienced in the heart of the wave—a regret made more keen by the slight movement that sent a bolt of white agony up my leg.

"I think your leg is broken, Sassenach," Jamie told me unnecessarily. "Ye likely shouldna move it much."

"Thanks for the advice," I said, through gritted teeth. "Where in bloody hell are we?"

He shrugged briefly. "I dinna ken. It's a fair-sized house, is all I could say. I wasna taking much note when they brought us in. One man said the place is called Les Perles." He held the cup to my lips and I swallowed gratefully.

"What happened?" So long as I was careful not to move, the pain in my leg was bearable. Automatically, I placed my fingers under the angle of my jaw to check my pulse; reassuringly strong. I wasn't in shock; my leg couldn't be badly fractured, much as it hurt.

Jamie rubbed a hand over his face. He looked very tired, and I noticed that his hand trembled with fatigue. There was a large bruise on his cheek, and a line of dried blood where something had scratched the side of his neck.

"The topmast snapped, I think. One of the spars fell and knocked ye overboard. When ye hit the water, ye sank like a stone, and I dived in after you. I got hold of you—and the spar, too, thank God. Ye had a bit of rigging

tangled round your leg, dragging ye down, but I managed to get that off.''
He heaved a deep sigh, and rubbed his head.

"I just held to ye; and after a time, I felt sand under my feet. I carried ye
ashore, and a bit later, some men found us and brought us here. That's all.''
He shrugged.

I felt cold, despite the warm breeze coming in through the windows.

"What happened to the ship? And the men? Ian? Lawrence?''

"Safe, I think. They couldna reach us, with the mast broken—by the time
they'd rigged a makeshift sail, we were long gone.'' He coughed roughly,
and rubbed the back of his hand across his mouth. "But they're safe; the
men who found us said they'd seen a small ketch go aground on a mud flat a
quarter-mile south of here; they've gone down to salvage and bring back the
men.''

He took a swallow of water, swished it about his mouth, and going to the
window, spat it out.

"I've sand in my teeth,'' he said, grimacing, as he returned. "And my ears.
And my nose, and the crack of my arse, too, I shouldna wonder.''

I reached out and took his hand again. His palm was heavily calloused, but
still showed the tender swelling of rising blisters, with shreds of ragged skin
and raw flesh, where earlier blisters had burst and bled.

"How long were we in the water?'' I asked, gently tracing the lines of his
swollen palm. The tiny "C" at the base of his thumb was faded almost to
invisibility, but I could still feel it under my finger. "Just how long did you
hold on?''

"Long enough,'' he said simply.

He smiled a little, and held my hand more tightly, despite the soreness of
his own. It dawned on me suddenly that I wasn't wearing anything; the linen
sheets were smooth and cool on my bare skin, and I could see the swell of my
nipples, rising under the thin fabric.

"What happened to my clothes?''

"I couldna hold ye up against the drag of your skirts, so I ripped them
off,'' he explained. "What was left didna seem worth saving.''

"I don't suppose so,'' I said slowly, "but Jamie—what about you?
Where's your coat?''

He shrugged, then let his shoulders drop, and smiled ruefully.

"At the bottom of the sea with my shoon, I expect,'' he said. And the
pictures of Willie and Brianna there, too.

"Oh, Jamie. I'm so sorry.'' I reached for his hand and held it tightly. He
looked away, and blinked once or twice.

"Aye, well,'' he said softly. "I expect I will remember them.'' He
shrugged again, with a lopsided smile. "And if not, I can look in the glass,
no?'' I gave a laugh that was half a sob; he swallowed painfully, but went on
smiling.

He glanced down at his tattered breeches then, and seeming to think of something, leaned back and worked a hand into the pocket.

"I didna come away completely empty-handed," he said, pulling a wry face. "Though I would as soon it had been the pictures I kept, and lost these."

He opened his hand, and I saw the gleam and glitter in his ruined palm. Stones of the first quality, cut and faceted, suitable for magic. An emerald, a ruby—male, I supposed—a great fiery opal, a turquoise blue as the sky I could see out the window, a golden stone like sun trapped in honey, and the strange crystal purity of Geilie's black diamond.

"You have the adamant," I said, touching it gently. It was still cool to the touch, in spite of being worn so close to his body.

"I have," he said, but he was looking at me, not at the stone, a slight smile on his face. "What is it an adamant gives ye? The knowledge of joy in all things?"

"So I was told." I lifted my hand to his face and stroked it lightly, feeling hard bone and lively flesh, warm to the touch, and joyful to behold above all things.

"We have Ian," I said softly. "And each other."

"Aye, that's true." The smile reached his eyes then. He dropped the stones in a glittering heap on the table and leaned back in his chair, cradling my hand between his.

I relaxed, feeling a warm peace begin to steal over me, in spite of the aches and scrapes and the pain in my leg. We were alive, safe and together, and very little else mattered; surely not clothes, nor a fractured tibia. Everything would be managed in time—but not now. For now, it was enough only to breathe, and look at Jamie.

We sat in a peaceful silence for some time, watching the sunlit curtains and the open sky. It might have been ten minutes later, or as much as an hour, when I heard the sound of light footsteps outside, and a delicate rap at the door.

"Come in," Jamie said. He sat up straighter, but didn't let go of my hand.

The door opened, and a woman stepped in, her pleasant face lit by welcome, tinged with curiosity.

"Good morning," she said, a little shyly. "I must beg your pardon, not to have waited upon you before; I was in the town, and learned of your— arrival"—she smiled at the word —"only when I returned, just now."

"We must thank ye, Madame, most sincerely, for the kind treatment afforded to us," Jamie said. He rose and bowed formally to her, but kept hold of my hand. "Your servant, ma'am. Have ye word of our companions?"

She blushed slightly, and bobbed a curtsy in reply to his bow. She was young, only in her twenties, and seemed unsure quite how to conduct herself